Mack Reynolds

The Greatest Sci-Fi Works
(Illustrated Edition)

OK Publishing 2021

Mack Reynolds
The Greatest Sci-Fi Works

(Illustrated Edition)

Ultima Thule, Black Man's Burden, Border, Breed nor Birth, Frigid Fracas, Adaptation

Published by
MUSAICUM
Books

- Advanced Digital Solutions & High-Quality book Formatting -

musaicumbooks@okpublishing.info

2021 OK Publishing

ISBN 978-80-272-7453-6

Contents

Ultima Thule

At least he'd got far enough to wind up with a personal interview. It's one thing doing up an application and seeing it go onto an endless tape and be fed into the maw of a machine and then to receive, in a matter of moments, a neatly printed rejection. It's another thing to receive an appointment to be interviewed by a placement officer in the Commissariat of Interplanetary Affairs, Department of Personnel. Ronny Bronston was under no illusions. Nine out of ten men of his age annually made the same application. Almost all were annually rejected. Statistically speaking practically nobody ever got an interplanetary position. But he'd made step one along the path of a lifetime ambition.

He stood at easy attention immediately inside the door. At the desk at the far side of the room the placement officer was going through a sheaf of papers. He looked up and said, "Ronald Bronston? Sit down. You'd like an interplanetary assignment, eh? So would I."

Ronny took the chair. For a moment he tried to appear alert, earnest, ambitious but not *too* ambitious, fearless, devoted to the cause, and indispensable. For a moment. Then he gave it up and looked like Ronny Bronston.

The other looked up and took him in. The personnel official saw a man of averages. In the late twenties. Average height, weight and breadth. Pleasant of face in an average sort of way, but not handsome. Less than sharp in dress, hair inclined to be on the undisciplined side. Brown of hair, dark of eye. In a crowd, inconspicuous. In short, Ronny Bronston.

The personnel officer grunted. He pushed a button, said something into his order box. A card slid into the slot and he took it out and stared gloomily at it.

"What're your politics?" he said.

"Politics?" Ronny Bronston said. "I haven't any politics. My father and grandfather before me have been citizens of United Planets. There hasn't been any politics in our family for three generations."

"Family?"

"None."

The other grunted and marked the card. "Racial prejudices?"

"I beg your pardon?"

"Do you have any racial prejudices? Any at all."

"No."

The personnel officer said, "Most people answer that way at first, these days, but some don't at second. For instance, suppose you had to have a blood transfusion. Would you have any objection to it being blood donated by, say, a Negro, a Chinese, or, say, a Jew?"

Ronny ticked it off on his fingers. "One of my greatgrandfathers was a French *colon* who married a Moroccan girl. The Moors are a blend of Berber, Arab, Jew and Negro. Another of my greatgrandfathers was a Hawaiian. They're largely a blend of Polynesians, Japanese, Chinese and Caucasians especially Portuguese. Another of my greatgrandfathers was Irish, English and Scotch. He married a girl who was half Latvian, half Russian." Ronny wound it up. "Believe me, if I had a blood transfusion from just anybody at all, the blood would feel right at home."

The interviewer snorted, even as he marked the card. "That accounts for three greatgrandfathers," he said lightly. "You seem to have made a study of your family tree. What was the other one?"

Rocky said expressionlessly, "A Texan."

The secretary shrugged and looked at the card again. "Religion?"

"Reformed Agnostic," Ronny said. This one was possibly where he ran into a brick wall. Many of the planets had strong religious beliefs of one sort or another. Some of them had state religions and you either belonged or else.

"Is there any such church?" the personnel officer frowned.

"No. I'm a one-man member. I'm of the opinion that if there are any greater-powers-that-be They're keeping the fact from us. And if that's the way They want it, it's Their business. If and when They want to contact me-one of Their puppets dangling from a string-then I suppose They'll do it. Meanwhile, I'll wait."

The other said interestedly, "You think that if there is a Higher Power and if It ever wants to get in touch with you, It will?"

"Um-m-m. In Its own good time. Sort of a *don't call Me*, thing, *I'll call you* ."

The personnel officer said, "There have been a few revealed religions, you know."

"So they said, so they said. None of them have made much sense to me. If a Super-Power wanted to contact man, it seems unlikely to me that it'd be all wrapped up in a lot of complicated gobbledegook. It would all be very clear indeed."

The personnel officer sighed. He marked the card, stuck it back into the slot in his order box and it disappeared.

He looked up at Ronny Bronston. "All right, that's all."

Ronny came to his feet. "Well, what happened?"

The other grinned at him sourly. "Darned if I know," he said. "By the time you get to the outer office, you'll probably find out." He scratched the end of his nose and said, "I sometimes wonder what I'm doing here."

Ronny thanked him, told him good-by, and left.

* * * * *

In the outer office a girl looked up from a card she'd just pulled from her own order box. "Ronald Bronston?"

"That's right."

She handed the card to him. "You're to go to the office of Ross Metaxa in the Octagon, Commissariat of Interplanetary Affairs, Department of Justice, Bureau of Investigation, Section G."

In a lifetime spent in first preparing for United Planets employment and then in working for the organization, Ronny Bronston had never been in the Octagon Building. He'd seen photographs, Tri-Di broadcasts and he'd heard several thousand jokes on various levels from pun to obscenity about getting around in the building, but he'd never been there. For that matter, he'd never been in Greater Washington before, other than a long ago tourist trip. Population Statistics, his department, had its main offices in New Copenhagen.

His card was evidently all that he needed for entry.

At the sixth gate he dismissed his car and let it shoot back into the traffic mess. He went up to one of the guard-guides and presented the card.

The guide inspected it. "Section G of the Bureau of Investigation," he muttered. "Every day, something new. I never heard of it."

"It's probably some outfit in charge of cleaning the heads on space liners." Ronny said unhappily. He'd never heard of it either.

"Well, it's no problem," the guard-guide said. He summoned a three-wheel, fed the co-ordinates into it from Ronny's card, handed the card back and flipped an easy salute. "You'll soon know."

The scooter slid into the Octagon's hall traffic and proceeded up one corridor, down another, twice taking to ascending ramps. Ronny had read somewhere the total miles of corridors in the Octagon. He hadn't believed the figures at the time. Now he believed them. He must have traversed several miles before they got to the Department of Justice alone. It was another quarter mile to the Bureau of Investigation.

The scooter eventually came to a halt, waited long enough for Ronny to dismount and then hurried back into the traffic.

He entered the office. A neatly uniformed reception girl with a harassed and cynical eye looked up from her desk. "Ronald Bronston?" she said.

"That's right."

"Where've you been?" She had a snappy cuteness. "The commissioner has been awaiting you. Go through that door and to your left."

Ronny went through that door and to the left. There was another door, inconspicuously lettered *Ross Metaxa, Commissioner, Section G*. Ronny knocked and the door opened.

Ross Metaxa was going through a wad of papers. He looked up; a man in the middle years, sour of expression, moist of eye as though he either drank too much or slept too little.

"Sit down," he said. "You're Ronald Bronston, eh? What do they call you, Ronny? It says here you've got a sense of humor. That's one of the first requirements in this lunatic department."

Ronny sat down and tried to form some opinions of the other by his appearance. He was reminded of nothing so much as the stereotype city editor you saw in the historical romance Tri-Ds. All that was needed was for Metaxa to start banging on buttons and yelling something about tearing down the front page, whatever that meant.

Metaxa said, "It also says you have some queer hobbies. Judo, small weapons target shooting, mountain climbing —" He looked up from the reports. "Why does anybody climb mountains?"

Ronny said, "Nobody's ever figured out." That didn't seem to be enough, especially since Ross Metaxa was staring at him, so he added, "Possibly we devotees keep doing it in hopes that someday somebody'll find out."

Ross Metaxa said sourly, "Not *too* much humor, please. You don't act as though getting this position means much to you."

Ronny said slowly, "I figured out some time ago that every young man on Earth yearns for a job that will send him shuttling from one planet to another. To achieve it they study, they sweat, they make all out efforts to meet and suck up to anybody they think might help. Finally, when and if they get an interview for one of the few openings, they spruce up in their best clothes, put on their best party manners, present themselves as the sincere, high I.Q., ambitious young men that they are-and then flunk their chance. I decided I might as well be what I am."

Ross Metaxa looked at him. "O.K.," he said finally. "We'll give you a try."

Ronny said blankly, "You mean I've got the job?"

"That's right."

"I'll be damned."

"Probably," Metaxa said. He yawned. "Do you know what Section G handles?"

"Well no, but as for me, just so I get off Earth and see some of the galaxy."

* * * * *

Metaxa had been sitting with his heels on his desk. Now he put them down and reached a hand into a drawer to emerge with a brown bottle and two glasses. "Do you drink?" he said.

"Of course."

"Even during working hours?" Metaxa scowled.

"When occasion calls."

"Good," Metaxa said. He poured two drinks. "You'll get your fill of seeing the galaxy," he said. "Not that there's much to see. Man can settle only Earth-type planets and after you've seen a couple of hundred you've seen them all."

Ronny sipped at his drink, then blinked reproachfully down into the glass.

Metaxa said, "Good, eh? A kind of tequila they make on Deneb Eight. Bunch of Mexicans settled there."

"What," said Ronny hoarsely, "do they make it out of?"

"Lord only knows," Metaxa said. "To get back to Section G. We're Interplanetary Security. In short, Department Cloak and Dagger. Would you be willing to die for the United Planets, Bronston?"

That curve had come too fast. Ronny blinked again. "Only in emergency," he said. "Who'd want to kill me?"

Metaxa poured another drink. "Many of the people you'll be working with," he said.

"Well, *why* ? What will I be doing?"

"You'll be representing United Planets," Metaxa explained. "Representing United Planets in cases where the local situation is such that the folks you're working among will be teed off at the organization."

"Well, why are they members if they don't like the UP?"

"That's a good question," Metaxa said. He yawned. "I guess I'll have to go into my speech." He finished his drink. "Now, shut up till I give you some background. You're probably full of a lot of nonsense you picked up in school."

Ronny shut up. He'd expected more of an air of dedication in the Octagon and in such ethereal departments as that of Interplanetary Justice, however, he was in now and not adverse to picking up some sophistication beyond the ken of the Earth-bound employees of UP.

The other's voice took on a far away, albeit bored tone. "It seems that most of the times man gets a really big idea, he goes off half cocked. Just one example. Remember when the ancient Hellenes exploded into the Mediterranean? A score of different City-States began sending out colonies, which in turn sprouted colonies of their own. Take Syracuse, on Sicily. Hardly was she established than, bingo, she sent off colonists to Southern Italy, and they in turn to Southern France, Corsica, the Balearics. Greeks were exploding all over the place, largely without adequate plans, without rhyme or reason. Take Alexander. Roamed off all the way to India, founding cities and colonies of Greeks all along the way."

The older man shifted in his chair. "You wonder what I'm getting at, eh? Well, much the same thing is happening in man's explosion into space, now that he has the ability to leave the solar system behind. Dashing off half cocked, in all directions, he's flowing out over this section of the galaxy without plan, without rhyme or reason. I take that last back, he has reasons all right-some of the screwiest. Religious reasons, racial reasons, idealistic reasons, political reasons, altruistic reasons and mercenary reasons.

"Inadequate ships, manned by small numbers of inadequate people, setting out to find their own planets, to establish themselves on one of the numberless uninhabited worlds that offer themselves to colonization and exploitation."

Ronny cleared his throat. "Well, isn't that a good thing, sir?"

Ross Metaxa looked at him and grunted. "What difference does it make if it's good or not? It's happening. We're spreading our race out over tens of hundreds of new worlds in the most haphazard fashion. As a result, we of United Planets now have a chaotic mishmash on our hands. How we manage to keep as many planets in the organization as we do, sometimes baffles me. I suppose most of them are afraid to drop out, conscious of the protection UP gives against each other."

He picked up a report. "Here's Monet, originally colonized by a bunch of painters, writers, musicians and such. They had dreams of starting a new race" —Metaxa snorted —"with everybody artists. They were all so impractical that they even managed to crash their ship on landing. For three hundred years they were uncontacted. What did they have in the way of government by that time? A military theocracy, something like the Aztecs of Pre-Conquest Mexico. A matriarchy, at that. And what's their religion based on? That of ancient Phoenicia including plenty of human sacrifice to good old Moloch. What can United Planets do about it, now that they've become a member? Work away very delicately, trying to get them to at least eliminate the child sacrifice phase of their culture. Will they do it? Hell no, not if they can help it. The Head Priestess and her clique are afraid that if they don't have the threat of sacrifice to hold over the people, they'll be overthrown."

Ronny was surprised. "I'd never heard of a member planet like that. Monet?"

Metaxa sighed. "No, of course not. You've got a lot to learn, Ronny, my lad. First of all, what're Articles One and Two of the United Planets Charter?"

That was easy. Ronny recited. "Article One: *The United Planets organization shall take no steps to interfere with the internal political, socio-economic, or religious institutions of its member planets.* Article Two: *No member planets of United Planets shall interfere with the internal political, socioeconomic or religious institutions of any other member planet.* " He looked at the department head. "But what's that got to do with the fact that I was unfamiliar with even the existence of Monet?"

"Suppose one of the advanced planets, or even Earth itself," Metaxa growled, "openly discussed in magazines, on newscasts, or wherever, the religious system of Monet. A howl would go up among the liberals, the progressives, the do-gooders. And the howl would be heard on the other advanced planets. Eventually, the citizen in the street on Monet would hear about it and be affected. And before you knew it, a howl would go up from Monet's government. Why? Because the other planets would be interfering with her internal affairs, simply by discussing them."

"So what you mean is," Ronny said, "part of our job is to keep information about Monet's government and religion from being discussed at all on other member planets."

"That's right," Metaxa nodded. "And that's just one of our dirty little jobs. One of many. Section G, believe me, gets them all. Which brings us to your first assignment."

* * * * *

Ronny inched forward in his chair. "It takes me into space?"

"It takes you into space all right," Metaxa snorted. "At least it will after a few months of indoctrination. I'm sending you out after a legend, Ronny. You're fresh, possibly you'll get some ideas older men in the game haven't thought of."

"A legend?"

"I'm sending you to look for Tommy Paine. Some members of the department don't think he exists. I do."

"Tommy Paine?"

"A pseudonym that somebody hung on him way back before even my memory in this Section. Did you ever hear of Thomas Paine in American history?"

"He wrote a pamphlet during the Revolutionary War, didn't he?"

" 'Common Sense,' " Metaxa nodded. "But he was more than that. He was born in England but went to America as a young man and his writings probably did as much as anything to put over the revolt against the British. But that wasn't enough. When that revolution was successful he went back to England and tried to start one there. The government almost caught him, but he escaped and got to France where he participated in the French Revolution."

"He seemed to get around," Ronny Bronston said.

"And so does this namesake of his. We've been trying to catch up with him for some twenty years. How long before that he was active, we have no way of knowing. It was some time before we became aware of the fact that half the revolts, rebellions, revolutions and such that occur in the United Planets have his dirty finger stirring around in them."

"But you said some department members don't believe in his existence."

Metaxa grunted. "They're working on the theory that no one man could do all that Tommy Paine has laid to him. Possibly it's true that he sometimes gets the blame for accomplishments not his. Or, for that matter, possibly he's more than one person. I don't know."

"Well," Ronny said hesitantly, "what's an example of his activity?"

Metaxa picked up another report from the confusion of his desk. "Here's one only a month old. Dictator on the planet Megas. Kidnapped and forced to resign. There's still confusion but it looks as though a new type of government will be formed now."

"But how do they know it wasn't just some dissatisfied citizens of Megas?"

"It seems as though the kidnap vehicle was an old fashioned Earth-type helicopter. There were no such on Megas. So Section G suspects it's a possible Tommy Paine case. We could be wrong, of course. That's why I say the man's in the way of being a legend. Perhaps the others are right and he doesn't even exist. I think he does, and if so, it's our job to get him and put him out of circulation."

Ronny said slowly, "But why would that come under our jurisdiction? It seems to me that it would be up to the police of whatever planet he was on."

Ross Metaxa looked thoughtfully at his brown bottle, shook his head and returned it to its drawer. He looked at a desk watch. "Don't read into the United Planets organization more than there is. It's a fragile institution with practically no independent powers to wield. Every member planet is jealous of its prerogatives, which is understandable. It's no mistake that Articles One and Two are the basic foundation of the Charter. No member planet wants to be interfered with by any other or by United Planets as an organization. They want to be left alone.

"Within our ranks we have planets with every religion known to man throughout the ages. Everything ranging from primitive animism to the most advanced philosophic ethic. We have every political system ever dreamed of, and every socio-economic system. It can all be blamed on the crack-pot manner in which we're colonizing. Any minority, no matter how small-religious, political, racial, or whatever-if it can collect the funds to buy or rent a spacecraft, can dash off on its own, find a new Earth-type planet and set up in business.

"Fine. One of the prime jobs of Section G is to carry out, to enforce, Articles One and Two of the Charter. A planet with Buddhism as its state religion, doesn't want some die-hard Baptist missionary stirring up controversy. A planet with a feudalistic socio-economic systems doesn't want some hot-shot interplanetary businessman coming in with some big deal that would eventually cause the feudalistic nobility to be tossed onto the ash heap. A planet with a dictatorship doesn't want subversives from some democracy trying to undermine their institutions-and vice versa."

"And its our job to enforce all this, eh?" Ronny said.

"That's right," Metaxa told him sourly. "It's not always the nicest job in the system. However, if you believe in United Planets, an organization attempting to co-ordinate in such manner as it can, the efforts of its member planets, for the betterment of all, then you must accept Section G and Interplanetary Security."

Ronny Bronston thought about it.

Metaxa added, "That's why one of the requirements of this job is that you yourself be a citizen of United Planets, rather than of any individual planet, have no religious affiliations, no political beliefs, and no racial prejudices. You've got to be able to stand aloof."

"Yeah," Ronny said thoughtfully.

Ross Metaxa looked at his watch again and sighed wearily. "I'll turn you over to one of my assistants," he said. "I'll see you again, though, before you leave."

"Before I leave?" Ronny said, coming to his feet. "But where do I start looking for this Tommy Paine?"

"How the hell would I know?" Ross Metaxa growled.

* * * * *

In the outer office, Ronny said to the receptionist, "Commissioner Metaxa said for me to get in touch with Sid Jakes."

She said, "I'm Irene Kasansky. Are you with us?"

Ronny said, "I beg your pardon?"

She said impatiently, "Are you going to be with the Section? If you are, I've got to clear you with your old job. You were in statistics over in New Copenhagen, weren't you?"

Somehow it seemed far away now, the job he'd held for more than five years. "Oh, yes," he said. "Yes, Commissioner Metaxa has given me an appointment."

She looked up at him. "Probably to look for Tommy Paine."

He was taken aback. "That's right. How did you know?"

"There was talk. This Section is pretty well integrated." She grimaced, but on her it looked good. "One big happy family. High interdepartmental morale. That sort of jetsam." She flicked some switches. "You'll find Supervisor Jakes through that door, one to your left, two to your right."

He could have asked one *what* to his left and two *what* to his right, but evidently Irene Kasansky thought he had enough information to get him to his destination. She'd gone back to her work.

It was one turn to his left and two turns to his right. The door was lettered simply *Sidney Jakes*. He knocked and a voice shouted happily, "It's open. It's always open."

Supervisor Jakes was as informal as his superior. His attire was on the happy-go-lucky side, more suited for sports wear than a fairly high ranking job in the ultra-staid Octagon.

He couldn't have been much older than Ronny Bronston but he had a nervous vitality about him that would have worn out the other in a few hours. He jumped up and shook hands. "You must be Bronston. Call me Sid." He waved a hand at a typed report he'd been reading. "Now I've seen them all. They've just applied for entry to United Planets. Republic. What a name, eh?"

"What?" Ronny said.

"Sit down, sit down." He rushed Ronny to a chair, saw him seated, returned to the desk and flicked an order box switch. "Irene," he said, "do up a badge for Ronny, will you? You've got his code, haven't you? Good. Send it over. Bronze, of course."

Sid Jakes turned back to Ronny and grinned at him. He motioned to the report again. "What a name for a planet. Republic. Bunch of screw-balls, again. Out in the vicinity of Sirius. Based their system on Plato's *Republic*. Have to go the whole way. Don't even speak Basic. Certainly not. They speak Ancient Greek. That's going to be a neat trick, finding interpreters. How'd you like the Old Man?"

Ronny said, dazed at the conversational barrage, "Old Man? Oh, you mean Commissioner Metaxa."

"Sure, sure," Sid grinned, perching himself on the edge of the desk. "Did he give you that drink of tequila during working hours routine? He'd like to poison every new agent we get. What a character."

The grin was infectious. Ronny said carefully, "Well, I did think his method of hiring a new man was a little-cavalier."

"Cavalier, yet," Sid Jakes chortled. "Look, don't get the Old Man wrong. He knows what he's doing. He always knows what he's doing."

"But he took me on after only two or three minutes conversation."

Jakes cocked his head to one side. "Oh? You think so? When did you first apply for inter-planetary assignment, Ronny?"

"I don't know, about three years ago."

Jakes nodded. "Well, depend on it, you've been under observation for that length of time. At any one period, Section G is investigating possibly a thousand potential agents. We need men but qualifications are high."

He hopped down from his position, sped around to the other side of the desk and lowered himself into his chair. "Don't get the wrong idea, though. You're not in. You're on probation. Whatever the assignment the Old Man gave you, you've got to carry it out successfully before you're full fledged." He flicked the order-box switch and said, "Irene, where the devil's Ronny's badge?"

Ronny Bronston heard the office girl's voice answer snappishly.

"All right, all right," Jakes said. "I love you, too. Send it in when it comes." He turned to Ronny. "What *is* your assignment?"

"He wants me to go looking for some firebrand nicknamed Tommy Paine. I'm supposed to arrest him. The commissioner said you'd give me details."

* * * * *

Sid Jakes' face went serious. He puckered up his lips. "Wow, that'll be a neat trick to pull off," he said. He flicked the order-box switch again. Irene's voice snapped something before he could say anything and Sid Jakes grinned and said, "O.K., O.K., darling, but if this is the way you're going to be I won't marry you. Then what will the children say? Besides, that's not what I called about. Have ballistics do up a model H gun for Ronny, will you? Be sure it's adjusted to his code."

He flicked off the order box and turned back to Ronny. "I understand you're familiar with hand guns. It's in this report on you."

Ronny nodded. He was just beginning to adjust to this free-wheeling character. "What will I need a gun for?"

Jakes laughed. "Heavens to Betsy, you babe in the woods. Do you realize this Tommy Paine character has supposedly stirred up a couple of score wars, revolutions and revolts? Not to speak of having laid in his lap two or three dozen assassinations. He's a quick lad with a gun. A regular Nihilist."

"Nihilist?"

Jakes chuckled. "When you've been in this Section for a while, you'll be familiar with every screwball outfit man has ever dreamed up. The Nihilists were a European group, mostly Russian, back in the Nineteenth Century. They believed that by bumping off a few Grand Dukes and a Czar or so they could force the ruling class to grant reforms. Sometimes they were pretty ingenious. Blew up trains, that sort of thing."

"Look here," Ronny said, "what motivates this Paine fellow? What's he get out of all this trouble he stirs up?"

"Search me. Nobody seems to know. Some think he's a mental case. For one thing, he's not consistent."

"How do you mean?"

"Well, he'll go to one planet and break his back trying to overthrow, say, feudalism. Then, possibly after being successful, he goes to another planet and devotes his energies to establishing the same socio-economic system."

Ronny assimilated that. "You're one of those who believes he exists?"

"Oh, he exists all right, all right," Sid Jakes said happily. "Matter of fact, I almost ran into him a few years ago."

Ronny leaned forward. "I guess I ought to know about it. The more information I have, the better."

"Sure, sure," Jakes said. "This deal of mine was on one of the Aldebaran planets. A bunch of nature boys had settled there."

"Nature boys?"

"Um-m-m. Back to nature. The trouble with the human race is that it's got too far away from nature. So a whole flock of them landed on this planet. They call it Mother, of all things. They landed and set up a primitive society. Absolute stone age. No metals. Lived by the chase and by picking berries, wild fruit, that sort of thing. Not even any agriculture. Wore skins. Bows and arrows were the nearest thing they allowed themselves in the way of mechanical devices."

"Good grief," Ronny said.

"It was a laugh," Jakes told him. "I was assigned there as Section G representative with the UP organization. Picture it. We had to wear skins for clothes. We had to confine ourselves to two or three long houses. Something like the American Iroquois lived in before Columbus. Their society on Mother was based on primitive communism. The clan, the phratry, the tribe. Their religion was mostly a matter of knocking into everybody's head that any progress was taboo. Oh, it was great."

"Well, were they happy?"

"What's happiness? I suppose they were as happy as anybody ever averages. Frankly, I didn't mind the assignment. Lots of fishing, lots of hunting."

Ronny said, "Well, where does Tommy Paine come in?"

"He snuck up on us. Started way back in the boondocks away from any of the larger primitive settlements. Went around putting himself over as a holy man. Cured people of various things from gangrene to eye diseases. Given antibiotics and such, you can imagine how successful he was."

"Well, what harm did he do?"

"I didn't say he did any harm. But in that manner he made himself awfully popular. Then he'd pull some trick like showing them how to smelt iron, and distribute some corn and wheat seed around and plant the idea of agriculture. The local witch doctors would try to give him a hard time, but the people figured he was a holy man."

"Well, what happened finally?" Ronny wasn't following too well.

"Communications being what they were, before he'd been discovered by the central organiza-tion-they had a kind of Council of Tribes which met once a year-he'd planted so many ideas that they couldn't be stopped. The young people'd never go back to flint knives, once introduced to iron. We went looking for friend Tommy Paine, but he got wind of it and took off. We even found where he'd hidden his little space cruiser. Oh, it was Paine, all right, all right."

"But what harm did he do? I don't understand," Ronny scowled.

"He threw the whole shebang on its ear. Last I heard, the planet had broken up into three main camps. They were whaling away at each other like the Assyrians and Egyptians. Iron weapons, chariots, domesticated horses. Agriculture was sweeping the planet. Population was exploding. Men were making slaves out of each other, to put them to work. Oh, it was a mess from the viewpoint of the original nature boys."

A red light flickered on his desk and Sid Jakes opened a delivery drawer and dipped his hand into it. It emerged with a flat wallet. He tossed it to Ronny Bronston.

"Here you are. Your badge."

Ronny opened the wallet and examined it. He'd never seen one before, but for that matter he'd never heard of Section G before that morning. It was a simple enough bronze badge. It said on it, merely, *Ronald Bronston, Section G, Bureau of Investigation, United Planets*.

Sid Jakes explained. "You'll get co-operation with that through the Justice Department any-where you go. We'll brief you further on procedure during indoctrination. You in turn, of course, are to co-operate with any other agent of Section G. You're under orders of anyone with" —his hand snaked into a pocket and emerged with a wallet similar to Ronny's —"a silver badge, carried by a First Grade Agent, or a gold one of Supervisor rank."

Ronny noted that his badge wasn't really bronze. It had a certain sheen, a brightness.

Jakes said, "Here, look at this." He tossed his own badge to the new man. Ronny looked down at it in surprise. The gold had gone dull.

Jakes laughed. "Now give me yours."

Ronny got up and walked over to him and handed it over. As soon as the other man's hand touched it, the bronze lost its sheen.

Jakes handed it back. "See, it's tuned to you alone," he said. "And mine is tuned to my code. Nobody can swipe a Section G badge and impersonate an agent. If anybody ever shows you a badge that doesn't have its sheen, you know he's a fake. Neat trick, eh?"

"Very neat," Ronny admitted. He returned the other's gold badge. "Look, to get back to this Tommy Paine."

But the red light flickered again and Jakes brought forth from the delivery drawer a hand gun complete with shoulder harness. "Nasty weapon," he said. "But we'd better go on down to the armory and show you its workings."

He stood up. "Oh, yes, don't let me forget to give you a communicator. A real gizmo. About as big as a woman's vanity case. Puts you in immediate contact with the nearest Section G office, no matter how near or far away it is. Or, if you wish, in contact with our offices here in the Octagon. Very neat trick."

He led Ronny from his office and down the corridors beyond to an elevator. He said happily, "This is a crazy outfit, this Section G. You'll probably love it. Everybody does."

* * * * *

Ronny learned to love Section G —in moderation.

He was initially taken aback by the existence of the organization at all. He'd known, of course, of the Department of Justice and even of the Bureau of Investigation, but Section G was hush-hush and not even United Planets publications ever mentioned it.

The problems involved in remaining hush-hush weren't as great as all that. The very magnitude of the UP which involved more than two thousand member planets, allowed of departments and bureaus hidden away in the endless stretches of red tape.

In fact, although Ronny Bronston had spent the better part of his life, thus far, in studying for a place in the organization, and then working in the Population Statistics Department for some years, he was only now beginning to get the over-all picture of the workings of the mushrooming, chaotic United Planets organization.

It was Earth's largest industry by far. In fact, for all practical purposes it was her only major industry. Tourism, yes, but even that, in a way, was related to the United Planets organization. Millions of visitors whose ancestors had once emigrated from the mother planet, streamed back in racial nostalgia. Streamed back to see the continents and oceans, the Arctic and the Antarctic, the Amazon River and Mount Everest, the Sahara and New York City, the ruins of Rome and Athens, the Vatican, the Louvre and the Hermitage.

But the populace of Earth, in its hundreds of millions were largely citizens of United Planets and worked in the organization and with its auxiliaries such as the Space Forces.

Section G? To his surprise, Ronny found that Ross Metaxa's small section of the Bureau of Investigation seemed almost as great a secret within the Bureau as it was to the man in the street. At one period, Ronny wondered if it were possible that this was a department which had been lost in the wilderness of boondoggling that goes on in any great bureaucracy. Had Section G been set up a century or so ago and then forgotten by those who had originally thought there was a need for it? In the same way that it is usually more difficult to get a statute off the lawbooks than it was originally to pass it, in the same manner eliminating an office, with its employees can prove more difficult than originally establishing it.

But that wasn't it. In spite of the informality, the unconventional brashness of its personnel on all levels, and the seeming chaos in which its tasks were done, Section G was no make-work project set up to provide juicy jobs for the relatives of high ranking officials. To the contrary, it didn't take long in the Section before anybody with open eyes could see that Ross Metaxa was privy to the decisions made by the upper echelons of UP.

Ronny Bronston came to the conclusion that the appointment he'd received was putting him in a higher bracket of the UP hierarchy than he'd at first imagined.

His indoctrination course was a strain such as he'd never known in school years. Ross Metaxa was evidently of the opinion that a man could assimilate concentrated information at a rate several times faster than any professional educator ever dreamed possible. No threats were made, but Ronny realized that he could be dropped even more quickly than he'd seemed to have been taken on. There were no classes, to either push or retard the rate of study. He worked with a series of tutors, and pushed himself. The tutors were almost invariably Section G agents, temporarily in Greater Washington between assignments, or for briefing on this phase or that of their work.

Even as he studied, Ronny Bronston kept the eventual assignment, at which he was to prove himself, in mind. He made a point of inquiring of each agent he met, about Tommy Paine.

The name was known to all, but no two reacted in the same manner. Several of them even brushed the whole matter aside as pure legend. *Nobody* could accomplish all the trouble that Tommy Paine had supposedly stirred up.

To one of these, Ronny said plaintively, "See here, the Old Man believes in him, Sid Jakes believes in him. My final appointment depends on arresting him. How can I ever secure this job, if I'm chasing a myth?"

The other shrugged. "Don't ask me. I've got my own problems. O.K., now, let's run over this question of Napoleonic law. There are at least two hundred planets that base their legal system on it."

But the majority of his fellow employees in Section G had strong enough opinions on the interplanetary firebrand. Three or four even claimed to have seen him fleetingly, although no two descriptions jibed. That, of course, could be explained. The man could resort to plastic surgery and other disguise.

Theories there were in plenty, some of them going back long years, and some of them pure fable.

* * * * *

"Look," Ronny said in disgust one day after a particularly unbelievable siege with two agents recently returned from a trouble spot in a planetary system that involved three aggressive worlds which revolved about the same sun. "Look, it's impossible for one man to accomplish all this. He's blamed for half the *coups d'états*, revolts and upheavals that have taken place for the past quarter century. It's obvious nonsense. Why, a revolutionist usually spends the greater part of his life toppling a government. Then, once it's toppled, he spends the rest of his life trying to set up a new government-and he's usually unsuccessful."

One of the others was shaking his head negatively. "You don't understand this Tommy Paine's system, Bronston."

"You sure don't," the other agent, a Nigerian, grinned widely. "I've been on planets where he'd operated."

Ronny leaned forward. The three of them were having a beer in a part of the city once called Baltimore. "You have?" he said. "Tell me about it, eh? The more background I get on this guy, the better."

"Sure. And this'll give you an idea of how he operates, how he can get so much trouble done. Well, I was on this planet Goshen, understand? It had kind of a strange history. A bunch of colonists went out there, oh, four or five centuries ago. Pretty healthy expedition, as such outfits go. Bright young people, lots of equipment, lots of know-how and books. Well, through sheer bad luck everything went wrong from the beginning. Everything. Before they got set up at all they had an explosion that killed off all their communications technicians. They lost contact with the outside. O.K. Within a couple of centuries they'd gotten into a state of chattel slavery. Pretty well organized, but static. Kind of an Athenian Democracy on top, a hierarchy, but nineteen people out of twenty were slaves, and I mean real slaves, like animals. They were at this stage when a scout ship from the UP Space Forces discovered them and, of course, they joined up."

"Where does Tommy Paine come in?" Ronny said. He signaled to a waiter for more beer.

"He comes in a few years later. I was the Section G agent on Goshen, understand? No planet was keener about Articles One and Two of the UP Charter. The hierarchy understood well enough that if their people ever came to know about more advanced socio-economic systems it'd be the end of Goshen's Golden Age. So they allowed practically no intercourse. No contact whatsoever between UP personnel and anyone outside the upper class, understand? All right. That's where Tommy Paine came in. It couldn't have taken him more than a couple of months at most."

Ronny Bronston was fascinated. "What'd he do?"

"He introduced the steam engine, and then left."

Ronny was looking at him blankly. "Steam engine?"

"That and the fly shuttle and the spinning jenny," the Nigerian said. "That Goshen hierarchy never knew what hit them."

Ronny was still blank. The waiter came up with the steins of beer, and Ronny took one and drained half of it without taking his eyes from the storyteller.

The other agent took it up. "Don't you see? Their system was based on chattel slavery, hand labor. Given machinery and it collapses. Chattel slavery isn't practical in a mechanized society. Too expensive a labor force, for one thing. Besides, you need an educated man and one with some initiative-qualities that few slaves possess-to run an industrial society."

Ronny finished his beer. "Smart cooky, isn't he?"

"He's smart all right. But I've got a still better example of his fouling up a whole planetary socio-economic system in a matter of weeks. A friend of mine was working on a planet with a highly-developed feudalism. Barons, lords, dukes, counts and no-accounts, all stashed safely away in castles and fortresses up on the top of hills. The serfs down below did all the work in the fields, provided servants, artisans and foot soldiers for the continual fighting that the aristocracy carried on. Very similar to Europe back in the Dark Ages."

"So?" Ronny said. "I'd think that'd be a deal that would take centuries to change."

The Section G agent laughed. "Tommy Paine stayed just long enough to introduce gunpowder. That was the end of those impregnable castles up on the hills."

"What gets me," Ronny said slowly, "is his motivation."

The other two both grunted agreement to that.

* * * * *

Toward the end of his indoctrination studies, Ronny appeared one morning at the Octagon Section G offices and before Irene Kasansky. Watching her fingers fly, listening to her voice rapping and snapping, O.K.-ing and rejecting, he came to the conclusion that automation could go just so far in office work and then you were thrown back on the hands of the efficient secretary. Irene was a one-woman office staff.

She looked up at him. "Hello, Ronny. Thought you'd be off on your assignment by now. Got any clues on Tommy Paine?"

"No," he said. "That's why I'm here. I wanted to see the commissioner."

"About what?" She flicked a switch. When a light flickered on one of her order boxes, she said into it, "No," emphatically, and turned back to him.

"He said he wanted to see me again before I took off."

She fiddled some more, finally said, "All right, Ronny. Tell him he's got time for five minutes with you."

"Five minutes!"

"Then he's got an appointment with the Commissioner of Interplanetary Culture," she said. "You'd better hurry along."

Ronny Bronston retraced the route of his first visit here. How long ago? It already seemed ages since his probationary appointment. Your life changed fast when you were in Section G.

Ross Metaxa's brown bottle, or its twin, was sitting on his desk and he was staring at it glumly. He looked up and scowled.

"Ronald Bronston," Ronny said. "Irene Kasansky told me to say I could have five minutes with you, then you have an appointment with the Commissioner of Interplanetary Culture."

"I remember you," Metaxa said. "Have a drink. Interplanetary Culture, ha! The Xanadu Folk Dance Troupe. They dance nude. They've been touring the whole UP. Roaring success everywhere, obviously. Now they're assigned to Virtue, a planet settled by a bunch of Fundamentalists. They want the troupe to wear Mother Hubbards. The Xanadu outfit is in a tizzy. They've been insulted. They claim they're the most modest members of UP, that nudity has nothing to do with modesty. The government of Virtue said that's fine but they wear Mother Hubbards or they don't dance. Xanadu says it'll withdraw from United Planets."

Ronny Bronston said painfully, "Why not let them?"

Ross Metaxa poured himself a Denebian tequila, offered his subordinate a drink again with a motion of the bottle. Ronny shook his head.

Metaxa said, "If we didn't take steps to soothe these things over, there wouldn't be any United Planets. In any given century every member in the organization threatens to resign at least once. Even Earth. And then what'd happen? You'd have interplanetary war before you knew it. What'd you want, Ronny?"

"I'm about set to take up my search for this Tommy Paine."

"Ah, yes, Tommy Paine. If you catch him, there are a dozen planets where he'd be eligible for the death sentence."

Ronny cleared his throat. "There must be. What I wanted was the file on him, sir."

"File?"

"Yes, sir. I've got to the point where I want to cram up on everything we have on him. So far, all I've got is verbal information from individual agents and from Supervisor Jakes."

"Don't be silly, Ronny. There isn't any file on Tommy Paine."

Ronny just looked at the other.

Ross Metaxa said impatiently, "The very knowledge of the existence of the man is top secret. Isn't that obvious? Suppose some reporter got the story and printed it. If our member planets knew there was such a man and that we haven't been able to scotch him, why they'd drop out of UP so fast the computers couldn't keep up with it. There's not one planet in ten that feels secure enough to lay itself open to subversion. Why some of our planets are so far down the ladder of social evolution they live under primitive tribal society; their leaders, their wise men and witch-doctors, whatever you call them, are scared someone will come along and establish chattel slavery. Those planets that have a system based on slavery are scared to death of developing feudalism, and those that have feudalism are afraid of *creeping capitalism* . Those with an anarchistic basis-and we have several-are afraid of being subverted to statism, and those who have a highly developed government are afraid of anarchism. The socio-economic systems based on private ownership of property hate the very idea of socialism or communism, and vice versa, and those planets with state capitalism hate them both."

He glared at Ronny. "What do you think the purpose of this Section is, Bronston? Our job is to keep our member planets from being afraid of each other. If they found that Tommy Paine and his group, if he's got a group, were buzzing through the system subverting everything they can foul up, they'd drop out of UP and set up quarantines that a space mite couldn't get through. No sir, there is no file on Tommy Paine and there never will be. And if any news of him spreads to the outside, this Section will emphatically deny he exists. I hope that's clear."

"Well, yes sir," Ronny said. The commissioner had been all but roaring toward the end.

The order box clicked on Ross Metaxa's desk and he said loudly, "What?"

"Don't yell at me," Irene snapped back. "Ronny's five minutes are up. You've got an appointment. I'm getting tired of this job. It's a mad-house. I'm going to quit and get a job with Interplanetary Finance."

"Oh, yeah." Ross snarled back. "That's what you think. I've taken measures. Top security. I've warned off every Commissioner in UP. You can't get away from me until you reach retirement age. Although I don't know why I care. I hate nasty tempered women."

"Huh!" she snorted and clicked off.

"There's a woman for you," Ross Metaxa growled at Ronny. "It's too bad she's indispensable. I'd love to fire her. Look, you go in and see Sid Jakes. Seems to me he said something about Tommy Paine this morning. Maybe it's a lead." He came to his feet. "So long and good luck, Ronny. I feel optimistic about you. I think you'll get this Paine troublemaker."

Which was more than Ronny Bronston thought.

Sid Jakes already had a visitor in his office, which didn't prevent him from yelling, "It's open," when Ronny Bronston knocked.

He bounced from his chair, came around the desk and shook hands enthusiastically. "Ronny!" he said, his tone implying they were favorite brothers for long years parted. "You're just in time."

Ronny took in the office's other occupant appreciatively. She was a small girl, almost tiny. He estimated her to be at least half Chinese, or maybe Indo-Chinese, the rest probably European or North American.

She evidently favored her Asiatic blood, her dress was traditional Chinese, slit almost to the thigh Shanghai style.

Sid Jakes said, "Tog Lee Chang Chu-Ronny Bronston. You'll be working together. Bloodhounding old Tommy Paine. A neat trick if you can pull it off. Well, are you all set to go?"

Ronny mumbled something to the girl in the way of amenity, then looked back at the supervisor. "Working together?" he said.

"That's right. Lucky you, eh?"

Tog Lee Chang Chu said demurely, "Possibly Mr. Bronston objects to having a female assistant."

Sid Jakes snorted, and hurried around his desk to resume his seat. "Does he look crazy? Who'd object to having a cutey like you around day in and day out? Call him Ronny. Might as well get used to it. Two of you'll be closer than man and wife."

"Assistant?" Ronny said, bewildered. "What do I need an assistant for?" He turned his eyes to the girl. "No reflection on you, Miss ... ah, Tog."

Sid Jakes laughed easily. "Section G operatives always work in pairs, Ronny. Especially new agents. The advantages will come home to you as you go along. Look on Tog Lee Chang Chu as a secretary, a man Friday. This isn't her first assignment, of course. You'll find her invaluable."

The supervisor plucked a card from an order box. "Now here's the dope. Can you leave within four hours? There's a UP Space Forces cruiser going to Merlini, they can drop you off at New Delos. Fastest way you could possibly get there. The cruiser takes off from Neuve Albuquerque in, let's see, three hours and forty-five minutes."

"New Delos?" Ronny said, taking his eyes from the girl and trying to catch up with the grasshopper-like conversation of his superior.

"New Delos it is," Jakes said happily. "With luck, you might catch him before he can get off the planet." He chuckled at the other's expression. "Look alive, Ronny! The quarry is flushed and on the run. Tommy Paine's just assassinated the Immortal God-King of New Delos. A neat trick, eh?"

* * * * *

The following hours were chaotic. There was no indication of how long a period he'd be gone. For all he knew, it might be years. For that matter, he might never return to Earth. This Ronny

Bronston had realized before he ever applied for an interplanetary appointment. Mankind was exploding through this spiral arm of the galaxy. There was a racial enthusiasm about it all. Man's destiny lay out in the stars, only a laggard stayed home of his own accord. It was the ambition of every youth to join the snowballing avalanche of man into the neighboring stars.

It took absolute severity by Earth authorities to prevent the depopulation of the planet. But someone had to stay to administer the ever more complicated racial destiny. Earth became a clearing house for a thousand cultures, attempting, with only moderate success, to co-ordinate her widely spreading children. She couldn't afford to let her best seed depart. Few there were, any more, allowed to emigrate from Earth. New colonies drew their immigrants from older ones.

Lucky was the Earthling able to find service in interplanetary affairs, in any of the thousands of tasks that involved journey between member planets of UP. Possibly one hundredth of the population at one time or another, and for varying lengths of time, managed it.

Ronny Bronston was lucky and knew it. The thing now was to pull off this assignment and cinch the appointment for good.

He packed in a swirl of confusion. He phoned a relative who lived in the part of town once known as Richmond, explained the situation and asked that the other store his things and dispose of the apartment he'd been occupying.

Luckily, the roof of his apartment building was a copter-cab pickup point and he was able to hustle over to the shuttleport in a matter of a few minutes.

He banged into the reservations office, hurried up to one of the windows and said into the screen, "I've got to get to Neuve Albuquerque immediately."

The expressionless voice said, "The next rocket leaves at sixteen hours."

"Sixteen hours! I've got to be at the spaceport by that time!"

The voice said dispassionately, "We are sorry."

The bottom fell out of everything. Ronny said, desperately, "Look, if I miss my ship in Neuve Albuquerque, what is the next spaceliner leaving from there for New Delos?"

"A moment, citizen." There was an agonized wait, and then the voice said, "There is a liner leaving for New Delos on the 14th of next month. It arrives in New Delos on the 31st, Basic Earth calendar."

The 31st! Tommy Paine could be halfway across the galaxy by that time.

A gentle voice next to him said, "Could I help, Ronny?"

He looked around at her. "Evidently, nobody can," he said disgustedly. "There's no way of getting to Neuve Albuquerque in time to get that cruiser to New Delos."

Tog Lee Chang Chu fished in her bag and came up with a wallet similar to the one in which Ronny carried his Section G badge. She held it up to the screen. "Bureau of Investigation, Section G," she said calmly. "It will be necessary that Agent Bronston and myself be in Neuve Albuquerque within the hour."

The metallic voice said, "Of course. Proceed to your right and through Corridor K to Exit Four. Your rocket will be there. Identify yourself to Lieutenant Economou who will be at the desk at Exit Four."

Tog turned to Ronny Bronston. "Shall we go?" she said demurely.

He cleared his throat, feeling foolish. "Thanks, Tog," he said.

"Not at all, Ronny. Why, this is my job."

Was there the faintest of sarcasm in her voice? It hadn't been more than a couple of hours ago that he had been hinting rather heavily to Sid Jakes that he needed no assistance.

She even knew the layout of the West Greater Washington shuttleport. Her small body swiveled through the hurrying passengers, her small feet a-twinkle, as she led him to and down Corridor K and then to the desk at Exit Four.

Ronny anticipated her here. He flashed his own badge at the chair-borne Space Forces lieutenant there.

"Lieutenant Economou?" he said. "Ronald Bronston, of the Bureau of Investigation, Section G. We've got to get to Neuve Albuquerque soonest."

The lieutenant, only mildly impressed, said, "We can have you in the air in ten minutes, citizen. Just a moment and I'll guide you myself."

* * * * *

In the rocket, Ronny had time to appraise her at greater length. She was a delicately pretty thing, although her expression was inclined to the over-serious. There was only a touch of the Mongolian fold at the corner of her eyes. On her it looked unusually good. Her complexion was that which only the blend of Chinese and Caucasian can give. Her figure, thanks to her European blood, was fuller than Eastern Asia usually boasts; tiny, but full.

Let's admit it, he decided. My assistant is the cutest trick this side of a Tri-Di movie queen, and we're going to be thrown in the closest of juxtaposition for an indefinite time. This comes under the head of work?

He said, "Look here, Tog, you were with Sid Jakes longer than I was. What's the full story?"

She folded her slim hands in her lap, looking like a schoolgirl about to recite. "Do you know anything about the socio-economic system on New Delos?"

"Well, no," he admitted.

She said severely, "I'd think that they would have given you more background before an assignment of this type."

Ronny said impatiently, "In the past three months I've been filled in on the economic systems, the religious beliefs, the political forms, of a thousand planets. I just happened to miss New Delos."

Her mouth expressed disapproval by rucking down on the sides, which was all very attractive but also irritating. She said, "There are two thousand, four hundred and thirty-six member planets in the UP, I'd think an agent of Section G would be up on the basic situation on each."

He had her there. He said snidely, "Hate to contradict you, Tog, but the number is two thousand, four hundred and thirty-four."

"Then," she nodded agreeably, "membership has changed since this morning when Menalaus and Aldebaran Three were admitted. Have two planets dropped out?"

"Look," he said, "let's stop bickering. What's the word on New Delos?"

"Did you ever read Frazer's 'Golden Bough'?" she said.

"No."

"You should. At any rate, New Delos is a theocracy. A priesthood elite rules it. A God-King, who is immortal, holds absolute authority. The strongest of superstition plus an efficient inquisition, keeps the people under control."

"Sounds terrible," Ronny growled.

"Why? Possibly the government is extremely efficient and under it the planet progressing at a rate in advance of UP averages."

He stared at her in surprise.

She said, "Would you rather be ruled by the personal, arbitrary whims of supremely wise men, or by laws formulated by a mob?"

It stopped him momentarily. In all his adult years, he couldn't remember ever meeting an intelligent, educated person who had been opposed to the democratic theory.

"Wait a minute, now," he said. "Who decides that they're supremely wise men who are doing this arbitrary ruling? Let any group come to power, by whatever means, and they'll soon tell you they're an elite. But let's get back to New Delos, from what you've said so far, the people are held in a condition of slavery."

"What's wrong with slavery?" Tog said mildly.

He all but glared at her. "Are you kidding?"

"I seldom jest," Tog said primly. "Under the proper conditions, slavery can be the most suitable system for a people."

"Under *what* conditions!"

"Have you forgotten your Earth history to the point where Egypt, Greece and Rome mean nothing to you? Man made some of his outstanding progress under slavery. And do you contend that man's lot is necessarily miserable given slavery? As far back as Aesop we know of slaves who have reached the heights in their society. Slaves sometimes could and did become the virtual rulers in ancient countries." She shrugged prettily. "The prejudices which you hold today, on Earth, do not necessarily apply to all time, nor to all places."

He said, impatiently, "Look, Tog, we can go into this further, later. Let's get back to New Delos. What happened?"

Tog said, "The very foundation of their theocracy is the belief on the part of the populace that the God-King is immortal. No man conspires against his Deity. Supervisor Jakes informed me that it is understood by UP Intelligence, that about once every twenty years the priesthood secretly puts in a new God-King. Plastic surgery would guarantee facial resemblance, and, of course, the rank and file citizen would probably never be allowed close enough to discover that their God-King seemed different every couple of decades. At any rate, it's been working for some time."

"And there's been no revolt against this religious aristocracy?"

She shook her head. "Evidently not. It takes a brave man to revolt against both his king and his God at the same time."

"But what happened now?" Ronny pursued.

"Evidently, right in the midst of a particularly important religious ceremony, with practically the whole planet watching on TV, the God-King was killed with a bomb. No doubt about it, definitely killed. There are going to be a lot of people on New Delos wondering how it can be that an immortal God-King can die."

"And Sid thinks it's Tommy Paine's work?"

She shifted dainty shoulders in a shrug. "It's the sort of thing he does. I suppose we'll learn when we get there."

* * * * *

Even on the fast Space Forces cruiser, the trip was going to take a week, and there was precious little Ronny Bronston could do until arrival. He spent most of his time reading up on New Delos and the several other planets in the UP organization which had fairly similar regimes. More than a few theocracies had come and gone during the history of man's development into the stars.

He also spent considerable time playing Battle Chess or talking with Tog and with the ship's officers.

These latter were a dedicated group, high in morale, enthusiastic about their work which evidently involved the combined duties of a Navy, a Coast Guard, and a Coast and Geodetic Survey system, if we use the ocean going services of an earlier age for analogy.

They all had the dream. The enthusiasm of men participating in a race's expansion to glory. There was the feeling, even stronger here in space than back on Earth, of man's destiny being fulfilled, that humanity had finally emerged from its infancy, that the fledgling had finally found its wings and got off the ground.

After one of his studying binges, Ronny Bronston had spent an hour or so once with the captain of the craft, while that officer stood an easy watch on the ship's bridge. There was little enough to do in space, practically nothing, but there was always an officer on watch.

They leaned back in the acceleration chairs before the ship's controls and Ronny listened to the other's space lore. Stories of far planets, as yet untouched. Stories of planets that had seemingly been suitable for colonization, but had proved disastrous for man, for this reason or that.

Ronny said, "And never in all this time have we run into a life form that has proved intelligent?"

Captain Woiski said, "No. Not that I know of. There was an animal on Shangri-La of about the mental level of the chimpanzee. So far as I know, that's the nearest to it."

"Shangri-La?" Ronny said. "That's a new one."

There was an affectionate gleam in the captain's eye. "Yes," he said. "If and when I retire, I think that'd be the planet of my choice, if I could get permission to leave Earth, of course."

Ronny scowled in attempted memory. "Now that you mention it, I think I did see it listed the other day among planets with a theocratic government."

The captain grunted protest. "If you're comparing it to this New Delos you're going to, you're wrong. There can be theocracy and theocracy, I suppose. Actually, I imagine Shangri-La has the most, well *gentle* government in the system."

Ronny was interested. His recent studies hadn't led him to much respect for a priesthood in political power. "What's the particular feature that's seemed to have gained your regard?"

"Moderation," Woiski chuckled. "They carry it almost to the point of immoderation. But not quite. Briefly, it works something like this. They have a limited number of monks —I suppose you'd call them-who spend their time at whatever moves them. At the arts, at scientific research, at religious contemplation-any religion will do-as students of anything and everything, and at the governing of Shangri-La. They make a point of enjoying the luxuries in moderation and aren't a severe drain on the rank and file citizens of the planet."

Ronny said, "I have a growing distrust of hierarchies. Who decides who is to become a monk and who remain a member of the rank and file?"

The captain said, "A series of the best tests they can devise to determine a person's intelligence and aptitudes. From earliest youth, the whole populace is checked and rechecked. At the age of thirty, when it is considered that a person has become adult and has finished his basic education, a limited number are offered monkhood. Not all want it."

Ronny thought about it. "Why not? What are the shortcomings?"

The captain shrugged. "Responsibility, I suppose."

"The monks aren't allowed sex, booze, that sort of thing, I imagine."

"Good heavens, why not? In moderation, of course."

"And they live on a higher scale?"

"No, no, not at all. Don't misunderstand. The planet is a prosperous one. Exceedingly prosperous. There is everything needed for comfortable existence for everyone. Shangri-La is one planet where the pursuit of happiness is pursuable by all." Captain Woiski chuckled again.

Ronny said, "It sounds good enough, although I'm leery of benevolent dictatorships. The trouble with them is that it's up to the dictators to decide what's benevolent. And almost always, nepotism rears its head, favoritism of one sort or another. How long will it be before one of your moderate monks decides he'll moderately tinker with the tests, or whatever, just to be sure his favorite nephew makes the grade? A high I.Q. is no guarantee of integrity."

The captain didn't disagree. "That's always possible, I suppose. One guard against it, in this case, is the matter of motive. The *privilege* of being a monk isn't as great as all that. Materially, you aren't particularly better off than any one else. You have more leisure, that's true, but actually most of them are so caught up in their studies or research that they put in more hours of endeavor than does the farmer or industrial worker on Shangri-La."

"Well," Ronny said, "let's just hope that Tommy Paine never hears of this place."

"Who?" the captain said.

Ronny Bronston reversed his engines. "Oh, nobody important. A guy I know of."

Captain Woiski scowled. "Seems to me I've heard the name."

At first Ronny leaned forward with quick interest. Perhaps the cruiser's skipper had a lead. But, no, he sank back into his chair. That name was strictly a Section G pseudonym. No one used it outside the department, and he'd already said too much by using the term at all.

Ronny said idly, "Probably two different people. I think I'll go on back and see how Tog is doing."

* * * * *

Tog was at her communicator when he entered the tiny ship's lounge. Ronny could see in the brilliant little screen of the compact device, the grinning face of Sid Jakes. Tog looked up at Ronny and smiled, then clicked the device off.

"What's new?" Ronny said.

She moved graceful shoulders. "I just called Supervisor Jakes. Evidently there's complete confusion on New Delos. Mobs are storming the temples. In the capital the priests tried to present a new God-King and he was laughed out of town."

Ronny snorted cynically. "Sounds good to me. The more I read about New Delos and its God-King and his priesthood, the more I think the best thing that ever happened to the planet was this showing them up."

Tog looked at him, the sides of her mouth tucking down as usual when she was going to contradict something he said. "It sounds bad to me," she said. "Tommy Paine's work is done. He'll be off to some other place and we won't get there in time to snare him."

Ronny considered that. It was probably true. "I wonder," he said slowly, "if it's possible for us to get a list of all ships that have blasted off since the assassination, all ships and their destination from New Delos."

The idea grew in him. "Look! It's possible that a dictatorial government such as theirs would immediately quarantine every spaceport on the planet."

Tog said, "There's only one spaceport on New Delos. The priesthood didn't encourage trade or even communication with the outside. Didn't want its people contaminated."

"Holy smokes!" Ronny blurted. "It's possible that Tommy Paine's on that planet and can't get off. Look, Tog, see if you can raise the Section G representative on New Delos and —"

Tog said demurely, "I already have taken that step, Ronny, knowing that you'd want me to. Agent Mouley Hassan has promised to get the name and destination of every passenger that leaves New Delos."

Ronny sat down at a table and dialed himself a mug of stout. "Drink?" he said to Tog. "Possibly we've got something to celebrate."

She shook her head disapprovingly. "I don't use depressants."

There was nothing more to be discussed about New Delos, they simply would have to wait until their arrival. Ronny switched subjects. "Ever hear of the planet Shangri-La?" he asked her. He took a sip of his brew.

"Of course," she said. "A rather small planet, Earth type within four degrees. Noted for its near perfect climate and its scenic beauty."

"Captain was talking about it," Ronny said. "Sounds like a regular paradise."

Tog made a negative sound.

"Well, what's wrong with Shangri-La?" Ronny said impatiently.

"Static," she said briefly.

He looked at her. "It sounds to me as though it's developed a near perfect socio-economic system. What do you mean, static?"

"No push, no drive," Tog said definitely. "Everyone-what is the old term? —everyone has it made. The place is stagnating. I wouldn't be surprised to see Tommy Paine show up there sooner or later."

Ronny said, "Look, since we've known each other, have I ever said anything you agree with?"

Tog raised her delicate eyebrows. "Why, Ronny. You know perfectly well we both agreed that the eggs for breakfast were quite inedible."

Ronny came to his feet again. Considering her size, she certainly was an irritating baggage. "I think I'll go to my room and see if I can get any inspirations on tracking down our quarry."

"Good night, Ronny," she said demurely.

* * * * *

They ran into a minor difficulty upon arrival at New Delos. The captain called both Ronny Bronston and Tog Lee Chang Chu to the bridge.

He nodded in the direction of the communications screen. A bald headed, robed character—obviously a priest-scowled at them.

Captain Woiski said, "The Sub-Bishop informs me that the provisional government has ruled that any spacecraft landing on New Delos cannot take off again without permission and that every individual who lands, even United Planets personnel, will need an exit visa before being allowed to depart."

Ronny said, "Then you can't land?"

The captain said reasonably, "My destination is Merlini. I've gone out of my way slightly to drop you off here. But I can't afford to take the chance of having my ship tied up for what might be an indefinite period. Evidently, there's considerably civil disorder down there."

From the screen the priest snapped, "That is an inaccurate manner of describing the situation."

"Sorry," the captain said dryly.

Ronny Bronston said desperately, "But, captain, Miss Tog and I simply have to land." He reached for his badge. "High priority, Bureau of Investigation."

The captain shrugged his hefty shoulders. "Sorry, I have no instructions that allow me to risk tying up my ship. Here's a possibility. Can you pilot a landing craft? I could spare you one, then you and your assistant would be the only ones involved. You could turn it over to whatever Space Forces base we have here."

Ronny said miserably, "No. I'm not a space pilot."

"I am," Tog said softly. "The idea sounds excellent."

"We shall expect you," the Sub-Bishop said. The screen went blank.

Tog Lee Chang Chu piloted a landing craft with the same verve that she seemed to be able to handle any other responsibility. As he sat in the seat next to her, Ronny Bronston took in her practiced flicking of the controls from the side of his eyes. He wondered vaguely at the efficiency of such Section G officials as Metaxa and Jakes that they would assign an unknown quality such as himself to a task as important as running down Tommy Paine, and then as an assistant provide him with an experienced operative such as Tog. The bureaucratic mind can be a dilly, he decided. Was the fact that she was a rather delicately constructed girl a factor? He felt the weight of the Model-H gun nestled under his left armpit. Perhaps in the clutch Section G preferred men as agents.

They swooped into a landing that brought them as close to the control tower as was practical. In a matter of moments there was a guard of twenty or more sloppily uniformed men about their small craft.

Tog made a move. "Welcoming committee," she said.

They climbed out the circular port, and flashed their United Planets Bu-reau of Investigation badges to the

They climbed out the circular port, and flashed their United Planets Bureau of Investigation badges to the youngish looking soldier who seemed in command. He was indecisive.

"United Planets?" he said. "All I know is I'm supposed to arrest anybody landing."

Ronny snapped, "We're to be taken immediately to United Planets headquarters."

"Well, I don't know about that. I don't take orders from foreigners."

One of his men was nervously fingering the trigger of his submachine gun.

Ronny's mouth went dry. He had the feeling of being high, high on a rock face, inadequately belayed from above.

Tog said smoothly, "But, major, I'm sure whoever issued your orders had no expectation of a special delegation from the United Planets coming to congratulate your new authorities on their success. Of course, it's unknown to arrest a delegation from United Planets."

"It is?" he frowned at her. "I mean, you are?"

"Yes," Tog said sweetly.

Ronny took the hint. "Where can we find a vehicle, major, to get us to the capital and to United Planets headquarters? Evidently we arrived before we were expected. There should have been a big welcoming committee here."

"Oh," the obviously recently promoted lad said hesitantly. "Well, I suppose we can make arrangements. This way please." He grinned at Tog as they walked toward the administration building. "Do all girls dress like you on Earth?"

"Well, no," she said demurely.

"That's too bad," he said gallantly.

"Why, major!" Tog said, keeping her eyes on the tarmac.

At the administration building there was little of order, but eventually they managed to arrange for their transportation. Luckily, they were supplied with a chauffeur driven helio-car.

Luckily, because without the chauffeur to help them run the gauntlet they would have been held up by parades, demonstrations and monstrous street meetings a dozen times before they ever reached their destination. Twice, Ronny stopped short of drawing his gun only by a fraction when half drunken demonstrators stopped them.

The driver, a wispy, sad looking type, shook his head. "There's no going back now," he told them over his shoulder. "No going back. Last week I was all with the rest, I never did believe David the One was really Immortal. But you was just used to the idea, see? It'd always been that way, with the priests running everything and we was used to it. Now I wish we was still that way. At least you knew how you stood, see? Now, what's going to happen?"

"That's an interesting question," Tog said politely.

Ronny said, "Possibly you'll have the chance to build a better world, now."

The driver shot a contemptuous look over his shoulder. "Better world? What do I want with a better world? I just don't want to be bothered. I've been getting my three squares a day, got a nice little flat for my family. How do I know it's not going to be a worse world?"

"That's always a possibility," Tog told him. "Do most people seem to feel the same?"

"Practically everybody I know does," he said glumly. "But the fat's in the fire now. The priests are trying to hold on but their government is falling apart all over the place."

"Well," Ronny said, "at least you can figure just about anything in the way of a new government will be better than one based on superstition and inquisition. It couldn't get worse."

"Things can always get worse," the other contradicted him sadly.

* * * * *

They left the cab before an impressively tall, many windowed building in city center. As they mounted the steps, Ronny frowned at her. "You seemed to be encouraging that man in his pessimism. So far as I can see, the best thing that ever happened to this planet was toppling that phony priesthood."

"Perhaps," she said agreeably. "However, the man's mind was an ossified one. A surprisingly large percentage of people have them, especially when it comes to institutions such as religion and government. We weren't going to be able to teach him anything, but it was possible to learn from him."

Ronny grunted his disgust. "What could we possibly learn from him?"

Tog said mildly, "We could learn what people of the street were thinking. It might give us some ideas about what direction the new government will take."

They approached the portals of the building and were halted by an armed Space Forces guard of half a dozen men. Their sergeant saluted, taking in their obvious other-planet clothing.

"Identifications, please," he said briskly.

They showed their badges and were passed on through. Ronny said to him, "Much trouble, sergeant?"

The other shrugged. "No. Just precautions, sir. We've been here only three or four weeks. Civil disturbance. We're used to it. Were over on Montezuma two basic months ago. Now there was *real* trouble. Had to shoot our way out."

Tog called, "Coming Ronny? I have this elevator waiting."

He followed her, scowling. An idea was trying to work its way through. Somehow he missed getting it.

Headquarters of the Department of Justice were on the eighth floor. A receptionist clerk led them through three or four doors to the single office which housed Section G.

A red eyed, exhausted agent looked up from the sole desk and snarled a question at them. Ronny didn't get it, but Tog said mildly, "Probationary Agent Ronald Bronston and Tog Lee Chang Chu. On special assignment." She flicked open her badge so that the other could see it.

His manner changed. "Sorry," he said, getting up to shake hands. "I'm Mouley Hassan, in charge of Section G on New Delos. We've just had a crisis here, as you can imagine. The worst of it's now over." He added sourly, "I hope. All my assistants have already taken off for Avalon." He was a short statured, dark complected man, his features betraying his Semitic background.

Ronny shook hands with him and said, "Sorry to bother you at a time like this."

They found chairs and Mouley Hassan flicked a key on his order box and said to them, "How about a drink? They make a wonderful sparkling wine on this planet. Trust any theocracy to have top potables."

Ronny accepted the offer, Tog refused it politely. She sat demurely, her hands in her lap.

Mouley Hassan ran a weary hand through already mussed hair. "What's this special assignment you're on?"

Ronny said, "Commissioner Metaxa has sent me looking for Tommy Paine."

"Tommy Paine!" the other blurted. "At a time like this, when I haven't had three nights' sleep in the last three basic weeks, you come around looking for Tommy Paine?"

Ronny was taken aback. "Sid Jakes seemed to think this might be one of Paine's jobs."

Tog said mildly, "What better place to look for Tommy Paine, than in a situation like this, Agent Hassan?" Her eyebrows went up. "Or don't you think the quest for Paine is an important one?"

The other subsided somewhat. "I suppose you're right," he said. "I'm deathly tired. Do whatever you want. But don't expect much from me."

Tog said, just a trifle tartly, Ronny thought, "We'll have to call on you, as usual, Agent Hassan. There's probably no single job in Section G more important than the pursuit of Tommy Paine."

"All right, all right," Mouley Hassan admitted. "I'll co-operate. How long have you been away from Earth?" he said to Ronny.

"About one basic week."

"Oh," he grunted. "This is your first stop, eh? Well, I don't envy you your job." He brought a cool bottle from a delivery drawer in the desk along with two glasses. "Here's the wine."

Ronny leaned forward to accept the glass. "This situation here," he said, "do you think it can be laid to Paine?"

Mouley Hassan shrugged wearily. "I don't know."

Ronny sipped the drink, looking at the tired agent over the glass rim. "From what we understand, check has been kept on all persons leaving the planet since the bombing."

"Check is right. There's only one ship that took off and it carried nobody except my assistants. If you ask me, I still needed them, but some brass hat back on Earth decided they were more necessary over on Avalon." He was disgusted.

Ronny put the glass down. "You mean only one ship's left this planet since the God-King was killed?"

"That's right. It was like pulling teeth to get the visas."

"How many men aboard?"

Mouley Hassan looked at him speculatively. "Four-man crew and six Section G operatives."

Tog said brightly, "Why, that means, then, that either Tommy Paine is still on this planet, or he's one of the passengers or crew members of that ship." She added, "That is, of course, unless he had a private craft, hidden away somewhere."

Ronny slumped back into his chair as some of the ramifications came home to him. "If it was Tommy Paine at all," he said.

Mouley Hassan nodded. "That's always a point." He finished his glass and looked pleadingly at Tog. "Look, I have work. If I can finish some of it, I might have time for some sleep. Couldn't we postpone the search for Tommy Paine."

Tog said nothing to him.

Ronny came to his feet. "We'll get along. A couple of ideas occur to me. I'll check with you later."

"Fine," the agent said. He shook hands with them again. He said, somehow more to Tog than to Ronny, "I know how important your job is. It's just that I've been pushed to the point where I can't operate efficiently."

She smiled her understanding, gave him her small, delicate hand.

In the elevator, Ronny said to her, "Why should this sort of thing particularly affect Section G?"

Tog said, "It's times like this that planets drop out of the UP. Or, possibly, get into the hands of some jingoistic military group and start off halfcocked to provoke a war with some other planet, or to missionarize or propagandize it." She thought about it a moment. "A new revolution, in government or religion, seems almost invariably to want to spread the light. An absolute compulsion to bring to others the new truths that they've found." She added, her voice holding a trace of mockery, "Usually the new truths are rather hoary ones, and there are few interested in hearing them."

* * * * *

They spent their first day in getting accommodations in a centrally located hotel, in making arrangements, through the Department of Justice, for the local means of exchange-it turned out to be coinage, based on gold-and getting the feel of their surroundings.

Evidently Delos, the capital city of the planet New Delos, was but slowly emerging from the chaos that had taken over on the assassination. A provisional government, composed of representatives of half a dozen different organizations which had sprung up like mushrooms following the collapse of the regime, had assumed power. Elections had been promised and were to be brought off when arrangements could be made.

Meanwhile, the actual government was still largely in the hands of the lower echelons of the priesthood. A nervous priesthood it was, seemingly desirous of getting out from under while the going was good, afraid of being held responsible for former excesses.

Ronny Bronston, high hopes still in his head, looked up the Sub-Bishop who had given them landing orders while they were still aboard the Space Forces cruiser. Tog was off making arrangements for various details involved in their being in Delos in its time of crisis.

A dozen times, on his way over to keep his appointment with the official, Ronny had to step into doorways, or in other wise make himself inconspicuous. Gangs of demonstrators roamed the street, some of them drunken, looking for trouble, and scornful of police or the military. Twice, when it looked as though he might be roughed up, Ronny drew his gun and held it in open sight, ready for use, but not threateningly. The demonstrators made off.

His throat was dry by the time he reached his destination. The life of a Section G agent, on interplanetary assignment, had its drawbacks.

The Sub-Bishop had formerly been in charge of Interplanetary Communications which involved commerce as well as intercourse with United Planets. It must have been an ultra-responsible position only a month ago. Now his offices were all but deserted.

He looked at Ronny's badge, only vaguely interested. "Section G of the Bureau of Investigation," he said. "I don't believe I am aware of your responsibilities. However," he nodded with sour courtesy, "please be seated. You must forgive my lack of ability to offer refreshment. Isn't there an old tradition about rats deserting a sinking ship? I am afraid my former assistants had rodentlike instincts."

Ronny said, "Section G deals with Interplanetary Security, sir —"

"I am addressed as Holiness," the other said.

Ronny looked at him. "Sorry," he said. "I am a citizen of the United Planets, not any one planet, even Earth. UP citizens have complete religious freedom. In my case I am unaffiliated with any church."

The Sub-Bishop let it pass. He said sourly, "I am afraid that even here on New Delos, I am seldom honoured by my title any more. Go on, you say you deal with Interplanetary Security."

"That's correct. In cases like this we're interested in checking to see if there is any possibility that citizens of planets other than New Delos are involved in your internal affairs."

The other's eyes were suddenly slits. He said, heavily, "You suspect that David the One was assassinated by an alien?"

Ronny had to tread carefully here. "I make no such suggestion. I am merely here to check on the possibility. If such was the case, my duty would be to arrest the man, or men."

"If we got hold of him, you'd have small chance of asserting your authority," the priest growled. "What did you want to know?"

"I understand that no interplanetary craft have left New Delos since the assassination."

"None except a United Planets ship which was carefully inspected."

Ronny said tightly, "But what facilities do you have to check on secret spaceports, possibly located in some remote desert or mountain area?"

The New Delian laughed sourly. "There is no other planet in all the United Planets with our degree of security. We even imported the most recent developments in artificial satellites equipped with the most delicate of detection devices. I assure you, it is utterly impossible for a spacecraft to land or take off from New Delos without our knowledge."

Ronny Bronston's eyes lit with excitement. "These security measures of yours. To what extent do you keep under observation all aliens on the planet?"

The priest's chuckle had a nasty quality. "You are quite ignorant of our institutions, evidently. Every person on New Delos, in every way of life, was under constant survey from the cradle to the grave. Aliens were highly discouraged. When they appeared on New Delos at all, they were restricted in their movements to this, our capital city."

Ronny let air whistle from his lungs. "Then," he said triumphantly, "if any alien had anything to do with this, he is still on the planet. Can you get me a list of all aliens?"

The other laughed again, still sourly. "But there are none. None except you employees of United Planets. I'm afraid you're on a wild-goose chase."

Ronny stared at him blankly. "But commercial representatives, cultural exchange —"

The priest said flatly, "No. None at all. All commerce was handled through UP. We encouraged no cultural exchanges. We wished to keep our people uncorrupted. United Planets alone had the right to land on our one spaceport."

The Section G agent came to his feet. This was much simpler than he could ever have hoped for. He thanked the other, but avoided the necessity of shaking hands, and left.

* * * * *

He found a helio-cab and dialed it to the UP building, finding strange the necessity of slipping coins into the vehicle's slots until the correct amount for his destination had been deposited. Coinage was no longer in use on Earth.

At the UP building he retraced his steps of the day before to the single office of Section G.

To his surprise, not only Mouley Hassan was there, but Tog as well. Hassan had evidently had at least a few hours of sleep. He was in better shape.

They exchanged the usual amenities and took their chairs again.

Hassan said, "We were just gossiping. It's been years since I've been in Greater Washington. Lee Chang tells me that Sid Jakes is now a Supervisor. I worked with him for a while, when I first joined Section G. How about a glass of wine?"

Ronny said, "Look. If Tommy Paine was connected with this, and it's almost positive he was, we've got him."

The others looked at him.

"You've evidently been busy," Tog said mildly.

He turned to her. "He's trapped, Tog! He can't get off the planet."

Mouley Hassan rubbed a hand through his hair. "It'd be hard, all right. They've got the people under rein here such as you've never seen before. Or they did until this blew up."

Ronny sketched the situation to Tog, winding up with, "The only thing that makes sense is that it's a Tommy Paine job. The local citizens would never have been able to get their hands on such a bomb, or been able to have made the arrangements for its delivery. They're under too much surveillance."

Tog said thoughtfully, "but how did he escape all this surveillance?"

"Don't you understand? He's working here, in this building, as an employee of UP. There is no other alternative."

They stared at him.

"I think perhaps you're right," Tog said finally.

Ronny turned to Mouley Hassan. "Can you get a list of all UP employees?"

"Of course." He flicked his order box, barked a command into it.

Ronny said, "It's going to be a matter of eliminating the impossible. For instance, what is the earliest known case of Tommy Paine's activity?"

Tog thought back. "So far as we know definitely, about twenty-two years ago."

"Fine," Ronny said, increasingly excited. "That will eliminate all persons less than, say, forty years of age. We can assume he was at least twenty when he began."

Hassan said, "Can we eliminate all women employees?"

Ronny said, "I'd think so. The few times he's been seen, all reports are of a man. And that case on the planet Mother where he put himself over as a Holy Man. He could hardly have been a woman in disguise in a Stone Age culture such as that."

Hassan said, "And this Tommy Paine has been flitting around this part of the galaxy for years, so anyone who has been here steadily for a period of even a couple of years or so, can't be suspect."

Mouley Hassan thrust his hand into a delivery drawer and brought forth a handful of punched cards, possibly fifty in all.

"Surely there's more people than that working in this building," Ronny protested.

Mouley Hassan said, "No. I've eliminated already everyone who is a citizen of New Delos. Obviously, Tommy Paine is an alien. We have only forty-eight Earthlings and other United Planets citizens working here."

He carried the cards to a small collator and worked for a moment on its controls, as Tog and Ronny watched him with mounting tension. "Let's see," he muttered. "We eliminate all women, all those less than forty, all who haven't done a great deal of travel, those who have been here for several years."

The end of it was that they eliminated everyone employed in the UP building.

The cards were stacked back on Mouley Hassan's desk again, and the three of them sat around and looked glumly at them.

Ronny said, "He's tinkered with the files. He counterfeited fake papers for himself, or something. Possibly he's pulled his own card and it isn't in this stack you have."

Mouley Hassan said, "We'll double-check all those possibilities, but you're wrong. Possibly a few hundred years ago, but not today. Forgery and counterfeiting are things of the past. And, believe me, the Bureau of Investigation and especially Section G, may look on the slipshod side, but they aren't. We're not going to find anything wrong with those cards. Tommy Paine simply is not working for UP on New Delos."

"Then," Ronny said, "there's only one alternative. He's on this UP ship going to, what was the name of its destination?"

"Avalon," Mouley Hassan said, his face thoughtful.

Tog said, "Do you have any ideas on the men aboard?"

Mouley Hassan said, "There were four crew men, and six of our agents."

Tog said, "Unless one of them has faked papers, the six agents are eliminated. That leaves the crew members. Do you know anything about them?"

Hassan shook his head.

Ronny said, "Let's communicate with Avalon. Tell our representatives there to be sure that none of the occupants of that ship leaves Avalon until we get there."

Mouley Hassan said, "Good idea." He turned to his screen and said into it, "Section G, Bureau of Investigation, on the Planet Avalon."

In moment the screen lit up. An elderly agent, as Section G agents seemed to go, looked up at them.

Mouley Hassan held his silver badge so the other could see it and on the Avalon agent's nod said, "I'm Hassan from New Delos. We've just had a crisis here and there seems to be a chance that it's a Tommy Paine job. Agent Bronston here is on an assignment tracking him down. I'll turn it over to Bronston."

The Avalon agent nodded again, and looked at Ronny.

Ronny said urgently, "We haven't the time to give you details, but every indication is that Paine is on a UP spacecraft with Avalon as its destination. There are only ten men aboard, and six of them are Section G operatives."

The other pursed his lips. "I see. You think you have the old fox cornered, eh?"

"Possibly," Ronny said. "There are various ifs. Miss Tog and I can double check here. Then as soon as we can clear exit visas, we'll make immediate way for Avalon."

The Avalon Section G agent said, "I haven't the authority to control the movements of other agents, they have as high rank as I have," he added, expressionlessly, "and probably higher than yours."

Ronny said, "But the four-man crew?"

The other said, "These men are coming to Avalon to work on a job that will take at least six months. We'll make a routine check, and I'll try and make sure the whole ten will still be on Avalon when and if you arrive."

They had to be satisfied with that. They checked all ways from the middle, nor did it take long. There was no doubt. If this was a Tommy Paine job, and it almost surely was, then there was only one way in which he could have escaped from the planet and that was by the single spacecraft that had left, destination Avalon. He was not on the planet, that was definite Ronny felt. A stranger on New Delos was as conspicuous as a walrus in a goldfish bowl. There simply were no such.

They spent most of their time checking and rechecking United Planets personnel, but there was no question there either.

Mouley Hassan and others of UP personnel helped cut the red tape involved in getting exit visas from New Delos. It wasn't as complicated as it might have been a week or two before. No one seemed to be so confident of his authority in the new provisional government that he dared veto a United Planets request.

Mouley Hassan was able to arrange for a small space yacht, slower than a military craft, but capable of getting them to Avalon in a few days time. A one-man crew was sufficient, Ronny, and especially Tog, could spell him on the watches.

Time aboard was spent largely in studying up on Avalon, going over and over again anything known about the elusive Tommy Paine, and playing Battle Chess and bickering with Tog Lee Chang Chu.

If it hadn't been for this ability to argue against just about anything Ronny managed to say, he could have been attracted to her to the detriment of the job. She was a good traveler, few people are; she was an ultra-efficient assistant; she was a joy to look at; and she never intruded. But, Great Guns, the woman could bicker.

The two of them were studying in the ship's luxurious lounge when Ronny looked up and said, "Do you have any idea why those six agents were sent to Avalon?"

"No," she said.

He indicated the booklet he was reading. "From what I can see here, it sounds like one of the most advanced planets in the UP. They've made some of the most useful advances in industrial techniques of the past century."

"Oh, I don't know," Tog mused. "I haven't much regard for Industrial Feudalism myself. It starts off with a bang, but tends to go sterile."

"Industrial feudalism," he said indignantly. "What do you mean? The government is a constitutional monarchy with the king merely a powerless symbol. The standard of living is high. Elections are honest and democratic. They've got a three-party system...."

"Which is largely phony," Tog interrupted. "You've got to do some reading between the lines, especially when the books you're reading are turned out by the industrial feudalistic publishing companies in Avalon."

"What's this industrial feudalism, you keep talking about? Avalon has a system of free enterprise."

"A gobbledygook term," Tog said, irritatingly. "Industrial feudalism is a socio-economic system that develops when industrial wealth is concentrated into the hands of a comparatively few families. It finally gets to the point of a closed circle all but impossible to break into. These industrial feudalistic families become so powerful that only in rare instances can anyone lift himself into their society. They dominate every field, including the so-called labor unions, which amount to one of the biggest businesses of all. With their unlimited resources they even own every means of dispensing information."

"You mean," Ronny argued, "that on Avalon you can't start up a newspaper of your own and say whatever you wish?"

"Certainly you can, theoretically. If you have the resources. Unfortunately, such enterprises become increasingly expensive to start. Or you could start a radio, TV or Tri-Di station-if you had the resources. However, even if you overcame all your handicaps and your newspaper or broadcasting station became a success, the industrial feudalistic families in control of Avalon's publishing and broadcasting fields have the endless resources to buy you out, or squeeze you out, by one nasty means or another."

Ronny snorted. "Well, the people must be satisfied or they'd vote some fundamental changes."

Tog nodded. "They're satisfied, and no wonder. Since childhood every means of forming their opinions have been in the hands of industrial feudalistic families-including the schools."

"You mean the schools are private?"

"No, they don't have to be. The government is completely dominated by the fifty or so families which for all practical purposes own Avalon. That includes the schools. Some of the higher institutions of learning are private, but they, too, are largely dependent upon grants from the families."

* * * * *

Ronny was irritated by her know-all air. He tapped the book he'd been reading with a finger. "They don't control the government. Avalon's got a three-party system. Any time the people don't like the government, they can vote in an alternative."

"That's an optical illusion. There are three parties, but each is dominated by the fifty families, and election laws are such that for all practical purposes it's impossible to start another party. Theoretically it's possible, actually it isn't. The voters can vary back and forth between the three political parties but it doesn't make any difference which one they elect. They all stand for the same thing —a continuation of the status quo."

"Then you claim it isn't democracy at all?"

Tog sighed. "That's a much abused word. Actually, pure democracy is seldom seen. They pretty well had it in primitive society where government was based on the family. You voted for one of your relatives in your clan to represent you in the tribal councils. Every one in the tribe was equal so far as apportionments of the necessities of life were concerned. No one, even the tribal chiefs, ate better than anyone else, no one had a better home."

Ronny said, snappishly, "And if man had remained at that level, we'd never have gotten anywhere."

"That's right," she said. "For progress, man needed a leisure class. Somebody with the time to study, to experiment, to work things out."

He said, "We're getting away from the point. You said in spite of appearances they don't have democracy on Avalon."

"They have a pretense of it. But only free men can practice democracy. So long as your food, clothing and shelter are controlled by someone else, you aren't free. Wait until I think of an example." She put her right forefinger to her chin, thoughtfully.

Holy smokes, she was a cute trick. If only she wasn't so confounded irritating.

Tog said, "Do you remember the State of California in Earth history?"

"I think so. On the west coast of North America."

"That's right. Well, back in the Twentieth Century, Christian calendar, they had an economic depression. During it a crackpot organization called Thirty Dollars Every Thursday managed to get itself on the ballot. Times were bad enough but had this particular bunch got into power it would have become chaotic. At first no thinking person took them seriously, however a majority of people in California at that time had little to lose and in the final week or so of the election campaign the polls showed that Thirty Dollars Every Thursday was going to win. So, a few days before voting many of the larger industries and businesses in the State ran full page ads in the newspapers. They said substantially the same thing. *If Thirty Dollars Every Thursday wins this election, our concern will close its doors. Do not bother to come back to work Monday.*"

Ronny was scowling at her. "What's your point?"

She shrugged delicate shoulders. "The crackpots were defeated, of course, which was actually good for California. But my point is that the voters of California were not actually free since their livelihoods were controlled by others. This is an extreme case, of course, but the fact always applies."

A thought suddenly hit Ronny Bronston. "Look," he said. "Tommy Paine. Do you think he's merely escaping from New Delos, or is it possible that Avalon is his next destination? Is he going to try and overthrow the government there?"

She was shaking her head, but frowning. "I don't think so. Things are quite stable on Avalon."

"Stable?" he scowled at her. "From what you've been saying, they're pretty bad."

She continued to shake her head. "Don't misunderstand, Ronny. On an assignment like this, it's easy to get the impression that all the United Planets are in a state of socio-political confusion, but it isn't so. A small minority of planets are ripe for the sort of trouble Tommy Paine stirs up. Most are working away, developing, making progress, slowly evolving. Avalon is one of these. The way things are there, Tommy Paine couldn't make a dent on changing things, even if he wanted to, and there's no particular reason to believe he does."

Ronny growled. "From what I can learn of the guy he's anxious to stir up trouble wherever he goes."

"I don't know. If there's any pattern at all in his activities, it seems to be that he picks spots where things are ripe to boil over on their own. He acts as a catalyst. In a place like Avalon he wouldn't get to first base. Possibly fifty years from now, things will have developed on Avalon to the point where there is dissatisfaction. By that time," she said dryly, "we'll assume Tommy Paine will no longer be a problem to the Commissariat of Interplanetary Affairs for one reason or the other."

Ronny took up his book again. He growled, "I can't figure out his motivation. If I could just put my finger on that."

For once she agreed with him. "I've got an idea, Ronny, that once you have that, you'll have Tommy Paine."

* * * * *

They drew blank on Avalon.

Or, at least, it was drawn for them before they ever arrived.

The Section G agent permanently assigned to that planet had already checked and double checked the possibilities. None of the four-man crew of the UP spacecraft had been on New Delos at the time of the assassination of the God-King. They, and their craft, had been light-years away on another job.

Ronny Bronston couldn't believe it. He simply couldn't believe it.

The older agent, his name was Jheru Bulchand, was definite. He went over it with Ronny and Tog in a bar adjoining UP headquarters. He had dossiers on each of the ten men, detailed dossiers. On the face of it, none of them could be Paine.

"But one of them has to be," Ronny pleaded. He explained their method of eliminating the forty-eight employees of UP on New Delos.

Bulchand shrugged. "You've got holes in that method of elimination. You're assuming Tommy Paine is an individual, and you have no reason to. My own theory is that it's an organization."

Ronny said unhappily, "Then you're of the opinion that there is a Tommy Paine?"

The older agent was puffing comfortably on an old style briar pipe. He nodded definitely. "I believe Tommy Paine exists as an organization. Possibly once, originally, it was a single person, but now it's a group. How large, I wouldn't know. Probably not too large or by this time somebody would have betrayed it, or somebody would have cracked and we would have caught them. Catch one and you've got the whole organization what with our modern means of interrogation."

Tog said, "I've heard the opinion before."

Jheru Bulchand pointed at Ronny with his pipe stem. "If its an organization, then none of that eliminating you did is valid. Your assassin could have been one of the women. He could have been one of the men you eliminated as too young-someone recently admitted to the Tommy Paine organization."

Ronny checked the last of his theories. "Why did Section G send six of its agents here?"

"Nothing to do with Tommy Paine," Bulchand said. "It's a different sort of crisis."

"Just for my own satisfaction, what kind of crisis?"

Bulchand sketched it quickly. "There are two Earth type planets in this solar system. Avalon was the first to be colonized and developed rapidly. After a couple of centuries, Avalonians went over and settled on Catalina. They eventually set up a government of their own. Now Avalon has a surplus of industrial products. Her economic system is such that she produces more than she can sell back to her own people. There's a glut."

Tog said demurely, "So, of course, they want to dump it in Catalina."

Bulchand nodded. "In fact, they're willing to give it away. They've offered to build railroads, turn over ships and aircraft, donate whole factories to Catalina's slowly developing economy."

Ronny said, "Well, how does that call for Section G agents?"

"Catalina has evoked Article Two of the UP Charter. No member planet of UP is to interfere with the internal political, socio-economic or religious affairs of another member planet. Avalon claims the Charter doesn't apply since Catalina belongs to the same solar system and since she's a former colony. We're trying to smooth the whole thing over, before Avalon dreams up some excuse for military action."

Ronny stared at him. "I get the feeling every other sentence is being left out of your explanation. It just doesn't make sense. In the first place, why is Avalon as anxious as all that to give away what sounds like a fantastic amount of goods?"

"I told you, they have a glut. They've overproduced and, as a result, they've got a king-size depression on their hands, or will have unless they find markets."

"Well, why not trade with some of the planets that want her products?"

Tog said as though reasoning with a youngster, "Planets outside her own solar system are too far away for it to be practical even if she had commodities they didn't. She needs a nearby planet more backward than herself, a planet like Catalina."

"Well, that brings us to the more fantastic question. Why in the world doesn't Catalina accept? It sounds to me like pure philanthropy on the part of Avalon."

Bulchand was wagging his pipe stem in a negative gesture. "Bronston, governments are never motivated by idealistic reasons. Individuals might be, and even small groups, but governments never. Governments, including that of Avalon, exist for the benefit of the class or classes that control them. The only things that motivate them are the interests of that class."

"Well, this sounds like an exception," Ronny said argumentatively. "How can Catalina lose if the Avalonians grant them railroads, factories and all the rest of it?"

Tog said, "Don't you see, Ronny? It gives Avalon a foothold in the Catalina economy. When the locomotives wear out on the railroad, new engines, new parts, must be purchased. They won't be available on Catalina because there will be no railroad industry because none will have ever grown up. Catalina manufacturers couldn't compete with that initial free gift. They'll be dependent on Avalon for future equipment. In the factories, when machines wear out, they will be replaceable only with the products of Avalon's industry."

Bulchand said, "There's an analogy in the early history of the United States. When its fledgling steel industry began, they set up a high tariff to protect it against British competition. The British were amazed and indignant, pointing out that they could sell American steel products at one third the local prices, if only allowed to do so. The United States said no thanks, it didn't want to be tied, industrially, to Great Britain's apron strings. And in a couple of decades American steel production passed England's. In a couple of more decades American steel production was many times that of England's and she was taking British markets away from her all over the globe."

"At any rate," Ronny said, "it's not a Tommy Paine matter."

Just for luck, though, Ronny and Tog double checked all over again on Bulchand's efforts. They interviewed all six of the Section G agents. Each of them carried a silver badge that gleamed only for the individual who possessed it. All of which eliminated the possibility that Paine had assumed the identity of a Section G operative. So that was out.

They checked the four crew members, but there was no doubt there, either. The craft had been far away at the time of the assassination on New Delos.

On the third day, Ronny Bronston, disgusted, knocked on the door of Tog's hotel room. The door screen lit up and Tog, looking out at him said, "Oh, come on in, Ronny, I was just talking to Earth."

He entered.

Tog had set up her Section G communicator on a desk top and Sid Jakes' grinning face was in the tiny, brilliant screen. Ronny approached close enough for the other to take him in.

Jakes said happily, "Hi, Ronny, no luck, eh?"

Ronny shook his head, trying not to let his face portray his feelings of defeat. This after all was a probationary assignment, and the supervisor had the power to send Ronny Bronston back to the drudgery of his office job at Population Statistics.

"Still working on it. I suppose it's a matter of returning to New Delos and grinding away at the forty-eight employees of the UP there."

Sid Jakes pursed his lips. "I don't know. Possibly this whole thing was a false alarm. At any rate, there seems to be a hotter case on the fire. If our local agents have it straight, Paine is about to pull one of his coups on Kropotkin. This is a top-top-secret, of course, one of the few times we've ever detected him before the act."

Ronny was suddenly alert, his fatigue of disgust of but a moment ago, completely forgotten. "Where?" he said.

"Kropotkin," Jakes said. "One of the most backward planets in UP and seemingly a setup for Paine's sort of trouble making. The authorities, if you can use the term applied to Kropotkin, are already complaining, threatening to invoke Article One of the Charter, or to resign from UP." Jake looked at Tog again. "Do you know Kropotkin, Lee Chang?"

She shook her head. "I've heard of it, rather vaguely. Named after some old anarchist, I believe."

"That's the place. One of the few anarchist societies in UP. You don't hear much from them." He turned to Ronny again. "I think that's your bet. Hop to it, boy. We're going to catch this Tommy Paine guy, or organization, or whatever, soon or United Planets is going to know it. We can't keep the lid on indefinitely. If word gets around of his activities, then we'll lose member planets like Christmas trees shedding needles after New Year's." He grinned widely. "That's sounds like a neat trick, eh?"

* * * * *

Ronny Bronston had got to the point where he avoided controversial subjects with Tog even when provoked and she had a sneaky little way of provoking arguments. They had only one really knock down and drag-out verbal battle on the way to Kropotkin.

It had started innocently enough after dinner on the space liner on which they had taken passage for the first part of the trip. To kill time they were playing Battle Chess with its larger board and added contingents of pawns and castles.

Ronny said idly, "You know, in spite of the fact that I'm a third generation United Planets citizen and employee, I'm just beginning to realize how far out some of our member planets are. I had no idea before."

She frowned in concentration, before moving. She was advancing her men in echelon attack, taking losses in exchange for territory and trying to pen him up in such small space that he couldn't maneuver.

She said, "How do you mean?"

Ronny lifted and dropped a shoulder. "Well, New Delos and its theocracy, for instance, and Shangri-La and Mother and some of the other planets with extremes in government of socio-economic system. I hadn't the vaguest idea about such places."

She made a deprecating sound. "You should see Amazonia, or, for that matter, the Orwellian State."

"*Amazonia ,*" he said, "does that mean what it sounds like it does?"

She made her move and settled back in satisfaction. Her pawns were in such position that his bishops were both unusable. He'd tried to play a phalanx game in the early stages of her attack, but she'd broken through, rolling up his left flank after sacrificing a castle and a knight.

"Certainly does," she said. "A fairly recently colonized planet. A few thousand feminists no men at all-moved onto it a few centuries ago. And it's still an out and out matriarchy."

Ronny cleared his throat delicately. "Without men ... ah, how did they continue several centuries?"

Tog suppressed her amusement. "Artificial insemination, at first, so I understand. They brought their, ah, supply with them. But then there were boys among the first generation on the new planet and even the Amazonians weren't up to cold bloodedly butchering their children. So they merely enslaved them. Nice girls."

Ronny stared at her. "You mean all men are automatically slaves on this planet?"

"That's right."

Ronny made an improperly thought out move, trying to bring up a castle to reinforce his collapsing flank. He said, "UP allows *anybody* to join evidently," and there was disgust in his voice.

"Why not?" she said mildly.

"Well, there should be *some* standards."

Tog moved quickly, dominating with a knight several squares he couldn't afford to lose. She looked up at him, her dark eyes sparking. "The point of UP is to include all the planets. That way at least conflict can be avoided and some exchange of science, industrial techniques and cultural gains take place. And you must remember that while in power practically no socio-economic system will admit to the fact that it could possibly change for the better. But actually there is nothing less stable. Socio-economic systems are almost always in a condition of flux. Planets such as Amazonia might for a time seem so brutal in their methods as to exclude their right to civilized intercourse with the rest. However, one of these days there'll be a change-or one of these centuries. They all change, sooner or later." She added softly, "Even Han."

"Han?" Ronny said.

Her voice was quiet. "Where I was born, Ronny. Colonized from China in the very early days. In fact, I spent my childhood in a commune." She said musingly, "The party bureaucrats thought their system an impregnable, unchangeable one. Your move."

Ronny was fascinated. "And what happened?" He was in full retreat now, and with nowhere to go, his pieces pinned up for the slaughter. He moved a pawn to try and open up his queen.

"Why don't you concede?" she said. "Tommy Paine happened."

"Paine!"

"Uh-huh. It's a long story. I'll tell you about it some time." She pressed closer with her own queen.

He stared disgustedly at the board. "Well, that's what I mean," he muttered. "I had no idea there were so many varieties of crackpot politico-economic systems among the UP membership."

"They're not necessarily crackpot," she protested mildly. "Just at different stages of development."

"Not crackpot!" he said. "Here we are heading for a planet named Kropotkin which evidently practices anarchy."

"Your move," she said. "What's wrong with anarchism?"

He glowered at her, in outraged disgust. Was it absolutely impossible for him to say anything without her disagreement?

Tog said mildly, "The anarchistic ethic is one of the highest man has ever developed." She added, after a moment of pretty consideration. "Unfortunately, admittedly, it hasn't been practical to put to practice. It will be interesting to see how they have done on Kropotkin."

"Anarchist ethic, yes," Ronny snapped. "I'm no student of the movement but the way I understand it, there isn't any."

Tog smiled sweetly. "The belief upon which they base their teachings is that no man is capable of judging another."

Ronny cast his eyes ceilingward. "O.K., I give up!"

She began rapidly resetting the pieces. "Another game?" she said brightly.

"Hey! I didn't mean the game! I was just about to counterattack."

"Ha!" she said.

* * * * *

The Section G agent on Kropotkin was named Hideka Yamamoto, but he was on a field tour and wouldn't be back for several days. However, there wasn't especially any great hurry so far as Ronny Bronston and Tog Lee Chang Chu knew. They got themselves organized in the rather rustic equivalent of a hotel, which was located fairly near UP headquarters, and took up the usual problems of arranging for local exchange, meals, means of transportation and such necessities.

It was a greater problem than usual. In fact, hadn't it been for the presence of the UP organization, which had already gone through all this the hard way, some of the difficulties would have been all but insurmountable.

For instance, there was no local exchange. There was no medium of exchange at all. Evidently simple barter was the rule.

In the hotel-if it could be called a hotel-lobby, Ronny Bronston looked at Tog. "Anarchism!" he said. "Oh, great. The highest ethic of all. And what's the means of transportation on this wonderful planet? The horse. And how are we going to get a couple of horses with no means of exchange?"

She tinkled laughter.

"All right," he said. "You're the Man Friday. You find out the details and handle them. I'm going out to take a look around the town-if you can call this a town."

"It's the capital of Kropotkin," Tog said placatingly, though with a mocking background in her tone. "Name of Bakunin. And very pleasant, too, from what little I've seen. Not a bit of smog, industrial fumes, street dirt, street noises —"

"How could there be?" he injected disgustedly. "There isn't any industry, there aren't any cars, and for all practical purposes, no streets. The houses are a quarter of a mile or so apart."

She laughed at him again. "City boy," she said. "Go on out there and enjoy nature a little. It'll do you good. Anybody who has cooped himself up in that one big city, Earth, all his life ought to enjoy seeing what the great outdoors looks like."

He looked at her and grinned. She was cute as a pixie, and there were no two ways about that. He wondered for a moment what kind of a wife she'd make. And then shuddered inwardly. Life would be one big contradiction of anything he'd managed to get out of his trap.

He strolled idly along what was little more than a country path and it came to him that there were probably few worlds in the whole UP where he'd have been prone to do this within the first few hours he'd been on the planet. He would have been afraid, elsewhere, of anything from footpads to police, from unknown vehicles to unknown traffic laws. There was something bewildering about being an Earthling and being set down suddenly in New Delos or on Avalon.

Here, somehow, he already had a feeling of peace.

Evidently, although Bakunin was supposedly a city, its populace tilled their fields and provided themselves with their own food. He could see no signs of stores or warehouses. And the UP building, which was no great edifice itself, was the only thing in town which looked even remotely like a governmental building.

Bakunin was neat. Clean as a pin, as the expression went. Ronny was vaguely reminded of a historical Tri-Di romance he'd once seen. It had been laid in ancient times in a community of the Amish in old Pennsylvania.

He approached one of the wooden houses. The things would have been priceless on Earth as an antique to be erected as a museum in some crowded park. For that matter it would have been priceless for the wood it contained. Evidently, the planet Kropotkin still had considerable virgin forest.

An old-timer smoking a pipe, sat on the cottage's front step. He nodded politely.

Ronny stopped. He might as well try to get a little of the feel of the place. He said courteously, "A pleasant evening."

The old-timer nodded. "As evenings should be after a fruitful day's toil. Sit down, comrade. You must be from the United Planets. Have you ever seen Earth?"

Ronny accepted the invitation and felt a soothing calm descend upon him almost immediately. An almost disturbingly pleasant calm. He said, "I was born on Earth."

"Ai?" the old man said. "Tell me. The books say that Kropotkin is an Earth type planet within what they call a few degrees. But is it? Is Kropotkin truly like the mother planet?"

Ronny looked about him. He'd seen some of this world as the shuttle rocket had brought them down from the passing liner. The forests, the lakes, the rivers, and the great sections untouched by man's hands. Now he saw the areas between homes, the neat fields, the signs of human toil-the toil of hands, not machines.

"No," he said, shaking his head. "I'm afraid not. This is how Earth must once have been. But no longer."

The other nodded. "Our total population is but a few million," he said. Then, "I would like to see the mother planet, but I suppose I never shall."

Ronny said diplomatically, "I have seen little of Kropotkin thus far but I am not so sure but that I might not be happy to stay here, rather than ever return to Earth."

The old man knocked the ashes from his pipe by striking it against the heel of a work-gnarled hand. He looked about him thoughtfully and said, "Yes, perhaps you're right. I am an old man and life has been good. I suppose I should be glad that I'll unlikely live to see Kropotkin change."

"Change? You plan changes?"

* * * * *

The old man looked at him and there seemed to be a very faint bitterness, politely suppressed. "I wouldn't say *we* planned them, comrade. Certainly not we of the older generation. But the trend toward change is already to be seen by anyone who wishes to look, and our institutions won't long be able to stand. But, of course, if you're from United Planets you would know more of this than I."

"I'm sorry. I don't know what you're talking about."

"You are new indeed on Kropotkin," the old man said. "Just a moment." He went into his house and emerged with a small power pack. He indicated it to Ronny Bronston. "This is our destruction," he said.

The Section G agent shook his head, bewildered.

The old-timer sat down again. "My son," he said, "runs the farm now. Six months ago, he traded one of our colts for a small pump, powered by one of these. It was little use on my part to argue against the step. The pump eliminates considerable work at the well and in irrigation."

Ronny still didn't understand.

"The power pack is dead now," the old man said, "and my son needs a new one."

"They're extremely cheap," Ronny said. "An industrialized planet turns them out in multi-million amounts at practically no cost."

"We have little with which to trade. A few handicrafts, at most."

Ronny said, "But, good heavens, man, build yourselves a plant to manufacture power packs. With a population this small, a factory employing no more than half a dozen men could turn out all you need."

The old man was shaking his head. He held up the battery. "This comes from the planet Archimedes," he said, "one of the most highly industrialized in the UP, so I understand. On Archimedes do you know how many persons it takes to manufacture this power pack?"

"A handful to operate the whole factory, Archimedes is fully automated."

The old man was still moving his head negatively. "No. It takes the total working population of the planet. How many different metals do you think are contained in it, in all? I can immediately see what must be lead and copper."

Ronny said uncomfortably, "Probably at least a dozen, some in microscopic amounts."

"That's right. So we need a highly developed metallurgical industry before we can even begin. Then a developed transportation industry to take metals to the factory. We need power to run the factory, hydro-electric, solar, or possibly atomic power. We need a tool-making industry to equip the factory, the transport industry and the power industry. And while the men are employed in these, we need farmers to produce food for them, educators to teach them the sciences and techniques involved, and an entertainment industry to amuse them in their hours of rest. As their lives become more complicated with all this, we need a developed medical industry to keep them in health."

The old man hesitated for a moment, then said, "And, above all, we need a highly complicated government to keep all this accumulation of wealth in check and balance. No. You see, my friend, it takes *social labor* to produce products such as this, and thus far we have avoided that on Kropotkin. In fact, it was for such avoidance that my ancestors originally came to this planet."

Ronny said, scowling, "This gets ridiculous. You show me this basically simple power pack and say it will ruin your socio-economic system. On the face of it, it's ridiculous."

The old man sighed and looked out over the village unseeingly. "It's not just that single item, of course. The other day one of my neighbors turned up with a light bulb with built-in power for a year's time. It is the envy of the unthinking persons of the neighborhood most of whom would give a great deal for such a source of light. A nephew of mine has somehow even acquired a powered bicycle, I think you call them, from somewhere or other. One by one, item by item, these products of advanced technology turn up-from whence, we don't seem to be able to find out."

Under his breath, Ronny muttered, "*Paine!* "

"I beg your pardon," the old man said.

"Nothing," the Section G agent said. He leaned forward and, a worried frown working its way over his face, began to question the other more closely.

Afterwards, Ronny Bronston strode slowly toward the UP headquarters. There was only a small contingent of United Planets personnel on this little populated member planet but, as always, there seemed to be an office for Section G.

Ronny stood outside it for a moment. There were voices from within, but he didn't knock.

In fact, he cast his eyes up and down the short corridor. At the far end was a desk with a girl in the Interplanetary Cultural Exchange Department working away in concentration. She wasn't looking in his direction.

Ronny Bronston put his ear to the door. The building was primitive enough, rustic enough in its construction, to permit his hearing.

Tog Lee Chang Chu was saying seriously, "Oh, it was chaotic all right, but no, I don't really believe it could have been a Tommy Paine case. Actually I'd suggest to you that you run over to Catalina. When I was on Avalon I heard rumors that Tommy Paine's finger seemed to be stirring around in the mess there. Yes, I'd recommend that you take off for Catalina immediately. If Paine is anywhere in this vicinity at all, it would be Catalina."

For a moment, Ronny Bronston froze. Then in automatic reflex his hand went inside his jacket to rest over the butt of the Model H automatic there.

No, that wasn't the answer. His hand dropped away from the gun.

He listened, further.

Another voice was saying, "We thought we were on the trail for a while on Hector, but it turned out it wasn't Paine. Just a group of local agitators fed up with the communist regime there. There's going to be a blood bath on Hector, before they're through, but it doesn't seem to be Paine's work this time."

Tog's voice was musing. "Well, you never know, it sounds like the sort of muck he likes to play in."

The strange voice said argumentatively, "Well, Hector *needs* a few fundamental changes."

"It could be," Tog said, "but that's their internal affairs, of course. Our job in Section G is to prevent troubles between the differing socio-economic and religious features of member planets. Whatever we think of some of the things Paine does, our task is to get him."

Ronny Bronston pushed the door open and went through. Tog Lee Chang Chu was sitting at a desk, nonchalant and petitely beautiful as usual, comfortably seated in easy-chairs were two young men by their attire probably citizens of United Planets and possibly even Earthlings.

"Hello, Ronny," Tog said softly. "Meet Frederic Lippman and Pedro Nazaré, both Section G operatives. This is my colleague, Ronald Bronston, gentlemen. Fredric and Pedro were just leaving, Ronny."

The two agents got up to shake hands.

Ronny said, "You can't be in that much of a hurry. What's your assignment, boys?"

Lippman, an earnest type, and by his appearance not more than twenty-five or so years of age, began to answer, but Nazaré said hurriedly, "Actually, it's a confidential assignment. We're working directly out of the Octagon."

Lippman said, frowning, "It's not that confidential, Tog. Bronston's an agent, too. What's your assignment, Ronny?"

Ronny said very slowly, "I'm beginning to suspect that it's the same as yours and various pieces are beginning to fall into place."

Lippman was taken aback. "You mean you're looking for Tommy Paine?" His eyes went to his associate. "How could that be, Tog? I didn't know more than one of us were on this job. Why, that means if Bronston here finds him first, I won't get my permanent appointment."

Ronny looked at Tog Lee Chang Chu who was sitting demurely, hands in lap, and a resigned expression on her face. He said, "Nor if you find him first, will I. Look here, Tog, how many men does Sid Jakes have out on this assignment?"

"I wouldn't know," she said mildly.

He snapped, "A few dozen or so? Or possibly a few hundred?"

"It seems unlikely there could be that many," she said mildly. She looked at the other two agents. "I think you two had better run along. Take my suggestion I made earlier."

"Wait a minute," Ronny snapped. "You mean that they go to Catalina? That's ridiculous."

Tog Lee Chang Chu looked at Pedro Nazaré and he turned and started for the door followed by Fredric Lippman who was still scowling his puzzlement.

"Wait a minute!" Ronny snapped. "I tell you it's ridiculous. And why follow her suggestions? She's just my assistant."

Pedro Nazaré said, "Come on, Fred, let's get going, we'll have to pack." But Lippman wasn't having any.

"His assistant?" he said to Tog Lee Chang Chu.

Tog Lee Chang Chu's face changed expression in sudden decision. She opened her bag and brought forth a Section G identification wallet and flicked it open. The badge was gold. "I suggest you hurry," she said to the two agents.

They left, and Tog turned back to Ronny, her eyebrows raised questioningly.

Ronny sank down into one of the chairs recently occupied by the other two agents and tried to unravel thoughts. He said finally, "I suppose my question should be, why do Ross Metaxa and Sid Jakes send an agent of supervisor rank to act as assistant to a probationary agent? But that's not what I'm asking yet. First, Lippman just called his buddy Tog. How come?"

Tog took her seat again, rueful resignation on her face. "You should be figuring it out on your own by this time, Ronny."

He looked at her belligerently. "I'm too stupid, eh?" The anger was growing within him.

"Tog," she said. "It's a nickname, or possibly you might call it a title. Tog. T-O-G. The Other Guy. My name is Lee Chang Chu, and I'm of supervisor grade presently working at developing new Section G operatives. Considering the continuing rapid growth of UP, and the continuing crises that come up in UP activities, developing new operatives is one of the department's most pressing jobs. Each new agent, on his first assignment, is always paired with an experienced old-timer."

"I see," he said flatly. "Your principal job being to needle the fledging, eh?"

She lowered her eyes. "I wouldn't exactly word it that way," she said. She was obviously unrepentant.

He said, "You must get a lot of laughs out of it. If I say, it seems to me democracy is a good thing, you give me an argument about the superiority of rule by an elite. If I say anarchism is ridiculous, you dredge up an opinion that it's man's highest ethic. You must laugh yourself to sleep at nights. You and Metaxa and Jakes and every other agent in Section G. Everybody is in on the Tog gag but the sucker."

"Sometimes there are amusing elements to the work," Lee Chang conceded, demurely.

"Just one more thing I'd like to ask," Ronny rapped. "This first assignment, agents are given. Is it always to look for Tommy Paine?"

She looked up at him, said nothing, but her eyes were questioning.

"Don't worry," he snapped. "I've already found out who Paine is."

"Ah?" She was suddenly interested. "Then I'm glad I ordered that other probationary agent to leave. Evidently, he hasn't. Obviously, I didn't want the two of you comparing notes."

"No, that would never do," he said bitterly. "Well, this is the end of the assignment so far as you and I are concerned. I'm heading back for Earth."

"Of course," she said.

* * * * *

He had time on the way to think it all over, and over and over again, and a great deal of it simply didn't make sense. He had enough information to be disillusioned, sick at heart. To have crumbled an idealistic edifice that had taken a lifetime to build. A lifetime? At least three. His father and his grandfather before him had had the dream. He'd been weaned on the idealistic purposes of the United Planets and man's fated growth into the stars.

He was a third-generation dreamer of participating in the glory. His grandfather had been a citizen of Earth and gave up a commercial position to take a job that amounted to little more than a janitor in an obscure department of Interplanetary Financial Clearing. He wanted to get into the big job, into space, but never made it. Ronny's father managed to work up to the point where he was a supervisor in Interplanetary Medical Exchange, in the tabulating department. He, too, had wanted into space, and never made it. Ronny had loved them both. In a way fulfilling his own dreams had been a debt he owed them, because at the same time he was fulfilling theirs.

And now this. All that had been gold, was suddenly gilted lead. The dream had become contemptuous nightmare.

Finally back in Greater Washington, he went immediately from the shuttleport to the Octagon. His Bureau of Investigation badge was enough to see him through the guide-guards and all the way through to the office of Irene Kasansky.

She looked up at him quickly. "Hi," she said. "Ronny Bronston, isn't it?"

"That's right. I want to see Commissioner Metaxa."

She scowled. "I can't work you in now. How about Sid Jakes?"

He said, "Jakes is in charge of the Tommy Paine routine, isn't he?"

She shot a sharper look up at him. "That's right," she said warily.

"All right," Ronny said. "I'll see Jakes."

Her deft right hand slipped open a drawer in her desk. "You'd better leave your gun here," she said. "I've known probationary agents to get excited, in my time."

He looked at her.

And she looked back, her gaze level.

Ronny Bronston shrugged, slipped the Model H from under his armpit and tossed it into the drawer.

Irene Kasansky went back to her work. "You know the way," she said.

This time Ronny Bronston pushed open the door to Sid Jakes' office without knocking. The Section G supervisor was poring over reports on his desk. He looked up and grinned his Sid Jakes' grin.

"Ronny!" he said. "Welcome back. You know, you're one of the quickest men ever to return from a Tommy Paine assignment. I was talking to Lee Chang only a day or so ago. She said you were on your way."

Ronny grunted, his anger growing within him. He lowered himself into one of the room's heavy chairs, and glared at the other.

Sid Jakes chuckled and leaned back in his chair. "Before we go any further, just to check, who is Tommy Paine?"

Ronny snapped, "You are."

The supervisor's eyebrows went up.

Ronny said, "You and Ross Metaxa and Lee Chang Chu-and all the rest of Section G. Section G is Tommy Paine."

"Good man!" Sid Jakes chortled. He flicked a switch on his order box. "Irene," he said, "how about clearing me through to the commissioner? I want to take Ronny in for his finals."

Irene snapped back something and Sid Jakes switched off and turned to Ronny happily. "Let's go," he said. "Ross is free for a time."

Ronny Bronston said nothing. He followed the other. The rage within him was still mounting.

In the months that had elapsed since Ronny Bronston had seen Ross Metaxa the latter had changed not at all. His clothing was still sloppy, his eyes bleary with lack of sleep or abundance of alcohol-or both. His expression was still sour and skeptical.

He looked up at their entry and scowled, and made no effort to rise and shake hands. He said to Ronny sourly, "O.K., sound off and get it over with. I haven't too much time this afternoon."

Ronny Bronston was just beginning to feel tentacles of cold doubt, but he suppressed them. The boiling anger was uppermost. He said flatly, "All my life I've been a dedicated United Planets man. All my life I've considered its efforts the most praiseworthy and greatest endeavor man has ever attempted."

"Of course, old chap," Jakes told him cheerfully. "We know all that, or you wouldn't ever have been chosen as an agent for Section G."

Ronny looked at him in disgust. "I've resigned that position, Jakes."

Jakes grinned back at him. "To the contrary, you're now in the process of receiving permanent appointment."

Ronny snorted his disgust and turned back to Metaxa. "Section G is a secret department of the Bureau of Investigation devoted to subverting Article One of the United Planets Charter."

Metaxa nodded.

"You don't deny it?"

Metaxa shook his head.

"Article One," Ronny snapped, "is the basic foundation of the Charter which every member of UP and particularly every citizen of United Planets, such as ourselves, has sworn to uphold. But the very reason for the existence of this Section G is to interfere with the internal affairs of member planets, to subvert their governments, their economic systems, their religions, their ideals, their very way of life."

Metaxa yawned and reached into a desk drawer for his bottle. "That's right," he said. "Anybody like a drink?"

Ronny ignored him. "I'm surprised I didn't catch on even sooner," he said. "On New Delos Mouley Hassan, the local agent, knew the God-King was going to be assassinated. He brought in extra agents and even a detail of Space Forces guards for the emergency. He probably engineered the assassination himself."

"Nope," Jakes said. "We seldom go *that* far. Local rebels did the actual work, but, admittedly, we knew what they were planning. In fact, I've got a sneaking suspicion that Mouley Hassan provided them with the bomb. That lad's a bit too dedicated."

"But *why*," Ronny blurted. "That's deliberately interfering with internal affairs. If the word got out, every planet in UP would resign."

"Probably no planet in the system that needed a change so badly," Metaxa growled. "If they were ever going to swing into real progress, that hierarchy of priests had to go." He snorted. "An immortal God-King, yet."

Ronny pressed on. "That was bad enough, but how about this planet Mother, where the colonists had attempted to return to nature and live in the manner man did in earliest times."

"Most backward planet in the UP," Metaxa said sourly. "They just had to be roused."

"And Kropotkin!" Ronny blurted. "Don't you understand, those people were *happy* there. Their lives were simple, uncomplicated, and they had achieved a happiness that —"

Metaxa came to his feet. He scowled at Ronny Bronston and growled, "Unfortunately, the human race can't take the time out for happiness. Come along, I want to show you something."

He swung around the corner of his desk and made his way toward a ceiling-high bookcase. Ronny stared after him, taken off guard, but Sid Jakes was grinning his amusement.

Ross Metaxa pushed a concealed button and the bookcase slid away to one side to reveal an elevator beyond.

"Come along," Metaxa repeated over his shoulder. He entered the elevator, followed by Jakes.

There was nothing else to do. Ronny Bronston followed them, his face still flushed with the angered argument.

The elevator dropped, how far, Ronny had no idea. It stopped and they emerged into a plain, sparsely furnished vault. Against one wall was a boxlike affair that reminded Ronny of nothing so much as a deep-freeze.

For all practical purposes, that's what it was. Ross Metaxa led him over and they stared down into its glass-covered interior.

Ronny's eyes bugged. The box contained the partly charred body of an animal approximately the size of a rabbit. No, not an animal. It had obviously once been clothed, and its limbs were obviously those of a tool using life form.

Metaxa and Jakes were staring down at it solemnly, for once no inane grin on the supervisor's face. And that of Ross Metaxa was more weary than ever.

Ronny said finally, "What is it?" But he knew.

"You tell us," Metaxa growled sourly.

"It's an intelligent life form," Ronny blurted. "Why has it been kept secret?"

"Let's go on back upstairs," Metaxa sighed.

Back in his office he said, "Now I go into my speech. Shut up for a while." He poured himself a drink, not offering one to the other two. "Ronny," he said, "man isn't alone in the galaxy. There's other intelligent life. Dangerously intelligent."

In spite of himself Ronny reacted in amusement. "That little creature down there? The size of a small monkey?" As soon as he said it, he realized the ridiculousness of his statement.

Metaxa grunted. "Obviously, size means nothing. That little fellow down there was picked up by one of our Space Forces scouts over a century ago. How long he'd been drifting through space, we don't know. Possibly only months, but possibly hundreds of centuries. But however long he's proof that man is not alone in the galaxy. And we have no way of knowing when the expanding human race will come up against this other intelligence-and whoever it was fighting."

"But," Ronny protested, "you're assuming they're aggressive. Perhaps coming in contact with these aliens will be the best thing that ever happened to man. Possibly that little fellow down there is the most benevolent creature ever evolved."

Metaxa looked at him strangely. "Let's hope so," he said. "However, when found he was in what must have been a one-man scout. He was dead and his craft was blasted and torn-obviously from some sort of weapons' fire. His scout was obviously a military craft, highly equipped with what could only be weapons, most of them so damaged our engineers haven't been able to figure them out. To the extent they have been able to reconstruct them, they're scared silly. No, there's no two ways about it, our little rabbit sized intelligence down in the vault was killed in an interplanetary conflict. And sooner or later, Ronny, man in his explosion into the stars is going to run into either or both of the opponents in that conflict."

Ronny Bronston slumped back into his chair, his brain running out a dozen leads at once. Metaxa and Jakes remained quiet, looking at him speculatively.

Ronny said slowly, "Then the purpose of Section G is to push the member planets of UP along the fastest path of progress, to get them ready for the eventual, inevitable meeting."

"Not just Section G," Metaxa growled, "but all of the United Planets organization, although most of the rank and file don't even know our basic purpose. Section G? We do the dirty work, and are proud to do it, by every method we can devise."

Ronny leaned forward. "But look," he said. "Why not simply inform all member planets of this common danger? They'd all unite in the effort to meet the common potential foe. Anything standing in the way would be brushed aside."

Metaxa shook his head wearily. "Would they? Is a common danger enough for man to change his institutions, particularly those pertaining to property, power and religion? History doesn't show it. Delve back into early times and you'll recall, for an example, that in man's early discovery of nuclear weapons he almost destroyed himself. Three or four different socio-economic systems co-existed at that time and all would have preferred destruction rather than changes in their social forms."

Jakes said, in an unwonted quiet tone, "No, until someone comes up with a better answer it looks as though Section G is going to have to continue the job of advancing man's institutions, in spite of himself."

The commissioner made it clearer. "It's not as though we deal with all our member planets. It isn't necessary. But you see, Ronny, the best colonists are usually made up of the, well, crackpot element. Those who are satisfied, stay at home. America, for instance, was settled by the adventurers, the malcontents, the non-conformists, the religious cultists, and even fugitives and criminals of Europe. So it is in the stars. A group of colonists go out with their dreams, their schemes, their far-out ideas. In a few centuries they've populated their new planet, and often do very well indeed. But often not and a nudge, a push, from Section G can start them up another rung or so of the ladder of social evolution. Most of them don't want the push. Few cultures, if any, realize they are mortal; like Hitler's Reich, they expect to last at least a thousand years. They resist any change-even change for the better."

* * * * *

Ronny's defenses were crumbling, but he threw one last punch. "How do you know the changes you make are for the better?"

Metaxa shrugged heavy shoulders. "It's sometimes difficult to decide, but we aim for changes that will mean an increased scientific progress, a more advanced industrial technology, more and better education, the opening of opportunity for every member of the culture to exert himself to the full of his abilities. The last is particularly important. Too many cultures, even those that think of themselves as particularly advanced, suppress the individual by one means or another."

Ronny was still mentally reeling with the magnitude of it all. "But how can you account for the fact that these alien intelligences haven't already come in contact with us?"

Metaxa shrugged again. "The Solar System, our sun, is way out in a sparsely populated spiral arm of our galaxy. Undoubtedly, these others are further in toward the center. We have no way of knowing how far away they are, or how many sun systems they dominate, or even how many other empires of intelligent life forms there are. All we know is that there are other intelligences in the galaxy, that they are near enough like us to live on the same type planets. The more opportunity man has to develop before the initial contact takes place, the stronger bargaining position, or military position, as the case may be, he'll be in."

Sid Jakes summed up the Tommy Paine business for Ronny's sake. "We need capable agents badly, but we need dedicated and efficient ones. We can't afford anything less. So when we come upon potential Section G operatives we send them out with a trusted Tog to get a picture of these United Planets of ours. It's the quickest method of indoctrination we've hit upon; the agent literally teaches himself by observation and participation. Usually, it takes four or five stops, on this planet and that, before the probationary agent begins sympathizing with the efforts of this elusive Tommy Paine. Especially since every Section G agent he runs into, including the Tog, of course, fills him full of stories of Tommy Paine's activities.

"You were one of the quickest to stumble on the true nature of our Section G. After calling at only three planets you saw that we ourselves are Tommy Paine."

"But ... but what's the end?" Ronny said plaintively. "You say our job is advancing man, even in spite of himself when it comes to that. We start at the bottom of the evolutionary ladder in a condition of savagery, clan communism in government, simple animism in religion, and slowly we progress through barbarism to civilization, through paganism to the higher ethical codes, through chattel slavery and then feudalism and beyond. What is the final end, the Ultima Thule?"

Metaxa was shaking his head again. He poured himself another drink, offered the bottle this time to the others. "We don't know," he said wearily, "perhaps there is none. Perhaps there is always another rung on this evolutionary ladder." He punched at his order box and said, "Irene, have them do up a silver badge for Ronny."

Ronny Bronston took a deep breath and reached for the brown bottle. "Well," he said. "I suppose I'm ready to ask for my first assignment." He thought for a moment. "By the way, if there's any way to swing it, I wouldn't mind working with Supervisor Lee Chang Chu."

Black Man's Burden

"Take up the white man's burden
Send forth the best ye breed...."
—Kipling

The two-vehicle caravan emerged from the sandy wastes of the *erg* and approached the small encampment of Taitoq Tuareg which consisted of seven goat leather tents. They were not unanticipated, the camp's scouts had noted the strange pillars of high-flung dust which were set up by the air rotors an hour earlier and for the past fifteen minutes they had been visible to all.

Moussa-ag-Amastan, headman of the clan, awaited the newcomers at first with a certain trepidation in spite of his warrior blood. Although he hadn't expressed himself thus to his followers, his first opinion had been that the unprecedented pillars were djinn come out of the erg for no good purpose. It wasn't until they were quite close that it could be seen the vehicles bore resemblance to those of the Rouma which were of recent years spreading endlessly through the lands of the Ahaggar Tuareg and beggaring those who formerly had conducted the commerce of the Sahara.

But the vehicles traveling through the sand dunes! That had been the last advantage of the camel. No wheeled vehicle could cross the vast stretches of the ergs, they must stick to the hard ground, to the tire-destroying gravel.

They came to a halt and Moussa-ag-Amastan drew up his teguelmoust turban-veil even closer about his eyes. He had no desire to let the newcomers witness his shocked surprise at the fact that the desert lorries had no wheels, floated instead without support, and now that they were at a standstill settled gently to earth.

There was further surprise when the five who issued forth from the two seemingly clumsy vehicles failed to be Rouma. They looked more like the Teda to the south, and the Targui's eyes thinned beneath his teguelmoust. Since the French had pulled out their once dreaded Camel Corps there had been somewhat of a renaissance of violence between traditional foes.

However, the newcomers, though dark as Negro Bela slaves, wore Tuareg dress, loose baggy trousers of dark indigo-blue cotton cloth, a loose, nightgownlike white cotton shirt, and over this a *gandoura* outer garment. Above all, they wore the teguelmoust though they were shockingly lax in keeping it properly up about the mouth.

Moussa-ag-Amastan knew that he was backed by ten or more of his clansmen, half of whom bore rifles, the rest Tuareg broadswords, Crusader-like with their two edges, round points and flat rectangular cross-members. Only two of the strangers seemed armed and they negligently bore their smallish guns in the crooks of their arms. The clan leader spoke at strength, then, but he said the traditional "*La bas.*"

"There is no evil," repeated the foremost of the newcomers. His Tamabeq, the Berber language of the Tuareg confederations, seemed perfect.

Moussa-ag-Amastan said, "What do you do in the lands of the Taitoq Tuareg?"

The stranger, a tall, handsome man with a dominating though pleasant personality, indicated the vehicles with a sweep of his hand. "We are Enaden, itinerant smiths. As has ever been our wont, we travel from encampment to encampment to sell our products and to make repair upon your metal possessions."

Enaden! The traveling smiths of the Ahaggar, and indeed of the whole Sahara, were a despised and ragged lot at best. Few there were that ever possessed more than a small number of camels, a sprinkling of goats, perhaps a sheep or two. But these seemed as rich as Roumas, as Europeans or Americans.

Moussa-ag-Amastan muttered, "You jest with us at your peril, stranger." He pointed an aged but still strong hand at the vehicles. "Enaden do not own such as these."

The newcomer shrugged. "I am Omar ben Crawf and these are my followers, Abrahim el Bakr Ma el Ainin, Keni Ballalou and Bey-ag-Akhamouk. We come today from Tamanrasset and we are smiths, as we can prove. As is known, there is high pay to be earned by working in the oil fields, at the dams on the Niger, in the afforestation projects, in the sinking of the new wells whose pumps utilize the rays of the sun, in the developing of the great new oases.

There is much Rouma money to be made in such work and my men and I have brought these vehicles specially built in the new factories in Dakar for desert use."

"Slave work!" one of Moussa-ag-Amastan's kinsmen sneered.

Omar ben Crawf shrugged in obvious amusement, but there was a warmth and vitality in the man that quickly affected even strangers. "Perhaps," he said. "But times change, as every man knows and today there no longer need be hunger, nor illness, nor any want-if a man will but work a fraction of each day."

"Work is for slaves," Moussa-ag-Amastan barked.

The newcomer refused to argue. "But all slaves have been freed, and where in the past this meant nothing since the Bela had no place to go, no way to live save with his owner, today it is different and any man can go and find work on the many projects that grow everywhere. So the slaves slip away from the Tuareg, and the Teda and Chaamba. Soon there will be no more slaves to do the work about your encampments. And then what, man of the desert?"

"We'll fight!" Moussa-ag-Amastan growled. "We Tuareg are warriors, bedouin, free men. We will never be slaves."

"*Inshallah.* If God wills it," the smith agreed politely.

"Show us your wares," the old chieftain snapped. "We chatter like women. Talk can wait until the evening meal and in the men's quarters of my tent." He approached the now parked vehicles and his followers crowded after him. From the tents debouched women and children. The children were completely nude, and the Tuareg women were unveiled for such are the customs of the Ahaggar Tuareg that the men go veiled but women do not.

* * * * *

One of the lorries was so constructed that a side could be raised in such fashion to display a wide variety of tools, weapons, household utensils, and textiles. Ohs and ahs punctuated the air, women being the same in every land. Two of the smiths brought forth metal-working equipment of strange design and set up shop to one side. A broken bolt on an aged Lebel rifle was quickly repaired, a copper cooking pot brazed, some harness tinkered with.

Of a sudden, Moussa-ag-Amastan said, "But your women, your families, where are they?"

The one who had been introduced as Abrahim el Bakr, an open-faced man whose constant smiling seemed to take a full ten years off what must have been his age, explained. "On the big projects, one can find employment only if he allows his children to attend the new schools. So our wives and children remain near Tamanrasset while the children learn the lore of books."

"Rouma schools!" one of the warriors sneered.

"Oh, no. There are few Roumas remaining in all the land now," the smith said easily. "Those that are left serve us in positions our people as yet cannot hold, in construction of the dams, in the bringing of trees to the desert, but soon, even they will be unneeded."

"*Our* people?" Moussa-ag-Amastan rumbled ungraciously. "You are smiths. The smiths have no people. You are neither Kel Rela, Tégehé Mellet, Taitoq, nor even Teda, Chaambra, or Ouled Tidrarin."

One of the smiths said easily, "In the great new construction camps, in the new towns, with their many ways to work and become rich, the tribes are breaking up. Tuareg works next to Teda and a Moor next to a former Haratin serf." He added, as though unthinkingly, even as he displayed an aluminum pan to a wide-eyed Tuareg matron, "Indeed, even the clans break up and often Tuareg marries Arab or Sudanese or Rifs down from the north ...or even we Enaden."

The clansmen were suddenly silent, in shocked surprise.

"That cannot be true!" the elderly chief snapped.

Omar ben Crawf looked at him mildly. "Why should my follower lie?"

"I do not know, but we will talk of it later, away from the women and children who should not hear such abominations." The chief switched subjects. "But you have no flocks with you. How are we to pay for these things, these services?"

"With money."

The old man's face, what little could be seen through his teguelmoust, darkened. "We have little money in the Ahaggar."

The one named Omar nodded. "But we are short of meat and will buy several goats and perhaps a lamb, a chicken, eggs. Then, too, as you have noted, we have left our women at home. We will need the services of cooks, some one to bring water. We will hire servants."

The other said gruffly, "There are some Bela who will serve you."

The smith seemed taken aback. "Verily, El Hassan has stated that the product of the labor of the slave is accursed."

"El Hassan! Who is El Hassan and why should the work of a slave be accursed?"

One of the tribesmen said, "I have heard of this El Hassan. Rumors of his teachings spread through the land. He is to lead us all, Tuareg, Arab and Sudanese, until we are all as rich as Roumas."

Omar said, "It is well known that the Roumas and especially the Americans are all rich as Emirs but none of them ever possess slaves. The bedouin have slaves but fail to prosper. Verily, the product of the labor of the slave is accursed."

"Madness," Moussa-ag-Amastan muttered. "If you do not let our slave women do your tasks, then they will remain undone. No Tuareg woman will work."

* * * * *

But the headman of his clan was wrong.

The smiths remained four days in all, and the abundance of their products was too much. What verbal battles might have taken place in the tent of Moussa-ag-Amastan, and in those of his followers, the smiths couldn't know, but Tuareg women are not dominated by their men. On the second day, three Tuareg women applied for the position of servants, at surprisingly high pay. Envy ran roughshod when they later displayed the textiles and utensils they purchased with their wages.

Nor could the aged Tuareg chief prevent in the evening discussions between the men, a thorough pursuing of the new ideas sweeping through the Ahaggar. Though these strangers proclaimed themselves lowly Enaden-itinerant desert smiths-they were obviously not to be dismissed as a caste little higher than Haratin serfs. Even the first night they were invited to the tent of Moussa-ag-Amastan to share the dinner of shorba soup, cous cous and the edible paste *kaboosh*, made of cheese, butter and spices. It was an adequate desert meal, meat being eaten not more than a few times a year by such as the Taitoq Tuareg who couldn't afford to consume the animals upon which they lived.

After mint tea, one of the younger Tarqui leaned forward. He said, "You have brought strange news, oh Enaden of wealth, and we would know more. We of the Ahaggar hear little from outside."

Moussa-ag-Amastan scowled at his clansman, for his presumption, but Omar answered, his voice sincere and carrying conviction. "The world moves fast, men of the desert, and the things that were verily true even yesterday, have changed today."

"To the sorrow of the Tuareg!" snapped Moussa-ag-Amastan.

The other looked at him. "Not always, old one. Surely in your youth you remember when such diseases as the one the Roumas once called the disease of Venus, ran rampant through the tribes. When trachoma, the sickness of the eyes, was known as the scourge of the Sahara. When half the children, not only of Bela slaves and Haratin serfs, but also of the Surgu noble clans, died before the age of ten."

"Admittedly, the magic of the Roumas cured many such ills," an older warrior growled.

"Not their magic, their learning," the smith named El Ma el Ainin put in. "And, verily, now the schools are open to all the people."

"Schools are not for such as the Bela and Haratin," the clan chief protested. "The Koran should not be taught to slaves."

El Ma el Ainin said gently, "The Koran is not taught at all in the new schools, old one. The teachings of the Prophet are still made known to those interested, in the schools connected with the mosques, but only the teachings of science are made in the new schools."

"The teachings of the Rouma!" a Tuareg protested, carefully slipping his glass of tea beneath his teguelmoust so that he could drink without his mouth being obscenely revealed.

Omar ben Crawf laughed. "That is what we have allowed the Roumas to have us believe for much too long," he stated. "El Hassan has proven otherwise. Much of the wisdom of science has its roots in the lands of Asia and of Africa. The Roumas were savages in skins while the earliest civilizations were being developed in Africa and Asia Minor. Hardly a science now developed by the Roumas of Europe and America but had its beginning with us." He turned to the elderly chief.

"You Tuareg are of Berber background. But a few centuries ago, the Berbers of Morocco, known as the Moors to the Rouma, leavened only with a handful of Jews and Arabs, built up in Spain the highest civilization in all the world of that time. We would be foolish, we of Africa, to give credit to the Rouma for so much of what our ancestors presented to the world."

The Tuareg were astonished. They had never heard such words.

Moussa-ag-Amastan was not appeased. "You sound like a Rouma, yourself," he said. "Where have you learned of all this?"

The smiths chuckled their amusement.

Abrahim el Bakr said, "Verily, old one, have you ever seen a black Rouma?"

Omar ben Crawf, the headman of the smiths, went on. "El Hassan has proclaimed great new beliefs that spread through all North Africa, and eventually, *Inshallah*, throughout the continent. Through his great learning he has assimilated the wisdom of all the prophets, all the wisemen of all the world, and proclaims their truths."

The Tuareg chief was becoming increasingly irritated. Such talk as this was little short of blasphemy to his ears, but the fascination of the discussion was beyond him to ignore. And he knew that even if he did his young men, in particular, would only seek out the strangers on their own and then he would not be present to mitigate their interest. In spite of himself, now he growled, "What beliefs? What truths? I know not of this El Hassan of whom you speak."

Omar said slowly, "Among them, the teachings of a great wise man from a far land. That all men should be considered equal in the eyes of society and should have equal right to life, liberty and the pursuit of happiness."

"Equal!" one of the warriors ejaculated. "This is not wisdom, but nonsense. No two men are equal."

Omar waggled a finger negatively. "Like so many, you fail to explore the teaching. Obviously, no man of wisdom would contend that all men are equally tall, or strong, or wise, or cunning, nor even fortunate. *No* two men are equal in such regards. But all men should have equal right to life, liberty and the pursuit of happiness, whatever that might mean to him as an individual."

One of the Tuareg said slyly, "And the murderer of one of your kinsmen, should he, too, have life and liberty, in the belief of El Hassan?"

"Obviously, the community must protect itself against those who would destroy the life or liberty of others. The murderer of a kinsman of mine, as well as any other man, myself included, should be subject equally to the same law."

It was a new conception to members of a tribal society such as that of the Ahaggar Tuareg. They stirred under both its appeal and its negation of all they knew. A man owed alliance to his immediate family, to his clan, his tribe, then to the Tuareg confederation-in decreasing degree. Beyond that, all were enemies, as all men knew.

One protested slowly, seeking out his words, "Your El Hassan preaches this equality, but surely the wiser man and the stronger man will soon find his way to the top in any land, in any tribe, even in the nations of the Rouma."

Omar shrugged. "Who could contend otherwise? But each man should be free to develop his own possibilities, be they strength of arm or of brain. Let no man exploit another, nor suppress another's abilities. If a Bela slave has more ability than a Surgu Tuareg noble, let him profit to the full by his gifts."

There was a cold silence.

Omar finished gently by saying, "Or so El Hassan teaches, and so they teach in the new schools in Tamanrasset and Gao, in Timbuktu and Reggan, in the big universities at Kano, Dakar, Bamako, Accra and Abidian. And throughout North Africa the wave of the future flows over the land."

"It is a flood of evil," Moussa-ag-Amastan said definitely.

* * * * *

But in spite of the antagonism of the clan headman and of the older Tuareg warriors, the stories of the smiths continued to spread. It was not even beyond them to discuss, long and quietly, with the Bela slaves the ideas of the mysterious El Hassan, and to talk of the plentiful jobs, the high wages, at the dams, the new oases, and in the afforestation projects.

Somehow the news of their presence spread, and another clan of nomad Tuareg arrived and pitched their tents, to handle the wares of the smiths and to bring their metal work for repair. And to listen to their disturbing words.

As amazing as any of the new products was the solar powered, portable television set which charged its batteries during the daylight hours and then flashed on its screen the images and the voices and music of entertainers and lecturers, teachers and storytellers, for all to see. In the beginning it had been difficult, for the eye of the desert man is not trained to pick up a picture. He has never seen one, and would not recognize his own photograph. But in time, it came to them.

The programs originated in Tamanrasset and in Salah, in Zinder and Fort Lamy and one of the smiths revealed that the mysterious waves, that fed the device its programs, were bounced off tiny moons which the Rouma had rocketed up into the sky for that purpose. A magic understandable only to marabouts and such, without doubt.

At the end of their period of stay, the smiths, to the universal surprise of all, gave the mystery device to two sisters, kinswomen of Moussa-ag-Amastan, who were particularly interested in the teachers and lecturers who told of the new world aborning. The gift was made in the full understanding that all should be allowed to listen and watch, and it was clear that if ever the set needed repair it was to be left untinkered with and taken to Tamanrasset or the nearest larger settlement where it would be fixed free of charge.

There were many strange features about the smiths, as each man could see. Among others, were their strange weapons. There had been some soft whispered discussion among the warriors in the first two days of their stay about relieving the strangers of their obviously desirable possessions-after all, they weren't kinsmen, not even Tuareg. But on the second day, the always smiling one named Abrahim el Bakr had been on the outskirts of the *erg* when a small group of gazelle were flushed. The graceful animals took off at a prohibitive rifle range, as usual, but Abrahim el Bakr had thrown his small, all but tiny weapon to his shoulder and *flic flic flic*, with a sound no greater than the cracking of a ground nut, had knocked over three of them before the others had disappeared around a dune.

Obviously, the weapons of the smiths were as great as their learning and their new instruments. It was discouraging to a raider by instinct.

Then, too, there was the strangeness of the night talks their leader was known to have with his secret *Kambu* fetish which was able to answer him in a squeaky but distinct voice in some unknown tongue, obviously a language of the djinn. The *Kambu* was worn on a strap on Omar's wrist, and each night at a given hour he was wont to withdraw to his tent and there confer.

On the fourth night, obviously, he was given instruction by the *Kambu* for in the morning, at first light, the smiths hurriedly packed, broke camp, made their good-byes to Moussa-ag-Amastan and the others and were off.

Moussa-ag-Amastan was glad to see them go. They were quite the most disturbing element to upset his people in many seasons. He wondered at the advisability of making their usual summer journey to the Tuareg sedentary centers. He had a feeling that if the clan got near enough to such centers as Zinder to the south, or Touggourt to the north, there would be wholesale desertion of the Bela, and, for that matter, even of some of his younger warriors and their wives.

However, there was no putting off indefinitely exposure to this danger. Even in such former desert centers as Tessalit and In Salah, the irrigation projects were of such magnitude that there was a great labor shortage. But always, of course, as the smiths had said, if you worked at the projects your children must needs attend the schools. And that way lay disaster!

The five smiths took out overland in the direction of Djanet on the border of what had once been known as Libya and famed for its cliffs which tower over twenty-five hundred feet above the town. Their solar powered, air cushion, hover-lorries, threw up their clouds of dust and sand to right and left, but they made good time over the *erg*. A good hovercraft driver could do much to even out a rolling landscape, changing his altitude from a few inches here to as much as twenty-five feet there, given, of course, enough power in his solar batteries, although that was little problem in this area where clouds were sometimes not seen for years on end.

This was back of the beyond, the wasteland of earth. Only the interior of the Arabian peninsula and the Gobi could compete and, of course, even the Gobi was beginning to be tamed under the afforestation efforts of the teeming multitudes of China who had suffered its disastrous storms down through the millennia.

* * * * *

Omar checked and checked again with the instrument on his wrist, asking and answering, his voice worried.

Finally they pulled up beside a larger than usual wadi and Omar ben Crawf stared thoughtfully out over it. The one they had named Abrahim el Bakr stood beside him and the others slightly to the rear.

Abrahim el Bakr nodded, for once his face unsmiling. "Those cats'll come down here," he said. "Nothing else would make sense, not even to an Egyptian."

"I think you're right," Omar growled. He said over his shoulder, "Bey, get the trucks out of sight, over that dune. Elmer, you and Kenny set the gun up over there. Solid slugs, and try to avoid their cargo. We don't want to set off a Fourth of July here. Bey, when you're finished with the trucks, take that Tommy-Noiseless of yours and flank them from over behind those rocks. Take a couple of clips extra, for good luck-you won't need them, though."

"How many are there supposed to be?" Abrahim el Bakr asked, his voice empty of humor now.

"Eight half-trucks, two armed jeeps, or land-rovers, one or the other. Probably about forty men, Abe."

"All armed," Abe said flatly.

"Um-m-m. Listen, that's them coming. Right down the *wadi*. Get going men. Abe, you cover me."

Abe Bakr looked at him. "Wha'd'ya mean, cover you, man? You slipped all the way round the bend? Listen, let me plant a couple quick land mines to stop 'em and we'll get ourselves behind these rocks and blast those cats half way back to Cairo."

"We'll warn them as per orders."

"Crazy man, like you're the boss, Homer," Abe growled. "But why'd I ever leave New Jersey?" He made his way to the right, to the top of the wadi's bank and behind a clump of thorny bush. He made himself comfortable, the light Tommy-Noiseless with its clip of two hundred .10 caliber, ultra-high velocity shells resting before him on a flat rock outcropping. He thoughtfully flicked the selector to the explosive side of the clip. Let Homer Crawford say what he would about not setting off a Fourth of July, but if he needed covering in the moments to come, he'd need it bad.

The chips were down now.

The convoy, the motors growling their protests of the hard going even here at the gravel bottomed wadi river bed, made its way toward them at a pace of approximately twenty kilometers per hour.

The lead jeep-Skoda manufacture, Homer Crawford noted cynically-was some thirty meters in advance. It drew to a halt upon seeing him and a turbaned Arab Union trooper swung a Brenn gun in his direction.

An officer stood up in the jeep and yelled at Crawford in Arabic.

The American took a deep breath and said in the same language, "You're out of your own territory."

The officer's face went poker-expressionless. He looked at the lone figure, dressed in the garb of the Tuareg, even to the turban-veil which covers all but the eyes of these notorious Apaches of the Sahara.

"This is no affair of yours," the lieutenant said. "Who are you?"

Homer Crawford said very clearly, "Sahara Division, African Development Project, Reunited Nations. You're far out of your own territory, lieutenant. I'll have to report you, and also to demand that you turn and go back to your origin."

The lieutenant flicked his hand, and the trooper behind the Brenn gun sighted the weapon and tightened his trigger finger.

Crawford dropped to the ground and rolled desperately for a slight depression that would provide cover. He could have saved himself the resultant bruises and scratches. Before the Brenn gun spoke even once, there was a *Götterdammerung* of sound and the three occupants of the jeep, driver, lieutenant and gunner were swept from the vehicle in a nauseating obscenity of exploding flesh, uniform cloth, blood and bone.

To the side, Abe Bakr behind his thorn bush and rock vantage point turned the barrel of his Tommy-Noiseless to the first of the half tracks. Already Arab Union troopers were debouching from them, some firing at random and at unseen targets. However, the so-called Enaden smiths were well concealed, their weapons silenced except for the explosion of the tiny shells upon reaching their target.

It wasn't much of a fight. The recoilless automatic rifle manned by Elmer Allen and Kenny Ballalou swept the wadi, swept it of life, at least, but hardly swept it clean. What few individuals were left, in what little shelter was to be found in the dry river's bottom, were picked off easily, if not neatly by the high velocity automatics in the hands of Abe Bakr and Bey-ag-Akhamouk.

Afterwards, the five of them, standing at the side of the wadi, stared down at their work.

Elmer Allen muttered a bitter four-letter obscenity. He had once headed a pacifist group at the University in Kingston, Jamaica. Now his teeth were bared, as they always were when he went into action. He hated it.

Of them all, Bey-ag-Ahkamouk was the least moved by the slaughter. He grumbled, "Guns, explosives, mortar, flame throwers. If there is anything in the world my people don't need in the way of *aid*, it's weapons."

"Our people," Homer Crawford said absently, his eyes-taking in the scene beneath them-empty, as though unseeing. He hated the need for killing, almost as badly as did Elmer Allen.

Bey looked at him, scowling slightly, but said nothing. There had been mild rebuke in his leader's voice.

"Well," Abe Bakr said with a tone of mock finality in his voice, as though he was personally wiping his hands of the whole affair, "how are you going to explain all this jazz to headquarters, man?"

Homer said flatly, "We were attacked by this unidentified group of, ah, gun runners, from some unknown origin. We defended ourselves, to the best of our ability."

Elmer Allen looked at the once human mess below them. "We certainly did," he muttered, scowling.

"Crazy man," Abe said, nodding his agreement to the alibi.

The others didn't bother to speak. Homer Crawford's unit was well knit.

He said after a moment. "Abe, you and Kenny get some dynamite and plant it in this wadi wall in a few spots. We'll want to bury this whole mess. It wouldn't do for someone to come along and blow himself up on some of these scattered land mines, or find himself a bazooka or something to use on his nearest blood-feud neighbor."

II

The young woman known as Izubahil was washing clothes in the Niger with the rest but slightly on the outskirts of the chattering group of women, which was fitting since she was both a comparative stranger and as yet unselected by any man to grace his household. Which, in a way, was passingly strange since she was comely enough. Clad as the rest with naught but a wrap of colored cloth about her hips, her face and figure were openly to be seen. Her complexion was not quite so dark as most. She came from up-river, so she said, the area of the Songhoi, but by the looks of her there was more than average Arab or Berber blood in her veins. Her lips and nose were thinner than those of her neighbors.

Yes, it was strange that no man had taken her, though it was said that in her shyness she repulsed any advances made by either the young men, or their wealthier elders who could afford more than one wife. She was a nothing-woman, really, come out of the desert alone, and without relatives to protect her interests, but still she repulsed the advances of those who would honor her with a place in their house, or tent.

She had come out of the desert, it was known, with her handful of possessions done up in a packet, and had quietly and unobtrusively taken her place in the Negro community of Gao. Little better than a slave or Gabibi serf, she made her meager living doing small tasks for the better-off members of the community.

But she knew her place, was dutifully shy and quiet spoken, and in the town or in the presence of men, wore her haik and veil. Yes, it was passing strange that she found no man. On the face of it, she was getting no younger, surely she must be into her twenties.

Up to their knees in the waters of the Niger, out beyond the point where the dugout canoes were pulled up to the bank, their ends resting on the shore, they pounded their laundry. Laughing, chattering, gossiping. Life was perhaps poor, but still life was good.

Someone pretended to see a crocodile and there was a wild scampering for the shore. And then high laughter when the jest was revealed. Actually, all the time they had known it a jest, since it was their most popular one-there were seldom crocodiles this far north in the Niger bend.

There was a stir as two men dressed in the clothes of the Rouma approached the river bank. It was not forbidden, but good manners called for males to refrain from this area while the woman bathed and washed their laundry, without veil or upper garments. These mean were obviously shameless, and probably had come to stare. From their dress, their faces and their bearing, they were strangers. Possibly Senegalese, up from the area near Dakar, products of the new schools and the new industries mushrooming there. Strange things were told of the folk who gave up the old ways, worked on the dams and the other new projects, sent their little ones to the schools, and submitted to the needle pricks which seemed to compose so much of the magic medicine being taught in the medical schools by the Rouma witchmen.

One of them spoke now in Songhoi, the *lingua franca* of the vicinity. Shamelessly he spoke to them, although none were his women, nor even his tribal kin. None looked at him.

"We seek a single woman, an unwed woman, who would work for pay and learn the new ways."

They continued their laundry, not looking up, but their chatter dribbled away.

"She must drop the veil," the man continued clearly, "and give up the haik and wear the new clothes. But she will be well paid, and taught to read and be kept in the best of comfort and health."

There was a low gasp from several of the younger women, but one of the eldest looked up in distaste. "Wear the clothes of the Rouma!" she said indignantly. "Shameless ones!"

The man's voice was testy. He himself was dressed in the clothing worn always by the Rouma, when the Rouma had controlled the Niger bend. He said, "These are not the clothes of the Rouma, but the clothes of civilized people everywhere."

The women's attention went back to their washing. Two or three of them giggled.

The elderly woman said, "There are none here who will go with you, for whatever shameless purpose you have in your mind."

But Izubahil, the strange girl come out of the desert from the north, spoke suddenly. "I will," she said.

There was a gasp, and all looked at her in wide-eyed alarm. She began making her way to the shore, her unfinished washing still in hand.

The stranger said clearly, "And drop the veil, discard the haik for the new clothing, and attend the schools?"

There was another gasp as Izubahil said definitely, "Yes, all these things." She looked back at the women. "So that I may learn all these new ways."

The more elderly sniffed and turned their backs in scorn, but the younger stared after her in some amazement and until she disappeared with the two strangers into one of the buildings which had formerly housed the French Administration officers back in the days when the area was known as the French Sudan.

Inside, the boy strangers turned to her and the one who had spoken at the river bank said in English, "How goes it?"

"Heavens to Betsy," Isobel Cunningham said with a grin, "get me a drink. If I'd known majoring in anthropology was going to wind up with my doing a strip tease with a bunch of natives in the Niger River, I would have taken up Home Economics, like my dear old mother wanted!"

They laughed with her and Jacob Armstrong, the older of the two, went over to a sideboard and mixed her a cognac and soda. "Ice?" he said.

"Brother, you said it," she told him. "Where can I change out of these rags?"

"On you they look good," Clifford Jackson told her. He looked surprisingly like the Joe Louis of several decades earlier.

"That's enough out of you, wise guy," Isobel told him. "Why doesn't somebody dream up a role for me where I can be a rich paramount chief's favorite wife, or something? Be loaded down with gold and jewelry, that sort of thing."

Jake brought her the drink. "Your clothes are in there," he told her, motioning with his head to an inner room. "It wouldn't do the job," he added. "What we're giving them is the old Cinderella story." He looked at his watch. "If we get under way, we can take the jet to Kabara and go into your act there. It's been nearly six months since Kabara and they'll be all set for the second act."

She knocked back the brandy and made her way to the other room, saying over her shoulder, "Be with you in a minute."

"Not that much of a hurry," Cliff called. "Take your time, gal, there's a bath in there. You'll probably want one after a week of living the way you've been."

"Brother!" she agreed.

Jake was making himself a drink. He said easily to Cliff Jackson, "That's a fine girl. I'd hate her job. We get the easy deal on this assignment."

Cliff said, "You said it, Nigger. How about mixing me a drink, too?"

"Nigger!" Jake said in mock indignation. "Look who's talking." His voice took on a burlesque of a Southern drawl. "Man when the Good Lawd was handin' out *cullahs*, you musta thought he said *umbrellahs*, and said give me a nice black one."

Cliff laughed with him and said, "Where do we plant poor Isobel next?"

Jake thought about it. "I don't know. The kid's been putting in a lot of time. I think after about a week in Kabara we ought to go on down to Dakar and suggest she be given another assignment for a while. Some of the girls, working out of our AFAA office don't do anything except drive around in recent model cars, showing off the advantages of emancipation, tossing money around like tourists, and living it up in general."

* * * * *

On the flight up-river to Kabara, Isobel Cunningham went through the notes she'd taken on that town. It was also on the Niger, and the assignment had been almost identical to the Gao one. In fact, she'd gone through the same routine in Ségou, Ké-Macina, Mopti, Gôundam and Bourem, above Gao, and Ansongo, Tillabéri and Niamey below. She was stretching her luck, if you asked her. Sooner or later she was going to run into someone who knew her from a past performance.

Well, let the future take care of the future. She looked over at Cliff Jackson who was piloting the jet and said, "What're the latest developments? Obviously, I haven't seen a paper or heard a broadcast for over a week."

Cliff shrugged his huge shoulders. "Not much. More trouble with the Portuguese down in the south."

Jake rumbled, "There's going to be a bloodbath there before it's over."

Isobel said thoughtfully, "There's been some hope that fundamental changes might take place in Lisbon."

Jake grunted his skepticism. "In that case the bloodbath would take place there instead of in Africa." He added, "Which is all right with me."

"What else?" Isobel said.

"Continued complications in the Congo."

"That's hardly news."

"But things are going like clockwork in the west. Kenya, Uganda, Tanganyika." Cliff took his right hand away from the controls long enough to make a circle with its thumb and index finger. "Like clockwork. Fifty new fellows from the University of Chicago came in last week to help with the rural education development and twenty or so men from Johns Hopkins in Baltimore have wrangled a special grant for a new medical school."

"All ... Negroes?"

"What else?"

Jake said suddenly, "Tell her about the Cubans."

Isobel frowned. "Cubans?"

"Over in the Anglo-Egyptian Sudan area. They were supposedly helping introduce modern sugar refining methods —"

"Why supposedly?"

"Why not?"

"All right, go on," Isobel said.

Cliff Jackson said slowly, "Somebody shot them up. Killed several, wounded most of the others."

The girl's eyes went round. "Who ... and why?"

The pilot shifted his heavy shoulders again.

Jake said, "Nobody seems to know, but the weapons were modern. Plenty modern." He twisted in his bucket seat, uncomfortably. "Listen, have you heard anything about some character named El Hassan?"

Isobel turned to face him. "Why, yes. The people there in Gao mentioned him. Who is he?"

"That's what I'd like to know," Jake said. "What did they say?"

"Oh, mostly supposed words of wisdom that El Hassan was alleged to have made with. I get it that he's some, well you wouldn't call him a nationalist since he's international in his appeal, but he's evidently preaching union of all Africans. I get an undercurrent of anti-Europeanism in general, but not overdone." Isobel's expressive face went thoughtful. "As a matter of fact, his program seems to coincide largely with our own, so much so that from time to time when I had occasion to drop a few words of propaganda into a conversation, I'd sometimes credit it to him."

Cliff looked over at her and chuckled. "That's a coincidence," he said. "I've been doing the same thing. An idea often carries more weight with these people if it's attributed to somebody with a reputation."

Jake, the older of the three said: "Well, I can't find out anything about him. Nobody seems to know if he's an Egyptian, a Nigerian, a MOR … or an Eskimo, for that matter."

"Did you check with headquarters?"

"So far they have nothing on him, except for some other inquiries from field workers."

Below them, the river was widening out to the point where it resembled swampland more than a waterway. There were large numbers of waterbirds, and occasional herds of hippopotami. Isobel didn't express her thoughts, but a moment of doubt hit her. What would all this be like when the dams were finished, the waters of this third largest of Africa's rivers, ninth largest of the world's, under control?

She pointed. "There's Kabara." The age-old river port lay below them. Cliff slapped one of his controls with the heel of his hand and the craft began to sink earthward.

* * * * *

They took up quarters in the new hotel which adjoined the new elementary school, and Isobel immediately went into her routine.

Dressed and shod immaculately, her head held high in confidence, she spent considerable time mingling with the more backward of the natives and especially the women. Six months ago, she had given a performance similar to that she had just finished in Gao, several hundred miles down river.

Now she renewed old acquaintances, calling them by name-after checking her notes. Invariably, their eyes bugged. Their questions came thick, came fast in the slurring Songhoi and she answered them in detail. They came quickly under her intellectual domination. Her poise, her obvious well being, flabbergasted them.

In all, they spent a week in the little river town, but even the first night Isobel slumped wearily in the most comfortable chair of their small suite's living room.

She kicked off her shoes, and wiggled weary toes.

"If my mother could see me now," she complained. "After giving her all to get the apple of her eye through school, her wayward daughter winds up living with two men in the wilds of deepest Africa." She twisted her mouth puckishly.

Cliff grunted, poking around in a bag for the bottle of cognac he couldn't remember where he had packed. "Huh!" he said. "The next time you write her you might mention the fact that both of them are continually proposing to you and you brush it all off as a big joke."

"Huh, indeed!" Isobel answered him. "Proposing, or propositioning? If either of you two Romeos ever rattle the doorknob of my room at night again, you're apt to get a bullet through it."

Jake winced. "Wasn't me. Look at my gray hair, Isobel. I'm old enough to be your daddy."

"Sugar daddy, I suppose," she said mockingly.

"Wasn't me either," Cliff said, criss-crossing his heart and pointing upward.

"Huh!" said Isobel again, but she was really in no mood for their usual banter. "Listen," she said, "what're we accomplishing with all this masquerade?"

Cliff had found the French brandy. He poured three stiff ones and handed drinks to Isobel and Jake.

He knew he wasn't telling her anything, but he said, "We're a king-size rumor campaign, that's what we are. We're breaking down institutions the sneaky way." He added reflectively. "A kinder way, though, than some."

"But this … what did you call it earlier, Jake?… this Cinderella act I go through perpetually. What good does it do, really? I contact only a few hundreds of people at most. And there are millions here in Mali alone."

"There are other teams, too," Jake said mildly. "Several hundreds of us doing one thing or another."

"A drop in the bucket," Isobel said, her piquant sepian face registering weariness.

Cliff sipped his brandy, shaking his big head even as he did so. "No," he said. "It's a king-size rumor campaign and it's amazing how effective they can be. Remember the original dirty-rumor campaigns back in the States? Suppose two laundry firms were competing. One of them, with a manager on the conscience-less side, would hire two or three professional rumor spreaders. They'd go around dropping into bars, barber shops, pool rooms. Sooner or later, they'd get a chance to drop some line such as *did you hear about them discovering that two lepers worked at the Royal Laundry?* You can imagine the barbers, the bartenders, and such professional gossips, passing on the good word."

Isobel laughed, but unhappily. "I don't recognize myself in the description."

Cliff said earnestly, "Sure, only few score women in each town you put on your act, really witness the whole thing. But think how they pass it on. Each one of them tells the story of the miracle. A waif comes out of the desert. Without property, without a husband or family, without kinsfolk. Shy, dirty, unwanted. Then she's offered a good position if she'll drop the veil, discard the haik, and attend the new schools. So off she goes-everyone thinking to her disaster. Hocus-pocus, six months later she returns, obviously prosperous, obviously healthy, obviously well adjusted. Fine. The story spreads for miles around. Nothing is so popular as the Cinderella story, and that's the story you're putting over. It's a natural."

"I hope so," Isobel said. "Sometimes I think I'm helping put over a gigantic hoax on these people. Promising something that won't be delivered."

Jake looked at her unhappily. "I've thought the same thing, sometimes, but what are you going to be with people at this stage of development —*subtle?*"

Isobel dropped it. She held out her glass for more cognac. "I hope there's something decent to eat in this place. Do you realize what I've been putting into my tummy this past week?"

Cliff shuddered.

Isobel patted her abdomen. "At least it keeps my figure in trim."

"Um-m-m," Jake pretended to leer heavily.

Isobel chuckled at him in a return to good humor. "Hyena," she accused.

"Hyena?" Jake said.

"Sure, there aren't any wolves in these parts," she explained. "How long are we going to be here?"

The two men looked at each other. Cliff said, "Well, we'd like to finish out the week. Guy named Homer Crawford has been passing around the word to hold a meeting in Timbuktu the end of this week."

"Crawford?"

"Homer Crawford, some kind of sociologist from the University of Michigan, I understand. He's connected with the Reunited Nations African Development Project, heads one of their cloak and dagger teams."

Jake grunted. "Sociologist? I also understand that he put in a hitch with the Marines and spent kind of a shady period of two years fighting with the FLN in Algeria."

"On what side?" Cliff said interestedly.

"Darn if I know."

Isobel said, "Well, we have nothing to do with the Reunited Nations."

Cliff shook his large head negatively. "Of course not, but Crawford seems to think it'd be a good idea if some of us in the field would get together and ...well, have sort of a bull session."

Jake growled, "We don't have much in the way of co-operation on the higher levels. Everybody seems to head out in all directions on their own. It can get chaotic. Maybe in the field we could give each other a few pointers. For one, I'd like to find out if any of the rest of these jokers know anything about that affair with the Cubans over in the Sudan."

"I suppose it can't hurt," Isobel admitted. "In fact, it might be fun swapping experiences with some of these characters. Frankly, though, the stories I've heard about the African Development teams aren't any too palatable. They seem to be a ruthless bunch."

Jake looked down into his glass. "It's a ruthless country," he murmured.

* * * * *

Dolo Anah, as he approached the ten Dogon villages of the Canton de Sangha, was first thought to be a small bird in the sky. As he drew nearer, it was decided, instead, that he was a larger creature of the air, perhaps a vulture, though who had ever seen such a vulture? As he drew nearer still, it was plain that in size he was more nearly an ostrich than vulture, but who had ever heard of a flying ostrich, and besides —

No! It was a man! But who in all the Dogon had ever witnessed such a *juju* man? One whose flailing limbs enabled him to fly!

The ten villages of the Dogon are perched on the rim of the Falaise de Bandiagara. The cliffs are over three hundred feet high and the villages are similar to Mesa Verde of Colorado, and as unaccessible, as impregnable to attack.

But hardly impregnable to arrival by helio-hopper.

When Dolo Anah landed in the tiny square of the village of Irèli, the first instinct of Amadijuè the village witchman was to send post haste to summon the Kanaga dancers, but then despair overwhelmed him. Against powers such as this, what could prevail? Besides, Amadijuè had not arrived at his position of influence and affluence through other than his own true abilities. Secretly, he rather doubted the efficacy of even the supposedly most potent witchcraft.

But this!

Dolo Anah unstrapped himself from the one man helio-hopper's small bicyclelike seat, folded the two rotors back over the rest of the craft, and then deposited the seventy-five pound vehicle in a corner, between two adobe houses. He knew perfectly well that the local inhabitants would die a thousand deaths of torture rather than approach, not to speak of touching it.

Looking to neither right nor left, walking arrogantly and carrying only a small bag-undoubtedly housing his *gris gris*, as Amadijuè could well imagine-Dolo Anah headed for the largest house. Since the whole village was packed, bug-eyed, into the square watching him there were no inhabitants within.

He snapped back over his shoulder, "Summon all the headmen of all the villages, and all of their eldest sons; summon all the Hogons and all the witchmen. Immediately! I would speak with them and issue orders."

He was a small man, clad only in a loincloth, and could well have been a Dogon himself. Surely he was black as a Dogon, clad as a Dogon, and he spoke the native language which is a tongue little known outside the semi-desert land of Dogon covered with its sand, rocks, scrub bush and baobab trees. It is not a land which sees many strangers.

The headmen gathered with trepidation. All had seen the juju man descend from the skies. It had been with considerable relief that most had noted that he finally sank to earth in the village of Irèli instead of their own. But now all were summoned. Those among them who were Kanaga dancers wore their masks and costumes, and above all their gris gris charms, but it was a feeble gesture. Such magic as this was unknown. To fly through the air *personally*!

Dolo Anah was seated to one end of the largest room of the largest house of Irèli when they crowded in to answer his blunt summons. He was seated cross-legged on the floor and staring at the ground before him.

The others seemed tongue-tied, both headmen and Hogons, the highly honored elders of the Dogon people. So Amadijuè as senior witchman took over the responsibility of addressing this mystery juju come out of the skies.

"Oh, powerful stranger, how is your health?"

"Good," Dolo Anah said.

"How is the health of thy wife?"

"Good."

"How is the health of thy children?"

"Good."

"How is the health of thy mother?"

"Good."

"How is the health of thy father?"

"Good."

"How is the health of thy kinswomen?"

"Good."

"How is the health of thy kinsmen?"

"Good."

To the traditional greeting of the Dogon, Amadijuè added hopefully, "Welcome to the villages of Sangha."

His voice registering nothing beyond the impatience which had marked it from the beginning, Dolo Anah repeated the routine.

"Men of Sangha," he snapped, "how is your health?"

"Good," they chorused.

"How is the health of thy wives?"

"Good!"

"How is the health of thy children?"

"Good!"

"How is the health of thy mothers?"

"Good!"

"How is the health of thy fathers?"

"Good!"

"How is the health of thy kinswomen?"

"Good!"

"How is the health of thy kinsmen?"

"Good!"

"I accept thy welcome," Dolo Anah bit out. "And now heed me well for I am known as Dolo Anah and I have instructions from above for the people of the Dogon."

Sweat glistened on the faces and bodies of the assembled Dogon headmen, their uncharacteristically silent witchmen, the Hogons and the sons of the headmen.

"Speak, oh juju come out of the sky," Amadijuè fluttered, but proud of his ability to find speech at all when all the others were stricken dumb with fear.

* * * * *

Dolo Anah stared down at the ground before him. The others, their eyes fascinated as though by a cobra preparing to strike its death, focused on the spot as well.

Dolo Anah raised a hand very slowly and very gently and a sigh went through his audience. The dirt on the hut floor had stirred. It stirred again and slowly, ever so slowly, up through the floor emerged a milky, translucent ball. When it had fully emerged, Dolo Anah took it up in his hands and stared at it for a long moment.

It came to sudden light and a startled gasp flushed over the room, a gasp shared by even the witchmen, Amadijuè included.

Dolo Anah looked up at them. "Each of you must come in turn and look into the ball," he said.

Faltering, though all eyes were turned to him, Amadijuè led the way. His eyes rounded, he stared, and they widened still further. For within, mystery upon mystery, men danced in seeming celebration. It was as though it was a funeral party but of dimensions never known before, for there were scores of Kanaga dancers, and, yes, above all other wonders, some of the dancers were Dogon, without doubt, but others were Mosse and others were even Tellum!

Amadijuè turned away, shaken, and Dolo Anah spoke sharply, "The rest, one by one."

They came. The headmen, the Hogons, the witchmen and finally the sons of the headmen, and each in turn stared into the ball and saw the tiny men within, doing their dance of celebration, Dogon, Mosse and Tellum together.

When all had seen, Dolo Anah placed the ball back on the ground and stared at it and slowly it returned to from whence it came, and Dolo Anah gently spread dust over the spot. When the floor was as it had been, he looked up at them, his eyes striking.

"What did you see?" he spoke sharply to Amadijuè.

There was a tremor in the village witchman's voice. "Oh juju, come out of the sky, I saw a great festival and Dogon danced with their enemies the Mosse and the Tellum-and, all seemed happy beyond belief."

The stranger looked piercingly at the rest. "And what did you see?"

Some mumbled, "The same. The same," and others, terrified still, could only nod.

"That is the message I have come to give you. You will hold a great conference with the people of the Tellum and the people of the Mosse and there will be a great celebration and no longer will there be Dogon, Mosse and Tellum, but all will be one. And there will be trade, and there will be marriage between the tribes, and no longer will there be three tribes, but only one people and no longer will the headmen and witchmen of the tribes resist the coming of the new schools, and all the young people will attend."

Amadijuè muttered, "But, great juju come out of the sky, these are our blood enemies. For longer than the memory of the grandfathers of our eldest Hogon we have carried the blood feud with Tellum and Mosse."

"No longer," Dolo Anah said flatly.

Amadijuè held shaking hands out in supplication, to this dominating juju come out of the skies. "But they will not heed us. Tellum and Mosse have hated the Dogon for all time. They will wreak their vengeance on any delegation come to make such suggestions to them."

"I fly to see their headmen and witchmen immediately," Dolo Anah bit out decisively. "They will heed my message." His tone turned dangerous. "As will the headmen and witchmen of the Dogon. If any fail to obey the message from above, their eyes will lose sight, their tongues become dumb, and their bellies will crawl with worms."

Amadijuè's face went ashen.

At long last the headman of all the Sangha villages spoke up, his voice trembling its fear. "But the schools, oh great juju-as all the Dogon have decided, in tribal conference-the schools are evil for our youth. They teach not the old ways —"

Dolo Anah cut him short with the chop of a commanding hand. "The old ways are fated to die. Already they die. The new ways are the ways of the schools."

Amazed at his own temerity, the head chief spoke once more. "But, since the coming of the French, we have rejected the schools."

Dolo Anah looked at him in scorn. "These will not be schools of the French. They will be the schools of Bantu, Berber, Sudanese and all the other peoples of the land. And when your young people have attended the schools and learned their wisdom they in turn will teach in the schools and in all the land there will be wisdom and good life. Now I have spoken and all of you will withdraw save only the sons of the headmen."

They withdrew, making a point each and every one not to turn their backs to this bringer of disastrous news and leaving only the terror-stricken young men behind them.

* * * * *

When all were gone save the dozen youngsters, Dolo Anah looked at them contemplatively. He shrugged finally and said, pointing with his finger, "You, you and you may leave. The others will remain." The three darted out, glad of the reprieve.

He looked at the remainder. "Be unafraid," he snapped. "There is no reason to fear me. Your fathers and the Hogons and the so-called witchmen, are fools, nothing-men. Fools and cowards, because they are impressed by foolish tricks."

He pointed suddenly. "You, there, what is your name?"

The youth stuttered, "Hinnan."

"Very well, Hinnan. Did you see me approach by the air?"

"Yes ...yes ...juju man."

"Don't call me a juju man. There is no such thing as juju. It is nonsense made by the cunning to fool the stupid, as you will learn when you attend the schools."

Hinnan took courage. "But I saw you fly."

"Have you never seen the great aircraft of the white men of Europe and America go flying over? Or have none of you witnessed these craft sitting on the ground at Mopti or Niamey. Surely some of you have journeyed to Mopti."

"Yes, but they are great craft. And you flew alone and without the great wings and propellers of the white-man's aircraft."

Dolo Anah chuckled. "My son, I flew in a helio-hopper as they are called. They are the smallest of all aircraft, but they are not magic. They are made in the factories of the lands of Europe and America and after you have finished school and have found a position for yourself in the new industries that spread through Africa, then you will be able to purchase one quite cheaply, if you so desire. Others among you might even learn to build them, themselves."

Hinnan and the others gasped.

Dolo Anah went on. "And observe this." He dug into the ground before him and revealed the crystal ball that had magically appeared before. He showed to them the little elevator device beneath it which he manipulated with a small rubber bulb which pumped air underneath.

One or two of them ventured a scornful laugh, at the obviousness of the trick.

Dolo Anah took up the ball and unscrewed the base. Inside were a delicate arrangement of film on a continuous spool so that the scene played over and over again, and a combination of batteries and bulbs to project the scene on the ball's surface. He explained, in patient detail, the workings of the supposed magic ball. Two of the boys had seen movies on trips to Mopti, the others had heard of them.

Finally one, highly encouraged now, as were the others, said, "But why do you show us this and shame us for our foolishness?"

Dolo Anah nodded encouragement at the teen-ager. "I do not shame you, my son, but your fathers and the Hogons and the so-called witchmen. For long ages the Dogon have been led by the oldest members of the tribe, the Hogons. This can be nonsense because in spite of your traditions age does not necessarily bring wisdom. In fact, senility as it is called can bring childish nonsense. A people should be governed by the wisest and best among them, not by tradition, by often silly beliefs handed down from one generation to another."

Hinnan, who was eldest son of the head chief, said, "But why do you tell us this, after shaming our fathers and the old men of the Dogon?"

For the first time since the elders had left, Dolo Anah's eyes gleamed as before. "Because you will be the leaders of the Dogon tomorrow, most like. And it is necessary to learn these great truths. That you attend the schools and bring to the Dogon tomorrow what they did not have yesterday, and do not have today."

"But suppose we tell them of how you have deceived them?" the other articulate Dogon lad said.

Dolo Anah chuckled and shook his head. "They will not believe you, boy. They will be afraid to believe you. And besides, men are almost everywhere the same. It is difficult for an older man to learn from a younger one, especially his own son. It is vanity, but it is true." His mouth twisted in memory. "When I was a lad myself, on the beaches of an island far from here in the Bahamas, my father beat me on more than one occasion, indignant that I should wish to attend the white man's schools, while he and his father before him had been fishermen. Beneath his indignation was the fear that one day I would excel him."

"You are right," Hinnan said uncomfortably, "they would not believe us." Instinctively, the son of the head chief assumed leadership of the others. "We will keep this secret between us," he said to them.

Dolo Anah came to his feet, yawned, stretched his legs and began to pack his gadgets into the small valise he carried. "Good luck, boys," he said unthinkingly in English.

As he left the hut, he emerged into a respectfully cleared area around the hut. Without looking left or right he approached his folded helio-hopper, made the few adjustments that were needed to make it air-borne, strapped himself into the tiny saddle, flicked the start control and to the accompaniment of a gasp from the entire village of Irèli, took off in a swoop.

In a matter of moments, he had disappeared to the north in the direction of the Mosse villages.

III

The Emir Alhaji Mohammadu, the Galadima Dawakin, Kudo of Kano, boiled furiously within as his gold plated Rolls Royce progressed through the Saba N'Gari section of town, the quarter outside the dirt walls of the millennium old city. He rode seated alone in the middle of the rear seat and his single counselor sat beside the chauffeur. Before them, a jeep load of his bodyguard, dressed in their uniforms of red and green, cleared the way. Another jeep followed similarly laden.

They entered through one of the ancient gates and swept up the principal street. They stopped before the recently constructed luxury hotel in the center of town and the bodyguard leapt from the jeeps and took positions to each side of the entry. The counselor popped out from his side of the car and beat the chauffeur to the task of opening the Emir's door.

Emir Alhaji Mohammadu was a tall man and a heavy one, his white robed figure towered some six and a half feet and his scales put him over the three hundred mark. He was in his mid fifties and almost a quarter century of autocratic position had marked his face with permanent scowl. He stomped now into the western style hotel.

His counselor, Ahmadu Abdullah, had already procured the information necessary to locate the source of the Emir's ire and now scurried before his chief, leading the way to the suite occupied by the mysterious strangers. He banged heavily on the door, then stepped behind his master as it opened.

One of the strangers, clad western style, opened the door and stepped aside courteously motioning to the large inner room. The Emir strutted arrogantly inside and stared in high irritation at the second and elder stranger who sat there at a heavy table. This one came to his feet, but there was no sign of acknowledgment of the Emir's rank. It was not too long a time before that men prostrated themselves in Alhaji Mohammadu's presence.

He looked at them. Though both were of dark complexion, there seemed no manner of typing them. Certainly they were neither Hausa nor Fulani, there being no signs of Hamitic features, but neither were they Ibo or Yoruba from farther south. The Emir's eyes narrowed and he wondered if these two were Nigerians at all!

He barked at them in Hausa and the older answered him in the same language, though there seemed a certain awkwardness in its use.

Emir Alhaji Mohammadu blared, "You dare summon me, Kudo of this city? You presume —"

They had resumed seats behind the table and the two of them looked at him questioningly. The older one interrupted with a gently raised hand. "Why did you come?"

Still glaring, the Emir turned to the cringing Ahmadu Abdullah and motioned curtly for the counselor to speak. Meanwhile, the ruler's eyes went around the room, decided that the couch was the only seat that would accommodate his bulk, and descended upon it.

Ahmadu Abdullah brought a paper from the folds of his robes. "This lying letter. This shameless attack upon the Galadima Dawakin!"

The younger stranger said mildly, "If the charges contained there are incorrect, then why did you come?"

The Emir rumbled dangerously, ignoring the question. "What is your purpose? I am not a patient man. There has never been need for my patience."

The spokesman of the two, the older, leaned back in his chair and said carefully, "We have come to demand your resignation and self-exile."

A vein beat suddenly and wildly at the gigantic Emir's temple and for a full minute the potentate was speechless with outrage.

Ahmadu Abdullah said quickly, "Fantastic! Ridiculous! The Galadima Dawakin is lawful ruler and religious potentate of three million devoted followers. You are lying strangers come to cause dissention among the people of Kano and —"

The spokesman for the newcomers took up a sheaf of papers from the table and said, his voice emotionless, "The reason you came here at our request is because the charges made in that letter you bear are valid ones. For a quarter century, you, Alhaji Mohammadu, have milked your people to your own profit. You have lived like a god on the wealth you have extracted from them. You have gone far, far beyond the legal and even traditional demands you have on the local population. Funds supposedly to be devoted to education, sanitation, roads, hospitals and a multitude of other developments that would improve this whole benighted area, have gone into your private pocket. In short, you have been a cancer on your people for the better part of your life."

"All lies!" roared the Kudo.

The other shook his head. "No. We have carefully gathered proof. We can submit evidence to back every charge we have made. Above all, we can prove the existence of large sums of money you have smuggled out of the country to Switzerland, London and New York to create a reserve for yourself in case of emergency. Needless to say, these funds, too, were originally meant for the betterment of the area."

The Emir's eyes were narrow with hate. "Who are you? Whom do you represent?"

"What difference does it make? This is of no importance."

"You represent my son, Alhaji Fodio! This is what comes of his studies in England and America. This is what comes of his leaving Kano and spending long years in Lagos among those unbeliever communists in the south!"

The younger stranger chuckled easily. "That is about the last tag I would hang on your son's associates," he said in English.

But the older stranger was nodding. "It is true that we hope your son will take over the Emirate. He represents progress. Frankly, his plans are to end the office as soon as the people are educated to the point where they can accept such change."

"End the office!" the Emir snarled. "For a thousand years my ancestors —"

* * * * *

The spokesman of the strangers shook his head wearily. "Your ancestors conquered this area less than two centuries ago in a jehad led by Othman Dan. Since then, you Fulani have feudalistically dominated the Hausa, but that is coming to an end."

The Emir had come to his feet again, in his rage, and now he towered over the table behind which the two sat as though about to physically attack them. "You speak as fools," he raged.

"Are you so stupid as to believe that these matters you have brought up are understandable to my people? Have you ever seen my people?" He sneered in a caricature of humor. "My people in their grass and bush huts? With not one man in a whole village who can add sums higher than those he can work out on his fingers? With not one man who can read the English tongue, nor any other? Would you explain to these the matters of transferring gold to the Zürich banks? Would you explain to these what is involved in accepting dash from road contractors and from politicians in Lagos?"

He sneered at them again. "And do you realize that I am church as well as state? That I represent their God to my people? Do you think they would take your word against *mine*, their Kudo?"

In talking, he had brought a certain calm back to himself. Now he felt reassured at his own words. He wound it up. "You are fools to believe my people could understand such matters."

"Then actually, you don't deny them?"

"Why should I bother?" the Emir chuckled heavily.

"That you have taken for personal use the large sums granted this area from a score of sources for roads, hospitals, schools, sanitation, agricultural modernization?"

"Of course I don't deny it. This is my land. I am the Kudo, the Emir, the Galadima Dawakin. Whatever I choose to do in Kano and to all my people is right because I wish it. Schools? I don't want them corrupting my people. Hospitals for these Hausa serfs? Nonsense! Roads? They are bad for they allow the people to get about too easily and that leads to their exchanging ideas and schemes and leads to their corruption. Have I appropriated all such sums for my own use? Yes! I admit it. Yes! But you cannot prove it to such as my people, you who represent my son. So be-gone from Kano. If you are here tomorrow, you will be arrested by the same men of my bodyguard who even now seek my son, Alhaji Fodio. When he is captured, it will be of interest to revive some of the methods of execution of my ancestors."

The Emir turned on his heel to stalk from the room but the older of the two murmured, "One moment, please."

Alhaji Mohammadu paused, his face dark in scowl again.

The spokesman said agreeably, "It is true that your people, and particularly your Hausa serfs, have no understanding of international finance nor of national corruption methods such as the taking of *dash*. However, they are susceptible to other proof." The other man raised his voice. "John!"

From an inner room came another stranger, making their total number three. He was grinning and in one hand held a contraption which boasted a conglomeration of lenses, switches, microphones, wires and triggers. "Got it perfectly," he said. You'd think it had all been rehearsed.

While the Emir and his counselor stared in amazement, the spokesman of the strangers said, "How long before you can project?"

"Almost immediately."

The other young man left the room and returned with what was obviously a movie projector. He set it up at one end of the table, pointed at a white wall, and plugged it in to a convenient outlet.

Before the Emir had managed to control himself beyond the point of saying any more than, "What is all this?" the cameraman had brought a magazine of film from his instrument and inserted it in the projector.

The photographer said conversationally, to the hulking potentate, "You'd be amazed at the advances in cinema these past few years. Film speed, immediate development, portable sound equipment. You'd be amazed."

Someone flicked out the greater part of the room's light. The projector buzzed and on the wall was thrown a re-enactment of everything that had been said and done in the room for the past ten minutes.

When it was over, the lights went on again.

The spokesman said conversationally, "I assume that if this film were shown throughout the villages, even your Hausa serfs would be convinced that throughout your reign you have systematically robbed them."

Emir Alhaji Mohammadu, the Galadima Dawakin, Kudo of Kano, his face in shock, turned and stumbled from the room.

* * * * *

The gymkhana, or fantasia as it is called in nearby Morocco, was under full swing before Abd-el-Kader and the camel- and horse-mounted warriors of his Ouled Touameur clan came dashing in, rifles held high and with great firing into the air. The Ouled Touameur were the noblest clan of the Ouled Allouch tribe of the Berazga division of the Chaambra nomad confederation-the noblest and the least disciplined. There were whispered rumors going about the conference as to the identity of the mysterious raiders who were preying upon the new oases, the oil and road building camps and the endless other new projects springing up, all but magically, throughout the northwestern Sahara.

The gymkhana was in full swing with racing and feasting, and storytellers and conjurers, jugglers and marabouts. And in the air was the acrid distinctive odor of *kif*, for though Mohammed forbade alcohol to the faithful he had naught to say about the uses of *cannabis sativa* and what is a great festival without the smoking of *kif* and the eating of *majoun*?

The tribes of the Chaambra were widely represented, Berazga and Mouadhi, Bou Rouba and Ouled Fredj, and there was even a heavy sprinkling of the sedentary Zenatas come down from the towns of Metlili, El Oued and El Goléo. Then, of course, were the Haratin serfs, of mixed Arab-Negro blood, and the Negroes themselves, until recently openly called slaves, but now-amusingly-named servants.

The Chaambra were meeting for a great ceremonial gymkhanas, but also, as was widely known, for a *djemaa el kebar* council of elders and chiefs, for there were many problems throughout the Western Erg and the areas of Mzab and Bourara. Nor was it secret only to the inner councils that the meeting had been called by Abd-el-Kader, of Shorfu blood, direct descendent of the Prophet through his daughter Fatima, and symbol to the young warriors of Chaambra spirit.

Of all the Ouled Touameur clan Abd-el-Kader alone refrained from discharging his gun into the air as they dashed into the inner circle of khaima tents which centered the gymkhana and provided council chambers, dining hall and sleeping quarters for the tribal and clan heads. Instead, and with head arrogantly high, he slipped from his stallion tossing the reins to a nearby Zenata and strode briskly to the largest of the tents and disappeared inside.

Bismillah! but Adb-el-Kader was a figure of a man! From his turban, white as the snows of the Atlas, to his yellow leather boots, he wore the traditional clothing of the Chaambra and wore them with pride. Not for Abd-el-Kader the new clothing from the Rouma cities to the north, nor even the new manufactures from Dakar, Accra, Lagos and the other mushrooming centers to the south.

His weapons alone paid homage to the new ways. And each fighting man within eyesight noted that it was not a rifle slung over the shoulder of Abd-el-Kader but a sub-machine gun. Bismillah! This could not have been so back in the days when the French Camel Corps ruled the land with its hand of iron.

The djemaa el kebar was already in session, seated in a great circle on the rug and provided with glasses of mint tea and some with water pipes. They looked up at the entrance of the warrior clan chieftain.

* * * * *

El Aicha, who was of Maraboutic ancestry and hence a holy man as well as elder of the Ouled Fredj, spoke first as senior member of the conference. "We have heard reports that are disturbing of recent months, Abd-el-Kader. Reports of activities amongst the Ouled Touameur. We would know more of the truth of these. But also we have high interest in your reason for summoning the djemaa el kebar at such a time of year."

Abd-el-Kader made a brief gesture of obeisance to the Chaambra leader, a gesture so brief as to verge on disrespect. He said, his voice clear and confident, as befits a warrior chief, "Disturbing only to the old and unvaliant, O El Aicha."

The old man looked at him for a long, unblinking moment. As a youth, he had fought at the Battle of Tit when the French Camel Corps had broken forever the military power of the Ahaggar Tuareg. El Aicha was no coward. There were murmurings about the circle of elders.

But when El Aicha spoke again, his voice was level. "Then speak to us, Abd-el-Kader. It is well known that your voice is heard ever more by the young men, particularly by the bolder of the young men."

The fighting man remained standing, his legs slightly spread. The Arab, like the Amerind, likes to make speech in conference, and eloquence is well held by the Chaambra.

"Long years ago, and only shortly after the death of the Prophet, the Chaambra resided, so tell the scribes, in the hills of far away Syria. But when the word of Islam was heard and the true believers began to race their strength throughout all the world, the Chaambra came here to the deserts of Africa and here we have remained. Long centuries it took us to gain control of the wide areas of the northern and western desert and many were the battles we fought with our traditional enemies the Tuareg and the Moors before we controlled all the land between the Atlas and the Niger and from what is now known as Tunisia to Mauritania."

All nodded. This was tribal history.

Abd-el-Kader held up four fingers on which to enumerate. "The Chaambra were ever men. Warriors, bedouin; not for us the cities and villages of the Zenatas, and the miserable Haratin serfs. We Chaambra have ever been men of the tent, warriors, conquerors!"

El Aicha still nodded. "That was before," he murmured.

"That will always be!" Abd-el-Kader insisted. His four fingers were spread and he touched the first one. "Our life was based upon, one, war and the spoils of war." He touched the second finger. "Two, the toll we extracted from the caravans that passed from Timbuktu to the north and back again. Three, from our own caravans which covered the desert trails from Tripoli to Dakar and from Marrakech to Kano. And fourth"—he touched his last finger—"from our flocks which fed us in the wilderness." He paused to let this sink in.

"All this is verily true," muttered one of the elders, a *so-what* quality in his voice.

Abd-el-Kader's tone soured. "Then came the French with their weapons and their multitudes of soldiers and their great wealth with which to pursue the expenses of war. And one by one the Tuareg and the Teda to the south and the Moors and Nemadi, yes, and even the Chaambra fell before the onslaughts of the Camel Corps and their wild-dog Foreign Legion." He held up his four fingers again and counted them off. "The four legs upon which our life was based were broken. War and its spoils was prevented us. The tolls we charged caravans to cross our land were forbidden. And then, shortly after, came the motor trucks which crossed the desert in a week, where formerly the journey took as much as a year. Our camel caravans became meaningless."

Again all nodded. "Verily, the world changes," someone muttered.

The warrior leader's voice went dramatic. "We were left with naught but our flocks, and now even they are fated to end."

The elderly nomads stirred and some scowled.

"At every water hole in the desert teams of the new irrigation development dig their wells, install their pumps which bring power from the sun, plant trees, bring in Haratin and former slaves—our slaves-to cultivate the new oases. And we are forbidden the water for the use of our goats and sheep and camels."

"Besides," one of the clan chiefs injected, "they tell us that the goat is the curse of North Africa, nibbling as it does the bark of small trees, and they attempt to purchase all goats until soon there will be few, if any, in all the land."

"So our young people," Abd-el-Kader pressed on, "stripped of our former way of life, go to the new projects, enroll in the schools, take work in the new oases or on the roads, and disappear from the sight of their kinsmen." He came to a sudden halt and all but glared at them, maintaining his silence until El Aicha stirred.

"And —?" El Aicha said. This was all obviously but preliminary.

Abd-el-Kader spoke softly now, and there was a different drama in his voice. "And now," he said, "the French are gone. All the Rouma, save a handful, are gone. In the south the English are gone from the lands of the blacks, such as Nigeria and Ghana, Sierra Leone and Gambia. The Italians are gone from Libya and Somaliland and the Spanish from Rio de Oro. Nor will they ever return for in the greatest council of all the Rouma they have decided to leave Africa to the African."

They all stirred again and some muttered and Abd-el-Kader pushed his point. "The Chaambra are warriors born. Never serfs! Never slaves! Never have we worked for any man. Our ancestors carved great empires by the sword." His voice lowered again. "And now, once more, it is possible to carve such an empire."

He swept his eyes about their circle. "Chiefs of the Chaambra, there is no force in all the Sahara to restrain us. Let others work on the roads, planting the new trees in the new oases, damming the great Niger, and all the rest of it. We will sweep over them, and dominate all. We, the Chaambra, will rule, while those whom Allah intended to drudge, do so. We, the Chosen of Allah, will fulfill our destiny!"

* * * * *

Abd-el-Kader left it there and crossed his arms on his chest, staring at them challengingly.

Finally El Aicha directed his eyes across the circle of listeners at two who had sat silently through it all, their burnooses covering their heads and well down over their eyes. He said, "And what do you say to all this?"

"Time to go into your act, man," Abe Bakr muttered, under his breath.

Homer Crawford came to his feet and pushed back the hood of the burnoose. He looked over at the headman of the Ouled Touameur warrior clan, whose face was darkening.

In Arabic, Crawford said, "I have sought you for some time, Abd-el-Kader. You are an illusive man."

"Who are you, Negro?" the fighting man snapped.

Crawford grinned at the other. "You look as though you have a bit of Negro blood in your own veins. In fact, I doubt if there's a so-called Arab in all North Africa, unless he's just recently arrived, whose family hasn't down through the centuries mixed its blood with the local people they conquered."

"You lie!"

Abe chuckled from the background. The Chaambra leader was at least as dark of complexion as the American Negro. Not that it made any difference one way or the other.

"We shall see who is the liar here," Homer Crawford said flatly. "You asked who I am. I am known as Omar ben Crawf and I am headman of a team of the African Development Project of the Reunited Nations. As you have said, Abd-el-Kader, this great council of the headmen of all the nations of the world-not just the Rouma-has decided that Africa must be left to the Africans. But that does not mean it has lost all interest in these lands. It has no intention, warrior of the Chaambra, to allow such as you to disrupt the necessary progress Africa must make if it is not to become a danger to the shaky peace of the world."

Abd-el-Kader's eyes darted about the tent. So far as he could see, the other was backed only by his single henchman. The warrior chief gained confidence. "Power is for those who can assert it. Some will rule. It has always been so. Here in the Western Erg, the Chaambra will rule, and I, Abd-el-Kader will lead them!"

Homer Crawford was shaking his head, almost sadly it seemed. "No," he said. "The day of rule by the gun is over. It must be over because at long last man's weapons have become so great that he must not trust himself with them. In the new world which is still aborning so that half the nations of earth are in the pains of labor, government must be by the most wise and most capable."

In a deft move the sub-machine gun's sling slipped from the desert man's shoulder and the short, vicious gun was in hand. "The strong will always rule!" the Arab shouted. "Time was when the French conquered the Chaambra, but the French have allowed their strength to ebb away, and now, armed with such weapons as these, we of the Sahara will again assert our birthright as the Chosen of Allah!"

Abe Baker chuckled. "That cat sure can lay on a speech, man." As though magically, a snub-nosed hand weapon of unique design appeared in his dark hand.

El Aicha's voice was suddenly strong and harsh. "There shall be no violence at a djemaa el kebar."

Homer ignored the automatic weapon in the hands of the excited Arab. He said, and there was still a sad quality in his voice. "The gun you carry is a nothing-weapon, desert man. When the French conquered this land more than a century ago they were armed with single-shot rifles which were still far in advance of your own long barrelled flintlocks. Today, you are proud of that tommy gun you carry, and, indeed, it has the fire power of a company of the Foreign Legion of a century past. However, believe me, Abd-el-Kader, it is a nothing-weapon compared to those that will be brought against the Chaambra if they heed your words."

The desert leader put back his head and laughed his scorn.

He chopped his laughter short and snapped, more to the council of chiefs than to the stranger. "Then we will seize such weapons and use them against those who would oppose us. In the end it is the strong who win in war, and the Rouma have gone soft, as all men know. I, Abd-el-Kader will have these two killed and then I shall announce to the assembled tribes the new jedah, a Holy War to bring the Chosen of Allah once again to their rightful position in the Sahara."

"Man," Abe Baker murmured pleasantly, "you're going to be one awful disappointed cat before long."

El Aicha said mildly, "Such decisions are for the djemaa el kebar to make, O Abd-el-Kader, not for a single chief of the Ouled Touameur."

The desert warrior chief sneered openly at the old man. "Decisions are made by those with the strength to enforce them. The young men of the Chaambra support me, and my men surround this tent."

"So do mine," Homer Crawford said decisively. "And I have come to arrest you and take you to Columb-Béchar where you will be tried for your participation in recent raids on various development projects."

El Aicha repeated his earlier words. "There shall be no violence at a djemaa el kebar."

The Ouled Touameur chief's eyes had narrowed. "You are not strong enough to take me."

* * * * *

In English, Abe Baker said, "Like maybe these young followers of this cat need an example laid on them, man."

"I'm afraid you're right," Crawford growled disgustedly.

The younger American came to his feet. "I'll take him on," Abe said.

"No, he's nearer to my size," Crawford grunted. He turned to El Aicha, and said in Arabic, "I demand the right of a stranger in your camp to a trial by combat."

"On what grounds?" the old man scowled.

"That my manhood has been spat upon by this warrior who does his fighting with his loud mouth."

The assembled chiefs looked to Abd-el-Kader, and a rustling sigh went through them. A hundred times the wiry desert chieftain had proven himself the most capable fighter in the tribes. A hundred times he had proven it and there were dead and wounded in the path he had cut for himself.

Abd-el-Kader laughed aloud again. "Swords, in the open before the ascan."

Homer Crawford shrugged. "Swords, in the open before the assembled Chaambra so that they may see how truly weak is the one who calls himself so strong."

Abe said worriedly, in English, "Listen, man, you been checked out on swords?"

"They're the traditional weapon in the Arab *code duello*," Homer said, with a wry grin. "Nothing else would do."

"Man, you sound like you've been blasting pot and got yourself as high as those cats out there with their *kif*. This Abd-el-Kader was probably raised with a sword in his hand."

Abd-el-Kader smiling triumphantly, had spun on his heel and made his way through the tent's entrance. Now they could hear him shouting orders.

El Aicha looked up at Homer Crawford from where he sat. His voice without inflection, he said, "Hast thou a sword, Omar ben Crawf?"

"No," Crawford said.

The elderly tribal leader said, "Then I shall loan you mine." He hesitated momentarily, before adding, "Never before has hand other than mine wielded it." And finally, simply, "Never has it been drawn to commit dishonor."

"I am honored."

Outside, the rumors had spread fast and already a great arena was forming by the packed lines of Chaambra nomads. At the tent entrance, Elmer Allen, his face worried, said, his English in characteristic Jamaican accent, "What did you chaps do?"

"Duel," Abe growled apprehensively. "This joker here has challenged their top swordsman to a fight."

Elmer said hurriedly, "See here, gentlemen, the hovercraft are parked over behind that tent. We can be there in two minutes and away from —"

Crawford's eyes went from Elmer Allen to Abe Baker and then back again. He chuckled, "I don't think you two think I'm going to win this fight," he said.

"What do you know about swordsmanship?" Elmer Allen said accusingly.

"Practically nothing. A little bayonet practice quite a few years ago."

"Oh, great," Abe muttered.

Elmer said hurriedly, "See here, Homer, I was on the college fencing team and —"

Crawford grinned at him. "Too late, friend."

As they talked, they made their way to the large circle of men. In its center, Abd-el-Kader was stripping to his waist, meanwhile laughingly shouting his confidence to his Ouled Touameur tribesmen and to the other Chaambra of fighting age. No one seemed to doubt the final issue. Beneath his white burnoose he wore a gandoura of lightweight woolen cloth and beneath that a longish undershirt of white cotton, similar to that of the Tuareg but with shorter and less voluminous sleeves. This the desert fighter retained.

Crawford stripped down too, nude to the waist. His body was in excellent trim, muscles bunching under the ebony skin. A Haratin servant came up bearing El Aicha's sword.

Homer Crawford pulled it from the scabbard. It was of scimitar type, the weapon which had once conquered half the known world.

From within the huge circle of men, Abd-el-Kader swung his own blade in flashing arcs and called out something undoubtedly insulting, but which was lost in the babble of the multitude.

"Well, here we go," Crawford grunted. "You fellows better station yourselves around just on the off chance that those Ouled Touameur bully-boys don't like the decision."

"We'll worry about that," Abe said unhappily. "You just see you get out of this in one piece. Anything happens to you and the head office'll make me head of this team-and frankly, man I don't want the job."

Homer grinned at him, and began pushing his way through to the center.

* * * * *

The Arab cut a last switch in the air, with his whistling blade and started forward, in practiced posture. Homer awaited him, legs spread slightly, his hands extended slightly, the sword held at the ready but with point low.

Abe Baker growled, unhappily, "He said he didn't know anything about the swords, and the way he holds it bears him out. That Arab'll cut Homer to ribbons. Maybe we ought to do something about it." As usual, under stress, he'd dropped his beatnik patter.

Elmer Allen looked at him. "Such as what? There are at least three thousand of these tribesmen chaps here watching their favorite sport. What did you have in mind doing?"

Abd-el-Kader hadn't remained the victor of a score of similar duels through making such mistakes as underestimating his foe. In spite of the black stranger's seeming ignorance of his weapon, the Arab had no intention of being sucked into a trap. He advanced with care.

His sword darted forward, quickly, experimentally, and Homer Crawford barely caught its razor edge on his own.

Save for his own four companions, the crowd laughed aloud. None among them were so clumsy as this.

The Ouled Touameur chief was convinced. He stepped in fast, the blade flicked in and out in a quick feint, then flicked in again. Homer Crawford countered clumsily.

And then there was a roar as the American's blade left his hand and flew high in the air to come to the ground again a score of feet behind the desert swordsman.

For a brief moment Abd-el-Kader stepped back to observe his foe, and there was mockery in his face. "So thy manhood has been spat upon by one who fights only with his mouth! Almost, braggart, I am inclined to give you your life so that you may spend the rest of it in shame. Now die, unbeliever!"

Crawford stood hopelessly, in a semicrouch, his hands still slightly forward. The Arab came in fast, his sword at the ready for the death stroke.

Suddenly, the American moved forward and then jumped a full yard into the air, feet forward and into the belly of the advancing Arab. The heavily shod right foot struck at the point in the abdomen immediately below the sternum, the solar plexus, and the left was as low as the groin. In a motion that was almost a bounce off the other's body, Crawford came lithely back to his feet, jumped back two steps, crouched again.

But Abd-el-Kader was through, his eyes popping agony, his body writhing on the ground. The whole thing, from the time the Arab had advanced on the disarmed man for the kill, hadn't taken five seconds.

His groans were the only sounds which broke the unbelieving silence of the Chaambra tribesmen. Homer Crawford picked up the fallen leader's sword and then strolled over and retrieved that of El Aicha. Ignoring Abd-el-Kader, he crossed to where the tribal elders had assembled to watch the fight and held out the borrowed sword to its owner.

El Aicha sheathed it while looking into Homer Crawford's face. "It has still never been drawn to commit dishonor."

"My thanks," Crawford said.

Over the noise of the crowd which now was beginning to murmur its incredulity at their champion's fantastic defeat, came the voice of Abe Baker swearing in Arabic and yelling for a way to be cleared for him. He was driving one of the hovercraft.

He drew it up next to the still agonized Abd-el-Kader and got out accompanied by Bey-ag-Akhamouk. Silently and without undue roughness they picked up the fallen clan chief and put him into the back of the hover-lorry, ignoring the crowd.

Homer Crawford came up and said in English, "All right, let's get out of here. Don't hurry, but on the other hand don't let's prolong it. One of those Ouled Touameur might collect himself to the point of deciding he ought to rescue his leader."

Abe looked at him disgustedly. "Like, where'd you learn that little party trick, man?"

Crawford yawned. "I said I didn't know anything about swords. You didn't ask me about judo. I once taught judo in the Marines."

"Well, why didn't you take him sooner? He like to cut your head off with that cheese knife before you landed on him."

"I couldn't do it sooner. Not until he knocked the sword out of my hand. Until then it was a sword fight. But as soon as I had no sword then in the eyes of every Chaambra present, I had the right to use any method possible to save myself."

Bey-ag-Akhamouk looked up at the sun to check the time. "We better speed it up if we want to get this man to Columb-Béchar and then get on down over the desert to Timbuktu and that meeting."

"Let's go," Homer said. The second hovercraft joined them, driven by Elmer Allen, and they made their way through the staring, but motionless, crowds of Chaambra.

IV

Once the city of Timbuktu was more important in population, in commerce, in learning than the London, the Paris or the Rome of the time. It was the crossroads where African traffic, east and west, met African traffic, north and south; Timbuktu dominated all. In its commercial houses accumulated the wealth of Africa; in its universities and mosques the wisdom of Greece, Rome, Byzantium and the Near East-at a time when such learning was being destroyed in Dark Ages beset Europe.

Timbuktu's day lasted but two or three hundred years at most. By the middle of the Twentieth Century it had deteriorated into what looked nothing so much as a New Mexico ghost town, built largely of adobe. Its palaces and markets has melted away to caricatures of their former selves, its universities were a memory of yesteryear, its population fallen off to a few thousands. Not until the Niger Projects, the dams and irrigation projects, of the latter part of the Twentieth Century did the city begin to regain a semblance of its old importance.

Homer Crawford's team had come down over the Tanezrouft route, Reggan, Bidon Cinq and Tessalit; that of Isobel Cunningham, Jacob Armstrong and Clifford Jackson, up from Timbuktu's Niger River port of Kabara. They met in the former great market square, bordered on two sides by the one time French Administration buildings.

Isobel reacted first. "Abe!" she yelled, pointing accusingly at him.

Abe Baker pretended to cringe, then reacted. "Isobel! Somebody *told* me you were over here!"

She ran over the heavy sand, which drifted through the streets, to the hovercraft in which he had just pulled up. He popped out to meet her, grinning widely.

"Why didn't you look me up?" she said accusingly, presenting a cheek to be kissed.

"In Africa, man?" he laughed. "Kinda big, Africa. Like, I didn't know if you were in the Sahara, or maybe down in Angola, or wherever."

She frowned. "Heaven forbid."

Abe turned to the others of his team who had crowded up behind him. It had been a long time since any of them had seen other than native women.

"Isobel," he said, "I hate to do this, but let me introduce you to Homer Crawford, my immediate boss and slave driver, late of the University of Michigan where he must've found out where the body was-they gave him a doctorate. Then here's Elmer Allen, late of Jamaica-British West Indies, not Long Island-all he's got is a master's, also in sociology. And this is Kenneth Ballalou, hails from San Francisco, I don't think Kenny ever went to school, but he seems to speak every language ever." Abe turned to his final companion. "And this is our sole *real* African, Bey-ag-Akhamouk, of Tuareg blood, so beware, they don't call the Tuareg the Apaches of the Sahara for nothing."

Bey pretended to wince as he held out his hand. "Since Abe seems to be an education snob, I might as well mention the University of Minnesota and my Political Science."

Jake Armstrong and Cliff Jackson had come up behind Isobel, and were now introduced in turn. The older man said, "A Tuareg in a Reunited Nations team? Not that it makes any difference to me, but I thought there was some sort of policy."

"I was taken to the States when I was three," Bey said. "I'm an American citizen."

Isobel was chattering, in animation, with Abe Baker. It developed they'd both been reporters on the school paper at Columbia. At least, they'd both started as reporters, Isobel had wound up editor.

Since their introduction, Homer Crawford had been vaguely frowning at her. Now he said, "I've been trying to place where I'd seen you before. Now I know. Some photographs of Lena Horne, she was —"

Isobel dropped a mock curtsy. "Thank you, kind sir, you don't have to tell me about Lena Horne, she's a favorite. I have scads of tapes of her."

"Brother," Elmer Allen said dourly, "how's anybody going to top that? Homer's got the inside track now. Let's get over to this meeting. By the cars, helio-copters and hovercraft around here, you got more of a turnout than I expected, Homer."

The meeting was held in what had once been an assembly chamber of the officials of the former *Cercle de Tombouctou*, when this had all been part of French Sudan. It was the only room in the vicinity which would comfortably hold all of them.

* * * * *

Elmer Allen had been right, there was something like a hundred persons present, almost all men but with a sprinkling of women, such as Isobel. More than half were in native costume running the gamut from Nigeria to Morocco and from Mauritania to Ethiopia. They were a competent looking, confident voiced gathering.

Homer Crawford knocked with a knuckle on the table that stood at the head of the hall and called for silence. "Sorry we're late," he said, "Particularly in view of the fact that the idea of this meeting originated with my team. We had some difficulty with a nomad raider, up in Chaambra country."

Someone from halfway back in the hall said bitterly, "I suppose in typical African Development Project style, you killed the poor man."

Crawford said dryly, "*Poor man* isn't too accurate a description of the gentleman involved. However, he is at present in jail awaiting trial." He got back to the meeting. "I had originally thought of this being an informal get-together of a score or so of us, but in view of the numbers I suggest we appoint a temporary chairman."

"You're doing all right," Jake Armstrong said from the second row of chairs.

"I second that," an unknown called from further back.

Crawford shrugged. His manner had a cool competence. "All right. If there is no objection, I'll carry on until the meeting decides, if it ever does, that there is need of elected officers."

"I object." In the third row a white haired, but Prussian-erect man had come to his feet. "I wish to know the meaning of this meeting. I object to it being held at all."

Abe Baker called to him, "Dad, how can you object to it being held if you don't know what it's for?"

Homer Crawford said, "Suppose I briefly sum up our mutual situation and if there are any motions to be made-including calling the meeting quits-or decisions to come to, we can start from there."

There was a murmur of assent. The objector sat down in a huff.

Crawford looked out over them. "I don't know most of you. The word of this meeting must have spread from one group or team to another. So what I'll do is start from the beginning, saying little at first with which you aren't already familiar, but we'll lay a foundation."

He went on. "This situation which we find in Africa is only a part of a world-wide condition. Perhaps to some, particularly in the Western World as they call it, Africa isn't of primary importance. But, needless to say, it is to we here in the field. Not too many years ago, at the same period the African colonies were bursting their bonds and achieving independence, an international situation was developing that threatened future peace. The rich nations were getting richer, the poor were getting poorer, and the rate of this change was accelerating. The reasons were various. The population growth in the backward countries, unhampered by birth control and rocketing upward due to new sanitation, new health measures, and the conquest of a score of diseases that have bedeviled man down through the centuries, was fantastic. Try as they would to increase per capita income in the have-not nations, population grew faster than new industry and new agricultural methods could keep up. On top of that handicap was another; the have-not nations were so far behind economically that they couldn't get going. Why build a bicycle factory in Morocco which might be able to turn out bikes for, say, fifty dollars apiece, when you could buy them from automated factories in Europe, Japan or the United States for twenty-five dollars?"

Most of his audience were nodding agreement, some of them impatiently, as though wanting him to get on with it.

Crawford continued. "For a time aid to these backward nations was left in the hands of the individual nations-especially to the United States and Russia. However, in spite of speeches of politicians to the contrary, governments are not motivated by humanitarian purposes. The government of a country does what it does for the benefit of the ruling class of that country. That was the reason it was appointed the government. Any government that doesn't live up to this dictum soon stops being the government."

"That isn't always so," somebody called.

Homer Crawford grinned. "Bear with me a while," he said. "We can debate till the Niger freezes over-later on."

He went on. "For instance, the United States would *aid* Country X with a billion dollars at, say four per cent interest, stipulating that the money be spent in America. This is aid? It certainly is for American business. But then our friends the Russians come along and loan the same country a billion rubles at a very low interest rate and with supposedly no strings attached, to build, say, a railroad. Very fine indeed, but first of all the railroad, built Russian style and with Russian equipment, soon needs replacements, new locomotives, more rolling stock. Where must it come from? Russia, of course. Besides that, in order to build and run the railroad it became necessary to send Russian technicians to Country X and also to send students from Country X to Moscow to study Russian technology so that they could operate the railroad." Crawford's voice went wry. "Few countries, other than commie ones, much desire to have their students study in Moscow."

* * * * *

There was a slight stirring in his audience and Homer Crawford grinned slightly. "You'll pardon me if in this little summation, I step on a few ideological toes-of both East and West.

"Needless to say, under these conditions of *aid* in short order the economies of various countries fell under the domination of the two great collossi. At the same time the other have nations including Great Britain, France, Germany and the newly awakening China, began to realize that unless they got into the *aid* act that they would disappear as competitors for the tremendous markets in the newly freed former colonial lands. Also along in here it became obvious that philanthropy with a mercenary basis doesn't always work out to the benefit of the receiver and the world began to take measures to administer aid more efficiently and through world bodies rather than national ones.

"But there was still another problem, particularly here in Africa. The newly freed former colonies were wary of the nations that had formerly owned them and often for good reasons, always remembering that governments are not motivated by humanitarian reasons. England did not free India because her heart bled for the Indian people, nor did France finally free Algeria because the French conscience was stirred with thoughts of Freedom, Equality and Fraternity."

A voice broke in from halfway down the hall, a voice heavy with British accent. "I say, why did you Yanks free the Philippines?"

Homer Crawford laughed, as did several other Americans present. "That's the first time I've ever been called a Yankee," he said. "But the point is well taken. By freeing the islands we washed our hands of the responsibility of such expensive matters as their health and education, and at the same time we granted freedom we made military and economic treaties which perpetuated our fundamental control of the Philippines.

"The point is made. The distrust of the European and the white man as a whole was prevalent, especially here in Africa. However, and particularly in Africa, the citizens of the new countries were almost unbelievably uneducated, untrained, incapable of engineering their own destiny. In whole nations there was not a single lawyer or —"

"That's no handicap," somebody called.

There was laughter through the hall.

Homer Crawford laughed, too, and nodded as though in solemn agreement. "However, there were also no doctors, engineers, scientists. There were whole nations without a single college graduate."

He paused and his eyes swept the hall. "That's where we came in. Most of us here this afternoon are from the States, however, also represented to my knowledge are British West Indians, a Canadian or two, at least one Panamanian, and possibly some Cubans. Down in the southern part of the continent I know of teams working in the Portuguese areas who are Brazilian in background. All of us, of course, are Africans racially, but few if any of us know from what part of Africa his forebears came. My own grandfather was born a slave in Mississippi and didn't know his father; my grandmother was already a hopeless mixture of a score of African tribes.

"That, I assume, is the story of most if not all of us. Our ancestors were wrenched from the lands of their birth and shipped under conditions worse than cattle to the New World." He added simply, "Now we return."

There was a murmur throughout his listeners, but no one interrupted.

"When the great powers of Europe arbitrarily split up Africa in the Nineteenth Century they didn't bother with race, tribe, not even geographic boundaries. Largely they seemed to draw their boundary lines with ruler and pencil on a Mercator projection. Often, not only were native nations split in twain but even tribes and clans, and sometimes split not only one way but two or three. It was chaotic to the old tribal system. Of course, when the white man left various efforts were made from the very start to join that which had been torn apart a century earlier. Right here in this area, Senegal and what was then French Sudan merged to form the short-lived Mali Federation. Ghana and French Guinea formed a shaky alliance. More successful was the federation of Kenya, Tanganyika, Uganda and Zanzibar, which of course, has since grown.

"But there were fantastic difficulties. Many of the old tribal institutions had been torn down, but new political institutions had been introduced only in a half-baked way. African politicians, supposedly 'democratically' elected, had no intention of facing the possibility of giving up their individual powers by uniting with their neighbors. Not only had the Africans been divided tribally but now politically as well. But obviously, so long as they continued to be Balkanized the chances of rapid progress were minimized.

"Other difficulties were manifold. So far as socio-economics were concerned, African society ran the scale from bottom to top. The Bushmen of the Ermelo district of the Transvaal and the Kalahari are stone age people still-savages. Throughout the continent we find tribes at an ethnic level which American Anthropologist Lewis Henry Morgan called barbarism. In some places we find socio-economic systems based on chattle slavery, elsewhere feudalism. In comparatively few areas, Casablanca, Algiers, Dakar, Cairo and possibly the Union we find a rapidly expanding capitalism.

"Needless to say, if Africa was to progress, to increase rapidly her per capita income, to depart the ranks of the have-nots and become have nations, these obstacles had to be overcome. That is why we are here."

"Speak for yourself, Mr. Crawford," the white haired objector of ten minutes earlier, bit out.

* * * * *

Homer Crawford nodded. "You are correct, sir. I should have said that is the reason the teams of the Reunited Nations African Development Project are here. I note among us various members of this project besides those belonging to my own team, by the way. However, most of you are under other auspices. We of the Reunited Nations teams are here because as Africans racially but not nationally, we have no affiliation with clan, tribe or African nation. We are free to work for Africa's progress without prejudice. Our job is to remove obstacles wherever we find them. To break up log jams. To eliminate prejudices against the steps that must be taken if Africa is to run down the path of progress, rather than to crawl. We usually operate in teams of about half a dozen. There are hundreds of such teams in North Africa alone."

He rapped his knuckle against the small table behind which he stood. "Which brings us to the present and to the purpose of suggesting this meeting. Most of you are operating under other auspices than the Reunited Nations. Many of you duplicate some of our work. It occurred to me, and my team mates, that it might be a good idea for us to get together and see if there is ground for co-operation."

Jake Armstrong called out, "What kind of co-operation?"

Crawford shrugged. "How would I know? Largely, I don't even know who you represent, or the exact nature of the tasks you are trying to perform. I suggest that each group of us represented here, stand up and announce their position. Possibly, it will lead to something of value."

"I make that a motion," Cliff Jackson said.

"Second," Elmer Allen called out.

The majority were in favor.

Homer Crawford sat down behind the table, saying, "Who'll start off?"

Armstrong said, "Isobel, you're better looking than I am. They'd rather look at you. You present our story."

Isobel came to her feet and shot him a scornful glance. "Lazy," she said.

Jake Armstrong grinned at her. "Make it good."

Isobel took her place next to the table at which Crawford sat and faced the others.

She looked at the chairman from the side of her eyes and said, "After that allegedly *brief* summation Mr. Crawford made, I have a sneaking suspicion that we'll be here until next week unless I set a new precedent and cut the position of the Africa for Africans Association shorter."

Isobel got her laugh, including one from Homer Crawford, and went on.

"Anyway, I suppose most of you know of the AFAA and possibly many of you belong to it, or at least contribute. We've been called the African Zionist organization and perhaps that's not too far off. We are largely, but not entirely an American association. We send out our teams, such as the one my colleagues and I belong to, in order to speed up progress and, as our chairman put it, eliminate prejudices against the steps that must be taken if Africa is to run down the path of progress instead of crawl. We also advocate that Americans and other non-African-born Negroes, educated in Europe and the Americas, return to Africa to help in its struggles. We find positions for any such who are competent, preferably doctors, educators, scientists and technicians, but also competent mechanics, construction workers and so forth. We operate a school in New York where we teach native languages and lingua franca such as Swahili and Songhai, in preparation for going to Africa. We raise our money largely from voluntary contributions, and largely from American Negroes although we have also had government grants, donations from foundations, and from individuals of other racial backgrounds. I suppose that sums it up."

Isobel smiled at them, returned to her chair to applause, probably due as much to her attractive appearance as her words.

Crawford said, "When we began this meeting we had an objection that it be held at all. I wonder if we might hear from that gentleman next?"

The white haired, ramrod erect, man stood next to his chair, not bothering to come to the head of the room. "You may indeed," he snapped. "I am Bishop Manning of the United Negro Missionaries, an organization attempting to accomplish the only truly important task that cries for completion on this largely godless continent. Accomplish this, and all else will fall into place."

Homer Crawford said, "I assume you refer to the conversion of the populace."

"I do indeed. And the work others do is meaningless until that has been accomplished. We are bringing religion to Africa, but not through white missionaries who in the past lived *off* the natives, but through Negro missionaries who live *with* them. I call upon all of you to give up your present occupations and come to our assistance."

Elmer Allan's voice was sarcastic. "These people need less superstition, not more."

The bishop spun on him. "I am not speaking of superstition, young man!"

Elmer Allen said. "All religions are superstitions, except one's own."

"And yours?" the Bishop barked.

"I'm an agnostic."

The bishop snorted his disgust and made his way to the door. There he turned and had his last word. "All you do is meaningless. I pray you, again, give it up and join in the Lord's work."

Homer Crawford nodded to him. "Thank you, Bishop Manning. I'm sure we will all consider your words." When the older man was gone, he looked out over the hall again. "Well, who is next?"

* * * * *

A thus far speechless member of the audience, seated in the first row, came to his feet. His face was serious and strained, the face of a man who pushes himself beyond the point of efficiency in the vain effort to accomplish more by expenditure of added hours.

He came to the front and said, "Since I'm possibly the only one here who also has objections to the reason for calling this meeting, I might as well have my say now." He half turned to Crawford, and continued. "Mr. Chairman, my name is Ralph Sandell and I'm an officer in the Sahara Afforestation Project, which, as you know, is also under the auspices of the Reunited Nations, though not having any other connection with your own organization."

Homer Crawford nodded. "We know of your efforts, but why do you object to calling this meeting?" He seemed mystified.

"Because, like Bishop Manning, I think your efforts misdirected. I think you are expending tremendous sums of money and the work of tens of thousands of good men and women, in directions which in the long run will hardly count."

Crawford leaned back in surprise, waiting for the other's reasoning.

Ralph Sandell obliged. "As the chairman pointed out, the problem of population explosion is a desperate one. Even today, with all the efforts of the Reunited Nations and of the individual countries involved in African aid, the population of this continent is growing at a pace that will soon outstrip the arable portion of the land. Save only Antarctica, Africa has the smallest arable percentage of land of any of the continents.

"The task of the Afforestation Project is to return the Sahara to the fertile land it once was. The job is a gargantuan one, but ultimately quite possible. Here in the south we are daming the Niger, running our irrigation projects farther and farther north. From the Mauritania area on the Atlantic we are pressing inland, using water purification and solar pumps to utilize the ocean. In the mountains of Morocco, the water available is being utilized more efficiently than ever before, and the sands being pushed back. We are all familiar with Egypt's ever increasingly successful efforts to exploit the Nile. In the Sahara itself, the new solar pumps are utilizing wells to an extent never dreamed of before. The oases are increasing in a geometric progression both in number and in size." He was caught up in his own enthusiasm.

Crawford said, interestedly, "It's a fascinating project. How long do you estimate it will be before the job is done?"

"Perhaps a century. As the trees go in by the tens of millions, there will be a change in climate. Forest begets moisture which in turn allows for more forest." He turned back to the audience as a whole. "In time we will be able to farm these million upon million of acres of fertile land. First it must go into forest, then we can return to field agriculture when climate and soil have been restored. This is our prime task! This is our basic need. I call upon all of you for your support and that of your organizations if you can bring their attention to the great need. The tasks you have set yourselves are meaningless in the face of this greater one. Let us be practical."

"Crazy man," Abe Baker said aloud. "Let's be practical and cut out all this jazz." The youthful New Yorker came to his feet. "First of all you just mentioned it was going to take a century, even though it's going like a geometric progression. Geometric progressions get going kind of slow, so I imagine that your scheme for making the Sahara fertile again, won't really be under full steam until more than halfway through that century of yours, and not really ripping ahead until, maybe two thirds of the way. Meanwhile, what's going to happen?"

"I beg your pardon!" Ralph Sandell said stiffly.

"That's all right," Abe Baker grinned at him. "The way they figure, population doubles every thirty years, under the present rate of increase. They figure there'll be three billion in the world by 1990, then by 2020 there would be six billions, and in 2050, twelve billions and twenty-four by the time your century was up. Old boy, I suggest the addition of a Sahara of rich agricultural land a century from now wouldn't be of much importance."

"Ridiculous!"

"You mean me, or you?" Abe grinned. "I once read an article by Donald Kingsbury. It's reprinted these days because it finished off the subject once and for all. He showed with mathematical rigor that given the present rate of human population increase, and an absolutely unlimited technology that allowed instantaneous intergalactical transportation and the ability to convert anything and everything into food, including interstellar dust, stars, planets, everything, it would take only seven thousand years to turn the total mass of the total universe into human flesh!"

The Sahara Afforestation official gaped at him.

The room rocked with laughter.

Irritated, Sandell snapped again, "Ridiculous!"

"It sure is, man," Abe grinned. "And the point is that the job is educating the people and freeing them to the point where they can develop their potentialities. Educate the African and he will see the same need that does the intelligent European, American, or Russian for that matter, to limit our population growth." He sat down again, and there was a scattering of applause and more laughter.

Sandell, still glowering, took his seat, too.

Homer Crawford, who'd been hard put not to join in the amusement, said, "Thanks to both of you for some interesting points. Now, who's next? Who else do we have here?"

* * * * *

When no one else answered, a smallish man, dressed in the costume of the Dogon, to the south, came to his feet and to the head of the room.

In a clipped British accent, he said, "Rex Donaldson, of Nassau, the Bahamas, in the service of Her Majesty's Government and the British Commonwealth. I have no team. Although our tasks are largely similar to those of the African Development Project, we field men of the African Department usually work as individuals. My native pseudonym is usually Dolo Anah."

He looked out over the rest. "I have no objection to such meetings as this. If nothing else, it gives chaps a bit of an opportunity to air grievances. I personally have several and may as well state them now. Among other things, it becomes increasingly clear that though some of the organizations represented here are supposedly of the Reunited Nations, actually they are dominated by Yankees. The Yankees are seeping in everywhere." He looked at Isobel. "Yes, such groups as your Africa for Africans Association has high flown slogans, but wherever you go, there go Yankee ideas, Yankee products, Yankee schools."

Homer Crawford's eyebrows went up. "What is your solution? The fact is that the United States has a hundred or more times the educated Negroes than any other country."

Donaldson said, doggedly, "The British Commonwealth has done more than any other element in bringing progress to Africa. She should be given the lead in developing the continent. A good first step would be to make the pound sterling legal tender throughout the continent. And, as things are now, there are some *seven hundred* different languages, not counting dialects. I suggest that English be made the lingua franca of—"

An excitable type, who had been first to join in the laughter at Sandell, now jumped to his feet. "*Un moment, Monsieur!* The French Community long dominated a far greater portion of Africa than the British flag flew over. Not to mention that it was the most advanced portion. If any language was to become the lingua franca of all Africa, French would be more suitable. Your ultimate purpose, Mr. Donaldson, is obvious. You and your Commonwealth African Department wish to dominate for political and economic reasons!"

He turned to the others and spread his hands in a Gallic gesture. "I introduce myself, Pierre Dupaine, operative of the African Affairs sector of the French Community."

"Ha!" Donaldson snorted. "Getting the French out of Africa was like pulling teeth. It took donkey's years. And now look. This chap wants to bring them back again."

Crawford was knuckling the table. "Gentlemen, Gentlemen," he yelled. He finally had them quieted.

Wryly he said, "May I ask if we have a representative from the government of the United States?"

A lithe, inordinately well dressed young man rose from his seat in the rear of the hall. "Frederic Ostrander, C.I.A.," he said. "I might as well tell you now, Crawford, and you other American citizens here, this meeting will not meet with the approval of the State Department."

Crawford's eyes went up. "How do you know?"

The C.I.A. man said evenly, "We've already had reports that this conference was going to be held. I might as well inform you that a protest is being made to the Sahara Division of the African Development Project."

Crawford said, "I suppose that is your privilege, sir. Now, in accord with the reason for this meeting, can you tell us why your organization is present in Africa and what it hopes to achieve?"

Ostrander looked at him testily. "Why not? There has been considerable infiltration of all of these African development organizations by subversive elements...."

"Oh, Brother," Cliff Jackson said.

"...And it is not the policy of the State Department to stand idly by while the Soviet Complex attempts to draw Africa from the ranks of the free world."

Elmer Allen said disgustedly, "Just what part of Africa would you really consider part of the Free World?"

The C.I.A. man stared at him coldly. "You know what I mean," he rapped. "And I might add, we are familiar with your record, Mr. Allen."

Homer Crawford said, "You've made a charge which is undoubtedly as unpalatable to many of those present as it is to me. Can you substantiate it? In my experience in the Sahara there is little, if any, following of the Soviet Complex."

An agreeing murmur went through the room.

Ostrander bit out, "Then who is subsidizing this El Hassan?"

Rex Donaldson, the British Commonwealth man, came to his feet. "That was a matter I was going to bring up before this meeting."

Homer Crawford, fully accompanied by Abe Baker and the rest of their team, even Elmer Allen, burst into uncontrolled laughter.

V

When Homer Crawford, Abe Baker, Kenny Ballalou, Elmer Allen and Bey-ag-Akhamouk had laughed themselves out, Frederic Ostrander, the C.I.A. operative stared at them in anger. "What's so funny?" he snapped.

From his seat in the middle of the hall, Pierre Dupaine, operative for the French Community, said worriedly, "*Messieurs*, this El Hassan is not amusing. I, too, have heard of him. His followers are evidently sweeping through the Sahara. Everywhere I hear of him."

There was confirming murmur throughout the rest of the gathering.

Still chuckling, Homer Crawford said, a hand held up for quiet, "Please, everyone. Pardon the amusement of my teammates and myself. You see, there is no such person as El Hassan."

"To the contrary!" Ostrander snapped.

"No, please," Crawford said, grinning ruefully. "You see, my team *invented* him, some time ago."

Ostrander could only stare, and for once his position was backed by everyone in the hall, Crawford's team excepted.

Crawford said doggedly, "It came about like this. These people need a hero. It's in their nomad tradition. They need a leader to follow. Given a leader, as history has often demonstrated, and the nomad will perform miracles. We wished to spread the program of the African Development Project. Such items as the need to unite, to break down the old boundaries of clan and tribe and even nation, the freeing of the slave and serf, the upgrading of women's position, the dropping of the veil and haik, the need to educate the youth, the desirability of taking jobs on the projects and to take up land on the new oases. But since we usually go about disguised as Enaden itinerant smiths, a poorly thought of caste, our ideas weren't worth much. So we invented El Hassan and everything we said we ascribed to him, this mysterious hero who was going to lead all North Africa to Utopia."

Jake Armstrong stood up and said, sheepishly, "I suppose that my team unknowingly added to this. We heard about this mysterious El Hassan and he seemed largely to be going in the same direction, and for the same reason-to give the rumors we were spreading weight-we ascribed the things we said to him."

Somebody farther back in the hall laughed and said, "So did I!"

Homer Crawford extended his hands in the direction of Ostrander, palms upward. "I'm sorry, sir. But there seems to be your mysterious subversive."

Angered, Ostrander snapped, "Then you admit that it was you, yourself, who have been spreading these subversive ideas?"

"Now, wait a minute," Crawford snapped in return. "I admit only to those slogans and ideas promulgated by the African Development Project. If any so-called subversive ideas have been ascribed to El Hassan, it has not been through my team. Frankly, I rather doubt that they have. These people aren't at any ethnic period where the program of the Soviet Complex would appeal. They're largely in a ritual-taboo tribal society and no one alleging any alliance whatsoever to Marx would contend that you can go from that primitive a culture to what the Soviets call communism."

"I'll take this up with my department chief," Ostrander said angrily. "You haven't heard the last of it, Crawford." He sat down abruptly.

Crawford looked out over the room. "Anybody else we haven't heard from?"

A middle-aged, heavy-set, Western dressed man came to his feet and cleared his throat. "Dr. Warren Harding Smythe, American Medical Relief. I assume that most of you have heard of us. An organization supported partially by government grant, partially by contributions by private citizens and institutions, as is that of Miss Isobel Cunningham's Africa for Africans Association." He added grimly, "But there the resemblance ends."

He looked at Homer Crawford. "I am to be added to the number not in favor of this conference. In fact, I am opposed to the presence of most of you here in Africa."

Crawford nodded. "You certainly have a right to your opinion, doctor. Will you elucidate?"

Dr. Smythe had worked his way to the front of the room, now he looked out over the assemblage defiantly. "I am not at all sure that the task most of you work at is a desirable one. As you know, my own organization is at work bringing medical care to Africa. We build hospitals, clinics, above all medical schools. Not a single one of our hospitals but is a school at the same time."

Abe Baker growled, "Everybody knows and values your work, Doc, but what's this bit about being opposed to ours?"

Smythe looked at him distastefully. "You people are seeking to destroy the culture of these people, and, overnight thrust them into the pressures of Twentieth Century existence. As a medical doctor, I do not think them capable of assimilating such rapid change and I fear for their mental health."

There was a prolonged silence.

Crawford said finally, "What is the alternative to the problems I presented in my summation of the situation that confronts the world due to the backward conditions of such areas as Africa?"

"I don't know, it isn't my field."

There was another silence.

Elmer Allen said finally, uncomfortably, "It *is* our field, Dr. Smythe."

Smythe turned to him, his face still holding its distaste. "I understand that the greater part of you are sociologists, political scientists and such. Frankly, ladies and gentlemen, I do not think of the social sciences as exact ones."

He looked around the room and added, deliberately, "In view of the condition of the world, I do not have a great deal of respect for the product of your efforts."

There was an uncomfortable stirring throughout the audience.

Clifford Jackson said unhappily, "We do what we must do, doctor. We do what we can."

Smythe eyed him. He said, "Some years ago I was impressed by a paragraph by a British writer named Huxley. So impressed that I copied it and have carried it with me. I'll read it now."

The heavy-set doctor took out his wallet, fumbled in it for a moment and finally brought forth an aged, many times folded, piece of yellowed paper.

He cleared his throat, then read:

"*To the question* quis custodiet custodes? —*who will mount guard over our guardians, who will engineer the engineers? —the answer is a bland denial that they need any supervision. There seems to be a touching belief among certain Ph.Ds in sociology that Ph.Ds in sociology will never be corrupted by power. Like Sir Galahad's, their strength is the strength of ten because their heart is pure-and their heart is pure because they are scientists and have taken six thousand hours of social studies. Alas, high education is not necessarily a guarantee of higher virtue, or higher political wisdom.*"

The doctor finished and returned to his seat, his face still uncompromising.

* * * * *

Homer Crawford chuckled ruefully. "The point is well taken, I suppose. However, so was the one expressed by Mr. Jackson. We do what we must, and what we can." His eyes went over the assembly. "Is there any other group from which we haven't heard?"

When there was silence, he added, "No group from the Soviet Complex?"

Ostrander, the C.I.A. operative, snorted. "Do you think they would admit it?"

"Or from the Arab Union?" Crawford pursued. "Whether or not the Soviet Complex has agents in this part of Africa, we know that the Arab Union, backed by Islam everywhere, has. Frankly, we of the African Development Project seldom see eye to eye with them which results in considerable discussion at Reunited Nations meetings."

There was continued silence.

Elmer Allen came to his feet and looked at Ostrander, his face surly. "I am not an advocate of what the Soviets are currently calling communism, however, I think a point should be made here."

Ostrander stared back at him unblinkingly.

Allen snorted, "I know what you're thinking. When I was a student I signed a few peace petitions, that sort of thing. How-or why they bothered-the C.I.A. got hold of that information, I don't know, but as a Jamaican I am a bit ashamed of Her Majesty's Government. But all this is beside the point."

"What is your point, Elmer?" Crawford said. "You speak, of course, as an individual not as an employee of the Reunited Nations nor even as a member of my team."

"Our team," Elmer Allen reminded him. He frowned at his chief, as though surprised at Crawford's stand. But then he looked back at the rest. "I don't like the fact that the C.I.A. is present at all. I grow increasingly weary of the righteousness of the prying for what it calls subversion. The latest definition of subversive seems to be any chap who doesn't vote either Republican or Democrat in the States, or Conservative in England."

Ostrander grunted scorn.

Allen looked at him again. "So far as this job is concerned-and by the looks of things, most of us will be kept busy at it for the rest of our lives —I am not particularly favorable to the position of either side in this never-warming cold war between you and the Soviet Complex. I have suspected for some time that neither of you actually want an ending of it. For different reasons, possibly. So far as the States are concerned, I suspect an end of your fantastic military budgets would mean a collapse of your economy. So far as the Soviets are concerned, I suspect they use the continual *threat* of attack by the West to keep up their military and police powers and suppress the freedom of their people. Wasn't it an old adage of the Romans that if you feared trouble at home, stir up war abroad? At any rate, I'd like to have it on the record that I protest the Cold War being dragged into our work in Africa-by either side."

"All right, Elmer," Crawford said, "you're on record. Is that all?"

"That's all," Elmer Allen said. He sat down abruptly.

"Any comment, Mr. Ostrander?" Crawford said.

Ostrander grunted, "Fuzzy thinking." Didn't bother with anything more.

The chairman looked out over the hall. "Any further discussion, any motions?" He smiled and added, "Anything-period?"

Finally Jake Armstrong came to his feet. He said, "I don't agree with everything Mr. Allen just said; however, there was one item where I'll follow along. The fact that most of us will be busy at this job for the rest of our lives-if we stick. With this in mind, the fact that we have lots of time, I make the following proposal. This meeting was called to see if there was any prospect of we field workers co-operating on a field worker's level, if we could in any way help each other, avoid duplication of effort, that sort of thing. I suggest now that this meeting be adjourned and that all of us think it over and discuss it with the other teams, the other field workers in our respective organizations. I propose further that another meeting be held within the year and that meanwhile Mr. Crawford be elected chairman of the group until the next gathering, and that Miss Cunningham be elected secretary. We can all correspond with Mr. Crawford, until the time of the next meeting, giving him such suggestions as might come to us. When he sees fit to call the next meeting, undoubtedly he will have some concrete proposals to put before us."

Isobel said, *sotto voce*, "Secretaries invariably do all the work, why is it that men always nominate a woman for the job?"

Jake grinned at her, "I'll never tell." He sat down.

"I'll make that a motion," Rex Donaldson clipped out.

"Second," someone else called.

Homer Crawford said, "All in favor?"

Those in favor predominated considerably.

They broke up into small groups for a time, debating it out, and then most left for various places for lunch.

Homer Crawford, separated from the other members of his team, in the animated discussions that went on about him, finally left the fascinating subject of what had happened to the Cuban group in Sudan, and who had done it, and went looking for his own lunch.

He strolled down the sand-blown street in the general direction of the smaller market, in the center of Timbuktu, passing the aged, wind corroded house which had once sheltered Major Alexander Gordon Laing, first white man to reach the forbidden city in the year 1826. Laing remained only three days before being murdered by the Tuareg who controlled the town at that time. There was a plaque on the door revealing those basic facts. Crawford had read elsewhere that the city was not captured until 1893 by a Major Joffre, later to become a Marshal of France and a prominent Allied leader in the First World War.

By chance he met Isobel in front of the large community butcher shop, still operated in the old tradition by the local Gabibi and Fulbe, formerly Songhoi serfs. He knew of a Syrian operated restaurant nearby, and since she hadn't eaten either they made their way there.

The menu was limited largely to local products. Timbuktu was still remote enough to make transportation of frozen foodstuffs exorbitant. While they looked at the bill of fare he told her a story about his first trip to the city some years ago while he was still a student.

He had visited the local American missionary and had dinner with the family in their home. They had canned plums for desert and Homer had politely commented upon their quality. The missionary had said that they should be good, he estimated the quart jar to be worth something like one hundred dollars. It seems that some kindly old lady in Iowa, figuring that missionaries in such places as Timbuktu must be in dire need of her State Fair prize winning canned plums, shipped off a box of twelve quarts to missionary headquarters in New York. At that time, France still owned French Sudan, so it was necessary for the plums to be sent to Paris, and thence, eventually to Dakar. At Dakar they were shipped through Senegal to Bamako by narrow gauge railroad which ran periodically. In Bamako they had to wait for an end to the rainy season so roads would be passable. By this time, a few of the jars had fermented and blown up, and a few others had been pilfered. When the roads were dry enough, a desert freight truck took the plums to Mopti, on the Niger River where they waited again until the river was high enough that a tug pulling barges could navigate, by slow stages, down to Kabara. By this time, one or two jars had been broken by inexpert handling and more pilfered. In Kabara they were packed onto a camel and taken to Timbuktu and delivered to the missionary. Total time elapsed since leaving Iowa? Two years. Total number of jars that got through? One.

Isobel looked at Homer Crawford when he finished the story, and laughed. "Why in the world didn't that missionary society refuse the old lady's gift?"

He laughed in return and shrugged. "They couldn't. She might get into a huff and not mention them in her will. Missionary societies can't afford to discourage gifts."

She made her selection from the menu, and told the waiter in French, and then settled back. She resumed the conversation. "The cost of maintaining a missionary in this sort of country must have been fantastic."

"Um-m-m," Crawford growled. "I sometimes wonder how many millions upon millions of dollars, pounds and francs have been plowed into this continent on such projects. This particular missionary wasn't a medical man and didn't even run a school and in the six years he was here didn't make a single convert."

Isobel said, "Which brings us to our own pet projects. Homer—I can call you Homer, I suppose, being your brand new secretary...."

He grinned at her. "I'll make that concession."

"...What's your own dream?"

He broke some bread, automatically doing it with his left hand, as prescribed in the Koran. They both noticed it, and both laughed.

"I'm conditioned," he said.

"Me, too," Isobel admitted. "It's all I can do to use a knife and fork."

He went back to her question, scowling. "My dream? I don't know. Right now I feel a little depressed about it all. When Elmer Allen spoke about spending the rest of our lives on this job, I suddenly realized that was about it. And, you know"—he looked up at her—"I don't particularly like Africa. I'm an American."

She looked at him oddly. "Then why stay here?"

"Because there's so much that needs to be done."

"Yes, you're right and what Cliff Jackson said to the doctor was correct, too. We all do what we must do and what we can do."

"Well, that brings us back to your question. What is my own dream? I'm afraid I'm too far along in life to acquire new ones, and my basic dream is an American one."

"And that is—?" Isobel prompted.

He shrugged again, slightly uncomfortable under the scrutiny of this pretty girl. "I'm a sociologist, Isobel. I suppose I seek Utopia."

She frowned at him as though disappointed. "Is Utopia possible?"

"No, but there is always the search for it. It's a goal that recedes as you approach, which is as it should be. Heaven help mankind if we ever achieve it; we'll be through because there will be no place to go, and man needs to strive."

They had finished their soup and the entree had arrived. Isobel picked at it, her ordinarily smooth forehead wrinkled. "The way I see it, Utopia is not heaven. Heaven is perfect, but Utopia is an engineering optimum, the best-possible-human-techniques. Therefore we will not have *perfect* justice in Utopia, nor will *everyone* get the exactly proper treatment. We design for optimum-not perfection. But granting this, then attainment is possible."

She took a bite of the food before going on thoughtfully. "In fact, I wonder if, during man's history, he hasn't obtained his Utopias from time to time. Have you ever heard the adage that any form of government works fine and produces a Utopia provided it is managed by wise, benevolent and competent rulers?" She laughed and said mischievously, "Both Heaven and Hell are traditionally absolute monarchies-despotisms. The form of government evidently makes no difference, it's who runs it that determines."

Crawford was shaking his head. "I've heard the adage but I don't accept it. Under certain socio-economic conditions the best of men, and the wisest, could do little if they had the wrong form of government. Suppose, for instance, you had a government which was a military-theocracy which is more or less what existed in Mexico at the time of the Cortez conquest. Can you imagine such a government working efficiently if the socio-economic system had progressed to the point where there were no longer wars and where practically everyone were atheists, or, at least, agnostics?"

She had to laugh at his ludicrous example. "That's a rather silly situation, isn't it? Such wise, benevolent men, would change the governmental system."

Crawford pushed his point. "Not necessarily. Here's a better example. Immediately following the American Revolution, some of the best, wisest and most competent men the political world has ever seen were at the head of the government of Virginia. Such men as Jefferson, Madison, Monroe, Washington. Their society was based on chattel slavery and they built a Utopia *for themselves* but certainly not for the slaves who out-numbered them. Not that they weren't kindly and good men. A man of Jefferson's caliber, I am sure, would have done anything in the world for those darkies of his-except get off their backs. Except to grant them the liberty and the right to pursue happiness that he demanded for himself. He was blinded by self interest, and the interests of his class."

"Perhaps they didn't want liberty," Isobel mused. "Slavery isn't necessarily an unhappy life."

"I never thought it was. And I'm the first to admit that at a certain stage in the evolution of society, it was absolutely necessary. If society was to progress, then there had to be a class that was freed from daily drudgery of the type forced on primitive man if he was to survive. They needed the leisure time to study, to develop, to invent. With the products of their studies, they were able to advance all society. However, so long as slavery is maintained, be it necessary or not, you have no Utopia. There is no Utopia so long as one man denies another his liberty be it under chattel slavery, feudalism, or whatever."

Isobel said dryly, "I see why you say your Utopia will never be reached, that it continually recedes."

He laughed, ruefully. "Don't misunderstand. I think that particular goal can and will be reached. My point was that by the time we reach it, there will be a new goal."

* * * * *

The girl, finished with her main dish, sat back in her chair, and looked at him from the side of her eyes, as though wondering whether or not he could take what she was about to say in the right way. She said, slowly, "You know, with possibly a few exceptions, you can't enslave a man if he doesn't want to be a slave. For instance, the white man was never able to enslave the Amerind; he died before he would become a slave. The majority of Jefferson's slaves *wanted to be slaves*. If there were those among them that had the ability to revolt against slave psychology, a Jefferson would quickly promote such. A valuable human being will be treated in a manner proportionate to his value. A wise, competent, trustworthy slave became the major domo of the master's estate-with privileges and authority actually greater than that of free employees of the master."

Crawford thought about that for a moment. "I'll take that," he said. "What's the point you're trying to make?"

"I, too, was set a-thinking by some of the things said at the meeting, Homer. In particular, what Dr. Smythe had to say. Homer, are we sure these people *want* the things we are trying to give them?"

He looked at her uncomfortably. "No they don't," he said bluntly. "Otherwise we wouldn't be here, either your AFAA or my African Development Project. We utilize persuasion, skull-duggery, and even force to subvert their institutions, to destroy their present culture. Yes. I've known this a long time."

"Then how do you justify your being here?"

He grinned sourly. "Let's put it this way. Take the new government in Egypt. They send the army into some of the small back-country towns with bayoneted rifles, and orders to use them if necessary. The villagers are forced to poison their ancient village wells-one of the highest of imaginable crimes in such country, imposed on them ruthlessly. Then they are forced to dig new ones in new places that are not intimately entangled with their own sewage drainage. Naturally they hate the government. In other towns, the army has gone in and, at gun point, forced the parents to give up their children, taken the children away in trucks and 'imprisoned' them in schools. Look, back in the States we have trouble with the Amish, who don't want their children to be taught modern ways. What sort of reaction do you think the tradition-ritual-tabu-tribesmen of the six thousand year old Egyptian culture have to having modern education imposed on their children?"

Isobel was frowning at him.

Crawford wound it up. "That's the position we're in. That's what we're doing. Giving them things they need, in spite of the fact they don't want them."

"But *why*?"

He said, "You know the answer to that as well as I do. It's like giving medical care to Typhoid Mary, in spite of the fact that she didn't want it and didn't believe such things as typhoid microbes existed. We had to protect the community against her. In the world today, such backward areas as Africa are potential volcanoes. We've got to deal with them before they erupt."

The waiter came with the bill and Homer took it.

Isobel said, "Let's go Dutch on that."

He grinned at her. "Consider it a donation to the AFAA."

Out on the street again, they walked slowly in the direction of the old administration buildings where both had left their means of transportation.

Isobel, who was frowning thoughtfully, evidently over the things that had been said, said, "Let's go this way. I'd like to see the old Great Mosque, in the Dyingerey Ber section of town. It's always fascinated me."

Crawford said, looking at her and appreciating her attractiveness, all over again, "You know Timbuktu quite well, don't you?"

"I've just finished a job down in Kabara, and it's only a few miles away."

"Just what sort of thing do you do?"

She shrugged and made a moue. "Our little team concentrates on breaking down the traditional position of women in these cultures. To get them to drop the veil, go to school. That sort of thing. It's a long story and —"

Homer Crawford suddenly and violently pushed her to the side and to the ground and at the same time dropped himself and rolled frantically to the shelter of an adobe wall which had once been part of a house but now was little more than waist high.

"Down!" he yelled at her.

She bug-eyed him as though he had gone suddenly mad.

There was a heavy, stub-nosed gun suddenly in his hand. He squirmed forward on elbows and belly, until he reached the corner.

"What's the matter?" she blurted.

He said grimly, "See those three holes in the wall above you?"

She looked up, startled.

He said, grimly, "They weren't there a moment ago."

What he was saying, dawned upon her. "But ...but I heard no shots."

He cautiously peered around the wall, and was rewarded with a puff of sand inches from his face. He pulled his head back and his lips thinned over his teeth. He said to her, "Efficiently silenced guns have been around for quite a spell. Whoever that is, is up there in the mosque. Listen, beat your way around by the back streets and see if you can find the members of my team, especially Abe Baker or Bey-ag-Akhamouk. Tell them what happened and that I think I've got the guy pinned down. That mosque is too much out in the open for him to get away without my seeing him."

"But ...but who in the world would want to shoot you, Homer?"

"Search me," he growled. "My team has never operated in this immediate area."

"But then, it must be someone who was at the meeting."

VI

"That is was," Homer said grimly. "Now, go see if you can find my lads, will you? This joker is going to fall right into our laps. It's going to be interesting to find out who hates the idea of African development so much that they're willing to commit assassination."

But it didn't work out that way.

Isobel found the other teammates one by one, and they came hurrying up from different directions to the support of their chief. They had been a team for years and operating as they did and where they did, each man survived only by selfless co-operation with all the others. In action, they operated like a single unit, their ability to co-operate almost as though they had telepathic communication.

From where he lay, Homer Crawford could see Bey-ag-Akhamouk, Tommy-Noiseless in hands, snake in from the left, running low and reaching a vantage point from which he could cover one flank of the ancient adobe mosque. Homer waved to him and Bey made motions to indicate that one of the others was coming in from the other side.

Homer waited for a few more minutes, then waved to Bey to cover him. The streets were empty at this time of midday when the Sahara sun drove the town's occupants into the coolness of dark two-foot-thick walled houses. It was as though they were operating in a ghost town. Homer came to his feet and handgun in fist made a dash for the front entrance.

Bey's light automatic *flic flic flicked* its excitement and dust and dirt enveloped the wall facing Crawford. Homer reached the doorway, stood there for a full two minutes while he caught his breath. From the side of his eye he could see Elmer Allen, his excellent teeth bared as always when the Jamaican went into action, come running up to the right in that half crouch men automatically go into in combat, instinctively presenting as small a target as possible. He was evidently heading for a side door or window.

The object now was to refrain from killing the sniper. The important thing was to be able to question him. Perhaps here was the answer to the massacre of the Cubans. Homer took another deep breath, smashed the door open with a heavy shoulder and dashed inward and immediately to one side. At the same moment, Abe Baker, Tommy-Noiseless in hand, came in from the rear door, his eyes darting around trying to pierce the gloom of the unlighted building.

Elmer Allen erupted through a window, rolled over on the floor and came to rest, his gun trained.

"Where is he?" Abe snapped.

Homer motioned with his head. "Must be up in the remains of the minaret."

Abe got to the creaking, age-old stairway first. In cleaning out a hostile building, the idea is to move fast and keep on the move. Stop, and you present a target.

But there was no one in the minaret.

"Got away," Homer growled. His face was puzzled. "I felt sure we'd have him."

Bey-ag-Akhamouk entered. He grunted his disappointment. "What happened, anyway? That girl Isobel said a sniper took some shots at you and you figure it must've been somebody at the meeting."

"Somebody at the meeting?" Abe said blankly. "What kind of jazz is that? You flipping, man?"

Homer looked at him strangely.

"Who else could it be, Abe? We've never operated this far south. None of the inhabitants in this area even know us, and it certainly couldn't have been an attempt at robbery."

"There were some cats at that meeting didn't appreciate our ideas, man, but I can't see that old preacher or Doc Smythe trying to put the slug on you."

Kenny Ballalou came in on the double, gun in hand, his face anxious.

Abe said sarcastically, "Man, we'd all be dead if we had to wait on you."

"That girl Isobel. She said somebody took a shot at the chief."

Homer explained it, sourly. A sniper had taken a few shots at him, then managed to get away.

Isobel entered, breathless, followed by Jake Armstrong.

Abe grunted, "Let's hold another convention. This is like old home town week."

Her eyes went from one of them to the other. "You're not hurt?"

"Nobody hurt, but the cat did all the shooting got away," Abe said unhappily.

Jake said, and his voice was worried, "Isobel told me what happened. It sounds insane."

They discussed it for a while and got exactly nowhere. Their conversation was interrupted by a clicking at Homer Crawford's wrist. He looked down at the tiny portable radio.

"Excuse me for a moment," he said to the others and went off a dozen steps or so to the side. They looked after him.

Elmer Allen said sourly, "Another assignment. What we need is a union."

Abe adopted the idea. "Man! Time and a half for overtime."

"With a special cost of living clause —" Kenny Ballalou added.

"And housing and dependents allotment!" Abe crowed.

They all looked at him.

Bey tried to imitate the other's beatnik patter. "Like, you got any dependents, man?"

Abe made a mark in the sand on the mosque's floor with the toe of his shoe, like a schoolboy up before the principal for an infraction of rules, and registered embarrassment. "Well, there's that cute little Tuareg girl up north."

"Ha!" Isobel said. "And all these years you've been leading me on."

Homer Crawford returned and his face was serious. "That does it," he muttered disgustedly. "The fat's in the fire."

"Like, what's up, man?"

Crawford looked at his right-hand man. "There are demonstrations in Mopti. Riots."

"Mopti?" Jake Armstrong said, surprised. "Our team was working there just a couple of months ago. I thought everything was going fine in Mopti."

"They're going fine, all right," Crawford growled. "So well, that the local populace wants to speed up even faster."

They were all looking their puzzlement at him.

"The demonstrations are in favor of El Hassan."

Their faces turned blank. Crawford's eyes swept his teammates. "Our instructions are to get down there and do what we can to restore order. Come on, let's go. I'm going to have to see if I can arrange some transportation. It'd take us two days to get there in our outfits."

Jake Armstrong said, "Wait a minute, Homer. My team was heading back for Dakar for a rest and new assignments. We'd be passing Mopti anyway. How many of you are there, five? If you don't haul too much luggage with you; we could give you a lift."

"Great," Homer told him. "We'll take you up on that. Abe, Elmer, let's get going. We'll have to repack. Bey, Kenny, see about finding some place we can leave the lorries until we come back. This job shouldn't take more than a few days at most."

"Huh," Abe said. "I hope you got plans, man. How do you go about stopping demonstrations in favor of a legend you created yourself?"

* * * * *

Mopti, also on the Niger, lies approximately three hundred kilometers to the south and slightly west of Timbuktu, as the bird flies. However, one does not travel as the bird flies in the Niger bend. Not even when one goes by aircraft. A forced landing in the endless swamps, bogs, shallow lakes and river tributaries which make up the Niger at this point, would be suicidal. The whole area is more like the Florida Everglades than a river, and a rescue team would be hard put to find your wreckage. There are no roads, no railroads. Traffic follows the well marked navigational route of the main channel.

Homer Crawford had been sitting quietly next to Cliff Jackson who was piloting. Isobel and Jake Armstrong were immediately behind them and Abe and the rest of Crawford's team took up the remainder of the aircraft's eight seats. Abe was regaling the others with his customary chaff.

Out of a clear sky, Crawford said bitterly, "Has it occurred to any of you that what we're doing here in North Africa is committing genocide?"

The others stared at him, taken aback. Isobel said, "I beg your pardon?"

"Genocide," Crawford said bitterly. "We're doing here much what the white men did when they cleared the Amerinds from the plains, the mountains and forests of North America."

Isobel, Cliff and Jake frowned their puzzlement. Abe said, "Man, you just don't make sense. And, among other things, there're more Indians in the United States than there was when Columbus landed."

Crawford shook his head. "No. They're a different people. Those cultures that inhabited the United States when the first white men came, are gone." He shook his head as though soured by his thoughts. "Take the Sioux. They had a way of life based on the buffalo. So the whites deliberately exterminated the buffalo. It made the plains Indians' culture impossible. A culture based on buffalo herds cannot exist if there are no buffalo."

"I keep telling you, man, there's more Sioux now than there were then."

Crawford still shook his head. "But they're a different people, a different race, a different culture. A mere fraction, say ten per cent, of the original Sioux, might have adapted to the new life. The others beat their heads out against the new ways. They fought-the Sitting Bull wars took place after the buffalo were already gone-they drank themselves to death on the white man's firewater, they committed suicide; in a dozen different ways they called it quits. Those that survived, the ten per cent, were the exceptions. They were able to adapt. They had a built-in genetically-conferred self discipline enough to face the new problems. Possibly eighty per cent of their children couldn't face the new problems either and they in turn went under. But by now, a hundred years later, the majority of the Sioux nation have probably adapted. But, you see, the point I'm trying to make? They're not the *real* Sioux, the original Sioux; they're a new breed. The plains living, buffalo based culture, Sioux are all dead. The white men killed them."

Jake Armstrong was scowling. "I get your point, but what has it to do with our work here in North Africa?"

"We're doing the same thing to the Tuareg, the Teda and the Chaambra, and most of the others in the area in which we operate. The type of human psychology that's based on the nomad life can't endure settled community living. Wipe out the nomad way of life and these human beings must die."

Abe said, unusually thoughtful, "I see what you mean, man. *Fish gotta swim, bird gotta fly* —and nomad gotta roam. He flips if he doesn't."

Homer Crawford pursued it. "Sure, there'll be Tuareg afterward ... but all descended from the fraction of deviant Tuareg who were so abnormal-speaking from the Tuareg viewpoint-that they liked settled community life." He rubbed a hand along his jawbone, unhappily. "Put it this way. Think of them as a tribe of genetic claustrophobes. No matter what a claustrophobe promises, he can't work in a mine. He has no choice but to break his promise and escape ... or kill himself trying."

Isobel was staring at him. "What you say, is disturbing, Homer. I didn't come to Africa to destroy a people."

He looked back at her, oddly. "None of us did."

Cliff said from behind the aircraft's controls, "If you believe what you're saying, how do you justify being here yourself?"

"I don't know," Crawford said unhappily. "I don't know what started me on this kick, but I seem to have been doing more inner searching this past week or so than I have in the past couple of decades. And I don't seem to come up with much in the way of answers."

"Well, man," Abe said. "If you find any, let us know."

Jake said, his voice warm, "Look Homer, don't beat yourself about this. What you say figures, but you've got to take it from this angle. The plains Indians had to go. The world is developing too fast for a few thousand people to tie up millions of acres of some of the most fertile farm land anywhere, because they needed it for their game-the buffalo-to run on."

"Um-m-m," Homer said, his voice lacking conviction.

"Maybe it's unfortunate the *way* it was done. The story of the American's dealing with the Amerind isn't a pretty one, and usually comfortably ignored when we pat ourselves on the back these days and tell ourselves what a noble, honest, generous and peace loving people we are. But it did have to be done, and the job we're doing in North Africa has to be done, too."

Crawford said softly, "And sometimes it isn't very pretty either."

* * * * *

Mopti as a town had grown. Once a small river port city of about five thousand population, it had been a river and caravan crossroads somewhat similar to Timbuktu, and noted in particular for its spice market and its Great Mosque, probably the largest building of worship ever made of mud. Plastered newly at least twice a year with fresh adobe, at a distance of only a few hundred feet the Great Mosque, in the middle of the day and in the glare of the Sudanese sun, looks as though made of gold. From the air it is more attractive than the grandest Gothic cathedrals of Europe.

Isobel pointed. "There, the Great Mosque."

Elmer Allen said, "Yes, and there. See those mobs?" He looked at Homer Crawford and said sourly, "Let's try and remember who it was who first thought of the El Hassan idea. Then we can blame it on him."

Kenny Ballalou grumbled, "We all thought about it. Remember, we pulled into Tessalit and found that prehistoric refrigerator that worked on kerosene and there were a couple of dozen quarts of Norwegian beer, of all things, in it."

"And we bought them all," Abe recalled happily. "Man, we hung one on."

Homer Crawford said to Cliff, "The Mopti airport is about twelve miles over to the east of the town."

"Yeah, I know. Been here before," Cliff said. He called back to Ballalou, "And then what happened?"

"We took the beer out into the desert and sat on a big dune. You can just begin to see the Southern Cross from there. Hangs right on the horizon. Beautiful."

Bey said, "I've never heard Kenny wax poetic before. I don't know which sounds more lyrical, though, that cold beer or the Southern Cross."

Kenny said, "Anyway, that's when El Hassan was dreamed up. We kicked the idea around until the beer was all gone. And when we awoke in the morning, complete with hangover, we had the gimmick which we hung all our propaganda on."

"El Hassan is turning out to be a hangover all right," Elmer Allen grunted, choosing to misinterpret his teammate's words. He peered down below. "And there the poor blokes are, rioting in favor of the product of those beer bottles."

"It was crazy beer, man," Abe protested. "Real crazy."

Homer Crawford said, "I wish headquarters had more information to give us on this. All they said was there were demonstrations in favor of El Hassan and they were afraid if things went too far that some of the hard work that's been done here the past ten years might dissolve in the excitement; Dogon, Mosse, Tellum, Sonrai start fighting among each other."

Jake Armstrong said, "That's not my big worry. I'm afraid some ambitious lad will come along and supply what these people evidently want."

"How's that?" Cliff said.

"They want a leader. Someone to come out of the wilderness and lead them to the promised land." The older man grumbled sourly. "All your life you figure you're in favor of democracy.

You devote your career to expanding it. Then you come to a place like North Africa. You're just kidding yourself. Democracy is meaningless here. They haven't got to the point where they can conceive of it."

"And —" Elmer Allen prodded.

Jake Armstrong shrugged. "When it comes to governments and social institutions people usually come up with what they want, sooner or later. If those mobs down there want a leader, they'll probably wind up with one." He grunted deprecation. "And then probably we'll be able to say, Heaven help them."

Isobel puckered her lips. "A leader isn't necessarily a misleader, Jake."

"Perhaps not necessarily," he said. "However, it's an indication of how far back these people are, how much work we've still got to do, when that's what they're seeking."

"Well, I'm landing," Cliff said. "The airport looks free of any kind of manifestations."

"That's a good word," Abe said. "Manifestations. Like, I'll have to remember that one. Man's been to school and all that jazz."

Cliff grinned at him. "Where'd you like to get socked, beatnik?"

"About two feet above my head," Abe said earnestly.

* * * * *

The aircraft had hardly come to a halt before Homer Crawford clipped out, "All right, boys, time's a wasting. Bey, you and Kenny get over to those administration buildings and scare us up some transportation. Use no more pressure than you have to. Abe, you and Elmer start getting our equipment out of the luggage —"

Jake Armstrong said suddenly, "Look here, Homer, do you need any help?"

Crawford looked at him questioningly.

Jake said, "Isobel, Cliff, what do you think?"

Isobel said quickly, "I'm game. I don't know what they'll say back at AFAA headquarters, though. Our co-operating with a Sahara Development Project team."

Cliff scowled. "I don't know. Frankly, I took this job purely for the dough, and as outlined it didn't include getting roughed up in some riot that doesn't actually concern the job."

"Oh, come along, Cliff," Isobel urged. "It'll give you some experience you don't know when you'll be able to use."

He shrugged his acceptance, grudgingly.

Jake Armstrong looked back at Homer Crawford. "If you need us, we're available."

"Thanks," Crawford said briefly, and turned off the unhappy stare he'd been giving Cliff. "We can use all the manpower we can get. You people ever worked with mobs before?"

Bey and Kenny climbed from the plane and made their way at a trot toward the airport's administration buildings. Abe and Elmer climbed out, too, and opened the baggage compartment in the rear of the aircraft.

"Well, no," Jake Armstrong said.

"It's quite a technique. Mostly you have to play it by ear, because nothing is so changeable as the temper of a mob. Always keep in mind that to begin with, at least, only a small fraction of the crowd is really involved in what's going on. Possibly only one out of ten is interested in the issue. The rest start off, at least, as idle observers, watching the fun. That's one of the first things you've got to control. Don't let the innocent bystanders become excited and get into the spirit of it all. Once they do, then you've got a mess on your hands."

Isobel, Jake and Cliff listened to him in fascination.

Cliff said uncomfortably, "Well, what do we do to get the whole thing back to tranquillity? What I mean is, how do we end these demonstrations?"

"We bore them to tears," Homer growled.

They looked at him blankly.

"We assume leadership of the whole thing and put up speakers."

Jake protested, "You sound as though you're sustaining not placating it."

"We put up speakers and they speak and speak, and speak. It's almost like a fillibuster. You don't say anything particularly interesting, and certainly nothing exciting. You agree with the basic feeling of the demonstrating mob, certainly you say nothing to antagonize them. In this case we speak in favor of El Hassan and his great, and noble, and inspiring, and so on and so forth, teachings. We speak in not too loud a voice, so that those in the rear have a hard time hearing, if they can hear at all."

Cliff said worriedly, "Suppose some of the hotheads get tired of this and try to take over?"

Homer said evenly, "We have a couple of bully boys in the crowd to take care of them."

Jake twisted his mouth, in objection. "Might that not strike the spark that would start up violence?"

Homer Crawford grinned and began climbing out of the plane. "Not with the weapons we use."

"Weapons!" Isobel snapped. "Do you intend to use weapons on those poor people? Why, it was you yourself, you and your team, who started this whole El Hassan movement. I'm shocked. I've heard about your reputation, you and the Sahara Development Project teams. Your ruthlessness —"

Crawford chuckled ruefully and held up a hand to stem the tide. "Hold it, hold it," he said. "These are special weapons, and, after all, we've got to keep those crowds together long enough to bore them to the point where they go home."

Abe came up with an armful of what looked something like tent-poles. "The quarterstaffs, eh, Homer?"

"Um-m-m," Crawford said. "Under the circumstances."

"Quarterstaffs?" Cliff Jackson ejaculated.

Abe grinned at him. "Man, just call them pilgrim's staffs. The least obnoxious looking weapon in the world." He looked at Cliff and Jake. "You two cats been checked out on quarterstaffs?"

Jake said, "The more I talk to you people, the less I seem to understand what's going on. Aren't quarterstaffs what, well, Robin Hood and his Merry Men used to fight with?"

"That's right," Homer said. He took one from Abe and grasping it expertly with two hands whirled it about, getting its balance. Then suddenly, he drooped, leaning on it as a staff. His face expressed weariness. His youth and virility seemed to drop away and suddenly he was an aged religious pilgrim as seen throughout the Moslem world.

"I'll be damned," Cliff blurted. "Oop, sorry Isobel."

"I'll be damned, too," Isobel said. "What in the world can you do with that, Homer? I was thinking in terms of you mowing those people down with machine guns or something."

Crawford stood erect again laughingly, and demonstrated. "It's probably the most efficient handweapon ever devised. The weapon of the British yeoman. With one of these you can disarm a swordsman in a matter of seconds. A good man with a quarterstaff can unhorse a knight in armor and batter him to death, in a minute or so. The only other handweapon capable of countering it is another quarterstaff. Watch this, with the favorable two-hand leverage the ends of the staff can be made to move at invisibly high speeds."

Bey and Kenny drove up in an aged wheeled truck and Abe and Elmer began loading equipment.

Crawford looked at Bey who said apologetically, "I had to liberate it. Didn't have time for all the dickering the guy wanted to go through."

Crawford grunted and looked at Isobel. "Those European clothes won't do. We've got some spare things along. You can improvise. Men and women's clothes don't differ that much around here."

"I'll make out all right," Isobel said. "I can change in the plane."

"Hey, Isobel," Abe called out. "Why not dress up like one of these Dogon babes?"

"Some chance," Isobel hissed menacingly at him. "A strip tease you want, yet. You'll see me in a haik and like it, wise guy."

"Shucks," Abe grinned.

Crawford looked critically at the clothing of Jake and Cliff. "I suppose you'll do in western stuff," he said. "After all, this El Hassan is supposed to be the voice of the future. A lot of his potential followers will already be wearing shirts and pants. Don't look *too* civilized, though."

When Isobel returned, Crawford briefed his seven followers. They were to operate in teams of two. One of his men, complete with quarterstaff would accompany each of the others. Abe with Jake, Bey with Cliff, and he'd be with Isobel. Elmer and Kenny would be the other twosome, and, both armed with quarterstaffs would be troubleshooters.

"We're playing it off the cuff," he said. "Do what comes naturally to get this thing under control. If you run into each other, co-operate, of course. If there's trouble, use your wrist radios." He looked at Abe and Bey. "I know you two are packing guns underneath those *gandouras*. I hope you know enough not to use them."

Abe and Bey looked innocent.

Homer turned and led the way into the truck. "O.K., let's get going."

VII

Driving into town over the dusty, pocked road, Homer gave the newcomers to his group more background on the care and control of the genus *mob*. He was obviously speaking through considerable experience.

"Using these quarterstaffs brings to mind some of the other supposedly innoxious devices used by police authorities in controlling unruly demonstrations," he said. "Some of them are beauties. For instance, I was in Tangier when the Moroccans put on their revolution against the French and for the return of the Sultan. The rumor went through town that the mob was going to storm the French Consulate the next day. During the night, the French brought in elements of the Foreign Legion and entrenched the consulate grounds. But their commander had another problem. Journalists were all over town and so were tourists. Tangier was still supposedly an international zone and the French were in no position to slaughter the citizens. So they brought in some special equipment. One item was a vehicle that looked quite a bit like a gasoline truck, but was filled with water and armored against thrown cobblestones and such. On the roof of the cabin was what looked something like a fifty caliber but which was actually a hose which shot water at terrific pressure. When the mob came, the French unlimbered this vehicle and all the journalists could say was that the mob was dispersed by squirting water on it, which doesn't sound too bad after all."

Isobel said, "Well, certainly that's preferable to firing on them."

Homer looked at her oddly. "Possibly. However, I was standing next to the Moorish boy who was cut entirely in half by the pressure spray of water."

The expression on the girl's face sickened.

Homer said, "They had another interesting device for dispersing mobs. It was a noise bomb. The French set off several."

"A noise bomb?" Cliff said. "I don't get it."

"They make a tremendous noise, but do nothing else. However, members of the mob who aren't really too interested in the whole thing–just sort of along for the fun-figure that things are getting earnest and that the troops are shelling them. So they remember some business they had elsewhere and take off."

Isobel said suddenly, "You like this sort of work, don't you?"

Elmer Allen grunted bitterly.

"No," Homer Crawford said flatly. "I don't. But I like the goal."

"And the end justifies the means?"

Homer Crawford said slowly, "I've never answered that to my own satisfaction. But I'll say this. I've never met a person, no matter how idealistic, no matter how much he played lip service to the contention that the ends do not justify the means, who did not himself use the means he found available to reach the ends he believed correct. It seems to be a matter of each man feeling the teaching applies to everyone else, but that he is free to utilize any means to achieve his own noble ends."

"Man, all that jazz is too much for me," Abe said.

They were entering the outskirts of Mopti. Small groups of obviously excited Africans of various tribal groups, were heading for the center of town.

"Abe, Jake," Crawford said. "We'll drop you here. Mingle around. We'll hold the big meeting in front of the Great Mosque in an hour or so."

"Crazy," Abe said, dropping off the back of the truck which Kenny Ballalou, who was driving, brought almost to a complete stop. The older Jake followed him.

The rest went on a quarter of a mile and dropped Bey and Cliff.

Homer said to Kenny, "Park the truck somewhere near the spice market. Preferably inside some building, if you can. For all we know, they're already turning over vehicles and burning them."

Crawford and Isobel dropped off near the pottery market, on the banks of the Niger. The milling throngs here were largely women. Elements of half a dozen tribes and races were represented.

Homer Crawford stood a moment. He ran a hand back over his short hair and looked at her. "I don't know," he muttered. "Now I'm sorry we brought you along." He leaned on his staff and looked at her worriedly. "You're not very ... ah, husky, are you?"

She laughed at him. "Get about your business, sir knight. I spent nearly two weeks living with these people once. I know dozens of them by name. Watch this cat operate, as Abe would say."

She darted to one of the over-turned pirogues which had been dragged up on the bank from the river, and climbed atop it. She held her hands high and began a stream of what was gibberish to Crawford who didn't understand Wolof, the Senegalese lingua franca. Some elements of the crowd began drifting in her direction. She spoke for a few moments, the only words the surprised Homer Crawford could make out were *El Hassan*. And she used them often.

She switched suddenly to Arabic, and he could follow her now. The drift of her talk was that word had come through that El Hassan was to make a great announcement in the near future and that meanwhile all his people were to await his word. But that there was to be a great meeting before the Mosque within the hour.

She switched again to Songhoi and repeated substantially what she'd said before. By now she had every woman hanging on her words.

A man on the outskirts of the gathering called out in high irritation, "But what of the storming of the administration buildings? Our leaders have proclaimed the storming of the reactionaries!"

Crawford, leaning heavily on the pilgrim staff, drifted over to the other. "Quiet, O young one," he said. "I wish to listen to the words of the girl who tells of the teachings of the great El Hassan."

The other turned angrily on him. "Be silent thyself, old man!" He raised a hand as though to cuff the American.

Homer Crawford neatly rapped him on the right shin bone with his quarterstaff to the other's intense agony. The women who witnessed the brief spat dissolved in laughter at the plight of the younger man. Homer Crawford drifted away again before the heckler recovered.

He let Isobel handle the bulk of the reverse-rabble rousing. His bit was to come later, and as yet he didn't want to reveal himself to the throngs.

* * * * *

They went from one gathering place of women to another. To the spice market, to the fish and meat market, to the bathing and laundering locations along the river. And everywhere they found animated groups of women, Isobel went into her speech.

At one point, while Homer stood idly in the crowd, feeling its temper and the extent to which the girl was dominating them, he felt someone press next to him.

A voice said, "What is the plan of operation, Yank?"

Homer Crawford's eyebrows went up and he shot a quick glance at the other. It was Rex Donaldson of the Commonwealth African Department. The operative who worked as the witchman, Dolo Anah. Crawford was glad to see him. This was Donaldson's area of operations, the man must have got here almost as soon as Crawford's team, when he had heard of the trouble.

Crawford said in English, "They've been gathering for an outbreak of violence, evidently directed at the Reunited Nations projects administration buildings. I've seen a few banners calling for El Hassan to come to power, Africa for the Africans, that sort of thing."

The small Bahamian snorted. "You chaps certainly started something with this El Hassan farce. What are your immediate plans? How can I co-operate with you?"

A teenage boy who had been heckling Isobel, stooped now to pick up some dried cow dung. Almost absently, Crawford put his staff between the other's legs and tripped him up, when the lad sprawled on his face the American rapped him smartly on the head.

Crawford said, "Thanks a lot, we can use you, especially since you speak Dogon, I don't think any of my group does. We're going to hold a big meeting in front of the square and give them a long monotonous talk, saying little but sounding as though we're promising a great deal. When we've taken most of the steam out of them, we'll locate the ringleaders and have a big indoor meeting. My boys will be spotted throughout the gang. They'll nominate me to be spokesman, and nominate each other to be my committee and we'll be sent to find El Hassan and urge him to take power. That should keep them quiet for a while. At least long enough for headquarters in Dakar to decide what to do."

"Good Heavens," Donaldson said in admiration. "You Yanks are certainly good at this sort of thing."

"Takes practice," Homer Crawford said. "If you want to help, ferret out the groups who speak Dogon and give them the word."

Out of a sidestreet came running Abe Baker at the head of possibly two or three hundred arm waving, shouting, stick brandishing Africans. A few of them had banners which were being waved in such confusion that nobody could read the words inscribed. Most of them seemed to be younger men, even teen-agers.

"Good Heavens," Donaldson said again.

At first snap opinion, Crawford thought his assistant was being pursued and started forward to the hopeless rescue, but then he realized that Abe was heading the mob. Waving his staff, the New Yorker was shouting slogans, most of which had something to do with "El Hassan" but otherwise were difficult to make out.

The small mob charged out of the street and through the square, still shouting. Abe began to drop back into the ranks, and then to the edge of the charging, gesticulating crowd. Already, though, some of them seemed to be slowing up, even stopping and drifting away, puzzlement or frustration on their faces.

Those who were still at excitement's peak, charged up another street at the other side of the square.

In a few moments, Abe Baker came up to them, breathing hard and wiping sweat from his forehead. He grinned wryly. "Man, those cats are way out. This is really Endsville." He looked up at where Isobel was haranguing her own crowd, which hadn't been fazed by the men who'd charged through the square going nowhere. "Look at old Isobel up there. Man, this whole town's like a combination of Hyde Park and Union Square. You oughta hear old Jake making with a speech."

"What just happened?" Homer asked, motioning with his head to where the last elements of the mob Abe'd been leading were disappearing down a dead-end street.

"Ah, nothing," Abe said, still watching Isobel and grinning at her. "Those cats were the nucleus of a bunch wanted to start some action. Burn a few cars, raid the library, that sort of jazz. So I took over for a while, led them up one street and down the other. I feel like I just been star at a track meet."

"Good Heavens," Donaldson said still again.

"They're all scattered around now," Abe explained to him. "Either that or their tongues are hanging out to the point they'll have to take five to have a beer. They're finished for a while."

Isobel finished her little talk and joined them. "What gives now?" she asked.

Rex Donaldson said, "I'd like to stay around and watch you chaps operate. It's fascinating. However, I'd better get over to the park. That's probably where the greater number of the Dogon will be." He grumbled sourly, "I'll roast those blokes with a half dozen bits of magic and send them all back to Sangha. It'll be donkey's years before they ever show face around here again." He left them.

Homer Crawford looked after him. "Good man," he said.

Abe had about caught his breath. "What gives now, man?" he said. "I ought to get back to Jake. He's all alone up near the mosque."

"It's about time all of us got over there," Crawford said. He looked at Isobel as they walked. "How does it feel being a sort of reverse agent provocateur?"

Her forehead was wrinkled, characteristically. "I suppose it has to be done, but frankly, I'm not too sure just what we are doing. Here we go about pushing these supposed teachings of El Hassan and when we're taken up by the people and they actually attempt to accomplish what we taught them, we draw in on the reins."

"Man, you're right," Abe said unhappily. He looked at his chief. "What'd you say, Homer?"

"Of course she's right," Crawford growled. "It's just premature, is all. There's no program, no plan of action. If there was one, this thing here in Mopti might be the spark that united all North Africa. As it is, we have to put the damper on it until there is a definite program." He added sourly, "I'm just wondering if the Reunited Nations is the organization that can come up with one. And, if it isn't, where is there one?"

The mosque loomed up before them. The square before it was jam packed with milling Africans.

"Great guns," Isobel snorted, "there're more people here than the whole population of Mopti. Where'd they all come from?"

"They've been filtering in from the country," Crawford said.

"Well, we'll filter 'em back," Abe promised.

* * * * *

They spotted a ruckus and could see Elmer Allen in the middle of it, his quarterstaff flailing.

"On the double," Homer bit out, and he and Abe broke into a trot for the point of conflict. The idea was to get this sort of thing over as quickly as possible before it had a chance to spread.

They arrived too late. Elmer was leaning on his staff, as though needing it for support, and explaining mildly to two men who evidently were friends of a third who was stretched out on the ground, dead to the world and with a nasty lump on his shaven head.

Homer came up and said to Elmer, in Songhai, "What has transpired, O Holy One?" He made a sign of obeisance to the Jamaican.

The two Africans were taken aback by the term of address. They were unprepared to continue further debate, not to speak of physical action, against a holy man.

Elmer said with dignity, "He spoke against El Hassan, our great leader."

For a moment the two Africans seemed to be willing to deny that, but Abe Baker took up the cue and turned to the crowd that was beginning to gather. He held his hands out, palms upward questioningly, "And why should these young men beset a Holy One whose only crime is to love El Hassan?"

The crowd began to murmur and the two hurriedly picked up their fallen companion and took off with him.

Homer said in English, "What really happened?"

"Oh, this chap was one of the hot heads," Elmer explained. "Wanted some immediate action. I gave it to him."

Abe chuckled, "Holy One, yet."

Spotted through the square, holding forth to various gatherings of the mob were Jake Armstrong, Kenny Ballalou and Cliff Jackson. Even as Homer Crawford sized up the situation and the temper of the throngs of tribesmen, Bey entered the square from the far side at the head of two or three thousand more, most of whom were already beginning to look bored to death from talk, talk, talk.

Isobel came up and looked questioningly at Homer Crawford.

He said, "Abe, get the truck and drive it up before the entrance to the mosque. We'll speak from that. Isobel can open the hoe down, get the crowd over and then introduce me."

Abe left and Crawford said to Isobel, "Introduce me as Omar ben Crawf, the great friend and assistant of El Hassan. Build it up."

"Right," she said.

Crawford said, "Elmer first round up the boys and get them spotted through the audience. You're the cheerleaders and also the sergeants at arms, of course. Nail the hecklers quickly, before they can get organized among themselves. In short, the standard deal." He thought a moment. "And see about getting a hall where we can hold a meeting of the ringleaders, those are the ones we're going to have to cool out."

"Wizard," Elmer said and was gone on his mission.

Isobel and Homer stood for a moment, waiting for Abe and the truck.

She said, "You seem to have this all down pat."

"It's routine," he said absently. "The brain of a mob is no larger than that of its minimum member. Any disciplined group, almost no matter how small can model it to order."

"Just in case we don't have the opportunity to get together again, what happens at the hall meeting of ringleaders? What do Jake, Cliff and I do?"

"What comes naturally," Homer said. "We'll elect each other to the most important positions. But everybody else that seems to have anything at all on the ball will be elected to some committee or other. Give them jobs compiling reports to El Hassan or something. Keep them busy. Give Reunited Nations headquarters in Dakar time to come up with something."

She said worriedly, "Suppose some of these ringleaders are capable, aggressive types and won't stand for us getting all the important positions?"

Crawford grunted. "We're *more* aggressive and more capable. Let my team handle that. One of the boys will jump up and accuse the guy of being a spy and an enemy of El Hassan, and one of the other boys will bear him out, and a couple of others will hustle him out of the hall." Homer yawned. "It's all routine, Isobel."

Abe was driving up the truck.

Crawford said, "O.K., let's go, gal."

"Roger," she said, climbing first into the back of the vehicle and then up onto the roof of the cab.

Isobel held her hands high above her head and in the cab Abe bore down on the horn for a long moment.

Isobel shrilled, "Hear what the messenger from El Hassan has come to tell us! Hear the friend and devoted follower of El Hassan!"

At the same time, Jake, Kenny, and Cliff discontinued their own harangues and themselves headed for the new speaker.

* * * * *

They stayed for three days and had it well wrapped up in that time. The tribesmen, bored when the excitement fell away and it became obvious that there were to be no further riots, and certainly no violence, drifted back to their villages. The city dwellers returned to the routine of daily existence. And the police, who had mysteriously disappeared from the streets at the height of the demonstrations, now magically reappeared and began asserting their authority somewhat truculently.

At the hall meetings, mighty slogans were drafted and endless committees formed. The more articulate, the more educated and able of the demonstrators were marked out for future reference, but for the moment given meaningless tasks to keep them busy and out of trouble.

On the fourth day, Homer Crawford received orders to proceed to Dakar, leaving the rest of the team behind to keep an eye on the situation.

Abe groaned, "There's luck for you. Dakar, nearest thing to a good old sin city in a thousand miles. And who gets to go? Old sour puss, here. Got no more interest in the hot spots —"

Homer said, "You can come along, Abe."

Kenny Ballalou said, "Orders were only you, Homer."

Crawford growled, "Yes, but I have a suspicion I'm being called on the carpet for one of our recent escapades and I want backing if I need it." He added, "Besides, nothing is going to happen here."

"Crazy man," Abe said appreciatively.

Jake said, "We three were planning to head for Dakar today ourselves. Isobel, in particular, is exhausted and needs a prolonged rest before going out among the natives any more. You might as well continue to let us supply your transportation."

"Fine," Homer told him. "Come on Abe, let's get our things together."

"What do we do while you chaps are gone?" Elmer Allen said sourly. "I wouldn't mind a period in a city myself."

"Read a book, man," Abe told him. "Improve your mind."

"I've read a book," Elmer said glumly. "Any other ideas?"

* * * * *

Dakar is a big, bustling, prosperous and modern city shockingly set down in the middle of the poverty that is Africa. It should be, by its appearance, on the French Riviera, on the California coast, or possibly that of Florida, but it isn't. It's in Senegal, in the area once known as French West Africa.

Their aircraft swept in and landed at the busy airport.

They were assigned an African Development Project air-cushion car and drove into the city proper.

Dakar boasts some of the few skyscrapers in all Africa. The Reunited Nations occupied one of these in its entirety. Dakar was the center of activities for the whole Western Sahara and down into the Sudan. Across the street from its offices, a street still named Rue des Résistance in spite of the fact that the French were long gone, was the Hotel Juan-les-Pins.

Crawford and Abe Baker had radioed ahead and accommodations were ready for them. Their western clothing and other gear had been brought up from storage in the cellar.

At the desk, the clerk didn't blink at the Tuareg costume the two still wore. This was commonplace. He probably wouldn't have blinked had Isobel arrived in the costume of the Dogon. "Your suite is ready, Dr. Crawford," he said.

The manager came up and shook hands with an old customer and Homer Crawford introduced him to Isobel, Jake and Cliff, requesting he do his best for them. He and Abe then made their excuses and headed for the paradise of hot water, towels, western drink and the other amenities of civilization.

On the way up in the elevator, Abe said happily, "Man, I can just *taste* that bath I'm going to take. Crazy!"

"Personally," Crawford said, trying to reflect some of the other's typically lighthearted enthusiasm, "I have in mind a few belts out of a bottle of stone-age cognac, then a steak yea big and a flock of French fries, followed by vanilla ice cream."

Abe's eyes went round. "Man, you mean we can't get a good dish of cous cous in this town?"

"Cous cous," Crawford said in agony.

Abe made his voice so soulful. "With a good dollop of rancid camel butter right on top."

Homer laughed as they reached their floor and started for the suite. "You make it sound so good, I almost believe you." Inside he said, "Dibbers on the first bath. How about phoning down for a bottle of Napoleon and some soda and ice? When it comes, just mix me one and bring it in, that hand you see emerging from the soap bubbles in that tub, will be mine."

"I hear and obey, O Bwana!" Abe said in a servile tone.

By the time they'd cleaned up and had eaten an enormous western style meal in the dining room of the Juan-les-Pins, it was well past the hour when they could have made contact with their Reunited Nations superiors. They had a couple of cognacs in the bar, then, whistling happily, Abe Baker went out on the town.

Homer Crawford looked up Isobel, Jake and Cliff who had, sure enough, found accommodations in the same hotel.

Isobel stepped back in mock surprise when she saw Crawford in western garb. "Heavens to Betsy," she said. "The man is absolutely extinguished in a double-breasted charcoal gray."

He tried a scowl and couldn't manage it. "The word is *distinguished*, not extinguished," he said. He looked down at the suit, critically. "You know, I feel uncomfortable. I wonder if I'll be able to sit down in a chair instead of squatting." He looked at her own evening frock. "Wow," he said.

Cliff Jackson said menacingly, "None of that stuff, Crawford. Isobel has already been asked for, let's have no wolfing around."

Isobel said tartly, "Asked for but she didn't answer the summons." She took Homer by the arm. "And I just adore extinguish-oops, I mean distinguished looking men."

They trooped laughingly into the hotel cocktail lounge.

The time passed pleasantly. Jake and Cliff were good men in a field close to Homer Crawford's heart. Isobel was possibly the most attractive woman he'd ever met. They discussed in detail each other's work and all had stories of wonder to describe.

Crawford wondered vaguely if there was ever going to be a time, in this life of his, for a woman and all that one usually connects with womanhood. What was it Elmer Allen had said at the Timbuktu meeting? "... *most of us will be kept busy the rest of our lives at this.*"

In his present state of mind, it didn't seem too desirable a prospect. But there was no way out for such as Homer Crawford. What had Cliff Jackson said at the same meeting? "*We do what we must do.*" Which, come to think of it, didn't jibe too well with Cliff's claim at Mopti to be in it solely for the job. Probably the man disguised his basic idealism under a cloak of cynicism; if so, he wouldn't be the first.

They said their goodnights early. All of them were used to Sahara hours. Up at dawn, to bed shortly after sunset; the desert has little fuel to waste on illumination.

In the suite again, Homer Crawford noted that Abe hadn't returned as yet. He snorted deprecation. The younger man would probably be out until dawn. Dakar had much to offer in the way of civilization's fleshpots.

He took up the bottle of cognac and poured himself a healthy shot, wishing that he'd remembered to pick up a paperback at the hotel's newsstand before coming to bed.

He swirled the expensive brandy in the glass and brought it to his nose to savor the bouquet.

But fifteen-year-old brandy from the cognac district of France should not boast a bouquet involving elements of bitter almonds. With an automatic startled gesture, Crawford jerked his face away from the glass.

He scowled down at it for a long moment, then took up the bottle and sniffed it. He wondered how a would-be murderer went about getting hold of cyanide in Dakar.

Homer Crawford phoned the desk and got the manager. Somebody had been in the suite during his absence. Was there any way of checking?

He didn't expect satisfaction and didn't receive any. The manager, after finding that nothing seemed to be missing, seemed to think that perhaps Dr. Crawford had made a mistake. Homer didn't bother to tell him about the poisoned brandy. He hung up, took the bottle into the bathroom and poured it away.

In the way of precautions, he checked the windows to see if there were any possibilities of entrance by an intruder, locked the door securely, put his handgun beneath his pillow and fell off to sleep. When and if Abe returned, he could bang on the door.

* * * * *

In the morning, clad in American business suits and frankly feeling a trifle uncomfortable in them, Homer Crawford and Abraham Baker presented themselves at the offices of the African Development Project, Sahara Division, of the Reunited Nations. Uncharacteristically, there was no waiting in anterooms, no dealing with subordinates. Dr. Crawford and his lieutenant were ushered directly to the office of Sven Zetterberg.

Upon their entrance the Swede came to his feet, shook hands abruptly with both of them and sat down again. He scowled at Abe and said to Homer in excellent English, "It was requested that your team remain in Mopti." Then he added, "Sit down, gentlemen."

They took chairs. Crawford said mildly, "Mr. Baker is my right-hand man. I assume he'd take over the team if anything happened to me." He added dryly, "Besides, there were a few things he felt he had to do about town."

Abe cleared his throat but remained silent.

Zetterberg continued to frown but evidently for a different reason now. He said, "There have been more complaints about your ... ah ... cavalier tactics."

Homer looked at him but said nothing.

Zetterberg said in irritation, "It becomes necessary to warn you almost every time you come in contact with this office, Dr. Crawford."

Homer said evenly, "My team and I work in the field Dr. Zetterberg. We have to think on our feet and usually come to decisions in split seconds. Sometimes our lives are at stake. We do what we think best under the conditions. At any time your office feels my efforts are misdirected, my resignation is available."

The Swede cleared his throat. "The Arab Union has made a full complaint in the Reunited Nations of a group of our men massacring thirty-five of their troopers."

Homer said, "They were well into the Ahaggar with a convoy of modern weapons, obviously meant for adherents of theirs. Given the opportunity, the Arab Union would take over North Africa."

"This is no reason to butcher thirty-five men."

"We were fired upon first," Crawford said.

"That is not the way they tell it. They claim you ambushed them."

Abe put in innocently, "How would the Arab Union know? We didn't leave any survivors."

Zetterberg glared at him. "It is not easy, Mr. Baker, for we who do the paper work involved in this operation, to account for the activities of you hair-trigger men in the field."

"We appreciate your difficulties," Homer said evenly. "But we can only continue to do what we think best on being confronted with an emergency."

The Swede drummed his fingers on the desk top. "Perhaps I should remind you that the policy of this project is to encourage amalgamation of the peoples of the area. Possibly, the Arab Union will prove to be the best force to accomplish such a union."

Abe grunted.

Homer Crawford was shaking his head. "You don't believe that Dr. Zetterberg, and I doubt if there are many non-Moslems who do. Mohammed sprung out of the deserts and his religion is one based on the surroundings, both physical and socio-economic."

Zetterberg grumbled, argumentatively, though his voice lacked conviction, "So did its two sister religions, Judaism and Christianity."

Crawford waggled a finger negatively. "Both of them adapted to changing times, with considerable success. Islam has remained the same and in all the world there is not one example of a highly developed socio-economic system in a Moslem country. The reason is that in your country, and mine, and in the other advanced countries of the West, we pay lip service to our religions, but we don't let them interfere with our day by day life. But the Moslem, like the rapidly disappearing ultra-orthodox Jews, lives his religion every day and by the rules set down by the Prophet fifteen centuries ago. Everything a Moslem does from the moment he gets up in the morning is all mapped out in the Koran. What fingers of the hand to eat with, what hand to break bread with-and so on and so forth. It can get ludicrous. You should see the bathroom of a wealthy Moslem in some modern city such as Tangier. Mohammed never dreamed of such institutions as toilet paper. His followers still obey the rules he set down as an alternative."

"What's your point?"

"That North Africa cannot be united under the banner of Islam if she is going to progress rapidly. If it ever unites, it will be in spite of local religions-Islam and pagan as well; they hold up the wheels of progress."

Zetterberg stared at him. The truth of the matter was that he agreed with the American and they both knew it.

He said, "This matter of physically assaulting and then arresting the chieftain" —he looked down at a paper on his desk —"of the Ouled Touameur clan of the Chaambra confederation, Abd-el-Kader. From your report, the man was evidently attempting to unify the tribes."

Crawford was shaking his head impatiently. "No. He didn't have the ...dream. He was a raider, a racketeer, not a leader of purposeful men. Perhaps it's true that these people need a hero to act as a symbol for them, but he can't be such as Abd-el-Kader."

"I suppose you're right," the Swede said grudgingly. "See here, have you heard reports of a group of Cubans, in the Anglo-Egyptian Sudan to help with the new sugar refining there, being attacked?"

The eyes of both Crawford and Baker narrowed. There'd been talk about this at Timbuktu. "Only a few rumors," Crawford said.

The Swede drummed his desk with his nervous fingers. "The rumors are correct. The whole group was either killed or wounded." He said suddenly, "You had nothing to do with this, I suppose?"

Crawford held his palms up, in surprise, "My team has never been within a thousand miles of Khartoum."

Zetterberg said, "See here, we suspect the Cubans might have supported Soviet Complex viewpoints."

Crawford shrugged, "I know nothing about them at all."

Zetterberg said, "Do you think this might be the work of El Hassan and his followers?"

Abe started to chuckle something, but Homer shook his head slightly in warning and said, "I don't know."

"How did that affair in Mopti turn out, these riots in favor of El Hassan?"

Homer Crawford shrugged. "Routine. Must have been as many as ten thousand of them at one point. We used standard tactics in gaining control and then dispersing them. I'll have a complete written report to you before the day is out."

Zetterberg said, "You've heard about this El Hassan before?"

"Quite a bit."

"From the rumors that have come into this office, he backs neither East nor West in international politics. He also seems to agree with your summation of the Islamic problem. He teaches separation of Church and State."

"They're the same thing in Moslem countries," Abe muttered.

Zetterberg tossed his bombshell out of a clear sky. "Dr. Crawford," he snapped, "in spite of the warnings we've had to issue to you repeatedly, you are admittedly our best man in the field. We're giving you a new assignment. Find this El Hassan and bring him here!"

Zetterberg leaned forward, an expression of somewhat anxious sincerity in his whole demeanor.

VIII

Abe Baker choked, and then suddenly laughed.

Sven Zetterberg stared at him. "What's so funny?"

"Well, nothing," Abe admitted. He looked to Homer Crawford.

Crawford said to the Swede carefully, "Why?"

Zetterberg said impatiently, "Isn't it obvious, after the conversation we've had here? Possibly this El Hassan is the man we're looking for. Perhaps this is the force that will bind North Africa together. Thus far, all we've heard about him has been rumor. We don't seem to be able to find anyone who has seen him, nor is the exact strength of his following known. We'd like to confer with him, before he gets any larger."

Crawford said carefully, "It's hard to track down a rumor."

"That's why we give the assignment to our best team in the field," the Swede told him. "You've got a roving commission. Find El Hassan and bring him here to Dakar."

Abe grinned and said, "Suppose he doesn't want to come?"

"Use any methods you find necessary. If you need more manpower, let us know. But we must talk to El Hassan."

Homer said, still watching his words, "Why the urgency?"

The Reunited Nations official looked at him for a long moment, as though debating whether to let him in on higher policy. "Because, frankly, Dr. Crawford, the elements which first went together to produce the African Development Project, are, shall we say, becoming somewhat unstuck."

"The glue was never too strong," Abe muttered.

Zetterberg nodded. "The attempt to find competent, intelligent men to work for the project, who were at the same time altruistic and unaffected by personal or national interests, has always been a difficult one. If you don't mind my saying so, we Scandinavians, particularly those not affiliated with NATO come closest to filling the bill. We have no designs on Africa. It is unfortunate that we have practically no Negro citizens who could do field work."

"Are you suggesting other countries have designs on Africa?" Homer said.

For the first time the Swede laughed. A short, choppy laugh. "Are you suggesting they haven't? What was that convoy of the Arab Union bringing into the Sahara? Guns, with which to forward their cause of taking over all North Africa. What were those Cubans doing in Sudan, that someone else felt it necessary to assassinate them? What is the program of the Soviet Complex as it applies to this area, and how does it differ from that of the United States? And how do the ultimate programs of the British Commonwealth and the French Community differ from each other and from both the United States and Russia?"

"That's why we have a Reunited Nations," Crawford said calmly.

"Theoretically, yes. But it is coming apart at the seams. I sometimes wonder if an organization composed of a membership each with its own selfish needs can ever really unite in an altruistic task. Remember the early days when the Congo was first given her freedom? Supposedly the United Nations went in to help. Actually, each element in the United Nations had its own irons in the fire, and usually their desires differed."

The Swede shrugged hugely. "I don't know, but I am about convinced, and so are a good many other officers of this project, that unless we soon find a competent leader to act as a symbol around which all North Africans can unite, find such a man and back him, that all our work will crumble in this area under pressure from outside. That's why we want El Hassan."

Homer Crawford came to his feet, his face in a scowl. "I'll let you know by tomorrow, if I can take the assignment," he said.

"Why tomorrow?" the Swede demanded.

"There are some ramifications I have to consider."

"Very well," the Swede said stiffly. He came to his own feet and shook hands with them again. "Oh, there's just one other thing. This spontaneous meeting you held in Timbuktu with elements from various other organizations. How did it come out?"

Crawford was wary. "Very little result, actually."

Zetterberg chuckled. "As I expected. However, we would appreciate it, doctor, if you and your team would refrain from such activities in the future. You are, after all, hired by the Reunited Nations and owe it all your time and allegiance. We have no desire to see you fritter away this time with religious fanatics and other crackpot groups."

"I see," Crawford said.

The other laughed cheerfully. "I'm sure you do, Dr. Crawford. A word to the wise."

* * * * *

They remained silent on the way back to the hotel.

In the lobby they ran into Isobel Cunningham.

Homer Crawford looked at her thoughtfully. He said, "We've got some thinking to do and some ideas to bat back and forth. I value your opinion and experience, Isobel, could you come up to the suite and sit in?"

She tilted her head, looked at him from the side of her eyes. "Something big has happened, hasn't it?"

"I suppose so. I don't know. We've got to make some decisions."

"Come on Isobel," Abe said. "You can give us the feminine viewpoint and all that jazz."

They started for the elevator and Isobel said to Abe, "If you'd just be consistent with that pseudo-beatnik chatter of yours, I wouldn't mind. But half the time you talk like an English lit major when you forget to put on your act."

"Man," Abe said to her, "maybe I was wrong inviting you to sit in on this bull session. I can see you're in a bad mood."

In the living room of the suite, Isobel took an easy-chair and Abe threw himself full length on his back on a couch. Homer Crawford paced the floor.

"Well?" Isobel said.

Crawford said abruptly, "Somebody tried to poison me last night. Got into this room somehow and put cyanide in a bottle of cognac Abe and I were drinking out of earlier in the evening."

Isobel stared at him. Her eyes went from him to Abe and back. "But ...but, why?"

Crawford ran his hand back over his wiry hair in puzzlement. "I ...I don't know. That's what's driving me batty. I can't figure out why anybody would want to kill me."

"I can," Abe said bluntly. "And that interview we just had with Sven Zetterberg just bears me out."

"Zetterberg," Isobel said, surprised. "Is he in Africa?"

Crawford nodded to her question but his eyes were on Abe.

Abe put his hands behind his head and said to the ceiling, "Zetterberg just gave Homer's team the assignment of bringing in El Hassan."

"El Hassan? But you boys told us all in Timbuktu that there was no El Hassan. You invented him and then the rest of us, more or less spontaneously, though unknowingly, took up the falsification and spread your work."

"That's right," Crawford said, still looking at Abe.

"But didn't you tell Sven Zetterberg?" Isobel demanded. "He's too big a man to play jokes upon."

"No, I didn't and I'm not sure I know why."

"I know why," Abe said. He sat up suddenly and swung his feet around and to the floor.

The other two watched him, both frowning.

Abe said slowly, "Homer, you *are* El Hassan."

His chief scowled at him. "What is that supposed to mean?"

The younger man gestured impatiently. "Figure it out. Somebody else already has, the somebody who took a shot at you from that mosque. Look, put it all together and it makes sense.

"These North Africans aren't going to make it, not in the short period of time that we want them to, unless a leader appears on the scene. These people are just beginning to emerge from tribal society. In the tribes, people live by rituals and taboos, by traditions. But at the next step in the evolution of society they follow a Hero-and the traditions are thrown overboard. It's one step up the ladder of cultural evolution. Just for the record, the Heroes almost invariably get clobbered in the end, since a Hero must be perfect. Once he is found wanting in any respect, he's a false prophet, a cheat, and a new, perfect and faultless Hero must be found.

"O.K. At this stage we need a Hero to unite North Africa, but this time we need a real super-Hero. In this modern age, the old style one won't do. We need one with education, and altruism, one with the dream, as you call it. We need a man who has no affiliations, no preferences for Tuareg, Teda, Chaambra, Dogon, Moor or whatever. He's got to be truly neutral. O.K., you're it. You're an American Negro, educated, competent, widely experienced. You're a natural for the job. You speak Arabic, French, Tamabeq, Songhai and even Swahili."

Abe stopped momentarily and twisted his face in a grimace. "But there's one other thing that's possibly the most important of all. Homer, you're a born leader."

"Who *me?*" Crawford snorted. "I hate to be put in a position where I have to lead men, make decisions, that sort of thing.

"That's beside the point. There in Timbuktu you had them in the palm of your hand. All except one or two, like Doc Smythe and that missionary. And I have an idea even they'd come around. Everybody there felt it. They were in favor of anything you suggested. Isobel?"

She nodded, very seriously. "Yes. You have a personality that goes over, Homer. I think it would be a rare person who could conceive of you cheating, or misleading. You're so obviously sincere, competent and intelligent that it, well, *projects* itself. I noticed it even more in Mopti than Timbuktu. You had that city in your palm in a matter of a few hours."

Homer Crawford shifted his shoulders, uncomfortably.

Abe said, "You might dislike the job, but it's a job that needs doing."

Crawford ran his hand around the back of his neck, uncomfortably. "You think such a project would get the support of the various teams and organizations working North Africa, eh?"

"Practically a hundred per cent. And even if some organizations or even countries, with their own row to hoe, tried to buck you, their individual members and teams would come over. Why? Because it makes sense."

Homer Crawford said worriedly, "Actually, I've realized this, partially subconsciously, for some time. But I didn't put myself in the role. I …I wish there really was an El Hassan. I'd throw my efforts behind him."

"There will be an El Hassan," Abe said definitely. "And you can be him."

Crawford stared at Abe, undecided.

Isobel said, suddenly, "I think Abe's right, Homer."

* * * * *

Abe seemed to switch the tempo of his talk. He said, "There's just one thing, Homer. It's a long range question, but it's an important one."

"Yes?"

"What're your politics?"

"My politics? I haven't any politics here in North Africa."

"I mean back home. I've never discussed politics with you, Homer, partly because I haven't wanted to reveal my own. But now the question comes up. What is your position, ultimately, speaking on a world-wide basis?"

Homer looked at him quizzically, trying to get at what was behind the other's words. "I don't belong to any political party," he said slowly.

Abe said evenly, "I do, Homer. I'm a Party member."

Crawford was beginning to get it. "If you mean do I ultimately support the program of the Soviet Complex, the answer is definitely no. Whether or not it's desirable for Russia or for China, is up to the Russians and Chinese to decide. But I don't believe it's desirable for such advanced countries as the United States and most of Western Europe. We've got large problems that need answering, but the commies don't supply the answers so far as I'm concerned."

"I see," Abe said. He was far, far different than the laughing, beatnik jabbering, youngster he had always seemed. "That's not so good."

"Why not?" Homer demanded. His eyes went to where Isobel sat, her face strained at all this, but he could read nothing in her expression, and she said nothing.

Abe said, "Because, admittedly, North Africa isn't ready for a communist program as yet. It's in too primitive a condition. However, it's progressing fast, fantastically fast, and the coming of El Hassan is going to speed things up still more."

Abe said deliberately, "Possibly twenty years from now the area *will* be ready for a communist program. And at that time we don't want somebody with El Hassan's power and prestige against us. We take the long view, Homer, and it dictates that El Hassan has to be secretly on the Party's side."

Homer was nodding. "I see. So that's why you shot at me in Timbuktu."

Abe's eyes went wary. He said, "I didn't know you knew."

Crawford nodded. "It just came to me. It had to be you. Supposedly, you broke into the mosque from the back at the same moment I came in the front. Actually, you were already inside." Homer grunted. "Besides, it would have been awfully difficult for anyone else to have doped that bottle of cognac on me. What I couldn't understand, and still can't, was motive. We've been in the clutch together more than once, Abe."

"That's right, Homer, but there are some things so important that friendship goes by the board. I could see as far back as that meeting something that hadn't occurred to either you or the others. You were a born El Hassan. I figured it was necessary to get you out of the way and put one of our own-perhaps me, even-in your place. No ill feelings, Homer. In fact, now I've just given you your chance. You could come in with us —"

Even as he was speaking, his eyes moved in a way Homer Crawford recognized. He'd seen Abe Baker in action often enough. A gun flicked out of an under-the-arm holster, but Crawford moved in anticipation. The flat of his hand darted forward, chopped and the hand weapon was on the floor.

As Isobel screamed, Abe countered the attack. He reached forward in a jujitsu maneuver, grabbed a coat sleeve and a handful of suit coat. He twisted quickly, threw the other man over one hip and to the floor.

But Homer Crawford was already expertly rolling with the fall, rolling out to get a fresh start.

Abe Baker knew that in the long go, in spite of his somewhat greater heft, he wouldn't be able to take his former chief in the other man's own field. Now he threw himself on the other, on the floor. Legs and arms tangled in half realized, quickly defeated holds and maneuvers.

Abe called, "Quick, Isobel, the gun. Get the gun and cover him."

She shook her head, desperately. "Oh no. No!"

Abe bit out, his teeth grinding under the punishment he was taking, "That's an order, *Comrade Cunningham*! Get the gun!"

"No. No, I can't!" She turned and fled the room.

Abe muttered an obscenity, bridged and crabbed out of the desperate position he was in. And now his fingers were but a few inches from the weapon. He stretched.

Homer Crawford, heavy veins in his own forehead from his exertions, panted, "Abe, I can't let you get that gun. Call it quits."

"Can't, Homer," Abe gritted. His fingers were a few fractions of an inch from the weapon.

Crawford panted, "Abe, there's just one thing I can do. A karate blow. *I* can chop your windpipe with the side of my hand. Abe, if I do, only immediate surgery could save your —"

Abe's fingers closed about the gun and Crawford, calling on his last resources, lashed out. He could feel the cartilage collapse, a sound of air, for a moment, almost like a shriek filled the room.

The gun was meaningless now. Homer Crawford, his face agonized, was on his knees beside the other who was threshing on the floor. "Abe," he groaned. "You made me."

Abe Baker's face was quickly going ashen in his impossible quest for oxygen. For a last second there was a gleam in his eyes and his lips moved. Crawford bent down. He wasn't sure, but he thought that somehow the other found enough air to get out a last, "Crazy man."

When it was over, Homer Crawford stood again, and looked down at the body, his face expressionless.

From behind him a voice said, "So I got here too late."

Crawford turned. It was Elmer Allen, gun in hand.

Homer Crawford said dully, "What are you doing here?"

Elmer looked at the body, then back at his chief. "Bey figured out what must have happened at the mosque there in Timbuktu. We didn't know what might be motivating Abe, but we got here as quick as we could."

"He was a commie," Crawford said dully. "Evidently, the Party decided I stood in its way. Where are the others?"

"Scouring the town to find you."

Crawford said wearily, "Find the others and bring them here. We've got to get rid of poor Abe, there, and then I've got something to tell you."

"Very well, chief," Elmer said, holstering his gun. "Oh, just one thing before I go. You know that chap Rex Donaldson? Well, we had some discussion after you left. This'll probably surprise you Homer, but-hold onto your hat, as you Americans say-Donaldson thinks you ought to *become* El Hassan. And Bey, Kenny and I agree."

Crawford said, "We'll talk about it later, Elmer."

* * * * *

He knocked at her door and a moment later she came. She saw who it was, opened for him and returned to the room beyond. She had obviously been crying.

Homer Crawford said, but with no reproach in his voice, "You should have helped me, to be consistent."

"I knew you'd win."

"Nevertheless, once you'd switched sides, you should have attempted to help me. If you had, maybe Abe would still be alive."

She took a quick agonized breath, and sat down in one of the two chairs, her hands clasped tightly in her lap. She said, "I ... I've known Abe since my early teens."

He said nothing.

"In college, he was the cell leader. He enlisted me into the Party."

Crawford still didn't speak.

She said defiantly, "He was an idealist, Homer."

"I know that," Crawford said. "And along with it, he's saved my life, on at least three different occasions in the past few years. He was a good man."

It was her turn to hold silence.

Homer hit the palm of his left hand with the fist of his right. "That's what so many don't realize. They think this is all a kind of cowboys and Indians affair. The good guys and the bad guys fighting it out. And, of course, all the good guys are on our side and their side is composed of bad guys. They don't realize that many, even most, of the enemy are fighting for an ideal, too-and are willing to die for it, or do things sometimes even harder than dying."

He paced the floor for an agonized moment, before adding. "The fact that the ideal is a false one-or so, at least, is my opinion-is beside the point."

He suddenly dropped it and switched subjects. "This isn't as much a surprise to me as you possibly think, Isobel. There was only one way that episode in Timbuktu could have taken place. Abe was waiting for me to pass that mosque. But I had to pass. I had to be *fingered* as the old gangster expression had it. And you led me into the ambush."

He looked down at her. "But what changed his mind? Why did he offer, tonight, to let me take over the El Hassan leadership?"

Isobel said, her voice low. "In Timbuktu, when Abe saw the way things were going, he realized you'd have to be liquidated, otherwise El Hassan would be a leader the Party couldn't control. He tried to eliminate you, and then tried again with the cognac. Last night, however, he checked with local party leaders and they decided that he'd acted too precipitately. They suggested you be given the opportunity to line up with the Party."

"And if I didn't?" Homer said.

"Then you were to be liquidated."

"So the finger is still on me, eh?"

"Yes, you'll have to be careful."

He looked full into her face. "How do you stand now?"

She returned his frank look. "I'm the first follower to dedicate her services to El Hassan."

"So you want to come along?"

"Yes," she said simply.

"And you remember what Abe said? That in the end the Hero invariably gets clobbered? Sooner or later, North Africa will outgrow the need for a Hero to follow and then ... then El Hassan and his closest followers have a good chance of winding up before a firing squad."

"Yes, I know that."

Homer Crawford ran his hand back over his short hair, wearily. "O.K., Isobel. Your first instructions are to contact those two friends of yours, Jake Armstrong and Cliff Jackson. Try to convert them."

"What are you going to be doing ... El Hassan?"

"I'm going over to the Reunited Nations to resign from the African Development Project. I have a sneaking suspicion that in the future they will not always be seeing eye to eye with El Hassan. Nor will the other organizations currently helping to advance Africa-whilst still at the same time keeping their own irons in the fire. Possibly the commies won't be the only ones in favor of liquidating El Hassan's assets."

Border, Breed nor Birth

I

El Hassan, would-be tyrant of all North Africa, was on the run.

His followers at this point numbered six, one of whom was a wisp of a twenty-four year old girl. Arrayed against him and his dream, he knew, was the combined power of the world in the form of the Reunited Nations, and, in addition, such individual powers as the United States of the Americas, the Soviet Complex, Common Europe, the French Community, the British Commonwealth and the Arab Union, working both together and unilaterally.

Immediate survival depended upon getting into the Great Erg of the Sahara where even the greatest powers the world had ever developed would have their work cut out locating El Hassan and his people.

* * * * *

Bey-ag-Akhamouk who was riding next to Elmer Allen in the lead air cushion hover-lorry, held a hand high. Both of the solar powered desert vehicles ground to a halt.

Homer Crawford vaulted out of the seat of the second lorry before it had settled to the sand. "What's up, Bey?" he called.

Bey pointed to the south and west. They were in the vicinity of Tessalit, in what was once known as French Sudan, and immediately to the south of Algeria. They were deliberately avoiding what little existed in this area in the way of trails, the Tanezrouft route which crossed the Sahara from Colomb-Béchar to Gao, on the Niger, was some fifty miles to the west.

Homer Crawford stared up into the sky in the direction Bey pointed and his face went wan.

The others were piling out of the vehicles.

"What is it?" Isobel Cunningham said, squinting and trying to catch what the others had already spotted.

"Aircraft," Bey growled. "A rocket-plane."

"Which means the military in this part of the world," Homer said.

The rest of them looked to him for instructions, but Bey suddenly took over. He said to Homer, "You better get on over beneath that outcropping of rock. The rest of us will handle this."

Homer looked at him.

Bey said, flatly, "If one of the rest of us gets it, or even if all of us do, the El Hassan movement goes on. But if something happens to you, the movement dies. We've already taken our stand and too much is at stake to risk your life."

Homer Crawford opened his mouth to protest, then closed it. He reached inside the solar-powered lorry and fetched forth a Tommy-Noiseless and started for the rock outcropping at a trot. Having made his decision, he wasn't going to cramp Bey-ag-Akhamouk's style with needless palaver.

Isobel Cunningham, Cliff Jackson, Elmer Allen and Kenny Ballalou gathered around the tall, American educated Tuareg.

"What's the plan?" Elmer said. Either he or Kenny Ballalou could have taken over as competently, but they were as capable of taking orders as giving them, a desirable trait in fighting men.

Bey was still staring at the oncoming speck. He growled, "We can't even hope he hasn't seen the pillars of sand and dust these vehicles throw up. He's spotted us all right. And we've got to figure he's looking for us, even though we can hope he's not."

The side of his mouth began to tic, characteristically. "He'll make three passes. The first one high, as an initial check. The second time he'll come in low just to make sure. The third pass and he'll clobber us."

The aircraft was coming on, high but nearer now.

"So," Elmer said reasonably, "we either get him the second pass he makes, or we've had it." The young Jamaican's lips were thinned back over his excellent teeth, as always when he went into combat.

"That's it," Bey agreed. "Kenny, you and Cliff get the flac rifle, and have it handy in the back of the second truck. Be sure he doesn't see it on this first pass. Elmer, get on the radio and check anything he sends."

Kenny Ballalou and the hulking Cliff Jackson ran to carry out orders.

Isobel said, "Got an extra gun for me?"

Bey scowled at her. "You better get over there with Homer where it's safer."

She said evenly, "I've always considered myself a pacifist, but when somebody starts shooting at me, I forget about it and am inclined to shoot back."

"I haven't got time to argue with you," Bey said. "There aren't any extra guns except handguns and they'd be useless." As he spoke, he pulled his own Tommy-Noiseless from its scabbard on the front door of the air cushion lorry, and checked its clip of two hundred .10 caliber ultra-high velocity rounds. He flicked the selector to the explosive side of the clip.

* * * * *

The plane was roaring in on what would be its first pass, if Bey had guessed correctly. If he had guessed incorrectly, this might be the end. A charge of napalm would fry everything for a quarter of a mile around, or the craft might even be equipped with a mini-fission bomb. In this area a minor nuclear explosion would probably go undetected.

Bey yelled, "Don't anybody even try to fire at him at this range. He'll be back. It takes half the sky to turn around in with that crate, but he'll be back, lower next time."

Cliff Jackson said cheerlessly, "Maybe he's just looking for us. He won't necessarily take a crack at us."

Bey grunted. "Elmer?"

"Nothing on the radio," Elmer said. "If he was just scouting us out, he'd report to his base. But if his orders are to clobber us, then he wouldn't put it on the air."

The plane was turning in the sky, coming back.

Cliff argued, "Well, we can't fire unless we know if he's just hunting us out, or trying to do us in."

Elmer said patiently, "For just finding us, that first pass would be all he needed. He could radio back that he'd found us. But if he comes in again, he's looking for trouble."

"Here he comes!" Bey yelled. "Kenny-Cliff ... the rifle!"

Isobel suddenly dashed out into the sands a dozen yards or so from the vehicles and began running around and around in a circle as though demented.

Bey stared at her. "Get back here," he roared. "Under one of the trucks!"

She ignored him.

The rocket-plane was coming in, low and obviously as slow as the pilot could retard its speed.

The flac rifle began jumping and tracers reached out from it-inaccurately. The Tommy-Noiseless automatics in the hands of Bey and Elmer Allen gave their silenced *flic flic flic* sounds, equally ineffective.

On the ultra-stubby wings of the fast moving aircraft, a row of brilliant cherries flickered and a row of explosive shells plowed across the desert, digging twin ditches, miraculously going between the air cushion lorries but missing both. It was upon them, over and gone, before the men on the ground could turn to fire after.

Elmer Allen muttered an obscenity under his breath.

Cliff Jackson looked around in desperation. "What can we do now? He won't come close enough for us to even fire at him, next time."

Bey said nothing. Isobel had collapsed into the sand. Elmer Allen looked over at her. "Nice try, Isobel," he said. "I think he came in lower and slower than he would have otherwise-trying to see what the devil it was you were doing."

She shrugged, hopelessly.

"Hey!" Kenny Ballalou pointed.

The rocketcraft was wobbling, shuddering, in the sky. Suddenly it burst into a black cloud of fire and smoke and explosion.

At the same moment, Homer Crawford got up from the sand dune behind which he'd stationed himself and plowed awkwardly through the sand toward them.

Bey glared at him.

Homer shrugged and said, "I checked the way he came in the first time and figured he'd repeat the run. Then I got behind that dune there and faced in the other direction and started firing where I *thought* he'd be, a few seconds before he came over. He evidently ran right into it."

Bey said indignantly, "Look, wise guy, you're no longer the leader of a five-man Reunited Nations African Development Project team. Then, you were expendable. Now, you're El Hassan. You give the orders. Other people are expendable."

Homer Crawford grinned at him, somewhat ruefully and held up his hands as though in supplication. "Listen to the man, is that any way to talk to El Hassan?"

Elmer Allen said worriedly, "He's right, though, Homer. You shouldn't take chances."

Homer Crawford went serious. "Actually, none of us should, if we can avoid it. In a way, El Hassan isn't one person. It's this team here, and Jake Armstrong, who by this time I hope is on his way to the States."

Bey was shaking his head in stubborn determination. "No," he said. "I'm not sure that you comprehend this yourself, Homer, but you're Number One. You're the symbol, the hero these people are going to follow if we put this thing over. They couldn't understand a sextet leadership. They want a leader, someone to dominate and tell them what to do. A team you need, admittedly, but not so much as the team needs you. Remember Alexander? He had a team starting off with Aristotle for a brain-trust, and Parmenion, one of the greatest generals of all time for his right-hand man. Then he had a group of field men such as Ptolemy, Antipater, Antigonus and Seleucus-not to be rivaled until Napoleon built his team, two thousand years later. And what happened to this super-team when Alexander died?"

Homer looked at him thoughtfully.

Bey wound it up doggedly. "You're our Alexander. Our Caesar. Our Napoleon. So don't go getting yourself killed, damn it. Excuse me, Isobel."

Isobel grinned her pixielike grin. "I agree," she said. "Dammit."

Homer said, "I'm not sure I go all along with you or not. We'll think about it." His voice took a sharper note. "Let's go over and see if there's enough left in that wreckage to give us an idea of who the pilot represented. I can't believe it was a Reunited Nations man, and I'd like to know who, of our potential enemies, dislikes the idea of El Hassan so much that they figure we should all be bumped off before we even get under way."

* * * * *

It had begun-if there is ever a beginning-in Dakar. In the offices of Sven Zetterberg the Swedish head of the Sahara Division of the African Development Project of the Reunited Nations.

Homer Crawford, head of a five-man trouble-shooting team, had reported for orders. In one hand he held them, when he was ushered into the other's presence.

Zetterberg shook hands abruptly, said, "Sit down, Dr. Crawford."

Homer Crawford looked at the secretary who had ushered him in.

Zetterberg said, scowling, "What's the matter?"

"I think I have something to be discussed privately."

The secretary shrugged and turned and left.

Zetterberg, still scowling, resumed his own place behind the desk and said, "Claud Hansen is a trusted Reunited Nations man. What could possibly be so secret...?"

Homer indicated the orders he held. "This assignment. It takes some consideration."

Sven Zetterberg was not a patient man. He said, in irritation, "It should be perfectly clear. This El Hassan we've been hearing so much about. This mystery man come out of the desert attempting to unify all North America. We want to talk to him."

"Why?" Crawford said.

"Confound it," Zetterberg snapped. "I thought we'd gone into this yesterday. In spite of the complaints that come into this office in regard to your cavalier tactics in carrying out your assignments, you and your team are our most competent operatives. So we've given you the assignment of finding El Hassan."

"I mean, why do you want to talk to him?"

The Swede glared at him for a moment, as though the American was being deliberately dense. "Dr. Crawford," he said, "when the African Development Project was first begun we had high hopes. Seemingly all Reunited Nations members were being motivated by high humanitarian reasons. Our task was to bring all Africa to a level of progress comparable to the advanced nations. It was more than a duty, it was a crying need, a demand. Africa is and has been throughout history a *have-not* continent. While Europe, the Americas, Australia and now even Asia, industrialized and largely conquered man's old socio-economic problems, Africa lagged behind. The reasons were manifold, colonialism, lingering tribal society ... various others. Now that very lagging has become a potential explosive situation. With the coming of antibiotics and other break-throughs in medicine, the African population is growing with an all but geometric progression. So fast is it growing, that what advances were being made did less than keep up the level of per capita gross product. It was bad enough to have a per capita gross product averaging less than a hundred dollars a year, but it actually sank below that point."

Homer Crawford was nodding.

Zetterberg continued the basic lecture with which he knew the other was already completely familiar. "So the Reunited Nations took on the task of advancing as rapidly as possible the African economy and all the things that must be done before an economy *can* be advanced. It was self-preservation, I suppose. *Have-not* nations, not to speak of *have-not* races and *have-not* continents, have a tendency eventually to explode upon their wealthier neighbors."

The Swede pressed his lips together before continuing. "Unfortunately, the Reunited Nations as the United Nations and the League of Nations before it, is composed of members each with its own irons in the fire. Each with its own plans and schemes." His voice was bitter now. "The Arab Union with its desire to unite all Islam into one. The Soviet Complex with its ultimate dream of a soviet world. The capitalistic economies of the British Commonwealth, Common Europe, and your United States of the Americas, with their hunger for, positive need for, sources of raw materials and markets for their manufactured products. All, though playing lip service to the African Development Project, have still their own ambitions."

Sven Zetterberg waggled a finger at Homer Crawford. "I do not charge that your United States is attempting to take over Africa, or even any section of it, in the old colonialistic sense. Even England and France have discovered that it is much simpler to dominate economically than to go through all the expense and effort of governing another people. That is the basic reason they gave up their empires. No, your United States would love to so dominate Africa that her products, her entrepreneurs, would flood the continent to the virtual exclusion of such economic competitors as Common Europe. The Commonwealth feels the same, so does the French Community. The Soviets and Arabs have different motivations, but they, too, wish to take over. The result...." The Swede tossed up his hands in a gesture more Gallic than Scandinavian.

* * * * *

"What has all this got to do with El Hassan?" Homer Crawford asked softly.

The Swede leaned forward. "If we more devoted adherents of the Reunited Nations are ever to see our hopes come true, Africa must be united and made strong. And this must be done through the efforts of *Africans* not Russians, British, French, Arabs ... nor even Scandinavians. Socio-economic changes should not, possibly cannot, be inflicted upon a people from without. Look at the mess the Russians made in such countries as Hungary, or the Americans in such as South Korea."

"The people themselves must have the dream," Crawford said softly.

"I beg your pardon?"

"Nothing. Go on."

Zetterberg said, "On the surface, great progress seems to be continuing. Afforestation of the Sahara, the solar pumps creating new oases, the water purification plants on the Atlantic and Mediterranean, pushing back the desert, the oil fields, the mines, the roads, the damming of the Niger. But already cracks can be seen. A week or so ago, a team of Cubans, supposedly, at least, in the Sudan to improve sugar refining methods, were machine-gunned to death. By whom? By the Sudanese? Unlikely. No, this Cuban massacre was one of many recent signs of conflict between the great powers in their efforts to dominate. Our problem, of course, deals only with North Africa, but I have heard rumors in Geneva that much the same situation is developing in the south as well."

"At any rate, Dr. Crawford, when the rumors of El Hassan began to come into this office they brought with them a breath of hope. From all we have heard, he teaches our basic program — a breaking down of old tribal society, education, economic progress, Pan-African unity. Dr. Crawford, no one with whom this office is connected seems ever to have seen this El Hassan but we are most anxious to talk to him. Perhaps this is the man behind whom we can throw our support. Your task is to find him."

Homer Crawford raked the fingers of his right hand back over his short wiry hair, and grimaced. He said, "It won't be necessary."

"I beg your pardon, Doctor?"

Crawford said, "It won't be necessary to go looking for El Hassan."

The Swede scowled his irritation at the other. "See here...."

Crawford said, "I'm El Hassan."

Sven Zetterberg stared at him, uncomprehending.

Homer Crawford said, "I suppose it's your turn to listen and for me to do the talking." He shifted in his chair, uncomfortably. "Dr. Zetterberg, even before the Reunited Nations evolved the idea of the African Development Project, it became obvious that the field work was going to have to be in the hands of Negroes. The reason is doublefold. First, the African doesn't trust the white man, for good reason. Second, the white man is a citizen of his own country, first of all, and finds it difficult not to have motives connected with his own race and nation. But the African Negro, too, has his tribal and sometimes national affiliations and cannot be trusted not to be prejudiced in their favor. The answer? The educated American Negro, such as myself."

"I haven't the slightest idea from whence came my ancestors, from what part of Africa, what tribe, what nation. But I am a Negro and ... well, have the dream of bettering my race. I have no irons in the fire, beyond altruistic ones. Of course, when I say American Negroes I don't exclude Canadian ones, or those of Latin America or the Caribbean. It is simply that there are greater numbers of educated American Negroes than you find elsewhere."

Zetterberg said impatiently, "Please, Dr. Crawford. Come to the point. That ridiculous statement you made about El Hassan."

"Of course, I am merely giving background. Most of we field workers, not only the African Development teams, but such organizations as the Africa for Africans Association and the representatives of the African Department of the British Commonwealth, and of the French Community's African Affairs sector, are composed of Negroes."

Zetterberg was nodding. "All right, I know."

Homer Crawford said, "The teams of all these organizations do their best to spur African progress, in our case, in North Africa, especially the area between the Niger and the Mediterranean. Often we disguise ourselves as natives since in that manner we are more quickly trusted. We wear the clothes, speak the local language or lingua franca."

The American hesitated a moment, then plunged in. "Dr. Zetterberg, the African is still a primitive but newly beginning to move out of a tradition-ritual-taboo tribal society. He seeks a hero to follow, a man of towering prestige who knows the answers to all questions. We may not *like* this fact, we with our traditions of democracy, but it is so. The African is simply not yet at that stage of society where political democracy is applicable."

"My team does most of its work posing as Enaden-low caste itinerant smiths of the Sahara. As such we can go any place and are everywhere accepted, a necessary sector of the Saharan economy. As such, we continually spread the ... ah, propaganda of the Reunited Nations-the need for education, the need for taking jobs on the new projects, the need for casting aside old institutions and embracing the new. Early in the game we found our words had little weight coming from simple Enaden smiths so we ... well, *invented* this mysterious El Hassan, and everything we said we attributed to him."

"News spreads fast in the desert, astonishingly fast. El Hassan started with us but soon other teams, hearing about him and realizing that his message was the same as that they were trying to propagate, did the same thing. That is, attributed the messages they had to spread to El Hassan. It was amusing when a group of us got together last week in Timbuktu, to find that we'd all taken to kowtowing to this mythical desert hero who planned to unite all North Africa."

The Swede was staring at him unbelievingly. "But, a bit earlier you said you were El Hassan."

Homer Crawford looked into his chief's face and nodded seriously. "I've been conferring with various other field workers, both Reunited Nations and otherwise. The situation calls for a real El Hassan. If we don't provide him, someone else will. I propose to take over the position."

Sven Zetterberg's face was suddenly cold. "And why, Dr. Crawford, do you think you are more qualified than others?"

The American Negro could hardly fail to note the other's disapproval. He said evenly, but definitely, "Through experience. Through education. Through ... through having the dream, Dr. Zetterberg."

"The Reunited Nations cannot support such a project, Dr. Crawford. I absolutely forbid you to consider it."

"Forbid me?"

* * * * *

It was as though a strange something entered the atmosphere of the room, almost as though a new *presence* was there. And almost, it seemed to Sven Zetterberg, that the already tall, solidly built man across from him grew physically as his voice seemed to swell, to reach out, to dominate. There was a new, and all but unbelievable Homer Crawford here.

The Swedish official regathered his forces. This was ridiculous. He said again, "I forbid you to...." the sentence dribbled away under the cold disdain in the air now.

Homer Crawford said flatly, "You don't seem to understand, Zetterberg. The Reunited Nations has no control over El Hassan. Homer Crawford, as of this meeting, has resigned his post with the African Development Project. And El Hassan has begun his task of uniting all North Africa."

Sven Zetterberg, shaken by this new and unsuspected force the other seemed to be able to bring to his command, fought back. "It will be simple to discredit you, to let it be known that you are no more than an ambitious American out to seize power illegally."

Crawford's scorn held an element of amusement. "Try it. I suspect your attempts to discredit El Hassan will prove unsuccessful. He has already been rumored to be everything from an Ethiopian to the Second Coming of the Messiah. Your attempt to brand him an American adventurer will be swallowed up in the flood of other rumor."

The Swede was still shaken by the strange manner in which his once subordinate had suddenly dominated him. Sven Zetterberg was not a man to be dominated, to be made unsure.

Time folded back on itself and for a moment he was again a lad and on vacation with his father in Bavaria. They were having lunch in the famed Hofbraühaus, largest of the Munich beercellars, and even a ten-year-old could sense an anticipation in the air, particularly among the large number of brownshirted men who had gathered to one side of the ground level of the beer hall. His father was telling Sven of the history of the medieval building when a silence fell. Into the beer hall had come a pasty faced, trenchcoat garbed little man, his face set in stern lines but insufficiently to offset the ludicrous mustache. He was accompanied by an elderly soldier in the uniform of a Field Marshal, by a large tub of a man whose face beamed-but evilly-and by a pinch faced cripple. All were men of command, all except the pasty faced one, to whom they seemingly and surprisingly, deferred. And then he stood on a heavy chair and spoke. And then his *power* reached out and grasped all within reach of his shrill voice. Grasped them and compelled them and they became a shouting, red faced, arm brandishing mob, demanding to be led to glory. And Sven's father had bustled the shocked boy from the building.

It came back to him now, clearly and forcefully, and he realized that whatever it was with which the Beast of Berchtesgaden had enchanted his people, that power was on call in Homer Crawford. Whether he used it for good or evil, that enchanting power was on call. And again Sven Zetterberg was shaken.

Homer Crawford was on his feet, preparatory to leaving.

The Swede simply *had* to reassert himself. "Dr. Crawford, the Reunited Nations is not without resources. You'll be arrested before you leave Dakar."

An element of the tenseness left the air when Crawford smiled and said, "Doctor, for several years now I have been playing hide and seek in the Sahara, doing your work. You mentioned earlier that my team is the most experienced and capable. Just whom are you going to send to pick me up? Members of some of the other teams? Old friends and comrades in arms. Many of whom owe their lives to my team when all bets were down. Please do send them, Doctor, I am going to need recruits."

He swung and left the office and even as he went could hear the angry Reunited Nations chief blasting into an interoffice communicator. He decided he'd better see if there wasn't a back door or window through which to leave the building. He'd have to phone Bey, Isobel and the others and get together for a meeting to plan developments. El Hassan was getting off to a fast start, already he was on the lam.

* * * * *

Homer Crawford played it safe. From the nearest public phone he called Isobel Cunningham at the Hotel Juan-le-Pin. No matter how fast Sven Zetterberg swung into action, it would take his operatives some time to connect Isobel with Homer and his team. As an employee of the Africa for Africans Association, she would ordinarily come in little contact with the Reunited Nations teams.

He said, "Isobel? Homer here. Can you talk?"

She said, "Cliff and Jake are here."

He said, "Have you sounded them out? How do they feel about the El Hassan project?"

"They're in. At least, Jake is. We're still arguing with Cliff."

"O.K. Now listen, carefully. Zetterberg turned thumbs down on the whole deal, for various reasons we can discuss later. In fact, he's incensed and threatened to take steps to keep us from leaving Dakar."

Isobel was alerted but she snorted deprecation. "What do you want?"

"They're probably already looking for me, and in a matter of minutes will probably try to pick up Bey-ag-Akhamouk, Elmer Allen and Kenny Ballalou, the other members of my team. Get in touch with them immediately and tell them to get into native costume and into hiding. You and Jake-and Cliff-do the same."

"Right. Where do we meet and when?"

"In the *souk*, in the food market. There's a native restaurant there, run by a former Vietnamese. We'll meet there at approximately noon."

"Right. Anything else?"

Homer said, "Tell Bey to bring along an extra 9mm Recoilless for me."

"Yes, El Hassan," she said, her voice expressionless. She didn't waste time. Homer Crawford heard the phone click as she hung up.

He was in a branch building of the post and telegraph network on the Rue des Resistance. Before leaving it, he looked out a window. Half a block away was the office of the Sahara Division of the African Development Project. Even as he watched, a dozen men hurried out the front door, fanned out in all directions.

Homer grinned sourly. Old Sven was moving fast.

He shot a quick glance around the lobby of the building. He had to get going. Zetterberg had started with a dozen men to trail down El Hassan. He'd probably have a hundred involved before the hour was out.

A corridor turned off to the right. Homer hurried down it. At each door he looked inside. To whoever occupied the room he murmured a few words of apology in Wolof, the Sengalese lingua franca. The fourth office was empty.

Homer stood there before it for a long, agonizing moment, waiting for the right person to pass. Finally, the man he needed came along. About six feet tall, about a hundred and eighty; dressed in the local native dress and on the ragged side.

Homer said to him authoritatively, in the Wolof tongue, "You there, come in here!" He opened the door, and pointed into the office.

The other, taken aback, demurred.

Homer's face and tone went still more commanding. "Step in here, before I call the police."

It was all a mistake, of course. The Senegalese made the gesture equivalent to the European's shrug, and entered the office.

Homer came in behind him, closed the door. He wasted no time in preliminaries. Before the native turned, the American's hand lashed out in a karate blow which stunned the other. Homer Crawford caught him, even as he fell, and lowered him gently to the floor.

"Sorry, old boy," he muttered, "but this is probably the most profitable thing that's happened to you this year."

He stripped off the other's clothes, as rapidly as he could make his hands fly. The other was still out and probably would be for another ten minutes, Crawford estimated. He stripped off his own clothes and donned the native's.

Last of all, he took his wallet from his pocket, divided the money it contained and stuffed a considerable wad of it into the European clothing he was abandoning.

"Don't spend all of that in one place," he growled softly.

Homer dragged the other to a side of the room so that the body could not be spotted from the entrance. Then he crossed to the door, opened it and stepped into the corridor beyond.

* * * * *

There was no need for sulking. He walked out the front door and headed away from the dock and administration buildings area and toward the native section, passing the Reunited Nations building on the way.

Dakar teems with multitudes of a dozen tribes come in from the jungles and the bush, the desert and the swamp areas of the sources of the Niger, to look for work on the new projects, to visit relatives, to market for the products of civilization-or to gawk. Homer Crawford disappeared into them. One among many.

Toward noon, he entered the cleared area which was the restaurant he had named to Isobel and squatted before the pots to the far end of the Vietnamese owned eatery, examining them with care. He chose a large chunk of barbequed goat and was served it with a half pound piece of unsalted Senegalese bread, torn from a monstrous loaf, and a twisted piece of newspaper into which had been measured an ounce or so of coarse salt. He took his meal and went to as secluded a corner as he could find.

Homer Crawford chuckled inwardly. That morning he had breakfasted in the most swank hotel in West Africa. He wished there was some manner in which he could have invited Sven Zetterberg to dine here with him. Or, come to think of it, a group of the students he had once taught sociology at the University of Michigan. Or, possibly, prexy Wallington, under whom he had worked while taking his doctor's degree.

Yes, it would have been interesting to have had a luncheon companion.

A native woman, on the stoutish side but with her hair done up in one of the fabulously ornate hair styles specialized in by the Senegalese, and wearing a flowing, shapeless dress of the garish textiles run off purposely for this market in Japan and Manchester, waddled up to take a place nearby. She bore a huge skewer of barbequed beef chunks, and a hunk of bread not unlike Homer's own.

She grumbled uncomfortably, her back to the American, as she settled into a position on the floor. And she mumbled as she began chewing at the meat.

No table manners, Homer Crawford grinned inwardly. He wondered how long it would take for the others to get here. He wasn't worried about Isobel, Cliff Jackson and Jake Armstrong. It would take time before Zetterberg's Reunited Nations cloak and dagger boys got around to them, but he wasn't sure that she'd be able to locate his own team in time. That bit he'd given the Swede official about his being so bully-bully with the other Reunited Nations teams was in the way of being an exaggeration, with the idea of throwing the other off. Actually, working in the field on definite assignments, it was seldom you ran into other African Development Project men. But perhaps it would tie Zetterberg up, wondering just who he could trust to send looking for El Hassan.

He finished off his barbequed goat and the bread and wiped his hands on his clothes. Nobody here yet. To have an excuse for staying, he would have to buy a bottle of Gazelle beer, the cheap Senegalese brew which came in quart bottles and was warm and on the gassy side.

It was then that the woman in front of him, without turning, said softly, "El Hassan?"

II

Homer Crawford stared at her, unbelievingly. The woman couldn't possibly be an emissary from Isobel or from one of his own companions. This situation demanded the utmost secrecy, they hadn't had time to screen any outsiders as to trustworthiness.

She turned. It was Isobel. She chuckled softly, "You should see your face."

His eyes went to her figure.

"Done with mirrors," Isobel said. "Or, at least, with pillows."

Homer didn't waste time. "Where are the others? They should be here by now."

"We figured that the fewer of us seen on the streets, the better. So they're waiting for you. Since I was the most easily disguised, the least suspicious looking, I was elected to come get you."

"Waiting where?"

She licked the side of her mouth, a disconcerting characteristic of hers, and looked at him archly. "Those pals of yours have quite a bit on the ball on their own. They decided that there was a fairly good chance that Sven Zetterberg wasn't exactly going to fall into your arms, so they took preliminary measures. Kenny Ballalou rented a small house, here in the native quarter. We've all rendezvoused there. See, you aren't the only one on the ball."

Homer frowned at her, for the moment being in no mood for humor. "What was the idea of sitting here for the past five minutes without even speaking? You must have recognized me, knowing what to look for."

She nodded. "I ... I wasn't sure, Homer, but I had the darnedest feeling I was being followed."

His glance was sharp now. First at her, then a quick darting around the vicinity. "Woman's intuition," he snapped, "or something substantial?"

She frowned at him. "I'm not a ninny, Homer."

His voice softened and he said quickly, "Don't misunderstand, Isobel. I know that."

She forgot about her objection to his tone. "Even intuition doesn't come out of a clear sky. Something sparks it. Subconscious psi, possibly, but a spark."

"However?" he prodded.

"I took all precautions. I can't seem to put my finger on anything."

"O.K.," he said decisively. "Let's go then." He came to his feet and reached a hand down for her.

"Heavens to Betsy," she said, "don't do that."

"What?"

"Help a woman in public. You'll look suspicious." She came to her own feet, without aid.

Damn, he thought. She was right. The last thing he wanted was to draw attention to a man who acted peculiarly.

* * * * *

They made their way out of the food market and into the *souk* proper, Homer walking three or four paces ahead of her, Isobel demurely behind, her eyes on the ground. They passed the native stands and tiny shops, and the even smaller venders and hucksters with their products of the mass production industries of East and West, side by side with the native handicrafts ranging from carved wooden statues, jewelry, *gris gris* charms and kambu fetishes, to ceramics whose designs went back to an age before the Portuguese first cruised off this coast. And everywhere was color; there are no people on earth more color conscious than the Senegalese.

Isobel guided him, her voice quiet and still maintaining its uncharacteristic demure quality.

He would never have recognized Isobel, Homer Crawford told himself. Isobel Cunningham, late of Columbia University where she'd taken her Master's in anthropology. Isobel Cunningham, whom he had told on their first meeting that she looked like the former singing star, Lena Horne. Isobel Cunningham, slight of build, pixie of face, crisply modern American with her tongue and wit. Was he in love with her? He didn't know. El Hassan had no time, at present, for those things love implied.

She said, "Here," and led the way down a brick paved passage to a small house, almost a hut, that lay beyond.

Homer Crawford looked about him critically before entering. He said, "I suppose this has been scouted out adequately. Where's the back entrance?" He scowled. "Haven't the boys posted a sentry?"

A voice next to his ear said pleasantly, "Stick 'em up, stranger. Where'd you get that zoot suit?"

He jerked his head about. There was a very small opening in the wooden wall next to him. It was Kenny Ballalou's voice.

"Zoot suit, yet!" Homer snorted. "I haven't heard that term since I was in rompers."

"You in rompers I'd like to see," Kenny snorted in his turn. "Come on in, everybody's here."

The aged, unpainted, warped, wooden house consisted of two rooms, the one three times as large as the second. The furniture was minimal, but there was sitting room on chair, stool and bed for the seven of them.

"Hail, O El Hassan!" Elmer Allen called sourly, as Homer entered.

"And the hail with you," Homer called back, then, "Oops, sorry, Isobel."

Isobel put her hands on her hips, greatly widened by the stuffing she'd placed beneath her skirts. "Look," she said. "Thus far, the El Hassan organization, which claims rule of all North Africa, consists of six men and one dame …ah, that is, one lady. Just so the lady won't continually feel that she's being a drag on the conversation, you are hereby allowed in moments of stress such shocking profanity as an occasional damn or hell. But only if said lady is also allowed such expletives during periods of similar stress."

Everyone laughed, and found chairs.

"I'm in love with Isobel Cunningham," Bey announced definitely.

"Second the motion," Elmer said.

The rest of them called, "Aye."

"O.K.," Homer Crawford said glumly, "I can see that this is going to be one tight knit organization. Six men in love with the one dame …ah, that is, lady. Kind of a reverse harem deal. Oh, this is going to lead to great co-operation."

* * * * *

They laughed again and then Jake said, "Well, what's the story, Homer? How does the El Hassan project sound to Zetterberg and the Reunited Nations?"

Cliff Jackson laughed bitterly. "Why do you think we're in hiding?" Only he and Jake Armstrong wore western clothing. Kenny Ballalou, Bey-ag-Akhamouk and Elmer Allen were in native dress, similar to that of Homer Crawford. Elmer Allen even bore a pilgrim's staff.

Crawford, glad that the edge of tenseness had been taken off the group by the banter with Isobel, turned serious now.

He said, "This is where we each take our stand. You can turn back at this point, any one of you, and things will undoubtedly go on as before. You'll keep your jobs, have no marks against you. Beyond this point, and there's no turning back. I want you all to think it over, before coming to any snap decisions."

Elmer Allen said, his face wearing its usual all but sullen expression. "How about you?"

Homer said evenly, "I've already taken my stand."

Kenny Ballalou yawned and said, "I've been in this team for three or four years, I'm too lazy to switch now Besides, I've always wanted to be a corrupt politician. Can I be treasurer in this El Hassan regime?"

"No," Homer said. "Bey?"

Bey-ag-Akhamouk said, "I've always wanted to be a general. I'll come in under those circumstances."

Homer said, his voice still even. "That's out. From this point in, you're a Field Marshal and Minister of Defense."

"Shucks," Bey said. "I'd always wanted to be a general."

Homer Crawford said dryly, "Doesn't anybody take this seriously? It's probably going to mean all your necks before it's through, you know."

Elmer Allen said dourly, "I take it seriously. I spent the idealistic years, the school years, working for peace, democracy, a better world. Now, here I am, helping to attempt to establish a tyranny over half the continent of my racial background. But I'm in."

"Right," Homer said, the side of his mouth twitching. "You can be our Minister of Propaganda."

"Minister of Propaganda!" Elmer wailed. "You mean like Goebbels? Me!"

Homer laughed. "O.K., we'll call it Minister of Information, or Press Secretary to El Hassan. It all means the same thing." He looked at Jacob Armstrong and said, "How old are you, Jake?"

"That's none of your business," the white-haired Jake said aggressively. "I'm in. El Hassan is the only answer. North Africa has got to be united, both for internal and external purposes. If you ... if we ... don't do the job first, somebody else will, and off hand, I can't think of anybody else I trust. I'm in."

Homer Crawford looked at him for a long moment. "Yes," he said finally. "Of course you are. Jake, you've just been made our combined Foreign Minister and Plenipotentiary Extraordinary to the Reunited Nations. You'll leave immediately, first for Geneva, to present our demands to the Reunited Nations, then to New York."

"What do I do in New York?" Jake Armstrong said blankly, trying to assimilate the curves that were being thrown to him.

"You raise money and support from starry eyed Negro groups and individuals. You line up such organizations as the Africa for Africans Association behind El Hassan. You give speeches, and ruin your liver eating at banquets every night in the week. You send out releases to the press. You get all the publicity for the El Hassan movement you can. You send official protests to the governments of every country in the world, every time they do something that doesn't fit in with our needs. You locate recruits and send them here to Africa to take over some of the load. I don't have to tell you what to do. You can think on your feet as well as I can. Do what is necessary. You're our Foreign Minister. Don't let us see your face again until El Hassan is in control of North Africa."

Jake Armstrong blinked. "How will I prove I'm your representative? I'll need more than just a note *To Whom It May Concern*."

Homer Crawford thought about that.

* * * * *

Bey said, "One of our first jobs is going to have to be to capture a town where they have a broadcast station, say Zinder or In Salah. When we do, we'll announce that you're Foreign Minister."

Crawford nodded. "That's obviously the ticket. By that time you should be in New York, with an office opened."

Jake rubbed a black hand over his cheek as though checking his morning shave. "It's going to take some money to get started. Once started I can depend on contributions, perhaps, but at first...."

Homer interrupted with, "Cliff, you're Minister of the Treasury. Raise some money."

"Eh?" Cliff Jackson said blankly. The king-size, easy-going Californian looked more like the early Joe Louis than ever.

Everybody laughed. Elmer Allen came forth with his wallet and began pulling out such notes as it contained. "I don't know what we'd be doing with this in the desert," he said.

Isobel said, "I have almost three thousand dollars in a checking account in New York. Let's see if I have my checkbook here."

The others were going through their pockets. As bank notes in British pounds, American dollars, French francs and Common Europe marks emerged they were tossed to the center of the small table which wobbled on three legs in the middle of the room.

Elmer Allen said, "I have an account with the Bank of Jamaica in Kingston. About four hundred pounds, I think. I'll have it transferred."

Cliff took up the money and began counting it, making notations on a notebook pad as he went.

Bey said, "We're only going to be able to give Jake part of this."

"How's that?" Elmer growled. "What use have we for money in the Sahara? Jake's got to put up a decent front in Geneva and New York."

Bey said doggedly, "As Defense Minister, I'm opposed to El Hassan's followers *ever* taking anything without generous payment. We'll need food and various services. From the beginning, we're going to have to pay our way. We can't afford to let rumors start going around that we're nothing but a bunch of brigands."

"Bey's right," Homer nodded. "The El Hassan movement is going to have to maintain itself on the highest ethical level. We're going to take over where the French Camel Corps left off and police North Africa. There can't be a man from Somaliland to Mauretania who can say that one of El Hassan's followers liberated him from as much as a date."

Kenny Ballalou said, "You can always requisition whatever you need and give them a receipt, and then we'll pay off when we come to power."

"That's out!" Bey snapped. "Most of these people can't read. And even those that do don't trust what they read. A piece of paper, in their eyes, is no return for some goats, or flour, camels, horses, or whatever else it might be we need. No, we're going to have to pay our way."

Crawford raked a hand back through his wiry hair. "Bey's right, Kenny. It's going to be a rough go, especially at first."

Kenny snorted. "What do you mean, *at first?* What's going to happen, *at second* to make it any easier? Where're we going to get all this money we'll need to pay for even what we ourselves use, not to speak of the thousands of men we're going to have to have if El Hassan is ever to come to power?"

Bey's eyebrows went up in shocked innocence. "Kenny, dear boy, don't misunderstand. We don't requisition anything from individuals, or clans, or small settlements. But if we take over a town such as Gao, or Niamey, or Colomb-Béchar, or wherever, there is nothing to say that a legal government such as that of El Hassan, can't requisition the contents of the local banks."

Homer Crawford said with dignity, "The term, my dear Minister of Defense, currently is to *nationalize* the bank. Whether or not we wish to have the banks remain nationalized, after we take over, we can figure out later. But in the early stages, I'm afraid we're going to have to nationalize just about every bank we come in contact with."

Cliff Jackson said cautiously, "I haven't said whether or not I'll come in yet, but just as a point, I might mention issuing your own legal tender. As soon as you liberate a printing press somewhere, of course."

Everyone was charmed at the idea.

Isobel said, "You can see Cliff was *meant* to be Minister of Treasury. He's got *wholesale* larceny in his soul, none of this picayunish stuff such as robbing nomads of their sheep."

Elmer Allen was shaking his head sadly. "This whole conversation started with Bey protesting that we couldn't allow ourselves to be thought of as brigands. Now listen to you all."

Kenny Ballalou said with considerable dignity, "See here, friend. Don't you know the difference between brigandage and international finance?"

"No," Elmer said flatly.

"Hm-m-m," Kenny said.

"Let's get on with this," Homer said. "The forming of El Hassan's basic government is beginning to take on aspects of a minstrel show. Then we've all declared ourselves in ... except Cliff."

All eyes turned to the bulky Californian.

He sat scowling.

Homer said, easily, "You're not being urged, Cliff. You can turn back at this point."

Elmer Allen growled, "You came to Africa to help your race develop its continent. To conquer such problems as sufficient food, clothing and shelter for all. To bring education and decent medical care to a people who have had possibly the lowest living standards anywhere. Can you see any way of achieving this beyond the El Hassan movement?"

Cliff looked at him, still scowling stubbornly. "That's not why I came to Africa."

Their eyes were all on him, but they remained silent.

He said, defensively, "I'm no do-gooder. I took a job with the Africa for Africans Association because it was the best job I could find."

Isobel broke the silence by saying softly, "I doubt it, Cliff."

The big man stood up from where he'd been seated on the bed. "O.K., O.K. Possibly there were other angles. I wanted to travel. Wanted to see Africa. Besides, it was good background for some future job. I figured it wouldn't hurt me any, in later years, applying for some future job. Maybe with some Negro concern in the States. I'd be able to say I'd put in a few years in Africa. Something like a Jew in New York who was a veteran of the Israel-Arab wars, before the debacle."

They still looked at him, none of them accusingly.

He was irritated as he paced. "Don't you see? Everybody doesn't have this *dream* that Homer's always talking about. That doesn't mean I'm abnormal. I just don't have the interest you do. All I want is a good job, some money in the bank, security back in the States. I'm not interested in dashing all over the globe, getting shot at, dying for some ideal."

Homer said gently, "It's up to you, Cliff. Nobody's twisting your arm."

There was sweat on the big man's forehead. "All I came to Africa for was the job, the money I got out of it," he repeated, insisting.

* * * * *

To Homer Crawford suddenly came the realization that the other needed an out, an excuse. An explanation to himself for doing something he wanted to do but wouldn't admit because it went against the opportunistic code he told himself he followed.

Homer said, "All right. How much are you making as a field worker for the Africa for Africans Association?"

Cliff looked at him, uncomprehending. "Eight thousand dollars, plus expenses."

"O.K., we'll double that. Sixteen thousand to begin with, as El Hassan's Minister of Treasury and whatever other duties we can think of to hang on you."

There was a long moment of silence, unbroken by any of the others. Finally in a gesture of desperation, Cliff Jackson waved at the money and checks sitting on the center table. "Sixteen thousand a year! The whole organization doesn't have enough to pay me six months' salary."

Homer said mildly, "That's why your pay was doubled. You have to take risks to make money in this world, Cliff. If El Hassan does come to power, undoubtedly you'll get other raises-along with greater responsibility."

He looked into Cliff Jackson's face, and although his words had dealt with money, a man's dream looked out from his eyes. And the force of personality that could emanate from Homer Crawford, possibly unbeknownst to himself, flooded over the huge Californian. The others in the room could feel it. Elmer Allen cleared his throat; Isobel held her elbows to her sides, in a feminine protest against naked male psychic strength.

Kenny Ballalou said without inflection, "Put up or shut up, Cliff old pal."

Cliff Jackson sank back onto the spot on the bed he'd occupied before. "I'm in," he muttered, so softly as hardly to be heard.

"None of you are in," a voice from the doorway said.

The figure that stood there held a thin, but heavy calibered automatic in his hand.

* * * * *

He was a dapper man, neat, trim, smart. His clothes were those of Greater Washington, rather than Dakar and West Africa. His facial expression seemed overly alert, overly bright, and his features were more Caucasian than Negroid.

He said, "I believe you all know me. Fredric Ostrander."

"Of the Central Intelligence Agency," Homer Crawford said dryly. He as well as Bey, Elmer and Kenny had risen to their feet when the newcomer entered from the smaller of the hut's two rooms. "What's the gun for, Ostrander?"

"You're under arrest," the C.I.A. man said evenly.

Elmer Allen snorted. "Under whose authority are you working? As a Jamaican, I'm a citizen of the West Indies and a subject of Her Majesty."

"We'll figure that out later," Ostrander rapped. "I'm sure the appropriate Commonwealth authorities will co-operate with the State Department and the Reunited Nations in this matter." The gun unwaveringly went from one of them to the other, retraced itself.

Bey looked at Homer Crawford.

Crawford shook his head gently.

He said to the newcomer, "The question still stands, Ostrander. Under whose authority are you operating? I don't think you have jurisdiction over us. We're in Africa, not in the United States of the Americas."

Ostrander said tightly, "Right now I'm operating under the authority of this weapon in my hand. Dr. Crawford. Do you realize that all of you Americans here are risking your citizenship?"

Kenny Ballalou said, "Oh? Tell us more, Mr. State Department man."

"You're serving in the armed forces of a foreign power."

Even the dour Elmer Allen laughed at that one.

Crawford said, "The fact of the matter is, we *are* the foreign power."

"You're not amusing, Dr. Crawford," Ostrander said. "I've kept up with this situation since you had that conference in Timbuktu. The State Department has no intention of allowing some opportunist, backed by known communists and fellow travelers, to seize power in this portion of the world. In a matter of months the Soviets would be in here."

Isobel said evenly, "I was formerly a member of the Party. I no longer am. I am an active opponent of the Soviet Complex at the moment, especially in regard to its activity in Africa."

Ostrander snorted his disbelief.

Elmer Allen said, "You chaps never forget, do you?" He looked at the others and explained. "Back during college days, I signed a few peace petitions, that sort of thing. Ever since, every time I come in contact with these people, you'd think I was Lenin or Trotsky."

Homer Crawford said, "My opinion is, Ostrander, that you've had to move too quickly to check back with your superiors. Has the State Department actually instructed you to arrest me and my companions here on foreign soil, without a warrant?"

Ostrander clipped, "That's my responsibility. I'm taking you all in. We'll solve such problems as jurisdiction and warrants when I get you to the Reunited Nations headquarters."

"Ah?" Homer Crawford said. "And then what happens to us?"

Ostrander jiggled the gun, impatiently. "Sven Zetterberg is of the opinion that you should immediately be flown out of Africa and the case brought before the High Council of the African Development Project. What measures will be taken beyond that point I have no way of knowing."

Bey took a step to the left, Kenny Ballalou one to the right. Homer Crawford remained immediately before the C.I.A. operative, his hands slightly out from his sides, palms slightly forward.

Ostrander snapped, "I'm prepared to fire, you men. I don't underestimate the importance of this situation. If your crazy scheme makes any progress at all, it might well result in the death of thousands. I know your background, Crawford. You once taught judo in the Marines. I'm not unfamiliar with the art myself."

Isobel had a hand to her mouth, her eyes were wide. "Boys, don't ..." she began.

Elmer Allen had been leaning on his pilgrim's staff, as though weary with this whole matter. He said to Ostrander, interestedly, "So you've been checked out on judo? Know anything about the use of the quarterstaff?"

Ostrander kept his gun traversing between the four of them. "Eh?" he said.

Elmer Allen shifted his grip on his staff infinitesimally. Of a sudden, the end of the staff, now gripped with both hands near the center, moved at invisibly high speed. There was a crack of the wrist bone, and the gun went flying. The other end of the staff flicked out and rapped the C.I.A. operative smartly on the head.

Fredric Ostrander crumbled to the floor.

* * * * *

"Confound it, Elmer," Crawford said. "What'd you have to go and do that for? I wanted to talk to him some more and send a message back to Zetterberg. Sooner or later we've got to make our peace with the Reunited Nations."

Elmer said embarrassedly, "Sorry, it just happened. I was merely going to knock the gun out of his hand, but then I couldn't help myself. I was tired of hearing that holier-than-thou voice of his."

Kenny Ballalou looked down at the fallen man gloomily. "He'll be out for an hour. You're lucky you didn't crack his skull."

"Holy Mackerel," Cliff Jackson said. "I'm going to have to learn to operate one of those things."

Elmer Allen handed him the supposed pilgrim's staff. "Best hand-to-hand combat weapon ever invented," he said. "The British yeoman's quarterstaff. Of course, this is a modernized version. Made of epoxy resin glass-fiber material, treated to look like wood. That stuff can turn a high-velocity bullet, let alone a sword, and it can be bent in a ninety degree arc without the slightest effect, although it'd take a power-driven testing machine to do it."

"All right, all right," Homer said. "We haven't got time for lessons in the use of the quarterstaff. Let's put some thought to this situation. If Ostrander here was able to find us, somebody else would, too."

Isobel licked the side of her mouth. "He was probably following me. Remember, I told you Homer?"

Kenny said, "If he had anyone with him, he'd have brought them along to cover him. You've got to give him credit for bravery, taking on the whole bunch of us by himself."

"Um-m-m," Homer said. "I wish he was with us instead of against us."

Jake Armstrong said, "Well, this solves one problem."

They looked at him.

He said, "Just as sure as sure, he's got a car parked somewhere. A car with some sort of United States or Reunited Nations emblem on it."

"So what?" Kenny said.

"So you've got to get out of town before the search for you *really* gets under way. With such a car, you can get past any roadblock that might already be up between here and the Yoff airport."

Elmer Allen had sunk to his knees and was searching the fallen C.I.A. man. He came up with car keys and a wallet.

Homer said to Jake Armstrong, "Why the Yoff airport?"

"Our plane is there," Jake told him. "The one assigned Isobel, Cliff and me by the AFAA. You're going to have to make time. Get somewhere out in the ah, boondocks, where you can begin operations."

Bey said thoughtfully, "He's right, Homer. Anybody against us, like our friend here" — he nodded at Ostrander —"is going to try to get us quick, before we can get the El Hassan movement under way. We've got to get out of Dakar and into some area where they'll have their work cut out trying to locate us."

Homer Crawford accepted their council. "O.K., let's get going. Jake, you'll stay in Dakar, and at first play innocent. As soon as possible, take plane for Geneva. As soon as you're there, send out press releases to all the news associations and the larger papers. Announce yourself as Foreign Minister of El Hassan and demand that he be recognized as the legal head of state of all North Africa."

"Wow," Cliff Jackson said.

"Then play it by ear," Homer finished.

He turned to the others. "Bey, where'd you leave our two hover-lorries when you came here to Dakar?"

"Stashed away in the ruins of a former mansion in Timbuktu. Hired two Songhai to watch them."

"O.K. Cliff, you're the only one in European dress. Take this wallet of Ostrander's. You'll drive the car. If we run into any roadblocks between here and the Yoff airport, slow down a little and hold the wallet out to show your supposed identification. They won't take the time to check the photo. Bluff your way past, don't completely stop the car."

"What happens if they do stop us?" Cliff said worriedly.

Kenny Ballalou said, "That'll be just too bad for them."

Bey stooped and scooped up the fallen automatic of Fredric Ostrander and tucked it into the voluminous folds of his native robe. "Here we go again," he said.

III

The man whose undercover name was Anton, landed at Gibraltar in a BEA roco-jet, passed quickly through customs and immigration with his Commonwealth passport and made his way into town. He checked with a Bobby and found that he had a two-hour wait until the Mons Capa ferry left for Tangier, and spent the time wandering up and down Main Street, staring into the Indian shops with their tax-free cameras from Common Europe, textiles from England, optical equipment from Japan, and cheap souvenirs from everywhere. Gibraltar, the tourist's shopping paradise.

The trip between Gibraltar and Tangier takes approximately two hours. If you've never made it before, you stand on deck and watch Spain recede behind you, and Africa loom closer. This was where Hercules supposedly threw up his Pillars, Gibraltar being the one on the European shore. Those who have made the trip again and again, sit down in the bar and enjoy the tax-free prices. The man named Anton stood on the deck. He was African by birth, but he'd never been to Morocco before.

When he landed, he made the initial error of expecting the local citizenry to speak Arabic. They didn't. Rif, a Berber tongue, was the first language. The man called Anton had to speak French to make known his needs. He took a Chico cab up from the port to the El Minza hotel, immediately off the Plaza de France, the main square of the European section.

At the hotel entrance were two jet-black doormen attired in a pseudo-Moroccan costume of red fez, voluminous pants and yellow barusha slippers. They made no note of his complexion, there is no color bar in the Islamic world.

He had reservations at the desk. He left his passport there to go through the standard routine, including being checked by the police, had his bag sent up to his room and, a few minutes later, hands nonchalantly in pockets, strolled along the Rue de Liberté toward the casbah area of the medina. Up from the native section of town streamed hordes of costumed Rifs, Arabs, Berbers of a dozen tribes, even an occasional Blue Man. At least half the women still wore the haik and veil, half the men the burnoose. Africa changes slowly, the man called Anton admitted to himself all over again-so slowly.

Down from the European section, which could have been a Californian city, filtered every nation of the West, from every section of Common Europe, the Americas, the Soviet Complex. If any city in the world is a melting pot, it is Tangier, where Africa meets Europe and where East meets West.

He passed through the teaming Grand Zocco market, and through the gates of the old city. He took Rue Singhalese, the only street in the medina wide enough to accommodate a vehicle and went almost as far as the Zocco Chico, once considered the most notorious square in the world.

For a moment the man called Anton stood before one of the Indian shops and stared at the window's contents. Carved ivory statuettes from the Far East, cameras from Japan, ebony figurines, chess sets of water jade, gimcracks from everywhere.

A Hindu stood in the doorway and rubbed his hands in a gesture so stereotyped as to be ludicrous. "Sir, would you like to enter my shop? I have amazing bargains."

The man they called Anton entered.

He looked about the shop, otherwise empty of customers. Vaguely, he wondered if the other ever sold anything, and, if so, to whom.

He said, "I was looking for an ivory elephant, from the East."

The Indian's eyebrows rose. "A white elephant?"

"A red elephant," the man called Anton said.

"In here," the Hindu said evenly, and led the way to the rear.

The rooms beyond were comfortable but not ostentatious. They passed through a livingroom-study to an office beyond. The door was open and the Indian merely gestured in the way of introduction, and then left.

Kirill Menzhinsky, agent superior of the *Chrezvychainaya Komissiya* for North Africa, looked up from his desk, smiled his pleasure, came to his feet and held out his hand.

"Anton!" he said. "I've been expecting you."

The man they called Anton smiled honestly and shook. "Kirill," he said. "It's been a long time."

The other motioned to a comfortable armchair, resumed his own seat. "It's been a long time all right-almost five years. As I recall, I was slung over your shoulder, and you were wading through those confounded swamps. The..."

"The Everglades."

"Yes." The heavy-set Russian espionage chief chuckled. "You are much stronger than you look, Anton. As I recall, I ordered you to abandon me."

The wiry Negro grunted deprecation. "You were delirious from your wound."

The Russian came to his feet, turned his back and went to a small improvised bar. He said, his voice low, "No, Anton, I wasn't delirious. Perhaps a bit afraid, but then the baying of dogs is disconcerting."

The man they called Anton said, "It is all over now."

The Russian returned and said, "A drink, Anton? As I recall you were never the man to refuse a drink. Scotch, bourbon, vodka?"

The other shrugged. "I believe in drinking the local product. What is the beverage of Tangier?"

Kirill Menzhinsky took up a full bottle the contents of which had a greenish, somewhat *oily* tinge. "Absinthe," he said. "Guaranteed to turn your brains to mush if you take it long enough. What was the name of that French painter...?"

"Toulouse Lautrec," Anton supplied. "I thought the stuff was illegal these days." He watched the other add water to the potent liqueur.

The Russian chuckled. "Nothing is illegal in Tangier, my dear Anton, except the Party." He laughed at his own joke and handed the other his glass. He poured himself a jolt of vodka and returned to his chair. "To the world revolution, Anton."

The Negro saluted with his drink. "The revolution!"

They drank.

The Russian put down his glass and sighed. "I wish we were some place in our own lands, Anton. Dinner, many drinks, perhaps some girls, eh?"

Anton shrugged. "Another time, Kirill."

"Yes. As it is, we should not be seen together. Nor, for that matter should you even return here. The imperialists are not stupid. Very possibly, American and Common Europe espionage agents know of this headquarters. Not to speak of the Arab Union. I shall try to give you the whole story and your assignment in this next half hour. Then you should depart immediately."

* * * * *

The man they called Anton sipped his drink and relaxed in his chair. He looked at his superior without comment.

The Russian took another jolt of his water-clear drink. "Have you ever heard of El Hassan?"

The Negro thought a moment before saying, "Vaguely. Evidently an Arab, or possibly a Tuareg. North African nationalist. No, that wouldn't be the word, since he is international. At any rate, he seems to be drawing a following in the Sahara and as far south as the Sudan. Backs modernization and wants unity of all North Africa. Is he connected with the Party?"

The espionage chief was shaking his head. "That is the answer I expected you to give, and is approximately what anyone else would have said. Actually, there is no such person as El Hassan."

Anton frowned. "I'm afraid you're wrong there, Kirill. I've heard about him in half a dozen places. Very mysterious figure. Nobody seems to have seen him, but word of his program is passed around from Ethiopia to Mauretania."

The Russian was shaking his head negatively. "That I know. It's a rather strange story and one rather hard to believe if it wasn't for the fact that one of my operatives was in on the, ah, *manufacturing* of this Saharan leader."

"Manufacturing?"

"I'll give you the details later. Were you acquainted with Abraham Baker, the American comrade?"

"Were? I *am* acquainted with him. Abe is a friend as well as a comrade."

The Russian shook his head again. "Baker is dead, Anton. As you possibly know, his assignment for the past few years has been with a Reunited Nations African Development Project team, working in the Sahara region. We planted him there expecting the time to arrive when his services would be of considerable value. He worked with a five-man team headed by a Dr. Homer Crawford and largely the team's task was to eliminate bottlenecks that developed as the various modernization projects spread over the desert."

"But what's this got to do with *manufacturing* El Hassan?"

"I'm coming to that. Crawford's team, including Comrade Baker, usually disguised themselves as Enaden smiths. As such, their opinions carried little weight so in order to spread Reunited Nations propaganda, they hit upon the idea of imputing everything they said to this great hero of the desert, El Hassan."

"I see," the man called Anton said.

"Others, without knowing the origin of our El Hassan, took up the idea and spread it. These nomads are at an ethnic level where they want a hero to follow, a leader. So in order to give prestige to their teachings the various organizations trying to advance North Africa followed in Crawford's footsteps and attributed their teachings to this mysterious El Hassan."

"And it snowballed."

"Correct! But the point is that after a time Crawford came around to the belief that there should be a real El Hassan. That the primary task at this point is to unite the area, to break down the old tribal society and introduce the populace to the new world."

"He's probably right," the man called Anton growled. He finished his drink, got up from his chair and on his own went over and mixed another. "More vodka?" he asked.

"Please." The Russian held up his glass and went on talking. "Yes, undoubtedly that is what is needed at this point. As it is, things are trending toward a collapse. The imperialists, especially the Americans, of course, wish to dominate the area for their capitalistic purposes. The Arab Union wishes to take over *in toto* and make it part of their Islamic world. We, of course, cannot afford to let either succeed."

The Negro resumed his chair, sipped at his drink and listened, nodding from time to time.

Kirill Menzhinsky said, "As you know, Marx and Engels when founding scientific socialism had no expectation that their followers would first come to power in such backward countries as the Russia of 1917 or the China of 1949. In fact, the establishment of true socialism presupposes a highly developed industrial economy. It is simply impossible without such an economy. When Lenin came to power in 1917, as a result of the chaotic conditions that prevailed upon the military collapse of Imperial Russia, he had no expectation of going it alone, as the British would say. He expected immediate revolutions in such countries as Germany and France and supposed that these more advanced countries would then come to the assistance of the Soviet Union and all would advance together to true socialism."

* * * * *

"It didn't work out that way," the man called Anton said dryly.

"No, it didn't. And Lenin didn't live to see the steps that Stalin would take in order to build the necessary industrial base in Russia." Kirill Menzhinsky looked about the room, almost as though checking to see if anyone else was listening. "Some of our more unorthodox theoreticians are inclined to think that had Lenin survived the assassin's bullet, that Comrade Stalin would have found it necessary to, ah, liquidate him."

The Russian cleared his throat. "Be that as it may, basic changes were made in Marxist teachings to fit into Stalin's and later Khrushchev's new concepts of the worker's State. And the Soviet Union muddled through, as the British have it. Today, the Soviet Complex is as powerful as the imperialist powers."

The espionage leader knocked back his vodka with a practiced stiff wristed motion. "Which brings us to the present and to North Africa." He leaned forward in emphasis. "Comrade, if the past half century and more has taught us anything, it is that you cannot establish socialism in a really backward country. In short, communism is impossible in North Africa at this point in her social evolution. Impossible. You cannot go directly from tribal society to communism. At this historic point, there is no place for the party's program in North Africa."

The man called Anton scowled.

The Russian waggled his hand negatively. "Yes, yes. I know. Ultimately, the whole world must become Soviet. Only that way will we achieve our eventual goal. But that is the long view. Realistically, we must face it, as the Yankees say. This area is not at present soil for our seed."

"Things move fast these days," the Negro growled. "Industrialization, education, can be a geometric progression."

His superior nodded emphatically. "Of course, and as little as ten or fifteen years from now, given progress at the present rate, perhaps there will be opportunity for our movement. But now? No."

The other said, "What has all this to do with El Hassan, or Crawford, or whatever the man's name is?"

"Yes," the Russian said. "Homer Crawford has evidently decided to become El Hassan."

"Ahhh."

"Yes. At this point, in short, he is traveling in our direction. He is doing what we realize must be done."

"Then we will support him?"

"Now we come to the point, Anton. Homer Crawford is not sympathetic to the Party. To the contrary. Our suspicion, although we have no proof, is that he killed Comrade Abe Baker, when Baker approached him on his stand in regard to the Party's long view."

"I see," the man called Anton said.

The Russian nodded. "We must keep in some sort of touch with him-some sort of control. If this El Hassan realizes his scheme and unites all North Africa, sooner or later we will have to deal with him. If he is antagonistic, we will have to find means to liquidate him."

"And my assignment...?"

"He will be gathering followers at this point. Many followers, most of whom will be unknown to him. You will become one of them. Raise yourself to as high a rank as you find possible in his group. Become a close friend, if that can be done...."

"He killed Abe Baker, eh?"

The Russian frowned. "This is an assignment, Comrade Anton. There is no room for personal feelings. You are a good field man. Among the best. You are being given this task because the Party feels you are the man for it. Possibly it is an assignment that will take years in the fulfilling."

The Negro said nothing.

"Are there any questions?"

"Do we have any other operatives working on this?"

The frown became a scowl. "An Isobel Cunningham worked with Comrade Baker, but it has been suspected that she has been drifting away from the party these past few years. Her present status is unknown, but she is believed to be with Homer Crawford and his followers. Possibly she has defected. If so, you will take whatever measures seem necessary. You will be working almost completely on your own, Comrade. You must think on your feet, as the Yankees say."

The man called Anton thought a moment. He said, "You'd better give me as thorough a run down as possible on this Homer Crawford and his immediate followers."

* * * * *

Menzhinsky settled back in his chair and took up a sheaf of papers from the desk. "We have fairly complete dossiers. I'll give you the highlights, then you can take these with you to your hotel to study at leisure."

He took up the first sheet. "Homer Crawford. Born in Detroit of working-class parents. In his late teens interrupted his education to come to Africa where he joined elements of the F.L.N. in Morocco and took part in several forays into Algeria. Evidently was wounded and invalided back to the States where he resumed his education. When he came of military age, he joined the Marine Corps and spent the usual, ah, hitch I believe they call it. Following that, he resumed his education, finally taking a doctor's degree in sociology. He then taught for a time until the Reunited Nations began its African program. He accepted a position, and soon distinguished himself."

The Russian took up another paper. "According to Comrade Baker's reports, Crawford is an outstanding personality, dominating others, even in spite of himself. He would make a top party man. Idealistic, strong, clever, ruthless when ruthlessness is called for."

Menzhinsky paused for a moment, finding words hard to come by from an ultra-materialist. His tone went wry. "Comrade Baker also reported a somewhat mystical quality in our friend Crawford. An ability in times of emotional crisis to break down men's mental barriers against him. A *force* that..."

The other raised his eyebrows.

His superior chuckled, ruefully. "Comrade Baker was evidently much swayed by the man's personality. However, Anton, I might point out that similar reports have come down to us of such a dominating personality in Lenin, and, to a lesser degree, in Stalin." He twisted his mouth. "History leads us to believe that such personalities as Jesus and Mohammed seemed to have some power beyond that of we more mundane types."

"And the others?" Anton said.

The Russian took up still another paper. "Elmer Allen. Born of small farmer background on the outskirts of Kingston, on the island of Jamaica. Managed to work his way through the University of Kingston where he took a master's degree in sociology. At one time he was thought to be Party material and was active in several organizations that held social connotations, pacifist groups and so forth. However, he was never induced to join the Party. Upon graduation, he immediately took employment with the Reunited Nations and was assigned to Homer Crawford's team. He is evidently in accord with Crawford's aims as El Hassan."

The espionage chief took up another sheet. "Bey-ag-Akhamouk..."

The other scowled. "That can't be an American name."

"No. He is the only real African associated with Crawford at this point. He was evidently born a Taureg and taken to the States at an early age, three or four, by a missionary. At any rate, he was educated at the University of Minnesota where he studied political science. We have no record of where he stands politically, but Comrade Baker rated him as an outstanding intuitive soldier. A veritable genius in combat. He would seem to have had military experience somewhere, but we have no record of it. Our Bey-ag-Akhamouk seems somewhat of a mystery man."

The Russian sorted out another sheet. "Kenneth Ballalou, born in Louisiana, educated in Chicago. Another young man but evidently as capable as the others. He seems to be quite a linguist. So far as we know, he holds no political stand whatsoever."

Menzhinsky pursed his lips before saying, "The Isobel Cunningham I mentioned worked with the Africa for Africans Association with two colleagues, a Jacob Armstrong and Clifford Jackson. It is possible that these two, as well as Isobel Cunningham, have joined El Hassan. If so, we will have to check further upon them, although I understand Armstrong is rather elderly and hardly effective under the circumstances."

The man called Anton said evenly, "And this former comrade, Isobel Cunningham, has evidently joined with Crawford even though he …was the cause of Abe Baker's death?"

"Evidently."

The Negro's eyes narrowed.

The other said, "And evidently she is a most intelligent and attractive young lady. We had rather high hopes for her formerly."

The Negro party member came to his feet and gathered up the sheaf of papers from the desk. "All right," he said. "Is there anything else?"

The espionage chief shook his head. "You do not need a step by step blueprint, Anton, that is why you have been chosen for this assignment. You are strongly based in Party doctrine. You know what is needed, we can trust you to carry on the Party's aims." After a pause, the Russian added, "Without being diverted by personal feelings."

Anton looked him in the face. "Of course," he said.

* * * * *

Fredric Ostrander was on the carpet.

His chief said, "You seem to have conducted yourself rather precipitately, Fred."

Ostrander shrugged in irritation. "I didn't have time to consult anyone. By pure luck, I spotted the Cunningham girl and since I knew she had affiliated herself with Crawford, I followed her."

The chief said dryly, "And tried to arrest the seven of them, all by yourself."

"I couldn't see anything else to do."

The C.I.A. official said, "In the first place, we have no legal jurisdiction here and you could have caused an international stink. The Russkies would just love to bring something like this onto the Reunited Nations floor. In the second place, you failed. How in the world did you expect to take on that number of men, especially Crawford and his team?"

Ostrander flushed his irritation. "Next time …" he began.

His chief waved a hand negatively. "Let's hope there isn't going to be next time, of this type." He took up a paper from his desk. "Here's your new job, Fred. You're to locate this El Hassan and keep in continual contact with him. If he meets with any sort of success at all, and frankly our agency doubts that he will, you will attempt to bring home to Crawford and his followers the fact that they are Americans, and orientate them in the direction of the West. Above all, you are to keep in touch with us and keep us informed on all developments. Especially notify us if there is any sign that our El Hassan is in communication with the Russkies or any other foreign element."

"Right," Ostrander said.

His chief looked at him. "We're giving you this job, Fred, because you're more up on it than anyone else. You're in at the beginning, so to speak. Now, do you want me to assign you a couple of assistants?"

"White men?" Ostrander said.

His higher-up scowled. "You know you're the only Negro in our agency, Fred."

Fredric Ostrander, his voice still even, said, "That's too bad, because anyone you assigned me who wasn't a Negro would be a hindrance rather than an assistant."

The other drummed his fingers on the table in irritation. He said suddenly, "Fred, do you think I ought to do a report to Greater Washington suggesting they take more Negro operatives into the agency?"

Ostrander said dryly, "You'd better if this department is going to get much work done in Africa." He stood up. "I suppose that the sooner I get onto the job, the better. Do you have any idea at all where Crawford and his gang headed after they left me unconscious in that filthy hut?"

"No, we haven't the slightest idea of where they might be, other than that they left your car abandoned at the Yoff airport."

"Oh, great," Fredric Ostrander complained. "They've gone into hiding in an area somewhat twice the size of the original fifty United States."

"Good luck," his chief said.

* * * * *

Rex Donaldson, formerly of Nassau in the British Bahamas, formerly of the College of Anthropology, Oxford, now field man for the African Department of the British Commonwealth working at expediting native development, was taking time out for needed and unwonted relaxation. In fact, he stretched out on his back in the most comfortable bed, in the most comfortable hotel, in the Niger town of Mopti. His hands were behind his head, and his scowling eyes were on the ceiling.

He was a small, bent man, inordinately black even for the Sudan and the loincloth costume he wore was ludicrous in the Westernized comfort of the hotel room. He was attired for the bush and knew that it was sheer laziness now that kept him from taking off for the Dogon country of the Canton de Sangha where he was currently working to bring down tribal prejudices against the coming of the schools. He had his work cut out for him in the Dogon, the old men, the tribal elders they called Hogons, instinctively knew that the coming of education meant subversion of their institutions and the eventual loss of Hogon power.

His portable communicator, sitting on the bedside table, buzzed and the little man grumbled a profanity and swung his crooked legs around to the floor. His eyebrows went up when he realized it was a priority call which probably meant from London.

He flicked the reception switch and a girl's face faded onto the screen. She said, "A moment, Mr. Donaldson, Sir Winton wants you."

"Right," Rex Donaldson said. Sir Winton, yet. Head of the African Department. Other than photographs, Donaldson had never seen his ultimate superior, not to mention speaking to him personally.

The girl's face faded out and that of Sir Winton Brett-Homes faded in. The heavy-set, heavy-faced Englishman looked down, obviously checking something on his desk. He looked up again, said, "Rex Donaldson?"

"Yes, sir."

"I won't waste time on preliminaries, Donaldson. We've been discussing, here, some of the disconcerting rumors coming out of your section. Are you acquainted with this figure, El Hassan?"

The black man's eyes widened. He said, cautiously, "I have heard a good many stories and rumors."

"Yes, of course. They have been filtering into this office for more than a year. But thus far little that could be considered concrete has developed."

Rex Donaldson held his peace, waited for the other to go on.

Sir Winton said impatiently, "Actually, we are still dealing with rumors, but they are beginning to shape up. Evidently, this El Hassan has finally begun to move."

"Ahhh," the wiry little field man breathed.

The florid faced Englishman said, "As we understand it, he wishes to cut across tribal, national and geographic divisions in all North Africa, wishes to unite the whole area from Sudan to the Mediterranean."

"Yes," Donaldson nodded. "That seems to be his program."

Sir Winton said, "It has been decided that the interests of Her Majesty's government and that of the Commonwealth hardly coincide with such an attempt at this time. It would lead to chaos."

"Ahhh," Donaldson said.

Sir Winton wound it up, all but beaming. "Your instructions, then, are to seek out this El Hassan and combat his efforts with whatever means you find necessary. We consider you one of our most competent operatives, Donaldson."

Rex Donaldson said slowly, "You mean that he is to be stopped at all cost?"

The other cleared his throat. "You are given carte blanche, Donaldson. You and our other operatives in the Sahara and Sudan. Stop El Hassan."

Rex Donaldson said flatly, "You have just received my resignation, Sir Winton."

"What ... what!"

"You heard me," Donaldson said.

"But ... but what are you going to do?" The heavy face of the African Department head was going a reddish-purple, which rather fascinated Donaldson but he had no time to further contemplate the phenomenon.

"I'm going to round up a few of my colleagues, of similar mind to my own, and then I'm going to join El Hassan," the little man snapped. "Good-bye, Sir Winton."

He clicked the set off and then looked down at it. His dour face broke into a rare grin. "Now there's an ambition I've had for donkey's years," he said aloud. "To hang up on a really big mucky-muck."

IV

Following the attack of the unidentified rocketcraft, El Hassan's party was twice again nearly flushed by reconnoitering planes of unknown origin. They weren't making the time they wanted.

Beneath a projecting rock face over a gravel bottomed wadi, the two hover-lorries were hidden, whilst a slow-moving helio-jet made sweeping, high-altitude circlings above them.

The six stared glumly upward.

Cliff Jackson who was on the radio called out, "I just picked him up. He's called in to Fort Lamy reporting no luck. His fuel's running short and he'll be knocking off soon."

Homer Crawford rapped, "What language?"

"French," Cliff said, "but it's not his. I mean he's not French, just using the language."

Bey's face was as glum as any and there was a tic at the side of his mouth. He said now, "We've got to come up with something. Sooner or later one of them will spot us and this next time we won't have any fantastic breaks like Homer being able to knock him off with a Tommy-Noiseless. He'll drop a couple of neopalms and burn up a square mile of desert including El Hassan and his whole crew."

Homer looked at him. "Any ideas, Bey?"

"No," the other growled.

Homer Crawford said, "Any of the rest of you?"

Isobel was frowning, bringing something back. "Why don't we travel at night?"

"And rest during the day?" Homer said.

Kenny said, "Parking where? We just made it to this wadi. If we're caught out in the dunes somewhere when one of those planes shows up, we've had it. You couldn't hide a jackrabbit out there."

But Bey and Homer Crawford were still looking at Isobel.

She said, "I remember a story the Tuaregs used to tell about a raid some of them made back during the French occupation. They stole four hundred camels near Timbuktu one night and headed north. The French weren't worried. The next morning, they simply sent out a couple of aircraft to spot the Tuareg raiders and the camels. Like Kenny said, you couldn't hide a jackrabbit in dune country. But there was nothing to be seen. The French couldn't believe it, but they still weren't really worried. After all a camel herd can travel only thirty or so miles a day. So the next day the planes went out again, circling, circling, but they still didn't spot the thieves and their loot, nor the next day. Well, to shorten it, the Tuareg got their four hundred camels all the way up to Spanish Rio de Oro where they sold them."

She had their staring attention. "How?" Elmer blurted.

"It was simple. They traveled all night and then, at dawn, buried the camels and themselves in the sand and stayed there all day."

Homer said, "I'm sold. Boys, I hope you're in physical trim because there's going to be quite a bit of digging for the next few days."

Cliff groaned. "Some Minister of the Treasury," he complained. "They give him a shovel instead of a bankbook."

Everyone laughed.

Bey said, "Well, I suppose we stay here until nightfall."

"Right," Homer said. "Whose turn is it to pull cook duty?"

Isobel said menacingly, "I don't know whose turn it is, but I know I'm going to do the cooking. After that slumgullion Kenny whipped up yesterday, I'm a perpetual volunteer for the job of chef-strictly in self-defense."

"That was a cruel cut," Kenny protested, "however, I hereby relinquish all my rights to cooking for this expedition."

"And me!"

"And me!"

"O.K.," Homer said, "so Isobel is Minister of the Royal Kitchen." He looked at Elmer Allen. "Which reminds me. You're our junior theoretician. Are we a monarchy?"

Elmer Allen scowled sourly and sat down, his back to the wadi wall. "I wouldn't think so."

Isobel went off to make coffee in the portable galley in the rear of the second hovercraft. The others brought forth tobacco and squatted or sat near the dour Jamaican. Years in the desert had taught them the nomad's ability to relax completely given opportunity.

"So if it's not a monarchy, what'll we call El Hassan?" Kenny demanded.

Elmer said slowly, thoughtfully, "We'll call him simply *El Hassan*. Monarchies are of the past, and El Hassan is the voice of the future, something new. We won't admit he's just a latter-day tyrant, an opportunist seizing power because it's there crying to be seized. Actually,

El Hassan is in the tradition of Genghis Khan, Tamerlane, or, more recently, Napoleon. But he's a modern version, and we're not going to hang the old labels on him."

Isobel had brought the coffee. "I think you're right," she said.

"Sold," Homer agreed. "So we aren't a monarchy. We're a tyranny." His face had begun by expressing amusement, but that fell off. He added, "As a young sociologist, I never expected to wind up a literal tyrant."

Elmer Allen said, "Wait a minute. See if I can remember this. Comes from Byron." He closed his eyes and recited:

"The tyrant of the Chersonese

Was freedom's best and bravest friend.

That tyrant was Miltiades,

Oh that the present hour would lend

Another despot of the kind.

Such bonds as his were sure to bind."

Isobel, pouring coffee, laughed and said, "Why Elmer, who'd ever dream you read verse, not to speak of memorizing it, you old sourpuss."

Elmer Allen's complexion was too dark to register a flush.

Homer Crawford said, "Yeah, Miltiades. Seized power, whipped the Athenians into shape to the point where they were able to take the Persians at Marathon, which should have been impossible." He looked around at the others, winding up with Elmer. "What happened to Miltiades after Marathon and after the emergency was over?"

Elmer looked down into his coffee. "I don't remember," he lied.

* * * * *

There was a clicking from the first hover-lorry, and Cliff Jackson put down his coffee, groaned his resentment at fate, and made his way to the vehicle and the radio there.

Bey motioned with his head. "That's handy, our still being able to tune in on the broadcasts the African Development Project makes to its teams."

Kenny said, "Not that what they've been saying is much in the way of flattery."

Bey said, "They seem to think we're somewhere in the vicinity of Bidon Cinq."

"That's what worries me," Homer growled. He raked his right hand back through his short hair. "If they think we're in Southern Algeria, what are these planes doing around here? We're hundreds of miles from Bidon Cinq."

Bey shot him an oblique glance. "That's easy. That plane that tried to clobber us, and these others that have been trying to search us out, aren't really Reunited Nations craft. They're someone else."

They all looked at him. "Who?" Isobel said.

"How should I know? It could be almost anybody with an iron in the North African fire. The Soviet Complex? Very likely. The British Commonwealth or the French Community? Why not? There're elements in both that haven't really accepted giving up the old colonies and would like to regain them in one way or the other. The Arab Union? Why comment? Common Europe? Oh, Common Europe would love to have a free hand exploiting North Africa."

"You haven't mentioned the United States of the Americas," Elmer said dryly. "I hope you haven't any prejudices in favor of the land of your adoption, Mr. Minister of War."

Bey shrugged. "I just hadn't got around to her. Admittedly with the continued growth of the Soviet Complex and Common Europe, the States have slipped from the supreme position they occupied immediately following the Second War. The more power-happy elements are conscious of the ultimate value of control of Africa and doubly conscious of the danger of it falling into the hands of someone else. Oh, never fear, those planes that have been pestering us might belong to anybody at all."

Cliff Jackson hurried back from his radio, his face anxious. "Listen," he said. "That was a high priority flash, to all Reunited Nations teams. The Arab Union has just taken Tamanrasset. They pushed two columns out of Libya, evidently one from Ghat and one from further north near Ghademès."

Homer Crawford was on his feet, alert. "Well …why?"

Cliff had what amounted to accusation on his face. "Evidently, the El Hassan rumors are spreading like wildfire. There've been more riots in Mopti, and the Reunited Nations buildings in Adrar have been stormed by mobs demonstrating for him. The Arab Union is moving in on the excuse of protecting the country against El Hassan."

Kenny Ballalou groaned, "They'll have half their Arab Legion in here before the week's out."

Cliff finished with, "The Reunited Nations is throwing a wingding. Everybody running around accusing and threatening, and, as per usual, getting nowhere."

Homer Crawford's face was working in thought. He shook his head at Kenny. "I think you're wrong. They won't send the whole Arab Legion in. They'll be afraid to. They'll want to see first what everybody else does. They know they can't stand up to a slugging match with any of the really big powers. They'll stick it out for a while and watch developments. We have, perhaps, two weeks in which to operate."

"Operate?" Cliff demanded. "What do you mean, operate?"

Homer's eyes snapped to him. "I mean to recapture Tamanrasset from the Arab Union, seize the radio and television station there, and proclaim El Hassan's regime."

The big Californian's eyes bugged at him. "You mean the six of us? There'll be ten thousand of them."

"No," Homer said decisively. "Nothing like that number. Possibly a thousand, if that many. Logistics simply doesn't allow a greater number, not on such short notice. They've put a thousand or so of their crack troops into the town. No more."

Cliff wailed, "What's the difference between a thousand and twenty thousand, so far as five men and a girl are concerned?"

The rest were saying nothing, but following the debate.

Crawford explained, not to just Cliff but to all of them. "Actually, the Arab Union is doing part of our job for us. They've openly declared that El Hassan is attempting to take over North Africa, that he's raising the tribes. Well, good. We didn't have the facilities to make the announcement ourselves. But now the whole world knows it."

* * * * *

"That's right," Elmer said, his face characteristically sullen. "Every news agency in the world is playing up the El Hassan story. In a matter of days, the most remote nomad encampment in the Sahara will know of it, one way or the other."

Homer Crawford was pacing, socking his right fist into the palm of the left. "They've given us a rallying *raison d'etre*. These people might be largely Moslem, especially in the north, but they have no love for the Arab Union. For too long the slave raiders came down from the northeast. Given time, Islam might have moved in on the whole of North Africa. But not this way, not in military columns."

He swung to Bey. "You worked over in the Teda country, before joining my team, and speak the Sudanic dialects. Head for there, Bey. Proclaim El Hassan. Organize a column. We'll rendezvous at Tamanrasset in exactly two weeks."

Bey growled, "How am I supposed to get to Faya?"

"You'll have to work that out yourself. Tonight we'll drop you near In Guezzam, they have one of the big solar pump, afforestation developments there. You should be able to, ah, requisition a truck, or possibly even a 'copter or aircraft. You're on your own, Bey."

"Right."

Homer spun to Kenny Ballalou. "You're the only one of us who gets along in the dialect of Hassania. Get over to Nemadi country and raise a column. There are no better scouts in the world. Two weeks from today at Tamanrasset."

"Got it. Drop me off tonight with Bey, we'll work together until we liberate some transport."

Bey said, "It might be worth while scouting in In Guezzam for a day or two. We might pick up a couple of El Hassan followers to help us along the way."

"Use your judgment. Elmer!"

Elmer groaned sourly, "I knew my time'd come."

"Up into Chaambra country for you. Take the second lorry. You've got a distance to go. Try to recruit former members of the French Camel Corps. Promise just about anything, but only remember that one day we'll have to keep the promises. El Hassan can't get the label of phony hung on him."

"Chaambra country," Elmer said. "Oh great. Arabs. I can just see what luck I'm going to have rousing up Arabs to fight other Arabs, and me with a complexion black as..."

Homer snapped at him, "They won't be following you, they'll be following El Hassan ... or at least the El Hassan dream. Play up the fact that the Arab Union is largely not of Africa but of the Middle East. That they're invading the country to swipe the goats and violate the women. Dig up all the old North African prejudices against the Syrians and Egyptians, and the Saudi-Arabian slave traders. You'll make out."

Cliff said, nervously, "How about me, Homer?"

Homer looked at him. Cliff Jackson, in spite of his fabulous build, hadn't a fighting man's background.

Homer grinned and said, "You'll work with me. We're going into Tuareg country. Whenever occasion calls for it, whip off that shirt and go strolling around with that overgrown chest of yours stuck out. The Tuareg consider themselves the best physical specimens in the Sahara, which they are. They admire masculine physique. You'll wow them."

Cliff grumbled, "Sounds like vaudeville."

Isobel said softly, "And me, El Hassan? What do I do?"

Homer turned to her. "You're also part of headquarters staff. The Tuareg women aren't dominated by their men. They still have a strong element of descent in the matrilinear line and women aren't second-class citizens. You'll work on pressuring them. Do you speak Tamaheq?"

"Of course."

Homer Crawford looked up into the sky, swept it. The day was rapidly coming to an end and nowhere does day become night so quickly as in the ergs of the Sahara.

"Let's get underway," Crawford said. "Time's a wastin'."

* * * * *

The range of the Ahaggar Tuareg was once known, under French administration, as the Annexe du Hoggar, and was the most difficult area ever subdued by French arms-if it was ever subdued. At the battle of Tit on May 7, 1902 the Camel Corps, under Cottenest, broke the combined military power of the Tuareg confederations, but this meant no more than that the tribes and clans carried on nomadic warfare in smaller units.

The Ahaggar covers roughly an area the size of Pennsylvania, New York, Virginia and Maryland combined, and supports a population of possibly twelve thousand, which includes about forty-five hundred Tuareg, four thousand Negro serf-slaves, and some thirty-five hundred scorned sedentary Haratin workers. The balance of the population consists of a handful of Enaden smiths and a small number of Arab shopkeepers in the largest of the sedentary centers. Europeans and other whites are all but unknown.

It is the end of the world.

Contrary to Hollywood-inspired belief, the Sahara does not consist principally of sand dunes, although these, too, are present, and all but impassable even to camels. Traffic, through the millennia, has held to the endless stretches of gravelly plains and the rock ribbed plateaus which cover most of the desert. The great sandy wastes or ergs cover roughly a fifth of the entire Sahara, and possibly two thirds of this area consists of the rolling sandy plains dotted occasionally with dunes. The remaining third, or about one fifteenth of the total Sahara, is characterized by the dune formations of popular imagination.

It was through this latter area that Homer Crawford, now with but one hover-lorry, and accompanied by Isobel Cunningham and Clifford Jackson, was heading.

For although the spectacular major dune formations of the Great Erg have defied wheeled vehicles since the era of the Carthaginian chariots, and even the desert born camel limits his daily travel in them to but a few miles, the modern hovercraft, atop its air cushion jets, finds them of only passing difficulty to traverse. And the hovercraft leaves no trail.

Cliff Jackson scowled out at the identical scenery. Identical for more than two hundred miles. For twice that distance, they had seen no other life. No animal, no bird, not a sprig of cactus. This was the Great Erg.

He muttered, "This country is so dry even the morning dew is dehydrated."

Isobel laughed-she, too, had never experienced this country before. "Why, Cliff, you made a funny!"

They were sitting three across in the front seat, with Homer Crawford at the wheel, and now all three were dressed in the costume of the Kel Rela tribe of the Ahaggar Tuareg confederation. In the back of the lorry were the jerry-cans of water and the supplies that meant the difference between life and mummification from sun and heat.

Cliff turned suddenly to the driver. "Why here?" he said bitterly. "Why pick this for a base of operations? Why not Mopti? Ten thousand Sudanese demonstrated for El Hassan there less than two weeks ago. You'd have them in the palm of your hand."

Homer didn't look up from his work at wheel, lift and acceleration levers. To achieve maximum speed over the dunes, you worked constantly at directing motion not only horizontally but vertically.

He said, "And the twenty and one enemies of the El Hassan movement would have had us in their palms. Our followers in Mopti can take care of themselves. If this movement is ever going to be worth anything, the local characters are going to have to get into the act. The current big thing is not to allow El Hassan and his immediate troupe to be eliminated before full activities can get under way. For the present, we're hiding out until we can gather forces enough to free Tamanrasset."

"Hiding out is right," Cliff snorted. "I have a sneaking suspicion that not only will they never find us, but we'll never find them again."

Homer laughed. "As a matter of fact, we're not so far right now from Silet where there's a certain amount of water-if you dig for it-and a certain amount of the yellowish grass and woody shrubs that the bedouin depend on. With luck, we'll find the Amenokal of the Tuareg there."

"Amenokal?"

"Paramount chief of the Ahaggar Tuaregs."

* * * * *

The dunes began to fall away and with the butt of his left hand Crawford struck the acceleration lever. He could make more time now when less of his attention was drawn to the ups and downs of erg travel.

Patches of thorny bush began to appear, and after a time a small herd of gazelle were flushed and high tailed their way over the horizon.

Isobel said, "Who is this Amenokal you mentioned?"

"These are the real Tuareg, the comparatively untouched. They've got three tribes, the Kel Rela, the Tégéhé Mellet and the Taitoq, each headed by a warrior clan which gives its name to the tribe as a whole. The chief of the Kel Rela clan is also chief of the Kel Rela tribe and automatically paramount chief, or Amenokal, of the whole confederation. His name is Melchizedek."

"Do you think you can win him over?" Isobel said.

"He's a smart old boy. I had some dealings with him over a year ago. Gave him a TV set in the way of a present, hoping he'd tune in on some of our Reunited Nations propaganda. He's probably the most conservative of the Tuareg leaders."

Her eyebrows went up. "And you expect to bring him around to the most liberal scheme to hit North Africa since Hannibal?"

He looked at her from the side of his eyes and grinned. "Remember Roosevelt, the American president?"

"Hardly."

"Well, you've read about him. He came into office at a time when the country was going to economic pot by the minute. Some of the measures he and his so-called brain trust took were immediately hailed by his enemies as socialistic. In answer, Roosevelt told them that in times of social stress the true conservative is a liberal, since to preserve, you have to reform. If Roosevelt hadn't done the things he did, back in the 1930s, you probably would have seen some *real* changes in the American socio-economic system. Roosevelt didn't undermine the social system of the time, he preserved it."

"Then, according to you, Roosevelt was a conservative," she said mockingly.

Crawford laughed. "I'll go even further," he said. "When social changes are pending and for whatever reason are not brought about, then reaction is the inevitable alternative. At such a time then-when sweeping socio-economic change is called for-any reform measures proposed are concealed measures of reaction, since they tend to maintain the *status quo.*"

"Holy Mackerel," Cliff protested. "Accept that and Roosevelt was not only not a liberal, but a reactionary. Stop tearing down my childhood heroes."

Isobel said, "Let's get back to this Amenokal guy. You think he's smart enough to see his only chance is in going along with..."

Homer Crawford pointed ahead and a little to the right. "We'll soon find out. This is a favorite encampment of his. With luck, he'll be there. If we can win him over, we've come a long way."

"And if we can't?" Isobel said, her eyebrows raised again.

"Then it's unfortunate that there are only three of us," Homer said simply, without looking at her.

There were possibly no more than a hundred Tuareg in all in the nomad encampment of goat leather tents when the solar powered hovercraft drew up.

When the air cushion vehicle stopped before the largest tent, Crawford said beneath his breath, "The Amenokal is here, all right. Cliff, watch your teguelmoust. If any of these people see more than your eyes, your standing has dropped to a contemptible zero."

The husky Californian secured the lightweight cotton, combination veil and turban well up over his face. Earlier, Crawford had shown him how to wind the ten-foot long, indigo-blue cloth around the head and features.

Isobel, of course, was unveiled, Tuareg fashion, and wore baggy trousers of black cotton held in place with a braided leather cord by way of drawstring and a gandoura upper-garment consisting of a huge rectangle of cloth some seven to eight feet square and folded over on itself with the free corners sewed together so as to leave bottom and most of both sides open. A V-shaped opening for her head and neck was cut out of a fold at the top, and a large patch had been sewed inside to make a pocket beneath her left breast. She wasn't exactly a Parisian fashion plate.

Even as they stepped down from the hovercraft, immediately after it had drifted to rest on the ground, an elderly man came from the tent entrance.

He looked at them for a moment, then rested his eyes exclusively on Homer Crawford.

"*La Bas*, El Hassan," he said through the cloth that covered his mouth.

Homer Crawford was taken aback, but covered the fact. "There is no evil," he repeated the traditional greeting. "But why do you name me El Hassan?"

A dozen veiled desert men, all with the Tuareg sword, several with modern rifles, had formed behind the Tuareg chief.

Melchizedek made a movement of hand to mouth, in a universal gesture of amusement. "Ah, El Hassan," he said, "you forget you left me the magical instrument of the Roumi."

Crawford was mystified, but he stood in silence. What the Tuareg paramount chief said now made considerable difference. As he recalled his former encounter with the Ahaggar leader, the other had been neither friendly nor antagonistic to the Reunited Nations team Crawford had headed in their role as itinerant desert smiths.

The Amenokal said, "Enter then my tent, El Hassan, and meet my chieftains. We would confer with you."

The first obstacle was cleared. Subduing a sigh of relief, Homer Crawford turned to Cliff. "This, O Amenokal of all the Ahaggar, is Clif ben Jackson, my Vizier of Finance."

The Amenokal bowed his head slightly, said, "*La Bas*."

Cliff could go that far in the Tuareg tongue. He said, "*La Bas*."

The Amenokal said, looking at Isobel, "I hear that in the lands of the Roumi women are permitted in the higher councils."

Homer said steadily, "This I have also been amazed to hear. However, it is fitting that my followers remain here while El Hassan discusses matters of the highest importance with the Amenokal and his chieftains. This is the Sitt Izubahil, high in the councils of her people due to the great knowledge she has gained by attending the new schools which dispense rare wisdom, as all men know."

The Amenokal courteously said, "*La Bas*," but Isobel held her peace in decency amongst men of chieftain rank.

When Homer and the Tuaregs had disappeared into the tent, she said to Cliff, "Stick by the car, I'm going to circulate among the women. Women are women everywhere. I'll pick up the gossip, possibly get something Homer will miss in there."

A group of Tuareg women and children, the latter stark naked, had gathered to gape at the strangers. Isobel moved toward them, began immediately breaking the ice.

Under his breath, Cliff muttered, "What a gal. Give her a few hours and she'll form a Lady's Aid branch, or a bridge club, and where else is El Hassan going to pick up so much inside information?"

* * * * *

The tent, which was of the highly considered mouflon skins, was mounted on a wooden frame which consisted of two uprights with a horizontal member laid across their tops. The tent covering was stretched over this framework with its back and sides pegged down and the front, which faced south, was left open. It was ten feet deep, fifteen feet wide and five feet high in the middle.

The men entered and filed to the right of the structure where sheepskins and rugs provided seating. The women and children, who abided ordinarily to the left side, had vanished for this gathering of the great.

They sat for a time and sipped at green tea, syrup sweet with mint and sugar, the tiny cups held under the teguelmoust so as not to obscenely reveal the mouth of the drinker.

Finally, Homer Crawford said, "You spoke of the magical instrument of the Roumi which I gave you as gift, O Amenokal, and named me El Hassan."

Several of the Tuareg chuckled beneath their veils but Crawford could read neither warmth nor antagonism in their amusement.

The elderly Melchizedek nodded. "At first we were bewildered, O El Hassan, but then my sister's son, Guémama, fated perhaps one day to become chief of the Kel Rela and Amenokal of all the Ahaggar, recalled the tales told by the storytellers at the fire in the long evenings."

Crawford looked at him politely.

Melchizedek's laugh was gentle. "But each man has heard, in his time, O El Hassan, of the ancient Calif Haroun El Raschid of Baghdad."

Crawford's mind went into high gear, as the story began to come back to him. From second into high gear, and he could have blessed these bedouin for handing him a piece of publicity gobblydygook worthy of Fifth Avenue's top agency.

He held up a hand as though in amusement at being discovered. "Wallahi, O Amenokal, you have discovered my secret. For many months I have crossed the deserts disguised as a common Enaden smith to seek out all the people and to learn their wishes and their needs."

"Even as Haroun el Raschid in the far past," one of the subchiefs muttered in satisfaction, "used to disguise himself as a lowborn dragoman and wander the streets of Baghdad."

"But how did you recognize me?" Homer said.

The Amenokal said in reproof, "But verily, your name is on all lips. The Roumi have branded you common criminal. You are to be seized on sight and great reward will be given he who delivers you to the authorities." He spoke without inflection, and Crawford could read neither support nor animosity-nor greed for the reward offered by El Hassan's enemies. He gathered the impression that the Tuareg chief was playing his cards close to his chest.

"And what else do they say?"

The elderly Melchizedek went on slowly, "They say that El Hassan is in truth a renegade citizen of a far away Roumi land and that he attempts to build a great confederation in North Africa for his own gain."

One of the others chuckled and said, "The Roumi on the magical instrument are indeed great liars as all can see."

Homer looked at him questioningly.

The other said, laughing, "Who has ever heard of a black Roumi? And you, O El Hassan, are as black as a Bela."

The Amenokal finished off the mystery of Crawford's recognition. "Know, El Hassan, that whilst you were here before, one of the slaves that served you for pay shamelessly looked upon your face in the privacy of your tent. It was this slave who recognized your face when the Roumi presented it on the magic instrument, calling upon all men to see you and to brand you enemy."

So that was it. The Reunited Nations, and probably all the rest, had used their radio and TV stations to broadcast a warning and offer a reward for Homer and his followers. Old Sven was losing no time. This wasn't so good. A Tuareg owes allegiance to no one beyond clan, tribe and confederation. All others are outside the pale and any advantage, monetary or otherwise, to be gained by exploiting a stranger is well within desert mores.

He might as well bring it to the point. Crawford said evenly, "And I have entered your camp alone except for two followers. Your people are many. So why, O Amenokal, have you not seized me for the reward the Roumi offer?"

* * * * *

There was a moment of silence and Homer Crawford sensed that the sub-chieftains had leaned forward in anticipation, waiting for their leader's words. Possibly they, too, could not understand.

The Tuareg leader finished his tea.

"Because, El Hassan, we yet have not heard the message which the Roumi are so anxious that you not be allowed to bring the men of the desert. The Roumi are great liars, and great thieves, as each man knows. In the memory of those still living, they have stolen of the bedouin and robbed him of land and wealth. So now we would hear of what you say, before we decide."

"Spoken like a true Amenokal, a veritable Suliman ben Davud," Homer said with a heartiness he could only partly feel. At least they were open to persuasion.

For a long moment he stared down at the rug upon which they sat, as though deep in contemplation.

"These words I speak will be truly difficult to hear and accept, O men of the veil," he said at last. "For I speak of great change, and no man loves change in the way of his life."

"Speak, El Hassan," Melchizedek said flatly. "Great change is everywhere upon us, as each man knows, and none can tell how to maintain the ways of our fathers."

"We can fight," one of the younger men growled.

The Amenokal turned to him and grunted scorn. "And would you fight against the weapons of the djinn and afrit, O Guémama? Know that in my youth I was distant witness to the explosion of a great weapon which the accursed Franzawi discharged south of Reggan. Know, that this single explosion, my sister's son, could with ease have destroyed the total of all the tribesmen of the Ahaggar, had they been gathered."

"And the Roumi have many such weapons," Crawford added gently.

The eyes of the tribal headmen came back to him.

"As each man knows," Crawford continued, "change is upon the world. No matter how strongly one wills to continue the traditions of his fathers, change is upon us all. And he who would press against the sand storm, rather than drifting with it, lasts not long."

One of the subchiefs growled, "We Tuareg love not change, El Hassan."

Crawford turned to him. "That is why I and my viziers have spent long hours in *ekhwan*, in great council, devoted to the problems of the Tuareg and how they can best fit into the new Africa that everywhere awakes."

They stirred in interest now. The Tuareg, once the Scourge of the Sahara, the Sons of Shaitan and the Forgotten of Allah, to the Arab, Teda, Moroccan and other fellow inhabitants of North Africa, were of recent decades developing a tribal complex. Robbed of their nomadic-bandit way of life by first the French Camel Corps and later by the efforts of the Reunited Nations, they were rapidly descending into a condition of poverty and defensive bewilderment. Not only were large numbers of former bedouin drifting to the area's sedentary centers, an act beyond contempt within the memory of the elders, but the best elements of the clans were often deserting Tuareg country completely and defecting to the new industrial centers, the dam projects, the afforestation projects, the new oases irrigated with the solar-powered pumps.

"Speak, El Hassan," the Amenokal ordered. And unconsciously, he, too, leaned forward, as did his subchiefs. The Ahaggar Tuareg were reaching for straws, unconsciously seeking shoulders upon which to lay their unsolvable problems.

"Let me, O chiefs of the Tuareg, tell of a once strong tribe of warriors and nomads who lived in the far country in which I was born," Crawford said. The desert man loves a story, a parable, a tale of the strong men of yesteryear.

Melchizedek clapped his hands in summons and when a slave appeared, called for *narghileh* water pipes. When all had been supplied, they relaxed, bits in mouths and looked again at Homer Crawford.

"They were called," he intoned, "the Cheyenne. The Northern Cheyenne, for they had a sister tribe to the South. And on all the plains of this great land, a land, verily, as large as all that over which the Tuareg confederations now roam, they were the greatest huntsmen, the greatest warriors. All feared them. They were the lords of all."

"Ai," breathed one of the older men. "As were the Tuareg before the coming of the cursed Franzawi and the other Nazrani."

"But in time," Crawford pursued, "came the new ways to the plains, and these men who lived largely by the chase began to see the lands fenced in for farmers, began to see large cities erected on what were once tribal areas, and to see the iron railroads of the new ways begin to spread out over the whole of the territory which once was roamed only by the Cheyennes and such nomadic tribes."

"Ai," a muffled mouth ejected.

Homer Crawford looked at the younger Targui, Guémama, the Amenokal's nephew. "And so," he said, "they fought."

"Wallahi!" Guémama breathed.

Homer Crawford looked about the circle. "Never has tribe fought as did the Cheyenne. Never has the world seen such warriors, with the exception, of course, of the Ahaggar Tuareg. Never were such raids, never such bravery, never such heroic deeds as were performed by the warriors of the Cheyennes and their women, and their old people and their children. Over and over they defeated the cavalry and the infantry of the newcomers who would change the old ways and bring the new to the lands of the Cheyennes."

The bedouin were staring in fascination, their water pipes forgotten.

"And then...?" the Amenokal demanded.

"The new ways taught the enemy how to make guns, and artillery, and finally Gatling guns, which today we call machine guns. And once a brave warrior might prevail against a common man armed with the weapons of the new ways, and even twice he might. But the numbers of the followers of the new ways are as the sands of the Great Erg and in time bravery means nothing."

"It is even so," someone growled. "They are as the sands of the erg, and they have the weapons of the djinn, as each man knows."

"And what happened in the end, O El Hassan?"

His eyes swept them all. "They perished," Homer said. "Today in all the land where once the Cheyenne pursued the game there is but a handful of the tribe alive. And they have become nothing people, no longer warriors, no longer nomads, and they are scorned by all for they are poor, poor, poor. Poor in mind and spirits, and in property and they have not been able to adjust to the ways of the new world."

Air went out of the lungs of the assembled Tuareg.

The Amenokal looked at him. "This is verily the truth, El Hassan?"

"My head upon it," Crawford said.

"And why do you tell us of these Cheyenne, these great warriors of the plains of the land of your birth? The story fails to bring joy to hearts already heavy with the troubles of the Tuareg."

It was time to play the joker.

Crawford said carefully, "Because there was no need, O Amenokal of all the Ahaggar, for the Cheyenne to disappear before the sandstorm of the future. They could have ridden before it and today occupy a position of honor and affluence in their former land."

They stared at him.

"And give up the old ways?" Guémama demanded. "Become no longer nomads, no longer honorable warriors, but serfs, slaves, working with one's hands upon the land and with the oil-dirty machines of the Roumi?"

The chiefs muttered angrily.

Crawford said hurriedly, "No! Never! In our great conferences, my viziers and I decided that the Tuareg could never so change. The Tuareg must die, as did the Northern Cheyenne before he would become a city dweller, a worker of the land."

"Bismillah!" someone muttered.

"Too often," Crawford explained, "do the bringers of these things of the future, be they Roumi or others, fail to utilize the potential services of the people of the lands they over-sweep."

"I do not understand you, El Hassan," Melchizedek grumbled. "There is no room for the Tuareg in this new world of bringing trees to the desert, of the great trucks which speed across the erg a score of time the pace of a *hejin* racing camel, of larger and ever larger oases with their great towns, their schools, their new industries. If the Tuareg remains Tuareg, he cannot fit into this new world, it destroys the old traditions, the old way which is the Tuareg way."

Homer Crawford now turned on the pressure. His voice took on overtones of the positive, his personality seemed to reach out and seize them, and even his physical stature seemed to grow.

"Some indeed of the ways of the bedouin must go," he entoned, "but the Tuareg will survive under my leadership. A people who have throve a millennium and more in the great wastes of the Sahara have strong survival characteristics and will blossom, not die, in my new world. Know, O Melchizedek, that it has been decided that the Ahaggar Tuareg will be the heart of my Desert Legion. In times of conflict, armed with the new arms, and riding the new vehicles, they will adapt their old methods of warfare to this new age. In times of peace they will patrol the new forests, watching for fire and other disaster, they will become herdsmen of the new herds and be the police and rescue forces of this wide area. As the Cheyennes of the olden times of the land of my birth could have become herdsmen and forest rangers and have performed similar tasks had they been shown the way."

Homer Crawford let his eyes go from one of them to the next, and his personality continued to dominate them.

The Amenokal ran his thin, aged hand through the length of his white beard beneath his teguelmoust and contemplated this stranger come out of the ergs to lead his people to still greater changes than those they had thus far rebelled against.

* * * * *

Crawford realized that the Targui was divided in opinion and inwardly the American was in a cold sweat. But his voice registered only supreme confidence. "Under my banner, all North

Africa will be welded into one. And all the products of the land will be available in profusion to my faithful followers. The finest wheat for cous cous from Algeria and Tunis, the finest dates and fruits from the oases to the north, the manufactured products of the factories of Dakar and Casablanca. For Africa has always been a poor land but will become a rich one with the new machines and techniques that I will bring."

The Amenokal raised a hand to stem the tide of oratory. "And what do you ask of us now, El Hassan?"

Instead of to the older man, Crawford turned his eyes to the face of Guémama, the leader of the young clansmen. "Now my people are gathering to establish the new rule. Teda from the east, Chaambra from the north, Sudanese from the south, Nemadi, Moors and Rifs from the west. We rendezvous in ten days from now at Tamanrasset where the Arab Legion dogs have seized the city as they wish to seize all the lands of the Sahara and Sudan for the corrupt Arab Union politicians."

Crawford came to his feet. His voice took on an edge of command. "You will address your scouts and warriors and each will ride off on the swiftest camels at your command to raise the Tuareg tribes. And the clans of the Kel Rela will unite with the Taitoq and the Tégéhé Mellet in a great harka at this point and we will ride together to sweep the Arab Legion from the lands of El Hassan."

Guémama was on his feet, too. "Bilhana!" he roared. "With joy."

The others were arising in excitement, all but Melchizedek, who still stroked his gray streaked beard beneath his teguelmoust. The Amenokal had seen much of desert war in his day and knew the horror of the new weapons possessed by the crack troops of the Arab Legion.

But his aged shoulders shrugged against the inevitable.

Crawford said, the ring of authority in his voice. "What does the Amenokal of all the Ahaggar say?" He had no intention of antagonizing the Tuareg chief by going over his head and directly to the people.

"Thou art El Hassan," Melchizedek said, his voice low, "and undoubtedly it is fated that the Tuareg follow you, for verily there is no way else to go, as each man knows."

"Wallahi!" Guémama crowed jubilantly.

V

Guémama, nephew of Melchizedek the Amenokal of the Ahaggar Tuareg confederation and fighting chief of the Kel Rela clan of the Kel Rela tribe, brought his Hejin racing camel to an abrupt halt with a smack of his mish'ab camel stick. He barked, *"Adar-ya-yan,"* in command to bring it to its knees, and slid to the ground before his mount had groaned its rocking way to the sand.

The Tarqui was jubilant. His dark eyes sparked above his teguelmoust veil and he presented himself before Homer Crawford with the elan of a Napoleonic cavalryman before his emperor. Were red leather fil fil boots capable of producing a clicking of heels, that sound would have rung.

Crawford said with dignity, "Aselamu, Aleikum, Guémama. Greeting to you."

"Salaam Aleikum," the tribesman got out breathlessly. "Your message spreads, O El Hassan. My men ride to eastward and westward and never a tent from here to Silet, from In Guezzam to Timissao but knows that El Hassan calls. The Taitoq and the Tégéhé Mellet ride!"

Homer Crawford was standing before the hovercraft. The Amenokal's tribesmen had set up two large goat leather tents for his use and the three Americans had largely withdrawn to their shelter. Crawford was aware of the dangers of familiarity.

Cliff Jackson, who as usual had been monitoring the radio, came from the hover-lorry and growled, "What's he saying?"

"The tribesmen are gathering as per instructions," Homer said in English.

Jackson grunted, somewhat self-conscious of the Targui's admiring gaze. The Tuareg is the handsomest physical specimen of North Africa, often going to six foot of wiry manhood, but there was nothing in all the Sahara to rival the build of Homer Crawford, not to speak of the giant Cliff Jackson.

Crawford turned back to the Tuareg chieftain. "You please me well, O Guémama. Know that I have been in conference with my viziers on the Roumi device which enables one to speak great distances and that we have decided that you are to head all the fighting clans of the Ahaggar, and that you will ride at the left hand of El Hassan, as shield on shoulder rides."

The Targui, overwhelmed, made adequate pledges of fidelity, flowering words of thanks, and then hurried off to inform his fellow tribesmen of his appointment.

Isobel emerged from her tent. She looked at Homer obliquely, the sides of her mouth turning down. "As shield on shoulder rides," she translated from the Tamaheq Berber tongue into English. "Hm-m-m." She cast her eyes upward in memory. "You aren't plagiarizing Kipling, are you?"

Crawford grinned at her. "These people like a well turned phrase."

"And who could turn them better than Rudyard?" she said. Her voice dropped the bantering tone. "What's this bit about making Guémama war-chief of the Tuareg? Isn't he on the young and enthusiastic side?"

Cliff scowled. "You mean that youngster? Why he can't be more than in his early twenties."

Crawford was looking after the young Targui who was disappearing into his uncle's tent on the far side of the rapidly growing encampment.

"You mean the age of Napoleon in the Italian campaign, or Alexander at Issus?" he asked. Isobel began to respond to that, but he shook his head. "He's the Amenokal's nephew, and traditionally would probably get the position anyway. He's the most popular of the young tribesmen, and it's going to be they who do the fighting. Having the appointment come from El Hassan, and at this early point, will just bind him closer. Besides that, he's a natural born warrior. Typical. Enthusiastic, bold, brave and with the military mind."

"What's a military mind?" Cliff said.

"He can take off his shirt without unbuttoning his collar," Homer told him.

"Very funny," Cliff grumbled.

Isobel turned to the big Californian. "What's on the radio, Cliff?"

"Let's go get a cup of coffee," he said. "All hellzapoppin."

* * * * *

They went into the larger of the two Tuareg tents, and Isobel poured water from a girba into the coffee pot which she placed on a heat unit, flicking its switch. She said sarcastically, from the side of her mouth, "A message, O El Hassan, from the Department of Logistics, subdepartment Commissary of Headquarters of the Commander in Chief. Unless you get around to capturing some supplies in the near future, your food is going to be prepared over a camel dung fire. This heat unit is fading out on me."

"Don't bother me with trivialities," Homer told her. "I've got *big* things on my mind."

She looked at him suspiciously. "Hm-m-m. Such as what?"

"Such as whether to put my face on the postage stamps profile or full."

She said, under her breath, "I shoulda known. Already, delusions of grandeur."

"Holy Mackerel," Cliff protested. "Aren't we ever serious around this place? You two will wind up gagging with the firing squad."

Crawford chuckled softly but let his face go serious. "Sorry, Cliff. What's on your mind?"

Cliff said impatiently, "From the radio reports, the Arab Union is consolidating its position. El Hassan is being discredited by the minute. Your followers were in control for a time in Mopti and Bamako, but they're falling away because of lack of direction. The best way I can put reports together, the Reunited Nations is in complete confusion. Everybody accusing everybody of double-dealing."

Isobel said dryly, "Any other good news?"

Cliff said glumly, "Rumors, rumors, rumors. Half the marabouts in North Africa are proclaiming a jehad in support of the Pan-Islam program of the Arab Union. Listen, Homer, we've got to get the backing of the Moslem leaders."

Homer Crawford grunted. "We need Islam in this part of the world like we need a hole in the head. That's one of the things already wrong with North Africa."

"What's wrong with Islam? It was probably the most dynamic religion ever to sweep the world."

"*Was* is right," Crawford growled, now on one of his favorite peeve subjects. "The Moslem religion exploded out of Arabia with some new concepts that set the world in ferment from India to Southern France. For all practical purposes Islam *invented* science. Sure, the Greeks had logic and the Romans had engineering-without applying the Greek-style logic. But the Arabs amalgamated the two concepts to yield experimental science. They were able to take the intellectual products of a dozen cultures and wield them into one. For a hundred years or so it looked as though they had something."

When he hesitated for a moment, Isobel said, questioningly, "And..."

"And they couldn't get away from that Q'ran of theirs. They took it seriously. They started off in their big universities, such as those at Fez, being the greatest scientists and scholars the world had ever seen. But the fundamentalists won out, and in a couple of hundred years the only thing being taught at Fez was the Q'ran. To even suggest that all necessary information isn't contained therein, is enough to have you clobbered. Islam became the most reactionary force to suppress progress in the civilized world. In fact, by this period in world history, we don't even think of the Moslem world as particularly civilized."

Cliff said defensively, "The Bible doesn't encourage original thinking either. A fundamentalist..."

"Sure," Crawford interrupted. "Those elements who take the Bible the way Islam took the Q'ran wind up in the same rut. But *as a whole*, Europe was sparked enough by the original Islamic explosion that the Renaissance resulted, with what world results we all know. Be..."

* * * * *

There was a roar of confusion outside. A blasting of guns, a shrieking of *Ul-Ul-Ul-Allah Akbar!*

Crawford came to his feet unhappily. "Another contingent of Tuareg," he said. "I'll have to give them a quick welcoming to the colors speech."

The guns outside continued their booming.

"Confound it," he growled, "I wish I could break them of that habit of blasting away their ammunition. They'll have better targets before the week is out."

He pushed open the tent flap and, followed by Isobel and Cliff, emerged into the stretch of clearing between his tents and the hovercraft, and the growing Tuareg encampment. His diagnosis had been correct. A contingent of possibly two score Tuareg camelmen had come a-galloping up, shaking rifles above their heads in a small scale gymhana, or fantasia as the Moors called them.

"At least it's a larger group than usual," Cliff said from behind. "But at this rate, it'll still take a month for us to equal the Arab Legion in Tamanrasset." He added in disgust, "And look at this bunch of ragamuffins. Half of them are carrying muzzleloaders."

The booming muskets and the cracking rifles suddenly began to fall off in intensity and the camelmen and the hordes of Tuareg women and naked children who had swarmed from the tents to greet them were falling silent. Here and there a hand pointed upward.

Homer, Cliff and Isobel swung their own eyes up to the sky in dreaded anticipation. The hover-lorry was camouflaged to blend in with the sands and rock outcroppings of this area, but it was possible that an aircraft might have determined that this was El Hassan's base, possibly through some act of a traitor, in which case...

They found the spot in the sky that the tribesmen were pointing out. It seemed to move slowly for a military craft, but for that matter it might be a helio-jet and considerably more dangerous, so far as they being spotted was concerned, than a fast moving fighter.

Guémama, was barking to his men to take cover. Two days before Crawford had checked out several of the more bright-eyed on the flac rifle and now three of them ran to where it was set up at a high point.

But hardly had the confused milling got under way than it fell off again. Movement stopped, and the Tuareg faced the approaching dot in the sky.

"Djinn...!"

"Afrit...!"

Cliff had darted back into the tent, now he emerged with binoculars.

"What the devil is it?" Crawford snapped. Desert trained eyes were evidently considerably more effective than his own. He couldn't see what the tribesmen were gaping at.

"It's the smallest heliohopper *I've* ever seen," Cliff snorted. "It's so small practically all you can see are the rotors and the passenger. He doesn't even look as though he's got a seat."

Guémama came hurrying up, his eyes wide beneath his teguelmoust. "El Hassan! A witch-man ... come out of the sky!"

Homer said evenly, "It is nothing. Only post men ready to obey my commands."

Guémama hesitated as though to waver out another protest, but then spun and hurried off-military-like, glad to have an order to obey to keep his mind from the impossible.

"I'm beginning to have a sneaking suspicion —" Crawford began without finishing. "Come on Isobel, Cliff. We're going to have to make the most of this."

* * * * *

Rex Donaldson, ex-field man for the African Department of the British Commonwealth, dropped the lift lever of his heliohopper and settled to the ground immediately before Homer Crawford who stood there flanked by Isobel Cunningham and Cliff Jackson. Further back and in the form of a crescent were possibly two or three hundred Tuareg of all ages and both sexes.

Donaldson, in the garb of a Dogan juju man consisting of little more than a wisp of cloth about his loins, played it straight, not knowing the setup. On the face of it, he had just flown out of the sky *personally*. The size of his equipment so small as to be all but meaningless.

He unstrapped himself from the thin, bicyclelike seat, and, expressionlessly, folded the rotors of his tiny craft back over themselves and the engine, collapsed the whole thing into a manageable packet of some seventy-five pounds, the seat now becoming a handle, and then turned and faced Crawford.

Donaldson screwed his wizened face into an expression of respect and made a motion of obeisance. Then he waited.

Isobel said, "El Hassan bids you speak."

That was the tip-off, then. Crawford had already revealed himself to these people as El Hassan. Very well.

Donaldson spoke in Arabic, not knowing the Tamaheq tongue. "Aselamu, Aleikum, El Hassan. I come to obey your wishes."

A sigh had gone through the Tuareg. "Aiiiii." *Wallahi, even the djinn obeyed El Hassan!*

With dignity, Homer Crawford said, "Keif halak, all in my house is yours."

Rex Donaldson inclined his small bent body again, in respect.

Crawford said in English, "Let's not carry this *too* far. Come on into the tent."

Ignoring the Tuareg, who still gaped but held their distance, the four English-speaking Negroes headed for the larger of the two tents that had been set up for El Hassan.

As they passed Guémama who stood slightly aside from the other Tuareg with his uncle Melchizedek, the Amenokal, Crawford nodded and said, speaking to them both. "A messenger from my people to the south. Continue with your newly arrived warriors, O Guémama."

Cliff Jackson had picked up the folded heliohopper and was now carrying it easily.

Guémama looked at the device and blinked.

Crawford refrained from laughing at his commander of irregulars. "It is not a *kambu* device. My people deal not in magic. It is but one of the many of the things the new ways bring. One day, Guémama," Homer's face remained expressionless, "perhaps you will fly thus."

The teguelmoust hid the other's blanch.

In the tent, Homer turned to the Bahaman, motioned to what seating arrangements were available.

Isobel said, "I'll get some coffee."

Cliff blurted, "Holy Mackerel, if Donaldson, here, can drop in on us out of a clear sky, what keeps anybody else from doing it? Somebody with a couple of neopalm bombs in the way of calling cards."

The dried up little man grimaced in his equivalent of a grin and said, "Hold it, you chaps. I want to notify the others."

"The others? What others?" Crawford said.

Donaldson ignored him for a moment, unslung the small bag he carried over one shoulder and dipped into it for a tiny, two-way radio. He pressed the buzzer button, then held it up to his mouth. "Jack, Jimmy, Dave. Here we are. Took donkey's years, but I found them. You chaps zero-in here." He left the device on and set it to one side, then yawned and settled himself to the rug-covered ground, crosslegged, Dogon style.

Homer Crawford, even as he sat down himself on a footlocker, in lieu of a chair, rapped, "How did you find us? Who did you just radio? Where'd you come from?"

"I say, hold it," Donaldson chuckled sourly. "First of all, I've come to join up. I thought as far back as that time we co-operated in quelling the riots in Mopti that you ought to do this-proclaim yourself El Hassan. When I heard you'd taken the step, I came to join up."

"Oh, great," Cliff said. "What took you so long? We hardly get here, to our ultra-secret hideout, than here you are."

Isobel came with the coffee and handed it around, silently. Then she, too, settled to the rug which covered the sand of the floor.

Rex Donaldson turned to Cliff and there was a wrinkle of amusement in the older man's eyes. "I took so long, because I needed the time to recruit a few other chaps I knew would stand with us."

Crawford rapped, "That's who you just radioed?"

"Of course, old boy. I'd hardly bring the opposition down on us, would I?"

"Where are they?"

"In a couple of hovercraft, similar to your own, possibly twenty kilometers to the southwest."

"You still haven't told us how you found us?"

The little man shrugged. "After tendering my resignation to Sir Winton, I considered the possibilities, which narrowed down very quickly when I heard the Arab Legion had taken Tamanrasset."

"Why?" Isobel said.

Donaldson shot a glance at her. "Because, my dear, unless El Hassan is able to retake Tamanrasset, his movement has come a cropper." He turned his eyes back to Crawford, who was nervously running his hand through his hair. "I knew you had done considerable work in this area, so your whereabouts became obvious seeing that Tamanrasset is in Tuareg country. It was simply a matter of finding what Tuareg encampment was your base, and since your quickest manner of gathering support would be to swing the Amenokal to your banner, I headed for his usual encampment this time of year."

Cliff looked at Homer Crawford. "If Rex found us so easily, so will anybody else."

Isobel put in. "Not necessarily. Mr. Donaldson has information that most of El Hassan's opponents wouldn't."

* * * * *

Homer came to his feet unhappily and began pacing. "No, Isobel. Ostrander, for instance, has all the dope Rex has and is just as capable of working it through to a conclusion. It takes no great insight to realize El Hassan has to either put up or shut up when it comes to Tamanrasset. That's possibly why some of the other elements interested in North Africa have so far refrained from action against the Arab Union. They want to see what El Hassan is going to do-find out just what he has on the ball."

Rex Donaldson looked at him interestedly, "And? What are your plans?"

Homer Crawford's face worked. "My plans right at present are to stay alive, and you finding me so easily isn't heartening. However, it brings to mind some other problems which need solving, too."

The rest of them fell silent, looking at him. His usual casual humor had dropped away, and his personality gripped them.

He stopped his pacing, and frowned down at them.

"El Hassan is going to have to remain on the move. Always. There can be no capital city, no definite base, and it's going to be a poor idea to sleep twice in the same place." He shook his head emphatically as though to deny rebuttal, which they hadn't actually made. "El Hassan's enemies mustn't know his location within twenty miles."

"Twenty miles!" Cliff blurted.

Crawford stared at him, but unseeingly. "Yes. At least half a dozen of our opponents possess nuclear weapons."

Donaldson demured, sourly. "A nuclear weapon hasn't been exploded for donkey's years and —"

"Of course not," Homer snapped. "Nor would anyone dare, anywhere else except in the wastes of the Sahara. A nuclear explosion in the Ahaggar would not go undetected and a controversy might go up in the Reunited Nations. But who could prove who had done it? And who, actually, would care if in the explosion a common foe of all was eliminated? But let the Arab Union, or possibly the Soviet Complex, or even others, learn definitely where El Hassan is and a bomb could well devastate twenty square miles seeking him out." Crawford shook his head. "No, we've simply got to keep on the move."

Donaldson said, even as he nodded agreement, "And what other problems were you talking about?"

"Oh?" Homer said. "Well, keeping on the move will serve to add mystery to the El Hassan legend. It isn't good for this Tuareg encampment, for instance, to see too much of El Hassan. A leader claiming domination of half a continent looks small potatoes in a desert camp of a few score tents. On the move, showing up here, there, the other place, for only a day or two at a time, is another proposition."

He thought a moment. "Remember DeGaulle?"

"How could we forget?" Rex Donaldson said wryly.

"He had one angle that couldn't be more correct. He said a leader had to keep remote, ever mysterious. He can't afford to have real intimates. Napoleon, Hitler, Stalin. None of them had a real friend to their name. The nearest to friends that Adolph the Aryan ever had, his old comrades of the beerhall days, such as Rhoem, he butchered in the blood purge. And Stalin? He managed to do away with every Old Bolshevik he knew in the days before the Party came to power."

Cliff was staring at him. "Hey," he said. "The one other thing one of these mystical leader types needs is a belief in his own destiny. To the point of clobbering all his intimates if he thinks they stand in his way."

Homer broke into a sudden short laugh. "Any qualms, Cliff?"

Cliff growled, "I don't know. This dream of yours is growing. Where it might end —I don't know."

As they were talking the cries of *Ul-Ul-Ul-Allah Akbar!* had broken out again.

"Heavens to Betsy," Isobel said. "Another contingent of camelmen?"

* * * * *

But this time the newcomers were three in number and rode in air cushion hover-lorries, the twins of that used by Homer Crawford.

Rex Donaldson brought them up to the tent, saying, "I didn't think you chaps were quite so close."

Homer, Cliff and Isobel faced the new recruits. The three were dressed in khaki bushshirts, shorts and heavy walking shoes-British style. Two were so obviously relatives that they could have been twins except for an age discrepancy of two or three years. They were smaller in stature than the Americans present, almost chunky, but their faces held education and cultivation. The third was slight of build, almost as wiry as Rex Donaldson, and seemed ever at ease.

The small, bent Bahaman made introductions. "Gentlemen, let me present El Hassan-Homer Crawford to you-formerly of the Reunited Nations African Development Project, formerly of the United States of the Americas." His face twisted in his sour grimace of a grin. "Now running for the office of tyrant of North Africa."

"And these are two of his original and most trusted adherents, Isobel Cunningham and Cliff Jackson." Donaldson turned to the newcomers. "John and James Peters-that's Jack and Jimmy, of course-recently colleagues of mine with the African Department of the Commonwealth, working largely in the Nigeria area."

Homer shook hands, grinning. "You're a long way from home."

"Farther than that," the one labeled Jack said without a smile changing the seriousness of his face. "We're originally from Trinidad."

Donaldson said, "And this is David Moroka, late of South Africa."

The wiry South African said easily, "Not so very late. In fact, I haven't seen Jo-burg since I was a boy."

He was shaking hands with Isobel now. "Jo-burg?" she said.

"Johannesburg," he translated. "I got out by the skin of my teeth during the troubles in the 1950s."

"You sound like an American," Cliff said when it was his turn to shake.

"Educated in the States," Moroka said. "Best thing that ever happened to me was to be kicked out of the land of my birth."

Homer made a sweeping gesture at the floor and the few articles of furniture the tent contained that could be improvised as chairs. "I'm surprised you're up here instead of in your own neck of the woods," he said to the South African.

Moroka shrugged. "I was considering heading south when I ran into Jimmy and Jack, here. They'd already got the word on the El Hassan movement from Rex. Their arguments made sense to me."

Eyes went to the brothers from Trinidad and Jack Peters took over the position of spokesman. He said, seriously, as though trying to convince the others, "North Africa is the starting point, the beginning. Given El Hassan's success in uniting North Africa, the central areas and later even the south will fall into line. Perhaps one day there will be a union of *all* Africa."

"Or at least a strong confederation," Jimmy Peters added.

Homer nodded thoughtfully. "Perhaps. But we can't look that far forward now." He looked from one of the newcomers to the other. "I don't know to what extent you fellows understand what the rest of us have set out to accomplish but I suppose if you've been with Rex for the past week, you have a fairly clear idea."

"I believe so," Jack nodded, straight-faced.

Homer Crawford said slowly, "I don't want to give you the wrong idea. If you join up, you'll find it's no parade. Our chances were slim to begin, and we've had some setbacks. As you've probably heard, the Arab Union has stolen a march on us. And from what we can get on the radio, we have thus far to pick up a single adherent among the world powers."

"*Powers?*" Cliff snorted. "We haven't got a nation the size of Monaco on our side."

Moroka shot a quick glance at the big Californian.

Isobel caught it and laughed. "Cliff's a perpetual sourpuss," she said. "However, he's been in since the first."

The South African looked at her in turn. "We were hardly prepared to find a beautiful American girl in the Great Erg," he said.

Something about his voice caused her to flush. "We've all caught Homer's dream," she said, almost defensively.

* * * * *

David Moroka flung to his feet, viper fast, and dashed toward Homer Crawford, his hands extended.

Automatically, Cliff Jackson stuck forward a foot in an attempt to trip him-and missed.

The South African, moving with blurring speed, grasped the unsuspecting Crawford by the right hand and arm, swung with fantastic speed and sent the American sprawling to the far side of the tent.

Homer Crawford, old in rough and tumble, was already rolling out. Before the inertia of his fall had given way, his right hand, only a split second before in the grip of the other, was fumbling for the 9 mm Noiseless holstered at his belt.

Rex Donaldson, a small handgun magically in his hand, was standing, half crouched on his thin, bent legs. The two brothers from Trinidad hadn't moved, their eyes bugging.

Moroka was spinning with the momentum of the sudden attack he'd made on his new chief. Now there was a gun in his own hand and he was darting for the tent opening.

Cliff yelled indignantly, "Stop him!"

Isobel, on her feet by now, both hands to her mouth, was staring at the goatskin tent covering, against which, a moment earlier, Crawford had been gently leaning his back as he talked.

There was a vicious slash in the leather and even as she pointed, the razor-sharp arm dagger's blade disappeared. There was the sound of running feet outside the tent.

Homer Crawford had assimilated the situation before the rest. He, too, was darting for the tent entrance, only feet behind Moroka.

Donaldson followed, muttering bitterly under his breath, his face twisted more as though in distaste than in fighting anger.

Cliff, too, finally saw light and dashed after the others, leaving only Isobel and the Peters brothers. They heard the muffled coughing of a silenced gun, twice, thrice and then half a dozen times, blurting together in automatic fire.

Homer Crawford shuffled through the sand on an awkward run, rounding the tent, weapon in hand.

There was a native on the ground making final spasmatic muscular movements in his death throes, and not more than three feet from him, coolly, David Moroka sat, bracing his elbows on his knees and aiming, two-handed, as his gun emptied itself.

Crawford brought his own gun up, seeking the target, and clipping at the same time, "We want him alive —"

It was too late. Two hundred feet beyond, a running tribesman, long arm dagger still in hand, stumbled, ran another three or four feet with hesitant steps, and then collapsed.

Moroka said, "Too late, Crawford. He would have got away." The South African started to his feet, brushing sand from his khaki bush shorts.

The others were beginning to come up and from the Tuareg encampment a rush of Gué-mama's men started in their direction.

Crawford said unhappily, looking down at the dead native at their feet, "I hate to see un-necessary killing."

Moroka looked at him questioningly. "Unnecessary? Another split second and his knife would have been in your gizzard. What do you want to give him, another chance?"

Crawford said uncomfortably, "Thanks, Dave, anyway. That was quick thinking."

"Thank God," Donaldson said, coming up, his wrinkled face scowling unhappily, first at the dead man at their feet, and then at the one almost a hundred yards away. "Are these local men? Where were your bodyguards?"

Cliff Jackson skidded to a halt, after rounding the tent. He'd heard only the last words. "What bodyguards?" he said.

Moroka looked at Crawford accusingly. "El Hassan," he said. "Leader of all North Africa. And you haven't even got around to bodyguards? Do you fellows think you're playing children's games? Gentlemen, I assure you, the chips are down."

VI

El Hassan's Tuaregs were on the move. After half a century and more of relative peace the Apaches of the Sahara, the Sons of Shaitan and the Forgotten of Allah were again disappearing into the ergs to emerge here, there, and ghostlike to disappear again. They faded in and faded away again, and even in their absence dominated all.

El Hassan was on the move, as all men by now knew, and he, who was not for the amalgamation of all North Africa, was judged against him. And who, in the Sahara, could afford to be against El Hassan when his Tuaregs were everywhere?

Refugees poured into Tamanrasset for the security of Arab Legion arms, or into In Salah and Reggan to the north, or Agades and Zinder to the south. Refugees who had already taken their stand with the Arab Union and Pan-Islam. Refugees who were men of property and would know more of this El Hassan before risking their wealth. Refugees who took no stand, but dreaded those who drank the milk of war, no matter the cause for which they fought. Refugees who fled simply because others fled, for terror is a most contagious disease.

Colonel Midan Ibrahim of the crack motorized units of the Arab Legion which occupied Tamanrasset, was fuming. His task was a double one. First, to hold Tamanrasset and its former French stronghold Fort Laperrine; second, to keep open his lines of communication with Ghademès and Ghat, in Arab Union dominated Libya. To hold them until further steps were decided upon by his superiors in Cairo and the Near East-whatever these steps might be. Colonel Midan Ibrahim was too low in the Arab Union hierarchy to be in on such privy matters.

His original efforts, in pushing across the Sahara from Ghademès and Ghat, had been no more than desert maneuvers. There had been no force other than nature's to say him nay. The Reunited Nations was an organization composed possibly of great powers, but in supposedly acting in unison they became a shrieking set of hair-tearing women; the whole being less than any of its individual parts. And El Hassan? No more than a rumor. In fact, an asset because this supposed mystery man of the desert, bent on uniting all North Africa under his domination, gave the Arab Union, its alibi for stepping in with Colonel Ibrahim's men.

Yes, the original efforts had been but a drill. But now his Arab Legion troopers were beginning to face reality. The supply trucks, coming down under convoy from Ghademès, reported the water source at Ohanet destroyed. The major well would take a week or more to repair. Who had committed the sabotage? Some said the Tuareg, some said local followers of El Hassan, others, desert tribesmen resentful of *both* the Arab Union and El Hassan.

One of his routine patrols, feeling out toward Meniet to the north, had suddenly dropped radio communication, almost in mid-sentence. A relieving patrol had thus far found nothing, the armored car's tracks covered over by the sands.

And rumors, rumors, rumors, Colonel Midan Ibrahim, born of aristocratic Alexandrian blood, though trained to a sharp edge in Near Eastern warfare, was basically city bred. The gloss of desert training might take on him, but the bedouin life itself was not in his experience, and it was hard for him to trace the dividing line between possibility and fantasy.

Rumors, rumors, rumors. They seemed capable of sweeping from one end of the Sahara to the other in a matter of hours. Faster, it would seem than the information could be dispensed by radio. El Hassan was here. El Hassan was there. El Hassan was marching on Rabat, in

Morocco; El Hassan had just signed a treaty with the Soviet Complex; El Hassan had been assassinated by a disgruntled follower. Or El Hassan was a renegade Christian; El Hassan was a Moslem of Sheriffian blood, a direct descendant of the Prophet; El Hassan was a pagan come up from Dahomey and practiced ritual cannibalism; El Hassan was a Jew, a veteran of the Israel debacle.

But this Colonel Ibrahim knew-the Tuareg had gone over to the new movement en masse. Something there was in El Hassan and his dream that had appealed to the Forgotten of Allah. The Tuareg, for the first time since the French Camel Corps had broken their strength, were united-united and on the move.

The Tuareg were everywhere. In most sinister fashion-everywhere. And all were El Hassan's men.

Colonel Ibrahim fumed and wondered what kept his superiors from sending in additional columns, additional armored elements. And, above all, adequate air cover. Ha! Give the colonel sufficient aircraft and he'd begin snuffing out bedouin life like candles-and bring the Peace of Allah to the Ahaggar.

So Colonel Ibrahim fumed, demanded further orders from mum superiors, and put his legionnaires to work on bigger and better gun emplacements, trenches and pillboxes surrounding Fort Laperinne and Tamanrasset.

E

l Hassan's personal entourage numbered exactly twenty persons. Of these, five were his immediate English-speaking, Western-educated supporters, Cliff, Isobel and the new Jack and Jimmy Peters and Dave Moroka. Rex Donaldson had been sent south again to operate in Senegal and Mali, to take over direction of the rapidly spreading movement in such centers as Bamako and Mopti and later, if possible, in Dakar.

The other fifteen were carefully selected Tuareg, picked from among Guémama's tribesmen taking care to show no preference to any tribe or clan, and taking particular care to choose men who fought coolly, unexcitedly, and didn't froth at the mouth when in action; men who were slow to charge wildly into the enemy's guns-but slower still to retreat when the going was hot. El Hassan was prone to neither hero nor coward in his personal bodyguard.

They kept under movement. In Abelessa one day, almost in range of the mobile artillery of the Arab Legion; in Timassao the next, checking the wells that meant everything to a desert force; the following day as far south as the Tamesna region to rally the less warlike Irreguenaten, a half-breed Tuareg people largely held in scorn by those of the Ahaggar.

Homer Crawford was killing time whilst stirring up as much noise and dust as his handful of followers could manage. Killing time until Elmer Allen from the Chaambra country, Bey-ag-Akhamouk from the Teda, and Kenny Ballalou from the west could show up with their columns. He had no illusions of how things now stood. At best, he could hold together a thousand Tuareg fighting men. No more. The economics of desert life prevented him a larger force, unless he had the resources of the modern world at hand, and he didn't. Besides that, the Tuareg confederation could provide no larger number of fighting men and at the same time continue their desert economy.

He stood now with Isobel, Cliff and Dave Moroka in one of the western type tents which the Peters brothers had brought with them in their hover-lorries, and poured over the half-adequate maps which covered the area.

Dave Moroka traced with a finger. "If we could dominate these wells running to Djanet, our Arab Union friends would have only their one line of supply going through Temassinine to Ghademès. That's a long haul, Homer."

Homer Crawford scowled thoughtfully. "That involves only four wells. If Ibrahim's legionnaires staked out only three armored vehicles at each water hole, they could hold them. Our camelmen could never take armor."

Moroka frowned, too. "We've got to start *some* sort of action, or the men will start dribbling away."

Cliff Jackson said, "Bey and Kenny and Elmer should be coming soon. I heard a radio item this morning about a big pro-El Hassan movement starting in the Sudan among the Teda."

Moroka said, "We need some sort of quick, spectacular victory. The bedouin can lose interest as quickly as they can get steamed up, and thus far we haven't given them anything but words-promises."

"You're right," Homer growled, "but there's nothing we can do right now but mark time. Irritate the Arabs a bit. Keep them from spreading out."

Isobel brought coffee, handing around the small Moroccan cups. She said, "Well, one thing is certain. We get supplies soon or start eating jerked goat and camel milk curds."

Moroka said in irritation, "It's not funny."

Isobel raised her eyebrows. "I didn't mean it to be. Have you ever been on a camel curd diet?"

"Yes, I have," Moroka said impatiently. He turned back to Homer Crawford. "How about waylaying an armored car or so, just in the way of giving the men something exciting to do?"

Crawford ran a hand back through his short hair. "Confound it, Dave, can you picture what a Recoilless-Brenn gun would do to a harka of our charging camelmen? We can't let these people be butchered."

"I wasn't thinking of wild charges," Moroka argued.

They had both turned away from Isobel, in their discussion. Now she looked at them, strangely. And especially at Homer Crawford. His brusqueness toward her didn't seem the old Homer.

* * * * *

There was a bustle from outside and a guardsman stuck his head in the tent entrance and reported in Tamaheq that a small camel patrol approached.

The four of them went out. Coming up were a dozen Tuareg and two motor vehicles.

Cliff said, "Something new."

Moroka said, "We can use the transport."

"Let's see who they are, before we start requisitioning their property," Homer said dryly.

The two desert trucks had hardly come to a halt before the camouflaged tents and hover-lorries of El Hassan's small encampment before a heavy-set, gray haired Negro, whose energy belied his weight, bounced down from the seat adjacent to the driver's in the lead vehicle and stomped belligerently to the group before the tent.

"What is the meaning of this?" he snapped.

Homer Crawford looked at him. "I'm sure I don't know as yet, Dr. Smythe. Neither you nor these followers of mine have informed me as to what has transpired. Won't you enter my quarters here and we'll go into it under more comfortable conditions?" He glanced upward at the midday Saharan sun.

The other seemed taken aback at Crawford calling him by name. He squinted at the man who was seemingly his captor.

"Crawford!" he snapped. "Dr. Homer Crawford! See here, what is the meaning of this?"

Homer said, "Dr. Warren Harding Smythe, may I present Isobel Cunningham, Clifford Jackson and David Moroka, of my staff?"

"Huuump. I met Miss Cunningham and, I believe, Mr. Jackson at that ridiculous meeting in Timbuktu, a short time ago." The doctor peered over his glasses at Moroka.

The wiry South African nodded his head. "A pleasure, Doctor." He held open the tent entrance.

Smythe snorted again and stomped inside to escape the sun's glare.

In the shade of the tent's interior, Isobel clucked at him and hurried to get a drink of water from a moist water cooler. Homer Crawford motioned the other to a seat, and took one himself. "Now then, Dr. Smythe."

The indignant medic blurted, "Those confounded bandits out there —"

"Irregular camel cavalry," Crawford amended gently.

"They've kidnapped me and my staff. I demand that you intercede, if you have any influence with them."

"What were you doing?" Crawford was frowning at the other. Actually, he had no idea of the circumstances under which the probably overenthusiastic Tuareg troopers had rounded up the American medical man.

"Doing? You know perfectly well I represent the American Medical Relief. My team has been in the vicinity of Silet, working with the nomads. The country is rife with everything from rickets to syphilis! Eighty per cent of these people suffer from trachoma. My team —"

"Just a moment," Moroka said. "You mean out in those two trucks you have a complete American medical setup? Assistants and all?"

Smythe said stiffly, "I have two American nurses with me and four Algerians recruited in Oran. This sort of interference with my work is insufferable and —"

The South African was staring at Homer Crawford.

Cliff Jackson cleared his throat. "It seems as though El Hassan has just acquired a Department of Health."

"El Hassan?" Smythe stuttered. "What, what?"

Isobel said softly, "Dr. Smythe, surely you have heard of El Hassan."

"Heard of him? I've heard of nothing else for the past month! Confounded ignorant barbarian. What this part of the world needs is *less* intertribal, interracial, international fighting, not more. The man's a raving lunatic and —"

Isobel said gently, "Doctor ... may I introduce you to El Hassan?"

"What ... what —?" For the briefest of moments, there was an element of timorness in the sputtering doctor's voice. Then suddenly he comprehended.

He pointed at Homer Crawford accusingly. "You're El Hassan!"

Homer nodded, seriously, "That's correct, Doctor."

The doctor's eyes went around the four of them. "You've done what you were driving at there at that meeting in Timbuktu. You're trying to unite these people in spite of themselves and then drag them, willy-nilly, into the twentieth century."

Homer still nodded.

Smythe shook an indignant finger at him. "I told you then, Crawford, and I tell you now. These natives are not suited for such sudden change. Already they are subject to mass neurosis because they cannot adjust to a world that changes too quickly."

"I wonder if that doesn't apply to the rest of us as well," Cliff said unhappily. "But the changes go on, if we like them or not. Can you think of any way to turn them off?"

The doctor snorted.

Homer Crawford said, "Dr. Smythe, the die is already cast. The question now becomes, will you join us?"

"Join you! Certainly not!"

Crawford said evenly, "Then I might suggest that, first, you will not be allowed to operate in my territory." He considered for a moment, grinning inwardly, but on the surface his expression serene. He added, "And second, that you will probably have difficulties procuring an exit visa from my domains."

"Exit visa! Are you jesting? See here, my good man, you realize I am a citizen of the United States of the Americas and —"

"A country," Homer yawned, "with which I have not as yet opened diplomatic relations, and hence has little representation in North Africa."

The doctor was bug-eying him. He began sputtering again. "This isn't funny. You're an American citizen yourself. And you, Miss Cunningham and —"

Isobel said sadly, "As a matter of fact, the last we heard, the State Department representative told us our passports were invalid."

Crawford leaned forward. "Look here, Doctor. You don't see eye to eye with us on matters socio-economic. However, as a medical man, I submit that joining my group ... ah, that is, until you can secure an exit visa from my authorities ... will give you an excellent opportunity to practice your science here in the Sahara under the wing of El Hassan. I'll assign a place for your trucks and tents. Please consider the question and let me have your answer at your leisure. Meanwhile, we will prepare a desert feast suitable to the high esteem in which we hold you."

* * * * *

They looked after the doctor, as he left, and Moroka chuckled. However, Isobel was watching Homer Crawford quizzically.

She said finally, "We rode over him a little in the roughshod manner, didn't we?"

Homer Crawford growled uncomfortably, "Particularly when we finally have our showdown with the Arab Legion, a medic will be priceless."

Isobel said softly, "And the end justifies the means —"

Homer shot a quick, impatient look at her. "The good doctor and his people are in the Sahara to work with the Tuareg and the Teda and the rest of the bedouin. Beyond that, he has the same dream we have-of developing this continent of our racial background."

"But he doesn't believe in your methods, Homer, and we're forcing him to follow El Hassan's road in spite of his beliefs."

Moroka had been peering at the two of them narrowly. "You don't make omelets without breaking eggs," he said, his voice on the overbearing side.

She spun on him. "But the omelets don't turn out so well if some of the eggs you use are rotten."

The South African's voice turned gentle. "Miss Cunningham," he said, "working in the field, like this, can have its rugged side for a young and delicate woman —"

"*Delicate!*" she snapped. "I'll have you know —"

"Hey, everybody, hold it," Cliff injected. "What goes on?"

Dave Moroka shrugged. "It just seems to me that Isobel might do better back in Dakar, or in New York with your friend Jake Armstrong. Somewhere where her sensibilities wouldn't be so bruised, and where her assets" —his eyes went up and down her lithe body —"could be put to better use."

Isobel's sepia face had gone a shade or more lighter. She said, very flatly, "My assets, Mr. Moroka, are in my head."

Homer Crawford said disgustedly, "O.K., O.K., let's all knock it off."

His eyes flicked back and forth between them, in definite command. "I don't want to hear any more in the way of personalities between you two."

Moroka shrugged again. "Yes, sir," he said without inflection.

Isobel turned away and took up some paperwork, without further words. She suppressed her feeling of seething indignation.

Homer Crawford, under his pressures, was changing. Possibly, she had told herself before, it was change for the better. The need was for a *strong* man, perhaps even a ruthless one.

The Homer Crawford she had first known was an easier going man than he who had snapped an abrupt order to her a moment ago. The Homer she had first known requested things of his teammates and friends. El Hassan had learned to command.

The Homer she had first known could never have ridden, roughshod, over the basically gentle Dr. Smythe.

The Homer she had first known, when the El Hassan scheme was still aborning, had thought of himself as a member of a team. He was quick to ask advice of all, and quick to take it if it had validity. Now Homer, as El Hassan, was depending less and less upon the opinions of those surrounding him, more and more upon his own decisions which he seemed to sometimes reach purely through intuition.

The El Hassan dream was still upon her, but, womanlike, she wondered if she liked the would-be tyrant of all North Africa as well as she had once liked the easy-going American idealist, Homer Crawford.

Jack and Jimmy Peters, the brothers from Trinidad, entered, the former carrying a couple of books.

They'd evidently failed to note the raised voices and wore their customary serious expressions. Jack looked at Homer and said, "*Cu vi scias Esperanton?*"

Homer Crawford's eyebrows went up but he said, "*Jes, mi parolas Esperanto tre bona, mi pensas.*"

"*Bona,*" Jack said, "*Tre bona.*"

"*Jes, estas bele,*" his brother said.

Moroka was scowling back and forth from one of them to the other. "I thought I had a fairly good working knowledge of the world's more common languages," he said, "but that goes by me. It sounds like a cross between Italian and pig-Latin."

Homer said to the Peters brothers, "Let's drop Esperanto so that Dave, Isobel and Cliff can follow us. We can give it a whirl later, if you'd like, just for the practice."

Isobel said slowly, "*Mi parolas Esperanto, malgranda.*" Then in English, "I took it for kicks while I was still in school. Kind of rusty now, though."

"Esperanto?" Cliff said. "You mean that gobblydygook so-called international language?"

Jack Peters looked at him, serious faced as always. "What is wrong with an international language, Mr. Jackson?"

Cliff was taken aback. "Search me. But it doesn't seem to have proved very practical. It didn't catch on."

"Well, more than you might think," Isobel told him. "There are probably hundreds of thousands of persons in one part of the world or another who can get along in Esperanto."

Moroka said impatiently, "What're a few hundred thousands of people in a world population like ours? Cliff's right. It never took hold."

Homer said, "All right, Jack and Jimmy. You boys evidently have something on your minds. Let everybody sit down and listen to it."

* * * * *

Even before they got thoroughly settled, Jack Peters was launching into his pitch.

"We need an official language," he said. "The El Hassan movement has set as a goal the uniting of all North Africa. We might start here in the Sahara, but it's just a start. Ultimately, the idea is to reach from Morocco to Egypt and from the Mediterranean to ... to where? The Congo?"

"Actually, we've never set exact limits," Homer said.

"Ultimately *all Africa*," Dave Moroka muttered softly. He ignored the manner in which Isobel contemplated him from the side of her eyes.

"All right," the West Indian said. "There are more than seven hundred major languages, not counting dialects, in Africa. Sooner or later, we need an official language, what is it going to be?"

"Why *one* official language? Why not several?" Cliff scowled. "Say Arabic, here in this area. Swahili on the East coast. And, say, Songhoi along the Niger, and Wolof, the Senegalese lingua franca, and —"

"You see," Peters interrupted. "Already you have half a dozen and you haven't even got out of this immediate vicinity as yet. Let me develop my point."

186

Homer Crawford was becoming interested. "Go on, Jack," he said.

Jack Peters pointed a finger at him. "To be the hero-symbol we have in mind, El Hassan is going to have to be able to communicate with *all* of his people. He's not going to be able to speak Arabic to, say, a Masai in Kenya. They hate the Arabs. He's not going to be able to speak Swahili to a Moroccan, they've never heard of the language. He can't speak Tamaheq to the Imraguen, they're scared to death of the Tuareg."

Homer said thoughtfully, "A common language would be fine. It'd solve a lot of problems. But it doesn't seem to be in the cards. Why not adopt as our official language the one in which the *most* of our people will be able to communicate? Say, Arabic?"

Jack was shaking his head seriously. "And antagonize all the Arab hating Bantu in Africa? It's no go, Homer."

"Well, then, say French-or English."

"English is the most international language in the world," Moroka said. But his face was thoughtful, as those of the others were becoming.

The West Indian was beginning to make his points now. "No, any of the European languages are out. The white man has been repudiated. Adopting English, French, Spanish, Portuguese or Dutch, as our official language would antagonize whole sections of the continent."

"Why Esperanto?" Cliff scowled. "Why not, say, Nov-Esperanto, or Ido, or Interlingua?"

Jimmy Peters put in a word now. "Actually, any one of them would possibly do, but we have a head start with Esperanto. Some years ago both Jack and I became avid Esperantists, being naïve enough in those days to think an international language would ultimately solve all man's problems. And both Homer and Isobel seem to have a working knowledge of the language."

Homer said, "So have the other members of my former Reunited Nations team. That's where those books you found came from. Elmer, Bey, Kenny ... and Abe ... and I used to play around with it when we were out in the desert, just to kill time. We also used it as sort of a secret language when we wanted to communicate and didn't know if those around us might understand some English."

"I still don't get the picture," Cliff argued. "If we picked the most common half a dozen languages in the territory we cover, then millions of these people wouldn't have to study a second language. But if you adapt Esperanto as an official language then *everybody* is going to have to learn something new. And that's not going to be easy for our ninety-five per cent illiterate followers."

Isobel said thoughtfully, "Well, it's a darn sight easier to learn Esperanto than any other language we decided to make official."

"Why?" Cliff said argumentatively.

* * * * *

Jack Peters took over. "Because it's almost unbelievably easy to learn. English, by the way, is extremely difficult. For instance, spelling and pronunciation are absolutely phonetic in Esperanto and there are only five vowel sounds where most national languages have twenty or so. And each sound in the alphabet has one sound only and any sound is always rendered by the same letter."

Dave Moroka said, "Actually, I don't know anything at all about this Esperanto."

The West Indian took him in, with a dominating glance. "Take grammar and syntax which can take up volumes in other languages. Esperanto has exactly sixteen short rules. And take vocabularies. For instance, in English we often form the feminine of a noun by adding *ess-actor-actress, tiger-tigress*. But not always. We don't say *bull-bulless* or *ghost-ghostess*. In Esperanto you simply add the feminine ending to any noun-there's no exception to any rule."

Jack Peters was caught up in his subject. "Still comparing it to English, realize that spelling and pronunciation in English are highly irregular and one letter can have several different sounds, and one sound may be represented by different letters. And there are even silent letters which are written but not pronounced like the *ugh* in *though*. There are none of these irregularities in Esperanto. And the sounds are all sharp with none of such subtle differences as, say, *bed/bad/bard/bawd*, that sort of thing."

Jimmy Peters said, "The big item is that any averagely intelligent person can begin speaking Esperanto within a few hours. Within a week of even moderate study, say three or four hours a day, he's astonishingly fluent."

Isobel said thoughtfully, "There'd be international advantages. It's always been a galling factor in Africans dealing with Europeans that they had to learn the European language involved. You couldn't expect your white man to learn kitchen kaffir, or Swahili, or whatever, not when you got on the diplomatic level."

Cliff Jackson was thinking out loud. "So far, El Hassan is an unknown. Rumor has it that he's everything from a renegade Egyptian, to an escaped Mau-Mau chief, to a Senegalese sergeant formerly in the French West African forces. But when he starts running into the press and they find that Homer and his closest associates all speak English, and most of them with an American accent, there's going to be some fat in the fire."

"And El Hassan will have lost some of his mysterious glamour," Homer added thoughtfully.

Even Moroka, the South African, was beginning to accept the idea. "If El Hassan, himself, refused in the presence of foreigners ever to speak anything but Esperanto, the aura of mystery would continue."

Jimmy Peters, elaborating and obviously pushing an opinion he and his brother had already discussed, said, "We make it a rule that every school, both locally taught and foreign, must teach Esperanto as a required subject. All El Hassan governmental affairs would be conducted in that language. Anybody at all trying to get anywhere in the new regime would have to learn the official inter-African tongue."

"Oh, brother," Cliff groaned, "that means me." He brightened. "We haven't any books or anything, as yet."

Isobel laughed at him. "I'll take on your studies, Cliff. We have a few books. Those that Homer and his team used to kill time with. And as soon as we're in a position to make requests for foreign aid of the great powers, Esperanto grammars, dictionaries and so forth can be high on the list."

With a sharp cry, almost a bark, a figure jumped into the entrance and with a bound into the center of the tent, sub-machinegun in hand. *"All right, everybody. On your feet. The place is raided!"*

Dave Moroka leaped to his feet, his hand tearing with blurring speed for his holstered hand gun. "Where's that bodyguard?" he yelled.

VII

Hold it," Homer Crawford roared, jumping to his own feet and grabbing the South African in his arms. He glared at the newcomer. "Kenny, you idiot, you're lucky you don't have a couple of holes in you."

Kenny Ballalou, grinning widely, stared at Dave Moroka. "Jeepers," he said, "you got that gun out fast. Don't you ever stick 'em up when somebody has the drop on you?"

Dave Moroka relaxed, the side arm dropping back into its holster. Homer Crawford released him and the South African ran a hand over his mouth and shook his head ruefully at Kenny.

Isobel and Cliff crowded up, the one to kiss Kenny happily, the other to pound him on the back.

Homer made introductions to Dave Moroka and the Peters brothers.

"I've told you about Kenny," he wound it up. "I sent him over to the west to raise a harka of Nemadi to help in taking Tamanrasset." He joined Cliff Jackson in giving the smaller man an affectionate blow on the shoulder. "What luck did you have, Kenny?"

Kenny Ballalou rubbed himself ruefully. "If you two will stop beating, I'll tell you. I didn't recruit a single Nemadi."

Homer Crawford looked at him.

Kenny said to the tent at large. "Anybody got a drink around here? Good grief, have I been covering ground."

Isobel bustled off to a corner where she'd amassed most of their remaining European type supplies, but she kept her attention on him.

Dave Moroka said, his voice unbelieving, "You mean you haven't brought any assistance *at all?*"

Kenny grinned around at them. "I didn't say that. I said I didn't recruit any of the Nemadi. I never even got as far as their territory."

Homer Crawford sank back onto the small crate he'd been using as a chair before Kenny's precipitate entrance. "O.K.," he said, "stop dramatizing and let us know what happened."

Kenny spread his hands in a sweeping gesture. "The country's alive from here to Bidon Cinq and south to the Niger. Bourem and Gao have gone over to El Hassan and a column of followers was descending on Niamey. They should be there by now. I never got as far as Nemadi country. I could have recruited ten thousand fighting men, but I didn't know what we'd do with them in this country. So I weeded through everybody who volunteered and took only veterans. Men who'd formerly been in the French forces, or British, or whatever. Louis Wallington and his team were in Bourem when I got there and —"

"Who is Louis Wallington?" Jack Peters said.

Homer looked over at the Peters brothers and Dave Moroka. "Head of a six-man Sahara Development Project team like the one I used to head." His eyes went back to Kenny. "What about Louis?"

"He's come in with us. Didn't know how to get in touch, so he was working on his own. And Pierre Dupaine. Remember him, the fellow from Guadeloupe in the French West Indies, used to be an operative of the African Affairs sector of the French Community? Well, he and a half dozen of his colleagues have come in and were leading an expedition on Timbuktu. But Timbuktu had already joined up too, before they got there —"

"Wow," Homer said. "It's really spreading."

Cliff said, "Why isn't all this on the radio?"

Isobel had brought Kenny a couple of ounces of cognac from their meager supply. He knocked it back thankfully.

Kenny said to Cliff, "Things are moving too fast, and communications have gone to pot." He looked at Homer. "Have any of these journalists found you yet?"

"What journalists?"

Kenny laughed. "You'll find out. Half the newspapers, magazines, newsreels and TV outfits in the world are sending every man they can release into this area. They're going batty trying to find El Hassan. Man, do you realize the extent of the country your followers now dominate?"

Homer said blankly, "I hadn't thought of it. Besides, most of what you've been saying is news to us here. We've been keeping on the prod."

Kenny grinned widely. "Well, the nearest I can figure it, El Hassan is ruler of an area about the size of Mexico. At least it was yesterday. By today, you can probably tack on Texas."

Jimmy Peters, serious faced as usual, said, "Things are moving so fast, we're going to have to run to keep ahead of El Hassan's followers. One thing, Homer, we're going to have to have a press secretary."

"Elmer Allen was going to handle that, but he's still up north," Isobel said.

"I'll do it. Used to be a newspaperman, when I was younger," Dave Moroka said quickly.

Isobel frowned and began to say something, but Homer said, "Great, you handle that, Dave." Then to Kenny, "Where're your men and how well are they armed?"

"Well, that's one trouble," Kenny said unhappily. "We requisitioned motor transport from some of the Sahara Afforestation Project oases down around Tessalit. In fact, Ralph Sandell, their chief mucky-muck in those parts, has come over to us. But we haven't got much in the way of shooting irons."

Homer Crawford closed his eyes wearily. "What it boils down to, still, is that a hundred of those Arab Legionnaires, with their armor, could finish us all off in ten minutes if it came to open battle."

* * * * *

El Hassan continued moving his headquarters, usually daily, but he eluded the journalists only another twelve hours. Then they were upon the mobile camp like locusts.

And David Moroka took over with a calm efficiency that impressed all. In the first place, he explained, El Hassan was much too busy to handle the press except for one conference a week. In the second place, he spoke only Esperanto to foreigners. Meanwhile, he, Dave Moroka, would handle all their questions, make arrangements for suitable photographs, and for the TV and newsreel boys to trundle their equipment as near the front lines as possible. And, meanwhile, James and John Peters of El Hassan's staff had prepared press releases covering the El Hassan movement and its program.

Homer, to the extent possible, was isolated from the new elements descending upon his encampment. Attempting anything else would have been out of the question. At this point, he was getting approximately four hours of sleep a night.

Kenny Ballalou was continually coming and going in a mad attempt to handle the logistics of supplying several thousand men in a desert area all but devoid of either water or graze, not to speak of food, petroleum products and ammunition.

Isobel and Cliff were thrown into the positions of combination secretaries, ministers of finance, assistant bodyguards, and all else that nobody else seemed to handle, *including* making coffee.

It was Isobel who approached a subject which had long worried her, as they drove across country, the only occupants of one of the original hover-lorries, during a camp move.

She said, hesitantly, "Homer, is it a good idea to give Dave such a free hand with the press? You know, there are some fifty or so of them around now and they must be influencing the TV, radio, magazines and newspapers of the world."

"He seems to know more about it than any of the rest of us," Homer said, his eyes on the all but sand-obliterated way. "We're going to have to move more of the men south. We simply haven't got water enough for them. There'd be enough in Tamanrasset, but not out here. Make a note to cover this with Kenny. I wonder where Bey is, and Elmer."

Isobel made a note. She said, "Yes, but the trouble is, he's a comparative newcomer. Are you *sure* he's in complete accord with the original plan, Homer? Does the El Hassan dream mean the same to him as it does to you, and ... well, me?"

He shot her an impatient glance, even as he hit the lift lever to raise them over a small dune. "You and Dave don't hit it off very well. He's a good man, so far as I can see."

Her delicate forehead wrinkled and her pixie face showed puzzlement. "I don't know why. I get along with most people, Homer."

He patted her hand. "You can't please everybody, Isobel. Listen, something's got to be done about this king-size mob of camp followers we've got. Did you know Common Europe sent in a delegation this morning?"

"Delegation? Common Europe —?"

"Yeah. Haven't had time to discuss it with you. They found us just before we raised camp. Evidently, the British Commonwealth and possibly the Soviet Complex-some Chinese, I think-are also trying to locate us. Half of these people are without their own equipment and supplies, but that's not what worries me right now. We used to be able to camouflage our headquarters camp. Dig into the desert and avoid the aircraft. But if a group of bungling Common Market diplomats can locate us, what's to keep the Arab Legion from doing it and blessing us with a stick of neopalm bombs?"

Isobel said, "Look, before we leave Dave. Did you know he was confiscating all radio equipment brought into our camp by the newsmen and whoever else?"

Homer frowned. "Well, why?"

"Espionage, Dave says. He's afraid some of these characters might be in with the Arab Union and inform on us."

"Well, that makes some sense," Homer nodded.

"Does it?" Isobel grumbled.

He shot an irritated glance at her again and said impatiently, "Can't the poor guy do anything right?"

"My woman's intuition is working," Isobel grumbled.

* * * * *

Dave Moroka came into headquarters tent without introduction. He was one of the half dozen who had permission for this. He had a sheaf of papers in his left hand and was frowning unhappily.

"What's the crisis?" Homer said.

"Scouts coming up say your pal Bey-ag-Akhamouk is on the way. Evidently, with a big harka of Teda from the Sudan."

"Great." Homer crowed. "Now we'll get going."

"Ha!" Dave said. "From what we hear, a good many are camel mounted. How are we going to feed them? Already some of the Songhai Kenny brought up from the south have drifted away, unhappy about supplies."

"Bey's a top man," Homer told him. "The best. He'll have some ideas on our tactics. Meanwhile, we can turn over most of his men to one of the new recruits, and head them down to take Fort Lamy. With Fort Lamy and Lake Chad in our hands we'll control a chunk of Africa so big everybody else will start wondering why they shouldn't jump on the bandwagon while the going is good."

Dave said, "Well, that brings up something else, Homer. These new recruits. In the past couple of days, forty or fifty men who used to be connected with African programs sponsored by everybody from the Reunited Nations to this gobblydygook outfit Cliff and Isobel once worked for, the AFAA, have come over to El Hassan. The number will probably double by tomorrow, and triple the next day."

"Fine," Homer said. "What's wrong with that? These are the people that will really count in the long run."

"Nothing's wrong with it, within reason. But we're going to have to start becoming selective, Homer. We've got to watch what jobs we let these people have, how much responsibility we give them."

Homer Crawford was frowning at him. "How do you mean?"

"See here," the wiry South African said plaintively, "when El Hassan started off there were only a half dozen or so who had the dream, as you call it. O.K. You could trust any one of them. Bey, Kenny, Elmer, Cliff, this Jake Armstrong that you've sent to New York, Rex Donaldson, then Jimmy and Jack Peters and myself. We all came in when the going was rough, if not impossible. But now things are different. *It looks as though El Hassan might actually win.*"

"So?" Homer didn't get it.

"So from now on, you're going to have an infiltration of cloak and dagger lads from every outfit with an interest in North Africa. Potential traitors, potential assassins, subversives and what not."

Homer was scowling at him. "Confound it, what do you suggest? That these Johnny-Come-Latelies be second-class citizens?"

"Not exactly that, but this isn't funny. We've got to screen them. The trouble with this movement is that it's a one-man deal, and has to be. The average African is either a barbarian or an actual savage, one ethnic degree lower. He wants a hero-symbol to follow. O.K., you're it. But remember both Moctezuma and Atahualpa. Their socio-economic systems pyramided up to them. The Spanish conquistadores, being old hands at sophisticated European-type intrigue, quickly sized up the situation. They kidnaped the hero-symbol, the big cheese, and later killed him. And the Inca and the Aztec cultures collapsed."

Homer was scowling at him unhappily.

Dave summed it up. "All we need is one fuzzy minded commie from the Soviet Complex, or one super-dooper democrat who thinks that El Hassan stands in the way of *freedom*, whatever that is, and bingo a couple of bullets in your tummy and the El Hassan movement folds its tents like the Arabs and takes a powder, as the old expression goes."

"You have your point," Homer Crawford admitted. "Follow through, Dave. Figure out some screening program."

* * * * *

Cliff came in. "Hey, Homer. Guess what old Jake has done."

"Jake Armstrong?"

"He's swung the Africa for Africans Association in New York over to us. They've raised a million bucks. What'll we do with it? How can he get anything to us?"

"We'll have him plow it back into publicity and further fund raising campaigns," Homer said. "That's the way it's done. You raise some money for some cause and then spend it all on a bigger campaign to raise still more money, and what you get from that one you plow into a still bigger campaign."

Cliff said, "Don't you *ever* get anything out of it?"

Dave and Homer both laughed.

Cliff said, "I've got some still better news."

"Good news, we can use," Homer said.

* * * * *

The big Californian looked at him in pretended awe. "A poet no less," he said.

"Shut up," Homer said. "What's the news?"

The fact of the matter was, he was becoming increasingly impatient of the continual banter expected of him by Cliff and even the others. As original members of the team, they expected an intimacy that he was finding it increasingly difficult to deliver. Among other things, he wished that Cliff, in particular, would mind his attitude when such followers as Guémama were present. The El Hassan posture could be maintained only in never to be compromised dignity.

Bey had once compared him to Alexander, to Homer's amusement at the time. But now he was beginning to sympathize with the position the Macedonian leader had found himself in, betwixt the King-God conscious Persians, and the rough and ready Companions who formed his bodyguard and crack cavalry units. A King-God simply didn't banter with his subordinates, not even his blood-kin.

Cliff scowled at him now, at the sharpness of Homer's words, but he made his report.

"Our old pal, Sven Zetterberg. He's gone out on a limb. Because of the great danger of this so-far localized fight spreading into world-wide conflict-says old Sven-the Reunited Nations will not tolerate the combat going into the air. He says that if *either* El Hassan or the Arab Legion resort to use of aircraft, the Reunited Nations will send in its air fleet."

"Wow," Homer said. "All the aircraft we've got are a few slow-moving heliocopters that Kenny brought up with him."

Dave Moroka snapped his fingers in a gesture of elation. "That means Zetterberg is throwing his weight to our side."

Homer was on his feet. "Send for Kenny and Guémama and send a heliocopter down to pick up Bey and rush him here. He shouldn't be more than a day's march away. I wonder what Elmer is up to. No word at all from him. At any rate, we want an immediate council of war. With Arab Legion air cover eliminated, we can move in."

Cliff said sourly, "It's still largely rifles against armored cars, tanks, mobile artillery and even flame throwers."

* * * * *

All the old hands were present. They stood about a map table, Homer and Bey-ag-Akhamouk at one end, the rest clustered about. Isobel sat in a chair to the rear, stenographer's pad on her knees.

Bey was clipping out suggestions.

"We have them now. Already our better trained men are heading up for Temassinine to the north and Fort Charlet to the east. We'll lose men but we'll knock out every water hole between here and Libya. We'll cut every road, blow what few bridges there are."

Jack Peters said worriedly, "But the important thing is Tamanrasset. What good —"

"We're cutting their supply line," Bey told him. "Can't you see? Colonel Ibrahim and his motorized column will be isolated in Tamanrasset. They won't be able to get supplies through without an air lift and Sven Zetterberg's ultimatum kills that possibility. They're blocked off."

Jimmy Peters was as confused as his brother. "So what? to use the Americanism. They have both food and water in abundance. They can hold out indefinitely. Meanwhile, our forces are undisciplined irregulars. We gain a thousand recruits a day. They come galloping in on camel-back or in beat-up old vehicles, firing their hunting rifles into the air. But we also lose a thousand a day. They get bored, or hungry, and decide to go back to their flocks, or their jobs on the new Sahara projects. At any rate, they drift off again. It looks to me that, if Colonel Ibrahim can hold out another week or so, our forces might melt away-all except the couple of hundred or so European and American educated followers. And, cut down to that number, they'll eliminate us in no time flat."

Homer Crawford was eying him in humor. "You're no fighting man, Peters. Tell me, what is the single most fearsome enemy of an ultra-mechanized soldier with the latest in military equipment and super-firepower weapons?"

Jimmy Peters was blank. "I suppose a similarly armed opponent."

Homer smiled at him. "Rather, a man with a knife."

The expressions of the Peters brothers showed resentment. "We weren't jesting."

"Neither was I," Homer rapped. He looked around at the rest, including Bey and Kenny. "What happens to a modern mechanized army when it runs out of gasoline? What happens to a water-cooled machine gun when there is no water? What use is a howitzer when the target is a single man in ten acres of cover? Gentlemen, have any of you ever studied the tactics of Abd-el-Krim or, more recently still, Tito? Bey, I assume you have."

He had their attention.

"During the Second War," Homer continued, "this Yugoslavian Tito tied up two Nazi army corps with a handful of partisans-guerrillas. The most modern army in the world, the German Panzers, tried to ferret him out for five years, and couldn't. There are other examples. The Chinese operating against the Japs in the same war. Or one of the classic examples is Abd-el-Krim destroying two different Spanish armies in the Moroccan Rif in the 1920s. His barefoot men, armed with rifles, took on Primo de Rivera's modernized Spanish armies and trounced them."

Bey said, "Homer's right. Our only tactics are guerrilla ones."

Homer Crawford looked at Guémama, who had been standing in the background, unfamiliar with the language these others spoke, but holding his dignity. Crawford said, diplomatically, "And what sayest thou, O chieftain of the Tuareg?"

Guémama was gratified at the attention. He said in Tamaheq, "As all men know, O El Hassan, we now outnumber by thrice the Arab *giaours* may they burn in Gehennum. Therefore, let us rush in and kill them all."

Bey shuddered.

Homer Crawford nodded seriously. "Ai, Guémama, that would be the valorous way of the Tuareg. But the heart of El Hassan forbids him to sacrifice the lives of his people. Consequently, we shall use the tactics of the desert jackal. Instruct those of your people who are most cunning, to infiltrate Tamanrasset in the night. Let them not carry arms for they may well be searched by the Arab *meleccha*."

The Tuareg chieftain was intrigued. "And what shall they do in Tamanrasset, El Hassan? Suddenly seize arms, one night, and rise up in wrath against the Arab dogs and kill them all?"

Homer was shaking his head. "They will address themselves to the Haratin serfs and spread to them the message of El Hassan. They will be told that in the world of El Hassan each man shall be free to seek his own destiny to the extent his mind and abilities allow. And no man shall be the less because he was born a serf, and no man the more because he was born to wealth or power in the old days."

"Aiii," Guémama all but moaned. "But such a message —"

"Is the message of El Hassan, as all men know," Homer Crawford said flatly. He turned to Kenny Ballalou. "Kenny, take over this angle. We want as many propagandists in that town as possible. It's already choked with refugees, most of them not knowing what they're fleeing. We might get recruits there, too. But mostly we want to appeal to the sedentary natives in town. They've got to get the dreams, too. Promise them schools, land ...I don't have to tell you."

"Right," Kenny said.

Isobel said, "Maybe I ought to get in on this, too. The women might do a better job than men on this slant. It's going to take a lot to get a Tuareg bedouin to sink to talking to a Haratin on an equal basis."

Bey and Homer had bent back over the maps, but before they could get back into the details of guerrilla warfare against Colonel Ibrahim and his legionnaires, they were halted by a controversy from without.

"What now?" Homer growled. "This camp is getting to be like a three-ring circus."

The entrance flap was pushed aside and three of Bey's Sudanese tribesmen half escorted, half pushed a newcomer front and center.

It was Fredric Ostrander, natty as usual, but now in khaki desert wear. He was obviously in a rage at the three rifle-carrying nomads who had him in charge.

Bey spoke to the Teda warriors in their own tongue. Then to Homer in Tamaheq, which he assumed the C.I.A. man didn't know, "They picked him up in the desert in a hover-jeep. He was evidently looking for our camp." He dismissed the three bedouin with a gesture.

Ostrander was outraged. He snapped at Homer Crawford, "I demand an explanation of this cavalier attack upon —"

His face expressionless, Homer held up a hand to quiet the smaller man. He looked at Jack Peters and raised his eyebrows. *Kion li la fremdul diras?*"

Jack, serious as ever, replied in Esperanto, then turned to the American C.I.A. man and said, "El Hassan has requested that I translate for him. He speaks only the official language of North Africa to foreign representatives. Undoubtedly, sir, you have proper credentials?"

Had Fredric Ostrander been of lighter complexion, his color would have undoubtedly gone dark red.

"Look here, Crawford," he snapped. "I'm in no mood for nonsense. The State Department has sent me to your headquarters to make another attempt to bring some sense home to you. As an American citizen, owing alliance —"

Homer Crawford spoke in Esperanto to Jack Peters who nodded seriously and said to Ostrander, "El Hassan informs you he owes alliance only to the people of North Africa whose chosen leader he is."

Ostrander knew they were kidding him, but at the same time the stand being taken was actuality. He glared at the Americans present whom he knew, Bey, Isobel, Cliff and Kenny. He snapped, "Very well, but I repeat what I told you when last we met. The State Department of the United States of the Americas will not stand idly by and see this area taken over by elements dominated by red subversives."

"Holy Mackerel," Cliff growled, "are you still tooting that horn?"

Dave Moroka said sarcastically, "It's an old wheeze. The definition of a red subversive is anybody who doesn't see eye to eye with the United States. They've been pulling the gag for decades. Remember Guatemala and Cuba? Do anything that interferes with American business abroad and the cry goes up, *he's an enemy of the free world!"*

Ostrander spun on him, his eyes narrowing.

Dave laughed. "The definition of members of the free world, of course, being anybody who follows the American line. Anybody is free, Spanish and Portuguese dictators, absolute monarchs in Arabia, Chinese warlords, if they're on the American side."

Ostrander snapped, "I don't believe we've met."

Moroka made a sweeping bow. "I'm afraid we don't move in the same circles. I've spent possibly a third of my life in prison —"

"Undoubtedly," Ostrander snorted.

"…Put there by people such as yourself-in various countries-because I was fighting for my own version of freedom."

"Communism, undoubtedly!"

Moroka said softly, "I'm a South African, sir. Both my parents were killed in the 1960 riots. It seems that they had dark skins-even as you and I —and weren't able to see why that should keep them from *freedom*."

Fredric Ostrander spun back to Homer Crawford. "I'm not here to quibble with self-confessed malcontents. I've been sent to represent the State Department, to report to them, and, above all, to do what I can to prevent your activities from redounding to the further advantage of the Soviet Complex. I assume you can assign me quarters."

Straight-faced, Jack Peters translated this into Esperanto, and, straight-faced, Homer answered in the same language.

Jack turned back to the impatient C.I.A. man. "El Hassan welcomes the representative of the United States of the Americas and hopes this will be the first step toward diplomatic recognition between North Africa and your great country. He has instructed me to find you quarters, which, possibly you may have to share with delegations from Common Europe or" —Peters cleared his throat —"the Soviet Complex. He further suggests that it might be well, if you maintain communications with your superiors, to have sent to you books on Esperanto, the official language of North Africa."

Dave Moroka put in, "By the way, we'll have to go through your things. We can't allow any radio communication from El Hassan's camp, except through official El Hassan channels-for obvious military reasons."

Ostrander snorted, stared indignantly at Homer again, spun on his heel and stalked from the tent. Jack Peters followed him but not before tipping an uncharacteristic wink at Homer.

When they were gone, Homer sighed and looked at Dave Moroka. "That reminds me, how are our other delegations coming?"

The South African grinned ruefully. "They're playing it cool. Waiting to see what way to jump. Give El Hassan some real success, and they'll probably jump at the chance to be first to recognize him. Especially these Soviet Complex opportunists. They'd just love to suck you into their camp."

Isobel looked at him. "After that tearing down you gave poor Ostrander about the United States, now you rip into the Soviet Complex. Just where do you stand, Dave?"

Dave shrugged her question off, as though there were more important things. "I'm an El Hassan man," he said. "Let those two overgrown powers handle their own troubles."

Jimmy Peters spoke up for the first time since Ostrander entered the tent. "You know," he said, seriously, "I'm beginning to wonder if the world can afford nationalistic patriotism. Haven't we gone too far along the road to think of ourselves any longer as Americans, or Russians, or French, or West Indians, or whatever? Hasn't the human race grown up beyond that point?"

Kenny said mockingly, "What! Aren't you proud of being a West Indian, and a loyal subject of Her Majesty?"

Peters ignored his tone. "Why should I be proud of my country? It was an accident of birth with which I had nothing to do, that made me a West Indian, rather than a Canadian, a Chinese, a Norwegian, or whatever. Intelligently, I should be proud only of things that I, myself, have accomplished."

Bey said, "If we can stop waxing philosophic for a while and get back to how most efficiently to clobber these Arabs —"

* * * * *

The Hindu entered Kirill Menzhinsky's small office behind the Indian souvenir shop in the Tangier Zocco Chico and said, "The operative Anton is on the receiver."

The agent superior of the *Chrezvychainaya Komissiya* for North Africa looked up from his desk and grunted acceptance of the message. He came to his feet and followed the other into a back room and took his place before a mouthpiece and screen.

The man whose party name was Anton nodded a greeting.

Kirill Menzhinsky said, "It's about time I heard from you, Anton."

"Yes. But the situation has been such that it was not easy to report."

"And now?"

"Briefly, I am at El Hassan's headquarters. You were correct. He is in actuality Homer Crawford. The others you mentioned are also with him, including the traitor Isobel Cunningham."

The Soviet Complex's agent allowed his eyebrows to rise.

Anton said flatly, "The dame has evidently renounced the party and now holds high rank in Crawford's inner circle."

"And you?"

"I am rapidly becoming his right-hand man. I am his press secretary and in charge of communications. Early in our acquaintanceship I was able to engineer an attempted assassination. I was able to, ah, save the life of El Hassan."

The Russian's eyes narrowed. "The assassins? Is there any chance that they might reveal your little trick?"

Anton grimaced. "I am not a fool, Kirill. Both of them were killed in the assassination attempt. El Hassan was most grateful."

"I see. And how would you sum up the present situation?"

"This area is swinging rapidly to El Hassan, but any sort of defeat and undoubtedly his followers would melt away. The bedouin are too volatile. Before he ever makes any real headway he will have to take the major commercial and industrial cities such as Dakar, Kano, Lagos, Accra, Freetown, Khartoum, and eventually, of course, Cairo, Casablanca, Algiers and so forth."

"And our friend El Hassan leans not at all in our direction?"

The man the Party called Anton shook his head. "He leans in no direction, except that which will unite and modernize North Africa. Neither do his immediate followers. They're a well-knit group and it seems unlikely that I could pry any of them away from him in case it became desirable."

"I see," Kirill Menzhinsky muttered. "I understand that a delegation from Moscow has arrived in El Hassan's camp. Have you contacted them?"

"Certainly not. My orders were to rise in the El Hassan hierarchy and await further orders. None of my current, ah, colleagues have any suggestion that I am identified with the Party. Which reminds me, an American C.I.A. man, Fredric Ostrander, has shown up. The fool seems to be under the impression that El Hassan is a Party tool."

"I know this Ostrander. Don't underestimate him, Anton. He's an extremely competent operative in the clutch, as the Americans call it."

"Perhaps. But nevertheless, there is no indication that the El Hassan movement leans either to East or West, nor do I see any signs that it is apt to in the future."

The Russian was scowling. "I see. Then perhaps it will be necessary for us to do something to topple our El Hassan before he becomes much stronger, and to find another to unite North Africa."

Anton frowned in his turn. "I don't know. This man Crawford-and his followers, for that matter-are motivated by high ideals. As you have said, North Africa is not ready for our socio-economic system. Men of the caliber of Homer Crawford could bring it into the modern age perhaps more quickly than another."

Menzhinsky chuckled. "Don't worry about it, Anton. Such matters of policy will be decided by others than you, or even me. Keep in touch with me more often, in the future, Anton."

"Yes, Comrade." His face faded from the screen.

* * * * *

Tamanrasset lies at an altitude of approximately 4,600 feet, about average for the Ahaggar plateau. Around it, such peaks as the Tahat reach 9,600 feet above sea level. The country is rugged, jagged, bleak beyond belief. With the possible exception of Southern Afghanistan in the Khyber area, there is no place in the world more suited for guerrilla warfare, less suited for the proper utilization of modern armor, particularly when the latter is forced to work without air cover.

Homer Crawford, equipped with an old-style telescope, was spread-eagled on top a rock outcropping, his only companion Isobel Cunningham. Directly before him, possibly two miles in distance, was the desert city of Tamanrasset, to the right, a kilometer or so, Amsel where palatable water was to be found at eighteen meters depth.

"Our friend, the colonel, is up to something," he grumbled.

She had a pair of binoculars, of considerably less power than his glass.

"It looks as though Guémama's boys are on the run," she said.

"As per orders. The primary theory of partisan warfare is not to get killed. The guerrilla never stands and fights. If the regular forces he opposes can bring him to bay, they've got him." He interrupted himself to clip out, "Look at that tank, darling! There on the left!"

Isobel tightened, looked at him quickly from the side of her eyes. No. He'd said it inadvertently, his mind concentrated on the fighting men below. She had often wondered where she stood with Homer Crawford the man, as opposed to El Hassan the idealist. The tip of her tongue licked the side of her mouth, as she surreptitiously took him in. But Crawford the man would have to wait, there was no time, no time.

Isobel swung her glasses. "The one starting to go in a circle? There, it stopped."

"One of the snipers got its commander," Homer said. "You can't fight a tank without the commander's head being up through the hatch. That's a popular fallacy. You can't see well enough to fight your tank unless you've got your head up. And that's suicide when you're against guerrillas. The colonel ought to send his infantry out first."

Isobel said, "What did you mean when you said that he's up to something?"

Homer's eye was still glued to the eyepiece of his glass. "He's leaving his entrenchments and sending his vehicles out to capture our ... our strong points."

"You mean our water, don't you?"

Bey came snaking up to them on his belly. He came abreast of Homer and brought forth his own binoculars. He watched for a moment and then muttered a curse under his breath.

"Guémama better start pulling back those men more quickly," he said.

"He will. He's a good man," Homer told him. "What's up?"

"Evidently, Colonel Ibrahim has decided to come out of retirement. He's sent small motorized elements to Effok, In Fedjeg, Otoul and even to Tahifet."

"And —?"

"And has taken them all, of course. Our men fall back, fighting a stubborn rear-guard action, taking as few casualties as possible."

"I don't get it," Homer bit out. "He's using up his fuel and ammunition and losing more men than we are. Certainly he can't figure, with the thousand odd troops he has, to be able to take and hold enough of the oases and water holes in this vicinity to push us out completely."

Bey said, "What worries me is the possibility that he knows something we don't. That he's figuring on being relieved or has a new source of fuel, ammunition and men on tap."

"The roads are cut. Our men hold every source of water from here to Libya and the Reunited Nations has put thumbs down on aircraft which eliminates an air lift."

"Yeah," Bey said, unhappily.

* * * * *

That evening, following the day's last meal, Cliff came into the headquarters tent grinning, broadly. "Hey, guess what we've liberated."

"A bottle of Scotch?" Kenny said hopefully.

"A king-size portable radio transmitter. Ralph Sandell knew about it. The Sahara Afforestation Project people were going to use it to propagandize the tribesmen into coming in and taking jobs in the new oases."

Dave Moroka, who'd been censoring press releases, shook his head. "That's why we need an El Hassan in this country," he complained. "They put a couple of million dollars into a radio transmitter, never asking themselves how many of the bedouin own radios."

Jack Peters said, "Wait a moment, you chaps. Didn't Bey capture a couple of Arab Legion radio technicians today?"

"They defected to us," Homer Crawford said, looking up from an improvised desk where he was poring over some supply papers with Isobel. "What did you have in mind, Jack?"

"There are radios in Tamanrasset. In fact, there's probably a radio in every one of those military vehicles of Ibrahim's. Why can't we blanket these Arab Union chaps with El Hassan propaganda? Quite a few of them are from Libya, Tunisia and Egypt. In short, they're Africans and susceptible to El Hassan's dream."

"Good man. Take over the details, Jack," Homer said. He went back to his work with Isobel.

Jimmy Peters entered with some papers in hand. He said, seriously, "The temperature is rising in the Reunited Nations-and everywhere else, for that matter. Damascus and Cairo have been getting increasingly belligerent. Homer, it looks as though the Arab Union is getting ready to go out on a limb. Weeks have passed since Colonel Ibrahim first took Tamanrasset and the Reunited Nations, the United States, the Soviet Complex and all others interested in North Africa, have failed to do anything. Everybody, evidently, afraid of precipitating something that couldn't be ended."

All eyes went to Homer Crawford who ran a black hand back over his hair in weariness. "I know," he said. "Something is about to blow. Dave has sent some of his best men into Tamanrasset to pick up gossip in the souks. Morale was dragging bottom among the legionnaires just a couple of days ago. Now they seem to have a new lease."

"In spite of the sabotage our people have been committing?" Isobel said.

"That's falling off somewhat," Cliff said. "At first our more enthusiastic followers were able to pull everything from heaving Molotov Cocktails into tanks, to pouring sugar in hover-jeep gas tanks, but the legionnaires have both smartened up and gotten very tough."

"Good," Dave Moroka said now.

They looked at him.

"Atrocities," he said. "In order to guard against sabotage, the legionnaires will be taking measures that will antagonize the people in Tamanrasset. They'll shoot a couple of teenage kids, or something, then they'll have a city-wide mess on their hands."

Isobel said unhappily, "It seems a nasty way to win a war."

Dave grunted his contempt of her opinion. "There is no way of winning a war other than a nasty one."

Bey came in, yawning hugely. His energy was inconceivable to the others. So far as was known, he hadn't slept, other than sitting erect in a moving vehicle, for the past four days. He said to Homer, "Fred Ostrander has bending my ear for the past hour or so. Do you want to talk to him?"

"About what?" Homer said.

"I don't know. He has a lot of questions. I think he's beginning to suspect-just *suspect*, understand-that possibly the whole bunch of us aren't receiving our daily instructions from either Moscow or Peking."

Dave and Cliff both laughed.

Homer sighed and said, "Show him in. He's the only thing we have in the way of a contact with the United States of the Americas and sooner or later we're going to have to make our peace with both them and the Soviet Complex. In fact, what we're probably going to have to do is play one against the other, getting grants, loans, economic assistance —"

"Technicians, teachers, arms," Bey continued the list.

Kenny Ballalou looked at him and snorted. "Arms! If there's anything this part of the world doesn't need it's more arms. In fact, that goes for the rest of the world, too. In the old days when the great nations were first beginning to attempt to line up the neutrals they sent aid to such countries by the billions-and most of it in arms. How ridiculous can you get? Putting arms in the hands of most of the governments of that time was like handing a loaded pistol to an idiot."

Bey hung his head in mock humility. "I bow before your wisdom," he said. He left the room to get Ostrander.

* * * * *

The C.I.A. man had lost a fraction of his belligerence, but none of his arrogance and natty appearance. Homer wondered vaguely how the other managed to remain so spruce in the inadequate desert camp.

Jack Peters said, "What did you wish to ask El Hassan? I will translate."

"Never mind that, Jack," Homer said. "We'll get tougher about using our official language when we've gone a little further in building our new government." He said to Ostrander, "What can I do for you? Obviously, my time, is limited."

Fredric Ostrander said, "I've been gathering material for reports to my superiors. I've been doing a good deal of questioning, and, frankly, even prying around."

Cliff grunted.

Ostrander went on. "I've also read the various press releases, manifestoes and so forth that your assistants have been compiling."

"We know," Homer said. "We haven't put any obstacles in your way. We haven't any particular secrets, Mr. Ostrander."

"You disguise the fact that you are an American," the C.I.A. man said accusingly.

Homer said slowly, "Only because El Hassan *is not* an American, Mr. Ostrander. He is an African with African solutions to African problems. That is what he must be if he is to accomplish his task."

Ostrander seemed to switch subjects. "See here, Crawford, the State Department is not completely opposed to the goal of uniting North Africa. It would solve many problems, both African and international."

Kenny Ballalou laughed softly. "You mean, you're on our side?"

Ostrander turned to him, for once not incensed at being needled. "Possibly more than you'd think," he rapped. He turned back again to Homer Crawford. "The question becomes, why do you think that *you* are the man for the job? Who gave *you* the go-ahead?"

Bey, who had settled down into a folding camp chair, now came to his feet, his tired face angry.

But Homer waved him to silence. "Hold it," he said. Then to Ostrander. "It doesn't work that way. It's not something you decide to do because you're thirsty for power, or greedy for money. You're pushed into it. Do you think Washington, a retired Virginian planter wrapped up in his estate and his family, wanted to spend years leading the revolutionary armies through the wilderness that was America in those days? He was thrust into the job, there was no one else more competent to take it. Men make the times, Ostrander, but the times also make the men. Look at Lenin and Trotsky. Three months before the October Revolution, Lenin wrote that he never expected to see in his lifetime the Bolsheviks come to power. Within those months he was at the head of government and Trotsky, a former bookworm who had never fired a gun in his life, was head of the Red Army and being proclaimed a military genius."

Ostrander was scowling at him, but his face was thoughtful.

Homer said quietly, "It's not always an easy thing, to have power thrust into your hands. Not always a desirable thing." His voice went quieter still. "Only a short time ago it led me to the necessity of ... killing ... my best friend."

"And mine," Isobel said softly, almost under her breath.

Dave Moroka said, "Abe Baker," before he caught himself.

Kenny Ballalou looked at him strangely. "Did you know Abe?"

The South African recovered. "I've heard several of you mention him from time to time. He was a commie, wasn't he?"

"Yes," Homer said without inflection. "And a man. He saved my life on more than one occasion. As long as we worked together with only Africa in mind, there was no conflict. But Abe had a further, and, to him, greater alliance."

He turned his attention back to the C.I.A. man. "A man does what he must do," he finished simply. "I did not ask to become El Hassan."

Ostrander said, "Your motivation is possibly beside the point. The thing is that the battle for men's minds continues and your program, eventually, must align with the West."

"And get clobbered in the stampeding around between the two great powers," Kenny said dryly.

"You've got to take your stand," Ostrander said. "I'd rather die under the neutron bomb, than spend the rest of my life on my knees under a Soviet Complex government. Wouldn't you?" His eyes went from one of them to the other, defiantly.

Homer said slowly. "No, even though that was the only alternative, which is unlikely. Not if it meant finishing off the whole human race at the same time." He shook his head. "If it were only me, it might be different. But if it was a matter of nuclear war the whole race might well end. Given such circumstances, I'd be proud to remain on my knees the rest of my life. You see, Ostrander, you make the mistake of thinking the Soviet socio-economic system is a permanent thing. It isn't. It's changing daily, even as our own socio-economic system is. Even if the Soviet Complex were to dominate the whole world, it would be but a temporary phase in man's history. Their regime, in its time, right or wrong, will go under in man's march to whatever his destiny might be. Some day it will be only a memory, and so will the socio-economic systems of the West. No institutions are less permanent than politico-economic ones."

"I don't agree with you," Ostrander snapped.

"Obviously," Homer shrugged. "However, this is another problem. El Hassan deals with North Africa. The other problems you bring up we admit, but at this stage are not dealing with them. Our dream is in Africa. Perhaps the Africans will be forced to taking other stands, to dreaming new dreams, twenty or thirty years from now. When that time comes, I assume the new problems will be faced. By that time there will probably be no need for El Hassan."

Ostrander looked at him and bit his lip in thought.

It came to him now that he had never won in his contests with Homer Crawford, and that he would probably never win. No matter how strong his convictions, in the presence of the other man, something went out of him. There was strength in Crawford that must be experienced to be understood. When he talked, he held you, and your own opinions became nothing-stupidities on your lips. He had a dream, and in conversation with him, all other things dropped away and nothing was of importance but that dream. A dream? Possibly *disease* was the better word. And so highly contagious.

While they talked, an aide had entered and handed a report to Bey-ag-Akhamouk. He read it and closed his eyes in weariness.

"What's up, Bey," Homer asked.

"I don't know. Colonel Ibrahim has stepped up his attacks in all directions. At least two thirds of his force is on the offensive. It doesn't make much sense. But it must make sense to *him*, or he wouldn't be doing it."

Ostrander said, and to everyone's surprise there seemed to be an element of worry in his voice too, "I know Colonel Midan Ibrahim, met him in Cairo and in Baghdad on various occasions. He's considered one of the best men in the Arab Legion. He doesn't make military blunders."

Bey said, "Come on, Kenny. Let's round up Guémama and take a look at the front." He led the way from the tent.

* * * * *

There was a guard posted before the tent which doubled as press and communications center, and the private quarters of David Moroka.

The figure that approached timidly was garbed in the traditional clothing of the young women of the Tégéhé Mellet tribe of the Tuareg and bore an *imzad* in her left hand, while her right held a corner of her gandoura over her face.

The guard, of the Kel Rela tribe, eyed the one-stringed violin with its string of hair and sounding box made of half a gourd covered with a thin membrane of skin, and grinned. A Tuareg maid was accustomed to sing and to make the high whining tones of desert music on the *imzad* before submitting to her lover's embrace. *Wallahi!* but these women of the Tégéhé Mellet were shameless.

"Where do you go?" he said gruffly. "El Hassan's vizier has ordered that he is occupied and none should approach."

"He awaits me," she wavered. There was *kohl* about her eyes, and indigo at the corners of her mouth. "We met at the *tendi* last night and he bid me come to his tent. It is for me he waits."

Wallahi! but his leader had taste, the sentry decided.

"Pass," he said gruffly. Even a vizier of such importance as this one must need solace at times, he decided philosophically.

She slipped past silently to the tent entrance where the Tuareg guard noticed she paused for a long moment before entering. He grinned into his teguelmoust. Aiii, the little bird was timid before the hawk.

She stood for a moment listening, and then slipped inside, dropping the desert musical instrument to the ground. Dave Moroka's back was to her and even as she entered he flicked off the switch of the video-radio into which he had been speaking and scowled at it.

When he stood and began to turn, she covered him with the small pocket pistol. She had an ease in handling it which denoted competence.

His eyebrows went up, but he remained silent, waiting for her gambit.

Isobel said evenly, "You're a Party member, aren't you, Dave?"

"Why do you say that?"

She nodded infinitesimally to the set. "You were reporting just now. I heard enough just as I came in."

He took in her disguise. "My guard isn't as efficient as I had thought," Dave said wryly.

Isobel said, "You knew Abe Baker, didn't you?"

He looked at her, expressionlessly.

She said, "I already knew you belonged to the Party, Dave. No matter how competent an agent, it's something difficult to hide from any other long-time member. There's a terminology you use-such as calling it the Soviet Union, rather than Russia. No commie ever says Russia, it's always *the Soviet Union*. You can tell, just as a Roman Catholic can tell a person raised in the Church, even though the other has dropped away, or even as one Jew can tell another. Yes, I've known you were a Party member for some time, Dave."

"And?" the South African said.

"Why are you here?"

Dave Moroka said, "For the same reason you are, to further the El Hassan dream, the uniting and modernization of the continent of my racial heritage."

"But you are still a Party member and still report to your superiors."

Dave Moroka looked at the tiny gun she held in her hand.

"Don't try it," she said. "I have seen you in action, Dave. I have never seen a man move so ruthlessly fast ... but don't try it."

"No reason to," he bit out. "Come on, let's go see Homer."

She was slightly taken aback, but not enough to release her control for even a split second. "Lead the way," she said.

* * * * *

Even at this time of evening, the headquarters tent was brightly lit and most of the immediate El Hassan staff still at work. Homer Crawford looked up as they entered.

Cliff Jackson saw the gun first and said, "Holy Mackerel, Isobel."

Fredric Ostrander was sitting to one side in discussion with the sober faced Jack Peters. He took in the gun and slowly came to his feet, obviously expecting climax.

Isobel said, "Dave's taking over control of communications had method. I just found him reporting to what must have been a superior ... in the Party."

Homer Crawford looked from the South African to Isobel, then back to Dave again, without speaking. His eyes were questioning.

Dave said, his voice sharp. "I haven't time for details now. Isobel's right. I was a Party member."

"Was?" Ostrander chuckled. "That's the understatement of the year. I hadn't got around to revealing the fact as yet, but our friend Dave is the notorious Anton, one of the Soviet Complex's most competent hatchetmen."

Dave looked at him only briefly. "Was," he reiterated. He turned his attention to Homer and to Bey, who was staring tired dismay at this new addition to the load.

Homer still held his peace, waiting for the other to go on.

"I found out tonight why Colonel Ibrahim is attacking, instead of pulling in his horns as reason would dictate." Dave paused for emphasis. "The Soviet Complex has thrown its weight, in this matter at least, on the side of the Arab Union. They have insisted that Sven Zetterberg be dismissed as head of the Sahara Division of the African Development Project and that his threat to use Reunited Nations aircraft if the local fighting spreads to the air, be repudiated."

Kenny blurted, "Good grief ... that means —"

Dave looked around at them, one by one. "It means," he said, "that the Arab Legion is going to be reinforced tomorrow morning by a full regiment of paratroopers."

"Holy Mackerel," Cliff groaned. "We've had it. Another regiment of crack troops in Tamanrasset and we'll *never* take the town."

Dave shook his head. "That's not the big thing. The paratroopers aren't going to drop in Tamanrasset. They're going to hit every oasis, every water hole, in a circumference of two hundred miles."

There was an empty silence.

Homer Crawford said finally, evenly, "In the expectation that every follower of El Hassan in the Sahara will either surrender or die of thirst, eh?" He didn't seem sufficiently impressed by the threatening disaster. He looked at Dave questioningly. "Why do you bother to tell us, Dave, if you're on the other side?"

Dave grunted sour amusement. "Because I've just become a full member of the team. I resigned from the Party tonight."

"Brother," Bey said, "you sure pick a helluva time to join up." He obviously was expressing the opinions of the majority.

Homer Crawford came to his feet and looked around at them. "All right," he said. "A new complication. Let's face up to it. There's always an answer. We're in the clutch, let's fight our way out."

Largely, they stared at him, but he ignored their dismay. He looked from one to the other. "We need some ideas. Let's kick it around. Isobel, Cliff, Jack, Kenny —?" His eyes went from one to the other. Obviously his own mind was churning.

They shook their heads dumbly.

Kenny said, "Ideas! We've had it, Homer!"

Homer Crawford spun on him and now the force they all knew was emanating from him. He laughed his scorn. "A month ago we were half a dozen fugitives. Now we're an army besieging a city. And you say we've had it? Listen, Kenny, if we have to we'll go back to being half a dozen fugitives again-those of us that are left. But the dream goes on! However, we're not going to have to. We're too near victory in this stage of the operation to sit down on the job because of a threatened reverse. Now then, let's kick it around. Jimmy! Dave! Kenny! Ostrander!"

Fredric Ostrander raised his eyebrows only slightly at being included in their number.

* * * * *

Bey, for once, was seemingly too exhausted to be brought to new enthusiasm. He tossed a detail map of Tamanrasset to the table. "And I'd just worked out a bang-up scheme for infiltrating into town, joining up with our adherents there, and seizing it while most of Ibrahim's men were out in the desert, trying to capture our nearer water holes."

Homer snapped, "It sounds like it still might have possibilities."

Ostrander looked down at the map, his face very tight. "How long would it take?"

Bey scowled at him, defeat dulling his mind. "What?"

"How long do you figure it would take to infiltrate Tamanrasset and capture it? Behind Ibrahim's back, so to speak."

Bey grunted. "A couple of hours in the early morning. I had a beautiful picture of the colonel's armor out in the desert, cut off from its petroleum supplies and ammunition dump while we held the town. Some of our men, the former veterans of the French West African forces, could have even operated the antitank guns he has mounted at Fort Laperrine."

The C.I.A. man's mouth worked.

Homer Crawford's eyes pierced him.

Ostrander walked over to the radio before which Kenny Ballalou sat. "See if you can raise Colonel Ibrahim for me."

Kenny scowled at him. "Why?"

"Do it."

Kenny looked at Homer Crawford.

Homer said, "O.K. Do it."

Kenny shrugged and turned to the set. While the others watched, Crawford's face alert, his eyes narrowed, the rest of them dull in apathy, the face of Colonel Ibrahim finally faded in on the screen.

Fredric Ostrander took his place at the instrument. He nodded, formally. "Greetings, Colonel, it seems a long time since last we met in Amman."

The Arab Legion officer smiled politely. "I had heard that you represented the State Department in this area, Mr. Ostrander, and have been somewhat surprised that you failed to make Tamanrasset your headquarters. It would have been pleasant to have renewed old friendship."

Ostrander cleared his throat. "I am afraid that would have been difficult, Colonel, particularly in view of the stand of my government at this time."

On the screen, the other's eyebrows went up.

Ostrander said evenly, "Colonel, we have just been informed that a regiment of paratroopers has been put at your disposal and that they plan to land at various points in the Sahara in the morning."

The colonel said stiffly, "This is military information which I am not free to discuss, Mr. Ostrander."

Frederic Ostrander went on, his voice still even. "We have further been informed that the Reunited Nations has withdrawn its ban on aircraft, which would seem to free your paratroop carrying planes."

The colonel remained silent, waiting for the bombshell. It was obvious that he expected a bombshell.

Ostrander said, "As representative of the State Department I warn you that if these paratroop carrying planes take off tomorrow morning, the Seventh Airfleet of the United States of the Americas will enter the conflict on the side of El Hassan. Good evening, Colonel."

The C.I.A. man reached out and flicked the switch that killed the set. Then he took the snowy white handkerchief from the breast pocket of his jacket and wiped his mouth.

Isobel said, "Heavens to Betsy."

Kenny said indignantly, "Good grief, you fool, it won't take more than hours for your superiors to repudiate you. Then what happens?"

"By then, I assume, the battle will be over and Tamanrasset in El Hassan's hands. The Arab Union will then think twice before committing their paratroopers, particularly with captured armor in El Hassan's hands."

"And your name will be mud," Kenny blurted.

Ostrander looked at Homer Crawford. "Gentlemen, you must remember that I, too, am an African. I had thought that perhaps there would be a position for me on El Hassan's staff."

Crawford reached for the Tommy-Noiseless that leaned up against the improvised desk at which he worked. He said, "Let's get moving, Bey. We haven't much time. We're going to have to be able to announce its capture *from* Tamanrasset in a couple of hours."

"Not you," Bey said, grabbing up his own weapon and motioning with his head for Kenny and Cliff to come along. "You're El Hassan and can't be risked."

"I'm coming," Homer said flatly. "It's about time El Hassan began taking some of the same risks his followers seem to be willing to face. Besides, the men will fight better with me out in front. Got a gun, Fred?"

Ostrander said, "No. Where am I issued one?"

"I'll show you," Homer said, stuffing extra clips in his bush jacket pockets. "Come on, Dave."

The whole group began heading for the open air, Bey already yelling orders.

Fredric Ostrander looked at Dave Moroka. "Strange bedfellows," he said.

Moroka grinned wryly. "My long view hasn't changed," he said. "It's just that this African matter takes precedence right now."

"Nor mine, of course," Ostrander said. He cleared his throat. "However, I hope you last out the night. El Hassan needs strong men."

"Same to you," Moroka said gruffly. "Let's get going, or the fight will be over while we hand each other flowers."

Epilogue

El Hassan stood in the smoking, war-wasted ruin of Fort Laperine, his mind empty. The body of Jack Peters was ten feet to his left, burned beyond recognition and crumpled over a flame thrower which he'd eliminated in the last few moments of the fighting. Had he let his eyes go out the gun port before which he stood, it might have been possible for El Hassan to have picked out the bodies of David Moroka and Fredric Ostrander amidst those of the several hundred Haratin serfs who had swarmed out of the souk area at the crucial moment and stormed the half manned fort-unarmed save for knives and farm implements.

To his right, Dr. Warren Harding Smythe supervised two Tuareg who were carrying off the broken body of Kenny Ballalou; there was still faint life in it.

The doctor looked at him. "You are satisfied, I assume?"

El Hassan failed to hear him.

Smythe turned and stomped off, following his impressed nurses.

In the distance, Bey-ag-Akhamouk called hoarse orders from an over-strained throat, placing guns for a counterattack that would never come. The Arab Legion was broken and Colonel Ibrahim a prisoner. Large numbers of the survivors were defecting to the banner of El Hassan.

He threw his empty Tommy-Noiseless to the side. All he wanted now was sleep, the surcease of a few hours of oblivion.

Isobel, her face wan from the horror of the agony of the combat whose result was everywhere visible, was picking her way through the wreckage with Cliff Jackson.

El Hassan looked at her absently. Whatever message she bore held little interest to him.

Cliff said, "India has recognized El Hassan as legal head of state of all North Africa. It is expected that Australia will follow before the week is out."

El Hassan nodded. For the time, not caring.

Isobel said, "We have other word. It came by messenger." She closed her eyes in pain and handed him a small box.

He opened it and recognized the ring on the enclosed finger. He looked up at them.

Cliff Jackson growled low in his throat. "Elmer Allen. He's been captured by a leader of the Ouled Touameur clan of the Ouled Allouch tribe. You know this Abd-el-Kader?"

El Hassan was staring down at the finger, his mind slowly clearing of its fatigue. "He belongs to the Berazga division of the Chaambra confederation. I had a run-in with him a few months ago and had him jailed. He's nothing but a desert bandit on the make."

Cliff said, "He's escaped, has thrown his weight behind the Arab Union, proclaimed himself the Mahdi and is uniting Algeria and parts of Morocco and Tunisia like a wildfire. The marabouts and Shorfa are backing him."

"Proclaimed himself the Mahdi?" Isobel said in question.

El Hassan turned to the girl and took a deep breath. "The original Mahdi was the holiest prophet since Mohammed and according to the more superstitious Moslems, he's still alive. According to Islamic tradition, he periodically shows up again in the desert and makes various predictions. When he does, it almost always winds up with a jehad, a holy war. Don't you remember in history the anti-British Mahdi at Khartoum, the killing of Chinese Gordon and so forth? That Mahdi was the son of a Dongola carpenter and he managed to conquer two million square miles in two years."

"But, what has this got to do with this Abd-el-Kader?"

"He's evidently proclaimed himself sort of a reincarnation of the original Mahdi. He's out to do the same thing we are-to unite North Africa. But in his case he doesn't exactly have the same dream and he's working under the green ensign of the Pan-Islamic Arab Union."

"And has Elmer Allen captive."

"Yes, he has Elmer." El Hassan's tone of voice turned sharp. "Cliff, go get Bey. Tell him we're forming a flying column and heading north."

Cliff was gone. El Hassan turned back to the girl. "You know, Isobel," he said softly, slowly, "in history there is no happy ending, ever. There is no ending at all. It goes from one crisis to another, but there is no ending."

Frigid Fracas

To my loyal fans.
Major Joe Madden

I

In other eras he might have been described as swacked, stewed, stoned, smashed, crocked, cock-eyed, soused, shellacked, polluted, potted, tanked, lit, stinko, pie-eyed, three sheets in the wind, or simply drunk.

In his own time, Major Joseph Mauser, Category Military, Mid-Middle Caste, was drenched. Or at least rapidly getting there.

He wasn't happy about it. It wasn't that kind of a binge.

He lowered one eyelid and concentrated on the list of potables offered by the auto-bar. He'd decided earlier in the game that it would be a physical impossibility to get through the whole list but he was making a strong attempt on a representative of each subdivision. He'd had a cocktail, a highball, a sour, a flip, a punch and a julep. He wagged forth a finger to dial a fizz, a Sloe Gin Fizz.

Joe Mauser occupied a small table in a corner of the Middle Caste Category Military Club in Greater Washington. His current fame, transient though it might be, would have made him welcome as a guest in the Upper Caste Club, located in the swank Baltimore section of town. Old pros in the Category Military had comparatively small sufferance for caste lines among themselves; rarified class distinctions meant little when you were in the dill, and you didn't become an old pro without having been in spots where matters had pickled. Joe would have been welcome on the strength of his performance in the most recent fracas in which he had participated as a mercenary, that between Vacuum Tube Transport and Continental Hovercraft. But he didn't want it that way.

You didn't devote the greater part of your life to pulling your way up, pushing your way up, fighting your way up, the ladder of status to be satisfied to associate with your social superiors on the basis of being a nine-day-wonder, an oddity to be met at cocktail parties and spoken to for a few democratic moments.

No, Joe Mauser would stick to his own position in the scheme of things until through his own efforts he won through to that rarefied altitude in society which his ambition demanded.

A sour voice said, "Celebrating, captain? Oops, major, I mean. So you did get something out of the Catskill Reservation fracas. I'm surprised."

A scowl, Joe decided, would be the best. Various others, in the course of the evening, had attempted to join him. Three or four comrades in arms, one journalist from some fracas buff magazine, some woman he'd never met before, and Zen knew how she'd ever got herself into the club. A snarl had driven some away, or a growl or sneer. This one, he decided, called for an angered scowl, particularly in view of the tone of voice which only brought home doubly how his planning of a full two years had come a cropper.

He looked up, beginning his grimace of discouragement. "Go away," he muttered nastily. The other's identity came through slowly. One of the Telly news reporters who'd covered the fracas; for the moment he couldn't recall the name.

Joe Mauser held the common prejudices of the Category Military for Telly and all its ramifications. Not only for the drooling multitudes who sat before their sets and vicariously participated in the sadism of combat while their trank bemused brains refused contemplation of the reality of their way of life. But also for Category Communications, and particularly its Sub-division Telly, Branch Fracas News, and all connected with it. His views, perhaps, were akin to those of the matador facing the moment of truth, the crowds screaming in the arena seats for him to go in and the promoters and managers watching from the *barrera* and possibly wondering if he were gored if next week's gate would improve.

The Telly cameras which watched you as, crouched almost double, you scurried into the fire area of a mitrailleuse or perhaps a Maxim; the Telly cameras which swung in your direction speedily, avidly, when a blast of fire threw you back and to the ground; the Telly cameras with their zoom lenses which focused full into your face as life leaked away. The Spanish aficionados never had it so good. The close-up expression of the dying matador had been denied them.

The other undeterred, sank into the chair opposite, his face twisted cynically. Joe placed him now. Freddy Soligen. Give the man his due, he and his team were right in there when the going got hot. More than once, in the past fifteen years, Joe had seen the little man lugging his cameras into the center of the fracas, taking chances expected only of combatants. Vaguely, he wondered why.

He demanded, "Why?"

"Eh?" Soligen said. "Major, by the looks of you, you're going to have a beaut, comes morning. Why don't you stick to trank?"

"Cause I'm not a slob," Joe sneered. "Why?"

"Why, what? Listen, you want me to help you on home?"

"Got no home. Live in hotels. Military clubs. In barracks. Got nothing but my rank and caste." He sneered again. "Such as they are."

Soligen said, "Mid-Middle, aren't you? And a major. Zen, most would say you haven't much to complain about."

Joe grunted contempt, but dropped that angle of it. However, he could have mentioned that he was well into his thirties, that he had copped many a one in his day and that now time was borrowed. When you had been in the dill as often as had Joe Mauser, the days you lived were borrowed. Borrowed from some lad who hadn't used up all that nature had originally allotted him. He was well into the thirties and his life's goal was still tantalizingly far before him, and he living on borrowed time.

He said, "Why're you ... exception? How come you get right into the middle of it, like that time on the Panhandle Reservation. You coulda copped one there."

Soligen chuckled abruptly, and as though in self-deprecation. "I *did* cop one there. Hospitalized three months. Didn't read any of the publicity I got? No, I guess you didn't, it was mostly in the Category Communications trade press. Anyway, I got bounced not only in rank on the job, but up to Low-Middle in caste." There was the faintest edge of the surly in his voice as he added, "I was born a Lower, major."

Joe snorted. "So was I. You didn't answer my question, Soligen. Why stick your neck out? Most of you Telly reporters, stick it out in some concrete pillbox with lots of telescopic equipment." He added bitterly, "And usually away from what's really going on."

The Telly reporter looked at him oddly. "Stick my neck out?" he said with deliberation. "Possibly for the same reason you do, major. In fact, it's kinda the reason I looked you up. Trouble is, you're probably too drenched, right now, to listen to my fling."

Joe Mauser's voice attempted cold dignity. He said, "In the Category Military, Soligen, you never get so drenched you can't operate."

The other's cynical grunt conveyed nothing, but he reached out and dialed the auto-bar. He growled, "O.K., a Sober-Up for you, an ale for me."

"I don't want to sober up. I'm being bitter and enjoying it."

"Yes, you do," the little man said. "I have the answer to your bitterness." He handed Joe the pill. "You see, what's wrong with you, major, is you've been trying to do it alone. What you need is help."

Joe glowered at him, even as he accepted the medication. "I make my own way, Soligen. I don't even know what you're talking about."

"That's obvious," the other said sourly. He waited, sipping his brew, while the Sober-Up worked its miracle. He was compassionate enough to shudder, having been through, in his time, the speeding up of a hangover so that full agony was compressed into mere minutes rather than dispensed over a period of hours.

Joe groaned, "It better be good, whatever you want to say."

Freddy Soligen asked, at long last, tilting his head to one side and taking Joe in critically. "You know one of the big reasons you're only a major?"

Joe Mauser looked at him.

The Telly reporter said, "You haven't got any mustache."

Joe Mauser stared at him.

The other laughed cynically. "You think I'm drivel-happy, eh? Well, maybe a long scar down the cheek would do even better. Or, possibly, you ought to wear a monocle, even in action."

Joe continued to stare, as though the little man had gone completely around the bend.

Freddy Soligen had made his first impression. He finished the ale, put the glass into the chute and turned back to the professional mercenary. His voice was flat now, all expression gone from his face. "All right," he said. "Now listen to my fling. You've got a lot to learn."

* * * * *

Joe held his peace, if only in pure amazement. He ranked the little man opposite him in both caste and in professional attainments. Besides which, he was a combat officer and unused to being addressed with less than full respect, even from superiors. For unlucky Joe Mauser might be in his chosen field, but respected he was.

Freddy Soligen pointed a finger at him, almost mockingly. "You're on the make, Mauser. In a world where few bother, any more, you're on the way up. The trouble is, you took the wrong path many years ago."

Joe snorted his contempt of the other's lack of knowledge. "I was born into the Clothing Category, Sub-division Shoes, Branch Repair. In the old days they called us cobblers. You think you could work your way up from Mid-Lower to Upper caste with that beginning, Soligen? Zen! we don't even have cobblers any more, shoes are thrown away as soon as they show wear. Sure, sure, sure. Theoretically, under People's Capitalism, you can cross categories into any field you want. But have you ever heard of anybody doing any real jumping of caste levels in any category except Military or Religion? I didn't take the wrong path, religion is a little too strong for even my stomach, which left the Category Military the only path available."

Freddy had heard him out, his face twisted sourly. He said now, "You misunderstand. I realize that the military's the only quick way of getting a bounce in caste. I wish I'd figured that out sooner, before I made a trade out of the one I was born into, Communications. It's too late now, I'm into my forties with a busted marriage but the proud papa of a kid." He twisted his face again in another grimace. "By the way, the boy's a novitiate in Category Religion."

Some elements were clearing up in Joe's mind. He said, in comprehension, "So ... we're both ambitious."

"That's right, major. Now, let's get back to fundamentals. Your wrong path is the *manner* in which you're trying to work your way up into the elite. You've got to become a celebrated hero, major. And it's the Telly fan, the fracas-buff, who decides who the Category Military heroes are. Those are the slobs you have to toady to. In the long run, nobody else counts. I know, I know. All the old pros, even big names like Stonewall Cogswell and Jack Alshuler, think you're a top man. Great! But how many buff-clubs you got to your name? How often do the buff magazines run articles about you? How often do you get interviewed on Telly, in between fracases? Have the movies ever done 'The Joe Mauser Story'?"

Joe twisted uncomfortably. "All that stuff takes a lot of time. I've been keeping myself busy."

"Right. Busy getting shot at."

"I'm a mercenary. That's my trade."

Freddy spread his hands. "O.K. If that's all you're interested in, shooting lads signed up on the other side, or getting shot by them, that's fine. But you know, major" —he cocked his head to one side, and peered knowingly at Joe —"I've got a sneaking suspicion that you don't particularly like combat. Some do, I know. Some love it. I don't think you do."

Joe looked at him.

Freddy said, "You're in it because of the chance for promotion, nothing else counts."

Joe remained silent.

Freddy pushed him. "Who're the names every fracas buff knows? Jerry Sturgeon, captain at the age of twenty-one, and so damned pretty in those fancy uniforms he wears. How many times have you ever heard of him really being in the dill? He knows better! Captain Sturgeon spends his time prancing around on that famous palomino of his in front of the Telly lenses, not dodging bullets. Or Ted Sohl. Colonel Ted Sohl. The dashing Sohl with his two western style six-shooters, slung low on his hips, and that romantic limp and craggy face. My, do the female buffs go for Colonel Sohl! I wonder how many of them know he wears a special pair of boots to give him that limp. Old Jerry's a long time drinking pal of mine, he's never copped one in his life. What's more, another year or so and he'll be a general and you know what that means. Almost automatic jump to Upper caste."

Joe's face was working. All this was not really news to him. Like his fellow old pros, Joe Mauser was fully aware of the glory grabbers. There had always been the glory grabbers from mythological Achilles, who sulked in his tent while his best friend died before the walls of Troy, to Alexander, who conquered the world with an army conceived and precision trained by another man whose name is all but forgotten, to the swashbuckling Custer who sacrificed self and squadron rather than wait for assistance.

Freddy pushed him. "How come you're never on lens when you're in there going good, major? Ever thought about that? When you're commanding a rear-guard action, maybe, trying to extract your lads when the situation's pickled, who's in the Telly lens where all the stupid buffs can see him? One of the manufactured heroes."

Joe scowled. "The who?"

"Come off it, major. You've been around long enough to know heroes are made, not born. We stopped having much regard for real heroes a long time ago. Lindbergh and Byrd were a couple of the last we turned out. After that, we left it to the Norwegians to do such things as crew the *Kon-Tiki*, or to the English to top Everest-whether or not the Britisher made the last hundred feet slung over the shoulder of a Sherpa. I don't know if it was talking movies, the radio, the coming of Telly, or what. Possibly all three. But we got away from real heroes, they're not exciting enough. Telly actors can do it better. Real heroes are apt to be on the dull side, they're men who do things rather than being showmen. Actually, most adventure can be on the monotonous side, nine-tenths of the time. When a Stanley goes to find a Livingston, he doesn't spend twenty-four hours a day killing rogue elephants or fighting off tribesman; most of the time he's plodding along in the swamps, getting bitten by mosquitoes, or through the bush getting bitten by tsetse flies. So, as a people, we turned it over to the movies, and Telly, where they can do it better."

Joe Mauser's mind was working now, but he held silence.

Freddy Soligen went on, "Your typical fracas buff, glued to his Telly set, wants two things. First, lots of gore, lots of blood, lots of sadistic thrill. And the Lower-Lower lads, who are silly enough to get into the Military Category for the sake of glory or the few shares of common stock they might secure, provide that gore. Second, your Telly fan wants some Good Guys whose first requirement is to be easily recognized. Some heroes, easily identified with. Anybody can tell a Telly hero when he sees one. Handsome, dashing, distinctively uniformed, preferably tall, and preferably blond and blue-eyed, though we'll eliminate those requirements in your case, if you'll grow a mustache." He cocked his head to one side. "Yes, sir. A very dashing mustache."

Joe said sourly, "You think that's all I need to hit the big time. A dashing mustache, eh?"

"No," Freddy Soligen said, very slowly and evenly. "We're also going to need every bit of stock you've accumulated, major. We're going to have to buy your way into the columns of the fracas buff magazine. We're going to have to bribe my colleagues, the Telly camera crews, to keep you on lens when you're looking good and, more important still, off it when you're not. We're going to have to spend every credit you've got."

"I see," Joe said. "And when it's all been accomplished, what do you get out of this, Freddy?"

Freddy Soligen laid it on the line. "When it's all been accomplished, you'll be an Upper. I'm ambitious, too, Joe. Just as ambitious as you are. I need an *In*. You'll be it. I'll make you. I have the know-how. I can do it. When you're made, you'll make me."

II

When Major Mauser, escorting Dr. Nadine Haer, daughter of the late Baron Haer of Vacuum Tube Transport, entered the swank Exclusive Room of the Greater Washington branch of the Ultra Hotels, the orchestra ceased the dreamy dance music it had been playing and struck up the lilting "The Girl I Left Behind Me."

As they followed the maître d'hôtel to their table, Nadine frowned in puzzled memory and after they were seated, she said, "That piece, where have I heard it before?"

Joe cleared his throat uncomfortably. "An old marching song, come down from way back. Popular during the Civil War. The seventh Cavalry rode forth to that tune on the way to their rendezvous with the Sioux at the Little Big Horn."

She frowned at him, puzzled still, "You seem to know an inordinate amount about a simple tune, Joe." Then she said, "Why, now I remember where I've heard it recently. Wednesday, when I was waiting for you at the Agora Bar. The band played it when you entered."

He picked up the menu, hurriedly. The Exclusive Room was ostentatious to the point of menus and waiters. "What'll you have, Nadine?" He still wasn't quite at ease with her first name. Offhand, he could never remember having been on a first name basis with a Mid-Upper, certainly not one of the female gender.

But she was not to be put off. "Why, Joe Mauser, you've acquired a theme song, or whatever you call it. I didn't know you were that well known amount the nit-wits who follow the fracases. Why next they'll be forming those ridiculous buff-clubs." Her laughter tinkled. "The Major Joe Mauser Club."

Joe flushed. "As a matter of fact, there are three," he said unhappily. "One in Mexico City, one in Bogota and one in Portland. I've forgotten if it's Oregon or Maine."

She was puzzled still, and ignored the waiter who, standing there, made Joe nervous. Establishments which boasted live waiters, were rare enough in Joe Mauser's experience that he could easily remember the number of occasions he'd attended them. Nadine Haer, to the contrary, an hereditary aristocrat born, was totally unaware of the flunky's presence and would remain so until she required him.

She looked at Joe from the side of her eyes, suspiciously. "That new mustache which gives you such a romantic air. Your new uniform, very gallant. You look like one of those Imperial Hussars or something. And your Telly interviews. By a stretch of chance, I saw one of them the other day. That master of ceremonies seemed to think you are the most dashing soldier since Jeb Stuart."

Joe said to the waiter, "Champagne, please."

That worthy said apologetically, "May I see your credit card, major? The Exclusive Room is limited to Upper —"

Nadine said coldly, "The major is my guest. I am Dr. Nadine Haer." Her voice held the patina of those to the manor born, and not to be gainsaid. The other bowed hurriedly, murmured something placatingly, and was gone.

There was a tic at the side of Joe's mouth which usually manifested itself only in combat. He said stiffly, "I am afraid we should have gone to a Middle establishment."

"Nonsense. What difference does it make? Besides, don't change the subject. I am not to be fooled, Joe Mauser. Something is afoot. Now, just what?"

The tic had intensified. Joe Mauser looked at the woman he loved, realizing that it could never occur to her that he, a Mid-Middle, would presume to think in terms of wooing her. That even in her supposed scorn of rank, privilege and status, she was still, subconsciously perhaps, a noble and he a serf. Evolution there was in society, and the terms were different, but it was still a world of class distinction and she was of the ruling class, and he the ruled, she a patrician, he a pleb.

His voice went very even, very flat, almost as though he was speaking to a foe. "When we first met, Nadine, I told you that I had been born a Mid-Lower. Why, I don't know, but from my earliest memories I revolted against the strata in which birth placed me. History—I have had lots of time to read history, in hospital beds-tells me there have been few socio-economic systems under which the strong, intelligent, aggressive, cunning or ruthless couldn't work their way to the top. Very well, I intend to do it under People's Capitalism."

"Industrial Feudalism," she murmured.

"Call it what you will. I won't be happy until I'm a member of that one per cent on top."

She looked into his face. "Are you sure you will be then?"

"I don't know," he said angrily. "But I've heard the argument before. It's been used down through the ages by apologists for the privileged classes. Pity the poor rich man. While the happy slaves are sitting down on the levee, strumming their banjos, the poor plantation owner is up in his mansion drowning his sorrows in mint juleps."

She had an edge of anger, too. "All right," she snapped. "But I'll tell you this, Joe Mauser. The world is out of gear, but the answer isn't for individuals to better their material lot by jumping their caste statuses."

The waiter brought their wine, and, both angry, both held their peace until he had served it and left.

"What *is* the answer?" he said, mock in his voice. "It's easy enough for you, on top, to tell me, below, that the answer isn't in making my way to your level."

She was interrupted in her hot reply by a rolling of the orchestra's drums and the voice of a domineering M.C. who managed effectively to drown all vocal opposition at the tables.

* * * * *

Grinning inanely, holding onto his portable, wireless mike, he babbled along about the wonderful people present tonight and the good time being had by all. The Exclusive Room being founded on pure snobbery, he made great todo about the celebrities present. This politician, that actress, this currently popular songstress, that baron of industry.

Joe and Nadine ignored most of his chatter, still glaring at each other, until he came to....

"And those among us who are fracas buffs, and who isn't a fracas buff these days, given the merest drop of red blood? Fracas buffs will be thrilled to know that they are spending the evening in the company of the intrepid Major Joseph Mauser...."

Behind him, the orchestra broke into the quick strains of "The Girl I Left Behind Me."

"...Whose most recent act of sheer military genius and derringdo combined resulted in his all but single-handed winning of the fracas between Continental Hovercraft and Vacuum Tube Transport, and thus inflicting defeat upon none other than Marshal Stonewall Cogswell for the first time in more than a decade."

The M.C. babbled on, now about another present celebrity, a retired pugilist, once a champion.

Nadine looked into his face. "I think I understand now. You mentioned that in any society the ... how did you put it? ... the strong, intelligent, aggressive, cunning or ruthless could work their way to the top. You've tried strength, intelligence, and aggressiveness, haven't you, Joe? They didn't work. At least, not fast enough. So now you're giving cunning a try. Will ruthlessness be next, Joe Mauser?"

He was saved an answer.

A hulking body in evening wear stood next to their table, swaying. Joe looked up into a face glazed by either trank or alcohol. He didn't know the other man and for a moment failed to realize the other's purpose. The man was mumbling something that didn't come through.

Joe, irritated, said, "What in Zen do you want?"

The stranger shook his head, as though to clear it. He sneered, "The famous Joe Mauser, eh? The brave soldier-boy. Well, lemme tell you something, soldier-boy, you don't look so tough to me with your cute little mustache and your fancy-pants uniform. You look like a molly to me."

"That's too bad," Joe bit out. "And now, if you'll just go away." He turned his face from the other.

"Joe...!" Nadine said in an alarmed warning.

The other's contemptuous cuff, unsuspected, nearly bowled Joe completely from his chair. As it was, he barely caught himself.

His attacker shuffled backward and Joe recognized the trained step of the professional boxer. The other's identity now came to him, although he was no follower of pugilism, a sport largely out of favor since the rapid growth of Telly scanned fracases. Boxing at its top had never been more than an inadequate replacement of the games once held in the Roman area.

Joe was on his feet, instantly the fighting man under attack. The table that he and Nadine occupied was a ringside one, and in open view of half the room, but that meant nothing. He was under attack and for the nonce surprised, on the defensive.

"How'd you like them apples, soldier-boy?" the professional pugilist chuckled nastily. His left flicked forward and Joe barely avoided its connecting with his face.

He threw aside, for the time, any attempt to explain the other's uncalled for aggression. Unless he did something, and quick, he was going to be a laughing stock, rather than the hero into which Freddy Soligen was trying to build him.

Nadine said, Anxiously, "Joe … please … the waiters will deal with —".

He didn't hear her.

Joe Mauser, with all his hospital studies, had never heard of the Marquis of Queensbury. But even if he had, it would never have occurred to him to be bound by that arbiter of fisticuffs. In fact, he had no intention even of being restricted to the use of his hands as fists. The Japanese, long centuries before, had proven the fist less than the most effective manner in which to pursue hand-to-hand combat.

Joe Mauser, working coolly, fast and ruthlessly, now, a trained combat man exercising his profession, moved in for the kill, his shoulders hunched slightly forward, his hands forward and to the sides, choppers rather than sledges.

Joe stepped closer, as quick as a jungle cat. His left hand leapt forward to the other's neck, hacked, came back into another blurring swing, hacked again. His opponent grunted agony.

But a man does not become heavyweight champion without being able to take as well as give punishment. Joe's attacker tucked his chin into his shoulder, fighter style, and moved in throwing off the effects of the karate blows. Somehow, he seemed considerably less drunk or over-tranked than he had short moments before, and there was rage in his face, rather than glaze.

One of the blows caught Joe on a shoulder and sent him reeling back. At the same time, behind the other, Joe could see the maître d'hôtel flanked by three waiters, hurrying up. He was going to have to do something, and do it quickly, or be branded a boorish Middle who had intruded into a domain of the Uppers only to participate in a brawl and have to be expelled by the establishment's servants.

The former champ, his eyes narrowed in confidence of victory, came boring in, on his toes, quick for all of his bulk. Joe turned sideways, his movements lithe. He lashed out with his right foot, at this angle getting double the leverage he would have otherwise, and caught the other on the kneecap. The pugilist bent forward in agony, his mouth opening as though in protest.

Joe stepped forward, quickly, efficiently. His hands were now knitted together in a huge double fist. He brought them upward, crushingly, into his opponent's face, with all the force he could achieve, and felt bone and cartilage crush. Before even waiting for the other to fall, he turned, righted his chair, and resumed his seat facing Nadine, his breath coming only inconsiderably faster than before.

Her eyes were wide, but she hadn't organized herself as yet to the point of either protest or praise.

The maître d' was at their table. "Sir ——" he began.

Joe said curtly, "This barroom brawler attacked me. I'm surprised you allow your patrons to get into the shape he is. Please bring our bill."

The head waiter stuttered, his eyes going about in despair, even as his assistants were lifting the fallen champion to his feet and hustling him away.

An occupant of one of the nearby tables spoke up, collaborating Joe's words. The action had been fast, though brief, and had won the fascinated attention of that half of the patrons of the Exclusive Room near enough to see. Somebody else called out, too. And it came to Joe cynically, that a brawl in an establishment exclusive to Uppers, differed little from on of Middle or even Lower caste.

But it was impossible that they remain. He had looked forward to this evening with Nadine Haer, had planned to lay the foundations for a future campaign, when, as a newly created Upper, he would be in the position to mention marriage. He fumed, inwardly, even as he helped her with her wrap, preparatory to leaving.

Nadine, now that she had recovered composure, said coldly, "I suppose you realize you broke that man's nose and injured his eye to an extent I'd have to examine him to evaluate?"

Behind her, he rolled his eyes upward in mute protest. He said, "What was I supposed to do, hand him a rose from our table bouquet?"

"Violence is the resort of the incompetent."

"You must tell that, some time, to a jungle animal being attacked by a lion."

"Oh, you're impossible!"

III

When Freddy Soligen entered his living room, he automatically switched off the Telly screen which was the entire north wall. The room's lights automatically went brighter.

His perpetual air of sour cynicism was absent as he chuckled to the room's sole inhabitant, "What! A son of mine gawking at Telly? Next I'll be finding tranks by the bowl full, sitting on the tea table."

His son grinned at him. Already, at the ago of sixteen, Samuel Soligen was a good three inches taller than his father, at least ten pounds heavier. The boy was bright of eye, toothy of smile, gawky as only a teen-ager can be gawky, and obviously the proverbial apple of his father's eye.

Sam said, the faintest note of apology in his tone, "Just finished my assignments, Papa. Thought I'd see if there was anything worthwhile on the air."

"An incurable optimist," Freddy chuckled. "You take after your mother. Believe me, Sam. There's *never* anything worthwhile on Telly."

"Not even when you're casting?"

"*Especially* when I'm casting, boy. What've you been getting at the Temple school these days? Zen! I've been so busy on a special project I've been working on, I haven't had time to keep check on whether or not you're even still living here."

The boy shrugged, picked up an apple from the sideboard and began to munch. His voice was disinterested. "Aw, Comparative Religion, mostly. We gotta go way back and study about the Greeks and the Triple-Goddess, and then the Olympians, and all that curd."

"Hey, watch your language, Sam. Remember, you're going to wind up a priest."

"Yeah," the boy grumbled, "that'll be the day. You ever heard of a Lower becoming a full priest? I'll be lucky if I ever get to monk."

Freddy Soligen sat down suddenly, across from his son, and his voice lost its edge of good-natured humor and became deadly serious. "Listen, son. You were born a High-Lower, just like your father. Unfortunately, I wasn't jumped to Low-Middle until after your birth. But you're not going to stay a High-Lower, any more than I'm going to stay a Low-Middle."

The boy shrugged, his expression almost surly, now. "Aw, what difference does it make? High-Lower isn't too bad. It's sure better than Low-Lower. I got enough stock issued me for anything I'll ever need. Or, if not, I can work a while, just like you've done, and earn a few more shares."

Freddy Soligen's face worked, in alarm. "Hey, Sam, listen here. We've been over this before, but may be not as thoroughly as we should've. Sure, this is People's Capitalism and on top of that the Welfare State; they got all sorts of fancy names to call it. You've got cradle to the grave security. Instead of waiting for old age, or thirty years of service, or something, to get your pension, it starts at birth. At long last, the jerks have inherited the earth."

The boy said plaintively, as though in objection to his father's sneering words. "You aren't talking against the government, or the old time way of doing things, are you Papa? What's wrong with what we got? Everybody's got it made. Nobody hasta —".

His father was impatiently waving a hand at him in negation. "No, everybody doesn't have it made. Almost everybody's bogged down. That's the trouble Sam. The guts have been taken out of us. And ninety-nine people out of a hundred don't care. They've got bread and butter security. They've got trank to keep them happy. And they've got the fracases to watch, the sadistic, gory death of others to keep them amused, and their minds off what's really being done to them. We're not part of that ninety-nine out of a hundred, Sam. We're two of those who aren't jerks. We're on our way up out of the mob, to where life can be full. Got it, son? A full life. Doing things worth doing. Thinking things worth thinking. Associating with people who have it on the ball."

He had come to his feet in his excitement and was pacing before the boy who sat now, mouth slightly agape at his father's emphasis.

"Sam, listen. I'm getting along. Already in my forties, and I never did get much education back when I was your age. Maybe I'll never make it. But you can. That's why I insisted you switch categories. You were born into Communications, like me, but you've switched to Religion. Why'd you think I wanted that?"

"Aw, I don't know, Papa. I thought maybe —".

His father snorted. "Look, son, I haven't spent as much time with you as I should. Especially since your mother left us. She just couldn't stand what she called my being against everything. She was one of the jerks, Sam —".

"You oughtn'ta talk about my mother that way," Sam said sullenly.

"All right, all right. I just meant that she was willing to spend her life sucking on trank, watching Telly, and living on the pittance income from the unalienable stock shares issued her at birth. But let's get to this religious curd. Son, whatever con man first thought up the idea of gods put practically the whole human race on the sucker list. You say they're giving you comparative religion in your classes at the Temple now, eh? O.K., have you ever heard of a major religion where the priests didn't do just fine for themselves?"

"But Papa.... Well, shucks, there's always been —"

"Certainly, certainly, individuals. Crackpots, usually, out of tune with the rest of the priesthood. But the rank and file do pretty well for themselves. Didn't you point out earlier that a Lower, in our society, never makes full priest? Not to speak of bishop, or ultra-bishop. They're Uppers, part of the ruling hierarchy."

"Well, what's all this got to do with me getting into Category Religion? I'd think it'd be more fun in Communications, like you. Gee, Papa, going around meeting all those famous —"

Freddy Soligen's face worked. "Look, son. Sure, I meet lots of people on top. But the thing is, eventually you're going to become one of those people, not just interview them." He began pacing again in nervous irritation.

"Sam, those on top want to stay there. Like always. They freeze things so they, and their kids, will remain on top. In our case, they've made it all but impossible for anybody to progress from the caste they were born in. Not impossible, but almost. They've got to allow for the man with extraordinary ability, like, to bust out to the top, if he's got it on the ball. Otherwise, there'd be an explosion."

"That's not the way they say in school."

"It sure isn't. The story is that anybody can make Upper-Upper if he has the ability. But the thing is, Sam, you can't make a jerk realize he's a jerk. If he sees somebody else rise in caste, he can't see why he shouldn't. That's why real rising has been restricted to Category Military and Category Religion. In the military, a man gives up his security, obviously, and if he's a jerk he dies.

"In Category Religion they've got another way to sort out the jerks and make sure they never get further than monk and beyond the caste of High-Lower. Gods always work in mysterious ways and anybody in Category Religion who doesn't have faith in the wisdom of the God's mysterious choices of who to ordain and who to reject, obviously shows that he's not really got the *true faith* which is, of course, essential to a priest, not to speak of bishop or ultra-bishop. So obviously, the Gods were wise in rejecting him. In simpler words, the would-be priest who simply hasn't got what it takes, can be given the heave-ho without it being necessary for him, or his family or friends, to understand why. It's all very simple; he lacked the humility essential in a priest of the Gods, as proven by his rebellious reaction."

Sam said, unhappily, "I don't get all this."

Freddy Soligen came to a pause before the boy, sat down again abruptly and patted his son's knee. "You're young, Sam. Too young to understand some of it. Trust your father. Stick to your studies now. You have to get the basic gobbledygook. But you're on your way up the ladder, son. I've got a deal cooking that's going to give us an in. Can't tell you about it now, but it's going to mean an important break for us."

It was then that the door announced, "Major Joseph Mauser, calling on Fredric Soligen."

IV

Joe Mauser shook hands with the Telly reporter in an abrupt, impatient manner.

Freddy said, "Major, I'd like to introduce my son, Samuel. Sam, this is Major Joe Mauser. You don't follow the fracases, but the major's one of the best mercenaries in the field."

Sam scrambled to his feet and shook hands. "Gee, Joe Mauser."

Joe looked at him questioningly. "I thought you didn't follow the fracases."

Sam grinned awkwardly. "Well, gee, you can't miss picking up some stuff about the fighting. All the other guys are buffs."

Joe said to Freddy, "Could I speak to you alone?"

"Certainly, certainly. Sam, run along the major and I have business."

When the boy was gone, Joe sank into a chair and looked up at the Telly reporter accusingly. He said, "This fancy uniform, I stood still for. That idea of picking a song to identify me with and bribing the orchestra leaders to swing into it whenever I enter some restaurant or nightclub, might have its advantages. Getting me all sorts of Telly interviews, between fracases, and all those write-ups in the fracas buff magazines, I can see the need for, in spite of what it's costing. But what in Zen" —his voice went dangerous —"was the idea of sticking that punch-drunk prizefighter on me in the most respectable nightclub in Greater Washington?"

Freddy grinned ruefully. "Oh, you figured that out, eh?"

"Did you think I was stupid?"

Freddy rubbed his hands together, happily. "He used to be world champion, and you flattened him. It was in every gossip column in the country, every news reporter, played it up. And hell all it cost us was five shares of your Vacuum Tube Transport stock."

"Five shares!"

"Why not? He used to be champ. Now, he's so broke he's got to live on stock he isn't allowed to sell. His basic government issue at birth. He was willing to take a dive cheap, if you ask me."

Joe growled at him unhappily. "I've got news for you, Freddy. Your hired brawler started off as per instructions, evidently, but after a couple of blows had been exchanged his slap-happy brain lost the message and he tried to take me. We're lucky he didn't splatter me all over the dance floor of the Exclusive Club. He didn't take a dive. I had to scuttle him."

Freddy blinked. "Zen!"

"Sure, sure, sure," Joe growled. "Look, next time you decide to spend five shares of my stock on some deal like this, let me know, eh?"

Freddy walked to the sideboard and got glasses. "Whiskey?" he said.

"Tequila, if you've got it," Joe said. "Look, I'm beginning to have second thoughts about this campaign. Where's it got us, so far?"

Freddy brought the fiery Mexican drink and handed it to him, and took a place in the chair opposite. His voice went persuasive. "It's going fine. You're on everybody's lips. First thing you know, some of the armaments firms will be having you indorse their guns, swords, cannon, or whatever."

"Oh, great," Joe growled. "Already my friends are ribbing me about this fancy uniform and all the plugs I've been getting. The glory-grabber isn't any more popular today among real pros than he's ever been."

"Who gives a damn?" Freddy sneered, cynically. "We're not in this to please your lame-brain mercenary pals with their soldier-of-fortune codes of behavior. We're in this for Number One, Joe Mauser, and Number Two, Freddy Soligen."

Joe put away the greater part of his drink. "Sure, sure, sure. But where are we now? Your campaign has been in full swing for months. What's accomplished?"

The small Telly reporter was indignant. "What's accomplished? We've got three Major Joe Mauser buff clubs in full swing and five more starting up. And next month you're going to be on the cover of the *Fracas Times*."

"And I'm still a major and still Mid-Middle caste. And my stock shares available for bribery are running short."

Freddy twisted his mouth and looked worriedly down into his glass. He said unhappily, "We need a gimmick to climax all this. Some kind of gimmick to bring you absolutely to the top."

"A gimmick?" Joe demanded. "What do you mean, a gimmick?"

"You're going to have to do something really spectacular. Make you the biggest Telly hero of them all. We'll have to get you into a real fracas and pull something dramatic. I don't know what, I don't seem to be able to come up with an angle. But when I do, I'll guarantee that every Telly camera covering the fracas will be zeroed in on Joe Mauser."

"Great," Joe growled. "I've got just the gimmick. It'll wow them."

The Telly reported looked up, hopefully.

"I'll get killed in a burst of glory," Joe said.

V

A servant took Joe Mauser's cap at the door and requested that Joe follow him. Joe trailed behind on the way to the living room of the mansion, somewhat taken aback by the, to him, ostentation of the display of the luxuries of yesteryear. Among them was to be numbered the butler. Servants, other than military batmen, were simply not in Joe's world. Only the Uppers were in position to utilise the full time of individuals. Long years past, those tasks which once called for servants had been automated, from automated elevators to automated baby-sitters.

>

The servant announced him and then seemingly disappeared in the brief moment while Joe was bowing formally over Nadine Haer's hand. Even while murmuring the appropriate banalities,

226

Joe wondered how one acquired the ability to seemingly disappear, once one's services were no longer needed. Each man to his own trade, he decided.

He had a date with Nadine, but it turned out that the piquant Upper was not alone. In fact, it was obvious that she had not as yet got around to dressing for her appointment with Joe. He had promised to take her soaring in his sailplane. She was attired, as always, as those dress who have never considered the cost of clothing. And, as ever, when Joe saw her newly, after a period of a day or more away, he was taken with her intensity and her almost brittle beauty. What was it that the aristocrat seemed able to acquire after but a generation or two of what they were pleased to call breeding? That aloof quality, the exquisite gentility.

"Joe," Nadine said, "you'll be pleased to meet Philip Holland, Category Government, Rank Secretary. Phil, Major Joseph Mauser."

The other, possibly forty, shook hands firmly and looked into Joe's face. He had a crisp manner. "Good heavens, yes," he said. "That remarkable innovation of using an engineless aircraft for reconnaissance. My old friend, Marshal Cogswell, was speaking of it the other day. I assume that in advance you purchased stock in the firms which manufacture such craft, major. They must be booming."

Joe grimaced wryly. "No, sir. I wasn't smart enough to think of that. Professional soldiers are traditionally stupid. What was the old expression? They can take their shirts off without unbuttoning their collars."

Philip Holland cocked his head, even as he chuckled. "I detect a note of bitterness, major."

Nadine said airily, "Joe is ambitious, thinking the answer to all his problems lies in jumping his caste to Upper."

Joe looked at her impatiently to where she sat on a Mid-Twentieth Century type sofa.

Philip Holland said, "Possibly he's right, my dear. Each of us have different needs to achieve such happiness as is possible to man."

To Joe, he sounded just vaguely on the stuffy side, even through the crispness. By nature nervous and quick moving, Holland seemed to try and project an air of calm which didn't quite come off. Joe wondered what his relationship to Nadine could be, a twinge of jealousy there. But that was ridiculous. Nadine must be in the vicinity of thirty. Obviously, she knew, and had known, many men as attracted to her as was Joe Mauser-And men in her own caste, at that. Somehow, though, he felt Holland was no Upper. The other simply didn't have the air.

Joe said to him, "Nadine doesn't get my point. I contend that in a strata divided society, it's hard to realize yourself fully until you're a member of the upper caste. Admittedly, perhaps you won't even if you are such a member, but at least you haven't the obstacles with which the lower class or classes are beset."

"Interestingly stated," Holland said briskly. He returned to his chair from which he had arisen to shake hands with Joe, and looked at Nadine. "You said, on introducing us, that Joe would be glad to meet me, my dear. Why, especially?"

Nadine laughed. "Because I have been practicing your arguments upon him."

Both of the men frowned at her.

Nadine looked at Joe. "Phil Holland's the most interesting man I know, I do believe. He's secretary to Marlow Mannerheim, the Minister of Foreign Affairs, and simply couldn't be more privy to the inner workings of government. It was Phil who convinced me that something is wrong with our socio-economic system."

"Oh?" Joe said. He wasn't really interested. Let society solve its problems. He had his own. And they were sufficient unto themselves as well as the day thereof. However, conversation was to be kept moving. He needled the other. "I've heard it contended that any type of government is good given capable, intelligent personnel to run it, or bad if not so managed. What was the example I read somewhere? Both heaven and hell are despotisms."

Phil Holland shrugged. "An interesting observation. However, institutions, including socio-political ones, can become outdated. When they do, no matter how intelligent, capable and honest the governmental heads, that socio-political system can be a hell. If, at such time there are capable, intelligent persons available, they will take such measures as are necessary to change the institutions."

Nadine had come to her feet. "The subject is my favorite, but I must change. Joe is taking me a-gliding, and I'm sure this frock isn't *de rigueur*. You gentlemen will excuse me?" She was off before they had time to come to their feet.

* * * * *

Joe Mauser settled himself again, crossing his legs. He said, idly, "And you think our basic institutions have reached the state of needing change?"

"Perhaps, although as a member of the Government Category, it should hardly be my position to advocate such." He seemed to switch subjects. "Have you read much of the Roman *ludi*, the games as we call them?"

"The gladiators and such?" Joe shrugged. "I've read a bit about them. It's been pointed out, in fact by Dr. Haer, among others, that basically our present day fracases serve the same purposes. That instead of bread and circuses, provided by the Roman patricians to keep the unemployed Roman mob from becoming restive, we give them trank pills and Telly violence."

"Um-m-m," Holland nodded, "but that isn't the point I was making right now. What I was thinking was that at first the Roman games were athletic affairs without bloodshed. It wasn't until 264 B.C. that three pairs of slaves were sent in to fight with swords. By 183 B.C. the number had gone up to sixty pairs. By 145 B.C. ninety pairs fought for three days. But that was just the beginning. They really got under way with the dictators. Sulla put a hundred lions into the arena, but Julius Caesar topped that with four hundred and Pompey that with six hundred, plus over four hundred leopards and twenty elephants. Augustus beat them all with three thousand five hundred elephants and ten thousand men killed in a series of games. But it was the emperors who really expanded the ludi. Trajan had ten thousand animals killed in the arena to celebrate his victory over the Dacians, not to mention eleven thousand people.

"Are you surprised at my memory? The subject has always fascinated me. For one thing, I am a great believer in the theory that history repeats itself. As time went on, arenas were built all over the empire, even small towns boasted their own. In Rome, the number of them grew so that eventually an avid follower could attend every day, the year around. And as they increased in quantity they also had to grow more extreme to hold the fan's attention. The Emperor Philip, in celebrating the thousandth anniversary of the founding of Rome, had killed a thousand pair of gladiators, a rhinoceros, six hippopotami, ten hyenas, ten giraffes, twenty wild asses, ten tigers, ten zebras, thirty leopards, sixty lions, thirty-two elephants, forty wild horses. I am afraid I forgot the rest."

Joe stirred in his chair. The other's personality grew on him. The crisp voice had a certain magnetic quality that made what he said important, somehow. However, Joe's interest in Roman history wasn't exactly paramount.

Holland said, "You wonder at what I am driving, eh? Do you realize the expense involved in getting a rhinoceros to Rome in those days? Not to speak of hippopotami, tigers, lions and leopards. Few people realize the extent to which the Romans went to acquire exotic animals to be slaughtered for the edification of the mob. They penetrated as far south as Kenya, there are still the ruins of a Roman fort there; as far east as Indonesia; as far north as the Baltic, and there is even evidence that they brought polar bears from Iceland."

Philip Holland snorted, as though in contempt. "But the mob wearied of even such spectacle as giraffes being killed by pigmies from the Iturbi forest. The games had started as fights between skilled swordsmen, being observed by knowledgeable combat soldiers of a warrior people. But as the Romans lost their warlike ardor and became a worthless mob performing no useful act for either themselves or the State, they no longer appreciated a drawn-out duel between equals. They wanted quick blood, and lots of it, and turned to mass slaughter of Christians, runaway slaves, criminals and whoever else they could find to throw to the lions, crocodiles or whatever.

Even this became old hat, and they turned increasingly to more extreme sadism. Children were hung up by their heels and animals turned loose to pull them down. Men were tied face to face with rotting corpses and so remained until death. Animals were taught to rape virgins."

Joe Mauser stirred again. What in Zen was this long monologue on the Roman games leading to?

Holland said, "By the way, contrary to some belief, the games didn't end upon Christianity becoming the dominant faith and finally the State religion. Constantine legalized Christianity in 313 A.D. but it wasn't until 365 that Valentinian passed a law against sacrificing humans to animals in the arena and the gladiator schools remained in operation until 399. The arenas were finally closed in 404 A.D. but by that time the Roman Empire was a mockery. In all they last more than half a millennium, but things move faster these days."

The tone of voice changed abruptly and Holland snapped a question at Joe. "By your age, I would imagine you've participated in the present day fracases for some fifteen years. How have they changed in that time?"

Joe was taken aback. "Why ..." he said, hesitated as he got the other's point, then went on, nodding. "Yes. They used to be company size —a few hundred lads involved. After a while, a battalion size fracas became fairly commonplace, then about ten years ago a corporation of any size had to be able to put at least a regiment into the field and the biggies had brigades."

"And now?" Holland urged.

"Now a divisional size fracas is the thing."

"Yes, and if a corporation isn't among the top dozen or so, a single defeat can mean bankruptcy."

Joe nodded. He had known of such cases.

Holland leaned back in his chair, as though all his points had been made. He said, his voice less brisk, "Our People's Capitalism, our Welfare State, took the road of bringing the equivalent of the Roman ludi to keep our people in a state of stupefied acceptance of the *status quo*. And as in the case of Rome, the games are bankrupting it. Our present day patrician class, our Uppers, have a tiger by the tail, Joseph Mauser, and can't let go. We need those capable and intelligent people of whom you spoke earlier, to make some basic changes. Where are they? Nadine said that your great driving ambition is to be jumped to Upper in caste. But even though you make it, what will you have on your hands but these problems that the Uppers seem unable to solve?"

Joe said, impatiently, "Possibly you're right. What you say about the fracases becoming bigger and more expensive is true. They're also becoming more bloody. In the old days, a corporation or union going into a fracas was conscious of having a high casualty list among the mercenaries. Highly trained soldiers cost money. Insurance, indemnity, pensions, all the rest of it. Consequently, you'd fight a battle of movement, maneuver, brainwork on the part of the officer commanding, so that practically nobody was hurt on either side. One force or the other would surrender after being caught in an impossible situation. Not any more. These days, they want blood. Plenty of blood. And they want the Telly cameras to focus right into the middle of it."

Joe shook his head. "But it's not my problem to solve. I've got my goal. I'll worry about other ones when I've achieved it."

* * * * *

A voice behind him said superciliously, "I do believe it's the status hungry captain, ah, that is, major these days. To what do I owe this unexpected visit, Major Mauser?"

Joe came to his feet and faced the newcomer, Philip Holland doing the same, somewhat more leisurely.

Baron Balt Haer, wearing a colonel's uniform and flicking his swagger stick along his booted leg, stood in the doorway. His voice was lazily arrogant. "And Mr. Holland, I must say, the Middle caste seems to have taken over the house. Well, Major Mauser? I assume you do not labor under the illusion that you are welcome in this dwelling."

In Category Military rank is observed whilst in uniform, even though neither individual is currently on active service. Joe had automatically come to attention. He said, stiffly, "Sir, I am calling upon your sister, Dr. Haer."

"Indeed," Baron Haer said, his nostrils high in that attitude once perfected by grandees of medieval Spain, landed gentry of England, Prussian Junkers. "I find that my sister, in her capacity as medical scientist, seems to go to extreme in her research. What aspect of the lower classes is she studying in your case, major?"

Joe flushed. "Baron Haer," he said, "we seem to have got off on the wrong foot when we participated in that fracas against Continental Hovercraft under your father, the late Baron. I would appreciate an opportunity to start over again."

"Would you indeed?" Balt Haer said loftily. He turned his eye to Philip Holland, whose mouth bore the slightest suggestions of suppressed humor. "Unless I am mistaken, the conversation at the time of my entry seemed to have a distinctly subversive element. Shouldn't this be somewhat surprising in the secretary of the administration's foreign minister?"

Philip Holland said crisply, "You must have intruded, um-m-m, that is, entered, at the end of a sentence, Baron Haer. We were merely discussing the various methods, down through the ages, that ruling classes have utilized to perpetuate themselves in power."

Haer obviously disbelieved him. He said, "For example?"

"There are many examples," Holland said, reseating himself. "For instance, the medieval feudalistic class who dominated the ignorant and highly superstitious serfdom soon found it expedient to add to their titles *by grace of God*, as though it was God's wish that they be count or baron, prince or king. What serf would dare attempt the overthrow of his lord, in the face of God's wishes?"

"I see," Balt Haer said. "And other examples?"

Holland shrugged. "The Chinese Mandarins utilized possibly the most unique method of a governing class perpetuating itself ever known, certainly one of the most gentle."

Haer was scowling at him, obviously out of his depth, as was Joe Mauser for that matter.

Holland said crisply, "The mandarins devised a written language so complicated that it took at least ten years to master reading and writing, thus assuring that only the very well-to-do could afford to educate their sons. When invaded, as so often China has been invaded, only the mandarins were in the position to serve the conquerors by carrying on the paperwork so vital to any advanced society. So, still in control of the machinery of government, they continued to perpetuate themselves, and shortly-as history is reckoned-we found the conquerors assimilated and the mandarins still in power."

Balt Haer said impatiently, "I seem to be under the impression that you were speaking of more current times, when I entered, Mr. Holland."

From the door, Nadine said, "Good heavens, Balt, are you badgering my guests again?"

The three men faced her.

Balt said nastily, "I am astonished that you persist in bringing members of the lower orders into my home, Nadine."

"Our home, Balt. In fact, if you must bring up such matters before outsiders, you will recall that you converted your portion of the family estate into continental Hovercraft stock, shortly before father met Baron Zwerdling's forces in the recent fracas. No wonder you dislike Major Mauser. Through his efforts, our company won, rather than losing as you had expected."

Her brother, who could have been only slightly her senior, was obviously enraged. "Are you suggesting that I am not welcome to stay in this, our family home, simply because the property is in your name?"

"Not at all," she sighed. "You are always at home here, Balt, I simply demand that you exercise common courtesy to my guests."

He turned and walked stiff kneed from the room.

* * * * *

230

"Sorry," Joe said to Nadine.

"Why?" she said simply. "The fact of the matter is that Balt and I are continually at each other. He is quite the active member of the Nathan Hale society."

Joe frowned his ignorance and looked at Holland.

Holland chuckled. "An ultra-conservative —reactionary might be the better term-organization devoted to witch hunting and such in its efforts to maintain the *status quo*, major. Once again, history repeats itself. Such groups invariably evolve when basic change threatens a socio-economic system." He looked at Nadine. "I must be going, my dear. My, how charming you look. If this is the customary garb whilst going a-gliding, I shall have to take up the sport."

"Why Phil, inane words of flattery from serious old you?"

Joe squirmed inwardly, wondering again upon what basis was the friendship of Nadine Haer and Philip Holland.

The butler entered and said, "A call for Major Mauser, if you please."

Only Max Mainz, his batman during his last fracas and now permanently attached to Joe, knew that he might be found at this address. Joe said to Nadine, "Would you pardon me for a moment? I assume it's something important, or I wouldn't be disturbed."

She said, demurely, "Undoubtedly one of the feminine members of a Joe Mauser buff club."

He snorted amusement and followed the butler to the library and the tele-screen.

Max Mainz's face loomed in the viewing screen. As soon as Joe appeared, he said, "Major, sir, the marshal's been trying to get hold of you ever since you left the hotel."

"The marshal?" Joe scowled.

"Marshal Cogswell. That one they call Stonewall Cogswell. And when he wants somebody, he really wants 'em, and I got a feeling it's a good idea to come on the double."

Joe laughed. "Stonewall Cogswell's a tough one all right, Max."

"You ain't just a countin' down, major, sir. He says when I get hold of you to come on over to his headquarters soonest."

"All right, Max, thanks." Joe flicked the set off.

Actually, Max was right. You didn't ignore a summons from Marshal Cogswell. Not if you were in the Category Military and ambitious. The date with Nadine was off. And just when he was beginning to detect signs of her meeting him on his own level.

VI

It was the common practice among Category Military mercenaries of highest rank to maintain skeleton staffs between those periods when they were under hire by corporations or unions. That of Marshal Stonewall Cogswell was one of the most complete, he habitually keeping upward of a hundred officers in his private uniform. It paid off, for with such a skeleton force of highly skilled professionals as a cadre, the marshal could enlist veterans for his rank and file and whip together a trained fighting force in a fantastically short period.

And nothing was so of the essence as time, in the present Category Military. For when two corporations sued for permission to meet on a military reservation for trial by combat to settle their commercial differences, the sums involved were staggering. Joe Mauser had been correct in saying that the fracas had grown, even in his memory, from skirmishes involving a company or two of men, to full fledged battles with a division or even more on either side, forty thousand men at each other's throats.

So a commanding officer became noted not only for his abilities in the field, but also those of cutting financial corners, recruiting his force of mercenaries, whipping them into a unit and getting them into the action. In fact, corporations, these days, invariably stated the period of time to be involved when they petitioned the Category Military Department. Perhaps a month, three weeks of which would be used for recruiting and drill, the last week for the fracas itself. Nobody could excel Marshal Cogswell in using the three weeks to best advantage.

Major Joe Mauser came to attention before the desk of the lieutenant colonel of Marshal Cogswell's staff who was acting as receptionist before the sanctum sanctorum of the field genius. He saluted and snapped, "Joseph Mauser, sir. Category Military, Rank Major. On request to see the marshal."

Lieutenant Colonel Paul Warren answered the salute, but then came to his feet and grinned while extending his hand to be shaken. He said, "Good to see you again, Mauser. Hope you're in this one with us." His grin turned rueful. "That trick of yours with the glider cost me a pretty penny. I'd made the mistake of wagering heavily on Hovercraft. But the marshal is waiting. Right through that door, major. See you later."

Evidently, Joe decided, the marshal was recruiting for another fracas. Which was why Joe had been summoned, although when a field officer of Cogswell's stature was gathering officers to command a force, he seldom called upon them; they clamored for permission to serve with him. You weren't apt to find yourself in the dill, under Cogswell, and you practically never failed to collect your victory bonus. Victory was a habit.

Marshal Cogswell looked up from the desk at which he sat scowling at a military chart stretched before him. The scowl disappeared and his strong face lit with pleasure. The craggy marshal was a small man but strongly built, clipped of voice and with a tone that would suggest he had been born to command, had always commanded.

Joe snapped to the salute which the marshal acknowledged with a flick of his baton, then stood to shake hands. "Ah, Major Mauser. Bit of trouble locating you." His eyes narrowed momentarily. "Trust you are not at present affiliated with any company colors." He took in Joe's uniform and scowled vaguely, not placing it.

Joe said in self-deprecation, "This is my own devising, sir. I thought if I was going to have to present myself to be killed, for a living, that I might as well show up before the screens as distinctively as possible. I've been told that ultimately the fracas buffs make or break you, in our category."

The marshal frowned, as though unhappy and possibly surprised at Joe's words, however, he sat down again and repeated his question by merely looking at the other.

"No, sir, I'm free," Joe said. "However, frankly, I wasn't looking for a commission right at this time."

Cogswell stared at him. Mauser was a good junior officer and they'd been through half a dozen fracases together over the years, not always on the same side.

"Why not?" Cogswell barked. "Are you convalescing, major? Surely you didn't manage to cop one in that last farce?"

"Personal reasons, sir."

"Very well," Cogswell growled. "However, I'm going to attempt to sway you, major. Would seem that I am up against it, if I don't, and, in a manner it's your fault."

Joe was bewildered. "My fault, sir?"

The older man's voice went brisk. "This is the situation. I have been approached by the United Miners to command their forces in their trial by combat with Carbonaceous Fuel. Same old issues, of course. Contract between the union and corporation is usually for only two years. Each time it comes up again, the union officials try to get a larger cut of the pie and the hereditary heads of Carbonaceous Fuel resist. Automatically, the Category Military Department issues a permit. The fracases they've been fighting prove so popular that there'd be riots if the permit was refused. Frankly, I'm no great admirer of the group in control of United Miners, but —"

Joe was surprised enough to say, "Why not, sir?" Old pro mercenaries seldom concerned themselves as to the issues or principles involved in a fracas. They chose their side by more mundane considerations.

* * * * *

Marshal Cogswell looked at him testily. "Sit down, Joe. You're not on my staff, as yet, at least. Zen take the formality!" When Joe had accepted the chair, he growled again. "Suppose you didn't know I was born into Category Mining?"

"No, sir."

"Well, I was. But even as a boy this new industrial revolution was cutting the number of employees involved in the category each year that went by."

"That's happened in every field, sir. Including my original one." Joe Mauser was thinking, *so what?*

"Of course," Cogswell rapped. "My objection is what happened to the union. Unions were originally founded as an instinctive gathering together of employees to achieve as high a pay as they could get from the employer, with the strike as their weapon. But whatever the original purpose, and its virtue or lack of it, the union grew into something entirely different by the early and middle twentieth century. Such unions as the United Miners grew to such a size that they, themselves, became some of the largest business organizations in the country. And eventually they came to be run, like any other business, for the benefit of those who owned or controlled them. The professional labor leader evolved, motivated by his own interests and finally becoming, in his despotic control of the union, backed by goon squads and gangsters, as powerful a man as was to be found in the country. Seldom were strikes any longer held to better the condition of the individual union members. Instead, the issues were contracts which allowed for fabulous sums to go into the union coffers where they were at the disposal of the union officials."

The marshal grunted sourly. "Now that the whole industry of mining is all but completely automated and only a few thousands employed actively, there are confounded few miners not on the unemployed list, but the union officials wax as fat as ever, what with the percentages of each ton mined going into so-called welfare funds, and such."

He looked at Joe, evidently conscious that he had made an inordinary long speech for the supposedly taciturn Stonewall Cogswell. He cleared his throat and said, "Not that it's my affair. I switched categories to Military, in my youth. Let us get to the point. I've been caught napping, Joe."

That was an unlooked for confession to come from Stonewall Cogswell. Joe said nothing, waiting for more.

The marshal shook his baton at the younger officer. "By utilizing that confounded glider of yours as a reconnaissance craft, you revolutionized present warfare, major. Act of absolute ingenuity, and I admired it. Unfortunately, I failed to realize the speed with which every professional in our category would jump upon the bandwagon and secure gliders for himself."

Joe saw light.

"Been caught short," Cogswell rapped. "Short of gliders. Short of even one glider. And within a few weeks I'm committed to a divisional size fracas." He pushed back his chair, angrily. "General McCord is in command of the Carbonaceous Fuel forces. Met him before, and always brought up victory only by the skin of my teeth. But this time he has two gliders. I have none."

"But, sir, surely you can either buy or rent several craft on the market."

"Confound it! It's not the machines that are unavailable, but the trained pilots to operate them. The sport hasn't been popular in half a century. Not overly so, even then."

"But training a pilot —"

"Training a pilot, nonsense!" the marshal was shaking his baton at him again, in indignation. "A *pilot* won't do. He must also be a trained reconnaissance man. Must be able to follow terrain from the air. Identify military forces both in nature and number. I needn't tell you this, major. You above all know the problem."

It hadn't occurred to Joe, but the other was obviously right. There couldn't be more than a few dozen men in Category Military who could hold down both the job of pilot and reconnaissance officer. In another six months, the situation would have changed. Officers would quickly be trained. But now? As Cogswell said, he was caught short.

Joe came to his feet. "Sir, I'll have to consider the commission. Frankly, my plans were otherwise."

Cogswell started at him grimly. "Mauser, you've always been one of the best. An old pro, in every sense of the word. However, there have been some rumors going around about your ambitions."

Joe said stiffly, "Sir, my ambitions are my own business, whatever these rumors."

"Didn't say I believed them, major. We've been together too often when the situation has pickled for me to judge you without more evidence than gossip. What I was leading up to, is this. There's nothing wrong with ambition. If you see me through in this, I'll do what I can toward pushing your promotion."

Joe came to the salute again. "Thank you, sir. I'll consider the commission and let you know by tomorrow."

Cogswell flicked the baton, in his nonchalant answer to salute. "That will be all, then, major."

VII

Freddy Soligen wasn't at home when Joe Mauser called. The Category Military officer was met, instead, by young Sam Soligen, clothed this day in the robes of a novitiate of the Temple. Joe remembered now that Freddy had mentioned the boy in training in Category Religion.

Sam led him back into the living room, switching off the Telly screen which had been tuned in on one of the fictionalized fracases of the past. Poor entertainment, when compared to the real thing, for any fracas buff, but better than nothing. In fact, it was even contended by some that if you got yourself properly tranked you could get almost as much emotion from a phony-fracas, as they were called, as for the genuine.

"Gee, sir," Sam said, "Papa was supposed to be back by now. I don't know where he is. If you wanta wait —"

Joe shrugged and picked himself a chair. He took in Sam's robes and made conversation. "Studies tough in the Temple schools?" he asked.

The teen-ager realized it was a make-talk question. He said, "Aw, not much. A lot of curd about rituals and all. You hafta memorize it."

"Curd, yet," Joe laughed. "You don't sound particularly pious, Sam. Come to think of it, I suppose any child of Freddy's could hardly be."

Sam said, his young voice urgent, "Papa said you were on your way up, Major Mauser. Just like us. Gee, how come you chose Category Military, instead of Religion?"

Joe Mauser looked at the other. It was his policy to treat young people either as children or adults. If he was to deal with a teen-ager as an adult, he didn't believe in pulling punches any more than had he been dealing with a person of sixty. He said, flatly, "I've never had much regard for those categories in which a man makes his living battening on human sorrow or fear, Sam. That includes in my book such fields as religion, undertakers and their affiliates, and even most doctors, for that matter." He added, to explain the last inclusion, "They profit too much from illness, for my satisfaction."

Major Mauser was enough of a current celebrity for practically anything he said to be impressive to young Sam Soligen. That youngster blinked. He said, "Well, gee, don't you believe in any gods at all? If you believe in any god at all, you gotta have a religious category, and that means priests."

"Why?" Joe said. Inwardly, he was amused at himself for getting into a debate with this youngster and even a trifle ashamed of needling the boy about his chosen field. But he said, "If there are gods, I doubt if they'd intrust a priesthood to threaten their created humanity with hellfire."

Sam was taken aback. "Well, why not?"

"Gods couldn't be bothered with such triviality. In fact, I'd think it unlikely they could be bothered with priests. If I was a god, certainly I couldn't."

The boy's face was intent, its youthfulness somewhat ludicrous in view of the dark robes he wore. He leaned forward, "Yeah, you talk about priests and undertakers and all battening on human sorrow, but how about you? How about the Category Military? How many men you killed, major?"

Joe winced. "Too many," he said abruptly. The tic was at the side of his mouth, unbeknownst to him. He added, "But mercenaries have deliberately chosen their path. They know what they're going into and they do it willingly, they haven't been drafted."

He thought a moment, and Phil Holland's talk about the Roman *ludi* came back to him. He said, "It's like the difference between throwing a bunch of Christians to some wild bulls in a Roman arena, to being a torero in Spain, a matador who has chosen his profession and enters the bullring to make money."

Then the boy said something that gave him greater depth than Joe had expected. "Yeah," he said, "but maybe the torero was forced into becoming a bullfighter on account of how bad he needed the money." In the heat of the discussion, he was emboldened to add, "And these new Rank Privates that go into a fracas, not knowing what it's all about, just filled with all the stuff we see on Telly and all. How much of a chance does one of them have if he runs into an old-timer like Joe Mauser, out there in no-man's-land?"

Touché, Joe thought.

* * * * *

There was the action that sometimes came back to him in his dreams. He had been a sergeant then, but already the veteran of five years or more standing, and a double score of fracases. The force of which he was a member had been in full retreat, and Joe's squad was part of the rear-guard. The terrain had been mountainous, the High Sierra Military Reservation. Four of his men had copped one, two so badly that they had to be left behind, incapable of being moved. Joe, under the pressure of long hours of retreat under fire, had finally sent the others on back, and found himself a crevice, near the top of a sierra, which was all but impregnable.

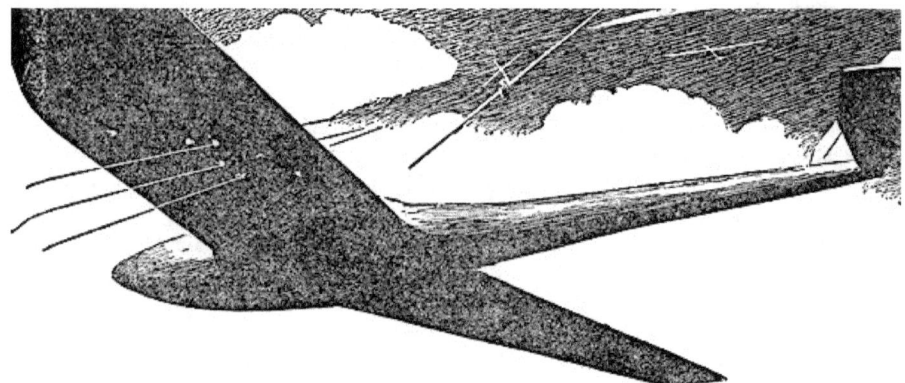

His rifle had been a .45-70 Springfield, with its ultra-heavy slug, but slow muzzle velocity. And Joe had a telescope mounted upon it, an innovation that barely made the requirement of predating the year 1900 and thus subscribing to the Universal Disarmament Pact between the Sov-world and the West-world. It had taken the enemy forces a long time to even locate him, a long time and half a dozen casualties that Joe had coolly inflicted. The way to get to him, the only way, involved exposure. Joe could see the enemy officers, through his scope, at a distance just out of his range. They knew the situation, being old pros. He found considerable satisfaction in the rage he knew they were feeling. He was dominating a considerable section of the front, due to the terrain, and there was but one way to root him out, direct frontal attack.

They had sent in Rank Privates; Low-Lowers, most of them in their first fracas. Low-Lowers, the dregs of society, seldom employed and then at the rapidly disappearing, all but extinct, unskilled labor jobs. Low-Lowers, most of them probably in this fracas in hopes of the unlikelihood of so distinguishing themselves that they would be jumped a caste, or at least acquire an extra share or two of common stock to better the basic living guaranteed by the State. Rank Privates, most in their first fracas, unknowledgeable about taking cover and not even in the physical condition this sort of combat demanded.

They came in time and again, surprisingly courageous, Joe had to admit, and time and again he decimated them. One by one, coolly, seldom wasting a shot. Not that he had to watch his ammunition, he had the squad's full supply. He estimated that before it was through he had inflicted approximately thirty casualties. Hits in the head, in the torso, the arms, legs. He had inflicted enough casualties to fill a field hospital. And it had all ended, finally, when a senior officer below had arrived on the scene, took in the irritating situation, and sent a dozen noncoms and junior officers, experienced men, to dig Joe out. Joe had remained only long enough for a few final shots, none of them effective, at long range, and had then hauled out and followed after his squad. He might possibly have got two or three more of his opponents, but only at his own risk. Besides, already the irritation and hate that he had built up while on the run, and while his squad mates were copping wounds, had left him and there was nausea in his belly at the slaughter he had perpetrated.

Or that time on the Louisiana Reservation in the fracas between Allied Petroleum and United Oil. Joe had been a lieutenant then and —

But he rejected this trend of thought and brought his attention back to Sam Soligen.

"Perhaps you're right," he admitted. "Some Low-Lower jerk, impressed by what he considers high pay and adventure, doesn't stand much of a chance against an old pro."

The gawky tee-ager broke into a toothy smile. "Gee, I wasn't arguing with you, major. I don't know anything about it. How about telling me about one of your fracases, eh? You know, some time you really got in the dill."

Joe snorted. He seldom met someone not of Category Military who didn't want a special detailed description of some gory action in which Joe had participated. And like all veterans of combat, there was nothing he liked less to do. Combat was something which, when done, you wished to leave behind you. Were brain washing really practicable, it was this you would wish to wash away.

But Joe, like others before him, down through the ages, had found a way out. He had a store of a dozen or so humorous episodes with which he could regale listeners. That time his horse's cinch had loosened when he was on a scouting mission and he had galloped around and around amidst a large company of enemy skirmishers, most of them running after him and trying to drag him from the horse's back, while he hung on for dear life.

But it occurred to him that the boy might better appreciate a tale which involved his father, the Telly reporter, and some act of daring the small man had performed the better to serve his fracas-buff audience.

He was well launched into the tale, boosting Freddy Soligen's part beyond reality, but not impossibly so, when that worthy entered the room, breaking it off.

While Freddy was shaking hands with his visitor, Sam said, "Hey, Papa, you never told me about that time you were surrounded by all the field artillery, and only you and Major Mauser and three other men got out."

Freddy grinned fondly at the boy and then looked his reproach at Joe. "What're you trying to do, make the life of a Telly reporter sound romantic to the kid? Stick to the priesthood, son, there's more chicken dinners involved." He saw Joe was impatient to talk to him. "How about leaving us alone for a while, Sam? We've got some business."

"Sure, Papa. I've got to memorize some Greek chants, anyway. How come they don't have all these rituals and all in some language everybody can understand?"

"Then everybody might understand them," Freddy said sourly. "Then what'd happen?"

His son said, "Major, maybe you can finish that story some other time, huh?"

Joe said, "Sure, sure, sure. It winds up with your father the hero and they bump him up to Upper-Upper and make him head of Category Communications."

"On the trank again," Freddy grumbled, but Joe sensed he wasn't particularly amused.

* * * * *

When the boy was gone, Joe Mauser told the Telly reporter of his interview with Stonewall Cogswell.

Freddy shook his head. "He wants you to fly that sailplane thing of yours again, huh? No. That won't do it. We need some gimmick, Joe. Something —"

Joe said impatiently, "You keep saying that. But, look, I'm a mercenary. A fighting man can't drop out of participation in the fracases if he expects the buffs to continue interest in him."

The little man tried to explain. "I'm not saying you're going to drop out of the fracases. But we need something where we can make you shine. Somewhere where you can be on every lens for a mile around."

Joe's face was still impatient.

Freddy said sourly, "Listen, you tried to handle all this by yourself, last time. You dreamed up that fancy glider gimmick and sold it to old Baron Haer. But did you do yourself any good with the buffs? Like Zen you did. All you did was louse up a perfectly promising fracas so far as they were concerned. Hardly a drop of blood was shed. Stonewall Cogswell just resigned when he saw what he was up against. Oh, sure, you won the battle for Vacuum Tube Transport, practically all by yourself, but that's not what the buff wants. He wants blood, he wants action, spectacular action. And you can't give it to him way up there in the air. Hey —!"

Joe looked at him, scowling questioningly.

Freddy said, slowly, "Why not?"

Joe Mauser growled, "What'd you mean, why not?"

Freddy said slowly, "Why can't you have some blood and guts combat, right up there in that glider?"

"Have you gone drivel-happy?"

But the little man was on his feet, pacing the floor quickly, irritably, but still happily. "A dogfight. A natural. Listen, you ever heard about dogfights, major?"

"You mean pitdogs, like in Wales, in the old days?"

"No, no. In the First War. All those early fighters. Baron Von Richthofen, the German, Albert Ball, the Englishman, René Fonck, the Frenchman. And all the rest. Werner Voss and Ernst Udet, and Rickenbacker and Luke Short."

Joe nodded at last. "I remember now. They'd have a Vickers or Spandau mounted so as to fire between the propeller blades. As I recall, that German, Richthofen, had some eighty victories to his credit."

"O.K. They called them dogfights. One aircraft against another. You're going to reintroduce the whole thing."

Joe was staring at him. Once again the Telly reporter sounded completely around the bend.

Freddy was impatiently patient. "We'll mount a gun on your sailplane and you'll attack those two gliders Cogswell says General McCord has."

Joe said, "The Sov-world observers would never stand still for it. In fact, there's a good chance that using gliders at all will be forbidden when the International Disarmament Commission convenes next month. If the Sov-world delegates vote against use of gliders as reconnaissance craft, the Neut-world will vote with them. Those Neut-world delegates vote against everything." Joe grunted. "It's true enough gliders were flown before the year 1900, but not the kind of advanced sailplanes you have to utilize for them to be practical. Certainly there were no gliders in use capable of carrying a machine gun."

Freddy demanded, "Look, what was the smallest machine gun in use in 1900?"

Joe considered. "Probably the little French Chaut-Chaut gun. It was portable by one man, the rounds were carried in a flat, circular pan. I think it goes back that far. They used them in the First War."

"Right! O.K., you had gliders. You had eight portable machine guns. All we're doing is combining them. It'll be spectacular. You'll be the most famous mercenary in Category Military and it'll be impossible for the Department not to bounce you to colonel and Low-Upper. Especially with me and every Telly reporter and fracas-buff magazine we've bribed yelling for it."

Joe's mouth manifested its tic, but he was shaking his head. "It wouldn't go, anyway. Suppose I caught one, or both, of those other gliders, busy at their reconnaissance and shot their tails off. So what? The fans still wouldn't have their blood and gore. We'd be so high they couldn't see the action. All they would be able to see would be the other glider falling."

Freddy stopped dramatically and pointed a finger at him in triumph. "That's where you're wrong. I'll be in the back seat of your sailplane with a portable camera. Get it! And every reporter on the ground will have the word, and his most powerful telescopic lens at the ready. Man, it'll be the most televized bit of fracas of this half of the century!"

VIII

When Major Joe Mauser entered the swank Agora Bar, the little afternoon dance band broke into a few bars of that tune which was beginning to pall on him.

"... I knew her heart was breaking,

And to my heart in anguish pressed,

The girl I left behind me."

Nadine looked up from the little table she occupied and caught the wry expression on his face and laughed.

"What price glory?" she said.

He took the chair across from her and chuckled ruefully. "All right," he said, "I surrender. However, if you think a theme song is bad, you'll be relieved at some of the other ideas my, ah, publicity agent had which I turned down."

She said, "Oh, did he want you to dash into some burning building and save some old lady's canary, or something?"

"Not exactly. However, he had a nightclub singer with a list of nine or ten victories behind her —"

"Victories?"

"Husbands. And I was to be seen escorting the singer around the nightclub circuit."

"A fate worse than death? But, truly, why did you turn him down?"

"I wanted to spend the time with you."

She made a moue. "So as to carry on our never-ending argument over the value of status?"

"No."

Her eyes dropped and there was a slight frown on her forehead. Joe interpreted it to mean that she took exception to one of Mid-Middle caste speaking to her in this wise. He said, flatly, "At least the tune is somewhat applicable tonight."

She looked up quickly, having immediately caught the meaning of his words. "Oh, Joe, you haven't taken another commission?"

"Why not? I'm a mercenary by trade, Nadine." He was vaguely irritated by her tone.

"But you admittedly made a small fortune on the last fracas. You were one of the very few investors in the whole country who expected Vacuum Tube Transport to boom, rather than go bankrupt. You simply don't *need* to risk your life further, Joe!"

He didn't bother to tell her that already the greater part of his small fortune had been siphoned off in Freddy Soligen's campaign to make him a celebrity. He said, instead, "The stock shares I'll make aren't particularly important, Nadine. But Stonewall Cogswell has pledged that if I'll fly for him in the Carbonaceous Fuel-United Miners fracas, he'll press my ambitions for promotion."

She said, her voice low, "Promotion in rank, or caste, Joe?"

"You know the answer to that."

"But, Joe, to risk your life, your *life*, Joe, for such a silly thing —"

He said softly, "Such a silly thing as attaining to a position which will enable me to court openly the girl I love?"

She flushed, looked into his face quickly. Her flush deepened and her eyes went to her folded hands, on the table.

He said nothing.

Nadine said finally, her voice so low as almost not to be heard, "Perhaps I would be willing to marry a man of Middle caste."

He was taken with surprise, but even in thrilling to the meaning of her words, his head was shaking in negation. "Nadine Haer, Category Medicine, Rank Doctor, Mid-Upper, married to Major Joseph Mauser, Category Military, Mid-Middle. Don't be ridiculous, Nadine. It would be as though back in the Twentieth Century you would have married a Negro or Oriental."

She was stirred with anger. "There is no law preventing marriage between castes!"

"Nor was there law, in most States, against marrying between races. But there were few who dared, and, of those, few who were allowed to be happy. It's no go, Nadine. Remember in the Exclusive Room the other night when the waiter questioned my presence in an Upper establishment and you had to tell him I was your guest? I don't desire to be your guest the rest of my life, Nadine."

The anger welled higher in her. "And do you think that in the remote case you do jump your caste to Upper, that I would marry you and then realize the rest of my life that our marriage was only possible due to your participation in mass slaughter for the sake of the slobbering multitudes of Telly fans?"

Joe said, "I wasn't going to bring the matter up until I had made Low-Upper caste."

"Well, sir, the matter is up. And I reject you in advance. Oh, Joe, if you have to persist in this status-hungry ambition of yours, drop the Category Military and get into something else. You have enough of a fortune to branch into various fields where your abilities would lead to advancement."

Again he didn't tell her that his fortune was all but dissipated. Instead, he said bitterly, "Those who have, get. The rich get richer, the poor get poorer. Things are rigged, these days, so that it's impossible to work your way to the top except in Military and Religion. The Uppers take care of their own, and at the same time make every effort to keep us of the lower orders from joining their sacred circle. I might make it in the Military, Nadine, but my chances in another field are so remote as to be laughable."

She stood and looked down at him emptily. "No," she said, "don't get up. I'm leaving, Major Mauser." He began to rise, to protest, but she said, her voice curt, "I have seen only one fracas on Telly in my entire life, and was so repelled that I vowed never to watch again. However, I am going to make an exception. I am going to follow this one, and if, as a result of your actions, even a single person meets death, I wish never to see you again. Do I make myself completely clear, Major Mauser?"

IX

Marshal Stonewall Cogswell looked impudently around at this staff officers gathered about the chart table. "Gentlemen," he said, "I assume you are all familiar with the battle of Chancellorsville?"

No one bothered to answer and he chuckled. "I know what you are thinking, that had any of you refrained from a thorough study of the campaigns of Lee and Jackson, he would not be a member of my staff."

The craggy marshal traced with his finger on the great military chart before them. "Then you will have noticed the similarity of today's dispensation of forces to that of Joseph Hooker's Army of the Potomac and Lee's Army of Northern Virginia, on May 2, 1863." He pointed with his baton. "Our stream, here, would be the Rappahannock, this woods, the Wilderness. Here would be Fredericksburg and here Chancellorsville."

One of his colonels nodded. "My regiment occupies a position similar to that of Jubal Early."

"Absolutely correct," the marshal said crisply. "Gentlemen, I repeat, our troop dispensations, those of Lieutenant General McCord and myself, are practically identical. Now then, if McCord continues to move his forces here, across our modern day Rappahannock, he makes the initial mistake that finally led to the opening which allowed Jackson's brilliant fifteen-mile flanking march. Any questions, thus far?"

There were some murmurs, no questions. The accumulated years of military service of this group of veterans would have totaled into the hundreds.

"Very interesting, eh?" the marshal pursued. "Jed, your artillery is massed here. It's a shame that General Jack Altshuler has taken a commission with Carbonaceous Fuel. We could use his cavalry. He would be our J.E.B. Stuart, eh?"

Lieutenant Colonel Paul Warren cleared his throat unhappily. "Sir, Jack Altshuler is the best cavalryman in North America."

"I would be the last to deny it, Paul."

"Yes, sir. And he's fought half his fracases under you, sir."

"Your point, Paul?" the marshal said crisply.

"He knows your methods, sir. For that matter, so does Lieutenant General McCord. He's fought you enough."

There was silence in the staff headquarters, broken suddenly by Cogswell's curt chuckle. "Paul, I'm going to recommend to the Category Military Department, your promotion to full colonel on the strength of that. You were the first to see what I have been getting to. Gentlemen, do you realize what General McCord and his staff are doing this very moment? I would wager my reputation that they are poring over a campaign chart of the battle of Chancellorsville."

The craggy veteran bent back over the map again, his voice dropped all humor and he stabbed with his baton. "Here, here, and here. They expect us to duplicate the movements of Lee. Very good, we shall. But the advances of Lee and Jackson, we will make feints. And the feints made by Lee and Jackson will be our attacks in force. Gentlemen, we are going to literally reverse the battle of Chancellorsville. Major Mauser!"

Joe Mauser had been in the background as befitted his junior rank. Now he stepped to the table's edge. "Yes, sir."

The marshal indicated a defile. "Were we actually duplicating the Civil War battle, this would have been the right flank of Sedgwick's two army corps. We're not dealing in army corps these days but only regiments, however, the position is relatively as important. Jack Altshuler's cavalry is largely concentrated here. When the action is joined, he can move in one of three ways. Through this defile, is least likely. However, if his heavy cavalry *does* work its way through here, I must know immediately. This is crucial, Joe. Any questions?"

"No, sir."

The marshal turned his attention to his chief of artillery. "Jed, when we need your guns, we're going to need them badly, but I doubt if that time will develop until the second or third day of the fracas. Going to want as clever a job of camouflage done as possible."

The other scowled. "Camouflage, sir?"

"Confound it, yes. French term, I believe. Going to want your guns so hidden that those two gliders of McCord's will fail to spot them." The marshal grimaced in the direction of Joe Mauser, who, having his instructions, had fallen back from the table again. "When you reintroduced aerial observation to the fracas, major, you set off a whole train of related factors. Camouflage is going to be in every field officer's lexicon from this day on. Which reminds me." He looked to his artilleryman.

"Yes, sir."

"Put your mind to work on devising Maxim gun mounts to be used to keep enemy gliders at as high altitude as possible, or preferably, of course, to bring them down. We'll need an antiaircraft squadron, in short. Better put young Wiley on it."

"Yes, sir."

X

The airport nearest to the Grant Memorial Military Reservation was some ten miles distance from the borders which, upon the scheduling of a fracas, were closed to all aircraft, and to all persons unconnected with the fracas, with the exception only of Telly crews and military observers from the Sov-world and the Neut-world, present to satisfy themselves that weapons of the post-1900 era were not being utilized.

The distance, however, wasn't of particular importance. The powered aircraft which would tow Joe Mauser's glider to a suitable altitude preliminary to his riding the air currents, as a bird rides them, could also haul him to a point just short of the military reservation's border.

Joe Mauser turned up on the opening day of the fracas, which was scheduled for a period of one week, or less, if one or the other of the combatants was able to achieve total victory in such short order. He was accompanied by Freddy Soligen, who, for once, was without a crew to help him with his cameras and equipment. Instead, he sweated it out alone, helped only by Max Mainz who was being somewhat huffy about this Telly reporter taking over his position as observer.

They approached the sailplane, and while Joe Mauser checked it out, in careful detail, Freddy Soligen and Max began loading the equipment into the graceful craft's second seat, immediately behind the pilot. Max growled, "How in Zen you going to be able to lift all this weight, major, sir?"

Joe said absently, testing the ailerons, "We'll make it. Freddy isn't any heavier than you are, Max. Besides, this sailplane is a workhorse. I sacrificed gliding angle for weight carrying potential."

That meant absolutely nothing to Max Mainz, so he took it out by awarding the Telly reporter with a rare combination of glower and sneer.

Freddy said, "Oh, oh, here they come, Joe." However, he kept his head low, storing away his equipment, and seemingly ignored the approach of the three distinctive uniformed officers.

Joe said from the side of his mouth, "Get that you-know-what out of sight, soonest." He turned as the trio neared, came to attention and saluted.

The foremost of the three, his tunic so small at the waist that he could only have been wearing a girdle, answered the salute by tapping his swagger stick against the visor of his cap. "Major Mauser," he said in acknowledgment. He made no effort to shake hands, turning instead to his two companions. He said, "Lieutenant Colonel Krishnalal Majumdur, of Bombay, Major Mohamed Kamil, of Alexandria, may I introduce the"—there was all but a giggle in his tone—"celebrated Major Joseph Mauser, who has possibly reintroduced aircraft to warfare."

Joe saluted and bowed in proper protocol. "Gentlemen, a pleasure." The two neutrals responded correctly, then stepped forward to shake his hand.

Colonel Lajos Arpid added, gently, "Or possibly he has not."

Joe looked at him. The Hungarian seemed to make a practice of turning up every time Joe Mauser was about to take off. The Sov-world representative said airily, "It will be up to the International Disarmament Commission to decide upon that when it convenes shortly, will it not?"

The Arab major was staring in fascination at the sailplane. He said to Joe, "Major Mauser, you are sure such craft were in existence before 1900? It would seem—"

Joe said definitely, "Designed as far back as Leonardo and flown in various countries in the Eighteenth Century." He looked at the Hungarian. "Including, so I understand, what was then Czarist Russia."

The Sov-world officer ignored the obvious needling, saying merely, "It is quite true that the glider was first flown by an obscure inventor in the Ukraine, however, that is not what particularly interests us today, major. Perhaps the commission will find that the use of the glider is permitted for observation, however, it is obvious that before the year 1900 by no stretch of the imagination could it be contended that they were, or could have been, used for, say, *bombing*."

He turned quickly and pointed at Freddy Soligen, who, already seated in the sailplane, was watching them, his face not revealing his qualms. "What has that man been hiding within the craft?"

Joe said formally, "Gentlemen, may I introduce Frederic Soligen, Category Communications, Sub-division Telly News, Rank Senior Reporter. Mr. Soligen has been assigned to cover the fracas from the air."

Freddy looked at the Sov-world officer and said innocently, "Hiding? You mean my portable camera, and my power pack, and my auxiliary lenses, and my —"

"All right, all right," Arpád snapped. The Hungarian was no fool and obviously smelled something wrong in this atmosphere. He turned to Joe. "I would remind you, major, that you as an individual are responsible for any deviations from the basic Universal Disarmament Pact. You, and any of your superiors who can be proven to have had knowledge of such deviation."

"I am familiar with the articles of war, as detailed in the pact," Joe said dryly. "And now, gentlemen, I am afraid my duty calls me." He bowed stiffly, saluted correctly. "A pleasure to make your acquaintance Colonel Majumdur, Major Kamil. Colonel Arpád, a pleasure to renew acquaintance."

They answered his salute and stared after him as he climbed into the sailplane and signaled to the pilot of the lightplane which was to tow him into the air. Max Mainz ran to the tip of one wing, lifting it from the ground and steadying the glider until forward motion gave direction and buoyancy.

Freddy Soligen growled, "Zen! If they'd known I had a machine gun tucked away in this tripod case."

Joe said unhappily, "The Sovs have obviously decided to put up a howl about the use of aircraft in the West-world."

He shifted his hand on the stick, gently, and the glider which had been sliding along on its single wheel, lifted ever so gently into the air. Joe kept it at an altitude of about six feet until the lightplane was air-borne.

Freddy growled, "How come the Hungarians have become so important in the Sov-world? I thought it was the Russians who started their whole shooting-match."

Joe said wryly, "That's something some of the early timers like Stalin didn't figure out when they began moving in on their neighbors. They could have learned a lesson from Hollywood about the Hungarians. What was the old saying? *If you've got a Hungarian for a friend, you don't need any enemies.*"

Freddy laughed, even as he looked apprehensively over the sailplane's side. He said, "Yeah, or that other one. The Hungarians are the only people who can enter a revolving door behind you and come out in front."

Joe said, "Well, that's what happened to the Russians." He pointed. "There's the reservation. We'll be cutting from the airplane in a moment now. Listen, were you able to find out who either of General McCord's glider pilots are?"

"Yeah," Freddy told him. "Both are captains. One named Bob Flaubert and the other Jimmy Hideka."

"Bob Flaubert?" Jeb growled. "He's an artilleryman. We've been in the dill together half a dozen times." Freddy was staring below, trying to understand the terrain from this perspective. While Joe was tripping the lever which let the tow rope drop away from the glider, the Telly reporter said, "Both of them used to fly lightplanes for sport. When you started this new glider angle, they must've seen the possibilities and took it up immediately. But you oughta be able to fly circles around them, they just haven't had the time for experience with planes without motors."

"Bob, eh?" Joe said softly. "He saved my life once. Five minutes later, I saved his."

Freddy looked at him quickly. "Zen!" he complained. "It's no time to be thinking of that. So now you're even with him. And you're both hired mercenaries in a fracas."

"But I've got a gun and he hasn't," Joe growled.

"Good!" Freddy snapped at him.

They had cut away from the lightplane and Joe headed for the area which Cogswell had ordered him particularly to keep scanned. Jack Altshuler was a fox, in combat. His heavy cavalry had more than once swung a fracas.

At the same time, he kept himself alert for the other gliders. It seemed probable, since the enemy forces had two, that they would use them in relays. Which meant, in turn, that it was unlikely Joe would find them both in the air at once. In other words, if he attacked the one, possibly shooting it down, then the other would be warned, would mount a gun of its own, and it would no longer be a matter of shooting a clay pigeon.

* * * * *

Joe turned to mention this over his shoulder to Freddy Soligen, just in time to catch the shadow above and behind him.

"Holy Zen!" he snapped, kicking right rudder, thrusting his stick to the right and forward.

"What the devil!" Freddy protested, looking up from adjusting a lens on his camera.

Three or four thirty-caliber slugs tore holes in their left wing, the rest of the burst missing completely.

Joe dove sharply, gained speed, winged over and reached desperately for altitude. The other—no, the *others* were above him. He yelled back at the cameraman, "Put that Chaut-Chaut gun together for me. Be ready to hand me pans of ammo. And if you want blood and gore on that Tellylens of yours, get going!"

It still hadn't got through to the smaller man. "What in devil's going on?"

Joe banked again, grabbing for a current rising along a hill slope, circled, circled, reaching for altitude before they could get over to him and make another pass. He snapped bitterly, "Did I say something about poor old Bob Flaubert not having a gun, while I did? Well, poor old Bob's obviously got at least as much fire power as we have. Freddy, I'm afraid matters have pickled."

The other was startled.

"Do I have to draw a picture?" Joe said. "Look." He pointed to where the other two crafts circled, possibly a hundred meters above and five hundred to the right of them. The other two gliders bore a single passenger apiece, and were seemingly moving as quietly as were Joe and Freddy, but gliders in motion are deceptive. Joe shot a glance at his rate of climb indicator. He was doing all right at six meters per second, a thousand feet a minute, considering his weight.

Freddy had at last awakened to the fact that they were in combat and even that the enemy had drawn first blood. The wound taken in their wing was not serious, from Joe's viewpoint, but the torn holes in the fabric were obvious. But the little man had not gained his intrepid reputation as a Telly cameraman without cause. He moved fast, both to get the small French machine gun into Joe's hands and to get himself into action as a cameraman.

He snapped, "What's the situation?"

Joe, circling, circling, praying the updraft wouldn't give out on him before it did on the others, on their opposite hill, said, "We weigh too much. Altitude counts. What've you got back there that can be thrown out?" As he talked, he was shrugging himself out of his leather flying jacket.

"Nothing," Freddy said in anguish. "I cut down my equipment to the barest, like you said."

"You've got extra lenses and stuff, out with them." Joe tossed his coat over the glider's side, began unlacing his shoes. "And all your clothes. Clothes are heavy."

"I need my equipment to get long-range shots, like when one of them crashes!" The little man was scanning the others through his view-finder, even as he argued, and shrugging out of his own jacket.

The updraft gave out and the rate of climb meter began to register a drop. Joe swore and shot a glance at his opponents. Happily, they, too, had lost their currents, both were now heading for him.

Joe clipped out to his companion. "We're not going to be getting shots of them crashing, unless we lose more weight. Overboard with everything you can possibly afford, Freddy. That's an order."

There was one thing in his favor. He had a year's flying experience, more than six months of it in this very glider. The stick and rudderbar were as though appendages of his body. One flies by the seat of his pants, in a soaring glider, and Joe flew his as though born in it. The others, obviously, were as yet not thoroughly used to engineless craft.

He banked away from them, flying as judiciously as possible, begrudging each foot dropped. He could feel the craft jump lightly each time the cursing Telly reporter jettisoned another article of equipment, his pants, or his shoes.

The others evidently had their guns fix-mounted, to fire straight ahead. Joe wondered, even as he slid away from them, how they managed to escape detection from the Sov-world and Neut-world field observers. Well, that could be worried about later.

One of them fired at him at too great a range, and then both, realizing that they were dropping altitude too quickly and that soon Joe would be on their level, turned away and sought a new updraft. As they banked, their faces were clearly discernible. One raised a hand in mocking salute.

"Look at that curd-loving Bob," Joe laughed grudgingly. "Here, let me have that gun."

He steadied the small mitrailleuse on the edge of the cockpit, holding the craft's stick between his knees, and squeezed off a burst which rattled through the other's fuselage without apparent damage. The foe glider slid away quickly, losing precious altitude in the maneuver.

"Ah, ha," Joe said wolfishly. "So now they know we've got a stinger too."

"I got that," Freddy crowed. "I got it perfectly. Listen, we're too high for the boys down below. Get lower so they can get you on lens, Joe. The other Telly teams. Every fracas buff in North America is watching this."

Joe snorted his disgust. "I hope every fracas buff in North America chokes on his trank pills," he snarled. "We're in the dill, Freddy. Understand? We're too heavy, and there's two of them and one of us. On top of that, those are Maxim guns they've got mounted, not peashooters like this Chaut-Chaut."

"That's your side of it," Freddy said, not unhappily. "I take care of the photography. Get closer, Joe. Get closer."

Joe had found another light updraft and gained a few hundred feet, but so had the others. They circled, circled. His experience balanced their advantage of the lesser weight. Happily, their glide ratios didn't seem to be any better than his own. Had they high performance gliders of forty, or even thirty-five, gliding angle ratios, he would have been lost.

"Nothing else you can toss out?" he growled at Freddy.

"What the Zen!" Freddy muttered nastily. "You want me to jump?"

"That's an idea," Joe growled wolfishly, even as he circled, circled. "I should have realized when you were giving me your fling about reintroducing aerial warfare, that it wasn't an idea that others couldn't have. It was just as easy for Bob to mount a gun as it was for us. Now we're both being kept from doing reconnaissance by the other and —"

Joe Mauser broke it off in mid-sentence and his face blanched. He shot a quick look downward. All three gliders had climbed considerably, and the terrain below was indistinct.

Joe snapped, "Hand me those glasses!"

"What glasses? What's the matter?" Freddy complained. "Try to get closer to them and let me get a close-up of you giving them a burst."

"My binoculars!" Joe snapped urgently. "I want to see what's going on below."

"Oh," Freddy said. "I threw them out. Along with all the rest of the equipment. Glasses, semaphore flags, that sun blinker you had. All of it went overboard with my extra lenses."

The craft was so banked as almost to have the wings perpendicular to earth. Joe shot an agonized look at the smaller man, then back again at the earth below, trying desperately to narrow his eyes for keener vision.

Freddy said, "What in Zen's the matter with you? What difference does it make what they're doing down below? We're all occupied up here, thanks."

"This is a frame-up," Joe growled. "Bob and that other pilot. They weren't out on reconnaissance, this morning. They were laying for me. They're out to keep me from seeing what's going on down there. And I know what's going on. Jack Altshuler's pulling a fast one. Here we go, Freddy, hang on!"

He slapped his flap brake lever with his left hand, winged over and began dropping like a shot as his gliding angle fell off from twenty-five to one to ten to one. In seconds the other two gliders were after him, riding his tail.

Freddy Soligen, his eyes bugging, shot a look of fear at the two trailing craft, both of which, periodically, showed brilliant cherries at their prows. Maxim guns, emitting their blessings.

The Telly reporter turned desperately back to Joe Mauser, pounding him on the shoulder. His physical fear was secondary to another. "Joe! You're on lens with every Telly team down there, and you're running!"

"Cut that out," Joe rapped. "Duck your head. Let me train this gun over you. I've got to keep those jokers from shooting off our tail before I can get to the marshal."

"The marshal!" Freddy yelled. "You can't get to him anyway. I told you I threw away your semaphore flags, your blinker-everything. This country's hilly. You can't get your message to him anyway. Listen, Joe, you've still got time. You can stunt these things better than those two can."

"Duck!" Joe snarled. He let loose a burst at the pursuing gliders over the smaller man's head, and just missing his own tail section.

They sped down almost to tree level at fantastic speed for a glider. The two enemy craft were hot after them, their guns *flac, flac, flacing* in continuous excitement, trying to catch Joe in sights, as he kicked rudder, right, left, right, in evasive maneuver.

He guess had been correct. The swashbuckling Jack Altshuler had know his many times commander even better than Cogswell had realized. Instead of three alternative maneuvers open to the wily cavalryman, he'd ferreted out a fourth and his full force, hauling mountain guns on mule back with them, were trailing over a supposedly impossible mountain path which originally could not have been more then a deer track.

Freddy Soligen, in back, was holding his head in his hands in surrender. He could have focused on the troops below, but the desire wasn't in him. Not one fracas buff in a hundred could comprehend the complications of combat, the need for adequate reconnaissance-the need for Joe to get through.

He made one last plea. "Joe, we've put everything into this. Every share of stock you've accumulated. All I have, too. Don't you realize what you're doing, so far as the buffs are concerned? Those two half-trained pilots behind have you on the run."

Joe growled, "And twenty thousands lads down below are depending on me to report on Altshuler's horse."

"But you can't win, anyway. You can't get your message to Cogswell!"

Joe shot him a wolfish grin. "Wanta bet? Ever heard of a crash landing, Freddy? Hang on!"

Stretched out on the convalescent bed in the Category Military rest home, Joe grinned up at his visitor and said ruefully, "I'd salute, sir, but my arms seem to be out of commission. And, come to think of it, I'm out of uniform."

Cogswell looked down at him, unamused. "You've heard the news?"

Joe caught the other's tone and his face straightened. "You mean the Disarmament Commission?"

Cogswell said brittlely, "They found against the use of aircraft, other than free balloons, in any military action. They threw the book, Mauser. The court ruled that you, Robert Flaubert and James Hideka be stripped of rank and forbidden the Category Military. You have also been fined all stock shares in your possession other than those unalienably yours as a West-world citizen."

Joe's face went empty. It was only then that he realized that the other was attired in the uniform of a brigadier general. The direction of his eyes was obvious.

Cogswell shrugged bitterly. "My Upper caste status helped me. I could pull just enough strings that the Category Military Department, in conjunction with the rulings of the International Disarmament Commission merely reduced me in rank and belted me with a stiff fine. Your friend—your former friend, I should say, Freddy Soligen, testified in my behalf. Testified that I had no knowledge of your mounting a gun."

The former marshal cleared his throat. "His testimony was correct. I had no such knowledge and would have issued orders against it, had I known. The fact that you enabled me to rescue the situation into which I'd been sucked, helps somewhat my feelings toward you, Mauser. But only somewhat."

Joe could imagine the other's bitterness. He had fought his way up the hard way to that marshal's baton. At his age, he wasn't going to regain it.

Brigadier general Stonewall Cogswell hesitated for a moment, then said, "One other thing. United Miners has repudiated your actions even to the point of refusing the cost of your hospitalization. I told the Category Medicine authorities to put your bill on my account."

Joe said quite stiffly, "That won't be necessary, sir."

"I'm afraid you'll find it is, Mauser." The former marshal allowed himself a grimace. "Besides, I owe you something for that spectacular scene when you came skimming over the treetops, the two enemy gliders right behind you, then stalling your craft and crashing into that tree not thirty feet from my open air headquarters. Admittedly, in forty years of fracases, I've never seen anything so confoundedly dramatic."

"Thank you, sir."

The old soldier grunted, turned and marched from the room.

XII

Freddy Soligen had been miraculously saved from the physical beating taken by Joe Mauser in the crash. The pilot, sitting so close before him, cushioned with his own body that of the Telly reporter.

For that matter, he had been saved the financial disaster as well, save for that amount he had contributed to the campaign to increase Mauser's stature in the eyes of the buffs. His Category Communications superiors had not even charged him for the cost of the equipment he had jettisoned from the glider during the flight, nor that which had been destroyed in the crash. If anything, his reputation with his higher-ups was probably better than ever. He'd been in there pitching, as a Telly reporter, right up until the end when the situation had completely pickled.

All that he had lost was his dream. It had been so close to the grasping. He could almost have tasted the sweetness of victory. Joe Mauser, at the ultimate top of the hero-heap. Joe Mauser accepting bounces in both rank and caste. And then, Joe Mauser being properly thankful and helpful to Freddy and Sam Soligen, in their turn. So near the realization of the dream.

He entered his house wearily, finally free of all the ridiculous questioning of the commission and the courts martial of Mauser and Cogswell, and Flaubert, Hideka and their commander, General McCord. All had been found guilty, though in different degrees. Using weapons of warfare which post-dated 1900. Than which there was no greater crime between nations.

He tossed the brief case he had carried to a table, and made his way to the living room, heading for the auto-bar and some straight spirits.

A voice said, "Hi, Papa."

He looked up, not immediately recognizing the Category Military, Rank Private, before him.

Then he said weakly, "Sam!" His legs gave way, and he sat down abruptly on the couch which faced the wall which was the Telly screen.

The boy said, awkwardly, "Surprise, Papa!"

His father said, very slowly, "What ... in ... Zen ... are ... you ... doing ... in ... that ... outfit?"

Sam grinned ruefully, albeit proudly. "Aw, it would've taken a century for me to make full priest, Papa. The only way to do is like Major Mauser. You didn't know this, but, I've been following the fracases all along. Especially when you were the reporter. I've watched every fracas you've covered for years. I guess you know I'm pretty proud of you."

"Sam! What are you doing in that uniform! Answer me!"

The boy flushed. "I'm old enough, Papa. I switched categories. I've signed up with Chrysler-Ford in their fracas with Hovercar Sports. They're taking me on as infantryman."

"Infantryman?" Freddy winced, and closed his eyes. "Listen, boy, where'd you get the idea that —" He started over again. "But all your life I've given you the inside on the Category Military, Sam. All your life. No trank in our home. No watching the Telly day in and out. You've gone to *school*. More than I ever did. You were going to be a Temple priest —"

Sam sat down too, vaguely surprised at this father's reaction. "Aw, Papa, everybody's a fracas buff now. Everybody. You can't get away from it. I ... well, I want to be like Major Mauser. Get so all the fans know me, want my autograph, all that. And all the excitement of being in a fracas, getting in the dill, and all. I just want to be like the other fellas, Papa."

Freddy could only stare at him.

Sam tried to explain. "Shucks, it was really you that made me want to become a mercenary. You're the best Telly reporter of them all. When *you* cover a fracas, Papa, you really do it. You can see *everything*." He shook his head in admiration. "Gosh, you really feel the emotion. It's the most exciting thing in the world."

"Yeah, son," Freddy Soligen said emptily. "I suppose it is."

Joe was able to get around on auto-crutches by the time she finally arrived —a stereotype visitor. Done up brightly, a box of candy in one hand, flowers in the other. He could see her coming across the lawn, from the visitor's offices. He wished that he had worn his other suit. His clothing was on the skimpy side when uniforms were subtracted.

She came up to him. "Well, Joe."

He looked at the flowers and attempted a grin. "Lilies would have been more appropriate, considering the shape I'm in."

Nadine said, "I've just been talking to the staff doctors. You're not in as bad shape as all that. Some bone mending, is all."

The grin turned wry. "I wasn't just thinking of the physical shape." He settled to the stone bench which stood to one side of the walk he had been exercising upon before her arrival. For a moment, she remained standing.

He looked up at her. "Well," he said. "I didn't break your condition," he said. "Am I still receivable?"

She frowned.

Joe said, bitterly, "You told me that you were going to take the fracas in and if my actions resulted in any casualties, you never wanted to see me again."

She took the place beside him. "I did watch. For a time, the rest of the battle going on below was ignored and you were full on lens for at least twenty minutes. I was never so frightened in my life."

Joe said, "The first step toward becoming a buff. First you're scared. Vicariously. But it's fun to become scared, when nothing can really happen to you. It becomes increasingly exciting to see others threatened with death-and then actually to die before you. After a while, you're hooked."

She looked carefully at the flowers. "That's not exactly what I meant. I was frightened for you, Joe. Not thrilled."

He looked at her for a long moment. Finally he breathed deeply and said, "Well, you'll never have to go through that again. I'm no longer in the Category Military, I suppose you know."

"It was on the news, Joe." She laughed without amusement. "In fact, I knew even before. Balt was tried, too."

"Balt? Your brother?"

She nodded. "You first used your glider in that fracas for father and Vacuum Tube Transport. Now that the commission has ruled against gliders, Balt, now head of the family, has been both fined and expelled from Category Military for life. It hasn't exactly improved his liking for you."

Joe hadn't heard of it, however, he had little sympathy for Balt Haer, nor interest in him. He said, "Why did you take so long to come?"

"I was thinking, Joe."

"And then you finally came."

"Yes."

He looked away and into unseen distances. Finally he cleared his throat and said, "Nadine, the first time I ever talked to you to any extent, I mentioned that I wanted to achieve the top in this status world of ours. I mentioned that I hadn't built this world, and possibly didn't even approve of it, but since I'm in it and have no other recourse, I must follow its rules."

She nodded. "I remember. And I said, why not try and change the rules?"

Joe nodded. He moistened his lips carefully. "O.K. Now I'm willing to listen. How do we go about changing the rules?"

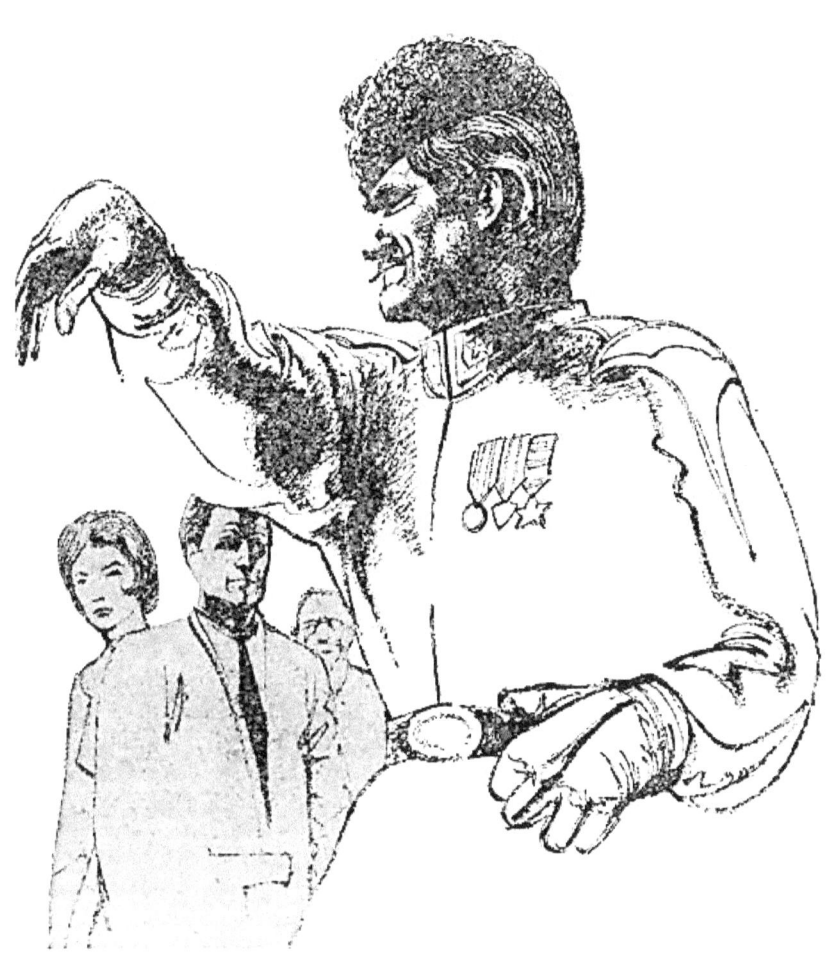

XIV

Dr. Nadine Haer, Category Medicine, Mid-Upper caste, was driving and with considerable enjoyment resultant not only from her destination, long desired, now to be realized, but also from the sheer exuberance of handling the vehicle. Since pre-history, man's pleasure in the physical control of a speedy vehicle has been superlative, particularly when that vehicle is known by the driver to be unique in its class. The Hittite charioteer, bowling across the landscape of Anatolia, a Sterling Moss carefully tooling his automobile around the multi-curves of the Upper Cornice on the Riviera, or a Nadine Haer delicately trimming the controls of a sports model Hovercar.

She shot a quick glance at Joe Mauser, formerly of Category Military, formerly Rank Major, now an unemployed Mid-Middle who slouched in the bucketseat next to her. He noticed neither speed nor direction.

Nadine called, above the wind, "Zen, Joe! Where did you ever acquire such a car? It must have been built entirely by hand, and by Swiss watchmakers."

Joe stirred and shrugged. Newly from the hospital, he was still deep in the gloom of his recent loss of the dream, the defeat of his life-long ambitions. He said, "A buff gave it to me."

She slowed down, the better to frown at him in amazement. "*Gave* it to you? Why the thing is priceless."

Joe sighed and told her the salient details. "Quite a few mercenaries manage to acquire a private fracas-buff." He defined the term for her. "He makes a hobby of your career. Winds up knowing more about it than you, yourself can possibly remember. He follows every fracas you get into. Knows every time you cop one, how serious it was, how long you were in hospital. He glories each time you get a promotion, is in gloom each time your side loses a fracas. He's got pictures of you in various poses taken from the fracas-buff magazines, and files away all articles in which your name appears."

"Zen!" Nadine laughed in deprecation.

"That's just the beginning. After a while he starts writing you fan letters, wanting auto-graphed portraits, wanting a souvenir-sometimes nothing more exciting than a button off your uniform. More often they want a gun, sword or combat knife, particularly one they saw you using in some fracas or other. They usually offer to pay for such, sometimes quite fabulous amounts. Other times they want a bit of bloody uniform, your own true blood from a time when you were in the dill and managed to cop one."

Nadine was astonished. Antagonistic as she was, herself, to the fracases, she wasn't partic-ularly knowledgeable about all their ramifications. She said, repelled, "But doesn't such mor-bidity disgust you? This fawning, this slobbering —"

Joe grunted. "All part of the game. A mercenary without buffs to boost him, to form fracas-buff clubs and such, hasn't much chance of promotion. So far as disgust is concerned, you'd have to see one of the really far-out ones. The gleam in an ordinarily fishlike eye when he recounts the time you killed three men in hand-to-hand combat, equipped only with an entrenching tool, when they came at you with bayonets. The trace of spittle, running down from the side of his mouth."

"And this buff of yours. Why did he give you this perfectly marvelous car?"

"It was a she, not a he," Joe said.

Nadine's voice changed infinitesimally. "You mean you accepted a gift of this value from a ... woman?"

Joe looked at her and grinned sourly. "I wasn't in much of a position to refuse. The gift was in her will. She was well into her nineties when she died. She was an Upper-Upper, by the way, and the most knowledgeable fracas buff I ever met. She knew the intimate details of every fracas since Tiglath-Pileser and his Assyrians captured Babylon. She could argue for an hour on whether Parmenion or Alexander the Great should have been given the credit for the victory over the Persians at Issus." Joe grunted. "I suppose there should be a moral somewhere about this kindly old lady who was the outstanding fracas buff of them all."

* * * * *

Nadine Haer was in the process of hitting the drop lever with her left hand as they slowed and headed for the entrance to a parking area. She said brittlely, "The moral is that you can have slobs at any level in society. Being an Upper doesn't guarantee anything."

Joe sighed, "Here we go again." He looked about him, scowling. "Which brings to mind. Where *are* we going? These are governmental buildings, aren't they?"

They were sinking quickly, below street level, now in the power of the auto-parker. Nadine turned off the engine and released the controls. She said, cryptogrammicly, "We are going to see about doing something with your abilities other than shooting at people, or being shot at."

When the car was parked, she led the way to an elevator.

Joe said wryly, "Oh, great. I love mysteries. When do we find out who killed the victim?"

Nadine looked at him from the side of her eyes. "I killed the victim," she said. "Major Mauser, mercenary by trade, is now no more."

There was bitterness in him and he found no ability to respond to what was meant as humor in her words. He followed her silently and his puzzlement grew with him. The office building through which they moved was as well done as any he could ever remember having observed, even on the Telly. Surely they couldn't be in the Octagon or the New White House. But, if so, why?

Nadine said. "Here we are," and indicated a door which opened at their approach.

There was a receptionist in the small office beyond, a bit of ostentation Joe Mauser seldom met with in the modern world. What in the name of Zen could anyone need with other than an auto-receptionist? Didn't efficiency mean anything here?

The receptionist said, "Good afternoon, Dr. Haer. Mr. Holland is expecting you."

It came to Joe now-Philip Holland, secretary to Harlow Mannerheim, the Minister of Foreign Affairs. He had met the man a few months ago at Nadine's home in that swank section of Greater Washington once known as Baltimore. But he had no idea what Nadine had in mind bringing him here. Evidently, she was well enough into the graces of the bureaucrat to barge into his office during working hours. Surprising in itself, since, although she was an Upper born, still governmental servants can't be at the beck of every hereditary aristocrat in the land.

Holland stood up briefly at their entrance and shook hands quickly, almost abruptly, held a chair for Nadine, motioned to another one for Joe. He sat down again and said into an inter-office telly-mike, "Miss Mikhail, the dossier on Joesph Mauser, and would you request Frank Hodgson to drop in?"

What was obviously the dossier slid from the desk chute and Holland leafed through it, as though disinterested. He said, "Joseph Mauser, born Mid-Lower, Clothing Category, Sub-division Shoes, Branch Repair." Holland looked up. "A somewhat plebian beginning, let us admit."

A tic manifested itself at the side of Joe Mauser's mouth, but he said nothing. If long years of the military had taught him anything, it was patience. The other man had the initiative now, let him use it.

Holland cast his eyes ceilingward, and, without referring to the dossier before him, said, "Crossed categories at the age of seventeen to Military, remaining a Rank Private for three years at which time promoted to corporal. Sergeant followed in another three years and upon reaching the rank of lieutenant, at the age of twenty-five was bounced in caste to High-Lower. After distinguishing himself in a fracas between Douglas-Boeing and Lockheed-Cessna was further raised to Low-Middle caste. By the age of thirty had reached Mid-Middle caste and Rank Captain. By thirty-three, the present, had been promoted to major, and had been under consideration for Upper-Middle caste."

That last, Joe had not know about, however, he said now, "Also at present, expelled from participation in future fracases on any level of rank, and fined his complete resources beyond the basic common stock issued him as a Mid-Middle." His voice was bitter.

Philip Holland said briskly, "The risks run by the ambitious."

* * * * *

The office door opened and a tall stranger entered. He had a strange gait, one shoulder held considerably lower than the other, to the point that Joe would have thought it the result of a wound hadn't the other obviously never been a soldier. The newcomer, office pallor heavily upon him, but his air of languor obviously assumed and artificial, darted his eyes around the room, to Holland, Nadine, and then to Joe where they rested for a moment.

He murmured some banality to Nadine, indicative of a long acquaintance and then approached Joe, who had automatically come to his feet, and extended a hand to be shaken. "I'm Frank Hodgson. You're Joe Mauser. I'm not fracas buff, but I know enough about current developments to know that. Welcome aboard, Joe."

Joe shook the hand offered, in some surprise.

"Welcome aboard?" he said.

Hodgson looked to Philip Holland, his eyebrows raised in question.

Holland said crisply, "You're premature, Frank. Dr. Haer and Mauser have just arrived."

"Oh." The newcomer found himself a chair, crossed his legs and fumbled in his pocket for a pipe, leaving it to the others to resume the conversation he had interrupted.

Philip Holland said to Joe, "Frank is assistant to Wallace Pepper." He looked at Hodgson and frowned. "I don't believe you have any other title do you, Frank?"

"I don't think so," Frank yawned. "Can't think of any."

Joe Mauser looked from one to the other, confusion adding to confusion within him. Wallace Pepper was the long time head of the North American Bureau of Investigation, having held that position under at least four administrations.

Nadine said dryly, "Which goes to show you, Joe, just how much titles mean. Commissioner Pepper has been all but senile for the past five years. Frank, here, is the true head of the bureau."

Frank Hodgson said mildly, "Why, Nadine, that's a rather strong statement."

Joe blurted, "Head of the Bureau of Investigation! I had gathered the impression I was being taken to meet some members of an underground, organized for the purpose of, as it was put, changing the present rules of government."

Frank Hodgson grinned at Nadine and laughed softly, "That's a gentle way of describing revolution."

Holland looked at Joe Mauser and said briskly, "I'll try to take you off the hook as quickly as possible, Joe. Tell me, when you hear the word revolution, what comes first to your mind?"

Joe, flustered, said, "Why, I don't know. Fighting, riots, people running around in the streets with banners. That sort of thing."

"Um-m-m," Holland nodded, "The common conception. However, a social revolution isn't, by definition, necessarily bloody. Picture a gigantic wheel, Joe. We'll call it the wheel of history. From time to time it makes a turn, forward, we hope, but sometimes backward. Such a turn is a revolution. Whether or not there is anybody under the wheel at the time of turning, is beside the point. The revolution takes place whether or not there is bloodshed."

He thought a moment. "Or you might compare it to childbirth. The fact that there is pain in childbirth, or, if through modern medical science, the pain is eliminated, is beside the point. Childbirth consists of a new baby coming into the world. The mother might even die, but childbirth has taken place. She might feel no pain whatsoever, under anesthetic, but childbirth has taken place."

Joe said carefully, "I'm no authority, but it seems to me that usually if changes take place in a socio-economic system without bloodshed, we call it evolution. Revolution is when they take place with conflict."

Holland shook his head. "No. Poor definitions. Among other things, don't confuse revolts, civil wars, and such with revolution. They aren't the same thing. You can have civil war, military revolts and various civil disturbances without having a socio-economic revolution. Let's use this for an example. Take a fertile egg. Inside of it a chick is slowly developing, slowly evolving. But it is still an egg. The chick finally grows tiny wings, a beak, even little feathers. Fine. But so far it's just evolution, within the shell of the egg. But one day that chick cannot develop further without breaking the shell and freeing itself of what was once its factor of defense but now threatens its very life. The shell must go. When that culminating action takes place, you have a revolutionary change and we are no longer dealing with an egg, but a chicken."

Joe, one by one, looked at the three of them. He said, finally, to Nadine, rather than to the men, "What's this got to do with me?"

She leaned forward in her earnestness. "All your life you've revolted against the *status quo*, Joe. You've beaten your head against the situation that confronted you, against a society you felt didn't allow you to develop your potentialities. But now you admit you've been wrong. What is needed is to" —she shot a defiant glance at Frank Hodgson, to his amusement —"change the rules if the race is to get back onto the road to progress." She shrugged. "Very well. You can't expect it to be done single handed. You need an organization. Others who feel the same way you do. Here we are."

He was truly amazed now. When he had finally admitted interest in what Nadine had hinted to be a subversive organization, he'd had in mind some secretive group, possibly making their headquarters in a hidden cellar, complete with primitive printing press, and possibly some weapons. He most certainly hadn't expected to be introduced to the secretary of the Foreign Minister, and the working head of the North American Bureau of Investigation.

Joe blurted, "But ... but you mean you Uppers are actually planning to subvert your own government?"

Holland said, "I'm not an Upper. I'm a Mid-Middle. What're you Frank?"

"Darned if I know," Hodgson said. "I forget. I think I was bounced up to Upper-Middle about ten years ago, for some reason or other, but I was busy at the time and didn't pay much attention. Every once in a while one of the Uppers I work with gets all excited about it and wants to jump me to Upper, but somehow or other we've never got around to it. What difference does it make?"

Joe Mauser was not the type to let his mouth fall agape, but he stared at the other, unbelievingly.

"What's the matter?" Hodgson said.

"Nothing," Joe said.

Philip Holland said briskly, "Let's get on with it. Nadine" —his voice had a dry quality —"is one of our most efficient talent scouts. It was no mistake I met you at her home, a few weeks back, Joe. She thought you were potentially one of us. I admit to having formed the same opinion, upon our brief meeting. I now put the question to you direct. Do you wish to join our organization, the purpose of which is admittedly, to change our present socio-economic system and, as Nadine put it, get back on the road to progress?"

"Yes," Joe said. "I do."

"Very well, welcome aboard, as Frank said. Your first assignment will take you to Budapest."

* * * * *

They were throwing these curves too fast for Joe. Noted among his senior officers as a quick man, thinking on his feet, he still wasn't up to this sort of thing. "Budapest!" he ejaculated. "The capital of the Sov-world? But ... but *why* —?"

Philip Holland looked at him patiently. "There are many ramifications to revolution, Joe. Particularly in this present day with its Frigid Fracas which has gone on for generations between the West-world and the Sov-world and with the Neut-world standing at the sidelines glaring at us both. You see, really efficient revolutions may simply not look like revolutions at all-just unusual results of historic accidents. And if we're going to make this one peacefully, we've got to take every measure to assure efficiency. One of these measures involves a thorough knowledge of where the Sov-world stands, and what it might do if there were any signs of a changing in the *status quo* here in the West-world."

Frank Hodgson said idly, "I believe you have met Colonel Lajos Arpád."

Joe said, puzzled still again, "Why, yes. One of their military attachés. An observer of our fracases to see whether or not the Universal Disarmament Pact is violated."

"But also, Colonel Arpád is probably the most competent espionage agent working out of Budapest."

"That corseted, giggling nincompoop!"

Frank Hodgson laughed softly. "If even an old pro like yourself hasn't spotted him, then we have one more indication of Arpád's abilities."

Philip Holland took up the ball again. "The presence of Colonel Arpád in Greater Washington is no coincidence. He is here for something, we're not sure what. However, rumors have been coming out of the Sov-world, and particularly Siberia, and the more backward countries to the south, such as Sinkiang. Rumors of an underground organized to overthrow the Sovs."

"And that religious thing," Nadine added.

Frank Hodgson murmured, "Yes, indeed. We received two more reports of it today."

All looked at him. He said to Joe, "Some fanatic in Siberia. A Tuvinian, one of the Turkic-speaking peoples in that area once called Tannu-Tuva, and now the Tuvinian Autonomous Oblast. He's attracting quite a following. Destroy the machines. Go back to the old way. Till the soil by hand. Let the women spin and weave, make clothing on the hand loom once more. Ride horses, rather than hovercraft and jets. That sort of thing. And, oh yes, kill those who stand in the way of this holy mission."

"And you mean this is catching hold in this day and age?" Joe said.

"Like wildfire," Hodges said easily. "And I wouldn't be too very surprised if it would do the same over here. Pressures are generating, in this world of ours. We'll either make changes peaceably or Zen knows what will happen. The Sovs haven't been exposed to religion for several generations, Joe. Probably the Party heads had forgotten it as a potential danger. Here in the West-world we do better. The Temple provides us with a pressure valve in that particular area, but I still wouldn't like to see our trank and Telly bemused morons subjected to a sudden blast of revival-type religion."

Joe looked back at Holland. "I still don't get my going to Budapest. How, why, when?"

Holland glanced at a desk watch and became brisk. "I have an appointment with the President," he said. "We'll have to turn this over to some of the other members of this group. They'll explain details, Joe. Nadine's going, too. In her case, as a medical attaché in our Embassy, in Budapest. You'll go as a military observer, check on potential violations of the Universal Disarmament Pact." A sudden thought struck him. "I imagine it would add to your prestige and possibly open additional doors to you, if you carried more status." He looked again at the telly-mike on his desk. "Miss Mikhail, in my office here is Joseph Mauser, now Mid-Middle in caste. Please take the necessary steps to raise him to Low-Upper, immediately. I'll clear this with Tom, and he'll authorize it as recommended through the White House. It that clear?"

In a daze, Joe could hear the receptionist's voice. "Yes, sir. Joseph Mauser to be raised to Low-Upper caste immediately."

XV

Budapest, basically, had changed little over half a millennium.

The Danube, seldom blue except when seen through the eyes of a twosome between whom spark has recently been struck, still wandered its way dividing the old, old town of Pest from the still older town of Buda. Where the stream widens there is room for the one hundred and twelve acres of Margitsziget, or Margaret Island to the West-world. Down through the ages, through Celts and Romans, Slavs and Hungs, Turks and Magyars, none have been so gross as to use Margitsziget for other than a park.

Buda, lying to the west of the Danube, is of rolling hills and bluffs and of ancient towers, fortresses, castles and walls which have suffered through a hundred wars, a score of revolutions. It dominates the younger, more dynamic, Pest which stretches out on the flat plains to the east so that though you stand on the Hármashatárhegy hill of Buda and strain your eyes, you are hard put to find the furtherest limits of Pest.

The jetport was on the outskirts of Pest, and the craft carrying Nadine Haer, Joseph Mauser and Max Mainz, settled in for a gentle landing, the autopilot more delicate far than human eye served by human hand.

Max, his eyes glued to the window, said, "Well, gee, it don't look much different than a lotta the other towns we passed over."

Nadine looked at him and laughed. She alone of the three of them had ever been outside the boundaries of the West-world having attended several international medical conventions. Over the years, the Frigid Fracas had laid its chill on tourism, so that now travel between West-world and Sov-world was all but unknown, and even visiting the Neut-world was considered a bit far out and somewhat suspect of going beyond the old time way of doing things-even among the Uppers. Securing a passport for a Middle's trip, not to speak of a Lower's, involved such endless bureaucratic red tape as to be nonsensical.

Nadine said to Joe's batman, "What did you expect, Max?"

"Well, I don't know, Miss Haer. I mean, Dr. Haer. Kind of gloomier, like. Shucks, I've seen this here town on Telly a dozen times."

"And seeing is believing," Joe muttered cynically. "It looks as though we have a reception committee." He looked at Nadine. "Are we supposed to know each other?"

She shrugged and made a moue. "It would be somewhat strange if we didn't, seeing that we flew over in the same aircraft, and were the only passengers to come this far."

He nodded and as the plane came to a halt, helped her from her chair, even as the plane's ladder slipped out and touched to the ground.

Joe grunted and said, as though to himself, "You realize that for all practical purposes there hasn't been any improvement in aircraft for a generation?"

Nadine looked at him from the side of her eyes, even as they descended. "That's what I keep telling you, Joe. We've become ossified. When a society, afraid of change, adopts a policy of maintaining the *status quo* at any cost, progress is arrested. Progress *means* change."

He grinned at her. "Sure, sure, sure. Please, no more lectures, teacher. Let what's already in my head stew a while."

* * * * *

On the ground, Nadine was met by one contingent from the Embassy and from the Sov-world authorities, and Joe and Max by another. Joe became occupied, hardly more than noticing that she had been whisked away in a hoverlimousine, ornately bedecked with official flags and stars.

Joe, no longer holding military rank, in spite of his mission, was in mufti, and restrained himself from returning the salute when greeted by two fresh young lieutenants from the Embassy and a be-medaled lieutenant colonel in Sov-world uniform, whose tight-waisted tunic reminded Joe of that worn by Colonel Lajos Arpád, the military attaché Joe had come across twice in West-world fracases, and who Frank Hodgson had branded an espionage agent. Joe swore again, inwardly, that these Hungarian officers must wear girdles under their uniforms, and wondered vaguely if they did so in combat.

The lieutenants, who could have been twins, so alike were they in size, bright smiling faces, uniform and words of welcome, saluted Joe, shook hands, and then turned to introduce him to the Sov-world officer.

One of them said, "Major Mauser, may we present you to Lieutenant Bela Kossuth of the Pink Army?"

They were, evidently using Joe's old title of rank, as if he were retired rather than dismissed from the Category Military. It meant little to Joe Mauser. The Sov officer clicked his heels, bowed from the waist, extended his hand to be shaken. His waist might be pinched in like that of a girl of the Nineteenth Century, but his hand was dry and firm.

"The fame of Joseph Mauser has penetrated to the Proletarian Paradise," he said, his voice conveying sincerity.

Joe shook and said, "Pink Army? I thought you called it —"

The colonel was indicating a hoverlimousine with a sweeping gesture that would have seemed overly graceful, had not Joe felt the grip of the man only a moment earlier. Kossuth interrupted him politely, "The plane was a trifle late and the banquet we have prepared awaits us, major. A multitude of my fellow officers are anxious to meet the famed Joseph Mauser. Would it surprise you to know that I have replayed, a score of times, your celebrated holding action on the Louisiana Military Reservation? Zut! Unbelievable. With but a single company of men!"

Joe was looking at him blankly. *Celebrated!* Joe couldn't but remember the fracas the mincing Hungarian was talking about. When the front had collapsed, Joe, then a captain, had held his position in the swamps while his superiors were supposedly reforming behind him, actually while they frantically tried to reach terms with the enemy.

One of the West-world lieutenants laughed at Joe's expression. "You're going to have to get used to the fact that there're as many fracas buffs over here, sir, as there are back home."

The Sov colonel waggled a finger at him. "But, no, you misunderstand completely, Lieutenant Andersen. We *study* the bloody fracases of the West. Following the campaigns of such tacticians as your Marshal Stonewall Cogswell goes far toward the training of our own Pink Army in its, ah, fracases."

That brought up a dozen questions in Joe's mind, but first he turned and indicated Max, who'd been standing behind, his eyes wide, and taking in the luxurious airport, the vehicles about it, the buildings, the airport workers, few in number though they be, the road leading to the city beyond.

Joe said, "Gentlemen, may I present Max Mainz?"

The faces of the lieutenants went blank, and one of them coughed as though apologetically.

The Sov colonel looked from Joe to Max, and then back again, his face assuming that expression so well known to Joe for so very long. The aristocrat looking at one of lower class as though wondering what made the fellow tick. Kossuth said, "But surely this, ah, chap, is a servant, one of your, what do you call them, a *Lower*."

Max blinked unhappily and looked at Joe.

Joe Mauser said evenly, "I had heard the Sov-world was the Utopia of the proletariat. However, gentlemen, Max Mainz is my friend as well as my ... assistant."

The three officers murmured some things stiffly to Max, who, a Lower born, was not overly nonplused by the situation. Zen, he knew the three were Upper caste, what was Major Mauser getting into a tissy about? He was given a seat in the front, where the chauffeur would have once been, and the others took places in the rear, one of the lieutenants dialing the hovercar's destination.

* * * * *

Joe Mauser said, "I am afraid my background is hazy, Colonel Kossuth. You mentioned the Pink Army. You also mentioned your own fracases. I knew you maintained an army, of course, but I thought the fracas was a West development, in fact, your military attachés are usually on the scornful side."

The two lieutenants grinned, but Kossuth said seriously, "Major, as always, nations which hold each other at arm's length, use different terminology to say much the same thing. It need not be confusing, if one digs below to find reality. Perhaps, for a moment, we four can lower barriers enough for me to explain that whilst in the West-world you hold your fracases to" — he began enumerating on his fingers —"One, settle disputes between business competitors, or between corporations and unions. Two, to train soldiers for your defense requirements. Three, to keep bemused a potentially dangerous lower class...."

"I object to that, colonel," one of the lieutenants said hotly.

The Sov officer ignored him. "Four, to dispose of the more aggressive potential rebels, by allowing them to kill each other off in the continual combat."

"That, sir, is simply not true," the lieutenant blurted. Joe couldn't remember if he was Andersen or Dickson, even their names were similar.

Joe said, evenly, "And your alternative?"

The Hungarian shrugged. "The Proletarian Paradise maintains two armies, major. One of veterans, for defense against potential foreign foes, and named the Glorious Invincible Red Army —"

"Or, the Red Army, for short," one of the lieutenants murmured dryly.

"...And the other composed of less experienced proletarians and their techno-intellectual, and sometimes even Party, officers. This is our Pink Army."

"Wait a moment," Joe said. "What's a proletarian?"

The lieutenant who had protested the Sov officer's summation of the reasons for the West-world fracases, laughed dryly.

Kossuth stared at Joe. "You *are* poorly founded in the background of the Sov-world, major."

Joe said, "Deliberately, Colonel Kossuth. When I learned of my assignment, I deliberately avoided cramming unsifted information. I decided it would be more desirable to get my information at the source, uncontaminated by our own West-world propaganda."

One of the stiff-necked twins, both of whom Joe was beginning to find a bit *too* stereotyped West-world adherents, said, "Sir, I must protest. The West does not utilize propaganda."

"Of course not," Kossuth said, taking his turn at a dry tone. He said to Joe, "I admire your decision. Obviously, a correct one. Major, a proletarian is, well, you could say, ah —"

"A Low-Lower," Andersen or Dickson said.

"Not exactly," the Sov protested. "Let us put it this way. Marx once wrote that when true Socialism had arrived, the formula would be from each according to his abilities and to each according to his needs. Unhappily, due to the fact that the Proletarian Paradise is surrounded by potential enemies, we have not as yet established this formula. Instead, it is now from each according to his abilities and to each according to his contribution. Consequently, the most useful members of our society are drawn into the ranks of the Party, and, contributing the most, are most highly rewarded. The Party consists of somewhat less than one per cent of the population."

"And is for all practical purposes, hereditary," Anderson or Dickson said.

Kossuth, in indignation, parroted, unknowingly, the lieutenant's earlier words. "That, sir, is simply not true."

Joe said, soothing over the ruffled waters, "And the ...what did you call them ... techno-intellectuals?"

"They are the second most useful members of society. Our technicians, scientists-although many of these are members of the Party, of course-teachers, artists, Pink and Red Army officers, and so forth."

Max looked around from the front seat. "Well, gee, that sounds just about like Uppers, Middles and Lowers to me."

Joe Mauser cleared his throat and said to the Hungarian who was glaring at Max. "And the Pink Army?"

But Kossuth bit out to Max, "Don't be silly, my man. There are no classes in the Proletarian Paradise."

"Yeah," Max said, "and back in the West-world we got People's Capitalism and the people own the corporations. Yeah."

"That'll be all, Max," Joe said, getting in before the two lieutenants could snap something at the fiesty little man. Joe had already decided that the lieutenants were both Uppers, and was somewhat surprised at their lowly rank.

Kossuth brought his attention back to Joe. "We're almost to our destination, Major Mauser. However, briefly, some of the more recent additions to the Sov-world, particularly in the more backward areas of southern Asia, have not quite adjusted to the glories of the Proletarian Paradise."

Both of the lieutenants chuckled softly.

Kossuth said, "So it is found necessary to dispatch punitive expeditions against them. A current such expedition is in the Kunlun Mountains in that area once known as Sinkiang to the north, Tibet to the south. Kirghiz and Kazakhs nomads in the region persist in rejecting the Party and its program. The Pink Army is in the process of eliminating these reactionary elements."

Joe was puzzled. He said, "You mean, in all these years you haven't been able to clean up such small elements of enemies?"

Kossuth said stuffily, "My dear major, please recall that we are limited to the use of weapons pre-1900 in accord with the Universal Disarmament Pact. To be blunt, it is quite evident that foreign elements smuggle weapons into Tibet and other points where rebellion flares, so that on some occasions our Pink Army is confronted with enemies better armed than themselves. These bandits, of course, are not under the jurisdiction of the International Commission and while we are limited, they are not."

"Besides," one of the lieutenants said, "They don't want to clean them up. If they did, the Sov equivalent of the fracas buff wouldn't be able to spend his time at the Telly watching the progress of the Glorious Pink Army against the reactionary foe."

Joe, under his breath, parroted the words of the Sov officer. "That, sir, is simply not true."

Max, who had largely been staring bug-eyed out the window at the passing scene, said, "Hey, the car's stopping. Is this it?"

XVI

Although in actuality working on a private mission for Philip Holland, Frank Hodgson and the others high in government responsibility who were planning fundamental changes in the West-world, Joseph Mauser was ostensibly a military attaché connected with the West-world Embassy to Budapest. As such, he spent several days meeting embassy personnel, his immediate superiors and his immediate inferiors in rank. He was, as a newcomer from home, wined, dined, evaluated, found an apartment, assigned a hovercar, and in general assimilated into the community.

Not ordinarily prone to the social life, Joe was able to find interest in this due to its newness. The citizen of the West-world, when exiled by duty to a foreign land, evidently did his utmost to take his native soil with him. Even house furnishings had been brought from North America. Sov food and drink were superlative, particularly for those of Party rank, but for all practical purposes all such supplies were flown in from the West. Hungarian potables, not to mention the products of a dozen other Sov political divisions including Russia, were of the best, but the denizens of the West-world Embassy drank bourbon and Scotch, or at most the products of the vines of California. The styles of Budapest rivaled those of Paris and Rome, New York and Hollywood, but a feminine employee of the embassy wouldn't have been caught dead in local fashions. It was a home away from home, an oasis of the West in the Sov-world.

Joe, figuring that in view of the double role, unknown even to the higher ranking officers of the embassy, he could best secure protective coloring by conforming and would have slipped into embassy routine without more than ordinary notice. But that wasn't Nadine's style.

From the first, she gloried in pörkölt, the veal stew with paprika sauce, in rostélyos, the round steak potted in a still hotter paprika sauce, in halászlé, the fish soup which is Hungary's challenge to French bouillabaisse, and threatened her lithe figure with her consumption of rétes, the Magyar strudel. All these washed down with Szamorodni or a Hungarian Riesling, the despair of a hundred generations of connoisseurs due to its inability to travel. When liqueurs were called for, barack, the highly distilled apricot brandy which was still the national tipple, was her choice, if not Tokay Aszú, the sweet nectar wine, once allowed only to be consumed by nobility so precious was it considered.

Her apartment became adorned with Hungarian, Bulgarian and Czech antiques, somewhat to the surprise even of the few Sovs with whom she and Joe associated. It had been long years since antiques were in vogue. She dressed in the latest styles from the dressing centers of Prague, Leningrad or from the local houses, ignoring the raised eyebrows of her embassy associates.

Joe, with an inner sigh, followed along in the swath she cut, Nadine being Nadine, and the woman he loved, to boot.

His being raised in caste to Upper through the easy efforts of Philip Holland, had made no observable difference in his relationship with Nadine. Of course, she was Mid-Upper, he told himself, while he was Low-Upper. Still it was far from unknown for romances to cross such comparatively little boundary. He couldn't quite figure out why she seemed to hold him at arm's length. Months had passed since she had told him, that day, she would marry him, even though he be a Middle. But now, when he tried to get her off by herself, for a moment of intimacy between them, she avoided the situation. When he brought their personal relationship into the conversation, she switched subjects. Joe, wedded for too long to his grim profession, inexperienced in the world of the lover, was out of his element.

His Upper caste rating also made little impression on the other embassy personnel, largely because it was the prevalent rank. In dealing with the Sovs, they came into contact almost exclusively with Party members and policy was that West-world officials never be put in the position to have to work with Sovs who ranked them. Only routine office workers were drawn from Middle caste, and largely they kept to themselves except during working hours.

Joe's immediate superior turned out to be a General George Armstrong, with whom Joe had once served some years earlier when the general had commanded a fracas between two labor unions fighting out a jurisdictional squabble. Although Joe hadn't particularly distinguished himself in that fray, the general remembered him well enough. Joe, recognized as the old pro he was, was taken in with open arms, somewhat to the surprise of older embassy military attachés who ranked him in caste, or seniority.

At the first, getting organized in apartment and office, getting his feeling of Budapest, its transportation system, its geographical layout, its offerings in entertainment, he came little in contact with either the Hungarians or the other officials of the Sov world, who teemed the city. In a way it was confusion upon confusion, since Budapest was the center of sovism and the languages of Indo-China, Outer Mongolia, Latvia, Bulgaria, Karelia, or Albania were as apt to be heard on street or in restaurant, as was Hungarian.

But Joe Mauser was in no hurry. His instructions were to take the long view. To take his time. To feel his way. Somewhere along the line, a door would open and he would find that for which he sought.

In a way, Max Mainz seemed to acclimate himself faster than either Nadine or Joe. The little man, completely without language other than Anglo-American, the lingua franca of the West, whilst Joe had both French and Spanish, and Nadine French and German, was still of such persistent social aggressiveness that in a week's time he knew every Hungarian of proletarian rank within a wide neighborhood of where they lived or worked. Within a month he had managed to acquire present tense, almost verbless, jargon with which he was able to conduct all necessary transactions pertaining to his household duties, and to get into surprisingly complicated arguments as well. Joe had to give up attempting to persuade him that discretion was called for in discussing the relative merits of West-world and Sov-world.

In fact, it was through Max that Joe Mauser made his breakthrough in his assignment to learn the inner workings of the Sov-world.

XVII

It was a free evening for Joe, but one that Nadine had found necessary to devote to her medical duties. Max had been gushing about a cabaret in Buda, a place named the Bécsikapu where the wine flowed as wine can flow only in the Balkans and where the gypsy music was as only gypsy music can be. Max had developed a tolerance for wine after only two or three attempts at what they locally called Sot and which he didn't consider exactly beer.

Joe said, only half interested, "For proletarians, Party members, or what?"

Max said, "Well, gee, I guess it's most proletarians, but in these little places, like, you can see almost anybody. Couple of nights ago when I took off I even seen a Russkie field marshal there. And was he drenched."

Joe was at loose ends. Besides, this was a facet of Budapest life he had yet to investigate. The intimate night spots, frequented by all strata of Sov society.

He came to a quick decision. "O.K., Max. Let's give it a look. Possibly it'll turn out to be a place I can take Nadine. She's a bit weary of the overgrown glamour spots they have here. They're more ostentatious than anything you find even in Greater Washington."

Max said, in his fiesty belligerence, "Does that mean better?"

Joe grunted amusement at the little man, even as he took up his jacket. "No, it doesn't," he said, "and take the chip off your shoulder. When you were back home you were continually beefing about what a rugged go you had being a Mid-Lower in the West-world. Now that you're over here the merest suggestion that all is not peaches at home and you're ready to fight."

Max said, his ugly face twisted in a grimace, even as he helped Joe with the jacket. "Well, all these characters over here are up to their tonsils in curd about the West. They think everybody's starving over there because they're unemployed. And they think the Lowers are, like, ground down, and all. And that there's lots of race troubles, and all."

Even as they left the apartment, Joe was realizing how much closer Max had already got to the actual people, than either he or Nadine. But he was still amused. He said, "And wasn't that largely what you used to think about things over here, when you were back home? How many starving have you seen?"

Max grunted. "Well, you know, that's right. They're not as bad off as I thought. Some of those Telly shows I used to watch was kind of exaggerated, like."

Joe said absently, "If international fracases would be won by newspapers and Telly reporters, the Sovs would have lost the Frigid Fracas as far back as when they still called it the Cold War."

The Bécsikapu turned out to be largely what Max had reported and Joe expected. A rather small cellar cabaret, specializing in Hungarian wines and such nibbling delicacies as túrós csusza, the cheese gnocchis; but specializing as well or even more so in romantic atmosphere dominated by heartstring touching of gypsy violins, as musicians strolled about quietly, pausing at this table or that to lean so close to a feminine ear that the lady was all but caressed. It came to Joe that there was more of this in the Sov world than at home. The Sov proletarians evidently spent less time at their Telly sets than did the Lowers in the West-world.

They found a table, crowded though the nightspot was, and ordered a bottle of chilled Feteasca. It wasn't until the waiter had recorded the order against Joe's international credit identification, that it was realized he and Max were of the West. So many non-Hungarians, from all over the Sov-world, were about Budapest that the foreigner was an accepted large percentage of the man-in-the street.

Max said, making as usual no attempt to lower his voice. "Well, look there. There's a sample of them not being as advanced, like, as the West-world. A waiter! Imagine using waiters in a beer joint. How come they don't have auto-bars and all?"

"Sure, sure, sure," Joe said dryly. "And canned music, and a big Telly screen, instead of a live show. Maybe they prefer it this way, Max. You can possibly carry automation too far."

"Naw," Max protested, taking a full half glass of his wine down in one gulp. "Don't you see how this takes up people's time? All these waiters and musicians and all could be home, relaxing, like."

"And watching Telly and sucking on tranks," Joe said, not really interested and largely arguing for the sake of conversation.

A voice from the next table said coldly in accented Anglo-American, "You don't seem to appreciate our entertainment, gentlemen of the west."

Joe looked at the source of the words. There were three officers, only one in the distinctive pinch-waisted uniform of the Hungarians, a captain. The other two wore the Sov epaulets which proclaimed them majors, but Joe didn't place the nationality of the uniforms. There were several bottles upon the table, largely empty.

Joe said carefully. "To the contrary, we find it most enjoyable, sir."

But Max had had two full glasses of the potent Feteasca and besides was feeling pleased and effervescent over his success in getting Joe Mauser, his idol, to spend a night on the town with him. He'd wanted to impress his superior with the extent to which he had get to know Budapest. Max said now, "We got places just as good as this in the West, and bigger too. Lots bigger. This joint wouldn't hold more then fifty people."

The one who had spoken, one of the majors who wore the boots of the cavalryman, said, nastily, "Indeed? I recognize now that when I addressed you both as gentlemen, I failed to realize that in the West gentlemen are not selective of their company and allow themselves to wallow in the gutter with the dregs of their society."

The Hungarian captain said lazily, "Are you sure, Frol, that *either* of them are gentlemen? There seems to be a distinctive *odor* about the lower classes whether in the West-world or our own."

Joe came to his feet quietly.

Max said, suddenly sobered, "Hey, major, sir ... easy. It ain't important."

Joe had picked up his glass of wine. With a gesture so easy as almost to be slow motion, he tossed it into the face of the foppish officer.

The Hungarian, aghast, took up his napkin and began to brush the drink from his uniform, meanwhile sputtering to an extent verging on hysteria. The major who had been seated immediately to his right, fumbled in assistance, meanwhile staring at Joe as though he were a madman.

The cavalryman, though, was of sterner stuff. In the back of his mind, Joe was thinking, even as the other seized a bottle by its long neck and broke off the base on the edge of the table, *Now this one's from the Pink Army, an old pro, and a Russkie, sure as Zen made green apples.*

The major came up, kicking a chair to one side. Joe hunched his shoulders forward, took up his napkin and with a quick double gesture, wrapped it twice around his left hand, which he extended slightly.

The major came in, the jagged edges of the bottle advanced much as a sword. His face was working in rage, and Joe, outwardly cool, decided in the back of his mind that he was glad he'd never have to serve under this one. This one gave way to rage and temper when things were pickling and there was no room for such luxuries in a fracas.

Max was yelling something from behind, something that didn't come through in the bedlam that had suddenly engulfed the Bécsikapu.

At the last moment, Joe suddenly struck out with his left leg, hooked with his foot the small table at which the three Sov officers had been sitting and twisted quickly, throwing it to the side and immediately into the way of his enraged opponent.

The other swore as his shins banged the side and was thrown slightly forward, for a moment off balance.

Joe stepped forward quickly, precisely, and his right chopped down and to the side of the other's prominent jawbone. The Russkie, if Russkie he was, went suddenly glazed of eye. His doubling forward, originally but an attempt to regain balance, continued and he fell flat on his face.

Joe spun around. "Come on, Max, let's get out of here. I doubt if we're welcome." He didn't want to give the other two time to organize themselves and decide to attack. Defeat the two, he and Max might be able to accomplish, but Joe wasn't at all sure where the waiters would stand in the fray, nor anyone else in the small cabaret, for that matter.

Max, at the peak of excitement now, yelled, "What'd you think I been saying? Come on, follow me. There's a rear door next to the rest room."

Waiters and others were converging on them. Joe Mauser didn't wait to argue, he took Max's word for it and hurried after that small worthy, going round and about the intervening tables and chairs like an old time broken field football player.

XVIII

Joe Mauser had assumed there would be some sort of reverberations as a result of his run-in with the Sov officers, but hadn't suspected the magnitude of them.

The next morning he had hardly arrived at the small embassy office which had been assigned him, before his desk set lit up with General Armstrong's habitually worried face. He said, without taking time for customary amenities, "Major Mauser, could you come to my office immediately?" It wasn't a question.

In General George Armstrong's office, beside the general himself, were his aide, Lieutenant Anderson who Joe had at long last sorted out from Lieutenant Dickson, Lieutenant colonel Bela Kossuth and another Sov officer whom Joe hadn't met before.

Everybody looked very stiff and formal.

The general said to Joe, "Major Mauser, Colonel Kossuth and Captain Petöfi have approached me, as your immediate superior, to request that your diplomatic immunity be waived so that you might be called upon on a matter of honor."

Joe didn't get it. He looked from one of the two Hungarians to the other, then back at Armstrong, scowling.

Lieutenant Anderson said, unhappily. "These officers have been named to represent Captain Sándor Rákóczi, major."

Bela Kossuth clicked his heels, bowed, said formally, "Our principal realizes, Major Mauser, that diplomatic immunity prevents his issuing request for satisfaction. However" —the Hungarian cleared his throat —"since honor *is* involved —"

At long last it got through to Joe. His own voice went coldly even. "General Armstrong, I —"

The general said quickly. "Mauser, as an official representative of the West-world, you don't have to respond to anything as dashed silly as a challenge to a duel."

The faces of the two Hungarians froze.

Joe finished his sentence. "...I would appreciate it if you and Lieutenant Anderson would act for me."

Kossuth clicked his heels again. "Gentlemen, the *code duello* provides that the challenged choose the weapons."

General Armstrong's face, usually worried, was now dark with anger. "Choice of weapons, eh? Against Sándor Rákóczi? If you will excuse us now, gentlemen, Lieutenant Anderson and I will consult with you in one hour in the Embassy Club and discuss the affair further. I say frankly, I have never heard of a diplomat being subjected to such a situation, especially on the part of officers of the country to which he is accredited."

The Hungarians were unfazed. Kossuth looked at his wrist chronometer. "One hour in the Embassy Club, gentlemen." The two of them clicked again, bowed from the waist, and were gone.

* * * * *

General Armstrong glared at Joe. "Dash it, if you hadn't been so confoundedly quick on the trigger, I could have warned you, Mauser."

Joe Mauser wasn't over being flabbergasted. "You mean to tell me," he said, "that those people still conduct duels? I thought duels had gone out back in the Nineteenth Century."

"Well, you're mistaken," Armstrong bit out. "It seems to be a practice that can crop up in any decadent society. Remember Hitler reviving it among the German universities? Well, it's all the rage now among the officers of the Sov world. Limited, however, to Party members, the lowly proletariat are assumed not to have honor."

Joe shrugged, "I'm not exactly an amateur at combat, you know."

The general snorted his disgust and turned to his aide. "Lieutenant, go find Dr. Haer for me. Then wait in the outer office until it's time for us to meet those heel-clicking Hungarians."

"Yes, sir," Andersen saluted, shot another look at Joe as though in commiseration, and left hurriedly.

"What's wrong with him?" Joe said.

Armstrong pulled open a desk drawer, brought forth a bottle and glass, poured himself a strong one and knocked it back without offering any to his junior officer. He replaced the bottle and glass and turned his scowl back to Joe. "Haven't you ever heard of Sándor Rákóczi?"

"No."

"He happens to be All-Sov-world Fencing Champion and has been for six years. He also is third from the top amongst the Red Army pistol and rifle marksmen. I once saw him put on an exhibition of trick handgun shooting. Uncanny. The man has abnormal reflexes."

* * * * *

The door opened and Nadine was there. "Joe," she said. "Dick Andersen says you've been challenged to a frame-up duel by Sándor Rákóczi." Her eyes hurried on to Armstrong. "George, this is ridiculous. Joe has diplomatic —"

Joe wasn't getting part of this. He broke in. "What do you mean, frame-up, Nadine? We got into a hassle in a nightspot last night."

Armstrong said. "Everybody simmer down, dash it!" His eyes went to Joe. "Sándor Rákóczi doesn't get into hassles in nightspots-not unless he's been ordered to. Captain Rákóczi is what in the old days was known as a hatchetman." He snorted in deprecation. "The Party no longer conducts purges amongst its own. Everything is all buddy-buddy now. Purges are something from the past. However, those on the very top sometimes find this unfortunate. One manner that has been devised to remove such Party members who have become a thorn in the side of the powers that be, is to have them challenged by such as Sándor Rákóczi."

Joe settled down into a chair, more dumbfounded than ever. "But that's ridiculous. *Why?* Why should they want me eliminated?"

Nadine said hurriedly, "You don't have to accept."

Joe said, "If I don't, I'll be laughed out of town. Remember that big banquet the Pink Army gave me when I first arrived? The celebrated Major Joseph Mauser fling? What happens to West-world prestige when the celebrated Joe Mauser backs down from a duel?"

General Armstrong mused, "If Mauser refuses the duel, he's right, he'll be laughed out of town. If he accepts it, and is killed, he is still removed from the scene." He looked from Joe to Nadine. "Somebody evidently doesn't want Joe Mauser in Budapest."

Pieces were beginning to fit in.

Joe looked at George Armstrong. "You're one of us, aren't you? One of the Phil Holland, Frank Hodgson group." He looked at Nadine. "Why wasn't I told? Am I a junior member or something, that I can't be trusted?"

Armstrong snorted. "You should study up on revolutionary routine, Joe. The smaller the unit of organization, the better. The fewer members you know, the fewer you can betray. Here in the Sov-world, back before the Sovs came to power, the size of their cells was five members, so the most any one person could betray was four."

The tic started at the side of Joe's mouth.

Armstrong said hurriedly. "Don't misunderstand. Your fortitude isn't being questioned. Bravery no longer enters into it. There are methods today under which nobody could hold up." He seemed to come to a sudden decision. "We can't let this take place. You'll have to back down, Mauser. Somehow, there's been a leak and your real purpose in being in Budapest is known. Very well, Phil Holland and the others will simply have to send someone else to replace you."

But Joe had had enough by now. "Look," he said. "Everybody seems to think I can't take care of myself with this foppish molly and his fancy swordsmanship. I've had fifteen years of combat."

"Joe!" Nadine said, "don't be silly. The man's a professional assassin. This is his field, not yours."

Joe said flatly, "On the other hand. I have a job to do and it doesn't involve being run out of Budapest."

General Armstrong said, "Dash it, don't go drivel-happy on us, Mauser. I've just told you, the man's the best swordsman in Europe and Asia combined, and the third best shot."

"How is he with Bowie knives?" Joe said.

XIX

To Mauser's surprise, the Sovs actually turned up two genuine Bowie knives. He had expected the duel, actually, to have to be conducted with trench knives or some other alternative. But the Sovs, ever great on museums, had located one of the weapons of the American Old West in a Prague exhibit of the American frontier, the other in Budapest itself in an extensive collection of fighting knives, down through the ages, in a military museum.

Formally correct, Lieutenant colonel Bela Kossuth appeared at Joe Mauser's apartment three days before the duel, a case in his hands. Max, in his role as batman, conducted him to Joe, doing little to keep his scowl of dislike for the Hungarian from his face. Max was getting fed up with the airs of Sov officers; caste lines were over here, if anything, more strictly drawn than at home.

Joe came to his feet on recognizing his visitor and answered the other's bow. "Colonel Kossuth," he said.

Bela Kossuth clicked heels. He held the case before him, opened it. Two heavy fighting knives lay within. Joe looked at them, then into the other's face.

Kossuth said, "Frankly, major, your somewhat unorthodox selection of weapons has been confusing. However, we have located two Bowie knives. Since it is assumed that the two gentlemen opponents are not thoroughly familiar with, ah, Bowie knives, it has been suggested that each be given his blade at this time."

Joe got it now. Sándor Rákóczi hadn't become the most celebrated duelist in the Sov-world by making such mistakes as underrating his opponents. The weapon was new to him. He wanted the opportunity to practice with it. It was all right with Joe.

Kossuth clicked his heels again. "Our selection, unfortunately, is limited to two weapons. Since you are the challenged, Captain Rákóczi insists you take first choice."

Joe shrugged and took up first one, then the other. It had been some time since he had held one of the famous frontier weapons in his hands. When still a sergeant in the Category Military, he had once become close companions with an old pro whose specialty was teaching hand-to-hand combat. Over a period of years, he and Joe had been comrades, going from one fracas to another as a team. He had taught Joe considerable, including the belief that of all blade hand weapons ever devised, the knife invented by Jim Bowie, whose frontier career ended at the Alamo, was the most efficient.

Joe ran his eyes over the blades carefully. On the back of one was stamped, *James Black, Washington, Arkansas.* Joe had found what he was looking for, however, he pretended to examine the other knife as well, ignoring the Sheffield, England stamp of manufacture.

The Bowie knife: Blade, eleven inches long by an inch and a half wide, the heel three eighths of an inch thick at the back. The point at the exact center of the width of the blade, which curved to the point convexly from the edge, and from the back concavely, both curves being as sharp as the edge itself. The crossguard was of heavy brass, rather than steel and a further backing of brass along the heel, up to the extent where the curve toward the point began. Brass, which is softer than steel, and could catch an opponent's blade, rather than allowing it to slip off and away.

Joe balanced the weapon he had selected, and shrugged. "This one will do," he said.

Kossuth clicked the case with the remaining knife shut. He could see no difference between the two. The selection of weapons had been a formality.

Max saw him to the door and returned to the living room. He said worriedly, "Major, sir, you sure you're checked out on that thing? I've been asking around, like, and they put these duels on Telly here, just like we got fracases back home. This here Captain Rákóczi's got one whopper of a reputation. He's quick as a snake. Kinda like a freak. He can move faster than most people."

"So they've been telling me," Joe mused, balancing the frontier weapon in his hand. It had a beautiful balance, this knife so big that it could be used as a hatchet or machete.

* * * * *

He was still contemplating the vicious looking blade when Nadine entered. He smiled up at her, put the knife aside on the table, and came to his feet.

She looked at Max, and the little man turned and left the room.

Nadine said, "Joe, a plane is leaving this afternoon. A West-world plane for London."

Joe looked at her speculatively. "I won't be on it."

"Joe, listen. A year ago you were an individual, trying to fight your way up to Upper caste. You weren't able to make it as an individual, Joe. But now you're a member of an organization, pledged to a high ideal. Joe, the organization doesn't need martyrs at this stage. It does need good, competent, highly trained members such as Joe Mauser."

He said nothing.

Nadine stepped suddenly closer to him. Her perfume, he noted, vaguely, was new, some sweet scent found here in the Sov world, undoubtedly. It had a heady quality, or was that merely the close presence of Nadine herself?

She put her arms around his neck and pulled his head down to her level. He had never realized that Nadine Haer was this much shorter then he. She pressed the softness of her lips to his.

Then she held back a foot or two, and said into his face, desperately serious, "Does this make any difference, Joe?"

He licked the edges of his lips, carefully, "It makes a great deal of difference." His voice was thick. His arms came up behind her.

"Then you'll be on the plane?"

He shook his head.

She wrenched herself suddenly free and stood back from him, infuriated. He had never seen anyone so infuriated.

He said, "Look, darling. If I had backed out of this, the way you want, you think you'd be happy. But you wouldn't. You want a man, not a coward."

"I want a *live* man! Not a dead hero."

He shook his head stubbornly. "You mentioned the organization. All right, they sent us to do a job here. They can't move in the West-world until they know where the Sov-world stands. They can't afford an attack, a sudden heating up of the Frigid Fracas, right in the middle of the confusion of a socio-economic change. They've got to know how the Sov-world stands, what it will do. They've got to know about this so-called underground, and the religious revival stuff out there in Siberia."

"You've been discovered," she said hotly. "They can send somebody else."

He was still stubborn. "No. There's a leak. If they send somebody else, the same thing will happen. And the next man might not be as much of a potential opponent to such as Sándor Rákóczi as even I am. If I run now, the West loses prestige, and the movement sponsored by Holland and Hodgson and the rest of us, loses prestige, too. Somewhere in Budapest, is some kind of a group that is watching us. We don't know who, or where, or what they stand for, but we can't afford to lose prestige with them."

"We're not exactly going to gain it, when and if this official assassin kills you." She looked down at the wicked knife, and shuddered. "Oh, Joe, your mercenary career is over. Miraculously, you stayed alive for fifteen years through it all. From the Rank Private all the way up to Rank Major. Now at long last, you're an Upper. You're not going to throw it all away, now."

He could say nothing.

She stamped a foot in uncharacteristic fury. "You silly clod. Suppose you do win? Don't you see? They'll simply send another killer after you. They're out to get you, Joe Mauser. Don't you see you can't win against the whole Sov-world? Next time, possibly they won't be quite so formal. Possibly a few footpads in the streets. Do you think they haven't the resources to kill a single man?"

The side of his mouth twitched. "I'm sure they have. But it will give me a few days before they come up with something else. It'd be too conspicuous if I fought their top duelist one day, and then was cut down on the streets the next."

She spun, in a fury, and all but ran from the room and from his apartment.

Joe looked after her ruefully. He growled in sour humor, "Every time matters pickle for me, my gal goes into a tissy and runs off."

XX

As Max had said, as one of their alternatives to the fracas of the West-world, the Sovs put on Telly such duels as were fought amongst their supposedly honor-conscious officer caste. Evidently, the lower caste of the Proletarian Paradise was well on the way to its own version of bread and circuses. In fact, Joe had already wondered what their version of trank was.

But though the Telly cameramen were highly evident, and for this inordinary affair had six cameras in all, placed strategically so that every phase of the fight could be recorded, they were not allowed to be so close as by any chance to interfere with the duel itself. Spaced well back from the action, they must needs depend upon zoom lenses.

Joe Mauser and Sándor Rákóczi stood stripped to the waist, both in tight, non-restricting trousers, both wearing tennis shoes. General Armstrong and Lieutenant Andersen, on one side, and Lieutenant colonel Kossuth and Captain Petöfi, on the other, stood at the sides of their principals.

Kossuth was saying formally, "It has been agreed, then, that the gentlemen participants shall be restricted to this ring measuring twenty feet across. Seconds will remain withdrawn to twenty feet beyond it. The conflict shall begin upon General Armstrong calling *commence*, and shall end upon one or the other, or both, of the gentlemen participants falling to the ground. Minor wounds shall not halt the conflict. This is understood?"

"Yes," Joe said. He had been sizing up his enemy. The man stripped well. He was almost a duplicate of Joe's build, perhaps slightly lighter, slightly taller. Like Joe, he bore a dozen scars about his upper torso. Sándor Rákóczi hadn't worked his way to the top in the dueling world without taking his share of punishment.

Rákóczi said something curtly, obviously affirmative, in Hungarian.

Lieutenant Andersen, his open face drawn worriedly, tendered Joe his Bowie knife. Captain Petöfi proffered Rákóczi his. The two men stepped into the arena, which had been floored with sand, its dimensions marked with blue chalk. Though nothing had been said, it was obvious that if a combatant stepped over this line he would have lost face.

They stood at opposite sides of the arena, both with arms loose at their sides, both holding their fighting knives in their right hands.

General Armstrong said, his voice tight and worried, "Ready, Captain Rákóczi?"

The Hungarian used his affirmative word again.

"Ready, Major Mauser?"

"Ready," Joe said. He felt like adding, *as ready as I'm ever going to be.* He was feeling qualms now. He'd been too long in the game not to recognize a superlative opponent when he saw one.

The four seconds drew back their twenty feet and joined the two doctors and half dozen hospital assistants who were there. Further back still, Joe knew, were emergency facilities. Two men by contemporary usage were going to be allowed to butcher each other, but moments after, all the facilities of modern medical science were going to be at their disposal. Joe felt a wry twinge of humor at the incongruity of it.

General Armstrong called, "Commence!"

Joe spread his legs, grasped the knife so that his thumb was along the side of the blade and held approximately waist high. He shuffled forward, slowly, feeling the consistency of the sand. There must be no slipping.

The Sov officer had assumed the stance of a swordsman. His smile was foxlike. For the first time, Joe noticed the scar along the other's cheek. It was white now, which brought it into prominence. Yes, Sándor Rákóczi, in his time, had copped one more than once. At least the man wasn't infallible.

As they came cautiously toward each other, the Hungarian grinned, fox-fashion, and said in his heavily accented Anglo-American, "Ah, our bad man from the West, you thought to choose a weapon unknown to Rákóczi, eh? But perhaps you have never heard of the Italian short sword, eh? Do you think this clumsy weapon is so different from the Italian short sword, eh?"

Joe had never heard of the Italian short sword, though now it came back to him that some of the phony-fracas films he had seen back home had depicted medieval duelists fighting with two swords, one long, one short. Obviously, his Sov opponent was thoroughly familiar with the usage. Joe swore inwardly.

They circled, warily, watching for an opening, sizing up the other. Each knew that once action was joined, events would most likely progress quickly. The Bowie knife was not built for finesse.

Like a flash, Sándor Rákóczi darted in, his blade flicked, he leapt back, instantly on guard again. There was a streak of red down Joe's arm.

Joe blinked. Somebody, General Armstrong, or was it Max? had said there was something freakish about this Hungarian. His reflexes were unbelievably fast. Now, Joe could believe it.

He attempted a slashing blow himself, and the other danced away so quickly that Joe had not come within feet of his opponent.

Rákóczi laughed insinuatingly. "Oaf," he said. "Is that the word? Clumsy, awkward, stumbling ... oaf. It is well to rid the world of such, eh?"

He was a talker. Joe had met the type before, especially in hand-to-hand combat. They talked, usually insultingly, sometimes bringing up such matters as your legitimacy, or the virtue of your wife or sister, or your own supposed perversions. They talked, and by so doing hoped to enrage you, provoke you into foolish attack. Joe was untouched by such tactics. He circled again, his mind moving quickly.

He had, he realized, no advantages on his side. He was neither stronger nor faster than the other, and he had no reason to believe that he had greater stamina. If anything, it might be the other way.

* * * * *

Rákóczi was in again, through Joe's guard, darting his blade as though it were a foil. A cut opening magically on Joe's chest from the left nipple to navel, and bled profusely.

The Sov duelist was back a good six feet, and laughing openly. Joe had had insufficient time even to move one foot in retreat at the other's offensive.

Joe Mauser wet his lips. The tic at the side of his mouth was in full evidence.

Rákóczi jeered, "Ah, my bad man from the West who throws wine in the face of gentlemen. You grow afraid, eh? Your mouth twitches. You feel in your stomach the fear of death, eh? No longer do you worry about locating the Sov-world underground and helping to overthrow the Party, eh? Now you worry about death."

Joe tried rushing him, plowing through the sand. But the Hungarian danced back, still jeering. He obviously knew the feel of sand beneath foot, as Joe did not. Joe had no time to wonder over Armstrong and Andersen agreeing to a sand deep arena. They had messed up on that one. For Joe, it was like trying to operate on a sandy beach, but Rákóczi seemed in his element.

Even as Joe's attack slowed in frustration, the other darted in, slashed once, twice, scoring on Joe's left arm, once, twice.

He has beginning to resemble a bloody mess. None of the wounds were overly deep, but combined they were costing him blood. He got the feeling that the Hungarian could finish him off at will. That Rákóczi had his number. That it was no longer a matter of the other being careful not to underestimate the foe. Joe had been correctly estimated and found wanting. He realized that only by sinking to the sand could he throw the fight. The duel ended upon one combatant or the other falling to the sand.

And then he could see the other's expression. There was to be no throwing in of the towel for Joe Mauser. At the first sign of such a move, the other would dart in, cobra-quick, and deal the finishing blow. The death blow. Rákóczi was fully capable of such speed. The man was a phenomenon, metabolically speaking.

Joe, his heels almost to the chalk line of the arena boundary, dashing suddenly forward again. His opponent, jeering, as before, darted backward with such speed, even through the sand, as to be unbelievable.

Joe Mauser grinned wolfishly. He tossed the Bowie knife suddenly into the air. It turned in a spin to come down blade in his hand.

He stepped forward with his left foot, threw with full might. The Bowie knife, balanced to turn once completely in thirty feet, blurred through the air and buried itself in the Hungarian's abdomen, up to the hilt.

The Sov officer grunted in agony, stared down at the protruding hilt unbelievingly. His eyes come up in hate, glaring at Joe who stood there across from him, hands now extended forward in the stance of a karate fighter.

Joe could follow the other's agonized thoughts in his expression. There were medics available and though the wound was a decisive one, it need not be fatal, not in this day of surgery and antibiotics. No, not fatal, the Sov Officer decided. He glared at Joe again, his teeth grinding in his pain and shock. To move across the ring at the American would be disastrous, stirring the heavy Bowie knife in his intestines.

Rákóczi knew he had only split seconds, then he must sink to the sand so that aid might come. But perhaps split seconds were sufficient. He reversed his own knife in hand, preparatory to throwing.

Joe watched him. The other's face was a mask of pure agony, but he was no quitter. He was going to make his own throw.

It came, blurringly fast, too fast to avoid. The heavy frontier knife turned over half in the air and struck Joe along the side, glancing off, ineffectively. Sándor Rákóczi fell to the sand and the medics came on the run, both toward him and to Joe.

And then the fog began to roll in on Joe Mauser, and he noted, as though distantly, that the medical assistance that General Armstrong had provided from the West-world Embassy was headed by Dr. Nadine Haer, who seemed to be crying, which was uncalled for in a doctor with a patient, after all.

XXI

His wounds were clean, straight slashes not overly deep and which should heal readily enough. In his time, Joe Mauser had copped many a more serious one. However, after bandaging, Nadine relegated him to the small embassy hospital. The West-world diplomats would not even trust the Sov-world medical care, preferring to import their own Category Medicine personnel.

He was, so Max informed him, the lion of the West-world colony in Budapest. And the Neut-world too, for that matter. It was quite a scandal that a diplomatic representative had been challenged to a duel by a known killer of Rákóczi's reputation. Informal protests were lodged. Joe, cynically, could imagine just how effective they would be, particularly at this late date.

A lion he might be, but Nadine was not allowing him visitors this first day of his recuperation. Max, to attend him, but no others. At least, so it was throughout the morning and early afternoon. Then, so obvious was it that his hurts were not of paramount importance, she relented to the extent of allowing General Armstrong to enter.

The general scowled down at him, as though to read just how badly Joe was feeling. He grumbled, finally, "Dash it, you looked nothing so much as an overgrown hamburger steak there for a while, Mauser."

Joe grinned wryly, "It's how I felt," he said. "I've never seen anyone move so fast."

Armstrong said curiously, "If you wanted to use throwing knives, why didn't you challenge him to a duel with throwing knives?"

Joe shifted his shoulders. "I figured my only chance with him was to use a weapon with which he wasn't familiar. The Bowie knife was it. It didn't occur to him that a knife build in that shape and as big as that, was a precisely constructed throwing knife as well as one to use hand to hand." Joe twisted his mouth. "Besides, if the Sovs think all the Machiavellians are on their side, they're wrong. Poor Captain Rákóczi got sucked in. *I* had a throwing knife, but he didn't."

Armstrong looked at him blankly.

Joe explained. "The knife designed by Jim Bowie was made by a smith named James Black, of Washington, Arkansas. Bowie made himself so notorious with it that the blade became world famous and Black made quite a few exact copies. Various other outfits tried to duplicate his work, but actually none succeeded in producing the perfect balance in such a large knife that made it practical for throwing. It turns over once in thirty feet, exactly. All I had to do was to get Rákóczi fifteen feet away from me, and he'd had it. And his own knife, when he tried to reciprocate, was off balance."

Armstrong said, "Zen!"

"By the way, how is he?" Joe said.

Armstrong said, soberly, "He's dead, Mauser."

"Dead! With all those doctors standing around?"

The general's face assumed its habitually worried expression "I rather doubt he died of your knife. The highest echelons of the Party do not approve of failures. You were correct when you said you would have lost prestige had you fled Rákóczi's challenge or even insisted upon your diplomatic immunity rights. As it is, the prestige has been lost on the other side. By the way, it occurs to me that no further effort will be made to eliminate you physically. It would be too blatant."

Joe said, "One of the things I wanted to talk to you about, general. While we were in there together, Rákóczi was sounding off in an effort to crack my nerve. Called me a lot of names, that sort of thing. But he also said, I'll try to repeat this exactly, *No longer do you worry about locating the Sov-world underground and helping overthrow the Party, eh?*"

Armstrong slumped down into the bedside chair. "Dash it! That makes it definite. They're fully aware of your mission, though they haven't got it exactly right. Your purpose isn't to aid the local underground but merely to size it up, get the overall picture." He snorted his disgust.

"I'll have to get in touch with our organization in Greater Washington. One thing certain, we're not going to be able to let you go into the field in your status as military attaché and observer."

Joe had been scheduled to observe some of the combat taking place in Chinese Turkestan with nomad rebels. He had looked forward to the experience, in view of his own background, wondering in what manners the Sov forces of the Pink Army differed from the mercenary armies of the West-world. He said now, "Why not?"

Armstrong snorted. "You'd never come out alive. There's be an accident, and the nomads would be given the dubious credit for having killed you." He came to his feet again. "I've got to think about this. I'll drop in later, Mauser."

Joe thought about it too, after the other had left. Obviously, the restrictions on his movements were a growing handicap on his abilities to serve the organization headed by Holland Hodgson. He wondered if he was becoming useless.

* * * * *

Max stuck his head in the door and said, "Major, sir, one of these here Hungarians wants to see you."

"Who?" Joe growled. "And why?"

"It's that Lieutenant Colonel Kossuth one, sir. I told him Doc Haer said you couldn't be bothered, but he don't seem to take no for an answer."

Kossuth, Joe Mauser knew, was assigned to the West-world Embassy military attaché department on a full time basis. It occurred to him that the Hungarian would be privy to the inner workings of the Party as they applied to Joseph Mauser and his associates.

"Show him in," he told Max.

"But the Doc —"

"Show him in, Max."

Lieutenant Colonel Bela Kossuth was solicitous. He clicked heels, bowed from the waist, inquired of Joe's well being.

Joe wasn't feeling up to military amenities after his framed-up near demise of the day before. He growled, "I'd think you'd be wishing I occupied Captain Rákóczi's place, rather than offering me sympathy."

The Hungarian's eyebrows went up, and uninvited he took the chair next to the bed. "But why?"

"You *were* the man's second."

Kossuth was expansive. "When asked to act, I could hardly refuse a brother officer. Besides, my superiors suggested that I take the part. As you probably have ascertained, major, there is considerable doubt the desirability of you remaining in Budapest."

Joe was astonished. "You mean to sit there and deliberately admit the duel was a planned attempt to eliminate me?"

The colonel coolly looked about the room. "Why not, major? There is no one here to witness our conversation."

"And you admit that your precious Party, the ruling organ of this Proletarian Paradise of yours, actually orders what amounts to assassination?"

Kossuth examined his finger nails with studied nonchalance. "Why not admit it? The party will do literally anything to maintain itself in its position, major. Certainly, the death of a junior officer of the West-world means nothing to them."

"But aren't you a Party member yourself?"

"Of course. One must be, if one is to operate as freely as circumstance allows in this best of all possible worlds, this paradise of ours."

Joe sank back on his pillow. He couldn't get used to the idea of this man, whom he had always thought of as the arch-stereotype Sov-world officer, speaking in this manner.

Kossuth crossed his legs comfortably. "See, here, major, you are all but naive in your understanding of our society. Let me, ah, brief you, on the history of this part of the world, and the organization which governs it. Have you studied Marx and Engels?"

"No," Joe said. "I've read a few short extracts, and a few criticisms, or criticisms of criticisms of short extracts. That sort of thing."

* * * * *

Kossuth nodded seriously. "That's all practically anybody does any more, even in the Sov-world where we give lip service to them. The point I was about to make is that the supposed founders of our society had nothing even remotely approaching this in mind when they did their research. It evidently never occurred to either that the first attempts to achieve the —" the Hungarian's voice went dry — "glorious revolution, would take place in such ultra-backward countries as Russia and China. The revolution of which they wrote presupposedly a highly industrialized, technical economy. Neither Russia nor, later China had this. The, ah, excesses that occurred in both countries, in the mid-Twentieth Century, were the result of efforts to rectify this. You follow me? The Party, in power as a result of the confusion following in one case the First World War, and in the second case, the Second World War, tried to lift the nations into the industrial world by the bootstraps."

The colonel cleared his throat. "Let us say that some elements resisted the sacrifices the Party demanded-the peasants, for instance."

Joe said, dryly himself, "If I am correctly informed on Sov-world history, you do not exaggerate."

"Exactly. Let us admit it. Stalin, in particular, but others too, both before and following him, were ruthless in their determination to achieve industrialization and raise the Sov-world to the level of the most advanced countries."

Joe said, "This isn't exactly news to me, colonel."

"Of course not. Bear with me, I was but making background. To accomplish these things, the Party had to, and did, become a strong, ruthless, even merciless organization, with all power safely-from its viewpoint, of course-in its hands. And, in spite of all handicaps and setbacks, eventually succeeded in the task it had set itself. That is the achieving of an industrialized nation."

The Hungarian pursed his lips. "But then comes the rub. Have you ever heard, Major Mauser, of a ruling class, caste, clique, call it what you will, which stepped down from power freely and willingly, handing over the reins of government to some other element?"

Joe vaguely remembered hearing similar words from some other source in the not too distant past, but by now he was fully taken up by the astonishing Sov officer. He shook his head, encouraging the other to continue.

* * * * *

Kossuth nodded. "They tell me that in ancient Greece and Rome, tyrants or dictators would assume full powers for a period long enough to meet some emergency, and would then relinquish such power. I do not know. I would think it doubtful. But whether or not such was done in ancient Greece, it has been a rare practice indeed, since.

"A ruling caste, like a socio-economic system itself, when taken as a whole, instinctively perpetuates its life, as though a living organism. It cannot understand, will not admit, that it is ever time to die."

The Hungarian waggled a finger at Joe. "At first, when there was insufficient even of the basics such as food, clothing and shelter, Party members soon learned to take care of their own, explaining this deviation from the original Party austerity, by various means. Nepotism reared its head, as always, almost from the very beginning. Party members wished their children to become Party members and saw to it that they secured the best of education, and the best of jobs. And ... how do you Americans put it ... the practice of you scratch my back and I'll scratch yours, became the rule. Soon we had a self-perpetuating hierarchy, jealous of its position, and jealous of the attempts of outsiders to break into the sanctified organization. Marx and Engels wrote that following the revolution the State would wither away." The colonel laughed acidly. "Instead, in the Sov-world it continually strengthened itself. A New Class, as the Yugoslavian Milovan Djilas called it, had been born."

The Hungarian seemed to switch subjects slightly. "And a new development manifested itself. At first, Russia alone was of the Sov-world but as she became increasingly powerful, she exported her revolution, taking over in such advanced countries as, let us say, Czechoslovakia and East Germany. Here, supposedly, would have been the conditions under which the original ideas of Marx and his collaborator would have flourished, but the Party moved in its heavy bureaucracy and prevented any such development."

Bela Kossuth laughed gently. "Ah, ha, but this led to one of the ironies of fate, my friend. Because as the Sov-world expanded its borders it assimilated peoples of far more, ah, sharpness, shall we say? than our somewhat dour Russkies. In time, bit by bit, inch by inch, intrigue by intrigue —"

"I know," Joe said. "The capital of the Sov-world is now not Moscow, but Budapest."

"Correct!" the Hungarian beamed. "At the very first, we Hungarians tried to fight them. When we found we couldn't prevail, we joined them-to their eventual sorrow. However, the central problem has not been erased. We have finally achieved, here in the Sov-world, to the point where we have the abundant life. The affluent society. But we have also reached stag-nation. The Party, like a living organism, refuses to die. Cannot even admit that its death is desirable."

He held his hands out, palms upward, as though at an impossible impasse.

Joe said, suddenly, "What's all this got to do with me, Colonel Kossuth?"

The Hungarian pretended surprise. "Why, nothing at all, Major Mauser. I was but making conversation. Small talk."

Joe didn't get it. "Well, why come here at all? Max said you were rather insistent about seeing me, in spite of doctor's orders."

"Ah, yes, of course." The Sov officer came to his feet again and clicked his heels. "My superiors have requested that I deliver this into your own hands, as well as copies to the West-world Ambassador, to General Armstrong and Dr. Haer." He handed a document to Joe.

Joe turned it over in hand, blankly. It was in Hungarian. He looked up at the other.

Lieutenant Colonel Bela Kossuth said formally, "The government of the Sov-world has found Major Joseph Mauser, Dr. Nadine Haer, and General George Armstrong, *persona non grata*. As soon as your health permits, Major, it is requested that you leave Budapest and all the lands of the Sov-world, never to return."

He clicked his heels, bowed again, and started for the door. Just as he reached it, he turned and said one last thing to Joe Mauser.

XXII

In spite of Nadine Haer's protests, Joseph Mauser insisted that they abide by the Sov government's expulsion order on the following day. A special plane took them to London, and they there caught the regular shuttle to Greater Washington. At least, Joe, Nadine and Max did, General Armstrong remained on in London.

The flight itself was largely uneventful, Joe having retreated into his thoughts. He had a great deal to think about. Not only in regard to the immediate collapse of his mission, but both of the past and future, as well.

Max, looking out the plane's window as they took off, bore an air of nostalgia. "Look there," he pointed. "You can see that big statue of the Magyar warriors, there in front of the Szepmuveszeti Museum, like." He sighed. "I had a date with a Croat girl, to meet her there tomorrow night. I was making good time with Carla. She thought it was romantic, me being from the West, and all."

"Max, my friend," Joe growled. "Save us the lurid details of your romances."

But his voice hadn't really borne irritation. Max went on, "You know, you kind of get used to these people. They aren't much different, like, than us. Take fracases, for instances. They don't have them like we do, but they got their Telly teams out there in Siberia, with the lads that go chasing the rebels and all. And they got their duels they cover on Telly. But I was thinking, why don't they get modern and have real fracases, like us? And then we could have, like, international meets, and they'd send a division, and we'd send one, and have it out. Zen! That'd be really something to watch."

Joe winced.

Nadine said, "Max, it took the human race ten thousand years to put even a temporary halt to the international war, now you want to bring it back for the sake of a sadistic Telly show."

"Yeah, but gee —"

Joe Mauser said, "Max, go on back to the bar and have yourself a drink. I want to talk to Nadine."

When the little man was gone, Joe said, in a conversational tone, "We can be married tomorrow, right after we've reported to Phil Holland and the others."

Her eyes widened, "Well, really! Don't you think you might ask me about it?"

He shook his head. "No, we've covered all the preliminaries. The trouble with me has been that I've continued to look *up* at you. I suppose the caste system is too deeply ingrained in me. But now ...you're my woman. Period. I suppose you've actually been wondering why I've been such a slow clod."

"Do you think you're looking *down* at me now?" She countered indignantly.

"No. Just evenly. We'll be married as soon as possible."

Her voice went strangely demure. "Yes, Joe," she said.

They drove immediately from the airport to the office of Philip Holland, stopping only long enough for Joe to make a phone call.

They retraced the route over which Nadine had taken him that day that seemed so long ago, but actually wasn't. Through the long corridors, and eventually to the small office with the receptionist.

Miss Mikhail said, brightly, "Dr. Haer, Major Mauser, Mr. Holland is expecting you. Go right in."

Just before pressing through the door, Nadine put her hand on Joe's arm and looked into his face ruefully. "Darling, you've had so much hard luck in your time, I'm sorry this first assignment for the organization had to be a failure."

Joe wet his lips, carefully, "Why'd you think it was?" he said, opening the door.

Nadine could only stare as he ushered her into Phil Holland's presence.

* * * * *

That crisp, efficient operator made much the same motions he had the first time Joe had met him here. Holding a chair for Nadine, shaking hands briskly with Joe and motioning to another chair for him. While they were getting settled, Frank Hodgson sauntered in, seemingly as lackadaisical and disinterested as ever. After a minimum of exchanged pleasantries, he subsided onto the couch and fished for pipe and tobacco.

Holland took in Joe's arm, still immobilized in a sling, and the other signs of his wounds. He said crisply, "I thought that we had removed you permanently from the field of combat, Joe."

Joe said sourly, "Some of the Sovs thought otherwise."

Holland said, an element of irritation in his voice, "It is hard to understand how you could have revealed yourself so quickly."

Joe pursed his lips and looked at Nadine. He said, "I think I've figured that out. It's practically impossible for Nadine to dissimulate. And I've never seen her and her brother together but that they weren't arguing."

Nadine was frowning at him. "What has Balt to do with it?"

Joe said, "I have a sneaking suspicion that in the heat of one of your arguments with your brother, the Baron, you revealed your, and my, mission and its real purpose."

Nadine's right hand went to her mouth.

Joe finished with, "And the Baron, after all, is a member of the Nathan Hale Society. I have no doubts that the organization has some connections with their equal number in the Sov-world."

Holland grunted. "Very possible. However, it's done now. The thing is, what is your opinion Joe, and yours, Nadine, on the advisability of sending other operatives on the same mission?"

Joe shook his head. "Unnecessary."

Frank Hodgson paused in lighting his pipe, to peer through the smoke.

Joe said, "In fact, it was unnecessary to send Nadine and me."

Holland's voice was testy. "I assure you, Joe, the particular assignment was quite important. We simply cannot afford to move, here in the West, until we know what the Sov-world will do. Your task was a delicate one, obviously. You simply couldn't go to their government and ask. There are strong elements in not only the Upper caste, but even the middle and Lower ones, here in this country, who would spring to the defense of present West-world society if they thought an attempt was being made to alter its structure. If the Sov government reported that it had been approached by elements of a revolutionary group, the fat would be in the fire."

Joe nodded. "I realize all that."

"You were expected to worm your way into their circles, to feel them out. To contact their own underground, if one exists. To ferret out definite information on how they would react if we began definite changes in the *status quo* here."

Joe continued to nod.

Holland was increasingly irritated. "Then why, good heavens, do you say your mission was unnecessary?"

"Because they had already sent a mission over here to contact us," Joe told him, evenly.

Had he suddenly got up from his chair, walked up the wall, across the ceiling, then down the other wall, they could not have stared at him the more.

The telly-mike on Phil Holland's desk squeaked something, and he took time enough to snap, "No. I told you, Miss Mikhail, I was not to be disturbed by *anyone*."

But Joe said, "If that's Colonel Lajos Arpád, I suggest you have him in. I took the liberty of phoning him and asking that he meet us here."

Frank Hodgson was the first to recover. "Arpád! That spy! I've just about gathered enough dope on him to have him declared *persona non grata* and ship him back to Budapest."

"As I was shipped back to Greater Washington," Joe said dryly. "Colonel Arpád and I seem to duplicate each other's activities in almost everything."

Phil Holland said crisply into the communicator, "Ask the colonel to come in, Miss Mikhail."

Ever the correct Sov-world officer, Colonel Arpád came to attention immediately upon entering the room, clicked heels, bowed from the waist. Except for Joe Mauser, none of them had met him, but he evidently knew all, greeting them by name.

The men had come to their feet. Joe said, "Meet Colonel Lajos Arpád, high in the ranks of the Sov-world Party, and at present on secret mission from the Sov-world underground revolutionary organization." Joe ended up wryly. "His mission being to determine what action the West-world might take if the secret group which has determined to make basic changes in the Sov-world socio-economic system was to take action."

It was the Hungarian who stared now. His eyes bored into Joe's face. "I do not, of course, admit that, Major Mauser. But where in the world did you receive that strange opinion?"

Joe sat down again. The blood he had lost still bothered him, and he tired easily.

He said, "From Colonel Kossuth, in Budapest. Another high ranking member of your group." Joe's eyes went back to Holland and Hodgson. Quick minded these two might be, but they were being asked to assimilate some shocking information.

Joe brought it all out. "I don't know why it didn't occur to any of us that the problems of the West-world and those of the Sov-world, at long last have become similar, almost identical. Both, following different paths, have achieved the affluent society, so called. But in doing it, both managed to inflict upon themselves a caste system that perpetuated itself, eventually to the detriment of progress. In the past, revolutions used to be accomplished by the masses, pushed beyond the point of endurance. A starving lower class, trying to change the rules of society so as to realize a better life. But now, in neither West nor in the Sov-world are there any starving. The majority of Lowers and Proletarians are well clothed, fed and housed, and bemused by fracases and trank pills, or their equivalent over there."

Joe shrugged, the weariness growing. Possibly Nadine had been right, he shouldn't have traveled so soon. "The best elements in both countries have finally realized that changes must be made. These elements, the more capable, more competent, more intelligent, already *are running* each country though they are not necessarily Uppers or Party members. Phil Holland here, supposedly a Middle secretary to the Foreign Minister, actually has performed that worthy's work for several administrations. Frank Hodgson is the working head of the Bureau of Investigation, though only a Middle. I assume a similar situation prevails in Budapest."

Arpád still stood. "It does."

Joe came to his feet, looking to Nadine. He said, "Gentlemen, I evidently have not recovered from my recent duel as much as I thought. I had better retire. Meanwhile, I suggest you exchange some notes."

Nadine hurried to his side, worried.

Holland, Hodgson and Arpád were staring at each other, somewhat like small boys, or strange dogs.

Hodgson grumbled, his voice, for once, forgetting to express laziness, "Our records show you to be a Sov espionage agent."

The Hungarian nodded, equally suspicious. "That is my official position. But I am also secretly a member of the executive committee of the organization of which Major Mauser speaks and have been attempting for some time to get in touch with the West-world underground, if one existed. I had about come to the conclusion that no such group was in existence, until today."

Joe said, "Relax boys, and let down your hair. You've got a lot in common. It looks as though, at long last, the Frigid Fracas is beginning to fade away."

Status Quo

In his income bracket and in the suburb in which he lived, government employees in the twenty-five to thirty-five age group were currently wearing tweeds. Tweeds were in. Not to wear tweeds was Non-U.

Lawrence Woolford wore tweeds. His suit, this morning, had first seen the light of day on a hand loom in Donegal. It had been cut by a Swede widely patronized by serious young career men in Lawrence Woolford's status group; English tailors were out currently and Italians unheard of.

Woolford sauntered down the walk before his auto-bungalow, scowling at the sportscar at the curb-wrong year, wrong make. He'd have to trade it in on a new model. Which was a shame in a way, he liked the car. However, he had no desire to get a reputation as a weird among colleagues and friends. What was it Senator Carey MacArthur had said the other day? Show me a weird and I'll show you a person who has taken the first step toward being a Commie.

Woolford slid under the wheel, dropped the lift lever, depressed gently the thrust pedal and took off for downtown Greater Washington. Theoretically, he had another four days of vacation coming to him. He wondered what the Boss wanted. That was the trouble in being one of the Boss' favorite trouble shooters, when trouble arose you wound up in the middle of it. Lawrence Woolford was to the point where he was thinking in terms of graduating out of field work and taking on a desk job which meant promotion in status and pay.

He turned over his car to a parker at the departmental parking lot and made his way through the entrance utilized by second-grade departmental officials. In another year, he told himself, he'd be using that other door.

The Boss' reception secretary looked up when Lawrence Woolford entered the anteroom where she presided. "Hello, Larry," she said. "Hear they called your vacation short. Darn shame."

LaVerne Polk was a cute little whizz of efficiency. Like Napoleon and his army, she knew the name of every member of the department and was on a first-name basis with all. However, she was definitely a weird. For instance, styles might come and styles might go, but LaVerne dressed for comfort, did her hair the way she thought it looked best, and wore low-heeled walking shoes on the job. In fact, she was ready and willing to snarl at anyone, no matter how kindly intentioned, who even hinted that her nonconformity didn't help her promotion prospects.

Woolford said, "Hi, LaVerne. I think the Boss is expecting me."

"That he is. Go right in, Larry."

She looked after him when he turned and left her desk. Lawrence Woolford cut a pleasant figure as thirty year old bachelors go.

The Boss looked up from some report on his desk which he'd been frowning at, nodded to his field man and said, "Sit down, Lawrence. I'll be with you in a minute. Please take a look at this while you're waiting." He handed over a banknote.

Larry Woolford took it and found himself a comfortable chair. He examined the bill, front and back. It was a fifty dollar note, almost new.

Finally the Boss, a stocky but impeccable career bureaucrat of the ultra-latest school, scribbled his initials on the report and tossed it into an Out chute. He said to Woolford, "I am sorry to cut short your vacation, Lawrence. I considered giving Walter Foster the assignment, but I think you're the better choice."

Larry decided the faint praise routine was the best tactic, said earnestly about his closest rival. "Walt's a good man, sir." And then, "What's the crisis?"

"What do you think of that fifty?"

His trouble shooter looked down at it. "What is there to think about it?"

The Boss grunted, slid open a desk drawer and brought forth another bill. "Here, look at this, please."

It was another fifty. Larry Woolford frowned at it, not getting whatever was going on.

"Observe the serial numbers," the Boss said impatiently.

They were identical.

Woolford looked up. "Counterfeit. Which one is the bad one?"

"That is exactly what we would like to know," the Boss said.

Larry Woolford stared at his superior, blinked and then examined the bills again. "A beautiful job," he said, "but what's it got to do with us, sir? This is Secret Service jurisdiction, counterfeiting."

"They called us in on it. They think it might have international ramifications."

Now they were getting somewhere. Larry Woolford put the two bills on the Boss' desk and leaned back in his chair, waiting.

His superior said, "Remember the Nazis turning out American and British banknotes during the Second War?"

"I was just a kid."

"I thought you might have read about it. At any rate, obviously a government-with all its resources-could counterfeit perfectly any currency in the world. It would have the skills, the equipment, the funds to accomplish the task. The Germans turned out hundreds of millions of dollars and pounds with the idea of confounding the Allied financial basics."

"And why didn't it work?"

"The difficulty of getting it into circulation, for one thing. However, they did actually use a quantity. For a time our people were so alarmed that they wouldn't allow any bills to come into this country from Mexico except two-dollar denomination-the one denomination the Germans hadn't bothered to duplicate. Oh, they had the Secret Service in a dither for a time."

Woolford was frowning. "What's this got to do with our current situation?"

The Boss said, "It is only a conjecture. One of those bills is counterfeit but such an excellent reproduction that the skill involved is beyond the resources of any known counterfeiter. Secret Service wants to know if it might be coming from abroad, and, if so, from where. If it's a governmental project, particularly a Soviet Complex one, then it comes into the ken of our particular cloak-and-dagger department."

"Yes, sir." Woolford said. He got up and examined the two bills again. "How'd they ever detect that one was bad?"

"Pure fortune. A bank clerk with an all but eidetic memory was going through a batch of fifties. It's not too commonly used a denomination, you know. Coincidence was involved since in that same sheaf the serial number was duplicated."

"And then?"

"The reproduction was so perfect that Secret Service was in an immediate uproar. Short of the Nazi effort, there has never been anything like it. A perfect duplication of engraving and paper identically the same. The counterfeiters have even evidently gone to the extent of putting a certain amount of artificial wear on the bills before putting them into circulation."

Larry Woolford said, "This is out of my line. How were they able to check further, and how many more did they turn up?"

"The new I.B.M. sorters help. Secret Service checked every fifty dollar bill in every institution in town both banking and governmental. Thus far, they have located ten bills in all."

"And other cities?"

"None. They've all been passed in Greater Washington, which is suspicious in itself. The amount of expense that has gone into the manufacture of these bills does not allow for only a handful of them being passed. They should be turning up in number. Lawrence, this reproduction is such that a pusher could walk into a bank and have his false currency changed by any clerk."

"Wow," Larry whistled.

"Indeed."

"So you want me to work with Secret Service on this on the off chance that the Soviet Complex is doing us deliberate dirt."

"That is exactly the idea, Lawrence. Get to work, please, and keep in touch with me. If you need support, I can assign Walter Foster or some of the other operatives to assist you. This might have endless ramifications."

* * * * *

Back in the anteroom, Woolford said to the Boss' receptionist, "I'm on a local job, LaVerne, how about assigning me a girl?"

"Can do," she said.

"And, look, tell her to get hold of every available work on counterfeiting and pile it on my desk."

"Right. Thinking of going into business, Larry?"

He grinned down at her. "That's the idea. Keeping up with the Jones clan in this man's town costs roughly twice my income."

LaVerne said disapprovingly, "Then why not give it up? With the classification you've got a single man ought to be able to save half his pay." She added, more quietly, "Or get married and support a family."

"Save half my pay?" Larry snorted. "And get a far out reputation, eh? No thanks, you can't afford to be a weird these days."

She flushed-and damn prettily, Larry Woolford decided. She could be an attractive item if it wasn't for obviously getting her kicks out of being individualistic.

Larry said suddenly, "Look, promise like a good girl not to make us conspicuous and I'll take you to the Swank Room for dinner tonight."

"Is that where all the bright young men currently have to be seen once or twice a week?" she snapped back at him. "Get lost, Larry. Being a healthy, normal woman I'm interested in men, but not necessarily in walking status-symbols."

It was his turn to flush, and, he decided wryly, he probably didn't do it as prettily as she did.

On his way to his office, he wondered why the Boss kept her on. Classically, a secretary-receptionist should have every pore in place, but in her time LaVerne Polk must have caused more than one bureaucratic eyebrow to raise. Efficiency was probably the answer; the Boss couldn't afford to let her go.

Larry Woolford's office wasn't much more than a cubicle. He sat down at the desk and banged a drawer or two open and closed. He liked the work, liked the department, but theoretically he still had several days of vacation and hated to get back into routine.

Had he known it, this was hardly going to be routine.

He flicked the phone finally and asked for an outline. He dialed three numbers before getting his subject. The phone screen remained blank.

"Hans?" he said. "Lawrence Woolford."

The Teutonic accent was heavy, the voice bluff. "Ah, Larry! you need some assistance to make your vacation? Perhaps a sinister, exotic young lady, complete with long cigarette holder?"

Larry Woolford growled, "How'd you know I was on vacation?"

The other laughed. "You know better than to ask that, my friend."

Larry said, "The vacation is over, Hans. I need some information."

The voice was more guarded now. "I owe you a favor or two."

"Don't you though? Look, Hans, what's new in the Russkie camp?"

The heartiness was gone. "How do you mean?"

"Is there anything big stirring? Is there anyone new in this country from the Soviet Complex?"

"Well now —" the other's voice drifted away.

Larry Woolford said impatiently, "Look, Hans, let's don't waste time fencing. You run a clearing agency for, *ah*, information. You're strictly a businessman, nonpartisan, so to speak. Fine, thus far our department has tolerated you. Perhaps we'll continue to. Perhaps the reason is that we figure we get more out of your existence than we lose. The Russkies evidently figure the same way, the proof being that you're alive and have branches in the capitals of every power on Earth."

"All right, all right," the German said. "Let me think a moment. Can you give me an idea of what you're looking for?" There was an undernote of interest in the voice now.

"No. I just want to know if you've heard anything new anti-my-side, from the other side. Or if you know of any fresh personnel recently from there."

"Frankly, I haven't. If you could give me a hint."

"I can't," Larry said. "Look, Hans, like you say, you owe me a favor or two. If something comes up, let me know. Then I'll owe you one."

The voice was jovial again. "It's a bargain, my friend."

After Woolford had hung up, he scowled at the phone. He wondered if Hans Distelmayer was lying. The German commanded the largest professional spy ring in the world. It was possible, but difficult, for anything in espionage to develop without his having an inkling.

The phone rang back. It was Steve Hackett of Secret Service on the screen.

Hackett said, "Woolford, you coming over? I understand you've been assigned to get in our hair on this job."

"Huh," Larry grunted. "The way I hear it, your whole department has given up, so I'm assigned to help you out of your usual fumble-fingered confusion."

Hackett snorted. "At any rate, can you drop over? I'm to work in liaison with you."

"Coming," Larry said. He hung up, got to his feet and headed for the door. If they could crack this thing the first day, he'd take up that vacation where it'd been interrupted and possibly be able to wangle a few more days out of the Boss to boot.

At this time of day, parking would have been a problem, in spite of automation of the streets. He left his car in the departmental lot and took a cab.

* * * * *

The Counterfeit Division of the Secret Service occupied an impressive section of an impressive governmental building. Larry Woolford flashed his credentials here and there, explained to guards and receptionists here and there, and finally wound up in Steve Hackett's office which was all but a duplicate of his own in size and decor.

Steve Hackett himself was a fairly accurate carbon copy of Woolford, barring facial resemblance alone. The fact was, Steve was almost Lincolnesque in his ugliness. Career man, about thirty, good university, crew cut, six foot, one hundred and seventy, earnest of eye. He wore Harris tweed. Larry Woolford made a note of that; possibly herringbone was coming back in. He winced at the thought of a major change in his wardrobe; it'd cost a fortune.

They'd worked on a few cases together before when Steve Hackett had been assigned to the presidential bodyguard and co-operated well.

Steve came to his feet and shook hands. "Thought that you were going to be down in Florida bass fishing this month. You like your work so well you can't stay away, or is it a matter of trying to impress your chief?"

Larry growled, "Fine thing. Secret Service bogs down and they've got to call me in to clean up the mess."

Steve motioned him to a chair and immediately went serious. "Do you know anything about pushing queer, Woolford?"

"That means passing counterfeit money, doesn't it? All I know is what's in the TriD crime shows."

"I can see you're going to be a lot of help. Have you got anywhere at all on the possibility that the stuff might be coming from abroad?"

"Nothing positive," Larry said. "Are you people accomplishing anything?"

"We're just getting underway. There's something off-trail about this deal, Woolford. It doesn't fit into routine."

Larry Woolford said, "I wouldn't think so if the stuff is so good not even a bank clerk can tell the difference."

"That's not what I'm talking about now. Let me give you a run down on standard counterfeiting." The Secret Service agent pushed back in his swivel chair, lit a cigarette, and propped his feet onto the edge of a partly open desk drawer. "Briefly, it goes like this. Some smart lad gets himself a set of plates and a platen press and —"

Larry interrupted, "Where does he get the plates?"

"That doesn't matter now," Steve said. "Various ways. Maybe he makes them himself, sometimes he buys them from a crooked engraver. But I'm talking about pushing green goods once it's printed. Anyway, our friend runs off, say, a million dollars worth of fives. But he doesn't try to pass them himself. He wholesales them around netting, say, fifty thousand dollars. In other words, he sells twenty dollars in counterfeit for one good dollar."

Larry pursed his lips. "Quite a discount."

"Um-m-m. But that's safest from his angle. The half dozen or so distributors he sold it to don't try to pass it either. They also are playing it carefully. They peddle it, at say ten to one, to the next rung down the ladder."

"And these are the fellows that pass it, eh?"

"Not even then, usually. These small timers take it and pass it on at five to one to the suckers in the trade, who take the biggest risks. Most of these are professional pushers of the queer, as the term goes. Some, however, are comparative amateurs. Sailors for instance, who buy with the idea of passing it in some foreign port where seamen's money flows fast."

Larry Woolford shifted in his chair. "So what are you building up to?"

Steve Hackett rubbed the end of his pug nose with a forefinger in quick irritation. "Like I say, that's standard counterfeit procedure. We're all set up to meet it, and do a pretty good job. Where we have our difficulties is with amateurs."

Woolford scowled at him.

Hackett said, "Some guy who makes and passes it himself, for instance. He's unknown to the stool pigeons, has no criminal record, does up comparatively small amounts and dribbles his product onto the market over a period of time. We had one old devil up in New York once who actually *drew* one dollar bills. He was a tremendous artist. It took us years to get him."

Larry Woolford said, "Well, why go into all this? We're hardly dealing with amateurs now."

Steve looked at him. "That's the trouble. We are."

"Are you batty? Not even your own experts can tell this product from real money."

"I didn't say it was being *made* by amateurs. It's being *pushed* by amateurs-or maybe amateur is the better word."

"How do you know?"

"For one thing, most professionals won't touch anything bigger than a twenty. Tens are better, fives better still. When you pass a fifty, the person you give it to is apt to remember where he got it." Steve Hackett said slowly, "Particularly if you give one as a tip to the *maître d'hôtel* in a first-class restaurant. A *maître d'* holds his job on the strength of his ability to remember faces and names."

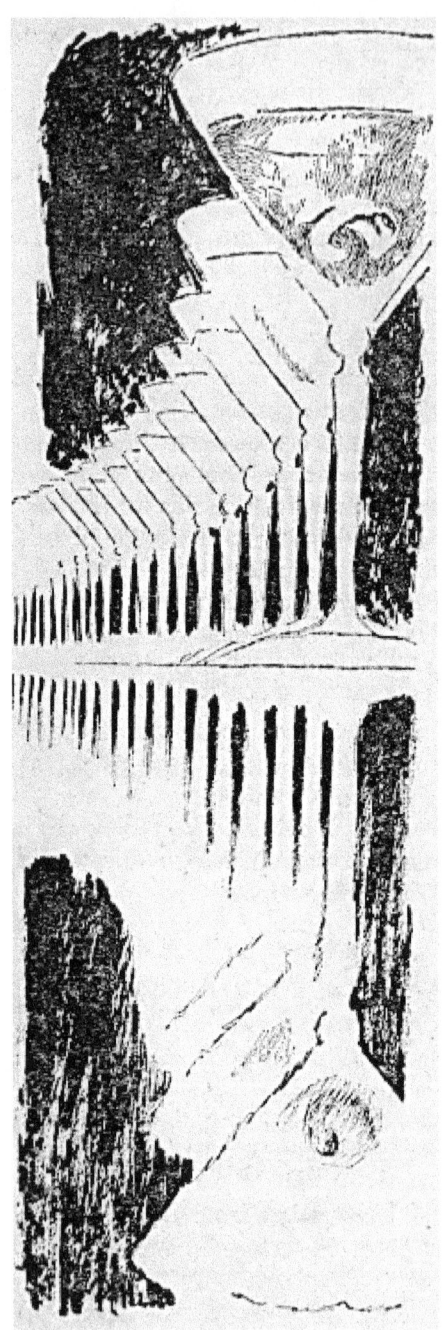

"What else makes you think your pushers are amateurs?"

"Amateur," Hackett corrected. "Ideally, a pusher is an inconspicuous type. The kind of person whose face you'd never remember. It's never a teenage girl who's blowing money."

It was time to stare now, and Larry Woolford obliged. "A teenager!"

"We've had four descriptions of her, one of them excellent. Fredrick, the *maître d'* over at La Calvados, is the one that counts, but the others jibe. She's bought perfume and gloves at Michel

Swiss, the swankiest shop in town, a dress at Chez Marie-she passed three fifties there-and a hat at Paulette's over on Monroe Street.

"That's another sign of the amateur, by the way. A competent pusher buys a small item and gets change from his counterfeit bill. Our girl's been buying expensive items, obviously more interested in the product than in her change."

"This doesn't seem to make much sense," Larry Woolford protested. "You have any ideas at all?"

"The question is," Hackett said, "where did she get it? Is she connected with one of the embassies and acquired the stuff overseas? If so, that puts it in your lap again possibly —"

The phone rang and Steve flicked the switch and grumbled, "Yeah? Steven Hackett speaking."

He listened for a moment then banged the phone off and jumped to his feet. "Come on, Larry," he snapped. "This is it."

Larry stood, too. "Who was that?"

"Fredrick, over at La Calvados. The girl has come in for lunch. Let's go!"

* * * * *

La Calvados was the swankiest French restaurant in Greater Washington, a city not devoid of swank restaurants. Only the upper-echelons in governmental circles could afford its tariffs; the clientele was more apt to consist of business mucky-mucks and lobbyists on the make. Larry Woolford had eaten here exactly twice. You could get a reputation spending money far beyond your obvious pay status.

Fredrick, the *maître de hôtel* , however, was able to greet them both by name. "Monsieur Hackett, Monsieur Woolford," he bowed. He obviously didn't approve of La Calvados being used as a hangout where counterfeiters were picked up the authorities.

"Where is she?" Steve said, looking out over the public dining room.

Fredrick said, unprofessionally agitated, "See here, Monsieur Hackett, you didn't expect to, ah, arrest the young lady *here* during our lunch hour?"

Steve looked at him impatiently. "We don't exactly beat them over the head with blackjacks, slip the bracelets on and drag them screaming to the paddywagon."

"Of course not, monsieur, but —"

Larry Woolford's chief dined here several times a week and was probably on the best of terms with Fredrick whose decisions on tables and whose degree of servility had a good deal of influence on a man's status in Greater Washington. Larry said wearily, "We can wait until she leaves. Where is she?"

Fredrick had taken them to one side.

"Do you see the young lady over near the window on the park? The rather gauche appearing type?"

It was a teenager, all right. A youngster up to her eyebrows in the attempt to project sophistication.

Steve said, "Do you know who she is?"

"No," Fredrick said. "Hardly our usual clientele."

"Oh?" Larry said. "She looks like money."

Fredrick said, "The dress appears as though it is of Chez Marie, but she wears it as though it came from Klein's. Her perfume is Chanel, but she has used approximately three times the quantity one would expect."

"That's our girl, all right," Steve murmured. "Where can we keep an eye on her until she leaves?"

"Why not at the bar here, Messieurs?"

"Why not?" Larry said. "I could use a drink."

Fredrick cleared his throat. "Ah, Messieurs, that fifty I turned over you. I suppose it turned out to be spurious?"

Steve grinned at him. "Afraid so, Fredrick. The department is holding it."

Larry took out his wallet. "However, we have a certain leeway on expenses on this assignment and appreciate your co-operation." He handed two twenties and a ten to the *maître d'*. Fredrick bowed low, the money disappearing into his clothes magically. "*Merci bien* , monsieur."

At the bar, Steve scowled at his colleague. "Ha!" he said. "Why didn't I think of that first? He'll get down on his knees and bump his head each time he sees you in the joint from now on."

Larry Woolford waggled a finger at the other. "This is a status conscious town, my boy. Prestige means everything. When I take over my Boss' job, maybe we can swing a transfer and I'll give you a position suitable to your attainments." He pursed his lips judiciously. "Although, come to think of it, that might mean a demotion from the job you're holding now."

"Vodka martini," Steve told the bartender. "Polish vodka, of course."

"Of course, sir."

Larry said, "Same for me."

The bartender left and Steve muttered, "I hate vodka."

"Yeah," Larry said, "But what're you going to do in a place like this, order some weird drink?"

Steve dug into his pocket for money. "We're not going to have to drink them. Here she comes."

She walked with her head held high, hauteur in every step. Ignoring the peasants at the tables she passed.

"Holy smokes," Steve grunted. "It's a wonder Fredrick let her in."

She hesitated momentarily before the doorway of the prestige restaurant allowing the passers-by to realize she'd just emerged, and then turned to her right to promenade along the shopping street.

Fifty feet below La Calvados, Steve said, "Let's go, Woolford."

One stepped to one elbow, the other to the other. Steve said quietly, "I wonder if we could ask you a few questions?"

Her eyebrows went up, "I *beg* your pardon!"

Steve sighed and displayed the badge pinned to his wallet, keeping it inconspicuous. "Secret Service, Miss," he murmured.

"Oh, devil," she said. She looked up at Larry Woolford, and then back at Steve.

Steve said, "Among other things, we're in charge of counterfeit money."

She was about five foot four in her heels, had obviously been on a round of beauty shops and had obviously instructed them to glamorize her. It hadn't come off. She still looked as though she'd be more at home as cheerleader of the junior class in small town high school. She was honey blond, green-blue of eye, and had that complexion they seldom carry even into the twenties.

"I ...I don't know what you're talking about." Her chin began to tremble.

Larry said gently, "Don't worry. We just want to ask you some questions."

"Well ... like what?" She was going to be blinking back tears in a moment. At least Larry hoped she'd blink them back. He'd hate to have her start howling here in public.

Larry said, "We think you can be of assistance to the government, and we'd like your help."

Steve rolled his eyes upward, but turned and waved for a street level cab.

In the cab, Larry said, "Suppose we go over to my office, Steve?"

"O.K. with me," Steve muttered, "but by the looks of the young lady here, I think it's a false alarm from your angle. She's obviously an American. What's your name, Miss?"

"It's Zusanette. Well, really, Susan."

"Susan what?"

"I ...I'm not sure I want to tell you. I ...I want a lawyer."

"A lawyer!" Steve snorted. "You mean you want the juvenile authorities, don't you?"

"Oh, what a mean thing to say," she sputtered.

In the corridor outside the Boss' suite of offices, Larry said to Steve, "You take Miss ...ah, Zusanette to my office, will you Steve. I'll be there in a minute."

He opened the door to the anteroom and said, "LaVerne, we've got a girl in my office —"

"Why, Larry!"

He glowered at her. "A suspect. I want a complete tape of everything said. As soon as we're through, have copies made, at least three or four."

"And, who, Mr. Woolford, was your girl Friday last year?"

"This is important, honey. I suppose you've supplied me with a secretary but I haven't even met her yet. Take care of it, will you?"

"Sure enough, Larry."

He followed Steve and the girl to his office.

Once seated, the girl and Steve in the only two extra chairs the cubicle boasted and Larry behind his desk, he looked at her in what he hoped was reassurance. "Just tell us where you got the money, Zusanette."

Steve reached out a hand suddenly and took her bag from her lap. She gasped and snatched at it, but he eluded her and she sat back, her chin trembling again.

Steve came up with a thick sheaf of bills, the top ones, at least, all fifties and tossed them to Larry's desk. He took out a school pass and read, "Susan Self, Elwood Avenue." He looked up at Larry and said, "That's right off Eastern, near Paterson Park in the Baltimore section of town, isn't it?"

Larry said to her, "Zusanette, I think you'd better tell us where you got all this money."

"I found it," she said defiantly. "You can't do anything to me if I simply found it. Anybody can find money. Finders keepers —"

"But if it's counterfeit," Steve interrupted dryly, "it might also be, finders weepers."

"Where did you find it, Zusanette?" Larry said gently.

She tightened her lips, and the trembling of her chin disappeared. "I ... I can't tell you that. But it's not counterfeit. Daddy ... my father said it was as good as any money the government prints."

"That it is," Steve said sourly. "But it's still counterfeit, which makes it very illegal indeed to spend, Miss Self."

She looked from one of them to the other, not clear about her position. She said to Larry, "You mean it's not *real* money?"

He kept his tone disarming, but shook his head, "I'm afraid not, Zusanette. Now, tell us, where did you find it?"

"I can't. I promised"

"I see. Then you don't know to whom it originally belonged?"

"It didn't belong to anybody."

Steve Hackett made with a disbelieving whistle. He was taking the part of the tough, suspicious cop; Larry the part of the understanding, sympathetic officer, trying to give the suspect a break.

Susan Self turned quickly on Steve. "Well, it didn't. You don't even know."

Larry said, "I think she's telling the truth, Steve. Give her a chance. She's playing fair." He looked back at the girl, and frowned his puzzlement. "All money belongs to *somebody* doesn't it?"

She had them now. She said superiorly. "Not necessarily to some*body* . It can belong to, like, an organization."

Steve grunted skepticism. "I think we ought to arrest her," he said.

Larry held up a hand, his face registering opposition. "I'll handle this," he said sharply. "Zusanette is doing everything she can to co-operate." He turned back to the girl. "Now, the question is, what organization did this money belong to?"

She looked triumphantly at Steve Hackett. "It belonged to the Movement."

They both looked at her.

Steve said finally, "What movement?"

She pouted in thought. "That's the only name they call it."

"Who's they?" Steve snapped nastily.

"I ... I don't know."

Larry said, "Well, you already told us your father was a member, Zusanette."

Her eyes went wide. "I did? I shouldn't have said that." But she evidently took him at his word.

Larry said encouragingly, "Well, we might as well go on. Who else is a member of this Movement besides your father?"

She shifted in her chair uncomfortably. "I don't know any of their names."

Steve looked down at the school pass in his hands. He said to Larry, "I'd better make a phone call."

He left.

* * * * *

Larry said, "Don't worry about him, Zusanette. Now then, this *movement* . That's kind of a funny name, isn't it? What does it mean?"

She was evidently glad that the less than handsome Steve Hackett had left the room. Her words flowed more freely. "Well, Daddy says that they call it the Movement rather than a revolution...."

An ice cube manifested itself in the stomach of Lawrence Woolford.

"...Because people get conditioned, like, to words. Like revolution. Everybody is against the word because they all think of killing and everything, and, Daddy says, there doesn't have to be any shooting or killing or anything like that at all. It just means a fundamental change in society. And, Daddy says, take the word propaganda. Everybody's got to thinking that it automatically means lies, but it doesn't at all. It just means, like, the arguments you use to convince people that what you stand for is right and it might be lies or it might not. And, Daddy says, take the word socialism. So many people have the wrong idea of what it means that the socialists ought to scrap the word and start using something else to mean what they stand for."

Larry said gently, "Your father is a socialist?"

"Oh, no."

He nodded in understanding. "Oh, a Communist, eh?"

Susan Self was indignant. "Daddy thinks the Communists are strictly awful, really weird."

Steve Hackett came back into the office. He said to Larry, "I sent a couple of the boys out to pick him up."

Susan was on her feet, a hand to mouth. "You mean my father! You're going to arrest him!"

Larry said soothingly, "Sit down, Zusanette. There's a lot of things about this that I'm sure your father can explain." He said to Steve, "She tells me that the money belonged to a movement. A revolutionary movement which doesn't use the term revolutionary because people react unfavorably to that word. It's not Commie."

Susan said indignantly, "It's American, not anything foreign!"

Steve growled, "Let's get back to the money. What's this movement doing with a lot of counterfeit bills and where did you find them?"

She evidently figured she'd gone too far now to take a stand. "It's not Daddy's fault," she said. "He took me to headquarters twice."

"Where's headquarters?" Larry said trying to keep his voice soothing.

"Well ... I don't know. Daddy was awfully silly about it. He tied his handkerchief around my eyes near the end. But the others complained about me anyway, and Daddy got awfully mad and said something about the young people of the country participating in their emancipation and all, but the others got mad too, and said there wasn't any kind of help I could do around headquarters anyway, and I'd be better off in school. Everybody got awfully mad, but after the second time Daddy promised not to take me to headquarters any more."

"But where did you find the money, Zusannette?" Larry said.

"At headquarters. There's tons and tons of it there."

Larry cleared his throat and said, "When you say tons and tons, you mean a great deal of it, eh?"

She was proudly definite. "I mean tons and tons. A ton is two thousand pounds."

"Look, Zusanette," Larry said reasonably. "I don't know how much money weighs, exactly, but let's say a pound would be, say, a thousand bills." He took up a pencil and scribbled on a pad before him. "A pound of fifties would be $50,000. Then if you multiply that by 2,000 pounds to make a ton, you'd have $100,000,000. And you say there's tons and tons?"

"And that's just the fifties," Susan said triumphantly. "So you can see the two little packages I picked up aren't really important at all. It's just like I found them."

"I don't think there's quite a thousand bills in a pound," Steve said weakly.

Larry said, "How much other money is there?"

"Oh, piles. Whole rooms. Rooms after rooms. And hundred dollar bills, and twenties, and fives, and tens —"

Larry said, "Look, Zusanette, I don't think you're in any position to be telling us whoppers. This whole story doesn't make much sense, does it?"

Her mouth tightened. "I'm not going to say anything more until Daddy gets here, anyway," she said.

Which was when the phone rang.

"I have an idea that's for me," Steve said.

The screen lit up and LaVerne Polk said, "Call for Steve Hackett, Larry."

Larry pushed the phone around so Steve could look into it. LaVerne flicked off and was replaced by a stranger in uniform. Steve said, "Yeah?"

The cop said, "He's flown the coop, sir. Must have got out just minutes before we arrived. Couldn't have taken more than a suitcase. Few papers scattered around the room he used for an office."

Susan gasped, "You mean Daddy?"

Steve Hackett rubbed a hand over his flattened nose. "Holy Smokes," he said. He thanked the cop and flicked off.

Larry said, "Look Zusanette, everything's going to be all right. Nothing will happen to you. You say you managed to pick up two packets of all this money they have at headquarters. O.K. So you thought it wouldn't be missed and you've always wanted to spend money the way you see the stars do on TriD and in the movies."

She looked at him, taken back. "How did you know?"

Larry said dryly, "I've always wanted to myself. But I would like to know one more thing. The Movement. What was it going to do with all this money?"

That evidently puzzled her. "The Professor said they were going to spend it on chorus girls. I guess ...I guess he was joking or something. But Daddy and I'd just been up to New York and we saw those famous precision dancers at the New Roxy Theatre and all and then when we got back the Professor and Daddy were talking and I heard him say it."

Steve said, carefully, "Professor who?"

Susan said, "Just the Professor. That's all we ever call him." Her chin went to trembling still again.

* * * * *

Larry summed it up for the Boss later.

His chief scoffed his disbelief. "The child is full of dreams, Lawrence. It comes from seeing an over-abundance of these TriD shows. I have a girl the same age. I don't know what is happening to the country. They have no sense of reality."

Larry Woolford said mildly, "Well, she might be full of nonsense, but she did have the fifties, and she's our only connection with whoever printed them whether it's a movement to overthrow the government, or what."

The Boss said tolerantly, "Movement, indeed. Obviously, her father produced them and she purloined a quantity before he was ready to attempt to pass them. Have you a run down on him yet?"

"Susan Self says her father, Ernest Self, is an inventor. Steve Hackett is working on locating him."

"He's an inventor indeed. Evidently, he has invented a perfect counterfeiting device. However, that is the Secret Service's headache, not ours. Do you wish to resume that vacation of yours, Lawrence?"

His operative twisted his face in a grimace. "Sure, I do, but I'm not happy about this, sir. What happens if there really is an organization, a Movement, like she said? That brings it back under our jurisdiction, anti-subversion."

The other shook his head tolerantly. "See here, Lawrence, when you begin scheming a social revolution you can't plan on an organization composed of a small number of persons who keep their existence secret. In spite of what a good many persons seem to believe, revolutions are not accomplished by handfuls of conspirators hiding in cellars and eventually overthrowing society by dramatically shooting the President, or King, or Czar, or whoever. Revolutions are precipitated by masses of people. People who have ample cause to be against whatever the current government happens to be. Usually, they are on the point of actual starvation. Have you ever read Machiavelli?"

Niccolo Machiavelli was currently *the thing* to read. Larry said with a certain dignity, "I've gone through 'The Prince,' the 'Discourses' and currently I'm amusing myself with his 'History of Florence.' "

"Anybody who can amuse himself reading Machiavelli," the Boss said dryly, "has a macabre sense of humor. At any rate, what I was alluding to was where he stated that the Prince cannot rule indefinitely in the face of the active opposition of his people. Therefore, the people always get a government that lies within the limits of their tolerance. It may be on one edge or the other of their limits of tolerance-but it's always within their tolerance zone."

Larry frowned and said, "Well, what's your point, sir?"

The Boss said patiently, "I'm just observing that cultures aren't overthrown by little handfuls of secret conspirators. You might eliminate a few individuals in that manner, in other words change the personnel of the government, but you aren't going to alter a socio-economic system. That can't be done until your people have been pushed outside their limits of tolerance. Very well then. A revolutionary organization must get out and propagandize. It has got to convince the people that they are being pushed beyond endurance. You have got to get the *masses* to moving. You have to give speeches, print newspapers, books, pamphlets, you have got to send your organizers out to intensify interest in your program."

Larry said, "I see what you mean. If this so-called Movement actually existed it couldn't expect to get anywhere as long as remained secret."

The Boss nodded. "That is correct. The *leaders* of a revolutionary movement might be intellectuals, social scientists, scholars-in fact they usually are-take our own American Revolution with Jefferson, Madison, Franklin, Washington. Or the French Revolution with Robespierre, Danton, Marat, Engels and Lenin. All were well educated intellectuals from the middle class. But the revolution itself, once it starts, comes from below, from the mass of people pushed beyond tolerance."

It came to Lawrence Woolford that his superior had achieved to his prominent office not through any fluke. He knew what he was talking about.

The Boss wound it up. "If there was such an organization as this Movement, then this department would know about it. You don't keep a revolutionary movement secret. It doesn't make sense to even try. Even if it is forced underground, it makes as much noise as it can."

His trouble shooter cleared his throat. "I suppose you're right, sir." He added hesitantly. "We could always give Susan Self a few drops of Scop-Serum, sir."

The Boss scowled disapprovingly. "You know how the Supreme Court ruled on that, Lawrence. And particularly since the medics revealed its effect on reducing sexual inhibitions. No, Mr. Hackett and Secret Service will have to get the truth out of the girl by some other means. At any rate, it is out of our hands."

Larry came to his feet. "Well, then, I'll resume my vacation, eh?"

His chief took up a report from his desk an frowned at it, his attention already passing to other matters. He grunted, "Clear it with LaVerne, please. Tell her I said to take another week to make up for our intruding on you in this manner."

* * * * *

In the back of his head, Larry Woolford had misgivings. For one thing, where had the kid, who on the face of her performance was no great brain even as sixteen or seventeen old's go, picked up such ideas as the fact that people developed prejudices against words like revolution and propaganda?

However, he was clear of it now. Let Steve Hackett and his people take over. He, Lawrence Woolford, was due for a quick return to Astor, Florida and the bass fishing on the St. John's River.

He stopped at LaVerne's desk and gave her his address to be, now that his vacation was resumed.

She said, smiling up at him. "Right. The boss already told me to get in touch with Secret Service and let them know we're pulling out. What happened to Susan Self?"

Larry looked at her. "How'd you know about Susan?"

Her tone was deprecating. "Remember? You had me cut some tapes on you and that hulking Steve Hackett grilling the poor kid."

Larry snorted. "Poor kid, yet. With her tastes for living-it-up, and that father she has, she'll probably spend the rest of her life getting in Steve's hair as a counterfeit pusher."

"What are they going to do with her? She's just a child."

The agent shrugged. "I feel sorry for her, too, LaVerne. Steve's got her in a suite at the Greater Washington Hilton, until things are cleared up. They don't want the newspapers to get wind of this until they've got that inventor father of hers and whatever he's cooked up to turn out perfect reproductions of Uncle Sam's money. Look, I won't be leaving until tomorrow. What'd you say we go out on the town tonight?"

"Why, Larry Woolford! How nice of you to ask me. Poor Little, Non-U me. What do you have in mind? I understand Mort Lenny's at one of the night clubs."

Larry winced. "You know what he's been saying about the administration."

She smiled sweetly at him.

Larry said, "Look, we could take in the Brahms concert, then —"

"Do you like Brahms? I go for popular music myself. Preferably the sort of thing they wrote back in the 1930s. Something you can dance to, something you know the words to. Corny, they used to call it. Remember 'Sunny Side of the Street,' and 'Just the Way You Look Tonight'."

Larry winced again. He said, "Look, I admit, I don't go for concerts either but it doesn't hurt you to —"

"I know," she said sweetly. "It doesn't hurt for a bright young bureaucrat to be seen at concerts."

"How about Dixieland?" he said. "It's all the thing now."

"I like corn. Besides, my wardrobe is all out of style. Paris, London, and Rome just got in a huddle a couple of weeks ago and antiquated everything I own. You wouldn't want to be seen with a girl a few weeks out of date, would you?"

"Oh, now, LaVerne, get off my back." He thought about it. "Look, you must have *something* you could wear."

"Get out of here, you vacant minded conformist! I *like* Mort Lenny, he makes me laugh; I *hate* vodka martinis, they give me sour stomach; I don't *like* the current women's styles, nor the men's either." LaVerne spun back to her auto-typer and began to dictate into it.

Larry glared down at her. "All right. O.K. What *do* you like?"

She snapped back irrationally, "I like what *I* like."

He laughed at her in ridicule.

This time she glared at him. "That makes more sense than you're capable of assimilating, Mr. Walking Status Symbol. My likes and dislikes aren't dictated by someone else. If I like corny music, I'll listen to it and the devil with Brahms or Dixieland or anything else that somebody else tells me is all the thing!"

He turned on his heel angrily. "O.K., O.K., it takes all sorts to make a world, weirds and all."

"One more label to hang on people," she snarled after him. "Everything's labels. Be sure and never come to any judgments of your own!"

What a woman! He wondered why he'd ever bothered to ask her for a date. There were so many women in this town you waded through them, and here he was exposing himself to be seen in public with a girl everybody in the department knew was as weird as they came. It didn't do your standing any good to be seen around with the type. He wondered all over again why the Boss tolerated her as his receptionist-secretary.

He got his car from the parking lot and drove home at a high level. Ordinarily, the distance being what it was, he drove in the lower and slower traffic levels but now his frustration demanded some expression.

* * * * *

Back at his suburban auto-bungalow, he threw all except the high priority switch and went on down into his small second cellar den. He didn't really feel like a night on the town anyway. A few vodka martinis under his belt and he'd sleep late and he wanted to get up in time for an early start for Florida. Besides, in that respect he agreed with the irritating wench. Vermouth was never meant to mix with Polish vodka. He wished that Sidecars would come back.

In his den, he shucked off his jacket, kicked off his shoes and shuffled into Moroccan slippers. He went over to his current reading rack and scowled at the paperbacks there. His culture status books were upstairs where they could be seen. He pulled out a western, tossed it over to the cocktail table that sat next to his chair, and then went over to the bar.

Up above in his living room, he had one of the new autobars. You could dial any one of more than thirty drinks. Autobars were all the rage. The Boss had one that gave a selection of a hundred. But what difference did it make when nobody but eccentric old-timers or flighty blondes drank anything except vodka martinis? He didn't like autobars anyway. A well mixed drink is a personal thing, a work of competence, instinct and art, not something measured to the drop, iced to the degree, shaken or stirred to a mathematical formula.

Out of the tiny refrigerator he brought a four-ounce cube of frozen pineapple juice, touched the edge with his thumbnail and let the ultra thin plastic peel away. He tossed the cube into his mixer, took up a bottle of light rum and poured in about two ounces. He brought an egg from the refrigerator and added that. An ounce of whole milk followed and a teaspoon of powdered sugar. He flicked the switch and let the conglomeration froth together.

He poured it into a king-size highball glass and took it over to his chair. Vodka martinis be damned, he liked a slightly sweet long drink.

He sat down in the chair, picked up the book and scowled at the cover. He ought to be reading that Florentine history of Machiavelli's, especially if the Boss had got to the point where he was quoting from the guy. But the heck with it, he was on vacation. He didn't think much of the Italian diplomat of the Renaissance anyway; how could you be that far back without being dated?

He couldn't get beyond the first page or two.

And when you can't concentrate on a Western, you just can't concentrate.

He finished his drink, went over to his phone and dialed *Department of Records* and then *Information* . When the bright young thing answered, he said, "I'd like the brief on an Ernest Self who lives on Elwood Avenue, Baltimore section of Greater Washington. I don't know his code number."

She did things with switches and buttons for a moment and then brought a sheet from a delivery chute. "Do you want me to read it to you, sir?"

"No, I'll scan it," Larry said.

Her face faded to be replaced by the brief on Ernest Self.

It was astonishingly short. *Records* seemed to have slipped up on this occasion. A rare occurrence. He considered requesting the full dossier, then changed his mind. Instead he dialed the number of the *Sun-Post* and asked for its science columnist.

Sam Sokolski's puffy face eventually faded in.

Larry said to him sourly, "You drink too much. You can begin to see the veins breaking in your nose."

Sam looked at him patiently.

Larry said, "How'd you like to come over and toss back a few tonight?"

"I'm working. I thought you were on vacation."

Larry sighed. "I am," he said. "O.K., so you can't take a night off and lift a few with an old buddy."

"That's right. Anything else, Larry?"

"Yes. Look, have you ever heard of an inventor named Ernest Self?"

"Sure I've heard of him. Covered a hassle he got into some years ago. A nice guy."

"I'll bet," Larry said. "What does he invent, something to do with printing presses, or something?"

"Printing presses? Don't you remember the story about him?"

"Brief me," Larry said.

"Well-briefly does it-it got out a couple of years ago that some of our rocketeers had bought a solid fuel formula from an Italian research outfit for the star probe project. Paid them a big hunk of Uncle's change for it. So Self sued."

Larry said, "You're being *too* brief. What d'ya mean, he sued? Why?"

"Because he claimed he'd submitted the same formula to the same agency a full eighteen months earlier and they'd turned him down."

"Had he?"

"Probably."

Larry didn't get it. "Then why'd they turn him down?"

Sam said, "Oh, the government boys had a good alibi. Crackpots turn up all over the place and you have to brush them off. Every cellar scientist who comes along and says he's got a new super-fuel developed from old coffee grounds can't be given the welcome mat. Something was wrong with his math or something and they didn't pay much attention to him. Wouldn't even let him demonstrate it. But it was the same formula, all right."

Larry Woolford was scowling. "Something wrong with his math? What kind of a degree does he have?"

Sam grinned in memory. "I got a good quote on that. He doesn't have any degree. He said he'd learned to read by the time he'd reached high school and since then he figured spending time in classrooms was a matter of interfering with his education."

"No wonder they turned him down. No degree at all. You can't get anywhere in science like that."

Sam said, "The courts rejected his suit but he got a certain amount of support here and there. Peter Voss, over at the university, claims he's one of the great intuitive scientists, whatever that is, of our generation."

"Who said that?"

"Professor Voss. Not that it makes any difference what he says. Another crackpot."

After Sam's less than handsome face was gone from the phone, Larry walked over to the bar with his empty glass and stared at the mixer for several minutes. He began to make himself another flip, but cut it short in the middle, put down the ingredients and went back to the phone to dial *Records* again.

He went through first the brief and then the full dossier on Professor Peter Luther Voss. Aside from his academic accomplishments, particularly in the fields of political economy and international law, and the dozen or so books accredited to him, there wasn't anything particularly noteworthy. A bachelor in his fifties. No criminal record of any kind, of course, and no military career. No known political affiliations. Evidently a strong predilection for Thorstein Veblen's theories. And he'd been a friend of Henry Mencken back when that old nonconformist was tearing down contemporary society seemingly largely for the fun involved in the tearing.

On the face of it, the man was no radical, and the term "crackpot" which Sam had applied was hardly called for.

Larry Woolford went back to the bar and resumed the job of mixing his own version of a rum flip.

But his heart wasn't in it. *The Professor* , Susan had said.

Before he'd gone to bed the night before, Larry Woolford had ordered a seat on the shuttle jet for Jacksonville and a hover-cab there to take him to Astor, on the St. Johns River. And he'd requested to be wakened in ample time to get to the shuttleport.

But it wasn't the saccharine pleasant face of the Personal Service operator which confronted him when he grumpily answered the phone in the morning. In fact, the screen remained blank.

Larry decided that sweet long drinks were fine, but that anyone who took several of them in a row needed to be candied. He grumbled into the phone, "All right, who is it?"

A Teutonic voice chuckled and said, "You're going to have to decide whether or not you're on vacation, my friend. At this time of day, why aren't you at work?"

Larry Woolford was waking up. He said, "What can I do for you, Distelmayer?" The German merchant-of-espionage wasn't the type to make personal calls.

"Have you forgotten so soon, my friend?" the other chuckled. "It was I who was going to do you a favor." He hesitated momentarily, before adding, "In possible return for future —"

"Yeah, yeah," Larry said. He was fully awake now.

The German said slowly, "You asked if any of your friends from, ah, abroad were newly in the country. Frol Eivazov has recently appeared on the scene."

Eivazov! In various respects, Larry Woolford's counterpart. Hatchetman for the *Chrezvychainaya Komissiya* . Woolford had met him on occasion when they'd both been present at international summit meetings, busily working at counter-espionage for their respective superiors. Blandly shaking hands with each other, blandly drinking toasts to peace and international co-existence, blandly sizing each other up and wondering if it'd ever come to the point where one would *blandly* treat the other to a hole in the head, possibly in some dark alley in Havana or Singapore, Leopoldville or Saigon.

Larry said sharply, "Where is he? How'd he get in the country?"

"My friend, my friend," the German grunted good-humoredly. "You know better than to ask the first question. As for the second, Frol's command of American-English is at least as good as your own. Do you think his *Komissiya* less capable than your own department and unable to do him up suitable papers so that he could be, perhaps, a 'returning tourist' from Europe?"

Larry Woolford was impatient with himself for asking. He said now, "It's not important. If we want to locate Frol and pick him up, we'll probably not have too much trouble doing it."

"I wouldn't think so," the other said humorously. "Since 1919, when they were first organized, the so-called Communists in this country, from the lowest to the highest echelons, have been so riddled with police agents that a federal judge in New England once refused to prosecute a case against them on the grounds that the party was a United States government agency."

Larry was in no frame of mind for the other's heavy humor. "Look, Hans," he said, "what I want to know is what Frol is over here for."

"Of course you do," Hans Distelmayer said, unable evidently to keep note of puzzlement from his voice. "Larry," he said, "I assume your people know of the new American underground."

"*What* underground?" Larry snapped.

The professional spy chief said, his voice strange, "The Soviets seem to have picked up an idea somewhere, possibly through their membership in this country, that something is abrewing in the States. That a change is being engineered."

Larry stared at the blank phone screen.

"What kind of a change?" he said finally. "You mean a change to the Soviet system?" Surely not even the self-deluding Russkies could think it possible to overthrow the American socio-economic system in favor of the Soviet brand.

"No, no, no," the German chuckled. "Of course not. It's not of their working at all."

"Then what's Frol Eivazov's interest, if they aren't engineering it?"

Distelmayer rumbled his characteristic chuckle with humor. "My dear friend, don't be naive. Anything that happens in America is of interest to the Soviets. There is delicate peace between you now that they have changed their direction and are occupying themselves largely with the economic and agricultural development of Asia and such portions of the world as have come under their hegemony, and while you put all efforts into modernizing the more backward countries among your satellites."

Larry said automatically, "Our allies aren't satellites."

The spy-master went on without contesting the statement. "There is immediate peace but surely governmental officials on both sides keep careful watch on the internal developments of the other. True, the current heads of the Soviet Complex would like to see the governments of all the Western powers changed-but only if they are changed in the direction of communism. They are hardly interested in seeing changes made which would strengthen the West in the, ah, Battle For Men's Minds."

Larry snorted his disgust. "What sort of change in government would strengthen the United States in —"

The German interrupted smoothly, "Evidently, that's what Frol seems to be here for, Larry. To find out more about this movement and —"

"This *what* ?" Larry blurted.

"The term seems to be *movement* ."

Larry Woolford held a long silence before saying, "And Frol is actually here in this country to buck this ... this movement."

"Not necessarily," the other said impatiently. "He is here to find out more about it. Evidently Peking and Moscow have heard just enough to make them nervous."

Larry said, "You have anything more, Hans?"

"I'm afraid that's about it."

"All right," Larry said. He added absently, "Thanks, Hans."

"Thank me some day with deeds, not with words," the German chuckled.

* * * * *

Larry Woolford looked at his watch and grimaced. He was either going to get going now or forget about doing any fishing in Florida this afternoon.

Grudgingly, he dialed the phone company's Personal Service and said to the impossibly cheerful blonde who answered, "Where can I find Professor Peter Voss who teaches over at the University in Baltimore? I don't want to talk with him, just want to know where he'll be an hour from now."

While waiting for his information, he dressed, deciding inwardly that he hated his job, the department in which he was employed, the Boss and Greater Washington. On top of that, he hated himself. He'd already been taken off this assignment, why couldn't he leave it lay?

The blonde rang him back. Professor Peter Voss was at home. He had no classes today. She gave him the address.

Larry Woolford raised his car from his auto-bungalow in the Brandywine suburb and headed northwest at a high level for the old Baltimore section of the city.

The Professor's house, he noted, was of an earlier day and located on the opposite side of Paterson Park from Elwood avenue, the street on which Susan Self and her father had resided. That didn't necessarily hold significance, the park was a large one and the Professor's section a well-to-do neighborhood, while Self's was just short of a slum these days.

He brought his car down to street level, and parked before the scholar's three-story, brick house. Baltimore-like, it was identical to every other house in the block; Larry wondered vaguely how anybody ever managed to find his own place when it was very dark out.

There was an old-fashioned bell at the side of the entrance and Larry Woolford pushed it. There was no identification screen in the door, evidently the inhabitants had to open up to see who was calling, a tiring chore if you were on the far side of the house and the caller nothing more than a salesman.

It was obviously the Professor himself who answered.

He was in shirtsleeves, tieless and with age-old slippers on his stockingless feet. He evidently hadn't bothered to shave this morning and he held a dog-eared pamphlet in his right hand, his forefinger tucked in it to mark his place. He wore thick-lensed, gold-rimmed glasses through which he blinked at Larry Woolford questioningly, without speaking. Professor Peter Voss was a man in his mid fifties, and, on the face of it, couldn't care less right now about his physical appearance.

A weird, Larry decided immediately. He wondered at the University, one of the nation's best, keeping on such a figure.

"Professor Voss?" he said. "Lawrence Woolford." He brought forth his identification.

The Professor blinked down at it. "I see," he said. "Won't you come in?"

The house was old, all right. From the outside, quite acceptable, but the interior boasted few of the latest amenities which made all the difference in modern existence. Larry was taken back by the fact that the phone which he spotted in the *entrada* hadn't even a screen-an old model for speaking only.

The Professor noticed his glance and said dryly, "The advantages of combining television and telephone have never seemed valid to me. In my own home, I feel free to relax, as you can observe. Had I a screen on my phone, it would be necessary for me to maintain the same appearance as I must on the streets or before my classes."

Larry cleared his throat without saying anything. This was a weird one, all right.

The living room was comfortable in a blatantly primitive way. Three or four paintings on the walls which were probably originals, Larry decided, and should have been in museums. Not an abstract among them. A Grant Wood, a Marin, and that over there could only be a Grandma Moses. The sort of things you might keep in your private den, but hardly to be seen as culture symbols.

The chairs were large, of leather, and comfortable and probably belonged to the period before the Second War. Peter Voss, evidently, was little short of an exhibitionist.

The Professor took up a battered humidor. "Cigar?" he said. "Manila. Hard to get these days."

A cigar? Good grief, the man would be offering him a chaw of tobacco next.

"Thanks, no," Larry said. "I smoke a pipe."

"I see," the Professor said, lighting his stogie. "Do you really like a pipe? Personally, I've always thought the cigar by far the most satisfactory method of taking tobacco."

What can you say to a question like that? Larry ignored it, as though it was rhetorical. Actually, he smoked cigarettes in the privacy of his den. A habit which was on the proletarian side and not consistent with his status level.

He said, to get things under way, "Professor Voss, what is an intuitive scientist?"

The Professor exhaled blue smoke, shook out the old-time kitchen match with which he'd lit it, and tossed the matchstick into an ashtray. "Intuitive scientist?"

"You once called Ernest Self a great intuitive scientist."

"Oh, Self. Yes, indeed. What is he doing these days?"

Larry said wryly, "That's what I came to ask you about."

The Professor was puzzled. "I'm afraid you came to the wrong place, Mr. Woolford. I haven't seen Ernest for quite a time. Why?"

"Some of his researches seem to have taken him rather far afield. Actually, I know practically nothing about him. I wonder if you could fill me in a bit."

Peter Voss looked at the ash on the end of his cigar. "I really don't know the man that well. He lives across the park. Why don't —"

"He's disappeared," Larry said.

The Professor blinked. "I see," he said. "And in view of the fact that you are a security officer, I assume under strange circumstances." Larry Woolford said nothing and the Professor sank back into his chair and pursed his lips. "I can't really tell you much. I became interested in Self two or three years ago when gathering materials for a paper on the inadequate manner in which our country rewards its inventors."

Larry said, "I've heard about his suit against the government."

The Professor became more animated. "Ha!" he snorted. "One example among many. Self is not alone. Our culture is such that the genius is smothered. The great contributors to our society are ignored, or worse."

Larry Woolford was feeling his way. Now he said mildly, "I was under the impression that American free enterprise gave the individual the best opportunity to prove himself and that if he had it on the ball he'd get to the top."

"Were you really?" the Professor said snappishly. "And did you know that Edison died a comparatively poor man with an estate somewhere in the vicinity of a hundred thousand dollars? An amount that might sound like a good deal to you or me, but, when you consider his contributions, shockingly little. Did you know that Eli Whitney realized little, if anything, from the cotton gin? Or that McCormick didn't invent the reaper but gained it in a dubious court victory? Or take Robert Goddard, one of the best examples of modern times. He developed the basics of rocket technology-gyroscopic stabilizers, fuel pumps, self-cooling motors, landing devices. He died in 1945 leaving behind twenty-two volumes of records that proved priceless. What did he get out of his researches? Nothing. It was fifteen years later that his widow won her suit against the government for patent infringements!"

Larry held up a hand. "Really," he said. "My interest is in Ernest Self."

The Professor relaxed. "Sorry. I'm afraid I get carried away. Self, to get back to your original question, is a great intuitive scientist. Unfortunately for him, society being what it is today, he fits into few grooves. Our educational system was little more than an irritation to him and consequently he holds no degrees. Needless to say, this interfered with his gaining employment with the universities and the large corporations which dominate our country's research, not to mention governmental agencies.

"Ernest Self holds none of the status labels that count. The fact that he is a genius means nothing. He is supposedly qualified no more than to hold a janitor's position in laboratories where his inferiors conduct experiments in fields where he is a dozenfold more capable than they. No one is interested in his genius, they want to know what status labels are pinned to him. Ernest has no respect for labels."

* * * * *

Larry Woolford figured he was picking up background and didn't force a change of subject. "Just what do you mean by intuitive scientist?"

"It's a term I have used loosely," the Professor admitted. "Possibly a scientist who makes a break-through in his field, destroying formerly held positions-in Self's case, without the math, without the accepted theories to back him. He finds something that works, possibly without knowing why or how and by using unorthodox analytical techniques. An intuitive scientist, if I may use the term, is a thorn in the side of our theoretical physicists laden down with their burden of a status label but who are themselves short of the makings of a Leonardo, a Newton, a Galileo, or even a Nicholas Christofilos."

"I'm afraid that last name escapes me," Larry said.

"Similar to Self's case and Robert Goddard's," Voss said, his voice bitter. "Although his story has a better ending. Christofilos invented the strong-focusing principle that made possible the multi-billion-volt particle accelerators currently so widely used in nuclear physics experimentation. However, he was nothing but a Greek elevator electrical system engineer and the supposed experts turned him down on the grounds that his math was faulty. It seems that he submitted the idea in straight-algebra terms instead of differential equations. He finally won through after patenting the discovery and rubbing their noses in it. Previously, none of the physics journals would publish his paper-he didn't have the right status labels to impress them."

Larry said, almost with amusement, "You seem to have quite a phobia against the status label, as you call it. However, I don't see how as complicated a world as ours could get along without it."

The Professor snorted his contempt. "Tell me," he said, "to which class do you consider yourself to belong?"

Larry Woolford shrugged. "I suppose individuals in my bracket are usually thought of as being middle-middle class."

"And you have no feeling of revolt in having such a label hung on you? Consider this system for a moment. You have lower-lower, middle-lower, and upper-lower; then you have lower-middle, middle-middle, upper-middle; then you have lower-upper, middle-upper, and finally we achieve to upper-upper class. Now tell me, when we get to that rarified category, who do we find? Do we find an Einstein, a Schweitzer, a Picasso; outstanding scientists, humanitarians, the great writers, artists and musicians of our day? Certainly not. We find ultra-wealthy playboys and girls, a former king and his duchess who eke out their income by accepting fees to attend parties, the international born set, bearers of meaningless feudalistic titles. These are your upper-upper class!"

Larry laughed.

The Professor snapped, "You think it funny? Let me give you another example of our status label culture. I have a friend whom I have known since childhood. I would estimate that Charles has an I.Q. of approximately 90, certainly no more. His family, however, took such necessary steps as were needed to get Charles through public school. No great matter these days, you'll admit, although on occasion he needed a bit of tutoring. On graduation, they recognized that the really better schools might be a bit difficult for Charles so he was entered in a university with a good name but without-shall we say? —the highest of scholastic ratings. Charles plodded along, had some more tutoring, probably had his thesis ghosted, and eventually graduated. At that point an uncle died and left Charles an indefinite amount to be used in furthering his education to any extent he wished to go. Charles, motivated probably by the desire to avoid obtaining a job and competing with his fellow man, managed to wrangle himself into a medical school and eventually even graduated. Since funds were still available, he continued his studies abroad, largely in Vienna."

The Professor wound it up. "Eventually, he ran out of schools, or his uncle's estate ran out —I don't know which came first. At any rate, my friend Charles, laden down with status labels, is today practicing as a psychiatrist in this fair city of ours."

Larry stared at him blankly.

The Professor said snappishly, "So any time you feel you need to have your brains unscrambled, you can go to his office and expend twenty-five dollars an hour or so. His reputation is of the highest." The Professor grunted his contempt. "He doesn't know the difference between an aspirin tablet and a Rorschach test."

Larry Woolford stirred in his chair. "We seem to have gotten far off the subject. What has this got to do with Self?"

The Professor seemed angry. "I repeat, I'm afraid I get carried away on this subject. I'm in revolt against a culture based on the status label. It eliminates the need to judge a man on his merits. To judge a person by the clothes he wears, the amount of money he possesses, the car he drives, the neighborhood in which he lives, the society he keeps, or even his ancestry, is out of the question in a vital, growing society. You wind up with nonentities as the leaders of your nation. In these days, we can't afford it."

He smiled suddenly, rather elfishly, at the security agent. "But admittedly, this deals with Self only as one of many victims of a culture based on status labels. Just what is it you wanted to know about Ernest?"

"When you knew him, evidently he was working on rocket fuels. Have you any idea whether he later developed a method of producing perfect counterfeit?"

The Professor said, "Ernest Self? Surely you are jesting."

Larry said unhappily, "Then here's another question. Have you ever heard him mention belonging to a movement, or, I think, he might word it *The Movement* ."

"Movement?" the Professor said emptily.

"Evidently a revolutionary group interested in the overthrow of the government."

"Good heavens," the Professor said. "Just a moment, Mr. Woolford. You interrupted me just as I was having my second cup of coffee. Do you mind if I —"

"Certainly not," Woolford shook his head.

"I simply can't get along until after my third cup," the Professor said. "You just wait a moment and I'll bring the pot in here."

He left Larry to sit in the combined study and living room while he shuffled off in his slippers to the kitchen. Larry Woolford decided that in his school days he'd had some far out professors himself, but it would really be something to study under this one. Not that the old boy didn't have some points, of course. Almost all nonconformists base their particular peeves on some actuality, but in this case, what was the percentage? How could you buck the system? Particularly when, largely, it worked.

* * * * *

The Professor returned with an old-fashioned coffeepot, two cups, and sugar and cream on a tray. He put them on a side table and said to Larry, "You'll join me? How do you take it?"

Larry still had the slightest of hang-overs from his solitary drinking of the night before. "Thanks. Make it black," he said.

The Professor poured, served, then did up a cup for himself. He sat back in his chair and said, "Now, where were we? Something about a revolutionary group. What has that to do with counterfeiting?"

Larry sipped the strong coffee. "It seems there might be a connection."

The Professor shook his head. "It's hard to imagine Ernest Self being connected with a criminal pursuit."

Larry said carefully, "Susan seemed to be of the opinion that you knew about a large amount of counterfeit currency that this Movement had on hand and that you were in favor of spending it upon chorus girls."

The Professor gaped at him.

Larry chuckled uncomfortably.

Professor Voss said finally, his voice very even, "My dear sir, I am afraid that I evidently can be of little assistance to you."

"Admittedly, it doesn't seem to make much sense."

"Susan-you mean that little sixteen year old? —said *I* was in favor of spending counterfeit money on chorus girls?"

Larry said unhappily, "She used the term *the Professor* ."

"And why did you assume that the title must necessarily allude to me? Even if any of the rest of the fantastic story was true."

Larry said, "In my profession, Professor Voss, we track down every possible clue. Thus far, you are the only professor of whom we know who was connected with Ernest Self."

Voss said stiffly, "I can only say, sir, that in my estimation Mr. Self is a man of the highest integrity. And, in addition, that I have never spent a penny on a chorus girl in my life and have no intention of beginning, counterfeit or otherwise."

Larry Woolford decided that he wasn't doing too well and that he'd need more ammunition if he was going to return to this particular attack. He was surprised that the old boy hadn't already ordered him from the house.

He finished the coffee preparatory to coming to his feet. "Then you think it's out of the question, Ernest Self belonging to a revolutionary organization?"

The Professor protested. "I didn't say that at all. Mr. Self is a man of ideals. I can well see him belonging to such an organization."

Larry Woolford decided he'd better hang on for at least a few more words. "You don't seem to think, yourself, that a subversive organization is undesirable in this country."

The Professor's voice was reasonable. "Isn't that according to what it means to subvert?"

"You know what I mean," Woolford said in irritation. "I don't usually think of revolutionists, even when they call themselves simply members of a *movement*, as exactly idealists."

"Then you're wrong," the Professor said definitely, pouring himself another cup of coffee. "History bears out that almost invariably revolutionists are men of idealism. The fact that they might be either right or wrong in their revolutionary program is beside the point."

Larry Woolford began to say, "Are you sure that you aren't interested in this *move* — "

But it was then that the knockout drops hit him.

* * * * *

He came out of the fog feeling nausea and with his head splitting. He groaned and opened one eye experimentally.

Steve Hackett, far away, said, "He's snapping out of it."

Larry groaned again, opened the other eye and attempted to focus.

"What happened?" he muttered.

"Now that's an original question," Steve said.

Larry Woolford struggled up into a sitting position. He'd been stretched out on a couch in the Professor's combined living room and study.

Steve Hackett, his hands on his hips, was looking down at him sarcastically. There were two or three others, one of whom Larry vaguely remembered as being a Secret Service colleague of Steve's, going about and in and out of the room.

Larry said, his fingers pressing into his forehead, "My head's killing me. Damn it, what's going on?"

Steve said sarcastically, "You've been slipped a mickey, my cloak and dagger friend, and the bird has flown."

"You mean the Professor? He's a bird all right."

"Humor we get, yet," Hackett said, his ugly face scowling. "Listen, I thought you people had pulled out of this case."

Larry sat up and swung his two feet around to the floor. "So did I," he moaned, "but there were two or three things that bothered me and I thought I'd tidy them up before leaving."

"You tidied them up all right," Steve grumbled. "This Professor Voss was practically the only lead I've been able to discover. An old friend of Self's. And you allowed him to get away before we even got here."

One of Hackett's men came up and said, "Not a sign of him, Steve. He evidently burned a few papers, packed a suitcase, and took off. His things look suspiciously as though he was ready to go into hiding at a moment's notice."

Steve growled to him, "Give the place the works. He's probably left some clues around that'll give us a line."

The other went off and Steve Hackett sat down in one of the leather chairs and glowered at Larry Woolford. "Listen," he said, "what did you people want with Susan Self?"

Larry shook his head for clarity and looked at him. "Susan? What are you talking about? You don't have any aspirin, do you?"

"No. What'd you mean, what am I talking about? You called Betsy Hughes and then sent a couple of men over to pick the Self kid up."

"Who's Betsy Hughes?"

Steve shook his head. "I don't know what kind of knockout drops the old boy gave you, but they sure worked. Betsy's the operative we had minding Susan Self over in the Greater Washington Hilton. About an hour ago you got her on the phone, said your department wanted to question Susan, and that you were sending two men over to pick her up. The two men turned up with an order from you, and took the girl."

Larry stared at him. Finally he said, "What time is it?"

"About two o'clock."

Larry said, "I came into this house in the morning, talked to the Professor for about half an hour and then was silly enough to let him give me some loaded coffee. He was such a weird old buzzard that it never occurred to me he might be dangerous. At any rate, I've been unconscious for several hours. I *couldn't've* called this Betsy Hughes operative of yours."

It was Steve Hackett's turn to stare.

"You mean your department doesn't have Susan Self?"

"Not so far as I know. The Boss told me yesterday that we were pulling out, that it was all in your hands. What would we want with Susan?"

"Oh, great," Steve snarled. "There goes our last contact. Ernest Self, Professor Voss, and now Susan Self; they've all disappeared."

"Look," Larry said unhappily, "let's get me some aspirin and then let's go and see my chief. I have a sneaking suspicion our department is back on this case."

Steve snorted sarcastically. "If you can foul things up this well when you're off the case, God only knows what you'll accomplish using your facilities on an all-out basis."

The Boss said slowly, "Whoever we are working against evidently isn't short of resources. Abducting that young lady was no simple matter." The career diplomat worked his lips in and out, in all but a pout.

Larry Woolford, who'd taken time out to go home, shower, change clothes and medicate himself out of his dope induced hangover, sat across the desk from him, flanked by Steve Hackett.

The Boss said sourly, "It would seem that I was in error. That our young Susan Self was not spouting fantasy. There evidently actually is an underground movement interested in changing our institutions." He stirred in his chair and his scowl went deeper. "And evidently working on a basis never conceived of by subversive organizations of the past. The fact that they have successfully remained secret even to this department is the prime indication that they are attempting to make their revolutionary changes in a unique manner."

Larry said, "The trouble is, we don't even know what it is they want."

"However," his superior said slowly, "we are beginning to get inklings."

Steve Hackett said, "What inklings, sir? This sort of thing might be routine for you people, but my field is counterfeit. I, frankly, don't know what it's all about."

The Boss looked at him. "We have a clue or two, Mr. Hackett. For one thing, we know that this Movement of ours has no affiliations with the Soviet Complex, nor, so far as we know, any foreign element whatsoever. If we take Miss Self's word, it is strictly an American phenomenon. From what little we know of Ernest Self and Peter Voss they might be in revolt against some of our current institutions but there is no reason to believe them, ah, *un-American* in the usually accepted sense of the word."

The two younger men looked at him as though he was joking.

He shook his heavy head negatively. "Actually, what do we have on this so-called Movement thus far? Aside from treating Lawrence, here, to some knockout drops-and let us remember that Lawrence was present in the Professor's home without a warrant-all we have is the suspicion that they have manufactured a quantity of counterfeit."

"A *quantity* is right," Steve Hackett blurted. "If we're to accept what that Self kid told us, they have a few billion dollars worth of perfect bills on hand."

"A strange amount for counterfeiters to produce," The Boss said uncomfortably. "That is what puzzles me. Any revolutionary movement needs funds. Remember Stalin as a young man? He used to be in charge of the Bolshevik gang which robbed banks to raise funds for their underground newspapers. But a billion dollars? What in the world can they expect to need that amount for?"

Larry said, "Sir, you keep talking as though these characters were a bunch of idealistic do-gooders bleeding for the sake of the country. Actually, from what we know, they're nothing but a bunch of revolutionists."

The Boss was shaking his head. "You're not thinking clearly, Lawrence. Revolution, *per se*, is not illegal in the United States. Our Constitution was probably the first document of its kind which allowed for its own amendment. The men who wrote it provided for changing it either slightly or *in toto*. Whenever the majority of the American people decide completely to abandon the Constitution and govern themselves by new laws, they have the right to do it."

"Then what's the whole purpose of this department, sir?" Larry argued. "Why've we been formed to combat foreign and domestic subversion?"

His chief sighed. "You shouldn't have to ask that, Lawrence. The present government cannot oppose the will of the majority if it votes, by constitutional methods, to make any changes it wishes. But we can, and do, unmask the activities of anyone trying to overthrow the government by force and violence. Any culture protects itself against that."

"What are we getting at, sir?" Steve Hackett said, impatiently.

The Boss shrugged. "I'm trying to point out that so far as my department is concerned, thus far we have little against this Movement. Secret Service may have, what with this wholesale counterfeiting, even though thus far they seem to have made no attempt to pass the currency they have allegedly manufactured. We wouldn't even know of it, weren't it for our young Susan pilfering an amount."

Larry said, desperately, "Sir, you just pointed out a few minutes ago that this Movement is a secret organization trying to make changes in some unique manner. In short, they don't figure on using the ballot to put over their revolution. That makes them as illegal as the Commies, doesn't it?"

The Boss said, "That's the difficulty; we don't know what they want. From your conversations with Susan Self and especially Professor Voss, evidently they think the country needs some basic changes. What these changes are, and how they expect to accomplish them, we don't know. Unless a foreign government is involved, or unless they plan to alter our institutions by violence, this department just doesn't have much jurisdiction."

Steve Hackett snorted, "Secret Service does! If those bales of money the Self kid told us about are ever put into circulation, there'll be hell to pay."

The Boss sighed. "Well," he said, "Lawrence can continue on the assignment. If it develops in such manner as to indicate that this department is justified in further investigation, we'll put more men on it. Meanwhile, it is obviously more a Secret Service matter. I am sorry to intrude upon your vacation again, Lawrence."

On awakening in the morning, Larry Woolford stared glumly at the ceiling for long moments before dragging himself from bed. This was, he decided, the strangest assignment he'd ever been on. In his day he'd trekked through South America, Common Europe, a dozen African states, and even areas of Southern Asia, combatting Commie pressures here, fellow-traveler organizations there, disrupting plots hatched in the Soviet Complex in the other place. On his home grounds in the United States he'd covered everything from out and out Soviet espionage, to exposing Communist activities of complexions from the faintest of pinks to the rosiest Trotskyite red. But, he decided he'd never expected to wind up after a bunch of weirds whose sole actionable activity to date seemed to be the counterfeiting of a fantastic amount of legal tender which thus far they were making no attempt to pass.

He got out of bed and went through the rituals of showering, shaving and clothing, of coffee, sausage, and eggs, toast and more coffee.

What amazed Larry Woolford was the shrug-it-off manner in which the Boss seemed to accept this underground Movement and its admitted subversive goals-whatever they were. Carry the Boss' reasoning to its ultimate and subversion was perfectly all right, just as it didn't involve force and violence. If he was in his chief's position, he would have thrown the full resources of the department into tracking down these crackpots. As it was, he, Larry Woolford was the only operative on the job.

He needed a new angle on which to work. Steve Hackett was undoubtedly handling the tracing down of the counterfeit with all the resources of the Secret Service. Possibly there was some way of detecting the source of the paper they'd used.

He finished his final cup of coffee in the living room and took up the pipe he was currently breaking in. He loaded it automatically from a humidor and lit it with his pocket lighter. Three drags, and he tossed it back to the table, fumbled in a drawer and located a pack of cigarettes. Possibly his status group was currently smoking British briars in public, but, let's face it, he hated the confounded things.

He sat down before the phone and dialed the offices of the *Sun-Post* and eventually got Sam Sokolski who this time beat him to the punch.

Sam said, "You shouldn't drink alone. Listen, Larry, why don't you get in touch with Alcoholics Anonymous. It's a great outfit."

"You ought to know," Larry growled. "Look, Sam, as science columnist for that rag you work for you probably come in touch with a lot of eggheads."

"Laddy-buck, you have said it," Sam said.

"Fine. Now look, what I want to know is have you ever heard-even the slightest of rumors-about an organization called the Movement?"

"What'd'ya mean, slightest of rumors? Half the weirds I run into are interested in the outfit. Get two or three intellectuals, scientists, technicians, or what have you, together and they start knocking themselves out on the pros and cons of the Movement."

Larry Woolford stared at him. "Are you kidding, Sam?"

The other was mystified. "Why should I kid you? As a matter of fact, I was thinking of doing a column one of these days on Voss and this Movement of his."

"*Voss* and this movement of his!"

"Sure," Sam said, "he's the top leader."

"Oh, great," Larry growled. "Look, Sam, eventually there is probably a story in this for you. Right now, though, we're trying to keep the lid on it. Could you brief me a little on this Movement? What are they trying to put over?"

"I seem to spend half my time briefing you in information any semi-moron ought to be up on," Sam said nastily. "However, *briefly*, they're in revolt against social-label judgments. They think it's fouling up the country and that eventually it'll result in the Russkies passing us in all the fields that really count."

"I keep running into this term," Larry complained. "What do you mean, social-label judgments, and how can they possibly louse up the country?"

Sam said, "I was present a month or so ago when Voss gave an informal lecture to a group of twenty or so. Here's one of the examples he used.

"Everybody today wants to be rated on a (1) personal, or, (2) social-label basis, depending on which basis is to his greatest advantage. The Negro who is a no-good, lazy, obnoxious person demands to be accepted because Negroes should not be discriminated against. The highly competent, hard working, honest and productive Negro wants to be accepted because he is hard-working, honest and productive-and should be so accepted.

"See what I mean? This social-label system is intended to relieve the individual of the necessity of judging, and the consequences of being judged. If you have poor judgment, and are forced to rely on your own judgment, you're almost sure to go under. So persons of poor judgment support our social-label system. If you're a louse, and are correctly judged as being a louse, you'd prefer that the social dictum 'Human beings are never lice' should apply."

Larry said, "What in the devil's this got to do with the race between this country and the Russkies?"

Sam said patiently, "Voss and the Movement he leads contend that a social-label system winds up with incompetents running the country in all fields. Often incompetent scientists are in charge of our research; incompetent doctors, in charge of our health; incompetent politicians run our government; incompetent teachers, laden with social-labels, teach our youth. Our young people are going to college to secure a degree, not an education. It's the label that counts, not the reality.

"Voss contends that it's getting progressively worse. That we're sinking into an equivalent of a ritual-taboo, tribal social-like situation. This is the system the low-level human being wants, yearns for and seeks. A situation in which no one's judgment is of any use. Then *his* lack of judgment is no handicap.

"According to members of the Movement, today the tribesman type is seeking to reduce civilization back to ritual-taboo tribalism wherein no one man's judgment is of any value. The union wants advancement based on seniority, not on ability and judgment. The persons with whom you associate socially judge you by the amount of money you possess, the family from which you come, the degrees you hold, by social-labels —not by your proven abilities. Down with judgment! is the cry."

"It sounds awfully weird to me," Larry grumbled in deprecation.

Sam shrugged. "There's a lot of sense in it. What the Movement wants is to develop a socio-economic system in which judgment produces a maximum advantage."

Larry said, "What gets me is that you talk as though half the country was all caught up in debating this Movement. But I haven't even heard of it, neither has my department chief, nor any of my colleagues, so far as I know. Why isn't anything about it in the papers or on the TriD?"

Sam said mildly, "As a matter of fact, I took in Mort Lenny's show the other night and he made some cracks about it. But it's not the sort of thing that's even meant to become popular with the man in the street. To put it bluntly, Voss and his people aren't particularly keen about the present conception of the democratic ideal. According to him, true democracy can only be exercised by peers and society today isn't composed of peers. If you have one hundred people, twenty of them competent, intelligent persons, eighty of them untrained, incompetent and less than intelligent, then it's ridiculous to have the eighty dictate to the twenty."

Larry looked accusingly at his long-time friend. "You know, Sam, you sound as though you approve of all this."

Sam said patiently, "I listen to it all, Larry my boy. I think Voss makes a lot of sense. There's only one drawback."

"And that is?"

"How's he going to put it over? This social-label system the Movement complains about was bad enough ten years ago. But look how much worse it is today. It's a progressive thing. And, remember, it's to the benefit of the incompetent. Since the incompetent predominates, you're going to have a hard time starting up a system based on judgment and ability."

Larry thought about it for a moment.

Sam said, "Look, I'm working, Larry. Was there anything else?"

Larry said, "You wouldn't know where I could get hold of Voss, would you?"

"At his home, I imagine, or at the University."

"He's disappeared. We're looking for him."

Sam laughed. "Gone underground, eh? The old boy is getting romantic."

"Does he have any particular friends who might be putting him up?"

Sam thought about it. "There's Frank Nostrand. You know, that rocket expert who was fired when he got in the big hassle with Senator McCord."

* * * * *

When Sam Sokolski had flicked off, Larry stared at the vacant phone screen for a long moment, assimilating what the other had told him. He was astonished that an organization such as the Movement could have spread to the extent it evidently had through the country's intellectual circles, through the scientifically and technically trained, without his department being keenly aware of it.

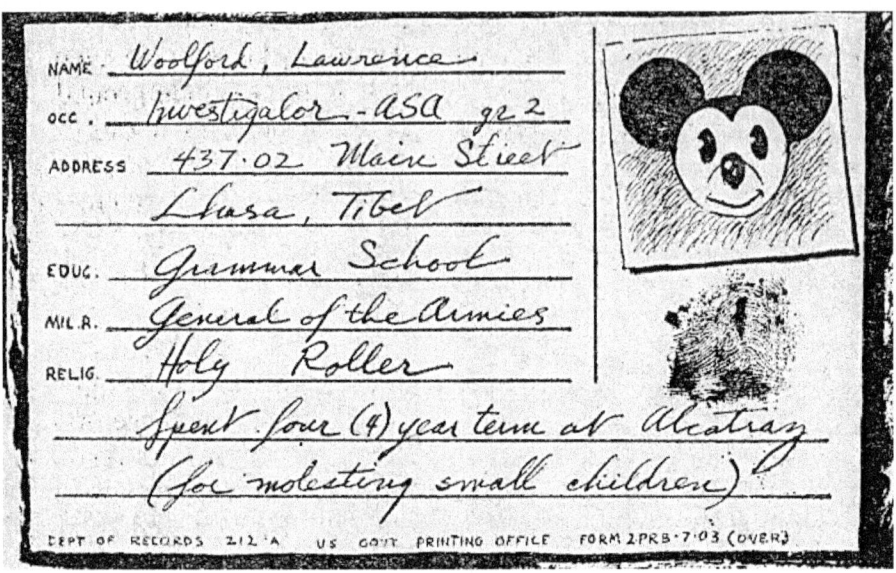

One result, he decided glumly, of labeling everything contrary to the *status quo* as *weird* and dismissing it with contempt. Admittedly, that would have been his own reaction only a week ago.

Suppose that he'd been at a cocktail party, and had drifted up to a group who were arguing about social-label judgments and the need to develop a *movement* to change society's use of them. The discussion would have gone in one ear, out the other, and he would have muttered inwardly, "Weirds," and have drifted on to get himself another vodka martini.

Larry snorted and dialed the Department of Records. He'd never heard of Frank Nostrand before, so he got Information.

The bright young thing who answered seemed to have a harried expression untypical of Records employees. Larry said to her, "I'd like the brief on a Mr. Frank Nostrand who is evidently an expert on rockets. The only other thing I know about him is that he recently got in the news as the result of a controversy with Senator McCord."

"Just a moment, sir," the bright young thing said.

She touched buttons and reached into a delivery chute. When her eyes came up to meet his again, they were more than ever harried. They were absolutely confused.

"Mr. Franklin Howard Nostrand," she said, "currently employed by Madison Air as a rocket research technician."

"That must be him," Larry said. "I'm in a hurry, Miss. What's his background?"

Her eyes rounded. "It says ... it says he's an Archbishop of the Anglican Church."

Larry Woolford looked at her.

She looked back, pleadingly.

Larry scowled and said, "His university degrees, please."

Her eyes darted to the report and she swallowed. "A bachelor in Home Economics, sir."

"Look here, Miss, how could a Home Economics degree result in his becoming either an Archbishop or a rocket technician?"

314

"I'm sorry, sir. That's what it says."

Larry was fuming but there was no point in taking it out on this junior employee of the Department of Records. He snapped, "Just give me his address, please."

She said agonizingly, "Sir, it says, Lhasa, Tibet."

A red light flicked at the side of his phone and he said to her, "I'll call you back. I'm getting a priority call."

He flicked her off, and flicked the incoming call in. It was LaVerne Polk. She seemed to be on the harried side, too.

"Larry," she said, "you better get over here right away."

"What's up, LaVerne?"

"This Movement," she said, "it seems to have started moving! The Boss says to get over here soonest."

* * * * *

The top of his car was retracted. Larry Woolford slammed down the walk of his auto-bungalow and vaulted over the side and into the seat. He banged the start button, dropped the lift lever, depressed the thrust pedal and took off at maximum acceleration.

He took the police level for maximum speed and was in downtown Greater Washington in flat minutes.

So the Movement had started moving. That could mean almost anything. It was just enough to keep him stewing until he got to the Boss and found out what was going on.

He turned his car over to a parker and made his way to the entrance utilized by the second-grade department officials. In another year, or at most two, he told himself all over again, he'd be using that other door. He had an intuitive feeling that if he licked this current assignment it'd be the opening wedge he needed and he'd wind up in a status bracket unique for his age.

LaVerne looked up when he hurried into her anteroom. She evidently had two or three calls going on at once, taking orders from one phone, giving them in another. Something was obviously erupting. She didn't speak to him, merely nodded her head at the inner office.

In the Boss' office were six or eight others besides Larry's superior. Their expressions and attitudes ran from bewilderment to shock. They weren't the men you'd expect to have such reactions. At least not those that Larry Woolford recognized. Three of them, Ben Ruthenberg, Bill Fraina and Dave Moskowitz were F.B.I. men with whom Larry had worked on occasion. One of the others he recognized as being a supervisor with the C.I.A. Walt Foster, Larry's rival in the Boss' affections, was also present.

The Boss growled at him, "Where in the heavens have you been, Lawrence?"

"Following our leads on this so-called Movement, sir," Larry told him. "What's going on?"

Ruthenberg, the Department of Justice man, grunted sour amusement. "So-called Movement, isn't exactly the correct phrase. It's a Movement, all right."

The Boss said, "Please dial Records and get your dossier, Lawrence. That'll be the quickest way to bring you up on developments."

Mystified, but already with a growing premonition, Larry dialed Records. Knowing his own classification code, he had no need of Information this time. He got the hundred-word brief and stared at it as it filled the screen. The only items really correct were his name and present occupation. Otherwise his education was listed as grammar school only. His military career had him ending the war as a General of the Armies, and his criminal career record included four years on Alcatraz for molesting small children.

Blankly, he faded the brief and dialed his full dossier. It failed to duplicate the brief, but that was no advantage. This time he had an M.D. degree from Johns Hopkins, but his military career listed him as a dishonorable discharge from the navy where he'd served in the steward department. His criminal record was happily nil, but his religion was listed as Holy Roller. Political affiliations had him down as a member of the Dixiecrats.

The others were looking at him, most of them blankly, although there were grins on the faces of Moskowitz and the C.I.A. man.

Moskowitz said, "With a name like mine, yet, they have me a Bishop of the Orthodox Greek Catholic Church."

Larry said, "What's it all about?"

Ruthenberg said unhappily, "It started early this morning. We don't know exactly when as yet." Which didn't seem to answer the question.

Larry said, "I don't get it. Obviously, the Records department is fouled up in some manner. How, and why?"

"How, we know," the Boss rumbled disgustedly. "Why is another matter. You've spent more time than anyone else on this assignment, Lawrence. Perhaps you can tell us." He grabbed up a pipe from his desk, tried to light it noisily, noticed finally that it held no tobacco and threw it to the desk again. "Evidently, a large group of these Movement individuals either already worked in Records or wriggled themselves into key positions in the technical end of the department. Now they've sabotaged the files."

"We've caught most of them already," one of the F.B.I. men growled, "but damn little good that does us at this point."

The C.I.A. supervisor made a gesture indicating that he gave it all up. "Not only here but in Chicago and San Francisco as well. All at once. Evidently perfectly rehearsed. Personnel records from coast to coast are bollixed. Why?"

Larry said slowly, "I think I know that now. Yesterday, I wouldn't have but I've been picking up odds and ends."

They all looked at him.

* * * * *

Larry sat down and ran a hand back through his hair. "The general idea is to change the country's reliance on social-label judgments."

"On *what* ," the Boss barked.

"On one person judging another according to social-labels. Voss and the others —"

"Who did you say?" Ruthenberg snapped.

"Voss. Professor Peter Voss from the University over in Baltimore section. He's the ring leader."

Ruthenberg snapped to Fraina, "Get on the phone and send out a pick-up order for him."

Fraina was on his feet. "What charge, Ben?"

Ben Ruthenberg snorted. "Rape, or something. Get moving, we'll figure out a charge later. The guy's a fruitcake."

Larry said wearily, "He's evidently gone into hiding. I've been trying to locate him. He managed to slip me some knockout drops and got away yesterday."

The Boss looked at him in disgust.

Ruthenberg said evenly, "We've had men go into hiding before. Get going, Fraina."

Fraina left the office and the others looked back to Larry.

The Boss said, "About this social-label nonsense —"

Larry said, "They think the country is going to pot because of it. People hold high office or places of responsibility not because of superior intelligence, or even acquired skill, but because of the social-labels they've accumulated, and these can be based on something as flimsy-from the Movement's viewpoint-as who your grandparents were, what school you attended, how much seniority you have on the job, what part of town you live in, or what tailor cuts your clothes."

Their expressions ran from scowls and frowns to complete puzzlement.

Walt Foster grumbled, "What's all this got to do with sabotaging the country's Records tapes?"

Larry shrugged. "I don't have the complete picture, but one thing is sure. It's going to be harder for a while to base your opinions on a quick hundred-word brief on a man. Yesterday, an employer, considering hiring somebody, could dial the man's dossier, check it, and form his opinions by the status labels the would-be employee could produce. Today, he's damn well going to have to exercise his own judgment."

LaVerne's face lit up the screen on the Boss' desk and she said, "Those two members of the Movement who were picked up in Alexandria are here, sir."

"Send them in," the Boss rumbled. He looked at Larry. "The F.B.I. managed to arrest almost everyone directly involved in the sabotage."

The two prisoners seemed more amused than otherwise. They were young men, in their early thirties-well dressed and obviously intelligent. The Boss had them seated side by side and glared at them for a long moment before speaking. Larry and the others took chairs in various parts of the room and added their own stares to the barrage.

The Boss said, "Your situation is an unhappy one, gentlemen."

One of the two shrugged.

The Boss said, "You can, ah, hedge your bets, by co-operating with us. It might make the difference between a year or two in prison-and life."

One of them grinned and then yawned. "I doubt it," he said.

The Boss tried a slightly different tack. "You have no reason to maintain a feeling of obligation to Voss and the others. You have obviously been abandoned. Had they any feeling for you there would have been more efficacious arrangements for your escape."

The more articulate of the two shrugged again. "We were expendable," he said. "However, it won't be long before we're free again."

"You think so?" Ruthenberg grunted.

The revolutionist looked at him. "Yes, I do," he said. "Six months from now and we'll be heroes since by that time the Movement will have been a success."

The Boss snorted. "Just because you deranged the Records? Why that's but temporary."

"Not so temporary as you think," the technician replied. "This country has allowed itself to get deeply enmeshed in punch-card and tape records. Oh, it made sense enough. With the population we have, and the endless files that result from our ultra-complicated society, it was simply a matter finally of developing a standardized system of records for the nation as a whole. Now, for all practical purposes, *all* of our records these days are kept with the Department of Records, confidential as well as public records. Why should a university, for instance, keep literally tons of files, with all the expense and space and time involved, when it can merely file the same records with the governmental department and have them safe and easily available at any time? Now, the Movement has completely and irrevocably destroyed almost all files that deal with the social-labels to which we object. An excellent first step, in forcing our country back into judgment based on ability and intelligence."

"First step!" Larry blurted.

The two prisoners looked at him. "That's right," the quieter of the two said. "This is just the first step."

"Don't kid yourselves," Ben Ruthenberg snapped at them. "It's also the last!"

The two members of the Movement grinned at him.

* * * * *

When the others had gone, the Boss looked at Larry Woolford. He said sourly, "When this department was being formed, I doubt anyone had in mind this particular type of subversion, Lawrence."

Larry grunted. "Give me a good old-fashioned Commie, any time. Look, sir, what are the Department of Justice boys going to do with those prisoners?"

"Hold them on any of various charges. We've conflicted with the F.B.I. in the past on overlapping jurisdiction, but thank heavens for them now. Their manpower is needed."

Larry leaned forward. "Sir, we ought to take all members of the Movement we've already arrested, feed them a dose of Scop-Serum, and pressure them to open up on the organization's operations."

His superior looked at him, waiting for him to continue.

Larry said urgently, "Those two we just had in here thought the whole thing was a big joke. The first step, they called it. Sir, there's something considerably bigger than this cooking. Uncle Sam might pride himself on the personal liberties guaranteed by this country, but unless we break this organization, and do it fast, there's going to be trouble that will make this fouling of the records look like the minor matter those two jokers seemed to think it."

The Boss thought about that. He said slowly, "Lawrence, the Supreme Court ruled against the use of Scop-Serum. Not that it is over efficient, anyway. Largely, these so-called truth serums don't accomplish much more than to lower resistance, slacken natural inhibitions, weaken the will."

"Sure," Larry said. "But give a man a good dose of Scop-Serum and he'd betray his own mother. Not because he's helpless to tell a lie, but because under the influence of the drug he figures it just isn't important enough to bother about. Sir, Supreme Court or not, I think those two ought to be given Scop-Serum along with all other Movement members we've picked up."

The Boss was shaking his head. "Lawrence, these men are not wide-eyed radicals picked up in a street demonstration. They're highly respected members of our society. They're educators, scientists, engineers, technicians. Anything done to them is going to make headlines. Those that were actually involved in the sabotage will have criminal charges brought against them, but they're going to get a considerable amount of publicity, and we're going to be in no position to alienate any of their constitutional rights."

Larry stood up, approached his chief's desk and leaned over it urgently. "Sir, that's fine, but we've got to move and move fast. Something's up and we don't even know what! Take that counterfeit money. From Susan Self's description, there's actually billions of dollars worth of it."

"Oh, come now, Lawrence. The child exaggerated. Besides, that's a problem for Steven Hackett and the Secret Service, we have enough on our hands as it is. Forget about the counterfeit, Lawrence. I think I shall put you in complete control of field work on this, to co-operate in liaison with Ben Ruthenberg and the F.B.I. So far as we're concerned, the counterfeit angle belongs to Secret Service, we're working on subversion, and until the Civil Liberties Union or whoever else proves otherwise, we'll consider this Movement an organization attempting to subvert the country by illegal means."

Larry Woolford made a hard decision quickly. He was shaking his head. "Sir, I'd rather you gave the administrative end to someone else and let me continue in the field. I've got some leads —I think. If I get bogged down in interdepartmental red tape, and in paper work here at headquarters, I'll never get to the heart of this and I'm laying bets that we either crack this within days or there are going to be some awfully big changes in this country."

The Boss glared at him. "You mean you're refusing this assignment, Woolford. Confound it, don't you realize it's a promotion?"

Larry was worriedly dogged. "Sir, I'd rather stay in the field."

"Very well," the other snapped disgustedly, "I hope you deliver some results, Woolford, otherwise I am afraid I won't feel particularly happy about your somewhat cavalier rejection of this opportunity." He flicked on the phone and snapped to LaVerne Polk, "Miss Polk, locate Walter Foster for me. He is to take over our end of this Movement matter."

LaVerne said, "Yes, sir," and her face was gone.

The Boss looked up, still scowling. "What are you waiting for, Woolford?"

"Yes, sir," Larry said. It was just coming home to him now, what he'd done. There possibly went his yearned for promotion in the department. There went his chance of an upgrading in status. And Walt Foster, of all people, in his place.

At LaVerne's desk, Larry stopped off long enough to say, "Did you ever assign that secretary to me?"

LaVerne shook her head at him. "She's come and gone, Larry. She sat around for a couple of days, after seeing you not even once, and then I gave her another assignment."

"Well, bring her back again, will you? I want her to do up briefs for me on all the information we accumulate on the Movement. It'll be coming in from all sides now. From the Press, from those members we've arrested, from our F.B.I. pals, now that they're interested, and so forth."

"I'll give you Irene Day," LaVerne said. "Where are you off to now, Larry?"

"Probably a wild goose chase," Larry growled. "Which reminds me. Do me a favor, LaVerne. Call Personal Service and find out where Frank Nostrand is. He's some kind of rocket technician at Madison Air Laboratories. I'll be in my office."

"Frank Nostrand," LaVerne said briskly. "Will do, Larry."

Back in his own cubicle, Larry stood for a moment in thought. He was increasingly aware of the uncomfortable feeling that time was running out on them. That things were coming to a dangerous head.

He stared down at the dozen or more books and pamphlets that his never seen secretary had heaped up for him. Well, he certainly didn't have time for them now.

He sat down at the desk and dialed an inter-office number.

The harassed looking face of Walter Foster faded in. On seeing Larry Woolford he growled accusingly, "My pal. You've let them dump this whole thing into my lap."

Larry grinned at him. "Better you than me, old buddy. Besides, it's a promotion. Pull this off and you'll be the Boss' right-hand man."

"That's a laugh," Foster said. "It's a madhouse. This Movement gang is as weird as they come."

"I bleed for you," Larry said. "However, here's a tip. Frol Eivazov, of the *Chrezvychainaya Komissiya* is somewhere in the country."

"Frol Eivazov!" Foster blurted. "What've the Commies got to do with this? Is this something the Boss knows about?"

"Haven't had time to go into it with him," Larry said. "However, it seems that friend Frol is here to find out what the Movement is all about. Evidently the big boys in Peking and Moscow are nervous about any changes that might take place over here. I suggest you have him picked up, Walt."

Walt Foster said, "O.K. I'll put some people on it. Maybe the F.B.I. can help."

Larry flicked off as he saw the red priority light on his phone shining. He pushed it and LaVerne's face faded in.

She said, "This Franklin Nostrand you wanted to know about. He's evidently working at the laboratories over in Newport News, Larry. He'll be on the job until five this afternoon."

"Fine," he said. Larry grinned at her. "When are we going to have that date, LaVerne?"

She made a face. "Some day when the program involves having fun instead of parading around in the right places, driving the right model car, dressed in exactly the right clothes, and above all associating with the right people."

It was his turn to grimace. "I'm beginning to think you ought to sign up with Voss and this Movement of his. You'd be right at home with his weirds."

She stuck out her tongue at him, and flicked off.

He looked at the empty screen and chuckled. He had half a mind to get a record of their conversation, strip out just the section where she'd stuck out her tongue, and then play it back to her. She'd be taken aback by being confronted by her own image making faces at her.

As he made his way to the parking lot for his car, something in their conversation nagged at him, but he couldn't put his finger on it. He considered the girl, all over again. She had almost all the qualities he looked for. She was attractive, without being overly so. He disliked women out of the ordinarily beautiful, it became too much to live up to. She was sharp, but not objectionably so. Not to the point of giving you an inferiority complex.

But, Holy Smokes, she'd never do as a career man's wife. He could just see the Boss' ultra-conservative better half inviting them to dinner. It would happen exactly once, never again.

He obtained his car, lifted it to one of the higher levels and headed for Newport News. It was a half-hour trip and he wasn't particularly expectant of results. The tip Sam Sokolski had given him, wasn't much to go by. Evidently, Frank Nostrand was a friend of the Professor's but that didn't necessarily mean he was connected with the movement, or that he knew Voss' whereabouts.

He might have saved himself the trip.

The bird had flown again. Not only was Frank Nostrand not at the Madison Air Laboratories, but he wasn't at home either. Larry Woolford, mindful of his departmental chief's words on the prestige these people carried, took a full hour in acquiring a search warrant before breaking into the Nostrand home.

Nostrand was supposedly a bachelor, but the auto-bungalow, similar to Larry Woolford's own, showed signs of double occupancy, and there was little indication that the guest had been a woman.

Disgruntled, Larry Woolford dialed the offices, asked for Walt Foster. It took nearly ten minutes before his colleague faded in.

"I'm up to my eyebrows, Larry. What'd you want?"

Larry gave him Frank Nostrand's address. "This guy's disappeared, Walt."

"So?"

"He was a close friend of Professor Voss. I got a warrant to search his house. It shows signs that he had a guest. Possibly it was the Professor. Do you want to get some of the boys down here to go through the place? Possibly there's some clue to where they took off for. The Professor's on the run and he's no professional at this. If we can pick *him* up, I've got a sneaking suspicion we'll have the so-called Movement licked."

Walt Foster slapped a hand to his face in anguish. "You knew where the Professor was hiding, and you tried to pick him up on your own let him get away. Why didn't you discuss this with either the Boss or me? I'm in charge of this operation! I would have had a dozen men down there. You've fouled this up!"

Larry stared at him. Already Walt Foster was making sounds like an enraged superior.

He said mildly, "Sorry, Walt. I came down here on a very meager tip. I didn't really expect it to pan out."

"Well, in the future, clear with either me or the Boss before running off half cocked into something, Woolford. Yesterday, you had this whole assignment on your own. Today, it's no longer a minor matter. Our department has fifty people on it. The F.B.I. must have five times as many and that's not even counting the Secret Service's interest. It's no longer your individual baby."

"Sorry," Larry repeated mildly. Then, "I don't imagine you've got hold of Frol Eivazov yet?"

The other was disgusted. "You think we're magicians? We just put out the call for him a few hours ago. He's no amateur. If he doesn't want to be picked up, he'll go to ground and we'll have our work cut out for us finding him. I can't see that it's particularly important anyway."

"Maybe you're right," Larry said. "But you never know. He might know things we don't. See you later."

Walt Foster stared at him for a moment as though about to say something, but then tightened his lips and faded off.

Larry looked at the phone screen for a moment. "Did that phony expect me to call him *sir* ," he muttered.

* * * * *

The next two days dissolved into routine.

Frustrated, Larry Woolford spent most of his time in his office digesting developments, trying to find a new line of attack.

For want of something else, he put his new secretary, a brightly efficient girl, as style and status conscious as LaVerne Polk wasn't, to work typing up the tapes he'd had cut on Susan Self and the various phone calls he'd had with Hans Distelmayer and Sam Sokolski. From memory, he dictated to her his conversation with Professor Peter Voss.

He carefully read the typed sheets over and over again. He continually had the feeling in this case that there were loose ends dangling around. Several important points he should be able to put his finger upon.

On the morning of the third day he dialed Steve Hackett and on seeing the other's worried, pug-ugly face fade in on the phone, decided that if nothing else the Movement was undermining the United States government by dispensing ulcers to its employees.

Steve growled, "What is it Woolford? I'm as busy as a whirling dervish in a revolving door."

"This is just the glimmer of an idea, Steve. Look, remember that conversation with Susan, when she described her father taking her to headquarters?"

"So?" Steve said impatiently.

"Remember her description of headquarters?"

"Go on," Steve rapped.

"What did it remind you of?"

"What are you leading to?"

"This is just a hunch," Larry persisted, "but the way she described the manner in which her father took her to headquarters suggests they're in the Greater Washington area."

Steve was staring at him disgustedly. How obvious could you get?

Larry hurried on. "What's the biggest business in this area, Steve?"

"Government."

"Right. And the way she described headquarters of the Movement, was rooms, after rooms, after rooms into which they'd stored the money."

"And?"

Larry said urgently, "Steve, I think in some way the Movement has taken over some governmental buildings, or storage warehouse. Possibly some older buildings no longer in use. It would be a perfect hideout. Who would expect a subversive organization to be in governmental buildings? All they'd need would be a few officials here and there who were on their side and —"

Steve said wearily, "You couldn't have thought of this two days ago."

Larry cut himself off sharply, "Eh?"

Steve said, "We found their headquarters. One of their members cracked. Ben Ruthenberg of the F.B.I. found he had a morals rap against him some years ago and scared him into talking by threats of exposure. At any rate, you're right. They had established themselves in some government buildings going back to Spanish-American War days. We've arrested eight or ten officials that were involved."

"But the money?"

"The money was gone," Steve said bitterly. "But Susan was right. There had evidently been room after room of it, stacked to the ceiling. Literally billions of dollars. They'd moved out hurriedly, but they left kicking around enough loose hundreds, fifties, twenties, tens and fives to give us an idea. Look, Woolford, I thought you'd been pulled off this case and that Walt Foster was handling it."

Larry said sourly, "I'm beginning to think so, too. They're evidently not even bothering to let me know about developments like this. See you later, Steve."

The other's face faded off.

Larry Woolford looked across the double desk at Irene Day. "Look," he said, "when you're offered a promotion, take it. If you don't, someone else will and you'll be out in the cold."

Irene Day said brightly, "I've always know that, sir."

He looked at her. The typical eager beaver. Sharp as a whip. Bright as a button. "I'll bet you have," he muttered.

"I beg your pardon, Mr. Woolford?"

The phone lit as LaVerne said, "The Boss wants to talk to you, Larry." Her face faded and Larry's superior was scowling at him.

He snapped, "Did you get anything on this medical records thing, Woolford?"

"Medical records?" Larry said blankly.

The Boss grunted in deprecation. "No, I suppose you haven't. I wish you would snap into it, Woolford. I don't know what has happened to you of late. I used to think that you were a good field man." He flicked off abruptly.

Larry dialed LaVerne Polk. "What in the world was the Boss just talking about, LaVerne? About medical records?"

LaVerne said, frowning, "Didn't you know? The Movement's been at it again. They've fouled up the records of the State Medical Licensing bureaus, at the same time sabotaging the remaining records of most, if not all, of the country's medical schools. They struck simultaneously, throughout the country."

He looked at her, expressionlessly.

LaVerne said, "We've caught several hundred of those responsible. It's the same thing. Attack of the social-label. From now on, if a man tells you he's an Ear, Eye and Throat specialist, you'd better do some investigation before letting him amputate your tongue. You'd better use your judgment before letting *any* doctor you don't really know about, work on you. It's a madhouse, Larry."

* * * * *

Larry Woolford, for long moments after LaVerne had broken the connection, stared unseeingly at his secretary across from him until she stirred.

He brought his eyes back to the present. "Another preliminary move, not the important thing, yet. Not the big explosion they're figuring on. Where have they taken that money, and why?"

Irene Day blinked at him. "I don't know, I'm sure, sir."

Larry said, "Get me Mr. Foster on the phone, Irene."

When Walt Foster's unhappy face faded in, Larry said, "Walt did you get Frol Eivazov?"

"Eivazov?" the other said impatiently. "No. We haven't spent much effort on it. I think this hunch of yours is like the other ones you've been having lately, Woolford. Frol Eivazov was last reported by our operatives as being in North Korea."

"It wasn't a hunch," Larry said tightly. "He's in this country on an assignment dealing with the Movement."

"Well, that's your opinion," Foster said snappishly. "I'm busy, Woolford. See here, at present you're under my orders on this job. In the way of something to do, instead of sitting around in that office, why don't you follow up this Eivazov thing yourself?" He considered it a moment. "That's an order, Woolford. Even if you don't locate him, it'll keep you out of our hair."

After the other was gone, Larry Woolford leaned back in his chair, his face flushed as though the other had slapped it. In a way, he had.

Larry said slowly, "Miss Day, dial me Hans Distelmayer. His offices are over in the Belmont Building."

As always, the screen remained blank as the German spy master spoke.

Larry said, "Hans, I want to talk to Frol Eivazov."

"Ah?"

"I want to know where I can find him."

The German's voice was humorously gruff. "My friend, my friend."

Larry said impatiently, "I'm not interested in arresting him at this time. I want to talk to him."

The other said heavily. "This goes beyond favors, my friend. On the face of it, I am not in business for my health. And what you ask is dangerous from my viewpoint. You realize that upon occasion my organization does small tasks for the Soviets...."

"Ha!" Larry said bitterly.

"...And," the German continued, unruffled, "it is hardly to my interest to gain the reputation of betraying my sometimes employers. Were you on an assignment in, say, Bulgaria or Hungary, would you expect me to betray you to the *Chrezvychainaya Komissiya* ?"

"Not unless somebody paid you enough to make it worth while," Larry said dryly.

"Exactly," the espionage chief said.

"Look," Larry said. "Send your bill to this department, Hans. I've been given carte blanche on this matter and I want to talk to Frol. Now, where is he?"

The German chuckled heavily. "At the Soviet Embassy."

"What! You mean they've got the gall to house their top spy right in —"

Distelmayer interrupted him. "Friend Eivazov is currently accredited as a military attaché and quite correctly. He holds the rank of colonel, you know. He entered this country quite legally, the only precaution taken was to use his second name, Kliment, instead of Frol, on his papers. Evidently, your people passed him by without a second look. Ah, I understand he went to the trouble of making some minor changes in his facial appearance."

"We'll expect your bill, Distelmayer," Larry said. "Good-by."

He got up and reached for his hat, saying to Irene Day, "I don't know how long I'll be gone." He added, wryly, "If either Foster or the Boss try to get in touch with me, tell them I'm carrying out orders."

He drove over to the Soviet Embassy, parked his car directly before the building.

* * * * *

The American plainclothesmen stationed near the entrance, gave him only a quick onceover as he passed. Inside the gates, the impassive Russian guards didn't bother to flicker an eyelid.

At the reception desk in the immense entrada, he identified himself. "I'd like to see Colonel Frol Eivazov."

"I am afraid —" the clerk began stiffly.

"I suppose you have him on the records as Kliment Eivazov."

The clerk had evidently touched a concealed button. A door opened and a junior embassy official approached them.

Larry restated his desire. The other began to open his mouth in denial, then shrugged. "Just a moment," he said.

He was gone a full twenty minutes. When he returned, he said briefly, "This way, please."

Frol Eivazov was in an inner office, in full uniform. He came to his feet when Larry Woolford entered and said to the clerk, "That will be all, Vova." He was a tall man, as Slavs go, but heavy of build and heavy of face.

He shook hands with Larry. "It's been a long time," he said in perfect English. "That conference in Warsaw, wasn't it? Have a chair, Mr. Woolford."

Larry took the offered chair and said, "How in the world did you expect to get by with this nonsense? We'll have you declared *persona non grata* in a matter of hours."

"It's not important," Eivazov shrugged. "I have found what I came to find. I was about to return to report any way."

"We won't do anything to hinder you, colonel," Larry said dryly.

Eivazov snapped his fingers. "It's all amusing," he said. "In our country we would quickly deal with this Movement nonsense. You Americans with your pseudo-democracy, your labels without reality, your —"

Larry said wearily, "Please, Frol, I promise not to convert you if you promise not to convert me. Needless to say, my department isn't happy about your presence in this country. You'll be watched from now on. We've been busy with other matters...."

Here the Russian laughed.

"...Or we'd already have flushed you." He allowed his voice to go curious. "We've wondered about your interest in this phase of our internal affairs."

The Russian agent let his facade slip over farther, his heavy lips sneering. "We are interested in all phases of your antiquated socio-economic system, Mr. Woolford. In the present peaceful economic competition between East and West, we would simply *loathe* to see anything happen to your present culture." He hesitated deliberately. "If you can call it a culture."

Larry said, unprovoked, "If I understand you correctly, you are not in favor of the changes the Movement advocates."

The Russian shrugged hugely. "I doubt if they are possible of achievement. The organization is a sloppy one. Revolutionary? Nonsense," he scoffed. "They have no plans to change the government. No plans for overthrowing the regime. Ultimately, what this country needs is true Communism. This so-called Movement doesn't have that as its eventual goal. It is laughable."

Larry said, interestedly, "Then perhaps you'll tell me what little you've found out about the group."

"Why not?" The Russian pursed his lips. "They are composed of impractical idealists. Scientists, intellectuals, a few admitted scholars and even a few potential leaders. Their sabotage of your Department of Records was an amusing farce, but, frankly, I have been unable to discover the purpose of their interest in rockets. For a time I contemplated the possibility that they had a scheme to develop a nuclear bomb, and to explode it over Greater Washington in the belief that in the resulting confusion they might seize power. But, on the face of it their membership is incapable of such an effort."

"Their interest in rockets?" Larry said softly.

"Yes, as you've undoubtedly discovered, half the rocket technicians of your country seem to have joined with them. We got the tip through" —the Russian cleared his throat —"several of our converts who happen to be connected with your space efforts groups."

"Is that so?" Larry said. "I wondered what you thought about their interest in money."

It was the other's turn to look blank. "Money?" he said.

"That's right. Large quantities of money."

The Russian said, frowning, "I suppose most citizens in your capitalist countries are interested largely in money. One of your basic failings."

* * * * *

Driving back to the office, Larry Woolford let it pile up on him.

Ernest Self had been a specialist in solid fuel for rockets. When Larry had questioned Professor Voss that worthy had particularly stressed his indignation at how Professor Goddard, the rocket pioneer, had been treated by his contemporaries. Franklin Nostrand had been employed as a technician on rocket research at Madison Air Laboratories. It was too darn much for coincidence.

And now something else that had been nagging away at the back of his mind suddenly came clear.

Susan Self had said that she and her father had seen the precision dancers at the New Roxy Theater in New York and later the Professor had said they were going to spend the money on chorus girls. Susan had got it wrong. The Rockettes-the precision chorus girls. The Professor had said they were going to spend the money on *rockets*, and Susan had misunderstood.

But billions of dollars expended on rockets? How? But, above all, to what end?

If he'd only been able to hold onto Susan, or her father; or to Voss or Nostrand, for that matter. Someone to work on. But each had slipped through his fingers.

Which brought something else up from his subconscious. Something which had been tugging at him.

At the office, Irene Day was packing her things as he entered. Packing as though she was leaving for good.

"What goes on?" Larry growled. "I'm going to be needing you. Things are coming to a head."

She said, a bit snippishly, Larry thought, "Miss Polk, in the Boss' office, said for you to see her as soon as you came in, Mr. Woolford."

"Oh?"

He made his way to LaVerne's office, his attention actually on the ideas churning in his mind. She looked up when he entered.

Larry said, "The Boss wanted to see me?"

LaVerne ducked her head, as though embarrassed. "Not exactly, Larry."

He gestured with his thumb in the direction of his own cubicle office. "Irene just said you wanted me."

LaVerne looked up into his face. "The Boss and Mr. Foster, too, are boiling about your authorizing that Distelmayer man to bill this department for information he gave you. The Boss hit the roof. Something about the Senate Appropriations Committee getting down on him if it came out that we bought information from professional espionage agents."

Larry said, "It was information we needed, and Foster gave me the go ahead on locating Frol Eivazov. Maybe I'd better see the Boss."

LaVerne said, "I don't think he wants to see you, Larry. They're up to their ears in this Movement thing. It's in the papers *now* and nobody knows what to do next. The President is going to make a speech on TriD, and the Boss has to supply the information. His orders are for you to resume your vacation. To take a month off and then see him when you get back."

Larry sank down into a chair. "I see," he said, "And at that time he'll probably transfer me to janitor service."

"Larry," LaVerne said, almost impatiently, "why in the world didn't you take that job Walt Foster has now when the Boss offered it to you?"

"Because I'm stupid, I suppose," Larry said bitterly. "I thought I could do more working alone than at an administrative post tangled in red tape and bureaucratic routine."

She said, "Sorry, Larry." She sounded as though she meant it.

Larry stood up. "Well, tonight I'm going to hang one on, and tomorrow it's back to Florida." He said in a rush, "Look LaVerne, how about that date we've been talking about for six months or more?"

She looked up at him. "I can't stand vodka martinis."

"Neither can I," he said glumly.

"And I don't get a kick out of prancing around, a stuffed shirt among fellow stuffed shirts, at some goings-on that supposedly improves my culture status."

Larry said "At the house I have every known brand of drinkable, and a stack of ... what did you call it? ... corny music. We can mix our own drinks and dance all by ourselves."

She tucked her head to one side and looked at him suspiciously. "Are your intentions honorable?"

"We can even discuss that later," he said sourly.

She laughed. "It's a date, Larry."

* * * * *

He picked her up after work, and they drove to his Brandywine auto-bungalow, largely quiet the whole way.

At one point she touched his hand with hers and said, "It'll work out, Larry."

"Yeah," he said sourly. "I've put ten years into ingratiating myself with the Boss. Now, overnight, he's got a new boy. I suppose there's some moral involved."

When they pulled up before his auto-bungalow, LaVerne whistled appreciatively. "Quite a neighborhood you're in."

He grunted. "A good address. What our friend Professor Voss would call one more status symbol, one more social-label. For it I pay about fifty per cent more rent than my budget can afford."

He ushered her inside and took her jacket. "Look," he said, indicating his living room with a sweep of hand. "See that volume of Klee reproductions there next to my reading chair? That proves I'm not a weird. Indicates my culture status. Actually, my appreciation of modern art doesn't go any further than the Impressionists. But don't tell anybody. See those books up on my shelves. Same thing. You'll find everything there that *ought* to be on the shelves of any ambitious young career man."

She looked at him from the side of her eyes. "You're really soured, Larry."

"Come along," he said. "I want to show you something."

He took her down the tiny elevator to his den.

"How hypocritical can you get?" he asked her. "This is where I really live. But I seldom bring anyone here. Wouldn't want to get a reputation as a weird. Sit down, LaVerne, I'll make a drink. How about a Sidecar?"

She sank onto the couch, kicked her shoes off and slipped her feet under her. "I'd love one," she said.

His back to her, he brought brandy and cointreau from his liquor cabinet, lemon and ice from the tiny refrigerator.

"What?" LaVerne said mockingly. "No auto-bar?"

"Upstairs with the rest of the status symbols," Larry grunted.

He put her drink before her and turned and went to the record player.

"In the way of corny music, how do you like that old-timer, Nat Cole?"

"King Cole? Love him," LaVerne said.

The strains of "For All We Know" penetrated the room.

Larry sat down across from her, finished half his drink in one swallow.

"I'm beginning to wonder whether or not this Movement doesn't have something," he said.

She didn't answer that. They sat in silence for a while, appreciating the drink. Nat Cole was singing "The Very Thought of You" now. Larry got up and made two more cocktails. This time he sat next to her. He leaned his head back on the couch and closed his eyes.

Finally he said softly, "When Steve Hackett and I were questioning Susan, there was only one other person who knew that we'd picked her up. There was only one person other than Steve and me who could have warned Ernest Self to make a getaway. Later on, there was only one person who could have warned Frank Nostrand so that he and the Professor could find a new hideout."

She said sleepily, "How long have you known about that, darling?"

"A while," Larry said, his own voice quiet. "I figured it out when I also decided how Susan Self was spirited out of the Greater Washington Hilton, before we had the time to question her further. Somebody who had access to tapes made of me while I was making phone calls cut out a section and dubbed in a voice so that Betsy Hughes, the Secret Service matron who was watching Susan, was fooled into believing it was I ordering the girl to be turned over to the two Movement members who came to get her."

LaVerne stirred comfortably and let her head sink onto his shoulder. "You're so warm and ... comfortable," she said.

Larry said softly, "What does the Movement expect to do with all that counterfeit money, LaVerne?"

She stirred against his shoulder, as though bothered by the need to talk. "Give it all away," she said. "Distribute it all over the country and destroy the nation's social currency."

It took him a long moment to assimilate that.

"What have the rockets to do with it?"

She stirred once again, as though wishing he'd be silent. "That's how it will be distributed. About twenty rockets, strategically placed, each with a *warhead* of a couple of tons of money. Fired to an altitude of a couple of hundred miles and then the money is spewed out. In falling, it will be distributed over cities and countryside, everywhere. Billions upon billions of dollars worth."

Larry said, so softly as hardly to be heard, "What will that accomplish?"

"Money is the greatest social-label of them all. The Professor believes that through this step the Movement will have accomplished its purpose. That people will be forced to utilize their judgment, rather than depend upon social-labels."

Larry didn't follow that, but he had no time to go further now. He said, still evenly soft, "And when is the Movement going to do this?"

La Verne moved comfortably. "The trucks go out to distribute the money tonight. The rockets are waiting. The firing will take place in a few days."

"And where is the Professor now?"

"Where the money and the trucks are hidden, darling. What difference does it make?" LaVerne said sleepily.

"And where is that?"

"At the Greater Washington Trucking Corporation. It's owned by one of the Movement's members."

He said. "There's a password. What is it?"

"Judgment."

Larry Woolford bounced to his feet. He looked down at her, then over at the phone. In three quick steps he was over to it. He grasped its wires and yanked them from the wall, silencing it. He slipped into the tiny elevator, locking the door to the den behind him.

As the door slid closed, her voice wailed, still sleepily husky, "Larry, darling, where are you —"

He ran down the walk of the house, vaulted into the car and snapped on its key. He slammed down the lift lever, kicked the thrust pedal and was thrown back against the seat by the acceleration.

Even while he was climbing, he flicked on the radio-phone, called Personal Service for the location of the Greater Washington Trucking Corporation.

Fifteen minutes later, he parked a block away from his destination, noting with satisfaction that it was still an hour or more to go until dark. His intuition, working doubletime now, told him that they'd probably wait until nightfall to start their money-laden trucks to rolling.

He hesitated momentarily before turning on the phone and dialing the Boss' home address.

When the other's face faded in, it failed to display pleasure when the caller's identity was established. His superior growled, "Confound it, Woolford, you know my privacy is to be respected. This phone is to be used only in extreme emergency."

"Yes, sir," Larry said briskly. "It's the Movement —"

The other's face darkened still further. "You're not on that assignment any longer, Woolford. Walter Foster has taken over and I'm sympathetic to his complaints that you've proven more a hindrance than anything else."

Larry ignored his words, "Sir, I've tracked them down. Professor Voss is at the Greater Washington Trucking Corporation garages here in the Alexandria section of town. Any moment now, they're going to start distribution of all that counterfeit money on some scatterbrain plan to disrupt the country's exchange system."

Suddenly alert, the department chief snapped, "Where are you, Woolford?"

"Outside the garages, sir. But I'm going in now."

"You stay where you are," the other snapped. "I'll have every department man and every Secret Service man in town over there within twenty minutes. You hang on. Those people are lunatics, and probably desperate."

Inwardly, Larry Woolford grinned. He wasn't going to lose this opportunity to finish up the job with him on top. He said flatly, "Sir, we can't chance it. They might escape. I'm going in!" He flicked off the set, dialed again and raised Sam Sokolski.

"Sam," he said, his voice clipped. "I've cornered the Movement's leader and am going in for the finish. Maybe some of you journalist boys better get on over here." He gave the other the address and flicked off before there were any questions.

From the dash compartment he brought a heavy automatic, and checked the clip. He put it in his hip pocket and left the car and walked toward the garages. Time was running out now.

He strode into the only open door, without shift of pace. Two men were posted nearby, neither of them truckmen by appearance. They looked at him in surprise.

Larry clipped out, "The password is *Judgment*. I've got to see Professor Voss immediately."

One of them frowned questioningly, but the other was taken up with the urgency in Woolford's voice. He nodded with his head. "He's over there in the office."

Now ignoring them completely, Larry strode past the long rows of sealed delivery vans toward the office.

He pushed the door open, entered and closed it behind him.

Professor Peter Voss was seated at a paper-littered desk. There was a cot with an army blanket in a corner of the room, some soiled clothing and two or three dirty dishes on a tray. The room was being lived in, obviously.

At the agent's entry, the little man looked up and blinked in distress through his heavy lenses.

Larry snapped, "You're under arrest, Voss."

The professor was obviously dismayed, but he said in as vigorous a voice as he could muster, "Nonsense! On what charge?"

"Counterfeiting, among many. Your whole scheme has fallen apart, Voss. You and your Movement, so-called, are finished."

The professor's eyes darted, left, right. To Larry Woolford's surprise, the Movement's leader was alone in here. Undoubtedly, he was awaiting others, drivers of the trucks, technicians involved in the rockets, other subordinates. But right now he was alone.

If Woolford correctly diagnosed the situation, Voss was playing for time, waiting for the others. Good enough, so was Larry Woolford. Had the Professor only known it, a shout would have brought at least two followers and the government agent would have had his work cut out for him.

Woodford played along. "Just what is this fantastic scheme of yours for raining down money over half the country, Voss? The very insanity of it proves your whole outfit is composed of a bunch of nonconformist weirds."

The Professor was indignant-and stalling for time. He said, "Nonconformists is correct! He who conforms in an incompetent society is an incompetent himself."

Larry stood, his legs apart and hands on hips. He shook his head in simulated pity at the angry little man. "What's all this about raining money down over the country?"

"Don't you see?" the other said. "The perfect method for disrupting our present system of social-labels. With billions of dollars, perfect counterfeit, strewing the streets, the fields, the trees, available for anyone to pick up, all social currency becomes worthless. Utterly unusable. And it's no use to attempt to print more with another design, because we can duplicate it as well. Our experts are the world's best, we're not a group of sulking criminals but capable, trained, dedicated men.

"Very well! We will have made it absolutely impossible to have any form of mass-produced social currency."

Larry stared at him. "It would completely foul the whole business system! You'd have chaos!"

"At first. Private individuals, once the value of money was seen to be zero, would have lost the amount of cash they had on hand. But banks and such institutions would lose little. They have accurate records that show the actual values they held at the time our money rains down."

Larry was bewildered. "But what are you getting at? What do you expect to accomplish?"

The Professor, on his favorite subject, said triumphantly, "The only form of currency that can be used under these conditions is the *personal* check. It's not mass produced, and mass-production can't duplicate it. It's immune to the attack. Business has to go on, or people will starve-so personal checks will have to replace paper money. Credit cards and traveler's checks won't do-we can counterfeit them, too, and will, if necessary. Realize of course that hard money will still be valid, but it can't be utilized practically for any but small transactions. Try taking enough silver dollars to buy a refrigerator down to the store with you."

"But what's the purpose?" Larry demanded, flabbergasted.

"Isn't it obvious? Our whole Movement is devoted to the destruction of social-label judgments. It's all very well to say: *You should not judge your fellow men* but when it comes to accepting another man's personal check, friend, you damn well have to! The bum check artist might have a field day to begin with-but only to begin with."

Larry shook his head in exasperation. "You people are a bunch of anarchists," he accused.

"No," the Professor denied. "Absolutely not. We are the antithesis of the anarchist. The anarchist says, 'No man is capable of judging another.' We say, 'Each man must judge his fellow, must demand proper evaluation of him.' To judge a man by his clothes, the amount of money he owns, the car he drives, the neighborhood in which he lives, or the society he keeps, is out of the question in a vital culture."

Larry said sourly, "Well, whether or not you're right, Voss, you've lost. This place is surrounded. My men will be breaking in shortly."

Voss laughed at him. "Nonsense. All you've done is prevent us from accomplishing this portion of our program. What will you do after my arrest? You'll bring me to trial. Do you remember the Scopes' Monkey Trial back in the 1920s which became a world appreciated farce and made Tennessee a laughingstock? Well, just wait until you get *me* into court backed by my organization's resources. We'll bring home to every thinking person, not only in this country, but in the world, the fantastic qualities of our existing culture. Why, Mr.-Secret-Agent-of-Anti-Subversive-Activity you aren't doing me an injury by giving me the opportunity to have my day in court. You're doing me a favor. Newspapers, radios, TriD will give me the chance to expound my program in the home of every thinking person in the world."

There was a fiery dedication in the little man's eyes. "This will be my victory, not my defeat!"

There were sounds now, coming from the other rooms-the garages. Some shouts and scuffling. Faintly, Larry Woolford could hear Steve Hackett's voice.

He was staring at the Professor, his eyes narrower.

The Professor was on his feet. He said in defiant triumph, "You think that you'll win prestige and honor as a result of tracking the Movement down, don't you, Mr. Woolford? Well, let me tell you, you won't! In six months from now, Mr. Woolford, you'll be a laughingstock."

That did it.

Larry said, "You're under arrest. Turn around with your back to me."

The Professor snorted his contempt, turned his back and held up his hands, obviously expecting to be searched.

In a fluid motion, Larry Woolford drew his gun and fired twice. The other with no more than a grunt of surprise and pain, stumbled forward to his knees and then to the floor, his arms and legs akimbo.

The door broke open and Steve Hackett, gun in hand, burst in.

"Woolford!" he barked. "What's up?"

Larry indicated the body on the floor. "There you are, Steve," he said. "The head of the counterfeit ring. He was trying to escape. I had to shoot him."

Behind Steve Hackett crowded Ben Ruthenberg of the F.B.I. and behind him half a dozen others of various departments.

The Boss came pushing his way through.

He glared down at the Professor's body, then up at Larry Woolford.

"Good work, Lawrence," he said. "How did you bring it off?"

Larry replaced the gun in his holster and shrugged modestly. "The Polk girl gave me the final tip-off, sir. I gave her some Scop-Serum in a drink and she talked. Evidently, she was a member of the Movement."

The Boss was nodding wisely. "I've had my eye on her, Lawrence. An obvious weird. But we will have to suppress that Scop-Serum angle." He slapped his favorite field man on the arm jovially. "Well, boy, this means promotion, of course."

Larry grinned. "Thanks, sir. All in a day's work. I don't think we'll have much trouble with the remnants of this Movement thing. The pitch is to treat them as counterfeiters, not subversives. Try them for that. Their silly explanations of what they were going to do with the money will never be taken seriously." He looked down at the small corpse. "Particularly now that their kingpin is gone."

A new wave of agents, F.B.I. men and prisoners washed into the room and Steve Hackett and Larry were for a moment pushed back into a corner by themselves.

Steve looked at him strangely and said, "There's one thing I'd like to know: Did you really have to shoot him, Woolford?"

Larry brushed it off. "What's the difference? He was as weird as they come, wasn't he?"

Dogfight – 1973

My radar picked him up when he was about five hundred miles to my north-northeast and about forty-five miles above me. I switched the velocity calculator on him as fast as I could reach it.

The enemy ship was doing sixteen, possibly even sixteen and a half. I took the chance that it was most likely an Ivar Interceptor, at that speed, and punched out a temporary evasion pattern with my right hand while with my left I snapped an Ivar K-12 card into my calculator along with his estimated speed, altitude and distance. It wasn't much to go on as yet but he couldn't have much more on me, if as much; inwardly I congratulated myself on the quick identification I'd managed.

He was near enough now for my visor screen to pick him up. At least he was alone, that was something. My nearest squadron mate was a good minute and a half away. It might as well have been a century.

Now, this is what is always hard to get over to a civilian; the time element. Understand, it will take me a while to tell this but it all took less than sixty seconds to happen.

He had guessed my evasion pattern already-either guessed it or had some new calculator that was far and beyond anything our techs were turning out. I could tell he'd anticipated me by the Bong-Sonic roll he slipped into.

I quickly punched up a new pattern based on the little material I had in the calculator. At least I'd caught the roll. I punched that up, hurriedly, slipped it into the IBM, guessed that his next probability was a pass, took a chance on that and punched it in.

I was wrong there. He didn't take his opportunity for a front-on pass. He was either newly out of their academy or insultingly confident. My lips felt tight as I canceled the frontal pass card, punched up two more to take its place.

The base supervisor cut in on the phone. "It looks like old Dmitri himself, Jerry, and he's flying one of the new K-12a models. Go get him, boy!"

I felt like snapping back. He knew better than to break in on me at a time like this. I opened my mouth, then shut it again. Did he say K-12a? *Did he say K-12a?*

I squinted at the visor screen. The high tail, the canopy, the oddly shaped wing tanks.

I'd gone off on the identification!

I slapped another evasion pattern into the controls, a standard set, I had no time to punch up an improvisation. But he was on me like a wasp. I rejected it, threw in another set. Reject. Another!

Even as I worked, I kicked the release on my own calculator, dumped it all, selected like a flash an Ivar K-12a card, and what other estimations I could make while my mind was busy with the full-time job of evasion.

My hands were still making the motions, my fingers were flicking here, there, my feet touching here, there. But my heart wasn't in it.

He already had such an advantage that it was all I could do to keep him in my visor screen. He was to the left, to the right. I got him for a full quarter-second in the wires, but the auto gunner was too far behind, much too far.

His own guns flicked red.

I punched half a dozen buttons, slapped levers, tried to scoot for home.

To the left of my cubicle two lights went yellowish and at the same time my visor screen went dead. I was blind.

I sank back in my chair, helpless.

* * * * *

The speed indicator wavered, went slowly, deliberately to zero; the altimeter died; the fuel gauge. Finally, even the dozen or so trouble-indicators here, there, everywhere about the craft. Fifteen million dollars worth of warcraft was being shot into wreckage.

I sat there for a long, long minute and took it.

Then I got to my feet and wearily opened the door of my cubicle. Sergeant Walters and the rest of the maintenance crew were standing there. They could read in my face what had happened.

The sergeant began, "Captain, I..."

I grunted at him. "Never mind, Sergeant. It had nothing to do with the ship's condition." I turned to head for the operations office.

Bill Dickson strolled over from the direction of his own cubicle. "Somebody said you just had a scramble with old Dmitri himself."

"I don't know," I said. "I don't know if it was him or not. Maybe some of you guys can tell a man's flying but I can't."

He grinned at me. "Shot you down, eh?"

I didn't answer.

He said, "What happened?"

"I thought it was an Ivar K-12, and I put that card in my calculator. Turned out it was one of those new models, K-12a. That was enough, of course."

Bill grinned at me again. "That's two this week. That flak got you near that bridge and now you get..."

"Shut up," I told him.

He counted up on his fingers elaborately. "The way I figure it, you lose one more ship and you're an enemy ace."

He was irrepressible. "Damn it," I said, "will you cut it out! I've got enough to worry about without you working me over. This means I'll have to spend another half an hour in operations going over the fight. And that means I'll be late for dinner again. And you know Molly."

Bill sobered. "Gee," he said, "I'm sorry. War is hell, isn't it?"

CAESAR HAD THE SAME PROBLEM AND NEVER SOLVED IT. LORD HELP US IF IT JUST CAN'T BE DONE!

Alexander the Great had not dreamed of India, nor even Egypt, when he embarked upon his invasion of the Persian Empire. It was not a matter of being like the farmer: "I ain't selfish, all I want is the land that jines mine." It was simply that after regaining the Greek cities of Asia Minor from Darius, he could not stop. He could not afford to have powerful neighbors that might threaten his domains tomorrow. So he took Egypt, and the Eastern Satrapies, and then had to continue to India. There he learned of the power of Cathay, but an army mutiny forestalled him and he had to return to Babylon. He died there while making plans to attack Arabia, Carthage, Rome. You see, given the military outlook, he could not afford powerful neighbors on his borders; they might become enemies some day.

Alexander had not been the first to be faced with this problem, nor was he the last. So it was later with Rome, and later with Napoleon, and later still with Adolf the Aryan, and still later —

It isn't travel that is broadening, stimulating, or educational. Not the traveling itself. Visiting new cities, new countries, new continents, or even new planets, *yes*. But the travel itself, *no*. Be it by the methods of the Twentieth Century-automobile, bus, train, or aircraft-or be it by spaceship, travel is nothing more than boring.

Oh, it's interesting enough for the first few hours, say. You look out the window of your car, bus, train, or airliner, or over the side of your ship, and it's very stimulating. But after that first period it becomes boring, monotonous, sameness to the point of redundance.

And so it is in space.

Markham Gray, free lance journalist for more years than he would admit to, was en route from the Neptune satellite Triton to his home planet, Earth, mistress of the Solar System. He was seasoned enough as a space traveler to steel himself against the monotony with cards and books, with chess problems and wire tapes, and even with an attempt to do an article on the distant earthbase from which he was returning for the *Spacetraveler Digest*.

When all these failed, he sometimes spent a half hour or so staring at the vision screen which took up a considerable area of one wall of the lounge.

Unless you had a vivid imagination of the type which had remained with Markham Gray down through the years, a few minutes at a time would have been enough. With rare exception, the view on the screen seemed almost like a still; a velvety blackness with pin-points of brilliant light, unmoving, unchanging.

But even Markham Gray, with his ability to dream and to discern that which is beyond, found himself twisting with ennui after thirty minutes of staring at endless space. He wished that there was a larger number of passengers aboard. The half-dozen businessmen and their women and children had left him cold and he was doing his best to avoid them. Now, if there had only been one good chess player —

Co-pilot Bormann was passing through the lounge. He nodded to the distinguished elderly passenger, flicked his eyes quickly, professionally, over the vision screen and was about to continue on his way.

Gray called idly, "Hans, I thought the space patrols very seldom got out here."

"Practically never, sir," the other told him politely, hesitating momentarily. Part of the job was to be constantly amiable, constantly watchful of the passengers out here in deep space-they came down with space cafard at the drop of a hat. Markham Gray reminded Bormann of pictures of Benjamin Franklin he'd seen in history books, and ordinarily he didn't mind spending a little time now and then talking things over with him. But right now he was hoping the old duffer wasn't going to keep him from the game going on forward with Captain Post and the steward.

"Just noticed one on the screen," the elderly journalist told him easily.

The co-pilot smiled courteously. "You must have seen a meteorite, sir. There aren't any —"

Markham Gray flushed. "I'm not as complete a space neophyte as your condescending air would indicate, Lieutenant. As a matter of fact, I'll stack my space-months against yours any day."

Bormann said soothingly, "It's not that, sir. You've just made a mistake. If a ship was within reasonable distance, the alarms would be sounding off right now. But that's not all, either. We have a complete record of any traffic within a considerable distance, and I assure you that —"

Markham Gray pointed a finger at the lower left hand corner of the screen. "Then what is that, Lieutenant?" he asked sarcastically.

The smile was still on the co-pilot's face as he turned and followed the direction of the other's finger. The smile faded. "I'll be a *makron*!" he blurted. Spinning on his heel, he hurried forward to the bridge, muttering as he went.

The older man snorted with satisfaction. Actually, he shouldn't have been so snappy with the young man; he hated to admit he was growing cranky with age. He took up his half completed manuscript again. He really should finish this article, though, space knew, he hadn't enough material for more than a few paragraphs. Triton was a barren satellite if he'd ever seen one-and he had.

He had almost forgotten the matter ten minutes later when the ship's public address system blurted loudly.

BATTLE STATIONS! BATTLE STATIONS! ALL CREW MEMBERS TO EMER-GENCY STATIONS. ALL PASSENGERS IMMEDIATELY TO THEIR QUARTERS. BATTLE STATIONS!

Battle Stations?

Markham Gray was vaguely familiar with the fact that every Solar System spacecraft was theoretically a warcraft in emergency, but it was utterly fantastic that —

He heaved himself to his feet, grunting with the effort, and, disregarding the repeated command that passengers proceed to their quarters, made his way forward to the bridge, ignoring the hysterical confusion in passengers and crew members hurrying up and down the ship's passageways.

It was immediately obvious, there at the craft's heart, that this was no farce, at least not a deliberate one. Captain Roger Post, youthful officer in command of the *Neuve Los Angeles*, Lieutenant Hans Bormann and the two crew members on watch were white-faced and shaken, momentarily confused in a situation which they had never expected to face. The two officers stood before the bridge vision screen watching, wide-eyed, that sector of space containing the other vessel. They had enlarged it a hundred-fold.

At the elderly journalist's entrance, the skipper had shot a quick, irritated glance over his shoulder and had begun to snap something; he cut it off. Instead, he said, "When did you first sight the alien ship, Mr. Gray?"

"*Alien?*"

"Yes, alien. When did you first sight it? It is obviously following us in order to locate our home planet." There was extreme tension in the captain's voice.

Markham Gray felt cold fingers trace their way up his back. "Why, why, I must have noticed it several hours ago, Captain. But ... an *alien*!... I...." He peered at the enlarged craft on the screen. "Are you sure, Captain? It seems remarkably like our own. I would say —"

The captain had spun back around to stare at the screen again, as though to reassure himself of what he had already seen.

"There are no other ships in the vicinity," he grated, almost as though to himself. "Besides that, as far as I know, and I should know, there are no Earth craft that look exactly like that. There are striking similarities, I'll admit, to our St. Louis class scouts, but those jets on the prow-there's nothing like them either in existence or projected."

His voice rose in an attempt to achieve decisiveness, "Lieutenant Bormann, prepare to attack."

Suddenly, the telviz blared.

Calling the Neuve Los Angeles. Calling the Neuve Los Angeles. Be unafraid. We are not hostile.

There was quiet on the bridge of the earth ship. Screaming quiet. It was seemingly hours before they had recovered even to the point of staring at one another.

Hans Bormann gasped finally, unbelievingly, "How could they possibly know the name of our ship? How could they possibly know the Amer-English language?"

The captain's face was white and frozen. He said, so quietly that they could hardly make it out, "That's not all. Our alarms still haven't been touched off, and our estimators aren't functioning; we don't know how large they are nor how far away. It's unheard of—.Somehow they've completely disrupted our instruments."

* * * * *

Markham Gray followed the matter with more than average interest, after their arrival at the New Albuquerque spaceport. Not that average interest wasn't high.

Finally man had come in contact with another intelligence. He had been dreading it, fearing it, for decades; now it was here. Another life form had conquered space, and, seemingly, had equipment, in some respects at least, superior to humanity's.

The court martial of Captain Roger Post had been short and merciless. Free access to the trial had been given to the press and telviz systems, and the newscasts had carried it in its entirety, partially to stress to the public mind the importance of the situation, and partially as a warning to other spacemen.

Post had stood before the raised dais upon which were seated SupSpaceCom Michell and four other high-ranking officers and heard the charge read-failure to attack the alien craft, destroy it, and thus prevent the aliens-wherever they might be from-returning to their own world and reporting the presence of man in the galaxy.

Markham Gray, like thousands of others, had sat on the edge of his chair in the living room of his small suburban home, and followed the trial closely on his telviz.

SupSpaceCom Michell had been blunt and ruthless. He had rapped out, bitingly, "Roger Post, as captain of the *Neuve Los Angeles*, why did you not either destroy the alien craft, or, if you felt it too strong for your ship, why did you not blast off into space, luring it away from your home planet?"

Post said hesitantly, "I didn't think it necessary, sir. His attitude was-well, of peace. It was as if we were two ships that had met by chance and dipped their flags in the old manner and passed on to their different destinations. They even were able to telviz us a message."

The SupSpaceCom snapped, "That was undoubtedly a case of telepathy. The alien is equipped in some manner to impose thoughts upon the human brain. You *thought* the telviz was used; actually the alien wasn't speaking Amer-English, he was simply forcing thoughts into your minds."

Markham Gray, watching and listening to this over his set, shook his head in dissatisfaction. As always, the military mind was dull and unreceptive. The ridiculousness of expecting Post to blast off into space in an attempt to fool the other craft in regard to his home planet was obvious. The whole affair had taken place within the solar system; obviously the alien would know that one of Sol's nine major planets was mankind's home. Finding out which one wouldn't be too difficult a job.

Roger Post was saying hesitantly, "Then it is assumed that the alien craft wasn't friendly?"

SupSpaceCom Michell indicated his disgust with an impatient flick of his hand. "Any alien is a potential enemy, Post; that should be elementary. And a potential enemy is an enemy in fact. Even though these aliens might seem amiable enough today, how do we know they will be in the future-possibly in the far future? There can be no friendship with aliens. We can't afford to have neighbors; we can't afford to be encircled by enemies."

"Nor even friends?" Captain Post had asked softly.

Michell glared at his subordinate. "That is what it amounts to, Captain; and the thing to remember is that they feel the same way. They must! They must seek us out and destroy us completely and as quickly as possible. By the appearance of things, and partially through your negligence, they've probably won the first round. They know our location; we don't know theirs."

The supreme commander of Earth's space forces dropped that point. "Let us go back again. When you received this telepathic message-or whatever it was-what was your reaction? Did it seem friendly, domineering, or what?"

Roger Post stood silent for a moment. Finally he answered, "Sir, I still think it was the telviz, rather than a telepathic communication, but the ... the tone of voice seemed to give me the impression of pitying."

"Pitying!" Michell ejaculated.

The captain was nervous but determined. "Yes, sir. I had the distinct feeling that the being that sent the message felt sorry for us."

The SupSpaceCom's face had gone red with indignation.

* * * * *

It was three years before another of the aliens was sighted. Three hurried, crowded, harassed years during which all the Solar System's resources were devoted to building and arming a huge space fleet and rushing space defenses. The total wars of the Twentieth Century paled in comparison to the all out efforts made to prepare for this conflict.

The second view of the alien ship was similar to the first. This, time the *Pendleton*, a four-man scout returning to the Venus base after a patrol in the direction of Sirius, held the intruder in its viewer for a full five minutes. Once again, no estimation of its distance nor size could be made. All instruments pertaining to such detection seemed to fail to function properly.

And again the alien had sent a message-seemingly, at least, by telviz. *We are no danger to you, mankind. Seek your destiny in peace. Your troubles are from within.*

The *Pendleton* would have attempted to follow the strange craft, but her fuel tanks were nearly dry and she had to proceed to Venus. Her captain's report made a sensation.

In a way, the whole business had been a good thing for Markham Gray. As a free lancing journalist, he'd had a considerable advantage. First, he was more than usually informed on space travel and the problems relating to it, second, he had been present at-in fact, had made himself-the first sighting of the aliens.

His articles were in continuous demand in both magazines and newspaper supplements; editors clamored for additional material from his voco-typer. There was but one complaint against his copy-it wasn't alarmist enough, sensational enough. Humanity had been whipped into a state of hysteria, an emotional binge, and humanity loved it.

And it was there that Markham Gray refused to go along. He had agreed with poor Captain Post, now serving a life sentence in the Martian prison camps; there had been no sign of hostility from the alien craft. It was man who was preparing for war-and Gray knew of no period in history in which preparations for war did not eventually culminate in one.

So it was not really strange that it was he the aliens chose to contact.

It came in the early hours of the morning. He awakened, not without a chill of fear, the sound of his telviz set in his ears. He had left it turned off, he knew that. He shook his head to clear it, impatient of the fact that with advancing years it was taking an increasing time to become alert after sleep.

He had not caught the message. For a brief moment he thought the sound had been a dream. Then the telviz spoke again. The screen was blank. It said, *You are awake, Mr. Gray?*

He stared at it, uncomprehending.

He said, "I ...I don't understand." Then, suddenly, he did understand, as though by an inspired revelation. Why they were able to speak Amer-English. Why their ship looked like a Terran one. Why they had been able to 'disrupt' the Earth ships instruments.

He said haltingly, "Why are you here?"

We are familiar with your articles. You alone, Mr. Gray, seem at least to seek understanding. Before we left, we felt it our duty to explain our presence and our purpose-that is, partially.

"Yes," he said. Then, in an attempt to check the conclusion at which he had just arrived, he added, "You are going from the Solar System-leaving your home for a new one?"

There was a long silence.

Finally: *As we said, we were going to explain partially our presence and purpose, but obviously you know more than we had thought. Would you mind revealing the extent of your knowledge?*

Gray reached to the foot of the bed and took up his night robe; partly because it was chilly, partly to give himself time to consider his answer. Perhaps he shouldn't have said that. He was alone in this small house; he had no knowledge of their intentions toward him.

But he had gone too far now. He said, "Not at all. I am not sure of where we stand, but things should be much clearer, shortly. First of all, your spaceships are tiny. Probably less than ten pounds."

About four, Mr. Gray.

"Which explains why our instruments did not record them; the instruments weren't disrupted, your ships were really too small to register. That's where we made our first mistake. We assumed, for no valid reason, that you were approximately our own size. We were willing to picture you as non-human and possessing limbs, organs, and even senses different from ours; but we have pictured 'aliens', as we've been calling you, as approximately our own size. Actually, you must be quite tiny."

Quite tiny, Markham Gray. Although, of course, the way we think of it is that you are quite huge.

He was becoming more confident now; widely awake, it was less strange to hear the words come from his commonplace home model telviz set. "Our second mistake was in looking for you throughout space," he said softly.

There was hesitation again, then, *And why was that a mistake, Markham Gray?*

Gray wet his lips. He might be signing his death warrant, but he couldn't stop now. "Because you are not really 'aliens,' but of Earth itself. Several facts point that way. For instance, your ships are minute models of Earth ships, or, rather, of human ships. You have obviously copied them. Then, too, you have been able to communicate with humans too easily. An alien to our world would have had much more trouble. Our ways, our methods of thinking, are not strange to you."

You have discovered a secret which has been kept for many centuries, Markham Gray.

He was more at ease now; somehow there was no threat in the attitude of the other. Gray said, "The hardest thing for me to understand is why it *has* been kept a secret. Obviously, you are a tiny form of Earth life, probably an insect, which has progressed intellectually as far beyond other insect forms as man beyond other mammals. Why have you kept this a secret from humans?"

You should be able to answer that yourself, Mr. Gray. As we developed, we were appalled by the only other form of life on our planet with a developed intelligence. Why, not even your own kind is safe from your bloodlust. The lesser animals on Earth have been either enslaved by man-or slaughtered to extinction. And even your fellows in the recent past were butchered; man killed man wholesale. Do you blame us for keeping our existence a secret? We knew that the day humans discovered there was another intelligence on Earth they would begin making plans to dominate or, even more likely, to destroy us. Our only chance was to find some refuge away from Earth. That is why we began to search the other stars for a planet similar to this and suitable to our form of life.

"You could have fought back, had we attempted to destroy you," Gray said uncomfortably.

The next words were coldly contemptuous. *We are not wanton killers, like man. We have no desire to destroy.*

Gray winced and changed the subject. "You have found your new planet?"

At last. We are about to begin transportation of our population to the new world. For the first time since our ancestors became aware of the awful presence of man on the Earth, we feel that we can look forward to security.

Markham Gray remained quiet for a long time. "I am still amazed that you were able to develop so far without our knowledge," he said finally.

There was an edge of amusement in the answering thought. *We are very tiny, Mr. Gray. And our greatest efforts have always been to keep from under man's eyes. We have profited greatly, however, by our suitability to espionage; little goes on in the human world of which we don't know. Our progress was greatly aided by our being able to utilize the science that man has already developed. You've noted, for instance, how similar our space ships are to your own.*

Gray nodded to himself. "But I'm also impressed by the manner in which you have developed some mechanical device to duplicate human speech. That involved original research."

At any rate, neither man nor we need dread the future any longer. We have escaped the danger that overhung us, and you know now that we are no alien enemies from space threatening you. We wish you well, mankind; perhaps the future will see changes in your nature. It is in this friendly hope that we have contacted humanity through you, Mr. Gray.

The elderly journalist said quietly, "I appreciate your thoughtfulness and hope you are correct. Good luck to you in your new world."

Thank you, Markham Gray, and goodbye.

The set was suddenly quiet again.

* * * * *

Markham Gray stood before the assembled Military Council of the Solar System. He had told his story without interruption to this most powerful body on Earth. They listened to him in silence.

When he had finished, he waited for their questions. The first came from SupSpaceCom Michell. He said, thoughtfully, "You believe their words to be substantially correct, Gray?"

"I believe them to be entirely truthful, your excellency," the journalist told him sincerely.

"Then they are on the verge of leaving the Earth and removing to this other planet in some other star system?"

"That is their plan."

The SupSpaceCom mused aloud. "We'll be able to locate them when they blast off en masse. Their single ships are so small that they missed being observed, but a mass flight we'll be able to detect. Our cruisers will be able to follow them all the way, blasting them as they go. If any get through to their new planet, we'll at least know where they are and can take our time destroying it."

The President of the Council added thoughtfully, "Quite correct, Michell. And in the early stages of the fight, we should be able to capture some of their ships intact. As soon as we find what kind of insect they are, our bacteriologists will be able to work on a method to eliminate any that might remain on Earth."

Markham Gray's face had paled in horror. "But why?" he blurted. "Why not let them go in peace? All they've wanted for centuries is to escape us, to have a planet of their own."

SupSpaceCom Michell eyed him tolerantly. "You seem to have been taken in, Mr. Gray. Once they've established themselves in their new world, we have no idea of how rapidly they might develop and how soon they might become a threat. Even though they may be peaceful today, they are potential enemies tomorrow. And a potential enemy *is* an enemy, who must be destroyed."

341

Gray felt sickness well through him "But ... but this policy.... What happens when man finally finds on his borders a life form more advanced than he-an intelligence strong enough to destroy rather than be destroyed?"

The tolerance was gone now. The SupSpaceCom said coldly, "Don't be a pessimistic defeatist, Gray."

He turned to the admirals and generals of his staff. "Make all preparations for the attack, gentlemen."

Off Course

First on the scene were Larry Dermott and Tim Casey of the State Highway Patrol. They assumed they were witnessing the crash of a new type of Air Force plane and slipped and skidded desperately across the field to within thirty feet of the strange craft, only to discover that the landing had been made without accident.

Patrolman Dermott shook his head. "They're gettin' queerer looking every year. Get a load of it-no wheels, no propeller, no cockpit."

They left the car and made their way toward the strange egg-shaped vessel.

Tim Casey loosened his .38 in its holster and said, "Sure, and I'm beginning to wonder if it's one of ours. No insignia and —"

A circular door slid open at that point and Dameri Tass stepped out, yawning. He spotted them, smiled and said, "Glork."

They gaped at him.

"Glork is right," Dermott swallowed.

Tim Casey closed his mouth with an effort. "Do you mind the color of his face?" he blurted. "How could I help it?"

Dameri Tass rubbed a blue-nailed pink hand down his purplish countenance and yawned again. "Gorra manigan horp soratium," he said.

Patrolman Dermott and Patrolman Casey shot stares at each other. "'Tis double talk he's after givin' us," Casey said.

Dameri Tass frowned. "Harama?" he asked.

Larry Dermott pushed his cap to the back of his head. "That doesn't sound like any language I've even *heard* about."

Dameri Tass grimaced, turned and reentered his spacecraft to emerge in half a minute with his hands full of contraption. He held a box-like arrangement under his left arm; in his right hand were two metal caps connected to the box by wires.

While the patrolmen watched him, he set the box on the ground, twirled two dials and put one of the caps on his head. He offered the other to Larry Dermott; his desire was obvious.

Trained to grasp a situation and immediately respond in manner best suited to protect the welfare of the people of New York State, Dermott cleared his throat and said, "Tim, take over while I report."

"Hey!" Casey protested, but his fellow minion had left.

"Mandaia," Dameri Tass told Casey, holding out the metal cap.

"Faith, an' do I look balmy?" Casey told him. "I wouldn't be puttin' that dingus on my head for all the colleens in Ireland."

"Mandaia," the stranger said impatiently.

"Bejasus," Casey snorted, "ye can't —"

Dermott called from the car, "Tim, the captain says to humor this guy. We're to keep him here until the officials arrive."

Tim Casey closed his eyes and groaned. "Humor him, he's after sayin'. Orders it is." He shouted back, "Sure, an' did ye tell 'em he's in technicolor? Begorra, he looks like a man from Mars."

"That's what they think," Larry yelled, "and the governor is on his way. We're to do everything possible short of violence to keep this character here. Humor him, Tim!"

"Mandaia," Dameri Tass snapped, pushing the cap into Casey's reluctant hands.

Muttering his protests, Casey lifted it gingerly and placed it on his head. Not feeling any immediate effect, he said, "There, 'tis satisfied ye are now, I'm supposin'."

The alien stooped down and flicked a switch on the little box. It hummed gently. Tim Casey suddenly shrieked and sat down on the stubble and grass of the field. "Begorra," he yelped, "I've been murthered!" He tore the cap from his head.

His companion came running, "What's the matter, Tim?" he shouted.

Dameri Tass removed the metal cap from his own head. "Sure, an' nothin' is after bein' the matter with him," he said. "Evidently the bhoy has niver been a-wearin' of a kerit helmet afore. 'Twill hurt him not at all."

* * * * *

"You can talk!" Dermott blurted, skidding to a stop.

Dameri Tass shrugged. "Faith, an' why not? As I was after sayin', I shared the kerit helmet with Tim Casey."

Patrolman Dermott glared at him unbelievingly. "You learned the language just by sticking that Rube Goldberg deal on Tim's head?"

"Sure, an' why not?"

Dermott muttered, "And with it he has to pick up the corniest brogue west of Dublin."

Tim Casey got to his feet indignantly. "I'm after resentin' that, Larry Dermott. Sure, an' the way we talk in Ireland is —"

Dameri Tass interrupted, pointing to a bedraggled horse that had made its way to within fifty feet of the vessel. "Now what could that be after bein'?"

The patrolmen followed his stare. "It's a horse. What else?"

"A horse?"

Larry Dermott looked again, just to make sure. "Yeah-not much of a horse, but a horse."

Dameri Tass sighed ecstatically. "And jist what is a horse, if I may be so bold as to be askin'?"

"It's an animal you ride on."

The alien tore his gaze from the animal to look his disbelief at the other. "Are you after meanin' that you climb upon the crature's back and ride him? Faith now, quit your blarney."

He looked at the horse again, then down at his equipment. "Begorra," he muttered, "I'll share the kerit helmet with the crature."

"Hey, hold it," Dermott said anxiously. He was beginning to feel like a character in a shaggy dog story.

Interest in the horse was ended with the sudden arrival of a helicopter. It swooped down on the field and settled within twenty feet of the alien craft. Almost before it had touched, the door was flung open and the flying windmill disgorged two bestarred and efficient-looking Army officers.

Casey and Dermott snapped them a salute.

The senior general didn't take his eyes from the alien and the spacecraft as he spoke, and they bugged quite as effectively as had those of the patrolmen when they'd first arrived on the scene.

"I'm Major General Browning," he rapped. "I want a police cordon thrown up around this, er, vessel. No newsmen, no sightseers, nobody without my permission. As soon as Army personnel arrives, we'll take over completely."

"Yes, sir," Larry Dermott said. "I just got a report on the radio that the governor is on his way, sir. How about him?"

The general muttered something under his breath. Then, "When the governor arrives, let me know; otherwise, nobody gets through!"

Dameri Tass said, "Faith, and what goes on?"

The general's eyes bugged still further. "*He talks!*" he accused.

"Yes, sir," Dermott said. "He had some kind of a machine. He put it over Tim's head and seconds later he could talk."

"Nonsense!" the general snapped.

Further discussion was interrupted by the screaming arrival of several motorcycle patrolmen followed by three heavily laden patrol cars. Overhead, pursuit planes zoomed in and began darting about nervously above the field.

"Sure, and it's quite a reception I'm after gettin'," Dameri Tass said. He yawned. "But what I'm wantin' is a chance to get some sleep. Faith, an' I've been awake for almost a *decal*."

* * * * *

Dameri Tass was hurried, via helicopter, to Washington. There he disappeared for several days, being held incommunicado while White House, Pentagon, State Department and Congress tried to figure out just what to do with him.

Never in the history of the planet had such a furor arisen. Thus far, no newspapermen had been allowed within speaking distance. Administration higher-ups were being subjected to a volcano of editorial heat but the longer the space alien was discussed the more they viewed with alarm the situation his arrival had precipitated. There were angles that hadn't at first been evident.

Obviously he was from some civilization far beyond that of Earth's. That was the rub. No matter what he said, it would shake governments, possibly overthrow social systems, perhaps even destroy established religious concepts.

But they couldn't keep him under wraps indefinitely.

It was the United Nations that cracked the iron curtain. Their demands that the alien be heard before their body were too strong and had too much public opinion behind them to be ignored. The White House yielded and the date was set for the visitor to speak before the Assembly.

Excitement, anticipation, blanketed the world. Shepherds in Sinkiang, multi-millionaires in Switzerland, fakirs in Pakistan, gauchos in the Argentine were raised to a zenith of expectation. Panhandlers debated the message to come with pedestrians; jinrikisha men argued it with their passengers; miners discussed it deep beneath the surface; pilots argued with their co-pilots thousands of feet above.

It was the most universally awaited event of the ages.

By the time the delegates from every nation, tribe, religion, class, color, and race had gathered in New York to receive the message from the stars, the majority of Earth had decided that Dameri Tass was the plenipotentiary of a super-civilization which had been viewing developments on this planet with misgivings. It was thought this other civilization had advanced greatly beyond Earth's and that the problems besetting us-social, economic, scientific-had been solved by the super-civilization. Obviously, then, Dameri Tass had come, an advisor from a benevolent and friendly people, to guide the world aright.

And nine-tenths of the population of Earth stood ready and willing to be guided. The other tenth liked things as they were and were quite convinced that the space envoy would upset their applecarts.

* * * * *

Viljalmar Andersen, Secretary-General of the U.N., was to introduce the space emissary. "Can you give me an idea at all of what he is like?" he asked nervously.

President McCord was as upset as the Dane. He shrugged in agitation. "I know almost as little as you do."

Sir Alfred Oxford protested, "But my dear chap, you've had him for almost two weeks. Certainly in that time —"

The President snapped back, "You probably won't believe this, but he's been asleep until yesterday. When he first arrived he told us he hadn't slept for a *decal*, whatever that is; so we held off our discussion with him until morning. Well-he didn't awaken in the morning, nor the next. Six days later, fearing something was wrong we woke him."

"What happened?" Sir Alfred asked.

The President showed embarrassment. "He used some rather ripe Irish profanity on us, rolled over, and went back to sleep."

Viljalmar Andersen asked, "Well, what happened yesterday?"

"We actually haven't had time to question him. Among other things, there's been some controversy about whose jurisdiction he comes under. The State Department claims the Army shouldn't —"

The Secretary General sighed deeply. "Just what *did* he do?"

"The Secret Service reports he spent the day whistling Mother Machree and playing with his dog, cat and mouse."

"Dog, cat and mouse? I say!" blurted Sir Alfred.

The President was defensive. "He had to have some occupation, and he seems to be particularly interested in our animal life. He wanted a horse but compromised for the others. I understand he insists all three of them come with him wherever he goes."

"I wish we knew what he was going to say," Andersen worried.

"Here he comes," said Sir Alfred.

Surrounded by F.B.I. men, Dameri Tass was ushered to the speaker's stand. He had a kitten in his arms; a Scotty followed him.

The alien frowned worriedly. "Sure," he said, "and what kin all this be? Is it some ordinance I've been after breakin'?"

McCord, Sir Alfred and Andersen hastened to reassure him and made him comfortable in a chair.

Viljalmar Andersen faced the thousands in the audience and held up his hands, but it was ten minutes before he was able to quiet the cheering, stamping delegates from all Earth.

Finally: "Fellow Terrans, I shall not take your time for a lengthy introduction of the envoy from the stars. I will only say that, without doubt, this is the most important moment in the history of the human race. We will now hear from the first being to come to Earth from another world."

He turned and gestured to Dameri Tass who hadn't been paying overmuch attention to the chairman in view of some dog and cat hostilities that had been developing about his feet.

But now the alien's purplish face faded to a light blue. He stood and said hoarsely. "Faith, an' what was that last you said?"

Viljalmar Andersen repeated, "We will now hear from the first being ever to come to Earth from another world."

The face of the alien went a lighter blue. "Sure, an' ye wouldn't jist be frightenin' a body, would ye? You don't mean to tell me this planet isn't after bein' a member of the Galactic League?"

Andersen's face was blank. "Galactic League?"

"Cushlamachree," Dameri Tass moaned. "I've gone and put me foot in it again. I'll be after getting *kert* for this."

Sir Alfred was on his feet. "I don't understand! Do you mean you aren't an envoy from another planet?"

Dameri Tass held his head in his hands and groaned. "An envoy, he's sayin', and meself only a second-rate collector of specimens for the Carthis zoo."

He straightened and started off the speaker's stand. "Sure, an' I must blast off immediately."

Things were moving fast for President McCord but already an edge of relief was manifesting itself. Taking the initiative, he said, "Of course, of course, if that is your desire." He signaled to the bodyguard who had accompanied the alien to the assemblage.

A dull roar was beginning to emanate from the thousands gathered in the tremendous hall, murmuring, questioning, disbelieving.

* * * * *

Viljalmar Andersen felt that he must say something. He extended a detaining hand. "Now you are here," he said urgently, "even though by mistake, before you go can't you give us some brief word? Our world is in chaos. Many of us have lost faith. Perhaps…"

Dameri Tass shook off the restraining hand. "Do I look daft? Begorry, I should have been a-knowin' something was queer. All your weapons and your strange ideas. Faith, I wouldn't be surprised if ye hadn't yet established a planet-wide government. Sure, an' I'll go still further. Ye probably still have wars on this benighted world. No wonder it is ye haven't been invited to join the Galactic League an' take your place among the civilized planets."

He hustled from the rostrum and made his way, still surrounded by guards, to the door by which he had entered. The dog and the cat trotted after, undismayed by the furor about them.

They arrived about four hours later at the field on which he'd landed, and the alien from space hurried toward his craft, still muttering. He'd been accompanied by a general and by the President, but all the way he had refrained from speaking.

He scurried from the car and toward the spacecraft.

President McCord said, "You've forgotten your pets. We would be glad if you would accept them as —"

The alien's face faded a light blue again. "Faith, an' I'd almost forgotten," he said. "If I'd taken a crature from this quarantined planet, my name'd be *nork*. Keep your dog and your kitty." He shook his head sadly and extracted a mouse from a pocket. "An' this amazin' little crature as well."

They followed him to the spacecraft. Just before entering, he spotted the bedraggled horse that had been present on his landing.

A longing expression came over his highly colored face. "Jist one thing," he said. "Faith now, were they pullin' my leg when they said you were after ridin' on the back of those things?"

The President looked at the woebegone nag. "It's a horse," he said, surprised. "Man has been riding them for centuries."

Dameri Tass shook his head. "Sure, an' 'twould've been my makin' if I could've taken one back to Carthis." He entered his vessel.

The others drew back, out of range of the expected blast, and watched, each with his own thoughts, as the first visitor from space hurriedly left Earth.

After Some Tomorrow

Before the first shots rang out, Alan had been sitting with some twenty young people of the Wolf clan in a grove of aspen approximately half way between the fields and the citadel on the hill-top. He had been teaching them myth-legend and, as usual, the girls were bored and unbelieving, the boys open mouthed.

He realized, even as he spoke, that the telling had changed even since his own youth. As a boy of ten, before it was definitely known whether or not he was a sterilie, he had sat at the feet of the Turtle clan's husband as open mouthed as those who sat at his feet now. But the telling was different. Now, had he spoken openly of when men bore weapons and women lived at home with the children, he would have crossed the boundaries of decency. It hadn't been so in his own youth, but then, when he was a boy, they had been one generation nearer to the old days, which weren't so far back after all.

Helen complained, "This is so silly, Alan. Why don't you tell us something about ... well, about hunting, or true fighting?"

He looked at her. Could this be a daughter of his? Tall for her fourteen years and straight, clear of eye, aggressive and brooking of no nonsense. The old books told of the femininity of women, but....

The shots went *bang, bang, bang*, from below, faint in the half mile or more of distance. And then *bang, bang* again and several *booms* from the new muzzle loading muskets.

Helen was on her feet first, her eyes flashing. Instantly she was in command. "Alan," she snapped. "Quick, to the citadel. All of you boys, hurry! To the citadel!"

She whirled to her older classmates. "Ruth, Margo, Jenny, Paula. Get stones, sharp stones. You younger girls go with Alan. See if you can help at the citadel. We'll come last. Hurry Alan."

Alan was already off, herding the boys before him. Possibly all of them were sterilies and so wouldn't count. But you never knew.

As they climbed the hill, he looked back over his shoulder. Down in the fields he could see the workers scattering for their weapons and for cover. One stumbled and was down. In the distance he couldn't make out whether she had fallen accidentally or been wounded. Further beyond the fields he could see the smoke from a half dozen or more places where the shots had originated. It didn't seem to be an attack in force.

Not far up the hill from the field workers, on a overhanging boulder in a lookout position, he could make out Vivian, the scout chief. She sat, seemingly in unconcerned ease, one elbow supported on a knee as her telescoped rifle went *crack, crack, crack*. If he knew Vivian there was more than one casualty among the raiders.

Who could it be this time? Deer from the south, Coyote or Horse from the east? Possibly Eagles, Crows or Dogs from Denver way. The clan couldn't stand much more of this pressure. It was the third raid in six months. They couldn't stand it and put in a crop, nor could the drain on the arsenal be maintained. He had heard that the Turtle clan, near Colorado Springs, the clan of his birth, had got to the point where they were using bows and arrows even for defense. If so, it wouldn't be long before they would be losing their husband.

He was puffing somewhat by the time they reached the citadel. Helen and her four girls were coming much more slowly, watching the progress of the fight below them, keeping their eyes peeled for a possible break through of individual enemies. The stones in their hands were pathetically brave.

The rounded citadel building, stone built, loopholed for rifles, loomed before them. He swung open the door and hurried inside.

"Hello, honey," a strange voice said pseudo-pleasantly. "Hey, you're kind of cute."

Alan's eyes went from the two figures before him, automatic rifles cuddled under their arms, to the two Wolf clan sentries collapsed in their own blood on the floor. They had paid for lack of vigilance with their lives.

He could see that the strangers were of different clans by their kilts, one a Horse the other a Crow. This would mean two clans had united in order to raid the Wolves and that, in turn, would mean the Wolves were outnumbered as much as two to one.

"Relax, darling," the second one said, a lewd quality in her voice. "Nothing's going to happen to *you*." Her eyes took in the dozen boys ranging in age from five to twelve. "Look like a bunch of steriles to me," she sneered. "Get them up above, and those girls too. You stay here where we can watch you, honey."

The Crow went to a small window, stared down below. "Wanda is holding them pretty well but they're beginning to work their way back in this direction." She laughed harshly. "These Wolves never could fight."

Her companion fingered the Bren gun which lay on the heavy table top in the round room's center. Aside from four equally heavily constructed chairs the table was the large room's sole furniture. While Alan was ushering the boys and younger girls up to the second floor where they would be safe, the Horse said musingly, "We could turn this loose on them even at this distance."

The Crow shook her head. "No. It'll be better to wait until they're closer. Besides, by that time Peggy and her group'll be coming up from the arroyo. There won't be a Wolf left half an hour from now."

Alan, his stomach empty, stared out the loophole nearest him.

One of the women said, grinning, "You better get away from there, honey. Make you sick. That's a mighty pretty suit you've got on. Make it yourself?"

"No," Alan said. As a matter of fact one of the steriles had made it.

She laughed. "Well, don't be so uppity. You're going to have to learn how to be nice to me, you know."

Both of them laughed, but Alan said nothing. He wondered how long the women of these clans had been without a husband.

Down below he could make out the progress of the fighting and then realized the battle plan of the aggressors. They must have planned it for months, waiting until the season was such that practically the whole Wolf clan, and particularly the fighters, would be at work in the fields. They'd sent these two scouts, probably their best warriors, to take the citadel by stealth. Only two of them, more would have been conspicuous.

They had then, with a limited force, opened fire on the field workers, pinning them down temporarily.

Meanwhile, the main body was ascending the arroyo to the left, completely hidden from the defending forces although they would have been in open sight from above had the citadel remained uncaptured.

Alan could see plainly what the next fifteen minutes would mean. The Wolf clan would draw back on the citadel, Vivian and her younger warriors bringing up the rear. When they broke into the clear and started the last dash for the safety of their fortress, they would be in the open and at the mercy of the crossfire from arroyo and citadel.

If only these two had failed in their attempt to....

The Crow woman said, "Look at this. Five young brats with stones in their hands. What do you say?"

It was Helen and her four girls.

Alan said, "They're only children! You can't...."

"You be quiet, sweetheart. We can't be bothered with you."

The Horse said, "Two years from now they'll all be warriors. Here, let me turn this on them."

Alan closed his eyes and he wanted to retch as he heard the automatic rifle speak out in five short bursts. In spite of himself he opened them again. Helen, his first born, Paula, his second. Ruth, Margo and Jenny, all his children. They were crumbled like rag dolls, fifty feet from the citadel door.

Now he was able to tell himself that he should have called out a warning. One or two of them, at least, might have escaped. Might have escaped to warn the approaching fighters of the trap behind them. Tradition had been too strong within him, the tradition that a man did not interfere in the business of the warriors, that war was a thing apart.

Jenny's body moved, stirred again, and she tried to drag herself away. Little Jenny, twelve years old. The rifle spat just once again and she slumped forward and remained quiet.

"Little bitch," the Crow woman said.

The heavy chair was in his hands and high above his head, he had brought it down on her before the rage of his hate had allowed him to think of what he was doing. The chair splintered but there was still a good half of it in his hands when he spun on the Horse woman. She stepped back, her eyes wide in disbelief. As her companion went down, the side of her face and her scalp welling blood, the Horse at first brought up her rifle and then, in despair, tried to reverse it to use its butt as a club.

* * * * *

* * * * *

She was stumbling backward, trying to get out of the way of his improvised weapon, when her heel caught on the body of one of the fallen Wolf sentries. She tried to catch herself, her eyes still staring horrified disbelief, even as he caught her over the head, and then once again. He beat her, beat her hysterically, until he knew she must be dead.

He worked now in a mental vacuum, all but unconsciously. He ran to the stair bottom and called, "Come down," his voice was shrill. "Alice, Tommy, all of you."

* * * * *

They came, hesitantly, and when they saw the shambles of the room stared at him with as much disbelief as had the enemy women. He pointed a finger at the oldest of the girls. "Alice," he said, "you've been given instruction by the warriors. How is the Bren gun fired?"

The eleven year old bug eyed at him. "But you're a husband, Alan...."

"How is it fired?" he shrilled. "Unless you tell me, there will be no Wolf clan left!"

He lugged the heavy gun to the window, mounted it there as he had seen the women do in practice.

"Tommy," he said to a thirteen year old boy. "Quick, get me a pan of ammunition."

"I can't," Tommy all but wailed.

"Get it!"

"I can't. It's ... it's *unmanly!*" Tommy melted into a sea of tears, utterly confused.

"Maureen," Alan snapped, cooler now. "Get me a pan of ammunition for the Bren gun. Quickly. Alice, show me how the gun is charged."

Alice was at his side, trying to explain. He would have let her take over had she been larger, but he knew she couldn't handle the bucking of the weapon. Maureen had returned with the ammunition, slipped it expertly into place. She too had had instructions in the gun's operation.

Alan ran his eyes down the arroyo. There were possibly forty of them, Horses and Crows-well armed, he could see. Less than a quarter of them had the new muzzle loaders being resorted to by many as ammunition stocks for the old arms became increasingly rare. The others had ancient arms, rifles, both military and sport, one or two tommy guns.

He waited another three or four minutes, one eye cocked on the progress of the running battle below. Vivian, the scout chief, had dropped back to take over command of the younger warriors. She was probably beginning to smell a rat. The intensity of fire wasn't such as to suggest a large body of enemy.

The women in the arroyo were placed now as he wanted them. He forced himself to keep his eyes open as he pressed the trigger.

Blat, blat, blat.

The gun spoke, kicking high the dust and gravel before the Horse and Crow warriors advancing up the arroyo.

They stopped, startled. The citadel was supposedly in their hands.

They reversed themselves and scurried back to get out of their exposed position.

He touched the trigger again. *Blat, blat, blat.* The heavy slugs tore up the arroyo wall behind them, they could retreat no further without running into his fire.

They stopped, confused.

Alan said, "Maureen, get another pan of ammunition. I'll have to hold them there until Vivian comes up. Alice, run down to the matriarch and tell her about the warriors in the arroyo. Quickly, now."

Little Alice said sourly, "A husband shouldn't interfere in warrior affairs," but she went.

* * * * *

When Vivian strode into the citadel she had her sniper rifle slung over her back and was admiring a tommy gun she had taken from one of the captured Horses. "Perfect," she said, stroking the stock. "Perfect shape. And they seem to have worlds of ammunition too. Must have made some kind of deal with the Denver clans."

Her eyes swept the room and her mouth turned down in sour amusement. The Horse woman was dead and the Crow had by now been marched off to take her place with the other prisoners who were being held in the stone corral.

"What warriors," she said contemptuously. "A *man* overcomes two of them. *Two* of them, mind you." She looked at Alan, the reaction was upon him now and he was white faced and couldn't keep his hands from trembling. "What a cutie you turned out to be. Who ever heard of such a thing?"

Alan said, defensively, "They didn't expect it. I took them unawares."

Vivian laughed aloud, her even white teeth sparkling in the redness of her lips. She was tall, shapely, a twenty-five year old goddess in her Wolf clan kilts. "I'll bet you did, sweetie."

One of the other warriors entered from behind Vivian, looked at the dead Horse woman and shuddered. "What a way to die, not even able to defend yourself." She said to Vivian worriedly, "They've got an awful lot of equipment, chief."

Vivian said, "Well, what're you worrying about, Jean? *We* have it now."

The girl said, "They have three tommy guns, four automatic rifles, twenty grenades and forty sticks of dynamite."

Vivian was impatient. "They had them, now they're ours. It's good, not bad."

Jean said doggedly, "These raids are coming more and more often. We've lost ten fighters in less than a year. And each time they come at us they're better equipped and there're more of them." She looked over at Alan. "If it hadn't been for this … this queer way things worked out, they'd have our husband now and we'd be done for."

"Well, it didn't happen that way," Vivian said abruptly, "and we still have our husband and we're going to keep him. This wasn't a bad action at all. They killed three of us, we've got more than forty of them."

"Not three, eight," Jean said. "You forget the five girls. In another couple of years they'd have been warriors. And besides, what difference does it make if we've got forty of them? There're always more of them where they came from. There must be a thousand women toward Denver without a husband between them."

Vivian quieted. "Let's hope they don't all decide on Alan at once," she said. "I wonder if the Turtles are having the same trouble."

"They're having more," Alan said. He had lowered himself wearily into one of the chairs.

The two warriors looked at him. "How do you know, sweetie?" Vivian asked him.

"I was talking to Warren, a few weeks ago. He's husband of the Turtle clan now, they traded him from the Foxes. Both clans were getting too interbred…."

"Get to the point, honey," Jean said, embarrassed at this man talk.

"The Turtles are having more trouble than we are. They have a stronger natural fortress at the center of their farm lands, but they've had so many raids that their arsenal is depleted and half their warriors dead or wounded. They're getting desperate."

"That's too bad," Vivian muttered. "They make good neighbors."

Jean said, "The matriarch told me to let you know there'd be a meeting this afternoon in the assembly hall. Clan meeting, all present."

"What about?" Vivian said, her attention going back to the beauty of her captured weapon again.

"About the prisoners. We've got to decide what to do with them."

"Do with them? We'll push them over the side of the canyon. Nobody thought we'd waste bullets on them did they?"

Alan said, mildly, "The question has come up whether we ought to destroy them at all."

Vivian looked at him in gentle annoyance. "Sweetie," she said, "don't bother your handsome head with these things. You've had enough excitement to last a nice looking fellow like you a lifetime."

Jean said, echoing her chief's disgust, "Anyway, that's what the meeting is about. Alan, here, has been talking to the matriarch and she's agreed to bring it up for discussion."

Vivian said nastily, "Sally is beginning to lose her grip. If there's anything a clan needs it's a strong matriarch."

"A wise matriarch," Alan amended, knowing he shouldn't.

Vivian stared at him for a moment, then threw her head back and laughed. "I'm going to have to spank your bottom one of these days," she told him. "You get awfully sassy for a man."

* * * * *

As chairman, Alan had a voice but not a vote in the meetings of the Wolf clan. He sometimes wondered at the institution which had come down from pre-bomb days. Why was it necessary to have a chair*man*. Of course, myth-legend had it that men were once just as numerous and active in society's economic (and even martial!) life as were women. But that was myth-legend. It all had a *basis* in reality, perhaps, but some of it was undoubtedly stretched all but to the breaking point.

Of course if all men *had* been fertile in the old days. But if you started with *if*, as a beginning point, you could go as far as you wished in any direction.

He called the meeting to order in the assembly hall which stood possibly a hundred feet below the citadel in one direction, another hundred from the stone corral which housed their prisoners, in the other. The Wolf clan was present in its entirety with the exception of children under ten and except for four scouts who were holding the prisoners. As chairman, Alan sat on the dais flanked by Sally, the matriarch, 35 years of age, tall, Junoesque, on one side and by Vivian the scout chief, on the other.

Before them sat, first, the active warrior-workers, some thirty-five of them. Second, the older women, less than a score. Further back were the steriles, possibly twenty of these and quite young, only within recent memory had they been allowed to become part of the clan, in the past they had been driven away or killed. Further back still were the children above ten but too young to join the ranks of either warrior-workers or steriles.

Alan called the meeting to order, quieted them somewhat and then invited the matriarch to take the floor.

Sally stood and looked out over her clan, the dignity of her presence silencing them where Alan's plea had not.

She said, "We have two matters to bring to our attention. First, I believe the clan should make it clear to Alan, our husband, that such interference in the affairs of women is utterly out of the question. I am speaking of his unmanly activities in the raid this morning."

There were mumblings of approval throughout the hall.

Alan came to his feet, his face bewildered. "But, Sally, what else could I do? If I hadn't overcome the enemy warriors and turned the Bren gun on the others you would all be gone now. Possibly none of you would have survived."

Sally quieted him with a chill look. "Let me repeat what is well known to every member of the clan. We consist of less than sixty women, a few more than thirty-five of whom are active. There are twenty steriles and twenty-five or so children. And one husband. A few more than one hundred in all."

Her voice slowed and lowered for the sake of emphasis. "All of our women-except for two or three-might die and the clan would live on. The steriles certainly might all die, and the clan live on. Even the children could all die and the clan live on. *But if our husband dies, the clan dies.* The greatest responsibility of every member of any clan is to protect the husband. Under no circumstances is he to be endangered. You know this, it should not have to be brought to your attention."

There was a strong murmur of assent from those seated before them.

Alan said, "But, Sally, I saved your lives! And if I hadn't, I would have been captured by the Crows and Horses and you would have lost me at any rate."

This was hard for Sally Wolf, but she said, "Then, at least, *they* would have had you. If you had died, in your foolhardiness, you would have been gone for all of us. Alan, two clans, husbandless clans, united in this attempt to capture you from us. While we fought to protect our husband, the life of our clan, we hold no rancor against them. In their position, we would have done the same. Much rather would we see you taken by them, than to see you dead. Even though the Wolf clan might die, the race must go on." She added, but not very believably, "If they had captured you, perhaps we could have, in our turn, captured a husband from some other clan."

"The reason we probably couldn't," Vivian said mildly, "is that since we've turned to agriculture and settled, our numbers have dropped off by half. We had more than sixty warriors while we were hunter-foragers."

"That's enough, Vivian," Sally snapped. "The question isn't being discussed this afternoon."

"Ought to be," somebody whispered down in front.

"Order," Alan said. He knew it was a growing belief in the clan that giving up the nomadic life had been a mistake. From raiders, they had become the raided.

Sally said, "The second order of business is the disposal of the Horse and Crow prisoners captured in the action today."

Vivian said, "We can't afford to waste valuable ammunition. I say shove them into the canyon."

Most of those seated in the hall approved of that. Some were puzzled of face, wondering why the matter hadn't been left simply in the scout chief's hands.

Sally said, dryly, "I haven't formed an opinion myself. However, our chairman has some words to say."

Vivian looked at Alan as though he was a precocious child. She shook her head. "You cutie, you. You're getting bigger and bigger for your britches every day."

Two or three of the warriors echoed her by chuckling fondly.

Alan said nothing to that, needing to maintain what dignity and prestige he could muster.

He stood and faced them and waited for their silence before saying, "You feminine members of the clan are too busy with work and with defense to pursue some of the studies for which we men find time."

Vivian murmured, "You ain't just a whistlin', honey. But we don't mind. You do what you want with your time, honey."

He tried to smile politely, but went on. "It has come to the point where few women read to any extent and most learning has fallen into the hands of the men-few as we are."

Sally said impatiently, "What has this got to do with the prisoners, Alan dear?"

It would seem that he had ignored her when he said, "I have been discussing the matter with Warren of the Turtle clan and two or three other men with whom I occasionally come in contact. At the rate the race is going, there will be no men left at all in another few generations."

There was quiet in the long hall. Deathly quiet.

Sally said, "How ... how do you mean, dear?"

"I mean our present system can't go on. It isn't working."

"Of course it's working," Vivian snapped. "Here we are aren't we? It's always worked, it always will. Here's the clan. You're our husband. After we've had you for twenty years, we'll trade you to another clan for their husband-prevents interbreeding. If you have a fertile son, the clan will either split, each half taking one husband, or we'll trade him off for land, or guns, or whatever else is valuable. Of course, it works."

He shook his head, stubbornly. "Things are changing. For a generation or two after bomb day, we were in chaos. By time things cleared we were divided as we are now, in clans. However, we were still largely able to exist on the canned goods, the animals, left over from the old days. There was food and guns for all and only a few of the men were steriles."

Vivian began to say something again, but he shook a hand negatively at her, pleading for silence. "No, I'm not talking about myth-legend now. Warren's great-grandfather, whom he knew as a boy, remembers when there were four times or more the number of men we have today and when the steriles were very few."

Vivian said impatiently, "What's this got to do with the prisoners? There they are. We can kill them or let them go. If we let them go, they'll be coming back, six months from now, to take another crack at us. Alan is cute as a button, but I don't think he should meddle in women's affairs."

But most of them were silent. They looked up at him, waiting for him to go on.

"I suppose," Sally said, "that you're coming to a point, dear?"

He nodded, his face tight. "I'm coming to the point. The point is that we've got to change the basis of clan society. This isn't working any more-if it ever did. There's such a thing as planned breeding ..." it had been hard to say this, and the younger women in the audience, in particular, tittered "... and we're going to have to think in terms of it."

Sally had flushed. She said now, "A certain dignity is expected at a clan meeting, Alan dear. But just what did you mean?"

Vivian said, "This is nonsense, I'm leaving," and she was up from the speaker's table and away. Two or three of her younger girls looked after, scowling, but they didn't follow her out of the hall.

"I mean," Alan said doggedly, "that one of those Crow women has been the mother of two fertile men. To my knowledge she is the only woman within hundreds of miles this can be said about. We men have been keeping records of such things."

Sally was as mystified as the rest of the clan.

Alan said, "I say bring these women into the clan. Unite with the Turtles and the Burros so that we'll have three clans, five counting the Horses and Crows. Then we'll have enough strength to fight off the forager-hunters, and we'll have enough men to experiment in selective breeding."

Half of the hall was on its feet in a roar.

"Share you with these ... these desert rats who just raided us, who killed eight of our clan?" Sally snapped, flabbergasted.

He stood his ground. "Yes. I'll repeat, one of those Crow women has borne two fertile men children. We can't afford to kill her. For all we know, she might have a dozen more. This haphazard method of a single husband for a whole clan must be replaced...."

The hall broke down into chaos again.

Sally held up a commanding hand for silence. She said, "And if we share you with another forty or fifty women, to what extent will the rest of us have any husband at all?"

He pointed out the steriles, seated silently in the back. "It would be healthier if you gave up some of this superior contempt you hold for sterile males and accept their companionship. Although they cannot be fathers, they can be mates otherwise. As it is, how much true companionship do you secure from me-any of you? Less than once a month do you see me more than from a distance."

"Mate with steriles?" someone gasped from the front row.

"Yes," Alan snapped back. "And let fertile men be used expressly for attempting to produce additional fertile men. Confound it, can't you warriors realize what I'm saying? I have reports that there is a woman among the Crows who has borne two fertile male children. Have you ever heard of any such phenomenon before? Do you realize that in the fifteen years I have been the husband of this clan, we have not had even one fertile man child born? Do you realize that in the past twenty years there has been born not one fertile man child in the Turtle clan? Only one in the Burro clan?"

He had them in the palm of his hand now.

"What-what does the Turtle clan think of this plan of yours?" Sally said.

"I was talking to Warren just the other day. He thinks he can win their approval. We can also probably talk the Burros into it. They're growing desperate. Their husband is nearly sixty years old and has produced only one fertile male child, which was later captured in a raid by the Denver foragers."

Sally said, "And we'd have to share you with all these, and with our prisoners as well?"

"Yes, in an attempt to breed fertile men back into the race."

Sally turned to the assembled clan.

A heavy explosion, room-shaking in its violence, all but threw them to the floor. Half a dozen of the younger warriors scurried to the windows, guns at the ready.

In the distance, from the outside, there was the chatter of a machine gun, then individual pistol shots.

"The corral," Jean the scout said, her lips going back over her teeth.

Vivian came sauntering back into the assembly hall, patting the stock of her new tommy gun appreciatively. "Works like a charm," she said. "That dynamite we captured was fresh too. Blew 'em to smithereens. Only had to finish off half a dozen."

Alan said, agonizingly, "Vivian! You didn't … the prisoners?"

She grinned at him. "Alan, you're as cute as a button, but you don't know anything about women's affairs. Now you be a honey and go back to taking care of the children."

Happy Ending

There were four men in the lifeboat that came down from the space-cruiser. Three of them were still in the uniform of the Galactic Guards.

The fourth sat in the prow of the small craft looking down at their goal, hunched and silent, bundled up in a greatcoat against the coolness of space —a greatcoat which he would never need again after this morning. The brim of his hat was pulled down far over his forehead, and he studied the nearing shore through dark-lensed glasses. Bandages, as though for a broken jaw, covered most of the lower part of his face.

He realized suddenly that the dark glasses, now that they had left the cruiser, were unnecessary. He slipped them off. After the cinematographic grays his eyes had seen through these lenses for so long, the brilliance of the color below him was almost like a blow. He blinked, and looked again.

They were rapidly settling toward a shoreline, a beach. The sand was a dazzling, unbelievable white such as had never been on his home planet. Blue the sky and water, and green the edge of the fantastic jungle. There was a flash of red in the green, as they came still closer, and he realized suddenly that it must be a *marigee*, the semi-intelligent Venusian parrot once so popular as pets throughout the solar system.

Throughout the system blood and steel had fallen from the sky and ravished the planets, but now it fell no more.

And now this. Here in this forgotten portion of an almost completely destroyed world it had not fallen at all.

Only in some place like this, alone, was safety for him. Elsewhere-anywhere-imprisonment or, more likely, death. There was danger, even here. Three of the crew of the space-cruiser knew. Perhaps, someday, one of them would talk. Then they would come for him, even here.

But that was a chance he could not avoid. Nor were the odds bad, for three people out of a whole solar system knew where he was. And those three were loyal fools.

The lifeboat came gently to rest. The hatch swung open and he stepped out and walked a few paces up the beach. He turned and waited while the two spacemen who had guided the craft brought his chest out and carried it across the beach and to the corrugated-tin shack just at the edge of the trees. That shack had once been a space-radar relay station. Now the equipment it had held was long gone, the antenna mast taken down. But the shack still stood. It would be his home for a while. A long while. The two men returned to the lifeboat preparatory to leaving.

And now the captain stood facing him, and the captain's face was a rigid mask. It seemed with an effort that the captain's right arm remained at his side, but that effort had been ordered. No salute.

The captain's voice, too, was rigid with unemotion. "Number One..."

"Silence!" And then, less bitterly. "Come further from the boat before you again let your tongue run loose. Here." They had reached the shack.

"You are right, Number..."

"No. I am no longer Number One. You must continue to think of me as *Mister* Smith, your cousin, whom you brought here for the reasons you explained to the under-officers, before you surrender your ship. If you *think* of me so, you will be less likely to slip in your speech."

"There is nothing further I can do-Mister Smith?"

"Nothing. Go now."

"And I am ordered to surrender the —"

"There are no orders. The war is over, lost. I would suggest thought as to what spaceport you put into. In some you may receive humane treatment. In others —"

The captain nodded. "In others, there is great hatred. Yes. That is all?"

"That is all. And, Captain, your running of the blockade, your securing of fuel *en route*, have constituted a deed of high valor. All I can give you in reward is my thanks. But now go. Goodbye."

"Not goodbye," the captain blurted impulsively, "but *hasta la vista, auf Wiedersehen, until the day* ...you will permit me, for the last time to address you and salute?"

The man in the greatcoat shrugged. "As you will."

Click of heels and a salute that once greeted the Caesars, and later the pseudo-Aryan of the 20th Century, and, but yesterday, he who was now known as *the last of the dictators*. "Farewell, Number One!"

"Farewell," he answered emotionlessly.

* * * * *

Mr. Smith, a black dot on the dazzling white sand, watched the lifeboat disappear up into the blue, finally into the haze of the upper atmosphere of Venus. That eternal haze that would always be there to mock his failure and his bitter solitude.

The slow days snarled by, and the sun shone dimly, and the *marigees* screamed in the early dawn and all day and at sunset, and sometimes there were the six-legged *baroons*, monkey-like in the trees, that gibbered at him. And the rains came and went away again.

At nights there were drums in the distance. Not the martial roll of marching, nor yet a threatening note of savage hate. Just drums, many miles away, throbbing rhythm for native dances or exorcising, perhaps, the forest-night demons. He assumed these Venusians had their superstitions, all other races had. There was no threat, for him, in that throbbing that was like the beating of the jungle's heart.

Mr. Smith knew that, for although his choice of destinations had been a hasty choice, yet there had been time for him to read the available reports. The natives were harmless and friendly. A Terran missionary had lived among them some time ago-before the outbreak of the war. They were a simple, weak race. They seldom went far from their villages; the space-radar operator who had once occupied the shack reported that he had never seen one of them.

So, there would be no difficulty in avoiding the natives, nor danger if he did encounter them. Nothing to worry about, except the bitterness.

Not the bitterness of regret, but of defeat. Defeat at the hands of the defeated. The damned Martians who came back after he had driven them halfway across their damned arid planet. The Jupiter Satellite Confederation landing endlessly on the home planet, sending their vast armadas of spacecraft daily and nightly to turn his mighty cities into dust. In spite of everything; in spite of his score of ultra-vicious secret weapons and the last desperate efforts of his weakened armies, most of whose men were under twenty or over forty.

The treachery even in his own army, among his own generals and admirals. The turn of Luna, that had been the end.

His people would rise again. But not, now after Armageddon, in his lifetime. Not under him, nor another like him. The last of the dictators.

Hated by a solar system, and hating it.

It would have been intolerable, save that he was alone. He had foreseen that-the need for solitude. Alone, he was still Number One. The presence of others would have forced recognition of his miserably changed status. Alone, his pride was undamaged. His ego was intact.

* * * * *

The long days, and the *marigees'* screams, the slithering swish of the surf, the ghost-quiet movements of the *baroons* in the trees and the raucousness of their shrill voices. Drums.

Those sounds, and those alone. But perhaps silence would have been worse.

For the times of silence were louder. Times he would pace the beach at night and overhead would be the roar of jets and rockets, the ships that had roared over New Albuquerque, his capitol, in those last days before he had fled. The crump of bombs and the screams and the blood, and the flat voices of his folding generals.

Those were the days when the waves of hatred from the conquered peoples beat upon his country as the waves of a stormy sea beat upon crumbling cliffs. Leagues back of the battered lines, you could *feel* that hate and vengeance as a tangible thing, a thing that thickened the air, that made breathing difficult and talking futile.

And the spacecraft, the jets, the rockets, the damnable rockets, more every day and every night, and ten coming for every one shot down. Rocket ships raining hell from the sky, havoc and chaos and the end of hope.

And then he knew that he had been hearing another sound, hearing it often and long at a time. It was a voice that shouted invective and ranted hatred and glorified the steel might of his planet and the destiny of a man and a people.

It was his own voice, and it beat back the waves from the white shore, it stopped their wet encroachment upon this, his domain. It screamed back at the *baroons* and they were silent. And at times he laughed, and the *marigees* laughed. Sometimes, the queerly shaped Venusian trees talked too, but their voices were quieter. The trees were submissive, they were good subjects.

Sometimes, fantastic thoughts went through his head. The race of trees, the pure race of trees that never interbred, that stood firm always. Someday the trees —

But that was just a dream, a fancy. More real were the *marigees* and the *kifs*. They were the ones who persecuted him. There was the *marigee* who would shriek *"All is lost!"* He had shot at it a hundred times with his needle gun, but always it flew away unharmed. Sometimes it did not even fly away.

"All is lost!"

At last he wasted no more needle darts. He stalked it to strangle it with his bare hands. That was better. On what might have been the thousandth try, he caught it and killed it, and there was warm blood on his hands and feathers were flying.

That should have ended it, but it didn't. Now there were a dozen *marigees* that screamed that all was lost. Perhaps there had been a dozen all along. Now he merely shook his fist at them or threw stones.

The *kifs*, the Venusian equivalent of the Terran ant, stole his food. But that did not matter; there was plenty of food. There had been a cache of it in the shack, meant to restock a space-cruiser, and never used. The *kifs* would not get at it until he opened a can, but then, unless he ate it all at once, they ate whatever he left. That did not matter. There were plenty of cans. And always fresh fruit from the jungle. Always in season, for there were no seasons here, except the rains.

But the *kifs* served a purpose for him. They kept him sane, by giving him something tangible, something inferior, to hate.

Oh, it wasn't hatred, at first. Mere annoyance. He killed them in a routine sort of way at first. But they kept coming back. Always there were *kifs*. In his larder, wherever he did it. In his bed. He sat the legs of the cot in dishes of gasoline, but the *kifs* still got in. Perhaps they dropped from the ceiling, although he never caught them doing it.

They bothered his sleep. He'd feel them running over him, even when he'd spent an hour picking the bed clean of them by the light of the carbide lantern. They scurried with tickling little feet and he could not sleep.

He grew to hate them, and the very misery of his nights made his days more tolerable by giving them an increasing purpose. A pogrom against the *kifs*. He sought out their holes by patiently following one bearing a bit of food, and he poured gasoline into the hole and the earth around it, taking satisfaction in the thought of the writhings in agony below. He went about hunting *kifs*, to step on them. To stamp them out. He must have killed millions of *kifs*.

But always there were as many left. Never did their number seem to diminish in the slightest. Like the Martians-but unlike the Martians, they did not fight back.

Theirs was the passive resistance of a vast productivity that bred *kifs* ceaselessly, overwhelmingly, billions to replace millions. Individual *kifs* could be killed, and he took savage satisfaction in their killing, but he knew his methods were useless save for the pleasure and the purpose they gave him. Sometimes the pleasure would pall in the shadow of its futility, and he would dream of mechanized means of killing them.

He read carefully what little material there was in his tiny library about the *kif*. They were astonishingly like the ants of Terra. So much that there had been speculation about their relationship-that didn't interest him. How could they be killed, *en masse*? Once a year, for a brief period, they took on the characteristics of the army ants of Terra. They came from their holes in endless numbers and swept everything before them in their devouring march. He wet his lips when he read that. Perhaps the opportunity would come then to destroy, to destroy, *and destroy*.

Almost, Mr. Smith forgot people and the solar system and what had been. Here in this new world, there was only he and the *kifs*. The *baroons* and the *marigees* didn't count. They had no order and no system. The *kifs* —

In the intensity of his hatred there slowly filtered through a grudging admiration. The *kifs* were true totalitarians. They practiced what he had preached to a mightier race, practiced it with a thoroughness beyond the kind of man to comprehend.

Theirs the complete submergence of the individual to the state, theirs the complete ruthlessness of the true conqueror, the perfect selfless bravery of the true soldier.

But they got into his bed, into his clothes, into his food.

They crawled with intolerable tickling feet.

Nights he walked the beach, and that night was one of the noisy nights. There were high-flying, high-whining jet-craft up there in the moonlight sky and their shadows dappled the black water of the sea. The planes, the rockets, the jet-craft, they were what had ravaged his cities, had turned his railroads into twisted steel, had dropped their H-Bombs on his most vital factories.

He shook his fist at them and shrieked imprecations at the sky.

And when he had ceased shouting, there were voices on the beach. Conrad's voice in his ear, as it had sounded that day when Conrad had walked into the palace, white-faced, and forgotten the salute. "There is a breakthrough at Denver, Number One! Toronto and Monterey are in danger. And in the other hemispheres —" His voice cracked. " —the damned Martians and the traitors from Luna are driving over the Argentine. Others have landed near New Petrograd. It is a rout. All is lost!"

Voices crying, "Number One, *hail*! Number One, *hail*!"

A sea of hysterical voices. "Number One, *hail*! Number One —"

A voice that was louder, higher, more frenetic than any of the others. His memory of his own voice, calculated but inspired, as he'd heard it on play-backs of his own speeches.

The voices of children chanting, "To thee, O Number One —" He couldn't remember the rest of the words, but they had been beautiful words. That had been at the public school meet in the New Los Angeles. How strange that he should remember, here and now, the very tone of his voice and inflection, the shining wonder in their children's eyes. Children only, but they were willing to kill and die, *for him*, convinced that all that was needed to cure the ills of the race was a suitable leader to follow.

"*All is lost!*"

And suddenly the monster jet-craft were swooping downward and starkly he realized what a clear target he presented, here against the white moonlit beach. They must see him.

The crescendo of motors as he ran, sobbing now in fear, for the cover of the jungle. Into the screening shadow of the giant trees, and the sheltering blackness.

He stumbled and fell, was up and running again. And now his eyes could see in the dimmer moonlight that filtered through the branches overhead. Stirrings there, in the branches. Stirrings and voices in the night. Voices in and of the night. Whispers and shrieks of pain. Yes, he'd shown them pain, and now their tortured voices ran with him through the knee-deep, night-wet grass among the trees.

The night was hideous with noise. Red noises, an almost *tangible* din that he could nearly *feel* as well as he could see and hear it. And after a while his breath came raspingly, and there was a thumping sound that was the beating of his heart and the beating of the night.

And then, he could run no longer, and he clutched a tree to keep from falling, his arms trembling about it, and his face pressed against the impersonal roughness of the bark. There was no wind, but the tree swayed back and forth and his body with it.

Then, as abruptly as light goes on when a switch is thrown, the noise vanished. Utter silence, and at last he was strong enough to let go his grip on the tree and stand erect again, to look about to get his bearings.

One tree was like another, and for a moment he thought he'd have to stay here until daylight. Then he remembered that the sound of the surf would give him his directions. He listened hard and heard it, faint and far away.

And another sound-one that he had never heard before-faint, also, but seeming to come from his right and quite near.

He looked that way, and there was a patch of opening in the trees above. The grass was waving strangely in that area of moonlight. It moved, although there was no breeze to move it. And there was an almost sudden *edge*, beyond which the blades thinned out quickly to barrenness.

And the sound-it was like the sound of the surf, but it was continuous. It was more like the rustle of dry leaves, but there were no dry leaves to rustle.

Mr. Smith took a step toward the sound and looked down. More grass bent, and fell, and vanished, even as he looked. Beyond the moving edge of devastation was a brown floor of the moving bodies of *kifs*.

Row after row, orderly rank after orderly rank, marching resistlessly onward. Billions of *kifs*, an army of *kifs*, eating their way across the night.

Fascinated, he stared down at them. There was no danger, for their progress was slow. He retreated a step to keep beyond their front rank. The sound, then, was the sound of chewing.

He could see one edge of the column, and it was a neat, orderly edge. And there was discipline, for the ones on the outside were larger than those in the center.

He retreated another step-and then, quite suddenly, his body was afire in several spreading places. The vanguard. Ahead of the rank that ate away the grass.

His boots were brown with *kifs*.

Screaming with pain, he whirled about and ran, beating with his hands at the burning spots on his body. He ran head-on into a tree, bruising his face horribly, and the night was scarlet with pain and shooting fire.

But he staggered on, almost blindly, running, writhing, tearing off his clothes as he ran.

This, then, was *pain*. There was a shrill screaming in his ears that must have been the sound of his own voice.

When he could no longer run, he crawled. Naked, now, and with only a few *kifs* still clinging to him. And the blind tangent of his flight had taken him well out of the path of the advancing army.

But stark fear and the memory of unendurable pain drove him on. His knees raw now, he could no longer crawl. But he got himself erect again on trembling legs, and staggered on. Catching hold of a tree and pushing himself away from it to catch the next.

Falling, rising, falling again. His throat raw from the screaming invective of his hate. Bushes and the rough bark of trees tore his flesh.

* * * * *

Into the village compound just before dawn, staggered a man, a naked terrestrial. He looked about with dull eyes that seemed to see nothing and understand nothing.

The females and young ran before him, even the males retreated.

He stood there, swaying, and the incredulous eyes of the natives widened as they saw the condition of his body, and the blankness of his eyes.

When he made no hostile move, they came closer again, formed a wondering, chattering circle about him, these Venusian humanoids. Some ran to bring the chief and the chief's son, who knew everything.

The mad, naked human opened his lips as though he were going to speak, but instead, he fell. He fell, as a dead man falls. But when they turned him over in the dust, they saw that his chest still rose and fell in labored breathing.

And then came Alwa, the aged chieftain, and Nrana, his son. Alwa gave quick, excited orders. Two of the men carried Mr. Smith into the chief's hut, and the wives of the chief and the chief's son took over the Earthling's care, and rubbed him with a soothing and healing salve.

But for days and nights he lay without moving and without speaking or opening his eyes, and they did not know whether he would live or die.

Then, at last, he opened his eyes. And he talked, although they could make out nothing of the things he said.

Nrana came and listened, for Nrana of all of them spoke and understood best the Earthling's language, for he had been the special protege of the Terran missionary who had lived with them for a while.

Nrana listened, but he shook his head. "The words," he said, "the words are of the Terran tongue, but I make nothing of them. His mind is not well."

The aged Alwa said, "Aie. Stay beside him. Perhaps as his body heals, his words will be beautiful words as were the words of the Father-of-Us who, in the Terran tongue, taught us of the gods and their good."

So they cared for him well, and his wounds healed, and the day came when he opened his eyes and saw the handsome blue-complexioned face of Nrana sitting there beside him, and Nrana said softly, "Good day, Mr. Man of Earth. You feel better, no?"

There was no answer, and the deep-sunken eyes of the man on the sleeping mat stared, glared at him. Nrana could see that those eyes were not yet sane, but he saw, too, that the madness in them was not the same that it had been. Nrana did not know the words for delirium and paranoia, but he could distinguish between them.

No longer was the Earthling a raving maniac, and Nrana made a very common error, an error more civilized beings than he have often made. He thought the paranoia was an improvement over the wider madness. He talked on, hoping the Earthling would talk too, and he did not recognize the danger of his silence.

"We welcome you, Earthling," he said, "and hope that you will live among us, as did the Father-of-Us, Mr. Gerhardt. He taught us to worship the true gods of the high heavens. Jehovah, and Jesus and their prophets the men from the skies. He taught us to pray and to love our enemies."

And Nrana shook his head sadly, "But many of our tribe have gone back to the older gods, the cruel gods. They say there has been great strife among the outsiders, and no more remain upon all of Venus. My father, Alwa, and I are glad another one has come. You will be able to help those of us who have gone back. You can teach us love and kindliness."

The eyes of the dictator closed. Nrana did not know whether or not he slept, but Nrana stood up quietly to leave the hut. In the doorway, he turned and said, "We pray for you."

And then, joyously, he ran out of the village to seek the others, who were gathering bela-berries for the feast of the fourth event.

When, with several of them, he returned to the village, the Earthling was gone. The hut was empty.

Outside the compound they found, at last, the trail of his passing. They followed and it led to a stream and along the stream until they came to the tabu of the green pool, and could go no farther.

"He went downstream," said Alwa gravely. "He sought the sea and the beach. He was well then, in his mind, for he knew that all streams go to the sea."

"Perhaps he had a ship-of-the-sky there at the beach," Nrana said worriedly. "All Earthlings come from the sky. The Father-of-Us told us that."

"Perhaps he will come back to us," said Alwa. His old eyes misted.

* * * * *

Mr. Smith was coming back all right, and sooner than they had dared to hope. As soon in fact, as he could make the trip to the shack and return. He came back dressed in clothing very different from the garb the other white man had worn. Shining leather boots and the uniform of the Galactic Guard, and a wide leather belt with a holster for his needle gun.

But the gun was in his hand when, at dusk, he strode into the compound.

He said, "I am Number One, the Lord of all the Solar System, and your ruler. Who was chief among you?"

Alwa had been in his hut, but he heard the words and came out. He understood the words, but not their meaning. He said, "Earthling, we welcome you back. I am the chief."

"You were the chief. Now you will serve me. I am the chief."

Alwa's old eyes were bewildered at the strangeness of this. He said, "I will serve you, yes. All of us. But it is not fitting that an Earthling should be chief among —"

The whisper of the needle gun. Alwa's wrinkled hands went to his scrawny neck where, just off the center, was a sudden tiny pin prick of a hole. A faint trickle of red coursed over the dark blue of his skin. The old man's knees gave way under him as the rage of the poisoned needle dart struck him, and he fell. Others started toward him.

"Back," said Mr. Smith. "Let him die slowly that you may all see what happens to —"

But one of the chief's wives, one who did not understand the speech of Earth, was already lifting Alwa's head. The needle gun whispered again, and she fell forward across him.

"I am Number One," said Mr. Smith, "and Lord of all the planets. All who oppose me, die by —"

And then, suddenly all of them were running toward him. His finger pressed the trigger and four of them died before the avalanche of their bodies bore him down and overwhelmed him. Nrana had been first in that rush, and Nrana died.

The others tied the Earthling up and threw him into one of the huts. And then, while the women began wailing for the dead, the men made council.

They elected Kallana chief and he stood before them and said, "The Father-of-Us, the Mister Gerhardt, deceived us." There was fear and worry in his voice and apprehension on his blue face. "If this be indeed the Lord of whom he told us —"

"He is not a god," said another. "He is an Earthling, but there have been such before on Venus, many many of them who came long and long ago from the skies. Now they are all dead, killed in strife among themselves. It is well. This last one is one of them, but he is mad."

And they talked long and the dusk grew into night while they talked of what they must do. The gleam of firelight upon their bodies, and the waiting drummer.

The problem was difficult. To harm one who was mad was tabu. If he was really a god, it would be worse. Thunder and lightning from the sky would destroy the village. Yet they dared not release him. Even if they took the evil weapon-that-whispered-its-death and buried it, he might find other ways to harm them. He might have another where he had gone for the first.

Yes, it was a difficult problem for them, but the eldest and wisest of them, one M'Ganne, gave them at last the answer.

"O Kallana," he said, "Let us give him to the *kifs*. If *they* harm him —" and old M'Ganne grinned a toothless, mirthless grin " —it would be their doing and not ours."

Kallana shuddered. "It is the most horrible of all deaths. And if he is a god —"

"If he is a god, they will not harm him. If he is mad and not a god, we will not have harmed him. It harms not a man to tie him to a tree."

Kallana considered well, for the safety of his people was at stake. Considering, he remembered how Alwa and Nrana had died.

He said, "It is right."

The waiting drummer began the rhythm of the council-end, and those of the men who were young and fleet lighted torches in the fire and went out into the forest to seek the *kifs*, who were still in their season of marching.

And after a while, having found what they sought, they returned.

They took the Earthling out with them, then, and tied him to a tree. They left him there, and they left the gag over his lips because they did not wish to hear his screams when the *kifs* came.

The cloth of the gag would be eaten, too, but by that time, there would be no flesh under it from which a scream might come.

They left him, and went back to the compound, and the drums took up the rhythm of propitiation to the gods for what they had done. For they had, they knew, cut very close to the corner of a tabu-but the provocation had been great and they hoped they would not be punished.

All night the drums would throb.

* * * * *

The man tied to the tree struggled with his bonds, but they were strong and his writhings made the knots but tighten.

His eyes became accustomed to the darkness.

He tried to shout, "I am Number One, Lord of —"

And then, because he could not shout and because he could not loosen himself, there came a rift in his madness. He remembered who he was, and all the old hatreds and bitterness welled up in him.

He remembered, too, what had happened in the compound, and wondered why the Venusian natives had not killed him. Why, instead, they had tied him here alone in the darkness of the jungle.

Afar, he heard the throbbing of the drums, and they were like the beating of the heart of night, and there was a louder, nearer sound that was the pulse of blood in his ears as the fear came to him.

The fear that he knew why they had tied him here. The horrible, gibbering fear that, for the last time, an army marched against him.

He had time to savor that fear to the uttermost, to have it become a creeping certainty that crawled into the black corners of his soul as would the soldiers of the coming army crawl into his ears and nostrils while others would eat away his eyelids to get at the eyes behind them.

And then, and only then, did he hear the sound that was like the rustle of dry leaves, in a dank, black jungle where there were no dry leaves to rustle nor breeze to rustle them.

Horribly, Number One, the last of the dictators, did not go mad again; not exactly, but he laughed, and laughed and laughed....

Unborn Tomorrow

Betty looked up from her magazine. She said mildly, "You're late."

"Don't yell at me, I feel awful," Simon told her. He sat down at his desk, passed his tongue over his teeth in distaste, groaned, fumbled in a drawer for the aspirin bottle.

He looked over at Betty and said, almost as though reciting, "What I need is a vacation."

"What," Betty said, "are you going to use for money?"

"Providence," Simon told her whilst fiddling with the aspirin bottle, "will provide."

"Hm-m-m. But before providing vacations it'd be nice if Providence turned up a missing jewel deal, say. Something where you could deduce that actually the ruby ring had gone down the drain and was caught in the elbow. Something that would net about fifty dollars."

Simon said, mournful of tone, "Fifty dollars? Why not make it five hundred?"

"I'm not selfish," Betty said. "All I want is enough to pay me this week's salary."

"Money," Simon said. "When you took this job you said it was the romance that appealed to you."

"Hm-m-m. I didn't know most sleuthing amounted to snooping around department stores to check on the clerks knocking down."

Simon said, enigmatically, "Now it comes."

* * * * *

There was a knock.

Betty bounced up with Olympic agility and had the door swinging wide before the knocking was quite completed.

He was old, little and had bug eyes behind pince-nez glasses. His suit was cut in the style of yesteryear but when a suit costs two or three hundred dollars you still retain caste whatever the styling.

Simon said unenthusiastically, "Good morning, Mr. Oyster." He indicated the client's chair. "Sit down, sir."

The client fussed himself with Betty's assistance into the seat, bug-eyed Simon, said finally, "You know my name, that's pretty good. Never saw you before in my life. Stop fussing with me, young lady. Your ad in the phone book says you'll investigate anything."

"Anything," Simon said. "Only one exception."

"Excellent. Do you believe in time travel?"

Simon said nothing. Across the room, where she had resumed her seat, Betty cleared her throat. When Simon continued to say nothing she ventured, "Time travel is impossible."

"Why?"

"Why?"

"Yes, why?"

Betty looked to her boss for assistance. None was forthcoming. There ought to be some very quick, positive, definite answer. She said, "Well, for one thing, paradox. Suppose you had a time machine and traveled back a hundred years or so and killed your own great-grandfather. Then how could you ever be born?"

"Confound it if I know," the little fellow growled. "How?"

Simon said, "Let's get to the point, what you wanted to see me about."

"I want to hire you to hunt me up some time travelers," the old boy said.

Betty was too far in now to maintain her proper role of silent secretary. "Time travelers," she said, not very intelligently.

The potential client sat more erect, obviously with intent to hold the floor for a time. He removed the pince-nez glasses and pointed them at Betty. He said, "Have you read much science fiction, Miss?"

"Some," Betty admitted.

"Then you'll realize that there are a dozen explanations of the paradoxes of time travel. Every writer in the field worth his salt has explained them away. But to get on. It's my contention that within a century or so man will have solved the problems of immortality and eternal youth, and it's also my suspicion that he will eventually be able to travel in time. So convinced am I of these possibilities that I am willing to gamble a portion of my fortune to investigate the presence in our era of such time travelers."

Simon seemed incapable of carrying the ball this morning, so Betty said, "But ...Mr. Oyster, if the future has developed time travel why don't we ever meet such travelers?"

Simon put in a word. "The usual explanation, Betty, is that they can't afford to allow the space-time continuum track to be altered. If, say, a time traveler returned to a period of twenty-five years ago and shot Hitler, then all subsequent history would be changed. In that case, the time traveler himself might never be born. They have to tread mighty carefully."

Mr. Oyster was pleased. "I didn't expect you to be so well informed on the subject, young man."

Simon shrugged and fumbled again with the aspirin bottle.

* * * * *

Mr. Oyster went on. "I've been considering the matter for some time and —"

Simon held up a hand. "There's no use prolonging this. As I understand it, you're an elderly gentleman with a considerable fortune and you realize that thus far nobody has succeeded in taking it with him."

Mr. Oyster returned his glasses to their perch, bug-eyed Simon, but then nodded.

Simon said, "You want to hire me to find a time traveler and in some manner or other-any manner will do-exhort from him the secret of eternal life and youth, which you figure the future will have discovered. You're willing to pony up a part of this fortune of yours, if I can deliver a bona fide time traveler."

"Right!"

Betty had been looking from one to the other. Now she said, plaintively, "But where are you going to find one of these characters-especially if they're interested in keeping hid?"

The old boy was the center again. "I told you I'd been considering it for some time. The *Oktoberfest*, that's where they'd be!" He seemed elated.

Betty and Simon waited.

"The *Oktoberfest*," he repeated. "The greatest festival the world has ever seen, the carnival, *feria*, *fiesta* to beat them all. Every year it's held in Munich. Makes the New Orleans Mardi gras look like a quilting party." He began to swing into the spirit of his description. "It originally started in celebration of the wedding of some local prince a century and a half ago and the Bavarians had such a bang-up time they've been holding it every year since. The Munich breweries do up a special beer, *Marzenbräu* they call it, and each brewery opens a tremendous tent on the fair grounds which will hold five thousand customers apiece. Millions of liters of beer are put away, hundreds of thousands of barbecued chickens, a small herd of oxen are roasted whole over spits, millions of pair of *weisswurst*, a very special sausage, millions upon millions of pretzels —"

"All right," Simon said. "We'll accept it. The *Oktoberfest* is one whale of a wingding."

* * * * *

"Well," the old boy pursued, into his subject now, "that's where they'd be, places like the *Oktoberfest*. For one thing, a time traveler wouldn't be conspicuous. At a festival like this somebody with a strange accent, or who didn't know exactly how to wear his clothes correctly, or was off the ordinary in any of a dozen other ways, wouldn't be noticed. You could be a four-armed space traveler from Mars, and you still wouldn't be conspicuous at the *Oktoberfest*. People would figure they had D.T.'s."

"But why would a time traveler want to go to a —" Betty began.

"Why not! What better opportunity to study a people than when they are in their cups? If *you* could go back a few thousand years, the things you would wish to see would be a Roman Triumph, perhaps the Rites of Dionysus, or one of Alexander's orgies. You wouldn't want to wander up and down the streets of, say, Athens while nothing was going on, particularly when you might be revealed as a suspicious character not being able to speak the language, not knowing how to wear the clothes and not familiar with the city's layout." He took a deep breath. "No ma'am, you'd have to stick to some great event, both for the sake of actual interest and for protection against being unmasked."

The old boy wound it up. "Well, that's the story. What are your rates? The *Oktoberfest* starts on Friday and continues for sixteen days. You can take the plane to Munich, spend a week there and —"

Simon was shaking his head. "Not interested."

As soon as Betty had got her jaw back into place, she glared unbelievingly at him.

Mr. Oyster was taken aback himself. "See here, young man, I realize this isn't an ordinary assignment, however, as I said, I am willing to risk a considerable portion of my fortune —"

"Sorry," Simon said. "Can't be done."

"A hundred dollars a day plus expenses," Mr. Oyster said quietly. "I like the fact that you already seem to have some interest and knowledge of the matter. I liked the way you knew my name when I walked in the door; my picture doesn't appear often in the papers."

"No go," Simon said, a sad quality in his voice.

"A fifty thousand dollar bonus if you bring me a time traveler."

"Out of the question," Simon said.

"But *why?*" Betty wailed.

"Just for laughs," Simon told the two of them sourly, "suppose I tell you a funny story. It goes like this:"

I got a thousand dollars from Mr. Oyster (Simon began) in the way of an advance, and leaving him with Betty who was making out a receipt, I hustled back to the apartment and packed a bag. Hell, I'd wanted a vacation anyway, this was a natural. On the way to Idlewild I stopped off at the Germany Information Offices for some tourist literature.

It takes roughly three and a half hours to get to Gander from Idlewild. I spent the time planning the fun I was going to have.

It takes roughly seven and a half hours from Gander to Shannon and I spent that time dreaming up material I could put into my reports to Mr. Oyster. I was going to have to give him some kind of report for his money. Time travel yet! What a laugh!

Between Shannon and Munich a faint suspicion began to simmer in my mind. These statistics I read on the *Oktoberfest* in the Munich tourist pamphlets. Five million people attended annually.

Where did five million people come from to attend an overgrown festival in comparatively remote Southern Germany? The tourist season is over before September 21st, first day of the gigantic beer bust. Nor could the Germans account for any such number. Munich itself has a population of less than a million, counting children.

And those millions of gallons of beer, the hundreds of thousands of chickens, the herds of oxen. Who ponied up all the money for such expenditures? How could the average German, with his twenty-five dollars a week salary?

In Munich there was no hotel space available. I went to the Bahnhof where they have a hotel service and applied. They put my name down, pocketed the husky bribe, showed me where I could check my bag, told me they'd do what they could, and to report back in a few hours.

I had another suspicious twinge. If five million people attended this beer bout, how were they accommodated?

The *Theresienwiese*, the fair ground, was only a few blocks away. I was stiff from the plane ride so I walked.

* * * * *

There are seven major brewers in the Munich area, each of them represented by one of the circuslike tents that Mr. Oyster mentioned. Each tent contained benches and tables for about five thousand persons and from six to ten thousands pack themselves in, competing for room. In the center is a tremendous bandstand, the musicians all *lederhosen* clad, the music as Bavarian as any to be found in a Bavarian beer hall. Hundreds of peasant garbed *fräuleins* darted about the tables with quart sized earthenware mugs, platters of chicken, sausage, kraut and pretzels.

I found a place finally at a table which had space for twenty-odd beer bibbers. Odd is right. As weird an assortment of Germans and foreign tourists as could have been dreamed up, ranging from a seventy- or eighty-year-old couple in Bavarian costume, to the bald-headed drunk across the table from me.

A desperate waitress bearing six mugs of beer in each hand scurried past. They call them *masses*, by the way, not mugs. The bald-headed character and I both held up a finger and she slid two of the *masses* over to us and then hustled on.

"Down the hatch," the other said, holding up his *mass* in toast.

"To the ladies," I told him. Before sipping, I said, "You know, the tourist pamphlets say this stuff is eighteen per cent. That's nonsense. No beer is that strong." I took a long pull.

He looked at me, waiting.

I came up. "Mistaken," I admitted.

A *mass* or two apiece later he looked carefully at the name engraved on his earthenware mug. "Löwenbräu," he said. He took a small notebook from his pocket and a pencil, noted down the word and returned the things.

"That's a queer looking pencil you have there," I told him. "German?"

"Venusian," he said. "Oops, sorry. Shouldn't have said that."

I had never heard of the brand so I skipped it.

"Next is the Hofbräu," he said.

"Next what?" Baldy's conversation didn't seem to hang together very well.

"My pilgrimage," he told me. "All my life I've been wanting to go back to an *Oktoberfest* and sample every one of the seven brands of the best beer the world has ever known. I'm only as far as Löwenbräu. I'm afraid I'll never make it."

I finished my *mass*. "I'll help you," I told him. "Very noble endeavor. Name is Simon."

"Arth," he said. "How could you help?"

"I'm still fresh-comparatively. I'll navigate you around. There are seven beer tents. How many have you got through, so far?"

"Two, counting this one," Arth said.

I looked at him. "It's going to be a chore," I said. "You've already got a nice edge on."

Outside, as we made our way to the next tent, the fair looked like every big State-Fair ever seen, except it was bigger. Games, souvenir stands, sausage stands, rides, side shows, and people, people, people.

The Hofbräu tent was as overflowing as the last but we managed to find two seats.

The band was blaring, and five thousand half-swacked voices were roaring accompaniment. *In Muenchen steht ein Hofbräuhaus!*

Eins, Zwei, G'sufa!

At the *G'sufa* everybody upped with the mugs and drank each other's health.

"This is what I call a real beer bust," I said approvingly.

Arth was waving to a waitress. As in the Löwenbräu tent, a full quart was the smallest amount obtainable.

A beer later I said, "I don't know if you'll make it or not, Arth."

"Make what?"

"All seven tents."

"Oh."

A waitress was on her way by, mugs foaming over their rims. I gestured to her for refills.

"Where are you from, Arth?" I asked him, in the way of making conversation.

"2183."

"2183 where?"

He looked at me, closing one eye to focus better. "Oh," he said. "Well, 2183 South Street, ah, New Albuquerque."

"New Albuquerque? Where's that?"

Arth thought about it. Took another long pull at the beer. "Right across the way from old Albuquerque," he said finally. "Maybe we ought to be getting on to the Pschorrbräu tent."

"Maybe we ought to eat something first," I said. "I'm beginning to feel this. We could get some of that barbecued ox."

Arth closed his eyes in pain. "Vegetarian," he said. "Couldn't possibly eat meat. Barbarous. Ugh."

"Well, we need some nourishment," I said.

"There's supposed to be considerable nourishment in beer."

That made sense. I yelled, *"Fräulein! Zwei neu bier!"*

* * * * *

Somewhere along in here the fog rolled in. When it rolled out again, I found myself closing one eye the better to read the lettering on my earthenware mug. It read Augustinerbräu. Somehow we'd evidently navigated from one tent to another.

Arth was saying, "Where's your hotel?"

That seemed like a good question. I thought about it for a while. Finally I said, "Haven't got one. Town's jam packed. Left my bag at the Bahnhof. I don't think we'll ever make it, Arth. How many we got to go?"

"Lost track," Arth said. "You can come home with me."

We drank to that and the fog rolled in again.

When the fog rolled out, it was daylight. Bright, glaring, awful daylight. I was sprawled, complete with clothes, on one of twin beds. On the other bed, also completely clothed, was Arth.

That sun was too much. I stumbled up from the bed, staggered to the window and fumbled around for a blind or curtain. There was none.

Behind me a voice said in horror, "Who ... how ... oh, *Wodo*, where'd you come from?"

I got a quick impression, looking out the window, that the Germans were certainly the most modern, futuristic people in the world. But I couldn't stand the light. "Where's the shade," I moaned.

Arth did something and the window went opaque.

"That's quite a gadget," I groaned. "If I didn't feel so lousy, I'd appreciate it."

Arth was sitting on the edge of the bed holding his bald head in his hands. "I remember now," he sorrowed. "You didn't have a hotel. What a stupidity. I'll be phased. Phased all the way down."

"You haven't got a handful of aspirin, have you?" I asked him.

"Just a minute," Arth said, staggering erect and heading for what undoubtedly was a bathroom. "Stay where you are. Don't move. Don't touch anything."

"All right," I told him plaintively. "I'm clean. I won't mess up the place. All I've got is a hangover, not lice."

Arth was gone. He came back in two or three minutes, box of pills in hand. "Here, take one of these."

I took the pill, followed it with a glass of water.

* * * * *

And went out like a light.

Arth was shaking my arm. "Want another *mass*?"

The band was blaring, and five thousand half-swacked voices were roaring accompaniment.

In Muenchen steht ein Hofbräuhaus!

At the *G'sufa* everybody upped with their king-size mugs and drank each other's health.

My head was killing me. "This is where I came in, or something," I groaned.

Arth said, "That was last night." He looked at me over the rim of his beer mug.

Something, somewhere, was wrong. But I didn't care. I finished my *mass* and then remembered. "I've got to get my bag. Oh, my head. Where did we spend last night?"

Arth said, and his voice sounded cautious, "At my hotel, don't you remember?"

"Not very well," I admitted. "I feel lousy. I must have dimmed out. I've got to go to the Bahnhof and get my luggage."

Arth didn't put up an argument on that. We said good-by and I could feel him watching after me as I pushed through the tables on the way out.

At the Bahnhof they could do me no good. There were no hotel rooms available in Munich. The head was getting worse by the minute. The fact that they'd somehow managed to lose my bag didn't help. I worked on that project for at least a couple of hours. Not only wasn't the bag at the luggage checking station, but the attendant there evidently couldn't make heads nor tails of the check receipt. He didn't speak English and my high school German was inadequate, especially accompanied by a blockbusting hangover.

I didn't get anywhere tearing my hair and complaining from one end of the Bahnhof to the other. I drew a blank on the bag.

And the head was getting worse by the minute. I was bleeding to death through the eyes and instead of butterflies I had bats in my stomach. Believe me, *nobody* should drink a gallon or more of Marzenbräu.

* * * * *

I decided the hell with it. I took a cab to the airport, presented my return ticket, told them I wanted to leave on the first obtainable plane to New York. I'd spent two days at the *Oktoberfest*, and I'd had it.

I got more guff there. Something was wrong with the ticket, wrong date or some such. But they fixed that up. I never was clear on what was fouled up, some clerk's error, evidently.

The trip back was as uninteresting as the one over. As the hangover began to wear off—a little—I was almost sorry I hadn't been able to stay. If I'd only been able to get a room I *would* have stayed, I told myself.

From Idlewild, I came directly to the office rather than going to my apartment. I figured I might as well check in with Betty.

I opened the door and there I found Mr. Oyster sitting in the chair he had been occupying four-or was it five-days before when I'd left. I'd lost track of the time.

I said to him, "Glad you're here, sir. I can report. Ah, what was it you came for? Impatient to hear if I'd had any results?" My mind was spinning like a whirling dervish in a revolving door. I'd spent a wad of his money and had nothing I could think of to show for it; nothing but the last stages of a grand-daddy hangover.

"Came for?" Mr. Oyster snorted. "I'm merely waiting for your girl to make out my receipt. I thought you had already left."

"You'll miss your plane," Betty said.

There was suddenly a double dip of ice cream in my stomach. I walked over to my desk and looked down at the calendar.

Mr. Oyster was saying something to the effect that if I didn't leave today, it would have to be tomorrow, that he hadn't ponied up that thousand dollars advance for anything less than immediate service. Stuffing his receipt in his wallet, he fussed his way out the door.

I said to Betty hopefully, "I suppose you haven't changed this calendar since I left."

Betty said, "What's the matter with you? You look funny. How did your clothes get so mussed? You tore the top sheet off that calendar yourself, not half an hour ago, just before this marble-missing client came in." She added, irrelevantly, "Time travelers yet."

I tried just once more. "Uh, when did you first see this Mr. Oyster?"

"Never saw him before in my life," she said. "Not until he came in this morning."

"This morning," I said weakly.

While Betty stared at me as though it was *me* that needed candling by a head shrinker preparatory to being sent off to a pressure cooker, I fished in my pocket for my wallet, counted the contents and winced at the pathetic remains of the thousand. I said pleadingly, "Betty, listen, how long ago did I go out that door-on the way to the airport?"

"You've been acting sick all morning. You went out that door about ten minutes ago, were gone about three minutes, and then came back."

"See here," Mr. Oyster said (interrupting Simon's story), "did you say this was supposed to be amusing, young man? I don't find it so. In fact, I believe I am being ridiculed."

Simon shrugged, put one hand to his forehead and said, "That's only the first chapter. There are two more."

"I'm not interested in more," Mr. Oyster said. "I suppose your point was to show me how ridiculous the whole idea actually is. Very well, you've done it. Confound it. However, I suppose your time, even when spent in this manner, has some value. Here is fifty dollars. And good day, sir!"

He slammed the door after him as he left.

Simon winced at the noise, took the aspirin bottle from its drawer, took two, washed them down with water from the desk carafe.

Betty looked at him admiringly. Came to her feet, crossed over and took up the fifty dollars. "Week's wages," she said. "I suppose that's one way of taking care of a crackpot. But I'm surprised you didn't take his money and enjoy that vacation you've been yearning about."

"I did," Simon groaned. "Three times."

Betty stared at him. "You mean —"

Simon nodded, miserably.

She said, "But *Simon*. Fifty thousand dollars bonus. If that story was true, you should have gone back again to Munich. If there was one time traveler, there might have been —"

"I keep telling you," Simon said bitterly, "I went back there three times. There were hundreds of them. Probably thousands." He took a deep breath. "Listen, we're just going to have to forget about it. They're not going to stand for the space-time continuum track being altered. If something comes up that looks like it might result in the track being changed, they set you right back at the beginning and let things start-for you-all over again. They just can't allow anything to come back from the future and change the past."

"You mean," Betty was suddenly furious at him, "you've given up! Why this is the biggest thing — Why the fifty thousand dollars is nothing. The future! Just think!"

Simon said wearily, "There's just one thing you can bring back with you from the future, a hangover compounded of a gallon or so of Marzenbräu. What's more you can pile one on top of the other, and another on top of that!"

He shuddered. "If you think I'm going to take another crack at this merry-go-round and pile a fourth hangover on the three I'm already nursing, all at once, you can think again."

I'm a Stranger Here Myself

The Place de France is the town's hub. It marks the end of Boulevard Pasteur, the main drag of the westernized part of the city, and the beginning of Rue de la Liberté, which leads down to the Grand Socco and the medina. In a three-minute walk from the Place de France you can go from an ultra-modern, California-like resort to the Baghdad of Harun al-Rashid.

It's quite a town, Tangier.

King-size sidewalk cafes occupy three of the strategic corners on the Place de France. The Cafe de Paris serves the best draft beer in town, gets all the better custom, and has three shoeshine boys attached to the establishment. You can sit of a sunny morning and read the Paris edition of the New York *Herald Tribune* while getting your shoes done up like mirrors for thirty Moroccan francs which comes to about five cents at current exchange.

You can sit there, after the paper's read, sip your expresso and watch the people go by.

Tangier is possibly the most cosmopolitan city in the world. In native costume you'll see Berber and Rif, Arab and Blue Man, and occasionally a Senegalese from further south. In European dress you'll see Japs and Chinese, Hindus and Turks, Levantines and Filipinos, North Americans and South Americans, and, of course, even Europeans-from both sides of the Curtain.

In Tangier you'll find some of the world's poorest and some of the richest. The poorest will try to sell you anything from a shoeshine to their not very lily-white bodies, and the richest will avoid your eyes, afraid *you* might try to sell them something.

In spite of recent changes, the town still has its unique qualities. As a result of them the permanent population includes smugglers and black-marketeers, fugitives from justice and international con men, espionage and counter-espionage agents, homosexuals, nymphomaniacs, alcoholics, drug addicts, displaced persons, ex-royalty, and subversives of every flavor. Local law limits the activities of few of these.

Like I said, it's quite a town.

* * * * *

I looked up from my *Herald Tribune* and said, "Hello, Paul. Anything new cooking?"

He sank into the chair opposite me and looked around for the waiter. The tables were all crowded and since mine was a face he recognized, he assumed he was welcome to intrude. It was more or less standard procedure at the Cafe de Paris. It wasn't a place to go if you wanted to be alone.

Paul said, "How are you, Rupert? Haven't seen you for donkey's years."

The waiter came along and Paul ordered a glass of beer. Paul was an easy-going, sallow-faced little man. I vaguely remembered somebody saying he was from Liverpool and in exports.

"What's in the newspaper?" he said, disinterestedly.

"Pogo and Albert are going to fight a duel," I told him, "and Lil Abner is becoming a rock'n'roll singer."

He grunted.

"Oh," I said, "the intellectual type." I scanned the front page. "The Russkies have put up another manned satellite."

"They have, eh? How big?"

"Several times bigger than anything we Americans have."

The beer came and looked good, so I ordered a glass too.

Paul said, "What ever happened to those poxy flying saucers?"

"What flying saucers?"

A French girl went by with a poodle so finely clipped as to look as though it'd been shaven. The girl was in the latest from Paris. Every pore in place. We both looked after her.

"You know, what everybody was seeing a few years ago. It's too bad one of these bloody manned satellites wasn't up then. Maybe they would've seen one."

"That's an idea," I said.

We didn't say anything else for a while and I began to wonder if I could go back to my paper without rubbing him the wrong way. I didn't know Paul very well, but, for that matter, it's comparatively seldom you ever get to know anybody very well in Tangier. Largely, cards are played close to the chest.

* * * * *

My beer came and a plate of tapas for us both. Tapas at the Cafe de Paris are apt to be potato salad, a few anchovies, olives, and possibly some cheese. Free lunch, they used to call it in the States.

Just to say something, I said, "Where do you think they came from?" And when he looked blank, I added, "The Flying Saucers."

He grinned. "From Mars or Venus, or someplace."

"Ummmm," I said. "Too bad none of them ever crashed, or landed on the Yale football field and said *Take me to your cheerleader*, or something."

Paul yawned and said, "That was always the trouble with those crackpot blokes' explanations of them. If they were aliens from space, then why not show themselves?"

I ate one of the potato chips. It'd been cooked in rancid olive oil.

I said, "Oh, there are various answers to that one. We could probably sit around here and think of two or three that made sense."

Paul was mildly interested. "Like what?"

"Well, hell, suppose for instance there's this big Galactic League of civilized planets. But it's restricted, see. You're not eligible for membership until you, well, say until you've developed space flight. Then you're invited into the club. Meanwhile, they send secret missions down from time to time to keep an eye on your progress."

Paul grinned at me. "I see you read the same poxy stuff I do."

A Moorish girl went by dressed in a neatly tailored gray jellaba, European style high-heeled shoes, and a pinkish silk veil so transparent that you could see she wore lipstick. Very provocative, dark eyes can be over a veil. We both looked after her.

I said, "Or, here's another one. Suppose you have a very advanced civilization on, say, Mars."

"Not Mars. No air, and too bloody dry to support life."

"Don't interrupt, please," I said with mock severity. "This is a very old civilization and as the planet began to lose its water and air, it withdrew underground. Uses hydroponics and so forth, husbands its water and air. Isn't that what we'd do, in a few million years, if Earth lost its water and air?"

"I suppose so," he said. "Anyway, what about them?"

"Well, they observe how man is going through a scientific boom, an industrial boom, a population boom. A boom, period. Any day now he's going to have practical space ships. Meanwhile, he's also got the H-Bomb and the way he beats the drums on both sides of the Curtain, he's not against using it, if he could get away with it."

Paul said, "I got it. So they're scared and are keeping an eye on us. That's an old one. I've read that a dozen times, dished up different."

I shifted my shoulders. "Well, it's one possibility."

"I got a better one. How's this. There's this alien life form that's way ahead of us. Their civilization is so old that they don't have any records of when it began and how it was in the early days. They've gone beyond things like wars and depressions and revolutions, and greed for power or any of these things giving us a bad time here on Earth. They're all like scholars, get it? And some of them are pretty jolly well taken by Earth, especially the way we are right now, with all the problems, get it? Things developing so fast we don't know where we're going or how we're going to get there."

* * * * *

I finished my beer and clapped my hands for Mouley. "How do you mean, *where we're going?*"

"Well, take half the countries in the world today. They're trying to industrialize, modernize, catch up with the advanced countries. Look at Egypt, and Israel, and India and China, and Yugoslavia and Brazil, and all the rest. Trying to drag themselves up to the level of the advanced countries, and all using different methods of doing it. But look at the so-called advanced countries. Up to their bottoms in problems. Juvenile delinquents, climbing crime and suicide rates, the loony-bins full of the balmy, unemployed, threat of war, spending all their money on armaments instead of things like schools. All the bloody mess of it. Why, a man from Mars would be fascinated, like."

Mouley came shuffling up in his babouche slippers and we both ordered another schooner of beer.

Paul said seriously, "You know, there's only one big snag in this sort of talk. I've sorted the whole thing out before, and you always come up against this brick wall. Where are they, these observers, or scholars, or spies or whatever they are? Sooner or later we'd nab one of them. You know, Scotland Yard, or the F.B.I., or Russia's secret police, or the French Sûreté, or Interpol. This world is so deep in police, counter-espionage outfits and security agents that an alien would slip up in time, no matter how much he'd been trained. Sooner or later, he'd slip up, and they'd nab him."

I shook my head. "Not necessarily. The first time I ever considered this possibility, it seemed to me that such an alien would base himself in London or New York. Somewhere where he could use the libraries for research, get the daily newspapers and the magazines. Be right in the center of things. But now I don't think so. I think he'd be right here in Tangier."

"Why Tangier?"

"It's the one town in the world where anything goes. Nobody gives a damn about you or your affairs. For instance, I've known you a year or more now, and I haven't the slightest idea of how you make your living."

"That's right," Paul admitted. "In this town you seldom even ask a man where's he's from. He can be British, a White Russian, a Basque or a Sikh and nobody could care less. Where are *you* from, Rupert?"

"California," I told him.

"No, you're not," he grinned.

I was taken aback. "What do you mean?"

"I felt your mind probe back a few minutes ago when I was talking about Scotland Yard or the F.B.I. possibly flushing an alien. Telepathy is a sense not trained by the humanoids. If they had it, your job-and mine-would be considerably more difficult. Let's face it, in spite of these human bodies we're disguised in, neither of us is humanoid. Where are you really from, Rupert?"

"Aldebaran," I said. "How about you?"

"Deneb," he told me, shaking.

We had a laugh and ordered another beer.

"What're you doing here on Earth?" I asked him.

"Researching for one of our meat trusts. We're protein eaters. Humanoid flesh is considered quite a delicacy. How about you?"

"Scouting the place for thrill tourists. My job is to go around to these backward cultures and help stir up inter-tribal, or international, conflicts-all according to how advanced they are. Then our tourists come in-well shielded, of course-and get their kicks watching it."

Paul frowned. "That sort of practice could spoil an awful lot of good meat."

Summit

Two king-sized bands blared martial music, the "*Internationale*" and the "Star-Spangled Banner," each seemingly trying to drown the other in a *Götterdämmerung* of acoustics.

Two lines of troops, surfacely differing in uniforms and in weapons, but basically so very the same, so evenly matched, came to attention. A thousand hands slapped a thousand submachine gun stocks.

Marshal Vladimir Ignatov strode stiff-kneed down the long march, the stride of a man for years used to cavalry boots. He was flanked by frozen visaged subordinates, but none so cold of face as he himself.

At the entrance to the conference hall he stopped, turned and waited.

At the end of the corridor of troops a car stopped and several figures emerged, most of them in civilian dress, several bearing brief cases. They in their turn ran the gantlet.

At their fore walked James Warren Donlevy, spritely, his eyes darting here, there, politician-like. A half smile on his face, as though afraid he might forget to greet a voter he knew, or was supposed to know.

His hand was out before that of Vladimir Ignatov's.

"Your Excellency," he said.

Ignatov shook hands stiffly. Dropped that of the other's as soon as protocol would permit.

The field marshal indicated the door of the conference hall. "There is little reason to waste time, Mr. President."

"Exactly," Donlevy snapped.

The door closed behind them and the two men, one uniformed and bemedaled, the other nattily attired in his business suit, turned to each other.

"Nice to see you again, Vovo. How're Olga and the baby?"

The soldier grinned back in response. "Two babies now-you don't keep up on the *real* news, Jim. How's Martha?" They shook hands.

"Not so good," Jim said, scowling. "I'm worried. It's that new cancer. As soon as we conquer one type two more rear up. How are you people doing on cancer research?"

Vovo was stripping off his tunic. He hung it over the back of one of the chairs, began to unbutton his high, tight military collar. "I'm not really up on it, Jim, but I think that's one field where you can trust anything we know to be in the regular scientific journals our people exchange with yours. I'll make some inquiries when I get back home, though. You never know, this new strain —I guess you'd call it-might be one that we're up on and you aren't."

"Yeah," Jim said. "Thanks a lot." He crossed to the small portable bar. "How about a drink? Whisky, vodka, rum-there's ice."

Vovo slumped into one of the heavy chairs that were arranged around the table. He grimaced, "No vodka, I don't feel patriotic today. How about one of those long cold drinks, with the cola stuff?"

"Cuba libra," Jim said. "Coming up. Look, would you rather speak Russian?"

"No," Vovo said, "my English is getting rusty. I need the practice."

Jim brought the glasses over and put them on the table. He began stripping off his own coat, loosening his tie. "God, I'm tired," he said. "This sort of thing wears me down."

Vovo sipped his drink. "Now there's as good a thing to discuss as any, in the way of killing time. The truth now, Jim, do you really believe in a God? After all that's happened to this human race of ours, do you really believe in divine guidance?" He twisted his mouth sarcastically.

The other relaxed. "I don't know," he said. "I suppose so. I was raised in a family that believed in God. Just as, I suppose, you were raised in one that didn't." He lifted his shoulders slightly in a shrug. "Neither of us seems to be particularly brilliant in establishing a position of our own."

Vovo snorted. "Never thought of it that way," he admitted. "We're usually contemptuous of anyone still holding to the old beliefs. There aren't many left."

"More than you people admit, I understand."

Vovo shook his heavy head. "No, not really. Mostly crackpots. Have you ever noticed how it is that the nonconformists in any society are usually crackpots? The people on your side that admit belonging to our organizations, are usually on the wild eyed and uncombed hair side —I admit it. On the other hand, the people in our citizenry who subscribe to your system, your religion, that sort of thing, are crackpots, too. Applies to religion as well as politics. An atheist in your country is a nonconformist-in mine, a Christian is. Both crackpots."

Jim laughed and took a sip of his drink.

Vovo yawned and said, "How long are we going to be in here?"

"I don't know. Up to us, I suppose."

"Yes. How about another drink? I'll make it. How much of that cola stuff do you put in?"

Jim told him, and while the other was on his feet mixing the drinks, said, "You figure on sticking to the same line this year?"

"Have to," Vovo said over his shoulder. "What's the alternative?"

"I don't know. We're building up to a whale of a depression as it is, even with half the economy running full blast producing defense materials."

Vovo chuckled, "Defense materials. I wonder if ever in the history of the human race anyone ever admitted to producing *offense* materials."

"Well, you call it the same thing. All your military equipment is for defense. And, of course, according to your press, all ours is for offense."

"Of course," Vovo said.

He brought the glasses back and handed one to the other. He slumped back into his chair again, loosened two buttons of his trousers.

"Jim," Vovo said, "why don't you divert more of your economy to public works, better roads, reforestation, dams-that sort of thing."

Jim said wearily, "You're a better economist than that. Didn't your boy Marx, or was it Engels, write a small book on the subject? We're already overproducing-turning out more products than we can sell."

"I wasn't talking about your government building new steel mills. But dams, roads, that sort of thing. You could plow billions into such items and get some real use out of them. We both know that our weapons will never be used-they can't be."

Jim ticked them off on his fingers. "We already are producing more farm products than we know what to do with; if we build more dams it'll open up new farm lands and increase the glut. If we build more and better roads, it will improve transportation, which will mean fewer men will be able to move greater tonnage-and throw transportation employees into the unemployed. If we go all out for reforestation, it will eventually bring down the price of lumber and the lumber people are howling already. No," he shook his head, "there's just one really foolproof way of disposing of surpluses and using up labor power and that's war-hot or cold."

Vovo shrugged, "I suppose so."

"It amounts to building pyramids, of course." Jim twisted his mouth sourly. "And since we're asking questions about each other's way of life, when is your State going to begin to *wither away?*"

"How was that?" Vovo asked.

"According to your sainted founder, once you people came to power the State was going to wither away, class rule would be over, and Utopia be on hand. That was a long time ago, and your State is stronger than ours."

Vovo snorted. "How can we wither away the State as long as we are threatened by capitalist aggression?"

Jim said, "Ha!"

Vovo went on. "You know better than that, Jim. The only way my organization can keep in power is by continually beating the drums, keeping our people stirred up to greater and greater sacrifices by using you as a threat. Didn't the old Romans have some sort of maxim to the effect that when you're threatened with unease at home stir up trouble abroad?"

"You're being even more frank than usual," Jim said. "But that's one of the pleasures of these get-togethers, neither of us resorts to hypocrisy. But you can't keep up these tensions forever."

"You mean *we* can't keep up these tensions forever, Jim. And when they end? Well, personally I can't see my organization going out without a blood bath." He grimaced sourly, "And since I'd probably be one of the first to be bathed, I'd like to postpone the time. It's like having a tiger by the tail, Jim. We can't let go."

"Happily, I don't feel in the same spot," Jim said. He got up and went to the picture window that took up one entire wall. It faced out over a mountain vista. He looked soberly into the sky.

Vovo joined him, glass in hand.

"Possibly your position isn't exactly the same as ours but there'll be some awfully great changes if that military based economy of yours suddenly had peace thrust upon it. You'd have a depression such as you've never dreamed of. Let's face reality, Jim, neither of us can afford peace."

"Well, we've both known that for a long time."

They both considered somberly, the planet Earth blazing away, a small sun there in the sky.

Jim said, "I sometimes think that the race would have been better off, when man was colonizing Venus and Mars, if it had been a joint enterprise rather than you people doing one, and we the other. If it had all been in the hands of that organization..."

"The United Nations?" Vovo supplied.

"... Then when Bomb Day hit, perhaps these new worlds could have gone on to, well, better things."

"Perhaps," Vovo shrugged. "I've often wondered how Bomb Day started. Who struck the spark?"

"Happily there were enough colonists on both planets to start the race all over again," Jim said. "What difference does it make, who struck the spark?"

"None, I suppose." Vovo began to button his collar, readjust his clothes. "Well, shall we emerge and let the quaking multitudes know that once again we have made a shaky agreement? One that will last until the next summit meeting."

Revolution

Preface ... For some forty years critics of the U.S.S.R. have been desiring, predicting, not to mention praying for, its collapse. For twenty of these years the author of this story has vaguely wondered what would replace the collapsed Soviet system. A return to Czarism? Oh, come now! Capitalism as we know it today in the advanced Western countries? It would seem difficult after almost half a century of State ownership and control of the means of production, distribution, communications, education, science. Then what? The question became increasingly interesting following recent visits not only to Moscow and Leningrad but also to various other capital cities of the Soviet complex. A controversial subject? Indeed it is. You can't get much more controversial than this in the world today. But this is science fiction, and here we go.

Paul Koslovnodded briefly once or twice as he made his way through the forest of desks. Behind him he caught snatches of tittering voices in whisper.

"...That's him ...The Chief's hatchetman ...Know what they call him in Central America, a *pistola*, that means ...About Iraq ...And that time in Egypt ...Did you notice his eyes ...How would you like to date *him* ...That's him. I was at a cocktail party once when he was there. Shivery ...cold-blooded —"

Paul Koslov grinned inwardly. He hadn't asked for the reputation but it isn't everyone who is a legend before thirty-five. What was it *Newsweek* had called him? "The T. E. Lawrence of the Cold War." The trouble was it wasn't something you could turn off. It had its shortcomings when you found time for some personal life.

He reached the Chief's office, rapped with a knuckle and pushed his way through.

The Chief and a male secretary, who was taking dictation, looked up. The secretary frowned, evidently taken aback by the cavalier entrance, but the Chief said, "Hello, Paul, come on in. Didn't expect you quite so soon." And to the secretary, "Dickens, that's all."

When Dickens was gone the Chief scowled at his trouble-shooter. "Paul, you're bad for discipline around here. Can't you even knock before you enter? How is Nicaragua?"

Paul Koslov slumped into a leather easy-chair and scowled. "I did knock. Most of it's in my report. Nicaragua is ...tranquil. It'll stay tranquil for a while, too. There isn't so much as a parlor pink —"

"And Lopez —?"

Paul said slowly, "Last time I saw Raul was in a swamp near Lake Managua. The very last time."

The Chief said hurriedly, "Don't give me the details. I leave details up to you."

"I know," Paul said flatly.

His superior drew a pound can of Sir Walter Raleigh across the desk, selected a briar from a pipe rack and while he was packing in tobacco said, "Paul, do you know what day it is-and what year?"

"It's Tuesday. And 1965."

The bureau chief looked at his disk calendar. "Um-m-m. Today the Seven Year Plan is completed."

Paul snorted.

The Chief said mildly, "Successfully. For all practical purposes, the U.S.S.R. has surpassed us in gross national product."

"That's not the way I understand it."

"Then you make the mistake of believing our propaganda. That's always a mistake, believing your own propaganda. Worse than believing the other man's."

"Our steel capacity is a third again as much as theirs."

"Yes, and currently, what with our readjustment-remember when they used to call them *recessions*, or even earlier, *depressions* —our steel industry is operating at less than sixty per cent of capacity. The Soviets always operate at one hundred per cent of capacity. They don't have to worry about whether or not they can sell it. If they produce more steel than they immediately need, they use it to build another steel mill."

The Chief shook his head. "As long ago as 1958 they began passing us, product by product. Grain, butter, and timber production, jet aircraft, space flight, and coal —"

Paul leaned forward impatiently. "We put out more than three times as many cars, refrigerators, kitchen stoves, washing machines."

His superior said, "That's the point. While we were putting the product of our steel mills into automobiles and automatic kitchen equipment, they did without these things and put their steel into more steel mills, more railroads, more factories. We leaned back and took it easy, sneered at their progress, talked a lot about our freedom and liberty to our allies and the neutrals and enjoyed our refrigerators and washing machines until they finally passed us."

"You sound like a Tass broadcast from Moscow."

"Um-m-m, I've been trying to," the Chief said. "However, that's still roughly the situation. The fact that you and I personally, and a couple of hundred million Americans, prefer our cars and such to more steel mills, and prefer our personal freedoms and liberties is beside the point. We should have done less laughing seven years ago and more thinking about today. As things stand, give them a few more years at this pace and every neutral nation in the world is going to fall into their laps."

"That's putting it strong, isn't it?"

"Strong?" the Chief growled disgustedly. "That's putting it mildly. Even some of our allies are beginning to waver. Eight years ago, India and China both set out to industrialize themselves. Today, China is the third industrial power of the world. Where's India, about twentieth? Ten years from now China will probably be first. I don't even allow myself to think where she'll be twenty-five years from now."

"The Indians were a bunch of idealistic screwballs."

"That's one of the favorite alibis, isn't it? Actually we, the West, let them down. They couldn't get underway. The Soviets backed China with everything they could toss in."

Paul crossed his legs and leaned back. "It seems to me I've run into this discussion a few hundred times at cocktail parties."

The Chief pulled out a drawer and brought forth a king-size box of kitchen matches. He struck one with a thumbnail and peered through tobacco smoke at Paul Koslov as he lit up.

"The point is that the system the Russkies used when they started their first five-year plan back in 1928, and the system used in China, works. If we, with our traditions of freedom and liberty, like it or not, it works. Every citizen of the country is thrown into the grinding mill to increase production. Everybody," the Chief grinned sourly, "that is, except the party elite, who are running the whole thing. Everybody sacrifices for the sake of the progress of the whole country."

"I know," Paul said. "Give me enough time and I'll find out what this lecture is all about."

The Chief grunted at him. "The Commies are still in power. If they remain in power and continue to develop the way they're going, we'll be through, completely through, in another few years. We'll be so far behind we'll be the world's laughing-stock —and everybody else will be on the Soviet bandwagon."

He seemed to switch subjects. "Ever hear of Somerset Maugham?"

"Sure. I've read several of his novels."

"I was thinking of Maugham the British Agent, rather than Maugham the novelist, but it's the same man."

"British agent?"

"Um-m-m. He was sent to Petrograd in 1917 to prevent the Bolshevik revolution. The Germans had sent Lenin and Zinoviev up from Switzerland, where they'd been in exile, by a sealed train in hopes of starting a revolution in Czarist Russia. The point I'm leading to is that in one of his books, 'The Summing Up,' I believe, Maugham mentions in passing that had he got to Petrograd possibly six weeks earlier he thinks he could have done his job successfully."

Paul looked at him blankly. "What could he have done?"

The Chief shrugged. "It was all out war. The British wanted to keep Russia in the allied ranks so as to divert as many German troops as possible from the Western front. The Germans wanted to eliminate the Russians. Maugham had carte blanche. Anything would have gone. Elements of the British fleet to fight the Bolsheviks, unlimited amounts of money for anything he saw fit from bribery to hiring assassins. What would have happened, for instance, if he could have had Lenin and Trotsky killed?"

Paul said suddenly, "What has all this got to do with me?"

"We're giving you the job this time."

"Maugham's job?" Paul didn't get it.

"No, the other one. I don't know who the German was who engineered sending Lenin up to Petrograd, but that's the equivalent of your job." He seemed to go off on another bent. "Did you read Djilas' 'The New Class' about a decade ago?"

"Most of it, as I recall. One of Tito's top men who turned against the Commies and did quite a job of exposing the so-called classless society."

"That's right. I've always been surprised that so few people bothered to wonder how Djilas was able to smuggle his book out of one of Tito's strongest prisons and get it to publishers in the West."

"Never thought of it," Paul agreed. "How could he?"

"Because," the Chief said, knocking the ash from his pipe and replacing it in the rack, "there was and is a very strong underground in all the Communist countries. Not only Yugoslavia, but the Soviet Union as well."

Paul stirred impatiently. "Once again, what's all this got to do with me?"

"They're the ones you're going to work with. The anti-Soviet underground. You've got unlimited leeway. Unlimited support to the extent we can get it to you. Unlimited funds for whatever you find you need them for. Your job is to help the underground start a new Russian Revolution."

* * * * *

Paul Koslov, his face still bandaged following plastic surgery, spent a couple of hours in the Rube Goldberg department inspecting the latest gadgets of his trade.

Derek Stevens said, "The Chief sent down a memo to introduce you to this new item. We call it a Tracy."

Paul frowned at the wristwatch, fingered it a moment, held it to his ear. It ticked and the second hand moved. "Tracy?" he said.

Stevens said, "After Dick Tracy. Remember, a few years ago? His wrist two-way radio."

"But this is really a watch," Paul said.

"Sure. Keeps fairly good time, too. However, that's camouflage. It's also a two-way radio. Tight beam from wherever you are to the Chief."

Paul pursed his lips. "The transistor boys are really doing it up brown." He handed the watch back to Derek Stevens. "Show me how it works, Derek."

They spent fifteen minutes on the communications device, then Derek Stevens said, "Here's another item the Chief thought you might want to see:"

It was a compact, short-muzzled hand gun. Paul handled it with the ease of long practice. "The grip's clumsy. What's its advantage? I don't particularly like an automatic."

Derek Stevens motioned with his head. "Come into the firing range, Koslov, and we'll give you a demonstration."

Paul shot him a glance from the side of his eyes, then nodded. "Lead on."

In the range, Stevens had a man-size silhouette put up. He stood to one side and said, "O.K., let her go."

Paul stood easily, left hand in pants pocket, brought the gun up and tightened on the trigger. He frowned and pressed again.

He scowled at Derek Stevens. "It's not loaded."

Stevens grunted amusement. "Look at the target. First time you got it right over the heart."

"I'll be ...," Paul began. He looked down at the weapon in surprise. "Noiseless and recoilless. What caliber is it, Derek, and what's the muzzle velocity?"

"We call it the .38 Noiseless," Stevens said. "It has the punch of that .44 Magnum you're presently carrying."

With a fluid motion Paul Koslov produced the .44 Magnum from the holster under his left shoulder and tossed it to one side. "That's the last time I tote that cannon," he said. He balanced the new gun in his hand in admiration. "Have the front sight taken off for me, Derek, and the fore part of the trigger guard. I need a quick draw gun." He added absently, "How did you know I carried a .44?"

Stevens said, "You're rather famous, Koslov. The Colonel Lawrence of the Cold War. The journalists are kept from getting very much about you, but what they do learn they spread around."

Paul Koslov said flatly, "Why don't you like me, Stevens? In this game I don't appreciate people on our team who don't like me. It's dangerous."

Derek Stevens flushed. "I didn't say I didn't like you."

"You didn't have to."

"It's nothing personal," Stevens said.

Paul Koslov looked at him.

Stevens said, "I don't approve of Americans committing political assassinations."

Paul Koslov grinned wolfishly and without humor. "You'll have a hard time proving that even our cloak and dagger department has ever authorized assassination, Stevens. By the way, I'm not an American."

Derek Stevens was not the type of man whose jaw dropped, but he blinked. "Then what are you?"

"A Russian," Paul snapped. "And look, Stevens, we're busy now, but when you've got some time to do a little thinking, consider the ethics of warfare."

Stevens was flushed again at the tone. "Ethics of warfare?"

"There aren't any," Paul Koslov snapped. "There hasn't been chivalry in war for a long time, and there probably never will be again. Neither side can afford it. And I'm talking about cold war as well as hot." He scowled at the other. "Or did you labor under the illusion that only the Commies had tough operators on their side?"

* * * * *

Paul Koslov crossed the Atlantic in a supersonic TU-180 operated by Europa Airways. That in itself galled him. It was bad enough that the Commies had stolen a march on the West with the first jet liner to go into mass production, the TU-104 back in 1957. By the time the United States brought out its first really practical trans-Atlantic jets in 1959 the Russians had come up with the TU-114 which its designer, old Andrei Tupolev named the largest, most efficient and economical aircraft flying.

In civil aircraft they had got ahead and stayed ahead. Subsidized beyond anything the West could or at least would manage, the air lines of the world couldn't afford to operate the slower, smaller and more expensive Western models. One by one, first the neutrals such as India, and then even members of the Western bloc began equipping their air lines with Russian craft.

Paul grunted his disgust at the memory of the strong measures that had to be taken by the government to prevent even some of the American lines from buying Soviet craft at the unbelievably low prices they offered them.

* * * * *

In London he presented a card on which he had added a numbered code in pencil. Handed it over a desk to the British intelligence major.

"I believe I'm expected," Paul said.

The major looked at him, then down at the card. "Just a moment, Mr. Smith. I'll see if his lordship is available. Won't you take a chair?" He left the room.

Paul Koslov strolled over to the window and looked out on the moving lines of pedestrians below. He had first been in London some thirty years ago. So far as he could remember, there were no noticeable changes with the exception of automobile design. He wondered vaguely how long it took to make a noticeable change in the London street scene.

The major re-entered the room with a new expression of respect on his face. "His lordship will see you immediately, Mr. Smith."

"Thanks," Paul said. He entered the inner office.

Lord Carrol was attired in civilian clothes which somehow failed to disguise a military quality in his appearance. He indicated a chair next to his desk. "We've been instructed to give you every assistance Mr. ... Smith. Frankly, I can't imagine of just what this could consist."

Paul said, as he adjusted himself in the chair, "I'm going into the Soviet Union on an important assignment. I'll need as large a team at my disposal as we can manage. You have agents in Russia, of course?" He lifted his eyebrows.

His lordship cleared his throat and his voice went even stiffer. "All major military nations have a certain number of espionage operatives in each other's countries. No matter how peaceful the times, this is standard procedure."

"And these are hardly peaceful times," Paul said dryly. "I'll want a complete list of your Soviet based agents and the necessary information on how to contact them."

Lord Carrol stared at him. Finally sputtered, "Man, *why*? You're not even a British national. This is —"

Paul, held up a hand. "We're co-operating with the Russian underground. Co-operating isn't quite strong enough a word. We're going to *push* them into activity if we can."

The British intelligence head looked down at the card before him. "Mr. Smith," he read. He looked up. "John Smith, I assume."

Paul said, still dryly, "Is there any other?"

Lord Carrol said, "See here, you're really Paul Koslov, aren't you?"

Paul looked at him, said nothing.

Lord Carrol said impatiently, "What you ask is impossible. Our operatives all have their own assignments, their own work. Why do you need them?"

"This is the biggest job ever, overthrowing the Soviet State. We need as many men as we can get on our team. Possibly I won't have to use them but, if I do, I want them available."

The Britisher rapped, "You keep mentioning *our team* but according to the dossier we carry on you, Mr. Koslov, you are neither British nor even a Yankee. And you ask me to turn over our complete Soviet machinery."

Paul came to his feet and leaned over the desk, there was a paleness immediately beneath his ears and along his jaw line. "Listen," he said tightly, "if I'm not on this team, there just is no team. Just a pretense of one. When there's a real team there has to be a certain spirit. A team spirit. I don't care if you're playing cricket, football or international cold war. If there's one thing that's important to me, that I've based my whole life upon, it's this, understand? *I've* got team spirit. Perhaps no one else in the whole West has it, but *I* do."

Inwardly, Lord Carrol was boiling. He snapped, "You're neither British nor American. In other words, you are a mercenary. How do we know that the Russians won't offer you double or triple what the Yankees pay for your services?"

Paul sat down again and looked at his watch. "My time is limited," he said. "I have to leave for Paris this afternoon and be in Bonn tomorrow. I don't care what opinions you might have in regard to my mercenary motives, Lord Carrol. I've just come from Downing Street. I suggest you make a phone call there. At the request of Washington, your government has given me carte blanche in this matter."

* * * * *

Paul flew into Moscow in an Aeroflot jet, landing at Vnukovo airport on the outskirts of the city. He entered as an American businessman, a camera importer who was also interested in doing a bit of tourist sightseeing. He was traveling deluxe category which entitled him to a Zil complete with chauffeur and an interpreter-guide when he had need of one. He was quartered in the Ukrayna, on Dorogomilovskaya Quai, a twenty-eight floor skyscraper with a thousand rooms.

It was Paul's first visit to Moscow but he wasn't particularly thrown off. He kept up with developments and was aware of the fact that as early as the late 1950s, the Russians had begun to lick the problems of ample food, clothing and finally shelter. Even those products once considered sheer luxuries were now in abundant supply. If material things alone had been all that counted, the Soviet man in the street wasn't doing so badly.

He spent the first several days getting the feel of the city and also making his preliminary business calls. He was interested in a new "automated" camera currently being touted by the Russians as the world's best. Fastest lens, foolproof operation, guaranteed for the life of the owner, and retailing for exactly twenty-five dollars.

He was told, as expected, that the factory and distribution point was in Leningrad and given instructions and letters of introduction.

On the fifth day he took the Red Arrow Express to Leningrad and established himself at the Astoria Hotel, 39 Hertzen Street. It was one of the many of the Intourist hotels going back to before the revolution.

He spent the next day allowing his guide to show him the standard tourist sights. The Winter Palace, where the Bolshevik revolution was won when the mutinied cruiser *Aurora* steamed up the river and shelled it. The Hermitage Museum, rivaled only by the Vatican and Louvre. The Alexandrovskaya Column, the world's tallest monolithic stone monument. The modest personal palace of Peter the Great. The Peter and Paul Cathedral. The king-size Kirov Stadium. The Leningrad subway, as much a museum as a system of transportation.

He saw it all, tourist fashion, and wondered inwardly what the Intourist guide would have thought had he known that this was Mr. John Smith's home town.

The day following, he turned his business problem over to the guide. He wanted to meet, let's see now, oh yes, here it is, Leonid Shvernik, of the Mikoyan Camera works. Could it be arranged?

Of course it could be arranged. The guide went into five minutes of oratory on the desire of the Soviet Union to trade with the West, and thus spread everlasting peace.

An interview was arranged for Mr. Smith with Mr. Shvernik for that afternoon.

Mr. Smith met Mr. Shvernik in the latter's office at two and they went through the usual amenities. Mr. Shvernik spoke excellent English so Mr. Smith was able to dismiss his interpreter-guide for the afternoon. When he was gone and they were alone Mr. Shvernik went into his sales talk.

"I can assure you, sir, that not since the Japanese startled the world with their new cameras shortly after the Second War, has any such revolution in design and quality taken place. The

Mikoyan is not only the *best* camera produced anywhere, but since our plant is fully automated, we can sell it for a fraction the cost of German, Japanese or American —"

Paul Koslov came to his feet, walked quietly over to one of the pictures hanging on the wall, lifted it, pointed underneath and raised his eyebrows at the other.

Leonid Shvernik leaned back in his chair, shocked.

Paul remained there until at last the other shook his head.

Paul said, in English, "Are you absolutely sure?"

"Yes." Shvernik said. "There are no microphones in here. I absolutely know. Who are you?"

Paul said, "In the movement they call you Georgi, and you're top man in the Leningrad area."

Shvernik's hand came up from under the desk and he pointed a heavy military revolver at his visitor. "Who are you?" he repeated.

Paul ignored the gun. "Someone who knows that you are Georgi," he said "I'm from America. Is there any chance of anybody intruding?"

"Yes, one of my colleagues. Or perhaps a secretary."

"Then I suggest we go to a bar, or some place, for a drink or a cup of coffee or whatever the current Russian equivalent might be."

Shvernik looked at him searchingly. "Yes," he said finally. "There's a place down the street." He began to stick the gun in his waistband, changed his mind and put it back into the desk drawer.

As soon as they were on the open street and out of earshot of other pedestrians, Paul said, "Would you rather I spoke Russian? I have the feeling that we'd draw less attention than if we speak English."

Shvernik said tightly, "Do the Intourist people know you speak Russian? If not, stick to English. Now, how do you know my name? I have no contacts with the Americans."

"I got it through my West German contacts."

The Russian's face registered unsuppressed fury. "Do they ignore the simplest of precautions! Do they reveal me to every source that asks?"

Paul said mildly, "Herr Ludwig is currently under my direction. Your secret is as safe as it has ever been."

The underground leader remained silent for a long moment. "You're an American, eh, and Ludwig told you about me? What do you want now?"

"To help," Paul Koslov said.

"How do you mean, to help? How can you help? I don't know what you're talking about."

"Help in any way you want. Money, printing presses, mimeograph machines, radio transmitters, weapons, manpower in limited amounts, know-how, training, anything you need to help overthrow the Soviet government."

They had reached the restaurant. Leonid Shvernik became the Russian export official. He ushered his customer to a secluded table. Saw him comfortably into his chair.

"Do you actually know anything about cameras?" he asked.

"Yes," Paul said, "we're thorough. I can buy cameras from you and they'll be marketed in the States."

"Good." The waiter was approaching. Shvernik said, "Have you ever eaten caviar Russian style?"

"I don't believe so," Paul said "I'm not very hungry."

"Nothing to do with hunger." Shvernik said. From the waiter he ordered raisin bread, sweet butter, caviar and a carafe of vodka.

The waiter went off for it and Shvernik said, "To what extent are you willing to help us? Money, for instance. What kind of money, rubles, dollars? And how much? A revolutionary movement can always use money."

"Any kind," Paul said flatly, "and any amount."

Shvernik was impressed. He said eagerly, "Any amount within reason, eh?"

Paul looked into his face and said flatly, "Any amount, period. It doesn't have to be particularly reasonable. Our only qualification would be a guarantee it is going into the attempt to overthrow the Soviets-not into private pockets."

The waiter was approaching. Shvernik drew some brochures from his pocket, spread them before Paul Koslov and began to point out with a fountain pen various features of the Mikoyan camera.

The waiter put the order on the table and stood by for a moment for further orders.

Shvernik said, "First you take a sizable portion of vodka, like this." He poured them two jolts. "And drink it down, ah, bottoms up, you Americans say. Then you spread butter on a small slice of raisin bread, and cover it with a liberal portion of caviar. Good? Then you eat your little sandwich and drink another glass of vodka. Then you start all over again."

"I can see it could be fairly easy to get stoned, eating caviar Russian style," Paul laughed.

They went through the procedure and the waiter wandered off.

Paul said, "I can take several days arranging the camera deal with you. Then I can take a tour of the country, supposedly giving it a tourist look-see, but actually making contact with more of your organization. I can then return in the future, supposedly to make further orders. I can assure you, these cameras are going to sell very well in the States. I'll be coming back, time and again-for business reasons. Meanwhile, do you have any members among the interpreter-guides in the local Intourist offices?"

Shvernik nodded. "Yes. And, yes, that would be a good idea. We'll assign Ana Furtseva to you, if we can arrange it. And possibly she can even have a chauffeur assigned you who'll also be one of our people."

That was the first time Paul Koslov heard the name Ana Furtseva.

* * * * *

In the morning Leonid Shvernik came to the hotel in a Mikoyan Camera Works car loaded with cameras and the various accessories that were available for the basic model. He began gushing the advantages of the Mikoyan before they were well out of the hotel.

The last thing he said, as they trailed out of the hotel's portals was, "We'll drive about town, giving you an opportunity to do some snapshots and then possibly to my country dacha where we can have lunch —"

At the car he said, "May I introduce Ana Furtseva, who's been assigned as your guide-interpreter by Intourist for the balance of your stay? Ana, Mr. John Smith."

Paul shook hands.

She was blond as almost all Russian girls are blond, and with the startling blue eyes. A touch chubby, by Western standards, but less so than the Russian average. She had a disturbing pixie touch around the mouth, out of place in a dedicated revolutionist.

The car took off with Shvernik at the wheel. "You're actually going to have to take pictures as we go along. We'll have them developed later at the plant. I've told them that you are potentially a very big order. Possibly they'll try and assign one of my superiors to your account after a day or two. If so, I suggest that you merely insist that you feel I am competent and you would rather continue with me."

"Of course," Paul said. "Now then, how quickly can our assistance to you get underway?"

"The question is," Shvernik said, "just how much you can do in the way of helping our movement. For instance, can you get advanced type weapons to us?"

The .38 Noiseless slid easily into Paul's hands. "Obviously, we can't smuggle sizable military equipment across the border. But here, for instance, is a noiseless, recoilless hand gun. We could deliver any reasonable amount within a month."

"Five thousand?" Shvernik asked.

"I think so. You'd have to cover once they got across the border, of course. How well organized are you? If you aren't, possibly we can help there, but not in time to get five thousand guns to you in a month."

Ana was puzzled. "How could you possibly get that number across the Soviet borders?" Her voice had a disturbing Slavic throatiness. It occurred to Paul Koslov that she was one of the most attractive women he had ever met. He was amused. Women had never played a great part in his life. There had never been anyone who had really, basically, appealed. But evidently blood was telling. Here he had to come back to Russia to find such attractiveness.

He said, "The Yugoslavs are comparatively open and smuggling across the Adriatic from Italy, commonplace. We'd bring the things you want in that way. Yugoslavia and Poland are on good terms, currently, with lots of trade. We'd ship them by rail from Yugoslavia to Warsaw. Trade between Poland and U.S.S.R. is on massive scale. Our agents in Warsaw would send on the guns in well concealed shipments. Freight cars aren't searched at the Polish-Russian border. However, your agents would have to pick up the deliveries in Brest or Kobryn, before they got as far as Pinsk."

Ana said, her voice very low, "Visiting in Sweden at the Soviet Embassy in Stockholm is a colonel who is at the head of the Leningrad branch of the KGB department in charge of counter-revolution, as they call it. Can you eliminate him?"

"Is it necessary? Are you sure that if it's done it might not raise such a stink that the KGB might concentrate more attention on you?" Paul didn't like this sort of thing. It seldom accomplished anything.

Ana said, "He knows that both Georgi and I are members of the movement."

Paul Koslov gaped at her. "You mean your position is known to the police?"

Shvernik said, "Thus far he has kept the information to himself. He found out when Ana tried to enlist his services."

Paul's eyes went from one to the other of them in disbelief. "Enlist his services? How do you know he hasn't spilled everything? What do you mean he's kept the information to himself so far?"

Ana said, her voice so low as to be hardly heard, "He's my older brother. I'm his favorite sister. How much longer he will keep our secret I don't know. Under the circumstances, I can think of no answer except that he be eliminated."

It came to Paul Koslov that the team on this side could be just as dedicated as he was to his own particular cause.

He said, "A Colonel Furtseva at the Soviet Embassy in Stockholm. Very well. A Hungarian refugee will probably be best. If he's caught, the reason for the killing won't point in your direction."

"Yes," Ana said, her sensitive mouth twisting. "In fact, Anastas was in Budapest during the suppression there in 1956. He participated."

* * * * *

The dacha of Leonid Shvernik was in the vicinity of Petrodvorets on the Gulf of Finland, about eighteen miles from Leningrad proper. It would have been called a summer bungalow in the States. On the rustic side. Three bedrooms, a moderately large living-dining room, kitchen, bath, even a car port. Paul Koslov took a mild satisfaction in deciding that an American in Shvernik's equivalent job could have afforded more of a place than this.

Shvernik was saying, "I hope it never gets to the point where you have to go on the run. If it does, this house is a center of our activities. At any time you can find clothing here, weapons, money, food. Even a small boat on the waterfront. It would be possible, though difficult, to reach Finland."

"Right," Paul said. "Let's hope there'll never be occasion."

Inside, they sat around a small table, over the inevitable bottle of vodka and cigarettes, and later coffee.

Shvernik said, "Thus far we've rambled around hurriedly on a dozen subjects but now we must become definite."

Paul nodded.

"You come to us and say you represent the West and that you wish to help overthrow the Soviets. Fine. How do we know you do not actually represent the KGB or possibly the MVD?"

Paul said, "I'll have to prove otherwise by actions." He came to his feet and, ignoring Ana, pulled out his shirt tail, unbuttoned the top two buttons of his pants and unbuckled the money belt beneath.

He said, "We have no idea what items you'll be wanting from us in the way of equipment, but as you said earlier all revolutions need money. So here's the equivalent of a hundred thousand American dollars-in rubles, of course." He added apologetically, "The smallness of the amount is due to bulk. Your Soviet money doesn't come in sufficiently high denominations for a single person to carry really large amounts."

He tossed the money belt to the table, rearranged his clothing and returned to his chair.

Shvernik said, "A beginning, but I am still of the opinion that we should not introduce you to any other members of the organization until we have more definite proof of your background."

"That's reasonable," Paul agreed. "Now what else?"

Shvernik scowled at him. "You claim you are an American but you speak as good Russian as I do."

"I was raised in America," Paul said, "but I never became a citizen because of some minor technicality while I was a boy. After I reached adulthood and first began working for the government, it was decided that it might be better, due to my type of specialization, that I continue to remain legally not an American."

"But actually you are Russian?"

"I was born here in Leningrad," Paul said evenly.

Ana leaned forward, "Why then, actually, you're a traitor to Russia."

Paul laughed. "Look who's talking. A leader of the underground."

Ana wasn't amused. "But there is a difference in motivation. I fight to improve my country. You fight for the United States and the West."

"I can't see much difference. We're both trying to overthrow a vicious bureaucracy." He laughed again. "You hate them as much as I do."

"I don't know." She frowned, trying to find words, dropped English and spoke in Russian. "The Communists made mistakes, horrible mistakes and-especially under Stalin-were vicious beyond belief to achieve what they wanted. But they did achieve it. They built our country into the world's strongest."

"If you're so happy with them, why are you trying to eliminate the Commies? You don't make much sense."

She shook her head, as though it was he who made no sense. "They are through now, no longer needed. A hindrance to progress." She hesitated, then, "When I was a student I remember being so impressed by something written by Nehru that I memorized it. He wrote it while in a British jail in 1935. Listen." She closed her eyes and quoted:

"Economic interests shape the political views of groups and classes. Neither reason nor moral considerations override these interests. Individuals may be converted, they may surrender their special privileges, although this is rare enough, but classes and groups do not do so. The attempt to convert a governing and privileged class into forsaking power and giving up its unjust privileges has therefore always so far failed, and there seems to be no reason whatever to hold that it will succeed in the future."

Paul was frowning at her. "What's your point?"

"My point is that the Communists are in the position Nehru speaks of. They're in power and won't let go. The longer they remain in power after their usefulness is over, the more vicious they must become to maintain themselves. Since this is a police state the only way to get them out is through violence. That's why I find myself in the underground. But I am a patriotic Russian!" She turned to him. "Why do *you* hate the Soviets so, Mr. Smith?"

The American agent shrugged. "My grandfather was a member of the minor aristocracy. When the Bolsheviks came to power he joined Wrangel's White Army. When the Crimea fell he was in the rear guard. They shot him."

"That was your grandfather?" Shvernik said.

"Right. However, my own father was a student at the Petrograd University at that time. Left wing inclined, in fact. I think he belonged to Kerensky's Social Democrats. At any rate, in spite of his upper class background he made out all right for a time. In fact he became an instructor and our early life wasn't particularly bad." Paul cleared his throat. "Until the purges in the 1930s. It was decided that my father was a Bukharinist Right Deviationist, whatever that was. They came and got him one night in 1938 and my family never saw him again."

Paul disliked the subject. "To cut it short, when the war came along, my mother was killed in the Nazi bombardment of Leningrad. My brother went into the army and became a lieutenant. He was captured by the Germans when they took Kharkov, along with a hundred thousand or so others of the Red Army. When the Soviets, a couple of years later, pushed back into Poland he was recaptured."

Ana said, "You mean liberated from the Germans?"

"Recaptured, is the better word. The Soviets shot him. It seems that officers of the Red Army aren't allowed to surrender."

Ana said painfully, "How did you escape all this?"

"My father must have seen the handwriting on the wall. I was only five years old when he sent me to London to a cousin. A year later we moved to the States. Actually, I have practically no memories of Leningrad, very few of my family. However, I am not very fond of the Soviets."

"No," Ana said softly.

Shvernik said, "And what was your father's name?"

"Theodore Koslov."

Shvernik said, "I studied French literature under him."

Ana stiffened in her chair, and her eyes went wide. "Koslov," she said. "You must be Paul Koslov."

Paul poured himself another small vodka. "In my field it is a handicap to have a reputation. I didn't know it had extended to the man in the street on this side of the Iron Curtain."

* * * * *

It was by no means the last trip that Paul Koslov was to make to his underground contacts, nor the last visit to the dacha at Petrodvorets.

In fact, the dacha became the meeting center of the Russian underground with their liaison agent from the West. Through it funneled the problems involved in the logistics of the thing. Spotted through the rest of the vast stretches of the country, Paul had his local agents, American, British, French, West German. But this was the center.

The Mikoyan Camera made a great success in the States. And little wonder. Unknown to the Soviets, the advertising campaign that sold it cost several times the income from the sales. All they saw were the continued orders, the repeated visits of Mr. John Smith to Leningrad on buying trips. Leonid Shvernik was even given a promotion on the strength of his so ably cracking the American market. Ana Furtseva was automatically assigned to Paul as interpreter-guide whenever he appeared in the Soviet Union's second capital.

In fact, when he made his "tourist" jaunts to the Black Sea region, to the Urals, to Turkestan, to Siberia, he was able to have her assigned to the whole trip with him. It gave a tremendous advantage in his work with the other branches of the underground.

Questions, unthought of originally when Paul Koslov had been sent into the U.S.S.R., arose as the movement progressed.

On his third visit to the dacha he said to Shvernik and three others of the organization's leaders who had gathered for the conference, "Look, my immediate superior wants me to find out who is to be your top man, the chief of state of the new regime when Number One and the present hierarchy have been overthrown."

Leonid Shvernik looked at him blankly. By this stage, he, as well as Ana, had become more to Paul than just pawns in the game being played. For some reason, having studied under the older Koslov seemed to give a personal touch that had grown.

Nikolai Kirichenko, a higher-up in the Moscow branch of the underground, looked strangely at Paul then at Shvernik. "What have you told him about the nature of our movement?" he demanded.

Paul said, "What's the matter? All I wanted to know was who was scheduled to be top man."

Shvernik said, "Actually, I suppose we have had little time to discus the nature of the new society we plan. We've been busy working on the overthrow of the Communists. However, I thought..."

Paul was uneasy now. Leonid was right. Actually in his association with both Ana and Leonid Shvernik they had seldom mentioned what was to follow the collapse of the Soviets. It suddenly occurred to him how overwhelmingly important this was.

Nikolai Kirichenko, who spoke no English, said in Russian, "See here, we are not an organization attempting to seize power for ourselves."

This was a delicate point, Paul sensed. Revolutions are seldom put over in the name of reaction or even conservatism. Whatever the final product, they are invariably presented as being motivated by liberal idealism and progress.

He said, "I am familiar with the dedication of your organization. I have no desire to underestimate your ideals. However, my question is presented with good intentions and remains unanswered. You aren't anarchists, I know. You expect a responsible government to be in control after the removal of the police state. So I repeat, who is to be your head man?"

"How would we know?" Kirichenko blurted in irritation. "We're working toward a democracy. It's up to the Russian people to elect any officials they may find necessary to govern the country."

Shvernik said, "However, the very idea of a *head man*, as you call him, is opposed to what we have in mind. We aren't looking for a super-leader. We've had enough of leaders. Our experience is that it is too easy for them to become misleaders. If the history of this century has proven anything with its Mussolinis, Hitlers, Stalins, Chiangs, and Maos, it is that the search for a leader to take over the problems of a people is a vain one. The job has to be done by the people themselves."

Paul hadn't wanted to get involved in the internals of their political ideology. It was dangerous ground. For all he knew, there might be wide differences within the ranks of the revolutionary movement. There almost always were. He couldn't take sides. His only interest in all this was the overthrow of the Soviets.

He covered. "Your point is well taken, of course. I understand completely. Oh, and here's one other matter for discussion. These radio transmitters for your underground broadcasts."

It was a subject in which they were particularly interested. The Russians leaned forward.

"Here's the problem," Kirichenko said. "As you know, the Soviet Union consists of fifteen republics. In addition there are seventeen Autonomous Soviet Socialist Republics that coexist within these basic fifteen republics. There are also ten of what we call Autonomous Regions. Largely, each of these political divisions speak different languages and have their own cultural differences."

Paul said, "Then it will be necessary to have transmitters for each of these areas?"

"Even more. Because some are so large that we will find it necessary to have more than one underground station."

Leonid Shvernik said worriedly, "And here is another thing. The KGB has the latest in equipment for spotting the location of an illegal station. Can you do anything about this?"

Paul said, "We'll put our best electronics men to work. The problem as I understand it, is to devise a method of broadcasting that the secret police can't trace."

They looked relieved. "Yes, that is the problem," Kirichenko said.

* * * * *

He brought up the subject some time later when he was alone with Ana. They were strolling along the left bank of the Neva River, paralleling the Admiralty Building, supposedly on a sightseeing tour.

He said, "I was discussing the future government with Leonid and some of the others the other day. I don't think I got a very clear picture of it." He gave her a general rundown of the conversation.

She twisted her mouth characteristically at him. "What did you expect, a return to Czarism? Let me see, who is pretender to the throne these days? Some Grand Duke in Paris, isn't it?"

He laughed with her. "I'm not up on such questions," Paul admitted. "I think I rather pictured a democratic parliamentary government, somewhere between the United States and England."

"Those are governmental forms based on a capitalist society, Paul."

Her hair gleamed in the brightness of the sun and he had to bring his mind back to the conversation.

"Well, yes. But you're overthrowing the Communists. That's the point, isn't it?"

"Not the way you put it. Let's set if I can explain. To begin with, there have only been three bases of government evolved by man ... I'm going to have to simplify this."

"It isn't my field, but go on," Paul said. She wore less lipstick than you'd expect on an American girl but it went with her freshness.

"The first type of governmental system was based on the family. Your American Indians were a good example. The family, the clan, the tribe. In some cases, like the Iroquois Confederation, a nation of tribes. You were represented in the government according to the family or clan in which you were born."

"Still with you so far," Paul said. She had a very slight dimple in her left cheek. Dimples went best with blondes, Paul decided.

"The next governmental system was based on property. Chattel slavery, feudalism, capitalism. In ancient Athens, for example, those Athenians who owned the property of the City-State, and the slaves with which to work it, also governed the nation. Under feudalism, the nobility owned the country and governed it. The more land a noble owned, the larger his voice in government. I'm speaking broadly, of course."

"Of course," Paul said. He decided that she had more an American type figure than was usual here. He brought his concentration back to the subject. "However, that doesn't apply under capitalism. We have democracy. Everyone votes, not just the owner of property."

Ana was very serious about it. "You mustn't use the words capitalism and democracy interchangeably. You can have capitalism, which is a social system, without having democracy which is a political system. For instance, when Hitler was in power in Germany the government was a dictatorship but the social system was still capitalism."

Then she grinned at him mischievously. "Even in the United States I think you'll find that the people who own a capitalist country run the country. Those who control great wealth have a large say in the running of the political parties, both locally and nationally. Your smaller property owners have a smaller voice in local politics. But how large a lobby does your itinerant harvest worker in Texas have in Washington?"

Paul said, slightly irritated now, "This is a big subject and I don't agree with you. However, I'm not interested now in the government of the United States. I want to know what you people have in store for Russia, if and when you take over."

She shook her head in despair at him. "That's the point the others were trying to make to you. We have no intention of taking over. We don't want to and probably couldn't even if we did want to. What we're advocating is a new type of government based on a new type of representation."

He noticed the faint touch of freckles about her nose, her shoulders-to the extent her dress revealed them-and on her arms. Her skin was fair as only the northern races produce.

Paul said, "All right. Now we get to this third base of government. The first was the family, the second was property. What else is there?"

"In an ultramodern, industrialized society, there is your method of making your livelihood. In the future you will be represented from where you work. From your industry or profession. The parliament, or congress, of the nation would consist of elected members from each branch of production, distribution, communication, education, medicine —"

"Syndicalism," Paul said, "with some touches of Technocracy."

She shrugged. "Your American Technocracy of the 1930s I am not too familiar with, although I understand power came from top to bottom, rather than from bottom to top, democratically. The early syndicalists developed some of the ideas which later thinkers have elaborated upon, I suppose. So many of these terms have become all but meaningless through sloppy use. What in the world does Socialism mean, for instance? According to some, your Roosevelt was a Socialist. Hitler called himself a National Socialist. Mussolini once edited a Socialist paper. Stalin called himself a Socialist and the British currently have a Socialist government-mind you, with a Queen on the throne."

"The advantage of voting from where you work rather than from where you live doesn't come home to me," Paul said.

"Among other things, a person knows the qualifications of the people with whom he works," Ana said, "whether he is a scientist in a laboratory or a technician in an automated factory. But how many people actually know anything about the political candidates for whom they vote?"

"I suppose we could discuss this all day," Paul said. "But what I was getting to is what happens when your outfit takes over here in Leningrad? Does Leonid become local commissar, or head of police, or ...well, whatever new title you've dreamed up?"

Ana laughed at him, as though he was impossible. "Mr. Koslov, you have a mind hard to penetrate. I keep telling you, we, the revolutionary underground, have no desire to take over and don't think that we could even if we wished. When the Soviets are overthrown by our organisation, the new government will assume power. We disappear as an organization. Our job is done. Leonid? I don't know, perhaps his fellow employees at the Mikoyan Camera works will vote him into some office in the plant, if they think him capable enough."

"Well," Paul sighed, "it's your country. I'll stick to the American system." He couldn't take his eyes from the way her lips tucked in at the sides.

Ana said, "How long have you been in love with me, Paul?"

"What?"

She laughed. "Don't be so blank. It would be rather odd, wouldn't it, if two people were in love, and neither of them realized what had happened?"

"*Two* people in love," he said blankly, unbelievingly.

* * * * *

Leonid Shvernik and Paul Koslov were bent over a map of the U.S.S.R. The former pointed out the approximate location of the radio transmitters. "We're not going to use them until the last moment," he said. "Not until the fat is in the fire. Then they will all begin at once. The KGB and MVD won't have time to knock them out."

Paul said, "Things are moving fast. Faster than I had expected. We're putting it over, Leonid."

Shvernik said, "Only because the situation is ripe. It's the way revolutions work."

"How do you mean?" Paul said absently, studying the map.

"Individuals don't put over revolutions. The times do, the conditions apply. Did you know that six months before the Bolshevik revolution took place Lenin wrote that he never expected to live to see the Communist take over in Russia? The thing was that the conditions were there. The Bolsheviks, as few as they were, were practically thrown into power."

"However," Paul said dryly, "it was mighty helpful to have such men as Lenin and Trotsky handy."

Shvernik shrugged. "The times make the men. Your own American Revolution is probably better known to you. Look at the men those times produced. Jefferson, Paine, Madison, Hamilton, Franklin, Adams. And once again, if you had told any of those men, a year before the Declaration of Independence, that a complete revolution was the only solution to the problems that confronted them, they would probably have thought you insane."

It was a new line of thought for Paul Koslov. "Then what does cause a revolution?"

"The need for it. It's not just our few tens of thousands of members of the underground who see the need for overthrowing the Soviet bureaucracy. It's millions of average Russians in every walk of life and every strata, from top to bottom. What does the scientist think when some bureaucrat knowing nothing of his speciality comes into the laboratory and directs his work? What does the engineer in an automobile plant think when some silly politician decides that since cars in capitalist countries have four wheels, that Russia should surpass them by producing a car with five? What does your scholar think when he is told what to study, how to interpret it, and then what to write? What does your worker think when he sees the bureaucrat living in luxury while his wage is a comparatively meager one? What do your young people think in their continual striving for a greater degree of freedom than was possessed by their parents? What does your painter think? Your poet? Your philosopher?"

Shvernik shook his head. "When a nation is ready for revolution, it's the *people* who put it over. Often, the so-called leaders are hard put to run fast enough to say out in front."

* * * * *

Paul said, "After it's all over, we'll go back to the States. I know a town up in the Sierras called Grass Valley. Hunting, fishing, mountains, clean air, but still available to cities such as San Francisco where you can go for shopping and for restaurants and entertainment."

She kissed him again.

Paul said, "You know, I've done this sort of work-never on this scale before, of course-ever since I was nineteen. Nineteen, mind you! And this is the first time I've realized I'm tired of it. Fed up to here. I'm nearly thirty-five, Ana, and for the first time I want what a man is expected to want out of life. A woman, a home, children. You've never seen America. You'll love it. You'll like Americans too, especially the kind that live in places like Grass Valley."

Ana laughed softly. "But we're Russians, Paul."

"Eh?"

"Our home and our life should be here. In Russia. The New Russia that we'll have shortly."

He scoffed at her. "Live here when there's California? Ana, Ana, you don't know what living is. Why —"

"But, Paul, I'm a Russian. If the United States is a more pleasant place to live than Russia will be, when we have ended the police state, then it is part of my duty to improve Russia."

It suddenly came to him that she meant it. "But I was thinking, all along, that after this was over we'd be married. I'd be able to show you *my* country."

"And, I don't know why, I was thinking we both expected to be making a life for ourselves here."

They were silent for a long time in mutual misery.

Paul said finally, "This is no time to make detailed plans. We love each other, that should be enough. When it's all over, we'll have the chance to look over each other's way of life. You can visit the States with me."

"And I'll take you on a visit to Armenia. I know a little town in the mountains there which is the most beautiful in the world. We'll spend a week there. A month! Perhaps one day we can build a summer dacha there." She laughed happily. "Why practically everyone lives to be a hundred years old in Armenia."

"Yeah, we'll have to go there sometime," Paul said quietly.

* * * * *

He'd been scheduled to see Leonid that night but at the last moment the other sent Ana to report that an important meeting was to take place. A meeting of underground delegates from all over the country. They were making basic decisions on when to move-but Paul's presence wasn't needed.

He had no feeling of being excluded from something that concerned him. Long ago it had been decided that the less details known by the average man in the movement about Paul's activities, the better it would be. There is always betrayal and there are always counter-revolutionary agents within the ranks of an organization such as this. What was the old Russian proverb? When four men sit down to discuss revolution, three are police spies and the third a fool.

Actually, this had been astonishingly well handled. He had operated for over a year with no signs that the KGB was aware of his activities. Leonid and his fellows were efficient. They had to be. The Commies had been slaughtering anyone who opposed them for forty years now. To survive as a Russian underground you had to be good.

No, it wasn't a feeling of exclusion. Paul Koslov was stretched out on the bed of his king-size Astoria Hotel room, his hands behind his head and staring up at the ceiling. He recapitulated the events of the past months from the time he'd entered the Chief's office in Washington until last night at the dacha with Leonid and Ana.

The whole thing.

And over and over again.

There was a line of worry on his forehead.

He swung his feet to the floor and approached the closet. He selected his most poorly pressed pair of pants, and a coat that mismatched it. He checked the charge in his .38 Noiseless, and replaced the weapon under his left arm. He removed his partial bridge, remembering as he did so how he had lost the teeth in a street fight with some Commie union organizers in Panama, and replaced the porcelain bridge with a typically Russian gleaming steel one. He stuffed a cap into his back pocket, a pair of steel rimmed glasses into an inner pocket, and left the room.

He hurried through the lobby, past the Intourist desk, thankful that it was a slow time of day for tourist activity.

Outside, he walked several blocks to 25th of October Avenue and made a point of losing himself in the crowd. When he was sure that there could be no one behind him, he entered a *pivnaya*, had a glass of beer, and then disappeared into the toilet. There he took off the coat, wrinkled it a bit more, put it back on and also donned the cap and glasses. He removed his tie and thrust it into a side pocket.

He left, in appearance a more or less average workingman of Leningrad, walked to the bus station on Nashimson Volodarski and waited for the next bus to Petrodvorets. He would have preferred the subway, but the line didn't run that far as yet.

The bus took him to within a mile and a half of the dacha, and he walked from there.

By this time Paul was familiar with the security measures taken by Leonid Shvernik and the others. None at all when the dacha wasn't in use for a conference or to hide someone on the lam from the KGB. But at a time like this, there would be three sentries, carefully spotted.

This was Paul's field now. Since the age of nineteen, he told himself wryly. He wondered if there was anyone in the world who could go through a line of sentries as efficiently as he could.

He approached the dacha at the point where the line of pine trees came nearest to it. On his belly he watched for ten minutes before making the final move to the side of the house. He lay up against it, under a bush.

From an inner pocket he brought the spy device he had acquired from Derek Steven's Rube Goldberg department. It looked and was supposed to look considerably like a doctor's stethoscope. He placed it to his ears, pressed the other end to the wall of the house.

Leonid Shvernik was saying, "Becoming killers isn't a pleasant prospect but it was the Soviet who taught us that the end justifies the means. And so ruthless a dictatorship have they established that there is literally no alternative. The only way to remove them is by violence. Happily, so we believe, the violence need extend to only a small number of the very highest of the hierarchy. Once they are eliminated and our transmitters proclaim the new revolution, there should be little further opposition."

Someone sighed deeply-Paul was able to pick up even that.

"Why discuss it further?" somebody whose voice Paul didn't recognize, asked. "Let's get onto other things. These broadcasts of ours have to be the ultimate in the presentation of our program. The assassination of Number One and his immediate supporters is going to react unfavorably at first. We're going to have to present unanswerable arguments if our movement is to sweep the nation as we plan."

A new voice injected, "We've put the best writers in the Soviet Union to work on the scripts. For all practical purposes they are completed."

"We haven't yet decided what to say about the H-Bomb, the missiles, all the endless equipment of war that has accumulated under the Soviets, not to speak of the armies, the ships, the aircraft and all the personnel who man them."

Someone else, it sounded like Nikolai Kirichenko, from Moscow, said. "I'm chairman of the committee on that. It's our opinion that we're going to have to cover that matter in our broadcasts to the people and the only answer is that until the West has agreed to nuclear disarmament, we're going to have to keep our own."

Leonid said, and there was shock in his voice, "But that's one of the most basic reasons for the new revolution, to eliminate this mad arms race, this devoting half the resources of the world to armament."

"Yes, but what can we do? How do we know that the Western powers won't attack? And please remember that it is no longer just the United States that has nuclear weapons. If we lay down our defenses, we are capable of being destroyed by England, France, West Germany, even Turkey or Japan! And consider, too, that the economies of some of the Western powers are based on the production of arms to the point that if such production ended, overnight, depressions would sweep their nations. In short, they can't afford a world without tensions."

"It's a problem for the future to solve," someone else said. "But meanwhile I believe the committee is right. Until it is absolutely proven that we need have no fears about the other nations, we must keep our own strength."

Under his hedge, Paul grimaced, but he was getting what he came for, a discussion of policy, without the restrictions his presence would have put on the conversation.

"Let's deal with a more pleasant subject," a feminine voice said. "Our broadcasts should stress to the people that for the first time in the history of Russia we will be truly in the position to lead the world! For fifty years the Communists attempted to convert nations into adopting their system, and largely they were turned down. Those countries that did become Communist either did so at the point of the Red Army's bayonet or under the stress of complete collapse such as in China. But tomorrow, and the New Russia? Freed from the inadequacy and inefficiency of the bureaucrats who have misruled us, we'll develop a productive machine that will be the envy of the world!" Her voice had all but a fanatical ring.

Someone else chuckled, "If the West thought they had competition from us before, wait until they see the New Russia!"

Paul thought he saw someone, a shadow, at the side of the clearing. His lips thinned and the .38 Noiseless was in his hand magically.

False alarm.

He turned back to the "conversation" inside.

Kirichenko's voice was saying, "It is hard for me not to believe that within a period of a year or so half the countries of the world will follow our example."

"Half!" someone laughed exuberantly. "The world, Comrades! The new system will sweep the world. For the first time in history the world will see what Marx and Engels were *really* driving at!"

* * * * *

Back at the hotel, toward morning, Paul was again stretched out on the bed, hands under his head, his eyes unseeingly staring at the ceiling as he went through his agonizing reappraisal.

There was Ana.

And there was even Leonid Shvernik and some of the others of the underground. As close friends as he had ever made in a life that admittedly hadn't been prone to friendship.

And there was Russia, the country of his birth. Beyond the underground movement, beyond the Soviet regime, beyond the Romanoff Czars. Mother Russia. The land of his parents, his grandparents, the land of his roots.

And, of course, there was the United States and the West. The West which had received him in his hour of stress in his flight from *Mother* Russia. Mother Russia, ha! What kind of a mother had she been to the Koslovs? To his grandfather, his father, his mother and brother? Where would he, Paul, be today had he as a child not been sent fleeing to the West?

And his life work. What of that? Since the age of nineteen, when a normal teenager would have been in school, preparing himself for life. Since nineteen he had been a member of the anti-Soviet team.

A star, too! Paul Koslov, the trouble-shooter, the always reliable, cold, ruthless. Paul Koslov on whom you could always depend to carry the ball.

Anti-Soviet, or anti-Russian?

Why kid himself about his background. It meant nothing. He was an American. He had only the faintest of memories of his family or of the country. Only because people told him so did he know he was a Russian. He was as American as it is possible to get.

What had he told such Westerners, born and bred, as Lord Carrol and Derek Stevens? *If he wasn't a member of the team, there just wasn't a team.*

But then, of course, there was Ana.

Yes, Ana. But what, actually, was there in the future for them? Now that he considered it, could he really picture her sitting in the drug store on Montez Street, Grass Valley, having a banana split?

Ana was Russian. As patriotic a Russian as it was possible to be. As much a dedicated member of the Russian team as it was possible to be. And as a team member, she, like Paul, knew the chances that were involved. You didn't get to be a star by sitting on the bench. She hadn't hesitated, in the clutch, to sacrifice her favorite brother.

* * * * *

Paul Koslov propped the Tracy, the wristwatch-like radio before him, placing its back to a book. He made it operative, began to repeat, "Paul calling. Paul calling."

A thin, far away voice said finally, "O.K. Paul. I'm receiving."

Paul Koslov took a deep breath and said, "All right, this is it. In just a few days we're all set to kick off. Understand?"

"I understand, Paul."

"Is it possible that anybody else can be receiving this?"

"Absolutely impossible."

"All right, then this is it. The boys here are going to start their revolution going by knocking off not only Number One, but also Two, Three, Four, Six and Seven of the hierarchy. Number Five is one of theirs."

The thin voice said, "You know I don't want details. They're up to you."

Paul grimaced. "This is why I called. You've got to make-or someone's got to make-one hell of an important decision in the next couple of days. It's not up to me. For once I'm not to be brushed off with that 'don't bother me with details,' routine."

"Decision? What decision? You said everything was all ready to go, didn't you?"

"Look," Paul Koslov said, "remember when you gave me this assignment. When you told me about the Germans sending Lenin up to Petrograd in hopes he'd start a revolution and the British sending Somerset Maugham to try and prevent it?"

"Yes, yes, man. What's that got to do with it?" Even over the long distance, the Chief's voice sounded puzzled.

"Supposedly the Germans were successful, and Maugham failed. But looking back at it a generation later, did the Germans win out by helping bring off the Bolshevik revolution? The Soviets destroyed them for all time as a first-rate power at Stalingrad, twenty-five years afterwards."

The voice from Washington was impatient. "What's your point, Paul?"

"My point is this. When you gave me this assignment, you told me I was in the position of the German who engineered bringing Lenin up to Petrograd to start the Bolsheviks rolling. Are you *sure* that the opposite isn't true? Are you sure it isn't Maugham's job I should have? Let me tell you, Chief, these boys I'm working with now are sharp, they've got more on the ball than these Commie bureaucrats running the country have a dozen times over.

"Chief, this is the decision that has to be made in the next couple of days. Just who do we want eliminated? Are you sure you don't want me to tip off the KGB to this whole conspiracy?"

Combat

Henry Kuran answered a nod here and there, a called out greeting from a desk an aisle removed from the one along which he was progressing, finally made the far end of the room. He knocked at the door and pushed his way through before waiting a response.

There were three desks here. He didn't recognize two of the girls who looked up at his entry. One of them began to say something, but then Betty, whose desk dominated the entry to the inner sanctum, grinned a welcome at him and said, "Hank! How was Peru? We've been expecting you."

"Full of Incas," he grinned back. "Incas, Russkies and Chinks. A poor capitalist *conquistador* doesn't have a chance. Is the boss inside?"

"He's waiting for you, Hank. See you later."

Hank said, "Um-m-m," and when the door clicked in response to the button Betty touched, pushed his way into the inner office.

Morton Twombly, chief of the department, came to his feet, shook hands abruptly and motioned the other to a chair.

"How're things in Peru, Henry?" His voice didn't express too much real interest.

Hank said, "We were on the phone just a week ago, Mr. Twombly. It's about the same. No, the devil it is. The Chinese have just run in their new People's Car. They look something like our jeep station-wagons did fifteen years ago."

Twombly stirred in irritation. "I've heard about them."

Hank took his handkerchief from his breast pocket and polished his rimless glasses. He said evenly, "They sell for just under two hundred dollars."

"Two hundred dollars?" Twombly twisted his face. "They can't transport them from China for that."

"Here we go again," Hank sighed. "They also can't sell pressure cookers for a dollar apiece, nor cameras with f.2 lenses for five bucks. Not to speak of the fact that the Czechs can't sell shoes for fifty cents a pair and, of course, the Russkies can't sell premium gasoline for five cents a gallon."

Twombly muttered, "They undercut our prices faster than we can vote through new subsidies. Where's it going to end Henry?"

"I don't know. Perhaps we should have thought a lot more about it ten or fifteen years ago when the best men our universities could turn out went into advertising, show business and sales-while the best men the Russkies and Chinese could turn out were going into science and industry." As a man who worked in the field Hank Kuran occasionally got bitter about these things, and didn't mind this opportunity of sounding off at the chief.

Hank added, "The height of achievement over there is to be elected to the Academy of Sciences. Our young people call scientists egg-heads, and their height of achievement is to become a TV singer or a movie star."

Morton Twombly shot his best field man a quick glance. "You sound as though you need a vacation, Henry."

Henry Kuran laughed. "Don't mind me, chief. I got into a hassle with the Hungarians last week and I'm in a bad frame of mind."

Twombly said, "Well, we didn't bring you back to Washington for a trade conference."

"I gathered that from your wire. What *am* I here for?"

Twombly pushed his chair back and came to his feet. It occurred to Hank Kuran that his chief had aged considerably since the forming of this department nearly ten years ago. The thought went through his mind, *a general in the cold war. A general who's been in action for a decade, has never won more than a skirmish and is currently in full retreat.*

Morton Twombly said, "I'm not sure I know. Come along."

They left the office by a back door and Hank was in unknown territory. Silently his chief led him through busy corridors, each one identical to the last, each sterile and cold in spite of the bustling. They came to a marine guarded door, were passed through, once again obviously expected.

The inner office contained but one desk occupied by a youthfully brisk army major. He gave Hank a one-two of the eyes and said, "Mr. Hennessey is expecting you, sir. This is Mr. Kuran?"

"That's correct," Twombly said. "I won't be needed." He turned to Hank Kuran. "I'll see you later, Henry." He shook hands.

Hank frowned at him. "You sound as though I'm being sent off to Siberia, or something."

The major looked up sharply, "What was that?"

Twombly made a motion with his hand, negatively. "Nothing. A joke. I'll see you later, Henry." He turned and left.

The major opened another door and ushered Hank into a room two or three times the size of Twombly's office. Hank formed a silent whistle and then suddenly knew where he was. This was the sanctum sanctorum of Sheridan Hennessey. Sheridan Hennessey, right arm, hatchetman, *alter ego*, one man brain trust-of two presidents in succession.

And there he was, seated in a heavy armchair. Hank had known of his illness, that the other had only recently risen from his hospital bed and against doctor's orders. But somehow he hadn't expected to see him this wasted. TV and newsreel cameramen had been kind.

However, the waste had not as yet extended to either eyes or voice. Sheridan Hennessey bit out, "That'll be all, Roy," and the major left them.

* * * * *

"Sit down," Hennessey said. "You're Henry Kuran. That's not a Russian name is it?"

Hank found a chair. "It was Kuranchov. My father Americanized it when he was married." He added, "About once every six months some Department of Justice or C.I.A. joker runs into the fact that my name was originally Russian and I'm investigated all over again."

Hennessey said, "But your Russian is perfect?"

"Yes, sir. My mother was English-Irish, but we lived in a community with quite a few Russian born emigrants. I learned the language."

"Good, Mr. Kuran, how would you like to die for your country?"

Hank Kuran looked at him for a long moment. He said slowly, "I'm thirty-two years old, healthy and reasonably adjusted and happy. I'd hate it."

The sick man snorted. "That's exactly the right answer. I don't trust heroes. Now, how much have you heard about the extraterrestrials?"

"I beg your pardon?"

404

"You haven't heard the news broadcasts the past couple of days? How the devil could you have missed them?" Hennessey was scowling sourly at him.

Hank Kuran didn't know what the other was talking about. "Two days ago I was in the town of Machu Picchu in the Andes trying to peddle some mining equipment to the Peruvians. Peddle it, hell. I was practically trying to give it away, but it was still even-steven that the Hungarians would undersell me. Then I got a hurry-up wire from Morton Twombly to return to Washington soonest. I flew here in an Air Force jet. I haven't heard any news for two days or more."

"I'll have the major get you all the material we have to date and you can read it on the plane to England."

"Plane to England?" Hank said blankly. "Look, I'm in the Department of Economic Development of Neutral Nations, specializing in South America. What would I be doing in England?" He had an uneasy feeling of being crowded, and a suspicion that this was far from the first time Sheridan Hennessey had ridden roughshod over subordinates.

"First step on the way to Moscow," Hennessey snapped. "The major will give you details later. Let me brief you. The extraterrestrials landed a couple of days ago on Red Square in some sort of spaceship. Our Russkie friends clamped down a censorship on news. No photos at all as yet and all news releases have come from Tass."

Hank Kuran was bug-eying him.

Hennessey said, "I know. Most of the time I don't believe it myself. The extraterrestrials represent what the Russkies are calling a Galactic Confederation. So far as we can figure out, there is some sort of league, United Planets, or whatever you want to call it, of other star systems which have achieved a certain level of scientific development."

"Well ... well, why haven't they shown up before?"

"Possibly they have, through the ages. If so, they kept their presence secret, checked on our development and left." Hennessey snorted his indignation. "See here, Kuran, I have no details. All of our information comes from Tass, and you can imagine how inadequate that is. Now shut up while I tell you what little I do know."

Henry Kuran settled back into his chair, feeling limp. He'd had too many curves thrown at him in the past few minutes to assimilate.

"They evidently keep hands off until a planet develops interplanetary exploration and atomic power. And, of course, during the past few years our Russkie pals have not only set up a base on the Moon but have sent off their various expeditions to Venus and Mars."

"None of them made it," Hank said.

"Evidently they didn't have to. At any rate, the plenipotentiaries from the Galactic Confederation have arrived."

"Wanting what, sir?" Hank said.

"Wanting nothing but to help." Hennessey said. "Stop interrupting. Our time is limited. You're going to have to be on a jet for London in half an hour."

He noticed Hank Kuran's expression, and shook his head. "No, it's not farfetched. These other intelligent life forms must be familiar with what it takes to progress to the point of interplanetary travel. It takes species aggressiveness-besides intelligence. And they must have sense enough not to want the wrong kind of aggressiveness exploding into the stars. They don't want an equivalent of Attila bursting over the borders of the Roman Empire. They want to channel us, and they're willing to help, to direct our comparatively new science into paths that won't conflict with them. They want to bring us peacefully into their society of advanced life forms."

Sheridan Hennessey allowed himself a rueful grimace. "That makes quite a speech, doesn't it? At any rate, that's the situation."

"Well, where do I come into this? I'm afraid I'm on the bewildered side."

"Yes. Well, damn it, they've landed in Moscow. They've evidently assumed the Soviet complex-the Soviet Union, China and the satellites-are the world's dominant power. Our conflicts, our controversies, are probably of little, if any, interest to them. Inadvertently, they've put a weapon in the hands of the Soviets that could well end this cold war we've been waging for more than twenty-five years now."

The president's right-hand man looked off into a corner of the room, unseeingly. "For more than a decade it's been a bloodless combat that we've been waging against the Russkies. The military machines, equally capable of complete destruction of the other, have been stymied Finally it's boiled down to an attempt to influence the neutrals, India, Africa, South America, to attempt to bring them into one camp or the other. Thus far, we've been able to contain them in spite of their recent successes. But given the prestige of being selected the dominant world power by the extraterrestrials and in possession of the science and industrial know-how from the stars, they'll have won the cold war over night."

His old eyes flared. "You want to know where you come in, eh? Fine. Your job is to get to these Galactic Confederation emissaries and put a bug in their bonnet. Get over to them that there's more than one major viewpoint on this planet. Get them to investigate our side of the matter."

"Get to them how? If the Russkies —"

Hennessey was tired. The flash of spirit was fading. He lifted a thin hand. "One of my assistants is crossing the Atlantic with you. He'll give you the details."

"But why *me*? I'm strictly a —"

"You're an unknown in Europe. Never connected with espionage. You speak Russian like a native. Morton Twombly says you're his best man. Your records show that you can think on your feet, and that's what we need above all."

Hank Kuran said flatly, "You might have asked for volunteers."

"We did. You, you and you. The old army game," Hennessey said wearily. "Mr. Kuran, we're in the clutch. We can lose, forever-right now. Right in the next month or so. Consider yourself a soldier being thrown into the most important engagement the world has ever seen-combating the growth of the Soviets. We can't afford such luxuries as asking for volunteers. Now do you get it?"

Hank Kuran could feel impotent anger rising inside him. He was off balance. "I get it, but I don't like it."

"None of us do," Sheridan Hennessey said sourly. "Do you think any of us do?" He must have pressed a button.

From behind them the major's voice said briskly, "Will you come this way, Mr. Kuran?"

* * * * *

In the limousine, on the way out to the airport, the bright, impossibly cleanly shaven C.I.A. man said, "You've never been behind the Iron Curtain before, have you Kuran?"

"No," Hank said. "I thought that term was passé. Look, aren't we even going to my hotel for my things?"

The second C.I.A. man, the older one, said, "All your gear will be waiting for you in London. They'll be sure there's nothing in it to tip off the KGB if they go through your bags."

The younger one said, "We're not sure, things are moving fast, but we suspect that that term, Iron Curtain, applies again."

"Then how am I going to get in?" Hank said irritably. "I've had no background for this cloak and dagger stuff."

The older C.I.A. man said, "We understand the KGB has increased security measures but they haven't cut out all travel on the part of non-Communists."

The other one said, "Probably because the Russkies don't want to tip off the spacemen that they're being isolated from the western countries. It would be too conspicuous if suddenly all western travelers disappeared."

They were passing over the Potomac, to the right and below them Hank Kuran could make out the twin Pentagons, symbols of a military that had at long last by its very efficiency eliminated itself. War had finally progressed to the point where even a minor nation, such as Cuba or Portugal, could completely destroy the whole planet. Eliminated wasn't quite the word. In spite of their sterility, the military machines still claimed their million masses of men, still drained a third of the products of the world's industry.

One of the C.I.A. men was saying urgently, "So we're going to send you in as a tourist. As inconspicuous a tourist as we can make you. For fifteen years the Russkies have boomed their tourist trade-all for propaganda, of course. Now they're in no position to turn this tourist flood off. If the aliens got wind of it, they'd smell a rat."

Hank Kuran brought his attention back to them. "All right. So you get me to Moscow as a tourist. What do I do then? I keep telling you jokers that I don't know a thing about espionage. I don't know a secret code from judo."

"That's one reason the chief picked you. Not only do the Russkies have nothing on you in their files-neither do our own people. You're safe from betrayal. There are exactly six people who know your mission and only one of them is in Moscow."

"Who's he?"

The C.I.A. man shook his head. "You'll never meet him. But he's making the arrangements for you to contact the underground."

Hank Kuran turned in his seat. "What underground? In Moscow?"

The bright, pink faced C.I.A. man chuckled and began to say something but the older one cut him off. "Let me, Jimmy." He continued to Hank. "Actually, we don't know nearly as much as we should about it, but a Soviet underground is there and getting stronger. You've heard of the *stilyagi* and the *metrofanushka*?"

Hank nodded. "Moscow's equivalent to the juvenile delinquents, or the Teddy Boys, as the British call them."

"Not only in Moscow, they're everywhere in urban Russia. At any rate, our underground friends operate within the *stilyagi*, the so-called jet-set, using them as protective coloring."

"This is new to me," Hank said. "And I don't quite get it."

"It's clever enough. Suppose you're out late some night on an underground job and the police pick you up. They find out you're a juvenile delinquent, figure you've been out getting drunk, and toss you into jail for a week. It's better than winding up in front of a firing squad as a counterrevolutionary, or a Trotskyite, or whatever they're currently calling anybody they shoot."

The chauffeur rapped on the glass that divided their seat from his, and motioned ahead.

"Here's the airport," Jimmy said. "We'll drive right over to the plane. Hid your face with your hat, just for luck."

"Wait a minute, now," Hank said. "Listen, how do I contact these beat generation characters?"

"You don't. They contact you."

"How."

"That's up to them. Maybe they won't at all; they're plenty careful." Jimmy snorted without humor. "It must be getting to be an instinct with Russians by this time. Nihilists, Anarchists, Mensheviks, Bolsheviks, now anti-Communists. Survival of the fittest. By this time the Russian underground must consist of members that have bred true as revolutionists. There've been Russian undergrounds for twenty generations."

"Hardly long enough to affect genetics," the older one said wryly.

Hank said, "Let's stop being witty. I still haven't a clue as to how Sheridan Hennessey expects me to get to these Galactic Confederation people-or things, or whatever you call them."

"They evidently are humanoid," Jimmy said. "Look more or less human. And stop worrying, we've got several hours to explain things while we cross the Atlantic. You don't step into character until you enter the offices of Progressive Tours, in London."

* * * * *

The door of Progressive Tours, Ltd. 100 Rochester Row, was invitingly open. Hank Kuran entered, looked around the small room. He inwardly winced at the appearance of the girl behind the counter. What was it about Commies outside their own countries that they drew such crackpots into their camp? Heavy lenses, horn rimmed to make them more conspicuous, wild hair, mawkish tweeds, and dirty fingernails to top it off.

She said, "What can I do for you, Comrade?"

"Not *Comrade*," Hank said mildly. "I'm an American."

"What did you want?" she said coolly.

Hank indicated the travel folder he was carrying. "I'd like to take this tour to Leningrad and Moscow. I've been reading propaganda for and against Russia as long as I've been able to read and I've finally decided I want to see for myself. Can I get the tour that leaves tomorrow?"

She became businesslike as was within her ability. "There is no country in the world as easy to visit as the Soviet Union, Mr —"

"Stevenson," Hank Kuran said. "Henry Stevenson."

"Stevenson. Fill out these two forms, leave your passport and two photos and we'll have everything ready in the morning. The *Baltika* leaves at twelve. The visa will cost ten shillings. What class do you wish to travel?"

"The cheapest." *And least conspicuous*, Hank added under his breath.

"Third class comes to fifty-five guineas. The tour lasts eighteen days including the time it takes to get to Leningrad. You have ten days in Russia."

"I know, I read the folder. Are there any other Americans on the tour?"

A voice behind him said, "At least one other."

Hank turned. She was somewhere in her late twenties, he estimated. And if her clothes, voice and appearance were any criterion he'd put her in the middle-middle class with a bachelor's degree in something or other, unmarried and with the aggressiveness he didn't like in American girls after living the better part of eight years in Latin countries.

On top of that she was one of the prettiest girls he had ever seen, in a quick, red headed, almost puckish sort of way.

Hank tried to keep from displaying his admiration too openly. "American?" he said.

"That's right." She took in his five-foot ten, his not quite ruffled hair, his worried eyes behind their rimless lenses, darkish tinted for the Peruvian sun. She evidently gave him up as not worth the effort and turned to the fright behind the counter.

"I came to pick up my tickets."

"Oh, yes, Miss...."

"Moore."

The fright fiddled with the papers on an untidy heap before her. "Oh, yes. Miss Charity Moore."

"Charity?" Hank said.

She turned to him. "Do you mind? I have two sisters named Honor and Hope. My people were the Seventh Day Adventists. It wasn't my fault." Her voice was pleasant-but nature had granted that; it wasn't particularly friendly-through her own inclinations.

Hank cleared his throat and went back to his forms. The visa questionnaire was in both Russian and English. The first line wanted, *Surname, first name and patronymic.*

To get the conversation going again, Hank said, "What does patronymic mean?"

Charity Moore looked up from her own business and said, less antagonism in her voice, "That's the name you inherited from your father."

"Of course, thanks." He went back to his forms. Under *what type of work do you do*, Hank wrote, *Capitalist in a small sort of way. Auto Agency owner.*

He took the forms back to the counter with his passport. Charity Moore was putting her tickets, suitcase labels and a sheaf of tour instructions into her pocketbook.

Hank said, "Look, we're going to be on a tour together, what do you say to a drink?"

She considered that, prettily, "Well ... well, of course. Why not?"

Hank said to the fright, "There wouldn't be a nice bar around would there?"

"Down the street three blocks and to your left is Dirty Dick's." She added scornfully, "All the tourists go there."

"Then we shouldn't make an exception," Hank said. "Miss Moore, my arm."

* * * * *

On the way over she said, "Are you excited about going to the Soviet Union?"

"I wouldn't say excited. Curious, though."

"You don't sound very sympathetic to them."

"To Russia?" Hank said. "Why should I be? Personally, I believe in democracy."

"So do I," she said, her voice clipped. "I think we ought to try it some day."

"Come again?"

"So far as I can see, we pay lip service to democracy, that's about all."

Hank grinned inwardly. He'd already figured that during this tour he'd be thrown into contact with characters running in shade from gentle pink to flaming red. His position demanded that he remain inconspicuous, as *average* an American tourist as possible. Flaring political arguments weren't going to help this, but, on the other hand to avoid them entirely would be apt to make him more conspicuous than ever.

"How do you mean?" he said now.

"We have two political parties in our country without an iota of difference between them. Every four years they present candidates and give us a choice. What difference does it make which one of the two we choose if they both stand for the same thing? This is democracy?"

Hank said mildly, "Well, it's better than sticking up just one candidate and saying, which one of this one do you choose? Look, let's steer clear of politics and religion, eh? Otherwise this'll never turn out to be a beautiful friendship."

Charity Moore's face portrayed resignation.

Hank said, "I'm Hank, what do they call you besides Charity?"

"Everybody but my parents call me Char. You spell it C-H-A-R but pronounce it like Chair, like you sit in."

"That's better," Hank said. "Let's see. There it is, Dirty Dick's. Crummy looking joint. You want to go in?"

"Yes," Char said. "I've read about it. An old coaching house. One of the oldest pubs in London. Dickens wrote a poem about it."

The pub's bar extended along the right wall, as they entered. To the left was a sandwich counter with a dozen or so stools. It was too early to eat, they stood at the ancient bar and Hank said to her, "Ale?" and when she nodded, to the bartender, "Two Worthingtons."

While they were being drawn, Hank turned back to the girl, noticing all over again how impossibly pretty she was. It was disconcerting. He said, "How come Russia? You'd look more in place on a beach in Biarritz or the Lido."

Char said, "Ever since I was about ten years of age I've been reading about the Russian people starving to death and having to work six months before making enough money to buy a pair of shoes. So I've decided to see how starving, barefooted people managed to build the largest industrial nation in the world."

"Here we go again," Hank said, taking up his glass. He toasted her silently before saying, "The United States is still the largest single industrial nation in the world."

"Perhaps as late as 1965, but not today," she said definitely.

"Russia, plus the satellites and China has a gross national product greater than the free world's but no single nation produces more than the United States. What are you laughing at?"

"I love the way the West plasters itself so nicely with high flown labels. The *free world*. Saudi Arabia, Ethiopia, Pakistan, South Africa-just what is your definition of *free*?"

Hank had her placed now. A college radical. One of the tens of thousands who discover, usually somewhere along in the sophomore year, that all is not perfect in the land of their birth and begin looking around for answers. Ten to one she wasn't a Commie and would probably never become one-but meanwhile she got a certain amount of kicks trying to upset ideological applecarts.

For the sake of staying in character, Hank said mildly, "Look here, are you a Communist?"

She banged her glass down on the bar with enough force that the bartender looked over worriedly. "Did it ever occur to you that even though the Soviet Union might be wrong-if it is wrong-that doesn't mean that the United States is right? You remind me of that ... that *politician*, whatever his name was, when I was a girl. Anybody who disagreed with him was automatically a Communist."

"McCarthy," Hank said. "I'm sorry, so you're not a Communist."

She took up her glass again, still in a huff. "I didn't say I wasn't. That's my business."

The turboelectric ship *Baltika* turned out to be the pride of the U.S.S.R. Baltic State Steamship Company. In fact, she turned out to be the whole fleet. Like the rest of the world, the Soviet complex had taken to the air so far as passenger travel was concerned and already the *Baltika* was a left-over from yesteryear. For some reason the C.I.A. thought there might be less observation on the part of the KGB if Hank approached Moscow indirectly, that is by sea and from Leningrad. It was going to take an extra four or five days, but, if he got through, the squandered time would have been worth it.

An English speaking steward took up Hank's bag at the gangplank and hustled him through to his quarters. His cabin was forward and four flights down into the bowels of the ship. There were four berths in all, two of them already had bags on them. Hank put his hand in his pocket for a shilling.

The steward grinned and said, "No tipping. This is a Soviet ship."

Hank looked after him.

A newcomer entered the cabin, still drying his hands on a towel. "Greetings," he said. "Evidently we're fellow passengers for the duration." He hung the towel on a rack, reached out a hand. "Rodriquez," he said. "You can call me Paco, if you want. Did you ever meet an Argentine that wasn't named Paco?"

Hank shook the hand. "I don't know if I ever met an Argentine before. You speak English well."

"Harvard," Paco said. He stretched widely. "Did you spot those Russian girls in the crew? Blond, every one blond." He grinned. "Not much time to operate with them-but enough."

A voice behind them, heavy with British accent said, "Good afternoon, gentlemen."

He was as ebony as a negro can get and as nattily dressed as only Savile Row can turn out a man. He said, "My name is Loo Motlamelle." He looked at them expressionlessly for a moment.

Paco put out his hand briskly for a shake. "Rodriquez," he said. "Call me Paco. I suppose we're all Moscow bound."

Loo Motlamelle seemed relieved at his acceptance, clasped Paco's hand, then Hank's.

Hank shook his head as the three of them began to unpack to the extent it was desirable for the short trip. "The classless society. I wonder what First Class cabins look like. Here we are, jammed three in a telephone booth sized room."

Paco chucked, "My friend, you don't know the half of it. There are *five* classes on this ship. Needless to say, this is Tourist B, the last."

"And we'll probably be fed borsht and black bread the whole trip," Hank growled.

Loo Motlamelle said mildly, "I hear the food is very good."

Paco stood up from his luggage, put his hands on his hips, "Gentlemen, do you realize there is no lock on the door of this cabin?"

"The crime rate is said to be negligible in the Soviet countries," Loo said.

Paco put up his hands in despair. "That isn't the point. Suppose one of us wishes to bring a lady friend into the cabin for ...a drink. How can he lock the door so as not to be interrupted?"

Hank was chuckling. "What did you take this trip for, Paco? An investigation into the mores of the Soviets-female flavor?"

Paco went back to his bag. "Actually, I suppose I am one of the many. Going to the new world to see whether or not it is worth switching alliances from the old."

A distant finger of cold traced designs in Henry Kuran's belly. He had never heard the United States referred to as the Old World before. It had a strange, disturbing quality.

Loo, who was now reclined on his bunk, said, "That's approximately the same reason I visit the Soviet Union."

Hank said quietly, "Who's sending you, Paco? Or are you on your own?"

"No, my North American friend. My lips are sealed but I represent a rather influencial group. All is not jest, even though I find life the easier if one laughs often and with joy."

Hank closed his bag and slid it under his bunk. "Well, you should have had this influencial group pony up a little more money so you could have gone deluxe class."

Paco looked at him strangely. "That is the point. We are not interested in a red-carpet tour during which the very best would be trotted our for propaganda purposes. I choose to see the New World as humbly as is possible."

"And me," Loo said. "We evidently are in much the same position."

Hank brought himself into character. "Well, lesson number one. Did you notice the teeth in that steward's face? Steel. Bright, gleaming steel, instead of gold."

Loo shrugged hugely. "This is the day of science. Iron rusts, it's true, but I assume that the Soviet dentists utilize some method of preventing corrosion."

"Otherwise," Paco murmured reasonably, "I imagine the Russians expectorate a good deal of rusty spittal."

"I don't know why I keep getting into these arguments," Hank said. "I'm just going for a look-see myself. But frankly, I don't trust a Russian any farther than I can throw one."

"How many Russians have you met?" Loo said mildly. "Or are your opinions formed solely by what you have read in American publications?"

Hank frowned at him. "You seem to be a little on the anti-American side."

"I'm not," Loo said. "But not pro-American either. I find much that is ridiculous in the propaganda of both the Soviets and the West."

"Gentlemen," Paco said, "the conversation is fascinating, but I must leave you. The ladies, crowding the decks above, know not that my presence graces this ship. It shall be necessary that I enlighten them. *Adios amigos!*"

*   *   *   *   *

The *Baltika* displaced eight thousand four hundred ninety-six tons and had accommodations for three hundred thirty passengers. Of these, Hank Kuran estimated, approximately half were Scandinavians or British being transported between London, Copenhagen, Stockholm and Helsinki on the small liner's way to Leningrad.

Of the tourists, some seventy-five or so, Hank estimated that all but half a dozen were convinced that Russian skunks didn't stink, in spite of the fact that thus far they'd never been there to have a whiff. The few such as Loo Motlamelle, who was evidently the son of some African paramount chief, and Paco Rodriquez, had also never been to Russia but at least had open minds.

Far from black bread and borscht, he found the food excellent. The first morning they found caviar by the pound nestled in bowls of ice, as part of breakfast. He said across the table to Paco, "Propaganda. I wonder how many people in Russia eat caviar."

Paco spooned a heavy dip of it onto his bread and grinned back. "This type of propaganda I can appreciate. You Yankees should try it."

Char was also eating at the other side of the community type table. She said, "How many Americans eat as well as the passengers on United States Lines ships?"

It was as good an opportunity as any for Hank to place his character in the eyes of his fellow Progressive Tours pilgrims. His need was to establish himself as a moderately square tourist on his way to take a look-see at highly publicized Russia. Originally, the C.I.A. men had wanted him to be slightly pro-Soviet, but he hadn't been sure he could handle that convincingly enough. More comfortable would be a role as an averagely anti-Russian tourist-not fanatically so, but averagely. If there were any KGB men aboard, he wanted to dissolve into mediocrity so far as they were concerned.

Hank said now, mild indignation in his voice. "Do you contend that the average Russian eats as well as the average American?"

Char took a long moment to finish the bite she had in her mouth. She shrugged prettily. "How would I know? I've never been to the Soviet Union." She paused for a moment before adding, "However, I've done a certain amount of traveling and I can truthfully say that the worst slums I have ever seen in any country that can be considered civilized were in the Harlem district and the lower East Side of New York."

All eyes were turned to him now, so Hank said, "It's a big country and there are exceptions. But on the average the United States has the highest standard of living in the world."

Paco said interestedly, "What do you use for a basis of measurement, my friend? Such things as the number of television sets and movie theaters? To balance such statistics, I understand that per capita your country has the fewest number of legitimate theaters of any of—I use Miss Moore's term-the civilized countries."

A Londoner, two down from Hank, laughed nastily. "Maybe schooling is the way he measures. I read in the *Express* the other day that even after Yankees get out of college they can't read proper. All they learn is driving cars and dancing and togetherness-wotever that it."

Hank grinned inwardly and thought, *You don't sound as though you read any too well yourself, my friend.* Aloud he said, "Very well, in a couple of days we'll be in the promised land, I contend that free enterprise performs the greatest good for the greatest number."

"Free enterprise," somebody down the table snorted. "That means the freedom for the capitalists to pry somebody else out of the greatest part of what he produces."

By the time they'd reached Leningrad aside from Paco and Loo, his cabinmates, Hank had built an Iron Curtain all of his own between himself and the other members of the Progressive Tours trip. Which was the way he wanted it. He could foresee a period when having friends might be a handicap when and if he needed to drift away from the main body for any length of time.

Actually, the discussions he ran into were on the juvenile side. Hank Kuran hadn't spent eight years of his life as a field man working against the Soviet countries in the economic sphere without running into every argument both pro and con in the continuing battle between Capitalism and Communism. Now he chuckled to himself at getting into tiffs over the virtues of Russian black bread versus American white, or whether Soviet jets were faster than those of the United States.

With Char Moore, though she tolerated Hank's company, in fact, seemed to prefer it to that of whatever other males were aboard, it was continually a matter of rubbing fur the wrong way. She was ready to battle it out on any phase of politics, international affairs or West versus East.

But it was the visitors from space that actually dominated the conversation of the ship-crew, tourists, business travelers, or whoever. Information was still limited, and Taas the sole source. Daily there were multilingual radio broadcasts tuned in by the *Baltika* but largely they added little to the actual information on the extraterrestrials. It was mostly Soviet back-patting on the significance of the fact that the Galactic Confederation emissaries had landed in the Soviet complex rather than among the Western countries.

Hank learned little that he hadn't already known. The Kremlin had all but laughingly declined a suggestion on the part of Switzerland that the extraterrestrials be referred to that all but defunct United Nations. The delegates from the Galactic Confederation had chose to land in Moscow. In Moscow they should remain until they desired to go elsewhere. The Soviet implication was that the alien emissaries had no desire, intention nor reason to visit other sections of Earth. They had contacted the dominant world power and could complete their business within the Kremlin walls.

* * * * *

Leningrad came as only a mild surprise to Henry Kuran. With his knowledge of Russian and his position in Morton Twombly's department, he had kept up with the Soviet progress though the years.

As early as the middle 1950s unbiased travelers to the U.S.S.R. had commented in detail upon the explosion of production in the country. By the end of the decade such books as Gunther's "Inside Russia Today" had dwelt upon the ultra-cleanliness of the cities, the mushrooming of apartment houses, the easing of the restrictions of Stalin's day-or at least the beginning of it.

He actually hadn't expected peasant clad, half starved Russians furtively shooting glances at their neighbors for fear of the secret police. Nor a black bread and cabbage diet. Nor long lines of the politically suspect being hauled off to Siberia. But on the other hand he was unprepared for the prosperity he did find.

Not that this was any paradise, worker's or otherwise. But it still came as a mild surprise. Henry Kuran couldn't remember so far back that he hadn't had his daily dose of anti-Russianism. Not unless it was for the brief respite during the Second World War when for a couple of years the Red Army had been composed of heroes and Stalin had overnight become benevolent old Uncle Joe.

There weren't as many cars on the streets as in American cities, but there were more than he had expected nor were they 1955 model Packards. So far as he could see, they were approximately the same cars as were being turned out in Western Europe.

414

Public transportation, he admitted, was superior to that found in the Western capitals. Obviously, it would have to be, without automobiles, buses, streetcars and subways would have to carry the brunt of traffic. However, it was the spotless efficiency of public transportation that set him back.

The shops were still short of the pinnacles touched by Western capitals. They weren't empty of goods, luxury goods as well as necessities, but they weren't overflowing with the endless quantities, the hundred-shadings of quality and fashion that you expected in the States.

But what struck nearest to him was the fact that the people in the streets were not broken spirited depressed, humorless drudges. In fact, why not admit it, they looked about the same as people in the streets anywhere else. Some laughed, some looked troubled. Children ran and played. Lovers held hands and looked into each other's eyes. Some reeled under an overload of vodka. Some hurried along, business bent. Some dawdled, window shopped, or strolled along for the air. Some read books or newspapers as they shuffled, radar directed, and unconscious of the world about them.

They were only a day and half in Leningrad. They saw the Hermitage, comparable to the Louvre and far and above any art museum in America. They saw the famous subway-which deserved its fame. They were ushered through a couple of square miles of the Elektrosile electrical equipment works, claimed ostentatiously by the to be the largest in the world. They ate in restaurants as good as any Hank Kuran had been able to afford at home and stayed one night at the Astoria Hotel.

At least, Hank had the satisfaction of grumbling about the plumbing.

Paco and Loo, the only single bachelors on the tour besides himself, were again quartered with him at the Astoria.

Paco said, "My friend, there I agree with you completely. America has the best plumbing in the world. And the most."

Hank was pulling off his shoes after an arch-breaking day of sightseeing. "Well, I'm glad I've finally found some field where it's agreeable that the West is superior to the Russkies."

Loo was stretched out on his bed, in stocking feet, gazing at the ceiling which towered at least fifteen feet above him. He said "In the town where I was born, there were three bathrooms, one in the home of the missionary, one in the home of the commissioner, and one in my father's palace." He looked up at Hank. "Or is my country considered part of the Western World?"

Paco laughed. "Come to think of it, I doubt if one third the rural homes of Argentina have bathrooms. Hank, my friend, I am afraid Loo is right. You use the word *West* too broadly. All the capitalist world is not so advanced as the United States. You have been very lucky, you Yankees."

Hank sank into one of the huge, Victorian era armchairs. "Luck has nothing to do with it. America is rich because private enterprise *works*."

"Of course," Paco pursued humorously, "the fact that your country floats on a sea of oil, has some of the richest forest land in the world, is blessed with some of the greatest mineral deposits anywhere and millions of acres of unbelievably fertile land has nothing to do with it."

"I get your point," Hank said. "The United States was handed the wealth of the world on a platter. But that's only part of it."

"Yes," Loo agreed. "Also to be considered is the fact that for more than a hundred years you have never had a serious war, serious, that is, in that your land was not invaded, your industries destroyed."

"That's to our credit. We're a peace loving people."

Loo laughed abruptly. "You should tell that to the American Indians."

Hank scowled over at him. "What'd you mean by that Loo? That has all the elements of a nasty crack."

"Or tell it to the Mexicans. Isn't that where you got your whole South-west?"

Hank looked from Loo to Paco and back.

*　*　*　*　*

Paco brought out cigarettes and tossed one to each of the others. "Aren't these long Russian cigarettes the end? I heard somebody say that by the time the smoke got through all the filter, you'd lost the habit." He looked over at Hank. "Easy my friend, easy. On a trip like this it would be impossible not to continually be comparing East and West, dwelling continually on politics, the pros and cons of both sides. All of us are continually assimilating what we hear and see. Among other things, I note that on the newsstands there are no publications from western lands. Why? Because still, after fifty years, our Communist bureaucracy dare not allow its people to read what they will. I note, too, that the shops on 25th October Avenue are not all directed toward the Russian man on the street, unless he is paid unbelievably more than we have heard. Sable coats? Jewelery? Luxurious furniture? I begin to suspect that our Soviet friends are not quite so classless as Mr. Marx had in mind when he and Mr. Engels worked out the rough framework of the society of the future."

Loo said seriously, "Oh, there are a great many things of that type to notice here in the Soviet Union."

Hank had to grin. "Well, I'm glad you jokers still have open minds."

Paco waggled a finger negatively at him. "We've had open minds all along, my friend. It is yours that seems closed. In spite of the fact that I spent four years in your country I sometimes confess I don't understand you Americans. I think you are too immersed in your TV programs, your movies and your light fiction."

"I can feel myself being saddled up again," Hank complained. "All set for another riding."

Loo laughed softly, his perfect white teeth gleaming in his black face.

Paco said, "You seem to have the fictional *good guys and bad guys* outlook. And, in this world of controversy, you assume that you are the good guys, the heroes, and since that is so then the Soviets must be the bad guys. And, as in the movies, everything the good guys do is fine and everything the bad guys do, is evil. I sometimes think that if the Russians had developed a cure for cancer first you Americans would have refused to use it."

Hank had had enough. He said, "Look, Paco, there are two hundred million Americans. For you, or anyone else, to come along and try to lump that many people neatly together is pure silliness. You'll find every type of person that exists in the world in any country. The very tops of intelligence, and submorons living in institutions; the most highly educated of scientists, and men who didn't finish grammar school; you'll find saints, and gangsters; infant prodigies and juvenile delinquents; and millions upon millions of just plain ordinary people much like the people of Argentina, or England, or France or whatever. True enough, among all our two hundred million there are some mighty prejudiced people, some mighty backward ones, and some downright foolish ones. But if you think the United States got to the position she's in today through the efforts of a whole people who are foolish, then you're obviously pretty far off the beam yourself."

Paco was looking at him narrowly. "Accepted, friend Hank, and I apologize. That's quite the most effective outburst I've heard from you in this week we've known each other. It occurs to me that perhaps you are other than I first thought."

Oh, oh. Hank backtracked. He said, "Good grief, let's drop it."

Paco said, "Well, just to change the subject, gentlemen, there is one thing above all that I noted here in Leningrad."

"What was that?" Loo said.

"It's the only town I've ever seen where I felt an urge to kiss a cop," Paco said soulfully. "Did you notice? Half the traffic police in town are cute little blondes."

Loo rolled over. "A fascinating observation, but personally I am going to take a nap. Tonight it's the Red Arrow Express to Moscow and rest might be in order, particularly if the train has square wheels, burns wood and stops and repairs bridges all along the way, as I'm sure Hank believes."

Hank reached down, got hold of one of his shoes and heaved it.

"Missed!" Loo grinned.

* * * * *

The Red Arrow Express had round wheels, burned Diesel fuel and made the trip between Leningrad and Moscow overnight. In one respect, it was the most unique train ride Hank Kuran had ever had. The track contained not a single curve from the one city to the other. Its engineers must have laid the roadbed out with a ruler.

The cars like the rest of public transportation, were as comfortable as any Hank knew. Traveling second class, as the Progressive Tours pilgrims did, involved four people in a compartment for the night, with one exception. At the end of the car was a smaller compartment containing two bunks only.

The Intourist guide who had shepherded them around Leningrad took them to the train, saw them all safely aboard, told them another Intourist employee would pick them up at the station in Moscow.

It was late. Hank was assigned the two-bunk compartment. He put his glasses on the tiny window table, sat on the edge of the lower and began to pull off his shoes. He didn't look up when the door opened until a voice said, icebergs dominating the tone, "Just what are you doing in here?"

Hank blinked up at her. "Hello, Char. What?"

Char Moore snapped, "I said, what are you doing in my compartment?"

"Yours? Sorry, the conductor just assigned me here. Evidently there's been some mistake."

"I suggest you rectify it, Mr. Stevenson."

Out in the corridor a voice, heavy with Britishisms, complained plaintively, "Did you ever hear the loik? They put men and women into the same compartment. Oim expected to sleep with a loidy in the bunk under me."

Hank cleared his throat, didn't allow himself the luxury of a smile. He said, "I'll see what I can do, Char. Seems to me I did read somewhere that the Russkies see nothing wrong in putting strangers in the same sleeping compartment."

Char Moore stood there, saying nothing but breathing deeply enough to express American womanhood insulted.

"All right, all right," he said, retying his shoes and retrieving his glasses. "I didn't engineer this." He went looking for the conductor.

He was back, yawning by this time, fifteen minutes later. Char Moore was sitting on the side of the bottom bunk, sipping a glass of tea that she'd bought for a few kopecks from the portress. She looked up coolly as he entered, but her voice was more pleasant. "Get everything fixed?"

Hank said, "What bunk do you want, upper or lower?"

"That's not funny."

"It's not supposed to be." Hank pulled his bag from under the bunk and from it drew pajamas and his dressing gown. "Check with the rest of the tour if you want. The conductor couldn't care less. We were evidently assigned compartments by Intourist and where we were assigned we'll sleep. Either that or you can stand in the corridor all night. I'll be damned if I will."

"You don't have to swear," Char bit out testily. "What are we going to do about it?"

"I just told you what I was going to do." Taking up his things he opened the door. "I'll change in the men's dressing room."

"I'll lock the door," Char Moore snapped.

Hank grinned at her. "I'll bet that if you do the conductor either has a passkey or will break it down for me."

When he returned in slippers, nightrobe and pajamas, Char was in the upper berth, staring angrily at the compartment ceiling. There were no hooks or other facilities for hanging or storing clothes. She must have put all of her things back into her bag. Hank grinned inwardly, carefully folded his own pants and jacket over his suitcase before climbing into the bunk.

"Don't snore, do you?" he said conversationally.

No answer.

"Or walk in your sleep?"

"You're not funny, Mr. Stevenson."

"That's what I like about this country," Hank said. "Progressive. Way ahead of the West. Shucks, modesty is a reactionary capitalistic anachronism. Shove 'em all into bed together, that's what I always say." He laughed.

"Oh, shut up," Char said. But then she laughed, too. "Actually, I suppose there's nothing wrong with it. We are rather Victorian about such things in the States."

Hank groaned. "There you are. If a railroad company at home suggested you spend the night in a compartment with a strange man, you'd sue them. But here in the promised land it's O.K."

After a short silence Char said, "Hank, why do you dislike the Soviet Union so much?"

"Why? Because I'm an American!"

She said so softly as to be almost inaudible, "I've known you for a week now. Somehow you don't really seem to be the type who would make that inadequate a statement."

Hank said "Look, Char. There's a cold war going on between the United States and her allies and the Soviet complex. I'm on our side. It's going to be one or the other."

"No it isn't, Hank. If it ever breaks out into hot war, it's going to be both. That is, unless the extraterrestrials add some new elements to the whole disgusting situation."

"Let's put it another way. Why are you so pro-Soviet?"

She raised herself on one elbow and scowled down over the edge of her bunk at him. Inside, Hank turned over twice to see the unbound red hair, the serious green eyes. Imagine looking at that face over the breakfast table for the rest of your life. The hell with South American senoritas.

Char said earnestly, "I'm not. Confound it, Hank, can't the world get any further than this cowboys and Indians relationship between nations? Our science and industry has finally developed to the point where the world could be a paradise. We've solved all the problems of production. We've conquered all the major diseases. We have the wonders of eternity before us-and look at us."

"Tell that to the Russkies and their pals. They're out for the works."

"Well, haven't we been?"

"The United States isn't trying to take over the world."

"No? Possibly not in the old sense of the word, but aren't we trying desperately to sponsor our type of government and social system everywhere? Frankly, I'm neither pro-West nor pro-Soviet. I think they're both wrong."

"Fine," Hank said. "What is your answer?"

She remained silent for a long time. Finally, "I don't claim to have an answer. But the world is changing like crazy. Science, technology, industrial production, education, population all are mushrooming. For us to claim that sweeping and basic changes aren't taking place in the Western nations is just nonsense. Our own country's institutions barely resemble the ones we had when you and I were children. And certainly the Soviet Union has changed and is changing from what it was thirty or forty years ago."

"Listen, Char," Hank said in irritation, "you still haven't come up with any sort of an answer to the cold war."

"I told you I hadn't any. All I say is that I'm sick of it. I can't remember so far back that there wasn't a cold war. And the more I consider it the sillier it looks. Currently the United States and her allies spend between a third and a half of their gross national product on the military-ha! the military! —and in fighting the Soviet complex in international trade."

"Well," Hank said, "I'm sick of it, too, and I haven't any answer either, but I'll be darned if I've heard the Russkies propose one. And just between you and me, if I had to choose between living Soviet style and our style, I'd choose ours any day."

Char said nothing.

Hank added flatly, "Who knows, maybe the coming of these Galactic Confederation characters will bring it all to a head."

She said nothing further and in ten minutes the soft sounds of her breathing had deepened to the point that Hank Kuran knew she slept. He lay there another half hour in the full knowledge that probably the most desirable woman he'd ever met was sleeping less than three feet away from him.

* * * * *

Leningrad had cushioned the first impression of Moscow for Henry Kuran. Although, if anything, living standards and civic beauty were even higher here in the capital city of world Communism.

They pulled into the Leningradsky Station on Komsomolskaya Square in the early morning to be met by Intourist guides and buses.

Hank sat next to Char Moore still feeling on the argumentative side after their discussion of the night before. He motioned with his head at some excavation work going on next to the station. "There you are. Women doing manual labor."

Char said, "I'm from the Western states, it doesn't impress me. Have you ever seen fruit pickers, potato diggers, or just about any type of itinerant harvest workers? There is no harder work and women, and children for that matter, do half of it at home."

He looked at the husky, rawboned women laborers working shoulder to shoulder with the men. "I still don't like it."

Char shrugged. "Who does? The sooner we devise machines to do all the drudgery the better off the world will be."

To his surprise, Hank found Moscow one of the most beautiful cities he had ever observed. Certainly the downtown area in the vicinity of the Kremlin compared favorably with any.

The buses whisked them down through Lermontovskaya Square, down Kirov Street to Novaya and then turned right. The Intourist guide made with a running commentary. There was the famous Bolshoi Theater and there Sverdlova Square, a Soviet cultural center.

Hank didn't know it then but they were avoiding Red Square. They circled it, one block away, and pulled onto Gorky Street and before a Victorian period building.

"The Grand Hotel," the guide announced, "where you will stay during your Moscow visit."

Half a dozen porters began manhandling their bags from the top of the bus. They were ushered into the lobby and assigned rooms. Russian hotel lobbies were a thing apart. No souvenir stands, no bellhops, no signs saying *To the Bar*, *To the Barber Shop* or to anything else. A hotel was a hotel, period.

Hank trailed Loo and Paco and three porters to the second floor and to the room they were assigned in common. Like the Astoria's rooms, in Leningrad, it was king-sized. In fact, it could easily have been divided into three chambers. There were four full sized beds, six arm chairs, two sofas, two vanity tables, a monstrous desk-and one wash bowl which gurgled when you ran water.

Paco, hands on hips, stared around. "A dance hall," he said. "Gentlemen, this room hasn't changed since some Grand Duke stayed in it before the revolution."

Loo, who had assumed his usual prone position on one of the beds, said, "From what I've heard about Moscow housing, you could get an average family in this amount of space."

Hank was stuffing clothes into a dresser drawer. "Now who's making with anti-Soviet comments?"

Paco laughed at him. "Have you ever seen some of the housing in the Harlem district in New York? You can rent a bed in a room that has possibly ten beds, for an eight-hour period. When your eight hours are up you roll out and somebody else rolls in. The beds are kept warm, three shifts every twenty-four hours."

Hank shook his head and muttered, "They call me Dobbin, I've been ridden so much."

Paco laughed and rubbed his hands together happily. "It's still early. We have nothing to do until lunch time. I suggest we sally forth and take a look at Russian womanhood. One never knows."

Loo said, "As an alternative, I suggest we rest until lunch."

Paco snorted. "A rightest-Trotskyite wrecker, and an imperialist war-monger to boot."

Loo said, dead panned, "Smile when you say that stranger."

Hank said, "Hey, wait a minute."

He went down the room to the far window and bug-eyed. One block away, at the end of Gorky Street, was Red Square. St. Basil's Cathedral at the far end, and unbelievable candy-cane construction of fanciful spirals, and every-colored turrets; the red marble mausoleum, Mecca of world Communism, housing the prophet Lenin and his two disciples; the long drab length of the GUM department store opposite. But it wasn't these.

There on the square, nestled in the corner between St. Basil's and the mausoleum, squatted what Henry Kuran had never really expected to see, in spite of his assignment, in spite of news broadcasts, in spite of everything to the contrary. Boomerang shaped, resting on short stilts, six of them in all, a baby blue in color-an impossibly beautiful baby blue.

The spaceship.

Paco stood at one shoulder, Loo at the other.

For once there was no humor in Paco's words. "There it is," he said. "Our visitors from the stars."

"Possibly our teachers from the stars," Hank said huskily.

"Or our judges." Loo's voice was flat.

They stood there for another five minutes in silence. Loo said finally, "Undoubtedly our Intourist guides will take us nearer, if that's allowed, later during our stay. Meanwhile, my friends, I shall rest up for the occasion."

"Let's take our quick look at the city," Paco said to Hank. "Once the Intourist people take over they'll run our feet off. Frankly, I have little interest in where the first shot of the revolution was fired, the latest tractor factory, or where Rasputin got it in the neck. There are more important things."

"We know," Loo said from the bed. "Women."

"Right!"

* * * * *

Hank was wondering whether or not to leave the room. The *Stilyagi* were to contact him. Where? When? Obviously, he'd need their help. He had no idea whatsoever on how to penetrate to the Interplanetary emissaries.

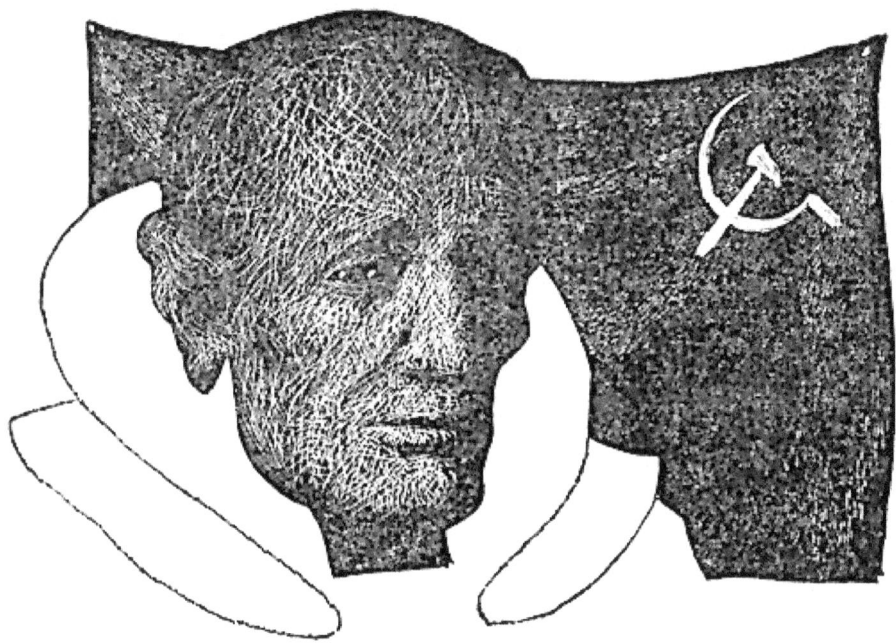

He spoke Russian. Fine. So what? Could he simply march up to the spacecraft and knock on the door? Or would he make himself dangerously conspicuous by just getting any closer than he now was to the craft?

As he stood now, he felt he was comparatively safe. He was sure the Russkies had marked him down as a rather ordinary American. Heavens knows, he'd worked hard enough at the role. A simple, average tourist, a little on the square side, and not even particularly articulate.

However, he wasn't going to accomplish much by remaining here in this room. He doubted that the *Stilyagi* would get in touch with him either by phone or simply knocking at the door.

"O.K., Paco," he said. "Let's go. In search of the pin-up girl-Moscow style."

They walked down to the lobby and started for the door.

One of the Intourist guides who had brought them from the railroad station stood to one side of the stairs. "Going for a walk, gentlemen? I suggest you stroll up Gorky Street, it's the main shopping center."

Paco said, "How about going over into Red Square to see the spaceship?"

The guide shrugged. "I don't believe the guards will allow you to get too near. It would be undesirable to bother the Galactic delegates to the Soviet Union."

That was one way of wording it, Hank thought glumly. *The Galactic delegates to the Soviet Union.* Not to the Earth, but to the Soviet Union. He wondered what the neutrals in such countries as India were thinking.

But at least there were no restrictions on Paco and him.

They strolled up Gorky Street, jam packed with fellow pedestrians. Shoppers, window-shoppers, men on the prowl for girls, girls on the prowl for men, Ivan and his wife taking the baby for a stroll, street cleaners at the endless job of keeping Moscow's streets the neatest in the world.

Paco pointed out this to Hank, Hank pointed out that to Paco. Somehow it seemed more than a visit to a western European nation. This was Moscow. This was the head of the Soviet snake.

And then Hank had to laugh inwardly at himself as two youngsters, running along playing tag in a grown-up world of long legs and stolid pace, all but tripped him up. Head of a snake it might be, but Moscow's people looked astonishingly like those of Portland, Maine or Portland, Oregon.

"How do you like those two, coming now?" Paco said.

Those two coming now consisted of two better than averagely dressed girls who would run somewhere in their early twenties. A little too much make-up by western standards, and clumsily applied.

"Blondes," Paco said soulfully.

"They're all blondes here," Hank said.

"Wonderful, isn't it?"

The girls smiled at them in passing and Paco turned to look after, but they didn't stop. Hank and Paco went on.

It didn't take Hank long to get onto Paco's system. It was beautifully simple. He merely smiled widely at every girl that went by. If she smiled back, he stopped and tried to start a conversation with her.

He got quite a few rebuffs but-Hank remembered an old joke-on the other hand he got quite a bit of response.

Before they had completed a block and a half of strolling, they were standing on a corner, trying to talk with two of Moscow's younger set-female variety. Here again, Paco was a wonder. His languages were evidently Spanish, English and French but he was in there pitching with a language the full vocabulary of which consisted of *Da* and *Neit* so far as he was concerned.

Hank stood back a little, smiling, trying to stay in character, but in amused dismay at the other's aggressive abilities.

Paco said, "Listen, I think I can get these two to come up to the room. Which one do you like?"

Hank said, "If they'll come up to the room, then they're professionals."

Paco grinned at him. "I'm a professional, too. A lawyer by trade. It's just a matter of different professions."

A middle-aged pedestrian, passing by, said to the girls in Russian, "Have you no shame before the foreign tourists?"

They didn't bother to answer. Paco went back to his attempt to make a deal with the taller of the two.

The smaller, who sported astonishingly big and blue eyes, said to Hank in Russian, "You're too good to associate with *metrofanushka* girls?"

Hank frowned puzzlement. "I don't speak Russian," he said.

She laughed lightly, almost a giggle, and, in the same low voice her partner was using on Paco, said, "I think you do, Mr. Kuran. In the afternoon, tomorrow, avoid whatever tour the Intourist people wish to take you on and wander about Sovietska Park." She giggled some more. The world-wide epitome of a girl being picked up on the street.

Hank took her in more closely. Possibly twenty-five years of age. The skirt she was wearing was probably Russian, it looked sturdy and durable, but the sweater was one of the new American fabrics. Her shoes were probably western too, the latest flared heel effect. A typical *stilyagi* or *metrofanushka* girl, he assumed. Except for one thing-her eyes were cool and alert, intelligent beyond those of a street pickup.

Paco said, "What do you think, Hank? This one will come back to the hotel with me."

"Romeo, Romeo," Hank sighed, "wherefore do thou think thou art?"

Paco shrugged. "What's the difference? Buenos Aires, New York, Moscow. Women are women."

"And men are evidently men," Hank said. "You do what you want."

"O.K., friend. Do you mind staying out of the room for a time?"

"Don't worry about me, but you'll have to get rid of Loo, and he hasn't had his eighteen hours sleep yet today."

Paco had his girl by the arm. "I'll roll him into the hall. He'll never wake up."

Hank's girl made a moue at him, shrugged as though laughing off the fact that she had been rejected, and disappeared into the crowds. Hank stuck his hands in his pockets and went on with his stroll.

The contact with the underground had been made.

* * * * *

Maintaining his front as an American tourist he wandered into several stores, picked up some amber brooches at a bargain rate, fingered through various books in English in an international bookshop. That was one thing that hit hard. The bookshops were packed. Prices were remarkably low and people were buying. In fact, he'd never seen a country so full of people reading and studying. The park benches were loaded with them, they read as the rode on streetcar and bus, they read as they walked along the street. He had an uneasy feeling that the jet-set kids were a small minority, that the juvenile delinquent problem here wasn't a fraction what it was in the West.

He'd expected to be followed. In fact, that had puzzled him when he first was given this unwanted assignment by Sheridan Hennessey. How was he going to contact this so-called underground if he was watched the way he had been led to believe Westerners were?

But he recalled their conducted tour of the Hermitage Museum in Leningrad. The Intourist guide had started off with twenty-five persons and had clucked over them like a hen all afternoon. In spite of her frantic efforts to keep them together, however, she returned to the Astoria Hotel that evening with eight missing-including Hank and Loo who had wandered off to get a beer.

The idea of the KGB putting tails on the tens of thousands of tourists that swarmed Moscow and Leningrad, became a little on the ridiculous side. Besides, what secret does a tourist know, or what secrets could he discover?

At any rate, Hank found no interference in his wanderings. He deliberately avoided Red Square and its spaceship, taking no chances on bringing himself to attention. Short of that locality, he wandered freely.

At noon they ate at the Grand and the Intourist guide outlined the afternoon program which involved a general sightseeing tour ranging from the University to the Park of Rest and Culture, Moscow's equivalent of Coney Island.

Loo said, "That all sounds very tiring, do we have time for a nap before leaving?"

"I'm afraid not, Mr. Motlamelle," the guide told him.

Paco shook his head. "I've seen a university, and I've seen a sport stadium and I've seen statues and monuments. I'll sit this one out."

"I think I'll lie this one out," Loo said. He complained plaintively to Hank. "You know what happened to me this morning, just as I was napping up in our room?"

"Yes," Hank said, "I was with our Argentine Casanova when he picked her up."

* * * * *

Hank took the conducted tour with the rest. If he was going to beg off the next day, he'd be less conspicuous tagging along on this one. Besides it gave him the lay of the land.

And he took the morning trip the next day, the automobile factories on the outskirts of town. It had been possibly fifteen years since Hank had been through Detroit but he doubted greatly that automation had developed as far in his own country as it seemed to have here. Or, perhaps, this was merely a showplace. But he drew himself up at that thought. That was one attitude the Western world couldn't afford-deprecating Soviet progress. This was the very thing that had led to such shocks as the launching of the early Sputniks. Underestimate your adversary and sooner or later you paid for it.

The Soviets had at long last built up a productive machine as great as any. Possibly greater. In sheer tonnage they were turning out more gross national product than the West. This was no time to be underestimating them.

All this was a double interest to a field man in Morton Twombly's department, working against the Soviets in international trade. He was beginning to understand at least one of the reasons why the Commies could sell their products at such ridiculously low prices. Automation beyond that of the West. In the Soviet complex the labor unions were in no position to block the introduction of ultra-efficient methods, and featherbedding was unheard of. If a Russian worker's job was *automated* out from under him, he shifted to a new plant, a new job, and possibly even learned a new trade. The American worker's union, to the contrary, did its best to save the job.

Hank Kuran remembered reading, a few months earlier, of a British textile company which had attempted to introduce a whole line of new automation equipment. The unions had struck, and the company had to give up the project. What happened to the machinery? It was sold to China!

Following the orders of his underground contact, he begged out of the afternoon tour, as did half a dozen of the others. Sightseeing was as hard on the feet in Moscow as anywhere else.

After lunch he looked up Sovietska Park on his tourist map of the city. It was handy enough. A few blocks up Gorky Street.

It turned out to be typical. Well done so far as fountains, monuments and gardens were concerned. Well equipped with park benches. In the early afternoon it was by no means empty, but, on the other hand not nearly so filled as he'd noticed the parks to be the evening before.

Hank stopped at one of the numerous cold drink stands where for a few kopecks you could get raspberry syrup fizzed up with soda water. While he sipped it, a teen-ager came up beside him and said in passable English, "Excuse me, are you a tourist? Do you speak English?"

This had happened before. Another kid practicing his school language.

"That's right," Hank said.

The boy said, "You aren't a ham, are you?" He brought some cards from an inner pocket. "I'm UA3-KAR."

For a moment Hank looked at him blankly, and then he recognized the amateur radio call cards the other was displaying. "Oh, a *ham*. Well, no, but I have a cousin who is."

Two more youngsters came up. "What's his call?"

Hank didn't remember that. They all adjourned to a park bench and little though he knew about the subject, international amateur radio was discussed in detail. In fifteen minutes he was hemmed in by a dozen or so and had about decided he'd better make his excuses and circulate around making himself available to the *stilyagi* outfit. He was searching for an excuse to shake them when the one sitting next to him reverted to Russian.

"We're clear now, Henry Kuran."

Hank said, "I'll be damned. I hadn't any idea —"

The other brushed aside trivialities. Looking at him more closely, Hank could see he was older than first estimate. Possibly twenty-two or so. Darker than most of the others, heavy-set, sharp and impatient.

"You can call me Georgi," he said. "These others will prevent outsiders from bothering us. Now then, we've been told you Americans want some assistance. What? And why should we give it to you?"

Hank said, worriedly, "Haven't you some place we could go? Where I could meet one of your higher-ups? This is important."

"Otherwise, I wouldn't be here," Georgi said impatiently. "For that matter there is no higher-up. We don't have ranks; we're a working democracy. And I'm afraid the day of the secret room in some cellar is past. With housing what it is, if there was an empty cellar in Moscow a family would move in. And remember, all buildings are State owned and operated. I'm afraid you'll have to tell your story here. Now, what is it you want?"

"I want an opportunity to meet the Galactic Confederation emissaries."

"Why?"

"To give them our side, the Western side, of the ... well, the controversy between us and the Soviet complex. We want an opportunity to have our say before they make any permanent treaties."

Georgi considered that. "We thought it was probably something similar," he muttered. "What do you think it will accomplish?"

"At least a delaying action. If the extraterrestrials throw their weight, their scientific progress, into the balance on the side of the Soviet complex, the West will have lost the cold war. Every neutral in the world will jump on the bandwagon. International trade, sources of raw materials, will be a thing of the past. Without a shot being fired, we'd become second-rate powers overnight."

Georgi said nothing for a long moment. A new youngster had drifted up to the group but one of those on the outskirts growled something at him and he went off again. Evidently, Hank decided, all of this dozen-odd cluster of youngsters were connected with the jet-set underground.

"All right, you want us to help you in the conflict between the Soviet government and the West," Georgi said. "Why should we?"

Hank frowned at him. "You're the anti-government movement. You're revolutionists and want to overthrow the Soviet government."

The other said impatiently, "Don't read something into our organization that isn't here. We don't exist for your benefit, but our own."

"But you wish to overthrow the Soviets and establish a democratic —"

Georgi was waggling an impatient hand. "That word democratic has been so misused this past half century that it's become all but meaningless. Look here, we wish to overthrow the present Soviet government, but that doesn't mean we expect to establish one modeled to yours. We're Russians. Our problems are Russian ones. Most of them you aren't familiar with-any more than we're familiar with your American ones."

"However, you want to destroy the Soviets," Hank pursued.

"Yes," Georgi growled, "but that doesn't necessarily mean that we wish *you* to win this cold war, as the term goes. That is, just because we're opposed to the Soviet government doesn't mean we like yours. But you make a point. If the Galactic Confederation gives all-out support to the Soviet bureaucracy it might strengthen it to the point where they could remain in office indefinitely."

* * * * *

Hank pressed the advantage. "Right. You'd never overthrow them then."

"On the other hand," Georgi muttered uncomfortably, "we're not interested in giving you Americans an opportunity that would enable you to collapse the whole fabric of this country and its allies."

"Look here," Hank said. "In the States we seem to know surprisingly little about your movement. Just what *do* you expect to accomplish?"

"To make it brief, we wish to enjoy the product of the sacrifices of the past fifty years. If you recall your Marx" —he twisted his face here in wry amusement —"the idea was that the State was to wither away once Socialism was established. Instead of withering away, it has become increasingly strong. This was explained by the early Bolsheviks in a fairly reasonable manner. Socialism presupposes a highly industrialized economy. It's not possible in a primitive nor even a feudalistic society. So our Communist bureaucracy remained in the saddle through a period of transition. The task was to industrialize the Soviet countries in a matter of decades where it had taken the Capitalist nations a century or two."

Georgi shrugged. "I've never heard of a governing class giving up its once acquired power of its own accord, no matter how incompetent they might be."

Hank said, "I wouldn't call the Soviet government incompetent."

"Then you'd be wrong," the other said. "Progress had been made but often in spite of the bureaucracy, not because of it. In the early days it wasn't so obvious, but as we develop the rule of the political bureaucrat becomes increasingly a hindrance. Politicians can't operate industries and they can't supervise laboratories. To the extent our scientist and technicians are interfered with by politicians, to that extent we are held up in our progress. Surely you've heard of the Lysenko matter?"

"He was the one who evolved the anti-Mendelian theory of genetics, fifteen or twenty years ago."

"Correct," Georgi snorted. "Acquired characteristics could be handed down by heredity. It took the Academy of Agricultural Science at least a decade to dispose of him. Why? Because his theories fitted into Stalin's political beliefs." The underground spokesman snorted again.

Hank had the feeling they were drifting from the subject. "Then you want to overthrow the Communist bureaucracy?"

"Yes, but that is only part of the story. Overthrowing it without something to replace the bureaucracy is a negative approach. We have no interest in a return to Czarist Russia, even if that were possible, and it isn't. We want to profit by what has happened in these years of ultra-sacrifice, not to destroy everything. The day of rule by politicians is antiquated, we look forward to the future." He seemed to switch subjects. "Do you remember Djilas' book which he wrote in one of Tito's prisons, "The New Class"?"

"Vaguely. I read the reviews. It was a best seller in the States some time ago."

Georgi made with his characteristic snort. "It was a best seller here-in underground circles. At any rate, that explains much. Our bureaucracy, no matter what its ideals might have been to begin with, has developed into a new class of its own. Russia sacrifices to surpass the West-but our bureaucrats don't. In Lenin's day the commissar was paid the same as the average worker, but today we have bureaucrats as wealthy as Western millionaires."

Hank said, "Of course, these are your problems. I don't pretend to have too clear a picture of them. However, it seems to me we have a mutual enemy. Right at this moment it appears that they are to receive some support that will strengthen them. I suggest you co-operate with me in hopes they'll be thwarted."

For the first time a near smile appeared on the young Russian's face. "A ludicrous situation. We have here a Russian revolutionary organization devoted to the *withering away* the Russian Communist State. To gain its ends, it co-operates with a Capitalist country's agent." His grin broadened. "I suspect that neither Nicolai Lenin nor Karl Marx ever pictured such contingencies."

Hank said, "I wouldn't know I'm not up on my Marxism. I'm afraid that when I went to school academic circles weren't inclined in that direction." He returned the Russian's wry smile.

Which only set the other off again. "Academic circles!" he snorted. "Sterile in both our countries. All professors of economics in the Soviet countries are Marxists. On the other hand, no American professor would admit to this. Coincidence? Suppose an American teacher was a convinced Marxist. Would he openly and honestly teach his beliefs? Suppose a Russian wasn't? Would he?" Georgi slapped his knee with a heavy hand and stood up. "I'll speak to various others. We'll let you know."

Hank said, "Wait. How long is this going to take? And *can* you help me if you want to? Where are these extraterrestrials?"

Georgi looked down at him. "They're in the Kremlin. How closely guarded we don't know, but we can find out."

"The Kremlin," Hank said. "I was hoping they stayed in their own ship."

"Rumor has it that they're quartered in the *Bolshoi Kremlevski Dvorets*, the Great Kremlin Palace. We'll contact you later-perhaps." He stuck his hands in his pockets and strode away, in all appearance just one more pedestrian without anywhere in particular to go.

One of the younger boys, the ham who had first approached Hank, smiled and said, "Perhaps we can talk a bit more of radio?"

"Yeah," Hank muttered, "Swell."

* * * * *

The next development came sooner than Henry Kuran had expected. In fact, before the others returned from their afternoon tour of the city. Hank was sprawled in one of the king-sized easy-chairs, turning what little he had to work on over in his mind. The principal decisions to make were, first, how long to wait on the assistance of the *stilyagi*, and, if that wasn't forthcoming, what steps to take on his own. The second prospect stumped him. He hadn't the vaguest idea what he could accomplish singly.

He wasn't even sure where the space aliens were. *The Bolshoi Kremlevski Dvorets*, Georgi had said. But was that correct, and, if so, where was the *Bolshoi Kremlevski Dvorets* and how did you get into it? For that matter, how did you get inside the Kremlin walls?

Under his breath he cursed Sheridan Hennessey. Why had he allowed himself to be dragooned into this? By all criteria it was the desperate clutching of a drowning man for a straw. He had no way to know, for instance, if he did reach the space emissaries, that he could even communicate with them.

He caught himself wishing he was back in Peru arguing with hesitant South Americans over the relative values of American and Soviet complex commodities-and then he laughed at himself.

There was a knock at the door.

Hank came wearily to his feet, crossed and opened it.

She still wore too much make-up, the American sweater and the flared heel shoes. And her eyes were still cool and alert. She slid past him, let her eyes go around the room quickly. "You are alone?" she said in Russian, but it was more a statement than question.

Hank closed the door behind them. He scowled at her, put a finger to his lips and then went through an involved pantomime to indicate looking for a microphone. He raised his eyebrows at her.

She laughed and shook her head. "No microphones."

"How do you know?"

"We know. We have contacts here in the hotel. If the KGB had to put microphones in the rooms of every tourist in Moscow, they'd have to increase their number by ten times. In spite of your western ideas to the contrary, it just isn't done. There are exceptions, of course, but there has to be some reason for it."

"Perhaps I'm an exception." Hank didn't like this at all. The C.I.A. men had been of the opinion that the KGB was once again thoroughly checking on every foreigner.

"If the KGB is already onto you, Henry Kuran, then you might as well give up. Your mission is already a failure."

"I suppose so. Will you have a chair? Can I offer you a drink? My roommate has a bottle of Stolichnaya vodka which he brought from the boat."

There was an amused light in her eyes even as she shook her head. "Your friend Paco is quite a man-so I understand. But no, I am here for business." She took one of the armchairs and Hank sank into another opposite her.

"The committee has decided to assist you to the point they can."

"Fine." Hank leaned forward.

"Tomorrow your Progressive Tours group is to have a conducted tour of the Kremlin museum, Ivan the Great's Tower, and the Assumption Cathedral."

"In the *Kremlin?*"

She was impatient. "The Kremlin is considerably larger than most Westerners seem to realize. Originally it was the whole city. The Kremlin walls are more then two kilometers long. In them are a great deal more than just government offices. Among other things, the Kremlin has one of the greatest museums and probably the largest in the world."

"What I meant was, with the space emissaries there, will tours still be held?"

"They *are* being held. It would be too conspicuous to stop them even if there was any reason to." She frowned and shook her head. "Just because you will be inside the Kremlin walls doesn't mean that you will be sitting in the lap of the extraterrestrials. They are probably well guarded in the palace. We don't know to what extent."

Hank said, "Then how can you help me?"

"Only in a limited way." She pulled a folder paper from her purse. "Here is a map of the Kremlin, and here one of the Palace. Both of these date from Czarist days but such things as the general layout of the Kremlin and the *Bolshoi Kremlevski Dvorets* do not change of course."

"Do you know where the extraterrestrials are?"

"We're not sure. The palace was built in the Seventeenth Century and was popular with various czars. It has been a museum for some time. We suspect that the Galactic Confederation delegates are housed in the *Sobstvennaya Plovina* which used to be the private apartments of Nicolas the First. It is quite define that the conferences are being held in the *Gheorghievskaya sala*; it's the largest and most impressive room in the Kremlin."

Hank stared at the two maps feeling a degree of dismay.

She said impatiently, "We can help you more than this. One of the regular guide-guards at the facade which leads to the main entrance of the palace is a member of our group. Here are your instructions."

They spent another fifteen minutes going over the details, then she shot a quick glance at her watch and came to her feet. "Is everything clear ...comrade?"

Hank frowned slightly at the use of the word, then understood. "I think so, and thanks ... comrade." He, as well as she, meant the term in its original sense.

He followed her to the door but before his hand touched the knob, it opened inwardly. Paco stood there, and behind him in the corridor was Char Moore.

The girl turned to Hank quickly, reached up and kissed him on the mouth and said, in English, "Good-bye, dollink." She winked at Paco, swept past Char and was gone.

Paco looked after her appreciatively, back at Hank and said, "Ah, ha. You are quite a dog after all, eh?"

Char Moore's face was blank. She mumbled something to the effect of, "See you later," directed seemingly to both of them, and went on to her room.

Hank said, "Damn!"

Paco closed the door behind him. "What's the matter, my friend?" he grinned. "Are you attempting to play two games at once?"

*   *   *   *   *

The morning tour was devoted to Red Square and the Kremlin. Immediately after breakfast they formed a column with two or three other tourist parties and were marched briskly to where Gorky Street debouched into Red Square. First destination was the mausoleum, backed against the Kremlin wall, which centered that square and served as a combined Vatican, Lhasa and Mecca of the Soviet complex. Built of dark red porphyry, it was the nearest thing to a really ultramodern building Hank had seen in Moscow.

As foreign tourists they were taken to the head of the line which already stretched around the Kremlin back into Mokhovaya Street along the western wall. A line of thousands.

Once the doors opened the line moved quickly. They filed in, two by two, down some steps, along a corridor which was suddenly cool as though refrigerated. Paco, standing next to Hank, said from the side of his mouth, "Now we know the secret of the embalming. I wonder if they're hanging on meathooks."

The line emerged suddenly into a room in the center of which were three glass chambers. The three bodies, the prophet and his two leading disciples flanking him. Lenin, Stalin, Khrushchev. On their faces, Hank decided, you could read much of their character. Lenin, the idealist and scholar. Stalin, utterly ruthless organization man. Khrushchev, energetic manager of what the first two had built.

They were in the burial room no more than two minutes, filed out by an opposite door. In the light of the square again, Paco grinned at him. "Nick and Joe didn't look so good, but Nikita is standing up pretty well."

Trailing back and forth across Red Square had its ludicrous elements. The guide pointed out this and that. But all the time his charges had their eyes glued to the spaceship, settled there at the far end of the square near St. Basil's. In a way it seemed no more alien than so much else here. Certainly no more alien to the world Hank knew than the fantastic St. Basil's Cathedral.

A spaceship from the stars, though. You still had to shake your head in effort to achieve clarity; to realize the significance of it. A spaceship with emissaries from a Galactic Confederation.

How simple if it had only landed in Washington, London or even Paris or Rome, instead of here.

They avoided getting very near it, although the Russians weren't being ostentatious about their guarding. There was a roped off area about the craft and twenty or so guards, not overly armed, drifting about within the enclosure. But the local citizenry was evidently well disciplined.

There were no huge crowds hanging on the ropes waiting for a glimpse of the interplanetary celebrities.

Nevertheless, the Intourist guide went out of his way to avoid bringing his charges too near. They retraced their steps back to Manezhnaya Square from which they had originally started to see the mausoleum, and then turned left through Alexandrovski Sad, the Alexander Park which ran along the west side of the Kremlin to the Borovikski Gate, on the Moskva River side of the fortress.

Paco said, "After this tour I'm in favor of us all signing a petition that our guide be awarded a medal, *Hero of Intourist*. You realize that thus far he has lost only two of us today?"

Some of the others didn't like his levity. They were about to enter the Communist shrine and wisecracking was hardly in order. Paco Rodriquez couldn't have cared less, being Paco Rodriquez.

The *stilyagi* girl had been correct about the Kremlin being an overgrown museum. Government buildings it evidently contained, but above all it provided gold topped cathedrals, fabulous palaces converted to art galleries and displays of the jeweled wealth of yesteryear and the tombs of a dozen czars including that of Ivan the Terrible.

* * * * *

They trailed into the Orushezhnaya Palace, through the ornate entrance hall displaying its early arms and banners.

Paco encouraged the harassed guard happily. "You're doing fine. You've had us out for more than two hours. We started with twenty-five in this group and still have twenty-one. Par for the course. What happens to a tourist who wanders absently around in the Kremlin and turns up in the head man's office?"

The guide smiled wanly. "And over here we have the thrones of the Empress Elizabeth and Czar Paul."

Unobtrusively, Hank dropped toward the tail of the group. He spent a long time peering at two silver panthers, gifts of the first Queen Elizabeth of England to Boris Godunov. The Progressive Tours assembly passed on into the next room.

A guard standing next to the case said, "Mr. Kuran?"

Without looking up, Hand nodded.

"Follow me, slowly."

No one from the Progressive Tours group was in sight. Hank wandered after the guard, looking into display cases as he went. Finally the other turned a corner into an empty and comparatively narrow corridor. He stopped and waited for the American.

"You're Kuran?" he asked anxiously in Russian.

"That's right."

"You're not afraid?"

"No. Let's go." Inwardly Hank growled, *Of course I'm afraid. Do I look like a confounded hero?* What was it Sheridan Hennessey had said? This was combat, combat cold-war style, but still combat. Of course he was afraid. Had there ever in the history of combat been a participant who had gone into it unafraid?

They walked briskly along the corridor. The guard said, "You have studied your maps?"

"Yes."

"I can take you only so far without exposing myself. Then you are on your own. You must know your maps or you are lost. These old palaces ramble —"

"I know," Hank said impatiently. "Brief me as we go along. Just for luck."

"Very well. We leave Orushezhnaya Palace by this minor doorway. Across there, to our right, is the *Bolshoi Kremlevski Dvorets*, the Great Kremlin Palace. It's there the Central Executive Committee meets, and the Assembly. The same hall used to be the czar's throne room in the old days. On the nearer side, on the ground floor, are the *Sobstvennaya Plovina*, the former private apartments of Nicholas First. The extraterrestrials are there."

"You're sure? The others weren't sure."

"That's where they are."

"How can we get to them?"

"*We* can't. Possibly *you* can. I can take you only so far. The front entrance is strongly guarded, we are going to have to enter the Great Palace from the rear, through the Teremni Palace. You remember your maps?"

"I think so."

They strode rapidly from the museum through a major courtyard. Hank to the right and a step behind the uniformed guard.

The other was saying, "The Teremni preceded the Great Palace. One of its walls was used to become the rear of the later structure. We can enter it fairly freely."

They entered through another smaller doorway a hundred feet or more from the main entrance, climbed a short marble stairway and turned right down an ornate corridor, tapestry hung. They passed occasionally other uniformed guards, none of whom paid them any attention.

They passed through three joined rooms, each heavily furnished in Seventeenth Century style, each thick with icons. The guide brought them up abruptly at a small door.

He said, an air almost of defiance in his tone, "I go no further. Through this door and you are in the Great Palace, in the bathroom of the apartments of Catherine Second. You remember your maps?"

"Yes," Hank said.

"I hope so." The guard hesitated. "You are armed?"

"No. We were afraid that my things might be thoroughly searched. Had a gun been found on me, my mission would have been over then and there."

The guard produced a heavy military revolver, offered it butt foremost.

But Hank shook his head. "Thanks. But if it comes to the point where I'd need a gun —I've already failed. I'm here to talk, not to shoot."

The guard nodded. "Perhaps you're right. Now, I repeat. On the other side of this door is the bathroom of the Czarina's apartments. Beyond it is her *paradnaya divannaya*, her dressing room and beyond that the *Ekaterininskaya sala*, the throne room of Catherine Second. It is probable that there will be nobody in any of these rooms. Beyond that, I do not know."

He ended abruptly with "Good luck," turned and scurried away.

"Thanks," Hank Kuran said after him. He turned and tried the door-knob. Inwardly he thought, *All right Henry Kuran. Hennessey said you had a reputation for being able to think on your feet. Start thinking. Thus far all you've been called on to do is exchange low-level banter with a bevy of pro-commie critics of the United States. Now the chips are down.*

* * * * *

The apartments of the long dead czarina were empty. He pushed through them and into the corridor beyond.

And came to a quick halt.

Halfway down the hall, Loo Motlamelle crouched over a uniformed, crumpled body. He looked up at Hank Kuran's approach, startled, a fighting man at bay. His lips thinned back over his teeth. A black thumb did something to the weapon he held in his hand.

Hank said throatily, "Is he dead?"

Loo shook his head, his eyes coldly wary. "No. I slugged him."

Hank said, "What are you doing here?"

Loo came erect. "It occurs to me that I'm evidently doing the same thing you are."

But the dull metal gun in his hand was negligently at the ready and his eyes were cold, cold. It came to Hank that banjos on the levee were very far away.

This lithe fighting man said tightly, "You know where we are? Exactly where we are? I'm not sure."

Hank said, "In the hall outside the *Sobstvennaya Plovina* of the *Bolshoi Kremlevski Dvorets*. The czar's private apartments. And how did you get here?"

"The hard way," Loo said softly. His eyes darted up and down the corridor. "I can't figure out why there aren't more guards. I don't like this. You're armed?"

"No," Hank said.

Loo grinned down at his own weapon. "One of us is probably making a mistake but we both seem to have gotten this far. By the way, I'm Inter-Commonwealth Security. You're C.I.A., aren't you? Talk fast, Hank, we're either a team from now on, or I've got to do something about you."

"Special mission for the President," Hank said. "Why didn't we spot each other sooner?"

Loo grinned again in deprecation. "Evidently because we're both good operatives. If I've got this right, the extraterrestrials are somewhere in here."

Hank started down the corridor. There was no time to go into the whys and wherefores of Loo's mission. It must be approximately the same as his own. "There are some private apartments in this direction," he said over his shoulder. "They must be quartered —"

A door off the corridor opened and a tall, thin, ludicrously garbed man —

Hank pulled himself up quickly, both mentally and physically. It was no man. It was almost a man-but no.

Loo's weapon was already at the alert.

The newcomer unhurriedly looked from one of them to the other. Then down at the Russian guard sprawled on the floor behind them.

He said in Russian, "Always violence. The sadness of violence. When faced with crisis, threaten violence if outpointed. Your race has much to learn." He switched to English. "But this is probably your language, isn't it?"

Loo gaped at him. The man from space was almost as dark complected as the Negro.

The extraterrestrial stepped to one side and indicated the room behind him "Please enter, I assume you've come looking for us."

They entered the ornate bedroom.

The extraterrestrial said, "Is the man dead?"

Loo said, "No. Merely stunned."

"He needs no assistance?"

"Nothing could help him for half an hour or more. Then he'll probably have a severe headache."

The extraterrestrial had even the ability to achieve a dry quality in his voice. "I am surprised at your forebearance." He took a chair before a baroque desk. "Undoubtedly you have gone through a great deal to penetrate to this point. I am a member of the interplanetary delegation. What is it that you want?"

Hank looked at Loo, received a slight nod, and went into his speech. The space alien made no attempt to interrupt.

When Hank had finished, the extraterrestrial turned his eyes to Loo. "And you?"

Loo said, "I represent the British Commonwealth rather than the United States, but my purpose in contacting you was identical. Her Majesty's government is anxious to consult with you before you make any binding agreements with the Soviet complex."

The alien turned his eyes from one to the other. His face, Hank decided, had a Lincolnesque quality, so ugly as to be beautiful in its infinite sadness.

"You must think us incredibly naive," he said.

Hank scowled. He had adjusted quickly to the space ambassador's *otherness*, both of dress and physical qualities, but there was an irritating something-He put his finger on it. He felt as he had, some decades ago, when brought before his grammar school principal for an infraction of school discipline.

Hank said, "We haven't had too much time to think. We've been desperate."

The alien said, "You have gone to considerable trouble. I can even admire your resolution. You will be interested to know that tomorrow we take ship to Peiping."

"Peiping?" Loo said blankly.

"Following two weeks there we proceed to Washington and following that to London. What led your governments to believe that the Soviet nations were to receive all our attention, and your own none at all?"

Hank blurted, "But you landed *here*. You made no contact with us."

"The size of our expedition is limited. We could hardly do everything at once. The Soviet complex, as you call it, is the largest government and the most advanced on Earth. Obviously, this was our first stop." His eyes went to Hank's. "You're an American. Do you know why you have fallen behind in the march of progress?"

"I'm not sure we have," Hank said flatly. "Do you mean in comparison with the Soviet complex?"

"Exactly. And if you don't realize it, then you've blinded yourself. You've fallen behind in a score of fields because a decade or so ago, in your years between 1957 and 1960, you made a disastrous decision. In alarm at Russian progress, you adopted a campaign of combating Russian science. You began educating your young people to combat Russian progress."

"We had to!"

The alien grunted. "To the contrary, what you should have done was try to excel Russian science, technology and industry. Had you done that you might have continued to be the world's leading nation, until, at least, some sort of world unity had been achieved. By deciding to *combat* Russian progress you became a retarding force, a deliberate drag on the development of your species, seeking to cripple and restrain rather than to grow and develop. The way to win a race is not to trip up your opponent, but to run faster and harder than he."

Hank stared at him.

The space alien came to his feet. "I am busy. Your missions, I assume, have been successfully completed. You have seen one of our group. Melodramatically, you have warned us against your enemy. Your superiors should be gratified. And now I shall summon a guide to return you to your hotels."

A great deal went out of Hank Kuran. Until now the tenseness had been greater than he had ever remembered in life. Now he was limp. In response, he nodded.

Loo sighed, returned the weapon which he had until now held in his hand to a shoulder holster. "Yes," he said, meaninglessly. He turned and looked at Hank Kuran wryly. "I have spent the better part of my life learning to be an ultra-efficient security operative. I suspect that my job has just become obsolete."

"I have an idea that perhaps mine is too," Hank said.

* * * * *

In the morning, the Progressive Tours group was scheduled to visit a co-operative farm, specializing in poultry, on the outskirts of Moscow. While the bus was loading Hank stopped off at the Grand Hotel's Intourist desk.

"Can I send a cable to the United States?"

The chipper Intourist girl said "But of course." She handed him a form.

He wrote quickly:

SHERIDAN HENNESSEY
WASHINGTON, D. C.
MISSION ACCOMPLISHED

MORE SATISFACTORILY

The girl checked it quickly. "But your name is Henry Stevenson."

"That," Hank said, "was back when I was a cloak and dagger man."

She blinked and looked after him as he walked out and climbed aboard the tourist bus. He found an empty seat next to Char Moore and settled into it.

Char said evenly, "Ah, today you have time from your amorous pursuits to join the rest of us."

He raised an eyebrow at her. Jealousy? His chances were evidently better than he had ever suspected. "I meant to tell you about that," he said, "the first time we're by ourselves."

"Hm-m-m," she said. Then, "We've been in Russia for several days now. What do you think of it?"

Hank said, "I think it's pretty good. And I have a sneaking suspicion that in another ten years, when a few changes will have evolved, she'll be better still."

She looked at him blankly. "You *do*? Frankly, I've been somewhat disappointed."

"Sure. But wait'll you see *our* country in ten years. You know, Char, this world of ours has just got started."

Medal of Honor

Don Mathers snapped to attention, snapped a crisp salute to his superior, said, "Sub-lieutenant Donal Mathers reporting, sir."

The Commodore looked up at him, returned the salute, looked down at the report on the desk. He murmured, "Mathers, One Man Scout V-102. Sector A22-K223."

"Yes, sir," Don said.

The Commodore looked up at him again. "You've been out only five days, Lieutenant."

"Yes, sir, on the third day I seemed to be developing trouble in my fuel injectors. I stuck it out for a couple of days, but then decided I'd better come in for a check." Don Mathers added, "As per instructions, sir."

"Ummm, of course. In a Scout you can hardly make repairs in space. If you have any doubts at all about your craft, orders are to return to base. It happens to every pilot at one time or another."

"Yes, sir."

"However, Lieutenant, it has happened to you four times out of your last six patrols."

Don Mathers said nothing. His face remained expressionless.

"The mechanics report that they could find nothing wrong with your engines, Lieutenant."

"Sometimes, sir, whatever is wrong fixes itself. Possibly a spot of bad fuel. It finally burns out and you're back on good fuel again. But by that time you're also back to the base."

* * * * *

The Commodore said impatiently, "I don't need a lesson in the shortcomings of the One Man Scout, Lieutenant. I piloted one for nearly five years. I know their shortcomings-and those of their pilots."

"I don't understand, sir."

The Commodore looked down at the ball of his thumb. "You're out in space for anywhere from two weeks to a month. All alone. You're looking for Kraden ships which practically never turn up. In military history the only remotely similar situation I can think of were the pilots of World War One pursuit planes, in the early years of the war, when they still flew singly, not in formation. But even they were up there alone for only a couple of hours or so."

"Yes, sir," Don said meaninglessly.

The Commodore said, "We, here at command, figure on you fellows getting a touch of space cafard once in a while and, ah, *imagining* something wrong in the engines and coming in. But," here the Commodore cleared his throat, "four times out of six? Are you sure you don't need a psych, Lieutenant?"

Don Mathers flushed. "No, sir, I don't think so."

The Commodore's voice went militarily expressionless. "Very well, Lieutenant. You'll have the customary three weeks leave before going out again. Dismissed."

Don saluted snappily, wheeled and marched from the office.

Outside, in the corridor, he muttered a curse. What did that chairborne brass hat know about space cafard? About the depthless blackness, the wretchedness of free fall, the tides of primitive terror that swept you when the animal realization hit that you were away, away, away from the environment that gave you birth. That you were alone, alone, *alone*. A million, a million-million miles from your nearest fellow human. Space cafard, in a craft little larger than a good-sized closet! What did the Commodore know about it?

Don Mathers had conveniently forgotten the other's claim to five years' service in the Scouts.

* * * * *

He made his way from Space Command Headquarters, Third Division, to Harry's Nuevo Mexico Bar. He found the place empty at this time of the day and climbed onto a stool.

Harry said, "Hi, Lootenant, thought you were due for a patrol. How come you're back so soon?"

Don said coldly, "You prying into security subjects, Harry?"

"Well, gee, no Lootenant. You know me. I know all the boys. I was just making conversation."

"Look, how about some more credit, Harry? I don't have any pay coming up for a week."

"Why, sure. I got a boy on the light cruiser *New Taos*. Any spaceman's credit is good with me. What'll it be?"

"Tequila."

Tequila was the only concession the Nuevo Mexico Bar made to its name. Otherwise, it looked like every other bar has looked in every land and in every era. Harry poured, put out lemon and salt.

Harry said, "You hear the news this morning?"

"No, I just got in."

"Colin Casey died." Harry shook his head. "Only man in the system that held the Galactic Medal of Honor. Presidential proclamation, everybody in the system is to hold five minutes of silence for him at two o'clock, Sol Time. You know how many times that medal's been awarded, Lootenant?" Before waiting for an answer, Harry added, "Just thirty-six times."

Don added dryly, "Twenty-eight of them posthumously."

"Yeah." Harry, leaning on the bar before his sole customer, added in wonder, "But imagine. The Galactic Medal of Honor, the bearer of which can do no wrong. Imagine. You come to some town, walk into the biggest jewelry store, pick up a diamond bracelet, and walk out. And what happens?"

Don growled, "The jewelry store owner would be over-reimbursed by popular subscription. And probably the mayor of the town would write you a letter thanking you for honoring his fair city by deigning to notice one of the products of its shops. Just like that."

"Yeah." Harry shook his head in continued awe. "And, imagine, if you shoot somebody you don't like, you wouldn't spend even a single night in the Nick."

Don said, "If you held the Medal of Honor, you wouldn't have to shoot anybody. Look, Harry, mind if I use the phone?"

"Go right ahead, Lootenant."

Dian Fuller was obviously in the process of packing when the screen summoned her. She looked into his face and said, surprised, "Why, Don, I thought you were on patrol."

"Yeah, I was. However, something came up."

She looked at him, a slight frown on her broad, fine forehead. "Again?"

He said impatiently, "Look, I called you to ask for a date. You're leaving for Callisto tomorrow. It's our last chance to be together. There's something in particular I wanted to ask you, Di."

She said, a touch irritated, "I'm packing, Don. I simply don't have time to see you again. I thought we said our goodbyes five days ago."

"This is important, Di."

She tossed the two sweaters she was holding into a chair, or something, off-screen, and faced him, her hands on her hips.

"No it isn't, Don. Not to me, at least. We've been all over this. Why keep torturing yourself? You're not ready for marriage, Don. I don't want to hurt you, but you simply aren't. Look me up, Don, in a few years."

"Di, just a couple of hours this afternoon."

Dian looked him full in the face and said, "Colin Casey finally died of his wounds this morning. The President has asked for five minutes of silence at two o'clock. Don, I plan to spend that time here alone in my apartment, possibly crying a few tears for a man who died for me and the rest of the human species under such extreme conditions of gallantry that he was awarded the highest honor of which man has ever conceived. I wouldn't want to spend that five minutes while on a date with another member of my race's armed forces who had deserted his post of duty."

Don Mathers turned, after the screen had gone blank, and walked stiffly to a booth. He sank onto a chair and called flatly to Harry, "Another tequila. A double tequila. And don't bother with that lemon and salt routine."

* * * * *

An hour or so later a voice said, "You Sub-lieutenant Donal Mathers?"

Don looked up and snarled. "So what? Go away."

There were two of them. Twins, or could have been. Empty of expression, heavy of build. The kind of men fated to be ordered around at the pleasure of those with money, or brains, none of which they had or would ever have.

The one who had spoken said, "The boss wants to see you."

"Who the hell is the boss?"

"Maybe he'll tell you when he sees you," the other said, patiently and reasonably.

"Well, go tell the boss he can go to the…"

The second of the two had been standing silently, his hands in his great-coat pockets. Now he brought his left hand out and placed a bill before Don Mathers. "The boss said to give you this."

It was a thousand-unit note. Don Mathers had never seen a bill of that denomination before, nor one of half that.

He pursed his lips, picked it up and looked at it carefully. Counterfeiting was a long lost art. It didn't even occur to him that it might be false.

"All right," Don said, coming to his feet. "Let's go see the boss, I haven't anything else to do and his calling card intrigues me."

At the curb, one of them summoned a cruising cab with his wrist screen and the three of them climbed into it. The one who had given Don the large denomination bill dialed the address and they settled back.

"So what does the boss want with me?" Don said.

They didn't bother to answer.

The Interplanetary Lines building was evidently their destination. The car whisked them up to the penthouse which topped it, and they landed on the terrace.

Seated in beach chairs, an autobar between them, were two men. They were both in their middle years. The impossibly corpulent one, Don Mathers vaguely recognized. From a newscast? From a magazine article? The other could have passed for a video stereotype villain, complete to the built-in sneer. Few men, in actuality, either look like or sound like the conventionalized villain. This was an exception, Don decided.

He scowled at them. "I suppose one of you is the boss," he said.

"That's right," the fat one grunted. He looked at Don's two escorts. "Scotty, you and Rogers take off."

They got back into the car and left.

The vicious-faced one said, "This is Mr. Lawrence Demming. I am his secretary."

Demming puffed, "Sit down, Lieutenant. What'll you have to drink? My secretary's name is Rostoff. Max Rostoff. Now we all know each other's names. That is, assuming you're Sub-lieutenant Donal Mathers."

Don said, "Tequila."

* * * * *

Max Rostoff dialed the drink for him and, without being asked, another cordial for his employer.

Don placed Demming now. Lawrence Demming, billionaire. Robber baron, he might have been branded in an earlier age. Transportation baron of the solar system. Had he been a pig he would have been butchered long ago; he was going unhealthily to grease.

Rostoff said, "You have identification?"

Don Mathers fingered through his wallet, brought forth his I.D. card. Rostoff handed him his tequila, took the card and examined it carefully, front and back.

Demming huffed and said, "Your collar insignia tells me you pilot a Scout. What sector do you patrol, Lieutenant?"

Don sipped at the fiery Mexican drink, looked at the fat man over the glass. "That's military information, Mr. Demming."

* * * * *

Demming made a move with his plump lips. "Did Scotty give you a thousand-unit note?" He didn't wait for an answer. "You took it. Either give it back or tell me what sector you patrol, Lieutenant."

Don Mathers was aware of the fact that a man of Demming's position wouldn't have to go to overmuch effort to acquire such information, anyway. It wasn't of particular importance.

He shrugged and said, "A22-K223. I fly the V-102."

Max Rostoff handed back the I.D. card to Don and picked up a Solar System sector chart from the short-legged table that sat between the two of them and checked it. He said, "Your information was correct, Mr. Demming. He's the man."

Demming shifted his great bulk in his beach chair, sipped some of his cordial and said, "Very well. How would you like to hold the Galactic Medal of Honor, Lieutenant?"

Don Mathers laughed. "How would you?" he said.

Demming scowled. "I am not jesting, Lieutenant Mathers. I never jest. Obviously, I am not of the military. It would be quite impossible for me to gain such an award. But you are the pilot of a Scout."

"And I've got just about as much chance of winning the Medal of Honor as I have of giving birth to triplets."

The transportation magnate wiggled a disgustingly fat finger at him, "I'll arrange for that part of it."

Don Mathers goggled him. He blurted finally, "Like hell you will. There's not enough money in the system to fiddle with the awarding of the Medal of Honor. There comes a point, Demming, where even *your* dough can't carry the load."

Demming settled back in his chair, closed his eyes and grunted, "Tell him."

Max Rostoff took up the ball. "A few days ago, Mr. Demming and I flew in from Io on one of the Interplanetary Lines freighters. As you probably know, they are completely automated. We were alone in the craft."

"So?" Without invitation, Don Mathers leaned forward and dialed himself another tequila. He made it a double this time. A feeling of excitement was growing within him, and the drinks he'd had earlier had worn away. Something very big, very, very big, was developing. He hadn't the vaguest idea what.

"Lieutenant, how would you like to capture a Kraden light cruiser? If I'm not incorrect, probably Miro class."

Don laughed nervously, not knowing what the other was at but still feeling the growing excitement. He said, "In all the history of the war between our species, we've never captured a Kraden ship intact. It'd help a lot if we could."

"This one isn't exactly intact, but nearly so."

Don looked from Rostoff to Demming, and then back. "What in the hell are you talking about?"

"In your sector," Rostoff said, "we ran into a derelict Miro class cruiser. The crew-repulsive creatures-were all dead. Some thirty of them. Mr. Demming and I assumed that the craft had been hit during one of the actions between our fleet and theirs and that somehow both sides had failed to recover the wreckage. At any rate, today it is floating, abandoned of all life, in your sector." Rostoff added softly, "One has to approach quite close before any signs of battle are evident. The ship looks intact."

Demming opened his eyes again and said, "And you're going to capture it."

Don Mathers bolted his tequila, licked a final drop from the edge of his lip. "And why should that rate the most difficult decoration to achieve that we've ever instituted?"

"Because," Rostoff told him, his tone grating mockery, "you're going to radio in reporting a Miro class Kraden cruiser. We assume your superiors will order you to stand off, that help is coming, that your tiny Scout isn't large enough to do anything more than to keep the enemy under observation until a squadron arrives. But you will radio back that they are escaping and that you plan to attack. When your reinforcements arrive, Lieutenant, you will have conquered the Kraden, single-handed, against odds of-what would you say, fifty to one?"

* * * * *

Don Mathers' mouth was dry, his palms moist. He said, "A One Man Scout against a Miro class cruiser? At least fifty to one, Mr. Rostoff. At least."

Demming grunted. "There would be little doubt of you getting the Galactic Medal of Honor, Lieutenant, especially since Colin Casey is dead and there isn't a living bearer of the award. Max, another drink for the Lieutenant."

Don said, "Look. Why? I think you might be right about getting the award. But why, and why me, and what's your percentage?"

* * * * *

Demming muttered, "Now we get to the point." He settled back in his chair again and closed his eyes while his secretary took over.

Max Rostoff leaned forward, his wolfish face very serious. "Lieutenant, the exploitation of the Jupiter satellites is in its earliest stages. There is every reason to believe that the new sources of radioactives on Callisto alone may mean the needed power edge that can give us the victory over the Kradens. Whether or not that is so, someone is going to make literally billions out of this new frontier."

"I still don't see..."

"Lieutenant Mathers," Rostoff said patiently, "the bearer of the Galactic Medal of Honor is above law. He carries with him an unalienable prestige of such magnitude that ... Well, let me use an example. Suppose a bearer of the Medal of Honor formed a stock corporation to exploit the pitchblende of Callisto. How difficult would it be for him to dispose of the stock?"

Demming grunted. "And suppose there were a few, ah, crossed wires in the manipulation of the corporation's business?" He sighed deeply. "Believe me, Lieutenant Mathers, there are an incredible number of laws which have accumulated down through the centuries to hamper the business man. It is a continual fight to be able to carry on at all. The ability to do no legal wrong would be priceless in the development of a new frontier." He sighed again, so deeply as to make his bulk quiver. "Priceless."

Rostoff laid it on the line, his face a leer. "We are offering you a three-way partnership, Mathers. You, with your Medal of Honor, are our front man. Mr. Demming supplies the initial capital to get underway. And I ..." He twisted his mouth with evil self-satisfaction. "I was present when the Kraden ship was discovered, so I'll have to be cut in. I'll supply the brains."

Demming grunted his disgust, but added nothing.

Don Mathers said slowly, looking down at the empty glass he was twirling in his fingers, "Look, we're up to our necks in a war to the death with the Kradens. In the long run it's either us or them. At a time like this you're suggesting that we fake an action that will eventually enable us to milk the new satellites to the tune of billions."

Demming grunted meaninglessly.

Don said, "The theory is that all men, all of us, ought to have our shoulders to the wheel. This project sounds to me like throwing rocks under it."

Demming closed his eyes.

Rostoff said, "Lieutenant, it's a dog-eat-dog society. If we eventually lick the Kradens, one of the very reasons will be because we're a dog-eat-dog society. Every man for himself and the devil take the hindmost. Our apologists dream up some beautiful gobbledygook phrases for it, such as free enterprise, but actually it's dog-eat-dog. Surprisingly enough, it works, or at least has so far. Right now, the human race needs the radioactives of the Jupiter satellites. In acquiring them, somebody is going to make a tremendous amount of money. Why shouldn't it be us?"

"Why not, if you-or we-can do it honestly?"

Demming's grunt was nearer a snort this time.

Rostoff said sourly, "Don't be naive, Lieutenant. Whoever does it, is going to need little integrity. You don't win in a sharper's card game by playing your cards honestly. The biggest sharper wins. We've just found a joker somebody dropped on the floor; if we don't use it, we're suckers."

Demming opened his pig eyes and said, "All this is on the academic side. We checked your background thoroughly before approaching you, Mathers. We know your record, even before you entered the Space Service. Just between the three of us, wouldn't you like out? There are a full billion men and women in our armed forces, you can be spared. Let's say you've already done your share. Can't you see the potentialities in spending the rest of your life with the Galactic Medal of Honor in your pocket?"

* * * * *

It was there all right, drifting slowly. Had he done a more thorough job of his patrol, last time, he should have stumbled upon it himself.

If he had, there was no doubt that he would have at first reported it as an active enemy cruiser. Demming and Rostoff had been right. The Kraden ship looked untouched by battle.

That is, if you approached it from the starboard and slightly abaft the beam. From that angle, in particular, it looked untouched.

It had taken several circlings of the craft to come to that conclusion. Don Mathers was playing it very safe. This thing wasn't quite so simple as the others had thought. He wanted no slip-ups. His hand went to a food compartment and emerged with a space thermo which should have contained fruit juice, but didn't. He took a long pull at it.

Finally he dropped back into the position he'd decided upon, and flicked the switch of his screen.

A base lieutenant's face illuminated it. He yawned and looked questioningly at Don Mathers.

Don said, allowing a touch of excitement in his voice, "Mathers, Scout V-102, Sector A22-K223."

"Yeah, yeah ..." the other began, still yawning.

"I've spotted a Kraden cruiser. Miro class, I think."

* * * * *

The lieutenant flashed into movement. He slapped a button before him, the screen blinked, to be lit immediately again.

440

A gray-haired Fleet Admiral looked up from papers on his desk.

"Yes?"

Don Mathers rapped, "Miro class Kraden in sector A22-K223, sir. I'm lying about fifty miles off. Undetected thus far —I think. He hasn't fired on me yet, at least."

The Admiral was already doing things with his hands. Two subalterns came within range of the screen, took orders, dashed off. The Admiral was rapidly firing orders into two other screens. After a moment, he looked up at Don Mathers again.

"Hang on, Lieutenant. Keep him under observation as long as you can. What're your exact coordinates?"

Don gave them to him and waited.

A few minutes later the Admiral returned to him. "Let's take a look at it, Lieutenant."

Don Mathers adjusted the screen to relay the Kraden cruiser. His palms were moist now, but everything was going to plan. He wished that he could take another drink.

The Admiral said, "Miro class, all right. Don't get too close, Lieutenant. They'll blast you to hell and gone. We've got a task force within an hour of you. Just hang on."

"Yes, sir," Don said. An hour. He was glad to know that. He didn't have much time in which to operate.

He let it go another five minutes, then he said, "Sir, they're increasing speed."

"Damn," the Admiral said, then rapid fired some more into his other screens, barking one order after another.

Don said, letting his voice go very flat, "I'm going in, sir. They're putting on speed. In another five minutes they'll be underway to the point where I won't be able to follow. They'll get completely clear."

The Admiral looked up, startled. "Don't be a fool."

"They'll get away, sir." Knowing that the other could see his every motion, Don Mathers hit the cocking lever of his flakflak gun with the heel of his right hand.

The Admiral snapped, "Let it go, you fool. You won't last a second." Then, his voice higher, "That's an order, Lieutenant!"

Don Mathers flicked off his screen. He grimaced sourly and then descended on the Kraden ship, his flakflak gun beaming it. He was going to have to expend every erg of energy in his Scout to burn the other ship up to the point where his attack would look authentic, and to eliminate all signs of previous action.

* * * * *

The awarding of the Galactic Medal of Honor, as always, was done in the simplest of ceremonies.

Only the President and Captain Donal Mathers himself were present in the former's office in the Presidential Palace.

However, as they both knew, every screen in the Solar System was tuned into the ceremony.

Don Mathers saluted and stood to attention.

The President read the citation. It was very short, as Medal of Honor citations were always.

...for conspicuous gallantry far and beyond the call of duty, in which you single-handedly, and against unbelievable odds, attacked and destroyed an enemy cruiser while flying a Scout armed only with a short-beam flakflak gun...

He pinned a small bit of ribbon and metal to Don Mathers' tunic. It was an inconspicuous, inordinately ordinary medal, the Galactic Medal of Honor.

Don said hoarsely, "Thank you, sir."

The President shook hands with him and said, "I am President of the United Solar System, Captain Mathers, supposedly the highest rank to which a man can attain." He added simply, "I wish I were you."

* * * * *

Afterwards, alone in New Washington and wanting to remain alone, Don Mathers strolled the streets for a time, bothered only occasionally when someone recognized his face and people would stop and applaud.

He grinned inwardly.

He had a suspicion already that after a time he'd get used to it and weary to death of it, but right now it was still new and fun. Who was the flyer, way back in history, the one who first flew the Atlantic in a propeller-driven aircraft? His popularity must have been something like this.

He went into O'Donnell's at lunch time and as he entered the orchestra broke off the popular tune they were playing and struck up the Interplanetary Anthem. The manager himself escorted him to his table and made suggestions as to the specialties and the wine.

When he first sat down the other occupants of the restaurant, men and women, had stood and faced him and applauded. Don flushed. There could be too much of a good thing.

After the meal, a fantastic production, Don finished his cigar and asked the head waiter for his bill, reaching for his wallet.

The other smiled. "Captain, I am afraid your money is of no value in O'Donnell's, not for just this luncheon but whenever you honor us." The head waiter paused and added, "in fact, Captain, I doubt if there is a restaurant in the Solar System where your money holds value. Or that there will ever be."

Don Mathers was taken aback. He was only beginning to realize the ramifications of his holding his Galactic Medal of Honor.

* * * * *

At Space Command Headquarters, Third Division, Don came to attention before the Commodore's desk and tossed the other a salute.

The Commodore returned it snappily and leaned back in his chair. "Take a seat, Captain. Nice to see you again." He added pleasantly, "Where in the world have you been?"

Don Mathers slumped into a chair, said wearily, "On a bust. The bust to end all busts."

The Commodore chuckled. "Don't blame you," he said.

"It was quite a bust," Don said.

"Well," the Commodore chuckled again, "I don't suppose we can throw you in the guardhouse for being A.W.O.L. Not in view of your recent decoration."

There was nothing to say to that.

"By the way," the Commodore said, "I haven't had the opportunity to congratulate you on your Kraden. That was quite a feat, Captain."

"Thank you, sir," Don added, modestly, "rather foolish of me, I suppose."

"Very much so. On such foolishness are heroic deeds based, Captain." The Commodore looked at him questioningly. "You must have had incredible luck. The only way we've been able to figure it was that his detectors were on the blink. That may be what happened."

"Yes, sir," Don nodded quickly. "That's the way I figure it. And my first blast must have disrupted his fire control or something."

The Commodore said, "He didn't get in any return fire at all?"

"A few blasts. But by that time I was in too close and moving too fast. Fact of the matter is, sir, I don't think they ever recovered from my first beaming of them."

"No, I suppose not," the Commodore said musingly. "It's a shame you had to burn them so badly. We've never recovered a Kraden ship in good enough shape to give our techs something to work on. It might make a basic difference in the war, particularly if there was something aboard that'd give us some indication of where they were coming from. We've been fighting this war in our backyard for a full century. It would help if we could get into *their* backyard for a change. It's problematical how long we'll be able to hold them off, at this rate."

Don Mathers said uncomfortably, "Well, it's not as bad as all that, sir. We've held them this far."

His superior grunted. "We've held them this far because we've been able to keep out enough patrol ships to give us ample warning when one of their task forces come in. Do you know how much fuel that consumes, Captain?"

"Well, I know it's a lot."

"So much so that Earth's industry is switching back to petroleum and coal. Every ounce of radioactives is needed by the Fleet. Even so, it's just a matter of time."

Don Mathers pursed his lips. "I didn't know it was that bad."

The Commodore smiled sourly at him. "I'm afraid I'm being a wet blanket thrown over your big bust of a celebration, Captain. Tell me, how does it feel to hold the system's highest award?"

* * * * *

Don shook his head, marveling. "Fantastic, sir. Of course, like any member of the services I've always known of the Medal of Honor, but ...well, nobody ever expects to get it." He added wryly, "Certainly not while he's still alive and in health. Why, sir, do you realize that I haven't been able to spend one unit of money since?" There was an element of awe in his voice. "Sir, do you realize that not even a beggar will take currency from me?"

The Commodore nodded in appreciation. "You must understand the position you occupy, Captain. Your feat was inspiring enough, but that's not all of it. In a way you combine a popular hero with an *Unknown Soldier* element. Awarding you the Galactic Medal of Honor makes a symbol of you. A symbol representing all the millions of unsung heroes and heroines who have died fighting for the human species. It's not a light burden to carry on your shoulders, Captain Mathers. I would imagine it a very humbling honor."

"Well, yes, sir," Don said.

The Commodore switched his tone of voice. "That brings us to the present, and what your next assignment is to be. Obviously, it wouldn't do for you to continue in a Scout. Big brass seems to be in favor of using you for morale and..."

Don Mathers cleared his throat and interrupted. "Sir, I've decided to drop out of the Space Service."

"Drop out!" The other stared at Mathers, uncomprehending. "We're at war, Captain!"

Don nodded seriously. "Yes, sir. And what you just said is true. I couldn't be used any longer in a Scout. I'd wind up selling bonds and giving talks to old ladies' clubs."

"Well, hardly that, Captain."

"No, sir, I think I'd really be of more use out of the services. I'm tendering my resignation and making arrangements to help in the developing of Callisto and the other Jupiter satellites."

The Commodore said nothing. His lips seemed whiter than before.

Don Mathers said doggedly, "Perhaps my prestige will help bring volunteers to work the new mines out there. If they see me, well, sacrificing, putting up with the hardships..."

The Commodore said evenly, "Mr. Mathers, I doubt if you will ever have to put up with hardships again, no matter where you make your abode. However, good luck. You deserve it."

* * * * *

Outside headquarters, Don Mathers summoned a cab and dialed his hotel. On the way over, he congratulated himself. It had gone easier than he had expected, really. Although, come to think of it, there wasn't a damn thing that the brass could do.

He had to laugh to himself.

Imagine if he'd walked in on the Commodore a month ago and announced that he was going to *drop out* of the Space Service. He would have been dropped all right, all right. Right into the lap of a squadron of psycho experts.

At the hotel he shucked his uniform, an action which gave him considerable gratification, and dressed in one of the score of civilian costumes that filled his closets to overflowing. He took pleasure in estimating what this clothing would have cost in terms of months of Space Service pay for a Sub-lieutenant or even a Captain. *Years, my boy, years.*

He looked at himself in the dressing-room mirror with satisfaction, then turned to the autobar and dialed himself a stone-age-old Metaxa. He'd lost his taste for the plebian tequila in the last few days.

He held the old Greek brandy to the light and wondered pleasurably what the stuff cost, per pony glass. Happily, he'd never have to find out.

He tossed the drink down and whistling, took his private elevator to the garages in the second level of the hotel's basement floors. He selected a limousine and dialed the Interplanetary Lines building.

He left the car at the curb before the main entrance, ignoring all traffic regulations and entered the building, still whistling softly and happily to himself. He grinned when a small crowd gathered outside and smiled and clapped their hands. He grinned and waved to them.

A receptionist hurried to him and he told her he wanted to see either Mr. Demming or Mr. Rostoff, and then when she offered to escort him personally he noticed her pixie-like cuteness and said, "What're you doing tonight, Miss?"

Her face went pale. "Oh, anything, sir," she said weakly.

He grinned at her. "Maybe I'll take you up on that if I'm not too busy."

He had never seen anyone so taken aback. She said, all flustered, "I'm Toni. Toni Fitzgerald. You can just call this building and ask for me. Any time."

"Maybe I'll do that," he smiled. "But now, let's see Old Man Demming."

* * * * *

That took her back too. Aside from being asked for a date-if asked could be the term-by the system's greatest celebrity, she was hearing for the first time the interplanetary tycoon being called *Old Man Demming*.

She said, "Oh, right this way, Captain Mathers."

Don said, "Mr. Mathers now, I'm afraid. I have new duties."

She looked up into his face. "You'll always be Captain Mathers to me, sir." She added, softly and irrelevantly, "My two brothers were lost on the *Minerva* in that action last year off Pluto." She took a deep breath, which only stressed her figure. "I've applied six times for Space Service, but they won't take me."

They were in an elevator now. Don said, "That's too bad, Toni. However, the Space Service isn't as romantic as you might think."

"Yes, sir," Toni Fitzgerald said, her soul in her eyes. "You ought to know, sir."

Don was somehow irritated. He said nothing further until they reached the upper stories of the gigantic office building. He thanked her after she'd turned him over to another receptionist.

Don Mathers' spirits had been restored by the time he was brought to the door of Max Rostoff's office. His new guide evidently hadn't even bothered to check on the man's availability, before ushering Mathers into the other's presence.

Max Rostoff looked up from his desk, wolfishly aggressive-looking as ever. "Why, Captain," he said. "How fine to see you again. Come right in. Martha, that will be all."

* * * * *

Martha gave the interplanetary hero one more long look and then turned and left.

As soon as the door closed behind her, Max Rostoff turned and snarled, "Where have you been, you rummy?"

He couldn't have shocked Don Mathers more if he'd suddenly sprouted a unicorn's horn.

444

"We've been looking for you for a week," Rostoff snapped. "Out of one bar, into another, our men couldn't catch up with you. Dammit, don't you realize we've got to get going? We've got a dozen documents for you to sign. We've got to get this thing underway, before somebody else does."

Don blurted, "You can't talk to me that way."

It was the other's turn to stare. Max Rostoff said, low and dangerously, "No? Why can't I?"

Don glared at him.

Max Rostoff said, low and dangerously, "Let's get this straight, Mathers. To everybody else, but Demming and me, you might be the biggest hero in the Solar System. But you know what you are to us?"

Don felt his indignation seeping from him.

"To us," Max Rostoff said flatly, "you're just another demi-buttocked incompetent on the make." He added definitely, "And make no mistake, Mathers, you'll continue to have a good thing out of this only so long as we can use you."

A voice from behind them said, "Let me add to that, period, end of paragraph."

It was Lawrence Demming, who'd just entered from an inner office.

He said, even his voice seemed fat, "And now that's settled, I'm going to call in some lawyers. While they're around, we conduct ourselves as though we're three equal partners. On paper, we will be."

"Wait a minute, now," Don blurted. "What do you think you're pulling? The agreement was we split this whole thing three ways."

Demming's jowls wobbled as he nodded. "That's right. And your share of the loot is your Galactic Medal of Honor. That and the dubious privilege of having the whole thing in your name. You'll keep your medal, and we'll keep our share." He growled heavily, "You don't think you're getting the short end of the stick, do you?"

Max Rostoff said, "Let's knock this off and get the law boys in. We've got enough paper work to keep us busy the rest of the week." He sat down again at his desk and looked up at Don. "Then we'll all be taking off for Callisto, to get things under way. With any luck, in six months we'll have every ounce of pitchblende left in the system sewed up."

* * * * *

There was a crowd awaiting his ship at the Callisto Spaceport. A crowd modest by Earth standards but representing a large percentage of the small population of Jupiter's moon.

On the way out, a staff of the system's best speech writers, and two top professional actors had been working with him.

Don Mathers gave a short preliminary talk at the spaceport, and then the important one, the one that was broadcast throughout the system, that night from his suite at the hotel. He'd been well rehearsed, and they'd kept him from the bottle except for two or three quick ones immediately before going on.

The project at hand is to extract the newly discovered deposits of pitchblende on these satellites of Jupiter.

He paused impressively before continuing.

It's a job that cannot be done in slipshod, haphazard manner. The system's need for radioactives cannot be overstressed.

In short, fellow humans, we must allow nothing to stand in the way of all out, unified effort to do this job quickly and efficiently. My associates and I have formed a corporation to manage this crash program. We invite all to participate by purchasing stock. I will not speak of profits, fellow humans, because in this emergency we all scorn them. However, as I say, you are invited to participate.

Some of the preliminary mining concessions are at present in the hands of individuals or small corporations. It will be necessary that these turn over their holdings to our single all-embracing organization for the sake of efficiency. Our experts will evaluate such holdings and recompense the owners.

Don Mathers paused again for emphasis.

This is no time for quibbling. All must come in. If there are those who put private gain before the needs of the system, then pressures must be found to be exerted against them.

We will need thousands and tens of thousands of trained workers to operate our mines, our mills, our refineries. In the past, skilled labor here on the satellites was used to double or even triple the wage rates on Earth and the settled planets and satellites. I need only repeat, this is no time for personal gain and quibbling. The corporation announces proudly that it will pay only prevailing Earth rates. We will not insult our employees by "bribing" them to patriotism through higher wages.

There was more, along the same lines.

It was all taken very well. Indeed, with enthusiasm.

* * * * *

On the third day, at an office conference, Don waited for an opening to say, "Look, somewhere here on Callisto is a young woman named Dian Fuller. After we get me established in an office, I'd like her to be my secretary."

Demming looked up from some reports he was scanning. He grunted to Max Rostoff, "Tell him," and went back to the papers.

Max Rostoff, settled back into his chair. He said to the two bodyguards, stationed at the door, "Scotty, Rogers, go and make the arrangements to bring that damned prospector into line."

When they were gone, Rostoff turned back to Don Mathers. "You don't need an office, Mathers. All you need is to go back to your bottles. Just don't belt it so hard that you can't sign papers every time we need a signature."

Don flushed angrily, "Look, don't push me, you two. You need me. Plenty. In fact, from what I can see, this corporation needs me more than it does you." He looked scornfully at Demming. "Originally, the idea was that you put up the money. What money? We have fifty-one percent of the stock in my name, but all the credit units needed are coming from sales of stock." He turned to Rostoff. "You were supposed to put up the brains. What brains? We've hired the best mining engineers, the best technicians, to do their end, the best corporation executives to handle that end. You're not needed."

Demming grunted amusement at the short speech, but didn't bother to look up from his perusal.

Max Rostoff's face had grown wolfishly thin in his anger. "Look, bottle-baby," he sneered, "you're the only one that's vulnerable in this set-up. There's not a single thing that Demming and I can be held to account for. You have no beefs coming, for that matter. You're getting everything you ever wanted. You've got the best suite in the best hotel on Callisto. You eat the best food the Solar System provides. And, most important of all to a rummy, you drink the best booze and as much of it as you want. What's more, unless either Demming or I go to the bother, you'll never be exposed. You'll live your life out being the biggest hero in the system."

It was Don Mathers' turn to sneer. "What do you mean, I'm the only one vulnerable? There's no evidence against me, Rostoff, and you know it. Who'd listen to you if you sounded off? I burned that Kraden cruiser until there wasn't a sign to be found that would indicate it wasn't in operational condition when I first spotted it."

Demming grunted his amusement again.

Max Rostoff laughed sourly. "Don't be an ass, Mathers. We took a series of photos of that derelict when we stumbled on it. Not only can we prove you didn't knock it out, we can prove that it was in good shape before you worked it over. I imagine the Fleet technician would have loved to have seen the inner workings of that Kraden cruiser-before you loused it up."

Demming chuckled flatly. "I wonder what kind of a court martial they give a hero who turns out to be a saboteur."

* * * * *

He ran into her, finally, after he'd been on Callisto for nearly eight months. Actually, he didn't remember the circumstances of their meeting. He was in an alcoholic daze and the fog rolled out, and there she was across the table from him.

Don shook his head, and looked about the room. They were in some sort of night spot. He didn't recognize it.

* * * * *

He licked his lips, scowled at the taste of stale vomit.

He slurred, "Hello, Di."

Dian Fuller said, "Hi, Don."

He said, "I must've blanked out. Guess I've been hitting it too hard."

She laughed at him. "You mean you don't remember all the things you've been telling me the past two hours?" She was obviously quite sober. Dian never had been much for the sauce.

Don looked at her narrowly. "What've I been telling you for the past two hours?"

"Mostly about how it was when you were a little boy. About fishing, and your first .22 rifle. And the time you shot the squirrel, and then felt so sorry."

"Oh," Don said. He ran his right hand over his mouth.

There was a champagne bucket beside him, but the bottle in it was empty. He looked about the room for a waiter.

Dian said gently, "Do you really think you need any more, Don?"

He looked across the table at her. She was as beautiful as ever. No, that wasn't right. She was pretty, but not beautiful. She was just a damn pretty girl, not one of these glamour items.

Don said, "Look, I can't remember. Did we get married?"

Her laugh tinkled. "Married! I only ran into you two or three hours ago." She hesitated before saying further, "I had assumed that you were deliberately avoiding me. Callisto isn't that big."

Don Mathers said slowly, "Well, if we're not married, let me decide when I want another bottle of the grape, eh?"

Dian flushed. "Sorry, Don."

* * * * *

The headwaiter approached bearing another magnum of vintage wine. He beamed at Don Mathers. "Having a good time, sir?"

"Okay," Don said shortly. When the other was gone he downed a full glass, felt the fumes almost immediately.

He said to Dian, "I haven't been avoiding you, Di. We just haven't met. The way I remember, the last time we saw each other, back on Earth, you gave me quite a slap in the face. The way I remember, you didn't think I was hero enough for you." He poured another glass of the champagne.

Di's face was still flushed. She said, her voice low, "I misunderstood you, Don. Even after your brilliant defeat of that Kraden cruiser, I still, I admit, think I basically misunderstood you. I told myself that it could have been done by any pilot of a Scout, given that one in a million break. It just happened to be you, who made that suicide dive attack that succeeded. A thousand other pilots might also have taken the million to one suicide chance rather than let the Kraden escape."

"Yeah," Don said. Even in his alcohol, he was surprised at her words. He said gruffly, "Sure anybody might've done it. Pure luck. But why'd you change your mind about me, then? How come the switch of heart?"

"Because of what you've done since, darling."

He closed one eye, the better to focus.

"Since?"

He recognized the expression in her eyes. A touch of star gleam. That little girl back on Earth, the receptionist at the Interplanetary Lines building, she'd had it. In fact, in the past few months Don had seen it in many feminine faces. And all for him.

Dian said, "Instead of cashing in on your prestige, you've been devoting yourself to something even more necessary to the fight than bringing down individual Kraden cruisers."

Don looked at her. He could feel a nervous tic beginning in his left eyebrow. Finally, he reached for the champagne again and filled his glass. He said, "You really go for this hero stuff, don't you?"

She said nothing, but the star shine was still in her eyes.

He made his voice deliberately sour. "Look, suppose I asked you to come back to my apartment with me tonight?"

"Yes," she said softly.

"And told you to bring your overnight bag along," he added brutally.

Dian looked into his face. "Why are you twisting yourself, your inner-self, so hard, Don? Of course I'd come—if that's what you wanted."

"And then," he said flatly, "suppose I kicked you out in the morning?"

Dian winced, but she kept her eyes even with his, her own moist now. "You forget," she whispered. "You have been awarded the Galactic Medal of Honor, the bearer of which can do no wrong."

"Oh, God," Don muttered. He filled his glass, still again, motioned to a nearby waiter.

"Yes, sir," the waiter said.

Don said, "Look, in about five minutes I'm going to pass out. See that I get back to my hotel, will you? And that this young lady gets to her home. And, waiter, just send my bill to the hotel too."

The other bowed. "The owner's instructions, sir, are that Captain Mathers must never see a bill in this establishment."

Dian said, *"Don!"*

He didn't look at her. He raised his glass to his mouth and shortly afterward the fog rolled in again.

* * * * *

When it rolled out, the unfamiliar taste of black coffee was in his mouth. He shook his head for clarity.

He seemed to be in some working class restaurant. Next to him, in a booth, was a fresh-faced Sub-lieutenant of the-Don squinted at the collar tabs-yes, of the Space Service. A Scout pilot.

Don stuttered, "What's ... goin' ... on?"

The pilot said apologetically, "Sub-lieutenant Pierpont, sir. You seemed so far under the weather, I took over."

"Oh, you did, eh?"

"Well, yes, sir. You were, well, reclining in the gutter, sir. In spite of your, well, appearance, your condition, I recognized you, sir."

"Oh." His stomach was an objecting turmoil.

The Lieutenant said, "Want to try some more of this coffee now, sir? Or maybe some soup or a sandwich?"

Don groaned. "No. No, thanks. Don't think I could hold it down."

448

The pilot grinned. "You must've thrown a classic, sir."

"I guess so. What time is it? No, that doesn't make any difference. What's the date?"

Pierpont told him.

It was hard to believe. The last he could remember he'd been with Di. With Di in some nightclub. He wondered how long ago that had been.

He fumbled in his clothes for a smoke and couldn't find one. He didn't want it anyway.

He growled at the Lieutenant, "Well, how go the One Man Scouts?"

Pierpont grinned back at him. "Glad to be out of them, sir?"

"Usually."

Pierpont looked at him strangely. "I don't blame you, I suppose. But it isn't as bad these days as it used to be while you were still in the Space Service, sir."

Don grunted. "How come? Two weeks to a month, all by yourself, watching the symptoms of space cafard progress. Then three weeks of leave, to get drunk in, and then another stretch in space."

The pilot snorted deprecation. "That's the way it used to be." He fingered the spoon of his coffee cup. "That's the way it still should be, of course. But it isn't. They're spreading the duty around now and I spend less than one week out of four on patrol."

Don hadn't been listening too closely, but now he looked up. "What'd'ya mean?"

Pierpont said, "I mean, sir, I suppose this isn't bridging security, seeing who you are, but fuel stocks are so low that we can't maintain full patrols any more."

There was a cold emptiness in Don Mathers' stomach.

He said, "Look, I'm still woozy. Say that again, Lieutenant."

The Lieutenant told him again.

Don Mathers rubbed the back of his hand over his mouth and tried to think.

He said finally, "Look, Lieutenant. First let's get another cup of coffee into me, and maybe that sandwich you were talking about. Then would you help me to get back to my hotel?"

* * * * *

By the fourth day, his hands weren't trembling any longer. He ate a good breakfast, dressed carefully, then took a hotel limousine down to the offices of the Mathers, Demming and Rostoff Corporation.

At the entrance to the inner sanctum the heavyset Scotty looked up at his approach. He said, "The boss has been looking for you, Mr. Mathers, but right now you ain't got no appointment, have you? Him and Mr. Rostoff is having a big conference. He says to keep everybody out."

"That doesn't apply to me, Scotty," Don snapped. "Get out of my way."

Scotty stood up, reluctantly, but barred the way. "He said it applied to everybody, Mr. Mathers."

Don put his full weight into a blow that started at his waist, dug deep into the other's middle. Scotty doubled forward, his eyes bugging. Don Mathers gripped his hands together into a double fist and brought them upward in a vicious uppercut.

* * * * *

Scotty fell forward and to the floor.

Don stood above him momentarily, watchful for movement which didn't develop. The hefty bodyguard must have been doing some easy living himself. He wasn't as tough as he looked.

Don knelt and fished from under the other's left arm a vicious-looking short-barreled scrambler. He tucked it under his own jacket into his belt, then turned, opened the door and entered the supposedly barred office.

Demming and Rostoff looked up from their work across a double desk.

Both scowled. Rostoff opened his mouth to say something and Don Mathers rapped, "Shut up."

Rostoff blinked at him. Demming leaned back in his swivel chair. "You're sober for a change," he wheezed, almost accusingly.

Don Mathers pulled up a stenographer's chair and straddled it, leaning his arms on the back. He said coldly, "Comes a point when even the lowest worm turns. I've been checking on a few things."

Demming grunted amusement.

Don said, "Space patrols have been cut far below the danger point."

Rostoff snorted. "Is that supposed to interest us? That's the problem of the military-and the government."

"Oh, it interests us, all right," Don growled. "Currently, Mathers, Demming and Rostoff control probably three-quarters of the system's radioactives."

Demming said in greasy satisfaction, "More like four-fifths."

"Why?" Don said bluntly. "Why are we doing what we're doing?"

They both scowled, but another element was present in their expressions too. They thought the question unintelligent.

Demming closed his eyes in his porcine manner and grunted, "Tell him."

Rostoff said, "Look, Mathers, don't be stupid. Remember when we told you, during that first interview, that we wanted your name in the corporation, among other reasons, because we could use a man who was above law? That a maze of ridiculously binding ordinances have been laid on business down through the centuries?"

"I remember," Don said bitterly.

"Well, it goes both ways. Government today is also bound, very strongly, and even in great emergency, not to interfere in business. These complicated laws balance each other, you might say. Our whole legal system is based upon them. Right now, we've got government right where we want it. This is free enterprise, Mathers, at its pinnacle. Did you ever hear of Jim Fisk and his attempt to corner gold in 1869, the so-called Black Friday affair? Well, Jim Fisk was a peanut peddler compared to us."

"What's this got to do with the Fleet having insufficient fuel to ..." Don Mathers stopped as comprehension hit him. "You're holding our radioactives off the market, pressuring the government for a price rise which it can't afford."

Demming opened his eyes and said fatly, "For triple the price, Mathers. Before we're through, we'll corner half the wealth of the system."

Don said, "But ... but the species is ... at ... *war.*"

Rostoff sneered, "You seem to be getting noble rather late in the game, Mathers. Business is business."

Don Mathers was shaking his head. "We immediately begin selling our radioactives at cost of production. I might remind you gentlemen that although we're supposedly a three-way partnership, actually, everything's in my name. You thought you had me under your thumb so securely that it was safe-and you probably didn't trust each other. Well, I'm blowing the whistle."

* * * * *

Surprisingly fast for such a fat man, Lawrence Demming's hand flitted into a desk drawer to emerge with a twin of the scrambler tucked in Don's belt.

Don Mathers grinned at him, even as he pushed his jacket back to reveal the butt of his own weapon. He made no attempt to draw it, however.

He said softly, "Shoot me, Demming, and you've killed the most popular man in the Solar System. You'd never escape the gas chamber, no matter how much money you have. On the other hand, if I shoot you ..."

He put a hand into his pocket and it emerged with a small, inordinately ordinary bit of ribbon and metal. He displayed it on his palm.

The fat man's face whitened at the ramifications and his hand relaxed to let the gun drop to the desk. "Listen, Don," he broke out. "We've been unrealistic with you. We'll reverse ourselves and split, honestly-split three ways."

Don Mathers laughed at him. "Trying to bribe me with money, Demming? Why don't you realize, that I'm the only man in existence who has no need for money, who can't spend money? That my fellow men-whom I've done such a good job of betraying-have honored me to a point where money is meaningless?"

Rostoff snatched up the fallen gun, snarling, "I'm calling your bluff, you gutless rummy."

Don Mathers said, "Okay, Rostoff. There's just two other things I want to say first. One —I don't care if I die or not. Two-you're only twenty feet or so away, but you know what? I think you're probably a lousy shot. I don't think you've had much practice. I think I can get my scrambler out and cut you down before you can finish me." He grinned thinly, "Wanta try?"

Max Rostoff snarled a curse and his finger whitened on the trigger.

Don Mathers fell sideward, his hand streaking for his weapon. Without thought there came back to him the long hours of training in hand weapons, in judo, in hand to hand combat. He went into action with cool confidence.

* * * * *

At the spaceport he took a cab to the Presidential Palace. It was an auto-cab, of course, and at the Palace gates he found he had no money on him. He snorted wearily. It was the first time in almost a year that he'd had to pay for anything.

Four sentries were standing at attention. He said, "Do one of you boys have some coins to feed into this slot? I'm fresh out."

A sergeant grinned, approached, and did the necessary.

Don Mathers said wearily, "I don't know how you go about this. I don't have an appointment, but I want to see the President."

"We can turn you over to one of the assistant secretaries, Captain Mathers," the sergeant said. "We can't go any further than that. While we're waiting, what's the chances of getting your autograph, sir? I gotta kid..."

It wasn't nearly as complicated as he'd thought it was going to be. In half an hour he was seated in the office where he'd received his decoration only-how long ago was it, really less than a year?

He told the story briefly, making no effort to spare himself. At the end he stood up long enough to put a paper in front of the other, then sat down again.

"I'm turning the whole corporation over to the government...."

* * * * *

The President said, "Wait a minute. My administration does not advocate State ownership of industry."

"I know. When the State controls industry you only put the whole mess off one step, the question then becomes, who controls the State? However, I'm not arguing political economy with you, sir. You didn't let me finish. I was going to say, I'm turning it over to the government to untangle, even while making use of the inventories of radioactives. There's going to be a lot of untangling to do. Reimbursing the prospectors and small operators who were blackjacked out of their holdings by our super-corporation. Reimbursing of the miners and other laborers who were talked into accepting low pay in the name of patriotism." Don Mathers cut it short. "Oh, it's quite a mess."

"Yes," the President said. "And you say Max Rostoff is dead?"

"That's right. And Demming off his rocker. I think he always was a little unbalanced and the prospect of losing all that money, the greatest fortune ever conceived of, tipped the scales."

The President said, "And what about you, Donal Mathers?"

Don took a deep breath. "I wish I was back in the Space Services, frankly. Back where I was when all this started. However, I suppose that after my court martial, there won't be..."

The President interrupted gently. "You seem to forget, Captain Mathers. You carry the Galactic Medal of Honor, the bearer of which can do no wrong."

Don Mathers gaped at him.

The President smiled at him, albeit a bit sourly. "It would hardly do for human morale to find out our supreme symbol of heroism was a phoney, Captain. There will be no trial, and you will retain your decoration."

"But I don't want it!"

"I'm afraid that is the cross you'll have to bear the rest of your life, Captain Mathers. I don't suppose it will be an easy one."

His eyes went to a far corner of the room, but unseeingly. He said after a long moment, "However, I am not so very sure about your not deserving your award, Captain."

Gun for Hire

Joe Prantera called softly, "Al." The pleasurable, comfortable, warm feeling began spreading over him, the way it always did.

The older man stopped and squinted, but not suspiciously, even now.

The evening was dark, it was unlikely that the other even saw the circle of steel that was the mouth of the shotgun barrel, now resting on the car's window ledge.

"Who's it?" he growled.

Joe Prantera said softly, "Big Louis sent me, Al."

And he pressed the trigger.

And at that moment, the universe caved inward upon Joseph Marie Prantera.

There was nausea and nausea upon nausea.

There was a falling through all space and through all time. There was doubling and twisting and twitching of every muscle and nerve.

There was pain, horror and tumultuous fear.

And he came out of it as quickly and completely as he'd gone in.

He was in, he thought, a hospital and his first reaction was to think, *This here California. Everything different.* Then his second thought was *Something went wrong. Big Louis, he ain't going to like this.*

He brought his thinking to the present. So far as he could remember, he hadn't completely pulled the trigger. That at least meant that whatever the rap was it wouldn't be too tough. With luck, the syndicate would get him off with a couple of years at Quentin.

A door slid open in the wall in a way that Joe had never seen a door operate before. *This here California.*

The clothes on the newcomer were wrong, too. For the first time, Joe Prantera began to sense an alienness —a something that was awfully wrong.

The other spoke precisely and slowly, the way a highly educated man speaks a language which he reads and writes fluently but has little occasion to practice vocally. "You have recovered?"

Joe Prantera looked at the other expressionlessly. Maybe the old duck was one of these foreign doctors, like.

The newcomer said, "You have undoubtedly been through a most harrowing experience. If you have any untoward symptoms, possibly I could be of assistance."

Joe couldn't figure out how he stood. For one thing, there should have been some kind of police guard.

The other said, "Perhaps a bit of stimulant?"

Joe said flatly, "I wanta lawyer."

The newcomer frowned at him. "A lawyer?"

"I'm not sayin' nothin'. Not until I get a mouthpiece."

The newcomer started off on another tack. "My name is Lawrence Reston-Farrell. If I am not mistaken, you are Joseph Salviati-Prantera."

Salviati happened to be Joe's mother's maiden name. But it was unlikely this character could have known that. Joe had been born in Naples and his mother had died in childbirth. His father hadn't brought him to the States until the age of five and by that time he had a stepmother.

"I wanta mouthpiece," Joe said flatly, "or let me outta here."

Lawrence Reston-Farrell said, "You are not being constrained. There are clothes for you in the closet there."

Joe gingerly tried swinging his feet to the floor and sitting up, while the other stood watching him, strangely. He came to his feet. With the exception of a faint nausea, which brought back memories of that extreme condition he'd suffered during ... during what? He hadn't the vaguest idea of what had happened.

He was dressed in a hospital-type nightgown. He looked down at it and snorted and made his way over to the closet. It opened on his approach, the door sliding back into the wall in much the same manner as the room's door had opened for Reston-Farrell.

Joe Prantera scowled and said, "These ain't my clothes."

"No, I am afraid not."

"You think I'd be seen dead wearing this stuff? What is this, some religious crackpot hospital?"

Reston-Farrell said, "I am afraid, Mr. Salviati-Prantera, that these are the only garments available. I suggest you look out the window there."

Joe gave him a long, chill look and then stepped to the window. He couldn't figure the other. Unless he was a fruitcake. Maybe he was in some kind of pressure cooker and this was one of the fruitcakes.

He looked out, however, not on the lawns and walks of a sanitarium but upon a wide boulevard of what was obviously a populous city.

And for a moment again, Joe Prantera felt the depths of nausea.

This was not his world.

He stared for a long, long moment. The cars didn't even have wheels, he noted dully. He turned slowly and faced the older man.

Reston-Farrell said compassionately, "Try this, it's excellent cognac."

Joe Prantera stared at him, said finally, flatly, "What's it all about?"

The other put down the unaccepted glass. "We were afraid first realization would be a shock to you," he said. "My colleague is in the adjoining room. We will be glad to explain to you if you will join us there."

"I wanta get out of here," Joe said.

"Where would you go?"

The fear of police, of Al Rossi's vengeance, of the measures that might be taken by Big Louis on his failure, were now far away.

Reston-Farrell had approached the door by which he had entered and it reopened for him. He went through it without looking back.

There was nothing else to do. Joe dressed, then followed him.

* * * * *

In the adjoining room was a circular table that would have accommodated a dozen persons. Two were seated there now, papers, books and soiled coffee cups before them. There had evidently been a long wait.

Reston-Farrell, the one Joe had already met, was tall and drawn of face and with a chainsmoker's nervousness. The other was heavier and more at ease. They were both, Joe estimated, somewhere in their middle fifties. They both looked like docs. He wondered, all over again, if this was some kind of pressure cooker.

But that didn't explain the view from the window.

Reston-Farrell said, "May I present my colleague, Citizen Warren Brett-James? Warren, this is our guest from ...from yesteryear, Mr. Joseph Salviati-Prantera."

Brett-James nodded to him, friendly, so far as Joe could see. He said gently, "I think it would be Mr. Joseph Prantera, wouldn't it? The maternal linage was almost universally ignored." His voice too gave the impression he was speaking a language not usually on his tongue.

Joe took an empty chair, hardly bothering to note its alien qualities. His body seemed to *fit* into the piece of furniture, as though it had been molded to his order.

Joe said, "I think maybe I'll take that there drink, Doc."

Reston-Farrell said, "Of course," and then something else Joe didn't get. Whatever the something else was, a slot opened in the middle of the table and a glass, so clear of texture as to be all but invisible, was elevated. It contained possibly three ounces of golden fluid.

Joe didn't allow himself to think of its means of delivery. He took up the drink and bolted it. He put the glass down and said carefully, "What's it all about, huh?"

Warren Brett-James said soothingly, "Prepare yourself for somewhat of a shock, Mr. Prantera. You are no longer in Los Angeles —"

"Ya think I'm stupid? I can see that."

"I was about to say, Los Angeles of 1960. Mr. Prantera, we welcome you to Nuevo Los Angeles."

"Ta where?"

"To Nuevo Los Angeles and to the year —" Brett-James looked at his companion. "What is the date, Old Calendar?"

"2133," Reston-Farrell said. "2133 A.D. they would say."

Joe Prantera looked from one of them to the other, scowling. "What are you guys talking about?"

Warren Brett-James said softly, "Mr. Prantera, you are no longer in the year 1960, you are now in the year 2133."

He said, uncomprehendingly, "You mean I been, like, unconscious for —" He let the sentence fall away as he realized the impossibility.

Brett-James said gently, "Hardly for one hundred and seventy years, Mr. Prantera."

Reston-Farrell said, "I am afraid we are confusing you. Briefly, we have *transported* you, I suppose one might say, from your own era to ours."

Joe Prantera had never been exposed to the concept of time travel. He had simply never associated with anyone who had ever even remotely considered such an idea. Now he said, "You mean, like, I been asleep all that time?"

"Not exactly," Brett-James said, frowning.

Reston-Farrell said, "Suffice to say, you are now one hundred and seventy-three years after the last memory you have."

Joe Prantera's mind suddenly reverted to those last memories and his eyes narrowed dangerously. He felt suddenly at bay. He said, "Maybe you guys better let me in on what's this all about."

Reston-Farrell said, "Mr. Prantera, we have brought you from your era to perform a task for us."

Joe stared at him, and then at the other. He couldn't believe he was getting through to them. Or, at least, that they were to him.

Finally he said, "If I get this, you want me to do a job for you."

"That is correct."

Joe said, "You guys know the kind of jobs I do?"

"That is correct."

"Like hell you do. You think I'm stupid? I never even seen you before." Joe Prantera came abruptly to his feet. "I'm gettin' outta here."

For the second time, Reston-Farrell said, "Where would you go, Mr. Prantera?"

Joe glared at him. Then sat down again, as abruptly as he'd arisen.

* * * * *

"Let's start all over again. I got this straight, you brought me, some screwy way, all the way ... here. O.K., I'll buy that. I seen what it looks like out that window —" The real comprehension was seeping through to him even as he talked. "Everybody I know, Jessie, Tony, the Kid, Big Louis, everybody, they're dead. Even Big Louis."

"Yes," Brett-James said, his voice soft. "They are all dead, Mr. Prantera. Their children are all dead, and their grandchildren."

The two men of the future said nothing more for long minutes while Joe Prantera's mind whirled its confusion.

Finally he said, "What's this bit about you wanting me to give it to some guy."

"That is why we brought you here, Mr. Prantera. You were ...you are, a professional assassin."

"Hey, wait a minute, now."

Reston-Farrell went on, ignoring the interruption. "There is small point in denying your calling. Pray remember that at the point when we ... *transported* you, you were about to dispose of a contemporary named Alphonso Annunziata-Rossi. A citizen, I might say, whose demise would probably have caused small dismay to society."

They had him pegged all right. Joe said, "But why me? Why don't you get some heavy from now? Somebody knows the ropes these days."

Brett-James said, "Mr. Prantera, there are no professional assassins in this age, nor have there been for over a century and a half."

"Well, then do it yourself." Joe Prantera's irritation over this whole complicated mess was growing. And already he was beginning to long for the things he knew-for Jessie and Tony and the others, for his favorite bar, for the lasagne down at Papa Giovanni's. Right now he could have welcomed a calling down at the hands of Big Louis.

Reston-Farrell had come to his feet and walked to one of the large room's windows. He looked out, as though unseeing. Then, his back turned, he said, "We have tried, but it is simply not in us, Mr. Prantera."

"You mean you're yella?"

"No, if by that you mean afraid. It is simply not within us to take the life of a fellow creature-not to speak of a fellow man."

Joe snapped: "Everything you guys say sounds crazy. Let's start all over again."

Brett-James said, "Let me do it, Lawrence." He turned his eyes to Joe. "Mr. Prantera, in your own era, did you ever consider the future?"

Joe looked at him blankly.

"In your day you were confronted with national and international, problems. Just as we are today and just as nations were a century or a millennium ago."

"Sure, O.K., so we had problems. I know whatcha mean-like wars, and depressions and dictators and like that."

"Yes, like that," Brett-James nodded.

The heavy-set man paused a moment. "Yes, like that," he repeated. "That we confront you now indicates that the problems of your day were solved. Hadn't they been, the world most surely would have destroyed itself. Wars? Our pedagogues are hard put to convince their students that such ever existed. More than a century and a half ago our society eliminated the reasons for international conflict. For that matter," he added musingly, "we eliminated most international boundaries. Depressions? Shortly after your own period, man awoke to the fact that he had achieved to the point where it was possible to produce an abundance for all with a minimum of toil. Overnight, for all practical purposes, the whole world was industrialized, automated. The second industrial revolution was accompanied by revolutionary changes in almost every field, certainly in every science. Dictators? Your ancestors found, Mr. Prantera, that it is difficult for a man to be free so long as others are still enslaved. Today the democratic ethic has reached a pinnacle never dreamed of in your own era."

"O.K., O.K.," Joe Prantera growled. "So everybody's got it made. What I wanta know is what's all this about me giving it ta somebody? If everything's so great, how come you want me to knock this guy off?"

Reston-Farrell bent forward and thumped his right index finger twice on the table. "The bacterium of hate —a new strain-has found the human race unprotected from its disease. We had thought our vaccines immunized us."

"What's that suppose to mean?"

Brett-James took up the ball again. "Mr. Prantera, have you ever heard of Ghengis Khan, of Tamerlane, Alexander, Caesar?"

Joe Prantera scowled at him emptily.

"Or, more likely, of Napoleon, Hitler, Stalin?"

"Sure I heard of Hitler and Stalin," Joe growled. "I ain't stupid."

The other nodded. "Such men are unique. They have a drive ...a drive to power which exceeds by far the ambitions of the average man. They are genii in their way, Mr. Prantera, genii of evil. Such a genius of evil has appeared on the current scene."

"Now we're getting somewheres," Joe snorted. "So you got a guy what's a little ambitious, like, eh? And you guys ain't got the guts to give it to him. O.K. What's in it for me?"

The two of them frowned, exchanged glances. Reston-Farrell said, "You know, that is one aspect we had not considered."

Brett-James said to Joe Prantera, "Had we not, ah, taken you at the time we did, do you realize what would have happened?"

"Sure," Joe grunted. "I woulda let old Al Rossi have it right in the guts, five times. Then I woulda took the plane back to Chi."

Brett-James was shaking his head. "No. You see, by coincidence, a police squad car was coming down the street just at that moment to arrest Mr. Rossi. You would have been apprehended. As I understand Californian law of the period, your life would have been forfeit, Mr. Prantera."

Joe winced. It didn't occur to him to doubt their word.

Reston-Farrell said, "As to reward, Mr. Prantera, we have already told you there is ultra-abundance in this age. Once this task has been performed, we will sponsor your entry into present day society. Competent psychiatric therapy will soon remove your present —"

"Waita minute, now. You figure on gettin' me candled by some head shrinker, eh? No thanks, Buster. I'm going back to my own —"

Brett-James was shaking his head again. "I am afraid there is no return, Mr. Prantera. Time travel works but in one direction, *with* the flow of the time stream. There can be no return to your own era."

Joe Prantera had been rocking with the mental blows he had been assimilating, but this was the final haymaker. He was stuck in this squaresville of a world.

* * * * *

Joe Prantera on a job was thorough.

Careful, painstaking, competent.

He spent the first three days of his life in the year 2133 getting the feel of things. Brett-James and Reston-Farrell had been appointed to work with him. Joe didn't meet any of the others who belonged to the group which had taken the measures to bring him from the past. He didn't want to meet them. The fewer persons involved, the better.

He stayed in the apartment of Reston-Farrell. Joe had been right, Reston-Farrell was a medical doctor. Brett-James evidently had something to do with the process that had enabled them to bring Joe from the past. Joe didn't know how they'd done it, and he didn't care. Joe was a realist. He was here. The thing was to adapt.

There didn't seem to be any hurry. Once the deal was made, they left it up to him to make the decisions.

They drove him around the town, when he wished to check the traffic arteries. They flew him about the whole vicinity. From the air, Southern California looked much the same as it had in his own time. Oceans, mountains, and to a lesser extent, deserts, are fairly permanent even against man's corroding efforts.

It was while he was flying with Brett-James on the second day that Joe said, "How about Mexico? Could I make the get to Mexico?"

The physicist looked at him questioningly. "Get?" he said.

Joe Prantera said impatiently, "The getaway. After I give it to this Howard Temple-Tracy guy, I gotta go on the run, don't I?"

"I see." Brett-James cleared his throat. "Mexico is no longer a separate nation, Mr. Prantera. All North America has been united into one unit. Today, there are only eight nations in the world."

"Where's the nearest?"

"South America."

"That's a helluva long way to go on a get."

"We hadn't thought of the matter being handled in that manner."

Joe eyed him in scorn. "Oh, you didn't, huh? What happens after I give it to this guy? I just sit around and wait for the cops to put the arm on me?"

Brett-James grimaced in amusement. "Mr. Prantera, this will probably be difficult for you to comprehend, but there are no police in this era."

Joe gaped at him. "No police! What happens if you gotta throw some guy in stir?"

"If I understand your idiom correctly, you mean prison. There are no prisons in this era, Mr. Prantera."

Joe stared. "No cops, no jails. What stops anybody? What stops anybody from just going into some bank, like, and collecting up all the bread?"

Brett-James cleared his throat. "Mr. Prantera, there are no banks."

"No banks! You gotta have banks!"

"And no money to put in them. We found it a rather antiquated method of distribution well over a century ago."

Joe had given up. Now he merely stared.

Brett-James said reasonably, "We found we were devoting as much time to financial matters in all their endless ramifications-including bank robberies-as we were to productive efforts. So we turned to more efficient methods of distribution."

*　*　*　*　*

On the fourth day, Joe said, "O.K., let's get down to facts. Summa the things you guys say don't stick together so good. Now, first place, where's this guy Temple-Tracy you want knocked off?"

Reston-Farrell and Brett-James were both present. The three of them sat in the living room of the latter's apartment, sipping a sparkling wine which seemed to be the prevailing beverage of the day. For Joe's taste it was insipid stuff. Happily, rye was available to those who wanted it.

Reston-Farrell said, "You mean, where does he reside? Why, here in this city."

"Well, that's handy, eh?" Joe scratched himself thoughtfully. "You got somebody can finger him for me?"

"Finger him?"

"Look, before I can give it to this guy I gotta know some place where he'll be at some time. Get it? Like Al Rossi. My finger, he works in Rossi's house, see? He lets me know every Wednesday night, eight o'clock, Al leaves the house all by hisself. O.K., so I can make plans, like, to give it to him." Joe Prantera wound it up reasonably. "You gotta have a finger."

Brett-James said, "Why not just go to Temple-Tracy's apartment and, ah, dispose of him?"

"Jest walk in, eh? You think I'm stupid? How do I know how many witnesses hangin' around? How do I know if the guy's carryin' heat?"

"Heat?"

"A gun, a gun. Ya think I'm stupid? I come to give it to him and he gives it to me instead."

Dr. Reston-Farrell said, "Howard Temple-Tracy lives alone. He customarily receives visitors every afternoon, largely potential followers. He is attempting to recruit members to an organization he is forming. It would be quite simple for you to enter his establishment and dispose of him. I assure you, he does not possess weapons."

Joe was indignant. "Just like that, eh?" he said sarcastically. "Then what happens? How do I get out of the building? Where's my get car parked? Where do I hide out? Where do I dump the heat?"

"Dump the heat?"

"Get rid of the gun. You want I should get caught with the gun on me? I'd wind up in the gas chamber so quick —"

"See here, Mr. Prantera," Brett-James said softly. "We no longer have capital punishment, you must realize."

"O.K. I still don't wanta get caught. What *is* the rap these days, huh?" Joe scowled. "You said they didn't have no jails any more."

"This is difficult for you to understand, I imagine," Reston-Farrell told him, "but, you see, we no longer punish people in this era."

That took a long, unbelieving moment to sink in. "You mean, like, no matter what they do? That's crazy. Everybody'd be running around giving it to everybody else."

"The motivation for crime has been removed, Mr. Prantera," Reston-Farrell attempted to explain. "A person who commits a violence against another is obviously in need of medical care. And, consequently, receives it."

"You mean, like, if I steal a car or something, they just take me to a doctor?" Joe Prantera was unbelieving.

"Why would anybody wish to steal a car?" Reston-Farrell said easily.

"But if I *give it* to somebody?"

"You will be turned over to a medical institution. Citizen Howard Temple-Tracy is the last man you will ever kill, Mr. Prantera."

A chillness was in the belly of Joe Prantera. He said very slowly, very dangerously, "You guys figure on me getting caught, don't you?"

"Yes," Brett-James said evenly.

"Well then, figure something else. You think I'm stupid?"

"Mr. Prantera," Dr. Reston-Farrell said, "there has been as much progress in the field of psychiatry in the past two centuries as there has in any other. Your treatment would be brief and painless, believe me."

Joe said coldly, "And what happens to you guys? How do you know I won't rat on you?"

Brett-James said gently, "The moment after you have accomplished your mission, we plan to turn ourselves over to the nearest institution to have determined whether or not we also need therapy."

"Now I'm beginning to wonder about you guys," Joe said. "Look, all over again, what'd'ya wanta give it to this guy for?"

The doctor said, "We explained the other day, Mr. Prantera. Citizen Howard Temple-Tracy is a dangerous, atavistic, evil genius. We are afraid for our institutions if his plans are allowed to mature."

"Well if you got things so good, everybody's got it made, like, who'd listen to him?"

The doctor nodded at the validity of the question. "Mr. Prantera, *Homo sapiens* is a unique animal. Physically he matures at approximately the age of thirteen. However, mental maturity and adjustment is often not fully realized until thirty or even more. Indeed, it is sometimes never achieved. Before such maturity is reached, our youth are susceptible to romantic appeal. Nationalism, chauvinism, racism, the supposed glory of the military, all seem romantic to the immature. They rebel at the orderliness of present society. They seek entertainment in excitement. Citizen Temple-Tracy is aware of this and finds his recruits among the young."

"O.K., so this guy is dangerous. You want him knocked off before he screws everything up. But the way things are, there's no way of making a get. So you'll have to get some other patsy. Not me."

"I am afraid you have no alternative," Brett-James said gently. "Without us, what will you do? Mr. Prantera, you do not even speak the language."

"What'd'ya mean? I don't understand summa the big words you eggheads use, but I get by O.K."

Brett-James said, "Amer-English is no longer the language spoken by the man in the street, Mr. Prantera. Only students of such subjects any longer speak such tongues as Amer-English, French, Russian or the many others that once confused the race with their limitations as a means of communication."

"You mean there's no place in the whole world where they talk American?" Joe demanded, aghast.

* * * * *

Dr. Reston-Farrell controlled the car. Joe Prantera sat in the seat next to him and Warren Brett-James sat in the back. Joe had, tucked in his belt, a .45 caliber automatic, once displayed in a museum. It had been more easily procured than the ammunition to fit it, but that problem too had been solved.

The others were nervous, obviously repelled by the very conception of what they had planned.

Inwardly, Joe was amused. Now that they had got in the clutch, the others were on the verge of chickening out. He knew it wouldn't have taken much for them to cancel the project. It wasn't any answer though. If they allowed him to call it off today, they'd talk themselves into it again before the week was through.

Besides, already Joe was beginning to feel the comfortable, pleasurable, warm feeling that came to him on occasions like this.

He said, "You're sure this guy talks American, eh?"

Warren Brett-James said, "Quite sure. He is a student of history."

"And he won't think it's funny I talk American to him, eh?"

"He'll undoubtedly be intrigued."

They pulled up before a large apartment building that overlooked the area once known as Wilmington.

Joe was coolly efficient now. He pulled out the automatic, held it down below his knees and threw a shell into the barrel. He eased the hammer down, thumbed on the safety, stuck the weapon back in his belt and beneath the jacketlike garment he wore.

He said, "O.K. See you guys later." He left them and entered the building.

An elevator-he still wasn't used to their speed in this era-whooshed him to the penthouse duplex occupied by Citizen Howard Temple-Tracy.

There were two persons in the reception room but they left on Joe's arrival, without bothering to look at him more than glancingly.

He spotted the screen immediately and went over and stood before it.

The screen lit and revealed a heavy-set, dour of countenance man seated at a desk. He looked into Joe Prantera's face, scowled and said something.

Joe said, "Joseph Salviati-Prantera to interview Citizen Howard Temple-Tracy."

The other's shaggy eyebrows rose. "Indeed," he said. "In Amer-English?"

Joe nodded.

"Enter," the other said.

A door had slid open on the other side of the room. Joe walked through it and into what was obviously an office. Citizen Temple-Tracy sat at a desk. There was only one other chair in the room. Joe Prantera ignored it and remained standing.

Citizen Temple-Tracy said, "What can I do for you?"

Joe looked at him for a long, long moment. Then he reached down to his belt and brought forth the .45 automatic. He moistened his lips.

Joe said softly, "You know what this here is?"

Temple-Tracy stared at the weapon. "It's a handgun, circa, I would say, about 1925 Old Calendar. What in the world are you doing with it?"

Joe said, very slowly, "Chief, in the line you're in these days you needa heavy around with wunna these. Otherwise, Chief, you're gunna wind up in some gutter with a lotta holes in you. What I'm doin', I'm askin' for a job. You need a good man knows how to handle wunna these, Chief."

Citizen Howard Temple-Tracy eyed him appraisingly. "Perhaps," he said, "you are right at that. In the near future, I may well need an assistant knowledgeable in the field of violence. Tell me more about yourself. You surprise me considerably."

"Sure, Chief. It's kinda a long story, though. First off, I better tell you you got some bad enemies, Chief. Two guys special, named Brett-James and Doc Reston-Farrell. I think one of the first jobs I'm gunna hafta do for you, Chief, is to give it to those two."

Freedom

Colonel Ilya Simonov tooled his Zil aircushion convertible along the edge of Red Square, turned right immediately beyond St. Basil's Cathedral, crossed the Moscow River by the Moskvocetski Bridge and debouched into the heavy, and largely automated traffic of Pyarnikskaya. At Dobryninskaya Square he turned west to Gorki Park which he paralleled on Kaluga until he reached the old baroque palace which housed the Ministry.

There were no flags, no signs, nothing to indicate the present nature of the aged Czarist building.

He left the car at the curb, slamming its door behind him and walking briskly to the entrance. Hard, handsome in the Slavic tradition, dedicated, Ilya Simonov was young for his rank. A plainclothes man, idling a hundred feet down the street, eyed him briefly then turned his attention elsewhere. The two guards at the gate snapped to attention, their eyes straight ahead. Colonel Simonov was in mufti and didn't answer the salute.

The inside of the old building was well known to him. He went along marble halls which contained antique statuary and other relics of the past which, for unknown reason, no one had ever bothered to remove. At the heavy door which entered upon the office of his destination he came to a halt and spoke briefly to the lieutenant at the desk there.

"The Minister is expecting me," Simonov clipped.

The lieutenant did the things receptionists do everywhere and looked up in a moment to say, "Go right in, Colonel Simonov."

Minister Kliment Blagonravov looked up from his desk at Simonov's entrance. He was a heavy-set man, heavy of face and he still affected the shaven head, now rapidly disappearing among upper-echelons of the Party. His jacket had been thrown over the back of a chair and his collar loosened; even so there was a sheen of sweat on his face.

He looked up at his most trusted field man, said in the way of greeting, "Ilya," and twisted in his swivel chair to a portable bar. He swung open the door of the small refrigerator and emerged with a bottle of Stolichnaya vodka. He plucked two three-ounce glasses from a shelf and pulled the bottle's cork with his teeth. "Sit down, sit down, Ilya," he grunted as he filled the glasses. "How was Magnitogorsk?"

Ilya Simonov secured his glass before seating himself in one of the room's heavy leathern chairs. He sighed, relaxed, and said, "Terrible, I loath those ultra-industrialized cities. I wonder if the Americans do any better with Pittsburgh or the British with Birmingham."

"I know what you mean," the security head rumbled. "How did you make out with you assignment, Ilya?"

Colonel Simonov frowned down into the colorlessness of the vodka before dashing it back over his palate. "It's all in my report, Kliment." He was the only man in the organization who called Blagonravov by his first name.

His chief grunted again and reached forward to refill the glass. "I'm sure it is. Do you know how many reports go across this desk daily? And did you know that Ilya Simonov is the most long-winded, as the Americans say, of my some two hundred first-line operatives?"

The colonel shifted in his chair. "Sorry," he said. "I'll keep that in mind."

His chief rumbled his sour version of a chuckle. "Nothing, nothing, Ilya. I was jesting. However, give me a brief of your mission."

Ilya Simonov frowned again at his refilled vodka glass but didn't take it up for a moment. "A routine matter," he said. "A dozen or so engineers and technicians, two or three fairly high-ranking scientists, and three or four of the local intelligentsia had formed some sort of informal club. They were discussing national and international affairs."

Kliment Blagonravov's thin eyebrows went up but he waited for the other to go on.

Ilya said impatiently, "It was the ordinary. They featured complete freedom of opinion and expression in their weekly get-togethers. They began by criticizing without extremism, local affairs, matters concerned with their duties, that sort of thing. In the beginning, they even sent a few letters of protest to the local press, signing the name of the club. After their ideas went further out, they didn't dare do that, of course."

He took up his second drink and belted it back, not wanting to give it time to lose its chill.

His chief filled in. "And they delved further and further into matters that should be discussed only within the party-if even there-until they arrived at what point?"

Colonel Simonov shrugged. "Until they finally got to the point of discussing how best to overthrow the Soviet State and what socio-economic system should follow it. The usual thing. I've run into possible two dozen such outfits in the past five years."

His chief grunted and tossed back his own drink. "My dear Ilya," he rumbled sourly, "I've *run into*, as you say, more than two hundred."

Simonov was taken back by the figure but he only looked at the other.

Blagonravov said, "What did you do about it?"

"Several of them were popular locally. In view of Comrade Zverev's recent pronouncements of increased freedom of press and speech, I thought it best not to make a public display. Instead, I took measures to charge individual members with inefficiency in their work, with corruption or graft, or with other crimes having nothing to do with the reality of the situation. Six or seven in all were imprisoned, others demoted. Ten or twelve I had switched to other cities, principally into more backward areas in the virgin lands."

"And the ringleaders?" the security head asked.

"There were two of them, one a research chemist of some prominence, the other a steel plane manager. They were both, ah, unfortunately killed in an automobile accident while under the influence of drink."

"I see," Blagonravov nodded. "So actually the whole rat's nest was stamped out without attention being brought to it so far as the Magnitogorsk public is concerned." He nodded heavily again. "You can almost always be depended upon to do the right thing, Ilya. If you weren't so confoundedly good a field man, I'd make you my deputy."

Which was exactly what Simonov would have hated, but he said nothing.

"One thing," his chief said. "The origin of this, ah, *club* which turned into a tiny underground all of its own. Did you detect the finger of the West, stirring up trouble?"

"No." Simonov shook his head. "If such was the case, the agents involved were more clever than I'd ordinarily give either America or Common Europe credit for. I could be wrong, of course."

"Perhaps," the police head growled. He eyed the bottle before him but made no motion toward it. He wiped the palm of his right hand back over his bald pate, in unconscious irritation. "But there is something at work that we are not getting at." Blagonravov seemed to change subjects. "You can speak Czech, so I understand."

"That's right. My mother was from Bratislava. My father met her there during the Hitler war."

"And you know Czechoslovakia?"

"I've spent several vacations in the Tatras at such resorts as Tatranski Lomnica since the country's been made such a tourist center of the satellites." Ilya Simonov didn't understand this trend of the conversation.

"You have some knowledge of automobiles, too?"

Simonov shrugged. "I've driven all my life."

His chief rumbled thoughtfully, "Time isn't of essence. You can take a quick course at the Moskvich plant. A week or two would give you all the background you need."

Ilya laughed easily. "I seem to have missed something. Have my shortcomings caught up with me? Am I to be demoted to automobile mechanic?"

Kliment Blagonravov became definite. "You are being given the most important assignment of your career, Ilya. This rot, this ever growing ferment against the Party, must be cut out, liquidated. It seems to fester worse among the middle echelons of … what did that Yugoslavian Djilas call us?… the *New Class*. Why? That's what we must know."

He sat farther back in his chair and his heavy lips made a *mout*. "Why, Ilya?" he repeated. "After more than half a century the Party has attained all its goals. Lenin's millennium is here; the end for which Stalin purged ten millions and more, is reached; the sacrifices demanded by Khrushchev in the Seven-Year Plans have finally paid off, as the Yankees say. Our gross national product, our per capita production, our standard of living, is the highest in the world. Sacrifices are no longer necessary."

There had been an almost whining note in his voice. But now he broke it off. He poured them still another drink. "At any rate, Ilya, I was with Frol Zverev this morning. Number One is incensed. It seems that in the Azerbaijan Republic, for one example, that even the Komsomols were circulating among themselves various proscribed books and pamphlets. Comrade Zverev instructed me to concentrate on discovering the reason for this disease."

Colonel Simonov scowled. "What's this got to do with Czechoslovakia-and automobiles?"

The security head waggled a fat finger at him. "What we've been doing, thus far, is dashing forth upon hearing of a new conflagration and stamping it out. Obviously, that's no answer. We must find who is behind it. How it begins. Why it begins. That's your job?"

"Why Czechoslovakia?"

"You're unknown as a security agent there, for one thing. You will go to Prague and become manager of the Moskvich automobile distribution agency. No one, not even the Czech unit of our ministry will be aware of your identity. You will play it by ear, as the Americans say."

"To whom do I report?"

"Only to me, until the task is completed. When it is, you will return to Moscow and report fully." A grimace twisted Blagonravov's face. "If I am still here. Number One is truly incensed, Ilya."

There had been some more. Kliment Blagonravov had evidently chosen Prague, the capital of Czechoslovakia, as the seat of operations in a suspicion that the wave of unrest spreading insidiously throughout the Soviet Complex owed its origins to the West. Thus far, there had been no evidence of this but the suspicion refused to die. If not the West, then who? The Cold War was long over but the battle for men's minds continued even in peace.

Ideally, Ilya Simonov was to infiltrate whatever Czech groups might be active in the illicit movement and then, if he discovered there was a higher organization, a center of the movement, he was to attempt to become a part of it. If possible he was to rise in the organisation to as high a point as he could.

Blagonravov, Minister of the *Chrezvychainaya Komissiya*, the Extraordinary Commission for Combating Counter-Revolution and Sabotage, was of the opinion that if this virus of revolt was originating from the West, then it would be stronger in the satellite countries than in Russia itself. Simonov held no opinion as yet. He would wait and see. However, there was an uncomfortable feeling about the whole assignment. The group in Magnitogorsk, he was all but sure, had no connections with Western agents, nor anyone else, for that matter. Of course, it might have been an exception.

He left the Ministry, his face thoughtful as he climbed into his waiting Zil. This assignment was going to be a lengthy one. He'd have to wind up various affairs here in Moscow, personal as well as business. He might be away for a year or more.

There was a sheet of paper on the seat of his aircushion car. He frowned at it. It couldn't have been there before. He picked it up.

It was a mimeographed throw-away.

It was entitled, *FREEDOM*, and it began: *Comrades, more than a hundred years ago the founders of scientific socialism, Karl Marx and Frederick Engels, explained that the State was incompatible with liberty, that the State was an instrument of repression of one class by another. They explained that for true freedom ever to exist the State must wither away.*

Under the leadership of Lenin, Stalin, Krushchev and now Zverev, the State has become ever stronger. Far from withering away, it continues to oppress us. Fellow Russians, it is time we take action! We must....

Colonel Simonov bounced from his car again, shot his eyes up and down the street. He barely refrained from drawing the 9 mm automatic which nestled under his left shoulder and which he knew how to use so well.

He curtly beckoned to the plainclothes man, still idling against the building a hundred feet or so up the street. The other approached him, touched the brim of his hat in a half salute.

Simonov snapped, "Do you know who I am?"

"Yes, colonel."

Ilya Simonov thrust the leaflet forward. "How did this get into my car?"

The other looked at it blankly. "I don't know, Colonel Simonov."

"You've been here all this time?"

"Why, yes colonel."

"With my car in plain sight?"

That didn't seem to call for an answer. The plainclothesman looked apprehensive but blank.

Simonov turned on his heel and approached the two guards at the gate. They were not more than thirty feet from where he was parked. They came to the salute but he growled, "At ease. Look here, did anyone approach my vehicle while I was inside?"

One of the soldiers said, "Sir, twenty or thirty people have passed since the Comrade colonel entered the Ministry."

The other one said, "Yes, sir."

Ilya Simonov looked from the guards to the plainclothes man and back, in frustration. Finally he spun on his heel again and re-entered the car. He slapped the elevation lever, twisted the wheel sharply, hit the jets pedal with his foot and shot into the traffic.

The plainclothes man looked after him and muttered to the guards, "Blagonravov's hatchet-man. He's killed more men than the plague. A bad one to have down on you."

Simonov bowled down the Kaluga at excessive speed. "Driving like a young *stilyagi*," he growled in irritation at himself. But, confound it, how far had things gone when subversive leaflets were placed in cars parked in front of the ministry devoted to combating counter revolution.

He'd been away from Moscow for over a month and the amenities in the smog, smoke and coke fumes blanketing industrial complex of Magnitogorsk hadn't been particularly of the best. Ilya Simonov headed now for Gorki Street and the Baku Restaurant. He had an idea that it was going to be some time before the opportunity would be repeated for him to sit down to Zakouski, the salty, spicy Russian hors d'oeuvres, and to Siberian pilmeny and a bottle of Tsinandali.

The restaurant, as usual, was packed. In irritation, Ilya Simonov stood for a while waiting for a table, then, taking the head waiter's advice, agreed to share one with a stranger.

The stranger, a bearded little man, who was dwaddling over his Gurievskaya kasha dessert while reading *Izvestia*, glanced up at him, unseemingly, bobbed his head at Simonov's request to share his table, and returned to the newspaper.

The harried waiter took his time in turning up with a menu. Ilya Simonov attempted to relax. He had no particular reason to be upset by the leaflet found in his car. Obviously, whoever had thrown it there was distributing haphazardly. The fact that it was mimeographed, rather than printed, was an indication of lack of resources, an amateur affair. But what in the world did these people want? What did they want?

The Soviet State was turning out consumer's goods, homes, cars as no nation in the world. Vacations were lengthy, working hours short. A four-day week, even! What did they *want*? What motivates a man who is living on a scale unknown to a Czarist boyar to risk his position, even his life! in a stupidly impossible revolt against the country's government?

The man across from him snorted in contempt.

He looked over the top of his paper at Smirnov and said, "The election in Italy. Ridiculous!"

Ilya Simonov brought his mind back to the present. "How did they turn out? I understand the depression is terrible there."

"So I understand," the other said. "The vote turned out as was to be expected."

Simonov's eyebrows went up. "The Party has been voted into power?"

"Ha!" the other snorted. "The vote for the Party has fallen off by more than a third."

The security colonel scowled at him. "That doesn't sound reasonable, if the economic situation is as bad as has been reported."

His table mate put down the paper. "Why not? Has there ever been a country where the Party was *voted* into power? Anywhere-at any time during the more than half a century since the Bolsheviks first took over here in Russia?"

Simonov looked at him.

The other was talking out opinions he'd evidently formed while reading the *Izvestia* account of the Italian elections, not paying particular attention to the stranger across from him.

He said, his voice irritated, "Nor will there ever be. They know better. In the early days of the revolution the workers might have had illusions about the Party and it goals. Now they've lost them. Everywhere, they've lost them."

Ilya Simonov said tightly, "How do you mean?"

"I mean the Party has been rejected. With the exception of China and Yugoslavia, both of whom have their own varieties, the only countries that have adopted our system have done it under pressure from outside-not by their own efforts. Not by the will of the majority."

Colonel Simonov said flatly, "You seem to think that Marxism will never dominate the world."

"Marxism!" the other snorted. "If Marx were alive in Russia today, Frol Zverev would have him in a Siberian labor camp within twenty-four hours."

Ilya Simonov brought forth his wallet and opened it to his police credentials. He said coldly, "Let me see your identification papers. You are under arrest."

The other stared at him for a moment, then snorted his contempt. He brought forth his own wallet and handed it across the table.

Simonov flicked it open, his face hard. He looked at the man. "Konstantin Kasatkin."

"Candidate member of the Academy of Sciences," the other snapped. "And bearer of the Hero of the Soviet Union award."

Simonov flung the wallet back to him in anger. "And as such, practically immune."

The other grinned nastily at him. "Scientists, my police friend, cannot be bothered with politics. Where would the Soviet Complex be if you took to throwing biologists such as myself into prison for making unguarded statements in an absent-minded moment?"

Simonov slapped a palm down on the table. "Confound it, Comrade," he snapped, "how is the Party to maintain discipline in the country if high ranking persons such as yourself speak open subversion to strangers."

The other sported his contempt. "Perhaps there's too much discipline in Russia, Comrade policeman."

"Rather, far from enough," Simonov snapped back.

The waiter, at last, approached and extended a menu to the security officer. But Ilya Simonov had come to his feet. "Never mind," he clipped in disgust. "There is an air of degenerate decay about here."

The waiter stared at him. The biologist snorted and returned to his paper. Simonov turned and stormed out. He could find something to eat and drink in his own apartment.

The old, old town of Prague, the *Golden City of a Hundred Spires* was as always the beautifully stolid medieval metropolis which even a quarter of a century and more of Party rule could not change. The Old Town, nestled in a bend of the Vltava River, as no other city in Europe, breathed its centuries, its air of yesteryear.

Colonel Ilya Simonov, in spite of his profession, was not immune to beauty. He deliberately failed to notify his new office of his arrival, flew in on a Ceskoslovenskè Aerolinie Tupolev rocket liner and spent his first night at the Alcron Hotel just off Wenceslas Square. He knew that as the new manager of the local Moskvich distribution agency he'd have fairly elaborate quarters, probably in a good section of town, but this first night he wanted to himself.

He spent it wandering quietly in the old quarter, dropping in to the age-old beer halls for a half liter of Pilsen Urquell here, a foaming stein of Smichov Lager there. Czech beer, he was reminded all over again, is the best in the world. No argument, no debate, the best in the world.

He ate in the endless automated cafeterias that line the Viclavské Námesi the entertainment center of Prague. Ate an open sandwich here, some crabmeat salad there, a sausage and another glass of Pilsen somewhere else again. He was getting the feel of the town and of its people. Of recent years, some of the tension had gone out of the atmosphere in Moscow and the other Soviet centers; with the coming of economic prosperity there had also come a relaxation. The *fear*, so heavy in the Stalin era, had fallen off in that of Khrushchev and still more so in the present reign of Frol Zverev. In fact, Ilya Simonov was not alone in Party circles in wondering whether or not discipline had been allowed to slip too far. It is easier, the old Russian proverb goes, to hang onto the reins than to regain them once dropped.

But if Moscow had lost much of its pall of fear, Prague had certainly gone even further. In fact, in the U Pinkasu beer hall Simonov had idly picked up a magazine left by some earlier wassailer. It was a light literary publication devoted almost exclusively to humor. There were various cartoons, some of them touching political subjects. Ilya Simonov had been shocked to see a caricature of Frol Zverev himself. Zverev, Number One! Ridiculed in a second-rate magazine in a satellite country!

Ilya Simonov made a note of the name and address of the magazine and the issue.

Across the heavy wooden community table from him, a beer drinker grinned, in typically friendly Czech style. "A good magazine," he said. "You should subscribe."

A waiter, bearing an even dozen liter-size steins of beer hurried along, spotted the fact that Simonov's mug was empty, slipped a full one into its place, gave the police agent's saucer a quick mark of a pencil, and hurried on again. In the U Pinkasu, it was supposed that you wanted another beer so long as you remained sitting. When you finally staggered to your feet, the nearest waiter counted the number of pencil marks on your saucer and you paid up.

Ilya Simonov said cautiously to his neighbor, "Seems to be quite, ah, brash." He tapped the magazine with a finger.

The other shrugged and grinned again. "Things loosen up as the years go by," he said. "What a man wouldn't have dared say to his own wife five years ago, they have on TV today."

"I'm surprised the police don't take steps," Simonov said, trying to keep his voice expressionless.

The other took a deep swallow of his Pilsen Urquell. He pursed his lips and thought about it. "You know, I wonder if they'd dare. Such a case brought into the People's Courts might lead to all sort of public reaction these days."

It had been some years since Ilya Simonov had been in Prague and even then he'd only gone through on the way to the ski resorts in the mountains. He was shocked to find the Czech state's control had fallen off to this extent. Why, here he was, a complete stranger, being openly talked to on political subjects.

His cross-the-table neighbor shook his head, obviously pleased. "If you think Prague is good, you ought to see Warsaw. It's as free as Paris! I saw a Tri-D cinema up there about two months ago. You know what it was about? The purges in Moscow back in the 1930s."

"A rather unique subject," Simonov said.

"Um-m-m, made a very strong case for Bukharin, in particular."

Simonov said, very slowly, "I don't understand. You mean this ... this film supported the, ah, Old Bolsheviks?"

"Of course. Why not? Everybody knows they weren't guilty." The Czech snorted deprecation. "At least not guilty of what they were charged with. They were in Stalin's way and he liquidated them." The Czech thought about it for a while. "I wonder if he was already insane, that far back."

Had he taken up his mug of beer and dashed it into Simonov's face, he couldn't have surprised the Russian more.

Ilya Simonov had to take control of himself. His first instinct was to show his credentials, arrest the man and have him hauled up before the local agency of Simonov's ministry.

But obviously that was out of the question. He was in Czechoslovakia and, although Moscow still dominated the Soviet Complex, there was local autonomy and the Czech police just didn't enjoy their affairs being meddled with unless in extreme urgency.

Besides, this man was obviously only one among many. A stranger in a beer hall. Ilya Simonov suspected that if he continued his wanderings about the town, he'd meet in the process of only one evening a score of persons who would talk the same way.

Besides, still again, he was here in Prague incognito, his job to trace the sources of this dry rot, not to run down individual Czechs.

But the cinema, and TV! Surely anti-Party sentiment hadn't been allowed to go this far!

He got up from the table shakily, paid up for his beer and forced himself to nod good-bye in friendly fashion to the subversive Czech he'd been talking to.

In the morning he strolled over to the offices of the Moskvich Agency which was located only a few blocks from his hotel on Celetna Hybernski. The Russian car agency, he knew, was having a fairly hard go of it in Prague and elsewhere in Czechoslovakia. The Czechs, long before the Party took over in 1948, had been a highly industrialized, modern nation. They consequently had their own automobile works, such as Skoda, and their models were locally more popular than the Russian Moskvich, Zim and Pobeda.

Theoretically, the reason Ilya Simonov was the newly appointed agency head was to push Moskvich sales among the Czechs. He thought, half humorously, half sourly, to himself, even under the Party we have competition and pressure for higher sales. What was it that some American economist had called them? a system of State-Capitalism.

At the Moskvich offices he found himself in command of a staff that consisted of three fellow Russians, and a dozen or so Czech assistants. His immediate subordinate was a Catherina Panova, whose dossier revealed her to be a party member, though evidently not a particularly active one, at least not since she'd been assigned here in Prague.

She was somewhere in her mid-twenties, a graduate of the University of Moscow, and although she'd been in the Czech capital only a matter of six months or so, had already adapted to the more fashionable dress that the style-conscious women of this former Western capital went in for. Besides that, Catherina Panova managed to be one of the downright prettiest girls Ilya Simonov had ever seen.

His career had largely kept him from serious involvement in the past. Certainly the dedicated women you usually found in Party ranks seldom were of the type that inspired you to romance but he wondered now, looking at this new assistant of his, if he hadn't let too much of his youth go by without more investigation into the usually favorite pastime of youth.

He wondered also, but only briefly, if he should reveal his actual identity to her. She was, after all, a party member. But then he checked himself. Kliment Blagonravov had stressed the necessity of complete secrecy. Not even the local offices of the ministry were to be acquainted with his presence.

He let Catherina introduce him around, familiarize him with the local methods of going about their business affairs and the problems they were running into.

She ran a hand back over her forehead, placing a wisp of errant hair, and said, "I suppose, as an expert from Moscow, you'll be installing a whole set of new methods."

It was far from his intention to spend much time at office work. He said, "Not at all. There is no hurry. For a time, we'll continues your present policies, just to get the feel of the situation. Then perhaps in a few months, we'll come up with some ideas."

She obviously liked his use of "we" rather than "I." Evidently, the staff had been a bit nervous upon his appointment as new manager. He already felt, vaguely, that the three Russians here had no desire to return to their homeland. Evidently, there was something about Czechoslovakia that appealed to them all. The fact irritated him but somehow didn't surprise.

Catherina said, "As a matter of fact, I have some opinions on possible changes myself. Perhaps if you'll have dinner with me tonight, we can discuss them informally."

Ilya Simonov was only mildly surprised at her suggesting a rendezvous with him. Party members were expected to ignore sex and be on an equal footing. She was as free to suggest a dinner date to him, as he was to her. Of course, she wasn't speaking as a Party member now. In fact, he hadn't even revealed to her his own membership.

As it worked out, they never got around to discussing distribution of the new Moskvich aircushion jet car. They became far too busy enjoying food, drink, dancing-and each other.

They ate at the Budapest, in the Prava Hotel, complete with Hungarian dishes and Riesling, and they danced to the inevitable gypsy music. It occurred to Ilya Simonov that there was a certain pleasure to be derived from the fact that your feminine companion was the most beautiful woman in the establishment and one of the most attractively dressed. There was a certain lift to be enjoyed when you realized that the eyes of half the other males present were following you in envy.

One thing led to another. He insisted on introducing her to barack, the Hungarian national spirit, in the way of a digestive. The apricot brandy, distilled to the point of losing all sweetness and fruit flavor, required learning. It must be tossed back just so. By the time Catherina had the knack, neither of them were feeling strain. In fact, it became obviously necessary for him to be given a guided tour of Prague's night spots.

It turned out that Prague offered considerably more than Moscow, which even with the new relaxation was still one of the most staid cities in the Soviet Complex.

They took in the vaudeville at the Alhambra, and the variety at the Prazské Varieté.

They took in the show at the U Sv Tomíse, the age old tavern which had been making its own smoked black beer since the fifteenth century. And here Catherina with the assistance of revelers from neighboring tables taught him the correct pronunciation of *Na zdraví!* the Czech toast. It seemed required to go from heavy planked table to table practicing the new salutation to the accompaniment of the pungent borovika gin.

Somewhere in here they saw the Joseph Skupa puppets, and at this stage, Ilya Simonov found only great amusement at the political innuendoes involved in half the skits. It would never had one in Moscow or Leningrad, of course, but here it was very amusing indeed. There was even a caricature of a security police minister who could only have been his superior Kliment Blagonravov.

They wound up finally at the U Kalicha, made famous by Hasek in "The Good Soldier Schweik." In fact various illustrations from the original classic were framed on the walls.

They had been laughing over their early morning snack, now Ilya Simonov looked at her approvingly. "See here," he said. "We must do this again."

"Fine," she laughed.

"In fact, tomorrow," he insisted. He looked at his watch. "I mean tonight."

She laughed at him. "Our great expert from Moscow. Far from improving our operations, there'll be less accomplished than ever if you make a nightly practice of carrying on like we did this evening."

He laughed too. "But tonight," he said insistently.

She shook her head. "Sorry, but I'm already booked up for this evening."

He scowled for the first time in hours. He'd seemingly forgotten that he hardly knew this girl. What her personal life was, he had no idea. For that matter, she might be engaged or even married. The very idea irritated him.

He said stiffly, "Ah, you have a date?"

Catherina laughed again. "My, what a dark face. If I didn't know you to be an automobile distributor expert, I would suspect you of being a security police agent." She shook her head. "Not a date. If by that you mean another man. There is a meeting that I would like to attend."

"A meeting! It sounds dry as —"

She was shaking her head. "Oh, no. A group I belong to. Very interesting. We're to be addressed by an American journalist."

Suddenly he was all but sober.

He tried to smooth over the short space of silence his surprise had precipitated. "An American journalist? Under government auspices?"

"Hardly." She smiled at him over her glass of Pilsen. "I forget," she said. "If you're from Moscow, you probably aren't aware of how open things are here in Prague. A whiff of fresh air."

"I don't understand. Is this group of yours, ah, illegal?"

She shrugged impatiently. "Oh, of course not. Don't be silly. We gather to hear various speakers, to discuss world affairs. That sort of thing. Oh, of course, *theoretically* it's illegal, but for that matter even the head of the Skoda plant attended last week. It's only for the more advanced intellectuals, of course. Very advanced. But, for that matter, I know a dozen or so Party members, both Czech and Russian, who attend."

"But an American journalist? What's he doing in the country? Is he accredited?"

"No, no. You misunderstand. He entered as a tourist, came across some Prague newspapermen and as an upshot he's to give a talk on freedom of the press."

"I see," Simonov said.

She was impatient with him. "You don't understand at all. See here, why don't you come along tonight? I'm sure I can get you in."

"It sounds like a good idea," Ilya Simonov said. He was completely sober now.

He made a written report to Kliment Blagonravov before turning in. He mentioned the rather free discussion of matters political in the Czech capital, using the man he'd met in the beer hall as an example. He reported-although, undoubtedly, Blagonravov would already have the information-hearing of a Polish Tri-D film which had defended the Old Bolsheviks purged in the 1930s. He mentioned the literary magazine, with its caricature of Frol Zverev, and, last of all, and then after hesitation, he reported party member Catherina Panova, who evidently belonged to a group of intellectuals who were not above listening to a talk given by a foreign journalist who was not speaking under the auspices of the Czech Party nor the government.

At the office, later, Catherina grinned at him and made a face. She ticked it off on her fingers. "Riesling, barack, smoked black beer, and borovika gin-we should have know better."

He went along with her, putting one hand to his forehead. "We should have stuck to vodka."

"Well," she said, "tonight we can be virtuous. An intellectual evening, rather than a carouse."

Actually, she didn't look at all the worse for wear. Evidently, Catherina Panova was still young enough that she could pub crawl all night, and still look fresh and alert in the morning. His own mouth felt lined with improperly tanned suede.

He was quickly fitting into the routine of the office. Actually, it worked smoothly enough that little effort was demanded of him. The Czech employees handled almost all the details.

Evidently, the word of his evening on the town had somehow spread, and the fact that he was prone to a good time had relieved their fears of a martinet sent down from the central offices. They were beginning to relax in his presence.

In fact, they relaxed to the point where one of the girls didn't even bother to hide the book she was reading during a period where there was a lull in activity. It was Pasternak's "Doctor Zhivago."

He frowned remembering vaguely the controversy over the book a couple of decades earlier. Ilya Simonov said, "Pasternak. Do they print his works here in Czechoslovakia?"

The girl shrugged and looked at the back of the cover. "German publisher," she said idly. "Printed in Frankfurt."

He kept his voice from registering either surprise or disapproval. "You mean such books are imported? By whom?"

"Oh, not imported by an official agency, but we Czechs are doing a good deal more travel than we used to. Business trips, tourist trips, vacations. And, of course, we bring back books you can't get here." She shrugged again. "Very common."

Simonov said blankly. "But the customs. The border police —"

She smiled in a manner that suggested he lacked sophistication. "They never bother any more. They're human, too."

Ilya Simonov wandered off. He was astonished at the extent to which controls were slipping in a satellite country. There seemed practically no discipline, in the old sense, at all. He began to see one reason why his superior had sent him here to Prague. For years, most of his work had been either in Moscow or in the newly opened industrial areas in Siberia. He had lost touch with developments in this part of the Soviet Complex.

It came to him that this sort of thing could work like a geometric progression. Give a man a bit of rope one day, and he expects, and takes, twice as much the next, and twice that the next. And as with individuals, so with whole populations.

This was going to have to be stopped soon, or Party control would disappear. Ilya Simonov felt an edge of uncertainty. Nikita Khrushchev should never have made those first motions of liberalization following Stalin's death. Not if they eventually culminated in this sort of thing.

He and Catherina drove to her meeting place that evening after dinner.

She explained as they went that the group was quite informal, usually meeting at the homes of group members who had fairly large places in the country. She didn't seem to know how it had originally begun. The meetings had been going on for a year of more before she arrived in Prague. A Czech friend had taken her along one night, and she'd been attending ever since. There were other, similar groups, in town.

"But what's the purpose of the organization?" Simonov asked her.

She was driving her little aircushion Moskvich. They crossed over the Vltava River by the Cechuv Bridge and turned right. On the hill above them loomed the fantastically large statue of Stalin which had been raised immediately following the Second War. She grimaced at it, muttered, "I wonder if he was insane from the first."

He hadn't understood her change of subject. "How do you mean?" he said.

"Stalin. I wonder how early it was in his career that he went insane."

This was the second time in the past few days that Ilya Simonov had run into this matter of the former dictator's mental condition. He said now, "I've heard the opinion before. Where did you pick it up?"

"Oh, it's quite commonly believed in the Western countries."

"But, have you ever been, ah, West?"

"Oh, from time to time! Berlin, Vienna, Geneva. Even Paris twice, on vacation, you know, and to various conferences. But that's not what I mean. In the western magazines and newspapers. You can get them here in Prague now. But to get back to your question. There is no particular purpose of the organization."

She turned the car left on Budenská and sped up into the Holesovice section of town.

The nonchalance of it all was what stopped Ilya Simonov. Here was a Party member calmly discussing whether or not the greatest Russian of them all, after Lenin, had been mad. The implications were, of course, that many of the purges, certainly the latter ones, were the result of the whims of a mental case, that the Soviet Complex had for long years been ruled by a man as unbalanced as Czar Peter the Great.

They pulled up before a rather large house that would have been called a dacha back in Moscow. Evidently, Ilya Simonov decided, whoever was sponsoring this night's get together, was a man of prominence. He grimaced inwardly. A lot of high placed heads were going to roll before he was through.

It turned out that the host was Leos Dvorak, the internationally famed cinema director and quite an idol of Ilya Simonov in his earlier days when he'd found more time for entertainment. It was a shock to meet the man under these circumstances.

Catherina Panova was obviously quite popular among this gathering. Their host gave her an affectionate squeeze in way of greeting, then shook hands with Simonov when Catherina introduced him.

"Newly from Moscow, eh?" the film director said, squinting at the security agent. He had a sharp glance, almost, it seemed to Simonov, as though he detected the real nature of the newcomer. "It's been several years since I've been to Moscow. Are things loosening up there?"

"Loosening up?" Simonov said.

Leos Dvorak laughed and said to Catherina, "Probably not. I've always been of the opinion that the Party's influence would shrivel away first at its extremities. Membership would fall off abroad, in the neutral countries and in Common Europe and the Americas. Then in the so-called satellite countries. Last of all in Russia herself. But, very last, Moscow-the dullest, stodgiest, most backward intellectually, capital city in the world." The director laughed again and turned away to greet a new guest.

This was open treason. Ilya Simonov had been lucky. Within the first few days of being in the Czech capital he'd contacted one of the groups which he'd been sent to unmask.

Now he said mildly to Catherina Panova, "He seems rather outspoken."

She chuckled. "Leos is quite strongly opinionated. His theory is that the more successful the Party is in attaining the goals it set half a century ago, the less necessary it becomes. He's of the opinion that it will eventually atrophy, shrivel away to the point that all that will be needed will be the slightest of pushes to end its domination."

Ilya Simonov said, "And the rest of the group here, do they agree?"

Catherina shrugged. "Some do, some don't. Some of them are of the opinion that it will take another blood bath. That the party will attempt to hang onto its power and will have to be destroyed."

Simonov said evenly, "And you? What do you think?"

She frowned, prettily. "I'm not sure. I suppose I'm still in the process of forming an opinion."

Their host was calling them together and leading the way to the garden where chairs had been set up. There seemed to be about twenty-five persons present in all. Ilya Simonov had been introduced to no more than half of them. His memory was good and already he was composing a report to Kliment Blagonravov, listing those names he recalled. Some were Czechs, some citizens of other satellite countries, several, including Catherina, were actually Russians.

The American, a newspaperman named Dickson, had an open-faced freshness, hardly plausible in an agent from the West trying to subvert Party leadership. Ilya Simonov couldn't quite figure him out.

Dickson was introduced by Leos Dvorak who informed his guests that the American had been reluctant but had finally agreed to give them his opinion on the press on both sides of what had once been called the Iron Curtain.

Dickson grinned boyishly and said, "I'm not a public speaker, and, for that matter, I haven't had time to put together a talk for you. I think what I'll do is read a little clipping I've got here-sort of a text-and then, well, throw the meeting open to questions. I'll try to answer anything you have to ask."

He brought forth a piece of paper. "This is from the British writer, Huxley. I think it's pretty good." He cleared his voice and began to read.

Mass communication ... is simply a force and like any other force, it can be used either well or ill. Used one way, the press, the radio and the cinema are indispensible to the survival of democracy. Used in another way, they are among the most powerful weapons in the dictator's armory. In the field of mass communications as in almost every other field of enterprise, technological progress has hurt the Little Man and helped the Big Man. As lately as fifty years ago, every democratic country could boast of a great number of small journals and local newspapers. Thousands of country editors expressed thousands of independent opinions. Somewhere or other almost anybody could get almost anything printed. Today the press is still legally free; but most of the little papers have disappeared. The cost of wood pulp, of modern printing machinery and of syndicated news is too high for the Little Man. In the totalitarian East there is political censorship, and the media of mass communications are controlled by the State. In the democratic West there is economic censorship and the media of mass communication are controlled by members of the Power Elite. Censorship by rising costs and the concentration of communication-power in the hands of a few big concerns is less objectionable than State Ownership and government propaganda; but certainly it is not something to which a Jeffersonian democrat could approve.

Ilya Simonov looked blankly at Catherina and whispered, "Why, what he's reading is as much an attack on the West as it is on us."

She looked at him and whispered back, "Well, why not? This gathering is to discuss freedom of the press."

He said blankly, "But as an agent of the West —"

She frowned at him. "Mr. Dickson isn't an agent of the West. He's an American journalist."

"Surely you can't believe he has no connections with the imperialist governments."

"Certainly, he hasn't. What sort of meeting do you think this is? We're not interested in Western propaganda. We're a group of intellectuals searching for freedom of ideas."

Ilya Simonov was taken back once again.

Colonel Ilya Simonov dismissed his cab in front of the Ministry and walked toward the gate. Down the street the same plainclothes man, who had been lounging there the last time he'd reported, once again took him in, then looked away. The two guards snapped to attention, and the security agent strode by them unnoticing.

At the lieutenant's desk, before the offices of Kliment Blagonravov, he stopped and said, "Colonel Simonov. I have no appointment but I think the Minister will see me."

"Yes, Comrade Colonel," the lieutenant said. He spoke into an inter-office communicator, then looked up. "Minister Blagonravov will be able to see you in a few minutes, sir."

Ilya Simonov stared nervously and unseeingly out a window while he waited. Gorki Park lay across the way. It, like Moscow in general, had changed a good deal in Simonov's memory. Everything in Russia had changed a good deal, he realized. And was changing. And what was the end to be? Or was there ever an end? Of course not. There is no end, ever. Only new changes to come.

The lieutenant said, "The Minister is free now, Comrade Colonel."

Ilya Simonov muttered something to him and pushed his way through the heavy door.

Blagonravov looked up from his desk and rumbled affectionately, "Ilya! It's good to see you. Have a drink! You've lost weight, Ilya!"

His top field man sank into the same chair he'd occupied nine months before, and accepted the ice-cold vodka.

Blagonravov poured another drink for himself, then scowled at the other. "Where have you been? When you first went off to Prague, I got reports from you almost every day. These last few months I've hardly heard from you." He rumbled his version of a chuckle. "If I didn't know you better, I'd think there was a woman."

Ilya Simonov looked at him wanly. "That too, Kliment."

"You are jesting!"

"No. Not really. I had hoped to become engaged-soon."

"A party member? I never thought of you as the marrying type, Ilya."

Simonov said slowly, "Yes, a Party member. Catherina Panova, my assistant in the automobile agency in Prague."

Blagonravov scowled heavily at him, put forth his fat lips in a thoughtful pout. He came to his feet, approached a file cabinet, fishing from his pocket a key ring. He unlocked the cabinet, brought forth a sheaf of papers with which he returned to his desk. He fumbled though them for a moment, found the paper he wanted and read it. He scowled again and looked up at his agent.

"Your first report," he said. "Catherina Panova. From what you say here, a dangerous reactionary. Certainly she has no place in Party ranks."

Ilya Simonov said, "Is that the complete file of my assignment?"

"Yes. I've kept it here in my own office. I've wanted this to be ultra-undercover. No one except you and me. I had hopes of you working your way up into the enemy's organization, and I wanted no possible chance of you being betrayed. You don't seem to have been too successful."

"I was as successful as it's possible to be."

The security minister leaned forward. "Ah ha! I knew I could trust you to bring back results, Ilya. This will take Frol Zverev's pressure off me. Number One has been riding me hard." Blagonravov poured them both another drink. "You were able to insert yourself into their higher circles?"

Simonov said, "Kliment, there are no higher circles."

His chief glared at him. "Nonsense!" He tapped the file with a pudgy finger. "In your early reports you described several groups, small organizations, illegal meetings. There must be an upper organization, some movement supported from the West most likely."

Ilya Simonov was shaking his head. "No. They're all spontaneous."

His chief growled, "I tell you there are literally thousands of these little groups. That hardly sounds like a spontaneous phenomenon."

"Nevertheless, that is what my investigations have led me to believe."

Blagonravov glowered at him, uncertainly. Finally, he said, "Well, confound it, you've spent the better part of a year among them. What's it all about? What do they want?"

Ilya Simonov said flatly, "They want freedom, Kliment."

"Freedom! What do you mean, freedom? The Soviet Complex is the most highly industrialized area of the world. Our people have the highest standard of living anywhere. Don't they understand? We've met all the promises we ever made. We've reached far and beyond the point ever dreamed of by Utopians. The people, all of the people, have it made as the Americans say."

"Except for freedom," Simonov said doggedly. "These groups are springing up everywhere, spontaneously. Thus far, perhaps, our ministry has been able to suppress some of them. But the pace is accelerating. They aren't inter-organized now. But how soon they'll start to be, I don't know. Sooner or later, someone is going to come up with a unifying idea. A new socio-political system to advocate a way of guaranteeing the basic liberties. Then, of course, the fat will be in the fire."

"Ilya! You've been working too hard. I've pushed you too much, relied on you too much. You need a good lengthy vacation."

Simonov shrugged. "Perhaps. But what I've just said is the truth."

His chief snorted heavily. "You half sound as though you agree with them."

"I do, Kliment."

"I am in no mood for gags, as the Yankees say."

Ilya Simonov looked at him wearily. He said slowly, "You sent me to investigate an epidemic, a spreading disease. Very well, I report that it's highly contagious."

Blagonravov poured himself more vodka angrily. "Explain yourself. What's this all about?"

His former best field man said, "Kliment —"

"I want no familiarities from you, colonel!"

"Yes, sir." Ilya Simonov went on doggedly. "Man never achieves complete freedom. It's a goal never reached, but one continually striven for. The moment as small a group as two or three gather together, all of them must give up some of the individual's freedom. When man associates with millions of his fellow men, he gives up a good many freedoms for the sake of the community. But always he works to retain as much liberty as possible, and to gain more. It's the nature of our species, I suppose."

"You sound as though you've become corrupted by Western ideas," the security head muttered dangerously.

Simonov shook his head. "No. The same thing applies over there. Even in countries such as Sweden and Switzerland, where institutions are as free as anywhere in the world, the people are continually striving for more. Governments and socio-economic systems seem continually to whittle away at individual liberty. But always man fights back and tries to achieve new heights for himself.

"In the name of developing our country, the Party all but eliminated freedom in the Soviet Complex, but now the goals have been reached and the people will no longer put up with us, sir."

"Us!" Kliment Blagonravov growled bitterly. "You are hardly to be considered in the Party's ranks any longer, Simonov. Why in the world did you ever return here?" He sneered fatly. "Your best bet would have been to escape over the border into the West."

Simonov looked at the file on the other's desk. "I wanted to regain those reports I made in the early days of my assignment. I've listed in them some fifty names, names of men and women who are now my friends."

The fat lips worked in and out. "It must be that woman. You've become soft in the head, Simonov." Blagonravov tapped the file beneath his heavy fingers. "Never fear, before the week is out these fifty persons will be either in prison or in their graves."

With a fluid motion, Ilya Simonov produced a small caliber gun, a special model designed for security agents. An unusual snout proclaimed its quiet virtues as guns go.

"No, Kliment," Ilya Simonov said.

"Are you mad!"

"No, Kliment, but I must have those reports." Ilya Simonov came to his feet and reached for them.

With a roar of rage, Kliment Blagonravov slammed open a drawer and dove a beefy paw into it. With shocking speed for so heavy a man, he scooped up a heavy military revolver.

And Colonel Ilya Simonov shot him neatly and accurately in the head. The silenced gun made no more sound than a pop.

Blagonravov, his dying eyes registering unbelieving shock, fell back into his heavy swivel chair.

Simonov worked quickly. He gathered up his reports, checked quickly to see they were all there. Struck a match, lit one of the reports and dropped it into the large ashtray on the desk. One by one he lit them all and when all were consumed, stirred the ashes until they were completely pulverized.

He poured himself another vodka, downed it, stiff wristed, then without turning to look at the dead man again, made his way to the door.

He slipped out and said to the lieutenant, "The Minister says that he is under no circumstances to be disturbed for the next hour."

The lieutenant frowned at him. "But he has an appointment."

Colonel Ilya Simonov shrugged. "Those were his instructions. Not to be bothered under any circumstances."

"But it was an appointment with Number One!"

That was bad. And unforeseen. Ilya Simonov said, "It's probably been canceled. All I'm saying is that Minister Blagonravov instructs you not to bother him under any circumstances for the next hour."

He left the other and strode down the corridor, keeping himself from too obvious, a quickened pace.

At the entrance to the Ministry, he shot his glance up and down the street. He was in the clutch now, and knew it. He had few illusions.

Not a cab in sight. He began to cross the road toward the park. In a matter of moments there, he'd be lost in the trees and shrubbery. He had rather vague plans. Actually, he was playing things as they came. There was a close friend in whose apartment he could hide, a man who owed him his life. He could disguise himself. Possibly buy or borrow a car. If he could get back to Prague, he was safe. Perhaps he and Catherina could defect to the West.

Somebody was screaming something from a window in the Ministry.

Ilya Simonov quickened his pace. He was nearly across the street now. He thought, foolishly, *Whoever that is shouting is so excited he sounds more like a woman than a man.*

Another voice took up the shout. It was the plainclothes man. Feet began pounding.

There were two more shouts. The guards. But he was across now. The shrubs were only a foot away.

The shattering blackness hit him in the back of the head. It was over immediately.

Afterwards, the plainclothes man and the two guards stood over him. Men began pouring from the Ministry in their direction.

Colonel Ilya Simonov was a meaningless, bloody heap on the edge of the park's grass.

The guard who had shot said, "He killed the Minister. He must have been crazy to think he could get away with it. What did he want?"

"Well, we'll never know now," the plainclothesman grunted.

Farmer

One of the auto-copters swooped in and landed. Johnny McCord emptied his pipe into the wastebasket, came to his feet and strolled toward the open door. He automatically took up a sun helmet before emerging into the Saharan sun.

He was dressed in khaki shorts and short-sleeved shirt, wool socks and yellow Moroccan babouche slippers.

The slippers were strictly out of uniform and would have been frowned upon by Johnny's immediate superiors. However, the Arabs had been making footwear suitable for sandy terrain for centuries before there had ever been a Sahara Reforestation Commission. Johnny was in favor of taking advantage of their know-how. Especially since the top brass made a point of staying in the swank air-conditioned buildings of Colomb-Bechar, Tamanrasset and Timbuktu, from whence they issued lengthy bulletins on the necessity of never allowing a Malian to see a Commission employee in less than the correct dress and in less than commanding dignity. While they were busily at work composing such directives, field men such as Johnny McCord went about the Commission's real tasks.

It was auto-copter 4, which Johnny hadn't expected for another half hour. He extracted the reports and then peered into the cockpit to check. There were two red lights flickering on the panel. Work for Reuben. This damned sand was a perpetual hazard to equipment. Number 4 had just had an overhaul a few weeks before and here it was throwing red lights already.

He took the reports back into the office and dumped them into the card-punch. While they were being set up, Johnny went over to the office refrigerator and got out a can of Tuborg beer. Theoretically, it was as taboo to drink iced beer in this climate, and particularly at this time of day, as it was to go out into the sun without a hat. But this was one place where the Commission's medics could go blow.

By the time he'd finished the Danish brew, the card-punch had stopped clattering so he took the cards from the hopper and crossed to the sorter. He gave them a quick joggling-cards held up well in this dry climate, though they were a terror further south-and sorted them through four code numbers, enough for this small an amount. He carried them over to the collator and merged them into the proper file.

He was still running off a report on the Alphabetyper when Derek Mason came in.

Johnny drawled in a horrible caricature of a New England accent, "I say, Si, did the cyclone hurt your barn any?"

Derek's voice took on the same twang. "Don't know, Hiram, we ain't found it yet."

Johnny said, "You get all your chores done, Si?"

Derek dropped the pseudo-twang and his voice expressed disgust. "I got a chore for you Johnny, that you're going to love. Rounding up some livestock."

Johnny looked up from the report he was running off and shot an impatient glance at him. "Livestock? What the hell are you talking about?"

"Goats."

Johnny McCord flicked the stop button on the Alphabetyper. "Where've you been? There isn't a goat within five hundred miles of here."

Derek went over to the refrigerator for beer. He said over his shoulder, "I was just making a routine patrol over toward Amérene El Kasbach. I'd estimate there were a hundred Tuareg in camp there. Camels, a few sheep, a few horses and donkeys. Mostly goats. Thousands of them. By the looks of the transplants, they've been there possibly a week or so."

* * * * *

Johnny said in agony, "Oh, Lord. What clan were they?"

Derek punched a hole in his beer can with the opener that hung from the refrigerator by a string. "I didn't go low enough to check. You can never tell with a Tuareg. They can't resist as beautiful a target as a helicopter, and one of these days one of them is going to make a hole in me, instead of in the fuselage or rotors."

Johnny McCord, furious, plunked himself down before the telephone and dialed Tessalit, 275 kilometers to the south. The girl on the desk there grinned at him and said, "Hello, Johnny."

Johnny McCord was in no mood for pleasantries. He snapped, "Who's supposed to be on Bedouin patrol down there?"

She blinked at him. "Why, Mohammed is in command of patrolling this area, Mr. McCord."

"Mohammed? Mohammed who? Eighty percent of these Malians are named Mohammed."

"Captain Mohammed Mohmoud ould Cheikh." She added, unnecessarily, "The Cadi's son."

Johnny grunted. He'd always suspected that the captain had got his ideas of what a cadi's son should be like from seeing Hollywood movies. "Look, Kate," he said. "Let me talk to Mellor, will you?"

Her face faded to be replaced by that of a highly tanned, middle-aged executive type. He scowled at Johnny McCord with a this-better-be-important expression, not helping Johnny's disposition.

He snapped, "Somebody's let several thousand goats into my eucalyptus transplants in my western four hundred."

Mellor was taken aback.

Johnny said, "I can have Derek back-trail them, if you want to be sure, but it's almost positive they came from the south, this time of year."

Mellor sputtered, "They might have come from the direction of Timmissao. Who are they, anyway?"

"I don't know. Tuareg. I thought we'd supposedly settled with all the Tuareg. Good Lord, man, do you know how many transplants a thousand goats can go through in a week's time?"

"A week's time!" Mellor rasped. "You mean you've taken a whole week to detect them?"

Johnny McCord glared at him. "A *whole* week! We're lucky they didn't spend the whole *season* before we found them. How big a staff do you think we have here, Mellor? There's just three of us. Only one can be spared for patrol."

"You have natives," the older man growled.

"They can't fly helicopters. Most of them can't even drive a Land Rover or a jeep. Besides that, they're scared to death of Tuaregs. They wouldn't dare report them. What I want to know is, why didn't you stop them coming through?"

Mellor was on the defensive. He ranked Johnny McCord, but that was beside the point right now. He said finally, "I'll check this all the way through, McCord. Meanwhile, I'll send young Mohammed Mohmoud up with a group of his men."

"To do what?" Johnny demanded.

"To shoot the goats, what else?"

* * * * *

Johnny growled, "One of these days a bunch of these Tuareg are going to decide that a lynching bee is in order, and that's going to be the end of this little base at Bidon Cinq."

Mellor said, "If they're Tuareg nomads then they have no legal right to be within several hundred miles of Bidon Cinq. And if they've got goats, they shouldn't have. The Commission has bought up every goat in this part of the world."

Johnny growled, "Sure, bought them up and then left it to the honor of the Tuareg to destroy them. The honor of the Tuareg! Ha!"

The other said pompously, "Are you criticizing the upper echelons, McCord?"

Johnny McCord snapped, "You're damned right I am." He slammed off the telephone and turned on Derek Mason. "What are you grinning about?"

Derek drawled, "I say, Hiram, I got a sneaky suspicion you ain't never gonna graduate off'n this here farm if you don't learn how to cotton up to the city slickers better."

"Oh, shut up," Johnny growled. "Let's have another beer."

Before Derek could bring it to him, the telephone screen lit up again and Paul Peterson, of the Poste Weygand base, was there. He said, "Hi. You guys look like you're having a crisis."

"Hello, Paul," Johnny McCord said. "Crisis is right. Those jerks down south let a clan of Tuareg, complete with a few thousand goats, camels and sheep through. They've been grazing a week or more in my west four hundred."

"Good grief." Paul grimaced. "At least that's one thing we don't have to worry about. They never get this far up. How'd it happen?"

"I don't know, but I'm going to find out. I haven't seen the mess yet, but it's certain to wreck that whole four hundred. Have you ever seen just one goat at work on the bark of three-year transplants?"

Paul shuddered sympathetically. "Look, Johnny," he said. "The reason I called you. There's an air-cushion Land Rover coming through. She just left."

Derek Mason looked over Johnny's shoulder into the screen. "What d'ya mean, *she*?"

Paul grinned. "Just that, and, Buster, she's stacked. A Mademoiselle Hélène Desage of *Paris Match*."

Johnny said, "The French magazine? What's she doing in a road car? Why doesn't she have an aircraft? There hasn't been a road car through here this whole year."

Paul shrugged. "She claims she's getting it from the viewpoint of how things must've been twenty years ago. So, anyway, we've notified you. If she doesn't turn up in eight or ten hours, you better send somebody to look for her."

"Yeah," Johnny McCord said. "Well, so long, Paul."

The other's face faded from the screen and Johnny McCord turned to his colleague. "One more extraneous something to foul up our schedule."

Derek said mildly, "I say, Hiram, what're you complaining about? Didn't you hear tell what Paul just said? She's stacked. Be just like a traveling saleswoman visitin' the farm."

"Yeah," Johnny growled. "And I can see just how much work I'll be getting out of you as long as she's here."

II

Poste Maurice Cortier, better known in the Sahara as Bidon Cinq, is as remote a spot on earth in which man has ever lived. Some 750 kilometers to the south is Bourem on the Niger river. If you go west of Bourem another 363 kilometers, you reach Timbuktu, the nearest thing to a city in that part of the Sudan. If you travel north from Bidon Cinq 1,229 kilometers you reach Colomb-Béchar, the nearest thing to a city in southern Algeria. There are no railroads, no highways. The track through the desert is marked by oil drums filled with gravel so the wind won't blow them away. There is an oil drum every quarter of a mile or so. You go from one to the next, carrying your own fuel and water. If you get lost, the authorities come looking for you in aircraft. Sometimes they find you.

In the latter decades of the Twentieth Century, Bidon Cinq became an outpost of the Sahara Reforestation Commission which was working north from the Niger, and south from Algeria as well as east from the Atlantic. The water table in the vicinity of Bidon Cinq was considerably higher than had once been thought. Even artesian wells were possible in some localities. More practical still were springs and wells exploited by the new solar-powered pumps that in their tens of thousands were driving back the sands of the world's largest desert.

Johnny McCord and Derek Mason ate in the officer's mess, divorced from the forty or fifty Arabs and Songhai who composed their work force. It wasn't snobbery, simply a matter of being able to eat in leisure and discuss the day's activities free of the chatter of the larger mess hall.

Derek looked down into his plate. "Hiram," he drawled, "who ever invented this here *cous cous?*"

Johnny looked over at the tall, easy-going Canadian who was his second in command and scowled dourly. He was in no humor for their usual banter. "What's the matter with *cous cous?*" Johnny growled.

"I don't know," Derek said. "I'm a meat and potatoes man at heart."

Johnny shrugged. "*Cous cous* serves the same purpose as potatoes do. Or rice, or spaghetti, or bread, or any of the other bland basic foods. It's what you put on it that counts."

Derek stared gloomily into his dish. "Well, I wish they'd get something more interesting than ten-year-old mutton to put on this."

Johnny said, "Where in the devil is Pierre? It's nearly dark."

"Reuben?" Derek drawled. "Why Reuben went out to check the crops up in the northeast forty. Took the horse and buggy."

That didn't help Johnny's irritation. "He took an air-cushion jeep, instead of a copter? Why, for heaven's sake?"

"He wanted to check quite a few of the pumps. Said landing and taking off was more trouble than the extra speed helped. He'll be back shortly."

"He's back now," a voice from the door said.

Pierre Marimbert, brushing sand from his clothes, pushed into the room and made his way to the mess-hall refrigerator. He said nothing further until he had a can of beer open.

Johnny said, "Damn it, Pierre, you shouldn't stay out this late in a jeep. If you got stuck out there, we'd have one hell of a time finding you. In a copter you've at least got the radio."

Pierre had washed the dust from his throat. Now he said quietly, "I wanted to check on as many pumps as I could."

"You could have gone back tomorrow. The things are supposed to be self-sufficient, no checking necessary more than once every three months. There's practically nothing that can go wrong with them."

Pierre finished off the can of beer, reached into the refrigerator for another. "Dynamite can go wrong with them," he said.

* * * * *

The other two looked at him, shocked silent.

Pierre said, "I don't know how many altogether. I found twenty-two of the pumps in the vicinity of In Ziza had been blown to smithereens-out of forty I checked."

Johnny rapped, "How long ago? How many trees...?"

Pierre laughed sourly. "I don't know how long ago. The transplants, especially the slash pine, are going to be just so much kindling before I get new pumps in."

Derek said, shocked, "That's our oldest stand."

Pierre Marimbert, a forty-year-old, sun-beaten Algerian *colon*, eldest man on the team, sank into his place at the table. He poured the balance of his can of beer into a glass.

Johnny said, "What ... what can we do? How many spare pumps can you get into there, and how soon?"

Pierre looked up at him wearily. "You didn't quite hear what I said, Johnny. I only checked forty. Forty out of nearly a thousand in that vicinity. Twenty-two of them were destroyed, better than fifty percent. For all I know, that percentage applies throughout the whole In Ziza area. If so, there's damn few of your trees going to be left alive. We have a few spare pumps on hand here, but we'd have to get a really large number all the way from Dakar."

Derek said softly, "That took a lot of men and a lot of dynamite. Which means a lot of transport-and a lot of money. We've had trouble before, but usually it was disgruntled nomads, getting revenge for losing their grazing land."

Johnny snorted, "Damn little grazing this far north."

Derek nodded. "I'm simply saying that even if we could blame our minor sabotage on the Tuareg in the past, we can't do it this time. There's money behind anything this big."

Johnny McCord said wearily, "Let's eat. In the morning we'll go out and take a look. I'd better call Timbuktu on this. If nothing else, the Mali Federation can send troops out to protect us."

Derek grunted. "With a standing army of about 25,000 men, they're going to patrol a million and a half square miles of desert?"

"Can you think of anything else to do?"

"No."

* * * * *

Pierre Marimbert began dishing *cous cous* into a soup plate, then poured himself a glass of *vin ordinaire*. He said, "I can't think of a better place for saboteurs. Twenty men could do millions of dollars of destruction and never be found."

Johnny growled, "It's not as bad as all that. They've got to eat and drink, and so do their animals. There are damned few places where they can."

From the door a voice said, "I am intruding?"

They hadn't heard her car come up. The three men scrambled to their feet.

"Good evening," Johnny McCord blurted.

"Hell ... o!" Derek breathed.

Pierre Marimbert was across the room, taking her in hand. *"Bonjour, Mademoiselle. Que puis-je faire pour vous? Voulez-vous une biere bien fraiche ou un apéritif? Il fait trés chaud dans le desert."* He led her toward the table.

"Easy, easy there, Reuben," Derek grumbled. "The young lady speaks English. Give a man a chance."

Johnny was placing a chair for her. "Paul Peterson, from Poste Weygand, radioed that you were coming. You're a little late, Mademoiselle Desage."

She was perhaps thirty, slim, long-legged, Parisian style. Even at Bidon Cinq, half a world away from the Champs Elysées, she maintained her chic.

She made a moue at Johnny, while taking the chair he held. "I had hoped to surprise you, catch you off guard." She took in the sun-dried, dour-faced American wood technologist appraisingly, then turned her eyes in turn to Derek and Pierre.

"You three are out here all alone?" she said demurely.

"Desperately," Derek said.

Johnny McCord said, "Mademoiselle Hélène Desage, I am John McCord, and these are my associates, Monsieur Pierre Marimbert and Mr. Derek Mason. Gentlemen, Mademoiselle Desage is with *Paris Match*, the French equivalent of *Life*, so I understand. In short, she is undoubtedly here for a story. So ixnay on the ump-pays."

"I would love cold beer," Hélène Desage said to Pierre, and to Johnny McCord, "These days a traveling reporter for *Paris Match* must be quite a linguist. My English, Spanish and Italian are excellent. My German passable. And while I am not fluent in Pig-Latin, I can follow it. What is this you are saying about the pumps?"

"Oh, Lord," Johnny said. "Perhaps I'll tell you in the morning. But for now, would you like to clean up before supper? You must be exhausted after that 260 kilometers from Poste Weygand."

Pierre said hurriedly, "I'll take Mademoiselle Desage over to one of the guest bungalows."

"Zut!" she said. "The sand! It is even worse than between Reggan and Poste Weygand. Do you realize that until I began coming across your new forests I saw no life at all between these two posts?"

The three forestry experts bowed in unison, as though rehearsed. "Mademoiselle," Derek, from the heart, "calling our transplant forests is the kindest thing you could have said in these parts."

They all laughed and Pierre led her from the room.

Derek looked at Johnny McCord. "Wow, that was a slip mentioning the pumps."

Johnny was looking through the door after her. "I suppose so," he said sourly. "I'll have to radio the brass and find out the line we're supposed to take with her. That's the biggest magazine in the French-speaking world and you don't get a job on it without knowing the journalistic ropes. That girl can probably smell a story as far as a Tuareg can smell water."

"Well, then undoubtedly she's already sniffing. Because, between that clan of Tuareg with its flocks and the pump saboteurs, we've got more stories around here than I ever expected!"

III

In the morning Hélène Desage managed to look the last word in what desert fashion should be, when she strolled into Johnny McCord's office. Although she came complete with a sun helmet that must have been the product of a top Parisian shop, she would have been more at place on the beaches at Miami, Honolulu or Cannes. Her shorts were short and fitting, her blouse silken, her walking shoes dainty.

He considered for a moment and then decided against informing her that Moslems, particularly in this part of the world, were little used to seeing semi-nude women strolling about. He'd leave the job of explanation to Pierre, as a fellow Frenchman and the oldest man present to boot.

"*Bonjour*," she said. "What a lovely day. I have been strolling about your little oasis. But you have made it a garden!"

"Thanks," Johnny said. "We've got to have something to do after working hours. Entertainment is on the scarce side. But it's more than a garden. We've been experimenting to see just what trees will take to this country-given water and care through the early years. Besides, we use it as a showplace."

"Showplace?"

"For skeptical politicians who come through," Johnny said, seating her in a chair near his desk. "We give them the idea that the whole Sahara could eventually be like this square mile or so at Bidon Cinq. Palm trees, fruit trees, pines, shade trees. The works."

"And could it?"

Johnny grinned sourly. "Well, not exactly. Not all in one spot, at least. You've got to remember, the Sahara covers an area of some three and a half million square miles. In that area you find almost everything."

"Everything except water, eh?" She was tapping a cigarette on a polish-reddened thumbnail. As he lit it for her, Johnny McCord realized that he hadn't seen fingernail polish for a year. He decided it was too long.

"Even water, in some parts," he said. "There's more water than most people realize. For instance, the Niger, which runs right through a considerable part of the Sahara, is the eleventh largest river in the world. But until our commission went to work on it, it dumped itself into the Gulf of Guinea, unused."

"The Niger is a long way from here," she said through her smoke.

He nodded. "For that matter, though, we have a certain amount of rain, particularly in the highland regions of the central massif. In the past, with no watershed at all, it ran off, buried itself in the sands, or evaporated."

"Mr. McCord," she said, "you are amazingly optimistic. Formerly, I must admit I had little knowledge of the Sahara Reforestation Commission. And I deliberately avoided studying up on the subject after receiving this assignment, because I wanted first impression to be received on the spot. However, I've just driven across the Sahara. My impression is that your Commission is one great —*Comment dit-on?* —boon-doggling project, a super-W.P.A. into which to plow your American resources and manpower. It is a fake, a delusion. This part of the world has never been anything but wasteland, and never will be."

Johnny McCord heard her out without change in expression.

He'd been through this before. In fact, almost every time a junketing congressman came through. There was danger in the viewpoint, of course. If the fantastic sums of money which were being spent were cut off, such pessimistic views would become automatically correct.

He took the paperweight from a stack of the correspondence on his desk and handed it to her.

She looked at it and scowled-very prettily, but still a scowl. "What is this? It's a beautiful piece of stone."

"I picked it up myself," Johnny said. "Near Reggan. It's a chunk of petrified wood, Miss Desage. From a tree that must have originally had a diameter of some ten feet. Not quite a redwood, of course, but big."

"Yes," she said, turning it over in her hand. "I can see this part, which must have once been bark. But why do you show it to me?"

"The Sahara was once a semi-tropical, moist area, highly wooded. It can become so again."

* * * * *

She put the piece of fossil back on his desk. "How long ago?" she said bluntly.

"A very long time ago, admittedly. During the last Ice Age and immediately afterwards. But, given man's direction, it can be done again. And it must be."

She raised pencilled eyebrows at him. "Must be?"

Johnny McCord shifted in his chair. "You must be aware of the world's population explosion, Miss Desage. The human race can't allow three and a half million square miles of land to be valueless." He grunted in deprecation. "And at the rate it was going, it would have been four million before long."

She didn't understand.

Johnny spelled it out for her. "A desert can be man-made. Have you ever been in the Middle East?" At her nod, he went on. "Visitors there usually wonder how in the world the ancient Jews could ever have thought of that area as a land of milk and honey. On the face of it, it's nothing but badlands. What was once the Fertile Crescent now looks like Arizona."

Hélène Desage was frowning at him. "And you suggest man did this-not nature?"

"The goat did it. The goat, and the use of charcoal as fuel. Along with ignorance of soil erosion and the destruction of the wonderful watershed based on the Cedars of Lebanon. Same thing applies to large areas of Libya and Tunisia, and to Morocco and Spain. Those countries used to be some of the richest agricultural areas of the Roman Empire. But you can't graze goats, probably the most destructive animal domesticated, and you can't depend on charcoal for fuel, unless you want to create desert."

"Those things happened a long time ago."

Johnny snorted. "When we first began operations, the Sahara was going south at the rate of two miles a year. Goats prefer twigs and bark even to grass. They strip a country."

"Well," the reporter said, shrugging shapely shoulders, "at any rate, the task is one of such magnitude as to be fantastic. Yesterday, I drove for nearly eight hours without seeing even a clump of cactus."

"The route you traveled is comparatively untouched by our efforts, thus far," Johnny nodded agreeably. "However, we're slowly coming down from Algeria, up from the Niger, and, using the new chemical methods of freshening sea water, east from Mauretania."

He came to his feet and pointed out spots on the large wall map. "Our territory, of course, is only this area which once was called French West Africa, plus Algeria. The battle is being fought elsewhere by others. The Egyptians and Sudanese are doing a fairly good job in their country, with Soviet Complex help. The Tunisians are doing a wonderful job with the assistance of Common Europe, especially Italy."

She stood beside him and tried to understand. "What is this area, here, shaded green?"

He said proudly, "That's how far we've got so far, heading north from the Niger. In the past, the desert actually came down to the side of the river in many places. The water was completely wasted. Now we've diverted it and are reforesting anywhere up to three miles a year."

"Three miles a year," she scoffed. "You'll take five centuries."

* * * * *

He shook his head and grinned. "It's a progressive thing. Water is admittedly the big problem. But as our forests grow, they themselves bring up the moisture content of the climate. Down in this area —" he made a sweeping gesture over the map which took in large sections north of the Niger —"we've put in hundreds of millions of slash pine, which is particularly good for sandy soil and fast growing. In ten years you've gone from two-year-old seedlings to a respectable forest."

Johnny pointed out Bidon Cinq on the map. "At the same time we found what amounts to a subterranean sea in this area. Not a real sea, of course, but a water-bearing formation or aquifer, deep down under the surface of the earth-layers of rock and gravel in which large quantities of water are lying. The hydro-geological technicians who surveyed it estimate that it holds reserves of several billion tons of water. Utilizing it, we've put in several hundred square miles of seedlings and transplants of various varieties. Where there are natural oases, of course, we stress a lot of date palm. In rocky areas it's *acacia tortila*. In the mountains we sometimes use varieties of the pinyon-they'll take quite a beating but are a little on the slow-growing side."

She was looking at him from the sides of her eyes. "You're all taken up by this, aren't you Mr. McCord?"

Johnny said, surprise in his voice. "Why, it's my work."

Derek came sauntering in and scaled his sun helmet onto his own desk. "Good morning, Mademoiselle," he said. And to Johnny, "Hiram, that city slicker from Timbuktu just came up with his posse."

Hélène said, "What is this *Si*, *Hiram* and *Reuben* which you call each other?"

Johnny smiled sourly, "In a way, Miss Desage, this is just one great tree farm. And all of us are farmers. So we make jokes about it." He thought for a moment. "Derek, possibly you better take over with Mohammed. I want to get over to In Ziza with Reuben."

"To see about the pumps?" Hélène said innocently.

Johnny frowned but was saved from an answer by the entrance of Mohammed Mohmoud. He was dark as a Saharan becomes dark, his original Berber blood to be seen only in his facial characteristics. He wore the rather flamboyant Mali Federation desert uniform with an air.

When he saw the girl, his eyebrows rose and he made the Moslem salaam with a sweeping flourish.

Johnny said, "Mademoiselle Desage, may I present Captain Mohammed Mohmoud ould Cheikh, of the Mali desert patrol." He added sourly, "The officer in charge of preventing nomads from filtering up from the south into our infant forests."

The Moslem scowled at him. "They could have come from the east, from Timmissao," he said in quite passable English. "Or even from Mauritania." He turned his eyes to Hélène Desage. "*Enchanté, Mademoiselle. Trés heureux de faire ta connaissance.*"

She gave him the full benefit of her eyes. "*Moi aussi, Monsieur.*"

Johnny wasn't through with the Malian officer. "There's a hundred of them," he snapped, "with several thousand head of goats and other livestock. It would have been impossible to push that number across from Mauritania or even from the east, and you know it."

A lighter complexion would have shown a flush. Mohammed Mohmoud's displeasure was limited in expression to a flashing of desert eyes. He said, "Wherever their origin, the task would seem to be immediately to destroy the animals. That is why my men and I are here."

Pierre Marimbert had entered while the conversation was going on. He said, "Johnny, weren't you going over to In Ziza with me?"

Hélène Desage said, the tip of her right forefinger to her chin as she portrayed thought, "I can't decide where to go. To this crisis of the Tuareg, or to the crisis of the pumps-whatever that is."

Johnny said flatly, "Sorry, but you'd just be in the way at either place."

Mohammed Mohmoud was shrugging. "Why not let her come with me? I can guarantee her protection. I have brought fifty men with me, more than a match for a few bedouin."

"Gracious," she said. "Evidently I was unaware of the magnitude of this matter. I absolutely *must* go."

Johnny said, "No."

She looked at him appraisingly. "Mr. McCord," she said, "I am here for a story. Has it occurred to you that preventing a *Paris Match* reporter from seeing your methods of operation is probably a bigger story than anything else I could find here?" She struck a mock pose. "I can see the headlines. *Sahara Reforestation Authorities Prevent Journalists from Observing Operations.*"

"Oh, Good Lord," Johnny growled. "This should happen to me, yet! Go on with Derek and the captain, if you wish."

* * * * *

Pierre Marimbert and Johnny McCord took one of the faster helicopters, Pierre piloting. With French élan he immediately raised the craft a few feet and then like a nervous horse it backed up, wheeled about and dashed forward in full flight.

Spread below them were the several dozen buildings which comprised Bidon Cinq; surrounding the buildings, the acres of palm and pine, eucalyptus and black locust. Quick-growing, dry-climate trees predominated, but there were even such as balsam fir, chestnut and elm. It made an attractive sight from the air.

The reforestation projects based on Bidon Cinq were not all in the immediate vicinity of the home oasis. By air, In Ziza was almost 125 kilometers to the northeast. By far the greater part of the land lying in between was still lacking in vegetation of any sort. The hydro-geological engineers who had originally surveyed the area for water had selected only the best sections for immediate sinking of wells, placement of solar power pumps, and eventually the importation of two-year seedlings and three- and four-year-old transplants. The heavy auto-planters, brought in by air transport, had ground their way across the desert sands in their hundreds, six feet between machines. Stop, dig the hole, set the seedling, splash in water, artfully tamp down the soil, move on another six feet, stop-and begin the operation all over again. Fifty trees an hour, per machine.

In less than two months, the planters had moved on to a new base further north. The mob of scientists, engineers, water and forest technicians, mechanics and laborers melted away, leaving Johnny McCord, his two assistants, his half dozen punch-card machines, his automated equipment and his forty or fifty native workers. It was one of a hundred such centers. It would eventually be one of thousands. The Sahara covered an area almost the size of Europe.

Johnny McCord growled, "Friend Mohammed seems quite taken with our reporter."

Pierre grinned and tried to imitate a New England twang. "Why not, Hiram? She's the first, eh, women folks seen in these parts for many a day." He looked down at the endless stretches of sand dunes, gravel and rock out-croppings. "Mighty dry farm land you've got around here, Hiram."

Johnny McCord grunted. "Derek said the other day it's so dry even the mirages are only mud holes." He pointed with his forefinger. "There's the first of our trees. Now, what pumps did you check?"

Pierre directed the copter lower, skimmed not much higher than the young tree tops. Some of them had already reached an impressive height. But Johnny McCord realized that the time was not too distant when they'd have to replant. Casualties were considerably higher than in forest planting at home. Considerably so. And replanting wasn't nearly so highly automated as the original work. More manpower was required.

"These pumps here seem all right," he said to Pierre.

"A little further north," Pierre said. "I came in over the track there, from the road that comes off the main route to Poste Weygand. Yes, there we are. Look! Completely destroyed."

Johnny swore. The trees that had depended on that particular pump wouldn't last a month, in spite of the fact that they were among the first set in this area.

He said, "Go higher. We should be able to spot the complete damage with glasses. You saw twenty-two, you say?"

"Yes, I don't know how many more there might be."

There were twenty-five destroyed pumps in all. And all of them were practically together.

It was sheer luck that Pierre Marimbert had located them so soon. Had his routine check taken place in some other section of the vast tree development, he would have found nothing untoward.

"This isn't nearly so bad as I had expected," Johnny growled. He was scowling thoughtfully.

"What's the matter?" Pierre said.

"I just don't get it," Johnny said. "Number one, nomads don't carry dynamite, unless it's been deliberately given them. Two, if it was given them by someone with a purpose, why only enough to blow twenty-five pumps? That isn't a drop in the bucket. A few thousand trees are all we'll lose. Three, where did they come from? Where are their tracks? And where have they gone? This job wasn't done so very long ago, probably within a week or two at most."

"How do you know that?"

"Otherwise those trees affected would already be dying. At their age, they couldn't stand the sun long without water."

Pierre said, his face registering disbelief, "Do you think it could be simple vandalism on the part of a small band of Tuareg?"

"Sure, if the pumps had been destroyed by hand. But with explosives? Even if your band of Tuareg did have explosives they wouldn't waste them on a few Sahara Reforestation Commission pumps."

"This whole thing just doesn't make sense," Pierre Marimbert decided.

"Let's land and take a look at one of those pumps," Johnny said. "You know, if you get the whole crew to work on this you might be able to replace them before we lose any of these transplants. It's all according to how long ago they were destroyed."

IV

Back at Bidon Cinq again that afternoon, Johnny McCord was greeted by the native office assistant he'd left in charge while all three of the officers were gone. Mellor, at the Tissalit base, had made several attempts to get in touch with him.

"Mellor!" Pierre grunted. "How do you Americans say it? Stuffed shirt!"

"Yeah," Johnny McCord said, sitting down to the telephone. "But my boss."

While Pierre was fishing two cans of beer from the refrigerator, Johnny dialed Tissalit. Kate's face lit up the screen. Johnny said, "Hi. I understand the old man wants to talk to me."

"That's right," the girl said, and moved a switch. "Just a minute, Johnny."

Her face faded to be replaced by that of Mellor. Johnny noted that as usual the other wore a business suit, complete with white shirt and tie-in the middle of the Sahara!

Mellor was scowling. "Where've you been, McCord?"

"Checking some pumps near In Ziza," Johnny said evenly.

"Leaving no one at all at camp?" the other said.

Johnny said, "There were at least a score of men here, Mr. Mellor."

"No officers. Suppose an emergency came up?"

Johnny felt like saying, *An emergency did come up, two of them in fact. That's why we were all gone at once.* But for some reason he decided against explaining current happenings at Bidon Cinq until he had a clearer picture. He said, "There are only three of us here, Mr. Mellor. We have to stretch our manpower. Derek Mason had to go over to Amérene el Kasbach with Mohammed Mohmoud and his men to clear out those nomads and their livestock."

"What did they find? Where were the Tuareg from?"

"They haven't returned yet." Automatically, Johnny took up his can of beer and took a swallow from it.

Mellor's eyebrows went up. "Drinking this early in the day, McCord?"

Johnny sighed deeply, "Look, Mr. Mellor, Pierre Marimbert and I just returned from several hours in the desert, inspecting pumps. We're dehydrated, so we're drinking cold beer. It tastes wonderful. I doubt if it will lead either of us to a drunkard's grave."

Mellor scowled pompously. He said finally, "See here, McCord-the reason I called-you can be expecting a reporter from one of the French publications —"

"She's here."

"Oh," Mellor said. "I just received notice this morning. Orders are to give her the utmost cooperation. Things are on the touchy side right now. Very touchy."

"How do you mean?" Johnny said.

"There are pressures on the highest levels," Mellor said, managing to put over the impression that these matters were above and beyond such as Johnny McCord but that he, Mellor, was privy to them.

"What pressures?" Johnny said wearily. "If you want me to handle this woman with kid gloves, then I've got to know what I'm protecting her against, or hiding from her, or whatever the hell I'm supposed to do."

Mellor glared at him. "I'm not sure I always appreciate your flippancy, McCord," he said. "However, back home the opposition is in an uproar over our expenditures. Things are very delicate. A handful of votes could sway the continuance of the whole project."

Johnny McCord closed his eyes in pain. This came up every year or so.

Mellor said, "That isn't all. The Russkies are putting up a howl in the Reunited Nations. They claim the West plans to eventually take over all northwest Africa. That this reforestation is just preliminary to make the area worth assimilating."

Johnny chuckled sourly, "Let's face it. They're right."

Mellor was shocked. "Mr. McCord! The West has never admitted to any such scheme."

Johnny sighed. "However, we aren't plowing billions into the Sahara out of kindness of heart. The Mali Federation alone has almost two million square miles in it, and less than twenty million population. Already, there's fewer people than are needed to exploit the new lands we've opened up."

"Well, that brings up another point," Mellor said. "The Southeast Asia Bloc is putting up a howl too. They claim they should be the ones allowed to reclaim this area and that it should go into farmland instead of forest."

"They're putting the cart before the horse," Johnny said. "At this stage of the game, the only land they could use really profitably for farming would be along the Niger. We're going to have to forest this whole area first, and in doing so, change the whole climate. *Then* it'll...."

Mellor interrupted him. "I'm as familiar with the program of the Sahara Reforestation Commission as you are, I am sure, McCord. I need no lecture. See that Miss Desage gets as sympathetic a picture of our work as possible. And, for heaven's sake, don't let anything happen that might influence her toward writing something that would change opinions either at home or in the Reunited Nations."

"I'll do my best," Johnny said sourly.

The other clicked off.

* * * * *

Pierre was handy with another can of beer, already opened. "So Mademoiselle Desage is to be handled with loving care."

Johnny groaned, "And from what we've seen so far of Mademoiselle Desage, she's going to take quite a bit of loving care to handle."

Outside, they could hear the beating of rotors coming in. Two helicopters, from the sound of it. Beer cans in hand they went over to the window and watched them approach.

"Derek and the girl in one, Mohammed in the other," Pierre said. "Evidently our good captain left the messy work of butchering goats to his men, while he remains on the scene to be as available to our girl Hélène as she will allow."

The copters swooped in, landed, the rotors came to a halt and the occupants stepped from the cockpits. The Arab ground crew came running up to take over.

Preceded by Hélène Desage, the two men made their way toward the main office. Even at this distance there seemed to be an aggressive lift to the girl's walk.

"Oh, oh, my friend," Pierre said. "I am afraid Mademoiselle Desage is unhappy about something."

Johnny groaned. "I think you're right. But smile, Reuben, smile. You heard the city slicker's orders. Handle her with all the care of a new-born heifer."

Hélène Desage stormed through the door and glared at Johnny McCord. "Do you realize what your men are doing?"

"I thought I did," Johnny said placatingly.

Derek and Mohammed Mohmoud entered behind her. Derek winked at Johnny McCord and made a beeline for the refrigerator. "Beer, everybody?" he said.

Mohammed Mohmoud said, "A soft drink for me, if you please, Mr. Mason."

Derek said, "Sorry, I forgot. Beer, Miss Desage?"

She turned and glared at him. "You did nothing whatsoever to prevent them!"

Derek shrugged. "That's why we went out there, honey. Did you notice how much damage those goats had done to the trees? Thousands of dollars worth."

Johnny said wearily, "What happened?" He sank into the chair behind his desk.

The reporter turned to him again. "Your men are shooting the livestock of those poverty-stricken people."

Mohammed Mohmoud said, "We are keeping an accurate count of every beast destroyed, Mr. McCord." His dark face was expressionless.

Johnny McCord attempted to explain to the girl. "As I told you, Miss Desage, goats are the curse of the desert. They prefer leaves, twigs and even the bark of young trees to grass.

The Commission before ever taking on this tremendous project arranged through the Mali Federation government to buy up and have destroyed every grazing animal north of the Niger. It cost millions upon millions. But our work couldn't even begin until it was accomplished."

"But why slaughter the livelihood of those poor people? You could quite easily insist that they return with their flocks to whatever areas are still available to them."

Derek offered her a can of beer. She seemed to be going to reject it, but a desert-born thirst changed her mind. She took it without thanking him.

The lanky Canadian said mildly, "I tried to explain to her that the Tuareg aren't exactly innocent children of the desert. They're known as the Apaches of the Sahara. For a couple of thousand years they've terrified the other nomads. They were slave raiders, bandits. When the Commission started its work the other tribes were glad to sell their animals and take up jobs in the new oases. Send their kids to the new schools we've been building in the towns. Begin fitting into the reality of modern life."

Her eyes were flashing now. "The Apaches of the Sahara, eh? *Bien sur!* If I remember correctly, the American Apaches were the last of the Indian tribes which you Americans destroyed. The last to resist. Now you export your methods to Africa!"

Johnny McCord said mildly, "Miss Desage, it seems to be the thing these days to bleed over the fate of the redman. Actually, there are a greater number of them in the United States today than there were when Columbus landed. But even if you do carry a torch for the noble Indian, picking the Apaches as an example is poor choice. They were bandit tribes, largely living off what they could steal and raid from the Pueblo and other harder working but less warlike Indians. The Tuareg are the North African equivalent."

"Who are you to judge?" she snapped back. "Those tribesmen out there are the last defenders of their ancient desert culture. Their flocks are their way of life. You mercilessly butcher them, rob their women and children of their sole source of food and clothing."

* * * * *

Johnny McCord ran his hand over his face in an unhappy gesture. "Look," he said plaintively. "Those goats and sheep have already been bought and paid for by the Commission. The Tuareg should have destroyed them, or sold them as food to be immediately butchered, several years ago. Where they've been hiding is a mystery. But they simply have no right to be in possession of those animals, no right to be in this part of the country, and, above all, no right to be grazing in our transplants."

"It's their country! What right have you to order them away?"

Johnny McCord held up his hands, palms upward. "This country is part of the Mali Federation, Miss Desage. It used to be called French Sudan and South Algeria. The government of the Federation gladly accepted the project of reforestating the Sahara. Why not? We've already succeeded in making one of the most poverty-stricken areas in the world a prosperous one. Far from there being unemployment here, we have a labor shortage. Schools have opened, even universities. Hospitals have sprung up. Highways have been laid out through country that hadn't even trails before. The Federation is booming. If there are a few Tuareg who can't adapt to the new world, it's too bad. Their children will be glad for the change."

She seated herself stiffly. "I am not impressed by your excuses," she said.

Johnny shrugged and turned to Mohammed Mohmoud who had been standing silently through all this, almost as though at attention.

Johnny said, "Did you learn where this band comes from? Where they had kept that many animals for so long without detection?"

The Moslem officer shook his head. "They wouldn't reveal that."

Johnny looked at Derek Mason. The Canadian shook his head. "None of them spoke French, Johnny. Or if they did, they wouldn't admit it. When we first came up they looked as though they were going to fight. Happily, the size of the captain's command made them decide otherwise. At any rate, they're putting up no resistance. I let them know through the captain, here, that when they got back to Tissalit, or Timbuktu, they could put in a demand for reimbursement for their animals–if the animals were legally theirs."

Johnny looked at the Malian officer again. "How come you've returned to camp? Shouldn't you be out there with your men?"

"There were a few things to be discussed," the Moslem said. He looked significantly at the French reporter.

Hélène Desage said, "Let me warn you, I will not tolerate being sent away. I want to hear this. If I don't, I demand you let me communicate immediately with my magazine and with the Transatlantic Newspaper Alliance for whom I am also doing a series of articles on the Sahara Reforestation *scheme*."

Johnny McCord winced. He said, "There is nothing going on around here, Miss Desage, that is secret. You won't be ordered away." He turned to Mohammed Mohmoud. "What did you wish to discuss, Captain?"

"First, what about the camels, asses and horses?"

"Shoot them. Practically the only graze between here and Tissalit are our trees."

"And how will they get themselves and their property out of this country?" the reporter snapped.

Johnny said wearily, "We'll truck them out, Miss Desage. They and all their property. And while we're doing it, we'll feed them. I imagine, before it's all over it will cost the Commission several thousand dollars." He turned back to the desert patrol captain. "What else?"

From a tunic pocket Mohammed Mohmoud brought a handgun and handed it to Johnny McCord. "I thought you might like to see this. They were quite well armed. At first I thought there might be resistance."

Johnny turned the automatic over in his hands, scowling at it. "What's there to see that's special? I don't know much about guns."

Mohammed Mohmoud said, "It was made in Pilsen."

Johnny looked up at him. "Czechoslovakia, eh?"

The other said, "So were most of their rifles."

Hélène Desage snorted in deprecation. "So, we'll drag in that old wheeze. The red menace. Blame it on *la Russie*."

Johnny McCord said mildly, "We haven't blamed anything on the Russkies, Miss Desage. The Tuareg have a right to bear arms, there are still dangerous animals in the Mali Federation. And they are free to purchase Czech weapons if they find them better or cheaper than western ones. Don't find an exciting story where there is none. Things are tranquil here."

Hélène Desage stared at him. So did Mohammed Mohmoud and Derek Mason for that matter.

Only Pierre Marimbert realized Johnny McCord's position, and he chuckled and went for more beer.

V

Johnny McCord was a man who didn't like to be thrown out of routine. He resented the interference with his schedule of the past few days. By nature he was methodical, not given to inspiration.

All of which was probably the reason that he spent a sleepless night trying to find rhyme and reason where seemingly there was none.

At dawn, he stepped from the door of his Quonset hut quarters and looked for a moment into the gigantic red ball which was the Saharan sun. Neither dawn nor sunset at Bidon Cinq were spectacular, nor would they become so until the Sahara Reforestation Commission began to return moisture to desert skies. Johnny wondered if he would live to see it.

He made his way over to the huge steel shed which doubled as garage and aircraft hanger. As yet, none of the native mechanics were stirring, although he could hear sounds of activity in the community kitchen.

Derek Mason looked up from his inspection of Hélène Desage's air-cushion Land Rover.

Johnny McCord scowled at him. "What in the hell are you doing here?"

The lanky Canadian came erect and looked for a long moment at his superior. He said finally, soberly, "It occurs to me that I'm probably doing the same thing you came to do."

"What have you found?"

"That a small bomb has been attached to the starter."

Johnny didn't change expression. It fitted in. "What else?" he said.

Derek handed him a steel ring.

Johnny McCord looked at it, recognized it for what it was and stuck it in his pocket. "Let's go back to the office. Yell in to the cook to send some coffee over, and call Pierre. We've got some notes to check."

Mademoiselle Desage was a late riser. When she entered the office, the three Sahara Reforestation Commission officers were already at work.

She said snappishly to Johnny McCord, "Today I would like to see these destroyed pumps."

Johnny said, his eyebrows questioning, "How did you know they were destroyed?"

"It doesn't seem to be much of a secret. The story is all about the camp."

"Oh?" Johnny sighed, then drawled to Derek, "I say, Si, you better go get the hired hand, we might as well finish this up so we can get back to work."

Derek nodded and left.

Johnny McCord left the collator he'd been working with, went around behind his desk and sat down. "Take a chair, Miss Desage. I want to say a few things in the way of background to you."

She sat, but said defiantly, "I have no need of a lengthy lecture on the glories of the Sahara Reforestation Commission."

"Coffee?" Pierre Marimbert said politely.

"No, thank you."

Johnny said, his voice thoughtful, "I imagine the real starting point was back about 1957 when the Chinese discovered that a nation's greatest natural resource is its manpower."

* * * * *

She frowned at him. "What in the world are you talking about?"

He ignored her and went on. "Originally, appalled by the job of feeding over half a billion mouths, they had initiated a birth control plan. But after a year or two they saw it was the wrong approach. They were going to succeed, if they succeeded, in their *Great Leaps Forward* by utilizing the labor of every man, woman and child in the country. And that's what they proceeded to do. The lesson was brought home to the rest of the world in less than ten years, when such other countries as India and Indonesia failed to do the same."

Johnny leaned back in his chair, and his eyes were thoughtful but unseeing. "Even we of the west learned the lesson. The most important factor in our leadership was our wonderful trained labor force. As far back as 1960 we had more than 65 million Americans working daily in industry and distribution. Even the Russkies, with their larger population, didn't begin to equal that number."

"What are you driveling about?" the reporter demanded.

"To sum it up," Johnny said mildly, "the battle for men's minds continues and each of the world's great powers has discovered that it can't afford to limit its population-its greatest resource. So population continues to explode and the world is currently frantically seeking sources of food for its new billions. The Amazon basin is being made into a tropical garden; the Japanese, landless, are devising a hundred methods of farming the sea; Australia is debouching into its long unpopulated interior, doing much the same things we are here in the Sahara. The Chinese are over-flowing into Sinkiang, Mongolia and Tibet; the Russkies into Siberia. We of the west, with the large underdeveloped areas of the western hemisphere have not been so greatly pushed as some others. However, there is always tomorrow."

Derek entered with Captain Mohammed Mohmoud. The latter day Rudolph Valentino had a puzzled expression on his dark face.

"Here's the hired man, Hiram," Derek drawled.

The desert patrol officer nodded questioningly to the men and said, *"Bonjour,"* to Hélène Desage.

Johnny went on. "Yes, there's tomorrow. And by the time we run out of *Lebensraum* in Brazil and Alaska, in Central America and the Argentine, in Texas and Saskatchewan, we're going to need the three million square miles of the Sahara."

She said in ridicule, "It will take you a century at least to reforest the desert."

"At least." Johnny nodded agreeably. "And we're willing and able to look that far ahead. Possibly by that time our opponents will also be looking for new lands for their expanding peoples. And where will they find them? The advantage will be ours, Miss Desage."

Mohammed Mohmoud looked from one to the other, frowning. "What are we discussing?" he said. "I should be getting back to my men."

Derek yawned and said, "Forget about it, pal. You're never going to be getting back to your men again."

* * * * *

The desert patrol officer's eyes widened. He turned his glare on Johnny McCord, "What is all this?"

Johnny said, "I'll tell it, Derek."

Hélène Desage was as surprised as the Malian. "What is going on? Are you trying to white-wash yourselves by casting blame on this gentleman?"

"Let me go on," Johnny said. "Needless to say, there are conflicting interests. The Soviet Complex obviously would as soon we didn't succeed. However, wars are impractical today, and the Russkies and Chinese are taken up with their own development. The Southeast Asia bloc wouldn't mind taking over here themselves, they desperately need land already. But they aren't our biggest opponents. There's another group even more involved-the *colons* of Algeria and Morocco and those of even such Mali cities as Dakar. I suppose it is this last element that you represent, Miss Desage."

She was staring unbelievingly at him now.

"Their interest is to get the Sahara Reforestation Commission out of the way so that they can immediately exploit the area. They are interested in the *now*, not the potentialities of the future. They resent the use of the Niger for reforestation, when they could use it for immediate irrigation projects. They would devote the full resources of the Mali Federation and Algeria to seeking oil and minerals and in the various other ways the country might be exploited. Finally, they rather hate to see the western schools, hospitals, and other means used to raise the local living standards. They liked the low wage rates that formerly applied."

Johnny nodded. "Yes, I imagine that's your angle."

Hélène Desage stormed to her feet. "I don't have to listen to this!"

Derek said, "Honey, we sure aren't holding you. You're free to go any time you want. And you can take this pal of yours along with you." He jerked his head contemptuously at Mohammed Mohmoud.

Pierre Marimbert said, "Mademoiselle, we have no idea of where you two met originally, nor how close your relationship, but the captain should have remembered that I too am French. A gentleman, on first meeting a lady, would never, never address her as *tu in our* language."

Johnny sighed again and looked at his watch. "Other things pile up too, Miss Desage. You let slip a few moments ago that you knew about the pumps being destroyed. You said the rumor was all around camp. But it couldn't be. The only persons who knew about it were myself, Pierre and Derek. On top of that, there were no signs of bedouin or animals near the exploded pumps; the person who did the job must have come in an aircraft or air-cushion car. And, besides, we found the pin of a hand grenade in your land rover this morning. We had thought at first that dynamite had been used, but evidently you smuggled your much more compact bombs across the desert with you. Obviously, no one would have dreamed of searching your vehicle.

"No, Miss Desage, it's obvious that you detoured from the track on the way down from Poste Weygand, went over to In Ziza, a comparatively short distance, and blew up twenty-five of our pumps."

Johnny turned to the Malian officer now. "At the same time you were coordinating with her, you and whatever gang is hiring you. Someone supplied those Tuareg with the livestock and paid them to trek up here. You, of course, turned your back and let them through. The same someone who supplied the livestock also supplied Czech weapons."

Hélène Desage was still sputtering indignation. "Ridiculous! Why? What would motivate me to such nonsense?"

Johnny grimaced. "The whole thing makes a beautiful story at a time when the American government is debating the practicality of the whole project. You could do quite a sob story on the poor, poverty-stricken Tuareg having their livestock destroyed. Then, quite a tale about the bedouin raiding our pumping stations and blowing them up. And quite a tale about the Tuareg being armed with Czech weapons. Oh, I imagine before it was through you'd have drawn a picture of civil war going on here between the nomads and the Commission. Blowing up your own car with a small bomb attached to the starter was just one more item. By the way, were you going to do it yourself? Or did you intend to allow one of our mechanics to kill himself?"

She flushed. "Don't be ridiculous. No one would have been hurt. The bomb is a very small one. More smoke and flash than anything else."

"Well, thanks for small favors," Derek said sarcastically.

* * * * *

She gave up. "Very well," she snapped. "There is nothing you can do. This whole project, as I said before, is nothing but American boon-doggling, a way of plowing endless resources into a hole. Your real motivation is an attempt to prevent depression and unemployment in your country."

Pierre Marimbert said softly, "So you admit to this whole scheme to discredit us?"

"Why not?" She turned to the door. "I will still write my articles. It's my word or yours."

Derek grinned at her. "I think I could fall in love with you, honey," he said. "Life would provide few dull moments. However, you didn't notice how nice and automated this office is. Card machines, electric typewriters, all the latest-including tape recorders for office conversations. You talked too much, honey."

"*Cochon!*" she shrilled at him. She whirled and was through the door.

Johnny turned to Mohammed Mohmoud. "I guess the best thing for you would be to turn in your commission, Captain."

Dark eyes snapped. "And if I say no?"

Johnny shook his head. "The Mali Federation passed some awfully strict laws when it was drawing up its constitution. Among them was one involving capital punishment for anyone destroying a source of water in the desert. Miss Desage did the actual work but you were hand in glove with her. I'd hate to have to report that to your superiors."

Derek jumped forward quickly. His hand snaked out and chopped the other's forearm. The heavy military pistol fell to the floor, and the Canadian kicked it to one side. "Shucks," he drawled, "the hired hand sure is tricky, ain't he?"

"Good Lord," Johnny McCord said disgustedly, "I didn't say I was going to report you. Just threatened to if you didn't resign. Now get out of here, we've got work to do. I'm three days behind on my reports!"

Mercenary

I

Joseph Mauser spotted the recruiting line-up from two or three blocks down the street, shortly after driving into Kingston. The local offices of Vacuum Tube Transport, undoubtedly. Baron Haer would be doing his recruiting for the fracas with Continental Hovercraft there if for no other reason than to save on rents. The Baron was watching pennies on this one and that was bad.

In fact, it was so bad that even as Joe Mauser let his sports hovercar sink to a parking level and vaulted over its side he was still questioning his decision to sign up with the Vacuum Tube outfit rather than with their opponents. Joe was an old pro and old pros do not get to be old pros in the Category Military without developing an instinct to stay away from losing sides.

Fine enough for Low-Lowers and Mid-Lowers to sign up with this outfit, as opposed to that, motivated by no other reasoning than the snappiness of the uniform and the stock shares offered, but an old pro considered carefully such matters as budget. Baron Haer was watching every expense, was, it was rumored, figuring on commanding himself and calling upon relatives and friends for his staff. Continental Hovercraft, on the other hand, was heavy with variable capital and was in a position to hire Stonewall Cogswell himself for their tactician.

However, the die was cast. You didn't run up a caste level, not to speak of two at once, by playing it careful. Joe had planned this out; for once, old pro or not, he was taking risks.

Recruiting line-ups were not for such as he. Not for many a year, many a fracas. He strode rapidly along this one, heading for the offices ahead, noting only in passing the quality of the men who were taking service with Vacuum Tube Transport. These were the soldiers he'd be commanding in the immediate future and the prospects looked grim. There were few veterans among them. Their stance, their demeanor, their … well, you could tell a veteran even though he be Rank Private. You could tell a veteran of even one fracas. It showed.

He knew the situation. The word had gone out. Baron Malcolm Haer was due for a defeat. You weren't going to pick up any lush bonuses signing up with him, and you definitely weren't going to jump a caste. In short, no matter what Haer's past record, choose what was going to be the winning side-Continental Hovercraft. Continental Hovercraft and old Stonewall Cogswell who had lost so few fracases that many a Telly buff couldn't remember a single one.

Individuals among these men showed promise, Joe Mauser estimated even as he walked, but promise means little if you don't live long enough to cash in on it.

Take that small man up ahead. He'd obviously got himself into a hassle maintaining his place in line against two or three heftier would-be soldiers. The little fellow wasn't backing down a step in spite of the attempts of the other Lowers to usurp his place. Joe Mauser liked to see such spirit. You could use it when you were in the dill.

As he drew abreast of the altercation, he snapped from the side of his mouth, "Easy, lads. You'll get all the scrapping you want with Hovercraft. Wait until then."

He'd expected his tone of authority to be enough, even though he was in mufti. He wasn't particularly interested in the situation, beyond giving the little man a hand. A veteran would have recognized him as an old-timer and probable officer, and heeded, automatically.

These evidently weren't veterans.

"Says who?" one of the Lowers growled back at him. "You one of Baron Haer's kids, or something?"

Joe Mauser came to a halt and faced the other. He was irritated, largely with himself. He didn't want to be bothered. Nevertheless, there was no alternative now.

The line of men, all Lowers so far as Joe could see, had fallen silent in an expectant hush. They were bored with their long wait. Now something would break the monotony.

By tomorrow, Joe Mauser would be in command of some of these men. In as little as a week he would go into a full-fledged fracas with them. He couldn't afford to lose face. Not even at this point when all, including himself, were still civilian garbed. When matters pickled, in a fracas, you wanted men with complete confidence in you.

* * * * *

The man who had grumbled the surly response was a near physical twin of Joe Mauser which put him in his early thirties, gave him five foot eleven of altitude and about one hundred and eighty pounds. His clothes casted him Low-Lower —nothing to lose. As with many who have nothing to lose, he was willing to risk all for principle. His face now registered that ideal. Joe Mauser had no authority over him, nor his friends.

Joe's eyes flicked to the other two who had been pestering the little fellow. They weren't quite so aggressive and as yet had come to no conclusion about their stand. Probably the three had been unacquainted before their bullying alliance to deprive the smaller man of his place. However, a moment of hesitation and Joe would have a trio on his hands.

He went through no further verbal preliminaries. Joe Mauser stepped closer. His right hand lanced forward, not doubled in a fist but fingers close together and pointed, spear-like. He sank it into the other's abdomen, immediately below the rib cage-the solar plexus.

He had misestimated the other two. Even as his opponent crumpled, they were upon him, coming in from each side. And at least one of them, he could see now, had been in hand-to-hand combat before. In short, another pro, like Joe himself.

He took one blow, rolling with it, and his feet automatically went into the shuffle of the trained fighter. He retreated slightly to erect defenses, plan attack. They pressed him strongly, sensing victory in his retreat.

The one mattered little to him. Joe Mauser could have polished off the oaf in a matter of seconds, had he been allotted seconds to devote. But the second, the experienced one, was the problem. He and Joe were well matched and with the oaf as an ally really he had all the best of it.

Support came from a forgotten source, the little chap who had been the reason for the whole hassle. He waded in now as big as the next man so far as spirit was concerned, but a sorry fate gave him to attack the wrong man, the veteran rather than the tyro. He took a crashing blow to the side of his head which sent him sailing back into the recruiting line, now composed of excited, shouting verbal participants of the fray.

However, the extinction of Joe Mauser's small ally had taken a moment or two and time was what Joe needed most. For a double second he had the oaf alone on his hands and that was sufficient. He caught a flailing arm, turned his back and automatically went into the movements which result in that spectacular hold of the wrestler, the Flying Mare. Just in time he recalled that his opponent was a future comrade-in-arms and twisted the arm so that it bent at the elbow, rather than breaking. He hurled the other over his shoulder and as far as possible, to take the scrap out of him, and twirled quickly to meet the further attack of his sole remaining foe.

That phase of the combat failed to materialize.

A voice of command bit out, "Hold it, you lads!"

The original situation which had precipitated the fight was being duplicated. But while the three Lowers had failed to respond to Joe Mauser's tone of authority, there was no similar failure now.

The owner of the voice, beautifully done up in the uniform of Vacuum Tube Transport, complete to kilts and the swagger stick of the officer of Rank Colonel or above, stood glaring at them. Age, Joe estimated, even as he came to attention, somewhere in the late twenties-an Upper in caste. Born to command. His face holding that arrogant, contemptuous expression once common to the patricians of Rome, the Prussian Junkers, the British ruling class of the Nineteenth Century. Joe knew the expression well. How well he knew it. On more than one occasion, he had dreamt of it.

Joe said, "Yes, sir."

"What in Zen goes on here? Are you lads overtranked?"

"No, sir," Joe's veteran opponent grumbled, his eyes on the ground, a schoolboy before the principal.

Joe said, evenly, "A private disagreement, sir."

"Disagreement!" the Upper snorted. His eyes went to the three fallen combatants, who were in various stages of reviving. "I'd hate to see you lads in a real scrap."

That brought a response from the non-combatants in the recruiting line. The *bon mot* wasn't that good but caste has its privileges and the laughter was just short of uproarious.

Which seemed to placate the kilted officer. He tapped his swagger stick against the side of his leg while he ran his eyes up and down Joe Mauser and the others, as though memorizing them for future reference.

"All right," he said. "Get back into the line, and you trouble makers quiet down. We're processing as quickly as we can." And at that point he added insult to injury with an almost word for word repetition of what Joe had said a few moments earlier. "You'll get all the fighting you want from Hovercraft, if you can wait until then."

The four original participants of the rumpus resumed their places in various stages of sheepishness. The little fellow, nursing an obviously aching jaw, made a point of taking up his original position even while darting a look of thanks to Joe Mauser who still stood where he had when the fight was interrupted.

The Upper looked at Joe. "Well, lad, are you interested in signing up with Vacuum Tube Transport or not?"

"Yes, sir," Joe said evenly. Then, "Joseph Mauser, sir. Category Military, Rank Captain."

"Indeed." The officer looked him up and down all over again, his nostrils high. "A Middle, I assume. And brawling with recruits." He held a long silence. "Very well, come with me." He turned and marched off.

Joe inwardly shrugged. This was a fine start for his pitch —a fine start. He had half a mind to give it all up, here and now, and head on up to Catskill to enlist with Continental Hovercraft. His big scheme would wait for another day. Nevertheless, he fell in behind the aristocrat and followed him to the offices which had been his original destination.

* * * * *

Two Rank Privates with 45-70 Springfields and wearing the Haer kilts in such wise as to indicate permanent status in Vacuum Tube Transport came to the salute as they approached. The Upper preceding Joe Mauser flicked his swagger stick in an easy nonchalance. Joe felt envious amusement. How long did it take to learn how to answer a salute with that degree of arrogant ease?

There were desks in here, and typers humming, as Vacuum Tube Transport office workers, mobilized for this special service, processed volunteers for the company forces. Harried noncoms and junior-grade officers buzzed everywhere, failing miserably to bring order to the chaos. To the right was a door with a medical cross newly painted on it. When it occasionally popped open to admit or emit a recruit, white-robed doctors, male nurses and half nude men could be glimpsed beyond.

Joe followed the other through the press and to an inner office at which door he didn't bother to knock. He pushed his way through, waved in greeting with his swagger stick to the single occupant who looked up from the paper- and tape-strewn desk at which he sat.

Joe Mauser had seen the face before on Telly though never so tired as this and never with the element of defeat to be read in the expression. Bullet-headed, barrel-figured Baron Malcolm Haer of Vacuum Tube Transport. Category Transportation, Mid-Upper, and strong candidate for Upper-Upper upon retirement. However, there would be few who expected retirement in the immediate future. Hardly. Malcolm Haer found too obvious a lusty enjoyment in the competition between Vacuum Tube Transport and its stronger rivals.

* * * * *

Joe came to attention, bore the sharp scrutiny of his chosen commander-to-be. The older man's eyes went to the kilted Upper officer who had brought Joe along. "What is it, Balt?"

The other gestured with his stick at Joe. "Claims to be Rank Captain. Looking for a commission with us, Dad. I wouldn't know why." The last sentence was added lazily.

The older Haer shot an irritated glance at his son. "Possibly for the same reason mercenaries usually enlist for a fracas, Balt." His eyes came back to Joe.

Joe Mauser, still at attention even though in mufti, opened his mouth to give his name, category and rank, but the older man waved a hand negatively. "Captain Mauser, isn't it? I caught the fracas between Carbonaceous Fuel and United Miners, down on the Panhandle Reservation. Seems to me I've spotted you once or twice before, too."

"Yes, sir," Joe said. This was some improvement in the way things were going.

The older Haer was scowling at him. "Confound it, what are you doing with no more rank than captain? On the face of it, you're an old hand, a highly experienced veteran."

An old pro, we call ourselves, Joe said to himself. *Old pros, we call ourselves, among ourselves.*

Aloud, he said, "I was born a Mid-Lower, sir."

There was understanding in the old man's face, but Balt Haer said loftily, "What's that got to do with it? Promotion is quick and based on merit in Category Military."

At a certain point, if you are good combat officer material, you speak your mind no matter the rank of the man you are addressing. On this occasion, Joe Mauser needed few words. He let his eyes go up and down Balt Haer's immaculate uniform, taking in the swagger stick of the Rank Colonel or above. Joe said evenly, "Yes, sir."

Balt Haer flushed quick temper. "What do you mean by —"

But his father was chuckling. "You have spirit, captain. I need spirit now. You are quite correct. My son, though a capable officer, I assure you, has probably not participated in a fraction of the fracases you have to your credit. However, there is something to be said for the training available to we Uppers in the academies. For instance, captain, have you ever commanded a body of lads larger than, well, a *company?*"

Joe said flatly, "In the Douglas-Boeing versus Lockheed-Cessna fracas we took a high loss of officers when the Douglas-Boeing outfit rang in some fast-firing French *mitrailleuse* we didn't know they had. As my superiors took casualties I was field promoted to acting battalion commander, to acting regimental commander, to acting brigadier. For three days I held the rank of acting commander of brigade. We won."

Balt Haer snapped his fingers. "I remember that. Read quite a paper on it." He eyed Joe Mauser, almost respectfully. "Stonewall Cogswell got the credit for the victory and received his marshal's baton as a result."

"He was one of the few other officers that survived," Joe said dryly.

"But, Zen! You mean you got no promotion at all?"

Joe said, "I was upped to Low-Middle from High-Lower, sir. At my age, at the time, quite a promotion."

* * * * *

Baron Haer was remembering, too. "That was the fracas that brought on the howl from the Sovs. They claimed those *mitrailleuse* were post-1900 and violated the Universal Disarmament Pact. Yes, I recall that. Douglas-Boeing was able to prove that the weapon was used by the French as far back as the Franco-Prussian War." He eyed Joe with new interest now. "Sit down, captain. You too, Balt. Do you realize that Captain Mauser is the only recruit of officer rank we've had today?"

"Yes," the younger Haer said dryly. "However, it's too late to call the fracas off now. Hovercraft wouldn't stand for it, and the Category Military Department would back them. Our only alternative is unconditional surrender, and you know what that means."

"It means our family would probably be forced from control of the firm," the older man growled. "But nobody has suggested surrender on any terms. Nobody, thus far." He glared at his officer son who took it with an easy shrug and swung a leg over the edge of his father's desk in the way of a seat.

Joe Mauser found a chair and lowered himself into it. Evidently, the foppish Balt Haer had no illusions about the spot his father had got the family corporation into. And the younger man was right, of course.

But the Baron wasn't blind to reality any more than he was a coward. He dismissed Balt Haer's defeatism from his mind and came back to Joe Mauser. "As I say, you're the only officer recruit today. Why?"

Joe said evenly, "I wouldn't know, sir. Perhaps freelance Category Military men are occupied elsewhere. There's always a shortage of trained officers."

Baron Haer was waggling a finger negatively. "That's not what I mean, captain. You are an old hand. This is your category and you must know it well. Then why are *you* signing up with Vacuum Tube Transport rather than Hovercraft?"

Joe Mauser looked at him for a moment without speaking.

"Come, come, captain. I am an old hand too, in my category, and not a fool. I realize there is scarcely a soul in the West-world that expects anything but disaster for my colors. Pay rates have been widely posted. I can offer only five common shares of Vacuum Tube for a Rank Captain, win or lose. Hovercraft is doubling that, and can pick and choose among the best officers in the hemisphere."

Joe said softly, "I have all the shares I need."

Balt Haer had been looking back and forth between his father and the newcomer and becoming obviously more puzzled. He put in, "Well, what in Zen motivates you if it isn't the stock we offer?"

Joe glanced at the younger Haer to acknowledge the question but he spoke to the Baron. "Sir, like you said, you're no fool. However, you've been sucked in, this time. When you took on Hovercraft, you were thinking in terms of a regional dispute. You wanted to run one of your vacuum tube deals up to Fairbanks from Edmonton. You were expecting a minor fracas, involving possibly five thousand men. You never expected Hovercraft to parlay it up, through their connections in the Category Military Department, to a divisional magnitude fracas which you simply aren't large enough to afford. But Hovercraft was getting sick of your corporation. You've been nicking away at them too long. So they decided to do you in. They've hired Marshal Cogswell and the best combat officers in North America, and they're hiring the most competent veterans they can find. Every fracas buff who watches Telly, figures you've had it. They've been watching you come up the aggressive way, the hard way, for a long time, but now they're all going to be sitting on the edges of their sofas waiting for you to get it."

Baron Haer's heavy face had hardened as Joe Mauser went on relentlessly. He growled, "Is this what everyone thinks?"

"Yes. Everyone intelligent enough to have an opinion." Joe made a motion of his head to the outer offices where the recruiting was proceeding. "Those men out there are rejects from Catskill, where old Baron Zwerdling is recruiting. Either that or they're inexperienced Low-Lowers, too stupid to realize they're sticking their necks out. Not one man in ten is a veteran. And when things begin to pickle, you want veterans."

Baron Malcolm Haer sat back in his chair and stared coldly at Captain Joe Mauser. He said, "At first I was moderately surprised that an old time mercenary like yourself should choose my uniform, rather than Zwerdling's. Now I am increasingly mystified about motivation. So all over again I ask you, captain: Why are you requesting a commission in my forces which you seem convinced will meet disaster?"

Joe wet his lips carefully. "I think I know a way you can win."

II

His permanent military rank the Haers had no way to alter, but they were short enough of competent officers that they gave him an acting rating and pay scale of major and command of a squadron of cavalry. Joe Mauser wasn't interested in a cavalry command this fracas, but he said nothing. Immediately, he had to size up the situation; it wasn't time as yet to reveal the big scheme. And, meanwhile, they could use him to whip the Rank Privates into shape.

He had left the offices of Baron Haer to go through the red tape involved in being signed up on a temporary basis in the Vacuum Tube Transport forces, and reentered the confusion of the outer offices where the Lowers were being processed and given medicals. He reentered in time to run into a Telly team which was doing a live broadcast.

Joe Mauser remembered the news reporter who headed the team. He'd run into him two or three times in fracases. As a matter of fact, although Joe held the standard Military Category prejudices against Telly, he had a basic respect for this particular newsman. On the occasions he'd seen him before, the fellow was hot in the midst of the action even when things were in the dill. He took as many chances as did the average combatant, and you can't ask for more than that.

The other knew him, too, of course. It was part of his job to be able to spot the celebrities and near celebrities. He zeroed in on Joe now, making flicks of his hand to direct the cameras. Joe, of course, was fully aware of the value of Telly and was glad to co-operate.

"Captain! Captain Mauser, isn't it? Joe Mauser who held out for four days in the swamps of Louisiana with a single company while his ranking officers reformed behind him."

That was one way of putting it, but both Joe and the newscaster who had covered the debacle knew the reality of the situation. When the front had collapsed, his commanders-of Upper caste, of course-had hauled out, leaving him to fight a delaying action while they mended their fences with the enemy, coming to the best terms possible. Yes, that had been the United Oil versus Allied Petroleum fracas, and Joe had emerged with little either in glory or pelf.

The average fracas fan wasn't on an intellectual level to appreciate anything other than victory. The good guys win, the bad guys lose-that's obvious, isn't it? Not one out of ten Telly followers of the fracases was interested in a well-conducted retreat or holding action. They wanted blood, lots of it, and they identified with the winning side.

Joe Mauser wasn't particularly bitter about this aspect. It was part of his way of life. In fact, his pet peeve was the *real* buff. The type, man or woman, who could remember every fracas you'd ever been in, every time you'd copped one, and how long you'd been in the hospital. Fans who could remember, even better than you could, every time the situation had pickled on you and you'd had to fight your way out as best you could. They'd tell you about it, their eyes gleaming, sometimes a slightest trickle of spittle at the sides of their mouths. They usually wanted an autograph, or a souvenir such as a uniform button.

Now Joe said to the Telly reporter, "That's right, Captain Mauser. Acting major, in this fracas, ah —"

"Freddy. Freddy Soligen. You remember me, captain —"

"Of course I do, Freddy. We've been in the dill, side by side, more than once, and even when I was too scared to use my side arm, you'd be scanning away with your camera."

"Ha ha, listen to the captain, folks. I hope my boss is tuned in. But seriously, Captain Mauser, what do you think the chances of Vacuum Tube Transport are in this fracas?"

Joe looked into the camera lens, earnestly. "The best, of course, or I wouldn't have signed up with Baron Haer, Freddy. Justice triumphs, and anybody who is familiar with the issues in this fracas, knows that Baron Haer is on the side of true right."

Freddy said, holding any sarcasm he must have felt, "What would you say the issues were, captain?"

"The basic North American free enterprise right to compete. Hovercraft has held a near monopoly in transport to Fairbanks. Vacuum Tube Transport wishes to lower costs and bring the consumers of Fairbanks better service through running a vacuum tube to that area. What could be more in the traditions of the West-world? Continental Hovercraft stands in the way and it is they who have demanded of the Category Military Department a trial by arms. On the face of it, justice is on the side of Baron Haer."

Freddy Soligen said into the camera, "Well, all you good people of the Telly world, that's an able summation the captain has made, but it certainly doesn't jibe with the words of Baron Zwerdling we heard this morning, does it? However, justice triumphs and we'll see what the field of combat will have to offer. Thank you, thank you very much, Captain Mauser. All of us, all of us tuned in today, hope that you personally will run into no dill in this fracas."

"Thanks, Freddy. Thanks all," Joe said into the camera, before turning away. He wasn't particularly keen about this part of the job, but you couldn't underrate the importance of pleasing the buffs. In the long run it was your career, your chances for promotion both in military rank and ultimately in caste. It was the way the fans took you up, boosted you, idolized you, worshipped you if you really made it. He, Joe Mauser, was only a minor celebrity, he appreciated every chance he had to be interviewed by such a popular reporter as Freddy Soligen.

* * * * *

Even as he turned, he spotted the four men with whom he'd had his spat earlier. The little fellow was still to the fore. Evidently, the others had decided the one place extra that he represented wasn't worth the trouble he'd put in their way defending it.

On an impulse he stepped up to the small man who began a grin of recognition, a grin that transformed his feisty face. A revelation of an inner warmth beyond average in a world which had lost much of its human warmth.

Joe said, "Like a job, soldier?"

"Name's Max. Max Mainz. Sure I want a job. That's why I'm in this everlasting line."

Joe said, "First fracas for you, isn't it?"

"Yeah, but I had basic training in school."

"What do you weigh, Max?"

Max's face soured. "About one twenty."

"Did you check out on semaphore in school?"

"Well, sure. I'm Category Food, Sub-division Cooking, Branch Chef, but, like I say, I took basic military training, like most everybody else."

"I'm Captain Joe Mauser. How'd you like to be my batman?"

Max screwed up his already not overly handsome face. "Gee, I don't know. I kinda joined up to see some action. Get into the dill. You know what I mean."

Joe said dryly, "See here, Mainz, you'll probably find more pickled situations next to me than you'll want-and you'll come out alive."

The recruiting sergeant looked up from the desk. It was Max Mainz's turn to be processed. The sergeant said, "Lad, take a good opportunity when it drops in your lap. The captain is one of the best in the field. You'll learn more, get better chances for promotion, if you stick with him."

Joe couldn't remember ever having run into the sergeant before, but he said, "Thanks, sergeant."

The other said, evidently realizing Joe didn't recognize him, "We were together on the Chihuahua Reservation, on the jurisdictional fracas between the United Miners and the Teamsters, sir."

It had been almost fifteen years ago. About all that Joe Mauser remembered of that fracas was the abnormal number of casualties they'd taken. His side had lost, but from this distance in time Joe couldn't even remember what force he'd been with. But now he said, "That's right. I thought I recognized you, sergeant."

"It was my first fracas, sir." The sergeant went businesslike. "If you want I should hustle this lad though, captain —"

"Please do, sergeant." Joe added to Max, "I'm not sure where my billet will be. When you're through all this, locate the officer's mess and wait there for me."

"Well, O.K.," Max said doubtfully, still scowling but evidently a servant of an officer, if he wanted to be or not.

"Sir," the sergeant added ominously. "If you've had basic, you know enough how to address an officer."

"Well, yessir," Max said hurriedly.

Joe began to turn away, but then spotted the man immediately behind Max Mainz. He was one of the three with whom Joe had tangled earlier, the one who'd obviously had previous combat experience. He pointed the man out to the sergeant. "You'd better give this lad at least temporary rank of corporal. He's a veteran and we're short of veterans."

The sergeant said, "Yes, sir. We sure are." Joe's former foe looked properly thankful.

* * * * *

Joe Mauser finished off his own red tape and headed for the street to locate a military tailor who could do him up a set of the Haer kilts and fill his other dress requirements. As he went, he wondered vaguely just how many different uniforms he had worn in his time.

In a career as long as his own from time to time you took semi-permanent positions in bodyguards, company police, or possibly the permanent combat troops of this corporation or that. But largely, if you were ambitious, you signed up for the fracases and that meant into a uniform and out of it again in as short a period as a couple of weeks.

At the door he tried to move aside but was too slow for the quick moving young woman who caromed off him. He caught her arm to prevent her from stumbling. She looked at him with less than thanks.

Joe took the blame for the collision. "Sorry," he said. "I'm afraid I didn't see you, Miss."

"Obviously," she said coldly. Her eyes went up and down him, and for a moment he wondered where he had seen her before. Somewhere, he was sure.

She was dressed as they dress who have never considered cost and she had an elusive beauty which would have been even the more hadn't her face projected quite such a serious outlook. Her features were more delicate than those to which he was usually attracted. Her lips were less full, but still — He was reminded of the classic ideal of the British Romantic Period, the women sung of by Byron and Keats, Shelly and Moore.

She said, "Is there any particular reason why you should be staring at me, Mr. —"

"Captain Mauser," Joe said hurriedly. "I'm afraid I've been rude, Miss-Well, I thought I recognized you."

She took in his civilian dress, typed it automatically, and came to an erroneous conclusion. She said, "Captain? You mean that with everyone else I know drawing down ranks from Lieutenant Colonel to Brigadier General, you can't make anything better than Captain?"

Joe winced. He said carefully, "I came up from the ranks, Miss. Captain is quite an achievement, believe me."

"Up from the ranks!" She took in his clothes again. "You mean you're a Middle? You neither talk nor look like a Middle, captain." She used the caste rating as though it was not *quite* a derogatory term.

Not that she meant to be deliberately insulting, Joe knew, wearily. How well he knew. It was simply born in her. As once a well-educated aristocracy had, not necessarily unkindly, named their status inferiors *niggers*; or other aristocrats, in another area of the country, had named theirs *greasers*. Yes, how well he knew.

He said very evenly, "Mid-Middle now, Miss. However, I was born in the Lower castes."

An eyebrow went up. "Zen! You must have put in many an hour studying. You talk like an Upper, captain." She dropped all interest in him and turned to resume her journey.

"Just a moment," Joe said. "You can't go in there, Miss —"

Her eyebrows went up again. "The name is Haer," she said. "Why can't I go in here, captain?"

Now it came to him why he had thought he recognized her. She had basic features similar to those of that overbred poppycock, Balt Haer.

"Sorry," Joe said. "I suppose under the circumstances, you can. I was about to tell you that they're recruiting with lads running around half clothed. Medical inspections, that sort of thing."

She made a noise through her nose and said over her shoulder, even as she sailed on. "Besides being a Haer, I'm an M.D., captain. At the ludicrous sight of a man shuffling about in his shorts, I seldom blush."

She was gone.

Joe Mauser looked after her. "I'll bet you don't," he muttered.

Had she waited a few minutes he could have explained his Upper accent and his unlikely education. When you'd copped one you had plenty of opportunity in hospital beds to read, to study, to contemplate-and to fester away in your own schemes of rebellion against fate. And Joe had copped many in his time.

III

By the time Joe Mauser called it a day and retired to his quarters he was exhausted to the point where his basic dissatisfaction with the trade he followed was heavily upon him.

He had met his immediate senior officers, largely dilettante Uppers with precious little field experience, and was unimpressed. And he'd met his own junior officers and was shocked. By the looks of things at this stage, Captain Mauser's squadron would be going into this fracas both undermanned with Rank Privates and with junior officers composed largely of temporarily promoted noncoms. If this was typical of Baron Haer's total force, then Balt Haer had been correct; unconditional surrender was to be considered, no matter how disastrous to Haer family fortunes.

Joe had been able to take immediate delivery of one kilted uniform. Now, inside his quarters, he began stripping out of his jacket. Somewhat to his surprise, the small man he had selected earlier in the day to be his batman entered from an inner room, also resplendent in the Haer uniform and obviously happily so.

He helped his superior out of the jacket with an ease that held no subservience but at the same time was correctly respectful. You'd have thought him a batman specially trained.

Joe grunted, "Max, isn't it? I'd forgotten about you. Glad you found our billet all right."

Max said, "Yes, sir. Would the captain like a drink? I picked up a bottle of applejack. Applejack's the drink around here, sir. Makes a topnotch highball with ginger ale and a twist of lemon."

Joe Mauser looked at him. Evidently his tapping this man for orderly had been sheer fortune. Well, Joe Mauser could use some good luck on this job. He hoped it didn't end with selecting a batman.

Joe said, "An applejack highball sounds wonderful, Max. Got ice?"

"Of course, sir." Max left the small room.

Joe Mauser and his officers were billeted in what had once been a motel on the old road between Kingston and Woodstock. There was a shower and a tiny kitchenette in each cottage. That was one advantage in a fracas held in an area where there were plenty of facilities. Such military reservations as that of the Little Big Horn in Montana and particularly some of those in the South West and Mexico, were another thing.

Joe lowered himself into the room's easy-chair and bent down to untie his laces. He kicked his shoes off. He could use that drink. He began wondering all over again if his scheme for winning this Vacuum Tube Transport versus Continental Hovercraft fracas would come off. The more he saw of Baron Haer's inadequate forces, the more he wondered. He hadn't expected Vacuum Tube to be in *this* bad a shape. Baron Haer had been riding high for so long that one would have thought his reputation for victory would have lured many a veteran to his colors. Evidently they hadn't bitten. The word was out all right.

Max Mainz returned with the drink.

Joe said, "You had one yourself?"

"No, sir."

Joe said, "Well, Zen, go get yourself one and come on back and sit down. Let's get acquainted."

"Well, yessir." Max disappeared back into the kitchenette to return almost immediately. The little man slid into a chair, drink awkwardly in hand.

His superior sized him up, all over again. Not much more than a kid, really. Surprisingly aggressive for a Lower who must have been raised from childhood in a trank-bemused, Telly-entertained household. The fact that he'd broken away from that environment at all was to his credit, it was considerably easier to conform. But then it is always easier to conform, to run with the herd, as Joe well knew. His own break hadn't been an easy one. "Relax," he said now.

Max said, "Well, this is my first day."

"I know. And you've been seeing Telly shows all your life showing how an orderly conducts himself in the presence of his superior." Joe took another pull and yawned. "Well, forget about it. With any man who goes into a fracas with me, I like to be on close terms. When things pickle, I want him to be on my side, not nursing some peeve brought on by his officer trying to give him an inferiority complex."

The little man was eying him in surprise.

Joe finished his highball and came to his feet to get another one. He said, "On two occasions I've had an orderly save my life. I'm not taking any chances but that there might be a third opportunity."

"Well, yessir. Does the captain want me to get him —"

"I'll get it," Joe said.

When he'd returned to his chair, he said, "Why did you join up with Baron Haer, Max?"

The other shrugged it off. "The usual. The excitement. The idea of all those fans watching me on Telly. The share of common stock I'll get. And, you never know, maybe a promotion in caste. I wouldn't mind making Upper-Lower."

Joe said sourly, "One fracas and you'll be over that desire to have the buffs watching you on Telly while they sit around in their front rooms sucking on tranks. And you'll probably be over the desire for the excitement, too. Of course, the share of stock is another thing."

"You aren't just countin' down, captain," Max said, an almost surly overtone in his voice. "You don't know what it's like being born with no more common stock shares than a Mid-Lower."

Joe held his peace, sipping at his drink, taking this one more slowly. He let his eyebrows rise to encourage the other to go on.

Max said doggedly, "Sure, they call it People's Capitalism and everybody gets issued enough shares to insure him a basic living all the way from the cradle to the grave, like they say. But let me tell you, you're a Middle and you don't realize how basic the basic living of a Lower can be."

Joe yawned. If he hadn't been so tired, there would have been more amusement in the situation.

Max was still dogged. "Unless you can add to those shares of stock, it's pretty drab, captain. You wouldn't know."

Joe said, "Why don't you work? A Lower can always add to his stock by working."

Max stirred in indignity. "Work? Listen, sir, that's just one more field that's been automated right out of existence. Category Food Preparation, Sub-division Cooking, Branch Chef. Cooking isn't left in the hands of slobs who might drop a cake of soap into the soup. It's done automatic. The only new changes made in cooking are by real top experts, almost scientists like. And most of them are Uppers, mind you."

Joe Mauser sighed inwardly. So his find in batmen wasn't going to be as wonderful as all that, after all. The man might have been born into the food preparation category from a long line of chefs, but evidently he knew precious little about his field. Joe might have suspected. He himself had been born into Clothing Category, Sub-division Shoes, Branch Repair-Cobbler —a meaningless trade since shoes were no longer repaired but discarded upon showing signs of wear. In an economy of complete abundance, there is little reason for repair of basic commodities. It was high time the government investigated category assignment and reshuffled and reassigned half the nation's population. But then, of course, was the question of what to do with the technologically unemployed.

* * * * *

Max was saying, "The only way I could figure on a promotion to a higher caste, or the only way to earn stock shares, was by crossing categories. And you know what that means. Either Category Military, or Category Religion and I sure as Zen don't know nothing about religion."

Joe said mildly, "Theoretically, you can cross categories into any field you want, Max."

Max snorted. "Theoretically is right ... sir. You ever heard about anybody born a Lower, or even a Middle like yourself, cross categories to, say, some Upper category like banking?"

Joe chuckled. He liked this peppery little fellow. If Max worked out as well as Joe thought he might, there was a possibility of taking him along to the next fracas.

Max was saying, "I'm not saying anything against the old time way of doing things or talking against the government, but I'll tell you, captain, every year goes by it gets harder and harder for a man to raise his caste or to earn some additional stock shares."

The applejack had worked enough on Joe for him to rise against one of his pet peeves. He said, "That term, the old time way, is strictly Telly talk, Max. We don't do things *the old time way*. No nation in history ever has-with the possible exception of Egypt. Socio-economics are in a continual flux and here in this country we no more do things in the way they did fifty years ago, than fifty years ago they did them the way the American Revolutionists outlined back in the Eighteenth Century."

Max was staring at him. "I don't get that, sir."

Joe said impatiently, "Max, the politico-economic system we have today is an outgrowth of what went earlier. The welfare state, the freezing of the status quo, the Frigid Fracas between the West-world and the Sov-world, industrial automation until useful employment is all but needless-all these things were to be found in embryo more than fifty years ago."

"Well, maybe the captain's right, but you gotta admit, sir, that mostly we do things the old way. We still got the Constitution and the two-party system and —"

Joe was wearying of the conversation now. You seldom ran into anyone, even in Middle caste, the traditionally professional class, interested enough in such subjects to be worth arguing with. He said, "The Constitution, Max, has got to the point of the Bible. Interpret it the way you wish, and you can find anything. If not, you can always make a new amendment. So far as the two-party system is concerned, what effect does it have when there are no differences between the two parties? That phase of pseudo-democracy was beginning as far back as the 1930s when they began passing State laws hindering the emerging of new political parties. By the time they were insured against a third party working its way through the maze of election laws, the two parties had become so similar that elections became almost as big a farce as over in the Sov-world."

"A farce?" Max ejaculated indignantly, forgetting his servant status. "That means not so good, doesn't it? Far as I'm concerned, election day is tops. The one day a Lower is just as good as an Upper. The one day how many shares you got makes no difference. Everybody has everything."

"Sure, sure, sure," Joe sighed. "The modern equivalent of the Roman Bacchanalia. Election day in the West-world when no one, for just that one day, is freer than anyone else."

"Well, what's wrong with that?" The other was all but belligerent. "That's the trouble with you Middles and Uppers, you don't know how it is to be a Lower and —"

Joe snapped suddenly, "I was born a Mid-Lower myself, Max. Don't give me that nonsense."

Max gaped at him, utterly unbelieving.

Joe's irritation fell away. He held out his glass. "Get us a couple of more drinks, Max, and I'll tell you a story."

By the time the fresh drink came, Joe Mauser was sorry he'd made the offer. He thought back. He hadn't told anyone the Joe Mauser story in many a year. And, as he recalled, the last time had been when he was well into his cups, on an election day at that, and his listener had been a Low-Upper, a hereditary aristocrat, one of the one per cent of the upper strata of the nation. Zen! How the man had laughed. He'd roared his amusement till the tears ran.

However, Joe said, "Max, I was born in the same caste you were-average father, mother, sisters and brothers. They subsisted on the basic income guaranteed from birth, sat and watched Telly for an unbelievable number of hours each day, took trank to keep themselves happy. And thought I was crazy because I didn't. Dad was the sort of man who'd take his belt off to a child of his who questioned such school taught slogans as *What was good enough for Daddy is good enough for me.*

"They were all fracas fans, of course. As far back as I can remember the picture is there of them gathered around the Telly, screaming excitement." Joe Mauser sneered, uncharacteristically.

"You don't sound much like you're in favor of your trade, captain," Max said.

Joe came to his feet, putting down his still half-full glass. "I'll make this epic story short, Max. As you said, the two actually valid methods of rising above the level in which you were born are in the Military and Religious Categories. Like you, even I couldn't stomach the latter."

Joe Mauser hesitated, then finished it off. "Max, there have been few societies that man has evolved that didn't allow in some manner for the competent or sly, the intelligent or the opportunist, the brave or the strong, to work his way to the top. I don't know which of these I personally fit into, but I rebel against remaining in the lower categories of a stratified society. Do I make myself clear?"

"Well, no sir, not exactly."

Joe said flatly, "I'm going to fight my way to the top, and nothing is going to stand in the way. Is that clearer?"

"Yessir," Max said, taken aback.

IV

After routine morning duties, Joe Mauser returned to his billet and mystified Max Mainz by not only changing into mufti himself but having Max do the same.

In fact, the new batman protested faintly. He hadn't nearly, as yet, got over the glory of wearing his kilts and was looking forward to parading around town in them. He had a point, of course. The appointed time for the fracas was getting closer and buffs were beginning to stream into town to bask in the atmosphere of threatened death. Everybody knew what a military center, on the outskirts of a fracas reservation such as the Catskills, was like immediately preceding a clash between rival corporations. The high-strung gaiety, the drinking, the overtranking, the relaxation of mores. Even a Rank Private had it made. Admiring civilians to buy drinks and hang on your every word, and more important still, sensuous-eyed women, their faces slack in thinly suppressed passion. It was a recognized phenomenon, even Max Mainz knew-this desire on the part of women Telly fans to date a man, and then watch him later, killing or being killed.

"Time enough to wear your fancy uniform," Joe Mauser growled at him. "In fact, tomorrow's a local election day. Parlay that up on top of all the fracas fans gravitating into town and you'll have a wingding the likes of nothing you've seen before."

"Well yessir," Max begrudged. "Where're we going now, captain?"

"To the airport. Come along."

Joe Mauser led the way to his sports hovercar and as soon as the two were settled into the bucket seats, hit the lift lever with the butt of his left hand. Aircushion-borne, he trod down on the accelerator.

Max Mainz was impressed. "You know," he said. "I never been in one of these swanky sports jobs before. The kinda car you can afford on the income of a Mid-Lower's stock aren't —"

"Knock it off," Joe said wearily. "Carping we'll always have with us evidently, but in spite of all the beefing in every strata from Low-Lower to Upper-Middle, I've yet to see any signs of organized protest against our present politico-economic system."

"Hey," Max said. "Don't get me wrong. What was good enough for Dad is good enough for me. You won't catch me talking against the government."

"Hm-m-m," Joe murmured. "And all the other cliches taught to us to preserve the status quo, our People's Capitalism." They were reaching the outskirts of town, crossing the Esopus. The airport lay only a mile or so beyond.

It was obviously too deep for Max, and since he didn't understand, he assumed his superior didn't know what he was talking about. He said, tolerantly, "Well, what's wrong with People's Capitalism? Everybody owns the corporations. Damnsight better than the Sovs have."

Joe said sourly. "We've got one optical illusion, they've got another, Max. Over there they claim the proletariat owns the means of production. Great. But the Party members are the ones who control it, and, as a result they manage to do all right for themselves. The Party hierarchy over there are like our Uppers over here."

"Yeah." Max was being particularly dense. "I've seen a lot about it on Telly. You know, when there isn't a good fracas on, you tune to one of them educational shows, like —"

Joe winced at the term *educational*, but held his peace.

"It's pretty rugged over there. But in the West-world, the people own a corporation's stock and they run it and get the benefit."

"At least it makes a beautiful story," Joe said dryly. "Look, Max. Suppose you have a corporation that has two hundred thousand shares out and they're distributed among one hundred thousand and one persons. One hundred thousand of these own one share apiece, but the remaining stockholder owns the other hundred thousand."

"I don't know what you're getting at," Max said.

Joe Mauser was tired of the discussion. "Briefly," he said, "we have the illusion that this is a People's Capitalism, with all stock in the hands of the People. Actually, as ever before, the stock is in the hands of the Uppers, all except a mere dribble. They own the country and they run it for their own benefit."

Max shot a less than military glance at him. "Hey, you're not one of these Sovs yourself, are you?"

They were coming into the parking area near the Administration Building of the airport. "No," Joe said so softly that Max could hardly hear his words. "Only a Mid-Middle on the make."

* * * * *

Followed by Max, he strode quickly to the Administration Building, presented his credit identification at the desk and requested a light aircraft for a period of three hours. The clerk, hardly looking up, began going through motions, speaking into telescreens.

The clerk said finally, "You might have a small wait, sir. Quite a few of the officers involved in this fracas have been renting out taxi-planes almost as fast as they're available."

That didn't surprise Joe Mauser. Any competent officer made a point of an aerial survey of the battle reservation before going into a fracas. Aircraft, of course, couldn't be used *during* the fray, since they postdated the turn of the century, and hence were relegated to the cemetery of military devices along with such items as nuclear weapons, tanks, and even gasoline-propelled vehicles of size to be useful.

Use an aircraft in a fracas, or even *build* an aircraft for military usage and you'd have a howl go up from the military attaches from the Sov-world that would be heard all the way to Budapest. Not a fracas went by but there were scores, if not hundreds, of military observers, keen-eyed to check whether or not any really modern tools of war were being illegally utilized. Joe Mauser sometimes wondered if the West-world observers, over in the Sov-world, were as hair fine in their living up to the rules of the Universal Disarmament Pact. Probably. But, for that matter, they didn't have the same system of fighting fracases over there, as in the West.

Joe took a chair while he waited and thumbed through a fan magazine. From time to time he found his own face in such publications. He was a third-rate celebrity, really. Luck hadn't been with him so far as the buffs were concerned. They wanted spectacular victories, murderous situations in which they could lose themselves in vicarious sadistic thrills. Joe had reached most of his peaks while in retreat, or commanding a holding action. His officers appreciated him and so did the ultra-knowledgeable fracas buffs-but he was all but an unknown to the average dim wit who spent most of his life glued to the Telly set, watching men butcher each other.

On the various occasions when matters had pickled and Joe had to fight his way out against difficult odds, using spectacular tactics in desperation, he was almost always off camera. Purely luck. On top of skill, determination, experience and courage, you had to have luck in the Military Category to get anywhere.

This time Joe was going to manufacture his own.

A voice said, "Ah, Captain Mauser."

Joe looked up, then came to his feet quickly. In automatic reflex, he began to come to the salute but then caught himself. He said stiffly, "My compliments, Marshal Cogswell."

The other was a smallish man, but strikingly strong of face and strongly built. His voice was clipped, clear and had the air of command as though born with it. He, like Joe, wore mufti and now extended his hand to be shaken.

"I hear you've signed up with Baron Haer, captain. I was rather expecting you to come in with me. Had a place for a good aide de camp. Liked your work in that last fracas we went through together."

"Thank you, sir," Joe said. Stonewall Cogswell was as good a tactician as freelanced and he was more than that. He was a judge of men and a stickler for detail. And right now, if Joe Mauser knew Marshal Stonewall Cogswell as well as he thought, Cogswell was smelling a rat. There was no reason why old pro Joe Mauser should sign up with a sure loser like Vacuum Tube when he could have earned more shares taking a commission with Hovercraft.

He was looking at Joe brightly, the question in his eyes. Three or four of his staff were behind a few paces, looking polite, but Cogswell didn't bring them into the conversation. Joe knew most by sight. Good men all. Old pros all. He felt another twinge of doubt.

Joe had to cover. He said, "I was offered a particularly good contract, sir. Too good to resist."

The other nodded, as though inwardly coming to a satisfactory conclusion. "Baron Haer's connections, eh? He's probably offered to back you for a bounce in caste. Is that it, Joe?"

Joe Mauser flushed. Stonewall Cogswell knew what he was talking about. He'd been born into Middle status himself and had become an Upper the hard way. His path wasn't as long as Joe's was going to be, but long enough and he knew how rocky the climb was. How very rocky.

Joe said, stiffly, "I'm afraid I'm in no position to discuss my commander's military contracts, marshal. We're in mufti, but after all—"

Cogswell's lean face registered one of his infrequent grimaces of humor. "I understand, Joe. Well, good luck and I hope things don't pickle for you in the coming fracas. Possibly we'll find ourselves aligned together again at some future time."

"Thank you, sir," Joe said, once more having to catch himself to prevent an automatic salute.

Cogswell and his staff went off, leaving Joe looking after them. Even the marshal's staff members were top men, any of whom could have conducted a divisional magnitude fracas. Joe felt the coldness in his stomach again. Although it must have looked like a cinch, the enemy wasn't taking any chances whatsoever. Cogswell and his officers were undoubtedly here at the airport for the same reason as Joe. They wanted a thorough aerial reconnaissance of the battlefield-to-be, before the issue was joined.

* * * * *

Max was standing at his elbow. "Who was that, sir? Looks like a real tough one."

"He is a real tough one," Joe said sourly. "That's Stonewall Cogswell, the best field commander in North America."

Max pursed his lips. "I never seen him out of uniform before. Lots of times on Telly, but never out of uniform. I thought he was taller than that."

"He fights with his brains," Joe said, still looking after the craggy field marshal. "He doesn't have to be any taller."

Max scowled. "Where'd he ever get that nickname, sir?"

"Stonewall?" Joe was turning to resume his chair and magazine. "He's supposed to be a student of a top general back in the American Civil War. Uses some of the original Stonewall's tactics."

Max was out of his depth. "American Civil War? Was that much of a fracas, captain? It musta been before my time."

"It was quite a fracas," Joe said dryly. "Lot of good lads died. A hundred years after it was fought, the *reasons* it was fought seemed about as valid as those we fight fracases for today. Personally I—"

He had to cut it short. They were calling him on the address system. His aircraft was ready. Joe made his way to the hangars, followed by Max Mainz. He was going to pilot the airplane himself and old Stonewall Cogswell would have been surprised at what Joe Mauser was looking for.

V

By the time they had returned to quarters, there was a message waiting for Captain Mauser. He was to report to the officer commanding reconnaissance.

Joe redressed in the Haer kilts and proceeded to headquarters.

The officer commanding reconnaissance turned out to be none other than Balt Haer, natty as ever, and, as ever, arrogantly tapping his swagger stick against his leg.

"Zen! Captain," he complained. "Where have you been? Off on a trank kick? We've got to get organized."

Joe Mauser snapped him a salute. "No, sir. I rented an aircraft to scout out the terrain over which we'll be fighting."

"Indeed. And what were your impressions, captain?" There was an overtone which suggested that it made little difference what impressions a captain of cavalry might have gained.

Joe shrugged. "Largely mountains, hills, woods. Good reconnaissance is going to make the difference in this one. And in the fracas itself cavalry is going to be more important than either artillery or infantry. A Nathan Forrest fracas, sir. A matter of getting there fustest with the mostest."

Balt Haer said amusedly. "Thanks for your opinion, captain. Fortunately, our staff has already come largely to the same conclusions. Undoubtedly, they'll be glad to hear your wide experience bears them out."

Joe said evenly, "It's a rather obvious conclusion, of course." He took this as it came, having been through it before. The dilettante amateur's dislike of the old pro. The amateur in command who knew full well he was less capable than many of those below him in rank.

"Of course, captain," Balt Haer flicked his swagger stick against his leg. "But to the point. Your squadron is to be deployed as scouts under my overall command. You've had cavalry experience, I assume."

"Yes, sir. In various fracases over the past fifteen years."

"Very well. Now then, to get to the reason I have summoned you. Yesterday in my father's office you intimated that you had some grandiose scheme which would bring victory to the Haer colors. But then, on some thin excuse, refused to divulge just what the scheme might be."

Joe Mauser looked at him unblinkingly.

Balt Haer said: "Now I'd like to have your opinion on just how Vacuum Tube Transport can extract itself from what would seem a poor position at best."

In all there were four others in the office, two women clerks fluttering away at typers, and two of Balt Haer's junior officers. They seemed only mildly interested in the conversation between Balt and Joe.

Joe wet his lips carefully. The Haer scion was his commanding officer. He said, "Sir, what I had in mind is a new gimmick. At this stage, if I told anybody and it leaked, it'd never be effective, not even this first time."

Haer observed him coldly. "And you think me incapable of keeping your secret, ah, *gimmick*, I believe is the idiomatic term you used."

Joe Mauser's eyes shifted around the room, taking in the other four, who were now looking at him.

Bait Haer rapped, "These members of my staff are all trusted Haer employees, Captain Mauser. They are not fly-by-night freelancers hired for a week or two."

Joe said, "Yes, sir. But it's been my experience that one person can hold a secret. It's twice as hard for two, and from there on it's a decreasing probability in a geometric ratio."

The younger Haer's stick rapped the side of his leg, impatiently. "Suppose I inform you that this is a command, captain? I have little confidence in a supposed gimmick that will rescue our forces from disaster and I rather dislike the idea of a captain of one of my squadrons dashing about with such a bee in his bonnet when he should be obeying my commands."

Joe kept his voice respectful. "Then, sir, I'd request that we take the matter to the Commander in Chief, your father."

"Indeed!"

Joe said, "Sir, I've been working on this a long time. I can't afford to risk throwing the idea away."

Bait Haer glared at him. "Very well, captain. I'll call your bluff, come along." He turned on his heel and headed from the room.

Joe Mauser shrugged in resignation and followed him.

* * * * *

The old Baron wasn't much happier about Joe Mauser's secrets than was his son. It had only been the day before that he had taken Joe on, but already he had seemed to have aged in appearance. Evidently, each hour that went by made it increasingly clear just how perilous a position he had assumed. Vacuum Tube Transport had elbowed, buffaloed, bluffed and edged itself up to the outskirts of the really big time. The Baron's ability, his aggressiveness, his flair, his political pull, had all helped, but now the chips were down. He was up against one of the biggies, and this particular biggy was tired of ambitious little Vacuum Tube Transport.

He listened to his son's words, listened to Joe's defense.

He said, looking at Joe, "If I understand this, you have some scheme which you think will bring victory in spite of what seems a disastrous situation."

"Yes, sir."

The two Haers looked at him, one impatiently, the other in weariness.

Joe said, "I'm gambling everything on this, sir. I'm no Rank Private in his first fracas. I deserve to be given some leeway."

Balt Haer snorted. "Gambling everything! What in Zen would *you* have to gamble, captain? The whole Haer family fortunes are tied up. Hovercraft is out for blood. They won't be satisfied with a token victory and a negotiated compromise. They'll devastate us. Thousands of mercenaries killed, with all that means in indemnities; millions upon million in expensive military equipment, most of which we've had to hire and will have to recompensate for. Can you imagine the value of our stock after Stonewall Cogswell has finished with us? Why, every two by four trucking outfit in North America will be challenging us, and we won't have the forces to meet a minor skirmish."

Joe reached into an inner pocket and laid a sheaf of documents on the desk of Baron Malcolm Haer. The Baron scowled down at them.

Joe said simply, "I've been accumulating stock since before I was eighteen and I've taken good care of my portfolio in spite of taxes and the various other pitfalls which make the accumulation of capital practically impossible. Yesterday, I sold all of my portfolio I was legally allowed to sell and converted to Vacuum Tube Transport." He added, dryly, "Getting it at an excellent rate, by the way."

Balt Haer mulled through the papers, unbelievingly. "Zen!" he ejaculated. "The fool really did it. He's sunk a small fortune into our stock."

Baron Haer growled at his son, "You seem considerably more convinced of our defeat than the captain, here. Perhaps I should reverse your positions of command."

His son grunted, but said nothing.

Old Malcolm Haer's eyes came back to Joe. "Admittedly, I thought you on the romantic side yesterday, with your hints of some scheme which would lead us out of the wilderness, so to speak. Now I wonder if you might not really have something. Very well, I respect your claimed need for secrecy. Espionage is not exactly an antiquated military field."

"Thank you, sir."

But the Baron was still staring at him. "However, there's more to it than that. Why not take this great scheme to Marshal Cogswell? And yesterday you mentioned that the Telly sets of the nation would be tuned in on this fracas, and obviously you are correct. The question becomes, what of it?"

The fat was in the fire now. Joe Mauser avoided the haughty stare of young Balt Haer and addressed himself to the older man. "You have political pull, sir. Oh, I know you don't make and break presidents. You couldn't even pull enough wires to keep Hovercraft from making this a divisional magnitude fracas-but you have pull enough for my needs."

Baron Haer leaned back in his chair, his barrel-like body causing that article of furniture to creak. He crossed his hands over his stomach. "And what are your needs, Captain Mauser?"

Joe said evenly, "If I can bring this off, I'll be a fracas buff celebrity. I don't have any illusions about the fickleness of the Telly fans, but for a day or two I'll be on top. If at the same time I had your all out support, pulling what strings you could reach —"

"Why then, you'd be promoted to Upper, wouldn't you, captain?" Balt Haer finished for him, amusement in his voice.

"That's what I'm gambling on," Joe said evenly.

The younger Haer grinned at his father superciliously. "So our captain says he will defeat Stonewall Cogswell in return for you sponsoring his becoming a member of the nation's elite."

* * * * *

"Good Heavens, is the supposed cream of the nation now selected on no higher a level than this?" There was sarcasm in the words.

The three men turned. It was the girl Joe had bumped into the day before. The Haers didn't seem surprised at her entrance.

"Nadine," the older man growled. "Captain Joseph Mauser who has been given a commission in our forces."

Joe went through the routine of a Middle of officer's rank being introduced to a lady of Upper caste. She smiled at him, somewhat mockingly, and failed to make standard response.

Nadine Haer said, "I repeat, what is this service the captain can render the house of Haer so important that pressure should be brought to raise him to Upper caste? It would seem unlikely that he is a noted scientist, an outstanding artist, a great teacher —"

Joe said, uncomfortably, "They say the military is a science, too."

Her expression was almost as haughty as that of her brother. "Do they? I have never thought so."

"Really, Nadine," her father grumbled. "This is hardly your affair."

"No? In a few days I shall be repairing the damage you have allowed, indeed sponsored, to be committed upon the bodies of possibly thousands of now healthy human beings."

Balt said nastily, "Nobody asked you to join the medical staff, Nadine. You could have stayed in your laboratory, figuring out new methods of preventing the human race from replenishing itself."

The girl was obviously not the type to redden, but her anger was manifest. She spun on her brother. "If the race continues its present maniac course, possibly more effective methods of birth control *are* the most important development we could make. Even to the ultimate discovery of preventing all future conception."

Joe caught himself in mid-chuckle.

But not in time. She spun on him in his turn. "Look at yourself in that silly skirt. A professional soldier! A killer! In my opinion the most useless occupation ever devised by man. Parasite on the best and useful members of society. Destroyer by trade!"

Joe began to open his mouth, but she overrode him. "Yes, yes. I know. I've read all the nonsense that has accumulated down through the ages about the need for, the glory of, the sacrifice of the professional soldier. How they defend their country. How they give all for the common good. Zen! What nonsense."

Balt Haer was smirking sourly at her. "The theory today is, Nadine, old thing, that professionals such as the captain are gathering experience in case a serious fracas with the Sovs ever develops. Meanwhile his training is kept at a fine edge fighting in our inter-corporation, inter-union, or union-corporation fracases that develop in our private enterprise society."

She laughed her scorn. "And what a theory! Limited to the weapons which prevailed before 1900. If there was ever real conflict between the Sov-world and our own, does anyone really believe either would stick to such arms? Why, aircraft, armored vehicles, yes, and nuclear weapons and rockets, would be in overnight use."

Joe was fascinated by her furious attack. He said, "Then, what would you say was the purpose of the fracases, Miss —"

"Circuses," she snorted. "The old Roman games, all over again, and a hundred times worse. Blood and guts sadism. The quest of a frustrated person for satisfaction in another's pain. Our Lowers of today are as useless and frustrated as the Roman proletariat and potentially they're just as dangerous as the mob that once dominated Rome. Automation, the second industrial revolution, has eliminated for all practical purposes the need for their labor. So we give them bread and circuses. And every year that goes by the circuses must be increasingly sadistic, death on an increasing scale, or they aren't satisfied. Once it was enough to have fictional mayhem, cowboys and Indians, gangsters, or G.I.s versus the Nazis, Japs or Commies, but that's passed. Now we need *real* blood and guts."

Baron Haer snapped finally, "All right, Nadine. We've heard this lecture before. I doubt if the captain is interested, particularly since you don't seem to be able to get beyond the protesting stage and have yet to come up with an answer."

"I have an answer!"

"Ah?" Balt Haer raised his eyebrows, mockingly.

"Yes! Overthrow this silly status society. Resume the road to progress. Put our people to useful endeavor, instead of sitting in front of their Telly sets, taking trank pills to put them in a happy daze and watching sadistic fracases to keep them in thrills, and their minds from their condition."

Joe had figured on keeping out of the controversy with this firebrand, but now, really interested, he said, "Progress to where?"

She must have caught in his tone that he wasn't needling. She frowned at him. "I don't know man's goal, if there is one. I'm not even sure it's important. It's the road that counts. The endeavor. The dream. The effort expended to make a world a better place than it was at the time of your birth."

Balt Haer said mockingly, "That's the trouble with you, Sis. Here we've reached Utopia and you don't admit it."

"Utopia!"

"Certainly. Take a poll. You'll find nineteen people out of twenty happy with things just the way they are. They have full tummies and security, lots of leisure and trank pills to make matters seem even rosier than they are-and they're rather rosy already."

"Then what's the necessity of this endless succession of bloody fracases, covered to the most minute bloody detail on the Telly?"

Baron Haer cut things short. "We've hashed and rehashed this before, Nadine and now we're too busy to debate further." He turned to Joe Mauser. "Very well, captain, you have my pledge. I wish I felt as optimistic as you seem to be about your prospects. That will be all for now, captain."

Joe saluted and executed an about face.

* * * * *

In the outer offices, when he had closed the door behind him, he rolled his eyes upward in mute thanks to whatever powers might be. He had somehow gained the enmity of Balt, his immediate superior, but he'd also gained the support of Baron Haer himself, which counted considerably more.

He considered for a moment, Nadine Haer's words. She was obviously a malcontent, but, on the other hand, her opinions of his chosen profession weren't too different than his own. However, given this victory, this upgrading in caste, and Joe Mauser would be in a position to retire.

The door opened and shut behind him and he half turned.

Nadine Haer, evidently still caught up in the hot words between herself and her relatives, glared at him. All of which stressed the beauty he had noticed the day before. She was an almost unbelievably pretty girl, particularly when flushed with anger.

It occurred to him with a blowlike suddenness that, if his caste was raised to Upper, he would be in a position to woo such as Nadine Haer.

He looked into her furious face and said, "I was intrigued, Miss Haer, with what you had to say, and I'd like to discuss some of your points. I wonder if I could have the pleasure of your company at some nearby refreshment —"

"My, how formal an invitation, captain. I suppose you had in mind sitting and flipping back a few trank pills."

Joe looked at her. "I don't believe I've had a trank in the past twenty years, Miss Haer. Even as a boy, I didn't particularly take to having my senses dulled with drug-induced pleasure."

Some of her fury was abating, but she was still critical of the professional mercenary. Her eyes went up and down his uniform in scorn. "You seem to make pretenses of being cultivated, captain. Then why your chosen profession?"

He'd had the answer to that for long years. He said now, simply, "I told you I was born a Lower. Given that, little counts until I fight my way out of it. Had I been born in a feudalist society, I would have attempted to batter myself into the nobility. Under classical capitalism, I would have done my utmost to accumulate a fortune, enough to reach an effective position in society. Now, under People's Capitalism..."

She snorted, "Industrial Feudalism would be the better term."

"...I realize I can't even start to fulfill myself until I am a member of the Upper caste."

Her eyes had narrowed, and the anger was largely gone. "But you chose the military field in which to better yourself?"

"Government propaganda to the contrary, it is practically impossible to raise yourself in other fields. I didn't build this world, possibly I don't even approve of it, but since I'm in it I have no recourse but to follow its rules."

Her eyebrows arched. "Why not try to change the rules?"

Joe blinked at her.

Nadine Haer said, "Let's look up that refreshment you were talking about. In fact, there's a small coffee bar around the corner where it'd be possible for one of Baron Haer's brood to have a cup with one of her father's officers of Middle caste."

VI

The following morning, hands on the pillow beneath his head, Joe Mauser stared up at the ceiling of his room and rehashed his session with Nadine Haer. It hadn't taken him five minutes to come to the conclusion that he was in love with the girl, but it had taken him the rest of the evening to keep himself under rein and not let the fact get through to her.

He wanted to talk about the way her mouth tucked in at the corners, but she was hot on the evolution of society. He would have liked to have kissed that impossibly perfectly shaped ear of hers, but she was all for exploring the reasons why man had reached his present impasse. Joe was for holding hands, and staring into each other's eyes, she was for delving into the differences between the West-world and the Sov-world and the possibility of resolving them.

Of course, to keep her company at all it had been necessary to suppress his own desires and to go along. It obviously had never occurred to her that a Middle might have romantic ideas involving Nadine Haer. It had simply not occurred to her, no matter the radical teachings she advocated.

Most of their world was predictable from what had gone before. In spite of popular fable to the contrary, the division between classes had become increasingly clear. Among other things, tax systems were such that it became all but impossible for a citizen born poor to accumulate a fortune. Through ability he might rise to the point of earning fabulous sums-and wind up in debt to the tax collector. A great inventor, a great artist, had little chance of breaking into the domain of what finally became the small percentage of the population now known as Uppers. Then, too, the rising cost of a really good education became such that few other than those born into the Middle or Upper castes could afford the best of schools. Castes tended to perpetuate themselves.

Politically, the nation had fallen increasingly deeper into the two-party system, both parties of which were tightly controlled by the same group of Uppers. Elections had become a farce, a great national holiday in which stereotyped patriotic speeches, pretenses of unity between all castes, picnics, beer busts and trank binges predominated for one day.

Economically, too, the augurs had been there. Production of the basics had become so profuse that poverty in the old sense of the word had become nonsensical. There was an abundance of the necessities of life for all. Social security, socialized medicine, unending unemployment insurance, old age pensions, pensions for veterans, for widows and children, for the unfit, pensions and doles for this, that and the other, had doubled, and doubled again, until everyone had security for life. The Uppers, true enough, had opulence far beyond that known by the Middles and lived like Gods compared to the Lowers. But all had security. They had agreed, thus far, Joe and Nadine. But then had come debate.

* * * * *

"Then why," Joe had asked her, "haven't we achieved what your brother called it? Why isn't this Utopia? Isn't it what man has been yearning for, down through the ages? Where did the wheel come off? What happened to the dream?"

Nadine had frowned at him-beautifully, he thought. "It's not the first time man has found abundance in a society, though never to this degree. The Incas had it, for instance."

"I don't know much about them," Joe admitted. "An early form of communism with a sort of military-priesthood at the top."

She had nodded, her face serious, as always. "And for themselves, the Romans more or less had it-at the expense of the nations they conquered, of course."

"And —" Joe prodded.

"And in these examples the same thing developed. Society ossified. Joe," she said, using his first name for the first time, and in a manner that set off a new count down in his blood, "a ruling caste and a socio-economic system perpetuates itself, just so long as it ever can. No matter what damage it may do to society as a whole, it perpetuates itself even to the point of complete destruction of everything.

"Remember Hitler? Adolf the Aryan and his Thousand Year Reich? When it became obvious he had failed, and the only thing that could result from continued resistance would be destruction of Germany's cities and millions of her people, did he and his clique resign or surrender? Certainly not. They attempted to bring down the whole German structure in a Götterdammerung."

Nadine Haer was deep into her theme, her eyes flashing her conviction. "A socio-economic system reacts like a living organism. It attempts to live on, indefinitely, agonizingly, no matter how antiquated it might have become. The Roman politico-economic system continued for centuries after it should have been replaced. Such reformers as the Gracchus brothers were assassinated or thrust aside so that the entrenched elements could perpetuate themselves, and when Rome finally fell, darkness descended for a thousand years on Western progress."

Joe had never gone this far in his thoughts. He said now, somewhat uncomfortably, "Well, what would replace what we have now? If you took power from you Uppers, who could direct the country? The Lowers? That's not even funny. Take away their fracases and their trank pills and they'd go berserk. They don't *want* anything else."

Her mouth worked. "Admittedly, we've already allowed things to deteriorate much too far. We should have done something long ago. I'm not sure I know the answer. All I know is that in order to maintain the status quo, we're not utilizing the efforts of more than a fraction of our people. Nine out of ten of us spend our lives sitting before the Telly, sucking tranks. Meanwhile, the motivation for continued progress seems to have withered away. Our Upper political circles are afraid some seemingly minor change might avalanche, so more and more we lean upon the old way of doing things."

Joe had put up mild argument. "I've heard the case made that the Lowers are fools and the reason our present socio-economic system makes it so difficult to rise from Lower to Upper is that you cannot make a fool understand he is one. You can only make him angry. If some, who are not fools, are allowed to advance from Lower to Upper, the vast mass who are fools will be angry because they are not allowed to. That's why the Military Category is made a channel of advance. To take that road, a man gives up his security and he'll die if he's a fool."

Nadine had been scornful. "That reminds me of the old contention by racial segregationalists that the Negroes *smelled* bad. First they put them in a position where they had insufficient bathing facilities, their diet inadequate, and their teeth uncared for, and then protested that they couldn't be associated with because of their odor. Today, we are born within our castes. If an Upper is inadequate, he nevertheless remains an Upper. An accident of birth makes him an aristocrat; environment, family, training, education, friends, traditions and laws maintain him in that position. But a Lower who potentially has the greatest of value to society, is born handicapped and he's hard put not to wind up before a Telly, in a mental daze from trank. Sure he's a fool, he's never been *allowed* to develop himself."

* * * * *

Yes, Joe reflected now, it had been quite an evening. In a life of more than thirty years devoted to rebellion, he had never met anyone so outspoken as Nadine Haer, nor one who had thought it through as far as she had.

He grunted. His own revolt was against the level at which he had found himself in society, not the structure of society itself. His whole *raison d'être* was to lift himself to Upper status. It came as a shock to him to find a person he admired who had been born into Upper caste, desirous of tearing the whole system down.

His thoughts were interrupted by the door opening and the face of Max Mainz grinning in at him. Joe was mildly surprised at his orderly not knocking before opening the door. Max evidently had a lot to learn.

The little man blurted, "Come on, Joe. Let's go out on the town!"

"Joe?" Joe Mauser raised himself to one elbow and stared at the other. "Leaving aside the merits of your suggestion for the moment, do you think you should address an officer by his first name?"

Max Mainz came fully into the bedroom, his grin still wider. "You forgot! It's election day!"

"Oh." Joe Mauser relaxed into his pillow. "So it is. No duty for today, eh?"

"No duty for anybody," Max crowed. "What'd you say we go into town and have a few drinks in one of the Upper bars?"

Joe grunted, but began to arise. "What'll that accomplish? On election day, most of the Uppers get done up in their oldest clothes and go slumming down in the Lower quarters."

Max wasn't to be put off so easily. "Well, wherever we go, let's get going. Zen! I'll bet this town is full of fracas buffs from as far as Philly. And on election day, to boot. Wouldn't it be something if I found me a real fracas fan, some Upper-Upper dame?"

Joe laughed at him, even as he headed for the bathroom. As a matter of fact, he rather liked the idea of going into town for the show. "Max," he said over his shoulder, "you're in for a big disappointment. They're all the same. Upper, Lower, or Middle."

"Yeah?" Max grinned back at him. "Well, I'd like the pleasure of finding out if that's true by personal experience."

VII

In a far away past, Kingston had once been the capital of the United States. For a short time, when Washington's men were in flight after the debacle of their defeat in New York City, the government of the United Colonies had held session in this Hudson River town. It had been its one moment of historic glory, and afterward Kingston had slipped back into being a minor city on the edge of the Catskills, approximately halfway between New York and Albany.

Of most recent years, it had become one of the two recruiting centers which bordered the Catskill Military Reservation, which in turn was one of the score or so population cleared areas throughout the continent where rival corporations or unions could meet and settle their differences in combat-given permission of the Military Category Department of the government. And permission was becoming ever easier to acquire.

It had slowly evolved, the resorting to trial by combat to settle disputes between competing corporations, disputes between corporations and unions, disputes between unions over jurisdiction. Slowly, but predictably. Since the earliest days of the first industrial revolution, conflict between these elements had often broken into violence, sometimes on a scale comparable to minor warfare. An early example was the union organizing in Colorado when armed elements of the Western Federation of Miners shot it out with similarly armed "detectives" hired by the mine owners, and later with the troops of an unsympathetic State government.

By the middle of the Twentieth-Century, unions had become one of the biggest businesses in the country, and by this time a considerable amount of the industrial conflict had shifted to fights between them for jurisdiction over dues-paying members. Battles on the waterfront, assassination and counter-assassination by gun-toting goon squads dominated by gangsters, industrial sabotage, frays between pickets and scabs-all were common occurrences.

But it was the coming of Telly which increasingly brought such conflicts literally before the public eye. Zealous reporters made ever greater effort to bring the actual mayhem before the eyes of their viewers, and never were their efforts more highly rewarded.

A society based upon private endeavor is as jealous of a vacuum as is Mother Nature. Give a desire that can be filled profitably, and the means can somehow be found to realize it.

* * * * *

At one point in the nation's history, the railroad lords had dominated the economy, later it became the petroleum princes of Texas and elsewhere, but toward the end of the Twentieth Century the communications industries slowly gained prominence. Nothing was more greatly in demand than feeding the insatiable maw of the Telly fan, nothing, ultimately, became more profitable.

And increasingly, the Telly buff endorsed the more sadistic of the fictional and nonfictional programs presented him. Even in the earliest years of the industry, producers had found that murder and mayhem, war and frontier gunfights, took precedence over less gruesome subjects. Music was drowned out by gunfire, the dance replaced by the shuffle of cowboy and rustler advancing down a dusty street toward each other, their fingertips brushing the grips of their six-shooters, the comedian's banter fell away before the chatter of the gangster's tommy gun.

And increasing realism was demanded. The Telly reporter on the scene of a police arrest, preferably a murder, a rumble between rival gangs of juvenile delinquents, a longshoreman's fray in which scores of workers were hospitalized. When attempts were made to suppress such broadcasts, the howl of freedom of speech and the press went up, financed by tycoons clever enough to realize the value of the subjects they covered so adequately.

The vacuum was there, the desire, the *need*. Bread the populace had. Trank was available to all. But the need was for the circus, the vicious, sadistic circus, and bit by bit, over the years and decades, the way was found to circumvent the country's laws and traditions to supply the need.

Aye, a way is always found. The final Universal Disarmament Pact which had totally banned all weapons invented since the year 1900 and provided for complete inspection, had not ended the fear of war. And thus there was excuse to give the would-be soldier, the potential defender of the country in some future inter-nation conflict, practical experience.

Slowly tolerance grew to allow union and corporation to fight it out, hiring the services of mercenaries. Slowly rules grew up to govern such fracases. Slowly a department of government evolved. The Military Category became as acceptable as the next, and the mercenary a valued, even idolized, member of society. And the field became practically the only one in which a status quo orientated socio-economic system allowed for advancement in caste.

Joe Mauser and Max Mainz strolled the streets of Kingston in an extreme of atmosphere seldom to be enjoyed. Not only was the advent of a divisional magnitude fracas only a short period away, but the freedom of an election day as well. The carnival, the Mardi Gras, the fete, the fiesta, of an election. Election Day, when each aristocrat became only a man, and each man an aristocrat, free of all society's artificially conceived, caste-perpetuating rituals and taboos.

Carnival! The day was young, but already the streets were thick with revelers, with dancers, with drunks. A score of bands played, youngsters in particular ran about attired in costume, there were barbeques and flowing beer kegs. On the outskirts of town were roller coasters and ferris wheels, fun houses and drive-it-yourself miniature cars. Carnival!

Max said happily, "You drink, Joe? Or maybe you like trank, better." Obviously, he loved to roll the other's first name over his tongue.

Joe wondered in amusement how often the little man had found occasion to call a Mid-Middle by his first name. "No trank," he said. "Alcohol for me. Mankind's old faithful."

"Well," Max debated, "get high on alcohol and bingo, a hangover in the morning. But trank? You wake up with a smile."

"And a desire for more trank to keep the mood going," Joe said wryly. "Get smashed on alcohol and you suffer for it eventually."

"Well, that's one way of looking at it," Max argued happily. "So let's start off with a couple of quick ones in this here Upper joint."

* * * * *

Joe looked the place over. He didn't know Kingston overly well, but by the appearance of the building and by the entry, it was probably the swankiest hotel in town. He shrugged. So far as he was concerned, he appreciated the greater comfort and the better service of his Middle caste bars, restaurants and hotels over the ones he had patronized when a Lower. However, his wasn't an immediate desire to push into the preserves of the Uppers; not until he had won rightfully to their status.

But on this occasion the little fellow wanted to drink at an Upper bar. Very well, it was election day. "Let's go," he said to Max.

In the uniform of a Rank Captain of the Military Category, there was little to indicate caste level, and ordinarily given the correct air of nonchalance, Joe Mauser, in uniform, would have been able to go anywhere, without so much as a raised eyebrow-until he had presented his credit card, which indicated his caste. But Max was another thing. He was obviously a Lower, and probably a Low-Lower at that.

But space was made for them at a bar packed with election day celebrants, politicians involved in the day's speeches and voting, higher ranking officers of the Haer forces, having a day off, and various Uppers of both sexes in town for the excitement of the fracas to come.

"Beer," Joe said to the bartender.

"Not me," Max crowed. "Champagne. Only the best for Max Mainz. Give me some of that champagne liquor I always been hearing about."

Joe had the bill credited to his card, and they took their bottles and glasses to a newly aban-doned table. The place was too packed to have awaited the services of a waiter, although poor

Max probably would have loved such attention. Lower, and even Middle bars and restaurants were universally automated, and the waiter or waitress a thing of yesteryear.

Max looked about the room in awe. "This is living," he announced. "I wonder what they'd say if I went to the desk and ordered a room."

Joe Mauser wasn't as highly impressed as his batman. In fact, he'd often stayed in the larger cities, in hostelries as sumptuous as this, though only of Middle status. Kingston's best was on the mediocre side. He said, "They'd probably tell you they were filled up."

Max was indignant. "Because I'm a Lower? It's *election* day."

Joe said mildly, "Because they probably are filled up. But for that matter, they might brush you off. It's not as though an Upper went to a Middle or Lower hotel and asked for accommodations. But what do you want, justice?"

Max dropped it. He looked down into his glass. "Hey," he complained, "what'd they give me? This stuff tastes like weak hard cider."

Joe laughed. "What did you think it was going to taste like?"

Max took another unhappy sip. "I thought it was supposed to be the best drink you could buy. You know, really strong. It's just bubbly wine."

A voice said, dryly, "Your companion doesn't seem to be a connoisseur of the French vintages, captain."

Joe turned. Balt Haer and two others occupied the table next to them.

Joe chuckled amiably and said, "Truthfully, it was my own reaction, the first time I drank sparkling wine, sir."

"Indeed," Haer said. "I can imagine." He fluttered a hand. "Lieutenant Colonel Paul Warren of Marshal Cogswell's staff, and Colonel Lajos Arpàd, of Budapest-Captain Joseph Mauser."

Joe Mauser came to his feet and clicked his heels, bowing from the waist in approved military protocol. The other two didn't bother to come to their feet, but did condescend to shake hands.

The Sov officer said, disinterestedly, "Ah yes, this is one of your fabulous customs, isn't it? On an election day, everyone is quite entitled to go anywhere. Anywhere at all. And, ah" —he made a sound somewhat like a giggle —"associate with anyone at all."

Joe Mauser resumed his seat then looked at him. "That is correct. A custom going back to the early history of the country when all men were considered equal in such matters as law and civil rights. Gentlemen, may I present Rank Private Max Mainz, my orderly."

Balt Haer, who had obviously already had a few, looked at him dourly. "You can carry these things to the point of the ludicrous, captain. For a man with your ambitions, I'm surprised."

The infantry officer the younger Haer had introduced as Lieutenant Colonel Warren, of Stonewall Cogswell's staff, said idly, "Ambitions? Does the captain have ambitions? How in Zen can a Middle have ambitions, Balt?" He stared at Joe Mauser superciliously, but then scowled. "Haven't I seen you somewhere before?"

Joe said evenly, "Yes, sir. Five years ago we were both with the marshal in a fracas on the Little Big Horn reservation. Your company was pinned down on a knoll by a battery of field artillery. The Marshal sent me to your relief. We sneaked in, up an arroyo, and were able to get most of you out."

"I was wounded," the colonel said, the superciliousness gone and a strange element in his voice above the alcohol there earlier.

Joe Mauser said nothing to that. Max Mainz was stirring unhappily now. These officers were talking above his head, even as they ignored him. He had a vague feeling that he was being defended by Captain Mauser, but he didn't know how, or why.

Balt Haer had been occupied in shouting fresh drinks. Now he turned back to the table. "Well, colonel, it's all very secret, these ambitions of Captain Mauser. I understand he's been an aide de camp to Marshal Cogswell in the past, but the marshal will be distressed to learn that on this occasion Captain Mauser has a secret by which he expects to rout your forces. Indeed, yes, the captain is quite the strategist." Balt Haer laughed abruptly. "And what good will this do the captain? Why on my father's word, if he succeeds, all efforts will be made to make the captain a caste equal of ours. Not just on election day, mind you, but all three hundred sixty-five days of the year."

Joe Mauser was on his feet, his face expressionless. He said, "Shall we go, Max? Gentlemen, it's been a pleasure. Colonel Arpàd, a privilege to meet you. Colonel Warren, a pleasure to renew acquaintance." Joe Mauser turned and, trailed by his orderly, left.

* * * * *

Lieutenant Colonel Warren, pale, was on his feet too.

Balt Haer was chuckling. "Sit down, Paul. Sit down. Not important enough to be angry about. The man's a clod."

Warren looked at him bleakly. "I wasn't angry, Balt. The last time I saw Captain Mauser I was slung over his shoulder. He carried, tugged and dragged me some two miles through enemy fire."

Balt Haer carried it off with a shrug. "Well, that's his profession. Category Military. A mercenary for hire. I assume he received his pay."

"He could have left me. Common sense dictated that he leave me."

Balt Haer was annoyed. "Well, then we see what I've contended all along. The ambitious captain doesn't have common sense."

Colonel Paul Warren shook his head. "You're wrong there. Common sense Joseph Mauser has. Considerable ability, he has. He's one of the best combat men in the field. But I'd hate to serve under him."

The Hungarian was interested. "But why?"

"Because he doesn't have luck, and in the dill you need luck." Warren grunted in sour memory. "Had the Telly cameras been focused on Joe Mauser, there at the Little Big Horn, he would have been a month long sensation to the Telly buffs, with all that means." He grunted again. "There wasn't a Telly team within a mile."

"The captain probably didn't realize that," Balt Haer snorted. "Otherwise his heroics would have been modified."

Warren flushed his displeasure and sat down. He said, "Possibly we should discuss the business before us. If your father is in agreement, the fracas can begin in three days." He turned to the representative of the Sov-world. "You have satisfied yourselves that neither force is violating the Disarmament Pact?"

Lajos Arpàd nodded. "We will wish to have observers on the field, itself, of course. But preliminary observation has been satisfactory." He had been interested in the play between these two and the lower caste officer. He said now, "Pardon me. As you know, this is my first visit to the, uh *West*. I am fascinated. If I understand what just transpired, our Captain Mauser is a capable junior officer ambitious to rise in rank and status in your society." He looked at Balt Haer. "Why are you opposed to his so rising?"

Young Haer was testy about the whole matter. "Of what purpose is an Upper caste if every Tom, Dick and Harry enters it at will?"

Warren looked at the door through which Joe and Max had exited from the cocktail lounge. He opened his mouth to say something, closed it again, and held his peace.

The Hungarian said, looking from one of them to the other, "In the Sov-world we seek out such ambitious persons and utilize their abilities."

Lieutenant Colonel Warren laughed abruptly. "So do we here *theoretically*. We are *free*, whatever that means. However," he added sarcastically, "it does help to have good schooling, good connections, relatives in positions of prominence, abundant shares of good stocks, that sort of thing. And these one is born with, in this free world of ours, Colonel Arpàd."

The Sov military observer clucked his tongue. "An indication of a declining society."

Balt Haer turned on him. "And is it any different in your world?" he said sneeringly. "Is it merely coincidence that the best positions in the Sov-world are held by Party members, and that it is all but impossible for anyone not born of Party member parents to become one? Are not the best schools filled with the children of Party members? Are not only Party members allowed to keep servants? And isn't it so that —"

Lieutenant Colonel Warren said, "Gentlemen, let us not start World War Three at this spot, at this late occasion."

VIII

Baron Malcolm Haer's field headquarters were in the ruins of a farm house in a town once known as Bearsville. His forces, and those of Marshal Stonewall Cogswell, were on the march but as yet their main bodies had not come in contact. Save for skirmishes between cavalry units, there had been no action. The ruined farm house had been a victim of an earlier fracas in this reservation which had seen in its comparatively brief time more combat than Belgium, that cockpit of Europe.

There was a sheen of oily moisture on the Baron's bulletlike head and his officers weren't particularly happy about it. Malcolm Haer characteristically went into a fracas with confidence, an aggressive confidence so strong that it often carried the day. In battles past, it had become a tradition that Haer's morale was worth a thousand men; the energy he expended was the despair of his doctors who had been warning him for a decade. But now, something was missing.

A forefinger traced over the military chart before them. "So far as we know, Marshal Cogswell has established his command here in Saugerties. Anybody have any suggestions as to why?"

A major grumbled, "It doesn't make much sense, sir. You know the marshal. It's probably a fake. If we have any superiority at all, it's our artillery."

"And the old fox wouldn't want to join the issue on the plains, down near the river," a colonel added. "It's his game to keep up into the mountains with his cavalry and light infantry. He's got Jack Alshuler's cavalry. Most experienced veterans in the field."

"I know who he's got," Haer growled in irritation. "Stop reminding me. Where in the devil is Balt?"

"Coming up, sir," Balt Haer said. He had entered only moments ago, a sheaf of signals in his hand. "Why didn't they make that date 1910, instead of 1900? With radio, we could speed up communications —"

His father interrupted testily. "Better still, why not make it 1945? Then we could speed up to the point where we could polish ourselves off. What have you got?"

Balt Haer said, his face in sulk, "Some of my lads based in West Hurley report concentrations of Cogswell's infantry and artillery near Ashokan reservoir."

"Nonsense," somebody snapped. "We'd have him."

The younger Haer slapped his swagger stick against his bare leg and kilt. "Possibly it's a feint," he admitted.

"How much were they able to observe?" his father demanded.

"Not much. They were driven off by a superior squadron. The Hovercraft forces are screening everything they do with heavy cavalry units. I told you we needed more —"

"I don't need your advice at this point," his father snapped. The older Haer went back to the map, scowling still. "I don't see what he expects to do, working out of Saugerties."

A voice behind them said, "Sir, may I have your permission —"

Half of the assembled officers turned to look at the newcomer.

Balt Haer snapped, "Captain Mauser. Why aren't you with your lads?"

"Turned them over to my second in command, sir," Joe Mauser said. He was standing to attention, looking at Baron Haer.

The Baron glowered at him. "What is the meaning of this cavalier intrusion, captain? Certainly, you must have your orders. Are you under the illusion that you are part of my staff?"

"No, sir," Joe Mauser clipped. "I came to report that I am ready to put into execution —"

"The great plan!" Balt Haer ejaculated. He laughed brittlely. "The second day of the fracas, and nobody really knows where old Cogswell is, or what he plans to do. And here comes the captain with his secret plan."

Joe looked at him. He said, evenly, "Yes, sir."

The Baron's face had gone dark, as much in anger at his son, as with the upstart cavalry captain. He began to growl ominously, "Captain Mauser, rejoin your command and obey your orders."

Joe Mauser's facial expression indicated that he had expected this. He kept his voice level however, even under the chuckling scorn of his immediate superior, Balt Haer.

He said, "Sir, I will be able to tell you where Marshal Cogswell is, and every troop at his command."

For a moment there was silence, all but a stunned silence. Then the major who had suggested the Saugerties field command headquarters were a fake, blurted a curt laugh.

"This is no time for levity, captain," Balt Haer clipped. "Get to your command."

A colonel said, "Just a moment, sir. I've fought with Joe Mauser before. He's a good man."

"Not that good," someone else huffed. "Does he claim to be clairvoyant?"

Joe Mauser said flatly. "Have a semaphore man posted here this afternoon. I'll be back at that time." He spun on his heel and left them.

Balt Haer rushed to the door after him, shouting, "Captain! That's an order! Return —"

But the other was obviously gone. Enraged, the younger Haer began to shrill commands to a noncom in the way of organizing a pursuit.

His father called wearily, "That's enough, Balt. Mauser has evidently taken leave of his senses. We made the initial mistake of encouraging this idea he had, or thought he had."

"*We?*" his son snapped in return. "I had nothing to do with it."

"All right, all right. Let's tighten up, here. Now, what other information have your scouts come up with?"

IX

At the Kingston airport, Joe Mauser rejoined Max Mainz, his face drawn now.

"Everything go all right?" the little man said anxiously.

"I don't know," Joe said. "I still couldn't tell them the story. Old Cogswell is as quick as a coyote. We pull this little caper today, and he'll be ready to meet it tomorrow."

He looked at the two-place sailplane which sat on the tarmac. "Everything all set?"

"Far as I know," Max said. He looked at the motorless aircraft. "You sure you been checked out on these things, captain?"

"Yes," Joe said. "I bought this particular soaring glider more than a year ago, and I've put almost a thousand hours in it. Now, where's the pilot of that light plane?"

A single-engined sports plane was attached to the glider by a fifty-foot nylon rope. Even as Joe spoke, a youngster poked his head from the plane's window and grinned back at them. "Ready?" he yelled.

"Come on, Max," Joe said. "Let's pull the canopy off this thing. We don't want it in the way while you're semaphoring."

A figure was approaching them from the Administration Building. A uniformed man, and somehow familiar.

"A moment, Captain Mauser!"

Joe placed him now. The Sov-world representative he'd met at Balt Haer's table in the Upper bar a couple of days ago. What was his name? Colonel Arpàd. Lajos Arpàd.

The Hungarian approached and looked at the sailplane in interest. "As a representative of my government, a military attache checking upon possible violations of the Universal Disarmament Pact, may I request what you are about to do, captain?"

Joe Mauser looked at him emptily. "How did you know I was here and what I was doing?"

The Sov colonel smiled gently. "It was by suggestion of Marshal Cogswell. He is a great man for detail. It disturbed him that an ...what did he call it? ...an old pro like yourself should join with Vacuum Tube Transport, rather than Continental Hovercraft. He didn't think it made sense and suggested that possibly you had in mind some scheme that would utilize weapons of a post 1900 period in your efforts to bring success to Baron Haer's forces. So I have investigated, Captain Mauser."

"And the marshal knows about this sail plane?" Joe Mauser's face was blank.

"I didn't say that. So far as I know, he doesn't."

"Then, Colonel Arpàd, with your permission, I'll be taking off."

The Hungarian said, "With what end in mind, captain?"

"Using this glider as a reconnaissance aircraft."

"Captain, I warn you! Aircraft were not in use in warfare until —"

But Joe Mauser cut him off, equally briskly. "Aircraft were first used in combat by Pancho Villa's forces a few years previous to World War I. They were also used in the Balkan Wars of about the same period. But those were powered craft. This is a glider, invented and in use before the year 1900 and hence open to utilization."

The Hungarian clipped, "But the Wright Brothers didn't fly even gliders until —"

Joe looked him full in the face. "But you of the Sov-world do not admit that the Wrights were the first to fly, do you?"

The Hungarian closed his mouth, abruptly.

Joe said evenly, "But even if Ivan Ivanovitch, or whatever you claim his name was, didn't invent flight of heavier than air craft, the glider was flown variously before 1900, including Otto Lilienthal in the 1890s, and was designed as far back as Leonardo da Vinci."

The Sov-world colonel stared at him for a long moment, then gave an inane giggle. He stepped back and flicked Joe Mauser a salute. "Very well, captain. As a matter of routine, I shall report this use of an aircraft for reconnaissance purposes, and undoubtedly a commission will meet to investigate the propriety of the departure. Meanwhile, good luck!"

Joe returned the salute and swung a leg over the cockpit's side. Max was already in the front seat, his semaphore flags, maps and binoculars on his lap. He had been staring in dismay at the Sov officer, now was relieved that Joe had evidently pulled it off.

Joe waved to the plane ahead. Two mechanics had come up to steady the wings for the initial ten or fifteen feet of the motorless craft's passage over the ground behind the towing craft.

Joe said to Max, "did you explain to the pilot that under no circumstances was he to pass over the line of the military reservation, that we'd cut before we reached that point?"

"Yes, sir," Max said nervously. He'd flown before, on the commercial lines, but he'd never been in a glider.

They began lurching across the field, slowly, then gathering speed. And as the sailplane took speed, it took grace. After it had been pulled a hundred feet or so, Joe eased back the stick and it slipped gently into the air, four or five feet off the ground. The towing airplane was still taxiing, but with its tow airborne it picked up speed quickly. Another two hundred feet and it, too, was in the air and beginning to climb. The glider behind held it to a speed of sixty miles or so.

At ten thousand feet, the plane leveled off and the pilot's head swiveled to look back at them. Joe Mauser waved to him and dropped the release lever which ejected the nylon rope from the glider's nose. The plane dove away, trailing the rope behind it. Joe knew that the plane pilot would later drop it over the airport where it could easily be retrieved.

In the direction of Mount Overlook he could see cumulus clouds and the dark turbulence which meant strong updraft. He headed in that direction.

Except for the whistling of wind, there is complete silence in a soaring glider. Max Mainz began to call back to his superior, was taken back by the volume, and dropped his voice. He said, "Look, captain. What keeps it up?"

Joe grinned. He liked the buoyancy of glider flying, the nearest approach of man to the bird, and thus far everything was going well. He told Max, "An airplane plows through the air currents, a glider rides on top of them."

"Yeah, but suppose the current is going down?"

"Then we avoid it. This sailplane only has a gliding angle ratio of one to twenty-five, but it's a workhorse with a payload of some four hundred pounds. A really high performance glider can have a ratio of as much as one to forty."

Joe had found a strong updraft where a wind ran up the side of a mountain. He banked, went into a circling turn. The gauge indicated they were climbing at the rate of eight meters per second, nearly fifteen hundred feet a minute.

Max hadn't got the rundown on the theory of the glider. That was obvious in his expression.

Joe Mauser, even while searching the ground below keenly, went into it further. "A wind up against a mountain will give an updraft, storm clouds will, even a newly plowed field in a bright sun. So you go from one of these to the next."

"Yeah, great, but when you're between," Max protested.

"Then, when you have a one to twenty-five ratio, you go twenty-five feet forward for each one you drop. If you started a mile high, you could go twenty-five miles before you touched ground." He cut himself off quickly. "Look, what's that, down there? Get your glasses on it."

Max caught his excitement. His binoculars were tight to his eyes. "Sojers. Cavalry. They sure ain't ours. They must be Hovercraft lads. And look, field artillery."

Joe Mauser was piloting with his left hand, his right smoothing out a chart on his lap. He growled, "What are they doing there? That's at least a full brigade of cavalry. Here, let me have those glasses."

With his knees gripping the stick, he went into a slow circle, as he stared down at the column of men. "Jack Alshuler," he whistled in surprise. "The marshal's crack heavy cavalry. And several batteries of artillery." He swung the glasses in a wider scope and the whistle turned into a hiss of comprehension. "They're doing a complete circle of the reservation. They're going to hit the Baron from the direction of Phoenicia."

X

Marshal Stonewall Cogswell directed his old fashioned telescope in the direction his chief of staff indicated.

"What is it?" he grunted.

"It's an airplane, sir."

"Over a military reservation with a fracas in progress?"

"Yes, sir." The other put his glasses back on the circling object. "Then what is it, sir? Certainly not a free balloon."

"Balloons," the marshal snorted, as though to himself. "Legal to use. The Union forces had them toward the end of the Civil War. But practically useless in a fracas of movement."

They were standing before the former resort hotel which housed the marshal's headquarters. Other staff members were streaming from the building, and one of the ever-present Telly reporting crews were hurriedly setting up cameras.

The marshal turned and barked, "Does anybody know what in Zen that confounded thing, circling up there, is?"

Baron Zwerdling, the aging Category Transport magnate, head of Continental Hovercraft, hobbled onto the wooden veranda and stared with the others. "An airplane," he croaked. "Haer's gone too far this time. Too far, too far. This will strip him. Strip him, understand." Then he added, "Why doesn't it make any noise?"

Lieutenant Colonel Paul Warren stood next to his commanding officer. "It looks like a glider, sir."

Cogswell glowered at him. "A what?"

"A glider, sir. It's a sport not particularly popular these days."

"What keeps it up, confound it?"

Paul Warren looked at him. "The same thing that keeps a hawk up, an albatross, a gull —"

"A vulture, you mean," Cogswell snarled. He watched it for another long moment, his face working. He whirled on his chief of artillery. "Jed, can you bring that thing down?"

The other had been viewing the craft through field binoculars, his face as shocked as the rest of them. Now he faced his chief, and lowered the glasses, shaking his head. "Not with the artillery of pre-1900. No, sir."

"What can you do?" Cogswell barked.

The artillery man was shaking his head. "We could mount some Maxim guns on wagon wheels, or something. Keep him from coming low."

"He doesn't have to come low," Cogswell growled unhappily. He spun on Lieutenant Colonel Warren again. "When were they invented?" He jerked his thumb upward. "Those things."

Warren was twisting his face in memory. "Some time about the turn of the century."

"How long can the things stay up?"

Warren took in the surrounding mountainous countryside. "Indefinitely, sir. A single pilot, as long as he is physically able to operate. If there are two pilots up there to relieve each other, they could stay until food and water ran out."

"How much weight do they carry?"

"I'm not sure. One that size, certainly enough for two men and any equipment they'd need. Say, five hundred pounds."

Cogswell had his telescope glued to his eyes again, he muttered under his breath, "Five hundred pounds! They could even unload dynamite over our horses. Stampede them all over the reservation."

"What's going on?" Baron Zwerdling shrilled. "What's going on Marshal Cogswell?"

Cogswell ignored him. He watched the circling, circling craft for a full five minutes, breathing deeply. Then he lowered his glass and swept the assembled officers of his staff with an indignant glare. "Ten Eyck!" he grunted.

An infantry colonel came to attention. "Yes, sir."

Cogswell said heavily, deliberately. "Under a white flag. A dispatch to Baron Haer. My compliments and request for his terms. While you're at it, my compliments also to Captain Joseph Mauser."

Zwerdling was bug-eyeing him. "Terms!" he rasped.

The marshal turned to him. "Yes, sir. Face reality. We're in the dill. I suggest you sue for terms as short of complete capitulation as you can make them."

"You call yourself a soldier —!" the transport tycoon began to shrill.

"Yes, sir," Cogswell snapped. "A soldier, not a butcher of the lads under me." He called to the Telly reporter who was getting as much of this as he could. "Mr. Soligen, isn't it?"

* * * * *

The reporter scurried forward, flicking signals to his cameramen for proper coverage. "Yes, sir. Freddy Soligen, marshal. Could you tell the Telly fans what this is all about, Marshal Cogswell? Folks, you all know the famous marshal. Marshal Stonewall Cogswell, who hasn't lost a fracas in nearly ten years, now commanding the forces of Continental Hovercraft."

"I'm losing one now," Cogswell said grimly. "Vacuum Tube Transport has pulled a gimmick out of the hat and things have pickled for us. It will be debated before the Military Category Department, of course, and undoubtedly the Sov-world military attaches will have things to say. But as it appears now, the fracas as we have known it, has been revolutionized."

"Revolutionized?" Even the Telly reporter was flabbergasted. "You mean by that thing?" He pointed upward, and the lenses of the cameras followed his finger.

"Yes," Cogswell growled unhappily. "Do all of you need a blueprint? Do you think I can fight a fracas with that thing dangling above me, throughout the day hours? Do you understand the importance of reconnaissance in warfare?" His eyes glowered. "Do you think Napoleon would have lost Waterloo if he'd had the advantage of perfect reconnaissance such as that thing can deliver? Do you think Lee would have lost Gettysburg? Don't be ridiculous." He spun on Baron Zwerdling, who was stuttering his complete confusion.

"As it stands, Baron Haer knows every troop dispensation I make. All I know of his movements are from my cavalry scouts. I repeat, I am no butcher, sir. I will gladly cross swords with Baron Haer another day, when I, too, have …what did you call the confounded things, Paul?"

"Gliders," Lieutenant Colonel Warren said.

XI

Major Joseph Mauser, now attired in his best off-duty Category Military uniform, spoke his credentials to the receptionist. "I have no definite appointment, but I am sure the Baron will see me," he said.

"Yes, sir." The receptionist did the things that receptionists do, then looked up at him again. "Right through that door, major."

Joe Mauser gave the door a quick double rap and then entered before waiting an answer.

Balt Haer, in mufti, was standing at a far window, a drink in his hand, rather than his customary swagger stick. Nadine Haer sat in an easy-chair. The girl Joe Mauser loved had been crying.

Joe Mauser, suppressing his frown, made with the usual amenities.

Balt Haer without answering them, finished his drink in a gulp and stared at the newcomer. The old stare, the aloof stare, an aristocrat looking at an underling as though wondering what made the fellow tick. He said, finally, "I see you have been raised to Rank Major."

"Yes, sir," Joe said.

"We are obviously occupied, major. What can either my sister or I possibly do for you?"

Joe kept his voice even. He said, "I wanted to see the Baron."

Nadine Haer looked up, a twinge of pain crossing her face.

"Indeed," Balt Haer said flatly. "You are talking to the Baron, Major Mauser."

Joe Mauser looked at him, then at his sister, who had taken to her handkerchief again. Consternation ebbed up and over him in a flood. He wanted to say something such as, "Oh *no*," but not even that could he utter.

Haer was bitter. "I assume I know why you are here, major. You have come for your pound of flesh, undoubtedly. Even in these hours of our grief—"

"I ...I didn't know. Please believe..."

"...You are so constituted that your ambition has no decency. Well, Major Mauser, I can only say that your arrangement was with my father. Even if I thought it a reasonable one, I doubt if I would sponsor your ambitions myself."

Nadine Haer looked up wearily. "Oh, Balt, come off it," she said. "The fact is, the Haer fortunes contracted a debt to you, major. Unfortunately, it is a debt we cannot pay." She looked into his face. "First, my father's governmental connections do not apply to us. Second, six months ago, my father, worried about his health and attempting to avoid certain death taxes, transferred the family stocks into Balt's name. And Balt saw fit, immediately before the fracas, to sell all Vacuum Tube Transport stocks, and invest in Hovercraft."

"That's enough, Nadine," her brother snapped nastily.

"I see," Joe said. He came to attention. "Dr. Haer, my apologies for intruding upon you in your time of bereavement." He turned to the new Baron. "Baron Haer, my apologies for *your* bereavement."

Balt Haer glowered at him.

Joe Mauser turned and marched for the door which he opened then closed behind him.

On the street, before the New York offices of Vacuum Tube Transport, he turned and for a moment looked up at the splendor of the building.

Well, at least the common shares of the concern had skyrocketed following the victory. His rank had been upped to Major, and old Stonewall Cogswell had offered him a permanent position on his staff in command of aerial operations, no small matter of prestige. The difficulty was, he wasn't interested in the added money that would accrue to him, nor the higher rank-nor the prestige, for that matter.

He turned to go to his hotel.

An unbelievably beautiful girl came down the steps of the building. She said, "Joe."

He looked at her. "Yes?"

She put a hand on his sleeve. "Let's go somewhere and talk, Joe."

"About what?" He was infinitely weary now.

"About goals," she said. "As long as they exist, whether for individuals, or nations, or a whole species, life is still worth the living. Things are a bit bogged down right now, but at the risk of sounding very trite, there's tomorrow."

Subversive

The young man with the brown paper bag said, "Is Mrs. Coty in?"

"I'm afraid she isn't. Is there anything I can do?"

"You're Mr. Coty? I came about the soap." He held up the paper bag.

"Soap?" Mr. Coty said blankly. He was the epitome of mid-aged husband complete to pipe, carpet slippers and office-slump posture.

"That's right. I'm sure she told you about it. My name's Dickens. Warren Dickens. I sold her—"

"Look here, you mean to tell me in this day and age you go around from door to door peddling soap? Great guns, boy, you'd do better on unemployment insurance. It's permanent now."

Warren Dickens registered distress. "Mr. Coty, could I come in and tell you about it? If I can make the first delivery to you instead of Mrs. Coty, shucks, it'll save me coming back."

Coty led him back into the living room, motioned him to a chair and settled into what was obviously his own favorite, handily placed before the telly. Coty said tolerantly, "Now then, what's this about selling soap? What kind of soap? What brand?"

"Oh, it has no name, sir. That's the point."

The other looked at him.

"That's why we can sell it for three cents a cake, instead of twenty-five." Dickens opened the paper bag and fished out an ordinary enough looking cake of soap and handed it to the older man.

Mr. Coty took it, stared down at it, turned it over in his hands. He was still blank. "Well, what's different about it?"

"There's nothing different about it. It's the same as any other soap."

"I mean, how come you sell it for three cents a cake, and what's the fact it has no name got to do with it?"

Warren Dickens leaned forward and went into what was obviously a strictly routine pitch. "Mr. Coty, have you ever considered what you're buying when they nick you twenty-five cents on your credit card for a bar of soap in an ultra-market?"

There was an edge of impatience in the older man's voice. "I buy soap!"

"No, sir. That's your mistake. What you buy is a telly show, in fact several of them, with all their expensive comedians, singers, musicians, dancers, news commentators, network vice presidents, and all the rest. Then you buy fancy packaging. You'll note, by the way, that our product hasn't even a piece of tissue paper wrapped around it. Fancy packaging designed by some of the most competent commercial artists and motivational research men in the country. Then you buy distribution. From the factory all the way to the retail ultra-market where your wife shops. And every time that bar of soap goes from one wholesaler or distributor to another, the price roughly doubles. You also buy a brain trust whose full time project is to keep you using their soap and not letting their competitors talk you into switching brands. The brain trust, of course, also works on luring away the competitor's customers to their product. Shucks, Mr. Coty, practically none of that twenty-five cents you spend to buy a cake of soap goes for soap. So small a percentage that you might as well forget about it."

Mr. Coty was obviously taken aback. "Well, how do I know this nameless soap you're peddling is, well, any good?"

Warren Dickens sighed deeply, and in such wise that it was obvious that he had so sighed before. "Sir, there is no difference between soaps. Oh, they might use a slightly different perfume, or tint it a slightly different color, but for all practical purposes common hand soap, common bath soap, is soap, period. All the stuff the copy writers dream up about secret ingredients and health for your skin, and cosmetic qualities, and all the rest, is Madison Avenue gobbledygook and applies as well to one brand as another. As a matter of fact, often two different soap companies, supposedly keen competitors, and using widely different advertising, have their products manufactured in the same plant."

Mr. Coty blinked at him. Shifted in his chair. Rubbed his chin as though checking his morning shave. "Well ... well, then where do you get *your* soap?"

"The same place. We buy in fantastically large lots from one of the gigantic automated soap plants."

Mr. Coty had him now. "Ah, ha! Then how come you sell it for three cents a cake, instead of twenty-five?"

"I've been telling you. Our soap doesn't even have a name, not to mention an advertising budget. Far from spending fortunes redesigning our packaging every few months in attempts to lure new customers, we don't package the stuff at all. It comes to you, in the simplest possible wrapping, through the mails. A new supply every month. Three cents a cake. No middlemen, no wholesalers, distributors. No nothing except soap at three cents a cake."

Mr. Coty leaned back in his chair. "I'll be darned." He thought it over. "Listen, do you sell anything besides soap?"

"Not right now, sir. But soap flakes are coming up next week and I think we'll be going into bread in a month or two."

"Bread?"

"Yes, sir, bread. Although we'll have to distribute that by truck, and have to have almost hundred per cent coverage in a given section before it's practical. A nickel a loaf."

"Five cents a loaf! You can't *make* bread for that much."

"Oh, yes we can. We can't advertise it, package it, and pay a host of in-betweens, is all. From the bakery to you, period."

Mr. Coty seemed fascinated. He said, "See here, what's the address of your office?"

Warren Dickens shook his head. "Sorry, sir. That's all part of it. We have no swanky offices with big, expensive staffs. We operate on the smallest of shoestrings. No brain trust. No complaint department. No public relations. No literature on how to beautify yourself. No nothing, except good soap at three cents a cake, plus postage. Now, if you'll sign this contract, we'll put you on our mailing list. Ten bars of soap a month, Mrs. Coty said. I brought this first supply so you could test it and see that the whole thing is bona fide."

Mr. Coty had to test it, but then he had to admit he couldn't tell any difference between the nameless soap and the product to which he was used. Eventually, he signed, made the first payment, shook hands with young Dickens and saw him to the door. He said, in parting, "I still wonder why you do this, rather than dragging down unemployment insurance like most young men fresh out of school."

Warren Dickens screwed up his face. This was a question that wasn't routine. "Well, I make approximately the same, if I stick to it and get enough contracts. And, shucks they're not hard to get. And, well, I'm working, not just bumming on the rest of the country. I'm doing something, something useful."

Coty pursed his lips and shrugged. "It's been a long time since anybody cared about that." He looked after the young man as he walked down the walk.

Then he turned and headed for the phone, and ten years seemed to drop away from him. He lit the screen with a flick, dialed and said crisply, "That's him, Jerry. Going down the walk now. Don't let him out of your sight."

Jerry's face was in the screen but he was obviously peering down, from the helio-jet, locating the subject. "O.K., Tracy, I make him. See you later." His face faded.

The man who had called himself Mr. Coty, dialed again, not bothering to light the screen. "All right," he said. "Thank Mrs. Coty and let her come home now."

* * * * *

Frank Tracy worked his way down an aisle of automated phono-typers and other office equipment. The handful of operators, their faces bored, periodically strolled up and down, needlessly checking that which seldom needed checking.

He entered the receptionist's office, flicked a hand at LaVerne Sandell, one of the few employees it seemed impossible to automate out of her position, and said, "The Chief is probably expecting me."

"That he is. Go right in, Mr. Tracy."

"I'm expecting a call from one of the operatives. Put it through, eh LaVerne?"

"Righto."

Even as he walked toward the door to the sanctum sanctorum, he grimaced sourly at her. *"Righto*, yet. Isn't that a bit on the maize side? Doesn't sound very authentic to me."

"I can see you don't put in your telly time, Mr. Tracy. Slang goes in cycles these days. They simply don't dream up a whole new set of expressions every generation anymore because everybody gets tired of them so soon. Instead, older periods of idiom are revived. For instance, scram is coming back in."

He stopped long enough to look at her, frowning. "Scram?"

She took him in quizzically, estimating. "Possibly *dust*, or *get lost*, was the term when you were a boy."

Tracy chuckled wryly, "Thanks for the compliment, but I go back to the days of *beat it*."

In the inner office the Chief looked up at him. "Sit down, Frank. What's the word? Another exponent of free enterprise, pre-historic style?"

Frank Tracy found a chair and began talking even while fumbling for briar and tobacco pouch. "No," he grumbled. "I don't think so, not this time. I'm afraid there might be something more to it."

His boss leaned back in the massive old-fashioned chair he affected and patted his belly, as though appreciative of a good meal just finished. "Oh? Give it all to me."

Tracy finished lighting his pipe, flicked the match out and put it back in his pocket, noting that he'd have to get a new one one of these days. He cleared his throat and said, "Reports began coming in of house to house canvassers selling soap for three cents a bar."

"Three cents a bar? They can't manufacture it for that. Will the stuff pass the Health Department?"

"Evidently," Tracy said wryly. "The salesman claimed it's the same soap as reputable firms peddle."

"Go on."

"We had to go to a bit of trouble to get a line on them without raising their suspicion. One of the boys lived in a neighborhood that was being canvassed for new customers and his wife had signed up. So I took her place when the salesman arrived with her first delivery-they deliver the first batch. I let him think I was Bob Coty and questioned him, but not enough to raise his suspicions."

"And?"

"An outfit selling soap and planning on branching into bread and heavens knows what else. No advertising. No middlemen. No nothing, as the salesman said, except standard soap at three cents a bar."

"They can't package it for that!"

"They don't package it at all."

The Chief raised his chubby right hand and wiped it over his face in a stereotype gesture of resignation. "Did you get his home office address? Maybe there's some way of buying them out-indirectly, of course."

"No, sir. It seemed to be somewhat of a secret."

The other's eyes widened. "Ridiculous. You can't hide anything like that. There's a hundred ways of tracking them down before the day is out."

"Of course. I've got Jerome Wiseman following him in a helio-jet. No use getting rough, as yet. We'll keep it quiet …assuming that meets with your approval."

"You're in the field, Frank. You make the decisions."

The phone screen had lighted up and LaVerne's piquant face faded in. "The call Mr. Tracy was expecting from Operative Wiseman."

"Put him on," the Chief said, lacing his plump fingers over his stomach.

Jerry's face appeared in the screen. He was obviously parked on the street now. He said, "Subject has disappeared into this office building, Tracy. For the past fifteen minutes he's kinda looked as though the day's work was through and since this dump could hardly be anybody's home, he must be reporting to his higher-up."

"Let's see the building," Tracy said.

The portable screen was directed in such manner that a disreputable appearing building, obviously devoted to fourth-rate businesses, was centered.

"O.K.," Tracy said. "I'll be over. You can knock off, Jerry. Oh, except for one thing. Subject's name is Warren Dickens. Just for luck, get a complete dossier on him. I doubt if he's got a criminal or subversive record, but you never know."

Jerry said, "Right," and faded.

Frank Tracy came to his feet and knocked the rest of his pipe out into the gigantic ashtray on his boss' desk. "Well, I suppose the next step's mine."

"Check back with me as soon as you know anything more," the Chief said. He wheezed a sigh as though sorry the interview was over and that he'd have to go back to his desk chores, but shifted his bulk and took up a sheaf of papers.

Just as Tracy got to the door, the Chief said, "Oh, yes. Easy on the rough stuff, Tracy. I've been hearing some disquieting reports about some of the overenthusiastic bullyboys on your team. We wouldn't want such material to get in the telly-casts."

Lard bottom, Tracy growled inwardly as he left. Did the Chief think he liked violence? Did anyone in his right mind like violence?

* * * * *

Frank Tracy looked up at the mid-century type office building. He was somewhat surprised that the edifice still remained. Where did the owners ever find profitable tenants? What business could be so small these days that it would be based in such quarters? However, here it was.

The lobby was shabby. There was no indication on the list of tenants of the firm he was seeking, nor was there a porter. The elevator was out of repair.

He did it the hard way, going from door to door, entering, hat in hand, apologetically, and saying, "Pardon me. You're the people who sell the soap?" They kept telling him no until he reached the third floor and a door to an office even smaller than usual. It was lettered *Freer Enterprises* and even as he knocked and entered, the wording rang a bell.

There was only one desk but it was efficiently equipped with the latest in office gadgetry. The room was quite choked with files and even a Mini-IBM tri-unit. The man behind the desk was old-fashioned enough to wear glasses, but otherwise seemed the average aggressive executive type you expected to meet in these United States of the Americas. He was possibly in his mid-thirties and one of those alert, over-eager characters irritating to those who believe in taking matters less than urgently.

He looked up and said snappily, "What can I do for you?"

Tracy dropped into an easy-going characterization. "You're the people who sell the soap?"

"That is correct. What can I do for you?"

Tracy said easily, "Why, I'd like to ask you a few questions about the enterprise."

"To what end, sir? You'd be surprised how busy a man I am."

Tracy said, "Suppose I'm from the Greater New York *News-Times* looking for a story?"

The other tapped a finger on his desk impatiently. "Pardon me, but in that case I would be inclined to think you a liar. The *News-Times* knows upon which side its bread is spread. Its advertisers include all the soap companies. It does not dispense free advertising through its news columns."

Tracy chuckled wryly, "All right. Let's start again." He brought forth his wallet, flicked through various identification cards until he found the one he wanted and presented it. "Frank Tracy is the name," he said. "Department of Internal Revenue. There seems to be some question as to your corporation taxes."

"Oh," the other said, obviously taken aback. "Please have a chair." He read the authentic looking, but spurious credentials. Tracy took the proffered chair and then sat and looked at the other as though it was his turn.

"My name is Flowers," the Freer Enterprises man told him, nervously. "Frederic Flowers. Frankly, this is my first month at the job and I'm not too well acquainted with all the ramifications of the business." He moistened his lips. "I hope there is nothing illegal —" He let the sentence fade away.

Tracy reclaimed his false identity papers and put them back into his wallet before saying easily, "I really couldn't say, as yet. Let's have a bit of questions and answers and I'll go further into the matter."

Flowers regained his confidence. "No reason why not," he said quickly. "So far as I know, all is above board."

Frank Tracy let his eyes go about the room. "Why are you established, almost secretly, you might say, in this business backwoods of the city?"

"No secret about it," Flowers demurred. "Merely the cheapest rent we could find. We cut costs to the bone, and then shave the bone."

"Um-m-m. I've spoken to one of your salesmen, a Warren Dickens, and I suppose he gave me the standard sales talk. I wonder if you could elaborate on your company's policies, its goals, that sort of thing."

"Goals?"

"You obviously expect to make money, somehow or other, though I don't see that peddling soap at three cents a bar has much of a future. There must be some further angle."

Flowers said, "Admittedly, soap is just a beginning. Among other things, it's given us a mailing list of satisfied customers. Consumers who can then be approached for future purchases."

* * * * *

Frank Tracy relaxed in his chair, reached for pipe and tobacco and let the other go on. But his eyes had narrowed, coldly.

Flowers wrapped himself up in his subject. "Mr. Tracy, you probably have no idea of the extent to which the citizens of Greater America are being victimized. Let me use but one example." He came quickly to his feet, crossed to a small toilet which opened off the office and returned with a power-pack electric shaver which he handed to Tracy.

Tracy looked at it, put it back on the desk and nodded. "It's the brand I have," he said agreeably.

"Yes, and millions of others. What did you pay for it?"

Frank Tracy allowed himself a slight smirk. "As a matter of fact, I got mine through a discount outfit, only twenty-five dollars."

"*Only* twenty-five dollars, eh, when the retail price is supposedly thirty-five?" Flowers was triumphant. "A great bargain, eh? Well, let me give you a rundown, Mr. Tracy."

He took a quick breath. "True, they're advertised to retail at thirty-five dollars. And stores that sell them at that rate make a profit of fifty per cent. The regional supply house, before them, knocks down from forty to sixty per cent, on the wholesale price. Then the trade name distributor makes at least fifty per cent on the sales to the regional supply houses."

"Trade name distributor?" Tracy said, as though ignorant of what the other was talking about. "You mean the manufacturer?"

"No, sir. That razor you just looked at bears a trade name of a company that owns no factory of its own. It buys the razors from a large electrical appliances manufacturing complex which turns out several other name brand electric razors as well. The trade name company does nothing except market the product. Its budget, by the way, calls for an expenditure of six dollars on every razor for national advertising."

"Well, what are you getting at?" Tracy said impatiently.

Frederic Flowers had reached his punch line. "All right, we've traced the razor all the way back to the manufacturing complex which made it. Mr. Tracy, that razor you bought at a discount bargain for twenty-five dollars cost thirty-eight cents to produce."

Tracy pretended to be dumfounded. "I don't believe it."

"It can be proven."

Frank Tracy thought about it for a while. "Well, even if true, so what?"

"It's a crime, that's so-what," Flowers blurted indignantly. "And that's where Freer Enterprises comes in. Very shortly, we're going to enter the market with an electric razor retailing for exactly one dollar. No name brand, no advertising, no nothing except a razor just as good as though selling for from twenty-five to fifty dollars."

Tracy scoffed his disbelief. "That's where you're wrong. No electric razor manufacturer would sell to you. They'd be cutting their own throats."

The Freer Enterprises official shook his head, in scorn. "That's where *you're* wrong. The same electric appliance manufacturer who produced that razor there will make a similar one, slightly different in appearance, for the same price for us. They don't care what happens to their product once they make their profit from it. Business is business. We'll be at least as good a customer as any of the others have ever been. Eventually, better, since we'll be getting electric razors into the hands of people who never felt they could afford one before."

He shook a finger at Tracy. "Manufacturers have been doing this for a long time. I imagine it was the old mail-order houses that started it. They'd get in touch with a manufacturer of, say, typewriters, or outboard motors, or whatever, and order tens of thousands of these, not an iota different from the manufacturer's standard product except for the nameplate. They'd then sell these for as little as half the ordinary retail price."

Tracy seemed to think it over for a long moment. Eventually he said, "Even then you're not going to break any records making money. Your distribution costs might be pared to the bone, but you still have some. There'll be darn little profit left on each razor you sell."

Flowers was triumphant again. "We're not going to stop at razors, once under way. How about automobiles? Have you any idea of the disparity between the cost of production of a car and what they retail for?"

"Well, no."

"Here's an example. As far back as about 1930 a barge company transporting some brand-new cars across Lake Erie from Detroit had an accident and lost a couple of hundred. The auto manufacturers sued, trying to get the retail price of each car. Instead, the court awarded them the cost of manufacture. You know what it came to, labor, materials, depreciation on machinery-everything? Seventy-five dollars per car. And that was around 1930. Since then, automation has swept the industry and manufacturing costs per unit have dropped drastically."

The Freer Enterprises executive was now in full voice. "But even that's not the ultimate. After all, cars were selling for as cheaply as $425 then. Let's take some items such as aspirin. You can, of course, buy small neatly packaged tins of twelve for twenty-five cents but supposedly more intelligent buyers will buy bottles for forty or fifty cents. If the druggist puts out a special for fifteen cents a bottle it will largely be refused since the advertising conditioned customer doesn't want an inferior product. Actually, of course, aspirin is aspirin and you can buy it, in one hundred pound lots in polyethylene film bags, at about fourteen cents a pound, or in carload lots under the chemical name of acetylsalicylic acid, for eleven cents a pound. And any big chemical corporation will sell you U.S.P. grade Milk of Magnesia at about six dollars a ton. Its chemical name, of course, is magnesium hydroxide, or $Mg(OH)_2$, and you'd have one thousand quarts in that ton. Buying it beautifully packaged and fully advertised, you'd pay up to a dollar twenty-five a pint in the druggist section of a modern ultra-market."

* * * * *

Tracy had heard enough. He said crisply, "All right, Mr. Flowers, of Freer Enterprises, now let me ask you something: Do you consider this country prosperous?"

Flowers blinked. Of a sudden, the man across from him seemed to have changed character, added considerable dynamic to his make-up. He flustered, "Yes, I suppose so. But it could be considerably more prosperous if—"

Tracy was sneering. "If consumer prices were brought down drastically, eh? Mr. Flowers, you're incredibly naïve when it comes to modern economics. Do you realize that one of the most significant developments, economically speaking, took place in the 1950s; something perhaps more significant than the development of atomic power?"

Flowers blinked again, mesmerized by the other's new domineering personality. "I ...I don't know what you're talking about."

"The majority of employees in the United States turned from blue collars to white."

Flowers looked pained. "I don't—"

"No, of course you don't or you wouldn't be participating in a subversive attack upon our economy, which, if successful, would lead to the collapse of Western prosperity and eventually to the success of the Soviet Complex."

Mr. Flowers gobbled a bit, then gulped.

"I'll spell it out for you," Tracy pursued. "In the early days of capitalism, back when Marx and Engels were writing such works as *Capital*, the overwhelming majority of the working class were employed directly in production. For a long time it was quite accurate when the political cartoonists depicted a working man as wearing overalls and carrying a hammer or wrench. In short, employees who got their hands dirty, outnumbered those who didn't.

"But with the coming of increased mechanization and eventually automation and the second industrial revolution, more and more employees went into sales, the so-called service industries, advertising and entertainment which has become largely a branch of advertising, distribution, and, above all, government which in this bureaucratic age is largely a matter of regulation of business and property relationships. As automation continued, fewer and fewer of our people were needed to produce all the commodities that the country could assimilate under our present socio-economic system. And I need only point out that the average American *still* enjoys more material things than any other nation, though admittedly the European countries, and I don't exclude the Soviet Complex, are coming up fast."

Flowers said indignantly, "But what's this charge that I'm participating in a subversive—"

"Mr. Flowers," Tracy overrode him, "let's not descend to pure maize in our denials of the obvious. If this outfit of yours, Freer Enterprises, was successful in its fondest dreams, what would happen?"

"Why, the consumers would be able to buy commodities at a fraction of the present cost!"

Tracy half came to his feet and pounded the table with fierce emphasis. *"What would they buy them with? They'd all be out of jobs!"*

Frederic Flowers bug-eyed him.

Tracy sat down again and seemingly regained control of himself. His voice was softer now. "Our social system may have its strains and tensions, Mr. Flowers, but it works and we don't want anybody throwing wrenches in its admittedly delicate machinery. Advertising is currently one of the biggest industries of the country. The entertainment industry, admittedly now based on advertising, is gigantic. Our magazines and newspapers, employing hundreds of thousands of employees from editors right on down to newsstand operators, are able to exist only through advertising revenue. Above all, millions of our population are employed in the service industries, and in distribution, in the stock market, in the commodity markets, in all the other branches of distribution which you Freer Enterprises people want to pull down. A third of our working force is now unemployed, but given your way, it would be at least two thirds."

Flowers, suddenly suspicious, said, "What has all this to do with the Department of Internal Revenue, Mr. Tracy?"

Tracy came to his feet and smiled ruefully, albeit a bit grimly. "Nothing," he admitted. "I have nothing at all to do with that department. Here is my real card, Mr. Flowers."

The Freer Enterprises man must have felt a twinge of premonition even as he took it up, but the effect was still enough to startle him. "Bureau of Economic Subversion!" he said.

"Now then," Tracy snapped. "I want the names of your higher ups, and the address of your central office, Flowers. Frankly, you're in the soup. As you possibly know, our hush-hush department has unlimited emergency powers, being answerable only to the President."

"I ... I've never even heard of it." Flowers stuttered. "But —"

Tracy held up a contemptuous hand. "Many people haven't," he said curtly.

* * * * *

Frank Tracy hurried through the outer office into LaVerne Sandell's domain, and bit out to her, "Tell the Chief I'm here. Crisis. And immediately get my team together, all eight of them. Heavy equipment. Have a jet readied. Chicago. The team will rendezvous at the airport."

LaVerne was just as crisp. "Yes, sir." She began doing things with buttons and switches.

Tracy hurried into the Chief's office and didn't bother with the usual amenities. He snapped, "Worse than I thought, sir. This outfit is possibly openly subversive. Deliberately undermining the economy."

His superior put down the report he was perusing and shifted his bulk backward. "You're sure? We seldom run into such extremes."

"I know, I know, but this could be it. Possibly a deliberate program. I've taken the initiative to have Miss Sandell summon my team."

"Now, see here, Frank —" The bureau head looked at him anxiously.

Tracy said, impatience there, "Chief, you're going to have to let your field men use their discretion. I tell you, this thing is a potential snowball. I'll play it cool. Arrange things so that there'll be no scandal for the telly-reporters. But we've got to chill this one quickly, or it'll be on a coast to coast basis before the year is out. They're even talking about going into automobiles."

The Chief winced, then said unhappily, "All right, Tracy. However, mind what I said. Curb those roughnecks of yours."

* * * * *

It proved considerably easier than Frank Tracy had hoped for. Adam Moncure's national headquarters turned out to be in a sparsely settled area not far from Woodstock, Illinois. The house, in the passé ranch style, must have once been a millionaire's baby, what with an artificial fishing lake in the back, a kidney shaped swimming pool, extensive gardens and an imposing approach up a corridor of trees.

"Right up to the front door," Tracy growled to the operative driving the first hover-car of their two-vehicle expedition. "The quicker we move, the better." He turned his head to the men in the rear seat. "We five will go in together. I don't expect trouble, they'll have had no advance warning. I made sure of that. Jerry has equipment in his car to blanket any radio sending. We'll take care of phones in the house. No rough stuff, we want to talk to these people."

One of the men growled, "Suppose they start shooting?"

Tracy snorted. "Then shoot back, of course. But just don't you start it. I shouldn't have to tell you these things."

"Got it," one of the others said. He shifted his shoulders to loosen the .38 Recoilless in its holster.

At the ornate doorway, the cars, which had been moving fast, a foot or so off the ground, came to a quick halt, settled, and the men disgorged, guns in hand.

Tracy called to the occupants of the other vehicle, "On the double. Surround the house. Don't let anybody leave. Come on, boys."

They scurried down the flagstone walk, banged on the door. It was opened by a houseman who stared at them uncomprehendingly.

"The occupants of this establishment are under arrest," Tracy snapped. He flashed a gold badge. "Take me to Adam Moncure." He turned to his men and gestured with his head. "Take over, boys. Jerry, you come with me."

The houseman was terrified, but not to the point of being unable to lead them to a gigantic former living room, now converted to offices.

There was an older man, and four assistants. All in shirt sleeves in concession to the mid-western summer, none armed from all Tracy could see. They looked up in surprise, rather than dismay. The older man snapped, "What is the meaning of this intrusion?"

Jerry chuckled sourly.

Frank Tracy said, "You're all under arrest. Jerry, herd these clerks, or whatever they are, into some other room. Get any other occupants of the house together, too. And watch them carefully, confound it. Don't underestimate these people. And make a search for secret rooms, cellars, that sort of thing."

"Right," Jerry growled.

The older of the five Freer Enterprises men was on his feet now. He was a thin, angry faced type, gray of hair and somewhere in his sixties. "I want to know the meaning of this!" he roared.

"Adam Moncure?" Tracy said crisply.

"That is correct. And to what do I owe this cavalier intrusion into my home and place of business?"

Jerry, at pistol point, was herding the four assistants from the room, taking the houseman along with them.

Tracy looked at Moncure, speculatively, then dipped into his pockets for pipe and tobacco. He gestured to a chair with his head. "Sit down, Mr. Moncure. The jig is up."

"The *jig?*" the other blurted in a fine rage. "I insist —"

"O.K., O.K., you'll get your explanation." Tracy sat down on a couch himself and sized up the older man, even as he lit his pipe.

Moncure, still breathing heavily in his indignation, took control of himself well enough to be seated. "Well, sir?" he bit out.

Tracy said curtly, "Frank Tracy, Bureau of Economic Subversion."

"Bureau of Economic Subversion!" Moncure said indignantly. "What in the name of all that's holy is the Bureau of Economic Subversion?"

Tracy pointed at him with the pipe stem. "I'll ask a few questions first, please. How many branches of your nefarious outfit are presently under operation?"

The other glared at him, but Tracy merely returned the pipe to his mouth and glowered back.

Finally Moncure snapped, "There is no purpose in hiding any of our affairs. We have opened preliminary offices only in Chicago and New York. Freer Enterprises is but in its infancy."

"Praise Allah for that," Tracy muttered sarcastically.

"And thus far we have dealt only in soap. However, as our organization gets under way we plan to branch out into a score, and ultimately hundreds of products."

Tracy said, "You can forget about that, Moncure. Freer Enterprises comes to a halt as of today. Do you realize that your business tactics would lead to a complete collapse of gainful employment and eventually to a depression such as this nation has never seen before?"

"Exactly!" Moncure snapped in return.

* * * * *

It was Tracy's turn to react. His eyes widened, then narrowed. "Do you mean that you are deliberately attempting to undermine the economy of the United States of the Americas? Remember, Mr. Moncure, you are under arrest and anything you say may be held against you."

"Undermine it!" Moncure said heatedly. "Bring it crashing to the ground is the better term. There has never been such an abortion developed in the history of political economy."

He came to his feet again and began storming up and down the room. "A full three quarters of our employed working at nothing jobs, gobbledygook jobs, non-producing jobs, make-work jobs, red-tape bureaucracy jobs. At a time when the nation is supposedly in a breakneck economic competition with the Soviet Complex, we put our best brains into advertising, entertainment and sales, while they put theirs into science and industry."

He stopped long enough to shake an indignant finger at the surprised Tracy. "But that isn't the worst of it. Have you ever heard of planned obsolescence?"

Tracy acted as though on the defensive. "Well ... sure ..."

"In the Soviet Complex, and, for that matter, in Common Europe and other economic competitors of ours, they simply don't believe in planned obsolescence and all its related nonsense. Razor blades, everywhere except in this country, don't go dull after two or three shaves. Cars don't fall apart after two or three years, or even become so out of style that the owner feels that he's losing status by being seen in it, the owners expect to keep them half a lifetime. Automobile batteries don't go to pieces after eighteen months, they last for a decade. And on and on!"

The old boy was really unwinding now. "Nor is even that the nadir of this socio-economic hodge-podge we've allowed to develop, this economy of production for sale, rather than production for use." He stabbed with his finger. "I think one of the best examples of what was to come was to be witnessed way back at the end of the Second War. The idea of the ball-bearing pen was in the air. The first one to hurry into production gave his pen a tremendous build-up. It had ink enough to last three years, it would make many carbon copies, you could use it under water. And so on and so forth. It cost fifteen dollars, and there was only one difficulty with it. It wouldn't write. Not that that made any difference because it sold like hotcakes what with all the promotion. He wasn't interested in whether or not it would write, but only in whether or not it would sell." Moncure threw up his hands dramatically. "I ask you, can such an economic system be taken seriously?"

"What's your point?" Tracy growled dangerously. He'd never met one this far out, before.

"Isn't it obvious? Continue this ridiculous economy and we'll lose the battle for men's minds. You can't have an economic system that allows such nonsense as large scale unemployment of trained employees, planned obsolescence, union featherbedding, and an overwhelming majority of those who are employed wasting their labor on unproductive employment."

Tracy said, "Then if I understand you correctly, Freer Enterprises was deliberately organized for the purpose of undermining the economy so that it will collapse and have to be reorganized on a different basis."

"That is *exactly* correct," Moncure said defiantly. "I am devoting my whole fortune to this cause. And there is nothing in American law that prevents me from following through with my plans."

"You're right there," Tracy said wryly. "There's nothing in American law that prevents you. However, you see, I have no connection whatsoever with the American government." He slipped the gun from its holster.

* * * * *

Frank Tracy made his way wearily into LaVerne's domain. She looked up from the desk. "Everything go all right, Mr. Tracy?"

"I suppose so. Tell Comrade Zotov that I'm back from Chicago, please."

She clicked switches, said something into an inner-office communicator, then looked up again. "He'll see you immediately, Mr. Tracy."

Pavel Zotov looked up from his endless paperwork and wheezed the sigh of a fat man. He correctly interpreted the expression of his field operative. "Pour us a couple of drinks, Frank, or would you rather have it *Frol*, today?"

His best field man grunted as he walked over to the bar. "Vodka, eh? *Chort vesmiot* how tired one can become of this everlasting bourbon." He reached into the refrigerator compartment and brought forth a bottle of iced Stolichnaya. He poured two three-ounce charges and brought them back to his bureau chief's desk.

They toasted silently, knocked back the colorless spirit. Pavel Zotov said, "Well, Frol?"

The man usually called Frank Tracy said, "The worst case yet. This one had quite a clear picture of the true situation. He saw the necessity-given *their* viewpoint, of course-of getting out of the fantastic rut their economy has fallen into." He ran his hand over his mouth in a gesture of weariness. "Chief, do you have any idea of how long it would take us to catch up to them, if we ever did, if they really turned this economy on full blast, as an alternative to their present foul-up?"

"That's why we're here," the Chief said heavily. "What did you do?"

The man sometimes called Tracy told him.

Zotov winced. "I thought I ordered you —"

"You did," the man called Tracy told him curtly, "but what alternative was there? The fire will completely destroy the records. I have the names and addresses of all the others connected with Freer Enterprises. We'll have to arrange car accidents, that sort of thing."

The fat man's lips worked. "We can't get by with this indefinitely, Frol. With such blatant tactics, sooner or later their C.I.A. or F.B.I. is going to get wind of us."

Tracy came to his feet angrily. "What alternative have we? We've been sent over here to do a job. We're doing it. If we're caught, who knows better than we that we're expendable? If you don't mind, I'm going on home."

As he left the office, through the secret door that led through the innocuous looking garage, the man they called Frank Tracy was inwardly thinking, "Zotov might be my superior, and a top man in the party, but he's too soft for this job. Perhaps I'd better send a report back to Moscow on him."

The Common Man

Frederick Braun, M.D., Ph.D., various other Ds, pushed his slightly crooked horn-rims back on his nose and looked up at the two-story wooden house. There was a small lawn before it, moderately cared for, and one tree. There was the usual porch furniture, and the house was going to need painting in another six months or so, but not quite yet. There was a three-year-old hover car parked at the curb of a make that anywhere else in the world but America would have been thought ostentatious in view of the seeming economic status of the householder.

Frederick Braun looked down at the paper in his hand, then up at the house again. He said to his two companions, "By Caesar, I will admit it is the most average-looking dwelling I have ever seen."

Patricia O'Gara said impatiently, "Well, do we or don't we?" Her hair should have been in a pony tail, or bouncing on her shoulders, or at least in the new Etruscan revival style, not drawn back in its efficient bun.

Ross Wooley was unhappy. He scratched his fingers back through his reddish crew cut. "This is going to sound silly."

Patricia said testily, "We've been through all that, Rossie, good heavens."

"Nothing ventured, nothing ..." Braun let the sentence dribble away as he stuffed the paper into a coat pocket, which had obviously been used as a waste receptacle for many a year, and led the way up the cement walk, his younger companions immediately behind.

He put his finger on the doorbell and cocked his head to one side. There was no sound from the depths of the house. Dr. Braun muttered, "Bell out of order."

"It would be," Ross chuckled sourly. "Remember? Average. Here, let me." He rapped briskly on the wooden door jamb. They stood for a moment then he knocked again, louder, saying almost as though hopefully, "Maybe there's nobody home."

"All right, all right, take it easy," a voice growled even as the door opened.

He was somewhere in his thirties, easygoing of face, brownish of hair, bluish of eye and moderately good-looking. His posture wasn't the best and he had a slight tummy but he was a goodish masculine specimen by Mid-Western standards. He stared out at them, defensive now that it was obvious they were strangers. Were they selling something, or in what other manner were they attempting to intrude on his well being? His eyes went from the older man's thin face, to the football hero heft of the younger, then to Patricia O'Gara. His eyes went up and down her figure and became approving in spite of the straight business suit she affected.

He said, "What could I do for you?"

"Mr. Crowley?" Ross said.

"That's right."

"I'm Ross Wooley and my friends are Patricia O'Gara and Dr. Frederick Braun. We'd like to talk to you."

"There's nobody sick here."

Patricia said impatiently, "Of course not. Dr. Braun isn't a practicing medical doctor. We are research biochemists."

"We're scientists," Ross told him, putting it on what he assumed was the man's level. "There's something on which you could help us."

Crowley took his eyes from the girl and scowled at Ross. "Me? Scientists? I'm just a country boy, I don't know anything about science." There was a grudging self-deprecation in his tone.

Patricia took over, a miracle smile overwhelming her air of briskness. "We'd appreciate the opportunity to discuss it with you."

Dr. Braun added the clincher. "And it might be remunerative."

Crowley opened the door wider. "Well, just so it don't cost me nothing." He stepped back for them. "Don't mind the place. Kind of mussed up. Fact is, the wife left me about a week ago and I haven't got around to getting somebody to come in and kind of clean things up."

He wasn't exaggerating. Patricia O'Gara had no pretensions to the housewife's art herself, but she sniffed when she saw the condition of the living room. There was a dirty shirt drooped over the sofa back and beside the chair which faced the TV set were half a dozen empty beer cans. The ashtrays hadn't been emptied for at least days and the floor had obviously not been swept since the domestic tragedy which had sent Mrs. Crowley packing.

Now that the three strangers were within his castle, Crowley's instincts for hospitality asserted themselves. He said, "Make yourself comfortable. Here, wait'll I get these things out of the way. Anybody like a drink? I got some beer in the box, or," he smirked at Patricia, "I got some port wine you might like, not this bellywash you buy by the gallon."

They declined the refreshments, it wasn't quite noon.

Crowley wrestled the chair which had been before the TV set around so that he could sit facing them, and then sat himself down. He didn't get this and his face showed it.

Frederick Braun came to the point. "Mr. Crowley," he said, "did it ever occur to you that somewhere amidst our nearly one hundred million American males there is the average man?"

Crowley looked at him.

Braun cleared his throat and with his thumb and forefinger pushed his glasses more firmly on the bridge of his nose. "I suppose that isn't exactly the technical way in which to put it."

Ross Wooley shifted his football shoulders and leaned forward earnestly. "No, Doctor, that's exactly the way to put it." He said to Crowley, very seriously, "We've done this most efficiently. We've gone through absolute piles of statistics. We've...."

"Done what?" Crowley all but wailed. "Take it easy, will you? What are you all talking about?"

Patricia said impatiently, "Mr. Crowley, you are the average American. The man on the street. The Common Man."

He frowned at her. "What'd'ya mean, common? I'm as good as anybody else."

"That's exactly what we mean," Ross said placatingly. "You are exactly as good as anybody else, Mr. Crowley. You're the average man."

"I don't know what the devil you're talking about. Pardon my language, Miss."

"Not at all," Patricia sighed. "Dr. Braun, why don't you take over? We seem to all be speaking at once."

* * * * *

The little doctor began to enumerate on his fingers. "The center of population has shifted to this vicinity, so the average American lives here in the Middle West. Population is also shifting from rural to urban, so the average man lives in a city of approximately this size. Determining average age, height, weight is simple with government data as complete as they are. Also racial background. You, Mr. Crowley, are predominantly English, German and Irish, but have traces of two or three other nationalities."

Crowley was staring at him. "How in the devil did you know that?"

Ross said wearily, "We've gone to a lot of trouble."

Dr. Braun hustled on. "You've had the average amount of education, didn't quite finish high school. You make average wages working in a factory as a clerk. You spent some time in the army but never saw combat. You drink moderately, are married and have one child, which is average for your age. Your I.Q. is exactly average and you vote Democrat except occasionally when you switch over to Republican."

"Now wait a minute," Crowley protested. "You mean I'm the only man in this whole country that's like me? I mean, you mean I'm the average guy, right in the middle?"

Patricia O'Gara said impatiently. "You are the nearest thing to it, Mr. Crowley. Actually, possibly one of a hundred persons would have served our purpose."

"O.K.," Crowley interrupted, holding up a hand. "That gets us to the point. What's this here purpose? What's the big idea prying, like, into my affairs till you learned all this about me? And what's this stuff about me getting something out of it? Right now I'm between jobs."

The doctor pushed his battered horn-rims back on his nose with his forefinger. "Yes, of course," he said reasonably. "Now we get to the point. Mr. Crowley, how would you like to be invisible?"

The three of them looked at him. It seemed to be his turn.

Crowley got up and walked into the kitchen. He came back in a moment with an opened can of beer from which he was gulping even as he walked. He took the can away from his mouth and said carefully, "You mean like a ghost?"

"No, of course not," Braun said in irritation. "By Caesar, man, have you no imagination? Can't you see it was only a matter of time before someone, possibly working away on an entirely different subject of research, stumbled upon a practical method of achieving invisibility?"

"Now, wait a minute," Crowley said, his voice belligerent. "I'm only a country boy, maybe, without any egghead background, but I'm just as good as the next man and just as smart. I don't think I like your altitude."

"Attitude," Ross Wooley muttered unhappily. He shot a glance at Patricia O'Gara but she ignored him.

Patricia turned on the charm. Her face opened into smile and she said soothingly, "Don't misunderstand, Mr. Crowley. May I call you Don? I'm sure we're going to be associates. You see, Don, we need your assistance."

This was more like it. Crowley sat down again and finished the can of beer. "O.K., it won't hurt to listen. What's the pitch?"

The older man cleared his throat. "We'll cover it quickly so that we can get to the immediate practical aspects. Are you interested in biodynamics ... umah ... no, of course not. Let me see. Are you at all familiar with the laws pertaining to refraction of ... umah, no." He cleared his throat again, unhappily. "Have you ever seen a medusa, Mr. Crowley? The gelatinous umbrella-shaped free swimming form of marine invertebrate related to the coral polyp and the sea anemone?"

Ross Wooley scratched his crew cut and grimaced. "Jellyfish, Doctor, jellyfish. But I think the Portuguese Man-of-War might be a better example."

"Oh, jellyfish," Crowley said. "Sure, I've seen jellyfish. I got an aunt lives near Baltimore. We used to go down there and swim in Chesapeake Bay. Sting the devil out of you. What about it?"

Patricia leaned forward, still smiling graciously. "I really don't see a great deal of point going into theory, gentlemen." She looked at Ross and Dr. Braun, then back at Crowley. "Don, I think that what the doctor was leading up to was an attempt to describe in layman's language the theory of the process onto which we've stumbled. He was using the jellyfish as an example of a life form all but invisible. But I'm sure you aren't interested in technical terminology, are you? A good deal of gobbledygook, really, don't you think?"

"Yeah, that's what I say. Let's get to the point. You mean you think it's possible to make a guy invisible. Nobody could see him, eh?"

"It's not a matter of thinking," Ross said sourly. "We've done it."

Crowley stared at him. "Done it? You mean, you, personal? You got invisible?"

"Yes. All three of us. Once each."

"And you come back all right, eh? So anybody can see you again."

The doctor said reasonably, "Here we are, quite visible. The effect of the usual dosage lasts for approximately twelve hours."

They let him assimilate it for a few minutes. Some of the ramifications were coming home to him. Finally he got up and went into the back again for another can of beer. By this time Ross Wooley was wishing he would renew his offer, but the other had forgotten his duties as a host.

He took the can away from his mouth and said, "You want to make me invisible. You want me to, like, kind of experiment on." His eyes thinned. "Why pick me?"

The doctor said carefully, "Because you're the common man, the average man, Mr. Crowley. Before we release this development, we would like to have some idea of the scope of the effects."

The beer went down chuck-a-luck. Crowley put the can aside and licked his bottom lip, then rubbed it with a fingertip. He said slowly, "Now take it easy while I think about this." He blinked. "Why you could just walk into a bank and...."

The three were watching him, empty-faced.

"Exactly," Dr. Braun said.

* * * * *

Frederick Braun stared gloomily from the hotel suite's window at the street below. He peered absently at his thin wrist, looked blank for a moment, then realized all over again that his watch was being cleaned. He stared down at the street once more, his wrinkled face unhappy.

The door opened behind him and Patricia O'Gara came in briskly and said, "No sign of the guinea pig yet, eh?"

"No."

"Where's Rossie?"

The doctor cleared his throat. "There was an item on the newscast. A humor bit. It seems that the head waiter of the Gourmet.... Have you ever eaten at the Gourmet, Patricia?"

"Do I look like a millionaire?"

"At any rate, a half pound of the best Caspian caviar disappeared, spoonful at a time, right before his eyes."

Patricia looked at him. "Good heavens."

"Yes. Well, Ross has gone to pay the tab."

Patricia looked at her watch. "The effects will be wearing off shortly. Crowley will probably be back at any time. We warned him about returning to visibility in the middle of some street, completely nude." She sank into a seat and looked up at the doctor. "I suppose you admit I was right." Her voice was crisp.

The other turned on her. "And just why do you say that?"

"This caviar bit. Our friend, Donald Crowley, has obviously walked into the Gourmet restaurant, having heard it was the most expensive in New York, and ate as much as he could stuff down of the most expensive item on the menu."

The elderly little doctor pushed his battered horn-rims farther back on his nose. "Tell me, Patricia, when you made the experiment, did you do anything ... umah ... anything at all, that saved you some money?"

Uncharacteristically, she suddenly giggled. "I had the time of my life riding on a bus without paying the fare."

Braun snorted. "Then Donald Crowley, in eating his caviar, did substantially the same thing. It's probably been a life's ambition of his to eat in an ultra-swank restaurant and then walk out without paying. To be frank," the doctor cleared his throat apologetically, "it's always been one of mine."

Patricia conceded him a chuckle, but then said impatiently, "It's one thing my saving fifteen cents on a bus ride, and his eating twenty-five dollars worth of caviar."

"Merely a matter of degree, my dear."

Patricia said in irritation, "Why in the world did we have to bring him to New York where he could pull such childish tricks? We could have performed the experiment right there in Far Cry, Nebraska."

Dr. Braun abruptly ceased the pacing he had begun and found a chair. He absently stuck a hand into a coat pocket, pulled out a crumbled piece of paper, stared at it for a moment, as though he had never seen it before, grunted, and returned it to the pocket. He looked at Patricia O'Gara. "We felt that on completely unknown territory he would feel less constrained, don't you remember? In his home town, his conscience would be more apt to restrict him."

Something suddenly came to her. She looked at her older companion suspiciously. "That newscast. Was there anything else on it? Don't look innocent, you know what I mean."

"Well, there was one item."

"Out with it," she demanded.

"The Hotel Belefonte threatens to sue that French movie star, Brigette whatever-her-name is."

"Brigette Loren," Patricia said, staring. "What's that got to do with Donald Crowley?"

The good doctor was embarrassed. "It seems that she came running out of her suite, umah, semi-dressed and screaming that the hotel was haunted."

"Good heavens," Patricia said with sudden vision. "That's one aspect I hadn't thought of."

"Evidently Crowley did."

Patricia O'Gara said definitely, "My point's been proven. Our average man is a slob. Give him the opportunity to exercise unlimited freedom without danger of consequence and he becomes an undisciplined and dangerous lout."

* * * * *

Ross Wooley had come in, scowling, just in time to catch most of that. He tossed his hat onto a table and fished in his pockets for pipe and tobacco. "Nuts, Pat," he said. "In fact, just the opposite's been proven. Don's just on a fun binge. Like a kid in a candy shop. He hasn't done anything serious. Went into a fancy restaurant and ate some expensive food. Sneaked into the hotel room of the world's most famous sex-symbol and got a close-up look." He grinned suddenly. "I wish I had thought of that."

"Ha!" Patricia snorted. "Our engagement is off, you Peeping Tom."

"Children, children," Braun chuckled. "I'll admit, though, I think Ross is correct. Don's done little we three didn't when first given the robe of invisibility. We experimented, largely playfully, even childishly."

Patricia bit out, "This experiment is ridiculous, anyway, and I don't know why I ever agreed to it. Scientific? Nonsense. Where are our controls? For it to make any sense we'd have to work with scores of subjects. Suppose we do agree that the manner in which Don Crowley has reacted is quite harmless. Does that mean we can release this discovery to the world? Certainly not."

Ross said sullenly, "But you agreed that we'd go by the results of this...."

"I agreed to no such thing, Rossie Wooley, you overgrown lug. All I agreed to do was consider the results. I was, and am, of the opinion that if the person our politicians so lovingly call the Common Man was released of the restrictions inhibiting him, he'd go hog wild and destroy both society and himself. What is to prevent murder, robbery, rape and a score of other crimes, given invisibility for anyone who has a couple of dollars with which to go into a drugstore and purchase our serum?"

Her fiancé sighed deeply, jamming tobacco fiercely into the bowl of his briar. He growled, "Look, you seem to think that the only thing that restricts man is the fear of being punished. There are other things, you know."

"Good heavens," she said sarcastically. "Name *one*."

"There is the ethical code in which he was raised, based on religion or otherwise. There is the fact that man is fundamentally good, to use a trite term, given the opportunity."

"My education has evidently been neglected," Patricia said, still argumentatively. "I've never seen evidence to support your claim."

"I'm not saying individuals don't react negatively, given opportunity to be antisocial," he all but snarled. "I'm just saying people in general, common, little people, trend toward decency, desire the right thing."

"Individuals my ... my neck," Patricia snapped back. "Did you ever hear of Rome and the games? Here a whole people, millions of them, were given the opportunity to indulge in sadistic spectacles to their heart's desire. How many of them stayed home from the games?" She laughed in ridicule.

Ross flushed. "Some of them did, confound it."

Dr. Braun had been taking in their debate, uncomfortably. As though in spite of himself, he said now, "Very few, I am afraid."

"Religious ethic," Patricia pursued, relentlessly. "The greatest of the commandments is Thou Shalt Not Kill, but comes along a war in which killing becomes not only permissible but an absolute virtue and all our good Christians, Jews, Mohammedans and even Buddhists, who supposedly are not even allowed to kill mosquitoes, wade in with sheer happiness."

"War releases abnormal passions," Ross said grudgingly.

"You don't need a war. Look at the Germans, supposedly one of our most highly civilized people. When the Nazi government released all restraints on persecution of the Jews, gypsies and others, you know what happened. This began in peace time, not in war."

Dr. Braun shifted in his chair. He said, his voice low, "We needn't look beyond our own borders. The manner in which our people conducted themselves against the Amerinds from the very beginning of the white occupation of North America was quite shocking."

Ross said to him, "I thought you were on my side. The Indian wars were a long time ago. We're more advanced now."

Dr. Braun said softly, "My father fought against Geronimo in Arizona. It wasn't so long ago as all that."

Ross Wooley felt the argument going against him and lashed back. "We've been over and over this, what's your point?"

Patricia said doggedly, "The same point I tried to make from the beginning. This discovery must not be generally released. We'll simply have to suppress it."

* * * * *

The door opened behind them. They turned. Nothing was there. Ross, scowling, lumbered to his feet to walk over and close it.

"Hey, take it easy," a voice laughed. "Don't walk right into a guy."

Ross stopped, startled.

Dr. Braun and Patricia stood up and stared, too.

Crowley laughed. "You all look like you're seeing a ghost."

Ross rumbled a grudging chuckle. "It'd be all right if we *saw* the ghost, it's not seeing you that's disconcerting."

The air began to shimmer, somewhat like heat on the desert's face.

Crowley said, "Hey, the stuff's wearing off. Where're my clothes?"

"Where you left them. There in that bedroom," Ross said. "We'll wait for you." He went back and rejoined his associates. The door to the bedroom opened, there was a shimmering, more obvious now, and then the door closed behind it.

"He rejoined us just in time," Dr. Braun murmured. "Another ten minutes and he would have ... umah ... *materialized* down on the street."

Ross hadn't finished the discussion. He said, his face in all but pout, "What you don't realize, Pat, is the world has gone beyond the point where scientific discoveries can be suppressed. If we try to keep the lid on this today, the Russians or Chinese, or somebody, will hit on it tomorrow."

Patricia said impatiently, "Good heavens, let's don't bring the Cold War into it."

Ross opened his mouth to snap something back at her, closed it again and shrugged his bulky shoulders angrily.

In a matter of less than ten minutes the bedroom door reopened and this time a grinning Crowley emerged, fully dressed. He said, "Man, that was a devil of an experience!"

They saw him to a chair and had him talk it all through. He was candid enough, bubbling over with it all.

In the some eleven and a half hours he'd been on his own, he had covered quite an area of Manhattan.

Evidently the first hour had been spent in becoming used to the startling situation. He couldn't even see himself, which, to his surprise affected walking and even use of his hands. You had to get used to it. Then there was the fact that he was nude and *felt* nude and hence uncomfortable walking about in mixed pedestrian traffic. But that phase passed. Early in the game he found that there was small percentage in getting into crowds. It led to all sorts of complications, including the starting of minor rows, one person thinking another was pushing when it was simply a matter of Crowley trying to get out from underfoot.

Then he went through a period of the wonder of it all. Being able to walk *anywhere* and observe people who had no suspicion that they were being observed. It was during that phase that he had sought out the hotel in which he had read the chesty French movie actress Brigette Loren was in residence. Evidently, he'd hit the nail right on the head. Brigette was at her toilette when he arrived on scene. In telling about this, Crowley leered amusedly at Patricia from the side of his eyes. She ignored him.

Then he'd gone through a period when the full realization of his immunity had hit him.

At this point he turned to Braun, "Hey, Doc, you ever eaten any caviar? You know, that Russian stuff. Supposed to be the most expensive food in the world."

The doctor cleared his throat. "Small amounts in hors d'oeuvres at cocktail parties."

"Well, maybe I'm just a country boy but the stuff tastes like fish eggs to me. Anyway, to get back to the story...."

He'd gone into Tiffany's and into some of the other swank shops. And then into a bank or two, and stared at the treasures of Manhattan.

At this point he looked at Ross. "You know, just being invisible don't mean all that. How you going to pick up a wad of thousand dollar bills and just walk out the front door with them? Everybody'd see the dough just kind of floating through the air."

"I came to the same conclusion myself, when I experimented," Ross said wryly.

He had ridden on the subways ... free. He had eaten various food in various swank restaurants. He had even had drinks in name bars, sampling everything from Metaxa to vintage champagne. He was of the opinion that even though he remained invisible for the rest of his years, he'd still stick to bourbon and beer.

He had gone down to Wall Street and into the offices of the top brokerage firms and into the sanctum sanctorums of the wealthiest of mucky-mucks but had been too impatient to stick around long enough to possibly hear something that might be profitable. He admitted, grudgingly, that he wouldn't have known what to listen for anyway. Frustrated there, he had gone back uptown and finally located the hangout of one of the more renown sports promoters who was rumored to have gangster connections and was currently under bail due to a boxing scandal. He had stayed about that worthy's office for an hour, gleaning nothing more than several dirty jokes he'd never heard before.

All this activity had wearied him so he went to the Waldorf, located an empty suite in the tower and climbed into bed for a nap after coolly phoning room service to give him a call in two hours. That had almost led to disaster. Evidently, someone on room service had found the suite to be supposedly empty and had sent a boy up to investigate. However, when he had heard the door open, Crowley had merely rolled out of the bed and left, leaving a startled bellhop behind staring at rumpled bedclothes which had seemed to stir of their own accord.

* * * * *

The rest of the day was little different from the first hours. He had gone about gawking in places he couldn't have had he been visible. Into the dressing room of the Roxie, into the bars of swank private clubs, into the offices of the F.B.I. He would have liked to have walked in on a poker game with some real high rollers playing, such as Nick the Greek, but he didn't have the time nor know-how to go about finding one.

Crowley wound it all up with a gesture of both hands, palms upward. "I gotta admit, it was fun, but what the devil good is it?"

They looked at him questioningly.

Crowley said, "I mean, how's it practical? How can you make a buck out of it, if you turn it over to the public, like? Everybody'd go around robbing everybody else and you'd all wind up equal."

Dr. Braun chuckled in deprecation. "There would be various profitable uses, Don. One priceless one would be scientific observation of wild life. For that matter there would be valid usage in everyday life. There are often personal reasons for not wishing to be observed. Celebrities, for instance, wishing to avoid crowds."

"Yeah," Crowley laughed, "or a businessman out with his secretary."

Dr. Braun frowned. "Of course, there are many other aspects. It would mean the end of such things as the Iron Curtain. And also the end of such things as American immigration control. There are many, many ramifications, Don, some of which frighten us. The world would be never quite the same."

Crowley leaned forward confidentially. "Well, I'll tell you. I was thinking it all out. What we got to do is turn it over to the Army and soak them plenty for it."

The others ignored his cutting himself a piece of the cake.

Ross Wooley merely grunted bitterly.

Patricia said impatiently, "We've thought most of these things through, Don. However, Dr. Braun happens to be quite a follower of Lord Russell."

Crowley looked at her blankly.

"He's a pacifist," she explained.

Braun pushed his glasses back more firmly on his nose and said, gently, "The military already have enough gadgets to destroy quite literally everything and I trust one set of them no more than the other. If *both* sides had our discovery, then, very well, each would go about attempting to find some manner of penetrating the invisibility, or taking various measures to protect their top secrets. But to give it to just one would be such an advantage that the other would have to embark immediately upon a desperate attack before the advantage could be fully realized. If we turn this over to the Pentagon, for exclusive use, the Soviets would have to begin a preventative war as soon as they learned of its existence."

"You a red?" Crowley said, scowling.

The doctor shrugged hopelessly. "No," he said.

Crowley turned to the other two. "If you think it's the patriotic thing to do, why don't one of you sell it to the government?"

Patricia said testily, "You don't understand, Don. Even if we were so thoroughly in disagreement that we would act unilaterally, we couldn't. You see, this is a three-way discovery. No one of us knows the complete process."

His face twisted. "Look, maybe some of this egghead stuff doesn't get through to me but I'm not stupid, see? You got the stuff, haven't you? You gave me that shot this morning."

Braun took over, saying reasonably, "Don, this discovery was hit upon by accident. The three of us are employed in the laboratories of a medical research organization. I am the department head. Patricia and Ross were doing some routine work on a minor problem when they separately stumbled upon some rather startling effects, practically at the same time. Each, separately, brought their discoveries to me, and, working you might say intuitively, I added some conclusions of my own, and ...well, I repeat, the discovery was stumbled upon."

Crowley assimilated that. "None of you knows how to do it, make those injections like, by himself?"

"That is correct. Each knows just one phase of the process. Each must combine with the other two."

Patricia said impatiently, "And thus far we wish to keep it that way. Rossie believes the discovery should be simultaneously revealed on a world-wide basis, and let man adapt to it as best he can. I think it should be suppressed until man has grown up a little-if he ever does. The doctor vacillates between the two positions. What he would truly like to see, is the method kept only for the use of qualified scientists, but even our good doctor realizes what a dream that is."

Crowley took them all in, one at a time. "Well, what the devil are you going to do?"

"That's a good question," Ross said unhappily.

"This experiment was a farce," Patricia said irritably. "After all our trouble locating Don, our *Common Man*, we have found out nothing that we didn't know before. His reactions were evidently largely similar to our own and...." She broke it off and frowned thoughtfully. The other three looked at her questioningly.

Patricia said, "You know, we simply haven't seen this thing through as yet."

"What do you mean, Pat?" Ross growled.

She turned to him. "We haven't given Don the chance to prove which one of us is right. One day is insufficient. Half the things he wished to do, such as sneaking around picking up stock tips in Wall Street and inside information on sporting events...."

"Hey, take it easy," Crowley protested. "I was just, like, curious."

Ross said heatedly, "That's not fair. I'll admit, I, too, thought of exactly the same possibilities. But *thinking* about them and going through with them are different things. Haven't you ever thought about what you'd do if given the chance to be world-wide supreme dictator? But, truly, if the job was offered, would you take it?"

"Good heavens," Patricia said disgustedly, "remind me to break off our engagement if I haven't already done it. I hate overpowering men. All I'm saying is that we'll have to give Don at least a week. One day isn't enough."

Dr. Braun cocked his head to one side and said uncomfortably, "I'm not sure but that in a week's time our friend Don might be able.... See here, Don, do you mind going on down to the hotel's bar while we three talk this through?"

Crowley obviously took umbrage at that, but there was nothing to be done. Frowning peevishly, he left.

The doctor looked from one to the other of his associates. "By Caesar, do you realize the damage friend Don could accomplish in a week's time?"

Patricia laughed at him. "That's what I keep telling the two of you. Do you realize the damage *any* person could do with invisibility? Not to speak of giving it to every Tom, Dick and Harry in the world."

Ross said, "We've started this, lets go through with it. I back Pat's suggestion, that we give Don sufficient serum to give him twelve hours of invisibility a day for a full week. However, we will ration it out to him day by day, so that if things get out of hand we can cut his supply."

"That's an idea," Patricia said. "And I suspect that within half the period we'll all be convinced that the process will have to be suppressed."

Ross leaned forward. "Good. I suggest we three keep this suite and get Don a room elsewhere, so he won't be inhibited by our continual presence. Once a day we'll give him enough serum for one shot and he can take it any time he wishes to." He ran his beefy hand back through his red crew cut in a gesture of satisfaction. "If he seems to get out of hand, we'll call it all off."

Dr. Braun cleared his throat unhappily. "I have premonitions of disaster, but I suppose if we've come this far we should see the experiment through."

Patricia said ungraciously, "At least the lout will be limited in his accomplishments by his lack of imagination. Imagine going into that French girl's dressing room."

"Yeah," Ross said ludicrously trying to make his big open face look dreamy.

"You wretch," Patricia laughed. "The wedding is off!"

* * * * *

But Crowley was no lout. He was full of the folk wisdom of his people.

God helps those who help themselves.

It's each man for himself and the devil take the hindmost.

Not to speak of.

Never give a sucker an even break.

If I didn't do it, somebody else would.

Had he been somewhat more of a student he might also have run into that nugget of the ancient Greek. *Morals are the invention of the weak to protect themselves from the strong.*

Once convinced that the three eggheads were incapable of realizing the potentialities of their discovery, he had little difficulty in arguing himself into the stand that he should. It helped considerably to realize that in all the world only four persons, including himself, were aware of the existence of the invisibility serum.

He spent the first day in what Marx called in "Das Kapital" the "original accumulation of capital," although it would seem unlikely that even in the wildest accusations of the most confirmed Marxist, no great fortune was ever before begun in such wise.

It was not necessary, he found, to walk into a large bank and simply seemingly levitate the money out the front door. In fact, that would have meant disaster. However, large sums of money are to be found elsewhere on Manhattan and for eleven hours Crowley used his native ingenuity and American know-how, most of which had been gleaned from watching TV crime shows. By the end of the day he had managed to accumulate in the neighborhood of a hundred thousand dollars and was reasonably sure that the news would not get back to his sponsors. The fact was, he had cleaned out the treasuries of several numbers rackets and those of two bookies.

It was important, he well realized, that he be well under way before the three eggheads decided to lower the boom.

The second day he spent making his preliminary contacts, an operation that was helped by his activities of the day before. He was beginning already to get the feel of the underworld element with which he had decided he was going to have to work, at least in the early stages of his operations.

Any leader, be he military, political or financial, knows that true greatness lies in the ability to choose assistants. Be you a Napoleon with his marshals, a Roosevelt with his brain trust, a J. P. Morgan with his partners, the truism applies. No great leader has ever stood alone.

But Crowley also knew instinctively that he was going to have to keep the number of his immediate associates small. They were going to have to know his secret, and no man is so naïve as not to realize that while one person can keep a secret, it becomes twice as hard for two and from that point on the likelihood fades in a geometric progression.

On the fifth day he knocked on the door of the suite occupied by Dr. Braun and his younger associates and pushed his way in without waiting for response.

The three were sitting around awaiting his appearance and to issue him his usual day's supply of serum. They greeted him variously, Patricia with her usual brisk, almost condescending smile; Dr. Braun with a gentle nod and a speaking of his first name; Ross Wooley sourly. Ross obviously had some misgivings, the exact nature of which he couldn't quite put his finger upon.

Crowley grinned and said, "Hello, everybody."

"Sit down, Don," Braun said gently. "We have been discussing your experiment."

While the newcomer was finding his seat, Patricia said testily, "Actually, we are not quite happy about your reports, Don. We feel an ... if you'll pardon us ... an evasive quality about them. As though you aren't completely frank."

"In short," Ross snapped, "have you been pulling things you haven't told us about?"

Crowley grinned at them. "Now you folks are downright suspicious."

Dr. Braun indicated some notes on the coffee table before him. "It seems hardly possible that your activities would be confined largely to going to the cinema, to the swankier night clubs and eating in the more famed restaurants."

Crowley's grin turned into a half embarrassed smirk. Patricia thought of a small boy who had been caught in a mischief but was still somewhat proud of himself. He said, "Well, I gotta admit that there's been a few things. Come on over to my place and I'll show you." He looked at Braun. "Hey, Doc, about how much is one of them Rembrandt paintings worth?"

Braun rolled his eyes toward the ceiling, "Great Caesar," he murmured. He came to his feet and looked around at the rest of them. "Let us go over there and learn the worst," he said.

At the curb, before the hotel, Ross Wooley looked up and down the street for a cab.

Crowley said, his voice registering self-deprecation, "Over here."

Over here was a several toned, fantastically huge hover-limousine, a nattily dressed, sharp-looking, expressionless-faced young man behind the wheel.

The three looked at Crowley.

He opened the door. "Climb in folks. Nothing too good for you scientists, eh?"

Inside, sitting next to a window with Patricia beside him and Dr. Braun at the far window, and with Ross in a jump seat, Crowley said expansively, "This is Larry. Larry, this is Doc Braun and his friends I was telling you about, Ross Wooley and Pat O'Gara. They're like scientists."

Larry said, "Hi," without inflection, and tooled the heavy car out into the traffic.

Ross spun on Crowley. "Don, where'd you get this car?"

Crowley laughed. "You'll see. Take it easy. You'll see a lot of things."

* * * * *

They were too caught up in their own thoughts and in the barrage of demands they were leveling at Crowley to notice direction. It wasn't until they were already on the George Washington Bridge that Patricia blurted, "Don, this isn't the way to your hotel!"

Crowley said tolerantly, "Take it easy, Pat. We're taking a short detour. Something I have to show you in Jersey."

"I don't like this," Ross snapped. The redhead shifted his heavy shoulders in a reflexive protest against the confining tweed coat he wore.

"Relax," Crowley told him reasonably. "I've been thinking things out quite a bit and I've got a lot to discuss with you folks."

They were across the bridge now and Larry headed into the maze which finally unraveled itself to the point that it was obvious they were heading north. Larry hit the lift lever and they rose ten feet from the surface.

Dr. Braun said evenly, "You had no intention of taking us to your room. You used that as a ruse to get us out of our hotel and, further, across the bridge until we are now in a position where it's quite impossible for us to summon police assistance."

Crowley grinned. "That's right, Doc. Didn't I tell you these three were real eggheads, Larry? Look how quick he figured that out."

Larry grunted in what might have been amusement.

Ross, growling low in his throat, turned suddenly in his jump seat and grabbed Crowley by the coat front. "What's going on here?"

Crowley snapped, "Larry!"

From seemingly nowhere, the chauffeur had produced a thin black automatic and was now lazily pointing it, not so much at Ross Wooley as at Dr. Braun and Patricia. He said evenly, softly, "Easy, friend."

Ross released his grip, "Put that thing away," he blurted.

"Sure, sure," Larry said, his voice all but disinterested. The gun disappeared.

Crowley, only slightly ruffled, said now, "Take it easy, Ross. Nothing's going to happen to you. I'm going to need you folks and I'm going to treat you right."

"Where are we going?" Ross growled.

"I had the boys rent me a big estate like up in the Catskills. Big place, nice and quiet. In fact, the last tenants used it for one of these rest sanitariums. You know, rich people with DTs or trying to get a monkey off their back."

"The boys?" Patricia said softly.

He looked at her and grinned again. Crowley was obviously enjoying himself. "I got a few people working for me," he explained.

Dr. Braun blurted, "You fool! You mean you've revealed the existence of the process Pat, Ross and I worked out to a group of ignoramuses?"

Crowley said angrily, "Now look, Doc, let's don't get on that bit. Maybe I'm just a country boy but I'm as smart as the next man. Just because some of you eggheads spend half your life in college don't mean you've got any monopoly on good common sense. I went to the school of hard knocks, understand, and I got plenty of diplomas to prove it. Take it easy on that ignoramus talk."

Patricia said suddenly, "Don's right, Dr. Braun. I think you've badly underestimated him."

Ross snorted sourly at that remark. "We've all underestimated him. Well, I think you'll agree that our friend Don will get no more injections of the invisibility serum."

Crowley chuckled.

They looked at him. Three sinkings of stomach taking place simultaneously.

"Now, you know I thought that might be your altitude...."

"Attitude," Ross muttered.

"...So I went to the trouble of coming up to your suite last night and sort of confiscating the supply. By the looks of it, I'd say there was enough for another ten shots or so."

"See," Patricia said to Ross. "You're not as smart as you thought you were. Don's one up on you."

* * * * *

571

The estate which the "boys" had secured for Crowley was two or three miles out of Tannersville on a mountainside and quite remote. He took considerable pride in showing them about, although it was obvious that he had been here before only once himself.

He was obviously enjoying the situation thoroughly and had planned it out in some detail. Besides the empty-faced Larry, who had driven the car, they were introduced to two more of Crowley's confederates, neither of whom gave any indication that the three were present under duress. The first was a heavy-set, moist palmed southerner with a false air of the jovial. He shook hands heartily, said nothing with a good many words for a few minutes and then excused himself. The third confidant was an older man of sad mien who would have passed easily in the swankest of Washington, New York or London private clubs. He was introduced simply as Mr. Whitely, greeted them pleasantly as though all were fellow guests, had a word to say about the weather then and passed on.

Patricia was frowning. "Your southern friend, Paul Teeter, it seems to me I've heard his name before."

Crowley grinned. "Oh, Paul's been in the news from time to time."

Ross was looking after Mr. Whitely who had disappeared into the main building. They were standing on the lawn, as part of the guided tour Crowley was giving them. He growled, "I suppose the two of them are experienced confidence men, or something."

"Take it easy with those cracks, Ross," Crowley said. "Whitely used to have a seat on the Stock Exchange. A real big shot. But that was before they disbarred him, or whatever they call it."

"See here," Dr. Braun said urgently. "We've had enough of all this, Don. I propose we go somewhere where it will be possible for us to bring you to your senses, and save you from disaster."

"Kind of a powwow, eh? O.K., Doc, come on in here." He led them to the entrance, conducted them inside and into a library that led off the main *entrada*. He said, "By the way, Larry has a few of his boys up here just kind of like estate watchmen. Some of them aren't much used to being out of the city and they get nervous. So...."

Ross growled, "All right, all right, don't try to make like a third-rate villain in a B-Movie. You have guards about and it would be dangerous to try to leave without your permission."

"How about that?" Crowley exclaimed as though amazed. "Man, you eggheads catch on quick. Nothing like a college education." He waved them to chairs. "I'm going to have to leave for a while. Whitely's got some big deal brewing and we got to work it out." He grinned suddenly. "And Larry's got a different kind of deal. One he's been planning for years but hasn't been able to swing one or two details. It's a caution how many details a little man who wasn't there can handle in one of these king-size capers."

He had used the pseudo-criminal term, caper, with considerable satisfaction. Crowley was obviously having the time of his life.

"Very well," Braun said, "we'll wait." When the other had left the room, leaving the door open behind him, the doctor turned to his two younger associates. "What children we've been."

Ross Wooley growled unhappily, "Brother, we couldn't have picked a worse so-called Common Man, if we'd tried. That character is as nutty as a stuffed date. Do you realize what he's in a position to do?"

Patricia twisted her mouth thoughtfully. "I wonder if any of us really realize. I am afraid even with all our speculation, we never truly thought this out."

Dr. Braun pushed his glasses back on his nose with a forefinger. He shook his head. "You make a mistake, Ross. We didn't make a bad choice in our selection of Don Crowley for our typical Common Man."

Ross looked at him and snorted.

Braun said doggedly, "Remember, we attempted to find the average man, the common man, the little man, the man in the street. Well, it becomes obvious to me that we did just that."

Patricia said thoughtfully, "I don't know. I'm inclined to think that from the beginning you two have underestimated Don. He has certainly shown considerable ingenuity. Do you realize that he's done all this in a matter of less than a week?"

"Done all *what?*" Ross said sarcastically.

She gestured. "Look at this establishment. He's obviously acquired considerable money, and he already has an organization, or at least the beginnings of one."

"That is beside the point," Braun said ruefully. "I say that he is reacting as would be expected. As the average man in the street would react given the opportunity to seize almost unlimited power, and with small chance of reprisal."

Patricia shrugged as though in disagreement.

Braun looked at Ross Wooley. "Close the door, Ross. Lord knows when we'll have another chance to confer. Obviously, something must be done."

Ross came quickly to his feet, crossed to the door, looked up and down the hallway which was empty and then closed the door behind him. He came back to the others and drew his chair in closer so that they could communicate in low voices.

Braun said, "One thing is definite. We must not allow him to secure further serum. For all we know, he might be planning to inject some of those gangsters he's affiliated himself with."

Patricia shook her head thoughtfully. "I still think you underestimate Don. He must realize he can't trust them. At this stage, he has had to confide in at least two or three, fully to utilize his invisibility. But in the long run it isn't to his advantage to have *anybody* know about it. If the authorities, such as the F.B.I., began looking for an invisible man, sooner or later they would penetrate the field of invisibility."

"You mean you think Crowley will use these men for a time and then … destroy them?"

"He'll have to, or sooner or later the secret will be out."

Braun said in soft logic, "If he can't allow anyone to know about it, then we, too, must be destroyed."

Ross growled, "Then we've got to finish him first."

Patricia said, "Now, I don't know. Don is showing considerably more sense than you two evidently give him credit for. I think in many ways what he's done is quite admirable. He's seen his chance-and has grasped it. Why, I wouldn't be surprised that Don will be the most powerful man in the country within months."

The two men were staring at her. Ross sputtered, "Have you gone completely around the bend? Are you defending this … this…."

* * * * *

A voice chuckled, "Mind your language, Buster. Just take it easy or you'll wind up with some missing teeth."

Ross jumped to his feet as though couched with an electric prod. Dr. Braun stiffened in his chair and his eyes darted about the room.

Patricia alone seemed collected. "Don Crowley!" she exclaimed. "You should be ashamed of yourself, listening in on private conversations."

"Yeah," the voice said. "However, it's handy to know what the other side is dreaming up in the way of a bad time for you. Sit down, Buster. I've got a few things to say."

Muttering, Ross resumed his place. The doctor sighed deeply and sank back onto the sofa he had been occupying. The three could see an indentation magically appear in the upholstery of an easy-chair across from them.

Crowley's voice said confidently, "You know, from the first, I've kept telling you eggheads that I'm not stupid, but none of you've bothered to listen. You think just because you spent six or eight years of your life in some college that you're automatically smarter than other people. But I got a theory, like, that it doesn't make any difference if you spent your whole life going to college, you still wouldn't wind up smart if you didn't start that way."

Ross began to mutter something, but Crowley snapped, "Shut up for a minute, I'm talking." He resumed his condescending tone. "Just for example, take a couple of guys who got to the top. Edison in science and Khrushchev in politics. For all practical purposes, neither of them went to school at all. Khrushchev didn't even learn to read until he was twenty-eight years old.

"Then take Dr. Braun here. He's spent half his life in school, and where's it got him? He'd make more dough if he owned the local garage and dealer franchise for one of the automobile companies in some jerkwater town. And look at Ross. He'd probably make more money playing pro football than he does messing around with all those test tubes and Bunsen burners and everything. What good has all the school done either?"

Dr. Braun said gently, "Could we get to the point?"

"Take it easy, Doc. I'm in charge here. You just sit and listen. The point is, you three with your smart-Aleck egghead education started off thinking Mr. Common Man, like you call me, is stupid. Well, it just so happens I'm not. Take Pat there. She's smarter than you two, but she had the same idea. That this here country boy isn't as smart as she is. She's going to fox him, see? As soon as she saw the way the cards were falling, she started buttering up to me. She even figured out that I was probably right in this room listening to you planning how to trip me up. So she pretended to take sides against you."

"Why, Don!" Patricia protested.

"Come off it, kid. You probably hate my guts worse than the others. You were the one who thought this *particular* average man was a slob. That all common people were slobs."

Patricia's face went expressionless, but Ross, knowing her well, could sense her dismay. Crowley was right. She had been trying to play a careful game but their supposedly average man had seen through her.

Crowley's voice went thoughtful. "I been doing a lot of thinking this week. A lot of it. And you want to know something? You know what I decided? I decided that everybody talks a lot about the Common Man but actually he's never had a chance to, like, express himself. He's never been able to put over the things he's always wanted."

"Haven't you ever heard of democracy?" Ross said sourly. "Who do you think elects our officials?"

"Shut up, I told you. I'm talking now. Sure, every four years the lousy politicians come around and they stick coonskin caps on their heads or Indian bonnets and start saying ain't when they make their speeches. Showing they're just folks, see? They go out into the country, and stick a straw in their mouth and talk about crops to the farmers, all that sort of thing. But they aren't *really* common folks. Most of them are lawyers or bankers or something. They run those political parties and make all the decisions themselves. The Common Man never really has anything to say about it."

Braun said reasonably, "You have your choice. If you think one candidate is opposed to your interests you can elect the other."

Crowley grunted his contempt. "But they're both the same. No, there hasn't been no common man in Washington since Lincoln, and maybe he wasn't. Well, I'll tell you something. The kind of talk I hear down in the corner saloon from just plain people makes a lot more sense to me than all this stuff the politicians pull."

Dr. Braun cleared his throat and stared at the seemingly empty chair from whence came the other's belligerent voice. "Are you thinking of entering politics, Don?"

"Maybe I am."

"Good heavens," Patricia ejaculated.

"Oh, I'm not smart enough, eh? Well, listen baby, the eggheads don't seem to be so great in there. Maybe it's time the Common Man took over."

Dr. Braun said reasonably, "But see here, Crowley, the ability to achieve invisibility doesn't give you any advantages in swinging elections or...." He broke off in mid-sentence and did a mental double take.

Crowley laughed in contempt. "The biggest thing you need to win elections, Doc, is plenty of dough. And I'll have that. But I'll also have the way to do more muck-raking than anybody in history. *I'll* sit in on every important private get-together those crook politicians have. I'll get the details of every scheme they cook up. I'll get into any safe or safe deposit box. I'll have the common people, you sneer so much about, screaming for their blood."

Ross rumbled, "What do you expect to accomplish in office, Crowley?"

The voice became expansive. "Lots of things. Take this Cold War. If you drop into any neighborhood bar, you'll hear what the common man thinks about it."

The three of them stared at the seemingly empty chair.

"Drop the bomb first!" Crowley snapped. "Finish those reds off before they start it. In fact, I'm not even sure they've got the bomb. They're not smart enough to...."

"There was sputnik, you know," Ross interrupted sourly.

"Yeah, but built by those captured German scientists. We're way ahead of those Russkies in everything. Hit 'em now. Finish 'em off. The eggheads in Washington are scared of their own shadows. Another thing I'd end is getting suckered in by those French and English politicians. What does America need with those countries? They always start up these wars and get us to bail them out. And I say stop all this foreign aid and keep the money in our own country.

"And we can do a lot of cleaning up right here, too. We got to kick all the commies out of the government. Make all the commies and socialists and these egghead liberals, illegal. In fact, I'm in favor of shooting them. When you got an enemy, finish him off. And take the Jews. I'm not anti-Semitic, like, understand. Some of my best friends are Jews. But you got to realize that wherever they go they cause trouble. They stick together and take over the best businesses and all. O.K., you know what I say? I say kick them out of the country. And they all came over here poor and made their money here. So let them leave the way they came. We'll, like, confiscate all their property except like personal things."

Patricia had closed her eyes in pain long before this. She said, softly, "I imagine somewhere along in here we'll get to the Negroes."

"I'm not against them. Just so they stay in their place. But this integration stuff is bunk. You got to face facts. Negroes aren't as smart as white people, neither are Chinks or Mexicans or Puerto Ricans. So, O.K., give them their own schools, up to high school is all they need, and let them have jobs like waiters and janitors and like that. They shouldn't take a white man's job and they shouldn't be allowed to marry white people. It deteriorates the race, like."

Crowley was really becoming wound up now. Wound up and expansive. "There's a lot of things I'd change, see. Take freedom of speech and press and like that. Sure I believe in that, I'm one hundred per cent American. But you can't allow people to talk against the government. Freedom of speech is O.K., but you can't let a guy jump up in the middle of a theater and yell fire."

"Why not?" Ross growled. "Freedom of speech is more important than a few movie houses full of people. Besides, if one man is allowed to jump up and yell fire, then somebody else can yell out 'You're a liar, there is no fire.'"

"You're not funny," Crowley said ominously.

"I wasn't trying to be," Ross muttered, and then blurred into sudden action. He shot to his feet, and then, arms extended, dashed toward the source of the voice. He hit the chair without slowing, grappled crazily.

"I've got him!" He wrestled awkwardly, fantastically, seemingly in an insane tumbling without opponent.

Patricia was on her feet. She grasped an antique bronze candle-holder and darted toward the now fallen chair and to where Ross was wrestling desperately on the floor. Crowley was attempting to shout, but was largely smothered.

Patricia held the candlestick at the ready, trying to find an opening, trying to locate the invisible Crowley's head.

Frederick Braun staggered to his own feet, bewildered, shaking.

A voice from the door said flatly, "O.K., that's it." Then, sharper, "I said cut it out. You all right, Mr. Crowley?"

It was Larry. His thin black automatic was held almost negligently in his right hand. He ran his eyes up and down Patricia, taking in the candlestick weapon. His ordinarily empty face registered a flicker of amused approval.

Patricia gasped, "Oh, no," dropped her bludgeon and sank into a chair, her head in her hands.

Ross, his face in dismay, came slowly to his feet. The redhead stared at the gunman, momentarily considering further attack. Larry, ignoring both Braun and Patricia, swung the gun to cover him exclusively. "I wouldn't," he said emptily.

Of a sudden, Ross' head jerked backward. His nose flattened, crushingly, and then spurted blood. He reeled back, his head flinging this way and that, bruises and cuts appeared magically.

Crowley's voice raged, "You asked for it, wise guy. How do you like these apples?"

The saturnine Larry chuckled sourly. "Hey, take it easy, chief. You'll kill the guy."

Ross had crumpled to the floor. There were still sounds of blows. Crowley raged, "You're lucky I'm not wearing shoes, I'd break every rib in your body!"

Patricia was staring in hopeless horror. She said sharply, "Don, remember you need Ross! You need all of us! Without all of us there can be no more serum."

The blows stopped.

"There will be no more serum anyway," Braun said shakily. The thin little man still stood before his chair having moved not at all since the action began.

Crowley's heavy breathing could be heard but he managed a snarl. "That's what you think, Doc."

Braun said, "By Caesar, I absolutely refuse to...."

Crowley interrupted ominously. "You know, Doc, that's where this particular common man has it all over you eggheads. You spend so much time reading, you don't take in the action shows on TV. Now what you're thinking is that even if we were going to twist your arm a little, you'd stick to your guns. But suppose, like, it was Pat we was working on, while you had to sit and watch."

The elderly man's brave front collapsed and his thin shoulders slumped.

Crowley barked a laugh.

Patricia by now, was bent over the unconscious Ross crying even as she tried to help him.

Crowley said to the silent, all but disinterested Larry, "Have these three put in separate rooms in that section they used for the violent wing when the place was a nuthouse. Have a good guard and see they don't talk back and forth."

"You're the boss," Larry said languidly.

* * * * *

Crowley was thorough. For that they had to give him credit. They were kept divided, each in a different room-cell and with at least two burly, efficient guards on constant watch. They were fed on army-type trays and their utensils checked carefully. There was no communication allowed-even with the guard.

The second day, Crowley took measures to see their disappearance raised no alarm at either their place of employment or at their residences. This raised few problems since all were single and all had already taken off both from the job and from their homes in order to carry out their experiment. Crowley forced them to write further notes and letters finding excuses for extending their supposed vacations. He also had Larry return to the hotel suite, pay their bill, pack their things and bring them to the Catskill estate which had become their prison.

He had them make up lists of materials and equipment they would need for further manufacture of the serum upon which they had stumbled, and sent off men to acquire the things.

And on three occasions during the following weeks he had them brought from their cells and spent an hour or so with them at lunch or dinner. Crowley evidently needed an audience beyond that of his henchmen. The release of his basic character, formerly repressed, was progressing geometrically and there seemed to be an urgency to crow, to brag, to boast.

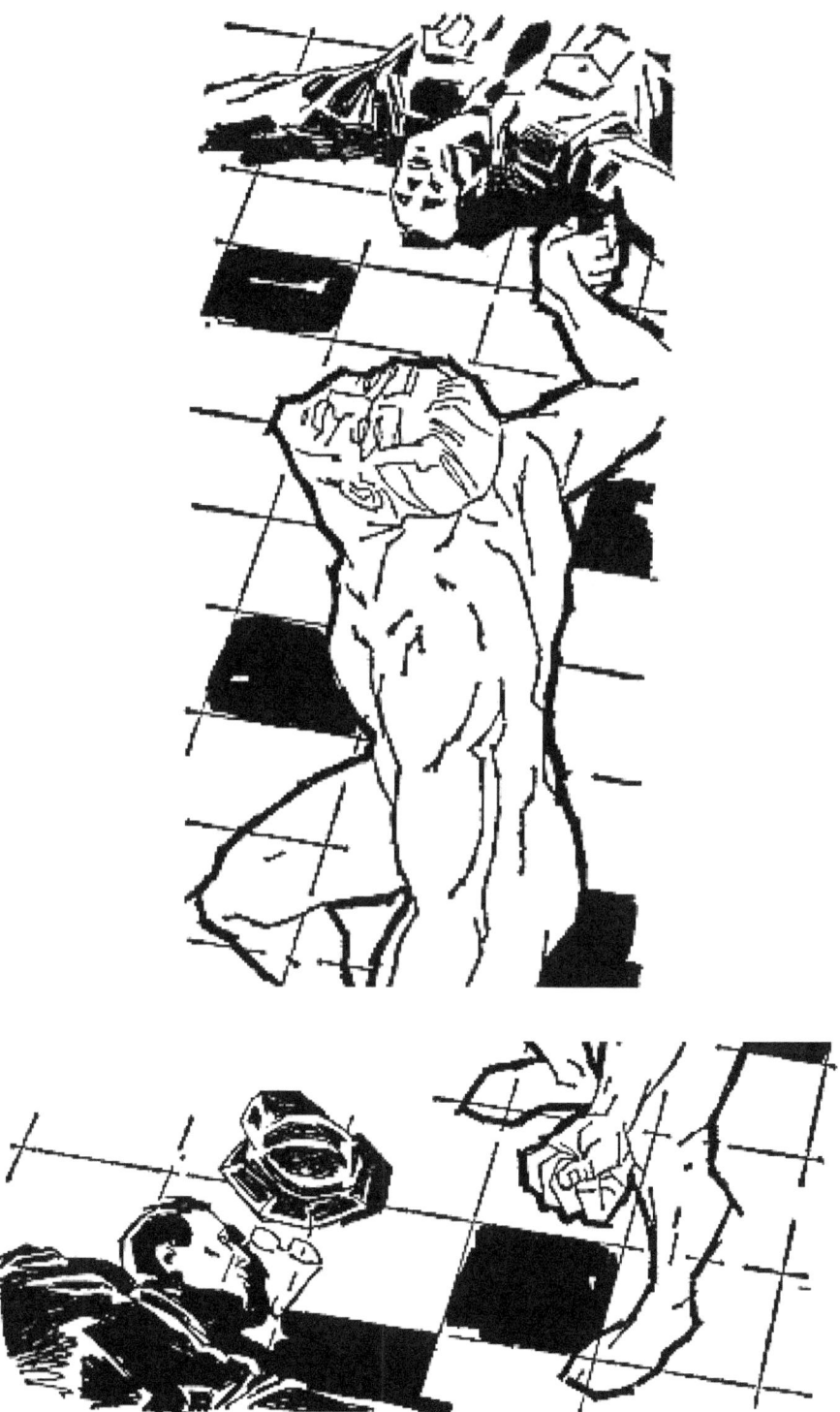

On the third of these occasions he was already seated at the table when they were ushered into the dining room. Crowley dismissed the guards with a wave of his hand as though they were liveried servants.

All had eaten but there were liqueurs and coffee, cigars and cigarettes on the broad table.

Ross sank into a chair and growled, "Well, what hath the great man wrought by now?"

Crowley grinned at him, poured coffee and then a dollop of Napoleon brandy into it. He gestured with a hand. "Help yourselves, folks. How you feeling? You been getting all the books you wanted? You look kind of peaked, Pat."

"Miss O'Gara to you, you ape with delusions of grandeur," she snapped. "When are you going to let us out of those prison cells?"

Crowley wasn't provoked. The strong can afford to laugh at the malcontented weak. "That's one of the things you never know," he said easily. "You sure you want out? Something the Doc said the other day had a lotta fact in it. The fewer people know about this secret of mine, the better off I'll be and the better off I am, the better off the whole country is going to be and I gotta think about that. I got responsibilities."

"A combination of Engine Charley and Louis XIV, eh?" Ross muttered, running his beefy hand back over his crew cut. It was a relief to get out of his room and talk with the others, but he didn't want Crowley to see that.

"What's that?" the other was impatient of conversation that went above his head.

Dr. Braun explained gently. "One said, *I am the State*, and the other, *anything that's good for my corporation is good for the United States* —or something quite similar."

Crowley sipped at his coffee royal. "Well, anyway, Pat, the day you're ready to leave that cell, you'd better start worrying cause that'll mean I don't need you any more."

Ross growled, "You didn't answer my question. Robbed any banks lately, great man?"

The other eyed him coldly. "Take it easy, Buster. Maybe in the early stages of the Common Man Movement we hafta take some strong-arm measures, but that stage's about finished."

Patricia O'Gara was interested in spite of herself. She said. "You mean you already have all the money you need?"

He was expansive. Obviously there was nothing to lose with these three and he liked a sounding board. In spite of his alleged contempt for eggheads there was an element in Crowley which wished to impress them, to grant him equal status in their own estimations.

"There's a devil of a lot to know about big finance. You need a starter, but once you get it, the stuff just rolls in automatic." He grinned suddenly, almost boyishly. "Especially when you got a certain little advantage, like me."

Braun said, interestedly, "How do you put your advantage to work?"

"Well, now, I gotta admit we aren't quite out of the woods. We need more capital to work with, but after tonight we'll have it. Remember that Brinks job up in New England a long time ago? Well, we got something lined up even bigger. I work with Larry and his boys to pull it. Then there's another thing cooking that Whitely's been keeping tabs on. It looks like IBM is going to split its stock, three for one. I gotta attend their next secret executive meeting and find out. If they do, we buy in just before, see? We buy on margin, buy options, all that sort of jazz. Whitely knows all about it. Then we got another big deal in Washington. Looks like the government might devaluate the dollar. Whitely explained it to me, kind of. Anyway, I got to sit in on a conference the President's gonna have. If they really decide to devalue, then Whitely and me, we go ahead and put every cent we got into Swiss gold. Then the day after devaluation, we switch it all back into dollars again. Double our money. Oh, we got all sorts of angles, Doc."

"By Caesar," Braun ejaculated. "You seem to have."

* * * * *

Patricia had poured herself some coffee and was sipping it, black, even as she stared at him. "But, Don, what do you need all this money for? You already have more than plenty. Why not call it all off. Get out from under."

Ross grunted, "Too late, Pat. Can't you see? He's got the power urge already."

Crowley ignored him and turned to her, pouring more coffee and cognac for himself. "I'm not running up all this dough just for me. You think you're the only one's got ideals, like? Let me tell you, I might just be a country boy but I got ambitions to put some things right in this world."

"Such as...." Patricia prodded, bitterness in her voice.

"Aw, we went through all that the other day. The thing is, now it's really under way. If you was seeing the newspapers these days, you'd know about the Common Man Party."

"Oh, oh," Ross muttered unhappily.

"It's just getting under way," Crowley said modestly, "but we're hiring two of the top Madison Avenue outfits to handle publicity and we're recruiting some of the best practical politicians in the field."

"Practical politicians!" Ross snorted. "Types like Huey Long, McCarthy, Pendergast, I suppose."

The other misunderstood him. "Yeah, and even better. We're going in big for TV time, full-page ads in the newspapers and magazines. That sort of thing. The average man's getting tired of the same old talk from the Republicans and Democrats. Paul Teeter thinks we might have a chance in the next election, given enough dough to plow into it."

Ross leaned back disdainfully. "What a combination. Whitely, the broker who has been barred from activity on Wall Street; Teeter, the crooked politician, but with connections from top to bottom; and Larry, whatever his name is...."

"Morazzoni," Crowley supplied. "You know where I first ran into his name? In one of them true crime magazines. He's a big operator."

"I'll bet he is," the redhead growled. "Probably with good Mafia connections. I'm surprised you haven't attempted to take over that outfit."

Crowley laughed abruptly. "We're working on that, pal. Just take it easy and all these things will work their way out. But meanwhile I didn't bring you jokers here to make snide remarks. I got work for you. I'm fresh out of that serum and you three are going to brew me up another batch."

They looked at him, Dr. Braun, Ross Wooley, Patricia O'Gara, their faces registering stubbornness, revolt and dismay.

He shook his head. "Larry and some of his boys have experience. I gotta admit, I wouldn't even want to watch."

"I'm for standing firm," Braun said stiffly. "There are but three of us. The most they can do is kill us. But if this man's insanity is released on the world...."

Crowley was shaking his head in deprecation. "Like when you say the worst we can do is kill you. Man, haven't you heard about the Nazis and commies and all? You oughta read some of the men's adventure magazines. How do you think Joe Stalin got all them early Bolsheviks to confess? You think they weren't tough buzzards? Why make us go to all the trouble, when you'd just cave in eventually anyway? Save yourself the grief."

Patricia said impatiently, "He's right, I'm afraid. I would collapse rather quickly under physical coercion. You might last a bit longer, Ross possibly longer still. But in the end we would concede."

Crowley said, as though in amazement, "You know, eggheads aren't as stupid as some would reckon. O.K., folks, I got a laboratory all fixed up with your things. Let's go. Ah, Ross, old pal, I'm carrying heat, as Larry would say, so let's don't have any trouble, eh?"

He had been as good as his word in regards to the laboratory. It was obviously one of the rooms used by the staff when the place had been a sanitarium. Now, each of the three had all the equipment and supplies they required.

Crowley took a seat at the far end of the room, facing them. There had been a guard outside the door when they entered and a call would bring him in seconds. Even so, Crowley sat in such wise that his right hand was ready to plunge inside his coat to the gun that evidently was holstered there. He said, "O.K., folks, let's get about it."

* * * * *

It took them half an hour or so to sort out those materials each needed in his own contribution to the end product.

Their captor looked at his watch impatiently. "Let's get a move on, here. I thought this was going to take a few minutes."

Patricia said testily, "What's the hurry, Don?"

He grinned at her. "Tonight's the big night. This evening, just before closing, I walk into.... Well, you don't have to know the name. Like I said, it'll make the Brinks job look like peanuts. They lock up the place and leave, see? O.K., about two o'clock in the morning, when the city's dead, Larry and the boys drive up into an alley, behind. I go around, one by one, and sock the four guards on the back of the head. Then I open up for Larry and they take their time and clear the place out. From then on, we got all the dough we need to start pyramiding it up on the Stock Exchange and like that."

Patricia had drawn on rubber gloves, pulled a lab apron around her. She began reaching for test tubes, measuring devices. She murmured softly, "What keeps you from telling yourself you're nothing but a crook, Don? When we first met you-it seems a terribly long time ago, back there in Far Cry-you didn't seem to be such a bad egg."

"We didn't know, then, he was a cracked egg," Ross muttered. He looked to where Crowley slouched, his eyes narrow as though considering his chances of rushing the other. Crowley grinned and shook his head. "Don't try it, Buster."

Crowley looked at Patricia. "You don't get it, sister. It's like somebody or other said. The ends, uh, justify the means. That means...."

"I know what it means," Patricia said impatiently.

Dr. Braun, who rather hopelessly was also beginning to work at the equipment their captor had provided, said reasonably, "Don, the greater number of the thinkers of the world have rejected that maxim. If you will, umah, analyze it, you will find that the end and the means are one."

"Yeah, yeah, a lot of complicated egghead gas. What I'm saying, Pat, is that what I'm eventually heading for is good for everybody. At least it's good for all real hundred per cent Americans. Everybody's going to go to college and guaranteed to come out with what you three got, a doctor's degree. Everybody's going to get a guaranteed annual wage, like, whether or not they can do any work. It's not a guy's fault if he gets sick or unemployed or something. Everybody...."

"Shades of all the social-reformers who ever lived," Ross muttered.

"By Caesar," Braun said in despair, "I have an idea you'll get the vote of every halfwit in the country."

Crowley came to his feet. "I don't like that kind of talk, Doc. Maybe I'm just a country boy, but I know what the common man wants and what I'm going to do is give it to him."

Patricia looked up from her work long enough to frown at him. "What special are you going to get out of this, Don?"

That took him back for a moment and he scowled at her.

"Come, come," she said. "You've already admitted to we three just what you think and are going to do. Now, how do you picture yourself, after all this has been accomplished?"

His face suddenly broke into its grin, a somewhat sly element in it now. "You know, when I get this all worked out, the folks are going to be pretty thankful."

"I'll bet," Ross muttered. He, too, was working at his element of compounding the serum.

"Yeah, they will, Buster," Crowley said truculently. "And they're going to want to show it. You ever seen one of those movies like 'Ben Hur' back in Roman days? Can you imagine everybody in the whole country thinking you were the best guy ever lived? You know, like an Emperor."

"Like Caligula," Dr. Braun said softly.

"I don't know any of their names, but they really had it made. Snap your fingers and there's a big banquet with the best floor show in the world. Snap your fingers and here comes the sexiest dames in Hollywood. Snap your fingers and some big entertainment like a chariot race, or something. Once I put this over, the Common Man Party, that's the way people are going to feel about me and want to treat me."

"And if they don't, you'll make them?" Ross said sarcastically.

"You're too smart for your own britches, egghead," Crowley snarled. He looked at his watch. "Let's get this rolling. I got to get on down to the city and start this caper going."

Ross handed a test tube to Dr. Braun and began stripping the gloves from his hands. "That's my contribution," he said.

Patricia had already delivered hers. Dr. Braun combined them, then heated the compound, adding a distillate of his own. He said, "When this cools...."

Crowley crossed the room to the door and said something to the guard there. He returned in a moment with an anthropoid ape in a cage. He sat it on the table and looked at them.

"O.K.," he said to Braun, his voice dangerous. "Let's see you inject the monk with this new batch of serum."

Braun raised his eyebrows.

The other watched him narrowly, saying nothing further.

Dr. Braun shrugged, located a hypodermic needle and prepared it. In a matter of moments, the animal was injected.

Ross Wooley said sourly, "Don't you trust your fellow man, Don?"

"No, I don't, and stop calling me Don. It's Dan. Daniel Crowley."

The three of them looked at him in bewilderment.

The ape was beginning to shimmer as though he was being seen through a window wet with driving rain.

"Don's my goody-goody brother. Used to live in the same house with me, but ever since we were kids and I got picked up on a juvenile delinquent rap for swiping a car, he's been snotty. Anyway, now he's moved out to Frisco."

Patricia blurted, "But ... but you let us believe you were Donald...."

He brushed it off with a flick of his hand. "You said you had some deal where I could make me some money. O.K., I was between jobs."

The ape was invisible now. Crowley peered in at him. "Seems to work, all right."

Dr. Braun sighed. "I am not a Borgia, Daniel Crowley."

"You're not a what?"

"Never mind. I wouldn't poison even you, if that is what you feared."

Daniel Crowley took up the new container of serum and put a lid on it. He said, "I got to get going. The guy out in front will get you back to your rooms. No tricks with him, Buster" —he was talking directly to Ross —"he's already beat a couple of homicide raps."

* * * * *

Back in their cell-rooms, they found that there was but one guard. Evidently, the all-out robbery attempt to be held this night involved practically all of Larry Morazzoni's forces. Beyond that, this guard did not seem particularly interested in keeping them from talking back and forth to each other through the peepholes that centered their doors.

After a couple of hours during which time they largely held silence, immersed in their own thoughts, Dr. Braun called out, "Patricia, Ross, I should tender my apologies. It was my less than brilliant idea to find the average man and use him as a guinea pig."

"No apology necessary," Patricia said impatiently. "We all went into it with open eyes."

"But you were correct, Pat," the doctor said unhappily. "Our common man turned out to be a Frankenstein monster."

Ross growled, "That's the trouble. It turned out he wasn't our common man but his brother, whose petty criminal record evidently goes back to juvenile days."

"Even that doesn't matter," Patricia said testily. "I've about come to the conclusion that it wouldn't have made any difference *who* we'd put in Don's ...I mean Daniel Crowley's position. Man is too near the animal, as yet at least, to be trusted with such power. Any man."

"Why, Pat," Dr. Braun said doggedly, "I don't quite believe you correct. For instance, do you feel the same about me? Would I have reacted like our friend Dan?" He chuckled in deprecation.

"That's my point," she said. "I think you would ...ultimately. Once again look at the Caesars, they held godlike power."

"You're thinking of such as Tiberius, Caligula, Nero, Commodus...."

"I'm also thinking of such as Claudius, the scholar who was practically forced to take the Imperial mantle. And Marcus Aurelius, the philosopher who although bound up in learning himself allowed his family free rein in their vices and finally turned the Empire over to his son Commodus, one of the most vicious men of all time. But take Caligula and Nero if you will. Both of them stepped into power comparatively clean and with the best of prospects. Well approved, well loved. What happened to them when given power without restraint?"

Ross grumbled, "I admit I missed the boat, but not for the reasons Pat presents. In a sane society, our serum would be a valuable contribution. But in a dog eat dog world, where it's each man for himself, then it becomes a criminal tool."

Patricia said sarcastically, "And can you point out a sane society?"

Ross grunted. "No," he said. After a moment he added, "You know, in a way Crowley was right. We three eggheads didn't do so well up against what he called his common sense. I tried to slug him, with negative results. Dr. Braun, you tried sweet reason on him. Forgive me if I laugh. Pat, you tried your womanly wiles, but he saw through that, too."

"The chickens have not all come home to roost," Patricia said mysteriously. "What time is it?"

Ross told her.

She called to the guard, "See here, you."

"Shut up. You ain't supposed to be talking at all. Go to sleep."

"I want to speak to Mr. Morazzoni. It's very important and you are going to be dreadfully sorry if you don't bring him."

"Larry can't be bothered. He's getting ready to go on down to the city."

"I know what he's doing, but if he doesn't listen to me, he's going to be very unhappy and probably full of bullet holes."

The guard came over to her door and stared at her for a long moment. He checked the lock on her door and then those of Dr. Braun and Ross Wooley. "We'll see who's going to be sorry," he grunted. He turned and left.

* * * * *

When he returned it was with both Larry Morazzoni and Paul Teeter, Dan Crowley's political adviser. Morazzoni growled, "What goes on? You squares looking for trouble?"

Patricia said testily, "I suggest you let us out of here, Mr. Morazzoni. If you do, we pledge not to press kidnaping charges against you. I believe you are aware of the penalty in this State."

"You trying to be funny?"

"Definitely not, Mr. Morazzoni," Patricia said icily. "Daniel Crowley bragged to us of your plans for tonight."

The hoodlum muttered a contemptuous obscenity under his breath.

Paul Teeter, the heavy-set southerner said jovially, "But what has this to do with releasing you, Miss O'Gara? Admittedly Dan is a bit indiscreet but...." He let the sentence fade away.

"Yes," Patricia said. "I realize that he is a nonprofessional in your ranks, and have little doubt that eventually you would have surmounted whatever precautions he has taken to keep you in underling positions. That's beside the point. The point is that by this time Daniel Crowley has, ah, infiltrated the institution you expected to burglarize tonight. He is inside, and you are still outside. There are four guards also inside, whom he is expected to eliminate before you can join him."

"He told you everything all right, the jerk," Larry said coldly. "But so what?"

"So Dan Crowley had us make up a new amount of serum tonight and tested it on a chimpanzee in the lab. If you'll go and check, you'll undoubtedly find the chimp is again visible."

The gunman looked at Paul Teeter blankly.

The other's reactions were quicker. "The serum lasts for twelve hours," Teeter barked.

"This batch lasts for three hours," Patricia said definitely. "Your friend Crowley is suddenly going to become visible right before the eyes of those four guards-and long before he had expected to eliminate them."

Teeter barked, "Larry, check that monkey."

Doc Braun spoke up for the first time since the appearance of the two. He said dryly, "You'll also notice that the animal is sound asleep. It seems that I added a slow-acting but rather potent sleeping compound to the serum."

The gunman started from the room in a rush.

Ross called after him, "If you'll look closely, you'll also note the chimp's skin has turned a brilliant red. There have been some basic changes in the pigment."

"Holy smokes," Paul Teeter protested, moping his face with a handkerchief. "Didn't he take any precautions against you people at all?"

Ross said, "He was too busy telling us how smart a country boy he happened to be."

Larry returned in moments, biting his lip in the first nervous manifestation any of them had ever seen in him. He took Teeter to one side.

Patricia called to them impatiently. "You have no time and no one to contact Crowley now. Don't be fools. Mend your bridges while you can. Let us out of here, and we'll prefer no charges."

Larry was a man of quick decisions. He snapped to the blank-faced guard who had assimilated only a fraction of all this, "Go on back to the boys and tell them to start packing to get out of here. Tell them the fix has chilled. It's all off. I'll be there in a few minutes."

"O.K., chief." The other had the philosophical outlook of those who were meant to take orders and knew it. He left.

Larry and Teeter opened the cell doors.

Teeter said, "How do we know we can trust you?"

Ross looked at him.

Larry said, "It's a deal. Give us an hour to get out of here. Then use the phone if you want to call a taxi, or whatever. I ain't stupid, this thing was too complicated to begin with."

When Teeter and Morazzoni were gone, the three stood alone in the corridor, looking at each other.

The doctor pushed his glasses back onto his nose with a thumb and forefinger. "By Caesar," he said.

Ross ran a hefty paw back through his red crew cut and twisted his face into a mock grimace. "Well," he said, "I have to revise my former statement. I used brute strength against Crowley, the doctor used sweet reason, and Pat her womanly wiles. And all failed. But as biochemists, each working without the knowledge of the others, we used science-and it paid off. I suppose the thing to do now is buy three jet tickets for California."

Braun and Patricia looked at him blankly.

Ross explained. "Didn't you hear what Crowley said? His brother, Donald, has moved out to San Francisco. He's our real Common Man, we'll have to start the experiment all over again."

Dr. Braun snorted.

Patricia O'Gara, hands on hips, snapped, "Ross Wooley, our engagement is off!"

Expediter

The knock at the door came in the middle of the night, as Josip Pekic had always thought it would. He had been but four years of age when the knock had come that first time and the three large men had given his father a matter of only minutes to dress and accompany them. He could barely remember his father.

The days of the police state were over, so they told you. The cult of the personality was a thing of the past. The long series of five-year plans and seven-year plans were over and all the goals had been achieved. The new constitution guaranteed personal liberties. No longer were you subject to police brutality at the merest whim. So they told you.

But fears die hard, particularly when they are largely of the subconscious. And he had always, deep within, expected the knock.

He was not mistaken. The rap came again, abrupt, impatient. Josip Pekic allowed himself but one chill of apprehension, then rolled from his bed, squared slightly stooped shoulders, and made his way to the door. He flicked on the light and opened up, even as the burly, empty faced zombi there was preparing to pound still again.

There were two of them, not three as he had always dreamed. As three had come for his father, more than two decades before.

His father had been a rightist deviationist, so the papers had said, a follower of one of whom Josip had never heard in any other context other than his father's trial and later execution. But he had not cracked under whatever pressures had been exerted upon him, and of that his son was proud.

He had not cracked, and in later years, when the cult of personality was a thing of the past, his name had been cleared and returned to the history books. And now it was an honor, rather than a disgrace, to be the son of Ljubo Pekic, who had posthumously been awarded the title Hero of the People's Democratic Dictatorship.

But though his father was now a hero, Josip still expected that knock. However, he was rather bewildered at the timing, having no idea of why he was to be under arrest.

The first of the zombi twins said expressionlessly, "Comrade Josip Pekic?"

If tremor there was in his voice, it was negligible. He was the son of Ljubo Pekic. He said, "That is correct. Uh ... to what do I owe this intrusion upon my privacy?" That last in the way of bravado.

The other ignored the question. "Get dressed and come with us, Comrade," he said flatly.

At least they still called him comrade. That was some indication, he hoped, that the charges might not be too serious.

He chose his dark suit. Older than the brown one, but in it he felt he presented a more self-possessed demeanor. He could use the quality. Five foot seven, slightly underweight and with an air of unhappy self-deprecation, Josip Pekic's personality didn't exactly dominate in a group. He chose a conservative tie and a white shirt, although he knew that currently some frowned upon white shirts as a bourgeois affectation. It was all the thing, these days, to look proletarian, whatever that meant.

The zombis stood, watching him emptily as he dressed. He wondered what they would have said had he asked them to wait in the hallway until he was finished. Probably nothing. They hadn't bothered to answer when he asked what the charge against him was.

He put his basic papers, his identity card, his student cards, his work record and all the rest in an inner pocket, and faced them. "I am ready," he said as evenly as he could make it come.

They turned and led the way down to the street and to the black limousine there. And in it was the third one, sitting in the front seat, as empty of face as the other two. He hadn't bothered to turn off the vehicle's cushion jets and allow it to settle to the street. He had known how very quickly his colleagues would reappear with their prisoner.

Josip Pekic sat in the back between the two, wondering just where he was being taken, and, above all, why. For the life of him he couldn't think of what the charge might be. True enough, he read the usual number of proscribed books, but no more than was common among other intellectuals, among the students and the country's avant garde, if such you could call it. He had attended the usual parties and informal debates in the coffee shops where the more courageous attacked this facet or that of the People's Dictatorship. But he belonged to no active organizations which opposed the State, nor did his tendencies attract him in that direction. Politics were not his interest.

At this time of the night, there was little traffic on the streets of Zagurest, and few parked vehicles. Most of those which had been rented for the day had been returned to the car-pool garages. It was the one advantage Josip could think of that Zagurest had over the cities of the West which he had seen. The streets were not cluttered with vehicles. Few people owned a car outright. If you required one, you had the local car pool deliver it, and you kept it so long as you needed transportation.

He had expected to head for the Kalemegdan Prison where political prisoners were traditionally taken, but instead, they slid off to the right at Partisan Square, and up the Boulevard of the November Revolution. Josip Pekic, in surprise, opened his mouth to say something to the security policeman next to him, but then closed it again and his lips paled. He knew where they were going, now. Whatever the charge against him, it was not minor.

A short kilometer from the park, the government buildings began. The Skupstina, the old Parliament left over from the days when Transbalkania was a backward, feudo-capitalistic power of third class. The National Bank, the new buildings of the Borba and the Politica. And finally, set back a hundred feet from the boulevard, the sullen, squat Ministry of Internal Affairs.

It had been built in the old days, when the Russians had still dominated the country, and in slavish imitation of the architectural horror known as Stalin Gothic. Meant to be above all efficient and imposing and winding up simply-grim.

Yes. Josip Pekic knew where they were going now.

* * * * *

The limousine slid smoothly on its cushion of air, up the curved driveway, past the massive iron statue of the worker struggling against the forces of reaction, a rifle in one hand, a wrench in the other and stopped before, at last, the well-guarded doorway.

Without speaking, the two police who had come to his room opened the car door and climbed out. One made a motion with his head, and Josip followed. The limousine slid away immediately.

Between them, he mounted the marble stairs. It occurred to him that this was the route his father must have taken, two decades before.

He had never been in the building of the Ministry of Internal Affairs, before. Few Transbalkanians had, other than those who were employed in the MVD, or who came under the Ministry's scrutiny.

Doors opened before them, closed behind them. Somewhat to Josip Pekic's surprise the place was copiously adorned with a surplus of metal and marble statues, paintings and tapestries. It had similarities to one of Zagurest's heavy museums.

Through doors and down halls and through larger rooms, finally to a smaller one in which sat alone at a desk a lean, competent and assured type who jittered over a heavy sheaf of papers with an electro-marking computer pen. He was nattily and immaculately dressed and smoked his cigarette in one of the small pipelike holders once made *de rigueur* through the Balkans by Marshal Tito.

The three of them came to a halt before his desk and, at long last, expression came to the faces of the zombis. Respect, with possibly an edge of perturbation. Here, obviously, was authority.

He at the desk finished a paper, tore it from the sheaf, pushed it into the maw of the desk chute from whence it would be transported to the auto-punch for preparation for recording. He looked up in busy impatience.

Then, to Josip Pekic's astonishment, the other came to his feet quickly, smoothly and with a grin on his face. Josip hadn't considered the possibility of being grinned at in the Ministry of Internal Affairs.

"Aleksander Kardelj," he said in self-introduction, sticking out a lean hand to be shaken. "You're Pekic, eh? We've been waiting for you."

Josip shook, bewildered. He looked at the zombi next to him, uncomprehendingly.

He who had introduced himself, darted a look of comprehension from Josip to the two. He said disgustedly, but with mild humor oddly mixed, "What's the matter, did these hoodlums frighten you?"

Josip fingered his chin nervously. "Of course not."

One of the zombis shifted his feet. "We did nothing except obey orders."

Kardelj grimaced in sour amusement. "I can imagine," he grunted. "Milka, you see too many of those imported Telly shows from the West. I suspect you see yourself as a present day Transbalkanian G-Man."

"Yes, Comrade," Milka said, and then shook his head.

"Oh, hush up and get out," Kardelj said. He flicked the cigarette butt from its holder with a thumb and took up a fresh one from a desk humidor and wedged it into the small bowl. He looked at Josip and grinned again, the action giving his face an unsophisticated youthful expression.

"You can't imagine how pleased I am to meet you, at last," he said. "I've been looking for you for months."

Josip Pekic ogled him blankly. The name had come through to him at last. Aleksander Kardelj was seldom in the news, practically never photographed, and then in the background in a group of Party functionaries, usually with a wry smile on his face. But he was known throughout the boundaries of the State, if not internationally. Aleksander Kardelj was Number Two. Right-hand man of Zoran Jankez himself, second in command of the Party and rumored to be the brains behind the throne.

The zombis had gone, hurriedly.

"Looking for me?" Josip said blankly. "I haven't been in hiding. You've made some mistake. All I am is a student of—"

"Of course, of course," Kardelj said, humorously impatient. He took up a folder from his desk and shook it absently in Josip's general direction. "I've studied your dossier thoroughly." He flicked his eyes up at a wall clock. "Come along. Comrade Jankez is expecting us. We'll leave explanations until then."

In a daze, Josip Pekic followed him.

Comrade Jankez, Number One. Zoran Jankez, Secretary General of the Party, President of the U.B.S.R., the United Balkan Soviet Republics. Number One.

Josip could hardly remember so far back that Zoran Jankez wasn't head of the Party, when his face, or sculptured bust, wasn't to be seen in every store, on the walls of banks, railroad stations, barber shops, or bars. Never a newsreel but that part of it wasn't devoted to Comrade Jankez, never a Telly newscast but that Number One was brought to the attention of the viewers. His coming to power had been a quiet, bloodless affair upon the death of the Number One who had preceded him, and he had remained in his position for a generation.

* * * * *

Josip Pekic followed Aleksander Kardelj in a daze, through a door to the rear of the desk, and into a somewhat bigger room, largely barren of furniture save for a massive table with a dozen chairs about it. At the table, looking some ten years older than in any photo Josip had ever seen, sat Zoran Jankez.

He looked ten years older, and his face bore a heavy weariness, a grayness, that never came through in his publicity shots. He looked up from a report he was perusing and grunted a welcome to them.

Kardelj said in pleasurable enthusiasm, "Here he is, Zoran. Our Comrade Josip Pekic. The average young citizen of Transbalkania."

Number One grunted again, and took in the less than imposing figure of Josip Pekic. Josip felt an urge to nibble at his fingernails, and repressed it. He had recently broken himself of the smoking habit and was hard put to find occupation for his hands when nervous.

Zoran Jankez growled an invitation for them to be seated and Kardelj adjusted his trousers to preserve the crease, threw one leg up along the heavy conference table, and rested on a buttock, looking at ease but as though ready to take off instantly.

Josip fumbled himself into one of the sturdy oaken chairs, staring back and forth at the two most powerful men of his native land. Thus far, no one had said anything that made any sense whatsoever to him since he had been hauled from his bed half an hour ago.

Zoran Jankez rasped, "I have gone through your dossier, Comrade. I note that you are the son of Hero of the People's Democratic Dictatorship, Ljubo Pekic."

"Yes, Comrade Jankez," Josip got out. He fussed with his hands, decided it would be improper to stick them in his pockets.

Number One grunted. "I knew Ljubo well. You must realize that his arrest was before my time. I had no power to aid him. It was, of course, after my being elected to the Secretary Generalship that he was exonerated and his name restored to the list of those who have gloriously served the State. But then, of course, you bear no malice at this late date. Ljubo has been posthumously given the hero's award."

It wasn't exactly the way Josip knew the story, but there was little point in his objecting. He simply nodded. He said, unhappily, "Comrades, I feel some mistake has been made. I ... I have no idea —"

Kardelj was chuckling, as though highly pleased with some development. He held up a hand to cut Josip short and turned to his superior. "You see, Zoran. A most average, laudable young man. Born under our regime, raised under the People's Democratic Dictatorship. Exactly our man."

Zoran Jankez seemed not to hear the other. He was studying Josip heavily, all but gloomily.

A beefy paw went out and banged a button inset in the table and which Josip had not noticed before. Almost instantly a door in the rear opened and a white-jacketed servant entered, pushing a wheeled combination bar and hors d'oeuvres cart before him. He brought the lavishly laden wagon to within reach of the heavy-set Party head, his face in servile expressionlessness.

Jankez grunted something and the waiter, not quite bowing and scraping, retreated again from the room. Number One's heavy lips moved in and out as his eyes went over the display.

Kardelj said easily, "Let me, Zoran." He arose and brought a towel-wrapped bottle from a refrigerated bucket set into the wagon, and deftly took up a delicate three-ounce glass which he filled and placed before his superior. He took up another and raised his eyebrows at Josip Pekic who shook his head —a stomach as queasy as his wasn't going to be helped by alcohol. Kardelj poured a short one for himself and resumed his place at the heavy conference table.

Jankez, his eyes small and piggish, took up a heavy slice of dark bread and ladled a full quarter pound of Danube caviar upon it. He took up the glass and tossed the chilled spirits back over his palate, grunted and stuffed the open sandwich into his mouth.

Josip's eyes went to the hors d'oeuvres wagon. The spread would have cost him six months' income.

Number One rumbled, his mouth full, "Comrade, I am not surprised at your confusion. We will get to the point immediately. Actually, you must consider yourself a very fortunate young man." He belched, took another huge bite, then went on. "Have you ever heard the term, expediter?"

"I ... I don't know ... I mean think so, Comrade Jankez."

The party head poured himself some more of the yellow spirits and took down half of it. "It is not important," he rasped. "Comrade Kardelj first came upon the germ of this project of ours whilst reading of American industrial successes during the Second World War. They were attempting to double, triple, quadruple their production of such war materiel as ships and aircraft in a matter of mere months. Obviously, a thousand bottlenecks appeared. All was confusion. So they resorted to expediters. Extremely competent efficiency engineers whose sole purpose was to seek out such bottlenecks and eliminate them. A hundred aircraft might be kept from completion by the lack of a single part. The expediter found them though they be as far away as England, and flew them by chartered plane to California. A score of top research chemists might be needed for a certain project in Tennessee, the expediter located them, though it meant the stripping of valued men from jobs of lesser importance. I need give no further examples. Their powers were sweeping. Their expense accounts unlimited. Their successes unbelievable." Number One's eyes went back to the piles of food, as though he'd grown tired of so much talk.

Josip fidgeted, still uncomprehending.

While the Party leader built himself a huge sandwich of Dalmatian ham and *pohovano pile* chicken, Aleksander Kardelj put in an enthusiastic word. "We're adapting the idea to our own needs, Comrade. You have been selected to be our first expediter."

If anything, Josip Pekic was more confused than ever. "Expediter," he said blankly. "To ... to expedite what?"

"That is for you to decide," Kardelj said blithely. "You're our average Transbalkanian. You feel as the average man in the street feels. You're our what the Yankees call, Common Man."

Josip said plaintively, "You keep saying that, but I don't know what you mean, Comrade. Please forgive me, perhaps I'm dense, but what is this about me being uh, the average man? There's nothing special about me. I...."

"Exactly," Kardelj said triumphantly. "There's nothing special about you. You're the average man of all Transbalkania. We have gone to a great deal of difficulty to seek you out."

Number One belched and took over heavily. "Comrade, we have made extensive tests in this effort to find our average man. You are the result. You are of average age, of average height, weight, of education, and of intelligence quotient. You finished secondary school, worked for several years, and have returned to the university where you are now in your second year. Which is average for you who have been born in your generation. Your tastes, your ambitions, your ... dreams, Comrade Pekic, are either known to be, or assumed to be, those of the average Transbalkanian." He took up a rich baklava dessert, saturated with honey, and devoured it.

Josip Pekic and his associates had wondered at some of the examinations and tests that had been so prevalent of recent date. He accepted the words of the two Party leaders. Very well, he was the average of the country's some seventy million population. Well, then?

* * * * *

Number One had pushed himself back in his chair, and Josip was only mildly surprised to note that the man seemed considerably paunchier than his photos indicated. Perhaps he wore a girdle in public.

Zoran Jankez took up a paper. "I have here a report from a journalist of the West who but recently returned from a tour of our country. She reports, with some indignation, that the only available eyebrow pencils were to be found on the black market, were of French import, and cost a thousand dinars apiece. She contends that Transbalkanian women are indignant at paying such prices."

The Party head looked hopelessly at first Josip and then Kardelj. "What is an eyebrow pencil?"

Kardelj said, a light frown on his usually easygoing face, "I believe it is a cosmetic."

"You mean like lipstick?"

Josip took courage. He flustered. "They use it to darken their eyebrows-women, I mean. From what I understand, it comes and goes in popularity. Right now, it is ultra-popular. A new, uh, fad originating in Italy, is sweeping the West."

Number One stared at him. "How do you know all that?" he rasped.

Josip fiddled with the knot of his tie, uncomfortably. "It is probably in my dossier that I have journeyed abroad on four occasions. Twice to International Youth Peace Conferences, once as a representative to a Trades Union Convention in Vienna, and once on a tourist vacation guided tour. On those occasions I ...ah ...met various young women of the West."

Kardelj said triumphantly, "See what I mean, Zoran? This comrade is priceless."

Jankez looked at his right-hand man heavily. "Why, if our women desire this ...this eyebrow pencil nonsense, is it not supplied them? Is there some ingredient we do not produce? If so, why cannot it be imported?" He picked at his uneven teeth with a thumbnail.

Kardelj held his lean hands up, as though in humorous supplication. "Because, Comrade, to this point we have not had expediters to find out such desires on the part of women comrades."

Number One grunted. He took up another report. "Here we have some comments upon service in our restaurants, right here in Zagurest, from an evidently widely published American travel reporter. He contends that the fact that there is no tipping leads to our waiters being surly and inefficient."

He glared up at his right-hand man. "I have never noticed when I have dined at the Sumadija or the Dva Ribara, that the waiters have been surly. And only last week I enjoyed *cigansko pecenje*, gypsy roast, followed by a very flaky cherry *strudla*, at the Gradski Podrum. The service was excellent."

Kardelj cleared his throat. "Perhaps you receive better service than the average tourist, Zoran."

Jankez growled, "The tourist trade is important. An excellent source of hard currencies." He glowered across at Josip. "These are typical of the weaknesses you must ferret out, Comrade."

He put the reports down with a grunt. "But these are comparatively minor. Last week a truck driver attached to a meat-packing house in Belbrovnik was instructed to deliver a load of frozen products to a town in Macenegro. When he arrived there, it was to find they had no refrigeration facilities. So he unloaded the frozen meat on a warehouse platform and returned to Belbrovnik. At this time of the year, obviously in four hours the meat was spoiled." He glowered at Kardelj and then at Josip Pekic. "Why do things like this continually happen? How can we overtake the United States of the Americas and Common Europe, when on all levels our workers are afraid to take initiative? That truck driver fulfilled his instructions. He delivered the meat. He washed his hands of what happened to it afterward. Why, Comrades? Why did he not have the enterprise to preserve his valuable load, even, if necessary, make the decision to return with it to Belbrovnik?"

He grunted heavily and settled back into his chair as though through, finished with the whole question.

Aleksander Kardelj became brisk. He said to Josip Pekic with a smile, "This is your job. You are to travel about the country, finding bottlenecks, finding shortages, ferreting out mistakes and bringing them to the attention of those in position to rectify them."

Josip said glumly, "But suppose ... suppose they ignore my findings?"

Number One snorted, but said nothing.

Kardelj said jovially, "Tomorrow the announcements will go out to every man, woman and child in the People's Democratic Dictatorship. Your word is law. You are answerable only to Comrade Jankez and myself. No restrictions whatsoever apply to you. No laws. No regulations. We will give you identification which all will recognize, and the bearer of which can do no wrong."

Josip was flabbergasted. "But ... but suppose I come up against some ... well, someone high in the Party, or, well ... some general or admiral? Some —"

Kardelj said jocularly, "You answer only to us, Comrade Pekic. Your power is limitless. Comrade Jankez did not exaggerate. Frankly, were cold statistics enough, Transbalkania has already at long last overtaken the West in per capita production. Steel, agriculture, the tonnage of coal mined, of petroleum pumped. All these supposed indications of prosperity." He flung up his hands again in his semihumorous gesture of despair. "But all these things do not mesh. We cannot find such a simple matter as ... as eyebrow pencils in our stores, nor can we be served acceptably in our restaurants and hotels. Each man passes the buck, as the Yankees say, and no man can care less whether or not school keeps. No man wants responsibility."

Josip was aghast, all over again. "But ... but me ... only me. What could you expect a single person to do?"

"Don't misunderstand, Comrade," Kardelj told him with amused compassion. "You are but an experiment. If it works out, we will seek others who are also deemed potential expediters to do similar work. Now, are there any further questions?"

Josip Pekic stared miserably back and forth between the two, wondering wildly what they would say if he turned the whole thing down. His eyes lit on the dour, heavy Number One, and inwardly he shook his head. No. There was no question about that. You didn't turn down Zoran Jankez. He looked at Aleksander Kardelj, and in spite of the other's smiling face, he decided you didn't turn down Number Two, either.

Josip said carefully, "From what you say, I ...I can override anyone in Transbalkania, except yourselves. But ... but what if I antagonize one of you? You know ... with something I think I find wrong?"

The second in command of the Party chuckled, even as he fitted a fresh cigarette into his curved holder. "We've provided even for that, Comrade. Fifty thousand Common Europe francs have been deposited to your account in Switzerland. At any time you feel your revelations might endanger yourself, you are free to leave the country and achieve sanctuary abroad." He chuckled whimsically again. "Given the position you will occupy, a man above all law, with the whole of the nation's resources at his disposal, I cannot imagine you wishing to leave. The Swiss deposit is merely to give you complete confidence, complete security."

* * * * *

Number One was radiating fury as he stalked heavily down the corridors of the Ministry of Internal Affairs. On the surface, his face displayed nothing-which meant nothing. There was simply a raging aura of trouble.

Veljko Gosnjak, posted with one other before the office of Aleksander Kardelj, winced when he saw the Party head approaching. He muttered from the side of his mouth, "Watch out. He's on a rampage. In this mood, he'd as well set you to filling salt shakers in the Nairebis mines as...."

But Zoran Jankez was now near enough that he might hear, and Veljko Gosnjak cut himself off abruptly and came to even stiffer attention.

Number One ignored them both and pushed on through the door.

Even as his right-hand man looked up from his work, Jankez was growling ominously. "Do you know the latest from that brain-wave experiment?"

Kardelj was close enough to the other personally to at least pretend lack of awe. He grinned and said, "You mean young Josip? Sit down, Zoran. A drink?"

The Number Two Party man swiveled slightly and punched out a code on a series of buttons. Almost immediately, an area of approximately one square foot sank down from the upper right-hand corner of his desk, to rise again bearing two chilled glasses.

Jankez snorted his anger but took up one of the glasses. "These everlasting gadgets from the West," he growled. "One of these days, this confounded desk of yours will give you an electric shock that will set me to looking for a new assistant." He threw the contents of the glass back over his palate. "If I don't start looking before that time," he added ominously.

However, he savored the drink, then put down the glass, pursed his lips and rumbled, "Where do you get this excellent slivovka, Aleksander?"

Kardelj sipped part of his own drink. He said lightly, "That is the only secret I keep from you, Zoran. However, I will give you this hint. Its proper name is sljivovica, rather than slivovka. It does not come from Slovenia. I am afraid, once you know its origin, I will no longer be of use to you."

He laughed again. "But what is it that young Josip has done?"

His superior's face resumed its dark expression. He growled, "You know Velimir Crvenkovski, of course."

Kardelj raised scanty eyebrows. "Of course, Vice chairman of the Secretariat of Agriculture."

Zoran Jankez had lowered his clumsy bulk into a chair. Now he said heavily, his voice danger-ous. "Velimir and I were partisans together. It was I who converted him to the Party, introduced him to the works of Lenin while we squatted in foxholes in Macenegro."

"Of course," the other repeated. "I know the story very well. A good Party man, Comrade Crvenkovski, never failing to vote with you in meetings of the Executive Committee."

"Yes," Jankez growled ominously. "And your precious Josip Pekic, your expediter, has removed him from his position as supreme presider of agriculture in Bosnatia."

Aleksander Kardelj cleared his throat. "I have just been reading the account. It would seem that production has fallen off considerably in the past five years in Bosnatia. Ah, Comrade Crvenkovski evidently had brought to his attention that wild life in the countryside, particularly birds, accounted for the loss of hundreds of thousands of tons of cereals and other produce annually."

"A well-known fact," Jankez rasped. He finished what remained of his drink, and reached forward to punch out the order for a fresh one. "What has that got to do with this pipsqueak using the confounded powers you invested him with to dismiss one of the best Party men in Transbalkania?"

His right-hand man had not failed to note that he was now being given full credit for the expediter idea. He said, still cheerfully, however, "It would seem that Comrade Crvenkovski issued top priority orders to kill off, by whatever means possible, all birds. Shotguns, poison, nets were issued by the tens of thousands to the peasants."

"*Well?*" his superior said ominously. "Obviously, Velimir was clear minded enough to see the saving in gross production."

"Um-m-m," Kardelj said placatingly. "However, he failed to respond to the warnings of our agriculturists who have studied widely in the West. It seems as though the balance of nature calls for the presence of wildlife, and particularly birds. The increase in destructive insects has more than counterbalanced the amount of cereals the birds once consumed. Ah, Zoran," he said with a wry smile, "I would suggest we find another position for Comrade Crvenkovski."

* * * * *

The secretary-receptionist looked up at long last at the very average looking young man before him. "Yes," he said impatiently.

The stranger said, "I would like to see Comrade Broz."

"Surely you must realize that the Commissar is one of the busiest men in Transbalkania, Comrade." There was mocking sneer in the tone. "His time is not at the disposal of every citizen."

The newcomer looked at the petty authority thoughtfully. "Do you so address everyone that enters this office?" he asked mildly.

The other stared at him flabbergasted. He suddenly banged upon a button on the desk.

When the security guard responded to the summons, he gestured curtly with his head at the newcomer. "Throw this fool out, Petar," he rapped.

Josip Pekic shook his head, almost sadly. "No," he said. "Throw *this* man out." He pointed at the secretary-receptionist.

The guard called Petar blinked at each of them in turn.

Josip brought forth his wallet, fidgeted a moment with the contents, then flashed his credentials. "State expediter," he said nervously. "Under direct authority of Comrade Zoran Jankez." He looked at the suddenly terrified receptionist. "I don't know what alternative work we can find to fit your talents. However, if I ever again hear of you holding down a position in which you meet the public, I will ... will, ah, see you imprisoned."

The other scurried from the room before Josip thought of more to say.

Josip Pekic looked at the guard for a long moment. He said finally, unhappy still, "What are you needed for around here?"

"Why yes, Comrade. I am the security guard."

Petar, obviously no brain at the best, was taken aback.

"You didn't answer my question." Josip's hands were jittering so he jammed them into his pockets.

Petar had to think back to remember the wording of the question in question. Finally he came up triumphantly with, "Yes, Comrade. I guard Comrade Broz and the others from assassins. I am armed." He proudly displayed the Mikoyan Noiseless which he had holstered under his left shoulder.

Josip said, "Go back to your superior and inform him that I say you are superfluous on this assignment. No longer are commissars automatically to be guarded. Only under special circumstances. If…well, if our people dislike individual commissars sufficiently to wish to assassinate them, maybe they need assassination."

Petar stared at him.

"Oh, get out," Josip said, with attempted sharpness. But then, "What door leads to Comrade Broz's office?"

Petar pointed, then got out. At least he knew how to obey orders, Josip decided. What was there about the police mentality? Were they like that before they became police, and the job sought them out? Or did the job make them all that way?

He pushed his way through the indicated door. The office beyond held but one inhabitant who stood, hands clasped behind his back, while he stared in obvious satisfaction at a wall of charts, maps and graphs.

The average young man looked at some of the lettering on the charts and shook his head. He said, his voice hesitant, "Commissar Broz?"

The other turned, frowning, not recognizing his caller and surprised to find him here without announcement. He said, "Yes, young man?"

Josip presented his credentials again.

Broz had heard of him. He hurried forth a chair, became expansive in manner. A cigar? A drink? A great pleasure to meet the Comrade Expediter. He had heard a great deal about the new experiment initiated by Comrade Jankez and ably assisted by Aleksander Kardelj. Happily, an expediter was not needed in the Transbalkanian Steel Complex. It was expanding in such wise as to be the astonishment of the world, both East and West.

"Yes," Josip began glumly, "but —"

Broz was back on his feet and to his wall of charts and graphs. "See here," he beamed expansively. "This curve is steel production. See how it zooms? A veritable Sputnik, eh? Our statistics show that we are rapidly surpassing even the most foremost of the Western powers."

Josip Pekic said, almost apologetically in view of the other's enthusiasm. "That's what I came to discuss with you, Comrade. You see, I've been sitting around, ah, in the local wineshops, talking it over with the younger engineers and the men on the job."

The other frowned at him. "Talking what over?"

"This new policy of yours." Josip's voice was diffident.

"You mean overtaking the steel production of the West, by utilizing *all* methods of production?" The commissar's voice dropped. "I warn you Comrade, the germ of this idea originated with Zoran Jankez himself. We are old comrades and friends from back before the revolution."

"I'm sure you are," Josip said pessimistically, and suppressing an urge to bite at the skin of his thumb. "However…well, I'm not so sure Number One will admit your program originated with him. At least, it hasn't worked out that way in the recent past when something soured."

The other bug-eyed. He whispered, "That approaches cynical treason, Comrade."

Josip half nodded, said discouragedly, "You forget. By Comrade Jankez's own orders I…I can do no wrong. But so much for that. Now, well, this steel program. I'm afraid it's going to have to be scrapped."

"Scrapped!" the Commissar of the Transbalkanian Steel Complex stared at his visitor as though the other was rabid. "You fool! Our steel progress is the astonishment of the world! Why, not only are our ultramodern plants, built largely with foreign assistance, working on a twenty-four hour a day basis, but thousands of secondary smelters, some so small as to be operated by a handful of comrade citizens, in backyard establishments, by schoolchildren, working smelters of but a few tons monthly capacity in the schoolyard, by —"

* * * * *

The newly created State Expediter held up a hand dispiritedly. "I know. I know. Thousands of these backyard smelters exist … uh … especially in parts of the country where there is neither ore nor fuel available."

The commissar looked at him.

The younger man said, his voice seemingly deprecating his words, "The schoolchildren, taking time off from their studies, of course, bring scrap iron to be smelted. And they bring whatever fuel they can find, often pilfered from railway yards. And the more scrap and fuel they bring, the more praise they get. Unfortunately, the so-called scrap often turns out to be kitchen utensils, farm tools, even, on at least on occasion, some railroad tracks, from a narrow gauge line running up to a lumbering project, not in use that time of the year. Sooner or later, Comrade Broz, the nation is going to have to replace those kitchen utensils and farm tools and all the rest of the scrap that isn't really quite scrap."

The commissar began to protest heatedly, but Josip Pekic shook his head and tried to firm his less than dominating voice. "But even that's not the worst of it. Taking citizens away from their real occupations, or studies, and putting them to smelting steel where no ore exists. The worst of it is, so my young engineer friends tell me, that while the steel thus produced might have been a marvel back in the days of the Hittites, it hardly reaches specifications today. Perhaps it might be used ultimately to make simple farm tools such as hoes and rakes; if so, it would make quite an endless circle, because that is largely the source of the so-called steel to begin with-tools, utensils and such. But it hardly seems usable in modern industry."

The commissar had gone pale with anger by now. He put his two fists on his desk and leaned upon them, staring down at his seated visitor. "Comrade," he bit out, "I warn you. Comrade Jankez is enthusiastic about my successes. Beyond that, not only is he an old comrade, but my brother-in-law as well."

Josip Pekic nodded, unenthusiastically, and his voice continued to quiver. "So the trained engineers under you, have already warned me. However, Comrade Broz, you are … well, no longer Commissar of the Steel Complex. My report has already gone in to Comrades Jankez and Kardelj."

* * * * *

The knock came at the door in the middle of the night as Aleksander Kardelj had always thought it would.

From those early days of his Party career, when his ambitions had sent him climbing, pushing, tripping up others, on his way to the top, he had expected it eventually.

Oh, his had been a different approach, on the surface, an easygoing, laughing, gentler approach than one usually connected with members of the Secretariat of the Executive Committee of the Party, but it made very little difference in the very long view. When one fell from the heights, he fell just as hard, whether or not he was noted for his sympathetic easy humor.

The fact was, Aleksander Kardelj was not asleep when the fist pounded at his door shortly after midnight. He had but recently turned off, with a shaking hand, the Telly-Phone, after a less than pleasant conversation with President of the United Balkan Soviet Republics, Zoran Jankez.

For the past ten years, Kardelj had been able to placate Zoran Jankez, even though Number One be at the peak of one of his surly rages, rages which seemed to be coming with increasing frequency of late. As the socio-economic system of the People's Democratic Dictatorship became increasingly complicated, as industrialization with its modern automation mushroomed in a geometric progression, the comparative simplicity of governing which applied in the past, was strictly of yesteryear. It had been one thing, rifle and grenades in hand, to seize the government, after a devastating war in which the nation had been leveled, and even to maintain it for a time, over illiterate peasants and unskilled proletarians. But industrialization calls for a highly educated element of scientists and technicians, nor does it stop there. One of sub-mentality can operate a shovel in a field, or even do a simple operation on an endless assembly line in a factory. But practically all workers must be highly skilled workers in the age of automation, and there is little room for the illiterate. The populace of the People's Dictatorship was no longer a dumb, driven herd, and their problems were no longer simple ones.

Yes, Number One was increasingly subject to his rages these days. It was Aleksander Kardelj's deepest belief that Jankez was finding himself out of his depth. He no longer was capable of understanding the problems which his planning bodies brought to his attention. And he who is confused, be he ditchdigger or dictator, is a man emotionally upset.

Zoran Jankez's face had come onto the Telly-Phone screen already enraged. He had snapped to his right-hand man, "Kardelj! Do you realize what that … that idiot of yours has been up to now?"

Inwardly, Kardelj had winced. His superior had been mountingly difficult of late, and particularly these past few days. He said now, cajolingly, "Zoran, I —"

"Don't call me Zoran, Kardelj! And please preserve me from your sickening attempts to fawn, in view of your treacherous recommendations of recent months." He was so infuriated that his heavy jowls shook.

Kardelj had never seen him this furious. He said placatingly, "Comrade Jankez, I had already come to the conclusion that I should consult you on the desirability of revoking this young troublemaker's credentials and removing him from the —"

"I am not interested in what you were *going* to do, Kardelj. I am already in the process of ending this traitor's activities. I should have known, when you revealed he was the son of Ljubo Pekic, that he was an enemy of the State, deep within. I know the Pekic blood. It was I who put Ljubo to the question. Stubborn, wrong headed, a vicious foe of the revolution. And his son takes after him."

Kardelj had enough courage left to say, "Comrade, it would seem to me that young Pekic is a tanglefoot, but not a conscious traitor. I —"

"Don't call me comrade, Kardelj!" Number One roared. "I know your inner motivation. The reason you brought this agent provocateur, this Trotskyite wrecker, to this position of ridiculous power. The two of you are in conspiracy to undermine my authority. This will be brought before the Secretariat of the Executive Committee, Kardelj. You've gone too far, this time!"

Aleksander Kardelj had his shortcomings but he was no coward. He said, wryly, "Very well, sir. But would you tell me what Josip Pekic has done now? My office has had no report on him for some time."

"What he has done! You fool, you traitorous fool, have you kept no record at all? He has been in the Macedonian area where my virgin lands program has been in full swing."

Kardelj cleared his throat at this point.

Jankez continued roaring. "The past three years, admittedly, the weather has been such, the confounded rains failing to arrive on schedule, that we have had our troubles. But this fool! This blundering traitorous idiot!"

"What has he done?" Kardelj asked, intrigued in spite of his position of danger.

"For all practical purposes he's ordered the whole program reversed. Something about a sandbowl developing, whatever that is supposed to mean. Something about introducing contour plowing, whatever nonsense that is. And even reforesting some areas. Some nonsense about watersheds. He evidently has blinded and misled the very men I had in charge. They are supporting him, openly."

Jankez, Kardelj knew, had been a miner as a youth, with no experience whatsoever on the soil. However, the virgin lands project had been his pet. He envisioned hundreds upon thousands of square miles of maize, corn as the Americans called it. This in turn would feed vast herds of cattle and swine so that ultimately the United Balkan Soviet Republics would have the highest meat consumption in the world.

Number One was raging on. Something about a conspiracy on the part of those who surrounded him. A conspiracy to overthrow him, Zoran Jankez, and betray the revolution to the Western powers, but he, Zoran Jankez, had been through this sort of plot before. He, Zoran Jankez, knew the answers to such situations.

Aleksander Kardelj grinned humorously, wryly, and reached to flick off the screen. He twisted a cigarette into the small pipelike holder, lit it and waited for the inevitable.

It was shortly after that the knock came on his door.

* * * * *

Zoran Jankez sat at his desk in the Ministry of Internal Affairs, a heavy military revolver close to his right hand, a half empty liter of sljivovica and a water tumbler, to his left. Red of eye, he pored over endless reports from his agents, occasionally taking time out to growl a command into his desk mike. Tired he was, from the long sleepless hours he was putting in, but Number One was in his element. As he had told that incompetent, Kardelj, he had been through this thing before. It was no mistake that he was Number One.

After a time he put a beefy hand down on the reports. He could feel the rage coming upon him. Of late, he realized, there most certainly had developed a plot to undermine his health by constant frustrations. Was there no one, no one at all, to take some of these trivialities off his shoulders? Must he do everything in the People's Democratic Dictatorship? Make every decision and see it through?

He snapped into the mike, "Give me Lazar Jovanovic." And then, when the police head's shaven poll appeared in the screen of the Telly-Phone, "Comrade, I am giving you one last chance. Produce this traitor, Josip Pekic, within the next twenty-four hours, or answer to me." He glared at the other, whose face had tightened in fear. "I begin to doubt the sincerity of your efforts, in this, Comrade Jovanovic."

"But ... but, Comrade, I —"

"That's all!" Number One snapped. He flicked off the instrument, then glowered at it for a full minute. If Jovanovic couldn't locate Pekic, he'd find someone who could. It was maddening that the pipsqueak had seemingly disappeared. To this point, seeking him had progressed in secret. There had been too much favorable publicity churned out in the early days of the expediter scheme to reverse matters to the point of having a public hue and cry. It was being done on the q.t.

But! Number One raged inwardly, if his police couldn't find the criminal soon enough, a full-scale hunt and purge could well enough be launched. There was more to all this than met the eye. Oh, he, Zoran Jankez had been through it before, though long years had lapsed since it had been necessary. The traitors, the secret conspiracies, and then the required purges to clean the Party ranks still once again.

The gentle summons of his Telly-Phone tinkled, and he flicked it on with a rough brush of his hand.

And there was the youthful face of Josip Pekic, currently being sought high and low by the full strength of the Internal Affairs Secretariat. Youthful, yes, but even as he stared his astonishment, Zoran Jankez could see that the past months had wrought their changes on the other's face. It was more mature, bore more of strain and weariness.

Before Jankez found his voice, Josip Pekic said diffidently, "I ... I understand you've been, well ... looking for me, sir."

"Looking for you!" the Party head bleated, his rage ebbing in all but uncontrollably. For a moment he couldn't find words.

Pekic said, his voice jittering, "I had some research to do. You see, sir, this ...this project you and Kardelj started me off on —"

"I had nothing to do with it! It was Kardelj's scheme, confound his idiocy!" Number One all but screamed.

"Oh? Well ...well, I had gathered the opinion that both of you concurred. Anyway, like I say, the project from the first didn't come off quite the way it started. I ...well ...we, were thinking in terms of finding out why waiters were surly, why workers and professionals and even officials tried to, uh, beat the rap, pass the buck, look out for themselves and the devil take the hindmost, and all those Americanisms that Kardelj is always using."

Jankez simmered, but let the other go on. Undoubtedly, his police chief, Lazar Jovanovic was even now tracing the call, and this young traitor would soon be under wraps where he could do no more damage to the economy of the People's Democratic Dictatorship.

"But, well, I found it wasn't just a matter of waiters, and truckdrivers and such. It ...well ... ran all the way from top to bottom. So, I finally felt as though I was sort of butting my head against the wall. I thought I better start at ...kind of ...fundamentals, so I began researching the manner in which the governments of the West handled some of these matters."

"Ah," Jankez said as smoothly as he was able to get out. "Ah. And?" This fool was hanging himself.

The younger man frowned in unhappy puzzlement. "Frankly, I was surprised. I have, of course, read Western propaganda to the extent I could get hold of it in Zagurest, and listened to the Voice of the West on the wireless. I was also, obviously, familiar with our own propaganda. Frankly ...well ...I had reserved my opinion in both cases."

* * * * *

This in itself was treason, but Number One managed to get out, almost encouragingly, "What are you driving at, Josip Pekic?"

"I found in one Western country that the government was actually paying its peasants, that is, farmers, not to plant crops. The same government subsidized other crops, keeping the prices up to the point where they were hard put to compete on the international markets."

Young Pekic made a moue, as though in puzzlement. "In other countries, in South America for instance, where the standard of living is possibly the lowest in the West and they need funds desperately to develop themselves, the governments build up large armies, although few of them have had any sort of warfare at all for over a century and have no threat of war."

"What is all this about?" Number One growled. Surely, Lazar Jovanovic was on the idiot traitor's trail by now.

Josip took a deep breath and hurried on nervously. "They've got other contradictions that seem unbelievable. For instance, their steel industry will be running at half capacity, in spite of the fact that millions of their citizens have unfulfilled needs, involving steel. Things like cars, refrigerators, stoves. In fact, in their so-called recessions, they'll actually close down perfectly good, modern factories, and throw their people out of employment, at the very time that there are millions of people who need that factory's product."

Josip said reasonably, "Why, sir, I've come to the conclusion that the West has some of the same problems we have. And the main one is politicians."

"What? What do you mean?"

"Just that," Josip said with dogged glumness. "I ...well, I don't know about the old days. A hundred, even fifty years ago, but as society becomes more complicated, more intricate, I simply don't think politicians are capable of directing it. The main problems are those of production and distribution of all the things our science and industry have learned to turn out. And politicians, all over the world, seem to foul it up."

Zoran Jankez growled ominously, "Are you suggesting that I am incompetent to direct the United Balkan Soviet Republics?"

"Yes, sir," Josip said brightly, as though the other had encouraged him. "That's what I mean. You or any other politician. Industry should be run by trained, competent technicians, scientists, industrialists-and to some extent, maybe, by the consumers, but not by politicians. By definition, politicians know about politics, not industry. But somehow, in the modern world, governments seem to be taking over the running of industry and even agriculture. They aren't doing such a good job, sir."

Jankez finally exploded. "Where are you calling from, Pekic?" he demanded. "You're under arrest!"

Josip Pekic cleared his throat, apologetically. "No, sir," he said. "Remember? I'm the average Transbalkanian citizen. And it is to be assumed I'd, well ... react the way any other would. The difference is, I had the opportunity. I'm in Switzerland."

"Switzerland!" Number One roared. "You've defected. I knew you were a traitor, Pekic. Like father, like son! A true Transbalkanian would remain in his country and help it along the road to the future."

The younger man looked worried. "Well, yes, sir," he said. "I thought about that. But I think I've done about as much as I could accomplish. You see, these last few months, protected by those 'can do no wrong' credentials, I've been spreading this message around among all the engineers, technicians, professionals, all the more trained, competent people in Transbalkania. You'd be surprised how they took to it. I think it's kind of ... well, snowballing. I mean the idea that politicians aren't capable of running industry. That if the United Balkan Soviet Republics are to ever get anywhere, some changes are going to have to be made."

Number One could no more than glare.

Josip Pekic, rubbed his nose nervously, and said, in the way of uneasy farewell, "I just thought it was only fair for me to call you and give a final report. After all, I didn't start all this. Didn't originate the situation. It was you and Kardelj who gave me my chance. I just ... well ... expedited things." His face faded from the screen, still apologetic of expression.

Zoran Jankez sat there for a long time, staring at the now dark instrument.

It was the middle of the night when the knock came at the door. But then, Zoran Jankez had always thought it would ... finally.

Spaceman on a Spree

I

They gave him a gold watch. It was meant to be symbolical, of course. In the old tradition. It was in the way of an antique, being one of the timepieces made generations past in the Alpine area of Eur-Asia. Its quaintness lay in the fact that it was wound, not electronically by power-radio, but by the actual physical movements of the bearer, a free swinging rotor keeping the mainspring at a constant tension.

They also had a banquet for him, complete with speeches by such bigwigs of the Department of Space Exploration as Academician Lofting Gubelin and Doctor Hans Girard-Perregaux. There was also somebody from the government who spoke, but he was one of those who were pseudo-elected and didn't know much about the field of space travel nor the significance of Seymour Pond's retirement. Si didn't bother to remember his name. He only wondered vaguely why the cloddy had turned up at all.

In common with recipients of gold watches of a score of generations before him, Si Pond would have preferred something a bit more tangible in the way of reward, such as a few shares of Variable Basic to add to his portfolio. But that, he supposed, was asking too much.

The fact of the matter was, Si knew that his retiring had set them back. They hadn't figured he had enough shares of Basic to see him through decently. Well, possibly he didn't, given their standards. But Space Pilot Seymour Pond didn't have their standards. He'd had plenty of time to think it over. It was better to retire on a limited crediting, on a confoundedly limited crediting, than to take the two or three more trips in hopes of attaining a higher standard.

He'd had plenty of time to figure it out, there alone in space on the Moon run, there on the Venus or Mars runs. There on the long, long haul to the Jupiter satellites, fearfully checking the symptoms of space cafard, the madness compounded of claustrophobia, monotony, boredom and free fall. Plenty of time. Time to decide that a one room mini-auto-apartment, complete with an autochair and built-in autobar, and with one wall a teevee screen, was all he needed to find contentment for a mighty long time. Possibly somebody like Doc Girard-Perregaux might be horrified at the idea of living in a mini-auto-apartment ... not realizing that to a pilot it was roomy beyond belief compared to the conning tower of a space craft.

No. Even as Si listened to their speeches, accepted the watch and made a halting little talk of his own, he was grinning inwardly. There wasn't anything they could do. He had them now. He had enough Basic to keep him comfortably, by his standards, for the rest of his life. He was never going to subject himself to space cafard again. Just thinking about it, now, set the tic to going at the side of his mouth.

They could count down and blast off, for all he gave a damn.

* * * * *

The gold watch idea had been that of Lofting Gubelin, which was typical, he being in the way of a living anachronism himself. In fact, Academician Gubelin was possibly the only living man on North America who still wore spectacles. His explanation was that a phobia against having his eyes touched prohibited either surgery to remould his eyeballs and cure his myopia, or contact lenses.

That was only an alibi so far as his closest associate, Hans Girard-Perregaux, was concerned. Doctor Girard-Perregaux was convinced Gubelin would have even worn facial hair, had he but a touch more courage. Gubelin longed for yesteryear, a seldom found phenomenon under the Ultrawelfare State.

Slumped in an autochair in the escape room of his Floridian home, Lofting Gubelin scowled at his friend. He said, acidly, "Any more bright schemes, Hans? I presume you now acknowledge that appealing to the cloddy's patriotism, sentiment and desire for public acclaim have miserably failed."

Girard-Perregaux said easily, "I wouldn't call Seymour Pond a cloddy. In his position, I am afraid I would do the same thing he has."

"That's nonsense, Hans. Zoroaster! Either you or I would gladly take Pond's place were we capable of performing the duties for which he has been trained. There aren't two men on North America-there aren't two men in the world! —who better realize the urgency of continuing our delving into space." Gubelin snapped his fingers. "Like that, either of us would give our lives to prevent man from completely abandoning the road to his destiny."

His friend said drily, "Either of us could have volunteered for pilot training forty years ago, Lofting. We didn't."

"At that time there wasn't such a blistering percentage of funkers throughout this whole blistering Ultrawelfare State! Who could foresee that eventually our whole program would face ending due to lack of courageous young men willing to take chances, willing to face adventure, willing to react to the stimulus of danger in the manner our ancestors did?"

Girard-Perregaux grunted his sarcasm and dialed a glass of iced tea and tequila. He said, "Nevertheless, both you and I conform with the present generation in finding it far more pleasant to follow one's way of life in the comfort of one's home than to be confronted with the unpleasantness of facing nature's dangers in more adventurous pastimes."

Gubelin, half angry at his friend's argument, leaned forward to snap rebuttal, but the other was wagging a finger at him negatively. "Face reality, Lofting. Don't require or expect from Seymour Pond more than is to be found there. He is an average young man. Born in our Ultrawelfare State, he was guaranteed his fundamental womb-to-tomb security by being issued that minimum number of Basic shares in our society that allows him an income sufficient to secure the food, clothing, shelter, medical care and education to sustain a low level of subsistence. Percentages were against his ever being drafted into industry. Automation being what it is, only a fraction of the population is ever called up. But Pond was. His industrial aptitude dossier revealed him a possible candidate for space pilot, and it was you yourself who talked him into taking the training ... pointing out the more pragmatic advantages such as complete retirement after but six trips, added shares of Basic so that he could enjoy a more comfortable life than most and the fame that would accrue to him as one of the very few who still participate in travel to the planets. Very well. He was sold. Took his training, which, of course, required long years of drudgery to him. Then, performing his duties quite competently, he made his six trips. He is now legally eligible for retirement. He was drafted into the working force reserves, served his time, and is now free from toil for the balance of his life. Why should he listen to our pleas for a few more trips?"

"But has he no spirit of adventure? Has he no feeling for...."

* * * * *

Girard-Perregaux was wagging his finger again, a gesture that, seemingly mild though it was, had an astonishing ability to break off the conversation of one who debated with the easy-seeming, quiet spoken man.

He said, "No, he hasn't. Few there are who have, nowadays. Man has always paid lip service to adventure, hardships and excitement, but in actuality his instincts, like those of any other animal, lead him to the least dangerous path. Today we've reached the point where no one need face danger-ever. There are few who don't take advantage of the fact. Including you and me, Lofting, and including Seymour Pond."

His friend and colleague changed subjects abruptly, impatiently. "Let's leave this blistering jabber about Pond's motivation and get to the point. The man is the only trained space pilot in the world. It will take months, possibly more than a year, to bring another novitiate pilot to the point where he can safely be trusted to take our next explorer craft out. Appropriations for our expeditions have been increasingly hard to come by-even though in *our* minds, Hans, we are near important breakthroughs, breakthroughs which might possibly so spark the race that a new dream to push man out to the stars will take hold of us. If it is admitted that our organization has degenerated to the point that we haven't a single pilot, then it might well be that the Economic Planning Board, and especially those cloddies on Appropriations, will terminate the whole Department of Space Exploration."

"So...." Girard-Perregaux said gently.

"So some way we've got to bring Seymour Pond out of his retirement!"

"Now we are getting to matters." Girard-Perregaux nodded his agreement. Looking over the rim of his glass, his eyes narrowed in thought as his face took on an expression of Machiavellianism. "And do not the ends justify the means?"

Gubelin blinked at him.

The other chuckled. "The trouble with you, Lofting, is that you have failed to bring history to bear on our problem. Haven't you ever read of the sailor and his way of life?"

"Sailor? What in the name of the living Zoroaster has the sailor got to do with it?"

"You must realize, my dear Lofting, that our Si Pond is nothing more than a latter-day sailor, with many of the problems and view-points, tendencies and weaknesses of the voyager of the past. Have you never heard of the seaman who dreamed of returning to the village of his birth and buying a chicken farm or some such? All the long months at sea-and sometimes the tramp freighters or whaling craft would be out for years at a stretch before returning to home port-he would talk of his retirement and his dream. And then? Then in port, it would be one short drink with the boys, before taking his accumulated pay and heading home. The one short drink would lead to another. And morning would find him, drunk, rolled, tattooed and possibly sleeping it off in jail. So back to sea he'd have to go."

Gubelin grunted bitterly. "Unfortunately, our present-day sailor can't be separated from his money quite so easily. If he could, I'd personally be willing to lure him down some dark alley, knock him over the head and roll him myself. Just to bring him back to his job again."

He brought his wallet from his pocket, and flicked it open to his universal credit card. "The ultimate means of exchange," he grunted. "Nobody can spend your money, but you, yourself. Nobody can steal it, nobody can, ah, *con* you out of it. Just how do you expect to sever our present-day sailor and his accumulated nest egg?"

The other chuckled again. "It is simply a matter of finding more modern methods, my dear chap."

II

Si Pond was a great believer in the institution of the spree. Any excuse would do. Back when he had finished basic education at the age of twenty-five and was registered for the labor draft, there hadn't been a chance in a hundred that he'd have the bad luck to have his name pulled. But when it had been, Si had celebrated.

When he had been informed that his physical and mental qualifications were such that he was eligible for the most dangerous occupation in the Ultrawelfare State and had been pressured into taking training for space pilot, he had celebrated once again. Twenty-two others had taken the training with him, and only he and Rod Cameroon had passed the finals. On this occasion, he and Rod had celebrated together. It had been quite a party. Two weeks later, Rod had burned on a faulty take-off on what should have been a routine Moon run.

Each time Si returned from one of his own runs, he celebrated. A spree, a bust, a bat, a wing-ding, a night on the town. A commemoration of dangers met and passed.

Now it was all over. At the age of thirty he was retired. Law prevented him from ever being called up for contributing to the country's labor needs again. And he most certainly wasn't going to volunteer.

He had taken his schooling much as had his contemporaries. There wasn't any particular reason for trying to excell. You didn't want to get the reputation for being a wise guy, or a cloddy either. Just one of the fellas. You could do the same in life whether you really studied or not. You had your Inalienable Basic stock, didn't you? What else did you need?

It had come as a surprise when he'd been drafted for the labor force.

In the early days of the Ultrawelfare State, they had made a mistake in adapting to the automation of the second industrial revolution. They had attempted to give everyone work by reducing the number of working hours in the day, and the number of working days in the week. It finally became ludicrous when employees of industry were working but two days a week, two hours a day. In fact, it got chaotic. It became obvious that it was more practical to have one worker putting in thirty-five hours a week and getting to know his job well, than it was to have a score of employees, each working a few hours a week and none of them ever really becoming efficient.

The only fair thing was to let the technologically unemployed remain unemployed, with their Inalienable Basic stock as the equivalent of unemployment insurance, while the few workers still needed put in a reasonable number of hours a day, a reasonable number of weeks a year and a reasonable number of years in a life time. When new employees were needed, a draft lottery was held.

All persons registered in the labor force participated. If you were drawn, you must need serve. The dissatisfaction those chosen might feel at their poor luck was offset by the fact that they were granted additional Variable Basic shares, according to the tasks they fulfilled. Such shares could be added to their portfolios, the dividends becoming part of their current credit balance, or could be sold for a lump sum on the market.

Yes, but now it was all over. He had his own little place, his own vacuum-tube vehicle and twice the amount of shares of Basic that most of his fellow citizens could boast. Si Pond had it made. A spree was obviously called for.

He was going to do this one right. This was the big one. He'd accumulated a lot of dollars these past few months and he intended to blow them, or at least a sizeable number of them. His credit card was burning a hole in his pocket, as the expression went. However, he wasn't going to rush into things. This had to be done correctly.

Too many a spree was played by ear. You started off with a few drinks, fell in with some second rate mopsy and usually wound up in a third rate groggery where you spent just as much as though you'd been in the classiest joint in town. Came morning and you had nothing to show for all the dollars that had been spent but a rum-head.

Thus, Si was vaguely aware, it had always been down through the centuries since the Phoenecian sailor, back from his year-long trip to the tin mines of Cornwall, blew his hard earned share of the voyage's profits in a matter of days in the wine shops of Tyre. Nobody gets quite so little for his money as that loneliest of all workers, he who must leave his home for distant lands, returning only periodically and usually with the salary of lengthy, weary periods of time to be spent hurriedly in an attempt to achieve the pleasure and happiness so long denied him.

Si was going to do it differently this time.

Nothing but the best. Wine, women, song, food, entertainment. The works. But nothing but the best.

* * * * *

To start off, he dressed with great care in the honorable retirement-rank suit he had so recently purchased. His space pin he attached carefully to the lapel. That was a good beginning, he decided. A bit of prestige didn't hurt you when you went out on the town. In the Ultrawelfare State hardly one person in a hundred actually ever performed anything of value to society. The efforts of most weren't needed. Those few who did contribute were awarded honors, decorations, titles.

Attired satisfactorily, Si double-checked to see that his credit card was in his pocket. As an after-thought, he went over to the auto-apartment's teevee-phone, flicked it on, held the card to the screen and said, "Balance check, please."

In a moment, the teevee-phone's robot voice reported, "Ten shares of Inalienable Basic. Twelve shares of Variable Basic, current value, four thousand, two hundred and thirty-three dollars and sixty-two cents apiece. Current cash credit, one thousand and eighty-four dollars." The screen went dead.

One thousand and eighty-four dollars. That was plenty. He could safely spend as much as half of it, if the spree got as lively as he hoped it would. His monthly dividends were due in another week or so, and he wouldn't have to worry about current expenses. Yes, indeedy, Si Pond was as solvent as he had ever been in his thirty years.

He opened the small, closet-like door which housed his vacuum-tube two-seater, and wedged himself into the small vehicle. He brought down the canopy, dropped the pressurizer and considered the dial. Only one place really made sense. The big city.

He considered for a moment, decided against the boroughs of Baltimore and Boston, and selected Manhattan instead. He had the resources. He might as well do it up brown.

He dialed Manhattan and felt the sinking sensation that presaged his car's dropping to tube level. While it was being taken up by the robot controls, being shuttled here and there preparatory to the shot to his destination, he dialed the vehicle's teevee-phone for information on the hotels of the island of the Hudson. He selected a swank hostelry he'd read about and seen on the teevee casts of society and celebrity gossip reporters, and dialed it on the car's destination dial.

"Nothing too good for ex-Space Pilot Si Pond," he said aloud.

The car hesitated for a moment, that brief hesitation before the shot, and Si took the involuntary breath from which only heroes could refrain. He sank back slowly into the seat. Moments passed, and the direction of the pressure was reversed.

Manhattan. The shuttling began again, and one or two more traversing sub-shots. Finally, the dash threw a green light and Si opened the canopy and stepped into his hotel room.

A voice said gently, "If the quarters are satisfactory, please present your credit card within ten minutes."

Si took his time. Not that he really needed it. It was by far the most swank suite he had ever seen. One wall was a window of whatever size the guest might desire and Si touched the control that dilated it to the full. His view opened in such wise that he could see both the Empire State Building Museum and the Hudson. Beyond the river stretched the all but endless city which was Greater Metropolis.

He didn't take the time to flick on the menu, next to the auto-dining table, nor to check the endless potables on the autobar list. All that, he well knew, would be superlative. Besides, he didn't plan to dine or do much drinking in his suite. He made a mock leer. Not unless he managed to acquire some feminine companionship, that was.

He looked briefly into the swimming pool and bath, then flopped himself happily onto the bed. It wasn't up to the degree of softness he presently desired, and he dialed the thing to the ultimate in that direction so that with a laugh he sank almost out of sight into the mattress.

He came back to his feet, gave his suit a quick patting so that it fell into press and, taking his credit card from his pocket, put it against the teevee-phone screen and pressed the hotel button so that registration could be completed.

For a moment he stood in the center of the floor, in thought. Take it easy, Si Pond, take it all easy, this time. No throwing his dollars around in second-class groggeries, no eating in automated luncheterias. This time, be it the only time in his life, he was going to frolic in the grand manner. No cloddy was Si Pond.

He decided a drink was in order to help him plan his strategy. A drink at the hotel's famous Kudos Room where celebrities were reputed to be a dime a dozen.

He left the suite and stepped into one of the elevators. He said, "Kudos Room."

The auto-elevator murmured politely, "Yes, sir, the Kudos Room."

* * * * *

At the door to the famous rendezvous of the swankiest set, Si paused a moment and looked about. He'd never been in a place like this, either. However, he stifled his first instinct to wonder about what this was going to do to his current credit balance with an inner grin and made his way to the bar.

There was actually a bartender.

Si Pond suppressed his astonishment and said, offhand, attempting an air of easy sophistication, "Slivovitz Sour."

"Yes, sir."

The drinks in the Kudos Room might be concocted by hand, but Si noticed they had the routine teevee screens built into the bar for payment. He put his credit card on the screen immediately before him when the drink came, and had to quell his desire to dial for a balance check, so as to be able to figure out what the Sour had cost him.

Well, this was something like it. This was the sort of thing he'd dreamed about, out there in the great alone, seated in the confining conning tower of his space craft. He sipped at the drink, finding it up to his highest expectations, and then swiveled slightly on his stool to take a look at the others present.

To his disappointment, there were no recognizable celebrities. None that he placed, at least-top teevee stars, top politicians of the Ultrawelfare State or Sports personalities.

He turned back to his drink and noticed, for the first time, the girl who occupied the stool two down from him. Si Pond blinked. He blinked and then swallowed.

"*Zo-ro-as-ter*," he breathed.

She was done in the latest style from Shanghai, even to the point of having cosmetically duplicated the Mongolian fold at the corners of her eyes. Every pore, but *every* pore, was in place. She sat with the easy grace of the Orient, so seldom found in the West.

His stare couldn't be ignored.

She looked at him coldly, turned to the bartender and murmured, "A Far Out Cooler, please, Fredric." Then deliberately added, "I thought the Kudos Room was supposed to be exclusive."

There was nothing the bartender could say to that, and he went about building the drink.

Si cleared his throat. "Hey," he said, "how about letting this one be on me?"

Her eyebrows, which had been plucked and penciled to carry out her Oriental motif, rose. "Really!" she said, drawing it out.

The bartender said hurriedly, "I beg your pardon, sir...."

The girl, her voice suddenly subtly changed, said, "Why, isn't that a space pin?"

Si, disconcerted by the sudden reversal, said, "Yeah ... sure."

"Good Heavens, you're a spaceman?"

"Sure." He pointed at the lapel pin. "You can't wear one unless you been on at least a Moon run."

She was obviously both taken back and impressed. "Why," she said, "you're Seymour Pond, the pilot. I tuned in on the banquet they gave you."

Si, carrying his glass, moved over to the stool next to her. "Call me Si," he said. "Everybody calls me Si."

She said, "I'm Natalie. Natalie Paskov. Just Natalie. Imagine meeting Seymour Pond. Just sitting down next to him at a bar. Just like that."

"Si," Si said, gratified. Holy Zoroaster, he'd never seen anything like this rarified pulchritude. Maybe on teevee, of course, one of the current sex symbols, but never in person. "Call me Si," he said again. "I been called Si so long, I don't even know who somebody's talking to if they say Seymour."

"I cried when they gave you that antique watch," she said, her tone such that it was obvious she hadn't quite adjusted as yet to having met him.

Si Pond was surprised. "Cried?" he said. "Well, why? I was kind of bored with the whole thing. But old Doc Gubelin, I used to work under him in the Space Exploration department, he was hot for it."

"*Academician* Gubelin?" she said. "You just call him *Doc*?"

Si was expansive. "Why, sure. In the Space Department we don't have much time for formality. Everybody's just Si, and Doc, and Jim. Like that. But how come you cried?"

* * * * *

She looked down into the drink the bartender had placed before her, as though avoiding his face. "I ... I suppose it was that speech Doctor Girard-Perregaux made. There you stood, so fine and straight in your space-pilot uniform, the veteran of six exploration runs to the planets...."

"Well," Si said modestly, "two of my runs were only to the Moon."

"... and he said all those things about man's conquest of space. And the dream of the stars which man has held so long. And then the fact that you were the last of the space pilots. The last man in the whole world trained to pilot a space craft. And here you were, retiring."

Si grunted. "Yeah. That's all part of the Doc's scheme to get me to take on another three runs. They're afraid the whole department'll be dropped by the Appropriations Committee on this here Economic Planning Board. Even if they can find some other patsy to train for the job, it'd take maybe a year before you could even send him on a Moon hop. So old man Gubelin, and Girard-Perregaux too, they're both trying to pressure me into more trips. Otherwise they got a Space Exploration Department, with all the expense and all, but nobody to pilot their ships. It's kind of funny, in a way. You know what one of those spaceships costs?"

"Funny?" she said. "Why, I don't think it's funny at all."

Si said, "Look, how about another drink?"

Natalie Paskov said, "Oh, I'd love to have a drink with you, Mr...."

"Si," Si said. He motioned to the bartender with a circular twist of the hand indicating their need for two more of the same. "How come you know so much about it? You don't meet many people who are interested in space any more. In fact, most people are almost contemptuous, like. Think it's kind of a big boondoggle deal to help use up a lot of materials and all and keep the economy going."

Natalie said earnestly, "Why, I've been a space fan all my life. I've read all about it. Have always known the names of all the space pilots and everything about them, ever since I was a child. I suppose you'd say I have the dream that Doctor Girard-Perregaux spoke about."

Si chuckled. "A real buff, eh? You know, it's kind of funny. I was never much interested in it. And I got a darn sight less interested after my first run and I found out what space cafard was."

She frowned. "I don't believe I know much about that."

Sitting in the Kudos Room with the most beautiful girl to whom he had ever talked, Si could be nonchalant about the subject. "Old Gubelin keeps that angle mostly hushed up and out of the magazine and newspaper articles. Says there's enough adverse publicity about space exploration already. But at this stage of the game when the whole ship's crammed tight with this automatic scientific apparatus and all, there's precious little room in the conning tower and you're the only man aboard. The Doc says later on when ships are bigger and there's a whole flock of people aboard, there won't be any such thing as space cafard, but...." Of a sudden the right side of Si Pond's mouth began to tic and he hurriedly took up his drink and knocked it back.

He cleared his throat. "Let's talk about some other angle. Look, how about something to eat, Natalie? I'm celebrating my retirement, like. You know, out on the town. If you're free...."

She put the tip of a finger to her lips, looking for the moment like a small girl rather than an ultra-sophisticate. "Supposedly, I have an appointment," she said hesitantly.

* * * * *

When the mists rolled out in the morning-if it was still morning-it was to the tune of an insistent hotel chime. Si rolled over on his back and growled, "*Zo-ro-as-ter*, cut that out. What do you want?"

The hotel communicator said softly, "Checking-out time, sir, is at two o'clock."

Si groaned. He couldn't place the last of the evening at all. He didn't remember coming back to the hotel. He couldn't recall where he had separated from, what was her name ...Natalie.

He vaguely recalled having some absinthe in some fancy club she had taken him to. What was the gag she'd made? Absinthe makes the heart grow fonder. And then the club where they had the gambling machines. And the mists had rolled in on him. Mountains of the Moon! but that girl could drink. He simply wasn't that used to the stuff. You don't drink in Space School and you most certainly don't drink when in space. His binges had been few and far between.

He said now, "I don't plan on checking out today. Don't bother me." He turned to his pillow.

The hotel communicator said quietly, "Sorry, sir, but your credit balance does not show sufficient to pay your bill for another day."

Si Pond shot up, upright in bed, suddenly cold sober.

His eyes darted about the room, as though he was seeing it for the first time. His clothes, he noted, were thrown over a chair haphazardly. He made his way to them, his face empty, and fished about for his credit card, finding it in a side pocket. He wavered to the teevee-phone and thrust the card against the screen. He demanded, his voice as empty as his expression, "Balance check, please."

In less than a minute the robot-voice told him: "Ten shares of Inalienable Basic. Current cash credit, forty-two dollars and thirty cents." The screen went dead.

He sank back into the chair which held his clothes, paying no attention to them. It couldn't be right. Only yesterday, he'd had twelve shares of Variable Basic, immediately convertible into more than fifty thousand dollars, had he so wished to convert rather than collect dividends indefinitely. Not only had he the twelve shares of Variable Basic, but more than a thousand dollars to his credit.

He banged his fist against his mouth. Conceivably, he might have gone through his thousand dollars. It was possible, though hardly believable. The places he'd gone to with that girl in the Chinese get-up were probably the most expensive in Greater Metropolis. But, however expensive, he couldn't possibly have spent fifty thousand dollars! Not possibly.

He came to his feet again to head for the teevee screen and demand an audit of the past twenty-four hours from Central Statistics. That'd show it up. Every penny expended. Something was crazy here. Someway that girl had pulled a fast one. She didn't seem the type. But something had happened to his twelve shares of Variable Basic, and he wasn't standing for it. It was his security, his defense against slipping back into the ranks of the cloddies, the poor demi-buttocked ranks of the average man, the desperately dull life of those who subsisted on the bounty of the Ultrawelfare State and the proceeds of ten shares of Inalienable Basic.

He dialed Statistics and placed his card against the screen. His voice was strained now. "An audit of all expenditures for the past twenty-four hours."

Then he sat and watched.

His vacuum-tube trip to Manhattan was the first item. Two dollars and fifty cents. Next was his hotel suite. Fifty dollars. Well, he had known it was going to be expensive. A Slivovitz Sour at the Kudos Room, he found, went for three dollars a throw, and the Far out Coolers Natalie drank, four dollars. Absinthe was worse still, going for ten dollars a drink.

He was impatient. All this didn't account for anything like a thousand dollars, not to speak of fifty thousand.

The audit threw an item he didn't understand. A one dollar credit. And then, immediately afterward, a hundred dollar credit. Si scowled.

And then slowly reached out and flicked the set off. For it had all come back to him.

At first he had won. Won so that the other players had crowded around him, watching. Five thousand, ten thousand. Natalie had been jubilant. The others had cheered him on. He'd bet progressively higher, smaller wagers becoming meaningless and thousands being involved on single bets. A five thousand bet on odd had lost, and then another. The kibitzers had gone silent. When he had attempted to place another five thousand bet, the teevee screen robot voice had informed him dispassionately that his current cash credit balance was insufficient to cover that amount.

Yes. He could remember now. He had needed no time to decide, had simply snapped, "Sell one share of Variable Basic at current market value."

The other eleven shares had taken the route of the first.

When it was finally all gone and he had looked around, it was to find that Natalie Paskov was gone as well.

* * * * *

Academician Lofting Gubelin, seated in his office, was being pontifical. His old friend Hans Girard-Perregaux had enough other things on his mind to let him get away with it, only half following the monologue.

"I submit," Gubelin orated, "that there is evolution in society. But it is by fits and starts, and by no means a constant thing. Whole civilizations can go dormant, so far as progress is concerned, for millennia at a time."

Girard-Perregaux said mildly, "Isn't that an exaggeration, Lofting?"

"No, by Zoroaster, it is not! Take the Egyptians. Their greatest monuments, such as the pyramids, were constructed in the earlier dynasties. Khufu, or Cheops, built the largest at Gizeh. He was the founder of the 4th Dynasty, about the year 2900 B. C. Twenty-five dynasties later, and nearly three thousand years, there was no greatly discernable change in the Egyptian culture."

Girard-Perregaux egged him on gently. "The sole example of your theory I can think of, offhand."

"Not at all!" Gubelin glared. "The Mayans are a more recent proof. Their culture goes back to at least 500 B. C. At that time their glyph-writing was already wide-spread and their cities, eventually to number in the hundreds, being built. By the time of Christ they had reached their peak. And they remained there until the coming of the Spaniards, neither gaining nor losing, in terms of evolution of society."

His colleague sighed. "And your point, Lofting?"

"Isn't it blisteringly obvious?" the other demanded. "We're in danger of reaching a similar static condition here and now. The Ultrawelfare State!" He snorted indignation. "The Conformist State or the Status Quo State, is more like it. I tell you, Hans, all progress is being dried up. There is no will to delve into the unknown, no burning fever to explore the unexplored. And this time it isn't a matter of a single area, such as Egypt or Yucatan, but our whole world. If man goes into intellectual coma this time, then all the race slows down, not merely a single element of it."

He rose suddenly from the desk chair he'd been occupying to pace the room. "The race must find a new frontier, a new ocean to cross, a new enemy to fight."

Girard-Perregaux raised his eyebrows.

"Don't be a cloddy," Gubelin snapped. "You know what I mean. Not a human enemy, not even an alien intelligence. But something against which we must pit our every wit, our every strength, our strongest determination. Otherwise, we go dull, we wither on the vine."

The other at long last chuckled. "My dear Lofting, you wax absolutely lyrical."

Gubelin suddenly stopped his pacing, returned to his desk and sank back into his chair. He seemed to add a score of years to his age, and his face sagged. "I don't know why I take it out on you, Hans. You're as aware of the situation as I. Man's next frontier is space. First the planets, and then a reaching out to the stars. This is our new frontier, our new ocean to cross."

His old friend was nodding. He brought his full attention to the discussion at last. "And we'll succeed, Lofting. The last trip Pond made gives us ample evidence that we can actually colonize and exploit the Jupiter satellites. Two more runs, at most three, and we can release our findings in such manner that they'll strike the imaginations of every Tom, Dick and Harry like nothing since Columbus made his highly exaggerated reports on his New World."

"Two or three more runs," Gubelin grunted bitterly. "You've heard the rumors. Appropriations is going to lower the boom on us. Unless we can get Pond back into harness, we're sunk. The runs will never be made. I tell you, Hans...."

* * * * *

But Hans Girard-Perregaux was wagging him to silence with a finger. "They'll be made. I've taken steps to see friend Seymour Pond comes dragging back to us."

"But he *hates* space! The funker probably won't consent to come within a mile of the New Albuquerque Spaceport for the rest of his life, the blistering cloddy."

A desk light flicked green, and Girard-Perregaux raised his eyebrows. "Exactly at the psychological moment. If I'm not mistaken, Lofting, that is probably our fallen woman."

"Our *what*?"

But Doctor Hans Girard-Perregaux had come to his feet and personally opened the door. "Ah, my dear," he said affably.

Natalie Paskov, done today in Bulgarian peasant garb, and as faultless in appearance as she had been in the Kudos Room, walked briskly into the office.

"Assignment carried out," she said crisply.

"Indeed," Girard-Perregaux said approvingly. "So soon?"

Gubelin looked from one to the other. "What in the blistering name of Zoroaster is going on?"

His friend said. "Academician Gubelin, may I present Operative Natalie of Extraordinary Services Incorporated?"

"Extraordinary Services?" Gubelin blurted.

"In this case," Natalie said smoothly, even while taking the chair held for her by Doctor Girard-Perregaux, "a particularly apt name. It was a dirty trick."

"But for a good cause, my dear."

She shrugged. "So I am often told, when sent on these far-out assignments."

Girard-Perregaux, in spite of her words, was beaming at her. "Please report in full," he said, ignoring his colleague's obvious bewilderment.

Natalie Paskov made it brief. "I picked up the subject in the Kudos Room of the Greater Metropolis Hotel, pretending to be a devotee of the space program as an excuse. It soon developed that he had embarked upon a celebration of his retirement. He was incredibly naive, and allowed me to over-indulge him in semi-narcotics as well as alcohol, so that his defensive inhibitions were low. I then took him to a gambling spot where, so dull that he hardly knew what he was doing, he lost his expendable capital."

Gubelin had been staring at her, but now he blurted, "But suppose he had won?"

She shrugged it off. "Hardly, the way I was encouraging him to wager. Each time he won, I urged him to double up. It was only a matter of time until ..." she let the sentence dribble away.

Girard-Perregaux rubbed his hands together briskly. "Then, in turn, it is but a matter of time until friend Pond comes around again."

"That I wouldn't know," Natalie Paskov said disinterestedly. "My job is done. However, the poor man seems so utterly opposed to returning to your service that I wouldn't be surprised if he remained in his retirement, living on his Inalienable Basic shares. He seems literally terrified of being subjected to space cafard again."

But Hans Girard-Perregaux wagged a finger negatively at her. "Not after having enjoyed a better way of life for the past decade. A person is able to exist on the Inalienable Basic dividends, but it is almost impossible to bring oneself to it once a fuller life has been enjoyed. No, Seymour Pond will never go back to the dullness of life the way it is lived by nine-tenths of our population."

Natalie came to her feet. "Well, gentlemen, you'll get your bill—a whopping one. I hope your need justifies this bit of dirty work. Frankly, I am considering my resignation from Extraordinary Services, although I'm no more anxious to live on my Inalienable Basic than poor Si Pond is. Good day, gentlemen."

She started toward the door.

The teevee-phone on Gubelin's desk lit up and even as Doctor Girard-Perregaux was saying unctuously to the girl, "Believe me, my dear, the task you have performed, though odious, will serve the whole race," the teevee-phone said:

"Sir, you asked me to keep track of Pilot Seymour Pond. There is a report on the news. He suicided this morning."

Adaptation

Forward

Hardly had man solved his basic problems on the planet of his origin than he began to fumble into space. Barely a century had elapsed in the exploration of the Solar System than he began to grope for the stars.

And suddenly, with an all but religious zeal, mankind conceived its fantasy dream of populating the galaxy. Never in the history of the race had fervor reached such a peak and held so long. The question of why was seemingly ignored. Millions of Earth-type planets beckoned and with a lemming-like desperation humanity erupted into them.

But the obstacles were frightening in their magnitude. The planets and satellites of Sol had proven comparatively tractable and those that were suited to man-life were quickly brought under his dominion. But there, of course, he had the advantage of proximity. The time involved in running back and forth to the home planet was meaningless and all Earth's resources could be thrown into each problem's solving.

But a planet a year removed in transportation or even communication? Ay! this was another thing and more than once a million colonists were lost before the Earthlings could adapt to new climates, new flora and fauna, new bacteria-or to factors which the most far out visionary had never fancied, perhaps the lack of something never before missed.

So, mad with the lust to seed the universe with his kind, men sought new methods. To a hundred thousand worlds they sent smaller colonies, as few as a hundred pioneers apiece, and there marooned them, to adapt, if adapt they could.

For a millennium each colony was left to its own resources, to conquer the environment or to perish in the effort.

A thousand years was sufficient. Invariably it was found, on those planets where human life survived at all, man slipped back during his first two or three centuries into a state of barbarism. Then slowly began to inch forward again. There were exceptions and the progress on one planet never exactly duplicated that on another, however the average was surprisingly close to both nadir and zenith, in terms of evolution of society.

In a thousand years it was deemed by the Office of Galactic Colonization such pioneers had largely adjusted to the new environment and were ready for civilization, industrialization and eventual assimilation into the rapidly evolving Galactic Commonwealth.

Of course, even from the beginning, new and unforeseen problems manifested themselves...
from "Man In Antiquity"

published in Terra City, Sol
Galactic Year 3,502.

the Co-ordinator said, "I suppose I'm an incurable romantic. You see, I hate to see you go." Academician Amschel Mayer was a man in early middle years; Dr. Leonid Plekhanov, his contemporary. They offset one another; Mayer thin and high-pitched, his colleague heavy, slow and dour. Now they both showed their puzzlement.

The Co-ordinator added, "Without me."

Plekhanov kept his massive face blank. It wasn't for him to be impatient with his superior. Nevertheless, the ship was waiting, stocked and crewed.

Amschel Mayer said, "Certainly a last minute chat can't harm." Inwardly he realized the other man's position. Here was a dream coming true, and Mayer and his fellows were the last thread that held the Co-ordinator's control over the dream. When they left, half a century would pass before he could again check developments.

The Co-ordinator became more businesslike. "Yes," he said, "but I have more in mind than a chat. Very briefly, I wish to go over your assignment. Undoubtedly redundant, but if there are questions, no matter how seemingly trivial, this is the last opportunity to air them."

What possible questions could there be at this late date? Plekhanov thought.

The department head swiveled slowly in his chair and then back again as he talked. "You are the first-the first of many, many such teams. The manner in which you handle your task will effect man's eternity. Obviously, since upon your experience we will base our future policies on interstellar colonization." His voice lost volume. "The position in which you find yourselves should be humbling."

"It is," Amschel Mayer agreed. Plekhanov nodded his head.

The Co-ordinator nodded, too. "However, the situation is as near ideal as we could hope. Rigel's planets are all but unbelievably Earthlike. Almost all our flora and fauna have been adaptable. Certainly our race has been.

"These two are the first of the seeded planets. Almost a thousand years ago we deposited small bodies of colonists upon each of them. Since then we have periodically checked, from a distance, but never intruded." His eyes went from one of his listeners to the other. "No comments or questions, thus far?"

Mayer said, "This is one thing that surprises me. The colonies are so small to begin with. How could they possibly populate a whole world in one millennium?"

The Co-ordinator said, "Man adapts, Amschel. Have you studied the development of the United States? During her first century and a half the need was for population to fill the vast lands wrested from the Amer-Inds. Families of eight, ten, and twelve children were the common thing, much larger ones were not unknown. And the generations crowded one against another; a girl worried about spinsterhood if she reached seventeen unwed. But in the next century? The frontier vanished, the driving need for population was gone. Not only were drastic immigration laws passed, but the family shrunk rapidly until by mid-Twentieth Century the usual consisted of two or three children, and even the childless family became increasingly common."

Mayer frowned impatiently, "But still, a thousand years. There is always famine, war, disease..."

Plekhanov snorted patronizingly. "Forty to fifty generations, Amschel? Starting with a hundred colonists? Where are your mathematics?"

The Co-ordinator said, "The proof is there. We estimate that each of Rigel's planets now supports a population of nearly one billion."

"To be more exact," Plekhanov rumbled, "some nine hundred million on Genoa, seven and a half on Texcoco."

Mayer smiled wryly. "I wonder what the residents of each of these planets call their worlds. Hardly the same names we have arbitrarily bestowed."

"Probably each call theirs *The World*," the Co-ordinator smiled. "After all, the basic language, in spite of a thousand years, is still Amer-English. However, I assume you are familiar with our method of naming. The most advanced culture on Rigel's first planet is to be compared to the Italian cities during Europe's feudalistic era. We have named that planet Genoa. The most advanced nation of the second planet is comparable to the Aztecs at the time of the conquest. We considered Tenochtitlán but it seemed a tongue twister, so Texcoco is the alternative."

"Modernizing Genoa," Mayer mused, "should be considerably easier than the task on semiprimitive Texcoco."

Plekhanov shrugged, "Not necessarily."

The Co-ordinator held up a hand and smiled at them. "Please, no debates on methods at present. An hour from now you will be in space with a year of travel before you. During that time you'll have opportunity for discussion, debate and hair pulling on every phase of your problem."

His expression became more serious. "You are acquainted with the unique position you assume. These colonists are in your control to an extent no small group has ever dominated millions of others before. No Caesar ever exerted the power that will be in your educated hands. For a half century you will be as gods. Your science, your productive know-how, your medicine-if it comes to that, your weapons-are many centuries in advance of theirs. As I said before, your position should be humbling."

Mayer squirmed in his chair. "Why not check upon us, say, once every decade? In all, our ship's company numbers but sixteen persons. Almost anything could happen. If you were to send a department craft each ten years…"

The Co-ordinator was shaking his head. "Your qualifications are as high as anyone available. Once on the scene you will begin accumulating information which we, here in Terra City, do not have. Were we to send another group in ten years to check upon you, all they could do would be interfere in a situation all the factors with which they would not be cognizant."

Amschel Mayer shifted nervously. "But no matter how highly trained, nor how earnest our efforts, we still may fail." His voice worried. "The department cannot expect guaranteed success. After all, we are the first."

"Admittedly. Your group is first to approach the hundreds of thousands of planets we have seeded. If you fail, we will use your failure to perfect the eventual system we must devise for future teams. Even your failure would be of infinite use to us." He lifted and dropped a shoulder. "I have no desire to undermine your belief in yourselves but-how are we to know? —perhaps there will be a score of failures before we find the ideal method of quickly bringing these primitive colonies into our Galactic Commonwealth."

The Co-ordinator came to his feet and sighed. He still hated to see them go. "If there is no other discussion…"

II.

Specialist Joseph Chessman stood stolidly before a viewing screen. Theoretically he was on watch. Actually his eyes were unseeing, there was nothing to see. The star pattern changed so slowly as to be all but permanent.

Not that every other task on board was not similar. One man could have taken the *Pedagogue* from the Solar System to Rigel, just as easily as its sixteen-hand crew was doing. Automation at its ultimate, not even the steward department had tasks adequately to fill the hours.

He had got beyond the point of yawning, his mind was a blank during these hours of duty. He was a stolid, bear of a man, short and massive of build.

A voice behind him said, "Second watch reporting. Request permission to take over the bridge."

Chessman turned and it took a brief moment for the blankness in his eyes to fade into life. "Hello Kennedy, you on already? Seems like I just got here." He muttered in self-contradiction, "Or that I've been here a month."

Technician Jerome Kennedy grinned. "Of course, if you want to stay..."

Chessman said glumly, "What difference does it make where you are? What are they doing in the lounge?"

Kennedy looked at the screen, not expecting to see anything and accomplishing just that. "Still on their marathon argument."

Joe Chessman grunted.

Just to be saying something, Kennedy said, "How do you stand in the big debate?"

"I don't know. I suppose I favor Plekhanov. How we're going to take a bunch of savages and teach them modern agriculture and industrial methods in fifty years under democratic institutions, I don't know. I can see them putting it to a vote when we suggest fertilizer might be a good idea." He didn't feel like continuing the conversation. "See you later, Kennedy," and then, as an afterthought, formally, "Relinquishing the watch to Third Officer."

As he left the compartment, Jerry Kennedy called after him, "Hey, what's the course!"

Chessman growled over his shoulder, "The same it was last month, and the same it'll be next month." It wasn't much of a joke but it was the only one they had between themselves.

In the ship's combination lounge and mess he drew a cup of coffee. Joe Chessman, among whose specialties were propaganda and primitive politics, was third in line in the expedition's hierarchy. As such he participated in the endless controversy dealing with overall strategy but only as a junior member of the firm. Amschel Mayer and Leonid Plekhanov were the center of the fracas and right now were at it hot and heavy.

Joe Chessman listened with only half interest. He settled into a chair on the opposite side of the lounge and sipped at his coffee. They were going over their old battlefields, assaulting ramparts they'd stormed a thousand times over.

Plekhanov was saying doggedly, "Any planned economy is more efficient than any unplanned one. What could be more elementary than that? How could anyone in his right mind deny that?"

And Mayer snapped, "*I* deny it. That term *planned economy* covers a multitude of sins. My dear Leonid, don't be an idiot..."

"I beg your pardon, sir!"

"Oh, don't get into one of your huffs, Plekhanov."

They were at that stage again.

* * * * *

Technician Natt Roberts entered, a book in hand, and sent the trend of conversation in a new direction. He said, worriedly, "I've been studying up on this and what we're confronted with is two different ethnic periods, barbarism and feudalism. Handling them both at once doubles our problems."

One of the junior specialists who'd been sitting to one side said, "I've been thinking about that and I believe I've got an answer. Why not all of us concentrate on Texcoco? When we've brought them to the Genoa level, which shouldn't take more than a decade or two, then we can start working on the Genoese, too."

Mayer snapped, "And by that time we'll have hardly more than half our fifty years left to raise the two of them to an industrial technology. Don't be an idiot, Stevens."

Stevens flushed his resentment.

Plekhanov said slowly, "Besides, I'm not sure that, given the correct method, we cannot raise Texcoco to an industrialized society in approximately the same time it will take to bring Genoa there."

Mayer bleated a sarcastic laugh at that opinion.

Natt Roberts tossed his book to the table and sank into a chair. "If only one of them had maintained itself at a reasonable level of development, we'd have had help in working with the other. As it is, there are only sixteen of us." He shook his head. "Why did the knowledge held by the original colonists melt away? How can an intelligent people lose such basics as the smelting of iron, gunpowder, the use of coal as a fuel?"

Plekhanov was heavy with condescension. "Roberts, you seem to have entered upon this expedition with a lack of background. Consider. You put down a hundred colonists, products of the most advanced culture. Among these you have one or two who can possibly repair an I.B.M. machine, but is there one who can smelt iron, or even locate the ore? We have others who could design an automated textile factory, but do any know how to weave a blanket on a hand loom?

"The first generation gets along well with the weapons and equipment brought with them from Earth. They maintain the old ways. The second generation follows along but already ammunition for the weapons runs short, the machinery imported from Earth needs parts. There is no local economy that can provide such things. The third generation begins to think of Earth as a legend and the methods necessary to survive on the new planet conflict with those the first settlers imported. By the fourth generation, Earth is no longer a legend but a fable..."

"But the books, the tapes, the films ..." Roberts injected.

"Go with the guns, the vehicles and the other things brought from Earth. On a new planet there is no leisure class among the colonists. Each works hard if the group is to survive. There is no time to write new books, nor to copy the old, and the second and especially the third generation are impatient of the time needed to learn to read, time that should be spent in the fields or at the chase. The youth of an industrial culture can spend twenty years and more achieving a basic education before assuming adult responsibilities but no pioneer society can afford to allow its offspring to so waste its time."

Natt Roberts was being stubborn. "But still, a few would carry the torch of knowledge."

Plekhanov nodded ponderously. "For a while. But then comes the reaction against these nonconformists, these crackpots who, by spending time at books, fail to carry their share of the load. One day they wake up to find themselves expelled from the group-if not knocked over the head."

* * * * *

Joe Chessman had been following Plekhanov's argument. He said dourly, "But finally the group conquers its environment to the point where a minimum of leisure is available again. Not for everybody, of course."

Amschel Mayer bounced back into the discussion. "Enter the priest, enter the war lord. Enter the smart operator who talks or fights himself into a position where he's free from drudgery."

Joe Chessman said reasonably, "If you don't have the man with leisure, society stagnates. Somebody has to have time off for thinking, if the whole group is to advance."

"Admittedly!" Mayer agreed. "I'd be the last to contend that an upper class is necessarily parasitic."

Plekhanov grumbled, "We're getting away from the subject. In spite of Mayer's poorly founded opinions, it is quite obvious that only a collectivized economy is going to enable these Rigel planets to achieve an industrial culture in as short a period as half a century."

Amschel Mayer reacted as might have been predicted. "Look here, Plekhanov, we have our own history to go by. Man made his greatest strides under a freely competitive system."

"Well now ..." Chessman began.

"Prove that!" Plekhanov insisted loudly. "Your so-called free economy countries such as England, France and the United States began their industrial revolution in the early part of the nineteenth century. It took them a hundred years to accomplish what the Soviets did in fifty, in the next century."

"Just a *moment*, now," Mayer simmered. "That's fine, but the Soviets were able to profit by the pioneering the free countries did. The scientific developments, the industrial techniques, were handed to her on a platter."

Specialist Martin Gunther, thus far silent, put in his calm opinion. "Actually, it seems to me the fastest industrialization comes under a paternal guidance from a more advanced culture. Take Japan. In 1854 she was opened to trade by Commodore Perry. In 1871 she abolished feudalism and encouraged by her own government and utilizing the most advanced techniques of a sympathetic West, she began to industrialize." Gunther smiled wryly, "Soon to the dismay of the very countries that originally sponsored bringing her into the modern world. By 1894 she was able to wage a successful war against China and by 1904 she took on and trounced Czarist Russia. In a period of thirty-five years she had advanced from feudalism to a world power."

Joe Chessman took his turn. He said obdurately, "Your paternalistic guidance, given an un-controlled competitive system, doesn't always work out. Take India after she gained independence from England. She tried to industrialize and had the support of the free nations. But what happened?"

Plekhanov leaned forward to take the ball. "Yes! There's your classic example. Compare India and China. China had a planned industrial development. None of this free competition nonsense. In ten years time they had startled the world with their advances. In twenty years —"

"Yes," Stevens said softly, "but at what price?"

Plekhanov turned on him. "At any price!" he roared. "In one generation they left behind the China of famine, flood, illiteracy, war lords and all the misery that had been China's through-out history."

Stevens said mildly, "Whether in their admitted advances they left behind all the misery that had been China's is debatable, sir."

Plekhanov began to bellow an angry retort but Amschel Mayer popped suddenly to his feet and lifted a hand to quiet the others. "Our solution has just come to me!"

Plekhanov glowered at him.

Mayer said excitedly, "Remember what the Co-ordinator told us? This expedition of ours is the first of its type. Even though we fail, the very mistakes we make will be invaluable. Our task is to learn how to bring backward peoples into an industrialized culture in roughly half a century."

The messroom's occupants scowled at him. Thus far he'd said nothing new.

Mayer went on enthusiastically. "Thus far in our debates we've had two basic suggestions on procedure. I have advocated a system of free competition; my learned colleague has been of the opinion that a strong state and a planned, not to say totalitarian, economy would be the quicker." He paused dramatically. "Very well, I am in favor of trying them both."

They regarded him blankly.

He said with impatience, "There are two planets, at different ethnic periods it is true, but not so far apart as all that. Fine, eight of us will take Genoa and eight Texcoco."

Plekhanov rumbled, "Fine, indeed. But which group will have the use of the *Pedagogue* with its library, its laboratories, its shops, its weapons?"

For a moment, Mayer was stopped but Joe Chessman growled, "That's no problem. Leave her in orbit around Rigel. We've got two small boats with which to ferry back and forth. Each group could have the use of her facilities any time they wished."

"I suppose we could have periodic conferences," Plekhanov said. "Say once every decade to compare notes and make further plans, if necessary."

Natt Roberts was worried. "We had no such instructions from the Co-ordinator. Dividing our forces like that."

Mayer cut him short. "My dear Roberts, we were given *carte blanche*. It is up to us to decide procedure. Actually, this system realizes twice the information such expeditions as ours might ordinarily offer."

"Texcoco for me," Plekhanov grumbled, accepting the plan in its whole. "The more backward of the two, but under my guidance in half a century it will be the more advanced, mark me."

"Look here," Martin Gunther said. "Do we have two of each of the basic specialists, so that we can divide the party in such a way that neither planet will miss out in any one field?"

Amschel Mayer was beaming at the reception of his scheme. "The point is well taken, my dear Martin, however you'll recall that our training was deliberately made such that each man spreads over several fields. This in case, during our half century without contact, one or more of us meets with accident. Besides, the *Pedagogue's* library is such that any literate can soon become effective in any field to the extent needed on the Rigel planets."

III.

Joe Chessman was at the controls of the space lighter. At his side sat Leonid Plekhanov and behind them the other six members of their team. They had circled Texcoco twice at great altitude, four times at a lesser one. Now they were low enough to spot man-made works.

"Nomadic," Plekhanov muttered. "Nomadic and village cultures."

"A few dozen urbanized cultures," Chessman said. "Whoever compared the most advanced nation to the Aztecs was accurate, except for the fact that they base themselves along a river rather than on a mountain plateau."

Plekhanov said, "Similarities to the Egyptians and Sumerians." He looked over his beefy shoulder at the technician who was photographing the areas over which they passed. "How does our geographer progress, Roberts?"

Natt Roberts brought his eyes up from his camera viewer. "I've got most of what we'll need for a while, sir."

Plekhanov turned back to Chessman. "We might as well head for their principal city, the one with the pyramids. We'll make initial contact there. I like the suggestion of surplus labor available."

"Surplus labor?" Chessman said, setting the controls. "How do you know?"

"Pyramids," Plekhanov rumbled. "I've always been of the opinion that such projects as pyramids, whether they be in Yucatan or Egypt, are make-work affairs. A priesthood, or other ruling clique, keeping its people busy and hence out of mischief."

Chessman adjusted a speed lever and settled back. "I can see their point."

"But I don't agree with it," Plekhanov said ponderously. "A society that builds pyramids is a static one. For that matter any society that resorts to make-work projects to busy its citizenry has something basically wrong."

Joe Chessman said sourly, "I wasn't supporting the idea, just understanding the view of the priesthoods. They'd made a nice thing for themselves and didn't want to see anything happen to it. It's not the only time a group in the saddle has held up progress for the sake of remaining there. Priests, slave-owners, feudalistic barons, or bureaucrats of a twentieth-century police state, a ruling clique will never give up power without pressure."

Barry Watson leaned forward and pointed down and to the right. "There's the river," he said. "And there's their capital city."

The small spacecraft settled at decreasing speed.

Chessman said, "The central square? It seems to be their market, by the number of people."

"I suppose so," Plekhanov grunted. "Right there before the largest pyramid. We'll remain inside the craft for the rest of today and tonight."

Natt Roberts, who had put away his camera, said, "But why? It's crowded in here."

"Because I said so," Plekhanov rumbled. "This first impression is important. Our flying machine is undoubtedly the first they've seen. We've got to give them time to assimilate the idea and then get together a welcoming committee. We'll want the top men, right from the beginning."

"The equivalent of the Emperor Montezuma meeting Cortez, eh?" Barry Watson said. "A real red carpet welcome."

The *Pedagogue's* space lighter settled to the plaza gently, some fifty yards from the ornately decorated pyramid which stretched up several hundred feet and was topped by a small temple-like building.

Chessman stretched and stood up from the controls. "Your anthropology ought to be better than that, Barry," he said. "There was no Emperor Montezuma and no Aztec Empire, except in the minds of the Spanish." He peered out one of the heavy ports. "And by the looks of this town we'll find an almost duplicate of Aztec society. I don't believe they've even got the wheel."

The eight of them clustered about the craft's portholes, taking in the primitive city that surrounded them. The square had emptied at their approach, and now the several thousand citizens that had filled it were peering fearfully from street entrances and alleyways.

Cogswell, a fiery little technician, said, "Look at them! It'll take hours before they drum up enough courage to come any closer. You were right, doctor. If we left the boat now, we'd make fools of ourselves trying to coax them near enough to talk."

Watson said to Joe Chessman "What do you mean, no Emperor Montezuma?"

Chessman said absently, as he watched, "When the Spanish got to Mexico they didn't understand what they saw, being musclemen rather than scholars. And before competent witnesses came on the scene, Aztec society was destroyed. The conquistadors, who did attempt to describe Tenochtitlán, misinterpreted it. They were from a feudalistic world and tried to portray the Aztecs in such terms. For instance, the large Indian community houses they thought were palaces. Actually, Montezuma was a democratically elected war chief of a confederation of three tribes which militarily dominated most of the Mexican valley. There was no empire because Indian society, being based on the clan, had no method of assimilating newcomers. The Aztec armies could loot and they could capture prisoners for their sacrifices, but they had no system of bringing their conquered enemies into the nation. They hadn't reached that far in the evolution of society. The Incas could have taught them a few lessons."

Plekhanov nodded. "Besides, the Spanish were fabulous liars. In Cortez's attempt to impress Spain's king, he built himself up far beyond reality. To read his reports you'd think the pueblo of Mexico had a population pushing a million. Actually, if it had thirty thousand it was doing well. Without a field agriculture and with their primitive transport, they must have been hard put to feed even that large a town."

A tall, militarily erect native strode from one of the streets that debouched into the plaza and approached to within twenty feet of the space boat. He stared at it for at least ten full minutes then spun on his heel and strode off again in the direction of one of the stolidly built stone buildings that lined the square on each side except that which the pyramid dominated.

Cogswell chirped, "Now that he's broken the ice, in a couple of hours kids will be scratching their names on our hull."

* * * * *

In the morning, two or three hours after dawn, they made their preparations to disembark. Of them all, only Leonid Plekhanov was unarmed. Joe Chessman had a heavy handgun holstered at his waist. The rest of the men carried submachine guns. More destructive weapons were hardly called for, nor available for that matter; once world government had been established on Earth the age-old race for improved arms had fallen away.

Chessman assumed command of the men, growled brief instructions. "If there's any difficulty, remember we're civilizing a planet of nearly a billion population. The life or death of a few individuals is meaningless. Look at our position scientifically, dispassionately. If it becomes necessary to use force-we have the right and the might to back it up. MacBride, you stay with the ship. Keep the hatch closed and station yourself at the fifty-caliber gun."

The natives seemed to know intuitively that the occupants of the craft from the sky would present themselves at this time. Several thousands of them crowded the plaza. Warriors, armed with spears and bronze headed war clubs, kept the more adventurous from crowding too near.

The hatch opened, the steel landing stair snaked out, and the hefty Plekhanov stepped down, closely followed by Chessman. The others brought up the rear, Watson, Roberts, Stevens, Hawkins and Cogswell. They had hardly formed a compact group at the foot of the spacecraft than the ranks of the natives parted and what was obviously a delegation of officials approached them. In the fore was a giant of a man in his late middle years, and at his side a cold-visaged duplicate of him, obviously a son.

Behind these were variously dressed others, military, priesthood, local officials, by their appearance.

Ten feet from the newcomers they stopped. The leader said in quite understandable Amer-English, "I am Taller, Khan of all the People. Our legends tell of you. You must be from First Earth." He added with a simple dignity, a quiet gesture, "Welcome to the World. How may we serve you?"

Plekhanov said flatly, "The name of this planet is Texcoco and the inhabitants shall henceforth be called Texcocans. You are correct, we have come from Earth. Our instructions are to civilize you, to bring you the benefits of the latest technology, to prepare you to enter the community of planets." Phlegmatically he let his eyes go to the pyramids, to the temples, the large community dwelling quarters. "We'll call this city Tula and its citizens Tulans."

Taller looked thoughtfully at him, not having missed the tone of arrogant command. One of the group behind the Khan, clad in gray flowing robes, said to Plekhanov, mild reproof in his voice, "My son, we are the most advanced people on ...Texcoco. We have thought of ourselves as civilized. However, we —"

Plekhanov rumbled, "I am not your son, old man, and you are far short of civilization. We can't stand here forever. Take us to a building where we can talk without these crowds staring at us. There is much to be done."

Taller said, "This is Mynor, Chief Priest of the People."

The priest bowed his head, then said, "The People are used to ceremony on outstanding occasions. We have arranged for suitable sacrifices to the gods. At their completion, we will proclaim a festival. And then—"

The warriors had cleared a way through the multitude to the pyramid and now the Earthlings could see a score of chained men and women, nude save for loin cloths and obviously captives.

Plekhanov made his way toward them, Joe Chessman at his right and a pace to the rear. The prisoners stood straight and, considering their position, with calm.

Plekhanov glared at Taller. "You were going to kill these?"

The Khan said reasonably, "They are not of the People. They are prisoners taken in battle."

Mynor said, "Their lives please the gods."

"There are no gods, as you probably know," Plekhanov said flatly. "You will no longer sacrifice prisoners."

A hush fell on the Texcocans. Joe Chessman let his hand drop to his weapon. The movement was not lost on Taller's son, whose eyes narrowed.

The Khan looked at the burly Plekhanov for a long moment. He said slowly, "Our institutions fit our needs. What would you have us do with these people? They are our enemies. If we turn them loose, they will fight us again. If we keep them imprisoned, they will eat our food. We ...Tulans are not poor, we have food aplenty, for we Tulans, but we cannot feed all the thousands of prisoners we take in our wars."

Joe Chessman said dryly, "As of today there is a new policy. We put them to work."

Plekhanov rumbled at him, "I'll explain our position, Chessman, if you please." Then to the Tulans. "To develop this planet we're going to need the labor of every man, woman and child capable of work."

Taller said, "Perhaps your suggestion that we retire to a less public place is desirable. Will you follow?" He spoke a few words to an officer of the warriors, who shouted orders.

* * * * *

The Khan led the way, Plekhanov and Chessman followed side by side and the other Earthlings, their weapons unostentatiously ready, were immediately behind. Mynor the priest, Taller's son and the other Tulan officials brought up the rear.

In what was evidently the reception hall of Taller's official residence, the newcomers were made as comfortable as fur padded low stools provided. Half a dozen teenaged Tulans brought a cool drink similar to cocoa; it seemed to give a slight lift.

Taller had not become Khan of the most progressive nation on Texcoco by other than his own abilities. He felt his way carefully now. He had no manner of assessing the powers wielded by these strangers from space. He had no intention of precipitating a situation in which he would discover such powers to his sorrow.

He said carefully, "You have indicated that you intend major changes in the lives of the People."

"Of all Texcocans," Plekhanov said, "you Tulans are merely the beginning."

Mynor, the aged priest, leaned forward. "But why? We do not want these changes-whatever they may be. Already the Khan has allowed you to interfere with our worship of our gods. This will mean —"

Plekhanov growled, "Be silent, old man, and don't bother to mention, ever again, your so-called gods. And now, all of you listen. Perhaps some of this will not be new, how much history has come down to you I don't know.

"A thousand years ago a colony of one hundred persons was left here on Texcoco. It will one day be of scholarly interest to trace them down through the centuries but at present the task does not interest us. This expedition has been sent to recontact you, now that you have populated Texcoco and made such adaptations as were necessary to survive here. Our basic task is to modernize your society, to bring it to an industrialized culture."

Plekhanov's eyes went to Taller's son. "I assume you are a soldier?"

Taller said, "This is Reif, my eldest, and by our custom, second in command of the People's armies. As Khan, I am first."

Reif nodded coldly to Plekhanov. "I am a soldier." He hesitated for a moment, then added, "And willing to die to protect the People."

"Indeed," Plekhanov rumbled, "as a soldier you will be interested to know that our first step will involve the amalgamation of all the nations and tribes of this planet. Not a small task. There should be opportunity for you."

Taller said, "Surely you speak in jest. The People have been at war for as long as scribes have records and never have we been stronger than today, never larger. To conquer the world! Surely you jest."

Plekhanov grunted ungraciously. He looked to Barry Watson, a lanky youth, now leaning negligently against the wall, his submachine gun, however, at the easy ready. "Watson, you're our military expert. Have you any opinions as yet?"

"Yes, sir," Watson said easily. "Until we can get iron weapons and firearms into full production, I suggest the Macedonian phalanx for their infantry. They have the horse, but evidently the wheel has gone out of use. We'll introduce the chariot and also heavy carts to speed up logistics. We'll bring in the stirruped saddle, too. I have available for study, works on every cavalry leader from Tamerlane to Jeb Stuart. Yes, sir, I have some ideas."

Plekhanov pursed his heavy lips. "From the beginning we're going to need manpower on a scale never dreamed of locally. We'll adopt a policy of expansion. Those who join us freely will become members of the State with full privileges. Those who resist will be made prisoners of war and used for shock labor on the roads and in the mines. However, a man works better if he has a goal, a dream. Each prisoner will be freed and become a member of the State after ten years of such work."

He turned to his subordinates. "Roberts and Hawkins, you will begin tomorrow to seek the nearest practical sources of iron ore and coal. Wherever you discover them we'll direct our first military expeditions. Chessman and Cogswell, you'll assemble their best artisans and begin their training in such basic advancements as the wheel."

Taller said softly, "You speak of advancement but thus far you have mentioned largely war and on such a scale that I wonder how many of the People will survive. What advancement? We have all we wish."

Plekhanov cut him off with a curt motion of his hand. He indicated the hieroglyphics on the chamber's walls. "How long does it take to learn such writing?"

Mynor, the priest, said, "This is a mystery known only to the priesthood. One spends ten years in preparation to be a scribe."

"We'll teach you a new method which will have every citizen of the State reading and writing within a year."

The Tulans gaped at him.

He moved ponderously over to Roberts, drew from its scabbard the sword bayonet the other had at his hip. He took it and slashed savagely at a stone pillar, gouging a heavy chunk from it. He tossed the weapon to Reif, whose eyes lit up.

"What metals have you been using? Copper, bronze? Probably. Well, that's steel. You're going to move into the iron age overnight."

He turned to Taller. "Are your priests also in charge of the health of your people?" he growled. "Are their cures obtained from mumbo-jumbo and a few herbs found in the desert? Within a decade, I'll guarantee you that not one of your major diseases will remain."

He turned to the priest and said, "Or perhaps this will be the clincher for some of you. How many years do you have, *old man?*"

Mynor said with dignity, "I am sixty-four."

Plekhanov said churlishly, "And I am two hundred and thirty-three." He called to Stevens, "I think you're our youngest. How old are you?"

Stevens grinned, "Hundred and thirteen, next month."

Mynor opened his mouth, closed it again. No man but would prolong his youth. Of a sudden he felt old, old.

Plekhanov turned back to Taller. "Most of the progress we have to offer is beyond your capacity to understand. We'll give you freedom from want. Health. We'll give you advances in every art. We'll eventually free every citizen from drudgery, educate him, give him the opportunity to enjoy intellectual curiosity. We'll open the stars to him. All these things the coming of the State will eventually mean to you."

Tula's Khan was not impressed. "This you tell us, man from First Earth. But to achieve these you plan to change every phase of our lives and we are happy with ... Tula ... the way it is. I say this to you. There are but eight of you and many, many of us. We do not want your ... State. Return from whence you came."

Plekhanov shook his massive head at the other. "Whether or not *you* want these changes they will be made. If you fail to co-operate, we will find someone who will. I suggest you make the most of it."

Taller arose from the squat stool upon which he'd been seated. "I have listened and I do not like what you have said. I am Khan of all the People. Now leave in peace, or I shall order my warriors..."

"Joe," Plekhanov said flatly. "Watson!"

Joe Chessman took his heavy gun from its holster and triggered it twice. The roar of the explosions reverberated thunderously in the confined space, deafening all, and terrifying the Tulans. Bright red colored the robes the Khan wore, colored them without beauty. Bright red splattered the floor.

Leonid Plekhanov stared at his second in command, wet his thick lips. "Joe," he sputtered. "I hadn't ... I didn't expect you to be so ... hasty."

Joe Chessman growled, "We've got to let them know where we stand, right now, or they'll never hold still for us. Cover the doors, Watson, Roberts." He motioned to the others with his head. "Cogswell, Hawkins, Stevens, get to those windows and watch."

Taller was a crumbled heap on the floor. The other Texcocans stared at his body in shocked horror.

All expect Reif.

Reif bent down over his father's body for a moment, and then looked up, his lips white, at Plekhanov. "He is dead."

Leonid Plekhanov collected himself. "Yes."

Reif's cold face was expressionless. He looked at Joe Chessman who stood stolidly to one side, gun still in hand.

Reif said, "You can supply such weapons to my armies?"

Plekhanov said, "That is our intention, in time."

Reif came erect. "Subject to the approval of the clan leaders, I am now Khan. Tell me more of this State of which you have spoken."

IV.

The sergeant stopped the small company about a quarter of a mile from the city of Bari. His detachment numbered only ten but they were well armed with short swords and blunderbusses and wore mail and steel helmets. On the face of it, they would have been a match for ten times this number of merchants.

It was hardly noon but the sergeant had obviously already been at his wine flask. He leered at them. "And where do you think you go?"

The merchant who led the rest was a thin little man but he was richly robed and astride a heavy black mare. He said, "To Bari, soldier." He drew a paper from a pouch. "I hold this permission from Baron Mannerheim to pass through his lands with my people and chattels."

The leer turned mercenary. "Unfortunately, city man, I can't read. What do you carry on the mules?"

"Personal property, which, I repeat, I have permission to transport over Baron Mannerheim's lands free from harassment from his followers." He added, in irritation, "The baron is a friend of mine, fond of the gifts I give him."

One of the soldiers grunted his skepticism, checked the flint on the lock of his piece, then looked at the sergeant suggestively.

The sergeant said, "As you say, merchant, my lord the baron is fond of gifts. Aren't we all? Unfortunately, I have received no word of your group. My instructions are to stop all intruders upon the baron's lands and, if there is resistance, to slay them and confiscate such properties as they may be carrying."

The merchant sighed and reached into a small pouch. The eyes of the sergeant drooped in greed. The hand emerged with two small coins. "As you say," the merchant muttered bitterly, "we are all fond of gifts. Will you do me the honor to drink my health at the tavern tonight?"

The sergeant said nothing, but his mouth slackened and he fondled the hilt of his sword.

The merchant sighed again and dipped once more into the pouch. This time his hand emerged with half a dozen bits of silver. He handed them down to the other, complaining, "How can a man profit in his affairs if every few miles he must pass another outstretched hand?"

The sergeant growled, "You do not seem to starve, city man. Now, on your way. You are fortunate I am too lazy today to bother going through your things. Besides," and he grinned widely, "the baron gave me personal instructions not to bother you."

The merchant snorted, kicked his heels into his beast's sides and led his half dozen followers toward the city. The soldiers looked after them and howled their amusement. The money was enough to keep them soused for days.

When they were out of earshot, Amschel Mayer grinned his amusement back over his shoulder at Jerome Kennedy. "How'd that come off, Jerry?"

The other sniffed, in mock deprecation. "You're beginning to fit into the local merchant pattern better than the real thing. However, just for the record, I had this, ah, grease gun, trained on them all the time."

Mayer frowned. "Only in extreme emergency, my dear Jerry. The baron would be up in arms if he found a dozen of his men massacred on the outskirts of Bari, and we don't want a showdown at this stage. It's taken nearly a year to build this part we act."

At this time of day the gates of the port city were open and the guards lounged idly. Their captain recognized Amschel Mayer and did no more than nod respectfully.

They wended their way through narrow, cobblestoned streets, avoiding the crowds in the central market area. They pulled up eventually before a house both larger and more ornate than its neighbors. Mayer and Kennedy dismounted from the horses and left their care to the others.

Mayer beat with the heavy knocker on the door and a slot opened for a quick check of his identity. The door opened wide and Technician Martin Gunther let them in.

"The others are here already?" Mayer asked him.

Gunther nodded. "Since breakfast. Baron Leonar, in particular, is impatient."

Mayer said over his shoulder, "All right, Jerry, this is where we put it to them."

They entered the long conference room. A full score of men sat about the heavy wooden table. Most of them were as richly garbed as their host. Most of them in their middle years. All of them alert of eye. All of them confidently at ease.

* * * * *

Amschel Mayer took his place at the table's end and Jerome Kennedy sank into the chair next to him. Mayer took the time to speak to each of his guests individually, then he leaned back and took in the gathering as a whole. He said, "You probably realize that this group consists of the twenty most powerful merchants on the continent."

Olderman nodded. "We have been discussing your purpose in bringing us together, Honorable Mayer. All of us are not friends." He twisted his face in amusement. "In fact, very few of us are friends."

"There is no need for you to be," Mayer said snappishly, "but all are going to realize the need for co-operation. Honorables, I've just come from the city of Ronda. Although I'd paid heavily in advance to the three barons whose lands I crossed. I had to bribe myself through a dozen road-blocks, had to pay exorbitant rates to cross three ferries, and once had to fight off supposed bandits."

One of his guests grumbled, "Who were actually probably soldiers of the local baron who had decided that although you had paid him transit fee, it still might be profitable to go through your goods."

Mayer nodded. "Exactly, my dear Honorable, and that is why we've gathered."

Olderman had evidently assumed spokesmanship for the others. Now he said warily, "I don't understand."

"Genoa, if you'll pardon the use of this name to signify the planet upon which we reside, will never advance until trade has been freed from these bandits who call themselves lords and barons."

Eyebrows reached for hairlines.

Olderman's eyes darted about the room, went to the doors. "Please," he said, "the servants."

"My servants are safe," Mayer said.

One of his guests was smiling without humor. "You seem to forget, Honorable Mayer, that I carry the title of baron."

Mayer shook his head. "No, Baron Leonar. But neither do you disagree with what I say. The businessman, the merchant, the manufacturer on Genoa today, is only tolerated. Were it not for the fact that the barons have no desire to eliminate such a profitable source of income, they would milk us dry overnight."

Someone shrugged. "That is the way of things. We are lucky to have wrested, bribed and begged as many favors from the lords as we have. Our twenty cities all have charters that protect us from complete despoilation."

Mayer twisted excitedly in his chair. "As of today, things begin to change. Jerry, that platen press."

Jerry Kennedy left the room momentarily and returned with Martin Gunther and two of the servants. While the assembled merchants looked on, in puzzled silence, Mayer's assistants set up the press and a stand holding two fonts of fourteen-point type. Jerry took up a printer's stick and gave running instructions as he demonstrated. Gunther handed around pieces of the type until all had examined it, while his colleague set up several lines. Kennedy transposed the lines to a chase, locked it up and placed the form to one side while he demonstrated inking the small press, which was operated by a foot pedal. He mounted the form in the press, took a score of sheets of paper and rapidly fed them, one by one. When they were all printed, he stopped pumping and Gunther handed the still wet finished product around to the audience.

Olderman stared down at the printed lines, scowled in concentration, wet his lips in sudden comprehension.

But it was merchant Russ who blurted, "This will revolutionize the inscribing of books. Why, it can well take it out of the hands of the Temple! With such a machine I could make a hundred books —"

Mayer was beaming. "Not a hundred, Honorable, but a hundred thousand!"

The others stared at him as though he was demented. "A hundred thousand," one said. "There are not that many literate persons on the continent."

"There will be," Mayer crowed. "This is but one of our levers to pry power from the barons. And here is another." He turned to Russ. "Honorable Russ, your city is noted for the fine quality of its steel, of the swords and armor you produce."

Russ nodded. He was a small man fantastically rich in his attire. "This is true, Honorable Mayer."

Mayer said, tossing a small booklet to the other, "I have here the plans for a new method of making steel from pig iron. The Bessemer method, we'll call it. The principle involved is the oxidation of the impurities in the iron by blowing air through the molten metal."

Amschel Mayer turned to still another. "And your town is particularly noted for its fine textiles." He looked to his assistants. "Jerry, you and Gunther bring in those models of the power loom and the spinning jenny."

While they were gone, he said, "My intention is to assist you to speed up production. With this in mind, you'll appreciate the automatic flying shuttle that we'll now demonstrate."

Kennedy and Gunther re-entered accompanied by four servants and a mass of equipment. Kennedy muttered to Amschel Mayer, "I feel like the instructor of a handicrafts class."

Half an hour later, Kennedy and Gunther wound up passing out pamphlets to the awed merchant guests. Kennedy said, "This booklet will give details on construction of the equipment and its operation."

Mayer pursed his lips. "Your people will be able to assimilate only so fast, so we won't push them. Later, you'll be interested in introducing the mule spinning frame, among other items."

He motioned for the servants to remove the printing press and textile machinery. "We now come to probably the most important of the devices I have to introduce to you today. Because of size and weight, I've had constructed only a model. Jerry!"

Jerry Kennedy brought to the heavy table a small steam engine, clever in its simplicity. He had half a dozen attachments for it. Within moments he had the others around him, as enthusiastic as a group of youngsters with a new toy.

"By the Supreme," Baron Leonar blurted, "do you realize this device could be used instead of waterpower to operate a mill to power the loom demonstrated an hour ago?"

Honorable Russ was rubbing the side of his face thoughtfully. "It might even be adapted to propel a coach. A coach without horses. Unbelievable!"

Mayer chuckled in excitement and clapped his hands. A servant entered with a toy wagon which had been slightly altered. Martin Gunther lifted the small engine, placed it in position atop the wagon, connected it quickly and threw a lever. The wagon moved smoothly forward, the first engine-propelled vehicle of Genoa's industrial revolution.

Martin Gunther smiled widely at Russ. "You mean like this, Honorable?"

Half an hour later they were re-seated, before each of them a small pile of pamphlets, instructions, plans, blueprints.

Mayer said, "I have just one more device to bring to your attention at this time. I wish it were unnecessary but I am afraid otherwise."

He held up for their inspection, a forty-five-caliber bullet. Jerry Kennedy handed around samples to the merchants. They fingered them in puzzlement.

"Honorables," Mayer said, "the barons have the use of gunpowder. Muskets and muzzleloading cannon are available to them both for their wars against each other and their occasional attacks upon our supposedly independent cities. However, this is an advancement on their weapons. This unit includes not only the bullet's lead, but the powder and the cap which will explode it."

They lacked understanding, and showed it.

Mayer said, "Jerry, if you'll demonstrate."

Jerry Kennedy said, "The bullet can be adapted to various weapons, however, this is one of the simplest." He pressed, one after another, a full twenty rounds into the gun's clip.

"Now, if you'll note the silhouette of a man I've drawn on the wooden frame at the end of the room." He pressed the trigger, sent a single shot into the figure.

Olderman nodded. "An improvement in firearms. But —"

Kennedy said, "However, if you are confronted with more than one of the bad guys." He grinned and flicked the gun to full automatic and in a Götterdämmerung of sound in the confines of the room, emptied the clip into his target sending splinters and chips flying and all but demolishing the wooden backdrop.

His audience sat back in stunned horror at the demonstration.

Mayer said now, "The weapon is simple to construct, any competent gunsmith can do it. It is manifest, Honorables, that with your people so equipped your cities will be safe from attack and so will trading caravans and ships."

Russ said shakily, "Your intention is good, Honorable Mayer, however it will be but a matter of time before the barons have solved the secrets of your weapon. Such cannot be held indefinitely. Then we would again be at their mercy."

"Believe me, Honorable," Mayer said dryly, "by that time I will have new weapons to introduce, if necessary. Weapons that make this one a very toy in comparison."

Olderman resumed his office as spokesman. "This demonstration has astounded us, Honorable Mayer, but although we admire your abilities it need hardly be pointed out that it seems unlikely all this could be the product of one brain."

"They are not mine," Mayer admitted. "They are the products of many minds."

"But where —?"

The Earthman shook his head. "I don't believe I will tell you now."

"I see." The Genoese eyed him emotionlessly. "Then the question becomes, *why?*"

Mayer said, "It may be difficult for you to see, but the introduction of each of these will be a nail in feudalism's coffin. Each will increase either production or trade and such increase will lead to the overthrow of feudal society."

Baron Leonar, who had remained largely silent throughout the afternoon, now spoke up. "As you said earlier, although I am a lord myself, my interests are your own. I am a merchant first. However, I am not sure I want the changes these devices will bring. Frankly, Honorable Mayer, I am satisfied with my world as I find it today."

Amschel Mayer smiled wryly at him. "I am afraid you *must* adapt to these new developments."

The baron said coldly, "Why? I do not like to be told I must do something."

"Because, my dear baron, there are three continents on the planet of Genoa. At present there is little trade due to inadequate shipping. But the steam engine I introduce today will soon propel larger craft than you have ever built before."

Russ said, "What has this to do with our being forced to use these devices?"

"Because I have colleagues on the other continents busily introducing them. If you don't adapt, in time competitors will invade your markets, capture your trade, drive you out of business."

Mayer wrapped it up. "Honorables, modernize or go under. It's each man for himself and the devil take the hindmost, if you'll allow a saying from another era."

They remained silent for a long period. Finally Olderman stated bluntly, "The barons are not going to like this."

Jerry Kennedy grinned. "Obviously, that's why we've introduced you to the tommy gun. It's not going to make any difference if they like it or not."

Russ said musingly, "Pressure will be put to prevent the introduction of this equipment."

"We'll meet it," Mayer said, shifting happily in his seat.

Russ added, "The Temple is ever on the side of the barons. The monks will fight against innovations that threaten to disturb the present way."

Mayer said, "Monks usually do. How much property is in the hands of the Temple?"

Russ admitted sourly, "The monks are the greatest landlords of all. I would say at least one third of the land and the serfs belong to the Temple."

"Ah," Mayer said. "We must investigate the possibilities of a Reformation. But that can come later. Now I wish to expand on my reason for gathering you.

"Honorables, Genoa is to change rapidly. To survive, you will have to move fast. I have not introduced these revolutionary changes without self-interest. Each of you are free to use them to his profit, however, I expect a thirty per cent interest."

There was a universal gasp.

Olderman said, "Honorable Mayer, you have already demonstrated your devices. What is there to prevent us from playing you false?"

Mayer laughed. "My dear Olderman, I have other inventions to reveal as rapidly as you develop the technicians, the workers, capable of building and operating them. If you cheat me now, you will be passed by next time."

Russ muttered, "Thirty per cent! Your wealth will be unbelievable."

"As fast as it accumulates, Honorables, it shall be invested. For instance, I have great interest in expanding our inadequate universities. The advances I expect will only be possible if we educate the people. Field serfs are not capable of running even that simple steam engine Jerry demonstrated."

Baron Leonar said, "What you contemplate is mind-shaking. Do I understand that you wish a confederation of all our cities? A joining together to combat the strength of the present lords?"

Mayer was shaking his head. "No, no. As the barons lose power, each of your cities will strengthen and possibly expand to become nations. Perhaps some will unite. But largely you will compete against each other and against the nations of the other continents. In such competition you'll have to show your mettle, or go under. Man develops at his fastest when pushed by such circumstance."

The Earthling looked off, unseeing, into a far corner of the room. "At least, so is my contention. Far away from here a colleague is trying to prove me wrong. We shall see."

V.

Leonid Plekhanov returned to the *Pedagogue* with a certain ceremony. He was accompanied by Joe Chessman, Natt Roberts and Barry Watson of his original group, but four young, hard-eyed, hard-faced and armed Tulans were also in the party. Their space lighter swooped in, nestled to the *Pedagogue's* hull in the original bed it had occupied on the trip from Terra City, and her port opened to the corridors of the mother ship.

Plekhanov, flanked by Chessman and Watson, strode heavily toward the ship's lounge. Natt Roberts and two of the Tulans remained with the small boat. Two of the other natives followed, their eyes darting here, there, in amazement, in spite of their efforts to appear grim and untouched by it all.

Amschel Mayer was already seated at the officer's dining table. His face displayed his irritation at the other's method of presenting himself. "Good Heavens, Plekhanov, what is this, an invasion?"

The other registered surprise.

Mayer indicated the Texcocans. "Do you think it necessary to bring armed men aboard the *Pedagogue*? Frankly, I have not even revealed to a single Genoese the existence of the ship."

Jerry Kennedy was seated to one side, the only member of Mayer's team who had accompanied him for this meeting. Kennedy winked at Watson and Chessman. Watson grinned back but held his peace.

Plekhanov sank into a chair, rumbling, "We hold no secrets from the Texcocans. The sooner they advance to where they can use our libraries and laboratories, the better. And the fact these boys are armed has no significance. My Tulans are currently embarked on a campaign to unite the planet. Arms are sometimes necessary, and Tula, my capital, is somewhat of an armed camp. All able-bodied men —"

Mayer broke in heatedly, "And is this the method you use to bring civilization to Texcoco? Is this what you consider the purpose of the Office of Galactic Colonization? An armed camp! How many persons have you slaughtered thus far?"

"Easy," Joe Chessman growled.

Amschel Mayer spun on him. "I need no instruction from you, Chessman. Please remember I'm senior in charge of this expedition and as such rank you."

Plekhanov thudded a heavy hand on the table. "I'll call my assistants to order, Mayer, if I feel it necessary. Admittedly, when this expedition left Terra City you were the ranking officer. Now, however, we've divided-at your suggestion, please remember. Now there are two independent groups and you no longer have jurisdiction over mine."

"Indeed!" Mayer barked. "And suppose I decide to withhold the use of the *Pedagogue's* libraries and laboratories to you? I tell you, Plekhanov —"

Leonid Plekhanov interrupted him coldly. "I would not suggest you attempt any such step, Mayer."

Mayer glared but suddenly reversed himself. "Let's settle down and become more sensible. This is the first conference of the five we have scheduled. Ten years have elapsed. Actually, of course, we've had some idea of each other's progress since team members occasionally meet on trips back here to the *Pedagogue* to consult the library. I am afraid, my dear Leonid, that your theories on industrialization are rapidly being proven inaccurate."

"Nonsense!"

Mayer said smoothly, "In the decade past, my team's efforts have more than tripled the Genoese industrial potential. Last week one of our steamships crossed the second ocean. We've located petroleum and the first wells are going down. We've introduced a dozen crops that had disappeared through misadventure to the original colonists. And, oh yes, our first railroad is scheduled to begin running between Bari and Ronda next spring. There are six new universities and in the next decade I expect fifty more."

"Very good, indeed," Plekhanov grumbled.

"Only a beginning. The breath of competition, of unharnessed enterprise is sweeping Genoa. Feudalism crumbles. Customs, mores and traditions that have held up progress for a century or more are now on their way out."

Joe Chessman growled, "Some of the boys tell me you've had a few difficulties with this crumbling feudalism thing. In fact, didn't Buchwald barely escape with his life when the barons on your western continent united to suppress all chartered cities?"

Mayer's thin face darkened. "Never fear, my dear Joseph, those barons responsible for shedding the blood of western hemisphere elements of progress will shortly pay for their crimes."

"You've got military problems too, then?" Barry Watson asked.

Mayer's eyes went to him in irritation. "Some of the free cities of Genoa are planning measures to regain their property and rights on the western hemisphere. This has nothing to do with my team, except, of course, in so far as they might sell them supplies or equipment."

The lanky Watson laughed lowly, "You mean like selling them a few quick-firing breech-loaders and trench mortars?"

Plekhanov muttered, "That'll be enough, Barry."

But Mayer's eyes had widened. "How did you know?" He whirled on Plekhanov. "You're spying on my efforts, trying to negate my work!"

Plekhanov rumbled, "Don't be a fool, Mayer. My team has neither the time nor interest to spy on you."

"Then how did you know—"

Barry Watson said mildly, "I was doing some investigation in the ship's library. I ran into evidence that you people had already used the blueprints for breech-loaders and mortars."

Jerry Kennedy came to his feet and rambled over to the messroom's bar. "This seems to be all out spat, rather than a conference to compare progress," he said. "Anybody for a drink? Frankly, that's the next thing I'm going to introduce to Genoa, some halfway decent likker. Do you know what those benighted heathens drink now?"

Watson grinned. "Make mine whisky, Jerry. You've no complaints. Our benighted heathens have a national beverage fermented from a plant similar to cactus. Ought to be drummed out of the human race."

He spoke idly, forgetful of the Tulan guards stationed at the doorway.

* * * * *

Kennedy passed drinks around for everyone save Mayer, who shook his head in distaste. If only for a brief spell, some of the tenseness left the air while the men from Earth sipped their beverages.

Jerry Kennedy said, "Well, you've heard our report. How go things on Texcoco?"

"According to plan," Plekhanov rumbled.

Mayer snorted.

Plekhanov said ungraciously, "Our prime effort is now the uniting of the total population into one strong whole, a super-state capable of accomplishing the goals set us by the Co-ordinator."

Mayer sneered, "Undoubtedly, this goal of yours, this super-state, is being established by force."

"Not always," Joe Chessman said. "Quite a few of the tribes join up on their own. Why not? The State has a lot to offer."

"Such as what?" Kennedy said mildly.

Chessman looked at him in irritation. "Such as advanced medicine, security from famine, military protection from more powerful nations. The opportunity for youth to get an education and find advancement in the State's government-if they've got it on the ball."

"And what happens if they don't *have it on the ball?*"

Chessman growled, "What happens to such under any society? They get the dirty-end-of-the-stick jobs." His eyes went from Kennedy to Mayer. "Are you suggesting you offer anything better?"

Mayer said, "Already on most of Genoa it is a matter of free competition. The person with ability is able to profit from it."

Joe Chessman grunted sour amusement. "Of course, it doesn't help to be the son of a wealthy merchant or a big politician."

Plekhanov took over. "In *any* society the natural leaders come to the top in much the same manner as the big ones come to the top in a bin of potatoes, they just work their way up."

Jerry Kennedy finished his drink and said easily, "At least, those at the top can claim they're the biggest potatoes. Remember back in the twentieth century when Hitler and his gang announced they were the big potatoes in Germany and men of Einstein's stature fled the country-being small potatoes, I suppose."

Amschel Mayer said, "We're getting away from the point. Pray go on, my dear Leonid. You say you are forcibly uniting all Texcoco."

"We are uniting all Texcoco," Plekhanov corrected with a scowl. "Not always by force. And that is by no means our only effort. We are ferreting out the most intelligent of the assimilated peoples and educating them as rapidly as possible. We've introduced iron..."

"And use it chiefly for weapons," Kennedy murmured.

"...Antibiotics and other medicines, a field agriculture, are rapidly building roads..."

"Military roads," Kennedy mused.

"...To all sections of the State, have made a beginning in naval science, and, of course, haven't ignored the arts."

"On the face of it," Mayer nodded, "hardly approaching Genoa."

Plekhanov rumbled indignantly, "We started two ethnic periods behind you. Even the Tulans were still using bronze, but the Genoese had iron and even gunpowder. Our advance is a bit slow to get moving, Mayer, but when it begins to roll —"

Mayer gave his characteristic snort. "A free people need never worry about being passed by a subjected one."

Barry Watson made himself another drink and while doing so looked over his shoulder at Amschel Mayer. "It's interesting the way you throw about that term *free*. Just what type of government do you sponsor?"

Mayer snapped, "Our team does not interfere in governmental forms, Watson. The various nations are free to adapt to whatever local conditions obtain. They range from some under feudalistic domination to countries with varying degrees of republican democracy. Our base of operations in the southern hemisphere is probably the most advanced of all the chartered cities, Barry. It amounts to a city-state somewhat similar to Florence during the Renaissance."

"And your team finds itself in the position of the Medici, I imagine."

"You might use that analogy. The Medici might have been, well, tyrants of Florence, dominating her finances and trade as well as her political government, but they were benevolent tyrants."

"Yeah," Watson grinned. "The thing about a benevolent tyranny, though, is that it's up to the tyrants to decide what's benevolent. I'm not so sure there's a great basic difference between your governing of Genoa and ours of Texcoco."

"Don't be an ass," Mayer snapped. "We are granting the Genoese political freedoms as fast as they can assimilate them."

Joe Chessman growled, "But I imagine it's surprising to find just how slowly they can assimilate. A moment ago you said they were free to form any government they wished. Now you say you feed them what you call freedom, only so fast as they can assimilate it."

"Obviously we encourage them along whatever path we think will most quickly develop their economies," Mayer argued. "That's what we've been sent here to do. We stimulate competition, encourage all progress, political as well as economic."

Plekhanov lumbered to his feet. "Amschel, obviously nothing new has been added to our respective positions by this conference. I propose we adjourn to meet again at the end of the second decade."

Mayer said, "I suppose it would be futile to suggest you give up this impossible totalitarian scheme of yours and reunite the expedition."

Plekhanov merely grunted his disgust.

Jerry Kennedy said, "One thing. What stand have you taken on giving your planet immortality?"

"Immortality?" Watson said. "We haven't it to give."

"You know what I mean. It wouldn't take long to extend the life span double or triple the present."

Amschel Mayer said, "At this stage progress is faster with the generations closer together. A man is pressed when he knows he has only twenty or thirty years of peak efficiency. We on Earth are inclined to settle back and take life as it comes; you younger men are all past the century mark, but none have bothered to get married as yet."

"Plenty of time for that," Watson grinned.

"That's what I mean. But a Texcocan or Genoese feels pressed to wed in his twenties, or earlier, to get his family under way."

"There's another element," Plekhanov muttered. "The more the natives progress the more nearly they'll equal our abilities. I wouldn't want anything to happen to our overall plans. As it is now, their abilities taper off at sixty and they reach senility at seventy or eighty. I think until the end we should keep it this way."

"A cold-blooded view," Kennedy said. "If we extended their life expectancy, their best men would live to be of additional use to planet development."

"But they would not have our dream," Plekhanov rumbled. "Such men might try to subvert us, and, just possibly, might succeed."

"I think Leonid is right," Mayer admitted with reluctance.

* * * * *

Later, in the space lighter heading back for Genoa, Mayer said speculatively, "Did you notice anything about Leonid Plekhanov?"

Kennedy was piloting. "He seems the same irascible old curmudgeon he's always been."

"It seems to me he's become a touch power mad. Could the pressures he's under cause his mind to slip? Obviously, all isn't peaches and cream in that attempt of his to achieve world government on Texcoco."

"Well," Kennedy muttered, "all isn't peaches and cream with us, either. The barons are far from licked, especially in the west." He changed the subject. "By the way, that banking deal went through in Pola. I was able to get control."

"Fine," Mayer chuckled. "You must be quite the richest man in the city. There is a certain stimulation in this financial game, Jerry, isn't there?"

"Uh huh," Jerry told him. "Of course, it doesn't hurt to have a marked deck."

"Marked deck?" the other frowned.

"It's handy that gold is the medium of exchange on Genoa," Jerry Kennedy said. "Especially in view of the fact that we have a machine on the ship capable of transmuting metals."

VI.

Leonid Plekhanov, Joseph Chessman, Barry Watson, Khan Reif and several of the Tulan army staff stood on a small knoll overlooking a valley of several square miles. A valley dominated on all sides but the sea by mountain ranges.

Reif and the three Earthlings were bent over a military map depicting the area. Barry Watson traced with his finger.

"There are only two major passes into this valley. We have this one, they dominate that."

Plekhanov was scowling, out of his element and knowing it. "How many men has Mynor been able to get together?"

Watson avoided looking into the older man's face. "Approximately half a million according to Hawkins' estimate. He flew over them this morning."

"Half a million!"

"Including the nomads, of course," Joe Chessman said. "The nomads fight more like a mob than an army."

Plekhanov was shaking his massive head. "Most of them will melt away if we continue to avoid battle. They can't feed that many men on the countryside. The nomads in particular will return home if they don't get a fight soon."

Watson hid his impatience. "That's the point, sir. If we don't break their power now, in a decisive defeat, we'll have them to fight again, later. And already they've got iron swords, the crossbow and even a few muskets. Given time and they'll all be so armed. Then the fat'll be in the fire."

"He's right," Joe Chessman said sourly.

Reif nodded his head. "We must finish them now, if we can. The task will be twice as great next year."

Plekhanov grumbled in irritation. "Half a million of them and something like forty thousand of our Tulans."

Reif corrected him. "Some thirty thousand Tulans, all infantrymen." He added, "And eight thousand allied cavalry only some of whom can be trusted." Reif's ten-year-old son came up next to him and peered down at the map.

"What's that child doing here?" Plekhanov snapped.

Reif looked into the other's face. "This is Taller Second, my son. You from First Earth have never bothered to study our customs. One of them is that a Khan's son participates in all battles his father does. It is his training."

Watson was pointing out features on the map again. "It will take three days for their full army to get in here." He added with emphasis, "In retreat, it would take them the same time to get out."

Plekhanov scowled heavily. "We can't risk it. If we were defeated, we have no reserve army. We'd have lost everything." He looked at Joe Chessman and Watson significantly. "We'd have to flee back to the *Pedagogue*."

Reif's face was expressionless.

Barry Watson looked at him. "We won't desert you, Reif, forget about that aspect of it."

Reif said, "I believe you, Barry Watson. You are a ... soldier."

Dick Hawkins' small biplane zoomed in, landed expertly at the knoll's foot. The occupant vaulted out and approached them at a half run.

Hawkins called as soon as he was within shouting distance. "They're moving in. Their advance cavalry units are already in the pass."

When he was with them, Plekhanov rubbed his hand nervously over heavy lips. He rumbled, "The cavalry, eh! Listen, Hawkins, get back there and dust them. Use the gas."

The pilot said slowly, "I have four bullet holes in my wings."

"Bullet holes!" Joe Chessman snapped.

Hawkins turned to him. "By the looks of things, MacBride's whole unit has gone over to the rebels. Complete with their double-barreled muskets. A full thousand of them."

Watson looked frigidly at Leonid Plekhanov. "You insisted on issuing guns to men we weren't sure of."

Plekhanov grumbled, "Confound it, don't use that tone of voice with me. We have to arm our men, don't we?"

Watson said, "Yes, but our still comparatively few advanced weapons shouldn't go into the hands of anybody but trusted citizens of the State, certainly not to a bunch of mercenaries. The only ones we can *really* trust even among the Tulans, are those that were kids when we first took over. The one's we've had time to indoctrinate."

"The mistake's made. It's too late now," Plekhanov said. "Hawkins go back and dust those cavalrymen as they come through the pass."

Reif said, "It was a mistake, too, to allow them the secret of the crossbow."

Plekhanov roared, "I didn't *allow* them anything. Once the crossbow was introduced it was just a matter of time before its method of construction got to the enemy."

"Then it shouldn't have been introduced," Reif said, his eyes unflinching from the Earthman's.

Plekhanov ignored him. He said, "Hawkins, get going on that dusting. Watson, pull what units we already have in this valley back through the pass we control. We'll avoid battle until more of their army has fallen away."

Hawkins said with deceptive mildness, "I just told you those cavalrymen have muskets. To fly low enough to use gas on them, I'd get within easy range. Point one, this is the only aircraft we've built. Point two, MacBride is probably dead, killed when those cavalrymen mutinied. Point three, I came on this expedition to help modernize the Texcocans, not to die in battle."

Plekhanov snarled at him. "Coward, eh?" He turned churlishly to Watson and Reif. "Start pulling back our units."

Barry Watson looked at Chessman. "Joe?"

Joe Chessman shook his head slowly. He said to Reif, "Khan, start bringing your infantry through the pass. Barry, we'll follow your plan of battle. We'll anchor one flank on the sea and concentrate what cavalry we can trust on the hills on the right. That's the bad spot, that right flank has to hold."

Plekhanov's thick lips trembled. He said in fury, "Is this insubordination?"

Reif turned on his heel and followed by young Taller and his staff hurried down the knoll to where their horses were tethered.

Chessman said to Hawkins, "If you've got the fuel, Dick, maybe it'd be a good idea to keep them under observation. Fly high enough, of course, to avoid gunfire."

Hawkins darted a look at Plekhanov, turned and hurried back to his plane.

Joe Chessman, his voice sullen, said to Plekhanov, "We can't afford any more mistakes, Leonid. We've had too many already." He said to Watson, "Be sure and let their cavalry units scout us out. Allow them to see that we're entering the valley too. They'll think they've got us trapped."

"They will have!" Plekhanov roared. "I countermand that order, Watson! We're withdrawing."

Barry Watson raised his eyebrows at Joe Chessman.

"Put him under arrest," Joe growled sourly. "We'll decide what to do about it later."

* * * * *

By the third day, Mynor's rebel and nomad army had filed through the pass and was forming itself into battle array. Rank upon rank upon rank.

The Tulan infantry had taken less than half a day to enter. They had camped and rested during the interval, the only action being on the part of the rival cavalry forces.

Now the thirty thousand Tulans went into their phalanx and began their march across the valley.

Joe Chessman, Hawkins, Roberts, Stevens and Khan Reif and several of his men again occupied the knoll which commanded a full view of the terrain. With binoculars and wrist radios from the *Pedagogue* they kept in contact with the battle.

Below, Barry Watson walked behind the advancing infantry. There were six divisions of five thousand men each, twenty-four foot *sarissas* stretched before their sixteen man deep line. Only the first few lines were able to extend their weapons; the rest gave weight and supplied replacements for the advanced lines' casualties. Behind them all the Tulan drums beat out the slow, inexorable march.

Cogswell, beside Watson with the wrist radio, said excitedly, "Here comes a cavalry charge, Barry. Reif says right behind it the nomad infantry is coming in." Cogswell cleared his throat. "All of them."

Watson held up a hand in signal to his officers. The phalanx ground to a halt, received the charge on the hedge of *sarissas*. The enemy cavalry wheeled and attempted to retreat to the flanks but were caught in a bloody confusion by the pressure of their own advancing infantry.

Cogswell, his ear to the radio, said, "Their main body of horse is hitting our right flank." He wet his lips. "We're outnumbered there something like ten to one. At least ten to one."

"They've got to hold," Watson said. "Tell Reif and Chessman that flank has to hold."

The enemy infantrymen in their hundreds of thousands hit the Tulan line in a clash of deafening military thunder. Barry Watson resumed his pacing. He signaled to the drummers who beat out another march. The phalanx moved forward slowly, and slowly went into an echelon formation, each division slightly ahead of the one following. Of necessity, the straight lines of the nomad and rebel front had to break.

The drums went *boom*, ah, *boom*, ah, *boom*, ah, *boom*.

The Tulan phalanx moved slowly, obliquely across the valley. The hedge of spears ruthlessly pressed the mass of enemy infantry before them.

The sergeants paced behind, shouting over the din. "Dress it up. You there, you've been hit, fall out to the rear."

"I'm all right," the wounded spearman snarled, battle lust in his voice.

"Fall out, I said," the sergeant roared. "You there, take his place."

The Tulan phalanx ground ahead.

One of the sergeants grinned wanly at Barry Watson as his men moved forward with the preciseness of the famed Rockettes of another era. "It's working," he said proudly.

Barry Watson snorted, "Don't give me credit. It belongs to a man named Philip of Macedon, a long ways away in both space and time."

Cogswell called, "Our right flank cavalry is falling back. Joe wants to know if you can send any support."

Watson's face went expressionless. "No," he said flatly. "It's got to hold. Tell Joe and the Khan it's got to hold. Suggest they throw in those cavalry units they're not sure of. The ones that threatened mutiny last week."

Joe Chessman stood on the knoll flanked by the Khan's ranking officers and the balance of the Earthmen. Natt Roberts was on the radio. He turned to the others and worriedly repeated the message.

Joe Chessman looked out over the valley. The thirty-thousand-man phalanx was pressing back the enemy infantry with the precision of a machine. He looked up the hillside at the point where the enemy cavalry was turning the right flank. Given cavalry behind the Tulan line and the battle was lost.

"O.K., boys," Chessman growled sourly, "we're in the clutch now. Hawkins!"

"Yeah," the pilot said.

"See what you can do. Use what bombs you have including the napalm. Fly as low as you can in the way of scaring their horses." He added sourly, "Avoiding scaring ours, if you can."

"You're the boss," Hawkins said, and scurried off toward his scout plane.

Joe Chessman growled to the others, "When I was taking my degree in primitive society and primitive military tactics, I didn't exactly have this in mind. Come on!"

It was the right thing to say. The other Earthmen laughed and took up their equipment, submachine guns, riot guns, a flame thrower, grenades, and followed him up the hill toward the fray.

Chessman said over his shoulder to Reif, "Khan, you're in the saddle. You can keep in touch with both Watson and us on the radio."

Reif hesitated only a moment. "There is no need for further direction of the battle from this point. A warrior is of more value now than a Khan. Come my son." He caught up a double-barreled musket and followed the Earthmen. The ten years old Taller scurried after with a revolver.

Natt Roberts said, "If we can hold their cavalry for only another half hour, Watson's phalanx will have their infantry pressed up against the pass they entered by. It took them three days to get through it, they're not going to be able to get out in hours."

"That's the idea," Joe Chessman said dourly, "Let's go."

VII.

Amschel Mayer was incensed.

"What's got into Buchwald and MacDonald?" he spat.

Jerry Kennedy, attired as was his superior in fur trimmed Genoese robes, signaled one of the servants for a refilling of his glass and shrugged.

"I suppose it's partly our own fault," he said lightly. He sipped the wine, made a mental note to buy up the rest of this vintage for his cellars before young Mannerheim or someone else did so.

"Our fault!" Mayer glared.

The old boy was getting decreasingly tolerant as the years went by, Kennedy decided. He said soothingly, "You sent Peter and Fred over there to speed up local development. Well, that's what they're doing."

"Are you insane!" Mayer squirmed in his chair. "Did you read this radiogram? They've squeezed out all my holdings in rubber, the fastest growing industry on the western continent. Why, millions are involved. Who do they think they are?"

Kennedy put down his glass and chuckled. "See here, Amschel, we're developing this planet by encouraging free competition. Our contention is that under such a socio-economic system the best men are brought to the lead and benefit all society by the advances they make."

"So! What has this got to do with MacDonald and Buchwald betraying my interests?"

"Don't you see? Using your own theory, you have been set back by someone more efficiently competitive. Fred and Peter saw an opening and, in keeping with your instructions, moved in. It's just coincidence that the rubber they took over was your property rather than some Genoese operator's. If you were open to a loss there, then if they hadn't taken over someone else could have. Possibly Baron Leonar or even Russ."

"That reminds me," Mayer snapped, "our Honorable Russ is getting too big for his britches in petroleum. Did you know he's established a laboratory in Amerus? Has a hundred or more chemists working on new products."

"Fine," Kennedy said.

"Fine! What do you mean? Dean is our man in petroleum."

"Look here, if Russ can develop the industry even faster than Mike Dean, let him go ahead. That's all to our advantage."

Mayer leaned forward and tapped his assistant emphatically on the knee. "Look here, yourself, Jerry Kennedy. At this stage we don't want things getting out of our hands. A culture is in the hands of those who control the wealth; the means of production, distribution, communication. Theirs is the real power. I've made a point of spacing our men about the whole planet. Each specializes, though not exclusively. Gunther is our mining man, Dean heads petroleum, MacDonald shipping, Buchwald textiles, Rykov steel, and so forth. As fast as this planet can assimilate we push new inventions, new techniques, often whole new sciences, into use. Meanwhile, you and I sit back and dominate it all through that strongest of power mediums, finance."

Jerry Kennedy nodded. "I wouldn't worry about old man Russ taking over Dean's domination of oil, though. Mike's got the support of all the *Pedagogue's* resources behind him. Besides, we've got to let these Genoese get into the act. The more the economy expands, the more capable men we need. As it is, I think we're already spread a little too thin."

Amschel Mayer had dropped the subject. He was reading the radiogram again and scowling his anger. "Well, this cooks MacDonald and Buchwald. I'll break them."

His assistant raised his eyebrows. "How do you mean?"

"I'm not going to put up with my subordinates going against my interests."

"In this case, what can you do about it? Business is business."

"You hold quite a bit of their paper, don't you?"

"You know that. Most of our team's finances funnel through my hands."

"We'll close them out. They've become too obsessed with their wealth. They've forgotten why the *Pedagogue* was sent here. I'll break them, Jerry. They'll come crawling. Perhaps I'll send them back to the *Pedagogue*. Make them stay aboard as crew."

Kennedy shrugged. "Well, Peter MacDonald's going to hate that. He's developed into quite a high liver-gourmet food, women, one of the swankiest estates on the eastern continent."

"Ha!" Mayer snorted. "Let him go back to ship's rations and crew's quarters."

A servant entered the lushly furnished room and announced, "Honorable Gunther calling on the Honorables Mayer and Kennedy."

Martin Gunther hurried into the room, for once his calm ruffled. "On the western continent," he blurted. "Dean and Rosetti. The Temple got them, they've been burned as witches."

Amschel Mayer shot to his feet. "That's the end," he swore shrilly. "Only in the west have the barons held out. I thought we'd slowly wear them down, take over their powers bit by bit. But this does it. This means we fight."

He spun to Kennedy. "Jerry, make a trip out to the *Pedagogue*. You know the extent of Genoa's industrial progress. Seek out the most advanced weapons this technology could produce."

Kennedy came to his own feet, shocked by Gunther's news. "But, Amschel, do you think it's wise to precipitate an intercontinental war? Remember, we've been helping to industrialize the west, too. It's almost as advanced as our continent. Their war potential isn't negligible."

"Nevertheless," Mayer snapped, "we've got to break the backs of the barons and the Temple monks. Get messages off to Baron Leonar and young Mannerheim, to Russ and Olderman. We'll want them to put pressure on their local politicians. What we need is a continental alliance for this war."

Gunther said, "Should I get in touch with Rykov? He's still over there."

Mayer hesitated. "No," he said. "We'll keep Nick informed but he ought to remain where he is. We'll still want our men in the basic positions of power after we've won."

"He might get hurt," Gunther scowled. "They might get him too, and we've only got six team members left now."

"Nonsense, Nick Rykov can take care of himself."

Jerry Kennedy was upset. "Are you sure about this war, chief? Isn't a conflict of this size apt to hold up our overall plans?"

"Of course not," Mayer scoffed. "Man makes his greatest progress under pressure. A major war will unite the nations of both the western continent and this one as nothing else could. Both will push their development to the utmost."

He added thoughtfully, "Which reminds me. It might be a good idea for us to begin accumulating interests in such industries as will be effected by a war economy."

Jerry Kennedy chuckled at him, "Merchant of death."

"What?"

"Nothing," Kennedy said. "Something I read about in a history book."

VIII.

At the decade's end, once again the representatives of the Genoese team were first in the *Pedagogue's* lounge. Mayer sat at the officer's table, Martin Gunther at his right. Jerry Kennedy leaned against the ship's bar, sipping appreciatively at a highball.

They could hear the impact of the space boat from Texcoco when it slid into its bed.

"Poor piloting," Gunther mused. "Whoever's doing that flying doesn't get enough practice."

They could hear ports opening and then the sound of approaching feet. The footsteps had a strangely military ring.

Joe Chessman entered, followed immediately by Barry Watson, Dick Hawkins and Natt Roberts. They were all dressed in heavy uniform, complete with decorations. Behind them were four Texcocans, including Reif and his teen-age son Taller.

Mayer scowled at them in way of greeting. "Where's Plekhanov?"

"Leonid Plekhanov is no longer with us," Chessman said dourly. "Under pressure his mind evidently snapped and he made decisions that would have meant the collapse of the expedition. He resisted when we reasoned with him."

The four members of the Genoese team stared without speaking. Jerry Kennedy put down his glass at last. "You mean you had to restrict him? Why didn't you bring him back to the ship!"

Chessman took a chair at the table. The others assumed standing positions behind him. "I'm afraid we'll have to reject your views on the subject. Twenty years ago this expedition split into two groups. My team will accomplish its tasks, your opinions are not needed."

Amschel Mayer glared at the others in hostility. "You have certainly come in force this time."

Chessman said flatly, "This is all of us, Mayer."

"All of you! Where are Stevens, Cogswell, MacBride?"

Barry Watson said, "Plekhanov's fault. Lost in the battle that broke the back of the rebels. At least Cogswell and MacBride were. Stevens made the mistake of backing Plekhanov when the showdown came."

Joe Chessman looked sourly at his military chief. "I'll act as team spokesman, Barry."

"Yes, sir," Watson said.

"Broke the back of the rebels," Jerry Kennedy mused. "That opens all sorts of avenues, doesn't it?"

Chessman growled. "I suppose that in the past twenty years your team had no obstacles. Not a drop of blood shed. Come on, the truth. How many of your team has been lost?"

Mayer shifted in his chair. "Possibly your point is well taken. Dean and Rosetti were burned by the formerly dominant religious group. Rykov was killed in a fracas with bandits while he was transporting some gold." He added, musingly, "We lost more than half a million Genoese pounds in that robbery."

"Only three men lost, eh?"

Mayer stirred uncomfortably, then flushed in irritation at the other's tone. "Something has happened to Buchwald and MacDonald. They must be insane. They've broken off contact with me, are amassing personal fortunes in the eastern hemisphere."

Hawkins laughed abruptly. "Free competition," he said.

Chessman growled, "Let's halt this bickering and get to business. First let me introduce Reif, Texcocan State Army Chief of Staff and his son Taller. And these other Texcocans are Wiss and Fokin, both of whom have gone far in the sciences."

The Tulans shook hands, Earth style, but then stepped to the rear again where they followed the conversation without comment.

Mayer said, "You think it wise to introduce natives to the *Pedagogue*?"

"Of course," Chessman said. "Following this conference, I'm going to take Fokin and Wiss into the library. What're we here for if not to bring these people up to our level as rapidly as possible?"

"Very well," Mayer conceded grudgingly. "And now I have a complaint. When the *Pedagogue* first arrived we had only so many weapons aboard. You have appropriated more than half in the past two decades."

Chessman shrugged it off. "We'll return the greater part to the ship's arsenal. At this stage we are producing our own."

"I'll bet," Kennedy said. "Look, any of you fellows want a real Earthside whisky? When we were crewing this expedition, why didn't we bring someone with a knowledge of distilling, brewing and such?"

Mayer snapped at him, "Jerry, you drink too much."

"The hell I do," the other said cheerfully. "Not near enough."

Barry Watson said easily, "A drink wouldn't hurt. Why're we so stiff? This is the first get-together for ten years. Jerry, you're putting on weight."

Kennedy looked down at his admittedly rounded stomach. "Don't get enough exercise," he said, then reversed the attack. "You look older. Are your taking your rejuvenation treatments?"

Barry Watson grimaced. "Sure, but I'm working under pressure. It's been one long campaign."

Kennedy passed around the drinks.

Dick Hawkins laughed. "It's been one long campaign, all right. Barry has a house as big as a castle and six or eight women in his harem."

Watson flushed, but obviously without displeasure.

Martin Gunther, of the Genoese team, cocked his head. "Harem?"

Joe Chessman said impatiently, "Man adapts to circumstances, Gunther. The wars have lost us a lot of men. Women are consequently in a surplus. If the population curve is to continue upward, it's necessary that a man serve more than one woman. Polygamy is the obvious answer."

Gunther cleared his throat smoothly, "So a man in Barry's position will have as many as eight wives, eh? You must have lost a *good many* men."

Watson grinned modestly. "Everybody doesn't have that many. It's according to your ability to support them, and, also, rank has its privileges. Besides, we figure it's a good idea to spread the best seed around. By mixing our blood with the Texcocan we improve the breed."

Behind him, Taller, the Tulan boy, stirred, without notice.

* * * * *

Kennedy finished off his highball and began to build another immediately. "Here we go again. The big potatoes coming to the top."

Watson flushed. "What do you mean by that, Kennedy?"

"Oh, come off it, Barry," Kennedy laughed. "Just because you're in a position to push these people around doesn't make you the prize stud on Texcoco."

Watson elbowed Dick Hawkins to one side in his attempt to get around the table at the other.

Chessman rapped, "Watson! That's enough. Knock it off or I'll have you under arrest." The Texcocan team head turned abruptly to Mayer and Kennedy. "Let's stop this nonsense. We've come to compare progress. Let's begin."

The three members of the Genoese team glared back in antagonism, but then Gunther said grudgingly, "He's right. There is no longer amiability between us, so let's forget about it. Perhaps when the fifty years is up, things will be different. Now let's merely be businesslike."

"Well," Mayer said, "our report is that progress accelerates. Our industrial potential expands at a rate that surprises even us. In the near future we'll introduce the internal combustion engine. Our universities still multiply and are turning out technicians, engineers, scientists at an ever-quickening speed. In several nations illiteracy is practically unknown and per capita production increases almost everywhere." Mayer paused in satisfaction, as though awaiting the others to attempt to top his report.

Joe Chessman said sourly, "Ah, almost everywhere per capita production increases. Why *almost?*"

Mayer snapped, "Obviously, in a system of free competition, all cannot progress at once. Some go under."

"Whole nations?"

"Temporarily whole nations can receive setbacks as a result of defeat in war, or perhaps due to lack of natural resources. Some nations progress faster than others."

Chessman said, "The whole Texcocan State is one great unit. Everywhere the gross product increases. Within the foreseeable future the standard of living will be excellent."

Jerry Kennedy, an alcoholic lisp in his voice now, said, "You mean you've accomplished a planet-wide government?"

"Well, no. Not as yet," Chessman's sullen voice had an element of chagrin in it. "However, there are no strong elements left that oppose us. We are now pacifying the more remote areas."

"Sounds like a rather bloody program-especially if Barry Watson, here, winds up with eight women," Martin Gunther said.

Watson started to say something but Chessman held up a restraining hand. "The Texcocan State is too strong to be resisted, Gunther. It is mostly a matter of getting around to the more remote peoples. As soon as we bring in a new tribe, we convert it into a commune."

"Commune!" Kennedy blurted.

Joe Chessman raised his thick eyebrows at the other. "The most efficient socio-economic unit at this stage of development. Tribal society is perfectly adapted to fit into such a plan. The principal difference between a tribe and a commune is that under the commune you have the advantage of a State above in a position to give you the benefit of mass industries, schools, medical assistance. In return, of course, for a certain amount of taxes, military levies and so forth."

Martin Gunther said softly, "I recall reading of the commune system as a student, but I fail to remember the supposed advantages."

Chessman growled, "They're obvious. You have a unit of tens of thousands of persons. Instead of living in individual houses, each with a man working while the woman cooks and takes care of the home, all live in community houses and take their meals in messhalls. The children are cared for by trained nurses. During the season all physically capable adults go out en masse to work the fields. When the harvest has been taken in, the farmer does not hole up for the winter but is occupied in local industrial projects, or in road or dam building. The commune's labor is never idle."

Kennedy shuddered involuntarily.

Chessman looked at him coldly. "It means quick progress. Meanwhile, we go through each commune and from earliest youth, locate those members who are suited to higher studies. We bring them into State schools where they get as much education as they can assimilate-more than is available in commune schools. These are the Texcocans we are training in the sciences."

"The march to the anthill," Amschel Mayer muttered.

Chessman eyed him scornfully. "You amuse me, old man. You with your talk of building an economy with a system of free competition. Our Texcocans are sacrificing today but their children will live in abundance. Even today, no one starves, no one goes without shelter nor medical care." Chessman twisted his mouth wryly. "We have found that hungry, cold or sick people cannot work efficiently."

He stared challengingly at the Genoese leader. "Can you honestly say that there are no starving people in Genoa? No inadequately housed, no sick without hope of adequate medicine? Do you have economic setbacks in which poorly planned production goes amuck and depressions follow with mass unemployment?"

"Nevertheless," Mayer said with unwonted calm, "our society is still far ahead of yours. A mere handful of your bureaucracy and military chiefs enjoy the good things of life. There are tens of thousands on Genoa who have them. Free competition has its weaknesses, perhaps, but it provides a greater good for a greater number of persons."

Joe Chessman came to his feet. "We'll see," he said stolidly. "In ten years, Mayer, we'll consider the position of both planets once again."

"Ten years it is," Mayer snapped back at him.

Jerry Kennedy saluted with his glass. "Cheers," he said.

* * * * *

On the return to Genoa Amschel Mayer said to Kennedy, "Are you sober enough to assimilate something serious?"

"Sure, chief, of course."

"Hm-m-m. Well then, begin taking the steps necessary for us to place a few men on Texcoco in the way of, ah, intelligence agents."

"You mean some of our team?" Kennedy said, startled.

"No, of course not. We can't spare them, and, besides, there'd be too big a chance of recognition and exposure. Some of our more trusted Genoese. Make the monetary reward enough to attract their services." He looked at his lieutenants significantly. "I think you'll agree that it might not be a bad idea to keep our eyes on the developments on Texcoco."

* * * * *

On the way back to Texcoco, Barry Watson said to his chief, "What do you think of putting some security men on Genoa, just to keep tabs?"

"Why?"

Watson looked at his fingers, nibbled at a hangnail. "It just seems to me it wouldn't hurt any." Chessman snorted.

Dick Hawkins said, "I think Barry's right. They can bear watching. Besides in another decade or so they'll realize we're going to beat them. Mayer's ego isn't going to take that. He'd go to just about any extreme to keep from losing face back on Earth."

Natt Roberts said worriedly, "I think they're right, Joe. Certainly it wouldn't hurt to have a few Security men over there. My department could train them and we'd ferry them over in this space boat."

"I'll make the decisions," Chessman growled at them. "I'll think about this. It's just possible that you're right though."

Behind them, Reif looked thoughtfully at his teen-age son.

IX.

Down the long palace corridor strode Barry Watson, Dick Hawkins, Natt Roberts, the aging Reif and his son Taller, now in the prime of manhood. Their faces were equally wan from long hours without sleep. Half a dozen Tulan infantrymen brought up their rear.

As they passed Security Police guards, to left and right, eyes took in their weapons, openly carried. But such eyes shifted and the guards remained at their posts. Only one sergeant opened his mouth in protest. "Sir," he said to Watson, hesitantly, "you are entering Number One's presence armed."

"Shut up," Natt Roberts rapped at him.

Reif said, "That will be all, sergeant."

The Security Police sergeant looked emptily after them as they progressed down the corridor.

Together, Watson and Reif motioned aside the two Tulan soldiers who stood before the door of their destination, and pushed inward without knocking.

Joe Chessman looked up wearily from his map and dispatch laden desk. For a moment his hand went to the heavy military revolver at his right but when he realized the identity of his callers, it fell away.

"What's up now?" he said, his voice on the verge of cracking.

Watson acted as spokesman. "It's everywhere the same. The communes are on the fine edge of revolt. They've been pushed too far; they've got to the point where they just don't give a damn. A spark and all Texcoco goes up in flames."

Reif said coldly, "We need immediate reforms. They've got to be pacified. An immediate announcement of more consumer goods, fewer State taxes, above all a relaxation of Security Police pressures. Given immediate promise of these, we might maintain ourselves."

Joe Chessman's sullen face was twitching at the right corner of his mouth. Young Taller made no attempt to disguise his contempt at the other's weakness in time of stress.

Chessman's eyes went around the half circle of them. "This is the only alternative? It'll slow up our heavy industry program. We might not catch up with Genoa as quickly as planned."

Watson gestured with a hand in quick irritation. "Look here, Chessman, don't we get through to you? Whether or not we build up a steel capacity as large as Amschel Mayer's isn't important now. Everything's at stake."

"Don't talk to me that way, Barry," Chessman growled truculently. "I'll make the decisions. I'll do the thinking." He said to Reif, "How much of the Tulan army is loyal?"

The aging Tulan looked at Watson before turning back to Joe Chessman. "All of the Tulan army is loyal-to me."

"Good!" Chessman pushed some of the dispatches on his desk aside, letting them flutter to the floor. He bared a field map. "If we crush half a dozen of the local communes ...crush them hard! Then the others..."

Watson said very slowly and so low as hardly to be heard, "You didn't bother to listen, Chessman. We told you, all that's needed is a spark."

Joe Chessman sat back in his chair, looked at them all again, one by one. Re-evaluating. For a moment the facial tic stopped and his eyes held the old alertness.

"I see," he said. "And you all recommend capitulation to their demands?"

"It's our only chance," Hawkins said. "We don't even know it'll work. There's always the chance if we throw them a few crumbs they'll want the whole loaf. You've got to remember that some of them have been living for twenty-five years or more under this pressure. The valve is about to blow."

"I see," Chessman grunted. "And what else? I can see in your faces there's something else."

The three Earthmen didn't answer. Their eyes shifted.

He looked to young Taller and then to Reif. "What else?"

"We need a scapegoat," Reif said without expression.

Joe Chessman thought about that. He looked to Barry Watson again.

Watson said, "The whole Texcocan State is about to topple. Not only do we have to give them immediate reform, but we're going to have to blame the past hardships and mistakes on somebody. Somebody has to take the rap, be thrown to the wolves. If not, maybe we'll all wind up taking the blame."

"Ah," Chessman said. His red-rimmed eyes went around them again, thoughtfully. "We should be able to dig up a few local chieftains and some of the Security Police heads."

They shook their heads. "It has to be somebody big," Natt Roberts said thickly, "a few of my Security Police won't do it."

Joe Chessman's eyes went to Reif. "The Khan is the highest ranking Texcocan of all," he said, finally. "The Khan and some Security Police heads would satisfy them."

Reif's face was as frigid as the Earthman's. He said, "I am afraid not, Joseph Chessman. You are Number One. It is your statue that is in every commune square. It is your portrait that hangs in every distribution center, every messhall, every schoolroom. You are the Number One-as you have so often pointed out to us. My title has become meaningless."

Joe Chessman spat out a curse, fumbled the gun into his hand and fired before the Tulan soldiers could get to him. In a moment they had wrested the weapon from his hand and had his arms pinioned. It was too late.

Reif had been thrown backward two paces by the blast of the heavy-calibered gun. Now he held a palm over his belly and staggered to a chair. He collapsed into it, looked at his son, let a wash of amusement pass over his face, said, "Khan," meaninglessly, and died.

Natt Roberts shrilled at Chessman, "You fool, we were going to give you a big, theatrical trial. Sentence you to prison and then, later, claim you'd died in your cell and smuggle you out to the *Pedagogue*."

Watson snapped to the guards, "Take him outside and shoot him."

The Tulans began dragging the snarling, cursing Chessman to the door.

Taller said, "A moment, please."

Watson, Roberts and Hawkins looked to him.

Taller said, "This perhaps can be done more effectively."

His voice was completely emotionless. "This man has killed both my father and grandfather, both of them Khans of Tula, heads of the most powerful city on all Texcoco, before the coming of you Earthlings."

The guards hesitated. Watson detained them with a motion of his hand.

Taller said, "I suggest you turn him over to me, to be dealt with in the traditional way of the People."

"No," Chessman said hoarsely. "Barry, Dick, Natt, send me back to the *Pedagogue*. I'll be out of things there. Or maybe Mayer can use me on Genoa."

They didn't bother to look in his direction. Roberts muttered savagely, "We told you all that was needed was a spark. Now you've killed the Khan, the most popular man on Texcoco. There's no way of saving you."

Taller said, "None of you have studied our traditions, our customs. But now, perhaps, you will understand the added effect of my taking charge. It will be a more ... profitable manner of using the downfall of this ... this power mad murderer."

Chessman said desperately, "Look, Barry, Natt, if you have to, shoot me. At least give me a man's death. Remember those human sacrifices the Tulans had when we first arrived? Can you imagine what went on in those temples? Barry, Dick-for old time's sake, boys..."

Barry Watson said to Taller, "He's yours. If this doesn't take the pressure off us, nothing will."

X.

At the end of the third decade, the Texcocan delegation was already seated in the *Pedagogue's* lounge when Jerome Kennedy, Martin Gunther, Peter MacDonald, Fredric Buchwald and three Genoese, Baron Leonar and the Honorables Russ and Modrin appeared.

The Texcocan group consisted of Barry Watson, Dick Hawkins and Natt Roberts to one side of him, Generalissimo Taller and six highly bemedaled Texcocans on the other.

Before taking a seat Barry Watson barked, "Where's Amschel Mayer? I've got some important points to cover with him."

"Take it easy," Kennedy slurred. "For that matter, where's Joe Chessman?"

Watson glared at the other. "You know where he is."

"That I do," Kennedy said. "He's purged, to use a term of yesteryear. At the rate you laddy-bucks are going, there won't be anything left of you by the time our half century is up." He snapped his fingers and a Genoese servant who'd been inconspicuously in the background, hurried to his side. "Let's have some refreshments here. What'll everybody have?"

"You act as though you've had enough already," Watson bit out.

Kennedy ignored him, insisted on everyone being served before he allowed the conversation to turn serious. Then he said, slyly, "I see we've been successful in apprehending all of your agents, or you'd know more of our affairs."

"Not all our agents," Watson barked. "Only those on your southern continent. What happened to Amschel Mayer?"

Peter MacDonald, who, with Buchwald, was for the first time attending one of the decade-end conferences, had been hardly recognized in his new girth by the Texcocan team. But his added weight had evidently done nothing to his keenness of mind. He said smoothly, "Our good Amschel is under arrest. Imprisoned, in fact." He shook his head, his double chin wobbling. "A tragedy."

"Imprisoned! By whom?" Taller scowled. "I don't like this. After all, he was your expedition's head man."

Barry Watson rapped, "Don't leave us there, MacDonald. What happened to him?"

MacDonald explained. "The financial and industrial empire he had built was overextended. A small crisis and it collapsed. Thousands of investors suffered. In brief, he was arrested and found guilty."

Watson was unbelieving. "There is nothing you could do? The whole team! Couldn't you bribe him out? Rescue him by force and get him back to the ship? With all the wealth you characters control —"

Jerry Kennedy laughed shortly. "We were busy bailing ourselves out of our own situations, Watson. You don't know what international finance can be. Besides, he dug his grave ... uh ... that is, he made his bed."

Kennedy signaled the servant for another drink, said, "Let's cut out this dismal talk. How about our progress reports?"

"Progress reports," Barry Watson said. "That's a laugh. You have agents on Texcoco, we have them on Genoa. What's the use of having these conferences at all?"

For the first time, one of the Genoese put in a word. Baron Leonar, son of the original Baron who had met with Amschel Mayer thirty years before, was a man in his mid-forties. He said quietly, "It seems to me the time has arrived when the two planets might profit by intercourse. Surely in this time one has progressed beyond the other in this field, but lagged in that. If I understand the mission of the *Pedagogue* it is to bring us to as high a technological level as possible in half a century. Already three decades have passed."

The Texcocans studied him thoughtfully, but Jerry Kennedy waved in negation with the hand that held his glass. "You don't get it, Baron. You see, the thing is we wanta find out what system is going to do the most the quickest. If we co-operate with Barry's gang, everything'll get all mixed up."

The Honorable Russ, now a wizened man of at least seventy, but still sharply alert, said, "However, Texcoco and Genoa might both profit."

Kennedy said happily, "What do we care? You gotta take the long view. What we're working out here is going to be used on half a million planets eventually." He tried to snap his fingers. "These two lousy planets don't count that much." He succeeded in snapping them this time. "Not that much."

Barry Watson said, "You're stoned, Kennedy."

"Why not?" Kennedy grinned. "Finally perfected a decent brandy. I'll have to send you a few cases, Barry."

"How would you go about that, Jerry?" Watson said softly.

"Shucks, man, our space lighter makes a trip to Texcoco every month or so. Gotta keep up with you boys. Maybe throw a wrench or so in the works once inna while."

Peter MacDonald said, "Shut up, Jerry. You talk too much."

"Don't talk to me that way. You'll find yourself having one helluva time floating that loan you need next month. How about another drink, everybody? This party's dead."

Watson said, "How about the progress reports? Briefly, we've all but completely united Texcoco. Minor setbacks have sometimes deterred us but the march of progress goes on. We —"

"Minor setbacks," Kennedy chortled. "Must of had to bump off five million of the poor slobs before that commune revolt was finished with."

Watson said coldly, "We always have a few reactionaries, religious fanatics, misfits, crackpots, malcontents to deal with. However, these are not important. Our industrial potential has finally begun to roll. We doubled steel production this year, will do the same next. Our hydro-electric installations tripled in the past two years. Coal production is four times higher, lumber production six times. We expect to increase grain harvest forty per cent next season. And —"

The Honorable Modrin put in gently, "Please, Honorable Watson, your percentage figures are impressive only if we know from what basis you start. If you produced but five million tons of steel last year, then your growth to ten million is very good but it is still not a considerable amount for an entire planet."

Buchwald said dryly, "If our agents are correct, Texcocan steel production is something like a quarter of our own. I assume your other basic products are at about the same stage of development."

Watson flushed. "The thing to remember is that our economy continues to grow each year. Yours spurts and stops, jerks ahead a few steps, then grinds to a halt or even retreats. Everything comes to a pause if you few on the top stop making a profit; all that counts in your economy is making money. Which reminds me, how in the world did you ever get out of that planet-wide depression you were in three years ago?"

Peter MacDonald grunted his disgust. "Planet-wide depression, indeed. A small recession. A temporary readjustment due to overextension in certain economic and financial fields."

From the other side of the table, Dick Hawkins laughed at him. "Where'd you pick up that line of gobbledygook, Peter?" he asked.

Peter MacDonald came to his feet. "I don't have to put up with this sort of impudence," he snapped.

Watson lurched to his own feet. "Nor do we have to listen to your snide cracks about the real progress Texcoco is making. We don't seem to be getting anywhere." He snapped to his associates, "Hawkins, Taller, Roberts! Let's go. Ten years from now, there'll be another story to tell. Even a blind man will see the difference."

They marched down the *Pedagogue's* corridor toward their space boat.

Kennedy called after them, "Ten years from now every family on Genoa'll have a car. Wait'll you see. Television, too. We're introducing TV next year. An' civil aviation. Be all over the place in two, three years —"

The Texcocans slammed the spaceport after them.

Kennedy sloshed some more drink into his glass. "Slobs can't stand the truth," he explained to the others.

XI.

With the exception of a few additional delegates composed of high-ranking Texcocan and Genoese political and scientific heads, the line-up at the end of forty years was the same as ten years earlier-except for the absence of Jerry Kennedy.

Extra tables had been set up, and chairs to accommodate the added numbers. To one side were the Genoese: Martin Gunther, Fredric Buchwald, Peter MacDonald, with such repeat delegates as Baron Leonar and the Honorables Modrin and Russ and half a dozen newcomers. On the other were Barry Watson, Dick Hawkins and Natt Roberts, Taller and such Texcocans as the scientists Wiss and Fokin, army heads, Security Police officials and other notables.

Note pads had been placed before each of them and both Watson and Gunther were equipped with gavels.

While chairs were still being shuffled, Barry Watson said over the table to Gunther, "Jerry?"

Martin Gunther shrugged "Jerry's indisposed. As a matter of fact, he's at one of the mountain sanitariums, taking a cure. He'll be all right."

"Good," Dick Hawkins said. "We've lost too many."

Watson pounded with his gavel. "Let's come to order. Gunther do you have anything to say in the way of preliminaries?"

"Not especially. I believe we all know where we stand, including the newcomers from Genoa and Texcoco. In brief, this is the fourth meeting of the Earth teams that were sent to these two planets to bring backward colonists to an industrialized culture. It would seem that we are both succeeding-possibly at different rates. Forty years have passed, ten remain to us."

For a moment there was silence.

Finally Roberts said, "Possibly you have already discovered this through your agents, but we have released the information on prolonging of life."

Peter MacDonald said wryly, "We, too, were pressured into such a step."

Baron Leonar said, "And why not?"

Taller, across the table from him, nodded.

Martin Gunther tapped twice on the table with his gavel. "The basic reason for our meeting is to report progress and to reconsider the possibilities of new elements having entered into the situation which might cause us to re-examine our policies. I think we already have a fairly good idea of each other's development." His voice went wry. "At least our agents do a fairly good job of reporting yours."

"And ours, yours," Watson rapped.

"However," MacDonald said, "now that we are drawing near the end of our half century, I think it becomes obvious that Amschel Mayer's original contention-that a freely competitive economy grows faster than one restricted by totalitarian bounds-has been proven."

Barry Watson snorted amusement. "Do you?" he said. "To the contrary, MacDonald. The proof is otherwise. On Genoa you still have comparative confusion. True enough, several of your nations, particularly those on your southern continent, are greatly advanced and with a high living and cultural standard-when times are good. But at the same time you have other whole peoples who are little, if any, better off, than when you arrived. On the western continent you even have a few feudalistic regimes that are probably worse off-mostly as a result of the wars you've crippled them with."

Natt Roberts said, his voice musing, "But even that isn't the important thing. The Co-ordinator sent us here to find a *method* of bringing backward cultures to industrialization. Have you got a blueprint to show him, when you return? Can you trace out the history of Genoa for this past half century and say, this war was necessary for progress-but that should have been avoided? Or is this whole *free competition* program of yours actually nothing but chaos which *sometimes* works out wonderfully for *some* nations, but actually destroys others? You have scorned our methods, our collectivized society-but when we return, we'll have a blueprint of how we arrived where we are."

Gunther banged the table with his gavel. "Just a moment. Is there any reason why we have to listen to these accusations when —"

Watson held up a hand, curtly, "Let us finish. If you have something to say, we'll gladly listen when we're through."

Gunther was flushed but he snapped, "Go ahead then, but don't think any of we Genoese are being taken in."

Watson said, "True enough, it took us a time to unite our people..."

"Time and blood," Peter MacDonald muttered.

"...But once underway the Texcocan State has moved on in a progression unknown in any of the Genoese nations. To industrialize a society you must reach a certain taking off point, a point where you have sufficient industry, particularly steel, sufficient power, sufficient scientists, technicians and skilled workers. Once that point has been reached you can move in almost a geometric progression. You build a steel mill and with the steel produced you build two more mills the following year, which in turn gives you the material for four the next year."

Buchwald grunted his disbelief.

Watson looked up and down the line of Genoese, the Earthmen as well as the natives. "On Texcoco we have now reached that point. We have a trained, eager population of over one billion persons. Our universities are turning out highly trained effectives at the rate of more than twenty million a year. We have located all the raw materials we will need. We are now under way." He looked at them in heavy amusement. "By the end of the next decade we will bury you."

Martin Gunther said calmly, "Are you through?"

"Yes. For the time," Watson nodded.

"Very well. Then this is *our* progress report. In the past forty years we have eliminated feudalism in all the more advanced countries. Even in the remote areas the pressures of our changing world are bringing them around. The populace of these countries will no longer stand to one side while the standard of living on the rest of Genoa grows so rapidly. On most of our planet, already the average family not only enjoys freedom but a way of life far in advance of that of Texcoco. Already modern housing and household appliances are everywhere. Already both land cars and aircraft are available to the majority. The nations have formed an Inter-Continental League of governments so that it is unlikely that war will ever touch us again. And this is merely a beginning. In ten years, continuing our freely competitive way of developing, all will be living on a scale that only the wealthy can afford today."

He came to an end and stared antagonistically at the Texcocans.

Taller said, "There seems to be no agreement."

Across the table from him the ancient Honorable Russ said, "It is difficult to measure. We seem to count refrigerators and privately owned automobiles. You seem to ignore personal standards and concentrate on steel tonnage."

The Texcocan scientist, Wiss, said easily, "Given the steel mills, and eventually automobiles and refrigerators will run off our assembly lines like water, and will be available for everyone, not just those who can afford to buy them."

"Hm-m-m, eventually," Peter MacDonald laughed nastily.

The atmosphere was suddenly hostile. Hostile beyond anything that had gone before in earlier conferences.

And then Martin Gunther said without inflection, "I note that you have removed from the *Pedagogue's* library the information dealing with nuclear fission."

"For the purpose of study," Dick Hawkins said smoothly.

"Of course," Gunther said. "Did you plan to return it in the immediate future?"

"I'm afraid our studies will take some time," Watson said flatly.

"I was afraid so," Gunther said. "Happily, I took the precaution of making microfilms of the material involved more than a year ago."

Barry Watson pushed his chair back. "We seem to have accomplished what was possible by this conference," he said. "If anything." He looked to right and left at his cohorts. "Let's go."

They came stiffly erect. Watson turned on his heel and started for the door.

As they left, Natt Roberts turned for a moment and said to Gunther, "One thing, Martin. During this next ten years you might consider whether or not half a century has been enough to accomplish our task. Should we consider staying on? I would think the Co-ordinator would accept any recommendation along this line that we might make."

The Genoese contingent looked after him, long after he was gone.

Finally Martin Gunther said, "Baron Leonar, I think it might be a good idea if you began putting some of your men to work on making steel alloys suitable for spacecraft. The way things are developing, perhaps we'll be needing them."

Buchwald and MacDonald looked at him unblinkingly.

XII.

It was fifty years to a day since the *Pedagogue* had first gone into orbit about Rigel. Five decades have passed. Half a century.

Of the original crew of the *Pedagogue*, six now gathered in the lounge of the spaceship. All of them had changed physically. Some of them softer to the point of flabbiness; some harder both of body and soul.

Barry Watson, Natt Roberts, Dick Hawkins, of the Texcocan team.

Martin Gunther, Peter MacDonald, Fredric Buchwald, of the Genoese.

The gathering wasn't so large as the one before. Only Taller and the scientist Wiss attended from Texcoco; only Baron Leonar and the son of Honorable Russ from Genoa.

From the beginning they stared with hostility across the conference table. Even the pretense of amiability was gone.

Watson rapped finally, "I am not going to dwell upon the measures you have been taking that can only be construed as military ones aimed eventually at the Texcocan State."

Martin Gunther laughed nastily. "Is your implication that your own people have not taken the same measures, in fact, inaugurated them?"

Watson said, "As I say, I have no intention of even discussing this. Surely we can arrive at no agreement. There is one point, however that we should consider on this occasion."

The corpulent Peter MacDonald wheezed, "Well, out with it!"

Natt Roberts said, "I mentioned the matter to you at the last meeting."

"Ah, yes," Gunther nodded. "Just as you left. We have considered it."

The Texcocans waited for him to go on.

"If I understand you," Gunther said, "you think we should reconsider returning to Terra City at this time."

"It should be discussed," Watson nodded. "Whatever the ... ah ... temporary difficulties between us, the original project of the *Pedagogue* is still our duty."

The three of the Genoese team nodded their agreement.

"And the problem becomes, have we accomplished completely what we set out to do? And, further, is it necessary, or at least preferable, for us to stay on and continue administration of the progress of the Rigel planets?"

They thought about it.

Buchwald said hesitantly, "It has been my own belief that Genoa is not quite ready for us to let loose the ... ah, reins. If we left now, I am not sure —"

Roberts said, "Same applies to Texcoco. The State has made fabulous strides, but I am not sure what would happen if we leaders were to leave. There might be a complete collapse."

Watson said, "We seem to be in basic agreement. Is a suggestion in order that we extend, for another twenty-five years, at least, this expedition's work?"

Dick Hawkins said, "The Office of Galactic Colonization —"

MacDonald said smoothly, "Will undoubtedly send out a ship to investigate. We shall simply inform them that things are not as yet propitious to our leaving, that another twenty-five years is in order. Since we are on the scene, undoubtedly our recommendation will be heeded."

Watson looked from one Earthman to the next. "We are in agreement?"

Each in turn nodded.

Peter MacDonald said, "And do you all realize that here we have a unique situation that might be exploited for the benefit of the whole race?"

They looked to him, questioningly.

"The dynamic we find in Genoa-and Texcoco, too, for that matter, though we disagree on so many fundamentals-is beyond that in the Solar System. These are new planets, new ambitions are alive. We have at our fingertips man's highest developments, evolved on Earth. But with this new dynamic, this freshness, might we not in time push even beyond old Earth?"

"You mean —" Natt Roberts said.

MacDonald nodded. "What particular of value is gained by our uniting Genoa and Texcoco with the so-called Galactic Commonwealth? Why not press ahead on our own? With the vigor of these new races we might well leave Earth far behind."

Watson mused, "Carrying your suggestion to the ultimate, who is to say that one day Rigel might not become the new center of the human race, rather than Sol?"

"A point well taken," Gunther agreed.

"No," Taller said softly.

The six Earthmen turned hostile eyes to him.

"This particular matter does not concern you, Generalissimo," Watson rapped at him.

Taller smiled his amusement at that and came to his feet.

"No," he said. "I am afraid that hard though it might be for you to give up the powers you have held so long, you Earthlings are going to have to return to Terra City, from whence you came."

Baron Leonar said in gentle agreement, "Obviously."

"What is this?" Watson rapped. "I'm not at all amused."

The Honorable Russ stood also. "There is no use prolonging this. I have heard you Earth-lings say, more than once, that man adapts to preserve himself. Very well, we of Genoa and Texcoco are adapting to the present situation. We are of the belief that if you are allowed to remain in power we of the Rigel planets will be destroyed, probably in an atomic holocaust. In self-protection we have found it necessary to unite, we Genoese and Texcocans. We bear you no ill will, far to the contrary. However, it is necessary that you all return to Earth. You have impressed upon us the aforementioned truism that *man adapts* but in the *Pedagogue's* library I have found another that also applies. Power corrupts, and absolute power corrupts absolutely."

There were heavy automatics in the hands of Natt Roberts and Dick Hawkins. Barry Watson leaned back in his chair, his eyes narrow. "How'd you ever expect to get away with this sort of treason, Taller?"

Martin Gunther blurted, "Or you, Russ?"

Wiss, the Texcocan scientist, held his wrist radio to his mouth and said, "Come in now."

Dick Hawkins thumbed back the hammer of his hand gun.

"Hold it a minute, Dick," Barry Watson said. "I don't like this." To Taller he rapped, "What goes on here? Talk up, you're just about a dead man."

And it was then that they heard the scraping on the outer hull.

The six Earthmen looked at the overhead, dumfounded.

"I suggest you put up your weapons," Taller said quietly. "At this late stage I would hate to see further bloodshed."

In moments they heard the opening and closing of locks and footsteps along the corridor. The door opened and in stepped,

Joe Chessman, Amschel Mayer, Mike Dean, Louis Rosetti, and an emaciated Jerry Kennedy. Their expressions ran the gamut from sheepishness to blank haughtiness.

MacDonald bug-eyed. "Dean ... Rosetti ... the Temple priests burned you at the stake!"

They grinned at him, shamefaced. "Guess not," Dean said. "We were kidnaped. We've been teaching basic science, in some phony monastery."

Watson's face was white. "Joe," he said.

"Yeah," Joe Chessman growled. "You sold me out. But Taller and the Texcocans thought I was still of some use."

Amschel Mayer snapped, bitterly, "And now if you fools will put down your stupid guns, we'll make the final arrangements for returning this expedition to Terra City. Personally, I'll be glad to get away!"

Behind the five resurrected Earthmen were a sea of faces representing the foremost figures of both Texcoco and Genoa in every field of endeavor. At least fifty of them in all.

As though protectively, the eleven Earthmen ganged together at the far side of the messtable they'd met over so often.

Martin Gunther, his expression dazed, said, "I ... I don't —"

Taller resumed his spokesmanship. "From the first the most progressive elements on both Texcoco and Genoa realized the value of your expedition and have been in fundamental sympathy with the aims the *Pedagogue* originally had. Primitive life is not idyllic. Until man is free from nature's tyranny and has solved the basic problems of sufficient food, clothing, shelter, medical care and education for all, he is unable to realize himself. So we co-operated with you to the extent we found possible."

His smile was grim. "I am afraid that almost from the beginning, and on both planets, your very actions developed an ... underground, I believe you call it. Not an overt one, since we needed your assistance to build the new industrialized culture you showed us was possible. We even protected you against yourselves, since it soon became obvious that if left alone you'd destroy each other in your addiction to power."

Baron Leonar broke in, "Don't misunderstand. It wasn't until the past couple of decades that this *underground* which had sprung up independently on both planets, amalgamated."

Barry Watson blurted, "But Joe ... Chessman —" he refused to meet the eye of the man he'd condemned.

Taller said, "From the first you made no effort to study our customs. If you had, you'd have realized why my father allied himself to you after you'd killed Taller First. And why I did not take my revenge on Chessman after he'd killed Reif. A Khan's first training is that no personal emotion must interfere with the needs of the People. When you turned Joe Chessman over to me, I realized his education, his abilities were too great to destroy. We sent him to a mountain university and have used him profitably all these years. In fact, it was Chessman who finally brought us to space travel."

"That's right," Buchwald blurted. "You've got a spaceship out there. How could you possibly —?"

Taller said mildly, "There are but a handful of you, you could hardly keep track of two whole planets and all that went on upon them."

Amschel Mayer said bitingly, "All this can be gone over on our return to Terra City. We'll have a full year to explain to ourselves and each other why we became such complete idiots. I was originally head of this expedition-before my supposed friends railroaded me to prison-does anyone object if I take over again?"

"No," Joe Chessman growled.

The others shook their heads.

Taller said, "There is but one other thing. In spite of how you may feel at this moment of embarrassment, basically you have succeeded in your task. That is, you have brought Texcoco and Genoa to an industrialized culture. We hold various reservations about how you accomplished this. However, when you return to your Co-ordinator of Galactic Colonization, please inform him that we are anxious to receive his ambassadors. The term is *ambassadors* and we will expect to meet on a basis of equality. Surely in all Earth's millennia of social evolution man has worked out something better than either of your teams have built here. We should like to be instructed."

Dick Hawkins said stiffly, "We can instruct you on Earth's present socio-economic system."

"I am afraid we no longer trust you, Richard Hawkins. Send others-uncorrupted by power, privilege or great wealth."

* * * * *

When they had gone and the sound of their departing spacecraft had faded, Amschel Mayer snapped, "We might as well get underway. And cheer up, confound it, we have lots of time to contrive a reasonable report for the Co-ordinator."

Jerry Kennedy managed a thin grin, almost reminiscent of the younger Kennedy of the first years on Genoa. "Say," he said, "I wonder if we'll be granted a good long vacation before being sent on another assignment."